Restoring Christmas

By Kate Kasch

For Mom,

Thanks for always making Christmas magical

Published by CreateSpace Independent Publishing Platform

ISBN: 978-1721070510

This book is a work of fiction. Names, characters, businesses, organizations, places and events other than those clearly in the public domain, are the product of the author's imagination. Any resemblance to actual events or places or persons, living or dead, is entirely coincidental.

CHAPTER ONE

Adrienne Harkins races down Fifth Avenue as fast as she can in 4-inch heels and a fitted skirt. Her phone rings inside her handbag and she stops short to answer it while carefully balancing four coffees in a cardboard tray. Commuters rush past her on the packed sidewalk bumping her from all sides.

"Hey, watch where you're going!" She yells to a man in a suit that almost knocks her into the street. An incoming bus barrels down the block. Only inches from the curb, the gust of air from the bus whizzing by blows her hair into her face and almost tosses the coffees.

New Yorkers.

"Hi Elaina. Yes, I'm on my way. I know I'm running late, there was a line at the coffee shop and then they got the order wrong . . . No, I'm not making excuses. I will be right there."

If you would stop calling me I could get there even faster, Adrienne thinks to herself as she puts her phone away and starts to hustle down the sidewalk. Just up ahead she can see the building entrance with the words "MORGAN LYNCH" etched above the double doors - almost there.

The lobby of the Morgan Lynch building is modern with two sets of security desks, one for employees and one for visitors. Adrienne typically enjoys the sleek décor when she enters through those large double doors. However today, on December 18th, it looks as though a Christmas bomb exploded, sending cheesy green wreaths, stiff red bows and shiny gold ball ornaments scattered around the once chic lobby. Walking right past the fifteen-foot Christmas trees, fake presents and faux pine garland that is wrapped around every visible column, Adrienne marches up to the employee security desk. She flashes her badge to Nico, one of the regular security guards, and ignores his wishes for her to "have a blessed day." Holidays or not, Adrienne is not in the mood. Or perhaps it is due to the holidays that she is not in the mood.

Aside from one small Christmas tree in the elevator bank area, there are no other signs that Christmas is one week away in the actual offices of Morgan Lynch. This is one thing she can appreciate about the financial institutions in New York; no one gets too caught up in the holidays. And she does not need any unnecessary distractions right now. Quickly dropping her coat and bag at her desk, she pulls her straight, blonde hair back into a bun, a nervous habit. Then grabbing the tray of coffees she heads toward the conference room.

Adrienne knocks gently on the conference door and without waiting for an answer, walks in.

"Do you have the coffees for Dan, Todd and Charles?" Elaina asks without even looking in Adrienne's direction.

"Um, you said to get coffee for you, Dan and Todd. I didn't get one for Charles."

Elaina stops passing out the paperwork at each seat and finally looks up at Adrienne, a scowl of disapproval on her face. "I see four coffees, one for Dan, Todd, Charlie and me. Put the coffees down at their usual seats, and make me ten photocopies of the agenda."

Adrienne does as she is told, putting the coffees down in the appropriate locations. With a black sharpie she scribbles out the name "Adrienne" on the one coffee cup and writes "Charles." She has never needed a cup of coffee so bad in her life. *Would it be totally awful if she stole just one sip? Charles wouldn't notice one sip missing.* As she struggles with this moral dilemma, Elaina disrupts her inner monologue, "Harkins -- photocopies!"

Walking back from the photocopy machine Adrienne passes by the kitchen area where the smell of coffee lures her in. Burnt drip coffee may not be the Gingerbread Latte she was expecting, but it is still caffeine. *Bad coffee is better than no coffee*, she convinces herself as she pours the steaming brew into a Styrofoam cup.

After sitting through an hour-long marketing meeting where Adrienne is responsible for taking notes and running the projector screen for Elaina's PowerPoint presentation, her mind starts to wander. She takes a sip of her coffee to stay focused. Gross. Maybe no coffee *is* better than bad coffee.

"Harkins. Harkins? HARKINS?!"

Adrienne jumps at the sound of her name being yelled across the boardroom and accidentally knocks her coffee cup over. The bitter coffee spills all over the table and the laptop Adrienne has been using to work the PowerPoint presentation. The laptop groans and green and purple zigzags flash across the screen. The projector screen goes blank. *Uh oh. That's not good.* Adrienne pops to her feet, attempting to wipe down the laptop with her hand, and then picks up the laptop and shakes it off, coffee dripping off the machine onto the table.

"Ohmygoodness, I am so, so, sorry. I can fix it, I promise. I have this great techie guy – he's amazing. Seriously, not a problem." Adrienne babbles on as she grabs napkins off the side buffet and tries to soak up some of the coffee.

"Harkins. Harkins! HARKINS!" Elaina yells over Adrienne's ramblings.

Adrienne looks up and sees nine solemn faces staring back at her in complete . . . disgust.

"Harkins, I think we are done for now. Why don't you go back to your desk and get cleaned up," Elaina says with forced patience. Adrienne looks down at her light gray skirt and suit jacket and for the first time realizes she is covered in coffee.

"Right. Okay. I'll just take the laptop and see what I can do. I will get it fixed, I promise. My guy is a miracle worker . . .."

"Adrienne. Just go."

At her cubicle, Adrienne slumps down in her desk chair and lays her head down on the desk. This cannot be happening. She has worked in the Marketing Department at Morgan Lynch for over three years now, and should be up for a promotion at the end of the year, which is only two weeks away. How is she going to show the team that she is ready for the next step? She has got to get this laptop fixed and save Elaina's presentation.

With a sense of purpose, Adrienne puts on her thankfully long wool coat, throws the laptop in her giant handbag and makes her way to the elevator bank. Out on the street the cold, crisp air is a welcome relief. Adrienne takes a deep breath and starts the ten-block walk to iTech. Her phone rings, and she answers hoping it's not Elaina calling to scold her some more.

"Adrienne, it's me. How are you?"

Jason.

"Jason, I'm so glad it's you. I have just had the worst morning."

"I heard. A complete meltdown like that and word gets around the office pretty fast. That's why I'm calling – I wanted to make sure you're okay. Where are you?"

Word of her coffee disaster has already spread to the bankers? This is worse than Adrienne thought. *Bye-bye promotion!*

"I am on my way to see my tech guy – I'm hoping he can fix the laptop. He has really helped me out in the past, so fingers crossed."

"Hey, it's fine. You are a young assistant – the guys will have a good laugh for a few days, but it will blow over. Maybe someone will get really drunk at the office holiday party and overshadow your coffee explosion."

"I wouldn't call it an explosion. I just spilled a cup of coffee . . . Why, people are calling it an explosion? Oh no . . ."

"Look, you're having a rough day. I think I can slip out of here for an hour or so around lunchtime. I have a great idea; can you meet me around one? I'll text you the address."

"That sounds perfect. Thank you, Jason."

Starting to feel better, Adrienne pulls open the glass door at iTech. Upon entering the store she is assaulted by a burst of warm air and the all-too-familiar sound of Christmas music. Thankfully, there are only seven more days of hearing this music everywhere she goes.

"Hi, can I speak with Michael please?" Adrienne asks the pretty woman at the counter.

"Oh honey, Michael is out sick today. Is there something I can help you with?"

Noooooooooo. This can't be happening. Not now. Adrienne throws her head down on the counter and moans.

"Is there any way we can call him? Maybe ask him to come in for a minute to look at something?"

"I'm afraid that's not possible, he is really not feeling well. Are you sure I can't help you? I am known to work a little magic," the woman says with a twinkle in her eye. Her dark hair is pulled back in a French twist, her eyes are a sparkling hazel and her light mocha skin is glowing – she is definitely not a native New Yorker. With white wool pants, a white soft sweater and a white furry scarf, she is taking the "winter white" thing to a whole new level. Adrienne has never seen anything like her before. And the woman can't seem to stop smiling – definitely from out of town.

"Well . . . Angela," Adrienne says as she reads the woman's nametag, "Michael has gotten me out of a jam before. He saved my iPhone from a near death experience. And I am currently desperate – walk-the-plank kind of desperate."

"Let's see what we can do."

Adrienne hands over the laptop figuring she's got nothing to lose.

"It really needed a caffeine boost this morning," Adrienne jokes.

"Just excuse me while I take it to the back room."

Adrienne pulls out her phone thinking she will check her email while she waits. In what could not be more than two minutes, Angela is walking back out with the laptop in her hands. That is probably not a good sign.

"Can't be saved, can it?"

"Oh honey, everything can be saved. It is good to go."

"Wait, what? Seriously? You fixed it that fast?"

"Just needed a little elbow grease," Angela says with a giggle.

Adrienne is just staring, mouth hanging open, in complete shock. Then she jumps across the counter and grabs Angela in a giant hug, squealing in delight.

"Thank you, thank you, thank you! You have no idea how much you have just helped me. You are a miracle worker!"

Still smiling, Angela says, "Now you should take the rest of the day off. Go get yourself a gingerbread latte, do a little Christmas shopping, see the tree at Rockefeller Center, maybe go buy a new dress . . . enjoy the magic of this holiday season."

With the mention of a new dress, Adrienne follows Angela's gaze to her coffee stained suit.

"You don't happen to have some magic stain remover back there, too, do you?"

"That I'm afraid I can't help you with."

"You know what? I think I'm going to take your advice. My boss does not want to see me right now. Although, the fixed laptop would cheer her up, not that she is ever 'cheery.' But, I am not going back to the office. I am going to go home and change . . . and then buy myself a latte."

With a little extra pep in her step, Adrienne hails a cab to take her to her apartment on the Upper East Side. She watches the city slide by in streaks of color – Christmas decorations light up the usually gray buildings, Santa Clauses ringing their bells every few blocks, and throngs of people bundled up in colorful scarves and hats. In a moment of weakness she thinks, *it really is a magical time of year.*

Adrienne rides the elevator up to the twelfth floor and walks down the hall to her apartment. As she pushes the door open she notices a red envelope on the floor behind the door. Since her mail is delivered to her mailbox in the lobby, Adrienne has no idea how the envelope got inside her apartment. She opens the envelope and scans the letter. Then she reads it again. Lightheaded and panicked, she feels as if the floor beneath her has dropped away. She stumbles toward the nearest chair and collapses on it with a thump.

Now she has to call Gretchen. Ugh. Worst. Day. Ever.

CHAPTER TWO

Not the garbage truck again! Gretchen thinks to herself as she rolls over in her bed and throws the blanket over her head. *It's only 9 a.m.! Don't the garbage men know that half of the people in New York City work nights?* Gretchen groans as the sound of metal on metal pierces through the quiet morning. The big crane lifts the giant garbage bin right outside her basement level apartment. Gretchen rolls over onto her back and stares up at the pockmarked ceiling. As the crane drops the container back onto the street, her whole apartment shakes. Coffee.

Shuffling in her fuzzy socks across the parquet floor over to her little kitchenette, she puts a pod into the Keurig machine and waits for the comforting aroma to fill her small home. With a shiver she throws her favorite over-sized sweater over her shoulders and checks out the thermometer. *Sixty-five degrees? Now that doesn't seem right.* She kicks the old radiator a few times and is relieved when she hears the clanging sound of the heat pumping through the pipes. Once the coffee is done dripping into her favorite mug that says, "I am an ARTIST, that does not mean I'll work for FREE," she adds cream to it and walks around the apartment to look at the framed photos stacked in every available space – which is not much. Aside from her full-size bed, one tiny desk and the kitchenette, which is so small it could never be called a kitchen, the rest of the 500 square feet is filled with a tripod, studio lights, a variety of camera lenses, black and white photographs scattered all over the desk, counter, and floor, and Gretchen's prized possession: her Canon 5D Mark IV DSLR. In other words, it's a really fancy camera.

Like most artists, Gretchen moved to the city full of hope and promise. She got a job bartending at night at McMurphy's Pub to pay the bills, and was happy to have her days to work on her craft. She gave herself four years to find success. Gretchen lets out a big sigh as she realizes the end of this year – December 31st, will mark her fourth year in the city. Unless she can find a miracle in the next 13 days, she has decided to give up on her dream.

In a quick decision, Gretchen decides she needs a pastry to cheer herself up. She switches her sweatpants for her favorite pair of jeans, and keeps on the thermal top and cozy sweater she slept in. In lieu of a brush, she just runs her fingers through her long wavy honey-blonde hair. That should be good enough. She throws on a knit beanie to hide the tangles. Outside on the sidewalk the wind seems to cut right through her sweater - she should have worn a coat.

"Excuse me," a voice from behind interrupts Gretchen's thoughts. She turns around to see a beautiful woman in a long white coat.

"Your shoe is untied, dear. I wouldn't want you to trip," her voice sings.

Gretchen looks down at her boot, and indeed her shoelace is untied.

"Oh, thank you. That is so nice of you, really."

As Gretchen bends down to tie her laces, she places her purse on the sidewalk next to her. Within seconds it's swiped from right next to her feet. She looks up quickly, half in shock her voice freezes up as she watches the young boy in the hoodie sweatshirt darting down the sidewalk with her bag.

"Stop! Thief!" She hears someone yell what she should be yelling. Gretchen follows the sound of the yelling to the mysterious woman in white.

Unfortunately, since this is New York City, very few people actually react to the fact that there is a thief running down the sidewalk. A few people may have glanced in her general direction, but Gretchen realizes she's on her own with this one – per usual. Her body seems to recover from the immediate shock and she starts to chase the boy down, yelling, "Stop! Thief," as she runs.

The world is whizzing by Gretchen as she zooms in on the gray hoodie. She sees him trying to cross the street, but the holiday traffic is insane. Just as Gretchen seems to be gaining on him, he slips between two big tour groups and turns left. Gretchen gets stuck in the middle of a group of Japanese tourists and tries to push through them, attempting to show her urgency without being too rude.

"Excuse me. Excuse me. I'm trying to get this man that stole my purse," she yells to the mob. But they all just smile at her and nod. "A thief! I'm trying to catch a thief!" Gretchen yells, elbowing her way through. Once on the other side of the group, she can see the hoodie, but he's so far ahead of her, she'll never catch him.

"If only he'd bump into that pretzel cart that's coming to set up on the corner," a voice behind her says. Gretchen turns around and there standing right behind her, and looking like she just stepped out of a limousine, is the woman in white.

"You? You followed me? That was so . . . thoughtful. You're definitely not a New Yorker, are you? How are you not out of breath?"

Before the woman can answer, there is a loud crash that can be heard above the traffic noise. Both Gretchen and the mystery woman's eyes dart down the sidewalk to where the pretzel cart was setting up. The boy and the cart have presumably collided. The pretzel cart man is yelling at the boy who is now pinned under the cart. Gretchen and the woman in white race down the block. Once at the scene of the collision, Gretchen looks at the boy who is too ashamed to look her in the eye, and she holds out her hand. He reluctantly hands Gretchen her purse, and then she and the woman in white try and help the pretzel cart operator lift the cart off of the boy. Once freed, the boy takes off running.

"Well, that was an eventful morning," Gretchen says to the woman. "Can I please buy you a coffee or a muffin, to thank you for your help?"

"That would be delightful, thank you!"

Gretchen holds out her hand, "I'm Gretchen Harkins. It's a pleasure to meet you . . .?"

"Angela. And the pleasure is all mine, I assure you."

After a nice chat over coffee and crumb cake, Gretchen and Angela say their good-byes and Gretchen heads home to get some work done editing her latest photographs. She wiggles the key in the sticky lock to her apartment until it finally decides to turn, and pushes the door open. There is a red envelope on the floor by the door. Her first thought is that it's an eviction notice – she's sure she's late paying the rent this month. Her heart begins to pound. As Gretchen reads the letter, her grip on the paper grows tighter and tighter until she's crumpling the paper in her hands. She then balls it up and throws it across the room.

Now she has to call Adrienne. Great.

CHAPTER THREE

Adrienne gathers her strength and leaving the red envelope on her kitchen countertop, slowly walks into her bedroom. Peeling off the coffee-stained skirt, blouse and suit jacket, Adrienne's mind goes over and over the words from the letter. An onslaught of memories of her family has her feeling dizzy. She opens her vast closet, which displays a variety of designer clothing all hung with velvet hangers and color-coded from dark to light.

Selecting a pair of jeans and a cozy cashmere sweater, Adrienne wants to snuggle onto her soft chaise lounge and eat a pint of ice cream. But the practical side of her realizes sitting alone in her apartment will do nothing but leave her brain free to roam around in thoughts from her past. What's that saying? *Idle hands are the devil's workshop.* Well, her memories are the devil.

Scanning her apartment for a particular pair of boots, Adrienne glances around and feels a sense of pride. She has made it this far all on her own. She got a good paying job and saved for this larger apartment and took months furnishing it with custom furniture and high-end appliances. If she gets this promotion at work, which is not looking good at the moment, but if she gets that promotion, she plans to try and move to an apartment in her building that is a few floors up with sweeping views of downtown and the Empire State Building. Currently, her only views are of a brick building a few feet away from her window. Thinking of work has her heart racing with anxiety. The light gray walls of her apartment now feel as if they are suffocating her.

Putting on a pair of comfortable low-heeled boots and a warm puffer jacket Adrienne leaves her apartment and walks straight toward the elevators. She needs to go for a walk. Out on the street, Adrienne thinks back to what Angela from iTech said to her, and decides to make her way over to Rockefeller Center. Due to the crowds, the tourists, the Christmas music and the cheery shoppers, Rockefeller Center is typically a place Adrienne avoids during the holidays. Perhaps it is Angela's energy or the red envelope encouraging her to go see the Rockefeller Center Christmas tree, Adrienne is not quite sure. Something deep down inside her is pushing her there, which is strange considering she hasn't been there in over four years.

On her way, Adrienne stops in a small café and orders herself that gingerbread latte she has been craving all day. Sipping the warm, spicy coffee, Adrienne wanders slowly down Fifth Avenue with its wide sidewalks and high-end retail stores, consumed by her own thoughts. *Maybe the incident at the office this morning was a good thing,* she thinks to herself. It has forced her to slow down for a minute, take in the fresh air, and really enjoy this city that she lives in. *The bells, the music, the ice skaters, the energy! How can anyone want to live anywhere else?*

Walking up to the edge of the viewing area with the ice skaters gliding around down below her, and the giant Christmas tree in front of her, Adrienne lets her mind slide back to when she was a child. She sees herself skating across the ice, hand-in-hand with her sister, giggling as they try to go faster and faster without falling. She can still hear her mother yelling to them, "Slow down! You're going to get hurt!" But the sisters just laugh, thrilled by the speed and the possible danger. Feeling a tear slip down her cold cheek, Adrienne quickly wipes it away and is brought back to the present.

"Excuse me? Excuse me, miss?" asks an unknown voice in a Russian accent. Adrienne turns to see a woman and a man, smiling broadly. The woman is holding up her phone and motioning for Adrienne to take their photo in front of the tree. Adrienne smiles and nods her head, reaching for the phone. She snaps a few photos of the happy tourists before she decides she has had enough of Rockefeller Center. She knows what she has to do now.

Walking a little further beyond all the holiday madness, the crowds begin to thin out, and the noise becomes muffled as Adrienne walks further and further east. It's as if her body is on a mission that her brain is unaware of – detached and focused she moves on. She walks and walks until she can walk no longer. She has come to the edge of the island and the East River shines ahead of her in the midday sun.

Choosing an empty bench along the water, Adrienne sits to rest her weary legs. She pulls her phone out of her pocket and stares at it for a moment. *I wonder if she still has the same number. Or if she even has a phone at all,* she thinks to herself. Taking a generous gulp of her now cold coffee, Adrienne pushes Gretchen's name on the screen and holds her breath. Will she even answer?

"Hi, Adrienne. I was just about to call you."

"Really? Then you got the letter too?"

"Yup. What are we going to do?"

"I have no idea. Maybe we should get together to discuss it – and try and come up with a solution?"

"Um, I guess so," Gretchen says hesitantly. "Want to have dinner tonight?"

"Okay. Oh, wait. I actually already have dinner plans. How about a drink after dinner?"

"I'm working tonight. Want to just come to McMurphy's? We can chat while I work. I'll save you a seat at the bar."

"Fine. I can't believe you still work at that dive."

"Don't start, Adrienne."

"Right. I'll see you later."

Well that went about as well as Adrienne could have hoped. Her belly swirls with the thought of seeing Gretchen later. It's been so long. Standing up slowly, Adrienne heads to the street to hail a cab and go meet Jason.

Unbeknownst to Adrienne, across town in a tiny apartment in Hell's Kitchen, her sister is also desperately in need of a little Christmas cheer.

CHAPTER FOUR

Holed up in her tiny basement flat, Gretchen sits back on her bed and leans against the wall. Staring at the balled up letter on the floor, she feels like the wind has been knocked out of her. Of course thoughts of her family sneak into her mind once in a while, but she does a pretty good job of keeping them buried in the shadows of her brain. This letter just brought everything back to the forefront with a giant bang.

Many of the people she works with at McMurphy's complain about working nights, but Gretchen is thankful for the late-night job. The constant drink making, pint filling, and wine pouring leaves little time for her to think. And when she does finally get home at two in the morning, she collapses on her bed and is asleep within seconds. If she had every night to just sit and think alone in her hovel, she would probably go insane.

What is Adrienne doing right now? She is most likely dressed in a perfectly tailored suit, with her hair pulled back in a bun sitting in her cubicle working diligently for twelve hours straight. There once was a time when Adrienne and Gretchen had fun together – when they would laugh with each other. Gretchen tries to hear the sound of Adrienne's laugh, but it has been too long – its sound is just another casualty of the accident and the time that has passed between them. Gretchen would do anything to hear that sound again.

Okay, that's enough of the pity party. Gretchen hops off the bed and picking up her phone, almost calls Adrienne, but decides to blast some music instead. Turning the volume on full blast in an attempt to drown out her thoughts, Gretchen turns on her laptop and opens the file that contains her most recent photographs. As she scans the photos of some gritty graffiti from the side of a building on the Lower East Side, Gretchen decides she really likes how they came out. Years ago when she first arrived in New York, she would walk up to Central Park every day in search of photographs that juxtaposed nature against the rough city backdrop. More recently she has started a series that highlights the glitz and glamour of New York City positioned next to the underground darker side of the city. She found a woman in a white fur coat walking down a sidewalk with the background covered in graffiti. It was perfect – just what she was looking for.

As she searches through photos she enlarges those that look interesting and plays with the lighting and different filters. So lost in her work when her phone dings it startles her so badly, she jumps. Glancing at her phone with one eye still on her computer screen, Gretchen sees a reminder blinking. *Oh no! The appointment!*

Leaping out of her desk chair so fast the chair falls to the ground, Gretchen runs over to her tiny closet, leaving the chair tipped over on the floor. She pulls open the closet door so fast she knocks a stack of folded sweaters off the top shelf and they all come raining down on her head. She throws the sweaters on the ground and quickly shuffles through them looking for one cardigan in particular. Then back to the closet, she pushes and pulls at the hanging clothes, which are squished in so tight they don't move when she pulls one item over to see the next. With no time to spare, Gretchen finds the long black casual dress she was searching for and puts it on as quickly as possible. She throws the cardigan sweater over the dress and pulls her hair up into a bun. Slipping boots onto her feet while simultaneously searching for her portfolio in the mound of photos and papers stacked on her desk, Gretchen frantically dumps the entire contents of her desk onto the floor. If someone were to walk into her apartment right now, they would think she had just been robbed.

With her portfolio and her bag in her hands, Gretchen rushes out the door and up the stairs onto the street level. *How could I forget about this appointment?* She says to herself, frustrated. Now, to avoid being late she needs to waste money she does not have on a cab ride. Thankfully, since it's not rush hour cabs are plentiful in Midtown. She hails a cab and then has to search through her emails on her phone to find the address of the art gallery. *I really need to get organized!*

After scrolling through a million emails, Gretchen finds the one she needs and gives the cab driver the address. On the ride downtown, Gretchen takes deep breaths and does her best to calm down and pull herself together. When the cab stops in front of the Gilmore Gallery, Gretchen steps out onto the sidewalk, smoothing her dress and hair, and walks through the glass doors with forced confidence.

The Gilmore Art Gallery has polished concrete floors and floor to ceiling windows allowing in an amazing amount of natural light. The walls are painted a bright white allowing the artwork that hangs on the walls to stand out. Gretchen can't help but scan the walls of artwork in awe of the talent. As she walks slowly around the main showroom taking it all in, she is approached by a woman in a tight-fitting black skirt and white button down blouse. The woman's hair is pulled back neatly and thick-rimmed black glasses sit perched on her pointy nose.

"Hello. Welcome to the Gilmore Gallery. Can I be of assistance in some way?"

"Hi, yes! I am here to see Eleanor Anderson. I have an appointment."

The woman with the thick glasses looks Gretchen up and down and with her lips held tight in a straight line nods her head and without saying a word turns around and walks away. Gretchen stands there puzzled, watching the woman until she disappears around a corner. *What does that mean?*

A minute or two later an older woman, possibly in her sixties, (Gretchen has never been great at guessing ages), with very short gray hair and bright red lipstick walks up to Gretchen and introduces herself.

"Hello, I am Eleanor Anderson," she says extending her right hand for a handshake.

"Hi, I'm Gretchen Harkins. It's a pleasure to meet you Ms. Anderson."

Just as quickly as the first woman disappeared, so does Ms. Anderson's smile. "So, what are you here for Ms. Harkins?" she asks.

"Right. Yes. I am a photographer and I have put together a series of photos that I call "Gritty Glam," which is a compilation of photos here in New York City where I juxtapose the conflicting worlds of, well, the gritty and the glam," Gretchen's palms start to sweat as she tries to open her portfolio standing up and hold it across her arms, while attempting to turn the pages and display her work. "You see, it's a statement about the gap between the wealthy and the poor, the powerful and the underprivileged and how we all live among each other in such close quarters," Gretchen feels as if she is rambling but she keeps talking because it appears that Eleanor Anderson is interested.

"You see this photo," Gretchen points at one of her favorite photos that is developed in black and white with only a woman's bright red lipstick in color. "You see here, she is in a floor length gown headed to a charity event and walking right by this homeless person . . .." Eleanor holds up her hand to signal for Gretchen to stop talking. Gretchen holds her breath.

"I think you have something there, but we are not looking for anything taking place in New York City right now. We are focusing on a multi-cultural theme at the moment and from the photography side are looking for work from Africa, South American, Russia – do you think you could bring us something from Siberia?"

Gretchen lets all the air out of her lungs she had been holding in and looks at Eleanor Anderson like she asked her to . . . well, like someone just asked her to go to Siberia to take photos.

"I don't think I can make it to Siberia, no." Gretchen says slowly, still looking at Eleanor perplexed. "Couldn't you have New York City as part of your mulit-cultural showcase? New York is full of people from all over the world . . .." Gretchen stops mid-sentence as she sees Eleanor's hand go up again.

"No, I'm afraid that is not what we are looking for at the moment. But you stick with it, you have a lot of potential," Eleanor says before she walks away, crushes Gretchen's dreams, and disappears around the corner.

Walking through the giant glass doors and back out onto the cold sidewalk, Gretchen is not sure she has ever felt so low. This appointment was her last chance to try and secure a showcase before the end of the year. *Maybe I am just not meant to be an artist.* Slowly moving one foot in front of the other, and with no money left for a cab ride, Gretchen begins the long trek back up to Midtown.

Pulling her sweater tight around her body, Gretchen feels the cold air seep into her bones. *Why do I keep forgetting to put on a coat? It's December! I really need to get organized.* Just ahead of her, two young women are leaving a coffee shop. Laughing and chatting with their coffees in hand, the women push the door open and knock straight into Gretchen; bumping her so hard she almost falls over. She looks over at the women and neither of them stops to acknowledge the collision or says,

"Excuse me" or "I'm sorry about crashing into you," – they say nothing, they do nothing. It's as if Gretchen isn't even there. *Can people not see me? Am I invisible? That would explain a lot.* Gretchen thinks to herself as she watches the two women giggling their way down the sidewalk.

Looking back toward the coffee shop, Gretchen makes an impulsive decision: she is getting herself a gingerbread latte. With her mind made up she marches over to the coffee shop doors, pulls them open, glancing through the glass first to be sure no one is on their way out, and walks inside. Shuddering at the initial burst of warm air, Gretchen takes a moment to appreciate the comfort of the heat and the smell of coffee and sweets. Ordering a latte to stay, Gretchen finds a seat and waits for her beverage. As she watches the many different types of people from all walks of life stroll past the window, she can't help but again be frustrated by Eleanor Anderson's remarks. *Siberia? Seriously?* And then her mind immediately goes back to the red envelope and Adrienne. She looks at her phone, contemplating whether or not to call her, and decides she will do it after she enjoys her latte.

Perhaps the barista can sense her dismal mood, because when her order arrives, Gretchen looks down at the big mug full of espresso and milk and sees a Christmas tree formed out of the foam. A wide smile spreads across her face as she looks up and around in search of who made her such a special treat. However, no one is in sight. Just then her phone rings, and forgetting about her angel barista, Gretchen looks at the phone and sees Adrienne's name on the screen.

"Hi, Adrienne. I was just about to call you."

CHAPTER FIVE

Adrienne steps out of the cab at the address Jason texted her and looks up at the buildings around her to see if anything looks familiar. When she sees an all-glass artsy looking building on the corner, a smile spreads across her face. And there, right in front of the big double doors, looking sharp in his navy suit and long wool coat is Jason.

"An art gallery. You must really feel bad for me," Adrienne says as she gives Jason a quick peck on the cheek.

"Can you believe I am not only going to an art gallery willingly, but I actually planned it? Now I know you don't believe in Christmas, but this would almost be considered a Christmas miracle."

"I believe in Christmas! Why do you think I don't believe in Christmas?

"Oh I don't know, maybe because you hate Christmas music, Christmas decorations and even Christmas trees. I have seen your apartment – nothing Christmas-y in sight."

"Well, I used to like Christmas. And, you don't have any Christmas decorations in your apartment either."

"That's true, but I'm a guy. It's different," and before Adrienne can disagree he says, "Can we go inside now. I can only be gone about an hour."

Letting the Christmas conversation drop, Adrienne walks into the Gilmore Art Gallery and unknowingly misses seeing her sister by only a few minutes. Walking past the abstract art that hangs on the bright white walls, Adrienne pauses in front of each piece, studying the interesting angles and colors. For a few minutes the heavy weight of her worries is lifted. The coffee debacle, Elaina, the red envelope and Gretchen are still there, but instead of sitting hard on her shoulders, they are floating above her head giving her a couple of minutes of peace.

"I still find it fascinating," Jason says.

"Find what fascinating? The art? Me too, doesn't it just transport you to another place altogether?"

"No, not the artwork. You. I find it fascinating that walking around looking at paintings on a wall is your idea of a good time."

Adrienne smiles at him, "You know my mom used to take my sister and me to art galleries all the time. She was an unbelievable sculptor and painter." Sometimes Jason has these moments where he surprises her with his thoughtfulness.

"I knew you would like it," Jason continues. "A guy at work asked that I come down here. He just started dating one of the women that works here and he wanted me to check her out and let him know what I think. He says she's pretty hot – do you mind if I wander toward the back and see if I can find her?"

Adrienne stops mid-walk to turn and look at him. "Are you serious?"

"What? What did I do?" he holds his hands up dumbfounded. "You're mad? I thought you would be thrilled we came to an art gallery. And it looks better if I'm not alone asking for this woman – I thought you coming was a win-win."

And then he has moments like this. Adrienne is no longer in the mood to be at the gallery, or with Jason. She gives him one last look letting him know how she feels about the fact that he only brought her here so he could check out some woman his friend is dating, and she starts to walk toward the door.

"Adrienne, don't leave. Come on, I still have a little time. Let me just go check her out and then I'll buy you a coffee – whatever that latte thing is you like."

Adrienne keeps walking, completely ignoring all the words coming out of his mouth. Jason stands there torn between finding his friend's new love interest and following Adrienne outside to apologize. Wisely, he starts to quickly walk after Adrienne.

Out on the sidewalk Adrienne is standing on the curb with her hand up to hail a cab. Jason rushes up behind her and starts to try and turn her around to look at him.

"Adrienne, I'm sorry. I didn't think you would mind. Let me make it up to you, please? Let me buy you coffee. No, let me buy you dinner. Let's go to Bandoli's tonight. We can have wine and good food, and we can forget all about your terrible day at work and what an idiot your boyfriend can be."

Feeling her anger start to dissipate, Adrienne slowly lowers her arm and turns around to face him. He is doing an excellent job of appearing remorseful with a sad face and pleading eyes – it's almost so pathetic that Adrienne can't help but want to laugh.

"Fine. I will meet you for dinner. As long as we're not really going to Bandoli's so you can check out some waitress that works there."

"Of course not. Meet me at eight. It will be amazing. I promise."

CHAPTER SIX

McMurphy's Pub is a typical Irish bar in Midtown Manhattan. Typically packed with men and women ranging from the college kid looking for a casual spot to hang to old-timers who want to enjoy a pint in a friendly place where no one cares if you stay for six hours straight. There are no judgments being made at McMurphy's, which is one of the things Gretchen appreciates about the place. Over the almost four years since she started working here it has become a second home for her. The people have stood in as her family, worrying about her if she's sick, checking up on the progress with her photography and keeping her company in this crowded lonely city. Sometimes Gretchen will even hang out at the bar when she is not working, just to avoid the solitude of her apartment.

On this particular Friday, December 18th, the pub fills up early with people looking for a warm place to celebrate the almost-holiday. Gretchen is thankful for the packed bar, since it is helping to keep her mind off the red envelope, her almost getting robbed today, being turned away at the gallery and the impending meeting with Adrienne. Gretchen can just picture Adrienne sauntering through the crowd in some gorgeous designer dress, not a hair out of place, and looking down at the worn, admittedly sometimes sticky, wood of the bar counter like it is covered in disease. She'll sit all high and mighty on her bar stool, sipping her Prosecco with her nose turned up at Larry, the local who parks his behind in the last stool near the wall, from open to close.

While Gretchen gets the tap started on a Guinness, pours a generous glass of red wine, and takes another order from a patron, out of the corner of her eye she sees a flash of white. When she looks up she is seeing, for the first time ever she's sure, a woman in McMurphy's dressed in white from head to toe and shining like a Christmas star. The crowd parts like the red sea as Angela makes her way toward the bar, graceful and smiling, of course. Gretchen is so surprised to see her again, she forgets about her Guinness pint and it starts to overflow under the tap.

"Oh my gosh, Angela? I can't believe it's you!" Gretchen says as she wipes up the spilled beer with a rag. "What on earth are you doing here?"

And just as miraculously as when the pretzel cart fell on the thief and pinned him down, a barstool opens up at the packed bar just as Angela arrives. She strolls on over and has a seat, front and center. Gretchen is beginning to realize that inexplicable extraordinary things tend to happen when Angela is around. She also has a contagious smile and positive energy that immediately perks up Gretchen's spirits.

Angela laughs, "This morning at coffee you mentioned you had to work tonight. I figured I would stop in and see how you are doing. I would think the robbery earlier must have been pretty traumatic for you."

"Well that is so sweet and thoughtful. And I'm fine. I wish I could say that it's the first time my bag has been stolen, but I'm afraid that's not the case."

"Oh dear, well it sounds like you need your luck to turn around," Angela's eyes twinkle.

"You have no idea," Gretchen says with a sigh as she excuses herself to take a few drink orders. A few minutes later she is back talking with Angela, "I am so sorry – I haven't even asked what you would like to drink!"

"I'll just have a club soda with a twist of lime, please. I have to say, I have been watching you, and you look worried. Is everything okay?"

"If you knew the day I have had, you would understand," Gretchen says, and Angela raises an eyebrow, signaling her to continue.

"Aside from being robbed and having to chase down a thief, which you already know, I received a strange letter that said I'm going to lose my childhood home, had all my career hopes and dreams crushed, and possibly worst of all, I have to meet with my sister."

Gretchen could think of a variety of different reactions that Angela would have after hearing about her day, however, the one she got was not one of them: laughter. Not sympathy, empathy, compassion, kindness – nope. Laughter. Giving Angela a look of complete astonishment and confusion only has Angela laughing harder.

"I am so sorry, I am not sure what has come over me!" Angela is somehow able to pull herself together.

"I'm glad you find the fact that my life is in ruins funny – hilarious, isn't it?" Gretchen can't help but show her irritation.

"I am not laughing at your heartache, I promise you. I'm laughing because you don't realize you are at the cusp of something amazing. You have nothing to lose at this point, right?" Gretchen continues to look puzzled.

"Alphonse Karr, an old French writer, once said, 'We can complain because rose bushes have thorns, or rejoice because thorns have roses.' Let's look on the bright side of things, you recovered your purse, you have shown strength in pursuing your hopes and dreams, and you have a sister - all things to be grateful for, in my opinion. But what do I know, anyway?"

Gretchen fills a few more drink orders thinking about what Angela said, and can't help but remember a time when she was a very positive thinking person. When did she lose that part of herself? Planning to ask that exact question to Angela, Gretchen walks over to where Angela was sitting, and instead of the beautiful woman in white, there is a young, male, twenty-something sitting there asking for a beer. Angela is gone. *Where did she go?*

CHAPTER SEVEN

In a black sheath dress that is tight in all the right places, leopard print pumps and a long black coat with a fur collar, Adrienne feels ready to make Jason forget all about the coffee fiasco earlier that morning and let him know she is willing to put the gallery incident behind them. It is 8 o'clock on the dot when she arrives at Bandoli's, which is a perfectly romantic Italian restaurant.

Just as Adrienne is about to pull open the door to the restaurant, she hears her cell phone ding, alerting her to a text message. She stops outside the restaurant and takes a peek at her phone – it is a text from Jason: *Running a little late, why don't you come meet me at Bar Ten*

Annoyed by the last minute change of plans, Adrienne texts back: *What about the dinner reservation?*

I will call them and change the reservation to 9:30.

Fully aware that this means Jason is hanging out with his guy friends from work and did not want to leave them in order to come meet her, Adrienne pauses for a minute and considers calling the whole night off. But then she looks down at her fabulous dress and heels, lets out a big sigh, and turns around back toward the street to hail a cab.

Walking into Bar Ten is like walking into a fraternity house for adults. Rowdy men of all ages are talking loudly above the blaring music, there is a large group of guys lining up shots at the bar and the few women in there are hoping since the odds are in their favor, they can possibly meet their husband-to-be. Adrienne is all too familiar with that strategy of hanging out in bars frequented by the after-work Wall Street crowd. She wishes she could pull the women in here aside and say, *"Leave. Go somewhere else. There may be a ton of guys here, but they are not looking for a serious relationship!"* Although, this is how she met Jason. Toward the back of the bar, Adrienne can see Jason and his group of friends. Always the life of the party, he has everyone's attention as he tells some story. When Adrienne is about ten feet away from the group, Jason must have reached the punch line because the entire crew erupts in uproarious laughter. The laughter is so loud it seems every person in the bar stops for a minute to see what the commotion is – probably hoping for a brawl. Once they realize everyone is laughing, not arguing, they all turn their attention back to their own conversations and Adrienne feels it's now safe to approach.

Walking up next to Jason she puts her hand on his arm to get his attention. He turns toward her and when he sees her his face lights up and he grabs her in a giant hug, lifting her off the ground.

"Hey guys, you all know Adrienne, right?" he says shouting to his friends. They all nod and say hello, or at least that is what it looks like they are saying, she certainly can't hear them and Adrienne is no lip reader.

"Let me get you a drink. Want a Cosmo? Martini?"

"Or a cup of coffee?" One of the guys says loud enough for everyone to hear, and the whole group erupts in laughter once again. Adrienne feels her cheeks burn and tries to laugh it off. She knows if she shows she is upset about it, they will just continue the assault. Jason puts his arm around her shoulders in an attempt to comfort her, and she is thankful for that. However, she is already ready to leave.

"I'll have a Cosmo," she screams. Jason nods his head and flags down a waitress who is somehow able to hear orders and navigate this crowd while carrying a tray full of drinks. As she waits for her drink to arrive, Adrienne does her best to participate in the conversation, however, with the noise and the mention of names of people she has never heard of, and the constant teasing each other, she ends up just people watching.

Sipping her cocktail, Adrienne feels herself growing more impatient by the minute. The story telling has moved on to a series of bets they are all coming up with for all types of different competitions. Who can bring in more accounts, who can work more hours, who can close a certain deal the fastest . . . these items are then assigned to specific men who then help come up with the winning bet and the losing bet. As the conversation continues, the stakes get higher for both winning the bet and losing the bet. Adrienne is bored. As one guy talks about having to show up for a week of work with a mustache drawn on with a sharpie if another guy loses the bet, Adrienne tugs on Jason's suit.

He looks down at her, still laughing from the current bet being made and gives her a quizzical look. She points to her wrist, letting him know it's time to go. He holds up his finger signaling one more minute and Adrienne rolls her eyes.

Finally, at about 9:20 Adrienne is able to drag Jason out of the bar. They hop in a cab and Adrienne is thankful for the quiet. Arriving at Bandoli's for the second time tonight, Adrienne takes a deep breath and shakes off the first half of the night. She really wanted this to be a nice intimate dinner where she could talk to Jason about all that is going on in her life right now, so she is going to try and start fresh – salvage what's left of their night.

Jason gives his name to the hostess who suggests they wait at the bar until their table is ready. The bar is cozy, with room enough for about six people to sit. It is made of dark mahogany and has small pendant lights hanging from the ceiling casting a soft glow on the patrons. Adrienne orders a glass of Cabernet and although she was all ready to focus on Jason and their night together, in the sudden quiet room all she can think about is Gretchen. She and Gretchen haven't seen each other in a few years, and seeing her is going to bring back a flood of memories, among other things. The letter. *What are they going to do?*

"Excuse me sir," the hostess taps Jason. "Your table is ready. You can follow me, please."

Once seated, Adrienne holds up her glass of wine in a toast, "Skoal," she says.

"Skoal?" Repeats Jason. "What does that mean?"

"Scandinavian countries say that as a toast to one's health. I don't know where that came from. I haven't said it in years. My Dad used to say it all the time . . ."

"Huh. That's weird. Why don't we just say 'cheers' like people in America do," Jason laughs.

Through most of the dinner Adrienne tries her best to listen as Jason goes on and on about his co-workers and all these crazy bets they were making at the bar earlier. Adrienne can't help but let her mind wander – Gretchen, her parents, her home . . . All things she hasn't allowed herself to think about in a long time.

"Hello? Earth to Adrienne! Are you still here?"

"Huh? Oh, sorry. Honestly, I'm a little distracted tonight. I've got a lot going on."

"Don't worry about the coffee explosion," Jason attempts to make her feel better. "It was an accident. It'll blow over."

"I'm not worried about the coffee – and it wasn't an explosion," Adrienne is annoyed now.

Jason holds up his hands in mock defense of himself, and makes a face at her that says, "Okay, if you say so."

"I'm not even thinking about that. I have to meet up with my sister later. We haven't seen each other in a long time."

Jason takes a hearty bite of his steak. "Ohhh, awkward family stuff. Want to know what I do in those situations? I drink. It really makes everything seem like it's no big deal!"

"That is your solution for everything," Adrienne rolls her eyes.

"Hey, don't knock it. It works. What's so bad about seeing your sister anyway? Do you two hate each other or something?"

"No. It's not that. Our family has been through a lot in the last few years, and today we got bad news."

"What news?"

"We both got a letter today that said we are going to lose our childhood home because we haven't been paying the taxes. The tax collector has a lien on the house and will sell it at auction unless we come up with the delinquent amount by the end of the year. Which, last I checked is in thirteen days."

"Whoa. That's heavy. You probably should have paid your taxes."

"Thanks Jason. That's very helpful."

"Sorry. Sorry. How much money are we talking about?"

"Well, with the taxes, interest, and fees . . . It's $25,000.00.

"Yikes. Can your parents help?"

"Jason, I've told you; my parents died four years ago."

"That's right, I forgot. Sorry. It's hard to keep up with all your family drama. So why did you stop paying the taxes?"

"I kept up with the payments for years, but then, well you know, living in this city is expensive! I skipped one month, and then another, and then the amount I owed just got bigger and bigger. . . .."

"What about your sister?"

"Ha! That's funny. She probably doesn't even own more than one pair of socks. She will not be helpful – in any way."

"Well, just let them sell it then. Done deal. Problem solved."

Adrienne looks at Jason and suddenly feels very alone. *Does he know her at all?*

"You know what, I have to go," Adrienne pops out of her seat. "Thank you for dinner, but I really need to go see my sister."

"Wait, what? Seriously?" Jason sits staring after her as she walks away. And then he takes another bite of his steak, followed by a long sip of wine.

CHAPTER EIGHT

Adrienne decides to walk from the restaurant to McMurphy's. The temperature has dropped significantly in the past few hours, but she doesn't notice. Her mind races flooded with memories. *Don't go there*, she warns herself. December 22nd is four days away, and on that one day every year she lets herself think briefly about her parents. This December 22nd it will officially be four years since they passed away. That day is one she will never forget. The sharp pain the memory causes makes it feel like it happened yesterday, but in so many ways it seems like a lifetime ago. She and Gretchen sipping warm spiced apple cider, sitting in the family room with the fire blazing, the Christmas tree lights sparkling, and *Hark! The Herald Angels Sing* softly filling the room. It was a magical feeling, their house at Christmastime. The four hand-knit stockings hung from the mantel, stretched and faded with time. The stocking holders spelled out NOEL, with Adrienne's monogrammed stocking hanging from the "E." Their parents had gone out to a Christmas party, and didn't plan to stay late. They said they would rather be spending time with "their girls."

It must have been about 10 p.m. when the girls heard a knock at the door. Gretchen was teasing that it was probably a singing telegram sent by Adrienne's then-boyfriend, Gabe Perkins. But the mood changed immediately when Adrienne looked into the eyes of Sheriff O'Doyle. The world stopped at that moment – Adrienne didn't even hear what the Sheriff said. It was as if someone was holding their hands over her ears -

the words were muffled. But she heard the few words that mattered: "car accident," "nothing anyone could do," and "so sorry."

From that December, four years ago until this very day, Adrienne and Gretchen's childhood home in Connecticut has been empty. The joy it once brought is in stark contrast to the aching sorrow it now brings.

Christmas of that year was not a celebration, nor has any Christmas been since. And the sisters quickly drifted apart – each other a reminder of what their family was and would never be again.

Adrienne reaches McMurphy's and takes a deep breath before pulling open the heavy door. Stepping inside she is greeted by the sound of pop Christmas music, groups of jovial men and women talking and laughing loudly over the noise, and the smell of stale beer and popcorn. But it's warm, and for this Adrienne is thankful.

She spots her sister quickly and sees that Gretchen has saved her a seat by putting caution tape around one of the bar stools. This makes Adrienne want to laugh, and cry, at the same time. *How did they let it get this way? Why did they focus so much on their differences?*

Adrienne weaves a path through the crowd to make her way to the bar. She gets to the tape-wrapped bar stool and starts ripping the tape enough so she can fit on the seat.

Gretchen hears the ripping tape from across the bar and whips around yelling, "Hey! That seat is spoken for . . .." Stopping mid-sentence as she sees Adrienne. The two lock eyes, both with their guard up waiting for each other's reaction.

"I'll have a vodka tonic with a twist of lime please," Adrienne offers a small smile.

"Vodka. Must have been a rough night. You're here earlier than I expected – dinner not go so well."

"That's the least of my worries. How are you doing? Your hair is so long!"

"Yeah, it is. Why, do you not like it?" She comments as she puts down Adrienne's drink.

"No, that's not what I . . .."

"Excuse me, bartender? Could I get a Heineken and a glass of red?" A middle-aged man interrupts the sisters.

Adrienne sits and nervously sips her vodka tonic as she waits for Gretchen to make the man's drinks. This is going to be even harder than she thought.

"So, what are we going to do?" Gretchen says as she walks back over to Adrienne.

"I have no idea. I don't have $25,000 – do you?"

Gretchen makes a face that says, *what do you think?*

"Right," Adrienne continues, "I could try and sell some of my stuff."

"Adrienne, you are not going to be able to sell $25,000 worth of stuff in thirteen days." Adrienne nods in agreement. "I was thinking maybe we could go back to Chestnut Ridge and talk to someone? Maybe someone will give us a break?" Gretchen offers.

"I can't imagine going back there," Adrienne says quietly.

"What? I can't hear you!" Gretchen yells over the noise.

"Nothing. Forget it. You're probably right – we should go back and see what we can do there. I wonder what the house looks like."

The two sisters look at each other, a thousand words passing through their silence.

"We should go soon. We don't have much time to figure this out," Adrienne says.

"Let's go tomorrow. Can you get off work?" Gretchen asks.

"Well, tomorrow is Saturday, so I can go. Can *you* get off work? Isn't Saturday one of your busiest nights?"

"Yeah, but I can get someone to cover for me. Are you going to come pick me up? Do you remember where I live?"

"I don't have a car, Gretchen. How do you suppose I come pick you up?"

"Rent a car."

"Right. Of course, that's my job. Always have to be the responsible one. You probably don't even have a license, or any money, or a working credit card . . . Geez Gretch, some things never change."

"Don't start with the high and mighty act, okay? At least I'm doing something I love, not like you – working for some corporate machine like a robot."

The two women are standing, red-faced and rigid, their faces only inches apart.

"Is everything okay over there ladies?" Another one of the bartenders asks.

"It's fine," Gretchen says backing away. Then she turns back to Adrienne, "So are you going to come get me tomorrow or what?"

"Do you still live in that dungeon?"

"Funny. Yes."

"I'll see you tomorrow then. Merry Christmas!" Adrienne says sarcastically as she throws a few dollars tip on the bar and grabs her coat.

CHAPTER NINE

Adrienne pulls the rental car up next to the curb in front of Gretchen's apartment building at 9 a.m. the next morning. It's probably the only time of day when the Hell's Kitchen neighborhood is anywhere close to quiet. She packed an overnight bag in case they want to stay the night, but the thought of sleeping in the house back in Chestnut Ridge makes her stomach hurt.

She honks twice -- *Gretchen better be awake*. It would definitely not surprise Adrienne if Gretchen were in her tiny apartment sound asleep. But much to her surprise, Adrienne sees the top of Gretchen's head coming up the stairs from the basement apartment. She's carrying a bulging bag that looks homemade, and another small black leather bag.

"You shouldn't honk your horn this early in the morning! Would it have killed you to come knock on my door? Not everyone is up at 6 a.m. showered and perfectly put together – some people have to work late you know?"

This is going to be a disaster.

"Good morning to you too. I'm stopping to get a coffee, do you want anything?"

"Um, no thanks."

"I'll buy you something."

"In that case, I'll have a chai tea latte and a cranberry scone."

"That's what I thought," Adrienne says as she pulls up to a coffee shop. The great thing about driving around the city early on a Saturday morning – parking spots!

"While I'm in ordering, pull up the GPS on your phone so we know the best route."

"I know how to get home."

"I know how to get home too. I'm just wondering about traffic and the fastest route out of the city. Just do it please!"

The drive out of the city is relatively easy . . . and quiet. Adrienne focuses on the road and Gretchen stares out the window watching the city go by in a blur. Both girls are lost in their own thoughts about going back to Chestnut Ridge. Just as they're about to get onto Route 95 North, a Christmas song comes on the radio. Gretchen quickly reaches for the dial and turns the station.

"Well that's something we can agree on," Adrienne says.

"There had to be something," Gretchen says, and the two sisters smile at each other.

"What's in the black leather bag?"

"It's my camera. I call her Heidi – she's the only thing of value I own."

"You have a name for your camera? Wow, you're further gone than I thought."

"You can tease me all you want, Heidi and I are not bothered by it."

"I can't believe we're going back to Oak Street. It's been so long. It's strange, so many years at that house full of joy – our entire childhoods. Our crazy teenage years and weekends home from college . . . so many happy memories," Adrienne then switches gears. "Yet, all I think about is December 22nd. I can't get past it."

"I know. It's not fair. So much of it isn't fair. I always felt so lucky living there -- I love that house on Oak Street. We had our family and great friends, and then Christmastime in Chestnut Ridge . . . I wonder if the town is still so Christmas crazy."

"I was wondering the same thing. Remember that year when our house was part of the Chestnut Ridge Christmas Home Tour and mom was a giant stress ball trying to make everything perfect?"

"Of course! Every square inch of the house was covered in garland and twinkle lights. It was blinding," Gretchen giggles.

"And then right when everyone is about to arrive, Mom forgot about the gingerbread cookies in the oven and the whole kitchen filled with smoke," Adrienne is now starting to laugh.

"And all the smoke alarms went off, and she and Dad were running around frantically waving brooms and towels in front of the smoke alarms," Gretchen is laughing so hard it's difficult to get the words out.

The two sisters laugh until tears are running down their cheeks and their stomachs hurt. It feels so good.

Before they know it, the girls see the exit off the highway for Chestnut Ridge. Adrienne looks over at Gretchen, "Are you ready?"

"Ready as I'll ever be."

Adrienne drives slowly down Main Street, trying to take it all in. In lots of ways not much has changed, but in other ways it has grown more than they could have imagined. There are twice as many shops and restaurants lining the quaint tree-lined street. Colorful lights are wrapped around every light post, storefronts are decorated with elaborate Christmas-themed displays, wreaths hang above every window, and people bustle along the sidewalks. It's more Christmas-y than the sisters remembered.

"Wow. This is . . . .."

"Yeah, right? Do you remember it being this . . . over-the-top?" Adrienne asks.

"They have definitely stepped it up a couple notches."

Soon the street sign for Oak Street is upon them, and Adrienne takes a slow right turn. They both quietly look out their windows at the houses they have known their whole lives: the Millers, Jacobsons, and Katz families. Mr. and Mrs. Burns are still putting up the giant inflatable Santa in their front yard. There is a lifetime of memories on this picturesque street in this beautiful small town. And one of those thousand memories overshadows all the rest.

Adrienne almost drives right past 22 Oak Street, and not because she doesn't know exactly where it is – but because she doesn't recognize it.

"No. Way." Gretchen says, her mouth hanging open in disbelief.

"What have we done?" Adrienne whispers, unable to take her eyes off the house. The two girls sit and stare at the once proud and beautiful home, which is now in shambles. The classic Georgian colonial now has chipping white paint which leaves gaping holes where the wood shows through, half the shutters are crooked, and one has totally fallen off and sits in the bushes, shingles are falling off the roof all around the three dormer windows, one of the pillars holding up the portico on the front porch looks like it might collapse on anyone who dares approach the front door, the gutters are overflowing with leaves, and the grass is knee-high. It looks . . . empty. Neglected. Sad.

"And I thought my apartment was a dump," Gretchen says.

"Oh, it is."

Gretchen shoots Adrienne a dirty look, "Let's go in and see if the inside looks as great as the outside."

The girls walk up the stone pathway that their father laid by hand one summer while Adrienne was in middle school. Turning the knob and preparing for the worst, Adrienne holds her breath, and can feel that Gretchen is doing the same.

Inside the house it's as if time has stood still. Framed family photographs line the walls and the piano sits in the corner covered in dust. In fact, every square inch of the place is covered in dust. The grand center staircase that Adrienne and Gretchen waltzed down in their prom dresses looks drab and faded - a shadow of its former self. The girls walk from room to room, each step echoing in the silence. It's cold and dark with the drapes closed tight. Gretchen stops in front of a framed photograph she took of the house. It was the Christmas the house was being featured in the Home Tour, and the house looked gorgeous from the street. Gretchen took a photo of it at night, all lit up and covered in garland – wreaths hanging from every window. She had the photo framed and gave it to her mom for Christmas that year. Her mom hung it in the family room every Christmas after that. The last Christmas in the house four years ago, no one ever took it down.

The girls meet back up in the living room in front of the fireplace.

"This is bad," Adrienne says.

"Really bad. What are we going to do? Maybe it looks so dilapidated that no one will want to buy it at auction?"

"People always want to buy on this street. It's a coveted location. It will sell."

"I can't imagine some other family living here," Gretchen says quietly.

"We can't let that happen. We've got to think of something. First, let's get a fire going and I'll run into town to get us some cleaning supplies, food, wine – you know, the essentials. Why don't you see if there's still any fire wood out back in the shed, while I go shopping."

With an initial plan decided on, the girls set off with a sense of determination. Gretchen goes out back for firewood and Adrienne gets back into her car and drives the few short minutes into town. She parks on Main Street in front of the small grocery store, Peas & Pickles. The sidewalk is full of energy and excitement. People shuffle by the Salvation Army Santa Claus on the corner, the tinkling of Santa's bells mixing in with chatter and laughter. The smell of gingerbread and coffee is wafting out of the Dreamy Bean coffee shop next door, and children run by sucking on candy canes, their eyes shining with anticipation. The Christmas spirit is alive and well in Chestnut Ridge – and it's contagious. Adrienne remembers back to her childhood when she walked this very same sidewalk full of wonder, and can't help but catch some of the spirit of the season.

On her way into Peas & Pickles, Adrienne is hit hard by a running child, who at full speed completely knocks her into a stand of poinsettias perched outside the grocery store. Doing her best to avoid knocking the whole stand over, Adrienne turns her body and sees the ground coming up on her fast. Just as she's about to eat pavement she is suddenly saved by someone who catches her under her arms and steadies the rack of plants at the same time. Adrienne gets her bearings, and then taking a deep breath turns around to thank the stranger. Stunned, Adrienne realizes she's staring right into the bright blue eyes of Gabe Perkins, her former boyfriend.

"Gabe?"

"Adrienne?"

"Oh my goodness, thank you so much. You saved me! How are you? It's been . . . It's been a long time."

"It sure has. How have you been? I hear you are still living in the city, working for some big time financial firm on Wall Street."

"Well, it's not as glamorous as it sounds. Believe me. And how about you? Last I knew you were in Law School? Is that right?"

"Yeah, graduated, thankfully," he says with a laugh. "And now I have my own practice here in town – see right over there next to the bank?" He points across the street.

"That's you?! Wow – so exciting! Congratulations! I'm really happy for you, Gabe."

"I see you are back in town for the holidays. That's . . .surprising."

"I know. We haven't been back since . . .well, we haven't been back in a long time."

"We? Who's with you?"

"Gretchen. Just the two of us."

"That's so great that the two of you are here together. You know, there's no place like Chestnut Ridge during the Christmas season."

"Well, isn't that the truth. This town is surely one of a kind. Unfortunately, it's not really a happy reason that we're back. Have you heard about our house?"

"I have. It was posted in the *Gazette*," Gabe says as he points to a rack holding copies of the local newspaper outside Peas & Pickles. "I am really sorry, Adrienne."

"They put it in the paper? I can't believe this is happening."

"Look, I have a meeting right now, but maybe I can help. Why don't you stop by my office later – around 4?"

"Really?!" Adrienne claps her hands together with hope. "That would be so amazing, Gabe. Thank you."

"No promises. But I'll see what I can do."

Adrienne and Gabe say good-bye and Adrienne walks into the grocery store. In a fog, Adrienne strolls through the aisles of the store. Her mind swarming with memories, emotions – this town, the house, Gabe . . . she's shocked by how good it feels to be here - to be home. She feels a warmth she hasn't felt in years. And although part of her wants to break down in tears, part of her also wants to jump with joy.

After getting her groceries and cleaning supplies, Adrienne pops into Corked, the wine shop across the street from the Peas & Pickles. She picks out a few bottles of Cabernet, loads everything into the car and heads back to Oak Street.

Back at the house, Gretchen has started a fire and is sitting on the couch looking through some old albums.

"What do you have there?" Adrienne asks as she walks the grocery bags into the kitchen and puts them on the counter with a thud.

"It's an old Christmas album."

"Uh oh," Adrienne says. "We have a problem."

"Another one? What now?"

"The refrigerator doesn't work, the lights won't switch on. We have no power."

"Oh no. We can't stay here if there's no power – that means no heat," Gretchen says as she walks into the kitchen. She opens the refrigerator and quickly slams it back shut, "Oh wow, that's disgusting."

"Yeah, it's pretty bad. I'll call the power company. What else do we need to do?"

"Oh just come up with $25,000 in twelve days," Gretchen says nonchalantly.

As Adrienne grabs her cell phone to start the process of getting their power turned back on, Gretchen starts to unload the groceries onto the counter. She notices a *Gazette* in one of the bags, and can't help but want to glance through it – for old times' sake. It might be interesting to see what's going on in Chestnut Ridge these days.

Adrienne comes back into the kitchen about ten minutes later and announces that the power company will be sending someone out to turn the power back on within the next few hours.

"Well that's good news.

"Yeah, well, it's amazing what paying your bills can do. But I don't know how much longer I can keep this up. It's just so expensive!"

"Well, no worries. I also have good news," Gretchen says with a mischievous smile.

"What?"

"I've figured out how we're going to get the $25,000."

"If you say rob a bank I'm going to kill you," says Adrienne annoyed.

"No, although the thought did cross my mind. Nope, look at this," Gretchen says holding up the front page of the *Gazette*.

Adrienne walks over and takes the paper from Gretchen, scans it. "You're kidding, right? The Chestnut Ridge Christmas Home Contest?"

"The winner gets $25,000!"

"Gretchen, have you looked around? The only contest our house could win right now is the spookiest Halloween house. Not to mention they are judging the houses on Christmas Eve, which is five days away. Do you know some sort of angel that can wave her magic wand and turn this dump of a house into a Christmas wonderland?"

"Well, no. I don't. But do you have a better idea? We have all the Christmas decorations that Mom used for the Christmas Home Tour that year – remember how beautiful this house used to look during the holidays? We just need to spruce things up a little."

"Well if that's not the understatement of the year, I don't know what is. We don't even have any money to put into it. I mean, the house needs to be painted, the shutters re-hung, the lawn mowed, the bushes trimmed . . . and that's just the exterior."

"Okay, so it'll be a challenge. But I think we can do it. We're Harkinses, remember? We can do anything we set our minds to," Gretchen says as she bumps hips with Adrienne and puts her arm around her shoulders.

Adrienne can't help but smile at Gretchen's enthusiasm and positive attitude. It reminds her of the Gretchen she knew long ago.

"I guess we have nothing to lose . . ." Adrienne starts to come around to the idea. "If we don't win, we're just right back to where we started, and we'll lose the house anyway."

"Now that's the spirit!"

"Okay, let's make a list of everything we need to do." Adrienne loves lists.

The two girls sit down in front of the fire and start their list, both of them excited about having a plan and bringing 22 Oak Street back to life.

Harkins Christmas List:

1. *Mow lawn*
2. *Trim bushes*
3. *Paint house*
4. *Clean gutters*
5. *Fix roof*
6. *Paint front door*
7. *Fix front porch/pillars*
8. *Paint and Re-hang shutters*
9. *Rake leaves*
10. *Dust*
11. *Wash floors*
12. *Clean refrigerator*
13. *Buy Christmas tree*
14. *Decorate interior*

15. Exterior Christmas lights, Wreaths

Sitting back, the girls take a long look at their Christmas List, and the reality sets in. There is a lot of work to do. A lot. And where to begin?

"Okay, so what should we start with?" Gretchen asks.

"Let's see. Well, we can't decorate a dirty house. I say we start with cleaning inside – I bought a bunch of cleaning supplies at Peas & Pickles. Oh my goodness! I forgot to tell you! You'll never guess who I ran into in town?"

"Who?" Gretchen asks, wide-eyed.

"Gabe."

"Gabe Perkins? Oh my – those eyes! Are they still so dreamy blue? How did he look? What's he doing now?"

"Whoa, slow down!" Adrienne laughs. "He's an attorney now – he opened a practice in town next to the bank."

"And my other questions?"

"And yes, he looks good. Really good," Adrienne says and both girls burst into giggles. "And the even better news, he said I should stop by his office later today to see if he can help us with any legal recourse we might have to save the house."

"That's amazing news! You have a date!"

"Gretchen! It's not a date! I have a boyfriend in the city, you know. This meeting with Gabe is strictly professional."

"Right. Of course it is. And this boyfriend in the city – is he the one you had dinner with the other night?"

"Yes. Jason."

"From what I remember, dinner with Jason ended preettttyy early. I'm just saying . . . ."

"Okay then, let's get going on the cleaning. Why don't you start with the refrigerator," Adrienne quickly changes the subject.

"No way. That's all you."

"Okay – let's settle it like we used to. Ready?"

The two girls do three games of "Rock, Paper, Scissors," and as per usual, Adrienne wins. "That refrigerator has your name all over it," Adrienne teases Gretchen. "Have fun!"

CHAPTER TEN

The afternoon is filled with scrubbing, sweeping, mopping and dusting. Gretchen tackles the kitchen and Adrienne works everywhere else. It's amazing what letting in some light can do, Adrienne thinks as she throws open the floor length drapes in the living room and dining room. It's as if the house opened its eyes after years of having them shut tight. Adrienne starts dusting all the furniture, followed by polishing the wood to make it shine. She then sweeps and mops all the wood floors on the main level, and vacuums the area rugs. There is a renewed sense of energy fueling both girls - the work giving them a sense of purpose. The feeling that they can *do* something about what once felt like a hopeless situation has replaced their feelings of desperation.

They stop only to allow themselves a quick bite to eat for lunch, and then they continue on with their work. Sometime during their cleaning a representative from the electric company comes and turns on the gas and electric. With electricity, the house warms up and out of nowhere, Gretchen blasts some Christmas music on the surround sound. She braces herself, thinking Adrienne is going to come yell at her to turn it off. But Adrienne never asks to switch the music, and if Gretchen could have seen her, she would have seen a small smile cross her sister's face.

At about 3:30 p.m., Adrienne walks into the kitchen to see the progress that Gretchen has made. The marble countertops are sparkling, the appliances and cabinets have all been scrubbed down and the floor is glistening. In the rear of the kitchen there is an eat-in kitchen area with floor-to-ceiling windows and a large chandelier. The windows have all been wiped clean and the room is aglow.

"Wow! Gretch – this is incredible! I wasn't sure the kitchen could look like this again," Adrienne says.

"I'm not done yet, but it's quite a transformation, isn't it?"

"Aside from the family room, this has always been my favorite room in the house."

"Well, it's where we spent most of our time. Our family has always liked to eat," Gretchen laughs.

The girls are quiet for a minute as they recall the happy times sitting around the kitchen island eating, drinking and laughing.

"I'm going to go see Gabe now. You should take a break while I'm gone. It's already been an exhausting day."

"Honestly, I'm fine. This is the most energy I've had in a long time."

"Why don't you see if you can find some of the Christmas decorations? I think Mom kept them all in the attic."

"Great idea - I'll do that. And good luck at your 'meeting' with Gabe," Gretchen says with a wink.

Adrienne freshens up quickly in the powder room, where she makes a mental note to come back and scrub . . . all of it, and then rushes out the door. As she pulls the rental car up to the front of Gabe's office, she can't quite calm the buzzing occurring in the pit of her stomach. She takes a few deep breaths and reminds herself that this is business – pretend it's something for work. *Be professional.*

The door chimes when she opens it, and an older woman in her mid-60's sits at the receptionist desk. Christmas music is playing softly, and there are a few tasteful holiday decorations creating an inviting office space. Is it strange that Adrienne no longer wants to tear up Christmas decorations and throw them in the garbage?

"Hello there, dear. Can I help you with something?" the woman asks sweetly.

"Hi. Yes, I have an appointment with Gabe . . . with Mr. Perkins."

"Of course, dear. I'm Louise, and your name is?"

"Oh, sorry. Adrienne Harkins."

"Nice to meet you Ms. Harkins," Louise says with a smile. "You aren't Tom and Elizabeth's daughter, are you?"

Hearing her parents' names spoken aloud for the first time in a long time, Adrienne stiffens. "Yes. Yes I am," she finally manages to squeak out.

"Your Dad was a loan officer at the Chestnut Ridge Bank, right?" Adrienne nods her head.

"Oh, they were such a lovely couple. I am so sorry for your loss, dear. Your Dad really helped my son out of a jam years back. My son wanted to start his own business so badly, but no banks were lending money at the time. But your Dad agreed to meet with him. Danny, that's my son, Danny worked so hard putting a business plan together, and then presented it to your Dad. He was so nervous. Anyway, your Dad saw how hard Danny worked on the presentation, thought Danny had a solid plan and he gave him a small business loan. It changed Danny's life. He has now been a successful business owner for ten years. All thanks to your Father."

"Thank you for telling me that," Adrienne says. "It's nice to hear stories about how my parents helped people."

"That's only one of many. Your Dad helped make this town what it is today. Very few of these businesses you see here on Main Street would exist if not for your Dad's help."

"He was a special guy," Adrienne agrees.

Louise picks up the phone and calls back to Gabe's office.

"He's expecting you, Ms. Harkins. You can go right in," she points toward a closed office door.

Gabe opens his office door before Adrienne can even knock. Adrienne can't help but smile. He really hasn't changed much at all in the years since she last saw him. If anything, he looks better than ever – mature and confident.

"Adrienne, it's so great to see you again," he says, pulling her into a quick hug.

Feeling suddenly hot, Adrienne starts to take off her coat and pull at the scarf around her neck.

"Is it hot in here, or is it just me?" She asks flustered.

Gabe takes her coat and scarf and hangs it on a coat rack.

"Come, have a seat, please," he says motioning toward a chair in front of his desk.

Adrienne sits down and tries to calm her nerves. Why is she so nervous?

"Okay, so tell me what's going on," he says sitting across from her, his face turning serious and concerned.

"Well, as I'm sure you know, no one has lived in the house on Oak Street for years. There is no mortgage on the house - thankfully that was settled with my parents' estate after the accident. However, I was still responsible for paying the taxes on it. And I'm sure you also know, that taxes in Chestnut Ridge are, well, exorbitant. So I fell behind, and then I fell even more behind, and then the amount I owed was just so much I guess I kind of gave up."

Gabe nods his head, and if he's judging Adrienne, he's not showing it.

"And now the tax collector wants to sell it at auction if we don't pay what we owe by the end of the year."

"Ok, so that would mean there is a lien on your home. The tax collector is required to send you three written notices before it can get to the point of an auction – did you receive three letters?"

"Weellll, I may have," Adrienne says meekly.

"What do you mean you *may* have?"

"I vaguely remember getting some letters and seeing the Tax Collector on the return address. A while ago I opened one of them and it was just a reminder that I was past due a few months, from that point forward I sort of ignored all other letters from them."

"And by ignore I'm assuming you mean throw in the garbage?" Gabe asks, lifting an eyebrow.

"Yes."

"Okay then, let's assume they sent you three official notices that you were delinquent and that they would be putting your house up for auction. The tax collector must also post the impending sale in the newspaper and file it with the county clerk's office. I called the clerk's office on your behalf, and it has indeed been posted. And I also saw it listed in the newspaper."

"Is there anything else we can do?"

"Well, once the house goes to auction, it will go to the highest bidder. However, if no one bids on the house they will then sell it to the municipality. This can buy you some time, and if the municipality does purchase it, you have six months to make good on what you owe and get the house back. So right now, let's just hope that most people in town know your story and no one will try and buy it at the auction."

"So we're hoping people feel bad for us and don't make an offer?"

"Yes."

"I'm okay with that," Adrienne says, and she and Gabe start laughing. They look at each other, surprised at how easily they can talk to each other after so much time has passed. The brief look turns into more of a stare, and suddenly feeling self-conscious, Adrienne stands up and walks to the door to get her coat and scarf.

"I don't want to take up too much of your time. I'm sure you have a busy schedule," Adrienne says fumbling to put her coat on.

"I just wish I could be of more help – I was hoping to get them on a technicality. But it seems the tax collector has followed everything to the letter. Literally. Do you have any type of plan B?" Gabe asks.

"You are not going to believe this, but Gretchen has thought of a plan. You know the town Christmas Home Decorating Contest?"

Gabe nods slowly, his face looking slightly confused.

"Well, we're going to enter Oak Street in the contest," Adrienne says sheepishly.

"Really?! I'm surprised . . . It's just that, last I saw 22 Oak it seemed . . . .."

"Like a dump?" Adrienne finishes his sentence for him.

"I don't want to be rude, but yeah, it looked pretty rough."

"You won't hurt my feelings. Honestly, Gretchen and I couldn't believe how bad we let things get. We almost didn't recognize the house when we pulled up to it this morning."

"And you know the contest gets judged on Christmas Eve?"

"Four days. I know."

"So what's the plan?"

"We've started cleaning the interior already, and we have a long to-do list. We're just going to try our best. It seems like our only chance. And I have to admit, so far it has been fun sprucing the place up."

"Your parents would be so happy," Gabe says softly.

Adrienne nods her head as the two of them walk to the receptionist area.

"Okay, then I only have one more question. What can I do to help?"

"Really? That would be amazing! Like I said, we have a huge to-do list. Want to come over later and take a look at it? See what you think you could help with?"

"Absolutely. I'll be there."

"Oh, and another thing - we have no budget."

"Right. I figured that."

Just as Adrienne is about to pull the door open, it's pushed in from the outside and almost hits her. She jumps back, startled.

"Excuse me," says a deep voice. "Didn't mean to getcha there."

"Mayor Jessup, to what do we owe the pleasure?" Gabe asks.

"Hello Gabe. And who is this lovely lady?"

Adrienne extends her hand for a handshake, "Adrienne Harkins. It's a pleasure to meet you, sir."

"Harkins? As in the Harkins from Oak Street?"

Nodding her head slowly, a dreadful feeling starts to form in the pit of her stomach.

"Well isn't this fortuitous! I came down here to talk to Gabe about your house," the Mayor says turning toward Gabe. "I was wondering if you had any information on the tax auction. I have always loved that house, and I plan to make an offer when the sale starts. Any idea of the day of the sale?"

"The house isn't for sale," Adrienne blurts out, louder than she had hoped.

"Oh, I'm sorry, was I misinformed? Is there no longer a lien on the house?"

"Technically, there is, but not for long. The house will not make it to auction."

Mayor Jessup smiles in a way that makes Adrienne want to pop him right in the nose.

"So you have some plan to come up with $25,000?"

"What Adrienne is saying, Mayor Jessup," Gabe steps in, "is that the Harkins girls love their home and plan to make every effort possible to keep it in their family."

"Well isn't that too bad," the Mayor says, although the smile has not left his face. "I'm so sorry you girls don't want to have to sell your home. But if you loved this home as much as you claim to, you probably should have paid your taxes, sweetheart."

Her face flushed and her hands clenched into tight fists, Adrienne musters all the restraint in her body to control herself.

"22 Oak Street will not make it to auction," Adrienne repeats herself, her voice cold and steady.

"Okay, sweetheart. You've got a few days – I hope you've got a plan."

"We're going to win the Christmas Home Decorating Contest, and . . ." But Adrienne is interrupted by the Mayor's obnoxiously loud laughter.

"Oh, that's rich," he says continuing to laugh. "Good luck with that." The Mayor then turns to Gabe, "It was nice seeing you Gabe, and meeting you Ms. Harkins. You both have a good day now," he says laughing all the way out the door.

"And don't call me sweetheart!" Adrienne yells after him

.

CHAPTER ELEVEN

Walking into 22 Oak Street, Adrienne looks around at the house that was once her home and feels the weight of what's at stake. The burst of positive energy she felt only a few hours earlier has been replaced by an overwhelming feeling of despair. The family room is crammed with green and red clear bins which are filled with Christmas decorations. Adrienne can't seem to push the Mayor's smug smile and wicked laugh out of her head. Are she and Gretchen just fooling themselves? Is entering this competition a ridiculous, desperate idea? If they lose the competition, they lose everything. The pressure of it all sits heavy on Adrienne, and she puts her hand on her chest where a deep ache is forming. Her breath is coming in short bursts, and sweat forms on her brow.

Unknowingly disrupting Adrienne's panic attack, Gretchen comes prancing into the family room carrying a glass of wine and singing "Rockin' Around the Christmas Tree" at the top of her lungs. She's swinging her hips and twirling around the boxes of holiday décor. Her long wavy hair is down and she looks so carefree. She looks like Gretchen again. The shock of seeing her sister so cheery and brimming with holiday spirit knocks the anxiety right out of Adrienne's body. Her own mood swings from new low to giddy and laughing. What a rollercoaster of a day it's been.

At the sound of Adrienne's laughter, Gretchen whips around and sees her sister staring at her.

"What, too early for wine?"

"Not at all. Just surprised to see you so . . . cheery," Adrienne says amidst her giggles.

"It must be this house, you know. I've been feeling it since we got to Chestnut Ridge – this feeling that we're supposed to be here. We're supposed to be doing this . . . do you know what I mean?"

"I think I do," Adrienne says, only half-believing it.

"How was the meeting with Gabe?"

"It was great – well, it started off great, and then took a turn. What do you want to hear first, the good news or the bad?"

"Good news first!"

"The good news is that Gabe is going to stop by later and see what he can do to help with the to-do list."

"Awesome! I don't know what I'm more excited about – the extra help which we desperately need, or getting to look into those beautiful blue eyes again," Gretchen swoons.

"Oh my goodness, Gretchen. You have lost your mind!"

"You are thinking it too. So, what's the bad news?"

"Unfortunately we have two pieces of bad news. First, it does not look like we have any legal recourse. The town dotted all their 'i's and crossed all their 't's, so to speak. And secondly, Mayor Jessup came to Gabe's office while I was there, and he plans to make an offer on the house when it goes to auction."

"You mean *if* it goes to auction. And I'm not going to worry about that, because we are going to win best Christmas house in Chestnut Ridge and everything is going to work out," Gretchen does another twirl around the family room.

"How much wine have you had?" Adrienne teases her.

"Not nearly enough. Why don't you grab a glass as well, and we'll start to dig through these Christmas boxes."

Pouring a glass of wine, Adrienne then turns up the Christmas music, her spirits lifted. *Everything is going to work out.* It has to.

The girls get deeply involved in taking inventory on their Mom's Christmas decorations. They have separate piles for outdoor lights, indoor lights, outdoor wreaths and garland, indoor garland, tree ornaments, mantel decorations, and the list goes on. It seems as though the boxes will never be emptied as hours go by and the girls sift and sort.

"I had no idea Mom had this much Christmas stuff!" Gretchen says.

"Me neither! She really did lose her mind when the house was featured in the home tour. I think she bought every Christmas decoration within twenty-five miles of Chestnut Ridge," Adrienne says with a laugh.

Gretchen holds up an ornament in the shape of a Christmas tree and with a wild smile on her face says, "You know what we need to get, don't you?"

"A Christmas tree? Oh my, I haven't had one in years! But I guess you're right, we can't win a Christmas house decorating competition without a Christmas tree."

"I need a break from these boxes anyway – let's go now!"

The two girls jump up and hurry to grab their coats. And without knowing why, neither of them can stop giggling. Bundled up in puffy coats, pom-pom hats and scarves they fling the front door open. In her haste, Adrienne smacks right into Gabe Perkins who was about to knock on the front door.

"Oh my goodness – I am so sorry!"

Gabe laughs and puts his hands on both Adrienne's arms, steadying her. "Where are you two off to?"

"We are going to get a Christmas tree! It's great to see you, Gabe," Gretchen leans in and gives Gabe a quick hug. "You should come with us!"

Gabe looks to Adrienne for her response, and when he doesn't get one he says, "I'm ready to work. I can get started without you two. Where's that to-do list I heard about?"

"Next item on the to-do list is to get a Christmas tree. I know we'll need help getting it onto the car. Actually, you have a truck?" She says looking at the shiny new pickup truck in the driveway. "That would be much easier to transport a tree than our little rental car. Right, Adrienne?"

Adrienne, who has been abnormally quiet throughout the whole exchange, suddenly smiles and says, "You should come. We could really use the help."

Thankfully Gabe's pickup truck has a backseat. Gretchen quickly hops in the back. Adrienne shoots her a knowing look, but is secretly thrilled to be sitting in the front seat with Gabe.

"This is a big upgrade from your old rusted Chevy," Adrienne says laughing. "How many times were we broken down on the side of some back road in that thing?"

"Hey, don't knock Larry – he was a great truck. I was so sad to have to get rid of him," Gabe says. "And to be honest, a lot of those times we 'broke down' it was really just me wanting to spend more time with you."

Adrienne blushes and looks away. Gabe fills the silence with commentary on the town and how it has changed over the years. He points out the jewelry store that his sister's friend opened, and the donut shop that a retired police officer opened. It's as if Adrienne and Gretchen are seeing their hometown through brand new eyes. Once they've reached their destination, Gabe pulls the truck into the gravel parking lot at St. Nick's Tree Lot.

"This place is new, too," Gretchen comments.

"Yeah, my buddy owns it," Gabe explains.

"Let's fan out and see what we can find," Adrienne is all business.

Gretchen heads off to the left and Adrienne goes right. It's dark and chilly, but the soft Christmas music, twinkle lights surrounding the lot, and the smell of pine has Adrienne feeling warm inside.

Sneaking up behind Adrienne, Gabe puts his arm around her shoulders, "So what's your favorite tree- Frasier Fir? Blue Spruce?"

Adrienne laughs. "It's been years since I had a Christmas tree, I'm not even sure anymore."

"You haven't had a tree in that long?! It sounds like it's been a rough few years."

Adrienne runs her fingers along a spiky tree branch, "I've just been really busy with work I guess."

"Right. Work. And you like working at Morgan Lynch?"

"It's okay. If I put the time in, the potential is there for me to make serious money. I'm pretty close to getting a promotion, and with that will come my own office, and the option to rent a bigger apartment."

"So you'll make more money, but then you'll just spend all that extra money on a bigger apartment?"

Adrienne shrugs.

"Why not work less, make less and just live a simpler life?"

"Ha! Now I see why you never moved to the city. That's not how things work on Wall Street, Gabe."

"I'm just saying, what's the point of it all if you don't even have time to get a Christmas tree? Or spend time with your family?"

The mention of the word 'family' and Adrienne's body tenses up. She stops in between two blue spruces and turns to face Gabe.

"Family? What family? Last I checked I don't have any."

"You have Gretchen. What's gone on with the two of you these past few years anyway? I can feel there's something different between you now."

"Nothing's 'gone on' between us," Adrienne snaps back defensively. "We are just very different people. We don't have much in common, and we live very different lives. We just drifted apart after my parents died. They were our common ground. And once they were gone, there didn't seem any point in trying to make something out of nothing."

"The point is that she's your sister. You have to make an effort for family."

"There's that word again. It must be nice to have a perfect family – you, your brother, sister and your parents all living close to each other. I bet you have brunch every Friday morning and Sunday dinner every week. We're not all so lucky, Gabe."

Pushing Gabe's arm off her shoulders, Adrienne stomps ahead of him to get lost in the maze of trees.

"Nice job, Gabe," he says to himself out loud.

Wandering through the sea of green, Gretchen is relishing in the smell of pine and hot apple cider. She turns a corner, and then stops short - there it is: the perfect Christmas tree. She walks up to it and leans in to smell it. It's a great shape, looks to be a perfect height, and is nice and full. She runs her fingers down the branches to make sure not too many needles fall off. Nope. It's perfect. But how much does it cost? She sees a tag on a high branch. As she reaches on her tippy toes to grab the tag a white coat-wearing shopper trying to get by her bumps into her from behind. The nudge from the woman is enough to knock Gretchen into the tree. Just as she and the tree are about to crash to the ground someone on the other side of the tree catches it mid-air, saving both Gretchen and the tree from disaster.

"Whoa, watch it now. We don't want anyone having to go to the emergency room right before Christmas," says a scruffy voice, with a hint of laughter.

The stranger pushes the tree back to standing, and Gretchen can then re-plant her feet firmly on the ground. Dusting the pine needles off her jacket she says to her hero on the other side of the tree, "Well that was unexpected! Thank you so much for catching us, whoever you are." The stranger walks around to Gretchen's side of the tree to make sure she has escaped unscathed.

"You might have to wash some sap out of your hair, but otherwise, I think you'll live," he says.

Gretchen looks up, and up, at the very tall man before her. He's got broad shoulders, shaggy dark blonde hair, hazel eyes and an easy smile. Gretchen can't seem to form any words.

The man holds out his hand, "Hi there, I'm Nick. And you are?"

Gretchen reaches out and shakes his hand slowly, unable to take her eyes off him, "I'm Gretchen. And clumsy," she says with a giggle. "Thank you again, Nick."

"Anytime, Gretchen." The sound of her name coming out of his mouth has Gretchen's belly doing flips.

"Can I help you with anything?" He asks her.

"I think you already have."

"I mean, with a tree. Did you find one you like?"

"Oh. Why – do you work here?"

"I do. This is my place."

"Oh, so you're Saint Nick?"

"That's me. I did just save you from a tree accident, didn't I?"

"You did. And since you mention it, I think this is *the* tree." She says pointing to the tree she just fell on. "The two of us are meant to be after that intimate meeting."

"You have to trust your gut with these things. Some things are definitely just meant to be."

Nick and Gretchen continue to stare at each other until they are interrupted.

"Gretchen, there you are," Adrienne says walking over to them. "Did you find a . . ." Adrienne stops mid-sentence as she notices the rugged, handsome guy standing with Gretchen.

"Hi. I'm Adrienne," she says smiling and holding out her hand for a handshake.

Finally, Nick pries his eyes away from Gretchen and introduces himself.

"Hey, Nick! Good to see you man," Gabe says coming up behind Adrienne.

"Gabe – how are you buddy?"

"Good, good. I see you've met Gretchen and Adrienne – old friends of mine. Ladies," Gabe says turning to Gretchen and Adrienne, "this is Nick, as in Saint Nick's Christmas Tree Lot."

"Ohhh, that Nick," Adrienne says. "You've got quite the place here. How long have you been in business?"

"About four years now, I guess. Wow, time sure flies when you're having fun," he says, turning to Gretchen and smiling.

"So Gretch, did you find a tree?"

"I did find a tree, and we're standing right in front of it," Gretchen steps to the side to reveal the tree.

"Hmmm, I like it," Adrienne nods her head as she looks the tree over. "I like the color, it smells great, and is a perfect size. Nice job, Gretchen."

"Well, let's get it wrapped up and in the car then," Gabe says. "Nick, you got us covered?"

"I sure do. What car is yours? I'll have one of my guys bring it over."

"It's my truck – you know it, right?" Gabe says.

Nick nods and instructs one of the young guys working the lot to prepare the tree and take it to the truck. Adrienne, Gretchen and Gabe follow Nick inside the little gift shop attached to the tree lot. As Nick rings up the tree at the register, Adrienne starts peppering him with questions.

"What do you do the rest of the year? You know, when you're not selling Christmas trees?"

"I own a construction company. A few years ago it was a slow winter for construction work, and I had always thought about having a tree lot here in Chestnut Ridge, or as I like to call it, "Christmas Ridge." Have you ever seen a town go so over the top for Christmas?"

"No, I haven't. This place is definitely one-of-a-kind."

"It sure is. I love it here. Anyway, I saw the need for a local tree lot, and made it happen. It's been a really fun side-business during the holidays. Really gets you in the holiday spirit," he says with a twinkle in his eyes.

"I just had a great idea," Gabe says from across the store. "Nick is in construction, which makes him really handy at fixing things . . .."

"Oh my goodness – you're right!" Adrienne says to Gabe, and then turning to Nick says, "We need your help."

Nick walks Adrienne, Gretchen and Gabe out to Gabe's truck as the sisters talk excitedly about the house and all the work that needs to be done to it. They leave with an initial plan for Nick to come over the next morning to see what he can help with. Now doubling their numbers with four people as part of the Christmas Home Competition, Adrienne and Gretchen have double the amount of hope that they just might be able to pull this off. Christmas is the season for miracles, after all.

On the car ride home, Adrienne peeks at her cell phone and sees a couple of missed texts. One is from Elaina and the other from Jason. So as not to spoil her joyful mood, Adrienne shuts her phone off without even reading them. She wants to savor this escape from reality as long as possible.

CHAPTER TWELVE

Pulling his pick-up truck into the driveway of his Craftsman-style home, Gabe sits for a moment trying to make sense of the events of the day. Of course, he has been driving by 22 Oak Street for years watching it slowly decline into the state it's in now. On many occasions he thought about trying to reach out to Adrienne and let her know what was happening, not only with the house, but the town too. But whenever he would pick up the phone to call her, he would remember showing up to her house that day four years ago and finding it empty. Adrienne was gone without a word – no good-bye, no explanation, just gone. Filled with anger and heartache, he would put the phone away, bury his feelings deep down and focus on his work.

And now, just as his business is beginning to take off, and he has been asked to work with the Mayor on a big real estate development deal, Adrienne reappears and turns his world upside down. She seems to have that effect on him. When she turned around today outside of Peas & Pickles, he could have sworn he felt his heart stop, and then once it started beating again it was thumping so loud he was afraid she might hear it. It was like seeing a ghost. Adrienne Harkins.

Being in that house felt like reliving a bad dream – everything looked eerily the same, but nothing is the same. Once a house filled with joy and life and happy memories there is now only sadness and thoughts of what could have been. Walking into his own house where he typically enjoys the peace and solitude, right now feels too quiet. Jittery energy has him pacing around the house not quite sure what to do with his hands that need to be busy. His stomach feels tight and knowing he won't be able to eat right now, he heads straight for his workshop.

The smell of timber, a layer of sawdust that blankets every flat surface, and a variety of wood in all shapes, sizes, and finishes are strewn about in Gabe's garage. Just after Adrienne left, Gabe's sister, Laura, suggested he find himself a hobby – something to keep his hands moving and his mind focused on a task. Gabe thought she was being dramatic, that he was fine dealing with things his way. However, when he stumbled upon a cabinetmaker that needed legal advice, the woodworking process quickly consumed him. By chance, a woman was selling a bunch of woodworking tools and he set up a shop in his garage and started learning to make furniture. Between the furniture making, law school and then setting up his law practice, Gabe has done a great job of staying busy these last few years.

Picking up a sander, Gabe starts to move it back and forth along the long piece of wormy maple. The repetitive motion has a calming effect after only a few minutes, and Gabe can feel his body start to relax. Underneath the sound of the sanding, Gabe can hear his phone start to ring, and he decides to ignore it. Deep down he thinks he knows who is calling, and Gabe is unsure how to deal with the situation. Mayor Jessup must not be happy with the fact that he saw Adrienne Harkins at his office earlier, and Gabe has been expecting the phone call all day. Gabe and Mayor Jessup have decided to partner up and start buying investment properties, and one of the properties on the list the Mayor made, is 22 Oak Street. Gabe thought he had time to figure out how to handle that property, but it looks like his time is running out.

CHAPTER THIRTEEN

Waking up in her childhood bedroom is like waking up in the twilight zone – a pink twilight zone, that is. Adrienne doesn't remember ever liking the color pink very much, so why does it look like a pink bomb exploded all over her room? Her walls are a pale pink, her sheets and bedding are all pink polka dots, and her drapes are long sheer pink panels. It must have been her mom who decided on the décor in here -- the thought sends a pang shooting to Adrienne's heart.

The heavenly smell of coffee is wafting up the stairs and beckoning for Adrienne to get out of bed. Wrapping a robe around her and stuffing her feet into fuzzy slippers, Adrienne follows the aroma. As she enters the kitchen, Adrienne decides she really must be in the twilight zone. Gretchen is up and moving around early, and has made coffee.

"Was waking up in your room as weird for you as it was for me?" Adrienne startles Gretchen.

"You're awake! And, yes. It was déjà vu – but not necessarily in a good way."

"I know, right? You know what is not déjà vu? You being awake before me and making a pot of coffee -- I'm not sure this has ever happened. Ever."

"Very funny. I can't explain it – I have this amazing amount of energy, and I can't wait to get the day started. We have so much to do! Thankfully Nick and Gabe are coming here today to help out."

"Ohhhhhh, now I see where this is all coming from – it all makes perfect sense now! Nick. Of course, Nick is coming over today and you are glowing at 7 a.m. Ha!" Adrienne is laughing at her sister.

"Hey – you won't be laughing when that big, strapping man who is also a construction professional is helping us fix this house."

"Did you just say big, strapping man? Wow – you are so smitten. Beyond smitten. This is going to be an interesting day."

"Right, let's focus on today, can we please? We need to go through our Christmas List and decide what we can do ourselves and what we're going to need help with."

"But first, coffee."

"Do you see what I've done over here?" Adrienne walks over to the big chalkboard that hangs on the far kitchen wall.

The sisters stare at the big number '4' written on the chalkboard.

"A different kind of countdown to Christmas," Adrienne says. "Only four more days to make this happen."

"Right. So, let's get to that Christmas list."

The girls sit at the kitchen island sipping their coffee and looking over the list.

Harkins Christmas List:

1. *Mow lawn*
2. *Trim bushes*
3. *Paint house*
4. *Clean gutters*
5. *Fix roof*
6. *Paint front door*
7. *Fix front porch/pillars*
8. *Paint and Re-hang shutters*
9. *Rake leaves*
10. *Dust*
11. *Wash floors*
12. *Clean refrigerator*
13. *Buy Christmas tree*
14. *Decorate interior*

15. Exterior Christmas lights, wreaths
16. Clean bathrooms

It feels good to be able to cross off a few of the chores they did yesterday – but then they also need to add one more item: clean bathrooms. There will definitely be a game of "Rock, Paper, Scissors," to decide which lucky sister gets to do that.

As Adrienne is re-filling her coffee cup, there is a knock at the door. Not wanting to be seen in her robe and slippers, Adrienne runs upstairs to get dressed while Gretchen, ever relaxed, rolls her eyes and goes to answer the door in her sweatpants. Upstairs in her pink room Adrienne quickly tugs on a pair of jeans and a sweater. She brushes her teeth and runs a brush through her pin-straight hair. Without thinking she starts to smooth her hair back into a bun, but then pauses, looking at herself in the (very dirty) mirror. Having a change of heart she decides to leave her hair down. After a light dusting of makeup she makes her way back downstairs.

Once at the bottom of the staircase, she can hear the sound of chatter and laughter emanating from the kitchen. Adrienne can't help but think that this is what was meant to fill this house: Laughter. Life. Love.

"What's going on in here?" Adrienne walks into the kitchen where she sees Gretchen, her face lit up like a Christmas tree. Nick and Gabe are around her laughing. Even having just woken up and still in her sweats, Gretchen looks beautiful. Her long wavy hair is half up in messy bun, the rest of it falling down her back. She's telling some story that has all of them in stitches. When they see Adrienne, all three of them try to cover up their chuckling – some are doing a better job than others.

"Okay, seriously Gretchen – what are you talking about?"

"Nothing. Nothing," she says starting to laugh again. "Definitely not about that time you insisted on putting lights on the roof so that Santa and his reindeer could find our house, and you slipped and were hanging off the house holding onto a string of lights for dear life. It definitely wasn't that," Gretchen is hysterically laughing at this point. Whatever restraint Gabe and Nick had, is gone, as the three of them laugh so hard they can barely breathe.

"Okay, I see what's going on. You all think the fact that I almost died falling off a roof is funny. Okay. Sure. Well, I just hope that never happens to any of you," Adrienne says. This only feeds their insatiable laughter.

Once the merriment dies down a bit, Gabe walks over to Adrienne who's standing with her arms folded across her chest, and holds out a latte from the Dreamy Bean, the coffee shop in town.

"Forgive me?" He asks her, doing his best to look contrite.

Hiding the smile trying to spread across her face, she says, "Maybe if you had also brought some pastries with my latte."

Just then, Nick smiles and holds up a box of pastries, "like these?"

"Well okay, you're forgiven." Adrienne smiles and reaches for a pastry.

"Now that all the goofing around is over, let's get down to business," Adrienne says. "I'd like to first thank you Gabe, and Nick, for coming here so early on a Sunday morning to help us try and figure this all out. As you may have guessed from when you pulled up to the house, we're in a little over our heads here."

"We're drowning," Gretchen pipes in.

"Gabe explained your situation to me on the ride over, so I'm all caught up," Nick says.

"Did Gabe also mention that we're broke?" Gretchen asks.

"Yes, he mentioned that."

"I will call in any and all favors that I can," Gabe says.

"As will I," Nick agrees. "And there's a lot here that Gabe and I can do on our own, that is, if you two help as well," Nick points to Gretchen and Adrienne.

"We're up for the challenge," Gretchen says, and Adrienne nods her head in agreement.

After further study of the list, it is decided that Gretchen and Adrienne will finish cleaning the house and start decorating inside. Instead of arguing over who has to clean the bathrooms, they decide each of them will clean two bathrooms, considering there are two bathrooms upstairs and two bathrooms downstairs. Since this is the worst item on the list, they choose to do it first and get it over with. The decorating, including trimming the tree they can do later, while sipping wine.

Gabe and Nick talk together for a while and then spend some time on their phones calling all types of friends and associates. Once they are satisfied with the plan, they both take off in separate directions looking for Adrienne and Gretchen.

The sound of muffled Christmas music is coming from the front of the house. Nick follows the sound, stopping by some of the photos hanging on the walls and studying them. When he reaches where the music is coming from, he steps back and watches the show. Gretchen is in one of the downstairs bathrooms, still in her sweatpants, with rubber gloves up to her elbows and all her hair piled on top of head in a giant bun. Music is blasting out of a small Bluetooth stereo and she is dancing around the bathroom sink as she scrubs it clean.

Once she notices she has an audience, Gretchen, embarrassed, stops mid-dance and turns the volume down on the stereo.

"I like to have music on while I clean. Makes it a little more enjoyable."

"You definitely looked like you were enjoying yourself," Nick laughs. "And I was enjoying watching you. You've got some good moves."

"Very funny. So, how's it going? Have you and Gabe figured anything out?"

"We have. The reason I came to find you however – do you know where there might be a lawn mower? And a weed trimmer? There's no way we can start off with the mower – the grass is too high."

"Hmmmm, whatever we have would be in the shed in the back yard. You're going to have to cut the entire lawn with a weed trimmer? And then mow the whole lawn too? Isn't that going to take forever?"

"Ah yeah. Probably. It's a big lawn."

"Okay, I have to ask," Gretchen leans against the sink. "Why are you doing this for us? We only just met you last night and you are going to spend your day cutting our lawn?"

"Honestly, I wasn't sure when I was going to tell you this – but I guess now is as good a time as any. Gabe told me the whole story about your family, and this house, and how things used to be here."

"What, and you feel bad for us? Look, I don't want your pity . . ." Gretchen starts to get upset.

"Let me finish," Nick says. "Gabe told me the whole story about your family, and when he was done I asked him your parents' names. He told me that your Dad was Tom Harkins, and I couldn't believe it."

"You knew my Dad?"

"Your Dad saved me. A little over four years ago, the construction industry around here was in a slump. That was when I had the idea to open up the tree lot for the off-season. I didn't know how I would make it through the winter otherwise. No one was lending money back then, but Gabe suggested I talk to your Dad. I went in and met with him, and he loved my idea. He convinced the bank to give me a small business loan."

Gretchen's eyes are starting to tear-up thinking of the special man her father was. She had really never thought about how his job affected people, and she is so grateful that after all these years she gets to see a whole new side of him.

"Without your Dad, I wouldn't have Saint Nick's – which floated me through that first winter until things picked up again. I only had the opportunity to know him for a short time, but he was a good man – a *great* man. And I feel honored to have the chance to help him the way he helped me."

Gretchen is so touched, without thinking she steps toward Nick and gives him a giant hug, burying her face into his chest.

"Thank you," she whispers.

"It's the least I can do."

As Gabe climbs the stairs to the second floor he still can't believe he is in this house again. Here with Adrienne again. At one point he was at the Harkins' house just as much as he was at his own. But after the accident, when Adrienne shut down and moved away, he never thought he would be back here again. He watched as the house slowly declined into the state it was in now – mirroring the state of the Harkins family.

Hearing movement in the hall bathroom, Gabe takes a peek inside. Adrienne is in there, furrowed brow, rubber gloves, scrubbing the bathtub vigorously.

"Be careful, if you scrub any harder you'll put a hole right through the porcelain."

Adrienne looks up, happy for the interruption.

"You know me, if I'm going to do something, I'm going to do it right."

"It's nice to know that some things about you haven't changed."

Adrienne smiles, "How are things going with you and Nick?"

"Great. We have a good plan, I think. I was wondering if you know where the lawn mower, weed trimmer, ladder, paint cans . . . where everything is. We need everything," Gabe laughs.

"Yeah, this is truly going to be a Christmas miracle if we pull this off."

"I happen to believe in miracles," Gabe's eyes sparkle.

"Well, that's one of us," Adrienne says just as her phone dings – a text message.

Gabe picks up her phone to hand it to her, and glances at the screen.

"Four missed text messages. Yikes – someone is really trying to get in touch with you."

"It's work. I'm ignoring it."

"Do you have to work tomorrow?" Gabe asks her, his voice going up at the end.

"I'm supposed to go in tomorrow. And I should go in, since I'm up for this promotion at the end of the year – which as you know is in a week or so. And I didn't exactly leave things on good terms last Friday."

"It's a family emergency – I'm sure they'll understand."

"Ha! No. No they won't understand. They really don't care. They just want me in the office doing my job and not bothering anyone with my personal life."

"Sounds like a great place to work," Gabe's voice is dripping with sarcasm.

Adrienne's phone dings again.

Picking up the phone to once again hand it to her, Gabe looks at the screen.

"Jason. Who's Jason? Someone you work with?"

Adrienne doesn't know what to say. Here Gabe is, going out of his way to help her and asking for nothing in return.

"Ummmm . . ." Adrienne freezes. She grabs the phone and holds it screen side to her chest. But her face says it all.

"Oh. It's not work."

"Look, Gabe . . .."

"No, it's okay. You don't owe me an explanation. We haven't seen each other in years. I'm not surprised you have a boyfriend. In fact, I would be surprised if you didn't."

Seeing the disappointment on his face, Adrienne wants so badly to tell him it's not true, but she can't lie to him.

"Okay, so where did you say you think all the lawn stuff and paint cans are?"

"In the back shed," Adrienne says quietly.

"Right. Thanks." Gabe turns around and leaves.

CHAPTER FOURTEEN

It takes Adrienne and Gretchen all morning and into the afternoon to clean the bathrooms. When it's done they celebrate with lunch from the great deli in town. They take lunch orders from Nick and Gabe and then Adrienne runs into town to pick up the food. When she returns, as she's pulling up to the house she can't help but feel her spirits lift when she sees Gabe and Nick and some of their crew working on the lawn. Two men used weed trimmers to get the grass down to a reasonable height, and someone else is pushing her Dad's old lawn mower back and forth across the lawn. That alone has made a drastic improvement on the curb appeal of the house – despite the house still being in shambles. Gretchen is walking around the front yard taking photos of everyone helping out. All the activity feels right.

The noise from the mower on the front lawn and the weed trimmer on the side of the yard make it impossible for anyone to hear Adrienne announce lunch. So she walks across the lawn waving one arm in the air as she balances the box of food in her other arm. She then dramatically points to the food to signal lunch. Everyone follows her into the house and back to the kitchen where she unpacks the box. Paper plates get passed around and Adrienne, Gretchen, Gabe, Nick and everyone else helping out dig in to the sandwiches, wraps, chips and drinks.

Adrienne and Gabe haven't spoken to each other since the conversation in the bathroom earlier. The dynamic between them has shifted, with Gabe being polite and cordial, but no longer warm and open. The disappointment Adrienne feels speaks volumes, but she's not ready to listen to what those feelings might mean – not yet. Gretchen, on the other hand, is one big bubble of positive energy bursting all over the place. She flirts and laughs with Nick every chance she gets, and is constantly making everyone feel appreciated, which Adrienne is grateful for, since she can't muster up that energy right now.

Finding Gabe alone for a minute, Adrienne walks over and says, "Looks like you guys made a lot of progress already."

"Yeah, it's coming along. Didn't know how big this lot was until I started trying to cut the grass with a tiny weed trimmer."

"Gabe, listen, you have already helped us so much, if you have more pressing work to do, I would totally understand if you can't come back here tomorrow."

"I'm doing this for your parents, Adrienne, not for you. They were a big part of my life for years, and I feel I owe them. So please, don't feel guilty or worry about me, which I'm sure you're doing. I'm fine. This is where I want to be."

As Gabe walks away, Adrienne stands in the hallway feeling foolish - like someone just punched her in the stomach. How could she have been so presumptuous, to think Gabe would be interested in getting back together with her? It has been years since she abruptly walked out on him. He could have a girlfriend for all she knows.

"What's wrong," Gretchen walks up beside her, "Is everything okay?"

"Yeah, it's fine. It's just Gabe . . .."

"Oh yeah, I see how you two look at each other," Gretchen smiles.

"No, no – it's not that. It's actually the opposite of that. I'm pretty sure he hates me."

"Um, no. Not possible," Gretchen shakes her head. "I hear he hasn't dated anyone seriously since you left."

"Really?" Adrienne asks, feeling a little better.

"Really," says Gretchen. "Now enough boy talk – let's get back to work."

"Right. Yes. What should we do next? Start decorating the family room?"

The two girls gather garland and bows and wreaths and start to decorate the family room. With Christmas music playing, the sisters continuously chitchat about each item they hold up – sharing memories and laughing. Gretchen holds up her and Adrienne's stockings and the sisters pause and stare at each other. Adrienne stops what she's doing, walks over to Gretchen and the two of them put up the stocking holders that spell out "NOEL" and place their Dad's under the N, their Mom's under the O, Adrienne's under the E and Gretchen's under the L. Then they both stand back and admire the mantel.

"It's just as I remember it," says Gretchen. Adrienne nods her head in agreement. They both take one more minute to savor the moment, and then move on.

Around 5 p.m. everyone is feeling exhausted. The few men Gabe and Nick had helping go home, and Adrienne and Gretchen plop themselves on the couch. The family room and dining room are decorated. There is garland wrapped around the staircase railings with big bows at the curved bottom of each side. Lighted garland illuminates the mantel with the stocking holders, ornaments and two large gold candles. Above it hangs a giant wreath with a large gold bow. Crystal snowflakes hang from the chandelier in the dining room. The dining room table is set with a gold runner down the center, and candles, pine cones, and silver and gold balls lining the runner. All the empty bins have been moved back up into the attic, and any other bins still filled with decorations have been moved to the back den. A warm glow fills the clean space, with candles and twinkle lights galore. Their mom would be proud.

When Gabe and Nick come inside they can't believe how amazing it looks.

"This is absolutely gorgeous," Nick says.

"It really takes me back," Gabe says quietly.

"But you know what you still desperately need?" Nick asks. The girls look at him confused.

"You need to decorate that poor Christmas tree!"

Everyone now turns to look at the sad looking bare Christmas tree, and they all start to laugh.

"I have an idea," Gretchen says with a smile. "Why don't we light a fire, pour some wine, order takeout Chinese food, and all decorate the tree together!"

A huge smile forms on Nick's face, "I love it. I'm in," he says.

But Gabe and Adrienne hesitate. "You've been here all day, Gabe. If you need to go . . ."

"You can't go!" Gretchen says. "You worked all day, now it's time for the fun. Come on!"

Gabe starts to come around, "Okay. Okay—I can stay for a little while."

"Yay! Okay, I'll go get the wine. Adrienne, you order the food."

Before long, all four friends are laughing and telling stories as they eat, drink and trim the tree. The fire is blazing, Christmas music plays in the background and the room is filled with warmth and happiness. It's one of the best nights Adrienne and Gretchen can remember in a very long time.

On the kitchen counter sits Adrienne's cell phone, buzzing constantly as she misses texts and emails from New York.

CHAPTER FIFTEEN

While sitting at the kitchen island with their coffee and leftover pastry, Adrienne and Gretchen stare at the chalkboard on the wall. There is a big number '3' looming over them and a long Christmas to-do list in front of them.

Harkins Christmas List:

1. ~~Mow lawn~~
2. Trim bushes
3. Paint house
4. Clean gutters
5. Fix roof
6. Paint front door
7. Fix front porch/pillars
8. Paint and Re-hang shutters
9. Rake leaves
10. ~~Dust~~
11. ~~Wash floors~~
12. ~~Clean refrigerator~~
13. ~~Buy Christmas tree~~

14. ~~Decorate interior~~
15. Exterior Christmas lights, wreaths
16. ~~Clean bathrooms~~

"It's a bit overwhelming, isn't it?" Adrienne says.

"We just have to focus on all the things we've gotten done already. Look what we've accomplished in two days!"

"But I feel like we've done the easy things. I'm pretty sure it takes a couple days to paint a house, or fix a roof . . . And you know what's not on there?"

"What?"

"Sign up for the contest. We need to go down to town hall today and officially sign up. We should probably go right at 9 a.m. when they open – it's usually less busy then."

"You're right," Gretchen agrees. "Well, there's no time like the present. Let's go get dressed and get moving – we have a busy day ahead."

While upstairs getting ready, Adrienne's phone rings, and without thinking she answers it.

"I assume you're on your way in to the office?"

Elaina.

"Oh my goodness, I forgot. It's Monday."

"You forgot it's Monday? Adrienne what is going on? We have a busy week, and you need to be here."

"I'm actually having a bit of a family emergency – and, so, I'm in Connecticut."

"Connecticut? Okay, family emergency – right. You can have today off – but I expect to see you here bright and early tomorrow morning. And we will be deducting this day from your time off."

"I've never taken time off."

"Now you have, haven't you? Fix whatever is going on, and get back to the city tomorrow."

Adrienne finishes getting dressed and meets Gretchen downstairs. They get into their rental car and drive into town.

"My boss just called me," Adrienne tells Gretchen.

"Oh, really? Is everything okay?"

"Not exactly. She says I need to be in the office tomorrow . . . and the rest of the week."

"You told her you couldn't go, right?"

"Not exactly. I don't know what I'm going to do."

"What do you mean? You can't leave, Adrienne. You know, this is so typical – you bailing out when things get hard – rushing off to work and work and work and not care about anything going on around you," Gretchen is surprised by her own anger.

Adrienne glances over at Gretchen. Her mouth is drawn in a straight line, eyes squinting with indignation.

"You can't just blame me for all the problems in your life, Gretchen. I had to work hard. And if I remember correctly, you took off too after mom and dad died."

Gretchen doesn't say anything; she just continues to stare out the front window.

"I'm not going into work tomorrow. Okay? I'm not going to leave. It's just that I'm up for this promotion that I've been working really hard for, and they announce it at the end of the year . . .But I am going to stay here and help out. I'll figure something out with work later."

Arriving at Chestnut Ridge Town Hall, Adrienne takes a moment to admire the old building's brick façade and large rounded columns. Right now, across the large triangular pediment hangs a big sign announcing the Christmas Home Decoration Contest. Upon seeing the sign, Adrienne and Gretchen smile at each other, doing their best to move past their argument in the car.

At the receptionist desk, a woman in a white blouse has her back to the girls, as she talks on the phone. Once she hangs up, she spins around and both girls' mouths drop open in surprise.

"It's you," they both say at the same time. And then, even more taken aback, say to each other, "You know her?"

"Ladies, what a lovely coincidence," Angela says with that dazzling smile.

"You work here in Chestnut Ridge? I thought you worked at iTech?" Adrienne asks, confused.

"Well, I am an independent contractor in the tech space, so I travel all over helping different companies with their systems. I was just filling in at iTech for the day, since I know the owner. And now, the Chestnut Ridge Town Hall has asked that I help them update their computer software – so here I am! Such a fun coincidence, don't you think?" She sings, her hazel eyes sparkling.

"It's wonderful!" Gretchen matches Angela's enthusiasm.

"Now, what can I do for the two of you?" she asks straightening out her perfectly white, perfectly tailored pantsuit.

"We would like to sign up for the Christmas Home Decoration Contest, please," Adrienne says.

"Well, isn't that exciting! All you need to do is fill out this paperwork here," Angela says, handing them a clipboard and pen.

As Adrienne starts to fill out the entrance form, Angela and Gretchen chat like old friends. Just as Adrienne is handing over the clipboard to Angela, the group of women is interrupted by a booming voice.

"I see you were serious about the competition, Ms. Harkins."

Adrienne looks over and standing there in his three-piece suit is Mayor Jessup.

"Oh, hello there Mayor," Angela says in her never-ending cheery voice. "Ladies, do you know Mayor Jessup? You should get to know him, since he is one of the judges of the Christmas Home Decoration Contest!"

"You are one of the judges?!" Adrienne practically yells.

"I am. Isn't that fantastic? And don't worry, Ms. Harkins, I am a fair man," he says with a crooked smile. "Good day to all of you, and Ms. Harkins, best of luck."

"He is creepy," Gretchen says as he walks away.

"Oh he's not that bad, once you get to know him," Angela says.

"Not bad? He's the worst. He wants to buy our house when it goes to auction. Now we have no chance of winning at all – we might as well not even enter." All the hope was just sucked right out of Adrienne's body within seconds. "It was already a long-shot, now it's just downright impossible."

"Don't think that way, Adrienne," Gretchen says. "There is more than one judge on the panel -Mayor Jessup does not get to decide alone."

"She's right," Angela pipes in. "There are five judges in the competition. The Mayor is only one of them."

"See! We can't give up now," Gretchen says.

Pulling their little red rental car up to 22 Oak Street, Adrienne and Gretchen sit and stare at the scene unfolding at their house. Adrienne blinks her eyes a few times to be sure they are not playing tricks on her. There are a whole slew of people on their front lawn. Two men standing on ladders cleaning out the gutters, one guy has a hedge trimmer and is shaping the hedges beautifully. Two men are on either side of the door raking leaves out of the bushes and collecting the leaves that are falling from the gutters.

Adrienne and Gretchen slowly get out of the car and stare in disbelief. Spotting Gabe, the two girls quickly rush up to him.

"What is all this? Did you do this?" Adrienne asks him.

"I just let people know what you two were trying to do – I didn't have to ask. You see over there?" He points to a man in buffalo plaid winter hat. "That's Pete Wallace. Your Dad gave him a loan to start his own landscaping business. He brought some of his employees over to help and show his appreciation. And over there," Gabe points to an older gentleman, "that's Charlie Matthews – your Dad gave him a loan over 20 years ago – he owns Matthews Garden Supply shop in town. He has offered to provide any type of greenery you need to spruce things up."

Adrienne and Gretchen are speechless. Gretchen grabs Gabe in a giant hug, and Adrienne has her hands clasped together at her heart.

"Let me continue," Gabe says. "Right over there where they have started prepping the house to be painted, is Kurt Jeffries and he owns an indoor/outdoor painting company – and you guessed it, your Dad gave him the loan to get started."

"I can't believe they would do this for us," Adrienne says quietly.

"Your family means a lot to this community," Gabe says. "And this is just the beginning."

Gretchen runs inside and a moment later emerges from the house with her camera. She walks around the yard taking photos of all the workers. Adrienne follows Gretchen around, stopping to thank each and every person who has shown up to help.

Adrienne spies Gabe helping pick up clippings from the bush trimming, and she smiles shyly. He offers a small smile back. The fact that there are still people in this world, right here in Chestnut Ridge, that are so generous and kind astonishes her. These people are helping out in the freezing cold, a few days before Christmas, donating their precious time to help her. And they expect nothing in return. The thought forms a lump in her throat, and Adrienne swallows hard to keep the tears away.

A little bubble of hope floats back up to the surface – and she has an idea. She runs in the house and up to her bedroom, grabs some old speakers she used to listen to in high school, and then hits up the garage for an extension cord. She runs the extension cord from the front family room out the door and plugs in her old speakers. Connecting her phone to the speakers, Adrienne blasts her favorite Christmas channel. As soon as "Jingle Bell Rock" blasts on, everyone working pauses for a moment, looking over at Adrienne. Within seconds the lawn is filled with singing, some dancing, mostly from Gretchen who miraculously found Nick and hasn't left his side since, and even a few cheers. Satisfied with herself, Adrienne walks over, grabs a rake and starts to pitch in.

After a long day of yard work in the frigid temperatures, Adrienne and Gretchen snuggle under blankets in front of the fireplace eating big bowls of pasta. The wind whistles outside, but the girls are warm and cozy as they sip wine and sink into the couches, their bodies exhausted.

"So much got done today, can you believe it?" Gretchen asks.

"I know, but I'm still nervous about how long it will take to paint the house. I think they mostly got it all prepped today, which now it looks even worse after they power-washed it and removed all the shutters. I'm worried about getting the whole exterior painted, the roof and the front porch pillars fixed in time – we only have two days left!"

"We just have to believe. We have to believe it will work out," Gretchen says with determination.

Adrienne smiles at Gretchen, wishing she could feel as confident.

"I don't want to upset you, but I feel like we should bring this up – what are you going to do tomorrow? Are you going into work?"

Adrienne pauses for a long time before she says, "I think I have to go in tomorrow. I'll leave really early and drive in, and try and be back in Chestnut Ridge by 6 p.m., that way . . ."

"Adrienne, why do you feel the need to do that? Aren't you allowed a few days off around the holidays?"

"It's my job, Gretchen. And I know I messed up this year keeping up with the bills, but for the three years before that, my job helped us keep this house. I have committed to something, and need to see it through. It's the responsible thing to do."

"And what about the house?"

"You'll have to run the show here tomorrow. It shouldn't be too hard – Gabe and Nick will be here to help, at least part of the day."

"Shouldn't be too hard? Weren't you just saying how many big projects still need to be finished, and that we only have two days?"

"Gretchen. You can do it. And I'll be home by six to help out."

Gretchen rolls her eyes.

A loud crash echoes through the quiet house. Adrienne and Gretchen jump up off the couch, eyes wide and ears alert.

"What was that?" Adrienne asks.

"I have no idea! It sounded like it was coming from the garage."

The girls quickly walk through the kitchen to the door that accesses the garage. Adrienne opens the door and her mouth drops open.

"Oh no!" she stares into the once empty garage.

"Is that a tree?!" Gretchen says in disbelief.

"It must be from the wind. Thank god we didn't park the rental car in here. It would be crushed."

"What are we going to do?" Gretchen starts to get panicky.

"This is the last thing we need right now – like our problems aren't bad enough."

"I'll call Nick. He'll know what to do."

CHAPTER SIXTEEN

Gabe and Nick sit at a high top table at the Chestnut Tavern, sipping their beers slowly and listening to a live band sing upbeat Christmas songs. The two met years ago when Nick was opening up Saint Nick's Tree Lot and needed a lawyer to help with the business. Both Giants fans and interested in working with their hands they discovered they had a lot in common and became fast friends. With Nick's family all living in Pennsylvania, the Perkins' family welcomed him with open arms. He is now at Sunday dinner every week with Gabe's parents and siblings, and is even the godfather to one of Gabe's nephews. They are now more like brothers than friends, and know each other better than anyone. That's why Nick can't help but notice that Gabe is extra quiet and distracted tonight.

"Okay, what's going on? You have been acting weird for days. Is your mom still mad we missed Sunday dinner last night? Or is it having Adrienne back here that's got you all freaked out? What's wrong?"

"I'm not freaking out. And yes, mom is still mad we didn't show up to dinner last night. I told her you met a girl and I was just being your wingman. I can't tell her it has anything to do with the Harkins family."

"Does your mom not like Adrienne?"

"She loved Adrienne, that's the problem. My mom always said Adrienne and I would find our way back to each other, or some crazy talk like that. 'Adrienne just needs time, she had a traumatic loss . . .' you get the picture. If I tell her Adrienne and I are back in touch she'll start planning the wedding."

"Look, I remember you after Adrienne left – that was right around the time we met. You were a mess, so I understand the significance of you seeing her again." Gabe looks down at his beer thinking back to that low point in his life. "How are you feeling about Adrienne?"

"I'm trying not to feel anything about her. I honestly don't know if I could ever trust her again after what she did to me. But we were together for a long time, and now we have these moments where it all just feels so . . . right. She has a boyfriend anyway. So it probably doesn't matter what I think about her."

Nick nods his head. "So, Adrienne's back in town and rocking your world, I get that. But there is something else going on, too. And we're not leaving this bar until you tell me. So you should just go ahead and let it out, man. Or it's going to be a loooong night," Nick smiles.

"Okay, but you can't tell anyone this – especially not Gretchen." Gabe looks to Nick for confirmation of secrecy, and Nick nods his head. "A few months ago I partnered up with Mayor Jessup on a joint venture to buy and sell real estate – investment properties. He came to me recently with a long list of properties he thought we should consider and look into. On that list was 22 Oak Street," Gabe looks at Nick whose eyes widen in surprise. "There were so many other properties on the list, I really didn't think I had to worry about Oak Street, until I saw the notice in the *Gazette* about it going to auction at the end of the year. I knew Adrienne and Gretchen hadn't been to it in years, so I figured maybe they would want to sell it. But obviously, things have changed. And I'm running out of time."

"Wow. That's heavy. Can I ask, and don't get mad at me here, but why on earth would you partner with a guy like Mayor Jessup? That was your first mistake, in my opinion."

"Thanks man, that's really helpful. It is a good, no, a great, business opportunity. And I figured I could keep the guy honest. But now, with Adrienne and Gretchen back, and all they are trying to do to save the house. I can't be part of buying it out from under them."

"You know you have to tell Adrienne this, right?"

"I know. I need to decide what I'm going to do first so that I have something to tell her. Right now, if the Mayor knew how much I have helped them try and fix the place up, the whole partnership would blow up."

"Well now I see why you are so stressed out. You're playing both sides here, Gabe. You are helping the girls try and save the house, and planning to buy it from them at the same time. That has got be weighing on your conscience. You need to make a decision. Like, yesterday."

Gabe rolls his eyes at Nick. "Thanks buddy. That makes me feel so much better."

CHAPTER SEVENTEEN

While Gretchen goes back in the house to call Nick, Adrienne goes in the garage to further inspect the damage. The tree that fell on the roof of the garage has caused an entire section of the garage to cave in. Glass, plaster, leaves, branches and splintered wood are everywhere – it's a total disaster. The wind is howling through the gaping hole in the structure whipping Adrienne's hair around. That little bubble of hope that had floated to the surface has now begun its descent back into despair.

Aware that there is absolutely nothing she can do at this point, Adrienne goes back inside.

"Nick is going to come over. He says not to go in the garage since it could be very unstable in there, and more could crash in."

Not saying a word, Adrienne walks over to the couch where she was sitting, picks up her wine glass and takes a long sip.

"This is a sign," Adrienne says.

"No, this is an old tree on a windy night. You don't believe in signs."

"I didn't believe in signs, but now I'm thinking I should. Just as we're starting to make progress, we get knocked back down again. Story of my life."

"I'm going to stop your little pity party right there," Gretchen says firmly. "This is just us being tested – to see how much we can overcome to make this happen. It's just another little bump in the road."

"This is more like a crater, Gretchen. I mean, how are we going to even pay for this? This isn't someone helping to mow the lawn or clean the gutters – this is major structural damage."

"I might be able to come up with some money," Gretchen says.

"Okay . . . and where might this mysterious money be coming from?"

"Don't worry about it. I'll see what I can do tomorrow."

"Tomorrow. Oh no! I'm supposed to go in to the office tomorrow. What am I going to do?"

Gretchen shrugs her shoulders, not wanting to tell Adrienne what she thinks she should do, for fear of upsetting her even further. She knows this is something Adrienne has to decide on her own.

Sooner than expected there is a knock at the door. Gretchen rushes to answer it, and there is a sense of relief when Nick and Gabe walk in.

"Are you two okay?" Nick asks.

"We're fine. Just shocked," Gretchen says.

"Thank you so much for coming – you didn't have to both come," Adrienne says looking at Gabe. "And how did you two get here so fast?"

"We were down at the Chestnut Tavern in town when Nick got the call, so we were only a few minutes away," Gabe answers.

"Let us go take a look. You two stay here," Nick says to the girls.

Although Adrienne would never admit it, it is a huge relief having the two guys here to help. She doesn't have the energy to deal with this right now - thinking about it just makes her feel tired. *And now what should she do about work?*

Adrienne's cell phone starts ringing, and with her mind racing she answers quickly without looking at the screen.

"Adrienne? Is this really you? I wasn't sure you were still alive."

Jason.

"Jason! How are you?" Adrienne walks into the family room and away from Gretchen's curious ears.

"*I'm* fine. Where have you been? No one has seen you since that Friday morning meeting, and then you don't show up to work today. People are starting to talk . . .."

"What do you mean people are starting to talk? What are they saying?"

"Oh you know, the typical gossip – nervous breakdown has been mentioned . . .."

"Nervous breakdown? You've got to be kidding me. I'm out one day and now I've had a nervous breakdown?"

"Once you come in tomorrow, everyone will see that you're fine and the rumors will go away. You are coming in tomorrow, right?"

"Ummmmm, well . . . .."

"Adrienne, I know you are having some issue with your sister, but you've been working toward this promotion for years. If you don't come in tomorrow you are risking everything – all that work will have been for nothing."

"I know. It's just that, this house – my house, we have a lot going on here, and I don't feel like I can just leave it all on Gretchen's shoulders."

"Who's Gretchen?"

Frustrated, Adrienne tries to answer patiently, "Gretchen is my sister."

"Right. Okay, here's what you're going to do: Sell the house, split the money with your sister – and come in and get that promotion. It all sounds pretty simple to me."

"I wish it were that simple."

Gabe, Nick and Gretchen walk into the family room talking about the garage.

"Look, I have to go – we've got an emergency here. I'm going to have to talk to you later," Adrienne says to Jason trying to quickly get off the phone.

"Okay, just remember to think about what's important to you. And what will be important to you in two weeks when this house stuff is all over with. I hope to see you tomorrow at the office."

Adrienne hangs up the phone and listens in on the conversation happening next to her.

"So what do we do next?" Gretchen is asking Nick.

Nick turns to Adrienne, "Do you have homeowner's insurance?"

"Yes! I kept paying that bill – I kept hearing my Dad's voice in my head telling me how important it is to have insurance – so that was one of the bills I paid every month!"

"Yay!" Gretchen cheers and grabs Adrienne in a bear hug. "I told you this would all work out!"

"This is great news, however, it would still be a miracle to finish fixing the roof on time – with or without insurance paying for it," the ever-practical Gabe says.

"Gabe's right," Nick agrees. "From a construction standpoint, this is a major job. We also need to call the tree people back over to chop down and clear out the tree."

"That I think shouldn't be a problem. I'll call Pete Wallace in the morning and I'm sure he'll be willing to come back over and help out. Hopefully he has some workers who can spare the time," Gabe says.

"I'll call the insurance company as soon as they open in the morning," Adrienne offers.

"And I'll get some of my guys over here tomorrow – but we won't be able to do anything until the tree is cleared out."

"Adrienne, since you will be dealing with the insurance company, I guess that means you can't go in to work tomorrow, right?" Gretchen says.

Nick and Gabe look over at Adrienne in surprise.

"You were going to go into work tomorrow?" Gabe says in an accusing tone.

"I was thinking about it. I hadn't yet decided. I do need to work you know."

"Don't you have some time off you could use?" Nick asks.

"I have a ton of time off I could use. That's not the problem. The problem is that taking the time off is frowned upon in my office. No one takes time off."

"Sounds like a great place to work," Gabe says sarcastically.

Adrienne shoots him a dirty look.

Taking a deep breath, Gretchen does her best to dissipate the growing tension in the room. "Nick and Gabe, thank you so much for everything. You two have been so amazing. But it's been a long day for everyone, so why don't we call it a night. Tomorrow is going to be another rough day. We should all try and get some sleep."

Everyone shakes their heads in agreement, and the girls follow Nick and Gabe to the front door and say good night. Once they are gone, Adrienne and Gretchen shut down all the lights and make their way upstairs to their bedrooms. Gretchen is asleep within minutes, unlike Adrienne who tosses and turns all night with the morning's decision looming. She thinks about how hard she has worked to get to this point at her job – *how can she miss another day?* But then she thinks about all these people in Chestnut Ridge who have donated their time to help her out, and she feels that if they are here, she should be here. It seems as though whatever she decides, she will be disappointing someone.

CHAPTER EIGHTEEN

The large number '2' written on the chalkboard in the morning causes the Harkins sisters' blood pressure to rise. It has become their morning ritual to sit at the kitchen island, drink coffee and look at their Christmas List.

Harkins Christmas List:

1. ~~Mow lawn~~
2. ~~Trim bushes~~
3. Paint house
4. ~~Clean gutters~~
5. Fix roof
6. Paint front door
7. Fix front porch/pillars
8. Paint and Re-hang shutters
9. ~~Rake leaves~~
10. ~~Dust~~
11. ~~Wash floors~~
12. ~~Clean refrigerator~~

13. *Buy Christmas tree*
14. *Decorate interior*
15. *Exterior Christmas lights, wreaths*
16. *Clean bathrooms*
17.   *Fix garage roof where tree fell*

"I was thinking about it, and I think you should go into the office today," Gretchen says out of the blue.

"Really? I wish I were so certain about it – one way or another. I have been weighing the options in my mind for days. What made you change your mind?"

"I was feeling bad for telling you not to go in – it's your job. You have worked so hard to get where you are – and the only reason this house is still in our family at all is due to your job and your dedication. So who am I to judge? I have nothing. I have no money, no career – I work at a bar for goodness sake."

"I know I tease you about McMurphy's, but the truth is – I envy you."

"*You* envy *me*?! You have got to be joking."

"No, not joking. I envy you for trying to do something you love, regardless of how hard that makes everything else. You are making big sacrifices in order to live a life where you are passionate about your work. You are beholden to no one, and you make all the decisions in your life with no one else to answer to. That is rare. Trust me."

"Thanks, Adrienne. That really means a lot to me. But actually, I've been thinking and I don't think I'm going to . . .."

Adrienne's phone rings – "Oh, it's the insurance company!" Adrienne says.

"This is early for them, isn't it?" Gretchen says.

"I left a message last night telling them it was an emergency," Adrienne says as she answers the phone. "Hello? Yes, this is Adrienne Harkins. Yes, okay great. We'll see you soon. Thank you," Adrienne hangs up the phone.

"They are coming at 9 a.m. Did you mean it when you said I should go in to the office today? Do you think you can handle the insurance company, and the Wallace tree guy, and the crew from Nick's construction company – oh, and Kurt Jeffries is coming back to continue working on painting the house, the shutters and the front door . . .."

Gretchen holds up her hand to signal Adrienne to stop talking. "Adrienne, go get ready for work. I got this."

Adrienne gives her sister a quick hug and rushes upstairs to get in the shower. Once she's ready, Adrienne takes one last look at the number '2' on the chalkboard and almost changes her mind. But, she feels she has to go in and fix things with Elaina at work.

The commute into the city is not as bad as Adrienne feared. Most likely due to the fact that Christmas is three days away, many people are not going into the office today, which means less traffic – at least that is one thing going her way. After spending the last three days in Chestnut Ridge, Adrienne finds that she has already gotten accustomed to the slower pace of life, and the rush of New York City catches her off guard. Although thrilling and full of energy, it does not appeal to Adrienne the same way it did only a few days ago.

Entering the Morgan Lynch building, Adrienne sings along with the Christmas music playing in the lobby. When Nico at the security desk tells her to "Have a blessed day," instead of sneering at him, she smiles and responds with "Thank you, and Merry Christmas!" Surprise registers on his face as he smiles after her.

Dropping her bag on her desk, Adrienne immediately searches out Elaina. She finds her in her office with her face buried in a folder.

"Knock, knock," Adrienne says announcing her arrival.

"Well, what a surprise - you actually decided to show up for work today. Should we be patting you on the back? Giving you an award?"

"I only missed one day, Elaina."

"A day and a half. And yes, everyone's keeping score."

"Right. So, what did I miss in the day and a half?"

"First, you could do your best to re-create that presentation you destroyed on the laptop last Friday."

"I have the original. I got the laptop fixed. It's good as new."

"You fixed that? Okay. Then I need you to do some market research on cell phone location technology. Our new pitch to the Board will be about creating an app for Morgan Lynch that will text our customers when they are close to one of our branches, and encourage them to come inside."

"Isn't that too creepy? Might it let people think we're watching their every move? Like a 'big brother' type issue? And our firm is not a typical bank. I like the idea of finding new ways to analyze data, and use technology, but I'm not sure about this one."

"Harkins, when I want your opinion I will ask you for it? Are we clear?"

Adrienne nods her head.

"I asked you to go do the research. So why don't you go do that, okay? Thank you."

Adrienne walks back to her desk and prepares for a long day sitting behind a desk staring at a computer. As she works gathering research on new cell phone location technology, her mind can't help but wander back to Oak Street, and if she's honest with herself, to Gabe.

The buzzing from Adrienne's cell phone knocks her out of her daydream. It's Gretchen.

"Gretch, hi! How are things at the house? Did everything go okay with the insurance guy?"

"Hi! Everything is okay here. I just met with the insurance guy and the good news is they will cover most of the cost to fix the garage."

"That's great, right!?"

"Well, it is. However, we will still owe a thousand dollars after the insurance pays. It doesn't cover 100 percent of the cost."

"A thousand dollars?"

"Yup. But don't worry – I think I can come up with the money."

"What, is there some other contest we can enter?" Adrienne teases.

"Ha. No. I think I can sell some stuff . . . but don't worry about it. I got it. You just focus on getting that promotion."

Of course once she was told not to worry, all Adrienne can do is worry. What could Gretchen be talking about – what could she possibly sell? Something she found in the house? She does her best to knock out a few more hours of work before she is interrupted once again.

"Hey look who's here! I knew you'd make the right decision."

"Jason, hi. How are you?"

"That is not a very warm greeting. Why is it you don't seem happy to see me?"

"I'm sorry. It's not you – of course I'm happy to see you. I just have a lot on my mind."

"Please tell me you're not still thinking about this house – I assumed since you were here today you sold the place. I was thinking we could go out to the martini bar on Fifth after work to celebrate."

"No, I didn't sell my childhood home – nor do I plan to. And no I can't go out partying after work today, because I need to get back to Chestnut Ridge as soon as I can. There is so much going on there, all these people . . . and I need to help. I can't believe I'm not there helping right now. And then a tree fell on the garage last night and destroyed the roof."

"What? A tree fell on your house last night? Why didn't you tell me that when I called you?"

"I don't know . . . honestly, I didn't think you would care. You don't seem to want to know anything about the house."

"Oh, so now it's my fault."

"That's not what I'm saying. It's just that you have made it clear you don't agree with my decision to try and keep the house – so I haven't told you about the contest we are entering to try and win $25,000 or all the work we're doing to fix the house up."

Jason stares at Adrienne like she has three heads. She is not even sure he understands anything she's saying – she is talking really fast.

"And all the people. The people who knew my father, they just keep coming over to help without me even having to ask. Gretchen has been taking photos of everyone helping, we're going to try and . . .."

"Wait, so who is Gretchen again?" Jason asks.

Adrienne is completely flabbergasted by this man standing in front of her right now. She looks around the office and it's as if the walls are closing in on her. Suddenly desperate for air, she grabs her coat and handbag and walks briskly to the elevators.

"The sister. That's right, I got it. Gretchen is the sister," Jason is calling after her. "Adrienne, where are you going? Don't be mad. You were just talking so fast . . .."

The elevator doors close and Adrienne is thankful for the peace and quiet. Once out on the street, the fresh air feels like it's breathing life back into her. Taking a deep breath, Adrienne closes her eyes and tries to organize her thoughts. She was thinking of something up there in the office while she was talking to Jason, but now she is having trouble recalling it. Walking down Fifth Avenue, Adrienne makes her way into a coffee shop. Coffee always helps – and Adrienne needs as much help as she can get. She has not felt this lost . . . ever. Stepping into the cozy café, Adrienne takes a big whiff of that wonderful aroma. Coffee feels like the only constant in her life at the moment, and if she ever spoke those words out loud, someone would think she was certifiably nuts. Heck, maybe she is nuts.

Stepping into line, she can't help but notice the woman in front of her wearing a long white coat.

"Angela?"

The woman spins around, and sure enough, there is Angela shining with that otherworldly glow. Wrapped up in a white faux fur snowball hat and matching fluffy scarf - looking at her is like staring into a bright light. She's so beautiful, it's blinding.

"Adrienne! How wonderful to bump into you again!"

"Yes, it is. I have to admit it's a little strange how you seem to keep appearing out of nowhere, everywhere I go. New York, Chestnut Ridge . . .."

"I was just going to say the same thing," Angela laughs. "How is it you keep popping up wherever I am – I guess the universe wants us to see each other."

"Huh, I guess it's something like that. So what brings you to the city today?"

"Today I am not here for work – today I am here to shop! Christmas is only a few days away you know. And I have not yet finished all the shopping on my list!"

"That sounds fun. I'm glad you are enjoying a day off."

"Oh yes, it has been wonderful. New York is a magical place."

"What's that book you're reading?" Adrienne points toward the book tucked into Angela's arm. Tilting her head sideways as to read it better, Adrienne says, "Mark Batterson? Who is he?"

"Oh, he's a preacher and an author. I find him inspiring. One of my favorite quotes of his is, 'You're always one decision away from a totally different life.' I find those words very powerful, don't you?"

"Hmmm, 'You're always one decision away from a totally different life,' Adrienne repeats quietly to herself. "That is powerful. It invokes the feeling that everyone has control over their life and their situation. I really wish that were true."

"Oh, but it is true, honey! You and only you can make decisions to create the life that you want to live."

"I'm not so sure. Sometimes you have responsibilities and bills to pay and people depending on you. Life is not that simple. At least not for me anyway."

"Well, think about that quote some more. Maybe it will be able to help you one day."

Adrienne nods her head respectfully, but feels frustrated on the inside.

"You know, I am so glad to run into you. Maybe you could help me?" Angela interrupts Adrienne's thoughts. "There is one gift on my list that is causing me some concern. You don't happen to know anything about photography, do you?"

"I'm afraid I don't. My sister, you met Gretchen, she is the photographer in the family."

"Oh, well – my niece wants some fancy camera, and I don't know anything about them. But, don't worry about me, sweetie - I'll figure it out."

Adrienne feels her heart skip a beat and her breath gets caught in her throat. *Gretchen's camera.*

"Excuse me, Angela, I have to leave."

"Is everything okay? I hope I haven't upset you in some way?"

"Not at all - quite the opposite actually. I have to get back to Chestnut Ridge."

"Okay, dear. You take care of yourself, okay?"

"Thanks Angela. And I guess I'll see you on Christmas Eve? Will you be a part of the Christmas Home Decorating Contest?"

"I sure am part of the contest! I will see you Christmas Eve!"

Adrienne races out of the café and runs as fast as she can on the overcrowded sidewalk. Once at the Morgan Lynch building she rushes up to Nico, flashing her badge on the fly. And just because she is in a hurry, the elevator stops on every floor on its way up to the 42nd, the ride feels like it will never end. When the elevator doors finally ease open, Adrienne pushes on each door with her two hands trying to get them to open faster. Running through her office she heads straight for Elaina's office.

"Elaina?"

"Harkins. Hi. How is the research going?"

"Fine. Fine. But I need to leave. I have a family emergency."

"Another family emergency? Geez Harkins, maybe you should find yourself a new family, one that's not so needy."

"I'm pretty sure it doesn't work that way."

Elaina rolls her eyes. "You are seriously leaving already?"

Adrienne gives one quick nod of her head.

"Then bring some work home with you, and I better see you bright and early tomorrow morning."

"But tomorrow is Christmas Eve eve."

"Is that even a thing?"

"Right. Well, I emailed you the research I started on the cell phone location technology. I will try and do some more tonight from home. And can I just say quickly – I found some really interesting information during my research regarding "Just-In-Time Marketing" and I was thinking it might be a good alternative to the cell phone location technology – less invasive maybe. You see, if someone cashes a check from a different company - they got a new job, well, we could then send them information on rolling over their 401K. Then it's not like we're watching their every move because they sent us a deposit and we just paid attention to it. And it's helpful . . .."

"Harkins – what did I ask you to research?" Elaina balls her hands into fists, frustrated.

"Cell phone location technology."

"Correct. So tonight after your fun family Christmas sugarplums with sparkly tinsel on them – what are you going to research and then send me?"

Adrienne has no idea why someone would eat sugarplums with tinsel on them, but she's knows better than to make that point. She says what Elaina wants to hear, "Information on cell phone location technology."

"You got it."

"Okay then. I guess I will see you tomorrow."

Making one quick stop at her desk to gather up her work to take home, Adrienne then hustles back to the elevator bank.

On the way to the elevator, Adrienne sees Jason walking toward her. She gives a quick wave and hops into an elevator before he has a chance to ask her any questions.

It seems to take three years for the valet to retrieve her car from the garage. As she waits, Adrienne continually tries to reach Gretchen on her cell phone, but for some reason Gretchen is not answering. Adrienne's car arrives and relief rushes over her. Finally. Finally she can head back home. Although, it's the middle of the day in New York City three days before Christmas, and the whole world seems to be driving through Midtown at this very moment. Inching her way through traffic, Adrienne's thoughts bounce between her conversations with Angela and Gretchen. She is praying that she can reach Gretchen before she does something really dumb.

After what feels like an eternity, Adrienne is on the Chestnut Ridge exit ramp, then driving down Main Street and turning right onto Oak Street. When she pulls up to the house, she is once again shocked by the amount of people and trucks and equipment flooding her front lawn. The main thing happening, and what Adrienne is the most concerned with, is the crew from Wallace Tree Company who are currently cutting down the tree that fell on the garage. There are chain saws and a chipper both on at the same time, and the sound is deafening. Covering her ears, Adrienne runs up to the first familiar face, unfortunately that is Gabe.

"Hi!" Adrienne yells over the noise.

Gabe yells something back, but Adrienne can't understand him.

"What?!" Adrienne asks.

"I said, you are back early," Gabe all but screams.

"Yeah, I am. Do you know where Gretchen is?"

Gabe gives her a look like he has no idea what she just said, so she just yells, "GRETCHEN?"

Gabe points inside.

Phew, Adrienne thinks – she hasn't done anything yet.

Inside, the house feels peaceful. Adrienne follows the sound of voices into the kitchen. She sees Nick talking to a few other men – but no Gretchen.

"Excuse me, Nick?"

Nick turns toward her, "Adrienne! You're back early – I'm so glad!"

"Thanks Nick. Have you seen Gretchen? She hasn't been answering her phone."

"Oh yeah, she took my truck to run some errand. I'm not really sure exactly what she is doing, but she said she wouldn't be long."

Panic sets in quickly, and Adrienne's face must show it.

"What's wrong, Adrienne? Are you okay?" Nick asks.

"Yeah, I'm fine. I just need to find Gretchen – now. If she calls you, will you tell her I'm looking for her and to please call me?"

"Of course. But there is one problem . . .."

Adrienne looks at Nick, confused.

"Gretchen won't be calling either of us – her phone was dead so she left it here to charge."

Ugh.

Adrienne immediately pulls out her phone and starts researching local pawnshops. There are three within ten miles of Chestnut Ridge. Which one would Gretchen try first?

She tries the closest one first – but it's only closer by one mile. She has to start somewhere though, right?

Racing back out through the noisy, busy lawn, Adrienne hops back into her car. Pulling up GPS, she types in the first address that will take her to Perfect Pawn in the next town over. The traffic is heavy everywhere she goes, so many people out and about running those last minute Christmas errands. Adrienne grips the steering wheel tightly hoping against hope that she can catch Gretchen in time. Adrienne parks her car in front of Perfect Pawn, but is already disappointed – she doesn't see Nick's truck parked in the parking lot. So she either has already missed her, or Gretchen never came to this particular shop. Either way, it's not great news.

Perfect Pawn is dark and dank inside. The only natural light is seeping in through two tiny windows high up close to the ceiling. Old matted down green carpet covers the floor. Adrienne walks up to the counter where a short, paunchy bald man is reading the newspaper.

"Hi there," Adrienne forces a calm smile as she approaches the man. "I was hoping you could help me."

"What can I do for ya dahlin'?"

"Right. Well, I was wondering if you were sold any cameras today – like within the last hour?"

"I did get a camera a little earlier. Why, are you interested in purchasing?"

Adrienne's heart sinks.

"Could I see it?"

"Of course," the little man hobbles over to a glass counter down a bit from the register, unlocks it from behind and holds up a camera.

Adrienne lets out a big sigh of relief. It's not Gretchen's camera.

"This is a really nice camera, and I can give you a great deal," the man starts his sales pitch.

"That's not the kind of camera I'm looking for, but thank you for your time."

"How about some jewelry? You look like you deserve a nice piece of jewelry to put under the tree this year. Or for that special man in your life? I have some very high-end watches, if you would like to see some of those?"

Adrienne just wants to get out of there. She declines the man's offers as politely as she can, and then races back out to her car. On her phone she pulls up the two remaining pawnshops that showed up in her search, and stares at them. Which one to choose? American Pawn Shop or EZ Pawn? She decides to go with American Pawn Shop since she likes the name better. It's all about luck at this point. She enters the address into her GPS and once again begins to silently pray that Gretchen doesn't go through with the sale.

Pulling up to American Pawn Shop Adrienne's heart sinks once again. Nick's truck is nowhere in sight. Doing her due diligence Adrienne walks into the shop. The bell dings as the door opens, and Adrienne feels like it's déjà vu all over again. This shop is dark with dirty carpet and a tall lanky young guy behind the counter. Another glass counter lines the back of the shop and Adrienne makes her way back to it.

"Hi there," Adrienne offers a half smile.

"Hey. You lookin' for somethin' in particular?" The guy asks.

"Actually yes, I'm looking for a camera. Did anyone happen to bring a camera by today to sell it to you? Recently perhaps?"

"Camera? Not today. But I could show you what I've got – maybe you'll take a likin' to one of em'."

"No. Thank you, anyway," Adrienne says as she turns around to walk back out into the fresh air. The heat must have been turned up to 90 degrees in that small shop. She steps back out into the cold fresh air and takes a deep breath. Cars zip by on the busy road the shop sits on. The cars are so close to the parking lot she can feel a gush of air that knocks her a little off balance with each vehicle that whizzes by. But she is too distracted by her thoughts to be worried about being hit by a car. Should she be disappointed or relieved that Gretchen didn't pawn her camera to either of these shops? Maybe Adrienne is wrong, maybe Gretchen doesn't plan to sell her camera after all. But she needs to find out either way. She needs to check the last shop, EZ Pawn, to be sure.

Driving to the third and final pawnshop, Adrienne spends the time on the road hoping she was wrong – that Gretchen never intended to sell the camera. But the tightening feeling deep down in her stomach is telling a different story. That part of her that is inexplicably still connected to her sister, can feel what Gretchen is feeling. So when Adrienne pulls her little red car up to EZ Pawn, she is not surprised to see Nick's truck sitting in the parking lot. EZ Pawn is about double the size of the first two pawn shops – Gretchen must have done her research.

Adrienne parks the car and runs toward front door of the building. Not only is this place bigger than the other two, it is also much nicer. With its sleek gray exterior and flashing signs advertising "best prices around" and "we buy gold" it is in stark contrast to the dark, dated holes in the wall Adrienne unfortunately had to visit. Just as Adrienne grabs the handle to the front door and pulls it toward her, there on the other side of the door pushing outward is Gretchen. The two sisters stare at each other for a moment until Adrienne snaps out of it, and pulls the door open, stepping to the side to let Gretchen out.

"Adrienne? What are you doing here?" Gretchen is completely surprised.

"I came to stop you – to stop you from selling Heidi."

"What do you? How did you?" Gretchen can't seem to complete a sentence.

"I just had a feeling. When you said you could come up with the money, that you could sell something, it didn't totally come together for me. But then I ran into Angela in the city . . .."

"You ran into Angela in the city? Geez, she gets around."

"I know, right? But yeah, when I ran into Angela, she mentioned something about photography or cameras, and it suddenly clicked. I knew what you were going to do – and I didn't want you to do it."

"Why do you care that I sold the camera?"

"Oh no. I'm too late! You sold it already? Maybe it's not too late – maybe we can go convince them to give it back to you. It could only have been a few minutes ago." Adrienne is desperate.

"It doesn't work that way, Adrienne. Once you sell it, it's gone. They own it, and the only way to get it back is to buy it back – for more money than they just gave you for it, of course. Honestly, I thought you would be happy about it."

"Happy about it?" it's Adrienne's turn to be surprised. "Why would you selling your camera make me happy?"

"I thought you would be happy that I am finally contributing to the house. I know you resent the fact that you always have had to pay for everything. I figured that resentment was the reason you didn't want anything to do with me after the accident."

Adrienne stares at her sister, guilt rising up from deep inside and settling just under her skin.

"I don't resent you, Gretchen. And although sometimes I do feel a bit smothered by the weight of all the responsibilities I have – that has nothing to do with why we have barely spoken in the last four years. I thought you felt the same way I did."

"And what way is that?"

"That our family was ruined after Mom and Dad died, and nothing would ever be the same again – so why bother even trying. You and I being together only highlights that they are not here with us. It was just too hard for me."

Gretchen's eyes well up with tears, but she somehow keeps them from spilling down her face.

"I thought you hated me. Hated that you had to handle everything after they were gone – the funeral arrangements, the paperwork, the house of course – paying for the taxes all those years. I would hate me too."

Adrienne shakes her head, "I could never hate you Gretch. I didn't mind handling everything after the accident – it gave me something to focus on – something to keep my mind away from the sadness, if only for a moment. And what I've realized the past few days is that you and I being together doesn't highlight that mom and dad are gone, it actually brings them back to life. My only regret is that it took me this long to figure it out – that it took me this long to come back to Chestnut Ridge. And that it took me this long to realize that you are the most important person in my life."

Now both sisters have tears streaming down their face as they hold each other in a tight hug.

"It's so cold out here – I'm freezing to death. Let's go home," Gretchen says with her arm still around Adrienne leading them both to the parking lot.

"But what about Heidi? That camera is everything to you," Adrienne stops them short.

"Heidi is helping pay to fix the house. I want to contribute, Adrienne. And this is the only way I can. And like you, I've realized there are more important things in my life than a camera. Please."

Adrienne looks into her sister's eyes and sees that her mind is made up. It's Gretchen's decision to make – and she has made it. Adrienne nods her head and the two girls walk to their cars to start the drive home.

CHAPTER NINETEEN

Adrienne is in the little red rental car following right behind Gretchen who is in Nick's big truck. At this point the two sisters have grown accustomed to pulling up to 22 Oak Street and seeing a flurry of activity. When Adrienne left for the pawnshop there were men everywhere taking down the tree that fell, power washing the house and repairing the front stoop. However, when the girls drive into the driveway they are once again surprised. There is no one there. No one. Wallace Tree Company is nowhere to be found. Nick and Gabe are gone. 22 Oak Street looks like all the workers suddenly dropped what they were doing and ran. Someone dropped an ax on the ground mid-swing, wood chips are strewn all over and around the half-chopped down tree, and ladders are still leaning against the house.

Getting out of their cars the girls give each other a puzzled look. They walk through the lawn looking at the disaster that has been left behind.

"What the heck happened here? Where is everyone?" Gretchen asks.

"I have no idea. When I left to go find you there were people everywhere. This is really strange."

Confirming that no one is outside in the yard, the girls go inside the house. They haven't even thought to lock the house because it's been full of people, but now everything feels exposed. The house is eerily quiet and as they do a lap around the main level, Adrienne and Gretchen don't say a word to each other. They convene back in the kitchen.

"Check your phone – maybe someone texted you," Adrienne tells Gretchen.

Gretchen picks up her phone that was charging on the counter. There are three missed texts. She clicks on them to read and her mouth falls open.

"What? What happened?" Adrienne is dying to know what Gretchen is reading.

"Ohmigoodness. You're not going to believe this!"

"WHAT?! Tell me!"

"Nick texted me three times, they didn't have time to leave us a note. There's been a fire. At Chestnut Ridge Town Hall."

"No!"

"Yes. Everyone that was here went there to help out. It is a serious emergency."

"That's so horrible! I hope everyone got out of the building safely!"

"I wonder if they need any more help?"

"Thankfully I know Angela wasn't in the building, since I saw her in the city earlier. Geez, that feels like a long time ago."

Adrienne and Gretchen are talking over each other, both their minds working overtime thinking of the repercussions. As with the beginning of any major tragedy there are more questions than answers at this point.

"We have to get down there," both girls say at the same time.

They rush out of the house and back into the red rental. Adrienne tries her best to follow the driving laws, but her anxiety has gotten the best of her and she is definitely driving over the speed limit, and maybe not stopping for the full eight seconds at stop signs. The sound of police cars and fire engine sirens can be heard long before the girls even get close to Town Hall. As they get closer they can see smoke billowing from the smoldering building. Parking as close as they can, Adrienne and Gretchen get out of the car and walk quickly toward the crowd surrounding the taped-off area.

"There's Nick," Gretchen points to an area of the crowd. Nick's height makes him easy to find, and upon further inspection Adrienne sees Gabe is standing next to him. The girls weave through the crowd in an attempt to reach them. Most of the people there are standing quietly watching the fire and the emergency workers who are running around with hoses. There is a mix of men and women – some with unblinking eyes and their hands covering their mouths in disbelief, some analyzing every move being made by emergency workers and others who have their eyes closed in prayer. It's a very stressful, anxious scene.

When Adrienne and Gretchen finally reach Nick and Gabe their concern has grown exponentially. The Chestnut Ridge Town Hall is a major landmark for the entire town. It is an historic building going back to the origination of the town back in the early 1800s and was even an Underground Railroad stop helping the slaves escape North to modern day Canada. The destruction of this building is truly a tragedy for the people of Chestnut Ridge.

"Hey," Gretchen says softly as she touches Nick's arm to get his attention.

Nick turns around and even despite the calamity, the two can't help but smile at each other.

"You got my texts, I'm so glad. We felt horrible leaving your house, but we had to come down and see if there was anything we could do."

"Oh, please. You don't have to explain. We understand completely. This is just so horrible."

"Do you know what happened?" Adrienne asks to both Nick and Gabe's general direction – too nervous to ask straight at Gabe. Things have been awkward between them ever since their conversation about Jason.

Thankfully, if Nick and Gretchen noticed the tension, they sure were good at appearing oblivious. "From what we hear it was an electrical fire. The wiring in these historical buildings is just so old – I'm not surprised," Nick says.

"I have always loved this building," Gabe says continuing to stare at the carnage.

"Me too," Adrienne agrees. "I hope they get everyone out safely."

"Look, over there. There's Pete Wallace," Gabe says pointing to the front left of the burning building. "I guess he's on stand-by to take care of any trees that are in danger."

"And over there – that's Kurt Jeffries. I see him and his crew have offered to help out," says Nick. "I think we should go find Bob Fiero, the Fire Chief, and see what we can do," Nick says. Gabe nods his head.

"Don't worry girls, as soon as we're finished up here we'll come back to your house and get back to work," Gabe says.

"Oh please, don't even think about us. Being here is more important," Adrienne reassures them.

Nick lingers for a brief second as he and Gretchen hold each other's eye contact. Adrienne can't help but notice the palpable feelings between them. It is as if they have known each other for years, not days – they can already look at each other and have a conversation with their eyes only. That is a special thing. Adrienne had that once.

Gabe and Nick leave to speak with the Fire Chief, and Adrienne and Gretchen stay for a bit longer making sure that everyone got out of the building safely. When they see that the fire is under control, and the building is now just a smoldering carcass of burnt wood and brick, Adrienne and Gretchen decide they should go home and deal with that reality. But first, coffee.

In downtown Chestnut Ridge, the sidewalks that were once buzzing with Christmas preparations, are now abuzz with talk of the fire. The girls start to walk toward The Dreamy Bean, when Adrienne stops short.

"I have an idea," she says turning to go into Peas & Pickles. Gretchen follows Adrienne into the store and once she sees where she is heading, Gretchen smiles in agreement. The girls load as many cases of water they can fit into two shopping carts. As they are paying for the waters at the register, Mrs. Cuthburt, the owner, asks the girls if they are taking those waters to the emergency workers at the fire. When the girls answer "yes," Mrs. Cuthburt asks them if they wouldn't mind waiting a few minutes. About five minutes later Mrs. Cuthburt is walking toward the girls with another shopping cart filled with premade sandwiches, bagels, giant containers of warm soup, and bags of rolls.

"Oh my goodness, thank you so much!" Gretchen exclaims.

"No, thank you so much. Let's remind everyone that although our beloved landmark is gone, our community is still as strong as ever."

With the help of some of the Peas & Pickles employees, Adrienne and Gretchen push the carts out to their little car and start loading up the trunk. In the end, the entire trunk and backseat are filled with waters and food. Gretchen is sitting with some of the soups on her lap in the passenger seat. With the food and water stacked tenuously throughout the car, Adrienne drives slowly. The crowd has started to dwindle a little, but the emergency workers and volunteers are still hard at work. Adrienne parks the car as close as she can get, and the girls each grab some bags of food and walk up to the yellow tape. Flagging down one of the police officers, Gretchen flashes her irresistible smile. The officer meanders over and asks, "What can I do for you Miss?"

"Hi there, Officer?"

"Kyle"

"Right, hi Officer Kyle. We have a car full of food and water for everyone working. Is there some way we could pull closer, and maybe even get some help unloading everything?"

And just like all the boys in high school, poor young Officer Kyle cannot say no to Gretchen's request. However, Adrienne is not complaining this time.

Officer Kyle pulls back some of the yellow tape and allows Adrienne to pull her car right up next to some of the police cars. He also rounds up a few volunteers who all start unloading the food and waters. Gabe walks over to the girls, he has his jacket off and Adrienne can see that despite the cold temperatures he has been working up a sweat. The remnants of the once beautiful building are still emanating heat regardless of the flames being out.

"This was really thoughtful of you two," Gabe says while opening a bottle of water.

"It is the least we can do," Adrienne says locking eyes with him.

"I don't like to bring this up, but you have less than two days to put your own house back together. You are spending some very precious time here."

"I know. I do understand that – it's just that when our house needed to be fixed the whole community gave up their own precious time to come help us. And well, I guess I feel like I need to return the favor. I *want* to return the favor. This building – what this building means to this community – that's all much more important than us winning some contest."

Gabe stares at Adrienne for a minute, thinking. "That's very admirable of you, Adrienne. And I know everyone here really appreciates all of this," he points at all the food and drinks. "But it's not just about winning some contest. It's about you being able to keep your childhood home in your family. And that's . . . big."

Adrienne slowly nods her head. She knows Gabe is right. What they are trying to do at 22 Oak Street is big. It's huge, actually. She looks over at Gretchen who is, of course, talking to Nick – it's as if each of them can feel when they are within one hundred feet of each other – and she says, "Gretch, we should probably get going. We have a lot of work to do."

Driving away from Town Hall, Adrienne watches the burnt building in the rear view mirror as it grows smaller and smaller. It has been a whirlwind of a day, and it's not even close to being over. She knows what she and Gretchen need before they go home -- a gingerbread latte from the Dreamy Bean. When she pulls the car up to the café, a smile spreads across Gretchen's face.

"Gingerbread latte?" She asks.

Adrienne nods her head. "I don't think I've ever needed one so bad in my life."

"It's on me this time," Gretchen says hopping out of the car.

Adrienne stays in the car and thinks about the emotional rollercoaster she and Gretchen have been on since those red envelopes showed up on their doorsteps. They have to find some way to make this work.

Refueling with their lattes, the girls drive home in silence. As they once again pull into the driveway at 22 Oak Street they stare at the work in progress and realize how far they are from finished.

"I think we should start to prepare ourselves for what happens if we don't win the prize money," Adrienne says quietly.

The girls stay sitting in the car, sipping their coffees and looking up at the white colonial.

"I have been so sure this was going to work out for the best. However, I will admit, right now with the tree falling on the garage, the fire at Town Hall and all our workers needing to leave to go help out there – I am feeling like the universe is doing all it can to stop us from succeeding. With less than 2 days until the contest, things are not looking good," Gretchen admits.

"Well, let's see – what still needs to be done?" Adrienne asks looking more closely at the house. "It appears that the pillars for the portico are fixed, just not painted. And the roof still needs some shingles fixed, the shutters need to be painted and re-hung, the front door and house need to be painted. And of course, there is a half-cut down tree and a hole in our garage . . ." Adrienne says.

"Well it's 3 p.m., we still have a few hours of daylight. Why don't we go inside and check out our list and see what you and I can do. Because like it or not, we are entered in this contest and judges will be at our house any time between 5 p.m. – 7 p.m. on Christmas Eve," Gretchen feels her determination growing again.

Inside the warm house, the girls' spirits lift. The interior of the house looks beautiful. Anyone entering the house would never know how horrible it looked only a few days ago. It's clean, and warm and glowing with Christmas sparkle. However, right now no one would want to enter the house judging from the outside. And everyone knows, first impressions are everything.

"So let's look at this list," Adrienne says.

Harkins Christmas List:

1. ~~Mow lawn~~
2. ~~Trim bushes~~
3. Paint house
4. ~~Clean gutters~~
5. Fix roof
6. Paint front door
7. ~~Fix~~ Paint front porch/pillars
8. Paint and Re-hang shutters
9. ~~Rake leaves~~
10. ~~Dust~~
11. ~~Wash floors~~
12. ~~Clean refrigerator~~
13. ~~Buy Christmas tree~~
14. ~~Decorate interior~~
15. Exterior Christmas lights, wreaths
16. ~~Clean bathrooms~~
17. Fix garage roof where tree fell

"Okay, so we can paint," Adrienne says.

"We can paint," Gretchen agrees. "That's about all we can do."

"There is a lot to paint. We can paint the house, the front door, the shutters, and the front pillars. There is a *lot* to paint."

"That is a lot. But we can start today, and work straight through tomorrow," Adrienne is feeling bolstered by the idea they can do something, anything, that will bring them closer to their goal.

"Tomorrow? You mean you're not going into work tomorrow?"

"Oh. Work. I forgot," Adrienne says. "I will deal with work later. Right now, let's get started."

"Okay. If we can get a lot of the painting done, the only other items on our list are replacing some of the shingles on our roof, fixing the giant gaping hole in the roof of our garage and decorating the exterior. We have all day and night tomorrow and until 5 p.m. the next day."

"Well, let's get started. I'll paint the pillars if you want to paint the shutters. The painting company laid them all out on the side lawn," Adrienne says as the girls start to walk outside.

"Ummmm, you should probably change your clothes," Gretchen laughs a little.

Adrienne looks down at her suit and heels and smiles. "Good point."

While Gretchen goes outside to figure out how to paint the shutters, Adrienne races upstairs to change into jeans and a sweatshirt. She grabs the portable speaker before going out to the shed to get the paint, and then brings everything to the front porch to begin painting.

Gretchen is already on the front lawn with a can of black spray paint and all the shutters lined up in a row.

"That was a good idea," Adrienne yells over to her.

"It is so much faster! There are about twenty shutters to paint and I didn't know how else I was going to be able to finish all of them. And it's just black over black – so it totally works."

The sisters spend the next few hours painting and painting and painting. Adrienne's arms ache and her toes are frozen but she pushes on. The sun goes down, and the girls continue in the dusk. Once Adrienne has the whole front porch painted a gleaming white, and Gretchen has all twenty shutters painted they decide to go inside and warm up.

"I think that's all we're going to be able to do today," Gretchen says as she stacks kindling in the fireplace to start a fire.

"I know. It really doesn't help that it gets dark so early. Although, I don't know that either of us are capable of hanging shutters or fixing roof shingles in the light or dark. What are we going to do?"

"We'll figure it out," Gretchen says still confident and positive. "Right now we're going to heat up some dinner and pour some wine. We deserve it."

"That sounds like heaven. And then I need to do some work for Elaina."

"You need to do work tonight?"

"Yeah, I have to gather some research for some presentation that she's working on. I don't even think it's a good idea, but what do I know, right?"

"I'm sorry, Adrienne. That must be rough hating your job."

"I don't hate my job. At least, I never thought I did. But lately, it just seems . . . empty. Like it doesn't mean anything. What am I actually doing? Who am I helping? All I'm doing right now is helping a giant corporation spy on their customers so they can plant ideas in their heads to spend more money. It all just seems . . . pointless."

Just then there is a knock on the door. Gretchen goes over to answer it, and by the way her face lights up, Adrienne knows who is there: Nick.

Surprisingly, Nick is not alone. Butterflies flutter around in Adrienne's belly as she stares at Gabe who is doing his best not to make eye contact with her.

"We wanted to come thank you both again for the food and waters you brought down to Town Hall. Or what was once Town Hall," Gabe says.

"Yeah, and we wanted to make sure you two were doing okay. I could smell the wet paint on the way in, so I see you did get a lot accomplished before nightfall," Nick smiles at them.

"We got the front porch and shutters painted – and we were just about to throw together some dinner. Would you two like to stay?" Gretchen asks.

"That sounds great," Nick says.

Gabe pauses for a moment, and looks at Adrienne, "Are you sure that would be okay?"

"Of course," Adrienne says quickly.

The foursome make their way into the kitchen, with Gretchen and Nick leading the pack. How strange that only a few days ago the four of them were practically strangers. And now here they are a team - a team all working toward a common goal, depending on each other, worrying about each other and taking care of one another.

"What's for dinner?" Nick asks, rubbing his belly. "I'm starved."

"I was thinking we would throw together a Harkins Hoop-dee-doo," Gretchen says with that mischievous smile.

"A what?" Gabe asks, already starting to laugh.

"A Harkins Hoop-dee-doo," Adrienne says, also laughing. "When we were growing up – if my Mom wasn't home and my Dad was responsible for dinner, my Dad would make a Harkins Hoop-dee-doo, which might sound fancy," Adrienne raises an eye brow, "but it really meant that my Dad would throw a bunch of leftovers into a frying pan and serve it to us on fancy plates."

The look of utter fear on both Gabe and Nick's faces is enough to send Adrienne and Gretchen into an eruption of laughter.

"Don't worry. I've gotten good at this over the years – you know, me being a starving artist and all. I have mastered the hoop-dee-doo."

"Now even I'm scared," Adrienne teases.

"Why don't you three take care of the wine, some music, and Adrienne maybe you could put out some cheese and crackers to hold big Nick over so he doesn't starve to death . . ."

The joking and laughing has eliminated any tension hanging in the air. The four friends get to work opening wine bottles, setting out nibbles and finding appropriate music. Of course, with Saint Nick in charge of the music – *All I Want For Christmas Is You* by Mariah Carey blasts from the surround sound. Adrienne watches Gretchen with initial skepticism until the kitchen begins to fill with delicious smells - Gretchen's face is relaxed and happy.

With the music, appetizers and wine flowing, Nick and Gabe give the girls an update on the fire. Once the flames were put out, the fire investigators were able to do some preliminary investigating and are pretty sure faulty wiring caused it. They determined the fire's place of origin was the kitchen in the back of the building. From there, they surmised that a very old refrigerator was the actual culprit. The old cord was plugged into an old outlet and the two caused friction, and then sparks. Due to the upcoming holiday there were very few people in the building so no one saw the sparks or smelled the acrid odor of something burning until it was too late. On a positive note, since there were so few people in the building, it was evacuated quickly and no one was hurt.

"Will they be able to save the building?" Adrienne asks Gabe.

"It's pretty much destroyed. My guess is that they will have to knock it down and completely rebuild it."

"It's such a shame," Adrienne says sadly.

"Okay everyone – who's ready for some Hoop-dee-doo?!" Gretchen interrupts the serious talk with her now constant state of cheeriness.

"I think I'm ready?" Nick says.

"Grab a plate and fork and we can all sit at the kitchen table," Gretchen instructs as she starts scooping something resembling a sloppy Joe onto plates. If the other three weren't so hungry maybe they would have hesitated. But, at this point, they are all in.

Adrienne waits for Nick's reaction to his first bite before taking one herself. Gabe seems to have the same strategy.

"I can't believe I'm saying this, but this is delicious," Nick says digging in for more.

"Really? Thanks, Nick!" Gretchen smiles. "It's sort of like a taco thingy with ground beef and onions and chopped tomatoes, cheese and avocado on top – here, dip some tortilla chips in it and it'll be even better."

Adrienne and Gabe follow suit, each of them taking a tortilla chip and dipping it into the "taco thingy." Perhaps their level of hunger has tricked their taste buds, but Adrienne and Gabe have to agree with Nick -- it tastes delicious.

"Wow, Gretchen – this is surprisingly tasty," Adrienne says. "I don't think Dad even made anything this good . . . ever."

Gretchen laughs, "Yeah, Dad pretty much just made pasta and threw some things on it."

Adrienne's phone dings and since anyone she would want to hear from is sitting with her at the moment, she really doesn't want to check who is trying to reach her.

"I meant to tell you, while I was cooking, your phone was beeping like crazy."

"Oh, okay. I'm sure it's work. I'll check it later."

The phone dinging is followed by another ding.

"Is that the doorbell?" Gretchen asks, surprised.

"I'll get it," Adrienne stands up and walks to answer the door. She pulls the door open expecting to see some type of delivery person or salesperson, and is instead shocked into silence by the tall, dark-haired man standing in front of her.

"Jason?! Oh my goodness, what are you doing here?" Adrienne's voice comes out in a high-pitched screech.

"It's nice to see you too," Jason says.

"I'm sorry – it's great to see you. Come in, come in – it's freezing out there."

"Thank you. So this is the house causing all the drama, huh," he says looking around. "I see you found time to decorate despite it being a time of great emergency," he teases her.

"We decorated because of the competition we entered. Remember the competition I was telling you about, or were you not paying attention?"

"Whoa, okay – I deserve that. I forgot how serious you were about this competition. No need to get angry, though."

"I'm not angry. I'm just . . . surprised, that's all. I didn't expect to see you of all people in the suburbs of Connecticut when you could be out at a club getting bottle service," Adrienne tries to make light of the situation despite her stomach being in knots.

"I sent you a bunch of texts today, and when I didn't hear back I figured I should go see what exactly is going on here in Chestridge."

"Chestnut Ridge."

"Right, whatever."

Gretchen walks into the family room, "Adrienne, who was at the . . .oh, hello . . ." she stops herself mid-sentence. "I don't think we've met. I'm Gretchen, Adrienne's sister."

Gretchen extends her hand in a handshake, and Jason does the same.

"I'm sorry, yes – Gretchen this is Jason. And Jason this is Gretchen, my sister."

"The famous sister Gretchen! It's nice to finally meet you," Jason says.

"Famous? I figured Adrienne never mentioned me."

"Well she hadn't until about a week ago. And then you were all I was hearing about."

"Jason, let me take your coat," Adrienne does her best to change the subject.

"We just sat down to eat, why don't you join us," Gretchen says, looking at Jason skeptically.

"Yes, right – please," Adrienne's words are coming out jumbled and rambling.

Jason follows the girls into the kitchen, and when Nick and Gabe see there is company, the two of them stand up.

Jason quickly takes in the scene and starts nodding his head.

"Nick, Gabe – this is Jason. My . . . we work together at Morgan Lynch."

Jason is still slowly nodding his head, "Well this looks cozy," his words soaked in sarcasm. "I didn't mean to interrupt this little date night."

"Don't be silly," Adrienne says. "Nick is a contractor and Gabe is an old friend – they have been helping us fix the house."

"I'm sure they have been," Jason turns to Adrienne, "maybe I should go."

"Don't go! You just got here – and look, you haven't tried Gretchen's Hoop-dee-doo!" Adrienne tries to lighten the mood. But the awkward silence cannot be broken, not even with hoop-dee-doo.

"Her what?" Jason looks confused.

"It's a family joke – never mind. But really, you just traveled all that way – stay. Please."

"Okay. Do you have anything to drink?" Jason makes his way over to the table and pulls out a chair – silently all three guys sit down simultaneously.

Adrienne finds another glass and shakily pours a generous amount of wine into it. Taking a giant sip of her own wine, she then walks back over to the table where she sees three men who look like they are having a staring contest – who will blink first?

"Jason, would you like some dinner?" Gretchen asks politely.

Looking at the pile of ground beef with tomatoes and avocado plopped on Adrienne's plate, Jason scrunches his nose with a look of disgust.

"I'm not really hungry. Thanks," he says.

Unfortunately, the rest of the group seems to have also lost their appetite. Gabe and Nick haven't touched their food since Jason arrived. However, the wine is going down like water after a marathon.

Quickly rising to his feet, Gabe excuses himself. "It's been a long day. Thank you Adrienne and Gretchen for the great food and company, but I'm tired. I think I'll head home."

Nick follows suit. "Yeah, I'm exhausted. Gretchen, thank you for the creative dinner, it is certainly one I will never forget," they smile at each other.

"I'll walk you two out," Gretchen says, grabbing Nick's hand.

Adrienne turns to Jason, "I'll be right back. Let me say good-bye."

Ignoring Jason's dramatic eye roll, Adrienne follows after Gabe, Nick and Gretchen. When she calls out to Gabe she is not even sure of what she's going to say, she just knows she does not want the night to end this way. Hearing his name, Gabe turns around to face her. Every inch of Adrienne's body wants to grab him and hold him close to her, but the indifference on his face stops her dead in her tracks.

"Did you need something?" Gabe finally asks her, as she stands there speechless and staring.

"I just wanted to say thank you. Thank you for everything you have done for us. And, I'm sorry about Jason – he doesn't mean to be so rude."

"Really? I think he does."

Adrienne looks up into Gabe's intense eyes and is at a loss for words.

"I wasn't kidding when I said I was tired – and Nick is waiting for me out there."

"Of course. I guess I'll just see you tomorrow?"

Gabe nods his head and Adrienne watches as he walks away.

"Are you okay?" Gretchen asks.

"I'm fine. I just wish there weren't so many things changing all at the same time. I need something beneath my feet that isn't shifting – something solid, or I'm just going to fall through the cracks."

"Well that's easy," Gretchen shrugs her shoulders. "You have me."

CHAPTER TWENTY

Gabe got in the passenger seat of Nick's truck in a huff, slamming the door shut he sat stewing, anger seeping out of his every pore. Looking over at him, Nick decides not to ask him any questions or bring up Adrienne; instead he puts the car in reverse and pulls out of the driveway. After a few minutes of driving in silence, Gabe finally says, "Can you believe that guy? I mean, seriously? *That* is who Adrienne is dating now? You have got to be kidding me."

"I don't mean to bring this up, but I thought you said you were not really interested in starting up a relationship with Adrienne again anyway."

"I'm not," Gabe says defensively. "It's just . . . it's just, she can do so much better."

"You have to trust that she will figure that out on her own. She and Jason are not a good fit for each other, we see that, and I have faith that she will see that too."

Gabe looks out the window, his stomach in knots, pent up energy building in his body to the point where he needs to either go for a run, or get in a boxing ring and throw some punches – preferably with Jason as his sparring partner.

The sound of a phone ringing breaks up Gabe's indignant thoughts about Jason. Reaching in his pocket he pulls out his cell phone and sees Mayor Bill Jessup's name flashing on his screen. *Perfect timing. This is just what I need right now.*

Tempted not to answer it, but knowing avoidance solves nothing, Gabe accepts the call, "Hey there Bill, what can I help you with?"

"Well Gabe, I just wanted to touch base and see what you were thinking regarding the Harkins house. Is it a go? Are we going to make 22 Oak Street our company's first investment property? You haven't really given me a solid answer."

Gabe pauses, looking over at Nick who is pretending not to listen. "Well, sir, to be honest, I think there are so many other properties on that list you sent me that are just as good of a deal, if not better, than 22 Oak Street. I plan to look at a couple of them more closely tonight and will get back to you with my thoughts on them tomorrow. If that sounds good?"

"Well, sure that list is a great starting point. But here we have a property in a perfect location, in a town where we understand the market, that has fallen into disrepair and we can most likely purchase at a more than fair price at auction. I don't see anything else on that list being a better option – especially not for our first property."

"Well, I don't think . . .."

"Listen Gabe," the Mayor interrupts him, "this is what I want you to do. If you want to be a part of this real estate development company with me, you need to make sure that house goes to auction. Am I being clear?"

And before Gabe can answer, the Mayor hangs up the phone. *Great. Now what am I going to do.*

CHAPTER TWENTY-ONE

"You didn't have to be so rude, Jason," Adrienne says, her patience worn thin.

"I'm sorry I wasn't making nice with your ex-boyfriend."

"How did you know Gabe is my ex-boyfriend?" Adrienne interrupts him.

"I do listen to you sometimes, Adrienne," Jason teases. "I mean, look at it from my point of view. I come all the way out here from the city after a long day of work, and I just wanted to see you and make sure you were okay."

"I know, and I understand that. And I am appreciative of that, Jason. But you have to understand how much Nick and Gabe have been helping us out the past few days. We truly could not have finished half of what we have done if it weren't for them."

"Fine. I'm sorry. I'm guessing they will be here tomorrow?" Jason asks her. Adrienne nods her head. "Well, I will apologize tomorrow when I see them, and thank them for helping you out this week."

"Thank you. That would be really great," Adrienne says and Jason walks over and puts his arms around her.

"Why don't we go out and get something to eat? I'm starving, and no offense to your sister, but there is no way I can eat that hoop-dee-whatever. That looked like dog food."

It's now Adrienne's turn to roll her eyes. "I guess we could go grab something to eat. The Chestnut Tavern usually has some live music, and the food is pub food, but it's pretty good."

"Now we're talking! A bar with live music – that's definitely more my speed."

The drive down to Main Street is quiet, with Adrienne lost in thought and Jason staring out the window, probably wondering how he ended up in the suburbs on a pretty big party night in New York. Entering the Chestnut Tavern, Adrienne can't help but smile as a flood of memories come roaring back from when she was in her early twenties. She and Gretchen and Gabe used to practically live at this bar. A live band is mixing it up playing some modern country songs, and some Christmas songs keeping the atmosphere light and fun.

"I can work with this," Jason says, leading them to a table close the stage. Usually Adrienne would prefer a table further back from the stage since the music can be so loud it makes it difficult to talk. But tonight, not being able to talk to Jason sounds like a good thing. The thought of trying to keep up a conversation with him just makes her tired.

They order drinks and appetizers and Jason orders a burger, and they sit listening to the music. He talks a little about what is happening at the office, of course talking about some of the crazy bets he and his co-workers have going about the office holiday party.

"You are going to come to the holiday party, right?" Jason asks her.

"When is it? Christmas Eve?" Jason nods his head. "I can't make it. I have to be here. That's the night of the Christmas Home Decorating Competition. That's when we find out if we won or not."

Jason shakes his head, "Adrienne, this is crazy. Now you are going to miss the holiday party? That's like the best party of the year! I really think you need to reconsider."

"Jason, I'm not going to the party. I have to be here," she says with finality. He doesn't press her any more on the subject. After another half hour, with their food and drinks finished, Jason asks, "Want another drink?"

"You know, it has been a long day. I think I just want to go home and go to bed."

"Okay, that sounds good. I know you probably have some work to do too, right?"

"I sure do. You know Elaina, never a minute's break."

Awake early the next morning, Adrienne sits in the family room watching the lighted tree sparkle in the morning light. Feeling like she is sitting in the middle of an intersection wondering which street she is supposed to turn down – her mind is a swirling whirlwind of thoughts. Her life before that red envelope appeared in her New York City apartment seems unfamiliar and unappealing. Like the little mouse that fell into the milk dish and struggled so hard until he churned that milk into butter – Adrienne's years of struggling in the city at her job were about to produce a successful result. But what does that next step even mean to her anymore? Does a promotion just mean more hours at the office and a slightly larger paycheck? The meaning of 'home' has changed. Adrienne isn't sure - is New York City home? Or is Chestnut Ridge home?

"Hey there," Jason's voice sounds sleepy.

"Hey, how did you sleep?"

"Not great. It's too quiet around here," he smiles.

"Ha – I know. When the sounds of the city aren't assaulting my ears all I can hear are my own thoughts – and they are yelling at me. I wish I had some city traffic to drown them out."

"Sounds like you couldn't sleep either."

"No. Not really."

"Look, I'm sorry about last night. It's just that I walk in to surprise you and try and show you some support, and I see you sitting down to date night in your kitchen with your ex-boyfriend."

"Yeah, I understand why the whole situation was awkward. I certainly never meant for that to be the case."

"What's your plan for today? I was thinking we could drive in together. Stop for some coffee, and then celebrate tonight – it is Christmas Eve eve."

"*You* want to celebrate Christmas Eve eve? I would not have expected to ever hear those words come out of your mouth?"

"Elaina told me about your conversation. We had a good laugh about it," Jason says with a chuckle.

"Elaina talked to you about our conversation?" Adrienne's voice is starting to rise. "And you *laughed* about it?"

"Don't get upset – I think it's cute that you are getting so into Christmas this year."

"Cute?" Adrienne stands up and starts to pace in front of the Christmas tree. "Wait a minute," she stops and turns to face Jason, "Elaina sent you here, didn't she?"

Jason looks down at his hands.

"She sent you here to talk to me. That's why last night you were encouraging me to work on that research, and why you are trying to convince me to drive in this morning?" Adrienne is practically yelling as she pieces together Jason and Elaina's devious plan.

"Okay, so yes, Elaina suggested I come here last night. But why is that a bad thing? She wants you to do well. She wants you to get that promotion – and this presentation she has you working on – which is today by the way – could be what finally gets you that promotion you deserve. That you have been working towards for years."

Adrienne is stunned into silence trying to process everything Jason is saying.

"I am sorry if you are mad that I would try and steer you back on the right path. I get that you were hit with this crazy house debacle – and that the timing is pretty bad – but you have completely lost yourself this week. I don't even recognize you," he says pointing at Adrienne's outfit as proof that she has lost her mind. Her silk pajamas have been replaced by an old pair of Chestnut Ridge lacrosse sweats with her hair pulled up in a messy ponytail.

She looks down and sees herself as Jason does at this moment and starts to laugh uncontrollably. Jason furrows his brow and looks at Adrienne like she belongs in the loony bin. This only makes Adrienne laugh even more. Bent over at the waist holding her stomach with tears streaming down her face, Adrienne feels as crazy as Jason thinks she is.

"I'm sorry," Adrienne says between big heaving breaths.

"I'm not sure what you find so funny about this situation, Adrienne. This is your future we are talking about right now."

"I know. I know, you're right," Adrienne regains her composure. "And I know why you say you don't even recognize me right now – it's because I am not the same person you knew a week ago. I've changed."

"You're telling me that we have been dating for a year, and then suddenly in one week you can completely change your personality?"

"My personality hasn't changed, but the things that are important to me have changed. My priorities have changed."

"I see that work is no longer a priority. And neither am I," Jason says quietly looking down at his hands again.

"I'm so sorry, Jason. But think about it, we have been dating for about a year, right?" Jason nods his head. "And what do we even really know about each other? Did you know anything about my family, or my childhood? I have never met anyone from your family – I may know your siblings names, but I don't know how you all get along, or what your family's Christmas traditions are?"

Jason opens his mouth to say something and then changes his mind.

"It's not either of our faults, we were just so focused on work and going out – we kept everything surface level. And I guess I just want something deeper."

After an awkward good-bye, Adrienne waves to Jason as he gets into his Uber and heads back into the city. Her spirit feels light and her mind clear. Although getting to the decision to break up with Jason was a difficult one, now that it's done Adrienne knows it was the right thing to do. Following a sleepless night and cloudy-headed morning, Adrienne now skips around the kitchen making another pot of coffee and putting some cinnamon rolls into the oven. Unaware that Gretchen is standing at the kitchen door watching her, Adrienne hums along to the Christmas music that is playing softly.

"What has gotten into you?" Gretchen laughs.

"Oh, you startled me," Adrienne jumps a little. "Nothing has gotten into me. I'm just getting ready for the day. Look at the chalkboard – do you notice that number one? We have a big day ahead of us if we want to win this contest. Can I get you some coffee?"

"It seems like you have maybe had too much coffee already? You are talking a mile a minute. And you know I am not a morning person," Gretchen says reaching for a coffee mug and pouring herself a generous amount.

"Where's Jason by the way? I figured he would already be dressed in his designer suit checking his emails," Gretchen teases.

"He left," Adrienne says slowly. Gretchen gives her a confused look.

"He left – for good?"

"Yes, for good. We broke up this morning."

"I'm so sorry, Adrienne. Are you okay?"

"Thanks, I'm okay. I am better than okay, actually."

"Phew, that is such good news!" Gretchen says with a big sigh of relief.

"What do you mean? He wasn't that bad!"

"I'll just say you two were not meant for each other, and leave it at that."

"Fine. Say what you want about him, but he *was* a good dresser," Adrienne laughs.

Gretchen giggles, "If you're into that look."

As Adrienne pulls the cinnamon buns out of the oven there is a knock at the door.

"Would you mind getting that, Gretch? I need to make a phone call."

"Of course," Gretchen says making her way to the front door. Adrienne snags her phone off the counter and quickly sneaks up the stairs.

Once Gretchen sees Nick's smiling face on the other side of the door, she perks right up.   "I could get used to this," she says.

"Used to what?" Nick asks.

"Used to seeing you right before I go to bed, and again when I wake up in the morning." Nick and Gretchen are so busy making googley eyes at each other they forget all about Gabe who is still standing outside in the cold.

"Excuse me? Lovebirds? Would you two mind if I came in now – maybe got some coffee?"

"Oh, I'm so sorry, Gabe. Come in, there's a pot of coffee and hot cinnamon buns in the kitchen."

Making himself at home in the kitchen away from the swooning couple, Gabe sits at the island sipping his coffee and hoping the sweet cinnamon bun will put him in a better mood. This to-do list on the counter certainly isn't helping. Adrienne comes down the stairs and is surprised to see Gabe sitting in the kitchen.

"Morning," she says.

Gabe turns around to face her and their eyes lock. "Morning."

"Thanks for coming back today. After last night, I wasn't sure you would."

"Actually, I wasn't sure I'd even see you here today. I thought you would be driving into New York with Jason."

The coldness in Gabe's voice makes it very clear that he is still angry.

"Well, I am not going in today. I just got off the phone with my boss to tell her just that, and I'll probably get fired for it. So that's great. As if the stakes for this contest weren't already high enough, just add on to it that I'll be unemployed," Adrienne's voice has gotten louder and louder as she speaks, to the point where she's yelling.

"Is everything okay in here?" Gretchen asks, walking into the kitchen with Nick right behind her.

"Everything is fine. Just fine," Adrienne says.

"Adrienne thinks she's going to get fired for not going into the office today," Gabe catches everyone up.

"Oh that would be amazing! First you dump that unbearable banker, and now you'll ditch that over-demanding job!" Gretchen cheers.

"Gretchen?!" Adrienne is stunned by her sister's response.

"You broke it off with Jason?" Gabe asks. Adrienne turns to him and nods her head. The two can't help but hold each other's stare for a moment, their eyes expressing more than they are willing to speak out loud.

"Isn't Gretchen kind of right, though?" Nick asks quietly.

Adrienne thinks about it for a minute. Then a smile spreads across her face and she says, "maybe."

"Okay everyone, let's move on, shall we?" Gabe says, now cheerful. "I have been looking at this to-do list and it appears that we have quite a bit of roof fixing and painting to do today."

Harkins Christmas List:

1. ~~Mow lawn~~
2. ~~Trim bushes~~
3. Paint house
4. ~~Clean gutters~~
5. Fix roof
6. ~~Paint front door~~
7. ~~Fix~~ ~~Paint front porch/pillars~~
8. ~~Paint and~~ Re-hang shutters
9. ~~Rake leaves~~
10. ~~Dust~~

11. ~~Wash floors~~
12. ~~Clean refrigerator~~
13. ~~Buy Christmas tree~~
14. ~~Decorate interior~~
15. Exterior Christmas lights, wreaths
16. ~~Clean bathrooms~~
17. Fix garage roof where tree fell

"Sorry to be the bearer of bad news, but that's actually why we are here so early this morning," Nick starts. "I don't think we are going to have any more help from Wallace's tree guy or Jeffries Painting – they are all hands on deck down at Town Hall."

"The four of us are going to have to try and do all of this ourselves today? It's not possible," Adrienne starts to panic.

"And I'm afraid that means that the tree that fell on the garage, which is only half removed at this point, will have to stay looking how it does. I don't have the equipment to completely remove it," Nick says apologetically.

"How bad is it right now?"

"Well, it's completely off the roof, and I would say it's still about my height, somewhere between six and seven feet tall."

"We'll figure something out," Gabe says.

"All we can do is try. What we get done is what we get done. That's it. And we do have up until around 5 p.m. tomorrow night," Gretchen says.

"I was thinking we save all the exterior decorations for tomorrow. You know, let the paint dry before we start wrapping lights and hanging wreaths on everything," Adrienne says.

"I think that's a great idea. So what's the plan then?" Gabe asks. "Nick obviously has to work on repairing the hole in the garage roof. Jeffries said he put all the roof shingles in the garage, so we can repair the ones on the main roof, and the garage roof with those."

"Nick, do you really think you can get the hole fixed in one day?" Gretchen asks.

"If all goes according to plan, I definitely can. But I really need to get started now. Gretch, you can be my assistant on the garage roof, and

Gabe and Adrienne can work on the main roof. Hopefully they can get that done by noon, and can then start painting the house.

Energized by their plan, the four friends finish their coffee and breakfast and get to work. After getting dressed Adrienne searches for Gabe – she finds him in the garage.

"Wow, this place is destroyed," Adrienne says looking around. She had not been in the garage since the tree fell on it. There is splintered wood, glass from a window that was smashed, sticks and leaves scattered all over the garage floor. Thankfully no car was parked in there at the time, and Adrienne's father did not keep his tools and things in the garage, or there would have been double the damage and expense.

"Yeah, it's pretty bad. Didn't Nick say the roof shingles were in here? I don't see them, do you?"

Adrienne scans the garage quickly - clearly there are no shingles in there.

"They are not in here. Let's go ask Nick if he knows where else they might be."

Gabe and Adrienne walk back through the house and outside into the cold. Pulling her jacket tighter around her body, Adrienne wishes she had worn a hat. Once they start work on the roof, she'll need to dress warmer.

Gabe can see Adrienne is cold and he longs to put his arm around her and pull her close. But his mind wanders back to that awful day four years ago when he arrived at 22 Oak Street to visit her, and she was gone. Poof. No good-bye, no explanation. Just gone. It was as if she vanished into thin air taking his heart with her. He needs to keep reminding himself of the pain Adrienne put him through, or risk going through that heartache all over again. He is not sure he could survive it.

Up ahead, Adrienne can see Nick and Gretchen giggling together as they position the ladder onto the garage.

"Are you two going to be able to get any work done together? Or are you going to be cuddling and giggling all day?" Adrienne knows she sounds bitter.

"Hey guys, how's it going?" Nick ignores Adrienne's question.

"Any idea where else Jeffries put the shingles? There's nothing in the garage but splintered wood, broken glass and tree branches," Gabe tells them.

"Really? I could have sworn he said he put the shingles in the garage. Let me call him and ask," Nick says grabbing his phone out of his jacket pocket.

"Kurt? Hey there, it's Nick. I'm over at the Harkins place and we are about to start replacing some of the broken roof shingles. Where did you say you put the shingles you had delivered?"

Nick pauses to listen and the look on his face changes from a smile to concern to a frown. Adrienne's heart starts to race as she and Gretchen look at each other, worried.

When Nick hangs up the phone, the other three are staring at him, anxiously awaiting the seemingly bad news.

"What is it? What happened?" Adrienne asks.

"Well, I must have misunderstood Kurt the other day. What he said was, when the shingles get delivered, have them put them in the good half of the garage."

"So they haven't been delivered yet? Who is supposed to deliver them?" Gabe asks.

"They have not been delivered -- should have been here yesterday. They are coming special order through some roofing distributor, Custom Roofing. Gabe, maybe you could find the number online and give them a call?" Nick says.

"Sure. I can do that. But if they don't come today, can't we just go down to the Hardware Store in town and buy some other shingles?"

"Unfortunately, we can't. You see these are custom multi-colored slate shingles – they aren't something you can buy in your average store. Since we didn't need a ton of them, Kurt called in a favor and got them donated to us – so it's even more difficult to give these people a hard time since we didn't even pay for them."

"Okay. I'll give them a call and see what I can do," Gabe says.

All that positive energy that was buzzing amongst the four of them has now come to a jarring halt. There is nothing more frustrating than having a bunch of work to do, the time to do it, but waiting for someone else to deliver in order to be able to get started.

"At least you two can continue what you're doing," Adrienne says to Nick and Gretchen as Gabe steps away to contact Custom Roofing.

Just then a gray pick-up truck pulls in front of the house. A middle-aged man holding a clipboard with a pencil tucked behind his right ear walks efficiently up the front path toward the group. *What now?* Adrienne thinks to herself.

"Hello there, I am looking for a Miss Harkins? Adrienne or Gretchen?" the man says.

"I am Adrienne Harkins."

"Hello Miss Harkins. My name is Seth Brower, and I work as an Inspector for the town of Chestnut Ridge. It has come to my attention that you have been having some work done on the property here at 22 Oak Street. Is this correct?"

"Yes, that's correct," Adrienne answers, instinctively feeling the need to defend herself.

"Well, from what I understand no construction permit application was ever filed with the town. In turn, this means that no permit has been issued allowing for said construction to legally begin."

Gabe walks out of the house and seeing the stunned expressions on Adrienne, Gretchen and Nick's faces he immediately puts on his lawyer hat.

"Is there a problem here?"

"This man is from the town and he says we don't have a construction permit to be able to do the work on the garage," Adrienne's voice is shaking.

"Can I see your identification, please?" Gabe asks. Mr. Brower's face is stone; he has not cracked a smile or a frown – completely expressionless. He hands his ID over to Gabe who inspects it quickly.

"You are with the Building Department, which means you report directly to Mayor Jessup," Gabe is more stating a fact than asking a question. But, Brower answers him anyway.

"That is correct. I am not sure how that is relevant."

"Trust me, it's relevant," Adrienne says coldly, putting it all together.

"So far all we have been doing is yard work, small repairs and painting. So what exactly are we required to have a permit for?" Gabe asks him.

"The construction work I see you are doing on your garage over there," he says pointing to where Nick and Gretchen were just working. "That you need a permit for."

"How long does it take to apply and get approved for a permit?" Adrienne asks.

"Well, the application process is not long, however the approval process could take anywhere from two to four weeks."

"Two to four weeks?!" Gretchen practically screams.

Adrienne hangs her head and puts her face in her hands.

"There has got to be something we can do to speed the process along . . . someone we can talk to?" Gabe says.

"You could try going directly to the Mayor, but until then, there is a stop order on this project and no work can be done on that garage until a licensed contractor has filed the appropriate paperwork and an Inspector comes out here to approve the work."

Handing Adrienne a stack of papers, Mr. Brower then turns on his heels and walks stiffly back to his truck - his last words hanging in the air.

The four friends look around at each other, stunned into silence. Mr. Brower, or Mayor Jessup for that matter, just took a sharp pin and stabbed the giant, fragile balloon of hope that had been floating among the friends. Its sudden burst stinging the faces of those holding it close.

"We can't give up," Gretchen, the first to speak, says quietly. "We've come this far! We can't give up."

"I just don't even know where to go from here. We can't fix the garage; we can't replace the tiles on the roof. All we can do is paint, but what is the point of that if the rest of the house is a disaster?! We can't win a house decorating competition with a house that looks like it could fall down at any moment!" Adrienne can no longer hold in her emotion. The more she rants, the angrier she becomes at one person in particular: Mayor Jessup.

Adrienne is so furious she doesn't notice another car has pulled in front of the Harkins home. A gleaming white luxury sedan stops at 22 Oak Street. Gretchen, Nick and Gabe stare at the wonder in white as she makes her way up the stone path. Adrienne, with her back to the street and continuing to vent sees the looks on the other three faces and turns to see what they are staring at.

"Angela?" Adrienne says, confused.

Angela seems to glide up the front walkway. Dressed in flowing white from head to toe, with her signature long white wool coat, furry white scarf and today, white fluffy earmuffs. Her presence has the already bewildered group, awe-struck.

With her bright smile and smooth voice, Angela says hello to the girls and gives them each a warm hug.

Gabe stares at Angela, a spark of recognition ignited in his brain, "Excuse me, do I know you from somewhere?" he asks her.

Before Angela can answer, Adrienne steps in, "I'm sorry I didn't introduce you all. Gabe and Nick this is Angela. Gretchen and I randomly met her in the city, and now she is here helping out at the Town Hall."

Nick and Gabe politely shake hands with Angela, and Adrienne can see they are also under her spell. Gabe stares at Angela, still trying to place her.

"Please tell me you're not here to deliver more bad news?" Adrienne pleads.

"Of course not, honey. I'm sure you heard about the fire at the Town Hall," they all nod their heads. "Such a tragedy. But if you could see how the community has responded, it would warm the heart of any Grinch this holiday season. Anyway, with the fire, all the paperwork from inside the office is gone – turned to ash. I am going around today to all the entrants in the Christmas Home Decorating Contest and asking that you re-fill out the paperwork. It will be a major help tomorrow – helping us to be sure we don't miss any contestant or get the wrong address for anyone . . . you understand."

"I understand, it's just that . . ." Adrienne is not sure how to finish the sentence.

"What is it sweetheart?" Angela asks concerned.

Adrienne looks around at Gretchen, Gabe and Nick hoping for some guidance. It seems they are all at a loss for words.

"It's just that we are not sure we are going to be able to compete in the contest after all," Adrienne says sadly.

"Why, whatever do you mean? Isn't it vital for you to win the contest in order to be able to keep the house in your family? I don't understand why you wouldn't enter?" Even with Angela being completely flabbergasted, her voice still sounds like a song, and her voice as smooth as butter.

Sensing Adrienne's emotional state, Gabe steps up and explains the situation as if he's giving his final arguments to a jury – reporting the facts of the problem in an orderly fashion. When he is done with stating his case, all four friends look to Angela, curious of her response.

After some careful thought, Angela turns to Adrienne, "Adrienne, do you remember that book I was reading when we bumped into each other at the café in the city?"

Adrienne nods her head, "Mark something that starts with a B?"

"Yes, Mark Batterson. Another thing he always says is 'All of us love miracles. We just don't like being in a situation that necessitates one.' This thought comes to me now, as you are in need of a miracle. And to this need, I say: have faith. This is the season for miracles and I truly believe what you are doing here is worthy of a miracle, don't you?"

Gretchen's face lights up. All she needed was someone else to believe this could work out, and she is right back on the positivity train. Adrienne, on the other hand, is a little more skeptical.

"Adrienne," Gretchen faces her sister and puts her hands on her shoulders, "I have no idea how this whole thing is going to come together, or if it will at all, but I do know that it feels right. It feels like this is what we are supposed to be doing right now. I am willing to take a leap of faith if you are. But whatever we decide, I want to make the decision together. So what do you say – want to create a Christmas miracle with me?"

Adrienne smiles at her sister whose eyes are full of hope and excitement – how can she say no?

"Let's do it," Adrienne says as the two girls hug each other.

"Yay! I am so excited for the both of you!" Angela says. "And now that you have made the decision to enter the contest, why don't you fill out that application and make it official."

With the Christmas Home Decorating Contest back on, now they just need to find a way to get a construction permit and find their lost-in-delivery roof shingles. That should be easy, right?

Adrienne, Gretchen, Nick and Gabe watch Angela gracefully walk down the path back to her car. Once she has driven away, it's back to work.

"Okay everyone, what's the plan?" Gretchen asks.

"It seems that the only thing we can do right now is paint," Adrienne says.

"Why don't the three of you get started on the painting – I have something I want to look into. I will be back as soon as I can to help out," Gabe says before quickly walking to his truck and driving off.

"And then there were three," Nick smiles. "And I don't know about the two of you, but I love to paint."

"Geez, you two glass-is-half-full people are meant for each other," Adrienne says as she walks toward the shed leaving Nick and Gretchen behind her blushing.

In the shed, Nick is hunting around looking for the correct paint to use on the front of the house. When he emerges with no paint cans in his hands and a pensive look on his face, Adrienne and Gretchen stop talking and brace themselves.

"What is it? What now?" Adrienne asks.

"It seems that you don't have the correct paint for the front of the house."

"Really? I swear I saw it in there," Adrienne says.

"I guess, yes, you do have paint that was used on the front of the house. The problem is, that paint was most likely used during warm weather – and well, last night the temperature dropped pretty significantly and although it has warmed up a bit today, you still need special paint to use in the winter."

Adrienne rolls her eyes. *Of course. Of course this would happen right now – just pile it on.*

"Is there somewhere we can buy the correct paint?" Gretchen asks.

"Yeah, we should be able to get it at the hardware store in town. Hopefully Bill has some. I'll go drive down there and see," Nick tells them.

"No, I'll go," Adrienne says. "You two stay here. I need to go for a drive. Really," she insists as Nick starts to disagree with her. But seeing her face, Gretchen and Nick realize she needs to get out of the house – a change of scenery can do wonders in situations like this.

Adrienne grabs her handbag and keys and drives into town. Although yesterday the fire seemed to put a damper on the Christmas festivities, today the town is back in full swing – mistletoe, twinkly lights, garland and carolers fill the sidewalks in anticipation of the big day. Adrienne has been so caught up in working on the house she has forgotten that tomorrow is Christmas Eve. Not Christmas Eve: the deadline for the contest. But *Christmas Eve*, the night before Christmas, which is the time to cherish all those close to you and celebrate giving. Adrienne needs to not only buy paint for Christmas Eve, but also a little something else to put under the tree.

CHAPTER TWENTY-TWO

Gabe hustles to his truck and with his heart racing, speeds downtown. Bursting through the front door of his office, Louise jumps in her seat, completely startled by the intrusion.

"Oh my goodness, Gabe, are you trying to give me a heart attack?"

"I am so sorry, Louise. I just have a lot on my mind. Can you do me a favor? Can you get Mayor Jessup on the line – I'll take it in my office."

Walking over to his desk, Gabe sits down and takes a deep breath to calm his nerves. Competing thoughts about what to do with his new business venture have been wrestling in his brain for days now, and he is completely worn out by it. It's time for him to make a decision. This latest stunt with the Mayor was the last straw. The phone rings once, letting Gabe know the Mayor is on the line.

"Bill, it's Gabe – we need to talk."

"Of course, what can I do for you Gabe?"

"I was just over at the Harkins residence, and a Mr. Brower showed up with a stop work order. He claims Adrienne and Gretchen can no longer do the construction repair work they need to do on their garage. I'm assuming you know about this."

"I know about everything going on in my town, Gabe. Just like I know how you have been practically living over at 22 Oak Street, helping them fix the house up. We had a deal, Gabe, and from my perspective, it doesn't look like you are honoring that agreement."

"You know what Mayor – I have been torn up about this partnership. And your little stunt today, well that's low, even for you. If I had known you were capable of stooping this low – of purposely trying to hurt members of our community for your own personal gain, well I never would have agreed to partner with you."

"Gabe, you need to grow up. This is how things work when you are an adult. Sometime in business you need to be willing to take things to the next level – it's just how it is. Now I'm sorry you are upset about it – if I had known you had a crush on Adrienne, maybe I would have approached things with you differently. But you weren't honest with me either. So why don't we agree that we both have made mistakes, and call it water under the bridge – let's move on."

"I'm afraid I can't do that, Bill. This partnership is over – terminated. And I'm going to need you to cancel that stop work order you put on the house. You know that is not the right thing to do."

"I'm afraid I can't do that, Gabe. You see, now with our terminated partnership, I now see you as the competition. One might even say, the enemy. Good luck to you and your little girlfriend, and I guess I will just see you tomorrow night at the Christmas Home Decorating Contest – you better change your attitude before I show up to judge."

Before Gabe can get another word in, the Mayor hangs up the phone. Gabe stands there listening to the dial tone drone on in his ear, and then he slams the phone down hard. So hard in fact, that poor Louise comes running into his office to be sure everything is okay. Seeing the anger on Gabe's face, Louise timidly asks, "Gabe, honey. Is everything all right? Is there anything I can do to help?"

Gabe looks up at Louise, and an idea flashes in his head. His anger is replaced by sheer determination. "Yes Louise, you can help," he starts to get excited. "We are going to do this my way – by the book. We are going to figure out a way to get this stop work order thrown out – and we'll do it using the law – all above board."

Louise looks at Gabe, puzzled. "Okay, sir. What is it you need me to do?"

"I need you to call in a favor for me."

CHAPTER TWENTY-THREE

Pushing open the door to the hardware store, Adrienne is overwhelmed. This place is definitely not in her comfort zone – she needs help. With no employees in site, Adrienne grabs a cart and starts wandering the aisles. As she makes a turn onto aisle eight, she is relieved to find paint cans and supplies. Scanning the million different kinds of paint, she finds the one Nick told her to buy: a premium oil based paint that is made for cold weather. Lifting the heavy gallons, she starts loading one after another into her cart. She then moves down the aisle a bit to check out paintbrushes. Adrienne's eyes start to glaze over reading all the different sizes and types of brushes, so she can't trust them when she looks up at the man standing three feet from her. Her eyes focus, and then her heart stops. Mayor Jessup.

"Why hello there, Miss Harkins. Funny running into you here."

"Hello. Why are you so surprised to see me here, Mayor Jessup? Is there some reason you didn't expect me to have any work to do on my house?"

Mayor Jessup stands up straight and looks her square in the eye. "Miss Harkins, is there something you would like to say to me?"

Adrienne's mind races – there are a million things she would *like* to say to him. But it's Christmas Eve eve and he is not worth her time.

"Looking forward to seeing you at the Christmas Home Decorating Competition," Adrienne's voice is as sweet as sugarplums. "Merry Christmas!"

"You should have seen the look on his face," Adrienne laughs to Gretchen and Nick back at the house. "I don't know if he was more surprised to see me buying paint or wishing him a Merry Christmas."

"I want to win this contest now more than ever," Gretchen says.

"Well let's get painting! I will start on the ladder near the roof line, you two start on the ground," Nick says.

Fueled by coffee, Christmas music and the desire to put Mayor Jessup in his place, the three friends begin the arduous task of painting the front of the large home. At around 11:30 a.m., after what seems like days, Adrienne steps back to look at their progress. Massaging her frozen, cramped hands she sighs, *this is going to take forever*. However, the relatively small section that has been painted looks amazing - only a million more hours to go.

"Anyone need a coffee?" she asks.

"Something warm and filled with caffeine? Yes, please!" Gretchen says.

"Yeah, that sounds great. Thanks, Adrienne," Nick yells down from up high near one of the second floor bedroom windows.

The entire drive into town Adrienne rotates her hands – one on the wheel and one in front of the heater, and then switch. The plan is to get some lunch to bring back from Peas & Pickles and then get three coffees from the Dreamy Bean. Walking out of Peas & Pickles with her grocery bags something across the street catches her eye. Adrienne stops moving and focuses on two people having what appears to be an intense conversation – it's Gabe. Gabe and a young woman with long blonde hair are sitting on a bench outside of a jewelry store. The pair is sitting so close their knees are touching.

Still holding her grocery bags, Adrienne hides behind one of the lampposts, which is wrapped in garland and lights, peering around it to watch Gabe and the mystery woman. Adrienne gasps when she sees Gabe put his hand on the woman's knee and lean in close. The woman nods her head, staring into his beautiful blue eyes. Simultaneously, they both stand up and hug for what seems to Adrienne like an extremely long time.

Feeling sick to her stomach, Adrienne hustles to her car and puts the groceries in the trunk. Not wanting to be seen by Gabe, she keeps her head turned away as she walks down the block to the Dreamy Bean. The delicious smell of coffee and scones does not have the calming effect it typically has for Adrienne. Why is she so upset? Is it at all surprising that Gabe has a girlfriend? Adrienne feels silly for thinking anything to the contrary. Of course he has a girlfriend – he's a successful, kind, thoughtful, handsome guy. After ordering the coffees, Adrienne does her best to not feel so dejected. Gabe is not the reason she is here, nor is he the reason she has stayed so long. Maybe this is a good thing – keeping her focused on the goal. She will keep reminding herself of that.

Back at the house, Gretchen and Nick are still painting away. Gretchen's excitement at the arrival of food and coffee shows how desperately she needs a break.

"What's wrong?" Gretchen immediately asks Adrienne.

"Huh? What do you mean? Nothing."

"You seem . . . sad. Did something happen?"

"No, I'm just worried, that's all."

"Okay," Gretchen says skeptically. And then switching gears asks, "We're only going to worry about painting the front of the house, right?"

"Definitely. We'll worry about the sides and back later – if the house is still ours."

"This house will always be ours."

CHAPTER TWENTY-FOUR

Stuck doing the monotonous painting, Adrienne does her best to focus on the positive, and not the fact that they very well might be painting the front of this house only to have it auctioned off to Mayor Jessup in a week. Because the truth is, they are halfway through the day and still don't have the new roof shingles, or the ability to fix the giant gaping hole in the garage. Despite how great the paint job might look, they will not win the contest having a disastrous roof and a hole in their house. No amount of garland and twinkly lights can detract from that crater in the garage.

But Adrienne is trying not to think about all of that. She is trying to have faith. She is trying to believe in miracles, like Gretchen and Angela. She does agree with Gretchen that what they are doing, this whole experience, has felt . . . right. It just feels right. And that's where her mind has circled back to when there is a loud engine roaring behind her. Holding their paintbrushes still, Adrienne, Gretchen and Nick all turn around to face the street in front of the house. Stopped on the road is a large white truck. Adrienne's heartbeat starts to quicken – could something actually go right today?

Nick hops down off the ladder and walks toward the man getting out of the truck.

"Can I help you?" Nick asks.

"I think you can. I apologize for the delay, but better late than never right?" The squat, jolly man says with a laugh. "I have some custom roof shingles here that were special ordered. Where would you like me to put them?"

Adrienne and Gretchen drop their paintbrushes and run up to Nick's side.

"Right over here on the driveway would be perfect. We are hoping to get them put up today," Nick tells the deliveryman.

Unable to hide their excitement, Adrienne and Gretchen are practically jumping up and down hugging each other. The roof shingles made it here in time!

"I knew they would come. We're going to do this," Gretchen whispers in her sister's ear.

Adrienne hugs her even tighter, a surge of hope emanating from their bodies.

Wrapping his tool belt around his waist, Nick instructs the sisters to continue painting while he gets up on the extension ladder and begins fixing the roof.

"How bad is it up there?" Gretchen yells up to him.

"It's not as bad as I feared," Nick yells down as he does a quick inspection. "It doesn't look like the actual roof has any damage, just shingles that need to be replaced. This is the best we could have hoped for."

With a renewed sense of purpose the three of them push on. Gretchen has to keep shaking her arm out to relieve the aching. Adrienne's mind has now wandered back to Gabe.

"Didn't you say earlier you didn't think Gabe had a girlfriend?" Adrienne asks Gretchen, seemingly out of the blue.

"That's what I had heard, but I guess I don't know for sure. Why are you thinking about that?"

"No reason," Adrienne starts to deny it, and then changes her mind. "Okay. I saw Gabe in town with a really pretty blonde. They seemed very . . . close. They definitely knew each other very well, and had some type of connection."

"Huh. You should ask him."

"I can't ask him! First of all, he's not even here," Adrienne looks over at Gretchen who is subtly motioning toward the driveway. Adrienne looks over, and as if he could sense she was talking about him, Gabe is walking up the lawn.

"Wow, this looks amazing guys! And, wait, are those roof shingles?"

"They sure are!" Nick leans over the edge of the house.

"Be careful, Nick!" Gretchen yells back. "The last thing we need is you falling off our roof right now!"

"Where were you?" Adrienne tries to sound nonchalant.

"Oh, I had some work to do. But I think I got it finished, so I can get back to work here now."

"Work? Really? On Christmas Eve eve? That's strange, isn't it?" Adrienne is annoyed at Gabe's dishonesty.

"You never know when people are going to need help," Gabe raises an eyebrow at Adrienne.

"Gretch, can you help me by hauling some of the shingles up the ladder?" Nick yells down.

"Gabe, it's all you," Gretchen hands Gabe her paintbrush, unable to hide her smile. She is pretty happy to take a break from the painting, and see Nick.

The crew works in relative silence for about an hour. Adrienne has to switch to using her left arm, since her right arm now feels like it might just give up and fall off.

"Remember that time we drove out to Falls Pond to go ice skating?" Adrienne breaks the silence.

"How could I forget?" Gabe smiles as he dips the tip of his brush into some paint. "It was the first, and only time I have been with someone who fell through the ice."

"I didn't exactly *fall* through the ice," Adrienne giggles. "I was just so sure that when that mitten fell off and into one of the cracks in the ice that I could reach down quickly and pull it right up. How was I supposed to know how cold that water was going to be?"

"It was partly frozen, so you know, that typically means freezing cold," Gabe chuckles.

"I thought you were going to have a heart attack," now Adrienne is really laughing. "I can still remember the look on your face when you saw me reaching down into the water. You were yelling 'No! Adrienne, no! Don't do it!' and then I did it. And I went in!"

"I had nightmares about you falling into that icy water for months after that day. For someone so smart, that was a really dumb thing to do," Gabe is laughing, too.

"Hey, that's not very nice! They were my favorite mittens – fuzzy, striped ones that were all different colors, and I thought I could reach in quickly and grab it. Maybe I wouldn't have fallen in if I didn't look over at you when you yelled at me. Did you ever think of that? That maybe the whole thing was your fault?" Adrienne teases him.

"Oh, don't even try and pin that one on me. I saved your life, if you haven't forgotten."

Adrienne stops painting and turns toward Gabe, "I haven't forgotten."

After a brief glance over at her, and before the moment can get too awkward, Gabe feels the need to break the silence. "I remember carrying you home wrapped in my winter coat with my favorite Giants hat on and rushing you into the house. I don't think I ever got that hat back, by the way. And you thought *I* was going to have a heart attack? How about your mom?"

"Yeah, she totally freaked out. I think that was only a week or two before the car accident."

"I think you're right. You left, without a word, two weeks later. Never to be heard from again – until last week, that is," Gabe's voice has turned cold. Adrienne can see the pain she caused him and she doesn't know how to fix it.

"I'm so sorry, Gabe. I just had to get out of here. It was too painful being in this house with their stuff all around me. I had to leave."

Gabe turns toward Adrienne, his paintbrush down by his side, "I could have helped you, Adrienne. I wanted to help you."

"I know. I'm sorry. It was almost as if I didn't want to feel anything after that – good or bad. I felt like my whole life was over. I knew nothing would ever be the same again."

"Of course it wouldn't. But I lost your parents too, you know. I had known them most of my life –heck, I practically lived in this house. And then they were gone, and you were gone too."

A single tear slides down Adrienne's cheek. "Not a single day has gone by that I haven't regretted how I handled the whole situation. And I wish I could do it all over again. But I can't." Adrienne pauses, and they both turn back to toward the house, and move their brushes up and down. But neither of them is paying any attention to how the paint looks.

"You know," Adrienne says a few moments later. "Angela told me a quote that seems to be so relevant to my life lately, she said 'you're always one decision away from a totally different life.' I originally took that to mean that I could make a decision now that could change my life for the better going forward. But what I am realizing now is that I've made decisions that changed my life forever - and they weren't good ones."

"Well, just like falling into a crack in a frozen pond, for someone so smart, that was a pretty dumb thing to do," a sad smile crosses Gabe's face.

"And leaving the way I did, I can't blame that one on you."

The sound of Gabe's cell phone breaks up the intense moment, and both Adrienne and Gabe breathe a small sigh of relief.

Adrienne attempts to get back to focusing on the darn white paint, while Gabe steps away to answer the call. A few minutes later he walks back over and picks up his paintbrush.

"Everything okay?" Adrienne does her best to sound nonchalant.

"Yeah, that was Louise. I have her working on something for me. I do have to work sometimes too you know."

"Of course – I'm sorry we have monopolized your time this week. I hope it isn't causing any problems for you."

"Don't worry about me, I've got it covered."

Gabe's phone rings again and he excuses himself once again.

Gretchen climbs down from the ladder, "How is it going over here?" she asks.

"Oh you know, still painting. I feel like this white paint is blinding me." Adrienne blinks her eyes a few times.

"Well, you have made a ton of progress! Take a step back and look at it!"

Adrienne and Gretchen walk toward the front of the lawn and look back at the house from the sidewalk.

"Wow, with the new roof shingles and the fresh paint – it doesn't even look like the same house it did this morning!" Adrienne exclaims.

"I know! It's incredible!" Gretchen agrees. "You should see Nick up there with these shingles, he is so fast! I don't know how he's doing it. But I have to say, he sure is a dream to watch," Gretchen's eyes glaze over into swoon-ville.

"I think we'll definitely be able to finish the painting and roof today, which is just so amazing. But what are we going to do with the giant gaping elephant in the room?" Adrienne worries.

"Oh, you mean the fact that our garage is basically caved in on one side? You can hardly notice!" Gretchen says and the two sisters start laughing uncontrollably.

"What is going on over here? Have you two breathed in too many paint fumes today?" Gabe smiles at the girls who are doubled over laughing hysterically.

"I guess sometimes things are so bad all you can do is laugh – either that or cry," Adrienne says between giggles.

"Well I have some news that might make things a little less bad," Gabe raises an eyebrow. "I did some research into your little permit problem and talked to a few people who are experts in the permit process in Chestnut Ridge, and well, as of this moment Adrienne and Gretchen Harkins from 22 Oak Street are officially able to continue construction work on their property."

Gretchen jumps up and down, "Eeeeeeekkk!! Ohmigod, Gabe, thank you, thank you, thank you! How did you do it? You are our hero! I knew this was all going to work out!"

"Whoa, Gretchen, calm down. Take a breath!" Adrienne chuckles, and then looking at Gabe asks, "Is this for real? We can continue fixing the garage?" She is almost unwilling to believe that they could have such good fortune.

Gabe nods his head up and down, a huge smile lighting up his face. Adrienne matches his smile, and throwing caution to the wind, grabs him and pulls him into a giant hug – her face buried into his neck so deep she can smell his spicy cologne. She wishes she could just set up a tent and move in right here, in this very spot.

"How did you do it?" Adrienne asks him when she finally pulls herself away from him.

"I realized our only hope was to find a loop hole, because there was no way we would be able to get someone to speed up the process for us, especially with the Mayor's influence and it being two days before Christmas. So after some initial research was getting me nowhere, I met up with a friend who works in the Building Department for the town," Gabe's excitement builds as he tells the story. "I explained the situation and she told me she would look into it. That was her right now on the phone, and apparently in the case of a natural disaster, like a storm causing a tree to fall on a house, the homeowner is allowed to immediately fix the damage. No permit necessary. I guess they figure they can't let people sit there with a hole in their house for a few weeks waiting for a permit. I, of course, then called Mr. Brower and explained this to him, and he reluctantly relented. Construction is back on!"

"I have to go tell Nick the good news," Gretchen is bursting with energy. She turns toward Gabe and gives him one more quick hug, "Thank you."

"And there it is – you saved my life once again," Adrienne says shyly.

"Not yet, I haven't. I may have gotten a green light to start construction. But there is still a lot of work to do, and we are almost out of daylight for today."

After another quick celebration that now includes Nick, the four friends get back to work with renewed energy. Nick and Gabe immediately start fixing the garage, and Adrienne and Gretchen are back at it: painting. Endless painting.

"Can I talk to you for a minute?" Gabe asks Adrienne a little while later.

"Of course, any excuse to take a break from painting," Adrienne smiles. But then looking at Gabe's serious expression, her smile fades and she immediately prepares herself for bad news. "What is it? Is everything okay? Is it the roof?"

"No, no – nothing like that. I just feel I need to be honest with you about something," Gabe looks down at his work gloves. "A few months ago, before you were back – before I had any idea you would ever come back, I partnered up with someone on a real estate development deal. The plan was to buy real estate at a low cost, renovate, and re-sell for a profit."

"Like flipping properties," Adrienne says, still unsure what this has to do with her.

"Exactly like that. Well, the person I partnered with was Mayor Jessup," Gabe pauses, letting this information sink in.

Puzzled, Adrienne looks at Gabe confused – and then her face slowly changes as she puts it all together. "You were going to be part of buying 22 Oak Street out from under us at the auction," Adrienne's face hardens.

"I was. But you have to understand – Oak Street was on a list with a ton of other properties, and I had no idea there was a lien on the home and that it would be going to auction now." Gabe looks at Adrienne apologetically.

"And what about now?"

"Well, now I am Team Harkins," he smiles. "I quickly realized Bill Jessup is not someone I want to get into business with. I tried to get him to cancel the stop work order, and he wouldn't do it. So I went around him and found another way to get it stopped. And trust me, this has all been a blessing. I saw his true colors before I got in too deep."

Adrienne looks over at the house, thinking. Gabe's news is surprising, and if she's honest with herself, disappointing. "So, why are you telling me this? Why now?"

"I just thought you should know everything – the whole truth. It has been eating me up inside, and I just want it all out in the open." Gabe searches Adrienne's expression for any clues to how she is feeling.

Having thought it all through, Adrienne turns her head back to look at Gabe, her face serious. And then breaks into a grin, "As long as you came around, I'm okay with it. I get it, I really do. Sometimes it takes a little while to commit to a decision you know is the right one all along. Team Harkins," she says and puts her hands up for a double high-five.

"Team Harkins," Gabe slaps both her hands, relieved.

As the sun sets on Christmas Eve eve, the fix-it crew of 22 Oak Street is wiped out. Completely exhausted.

"I'm not going to be able to move my arms for weeks," Gretchen complains as she massages her upper arms.

"I don't think my body has ever been this tired," Adrienne agrees.

The four of them have called it a day and have slumped their weary bodies on the sofas in the family room. Nick somehow musters up the energy to start a fire, and the four of them sit quietly watching the flames dance.

"I think we should have superhero names," Gretchen says.

Adrienne lets out a laugh.

"No, I am serious. What mere mortal can do what we have done in only three days? Three days!" Gretchen says. "Now I'm going in to make popcorn and open a bottle of wine, when I get back I want to know some superhero names."

The other three laugh at the idea, but don't want to disappoint Gretchen. When Gretchen saunters back into the family room a few minutes later, Adrienne, Gabe and Nick are laughing so hard no one can even get a word out, never mind a superhero nickname.

"So what did you come up with Miss Marketing guru?" Gretchen singles out Adrienne who does her best to stop laughing long enough to speak.

"Okay, this is what we've got," Adrienne giggles again, "Nick is PHANTOM FASTHAMMER, for obvious reasons."

"I like that . . ." Gretchen looks at Nick in that sticky sweet way that makes Adrienne want to throw popcorn at her.

"And what about Gabe?" Gretchen asks.

"Gabe is CAPTAIN PHENOMENAL, again for obvious reasons. He definitely saved the day, and he is definitely phenomenal." Gabe blushes at the compliment.

"And for you, Miss Gretchen," Gabe says. "You are the POSITIVITY PROTECTOR!" as soon as Gabe says this, Nick, Adrienne and Gabe burst out laughing.

"That's kinda lame guys," Gretchen says while handing out glasses of wine. "Why are Nick and Gabe's names so much cooler?"

"Sorry, our brains are fried. It was the best we could do with such time constraints," Adrienne says grabbing a handful of popcorn.

"And what about Adrienne's superhero name? We didn't get that far . . ." Gabe says, thinking.

"I actually came up with her name while I was in the kitchen," Gretchen says smiling. "Adrienne, the IRON VIXEN."

"That's amazing! Maybe you should apply to take over my position in marketing, Gretch," Adrienne says. "There should be an opening at Morgan Lynch soon."

"No thank you. I value my soul."

"Ha. Funny. Well, I love my superhero name. From here on out I expect you all to refer to me as the Iron Vixen," Adrienne says. "Now, Captain Phenomenal, I insist that you find us a Christmas movie, stat. And please make sure my wine does not get too low."

"It would be my pleasure, Ms. Vixen."

CHAPTER TWENTY-FIVE

The sun teems through the window so brightly; Adrienne can feel it on her closed eyelids. Cracking one eye open she looks around, not immediately realizing where she is. Braving the illuminated room she opens her eyes as far as they are willing to go and sits up. Popcorn is sprinkled all over the coffee table and floor, scattered wine bottles and wine glasses sit empty and the fireplace holds the ash remnants of a once roaring fire. And four, now three, adults are passed out on two sofas, their bodies contorted and squished under layers of blankets.

It's Christmas Eve! And although this year this day means <u>deadline</u> for something they are not even ready for, Adrienne feels the magic of this day fill her soul and warm her heart. This day will always bring back memories of her parent's tragedy, but for the first time Adrienne can look back and remember the good times too, not just the bad: the joy, the laughter, the love.

Ever so quietly Adrienne pushes the blanket off of her, and untangles her legs from Gabe's. Gabe. The thought of him makes her tingle from her belly up to her throat. Can life really be like this? Can she wake up feeling happy and light every morning? Tiptoeing into the kitchen she puts on some coffee, puts bacon in the oven and starts to mix up some pancake batter. Looking over at the chalkboard she knows what she has to do. Erasing the number one, Adrienne writes a big fat zero. There are no more days -- today is the day. It's 8 a.m., so the Harkins' family has nine hours before judges could start to arrive. And what needs to be done? Adrienne crosses off "Paint house" (hallelujah!) and "Fix roof" (yay!).

Harkins Christmas List:

1. ~~Mow lawn~~
2. ~~Trim bushes~~
3. ~~Paint house~~
4. ~~Clean gutters~~
5. ~~Fix roof~~
6. ~~Paint front door~~
7. ~~Fix~~ ~~Paint front porch/pillars~~
8. ~~Paint and~~ Re-hang shutters
9. ~~Rake leaves~~
10. ~~Dust~~
11. ~~Wash floors~~
12. ~~Clean refrigerator~~
13. ~~Buy Christmas tree~~
14. ~~Decorate interior~~
15. Exterior Christmas lights, wreaths
16. ~~Clean bathrooms~~
17. Fix garage roof where tree fell

Obviously, the biggest thing to get done today is the garage. Even once the hole is repaired, the garage will need to be painted a little, and its roof will need new shingles. The shutters still need to be hung . . . and then they can decorate – hooray! Adrienne has already chosen what her job will be today, on Christmas Eve. She will definitely be hanging lights, wreaths and garland -- creating a magical Christmas wonderland. She makes a mental note to check the basement to see if any of the lawn ornaments are down there.

"Good morning," Gabe's voice is just above a whisper.

"Good morning," Adrienne smiles. "Merry Christmas Eve. I hope I didn't wake you."

"No, you didn't. I feel like I'm in one of those coffee commercials where the smell of the coffee brewing wakes everyone up. That's me right now – and let me tell you, there's nothing better than being woken up to the smell of coffee and bacon . . . and having you be the first person I see. This might well be the best Christmas Eve ever."

Adrienne blushes, and nervously stirs the pancake batter. "You might be speaking a bit too soon – you haven't looked at the to-do list yet. It'll be a working Christmas Eve, unfortunately."

"I don't mind at all. I have to say I've been thinking about you, a lot actually, and wondering how you would deal with Christmas Eve. This must be a tough day for you."

Adrienne keeps busy making pancakes; afraid if she looks up and into Gabe's eyes, she will get too emotional.

"Honestly, the past few Christmas Eves were awful. I would sit alone in my apartment avoiding Christmas movies, avoiding anything to do with Christmas actually, which is no easy feat. And I would wallow in my misery. Gretchen and I would maybe send each other a text, but sometimes not even that. I can't believe I thought that was the best way to handle the pain."

"And what about this year?" Gabe asks.

"I am overwhelmed," Adrienne says quietly and Gabe looks at her concerned. "I am overwhelmed with . . . happiness. Family. Love," she speaks the last word barely above a whisper.

"What's going on in here? Ooohh Adrienne, are you making the traditional Harkins' Christmas Eve pancakes?" Gretchen all but barges in.

"I sure am," Adrienne takes a deep breath, smiling at Gabe.

"You know," Gretchen walks over and grabs a slice of bacon, "I made these by myself the last few years on Christmas Eve. I can tell you, they taste much better when shared with friends and family."

Adrienne plops pancakes on plates, gets out the butter and syrup and pours coffee all around. Nick walks in soon after and the four of them enjoy a big hearty breakfast before their busy day. They laugh as they reminisce about the night before, teasing each other with their Superhero names.

"I see that big zero on the chalkboard and I can't believe the day is really here. Sometimes it felt like it would never come, and sometimes it felt like it was coming too quickly," Gretchen says.

"I know I was skeptical, but I actually think we are going to pull this off," Adrienne smiles at the group.

"Wait, is that Adrienne being positive? Maybe we should be calling you the Positivity Protector?" Gretchen laughs and the rest join in.

Once everyone has showered and gotten dressed (for the guys, it was right back into the clothes they wore all yesterday and then slept in), the four of them meet outside for job assignment. Nick takes over as foreman and is all business, "Gabe, you will start by hanging shutters. I don't think this will take you more than a few hours, and then you can join me on the garage. Adrienne and Gretchen, I know you two will be so sad not to be painting today," the girls smile, "but instead, I'm afraid you are going to have to put up all the Christmas decorations. Now this is a very important job, you know. Think the Griswolds from *Christmas Vacation* – no skimping on the lights. And please, be careful on the ladder."

Adrienne and Gretchen are practically jumping up and down. Once again the girls bring out a portable speaker and blast Christmas music. Then they begin the search for all the outdoor lawn ornaments, lights, wreaths and garland. Some of the décor is in the boxes they have stored in the den, and some things are in the basement, and some are in the attic – it takes the girls quite a while to gather it all up on the front lawn and take inventory.

"I need a coffee break already," Gretchen laughs. "And do you know what would go perfect with hanging Christmas lights?" Adrienne stares at her blankly. "Gingerbread lattes from the Dreamy Bean!" Gretchen's eyes light up like twinkle lights.

"Okay, but you are going into town. I feel like I have been in and out of town a million times a day. I will get started with the front portico. I was thinking we wrap lighted garland around the columns, hang garland with a bow around the front door, and then a lighted wreath on the door. What do you think?"

"I think that sounds perfect. I will be super-fast at the Dreamy Bean, I promise. And it will totally be worth working alone for a bit once you taste the amazing gingerbread flavor."

Adrienne cannot argue with that. As she starts to wrap the lighted garland around the two front portico columns, she and Gabe keep passing each other by as he goes back and forth with the freshly painted shutters. The two of them can't seem to stop smiling at each other. *Does he have a girlfriend or not?* Keeps running through her mind as she puts one foot on the small stepladder to reach the top of the column. So distracted by her thoughts of Gabe, as she reaches up high on her tippy toes she loses her balance and can feel the ladder begin to tip. A small scream slips from her mouth and she squeezes her eyes tight, bracing herself for impact. Just as she should be hitting the hard cement, she is suddenly floating in someone's strong arms. Relief washes over Adrienne as she opens her eyes to thank her rescuer. However, words escape her when she finds herself inches from Gabe's face. They stare into each other's eyes and caught up in the moment, Adrienne leans in to kiss him.

Gabe quickly pulls away and plants Adrienne back on her feet.

"I am so sorry. I don't know what came over me! I know you have a girlfriend, and did that anyway. What is wrong with me?" Adrienne is incredibly embarrassed by the rejection, though.

"Girlfriend? What are you . . .? That's not why I . . .."

"It's okay, Gabe. I saw you two together in town. The pretty blonde sitting on the bench?"

"What? Oh, I see," Gabe says, finally understanding. "Jennifer."

"So that's her name," Adrienne feels nauseous.

"Yeah – Jennifer, my assistant Louise's daughter."

"You're dating your assistant's daughter?"

"No! We're not dating. We're just good friends. She works for the Department of Buildings. Jennifer is the person who helped us with the permit information."

"Ohhhhhh," Adrienne feels euphoric. "But wait, then why did you . . .?"

"Why did I pull away from you?" Gabe finishes her sentence. Adrienne nods her head.

"I am not sure I can put myself through that again. Through *this* again," he says moving his hand between the two of them. "When you left, it crushed me Adrienne. I'm not sure I could take going through that again. I mean once this contest is over, what is your plan? Are you picking back up with your old life with the apartment in the city, the high-stress job? I mean, do you have a plan?"

Adrienne stares at him blankly. She is unsure how to answer him.

"Until you know that, Adrienne, I can't let myself fall for you again." Her eyes wide, Adrienne stands stunned.

"Hey, what's with all the chit-chat over there? Let's get back to work, huh?" Nick yells from across the yard breaking up the tense moment. Gabe turns and walks back to the good side of the garage to grab another shutter to hang. Adrienne doesn't move for a few minutes, dizzy with thoughts zooming around her brain.

Gretchen walks over carrying the tray of coffees, and looking at Adrienne quizzically asks, "Adrienne, are you okay? What happened?" Adrienne continues to stare off into space.

"Helloooo? Earth to Adrienne! What's going on?"

Adrienne snaps back to life, "Oh, I'm sorry, I am a little out of it. I almost just fell off the stepladder and then I got hit with a truth bomb."

"Oh my, let's take one thing at a time. You almost fell off the ladder – and you're okay?" Gretchen gives Adrienne the once-over looking for injuries. Adrienne nods her head, letting Gretchen know she is not hurt.

"Okay, great. And now for the truth-bomb . . .I'm assuming that was from Gabe, since I don't think Saint Nick delivers truth-bombs on Christmas Eve," Gretchen tries to get a smile out of Adrienne. However, Adrienne seems to barely hear her.

"What did he say?" Gretchen asks quietly, almost reluctantly.

"I'm an idiot."

"He said you were an idiot?"

"No, I just am an idiot. I tried to kiss him, and he backed away." Gretchen grimaces. "And then he told me that he couldn't ever be with me again because of the way I treated him after Mom and Dad died. Unless I have a plan, or something like that . . .I'm pretty sure he thinks I'm an idiot and he hates me."

"Now, some of that sounds awful, some of that sounds, well, true, and some of it sounds crazy. He doesn't hate you, Adrienne. He's just trying to protect his heart from being broken again. I think you know a little about that, don't you? Why else would you have dated Jason for so long?"

Adrienne looks at Gretchen, confused.

"You dated him for so long because you were never at risk of falling in love with him, and therefore never at risk for getting hurt. I'm proud of you for trying to kiss Gabe. Personally, I think it's the bravest thing you've done in a long time – putting yourself out there like that."

Adrienne smiles at Gretchen, and then leans in for a quick hug. "You are really easy to talk to, do you know that?"

"Well, we should do it more often, then. Right? Here, this will make you feel better," she says handing Adrienne a gingerbread latte.

A few hours go by and the shutters are all hung up – Gabe did an amazing job. The girls are making the house Christmas spectacular. The portico and front door look gorgeous, and now Adrienne and Gretchen are moving on to hanging strings of lights along the roofline. This is not an easy job, even with hooks already there from previous years. Gretchen is doing most of the high ladder work, considering Adrienne already fell off a short stepladder.

Adrienne stands at the bottom of an extension ladder as Gretchen balances on one of the top rungs, reaching over to hook a light strand. Nick walks over and is watching the whole scene. "I can't even watch, it's making me so nervous!" Adrienne says to Nick. "I feel like she's going to come tumbling down any minute!"

"It is a bit nerve-wracking to watch. But I feel better with her up there than you, no offense," Nick teases.

After an eye roll, Adrienne asks, "How are things going over there on the garage?"

"We're moving along okay. I've got it cleaned up and Gabe is working on framing it out. Right now I need to run to the hardware store and pick up some sheathing, felt paper and more nails for my nail gun. Do you ladies need anything?"

"I have no idea what you just said, but it sure sounds good," Adrienne laughs. "We don't need anything, right Gretch?" Adrienne yells up to her sister.

"We need lunch! I'm hungry already!"

As Nick is walking down the front path a small sedan pulls up to the front of the house. Adrienne, Gretchen, Gabe and Nick all stop what they are doing to stare at the car. Historically they have not had much luck with surprise visitors, aside from Angela, of course. And it looks like they will keep the unlucky streak alive, as out walks Elaina.

Pulling her cashmere coat tightly around her, Elaina click clacks on four-inch heels up the walkway. Her face is pinched and stern - she is all business, as usual.

"Elaina? What are you doing here?" Adrienne asks.

"Hello Harkins, so this is what you've been doing instead of being at work? Hanging Christmas lights?" Before Adrienne can even answer, Elaina interrupts her, "Never mind, it doesn't matter. Can I speak to you in private please? And maybe somewhere that's not freezing cold?"

"Sure, come on inside."

As they two women walk inside, Elaina gasps at the décor. "Wow, it's like Christmas threw up in here. Harkins, what has gotten into you?"

"I think it's magical. But that is only one of many things we disagree on. Now, I know you didn't come all the way to Connecticut to talk about Christmas decorations. What do you want, Elaina?"

Elaina looks down at her feet sheepishly, "The truth, Harkins, is that I want you to come back to work. Remember that big important meeting regarding the cell phone location technology that you did all that research on? Well, the Board hated the idea. They thought it was creepy and invasive, just like you tried to tell me."

A contrite Elaina is something Adrienne never expected to see, ever. "Look Elaina, I am sorry the meeting didn't go well for you. I know you worked hard on it. But I still don't know what that has to do with me."

"You used excellent judgment, that I was lacking, in coming up with new marketing ideas for the company. Thankfully because of the Just-In-Time marketing you had told me about, I was able to save myself at the meeting. Everyone loved that idea of paying closer attention to what clients do with our company, and then offer them a relevant additional service. The Board thought that was a total win-win. So I guess I am here to thank you, firstly. And secondly, to say that you can have a little time off for the holidays, but then we would like you to come back to work as the new Marketing Manager."

"You are offering me the promotion?" Adrienne could not be more surprised if Santa himself jumped out from behind her Christmas tree right now.

"We are offering you the promotion, which you have worked hard for and deserve. You will have an actual office, not just a cubical, and a pay raise of course."

"Please email me the terms – I need to go over them and then think about it."

Although many expressions don't show on Elaina's face, Adrienne is pretty sure she saw a glimpse of surprise.

"Of course. I will email you the paperwork this afternoon for you to review. But we will need an answer by December 26th."

Adrienne walks Elaina out to her car, says good-bye and wishes her a Merry Christmas. Elaina looks as though no one has ever said those words to her, and even more surprisingly, she says them back. This certainly is the season for miracles.

As Adrienne walks back up toward the house after Elaina has driven off, she feels three sets of eyes boring into her. "What?" she asks all of them.

"Well, what was that all about? Did you get fired? Please say you got fired," Gretchen says.

"No, I didn't get fired, Gretchen. I actually got promoted. They offered me the Marketing Manager position."

"Congratulations?" Gretchen sounds less than excited.

"Yeah, Adrienne. Congratulations," Gabe says, also in more of a monotone voice.

"Let me guess, you have to start tomorrow, on Christmas day?" Gretchen teases.

"Well, no. But I have to give her an answer by the 26th."

"You didn't take the job?" Gretchen asks surprised.

"I told her I would like to think about it. And that's the truth – it is not a simple decision either way. So I am going to think about it – is that okay with everyone?"

All three of them nod their heads, afraid to say another word. Adrienne's tone has made it clear that she would like to change the subject.

"Okay, then!" Nick does just that. "I am going to run to the hardware store. Gabe is going to continue framing out the garage, and you two," he points to Adrienne and Gretchen, "are going to hang some Christmas lights and get into the spirit of the season. Does that sound good?"

Adrienne and Gretchen smile. Saint Nick.

Another hour of work flies by and then the famished crew heads inside for some lunch. The reality that there are only a few hours left until the start of the contest looms over all of them as they eat in thoughtful silence. Adrienne is thinking about the contest and her promotion, and Gretchen, Gabe and Nick are thinking about the contest and Adrienne's promotion. *What will she decide to do?*

"Gretch," Adrienne disturbs the quiet, "what is going on with your job? What does your boss from McMurphy's have to say about you being out?"

"It's no biggie. I told them I have a family emergency and need a week off. They were fine with it. This week is a super busy week, and tips are huge – trust me, people are happy to pick up the extra shifts."

"It's that easy, huh?" Adrienne surprises herself by envying her sister's more simple life. "What is your plan after Christmas?"

"I'm not totally sure yet. I guess it all depends on what happens tonight. The outcome of the contest will determine a lot."

Gretchen's words hang in the air, *the outcome of the contest will determine a lot*. It sure will.

After a quick lunch, the group makes their way back outside, back to their work. This is the homestretch – the last few hours to finish up the decorating and the garage. It is the last few hours of getting to work together all day and laugh together all night. Although Adrienne has wanted to finish the project, now the thought of it being over fills her with a bit of sadness. Despite the ups and downs, overall it has been a joyous, healing, learning experience.

Peeking at her watch, Adrienne takes a deep calming breath: 4:30 p.m. They have half an hour. All the lights are hung along the roofline and around the big pine tree on the front lawn. Five faux multi-colored presents sit beneath the tree invoking the feeling of Christmas morning. They too, light up. The front portico and front door are beautifully adorned in garland and lights, with a giant red bow pinned to the top of the triangle pediment. Charlie Matthews from Matthews Garden Supply wanted to contribute in some way, so he sent over a dozen natural pine wreaths. Adrienne and Gretchen hung the wreaths from red ribbon on all nine front-facing windows as well as the three dormer windows. A pair of light up reindeer sculptures stand perched on the left side of the lawn. The word NOEL is spelled out in large lighted letters on the right side.

Stepping back to the look at the house, Gretchen says, "It looks incredible. I am dying to see what it looks like with the lights turned on. And we should test it to be sure the lights actually work. You remember what happened in *National Lampoon's Christmas Vacation* movie, right?" She says referencing the hilarious scene in the movie where Chevy Chase's character puts up thousands of twinkle lights, and when he plugs the main cord in during the big dramatic reveal, the lights don't go on.

"Yeah, you're right. Did you check on Nick and Gabe? Are they done?"

"They are putting on the last of the roof shingles! You should see it, you would never believe there was a giant gaping hole there only this morning."

"Great," Adrienne says, still staring at the house. "I feel like something is missing."

"Really? I don't even know where we'd put anything else," Gretchen laughs.

"I got it!" Adrienne says as the idea springs to mind, "We forgot the candles in the windows!"

"Oh my goodness, you are right! Let's hurry, I know where they are inside."

The girls dash inside the house and down the stairs. They search around in a few of the boxes, which have only just recently been taken to the basement.

"I think I saw them in that box that had all the extra ribbon," Gretchen frantically pulls open box after box.

"Found them!" Adrienne holds up a couple of the single electric candles. "Let's hurry and get them plugged in and then we can do the big test on the lights."

The girls split the candles up and run up the stairs going room-to-room plugging a single candle in to each front-facing window.

"Make sure you test each one to be sure the bulb isn't burned out!" Adrienne yells up to Gretchen who is in one of the upstairs bedrooms.

"I need a bulb! One of them is burned out!" Gretchen yells back down.

Adrienne rushes back down to the basement to the box where they found the candles and frantically pulls everything out of it praying for extra bulbs. She finds a couple other candles in the box, and hoping at least one of them works she rushes back upstairs. Up in the front bedroom Adrienne hands Gretchen one of the candles, "Try this one," she says. Much to their dismay it does not turn on. "Okay, this is our last hope," Adrienne hands Gretchen the last candle. Gretchen sets it on the window sill and holding her breath, plugs it in. It turns on!

"Yay!" Gretchen cheers as the two girls jump up and down. "Okay, how much time do we have?"

"It is 4:50, we have ten minutes."

"Okay, let's quickly check on the guys, and then test the lights," Gretchen says.

"There is no time to check on the guys, at this point, whatever the garage looks like is how it will have to be. We need to make sure the lights work, because without the lights – we have nothing."

Dashing back outside Adrienne runs to the side of the house where there is an outdoor electrical outlet. She grabs the extension cord and yells to Gretchen, "Gretchen! Are you ready?"

Gretchen stands at the edge of the front yard, almost in the street.

"Wait! Gabe and Nick want to see too!" Gretchen yells back to Adrienne. Gabe and Nick run to where Gretchen is standing. "Okay! Now!"

Adrienne holds her breath, closes her eyes and says a little prayer. She then pushes the plug into the outlet . . . and hears nothing. *Does that mean they didn't come on? Did it not work? Noooooo!* She's thinking as she walks to the front yard to see. She immediately looks to Gretchen, Nick and Gabe and sees their faces alive with delight. Adrienne walks over to where they are standing and turns toward the house to take it all in. It is magical. The candles, the wreaths, and the garland are all beautiful, but now at dusk with the lights along the roof, the front portico, and the pine tree – the house is glowing. The presents and the reindeer and the word NOEL add to the absolute magnificence that is 22 Oak Street.

"It is absolutely amazing," Gretchen whispers, a tear sliding down her cheek. Nick wraps his arm around her shoulders and pulls her toward him.

"All I can say is: WOW," Nick says. "How did you two do this? And in one day?!"

"It was not just one day. And it certainly was not just us," Adrienne says, looking at Gabe. "We could never have done this without you two. I don't know how we will ever be able to repay you."

"It was not the way I thought I would be spending the days leading up to Christmas," Gabe smiles, "but I wouldn't change a thing."

The foursome stand with linked arms and continue to stare at the house in silence. They did it. They actually *did* it! Despite fires and permit problems and a tree falling on the house – they got it finished. 22 Oak Street has been brought back to life.

"We are *so* going to crush this contest," Gretchen says. "What house could look more beautiful than this one?"

Just as the words escape her lips, a series of five cars pull down Oak Street and stop in front of the house.

"They're here."

CHAPTER TWENTY-SIX

The foursome stands at the edge of the yard as the five-car entourage lines up on the street. The time has come, and Adrienne feels ready – well, almost ready.

"I have to run inside, you three get things started out here," Adrienne says quickly as she rushes into the house.

"Wait, where are you going? You can't leave me out here to fend for myself!" Gretchen panics. But Adrienne is already halfway up the lawn and pays her no attention.

One judge steps out of each of the five cars and they all begin to make their way over to Gretchen, Nick and Gabe. With Mayor Jessup leading the pack, Gretchen plasters a nervous smile on her face and turns on the charm.

"Why Mayor Jessup, what a pleasure to see you again," Gretchen holds out her hand for a handshake.

"Ms. Harkins, the pleasure is all mine, truly. I see you have really fixed the place up, and in such a short period of time. Impressive. You must have had a lot of help," he says looking Gabe straight in the eyes.

"We sure have been working hard, and we could not have done it without our friends and certain members of the community. It really does take a village, I guess," her voice shakes a little.

The Mayor shakes Nick's hand and then walking over to Gabe, he puts his hand out. Gabe reaches out and shakes the Mayor's hand, instantly regretting it when Mayor Jessup says, "Good luck tonight, Gabe. May the best man win."

The Mayor then turns to the other four judges who are making their way closer to Gretchen, Nick and Gabe. "This is the first house we will be seeing today, 22 Oak Street. You will see on your Scoring Sheet that all homes will be judged based on a combined score from five categories: Exterior Illumination, Curb Appeal, Creativity, Interior Décor, which is limited to the first floor of the home, and an Overall score that is a subjective score based on your own personal opinion – how the house makes you feel. Why don't we all take a minute to take in the house from the street, and then walk around the yard getting a closer look at all the details – okay?" Gretchen looks over at the four remaining judges for the first time, and much to her surprise, she recognizes someone.

Inside the house Adrienne is frantic, yet focused, as she pulls some last minute details together. She figures she has about ten minutes before the judges make their way inside. She throws a fire starter log in the fireplace and lights it, she puts Christmas music on the surround sound, lights a candle that smells like gingerbread, since there is no time to bake cookies, and fills a red platter with sugar cookies bought from the Dreamy Bean, placing it on the coffee table in front of the fireplace. She quickly warms up hot cocoa and pours the steaming liquid chocolate into five Christmas mugs, topping them each with a generous dollop of whipped cream. Giving the house a once-over, she thinks, *now that's better.* The house is warm, sparkly and a place where everyone would want to spend their Christmas Eve.

Just as she's topping off the final mug of hot cocoa, she hears the front door open and Gretchen speaking loudly, a warning that they are on their way inside. "Welcome to the Harkins' family Christmas home," Gretchen is saying.

That's my cue, Adrienne thinks. Walking over to the front door wearing the Santa Claus apron her mom used to wear every Christmas and holding a silver tray of steaming mugs of hot cocoa, Adrienne looks like Mrs. Claus herself.

Gretchen raises her eyebrows in surprise, but she keeps her thoughts to herself, thankfully.

"Welcome! Welcome! Please come in and make yourselves at home. Would anyone like some hot cocoa or a Christmas cookie?" Adrienne's voice is as sweet as honey.

The judges make their way one by one into the house, the first three people, one man and two women, Adrienne does not recognize. However, the fourth person to walk inside is a woman dressed in white from head-to-toe, and glowing like a star on top of a Christmas tree.

"Angela?" Adrienne is completely taken by surprise. "You are one of the judges for the contest?"

"Adrienne! How lovely to see you dear. Did I not mention that I was one of the judges? I'm sure I did!" She smiles that infectious smile while taking a mug off the tray.

"You definitely did not mention that, trust me, I would have remembered."

"One of the original judges came down with the flu, so last minute they asked me to step in, seeing that since I'm from out of town I can be impartial. So, here I am! Merry Christmas, dear."

"Merry Christmas. Please enjoy our home," Adrienne smiles.

And last to enter the house, is Mayor Jessup. He smiles a big ol' fake smile at Adrienne, who fake smiles right back at him.

"Mayor Jessup, nice to see you. Would you like some hot cocoa?"

"I would, thank you Ms. Harkins."

"I see you came to our home first. Isn't that interesting."

"Oh, I was just so anxious to see what you've done with the place. You know, since this house could be mine in a week."

Adrienne's mouth drops open in a shock that has rendered her completely speechless. She stands there holding the empty tray and anger starts to build. The anger starts in her toes and works itself all the way up to her stomach where it burns, and then as it rises higher, she closes her eyes, takes a deep breath and listens to the soft Christmas music playing the background. *Hark! The Herald Angel Sings* fills the house, and Adrienne smiles. *Thanks, Mom.*

Putting Mayor Jessup out of her mind, she walks back to the kitchen where Gabe, Nick and Gretchen are standing around the island.

Placing the tray on the counter, she asks the group, "So what do you think? What was their reaction outside? Did they seem to like everything?"

"Each judge seemed to love the outside decorations, and I heard so many comments about how beautiful the house is, I even heard one person say it was 'magnificent' but that was Angela, so you know . . ." Gretchen thinks aloud.

"I would say every judge loved it," Gabe says, "but honestly, I am worried about the Mayor. He has not said one word, either negative or positive, and I was listening for him."

"I have to agree. The Mayor is the issue, but we all knew that to be the case before they even showed up," Gretchen says.

"Yeah, he said something to me at the door about how glad he is that we fixed the place up just in time for him to buy it, or something like that," Adrienne looks down at her hands.

"He said what?! I'm going to march in there and tell him where he can stick the mistletoe!" Gretchen gets heated. As she starts toward the family room, Nick grabs her arm.

"Hold on there, Positivity Protector – the last thing you want to do right now is cause a scene and disrupt the peace. That's the reaction he is trying to get out of you two. The best thing you can do, and I know it's hard, is ignore him. Keep that smile on your face and wish everyone a Merry Christmas."

The judges walk around the first level of the home sipping their hot cocoa and commenting here and there about the garland, or a wreath or an ornament. They are definitely paying attention to every detail. Adrienne and Gretchen feel as if they are holding their breath the entire time the judges are in the house. The four friends watch the judges write notes and scores down using their clipboards, and after what feels like hours but is probably only five to ten minutes, they thank Adrienne and Gretchen for their time.

Adrienne and Gretchen thank all the judges for coming, wishing them all a Merry Christmas as they leave. Mayor Jessup pauses as he's leaving, turns around and says, "Good luck, ladies," with a crooked smile before he turns and walks out. Adrienne gives him the biggest smile she can force and says, "Merry Christmas, Mayor Jessup! And have a blessed day!"

The last judge to leave is Angela. She wraps both Adrienne and Gretchen into a giant hug and says, "What you two, or you four," nodding toward Gabe and Nick, "have done here, is truly spectacular. No matter the outcome, you should be so proud of yourselves. I know I'm proud of you, and I know your parents are smiling down at all of us right now. Now, what I want you to do while you await the results, is spend some time thinking about all you have gained from this experience. And then whether you take home that grand prize or not, you will feel like you've won. Is that a deal?"

Nodding their heads, both girls have tears in their eyes and they give Angela one last hug before she leaves.

Once the front door closes, the four friends look around at each other. There is nothing left for them to do. They gave it all they had – left it all out on the field. The rest is out of their hands. Adrienne feels like she can breathe easy for the first time in a week.

"We need wine," Gretchen says heading straight for the kitchen.

"We sure do! It's Christmas Eve and we have a lot to celebrate!" Adrienne follows her into the kitchen.

Nick walks into the family room and grabs the platter of cookies off the coffee table and brings them into the kitchen. "I'm starving. Anyone else hungry?"

"I'm starving," Gabe says opening the refrigerator and poking around. "Well it's not going to be a Harkins Hoop-dee-doo, but I think I can throw something together that resembles a meal."

"So, when do they announce the winner?" Nick asks with his mouth full of cookie.

"All the contestants received an email with the details, but I haven't even had time to read it!" Adrienne says picking up her phone off the counter. She opens her email and takes a minute to read through the message. And then summarizing for the group, "So, here is how it all goes down. The judges will go visit all homes in the contest, taking notes and scoring each home as they go. As they leave each house, that house will have a combined score that will be written down on some master sheet. Obviously the house with the highest score, wins. At 8 p.m. they will announce the winner live at what was supposed to be Town Hall, but due to the fire, now they will announce it in town, in front of the big Christmas tree near the train station. If the winners are not present at the live announcement, they will be notified via phone later this evening. However, they are encouraging all contestants to attend the live announcement. There will be a First Place winner and a Runner-up announced. All contestants will receive a gift certificate to Peas & Pickles for entering."

"Well, if we lose at least we can get some free groceries," Gretchen says.

"How are we going to keep busy until 8 p.m.? It's only 5:30 and I already feel like we have had to wait forever," Adrienne whines.

"First we are going to eat some food, drink some wine, and eat some cookies," Gabe says.

"That will take an hour tops," Adrienne says.

"We could watch a Christmas movie," Nick suggests.

"I think it will be hard for me to just sit still and watch a movie," Adrienne says. "Wait, I know what we can do! Charades!"

"You have got to be joking," Gabe looks up from the meat and cheese platter he just put together. "Charades?"

"Yes! It's so fun – I am totally in," Gretchen gets excited.

"We used to do this as a family all the time," Adrienne says. "Let me see if I can find the game in the game cupboard and then after we eat we can play charades until we have to leave. Trust me, it will make time fly by."

With the plan in place to take their minds off the contest, the foursome chat and laugh over cheese, meats, crackers, olives, dried apricots, and nuts – with a few cookies thrown in there too, of course. And then, led by Adrienne they all file into the family room and start to play charades, some of them reluctantly.

"We're in luck!" Adrienne says with a wicked smile, "I found the Christmas Charades game!" She ignores the groans and pulls out the first card. "If Gretchen and I are on the same team, we would crush you guys. It would be totally unfair. So, in the spirit of Christmas, Gabe and I will be on a team and then you two, Gretchen and Nick will be a team. Here we go!"

Adrienne does her best to act out the movie *The Polar Express*, but she soon realizes that Gabe is, well, Gabe is terrible at charades. Once their time is up, Gretchen and Nick have the chance to steal the points, and Gretchen guesses correctly immediately. Gretchen is up, and lucky for her and Nick, she has to act out chopping down a Christmas tree. Mr. Saint Nick's Tree Lot owner guesses the answer within seconds.

The group plays on for a while with lots of laughs and teasing, and with a score of 21 to 5, Gabe and Adrienne are losing big time. When it is once again Gabe's turn to act, he looks at his watch and his face lights up. "Although I am dying to act out another round of charades here, it looks as though we need to leave if we want to be there for the live announcement. And I so wanted to act this out, *A Charlie Brown Christmas*, that would have been so easy," he feigns disappointment.

Adrienne and Gretchen look at each other across the room, anxiety passes between their stares. Adrienne suddenly feels like she is going to be sick. The four of them quickly bundle up in warm coats, hats and mittens, and pile into Gabe's truck.

Down at the town square, the giant Christmas tree is lit up in thousands of multi-colored twinkle lights. The crowd waiting around the tree is buzzing with anticipation. There is a small platform in front of the tree with a microphone, and a group of carolers standing nearby singing "O Holy Night" as Adrienne, Gretchen, Nick and Gabe draw near. Nick does a great job of subtly making his way toward the front of the crowd. It seems that if you are as big as Nick, people just subconsciously move over for you if you are trying to get by. Before they know it, the four of them are in the front row, with Adrienne and Gretchen standing shoulder to shoulder and holding each other's hands. Adrienne is not sure she has ever been this nervous for anything in her life. She is pretty sure none of the other contestants have the fear of losing their home on the line. They have to win. *They just have to.*

After a few more songs from the carolers, which feel to Adrienne and Gretchen like they are ten minutes long each, the carolers stop singing and look toward the small stage. The crowd follows their eyes and sees the arrival of Mayor Jessup, Angela, and the other three judges. Adrienne is trying to look at Angela's facial expressions to see if she can read her thoughts. However, Angela is just smiling that angelic smile, as usual.

Mayor Jessup steps up to the microphone and introduces himself. He thanks all the contestants who put in so much time and effort into making their homes beautiful for the contest, and in turn, made the town shine that much brighter this Christmas season. He takes, way too much time, in Adrienne's opinion, thanking each and every judge personally and giving a background on each of them. The crowd cheers and claps for all the judges. And then, just when Adrienne and Gretchen think he is going to start to announce the winners, he rattles on thanking the Sponsors of the event who have put up the cash for the winner and runner-up. He also thanks Peas & Pickles for giving out gift certificates to all participants.

And then, finally, the tone of the Mayor's voice changes and he says, "Without further ado, let's get down to what we are all anxiously awaiting, the announcement of the winner of the Christmas Home Decoration Contest. Let me just say, this was a very difficult decision, as each home was so beautifully decorated and exuded the Christmas spirit. First we will announce the runner-up of the contest, who will win $10,000! Not too shabby a prize if you ask me. So here it is, the Runner-Up of the Chestnut Ridge Christmas Home Decorating Contest is! Adrienne and Gretchen Harkins of 22 Oak Street!"

The crowd erupts in cheers and clapping. Adrienne and Gretchen stand there, stunned. Adrienne feels like she's having an out-of-body experience as she tries to process what just happened amidst the chaos surrounding her. They wanted to hear their names called, and they were called, but they are the Runners-Up. They didn't win. *They didn't win.*

Adrienne turns to Gretchen as tears well up in her eyes. Gretchen looks just as shell-shocked with her wide eyes and confused expression.

"Well girls, are you going to come up and claim your prize?" The Mayor asks over the wild crowd. "If you don't want the $10,000 I'll certainly take it," he laughs and the crowd laughs with him.

"Adrienne. Adrienne, you have to go up on stage," someone is saying in her ear. She turns toward Gabe who is looking at her with growing concern. "Do you want me to claim it for you?" he asks.

Adrienne slowly shakes her head. She turns back to Gretchen, linking their arms together. She gently pulls Gretchen with her and they make their way up to the stage.

"Here they come!" The Mayor yells. "Let's all give a giant Chestnut Ridge congratulations to the Harkins' sisters! Come on now, you can do better than that," he encourages the crowd. The crowd screams louder and Adrienne can't hear herself think. She and Gretchen stand up on stage looking like two deer in the headlights of a Mack truck. They hold the large fake check up, and all five judges crowd around them as a photographer snaps photos. Adrienne can feel someone's arm go around her shoulders, she looks to her left, and sees Angela's shining face. At that moment, Adrienne is sure she is going to break down and cry right there up on stage for the whole town to see. Somehow, she manages to keep her emotions under control.

Once the photographs are finished and the crowd dies down, Adrienne and Gretchen are led off the stage. Their legs move without their brains telling them to – one foot after another. Adrienne is in front carrying the first half of the giant check, and Gretchen is right behind her sister, holding the back end of the check. They walk without even knowing where they are going – just away from the stage, away from the Mayor and away from all the cheering, happy people.

Gabe and Nick come running up beside them, "Are you two okay?" Gabe asks quietly. The girls keep walking, not acknowledging that anyone is there talking to them.

"Adrienne. Stop walking. Talk to me," Gabe says, touching Adrienne's shoulder gently.

Adrienne stops abruptly causing Gretchen to bump into her. She then turns too quickly toward Gabe taking the awkward giant check with her, which knocks into Gabe's stomach. It's like a slapstick comedy routine with all the bumping and hitting. She looks at Gabe who is slightly bent over holding his stomach, and she bursts out laughing. A domino effect occurs as Gabe starts to laugh, followed by Gretchen and Nick. Soon all four of them are hysterically laughing. Adrienne can no longer hold up her end of the check and she lets it drop to the ground. Bent over with their hands on their knees, Adrienne and Gretchen laugh until tears are streaming down their cheeks. It's another one of those moments where if you didn't laugh, you would cry. And Adrienne figures, she has cried on enough Christmas Eve nights. This year is going to be different.

Catching her breath, Adrienne wipes her eyes and takes a deep breath. She looks up at the starry sky and is overcome with emotion. Surprisingly, she feels . . . grateful. In the background she can hear the Mayor over the microphone announcing the Grand Prize Winner, "The Goody Family from View Point Drive have won $25,000! Their home was absolutely spectacular, and if you haven't done so yet, you have got to drive by and check their house out. With a light show timed to the instrumental of 'Hark Hear the Bells,' it is like nothing I have ever seen on someone's front lawn. Congratulations Goody Family!"

"Let's go home," Adrienne says to Gretchen, Nick and Gabe as the crowd's cheering assaults her ears. The three nod their heads and start the trek back to Gabe's truck, walking in silence.

As the truck pulls up to 22 Oak Street, the four friends sit and stare at the beautiful house for a moment, each lost in his or her own thoughts.

"It looks so amazing," Nick says, "Nobody can take that away from you. Nobody can take away what you two did to make this happen. You should both be so proud."

Gretchen lays her head on Adrienne's shoulder and Adrienne wraps her arm around her sister. They will be okay. Adrienne has never been so sure of it.

They walk into the house and Nick walks over to the fireplace and starts to light a fire. Gretchen disappears into the kitchen, and a few moments later "Hark! The Herald Angels Sing," is playing softly on the surround sound.

They all sit in what have become their unofficial assigned seats, with Gabe on the end of the sofa, Adrienne next to him and Gretchen then Nick on the other sofa. Adrienne sinks into the cushion, physically and emotionally drained.

"I can't believe this is going to be the last Christmas we have in this house," Gretchen says, her voice shaking.

No one responds. They all just sit and stare at the red and orange flames fluttering in the fireplace. And then Adrienne sits up with a start, "Okay, that's it. The pity party is officially over. It's Christmas Eve and we are all here, together. We have a lot to be thankful for, and I want to spend Christmas celebrating for once."

Gretchen, Gabe and Nick all stare at Adrienne like she has suddenly grown a second head.

"Who's with me?" She asks overflowing with enthusiasm.

A smile slowly starts to form on Gretchen's once melancholy face. And if it's one thing that is contagious on Christmas Eve, it's a smile. Soon all four of them are smiling at each other and thinking about all they are thankful for.

"I will pop the champagne I bought! Yeah, maybe I thought we would be celebrating something different, but Adrienne's right, we do have a lot to celebrate," Gretchen jumps out of her seat.

The doorbell rings and they all look at each quizzically. *Who could that be?*

Adrienne stands up, "You get the champagne, I'll get the door," she says to Gretchen as she walks toward the front door.

Adrienne pulls the door open to reveal the mysterious woman dressed in all white that always seems to show up at the most unexpected times.

"Angela, hello. Come on in," Adrienne steps aside to let Angela enter.

Angela wraps Adrienne in a warm hug, "I wanted to come check on you two. How are you doing?"

"Surprisingly, okay," Adrienne smiles. "Better than okay, actually," she looks at Gabe walking over to her. "I'm just trying to focus on the positive."

"Angela! You are just in time!" Gretchen walks over to them with a tray of champagne flutes. "Come in and join us in celebrating!"

"That sounds wonderful," Angela reaches for a glass of champagne, "What are we celebrating?"

Standing around in a circle, the five friends reach their glasses in for a toast.

"To wonderful family and friends," Adrienne says.

"To coming home," Gretchen chimes in.

"And to the magic of the holiday season," Angela finishes off the toast as they all clink glasses and sip the bubbly beverage.

Soon again there is another ringing of the doorbell. Gretchen answers the door and is surprised to find Pete Wallace from Wallace Landscaping & Tree Removal, Charlie Matthews from Matthews Garden Supply and Kurt Jeffries from Jeffries Painting Service. She invites them all into the family room, and hands them a glass of champagne. What started out as a small intimate gathering has turned into a full-blown Christmas Eve party.

The three men approach Adrienne and wish her a Merry Christmas. "We heard about the Christmas Home Decorating Contest, and we all feel terrible. Maybe if we had been able to help out more here we could have given you more of a chance," Charlie Matthews says.

"Yeah, I have seen what the Goodys do every year, I should have known they would enter the contest. I could have warned you what you were up against," Pete Wallace says.

Adrienne shakes her head, "Please don't feel bad about anything. The three of you helped us out so much, and encouraged us and motivated us when we thought we were trying to accomplish the impossible. I mean, look at what we did! Normally, a second place finish and $10,000 is an unbelievable prize. Perhaps Gretchen and I staying in this house was just not meant to be."

While Gretchen is chatting with Kurt Jeffries about the work taking place down at Town Hall, Angela walks over and asks to borrow her for a minute.

"Thanks so much for coming here tonight, Angela. It's always so nice to see you."

"It is my pleasure, trust me. Now Gretchen, you took a lot of photos of the house and all the people who helped you fix it up, correct?"

"I did! That is my way of guaranteeing the memories last forever."

"Do you think I would be able to see some of them? I would love to see the full transformation of the house."

"Of course! Who doesn't love before and after renovation photos? I have them all on a thumb drive that I can lend you. Some of them are just taken with the camera on my phone, so they definitely aren't going to win any awards, but it is a documentation of history."

Angela gives Gretchen a quick hug, "thank you so much! Would you mind going to get it now? I actually have to be on my way."

"Of course," Gretchen says as she runs into the kitchen to get the thumb drive. After handing it over to Angela, the two give each other yet another hug before saying good night.

The festivities continue on with Christmas music playing, the smell of pine and burning wood filling the house, and most importantly the chatter of good friends enjoying each other's company. As the party dwindles down, soon it's just Adrienne and Gretchen left in the big, old house.

"It seems so quiet now," Gretchen laughs.

"Yeah, that was such a fun, impromptu Christmas Eve celebration, you agree?"

"It was the best Christmas Eve I have had in . . . well, in a long time," Gretchen says as she gathers empty glasses and dishes and brings them to the sink.

"I can't believe it will be the last one we spend in this house."

"I know. But it was all worth it, don't you think?"

Adrienne nods her head, thoughtfully. "I can't stop thinking about our champagne toast tonight. You know the only thing I have toasted over in the past four years was work-related. How pathetic is that?"

"I'm not sure if pathetic is the word, but I can see where your priorities were."

"Exactly. I have realized that you can't put all your eggs into one basket and expect to be happy. Do you know what I mean?"

"Not really," Gretchen laughs. "I assume you are talking about balance?"

"Yes. Balance. Being in this house, surrounded by this community of *good* people – a balanced life is more easily achieved here. In the city I just work and work and work . . . and with every raise I just spend more money. So, it's like running in place. Does that make sense?"

"Are you saying you don't want to go back to the city? Do you want to move back here?"

Adrienne sighs. "I'm not sure. I mean, could I really live in Chestnut Ridge again?"

"I think I could," Gretchen smiles. "I too have been thinking a lot about my life since we have been back here. And, I am just so unhappy in the city. I thought that unhappiness was due to everything with mom and dad, but it's definitely more than that. I need a change. I feel so at peace here - even without my camera."

Adrienne gives her sister a big hug. "I have been cursing that red envelope that showed up on my doorstep, but now I am thankful for it. It brought us back together, and it brought us home."

CHAPTER TWENTY-SEVEN

The sound of a ringing bell is pounding in Adrienne's ears. She rolls over in bed, disoriented and groggy. Her bubblegum pink room is still dark, indicating it's either the middle of the night or waaayyy too early in the morning. She peeks over at the clock and sees that it's 6:45 a.m. *What the heck?*

Tangled up in pink sheets and blankets, she struggles to free herself from the grips of her warm, soft bed. She stumbles off the mattress and absentmindedly slips her feet into her slippers and wraps a robe around her shoulders. Opening her bedroom door, the sound of the ringing bell grows louder and louder. At the top of the stairs she runs into Gretchen who looks just as confused - her hair in a giant tangle of curls sticking out in every direction. The sisters slowly make their way down the stairs and try with no luck to spy through the window to see who might be at the door.

Finally giving up, Adrienne unlocks the deadbolt, grabs hold of the doorknob, and with one last look at Gretchen's worried eyes, pulls the door open quickly. And there stands Nick and Gabe, donned in Santa hats, giant smiles, and carrying a tray of coffee and a box of what smells like cinnamon buns.

"Merry Christmas!" They say in unison.

Adrienne pauses, waiting for her brain to catch up with her eyes and then she and Gretchen burst out laughing.

"You two are crazy! Do you know what time it is?" Adrienne says through her laughter.

"It's Christmas, that's what time it is! Didn't you always wake up at the crack of dawn on Christmas morning?" Gabe asks.

"When I was six years old! But it looks like you brought coffee and baked goods, so you are forgiven. Come on in."

"I feel like I only just went to bed," Gretchen says rubbing her eyes.

"Oh, Nick, there's something you should know about Gretchen," Gabe says, "I remember this from when we were growing up. She is *not* a morning person."

"Hey – leave me alone, Gabe. Nick doesn't believe you, right Nick?"

"I don't believe him – and even if I did, I don't mind at all. I think you're perfect," he says wrapping his arms around her waist and lifting her off her feet in a giant hug.

"Maybe if I could wake up to this, I *would* be a morning person. Maybe I just have never been able to wake up the right way, did anyone ever think of that?" She asks as Nick slowly lowers her back to the ground.

With the tree lights on and the fire blazing, Adrienne, Gretchen, Nick and Gabe sit around the family room chatting. There is something magical about Christmas morning, no matter how old you get. If you let it in, it's there.

"Why don't you see if there are any presents under the tree with your name on it," Gabe says.

"Did Santa come last night?" Adrienne's face lights up.

"I think he may have – it depends – were you a good girl this year?"

Adrienne hunts under the tree looking for a gift with her name on it. "Found it!" she says. "Hmmm, To: Adrienne, From: Santa," she walks back to the sofa smiling. "I wonder what it could be!"

"Well, open it already!" Gretchen can't hide her excitement.

Adrienne tears at the wrapping paper and as soon as the gift is revealed, she starts laughing. "Fuzzy, striped mittens! Just like the ones I lost under the ice at Falls Pond!" She immediately tries them on, and then leans over to Gabe and gives him a hug. "I love them. Thank you."

"Merry Christmas," Gabe says hugging her back. "And I have something else for you too. Put on a coat and come outside with me for a minute."

Filled with curiosity, Adrienne holds Gabe's hand as he leads her out the front door. She can't help but be hyper aware of the feel of his hand wrapped around hers, sending tingles down her spine. Out on the front porch, Gabe turns around so the two are face to face. They stare into each other's eyes and Adrienne has completely forgotten about whatever else Gabe is planning on giving her. She just stares into those baby blues and feels like *this* is Christmas.

"Okay, so I made you something – I hope you like it," Gabe steps to the side to reveal a wooden bench. Adrienne gasps, "It's so beautiful, you made this?" She asks him surprised. "When did you take up woodworking? This is amazing!" She leans down inspecting the craftsmanship and running her hand down the smooth seat.

"I started to learn right after you left. It kept my hands and mind busy, which I needed at the time. It's made out of maple, and I stained it a deep coffee brown, since I know you like coffee," he teases. "Take a look at the back."

Adrienne walks around the back of the bench and sees an inscription carved into the wood. Underneath a monogram of her initials, reads: *"To making decisions that fill your life with love and happiness"*

As Adrienne traces the words with her fingers, she looks up at Gabe filled with so much emotion she is sure her heart might burst. "I don't know what to say – it's the most beautiful gift I have ever received. You are incredible." Walking back around the bench, Adrienne doesn't take her eyes off Gabe's, and they stare at each other until she is inches in front of him. She puts her arms around his neck, and in her slippers, stands on her tippy toes and softly kisses him on his cheek. "Thank you," she whispers.

Back in the warm house, the Christmas morning fun continues.

"Okay, who is next?" Adrienne asks. "I think I saw something for Gretch under there," while keeping her mittens on, she walks back to the tree and finds a gift with Gretchen's name on it and hands it to her.

"For me?!" Gretchen asks, surprised. "To: Gretchen, From: St. Nick. I guess Santa did come last night," she smiles at Nick.

Ripping the paper off reveals a cardboard box. As she opens the box and gets a peek at what is inside, she gasps and tears fill her eyes.

"What is it?!" Adrienne asks.

Gretchen holds up her Canon 5D Mark IV DSLR and looks over at Nick. "How did you . . . it's too much! I can't accept it," she shakes her head.

"I'm pretty sure Santa doesn't take returns," Nick smiles. "Let's just say I know a guy, who knows a guy, who happens to own a pawn shop."

Gretchen puts the box down on the coffee table and jumps on Nick's lap wrapping him in a giant hug. "You are amazing."

"Okay, enough of the sappy stuff," Adrienne says. "Let's see what else I can find under this magical tree. Oh! Look at this – it has Gabe's name on it!"

After handing the gift to a very surprised looking Gabe, Adrienne then sits back down to watch him open it.

"Ha! A Giants hat just like the one Adrienne stole from me years ago - same pompom on top and everything. Santa must have known how much I missed this hat."

"Or he just likes the way the blue hat brings out the color in your eyes," Adrienne smiles.

"Thank you, it's perfect," Gabe says to Adrienne.

"I think Santa definitely likes when Gabe wears blue," Gretchen says laughing. "Okay, my turn to play Santa! She runs over to the tree, picks up a large rectangular gift and hands it to Nick.

"What could this be?" Nick asks. He opens the gift and his mouth drops open in surprise. He turns the large gift around so that Adrienne, Gabe and Gretchen can see it.

"This is incredible, Gretchen. Did you make this?" he asks her amazed.

"I did," Gretchen says shyly. "I used some of the branches that get trimmed off the Christmas trees before people take them home – you know, from Saint Nick's Tree Lot? And I made the frame with those. And then I painted this picture of a Christmas tree in it."

"I didn't know you could paint?" Nick says, now even more in awe of Gretchen than before.

"I took some classes in college and haven't done much with it since, but thought I would play around with it a little. My mom used to paint, remember Adrienne?" Gretchen looks over at Adrienne who nods. "I no longer had my camera, so I felt a little lost. But now, thanks to you, I am whole again," she looks deep into Nick's eyes.

"This is the best gift I have ever gotten on Christmas morning. Thank you," Nick says to Gretchen, who blushes at the compliment. "I will display it proudly."

"I have one more gift to hand out!" Adrienne feels the need to break up the intense staring happening between Nick and Gretchen. And to remind them that there are other people in the room, she takes a small little gift from under the tree and gives it to Gretchen. "From me," she smiles at her.

Gretchen tears off the paper to reveal a small red box. She opens the lid of the box and there resting on white satin is a shining gold locket. Gretchen pulls the locket out of the box and lets it dangle in her hand. "Adrienne, it's beautiful! I absolutely love it!"

Adrienne smiles at her, "Open it," she tells her.

Gretchen opens the locket and for the second time this morning, tears spring to her eyes. On one side of the locket is a tiny photo of their mom, and on the other side a photo of their dad. Gretchen clutches it to her chest and closes her eyes. "I will never take it off," she tells her.

Adrienne reaches around the neckline of her sweater and pulls out an identical locket. "I have the same exact one. This way, they will always be with us, whether we live in this house or not."

The sisters hold each other for a moment, filled with gratitude for each other.

"I have one more gift to give," Gretchen says as she slowly pulls out of the embrace. She picks up another large gift and hands it to Adrienne.

Adrienne opens the present and holding it on her lap she stares at it, breathless.

"Where did you get this?" Adrienne's voice comes out in a whisper as she continues to marvel at the framed photo in her lap.

"I found it in one of the boxes in the attic when I was looking for Christmas decorations. I had it blown up and printed in black and white. Isn't it beautiful?" Gretchen says looking over Adrienne's shoulder at the framed black and white photo of Adrienne and their mom. "I think you were probably about four years old, don't you think?"

"I was five years old – in Kindergarten. I remember that dress I have on; it would swish around when I would twirl. I wanted to wear it every day to school. Mom would ask me to dance for her and she would laugh and clap along with me. I remember it like it was yesterday. She had the most beautiful smile, didn't she?" Adrienne looks at Gretchen.

"She did. And that's why I chose this photo with Mom laughing and you dancing for her – so carefree and happy. This is the childhood I want us to remember. I want us to think about all the happy times we had together. I know that's what mom and dad would want for us."

Adrienne nods her head as a single tear slides down her cheek. "Thank you, Gretchen. It is just what I needed."

Adrienne wipes her eyes, and stands up. "Okay, I'm feeling a little bad here. We all gave and received such thoughtful gifts, and all I got Gabe was a winter hat."

Gretchen and Nick laugh as Adrienne looks at Gabe smiling apologetically.

"Can I make you breakfast to make up for it?" she asks him.

"That sounds perfect. And trust me, Adrienne, I love my hat."

The foursome spends the rest of the morning lazily, hanging around talking, laughing, and eating – just the way Christmas morning is meant to be.

"I have an idea," Gabe says. "Let's go ice skating! It has been so cold; Falls Pond is definitely frozen right now. Wouldn't that be fun?!"

"Are you serious?" Adrienne asks, laughing. "Are you hoping for a repeat of the last time we were there?"

"Ah, no - absolutely not. But I am hoping to skate around with you again. It's been a long time since we did that. Remember how much fun we used to have?"

"I'm not even sure I remember how to skate!" Gretchen laughs. "But I'm up for it!"

"Me too!" Nick chimes in. "The fresh air will do us all some good."

"I guess we're going then. I will go dig up some of our old skates in the basement," Adrienne says.

What seemed like an easy suggestion ends up being a giant production. Nick and Gabe have to both run home and get their skates. The girls have to find skates that fit and "feel right." And then as Gabe and Nick sit and read the paper in front of the fireplace for what seems like hours, Adrienne and Gretchen shower and get ready. Who knew ice-skating required so much primping? *And we can't forget the snacks and the drinks! God forbid that we be farther than an arm's length away from food or drink at any given moment.*

Finally, everyone is ready. The four of them are showered, dressed, bundled up, food and drinks packed, and skates slung over shoulders. It's a Christmas miracle. They pile into Gabe's truck and make the thankfully short drive over to Falls Pond. Each of them takes a seat on a tree trunk that has been turned on its side to form a makeshift bench. They all lace up their skates and are ready to go! Until Gretchen stands up and forgets that she is on ice – and immediately falls right on her backside. Adrienne bursts out laughing which causes her to wobble and then fall down too. Gabe and Nick skate around like they are competing for Gold in the figure skating Olympics, circling around Adrienne and Gretchen to tease them.

"Okay, that's it," Adrienne says trying to control her laughter. "I'm doing this. It's been a long time, but I have my lucky mittens on, and I'm going to crush this ice skating thing."

"I'm not quite sure I would call those mittens lucky," Gabe laughs.

"Adrienne has always been the competitive one," Gretchen says, "I think I'll just sit over here on the log and cheer you all on."

"Oh no you're not," Nick says to her. "Come on, give me your hands. Let me help."

Gretchen cannot resist the chance to hold Nick's hands so she lets him pull her up and lead her around slowly.

Wobbling to her feet, Adrienne starts to awkwardly shuffle around the ice.

"Do you need help?" Gabe asks her.

"No, I do not need help, thank you. I can do this. I used to be good at this, I'm not quite sure what happened."

"Oh Adrienne, some things never change. Why is it so hard for you to accept help?"

Ignoring Gabe's comment, Adrienne attempts to pick up speed. She is doing pretty well until her skate hits a bump in the ice and she almost face plants on the ice, but catches herself with her hands, actually, her mittens.

"See! What did I tell you? Lucky mittens!" she and Gabe laugh.

Before long, Adrienne has picked the skating right back up and gracefully glides along the ice. She and Gabe hold hands and let the wind push them across the frozen pond so it feels like they are flying. Adrienne closes her eyes and savors the moment.

"My toes are numb," Gretchen says a little while later. "Are you all ready to go back home and sit in front of the fire?"

"Yeah, I can't feel my face," Adrienne laughs. "Let's pack it up."

Sitting four across on the bench unlacing their skates, Gabe says to Adrienne, "Wouldn't it be nice to be able to do this all the time?"

She looks over at him, understanding the deeper meaning of the question. "It would," she says with little emotion.

"I don't really want to bring it up, mostly because I am afraid of the answer, but don't you have to let work know tomorrow whether or not you are accepting the promotion?" Gabe asks her.

Adrienne can feel Gretchen and Nick listening while trying to pretend they are too busy with their skates.

"I called Elaina while I was upstairs getting ready. I already gave them my answer."

"You did?!" Gretchen asks, shocked by this news.

"I did."

"Well, don't leave us in suspense, what did you tell her?" Gretchen asks. Gabe stays quiet, almost as if he is holding his breath.

"I turned the promotion down," Adrienne says firmly. Gretchen jumps on Adrienne and hugs her tightly.

"Yay! I'm so happy for you, Adrienne. I think that was a good decision."

Gabe seems to be able to breathe again. "So what does that mean exactly? Do you plan to try and work fewer hours? Or . . ."

"I gave my two weeks' notice as well," Adrienne says nonchalantly.

"Are you serious?!" Gretchen screeches. "You quit?! I can't believe it! I'm so proud of you, Adrienne!"

"Calm down, Gretchen. Yay for me, I'm unemployed."

"You are Adrienne Harkins. You'll figure it out," Gabe looks at Adrienne with a sparkle in his eyes. She can't help but smile at him.

When the four friends get back to Oak Street they are red-cheeked and weary. Nick immediately begins to start the fire back up, and Adrienne puts the kettle on for hot cocoa.

Alone in the kitchen, Gabe asks Adrienne, "So what *is* your plan going to be? Are you going to stay in your apartment in the city? What kind of job are you going to look for?"

Adrienne sighs, "I am not sure of anything right now. When things started to come together with the house, I really believed that maybe I could stay here. But now, it seems strange to move back to Chestnut Ridge and not live in this house." Adrienne gets out four mugs and starts to fill them with the warm milk. "I have to work in the city for the next two weeks. I said I would help train someone to take over for me, and wrap up some projects – things like that. I guess I will figure it out then?"

"That sounds like a good plan. And just so you know, I could definitely picture you back in Chestnut Ridge – whether you are living at 22 Oak Street or not," Gabe puts his hand on Adrienne's. "You can do anything. Think of this as an opportunity to do something you have always wanted to do. You do have the runner-up money from the contest to get you started . . ."

"You're always one decision away from a totally different life," Adrienne whispers to herself.

"What's that?" Gabe asks.

"Oh nothing. I think I told you – it was something Angela said to me once, and I can't seem to get it out of my head.

"Yes, I remember. And I have also been thinking about that quote. It's so true. So what decision are you going to make to change your life? You already made a big one quitting your job. What's next?"

"OHMIGOD! Adrienne! Gabe! Get in here!" Gretchen is screaming to the point of hysterics.

Adrienne and Gabe rush into the family room fearing the house is on fire, or they are being robbed at gunpoint, or Nick collapsed and is having a heart attack. They round the corner and see Gretchen standing on one of the sofas jumping up and down while holding an e-tablet.

"What? What's wrong?" Adrienne asks, panicked.

"You are never going to believe this! I can't believe this! Look at what Nick just found on the Internet?"

"Gretchen if this is some sort of cute kittens playing with yarn kind of thing, I'm going to kill you," Adrienne threatens.

"Oh no, this is so much better than that! Look," she thrusts the tablet at Adrienne.

It takes Adrienne a minute to realize what she is looking at. It is some sort of community crowd-funding page where people come together to raise money for charities and things, but the name of the page is 22 Oak Street.

22 Oak Street
The Harkins' Family needs your help!

Many of you knew Tom and Elizabeth Harkins who tragically died in a car accident four years ago. Longtime residents of Chestnut Ridge, they constantly gave back to the community. Tom helped most of the businesses on Main Street become what they are today. They also raised their two daughters, Adrienne and Gretchen, here.

Their family home was always a beautiful piece of Chestnut Ridge history having been around for over one hundred years. Tom and Elizabeth restored it to its original beauty. It was even once featured in the Chestnut Ridge House Tour one holiday season.

Unfortunately, since Tom and Elizabeth's passing the house had fallen into disrepair. That is, until about a week ago when Adrienne and Gretchen returned. I'm sure some of you have driven by and noticed the amazing transformation that has occurred in an unbelievably short amount of time.

22 Oak Street will be put up for auction if Adrienne and Gretchen don't raise $15,000 by December 31st!

Let's show one of our beloved families of Chestnut Ridge how our community helps those in need. We helped raise them, now let's help save their childhood home. Please donate what you can today!

*Below see photos taken of 22 Oak Street during the renovations this past week. Notice many of our community members donating their time and expertise.

As Adrienne scrolls the photos taken during the renovation, she sees Gabe and Nick, Pete Wallace, Charlie Matthews, Kurt Jeffries, and before and after photos of the house. Stunned that someone in their community would go out of their way like this to help them – people they have never met – her mouth hangs open and her heart pounds in her chest.

"Who did this?" Adrienne looks up at Gretchen.

"I don't know! Nick got an email about it – that's how he saw it."

"But the photos – aren't those the photos you took?

"Ohmigoodness, you're right. I know who did this! Angela! She asked me for the photos I took – she said she wanted to see the 'before and after' transformation. This has to be her."

"We need to find her. We need to thank her. Oh my, Gretchen, did you see how much money they have raised already?!"

"No, I got too excited. How much?"

"$8,000. And it's only been a few hours. I can't believe this!"

Gabe grabs Adrienne by the shoulders and turns her toward him. She looks up from the tablet, her eyes filling with tears. "Adrienne, whatever is not raised through this site, I'll cover it. You have the $10,000 from the contest, and $8,000 already from this fundraising campaign . . . you are keeping this house."

Adrienne feels like she has been knocked over the head and spun around in circles. No words can find themselves from her brain to her mouth; she just stands there wide-eyed and dumbfounded.

"I could never. . .."

"It would be a loan. I see a lot of potential in you, and I trust that you would be able to pay me back quickly," he smiles at her.

Gretchen comes over and takes the tablet out of Adrienne's hands, "It's already up to $9,000! And you have to read some of the comments people are posting -- Mom volunteering at the women's shelter, Dad helping someone start a business or get a loan to save their home. This is incredible . . . Oh my gosh, it's at $10,000!"

Adrienne has to sit down; her legs no longer have the strength to hold her weight.

"We need to find Angela. Does anyone know how to contact the Town Hall right now? Have they forwarded their calls somewhere? Gretchen, can I see the tablet for a minute?"

Adrienne uses the tablet to go on the Town Hall website. There is a phone number listed for questions or concerns. Adrienne rushes into the kitchen to get her phone, and dials the number. After a few rings a woman answers.

"Hello, could I speak to Angela, please? Um, I'm not quite sure of her last name. But you must know her -- Angela – beautiful, sparkly, always wearing white . . . she was contracted out to revamp the software program."

After a quick conversation with the receptionist, Adrienne hangs up the phone and is completely confused.

"Did you get to speak with Angela?" Gretchen asks.

"The receptionist said she knows exactly who I am talking about, but since the fire they have no contact information for people. And since Angela was just there temporarily as an independent contractor, she has no way of getting in touch with her."

"That's it! I know where I have seen Angela before!" Gabe exclaims. Hoping it will be some clue as to how to get ahold of her, Adrienne and Gretchen listen anxiously. "She is the person who gave me the woodworking tools all those years ago. I don't know how I didn't remember this. I couldn't believe the deal she was giving me, really expensive tools, and she sold them to me for practically nothing."

The girls stare at each other, bewildered.

"It's like she is some kind of fairy godmother," Gretchen says.

"Guys, the campaign is at $11,500. This is crazy!" Nick says, looking at the page on his phone. "I don't want to get ahead of myself, but I think you'll have reached the $15,000 by the end of today – never mind the end of the week."

"I don't know about all of you, but all this excitement has me starving. Anyone else hungry?" Gabe asks.

The others nod their heads, "I guess it is almost dinner time, and we sort of missed lunch," Adrienne agrees.

"Okay, here's the plan. Nick and I will run to Peas & Pickles, I know they're open on Christmas Day, and we'll pick up some dinner. Do we have champagne?"

"I think we drank it all last night," Gretchen answers.

"We'll get more. I think we are going to have a lot to celebrate tonight."

Adrienne and Gretchen follow Nick and Gabe to the front door, giving them last minute items to pick up at the store. Suddenly Nick and Gabe, who are leading the pack, both stop short causing Adrienne and Gretchen to bump into them.

"What is it? Is something wrong?" Adrienne asks.

When the guys don't respond, Adrienne walks around them and follows their eyes to something on the floor in front of the door. A red envelope.

Gretchen gasps and Adrienne freezes in place. The last time the two sisters saw a red envelope like that it was not good news. Everyone stands still, not getting too close – as if it is a bomb that might go off at any second.

"Adrienne, you open it. I can't do it. I can't look," Gretchen says.

Adrienne walks over to the envelope and slowly picks it up off the floor. Feeling three sets of eyes on her, she holds her breath as she tears open the thick envelope. She pulls out a bright white card with a big red "A" on the front, and opens it, reading silently as the other three look on anxiously.

> *Dear Adrienne and Gretchen,*
> *It has been a pleasure getting to know you both over the past few weeks. I am so pleased with the decisions you have made throughout this journey – your parents would be proud. I hope living in your home brings you the joy you both deserve and have worked hard for.*
> *Remember, one of the hardest decisions in life is choosing whether to walk away or try harder – you both chose to walk away from some things and try harder for others. That's what leads to a life filled with purpose and happiness.*
> *I will miss you both, but plan to check in on you from time to time -- especially around Christmastime.*
> *All my love, Angela*

When Adrienne is done reading the letter to herself, filled with emotion, she reads it out loud to the group. Gabe, Nick and Gretchen listen, astounded by Angela's words and filled with wonder about this mysterious woman in white. At the close of the letter, Adrienne looks up at Gretchen, shaking her head in disbelief. "Who *is* she?" Adrienne asks.

"I think she is our fairy godmother," Gretchen says.

"More like a Christmas angel," Adrienne smiles. They all nod their heads in agreement.

"The red envelope is exactly like the ones we received in our apartments in the city. Does that mean that Angela . . . did she put them under our doors?"

The foursome all look around at each other with eyes wide, letting the relevance of this new information sink in. *Our Christmas miracle.*

After shopping, prepping and cooking, the four friends feast on a dinner of juicy steaks, red potatoes and green beans.

"Well, I have to say, this has been the best Christmas ever," Gretchen says laying her head against Nick's arm.

Looking down at his phone, Gabe says, "I think it just got better. The fundraising campaign just reached $15,000. Congratulations Adrienne and Gretchen -- you are homeowners again!"

Gretchen and Adrienne jump up from their seats causing one of the chairs to tip over and crash loudly on the floor. The loud bang can barely be heard underneath the screams and cheers from the sisters. They run and hug each other, continuing to jump up and down while holding each other.

The pop of the champagne cork blasts through the celebration. Adrienne runs and brings champagne flutes back over to the table and Gabe fills each glass to the top.

"Cheers! To the Harkins sisters – and to the bravery it takes to make life-changing decisions."

"And to Angela, our very own Christmas Angel," Adrienne adds.

They clink their glasses and Adrienne feels like she might explode with happiness.

CHAPTER TWENTY-EIGHT

Two Weeks Later

Hopping off the train at the Chestnut Ridge station, Adrienne feels so light she would not be surprised if she just floated away. Having just completed her last day working for Morgan Lynch, this dreary January day appears brighter, and excitement from her newfound freedom is oozing out of every pore. Not since college has she felt like she has so much to look forward to – starting tonight with dinner plans with Gabe, Gretchen and Nick to celebrate her last day of work. She feels like, although they are taking things slowly, she and Gabe have really made progress in their relationship these past few weeks. Adrienne is really looking forward to seeing him tonight.

Perhaps the old Adrienne would have been annoyed when Gretchen asked if she and Nick could join Adrienne and Gabe for dinner, but today, nothing can spoil her good mood. She and Gretchen have some exciting news to share with Nick and Gabe, so it will be fun to be able to tell them both at the same time.

Unlocking the doors to her new car that she leased after she decided to move out of the city, she anxiously drives home to Oak Street to quickly change before dinner tonight. When she pulls into the driveway, she is happy to see a moving truck outside the house. Finally, all her things from her apartment in the city are here: her clothes, her furniture, and her shoes! *Now I will actually have something to wear tonight*, she thinks to herself as she walks in the front door.

She waits for the two movers who are carrying the headboard from her bed into the house.

"Would you mind putting that in the upstairs bedroom? It's the very pink bedroom," She asks the movers politely. She cannot wait to re-decorate that bedroom.

Once the movers have moved out of the way and disappeared up the stairs with her bed, she stops dead in her tracks as she sees the family room. It is filled from floor to ceiling with cardboard boxes of all shapes and sizes, the coffee table, sofa and chaise lounge from her city living room. *So much for being able to find an outfit for tonight.* She would be lucky to be able to find the kitchen.

"I thought you said you had a small apartment?" Gretchen's voice can be heard but Adrienne doesn't see her anywhere.

"Where are you?"

Gretchen pushes a stack of boxes out of the way, and steps out from behind them. I was trying to find a box labeled 'shoes.' I wanted to steal a pair of yours to wear tonight."

"Any luck? I wanted to find some of those boxes too."

"There is more than one box? Ooohhh I can't wait. We have to find them. And seriously though, I thought you had a small apartment? My stuff all fit in the back of Nick's pickup truck."

"Well, I guess 'small' is a relative term. Now let's continue to dig for some shoe boxes."

"There's more in the dining room. And still some out in the truck."

"Oh. Okay, I'll start in the dining room. You keep looking in here."

After about twenty minutes of searching, the girls found a couple of boxes labeled 'shoes' and Adrienne found a box of dresses. Excitedly, Adrienne and Gretchen rush upstairs to change and get ready for dinner. When they both are satisfied with their appearance, they meet at the bottom of the stairs.

"Looks like you are driving," Gretchen smiles at Adrienne.

"You know, at some point you are going to have to get a car. We are only going to be able to share for so long. You should go down to Freddie's, he gave me a great deal on my used car."

"I know, I know. I will. The one thing I miss from living in the city? Being able to walk everywhere."

Adrienne nods in agreement.

"Are you ready to tell them our news tonight?"

"I am. I can't wait! It has been so hard keeping it from Nick all week. Did you confirm everything with Mr. Cooper?"

"It's confirmed! It's a done deal. Okay, let's go before we're late."

Walking into Judy's Restaurant downtown, Adrienne and Gretchen spot Gabe and Nick right away. How could you miss two men that look like *that*? Nick and Gabe stand up as they see the sisters approaching the table. Nick lets out a low whistle, "Wow. You two look gorgeous!"

"Seriously. Wow," Gabe says, pulling Adrienne into a hug.

Adrienne and Gretchen are glowing. They both take their seats and can feel each other ready to burst with the news they have to share. Gabe pours each of them a glass of wine and holds his up in a toast.

"I know we have had a lot to celebrate lately, but today is extra special. Today is the first day of the rest of Adrienne's life. We are so happy for you. And so proud. Here's to the future – and it sure looks bright," Gabe says as they all toast Adrienne's last day of work.

"Thanks, Gabe. I really appreciate all the support the three of you have given me these past two weeks. Being back at Morgan Lynch when everyone knew I was leaving certainly was not easy."

"I have some news," Nick looks around at the table. "I just heard today that my construction company has been selected to lead the restoration project at the Town Hall. I am working with a local architect and he has some amazing ideas. It won't have the historical significance that the original building had, of course, but it will be an impressive building – one Chestnut Ridge can be proud of."

"Congratulations Nick! I am so excited for you -- it looks like your future is bright too!" Gretchen reaches over and puts her hand over his.

"Nick, that is such great news. It sounds like you are going to have a busy year ahead!" Adrienne says. "And speaking of the future, Gretchen and I have something we would like to tell you," Adrienne says making eye contact with Gretchen.

Gretchen nods her head, a huge smile lighting up her face. Nick and Gabe look on, curious.

"Gretchen and I are going to start our own business. We have been working with the Chestnut Ridge Bank, where, of course, my Dad used to work, and have received a small business loan from them. Mr. Cooper, the bank manager, confirmed our application was accepted today," Adrienne says bubbling over with enthusiasm.

"That is amazing news!" Gabe and Nick congratulate the girls, giving hugs all around.

"So what is this new venture? What kind of business?" Nick asks.

"It's going to be an art gallery, but so much more than that. We are going to offer art classes, for children and adults, painting, drawing, and photography. I'll hang some of my photographs that I have been working on over the years, just to get things started, of course. And then we hope to be able to showcase local artists," Gretchen explains.

"That is incredible. Such a great idea," Gabe says.

"I'll handle the finances and the marketing side of the business, and Gretchen will teach some of the classes and do all the creative part," Adrienne continues.

"You two are the ying to the other's yang. A perfect balance," Nick smiles.

"And considering how your dad felt about small businesses and how they are the backbone to every community, I'm pretty sure he would approve," Gabe says.

Adrienne and Gretchen look at each other and nod, their eyes filling with tears, "We thought the same thing. And we feel we are paying homage to our mom too, she so loved art galleries," Adrienne says.

The dinner continues on with talk about the gallery and all the different ideas the girls have for it, and then sometime around the dessert course, Nick asks for everyone's attention.

He turns to Gretchen and grabs her hand. She looks deep into his eyes, and suddenly it's as if no one else is in the room. Nick gets out of his seat, and bends down on one knee, keeping Gretchen's left hand in his. Gretchen's mouth drops open in surprise, and as the diamond ring is slipped on her finger she gasps. She looks from the ring to Nick and back again, unable to speak as her mind attempts to understand what is happening.

"Gretchen, I'm pretty sure I have been in love with you since the moment you knocked a Christmas tree on top of me."

Gretchen laughs nervously, tears filling her eyes.

"I know we have not known each other very long, but I also know I have never felt like this before. I know that I want your face to be the one I see when I wake up in the morning, and when I go to bed at night. If there's one thing I have realized, it's that life is short, and not a minute of it should be wasted. I don't want to waste another minute without you by my side. Will you marry me?"

"Yes, yes, yes!" Gretchen says jumping into Nick's arms as the entire restaurant cheers. "I know the perfect place for the wedding. Adrienne, do you think we can have Oak Street ready for a wedding this spring?"

About the Author

Kate Kasch is a displaced New Englander living in northern New Jersey with her (amazing) husband and four children.

Aside from *Restoring Christmas*, she has written two mystery/thriller novels: *Jane Street* and *The Dakota*.

More information can be found at www.katekasch.com.

Made in the USA
Lexington, KY
13 September 2018

Volume II
Since 1560

WESTERN CIVILIZATION

The Continuing Experiment

SECOND EDITION

Thomas F. X. Noble
University of Virginia

Barry S. Strauss
Cornell University

Duane J. Osheim
University of Virginia

Kristen B. Neuschel
Duke University

William B. Cohen
Indiana University

David D. Roberts
University of Georgia

Houghton Mifflin Company   Boston   New York

Executive Editor: Patricia A. Coryell
Senior Basic Book Editor: Elizabeth M. Welch
Senior Project Editor: Christina M. Horn
Editorial Assistant: Stewart S. Jester
Senior Production/Design Coordinator: Sarah Ambrose
Senior Manufacturing Coordinator: Marie Barnes
Marketing Manager: Sandra McGuire

Chapter opener credits begin on page A-1. Text credits begin on page A-1.

Volume II cover image: Reception of the Siamese Ambassadors. Jean-Léon Gerome (1824–1904), French. © Superstock.

Cover designer: Tony Saizon

Printed in the U.S.A.

Library of Congress Catalog Card Number: 97-93647

ISBN: 0-395-87069-0

1 2 3 4 5 6 7 8 9-VH-01 00 99 98 97

Brief Contents

Contents

15 Europe in the Age of Religious War, 1555–1648   547

16 Europe in the Age of Louis XIV, ca. 1610–1715   589

22 New Powers and New Tensions, 1850–1880   811

**25 War and Revolution,
1914–1919   917**

**26 The Illusion of Stability,
1919–1930   957**

30 The West and the World in the Late Twentieth Century   1113

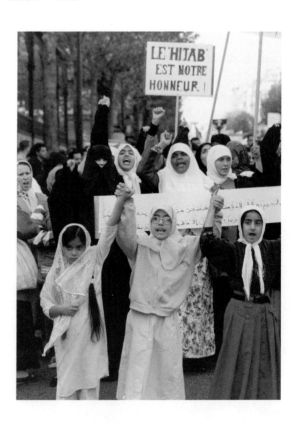

Maps

Documents

Chronologies, Genealogies, and Charts

Weighing the Evidence

Preface

Miles Davis was once asked what he thought jazz musicians would be playing in ten years, and he said that if he knew that, he would already be playing it. The authors of this book are committed teachers who never lost the thrill of being history students. We do not claim that we have seen into the future, but we can say with real conviction that we have tried to do better, for both instructors and students, than has been done in the past. And as we look back over nearly a decade, to the time when we were planning the first edition of *Western Civilization: The Continuing Experiment*, we can say with a mixture of pride and humility that we anticipated quite well what kind of history would be "playing" in ten years.

The purpose of a Western civilization textbook is to anchor a course that aims to inform students about essential developments within a tradition that has powerfully, although not always positively, affected everyone who is alive today. Although each of us finds something to admire in all of the existing textbooks, none of us was fully happy with any of them. We were disappointed with books that claimed "balance" but actually stressed a single kind of history. We regretted that so many texts were uneven in their command of recent scholarship. Although convinced of both the inherent interest of Western civilization and the importance of teaching the subject, we were disconcerted by the celebratory tone of some books, which portray the West as resting on its laurels instead of creatively facing its future.

As we were planning this book, momentous changes shook the Western world. Most obviously, the Soviet Union collapsed and the communist regimes of Eastern Europe tumbled one after another. Those who reflect on the West today must take account of Islamic minorities in the Slavic Balkans, Turkish workers in Germany, and African workers in France. Unprecedented economic prosperity—to be sure, unevenly distributed—marks all the lands from Ireland to Russia. Thus, the study of Western civilization at the dawn of a new millennium cannot focus narrowly on the peoples of Europe's western fringe, and it cannot take its bearings from a historical landscape whose most prominent features are the Depression of the 1930s, the world wars, and a global population divided by the iron curtain.

We decided to try very hard to produce a book that is balanced and coherent; that addresses the full range of subjects that a Western civilization text needs to address; that provides the student reader with interesting, timely material; that is up-to-date in terms of scholarship and approach; and that is handsome to look at—in short, a book that helps the instructor to teach and the student to learn. We have kept our common vision fresh through frequent meetings, correspondence, E-mail, critical mutual readings, and expert editorial guidance. Six authors have come together as one, and because each of us focused on his or her own area of specialization, we believe we have attained a rare blend of competence, confidence, and enthusiasm.

CENTRAL THEMES AND APPROACH

Western civilization is a story. We therefore aimed at a strong chronological narrative line. Our experience as teachers tells us that students appreciate this clear but gentle orientation. Our experience tells us, too, that an approach that is more chronological than thematic will leave instructors plenty of room to adapt our narrative to their preferred organization.

Although we maintain the familiar, large-scale divisions of a Western civilization book, we also present some innovative adjustments in arrangement. For instance, Chapter 2 treats early Greece together with the whole eastern Mediterranean region in the period from about 1500 to 750 B.C. This approach both links kindred cultures and respects chronological flow better than customary treatments, which take western Asia to a certain point and backtrack to deal with early Greece. We focus an entire chapter on Late Antiquity, the tumultuous and fascinating period from about A.D. 300 to 600 that witnessed the transformation of the Roman Empire into three successors: Byzantine, Islamic, and European. We introduce and analyze the industrial transformation in the middle of the nineteenth century, when it was at its high point, instead of scattering its account through several chapters. Our twentieth-century chapters reflect an understanding of the century formed in its closing years rather than in its middle decades. What is new in our organization represents adjustments grounded in the best scholarship, and what is old represents time-tested approaches.

A chronological narrative that respects the traditional divisions of ancient, medieval, early modern, and modern will inevitably reflect great people and great events. We make no apology for this, and we urge no particular ideology in doing it. Marx was surely right when he said that women and men make history without knowing they are doing so, but it is nonetheless true that Alexander, Charlemagne, Elizabeth I, Napoleon, and Hitler have had a more decisive impact on the development of the West than most ordinary individuals. That is true, but not interesting to teachers or to students until we say why it is true.

This book takes as its point of departure *power* in all its senses: public and private; economic, social, political, and cultural; symbolic and real. We continually ask who had power, and who did not. Through what public and private means was power gained, lost, and exercised in a given time and place? How did people talk about power? What kinds of rituals, ceremonies, or celebrations displayed power? What relationships existed among economic, social, political, and cultural power?

By using power, not old-fashioned high politics, as our organizing principle we believe we have achieved the kind of balance and integration that are frequently promised but seldom attained. We have deliberately avoided putting the occasional paragraph or section on women, children, families, religious minorities, eating habits, or marriage patterns in the middle of a discussion of something else entirely. We maintain a sustained interest in the history of women, often using gender as a tool of analysis and explanation, and we discuss such subjects as diet, clothing, or dwellings when Europeans themselves talked about them, or when there were important changes in these areas. Women are not relegated to a separate section in our account of the Middle Ages, for example, but instead are situated in accounts of politics, society, religion, and culture. Nineteenth-century women appear as workers, writers, or political activists and not under a single heading that would deprive them of contextual participation in their contemporary world.

Our focus on power permits a continuous, nuanced treatment of intellectual history. Major thinkers and key intellectual traditions are consistently integrated into the story rather than treated in-dependently as if they were *the* story of Western civilization, or else a sideshow to the main event. Any understanding of Plato and Aristotle, for instance, must begin in the Greek *polis.* Renaissance humanism cannot be understood apart from its late medieval Italian, urban context. We anchor the Scientific Revolution to Renaissance and Reformation intellectual life, court societies, patronage networks, and the expanding world created by Europe's first overseas empires. We root romanticism in its urban, industrial, nationalistic, and politically restless nineteenth-century world, and we treat existentialism as one response to modern war and totalitarianism.

We thought hard about another issue that textbooks usually take for granted: What is the West? This book was conceived and written after the end of the cold war and the fall of communist regimes in Eastern Europe. Both the West's understanding of itself at any point in time and the historical understanding of the West through succeeding generations have changed in interesting and important ways, never more so than today. Thus, we continually invite our readers to think about the precise object of their study.

In fashioning our picture of the West, we took two unusual steps. First, our West is bigger than the one found in most textbooks. We treat the Celtic world, Scandinavia, and the Slavic world as integral parts of the story. We look often at the lands that border the West—Anatolia/Turkey, western Asia, North Africa, the Eurasian steppes—in order to show the to-and-fro of peoples, ideas, technologies, and products. Second, we continually situate the West in its global context. We must be clear: This is not a world history book. But just as we recognize that the West has influenced the rest of the world, so too we carefully acknowledge that the rest of the world has influenced the West. We begin this story of mutual interaction with the Greeks and Romans, carry it through the European Middle Ages, focus on it in the age of European exploration and conquest, and analyze it closely in the modern world of industry, empire, diplomacy, and questions of citizenship and identity.

We ask, finally, that you note the subtitle of the book: "The Continuing Experiment." It was carefully chosen to convey our resolve to avoid a deterministic approach. For students and teachers, an appreciation of continuity and change, of unity and diversity, can foster sympathetic participation in our often bewildering world. We try to give individual actors, moments, and movements the sense of drama, possibility, and contingency that they actually possessed.

We, with faultless hindsight, always know how things came out. Contemporaries often hadn't a clue. We respect them. Much of the fascination, and the reward, of studying Western civilization lies precisely in its richness, diversity, changeability, unpredictability.

DISTINCTIVE FEATURES

To make this text as accessible as possible to students, we have constantly been aware of its place in a program of teaching. Each chapter begins with a thematic introduction that engages the reader's interest while pointing clearly and in some detail to what will follow. Chronologies help to organize and review major developments. Careful chapter summaries draw together major topics and themes and link the present chapter to the one that follows. To help students strike out on their own to new historical discoveries, we provide for each chapter an annotated reading list of scholarly classics and exciting new works.

In addition to a sound pedagogical framework, and to an engaging full-color design that clarifies and animates the illustrations and text, we have thoroughly integrated all the elements of the book. Our maps, for example, support the text in both traditional and novel ways. Teachers will find "old friends" among them but will make many new acquaintances too. Our diverse array of boxed primary sources—five per chapter—are referred to and tightly anchored in the text and support their surrounding discussion. Here again, classic documents are blended with fresh newcomers. Our photographs, many of which have not previously appeared in textbooks, are never merely decorative, and their captions seek to extend the discussions that they complement.

An example may help to illustrate this integration. The central theme of Chapter 9, which treats Europe from 900 to 1150, is "expansion." Thus the chapter explores population growth, economic development, and foreign military adventures—chiefly the Crusades. But this theme of expansion is developed to reinforce the book's central, unifying themes—power and the West within the wider world. For example, the text discusses the kinds of social and institutional structures that were created or refined to accommodate the expansion of territorial power and responsibility. The maps provide clear evidence of the territorial expansion of both old states (England, France, Germany) and new ones (in Celtic, Scandinavian, and Slavic areas). The pictures illustrate power in several ways. Kings are depicted on thrones, wearing crowns, holding orbs and scepters, and receiving gifts and obeisance. In other words, their symbolic and ceremonial manifestations of power are displayed. Castles, one of the great military and political technologies of the time, appear in Welsh, French, and Polish forms. A woman of immense power in central Italy is shown receiving the earnest entreaties for help of a German emperor. Boxed documents illustrate personal bonds of homage and fealty, key issues in the period's clashes between secular and ecclesiastical officials, and, on a lesser scale, the division of goods in Welsh law between men and women after a divorce. The various components of this chapter, as of all the chapters, continually reinforce one another, for a careful integration that promotes discussion and enhances learning.

Another important component of this book is the two-page feature "Weighing the Evidence," presented at the end of each chapter. These features introduce students to the fascinating variety of sources that historians use and invite them to think critically about the nature of historical information and inquiry. Each opens with a description of the evidence reproduced in the feature—sources ranging from images of Cleopatra, the Ravenna mosaics, Reformation woodcuts, eighteenth-century political symbols, the layout of the British Museum, and the poetry of World War I—and then discusses how the professional historian examines this evidence to reconstruct the past. When Samuel Butler said that God cannot change history but that historians can and often do, he meant that history itself arises from new or different acts of interpretation. With "Weighing the Evidence," students look over the shoulder of the historian to become active participants in this interpretive process. The sources examined are interesting and instructive in their own right, but the "Weighing the Evidence" features also contribute to the teaching program of the book. As always, they are carefully integrated into the text: There are references to them at appropriate points in the narrative; they themselves contain cross-references where appropriate to other sections or illustrations; and they support ongoing discussions.

This book is also flexible in format as well as substantive organization. Because schools use different academic calendars, organize Western civilization courses according to different chronologies, and require or recommend different parts of the course, we issue this book in four formats, three of which embrace the complete work:

- One-volume hardcover edition (Chapters 1–30)
- Two-volume paperback, Volume I: To 1715 (Chapters 1–17), Volume II: Since 1560 (Chapters 15–30)
- Three-volume paperback, Volume A: To 1500 (Chapters 1–12), Volume B: 1300–1715 (Chapters 11–19), Volume C: Since 1789 (Chapters 19–30)
- And new to this edition, Since 1300 (Chapters 11–30)

Volume II opens with a comprehensive introduction that situates the student reader in the late sixteenth century and surveys the course of Western civilization from ancient times to the early centuries of the modern era. This introduction is designed particularly for students who did not take the first semester of the course, or who are new to this book.

CHANGES IN THE NEW EDITION

In preparing our second edition we thought hard about our own experiences in using the book, and we paid strict attention to the advice given us by many instructors, including those who used the book and those who did not. Five main lines of revision guided our changes:

Organizational Changes

The most obvious change here is that we shrank our book from thirty-two to thirty chapters. The first-edition chapter on "The Frontiers of Latin Europe" was deleted, and its most important conceptual perspectives and substantive material were redistributed among Chapters 8, 9, and 10. Two chapters on later medieval Europe were tightened in focus and organization and turned into one new chapter (11). By cutting out two first-edition chapters in Volume I, it became possible to include Chapter 17 on the Scientific Revolution in both Volumes I and II, a change that accommodates many syllabuses.

Many other organizational changes are less visible but still significant. The revolution from the Gracchi to Caesar in Republican Rome has been moved to Chapter 5, which permits Chapter 6 to have a sharper focus on the crisis of the late Republic and the emergence of the Roman Empire. Some material on medieval church-state controversies that was earlier distributed over several chapters is now

consolidated in Chapter 10. Discussions of the late medieval economy are now sharply focused in Chapter 11, and former sections on late medieval and Renaissance art are now found together in Chapter 12. Sections treating the English Revolution, the French Revolution, and the revolutions of 1848 have undergone significant reorganization and revision. The book's final chapters have been rearranged and revised in light of shifting perspectives on postcommunist Eastern Europe.

Thematic Integration

Users and reviewers praised our book's two major themes—power and the shape of the West within the wider world—but in preparing this edition we felt we could do even better. Specifically, we saw opportunities to treat the second theme in more detail and to sharpen our use of gender as a means of explanation. Accordingly, we began at the beginning, so to speak, and incorporated material on Neolithic and Copper Age Europe to complement our treatment of the Mesopotamian and Mediterranean worlds. We paid more attention to the shifting frontiers of medieval Europe. In revising our account of the immensely important political and diplomatic history of the period from about 1500 to 1800, we included more extensive coverage of both Europe's immediate frontiers and the wider world. Our nineteenth-century chapters contain an expanded account of the growing power of the United States and the global significance of European emigration. Our nineteenth- and twentieth-century chapters now contain additional coverage of the mutual relations between Europe and its colonies. The Depression of the 1930s is anchored more firmly in a global context, and the multicultural implications of vast population movements in the late twentieth century are carefully considered.

From the start, our book paid serious attention to the experiences of women and to the exciting possibilities of using gender as a tool of analysis. We were very pleased that users and reviewers affirmed our intentions and achievements. Still, in revising we believed that we could improve our coverage. Readers of the first edition will detect many changes, as in the sections on the Roman Empire, Late Antiquity, the High Middle Ages, exploration and discovery, the Scientific Revolution, nineteenth-century ideologies and social movements, the welfare state, and the problems of identity politics in the very recent past.

New Primary-Source Chapter Feature

To help us achieve our goal of thematic integration, in this edition we have added the primary-source feature "Encounters with the West." Every chapter contains one readily identifiable document that portrays other people commenting on westerners or westerners commenting on the world around them. In these documents, students meet Egyptians and Romans reacting to foreigners, a Franciscan missionary telling about the Mongols, an Inca nobleman describing his civilization, the wife of a wealthy plantation owner stating her views on Haiti's slave revolt, a Moroccan commenting on French press freedoms, Gandhi talking about nonviolence, and the controversial, influential Edward Said discussing "Orientalism."

Improved Chapter Features

We have also revised our existing pedagogical framework to take every opportunity to tighten the book's integration and to enhance its teachability. Every chapter now opens with an arresting full-color illustration that is specifically referenced in the introduction on the facing page. This visual and textual device expresses the main themes and issues raised in that chapter and captures the interest and provokes the imagination of the student reader. To continue our book's close integration of text and artwork, we have replaced about one-third of the in-text illustrations. Each new picture and drawing was chosen specifically to enhance the book's pedagogical force. All maps were scrutinized for accuracy and pedagogical value, and many were revised in subtle ways. We incorporated a number of new boxed documents that work to illustrate or extend our themes. Most chapters, moreover, now contain at least one document that lends itself to a "gendered" reading to help students familiarize themselves with gender as a tool of analysis. About one-third of the "Weighing the Evidence" features are new in this edition. Some of the newcomers are attributable to exciting discoveries, such as "The Ice Man's World." Others, on topics ranging from the invention of modern cartography to the Crystal Palace and pop art, serve to bolster our themes and to provoke discussion.

Incorporation of Recent Scholarship

One important advantage of a six-person author team is that we can keep track of the latest publications across the whole course of Western civilization. Natu- rally, few periods or problems have been the subject of massive reinterpretation since our first edition, but many small changes in perspective have turned up all over. In line with the most recent, sound work, we have especially revised sections on the Greek phalanx and polis, the Etruscans and early Rome, Jesus and early Christianity, Late Antiquity, the Slavic world, vernacular culture in the Renaissance, the origins of the Reformation, the English Revolution, Napoleon, many aspects of the nineteenth century, the cold war, and the fall of Soviet communism. To incorporate recent findings and perspectives, we have updated all the lists of suggested readings.

SUPPLEMENTS

We have thoroughly revised our array of text supplements provided to aid students in learning and instructors in teaching. These supplements, including a *Study Guide*, a *Computerized Study Guide*, an *Instructor's Resource Manual*, *Test Items*, *Computerized Test Items*, *Map Transparencies*, a *Videodisc* and *Videodisc Guide*, and two new multimedia supplements: a *Power Presentation Manager* and a CD-ROM of interactive maps, are tied closely to the text and to one another, to provide a tightly integrated program of teaching and learning.

The *Study Guide*, written by Miriam Shadis of Ohio University, includes an introductory essay on how to make the best use of your Western Civilization course. For each chapter it gives learning objectives, an annotated outline of the chapter, multiple-choice questions keyed to the text, essay questions with guidelines, analytical questions, and map exercises. The *Study Guide* is published in two volumes, to correspond with Volumes I and II of the text: Volume I contains Chapters 1–17 and Volume II contains Chapters 15–30. The *Study Guide* is also available in a computerized version for use with IBM® PC or compatible computers. This *Computerized Study Guide* contains text page references for all questions and rejoinders to each multiple-choice question that explain why the student's response is or is not correct.

The *Instructor's Resource Manual*, prepared by Janice Liedl of Laurentian University, contains useful teaching strategies and tips for getting the most out of the text. Each chapter includes a summary and outline, learning objectives, lecture suggestions, discussion questions, recommended outside reading, and writing assignment and paper topics. For the new edition we have expanded the *Instructor's Resource Manual* to include recommended film, video, and multimedia resources, as well as collaborative learning activities for students.

Each chapter of the *Test Items,* written by Diane Moczar of Northern Virginia Community College, offers a list of 20 to 30 key terms, 10 to 15 short-answer and essay questions, 2 to 3 map questions, and 40 to 50 multiple-choice questions. Answers to the multiple-choice questions are located at the end of the *Test Items.* We also offer a computerized version of the *Test Items* for use with IBM® PC or compatible computers, to enable teachers to alter, replace, or add questions. Each item in the computerized test item file is numbered according to the printed test item file to ease the creation of customized tests.

An exciting addition to our map program is a CD-ROM of thirty interactive maps, available to both instructors and students. We also offer *The Western Civilization Videodisc/Videotape/Slide* program, a multimedia collection of visual images, as well as a set of full-color *Transparencies* of all the maps in the text.

In addition, we are pleased to provide the *Power Presentation Manager,* a software tool that enables teachers to prepare visual aids for lectures electronically, using both textual and visual materials. Instructors can customize their lectures by incorporating their own material onto the PPM and combining it with the electronic resources provided, including adaptable chapter outlines, tables, illustrations, and maps from the text.

Finally, we are proud to announce the creation of our on-line primary-source collection, *BiblioBase™: Custom Coursepacks in Western Civilization.* This resource will allow instructors to select from over 600 primary-source documents to create their own customized reader.

ACKNOWLEDGMENTS

From the first draft to the last, the authors have benefited from repeated critical readings by many colleagues. We have tried very hard to profit from the vast fund of experience and knowledge that has been placed generously at our disposal. Our thanks to the following instructors: **Lawrence Backlund,** Montgomery County Community College; **John Battick,** University of Maine—Orono; **F. E. Beemon,** Middle Tennessee State University; **Christopher M. Bellitto,** St. Joseph's Seminary, Dunwoodie; **Wayne Bledsoe,** University of Missouri—Rolla; **Donna Bohanan,** Auburn University; **RaGena De Aragon,** Gonzaga University; **Peter Diehl,** Western Wash-

ington University; **Katherine J. Haldane,** The Citadel; **Boyd Hill,** University of Colorado—Boulder; **James Lehning,** University of Utah; **Daniel Lewis,** California State Polytechnic University at Pomona; **Janice Liedl,** Laurentian University; **Raymond Mentzner,** Montana State University; **John Nicols,** University of Oregon; **Byron Nordstrom,** Gustavus Adolphus College; **Beth Plummer,** Wingate University; **Janet Polasky,** University of New Hampshire; **Donald Pryce,** University of South Dakota; **John Rosser,** Boston College; **Arnold Sherman,** Champlain College; **Tom Taylor,** Seattle University; and **James Walter,** Sinclair Community College.

Each of us has also benefited from the close readings and valuable criticisms of our coauthors, although we all assume responsibility for our own chapters. Barry Strauss has written Chapters 1–6; Thomas Noble, Chapters 7–10; Duane Osheim, Chapters 11–14; Kristen Neuschel, Chapters 15–19; William Cohen, Chapters 20–24; and David Roberts, Chapters 25–30.

Many colleagues, friends, and family members have helped us develop this work as well. Thomas Noble wishes to thank Linda L. Noble for her patience and kindness over the years devoted to this project. He is also grateful to John Contreni, Wendy Davies, Thomas Head, Elizabeth Meyer, Richard Sullivan, John Van Engen, Robert Wilken, and Ian Wood.

Barry Strauss is grateful to colleagues at Cornell and at other universities who offered advice and encouragement and responded to scholarly questions. He would also like to thank Sandra Kisner and Elaine Scott for their invaluable assistance. Most important has been the support and forbearance of his family. His daughter, Sylvie, his son, Michael, and, above all, his wife, Marcia, have truly been sources of inspiration.

Duane Osheim wishes to thank his family for support during the writing and revising of this book. He is also grateful to colleagues at the University of Virginia, who helped to clarify the many connections between Western civilization and the wider world. He would specifically like to thank Erik Midelfort, Arthur Field, Janis Gibbs, and Beth Plummer for comments and advice.

Kristen Neuschel thanks her colleagues at Duke University for sharing their expertise. She is especially grateful to Sy Mauskopf, Bill Reddy, John Richards, Tom Robisheaux, Alex Roland, John J. TePaske, Julius Scott, and Peter Wood. She also thanks her husband and fellow historian, Alan Williams, for his wisdom about Western civilization and his support throughout the project, and her children, Jesse and Rachel, for their patience, joy, and curiosity.

William Cohen thanks his wife, Christine Matheu, and his daughters, Natalie, Leslie, and Laurel, for their support and encouragement over the many years that this project has matured.

David Roberts wishes to thank Bonnie Cary, Linda Green, and Nancy Heaton for their able assistance and Joshua Cole, Karl Friday, Thomas Ganschow, John Haag, John Morrow, Miranda Pollard, Ronald Rader, William Stueck, Eve Troutt Powell, and Kirk Willis, colleagues at the University of Georgia, for sharing their expertise in response to questions. He also thanks Beth Roberts for her constant support and interest and her exceedingly critical eye, and Ellen, Trina, and Anthony, for their college-age perspective and advice.

All the authors wish to thank the thousands of students who helped us to learn and to teach Western civilization. Their questions and concerns have shaped much of this work.

We also wish to acknowledge and thank the editors who did so much to bring this book into being. Elizabeth Welch, our Senior Basic Book Editor, sifted our thoughts, sharpened our focus, and smoothed our prose. Christina Horn, our Senior Project Editor, displayed boundless patience and professionalism as she assembled this book from all its constituent parts. Carole Frohlich, our tireless and enterprising picture researcher, often knew better than we did just what we wanted. To Jean Woy, Editor-in-Chief for Social Sciences (and our original Sponsoring Editor), we are grateful for confidence in this project, and in us. Sean Wakely was the Sponsoring Editor who steered this ship safely into port on its first voyage. Patricia Coryell is on the bridge now. We are grateful to them both for smooth passages.

Thomas F. X. Noble

The authors (left to right): Kristen Neuschel, Bill Cohen, David Roberts, Tom Noble (in back), Duane Osheim, Barry Strauss.

About the Authors

Thomas F. X. Noble

After receiving his Ph.D. from Michigan State University, Thomas Noble has taught at Albion College, Michigan State University, Texas Tech University, and since 1980 at the University of Virginia. He is the author of *The Republic of St. Peter: The Birth of the Papal State, 680–825, Religion, Culture and Society in the Early Middle Ages*, and *Soldiers of Christ: Saints and Saints' Lives from Late Antiquity and the Early Middle Ages*. Noble's articles and reviews have appeared in many leading journals, including the *American Historical Review, Byzantinische Zeitschrift, Catholic Historical Review, Revue d'histoire ecclésiastique, Speculum,* and *Studi medievali*. He has also contributed chapters to several books and articles to three encyclopedias. Noble, who was a member of the Institute for Advanced Study in 1994, has been awarded fellowships by the National Endowment for the Humanities (twice) and by the American Philosophical Society.

Barry S. Strauss

Professor of history and Classics at Cornell University, where he is also Director of the Peace Studies Program, Barry S. Strauss holds a Ph.D. from Yale in history. He has been awarded fellowships by the National Endowment for the Humanities, the American School of Classical Studies at Athens, and the Killam Foundation of Canada. He is the recipient of the Clark Award for excellence in teaching from Cornell. His many publications include *Athens After the Peloponnesian War: Class, Faction, and Policy, 403–386 B.C.; Fathers and Sons in Athens: Ideology and Society in the Era of the Peloponnesian War; The Anatomy of Error: Ancient Military Disasters and Their Lessons for Modern Strategists* (with Josiah Ober); and *Hegemonic Rivalry from Thucydides to the Nuclear Age* (co-edited with R. Ned Lebow).

Duane J. Osheim

A Fellow of the American Academy in Rome with a Ph.D. in History from the University of California, Davis, Duane Osheim is a professor of history at the University of Virginia. A specialist in late Medieval and Renaissance social and institutional history, he is author of *A Tuscan Monastery and Its Social World* and *An Italian*

Lordship: The Bishopric of Lucca in the Late Middle Ages, as well as numerous studies of religious values and rural life in late Medieval Italy.

Kristen B. Neuschel

Associate professor of history at Duke University, Kristen B. Neuschel received the Ph.D. from Brown University. She is the author of *Word of Honor: Interpreting Noble Culture in Sixteenth-Century France* and articles on French social history and European women's history. In 1988 she received the Alumni Distinguished Undergraduate Teaching Award, which is awarded annually on the basis of student nominations for excellence in teaching at Duke.

William B. Cohen

After receiving his Ph.D. at Stanford University, William Cohen has taught at Northwestern University and Indiana University, where he is now professor of history. At Indiana, he served as chairman of the West European Studies and History departments. A previous president of the Society for French Historical Studies, Cohen has received several academic fellowships, among them a National Endowment for the Humanities and a Fulbright fellowship. Among his many publications are *Rulers of Empire, The French Encounter with Africans, European Empire Building, Robert Delavignette and the French Empire, The Transformation of Modern France,* and *Urban Government and the Rise of the City.*

David D. Roberts

After taking his Ph.D. in modern European history at the University of California, Berkeley, David Roberts taught at the Universities of Virginia and Rochester before becoming professor of history at the University of Georgia in 1988. At Rochester he chaired the Humanities Department of the Eastman School of Music, and he has chaired the History Department at Georgia since 1993. A recipient of Woodrow Wilson and Rockefeller Foundation fellowships, he is the author of *The Syndicalist Tradition and Italian Fascism, Benedetto Croce and the Uses of Historicism,* and *Nothing but History: Reconstruction and Extremity after Metaphysics,* as well as numerous articles and reviews.

The West Before 1560

Historians sometimes say that "History begins at Sumer," a region of ancient Mesopotamia located in the south of modern Iraq. For the reader of Volume II of *Western Civilization: The Continuing Experiment*, history begins forty-five hundred years after Sumer, in the sixteenth-century European world. Some orientation may therefore be helpful to situate the reader in time and place.

EUROPE AT 1560

Hindsight enables today's history student to detect three major features of the European scene at the middle of the sixteenth century. First, the state system was marked by ever larger empires and intricate alliances. Second, the European world was riven by religious differences that reflected old political and cultural divisions and generated new tensions. Third, Spanish and Portuguese explorers and conquerors had begun building vast overseas empires in North and South America and in the whole Indian Ocean basin. The globe was being brought within the orbit of Western civilization.

States and Empires

Europe's state system was dominated by two multi-ethnic empires. Through marriage alliances, the Habsburg family, originally from Switzerland, had established extensive claims: to Spain and its overseas empire, to parts of Italy and much of Austria, to the Crown of the Holy Roman Empire (as the German Empire had been called since the fourteenth century), to Burgundy, and to the Netherlands. At the opposite end of Europe, the empire of the Muslim Ottoman Turks reached from central Asia to the gates of Vienna.

The Habsburg dominions literally surrounded France. The chief dynamic in western Europe was continuing rivalry between the Habsburgs and the Valois rulers of France.

Other states in Europe sought a place alongside the greater ones. Scandinavia was dominated by Sweden, whose rulers continually entered the complicated politics of northern Germany. Those complications, and Sweden's opportunities, were directly tied to the fluctuating influence of the Holy Roman emperors. Prussia, a small Baltic state founded by German knights and adventurers, was hemmed in by other north German states, Sweden, Lithuania, and, on occasion, Russia. In the fifteenth century, the Russians threw off the yoke of the Mongols—a confederation of peoples from the northern frontiers of China who had begun raiding in central and western Asia, as well as in eastern Europe, in the thirteenth century—and turned increasingly to the east, to Asia, but never lost sight of their western frontier with Germanic and Slavic Europe or their southern frontier with the Turks. The Turks threatened, or at least contemporaries perceived them to threaten, the Holy Roman Empire in the northern Balkans, Russia in the Black Sea region, and Italian merchants all over the Mediterranean. The traders of Venice and Genoa, in particular, were anxious about their old commercial superiority after the Portuguese and the Spanish opened vast new economic opportunities as a result of their commercial exploitation of the Americas, Africa, and the Indian Ocean basin.

Religious Divisions

For hundreds of years after the Frankish emperor Charlemagne (r. 768–814), many people held up the ideal of Europe as "Christendom." Christianity was seen as a badge of citizenship in a world where the purpose of governments—indeed of organized societies—was to assist people in their quest for eternal salvation. Leadership in this Christendom was hotly contested between secular rulers, with the German emperor in the lead, and ecclesiastical powers arrayed behind the pope.

A truly Christian political order that transcended national boundaries was never really created in the Middle Ages (roughly the years from 500 to 1500), but a fundamentally Christian society certainly was. The beliefs of ordinary people were not their own private affair. Deviation from official beliefs brought swift punishment. "Correct" belief was nurtured, imposed, and reinforced

in countless ways. Most schools were run by the church to promote religious learning and culture. The ordinary rituals of daily life—birth, baptism, marriage, death—were attended by religious ceremonies. Celebrations, from royal feasts to humble village revels, were held on saints' days. Christianity, and churchmen, were literally and figuratively inescapable.

In the sixteenth century Europe's rich religious life and heritage were sundered in unprecedented ways. A series of religious reformers, most notably the German Martin Luther (1483–1546) and the French-born John Calvin (1509–1564), turned to the Bible and to their visions of the early Christian church to forge a program of religious renewal—now called the "Protestant Reformation"—that stripped the papacy and the Roman Catholic church of their control of important parts of Europe: England and Scotland, Scandinavia, the Netherlands, Switzerland, northern Germany. Although the uniformity of medieval Christianity should not be exaggerated, there was, after the Reformation of the sixteenth century, no possibility of the attainment or the enforcement of a single pattern of belief.

Religious divisions and the abandonment of the medieval ideal of Christendom had two important outcomes for Europe. First, much of the political and diplomatic controversy of the sixteenth century was intimately related to religious issues. The English crown vastly strengthened itself by promoting religious reform, and bitter religious quarrels threatened more than once to destroy France. Spain set itself up as the guardian of Catholic orthodoxy but usually lacked the power to impose its will in matters of religion. Holy Roman emperors were Catholic, and north German rulers were often Protestant. Religious divisions worsened old antagonisms and, in turn, generated new ones.

Second, the demise of the ideal of Christendom launched a quest for a new way to define the rationale for the state. If the state was not an agent of God's plan for humanity, if its essential ends were not religious, what was its purpose? Already in the thirteenth and fourteenth centuries thinkers had challenged the right of ecclesiastical authorities to exercise superior power in the state. The reformers agreed in denying to the pope any role in government, but often they sought to erect godly commonwealths based on their understanding of biblical truths. An Italian civic tradition, holding that states are free associations among people to promote their best interests, came to fruition in the writings of the French political thinker Jean Bodin (1530–1596), who would vest sovereign—that is, total—authority in the monarch. People later located sovereignty elsewhere in the body politic, but Bodin took a long step toward subordinating religion to government.

Europe and the Wider World

A glance at a map of the world today will show that Europe is not especially well placed for global domination. Its size is smaller than that of other continents, its population is no greater, and its material resources are not superior. One of the important questions in world history concerns exactly why it was Europeans, of all peoples, who turned outward in an attempt to explore and exploit the rest of the world.

Europeans long had contacts with non-Europeans. From ancient to modern times, trade routes running across Africa and Asia have brought the products of the whole world to Europe's markets. Occasional bursts of crusading ferocity or missionary zeal carried Europeans into the lands beyond their own frontiers. Travelers, such as the renowned Italian Marco Polo (1254–1324), were sometimes drawn by an irresistible urge to know what lay beyond the horizon. Nevertheless, most Europeans traveled little and knew almost nothing about the world.

In the fifteenth century an accumulation of factors changed forever Europe's place on earth. The popularity of travel literature may have aroused some people's curiosity. Real and imagined threats from the Turks may have fanned the remaining embers of crusading and missionary zeal. The Italian stranglehold on Mediterranean trade encouraged quests for alternative commercial routes. The slow, steady introduction of new technologies for sailing and navigation made possible long voyages away from the sight of familiar coastlines. New navigational devices, better maps and charts, and improved ship and sail designs—some of the latter borrowed from the non-European world—gave Europeans distinct advantages. The consolidation of powerful states like Spain

and, a century later, France and England put financial resources at the disposal of brave and ambitious seamen.

From modest explorations of the West African coast sponsored by the Portuguese royal family, European involvement with the rest of the world expanded to the creation of vast empires. By 1560 the Spanish had conquered southwestern North America, Central America, and South America, except for Brazil, which fell to Portugal. The Portuguese had established military and commercial bases in the Indian Ocean and in the South China Sea. The Dutch would eventually contest Portuguese control of the seas and islands lying to the south of China, as well as land colonists in southern Africa and North America. Yet the Dutch presence in North America would pale into insignificance before the territorial acquisitions of France and England.

Did Europeans bring real benefits to the rest of the world, or were they merely cruel exploiters? How has the non-Western world influenced the West? People argue over the answers to these questions. What cannot be argued is that during the sixteenth century Western civilization assumed a role in world history that it had never held before.

EUROPE TO 1560

In the fourteenth century the Florentine man of letters Francesco Petrarch (1304–1374) and his contemporaries, the first figures in a movement that we call the "Renaissance" (French for "rebirth"), explicitly stated their feeling that they were unlike the people and times that had just preceded them and were instead similar to the ancient Romans. Petrarch and the others created the traditional tripartite division of Western history into ancient, modern, and the part in the middle—the so-called Middle Ages, or Dark Ages.

Scholars today do not think Petrarch was right either in his denigration of the medieval period as the "Dark Ages" or in his assertion that he and his contemporaries were like the Romans. It is interesting that he said these things, but in doing so he revealed more about how people thought in his own period than about the realities of the past. Modern historians do not see sharp breaks between historical periods. For instance, scholars now discuss "Late Antiquity," a long period from roughly 300 to 600, as a transitional period between classical antiquity and the Middle Ages. Also absent today is any idea that the Middle Ages quickly gave way to the Renaissance. Historians now talk about continuity and change operating in tandem. Nevertheless, the old tripartite division persists because it represents the major way in which Westerners have reflected on their history and because broad chronological divisions accommodate academic programs of study.

Ancient Western Asia and Egypt

Let us return to Sumer. Historians usually begin their accounts of Western civilization with the Sumerians because they were, between about 3500 and 3000 B.C., the first people of ancient western Asia to attain civilization. The Egyptians achieved civilization at about the same time as the Sumerians. Sumer lies in Mesopotamia, the land "between the rivers" Tigris and Euphrates. After the Sumerians, a succession of peoples in Mesopotamia itself—Akkadians, Babylonians, and Assyrians, for example—and many other peoples in the lands bordering on Mesopotamia—Medes and Persians to the east, Hittites to the north, Phoenicians, Canaanites, and Hebrews to the west—also crossed the line that marks the beginnings of civilization.

All of these peoples are interesting and important in their own right, but they concern the continuing course of Western civilization in one particularly important way. They contributed much to the Greeks, who were a millennium behind them in developing civilization, and later to the Romans, who were another millennium behind the Greeks. Western Asia and Egypt contributed religious ideas, artistic norms, mathematical concepts, ways of reckoning time, and even the alphabet the Greeks adapted to their own language. Ideas, technologies, and practices from western Asia and Egypt radiated far beyond the Greek and Roman worlds and helped to spark the rise of civilization in Europe, where the Neolithic period (the "new stone" age, the time of carefully fashioned stone tools) gave way to civilization more slowly than in the Mediterranean world.

What, exactly, is civilization? No definition can win universal acceptance, but certain elements of a definition are widely accepted. Cities are crucial. With cities emerge complex social organizations that involve at least a minimal division of labor: Some people work in the fields, some in the home. Soldiers defend the city, and artisans provide for its daily goods. Governing institutions have a wide measure of acceptance and have the ability to enforce their will. Complex cultures appear with religious ideas and authorities, a literature and law that may be oral or written, and monumental architecture, especially fortifications, palaces, and temples.

Civilization emerged over a long time after about 3500 B.C. It appears that a slowly but steadily increasing population made it imperative to secure a predictable food supply. This need led to agriculture and animal husbandry, the taming of fields and flocks to the needs of a human community. The manifold processes involved in agriculture led to specialization of labor. The sharper definition of social and economic roles led to the delineation of gender roles. Communities defined certain tasks—government and war, for example—as essentially male, while reserving domestic responsibilities and some religious duties for women. The interests of self-sufficiency became subordinated to the needs of the community.

Because one person's predictable food supply is another person's temptation to plunder or conquer, government and military institutions were early products of agricultural societies. Settled communities began to develop cultures that helped men and women memorialize their past, explain their present, and point to their future.

Two words characterize well the historical experience of Mesopotamia: *invasion* and *diffusion*. Mesopotamia has no natural impediments to entry, and its fertile lands have long been a magnet for the peoples who live outside the region. Two groups of people have been especially influential. Semites, a linguistic community whose origins may lie in the Arabian desert, invaded Mesopotamia many times, usually from the southwest. Indo-Europeans, a vast group of peoples strewn from western Europe to northern India who share a common family of languages, invaded from the north and from the east somewhat later than the earliest Semites. The peoples who entered Mesopotamia were usually at a lower level of cultural development than the Sumerians. Thus, Sumer was conquered many times, but its culture survived. As conquerors built larger kingdoms, and even empires, they spread Sumerian culture throughout western Asia, providing in the process a common substratum of political, social, religious, artistic, and literary ideas.

The historical experience of Egypt was quite different. The Greek historian Herodotus (480–425 B.C.) called Egypt "the gift of the Nile." Historical Egypt is the fertile strip of land, ranging from 5 to 15 miles wide, that hugs the Nile along its 750-mile course. Whereas the Tigris and Euphrates flood irregularly, sometimes violently, the Nile usually floods annually and beneficently. Efforts to manage irrigation, grain production, and storage along the course of the river led to an early (just before 3000 B.C.) replacement of local autonomy by a unified monarchy under god-kings called pharaohs.

Under the pharaohs of the period that historians now call the "Old Kingdom" (2695–2160 B.C.), Egypt faced no foreign threats and built up its central institutions. The great monuments of this time, the pyramids—pharaonic tombs—symbolize the power, wealth, and security of Egypt. An invasion brought an end to the Old Kingdom, and the eventual overthrow of the invaders ushered in the Middle Kingdom (1963–1786 B.C.), a time of political innovation—pharaohs had to share power with aristocrats—and cultural stimulation from Mesopotamian sources. The Middle Kingdom yielded in turn to the New Kingdom (1550–1070 B.C.), when Egypt became an imperial state whose reach extended all the way to Mesopotamia. The treasures of Tutankhamon ("King Tut") exemplify the wealth and sophistication of this age. Imperial Egypt was eventually ground down in a series of wars with the Hittites, an Anatolian people whose efforts to dominate Mesopotamia were complicated by their battles with the Egyptians.

After the Egyptians and Hittites wore each other out, western Asia experienced a time of smaller, independent states. Phoenicia (roughly today's Lebanon) emerged as a major commercial power. The Phoenicians gathered up the goods of Asia and Arabia, which they received by means of land trade routes, and exchanged them for products acquired in colonies all over the Mediterranean. Such commercial ventures initiated the unification of the Mediterranean world.

Another small state of immense interest and importance was the kingdom created by the Hebrews. Oral traditions and much later writings tell a coherent story of Hebrew historical development. This fascinating story, so difficult either to verify or to refute, suggests that as early as 2000 B.C. a band of Hebrews under their tribal leader Abraham migrated from Mesopotamia to Palestine. Neither numerous nor united nor powerful, the Hebrews were often victimized by stronger neighbors. Around 1200 B.C. a group of Hebrews, slaves and workers in Egypt, cast off their bondage and returned to Palestine. This formative experience, remembered as the Exodus ("journey out" in Greek), forged a nation. For a century after 1000 B.C., kings Saul, David, and Solomon built a state that was a match for its neighbors. Later, fierce rivalries among the Hebrews led to the disintegration of the unified monarchy, and the fragmented Hebrew communities fell to powerful enemies.

The unique religious vision of the Hebrews makes them key founders of the Western tradition. The Jewish faith is very much alive in the world today and serves as the basis for two other major religious traditions: Christianity and Islam.

The Hebrew religious vision was the product of considerable historical evolution. It is revealed to us in a large collection of writings, the Hebrew Bible, which Christians call the Old Testament. These Hebrew Scriptures consist of historical writings that elaborate the unfolding relationship of the Hebrews with their God, legal books that lay down many rules for personal conduct and social organization, prophetic books that express some of humanity's deepest spiritual insights, and wisdom literature that is full of humane guidance for daily life.

Exclusive monotheism is the central truth revealed by these Scriptures. There is only one God. With this God the Hebrews have a covenant, a special pact. As long as the Hebrews do God's will, they will enjoy God's blessings and protection. God's will can be kept by observing the Law and by heeding the prophets, teachers who were believed to express God's will. Among legal provisions of the Scriptures the Ten Commandments are especially revealing. The first three of these pertain to the worship of God; the remaining seven relate to the formation of a just community.

The period of small states was concluded by the creation, one after another, of ever larger states culminating in the Persian Empire (ca. 550–334 B.C.). Here we meet once again the two concepts of invasion and diffusion. The Persians spread ideas and institutions through their vast empire, the largest the world had yet seen. The Persians were finally conquered by the Macedonian armies of Alexander the Great (r. 336–323 B.C.), the remnants of whose empire were swallowed up by the Romans. Rome was succeeded in the seventh century A.D. by the Islamic Arabs, whose empire fell in 1258 to the Mongols, who were in turn succeeded within a century by the Ottoman Turks, whose empire was dismantled in 1919 after World War I. Thus, invasion and diffusion have proceeded in Mesopotamia without interruption from Sumer to the twentieth century.

What was diffused? We have remarked on one example already: the religious vision of the Hebrews. Another is a style of rulership that we call "theocratic." This means that rulers are placed in office by, and are answerable only to, a god. In Mesopotamia rulers were generally believed to be the agents of the gods; in Egypt rulers were believed to be gods. In Alexander and his successors—Roman emperors and Islamic caliphs—theocratic rulership had a long run. The "divine right of kings" in seventeenth-century Europe, on the threshold of modernity, is a faint echo of Sumer. Egyptian ideas of a last judgment and of life after death circulated widely. Scientific and mathematical advances are another legacy. In building huge monuments like pyramids, in preserving human remains by mummification, in measuring fields, in observing the heavens, people in Mesopotamia and Egypt laid up a huge store of practical information from which later peoples, especially the Greeks, drew enthusiastically.

Classical Antiquity

Classical means normative, a standard by which to judge. In the nineteenth century intellectuals were fond of saying, "You were born in Greece." They meant that many cultural and aesthetic standards still prevalent in their own day had arisen in ancient Greece. So powerful has been the hold of Greece over architecture and sculpture, for example, that some modern movements have been deliberately "anticlassical."

The Greeks made fundamental—classical—contributions in two areas: political ideas and culture. The basic Greek institution was the *polis*, the city-state. The people of rugged, craggy Greece clustered in small territories; thus, numerous independent poleis arose in a land smaller than most American states. Each polis had a central urban zone and an agricultural hinterland. Often the urban zone featured an easily fortified hill: an *acropolis*. The acropolis sheltered people occasionally in times of attack and routinely in the conduct of civic and religious affairs.

The way to the polis is through Homer's epic poems, the *Iliad* and the *Odyssey*, probably composed not long after 800 B.C. but the products of a long oral development. They purport to tell of Greece in the days of the Trojan wars. Greek memory fixed those wars in about 1200 B.C., when there undoubtedly were some nasty commercial squabbles between the Greeks and their neighbors in the Aegean basin. It is grand to imagine, with Homer, that the beauty of Helen of Troy launched a thousand Greek ships. It is unlikely, however, that it is historically accurate to think so.

The *Iliad* and the *Odyssey* profess to describe actual events in the Greek world around the year 1200 B.C. That is, Homer seems to take us back to the Mycenaean period, so called because Mycenae was the greatest of that period's cities. Between about 1500 and 1200, several remarkable cities were built in the Greek lands by peoples who were the ancestors of the Greeks of the classical period. Before the Mycenaeans there had been a flourishing culture on the island of Crete. Historians call this culture "Minoan" after the legendary King Minos. But there is nothing legendary about the spectacular Minoan palaces, whose ruins are still impressive, or about the exquisite artistic remains of Minoan culture. The Minoan and Mycenaean periods played a key role in connecting the Greeks with the realms of western Asia and Egypt. The *Iliad*, after all, is a tale about a Greek expedition to Anatolia.

Homer sings of a world of kings and aristocrats. Huge armies are mentioned; individual warriors are described in minute detail. A common soldier could be flogged for speaking in the presence of his betters. This regal, aristocratic society, whose leaders were *Eupatrids*, "well-fathered men," dominated Greece for centuries.

Slowly the polis began to emerge, and its population began to grow. Many poleis outstripped the locally available food supplies and looked enviously at their neighbors'. Weaker poleis had to see to their defenses just as stronger ones had to beef up their capacity for attack. This competition resulted in the expansion of political and social participation in the public life of the polis. The infantryman, the hoplite, gained a role in defending his city and then insisted on a role in its government.

Some cities, most notably Athens, moved toward greater and greater participation until *demokratia,* the rule of the people, was achieved. Sparta, however, became a military juggernaut in which the rights of all were subordinated to the dictates of a small number of the oldest, most conservative citizens. Corinth, where large landowners invested in trade, became a commercial oligarchy. In all cases expanded or redefined participation belonged only to men. Women were excluded from active participation in public life. Yet in Sparta women exercised effective daily control over the private lands allotted to soldiers, and in Athens women played leading roles in the city's public religious celebrations.

In addition to reforming their own institutions, many Greek cities exported surplus population in colonies all over the Mediterranean world. As well as defusing Greek tensions, these colonies spread Greek culture far and wide.

While they were creating their basic political institutions between about 750 and 500 B.C., the Greeks also began to reflect systematically on political organization. Indeed, much of our political vocabulary is Greek in origin. Politics, after all, is what people do publicly in a polis.

Although Athens invented democracy, most Greek political thinkers were hostile to democratic ideas. Their criticisms alleged that democracy elevated the rabble over the best citizens and permitted the masses to satisfy their immediate desires, cast aside restraint, and neglect the long-term needs of the community as a whole. Curiously, the latter view was attacked by thinkers, whom we call "Sophists," who did not defend democracy but rather attacked the very idea that there were immutable standards of right and wrong in the conduct of public business. Everything, Sophists said, was convention. In one way or another, every Greek political thinker addressed an issue that has been critical in Western political discourse ever since: How can a person reconcile personal interests with the needs of the community?

The second Greek achievement lies in the realm of culture—more specifically in art, architecture, literature, science, and philosophy. Generalizations are difficult, but it may be fair to say that the Greeks, or at least the elite among them, set out very early to pursue truth and beauty. The Greeks were not unique in this quest. What sets them apart is the way they defined their objectives.

To a Greek thinker, beauty existed in the balance, order, and harmony that seemed to underlie everything really good. Thus, Greek scientific writers looked for a single, unchanging substance behind everything in existence. Failing in this search, they looked for theories capable of explaining everything. Failing in this, they explored the nature of thought and of language to see what could be known and communicated. The Greeks added, in relative terms, rather few concrete details to the huge fund of Mesopotamian and Egyptian discoveries. What the Greeks added was a vast mental edifice designed to systematize and explain what is known. In Classical Greece we see the birth of both science and philosophy.

Greek literature is full of memorable characters who present the reader, or the theater audience, with dilemmas of conscience. Oedipus, the main character of *Oedipus the Tyrant* by Sophocles (ca. 495–406 B.C.), whom Shakespeare called "the most tragic of poets," kills his father and marries his mother. He has absolutely no idea that he has done so. Is he nevertheless guilty of a hideous offense? Antigone, the central character in *Antigone,* by Euripides (ca. 485–406 B.C.), is one of the most powerful women in literature. It is to Greek literature that we must turn for insights into the roles of women, for they were excluded from formal, public positions. Antigone is forced to choose between the conflicting claims of country and family. What is justice; what does it mean to be just; is it possible to be just? Can a rule apply to one person alone, or must it apply to all? Do rules exist at all? Reading the best of Greek literature today produces exactly the effect it did then: gut-wrenching choices.

To look at a fine Greek statue or building is, first of all, to admire the astonishing technical skill that went into making it. Second, the viewer is moved by its beauty. Another look will usually prove disconcerting. The object in our gaze is *too* perfectly executed, *too* beautiful. It is like nothing we have ever seen, although it is vaguely like everything we see all the time. It is as if the object is meant less to remind us of things in this world than to provide a glimpse of a better, purer world.

Greek art opens up a vista on the greatest Greek philosophers. Plato (427–348 B.C.) distrusted the senses as guides to truth or reality. He believed that we are all prisoners of the world and of our human limitations. He said that ultimate reality existed in a transcendent world. In our world, and in this life, we can gain only hints of what really exists. We call Plato's way of thinking about things "idealism." His greatest pupil was Aristotle (384–322 B.C.), whose mania for classification has been the despair of many a biology student. Aristotle reminds us of the technical artistry of the Greek sculptor. For Aristotle, knowledge was perfectly possible right here in this world. But knowledge was the result of knowing what you wanted to find out, of working immensely hard to discover truth, and of living with the consequences of the truths you found.

Fame and success are not the same. Greek political ideas, institutions, and terminology have been famous for ages, but the Greeks were, finally, unsuccessful at politics. Only during the Persian Wars (490–479 B.C.) were the Greeks able to rally together, and even then they quarreled over strategy and leadership. Individual Greek states were notoriously unstable and violent, and most of the time the poleis of Greece found themselves forced to accept membership in leagues and alliances. Between 431 and 404 B.C., Sparta's Peloponnesian League and the Athenian Empire convulsed the whole Greek world in the Peloponnesian War.

Philip II of Macedon, an increasingly powerful and well-organized kingdom to the north of Greece, conquered the Greeks in 338 B.C. and bequeathed his prize to his remarkable son, Alexander the Great. After securing the Balkans, Alexander set off on a tour of military conquest unrivaled before his time. He conquered the Persian Empire and much more besides. His conquests ushered in a period that historians call "Hellenistic."

Hellenistic—"Greekish," as opposed to Hellenic, "purely Greek," the term applied to the period from about 750 to 323 B.C.—is a useful name for the period, roughly 323 to 30 B.C., when Greek language and culture dominated the Mediterranean world. Alexander's generals carved his vast empire into many smaller states that, despite many struggles, survived until one by one they fell to Rome. Greek leaders and elites mixed with local populations of many traditions to produce a rich, international culture that was everywhere recognizably, but nowhere purely, Greek. It was Hellenistic.

The expanding, fluid nature of Hellenistic culture and states provided unprecedented opportunities for women in commerce and in government. Unlike cities, which reserved offices to men, monarchies had courts in which women could be influential advisers and sometimes actual rulers. Cleopatra (r. 51–30 B.C.) is the most famous but by no means the only powerful Hellenistic woman.

The Roman poet Horace (65–8 B.C.) once said that "Captive Greece took her captor captive." Two points embedded in that remark serve well to open a discussion of Roman history. First, the Romans conquered Greece—and many more lands. Second, Greek culture deeply influenced the Romans, who in general were not so original and creative as the Greeks.

The Romans considered their history to have begun with the founding of Rome itself, an event that they dated to what we call 753 B.C. Actually, the historic Romans were in Rome's neighborhood long before that date, and Rome's familiar society and institutions arose long after it.

From 509 B.C., when the Romans believed that their Republic had been instituted, until 27 B.C., when that Republic was definitively transformed into a military monarchy, Rome was remarkably stable. Partly that stability was institutional. Rome had several magistrates with differing degrees of power, responsibility, and prestige, and several representative institutions with varying areas of authority. All adult males participated in important but very different ways. Partly, too, that stability was cultural. In society and politics, Rome was hierarchical and deferential in equal measure. Rome accorded responsibility for running the Republic to a small number of men. As in Greece, women in Rome were systematically excluded from public life. Roman literature depicts women as domestic and submissive.

Prominent Romans ruled through office and assembly and also through patronage and private influence. Leading Romans were dead set against innovation. The only good ways were the old ways, they believed. A Roman speech almost always began with an appeal to the "way our ancestors would have done things." Thus, it took a long time for the Roman system to emerge, and it seemed unchanged and unchanging.

There is a saying that "All roads lead to Rome." Slowly the Romans conquered their neighbors in Italy (509–265 B.C.). Then a series of wars (264–146 B.C.) against Carthage, an old Phoenician colony, gave Rome dominance in the western Mediterranean. Finally, a series of wars against the Hellenistic monarchies (200–31 B.C.) left Rome in control of the whole Mediterranean world.

Such wars came at a high price. Political and social stability was destroyed as personal and imperial ambition became regular weapons in domestic politics. Generals came to count for more than statesmen. Vast wealth, unevenly distributed, fractured the deferential structures of Roman society. Great wealth and shifting social realities also created unprecedented opportunities for women to influence public life through both family politics and artistic patronage. The culture of the Hellenistic world, as Horace correctly saw, overwhelmed the earnest Romans, who were less bumpkinish than they pretended but less sophisticated than most of their neighbors.

The Republic collapsed in a century of civil wars that produced a dramatically changed regime in the person of Augustus Caesar (r. 31 B.C.–A.D. 14). He inaugurated a two-century-long period, the *pax Romana* (the Roman peace), that brought the Mediterranean world as close as it has ever come to unity. It also brought peace and prosperity, good government, spectacular building projects, and a process of cultural diffusion now called "Romanization."

Augustus took the title of *Princeps* ("First Citizen"). The Augustan Principate rested on a few basic notions. Rome's ruler was now an emperor, a commander who pretended to be a magistrate, although his real power depended on his control of the military. The Roman Empire was now less and less an exclusively Roman entity: People from all over Italy and from the provinces shared in the benefits of empire. Augustus and the emperors who succeeded him forged a partnership with local elites everywhere. For instance, the Herods of

Judea are "bad guys" in the Christian Scriptures; but, from the Roman point of view, they were loyal, pliable, competent servants. And there were many like them. One of the ways in which such people showed their loyalty to Rome was by adopting the trappings of Roman culture—that is, by Romanizing.

Although the Romans were less innovative than the Greeks, they were by no means uncreative. Roman architecture achieved heights of complexity and sophistication. Roman law remains influential to this day. Cities from England to Mesopotamia still reveal their Roman street plans, and highway systems all over Europe lie atop Roman roads. No less an authority than Alfred, Lord Tennyson, called the poet Virgil (70–19 B.C.) "wielder of the stateliest measure ever formed by the mouth of man." Roman writers were learned, technically expert, verbally adroit, and at their best they ranged from moving to hilarious. Virgil's *Aeneid*, the story of Aeneas, one of the defeated at Troy and the legendary founder of Rome, presents the archetypal Roman hero: strong, familial, humble, loyal, and, above all else, perseverent.

The third century A.D. spelled the end for the Augustan Principate and for the classical order. The muses fell silent. From one end of the Roman Empire to the other, both the forms and the feelings of classical literature vanished. Large-scale building ceased. New religions, perhaps capable of explaining the difficulties of the age, proliferated. One prominent historian speaks of an "age of anxiety." What happened?

First, as the Roman historian Tacitus dryly observed in the first century A.D., "the army made the emperor." And, we might add, unmade him too, with alarming frequency. Civil war became endemic. The military was prominent because of its close relationship with the imperial office and also because, in the third century, the Roman Empire began to experience military threats along many of its long and exposed frontiers. Military and civil unrest contributed to a loosening of the old ties between the imperial government and the provincial elites. The economy was disrupted by political turmoil and was further weakened by uncontrollable inflation. At the end of the third century, Rome's prospects looked grim, but transformation edged out catastrophe.

The World of Late Antiquity

The years from about 300 to 600 witnessed changes in the structure of Roman institutions, alterations in the composition and functions of the social and political elite, and the elaboration of a Christian culture and a catholic church.

To survive, emperors such as Diocletian (r. 284–305) and Constantine (r. 306–337) radically expanded the imperial bureaucracy and army and created a second capital for the empire at Byzantium on the Bosporus. Constantine renamed the new capital after himself: Constantinople. However prudent these reforms may have seemed, they were costly in several senses. They necessitated higher taxes and more vigilant tax-collecting. Roman officials seemed more intrusive and, quite often, less honest. A larger army might solve border problems or worsen political ones. The armies themselves were increasingly recruited from Germanic peoples living along the frontiers. These people might be loyal to Rome, as foreigners had been in the early years of the pax Romana, or alienated, as many people had been in the third century. Military leaders in the fourth and fifth centuries were likely to be Germans. These men were usually loyal and competent, but divided allegiance could be a problem for them in ways unknown to the sturdy Romans of old.

The greatest change in the political landscape of Late Antiquity can be seen on a map. In 300 the western half of the Roman Empire consisted of a number of provinces governed by a hierarchy of Roman officials. In 600, several Germanic kingdoms stood in place of those provinces. One might suppose that Rome had "fallen," that the ancient world had ended. A closer look at those kingdoms, however, reveals some interesting continuities.

Western kings cultivated close relations with the eastern Roman Empire headquartered at Constantinople. Kings covered themselves with Roman titles, adapted Roman public ceremonies, and acted like imperial magistrates. They issued laws and recorded documents in Latin and maintained, under their own authority, features of Roman local administration. Given that most Germanic kings were the descendants of late antique Roman military officers, it is unlikely that most people detected much difference between provinces and kingdoms.

Who were these Germanic kings and their followers? The lands beyond the Rhine and Danube, the two rivers that formed Rome's northern frontier, held innumerable peoples with whom the Romans had long, complex relationships. Rome traded with, fought against, allied with, and recruited many Germanic peoples at one time or another. The Germanic peoples themselves were actually confederations, not ethnic groups. "Frank," the name of one Germanic people, applies not only to persons who were Frankish but also to a troupe of relatives by marriage, clients, allies, defeated foes, and hangers-on. Such peoples created kingdoms by violent encounters and by peaceful settlement, by usurpation and by delegation. One might say that the kingdoms were Germanized and militarized versions of formerly Roman provinces. In other words, Rome provided the framework within which its own transformation took place.

Continuity and change are also evident in the most important cultural transformation of Late Antiquity: the triumph of Christianity. Christianity arose in first-century Palestine among a dedicated band of followers of Jesus of Nazareth. Jesus, a Jewish teacher of great charisma and compassion, preached an uncompromising morality, a need for repentance, and preparation for a coming kingdom of God. Jesus's teachings were intimately connected to venerable strains in Jewish thought and life. His closest followers believed him to be the Son of God.

From unpromising beginnings among a minority sect of Jews in a small, poor province, Christianity rose by the end of the fourth century to a position as the dominant religion in the Roman world. Fundamental teachings, the basic message of Jesus as related in the New Testament books of Matthew, Mark, Luke, and John—four accounts of Jesus's life and teachings written a generation or two after his death—were critical in this success story. Jesus's teachings were universal. They were addressed to men and women, to people of every land, to persons of every status. Important too were institutional and intellectual structures.

Christianity spread through towns. In each town, individual communities of believers had officials whose customary titles in English are *bishop, priest,* and *deacon.* Bishops—the word means "overseers"—gradually came to have administrative, moral, and intellectual responsibilities in their towns. They controlled the local church and its property, recruited and trained priests and deacons, disciplined heretics (dissenters from official teachings), and preached. A growing Christian church adapted the administrative geography of the Roman Empire. Bishops from towns and provinces began to meet in councils to decide complex matters of theology and ordinary matters of Christian living.

Christians were at times persecuted, but in 314 Constantine granted Christianity legal equality with all other religions. In 380 Emperor Theodosius demanded that all Christians believe exactly as the bishop of Rome believed. By 400 the most august local personage in almost every town of the empire was the bishop. Bishops came from the same families that had long given Rome its greatest citizens. Following the lead of the bishops was not difficult for local populations. Leading people from the pulpit was easy for men long accustomed to authority and respect.

Christians were invited both to change the world around themselves and also to flee that world and all its temptations. The church's public institutions represented an effort to respond to the first of these invitations. Another institution, monasticism, responded to the second. All over the Roman world groups of men and women settled as monks or nuns in communities dedicated to prayer, study, self-denial, and work. Monasticism attracted people from every region, class, and level of education. This powerful spiritual force was one of Late Antiquity's most enduring legacies.

Christianity touched the lives of women in a variety of ways. Church teachings, held out to women two models. There was Eve, the eternal temptress, who tricked Adam and cost humanity the joys of paradise. Then there was Mary, the holy, obedient, and exemplary mother of Jesus. Women were gradually denied clerical positions in the church but gained great prominence in monasticism. Generally, Christian teachings accorded women more respect and dignity than secular laws did.

The bishop of Rome attained special prominence. This status owed something to the doctrine of apostolic succession, according to which all bishops inherited the teaching authority of the apostles, the twelve most prominent original followers of Jesus. In the Roman version of this doctrine, Peter was the leader of the apostles. Thus, Peter's successors, the bishops of Rome—they began to be called popes in the third century—remained the leaders in the church as a whole. Roman prominence is also attributable to the connection between the popes and the city of Rome itself, the capital of the empire to which all roads led. Finally, papal leadership matured during bitter theological struggles in the Christian community. Popes routinely intervened on behalf of, or entertained appeals from, persons they supported.

The quarrels were many but tended to gather around the problem of the Trinity and the person of Jesus. The majority of Christian thinkers argued that God was triune, three persons—Father, Son, and Holy Spirit—in one. It proved impossible, however, to find a formula that expressed this truth to everyone's satisfaction. Christian tradition also maintained that the second person of the Trinity, Jesus Christ, was true God and true man. This notion also proved very difficult to define.

Between about 350 and 450, Christian thinkers all over the Mediterranean world addressed themselves to solving such theological problems, to explaining both the Jewish and the Christian Scriptures (which Christians call the Old and the New Testaments), and to defining practical rules for living. We call such thinkers "Church Fathers" and their age "patristic" (from *pater,* the Latin word for "father"). The most famous of the Latin Church Fathers is Augustine (354–430), a North African who became a professor of rhetoric and converted to Christianity as an adult. Augustine's voluminous writings chronicled his own spiritual quest and commented on the religious issues of his day.

Late Antiquity no longer produced works in the classical tradition, but it was not sterile. The Church Fathers are among the most learned, prolific, accomplished, and influential writers in all of history. They were products of the Roman world, but they did not suppose, as Virgil did, that time would last only as long as Rome. For them, the source and goal of human existence was the heavenly Jerusalem, not the earthly Rome.

Many Medieval Civilizations

The Roman world left not one but three heirs. We have already encountered the Germanic kingdoms that replaced Rome's western provinces. We have also mentioned the eastern Roman Empire centered on Constantinople. We have not mentioned, and no one in Late Antiquity could have predicted, the emergence of the Islamic faith and the Muslim peoples.

Islam arose in Arabia, a large, barren land deeply influenced by all the currents of ancient culture but never wholly conquered by any ancient people. In 570 Muhammad was born in Mecca, a great commercial city. Tradition holds that when Muhammad was a young man his exquisite spiritual sensibilities were awakened by visits from the Archangel Gabriel, who commanded him to "recite" a holy text. That text revolved around one great truth: "There is no God but Allah, and Muhammad is his prophet."

Like many religious leaders, Muhammad gained both followers and foes. Enemies forced Muhammad to flee in 622 to Medina, a city about 200 miles from Mecca. There he gave full force to his religious and social vision. Before he died in 632, Muhammad saw that vision triumph in Mecca and throughout Arabia.

The faith of Muhammad is revealed in the Quran, a collection of Allah's revelations to the prophet. Muhammad's religion demands absolute surrender to Allah: *al-Islam*, "the surrender," whence the name of the faith. Like Judaism, Islam has two central components: faith and community. The faith is simple, direct, uncompromising. There is no God but Allah, the creator and ruler of all. Islam had no creeds, no statements of religious belief, and no hierarchical clergy. The community, the *umma muslima*, was the assemblage of all who had surrendered to Allah. Class, status, occupation, gender, ethnicity: None of these attributes mattered at all.

Shortly after Muhammad's death, his followers rallied to the standard of the caliph, the successor to the prophet and commander of the faithful, and in a century created an empire that extended from France to the frontiers of China. That empire, the caliphate, centering on Arabia plus the ancient lands of Mesopotamia and Egypt, hugged the Mediterranean, and embraced much of the Judeo-Christian and Hellenic heritages. As it expanded, the caliphate also folded in rich cultural ingredients from Persia, India, Africa, and Asia. Not for the first time was the Mediterranean the hub of a rich international culture—rich but perhaps too complex.

Internal rivalries and external threats eventually pulled the caliphate apart. Spain broke away first, then a series of small states across North Africa, then Egypt, then parts of Anatolia. Caliphs sat on their jeweled thrones until 1258 while a profusion of foreigners dominated the state. Roman armies, Italian merchants, and Turkish mercenaries were among the most prominent of the caliphate's external foes until the Mongols overwhelmed the caliphate in the thirteenth century and turned the Islamic world so that its back was to the Mediterranean and its face to Asia. Until then, the Islamic world had been very much a part of the West. Since that time, neither the Islamic world nor the West has been quite sure about their relationship.

In the sixth century, the Roman emperor Justinian (r. 527–565), based in Constantinople, attempted to regain Rome's former western provinces, reformed the imperial administration along traditional lines, issued a major codification and revision of Roman law, and regulated ecclesiastical affairs. In the next two centuries his successors created new military and administrative institutions to face Muslim threats in the east and Slavic threats in the Balkans. In 726 the emperor Leo III (r. 717–741) issued the first major revision of Roman law since Justinian's. Leo's code, a drastically abbreviated version of Justinian's, provided a simplified, unified body of law for provincial judges in the empire. In religion, the Orthodox tradition began clearly to emerge. This tradition was based on the writings of the Greek Church Fathers, Greek forms of worship and church discipline, and a close partnership between the emperors and the patriarchs of Constantinople, the highest religious officers. For almost a thousand years this eastern incarnation of the Roman Empire, usually called the Byzantine Empire, bore the Roman legacy.

In 867 a new and highly talented dynasty, the Macedonian, came to the throne in the person of Basil I (r. 867–886). Until 1025, rulers from this family rolled back the frontiers, carried out impressive legal and government reforms, and continued a close partnership with the Orthodox church. This was the high point of Byzantine political, military, and diplomatic influence.

The years after 1025 brought short reigns, disputed successions, aristocratic and ecclesiastical factionalism, a bitter feud with the papacy in Rome over theology and worship, and, worst of all, military threats from the Turks. In 1071 the Byzantines suffered a devastating defeat at Manzikert in central Anatolia. Appeals to western Europe for military assistance brought not mercenaries who would recapture Anatolia from the Turks but Crusaders intent on liberating the Holy Land—the Palestine of Jesus—from the Muslims. In 1204 a crusading army conquered Constantinople, and until 1261 there was a "Latin Empire" in the east. The Byzantines eventually rallied, expelled the Latins, and restored independent rule. Down to the fall of Constantinople to the Turks in 1453, however, Byzantium was a shadow of its former self.

In Late Antiquity the Roman West had become several Germanic kingdoms. Those that did not confront more powerful neighbors, did not suffer religious differences, and had room to expand managed to succeed. Thus, the late antique heritage fell to the Franks in Gaul and to the Anglo-Saxons in Britain.

By the middle of the eighth century, continental Europe was dominated by a single family: the Carolingian, which takes its name from *Carolus Magnus,* Charles the Great (or Charlemagne). Charlemagne's dynasty united France, the Low Countries, most of Germany, northern Italy, and northeastern Spain into a single empire that lasted in reality for a few generations and in memory for a millennium as "Christendom." By force of will the Carolingians imposed standards of worship, education, law, and institutions. Their success was very uneven, but much of the evident similarity in the later history of the western European countries derives from their common Carolingian past.

In Britain, Germanic Anglo-Saxons from continental Europe jostled with local Celts, especially in Wales and Scotland. Anglo-Saxon, or English, Britain was moving toward unity, as were Wales and Scotland, until attacks by the Vikings, seaborne raiders from Scandinavia, provoked a crisis of authority that was resolved to the advan-

tage of the central government only in Scotland. In 1013 and again in 1066, bands of Northmen actually conquered England.

Vikings attacked the Continent too, but so did Muslims in the south and Magyars, the ancestors of the Hungarians, in the east. The Carolingian Empire, already weakened by dynastic struggles, succumbed to these attacks. It was able to mount a defense only at the local level.

For more than two centuries social and political development was more creative at the local than at the central level. Powerful men (lords) forced lesser men (vassals) into bonds of dependence that we usually refer to as feudalism. Vassals pledged homage (honor), fealty (fidelity), and service; lords promised maintenance and protection. To maintain their vassals, lords usually gave them fiefs—estates consisting of farms and peasants.

Between the collapse of the Carolingian Empire around 900 and the first widespread renewal of central authority around 1150, Europe was by no means anarchic. In fact, counties, duchies, principalities, and cities displayed an amazing institutional creativity. The population of Europe was expanding dramatically, perhaps doubling in two and a half centuries. Trade expanded everywhere. In a sense, Europe grew physically. States emerged in new areas such as Scandinavia and the Slavic realms. The Crusades extended Europe's frontier to Muslim Palestine. People everywhere felled forests, drained marshes, and brought new land into cultivation.

Nor was Europe sterile culturally. Latin culture was primarily religious culture, fostered by the church. The church needed educated clergy to carry out its essential tasks of preaching and teaching. Moreover, religious leaders were conscious of belonging to a rich intellectual tradition that needed to be mastered and transmitted.

Schools and libraries were found in cathedrals, in bishops' churches, and in monasteries. Monasteries housed communities of men or women who had voluntarily separated themselves from the world in order to seek God in community with a few like-minded people. Monasticism arose in Egypt in the third century and eventually spread all over the Christian world. Monasteries preserved books and learning while serving as witnesses to a holy way of living. Convents of nuns were often intellectual centers and places where women could attain a control over their own lives that was denied to them in the male world of lords and vassals.

In addition to the Latin culture of the Catholic church, a vernacular culture flourished. Literature in Welsh and Irish appeared in the seventh century; Old English literature, topped by the epic poem *Beowulf,* came only a little later. French literature produced an epic—*Song of Roland*—around 1100, then romances and adventures. German literature preceded French but took longer to reach a high standard. Italian emerged last but was the first to produce a true masterpiece: Dante's *Divine Comedy* of the early fourteenth century.

In the realms of government and institutions, twelfth- and thirteenth-century Europe was marked by two major developments: quarrels between secular and ecclesiastical rulers, and the growth of central governments. A series of struggles between secular and religious authorities sought to find a solution to an ideological dilemma. If, as all seemed to agree, government existed to promote eternal salvation, who was to have final authority: the pope and the ecclesiastical hierarchy or the emperor and other secular rulers? No land in Europe escaped these battles between 1050 and 1300. The Catholic church, with its elaborate administration, its sophisticated canon law, and its command of people's spiritual loyalties, won most of the early battles. Then, slowly, secular governments began to define their responsibilities in other-than-religious terms and to treat churches as subordinate governing institutions. By 1300 the church was exhausted from decades of struggles with a variety of rulers, European society was becoming more secular, and public institutions were growing more effective. The advantageous position the church had enjoyed in, say, 1100 or 1200, had been reversed by 1300.

Central governments gained strength as kings promoted themselves through ceremonies, built up their financial resources, led armies to key military victories, reduced great aristocrats to submission, and allied themselves to rising urban and commercial movements. But Europe was a complex place, and the governments were fragile. England, France, and Spain were headed toward centralization by 1300 but suffered reverses in the years after that and differed sharply in their basic institutional structures. Germany collapsed. Italy

produced no large state but instead many urban communes—autonomous local regimes of infinite variety and robust creativity. In 1300, Europe was sumptuous in its political complexity.

Europe's culture was no less complex. Religious schools at the monastic and cathedral levels were not so prominent as before. A new kind of religious intellectual establishment, the university, had seized the day. Though changed in important ways since its twelfth-century origins, the university has never lost its position as the paramount intellectual institution in the West.

Medicine and law were important courses of study in some places, but university teaching and research were primarily focused on the key texts of the Christian tradition. The approach to those texts was increasingly through the logic of the Greek philosopher Aristotle. Scholasticism is the name for this encounter between Greek logic and Christian revelation. Thomas Aquinas (1225–1274), prolific author, immensely learned scholar, and gifted interpreter, was the greatest of the Scholastics.

Vernacular culture grew apace. More and more literatures appeared, especially in Scandinavian and Slavic lands. In addition to imaginative literature, lawbooks, ordinary legal documents, and other texts were written in languages other than Latin.

Architecture produced two stunning leaps forward. In Romanesque (after 1050) and Gothic (after 1150) cathedrals, all existing forms were recombined in buoyant new styles that have lost none of their power to move and inspire. Romanesque façades saw the reappearance of large-scale sculpture, lost since antiquity, and free-standing sculpture reappeared. Gothic stained glass is one of medieval Europe's crowning achievements.

Medieval Europe remained a challenging place for women. Public power was generally reserved for males in a society that prized military qualities. Ecclesiastical offices were confined to men, as were student and teaching positions in schools and universities. Nevertheless, on Europe's many expanding frontiers, where old conventions were observed less tightly, women had opportunities for social and political power. Bustling, innovative cities accorded women a wide range of occupations. Some women, such as the gifted theologian Hildegard of Bingen

(1098–1179), made distinguished contributions to Latin literature, and a number of women, such as Marie de France (worked ca. 1170), became prominent as vernacular authors. Women could not be priests and bishops but nevertheless played key roles in the many new religious movements of the Middle Ages. The thirteenth-century Beguines were the first religious movement created by and only for women in the history of Christianity.

Crisis and Recovery

The biblical Book of Revelation mentions Four Horsemen of the Apocalypse: war, slaughter, famine, and death. Those grim riders trod hard on fourteenth-century Europe.

Old hostilities dragged France and England into the conflict now known as the "Hundred Years' War" (1337–1453), which, before it ended, drained the talent and treasure of many parts of Europe. This international conflict was the most prominent but only one of the age's struggles. There were trade wars in the Baltic and North Seas, religious and ethnic battles in the Holy Roman Empire, continuing Christian-Muslim struggles in Spain, peasant rebellions in France and England, and workers' revolts in Flanders and Italy.

To all this slaughter must be added economic dislocation. Several problems combined to produce economic and social crisis. Population began leveling off in the thirteenth century. The weather turned foul. Most critically, though, Europe was visited in 1348 by an outbreak of bubonic plague that carried off perhaps one-third of the population and worked its cruelest ravages on the cities that were Europe's most creative, productive areas. Tragic and devastating as it was, the epidemic of 1348–1349 was only the first of many recurrences of the plague.

Some of the effects of the plague were psychological. A sense of despair fell over a Christian society convinced that God was punishing it. But for what? Moralists complained about dissolute living, and ecclesiastical powers worried about heresy. Jews sometimes became scapegoats to popular hysteria as people sought to blame others for their own misfortune.

The church could not salve Europe's wounds because it was going through deep struggles. By the end of the thirteenth century many people

were confused and angry because the papacy seemed focused more on political hegemony than on spiritual leadership. From 1305 to 1378 the popes resided not in Rome but in Avignon, in the south of what is now France. They had settled there temporarily to settle some outstanding controversies with the French monarchy but scandalized people all over Europe by staying for three-quarters of a century. When the popes tried to return to Rome, factions of cardinals, the aristocrats of the church, split. From 1378 to 1417 there was a "Great Schism" as two or more men claimed to be the legitimate pope. The schism was healed and the pope was enabled to return to Rome after a council that proclaimed a new vision of church government: "Conciliarism" maintained that the church was not a monarchy under the pope but a collegial body of all bishops. Churchmen argued over the implications of this finding for years.

Despite these trials, western Europe in the fifteenth and early sixteenth centuries experienced many positive developments. France emerged from its long war with England with a greatly strengthened royal government that could raise armies, collect taxes, and control nobles. England suffered through a civil war after the Hundred Years' War but then, after 1485, began a long, steady process of political consolidation under the Tudor dynasty. Major compromises in 1356 provided the Holy Roman Empire with a formula not for unity but at least for stability. The Spanish monarchies grew stronger by the year. In Italy a profusion of independent cities chose or were forced to defer to Florence, Milan, or Venice.

The years from about 1300 to about 1550 were both constructive and destructive in the political and material realms of life but were boundlessly creative in the cultural realms. This was the Renaissance. Italians, in particular, genuinely believed that they were calling back to life the spirit, the ideals, of classical Greece and Rome. They avidly sought out works of classical literature and combed through them for models of style and for bits of practical wisdom and guidance. Though by no means irreligious, Renaissance writers were more concerned with the ancient world, and with their own world, than they were with the next world. We call them "humanists" because of their interest in the humane disciplines. The "study of humanity" (*studia humanitatis*) that was central to the Renaissance was grounded in the seven liberal arts—grammar, rhetoric, logic, arithmetic, astronomy, geometry, and music—that had formed the core of Western education since antiquity. The "arts" were the skills or methods used by the "liberal"—literally, the free—in the conduct of their affairs in society. Armed with the liberal arts, the humanists sought beauty and harmony; they cultivated elegance in the spoken and written word. Their achievements in literature, art, and architecture betoken for many the dawn of modernity.

"They," however, were mostly men. A great historian has asked whether women had a Renaissance at all. Some women humanists have come to light, and the importance of prolific vernacular writers such as Christine de Pizan (1364–1430) and Marguerite de Navarre (1492–1549) has long been acknowledged. But women's daily lives do not seem to have improved during the Renaissance.

The Renaissance was disseminated from Italy—first by northerners who studied for a time in the south and then, after 1454, by printing, which made books and ideas more accessible than ever before. In northern Europe, Renaissance scholars turned to the sources of the Christian tradition—to the Scriptures and the Church Fathers—with the same zeal and scholarship that the Italians applied to classical sources. Study led some figures to harsh criticism of the institutional, intellectual, and moral failings of the late medieval Catholic church. These scholarly and critical streams joined in the religious flood that we call the "Protestant Reformation."

Central to that reformation were two fundamental beliefs. The first was that everything necessary for salvation had been revealed by God in the Bible; thus, the teachings of the Catholic church were as nothing compared to the word of God. The second was that salvation resulted from faith in God and from God's grace; thus, good works and upright behavior were no guarantees of salvation.

The sixteenth century witnessed many efforts to reform the medieval church. Protestant reformers such as Martin Luther and John Calvin sought to restore Christianity to the form they believed it had possessed in the first centuries of its existence. Royal reformers such as Henry VIII of England (r. 1509–1547) decreed the reform of the church in their lands. Fiery radicals wished to cast down the existing order of society in the name of a purified religion, and humble pietists sought to withdraw from all social and political entanglements. The Catholic church corrected many of the abuses that had offended its critics but reaffirmed its basic teachings at the Council of Trent (1545–1563). Europe was charged with religious feeling.

The Protestant Reformation did not dramatically alter the roles of women in European society or in the Christian churches. From the beginning, ambivalence marked women's participation in the Christian religion. On the one hand, the teachings of Jesus proclaimed the essential equality of women and men and opened heaven equally to both. On the other hand, both Protestant and Catholic churches denied official and educational roles to women. The reformers were not social revolutionaries. They said, for example, that a housewife was as pleasing to God as a nun, but they did not say that a woman could be a minister. And the Protestants' closing of convents denied some women the intellectual and administrative opportunities long available in those houses.

Scholarly or spiritual, political or institutional, experimentation was everywhere. Nowhere is this more evident than in the European rush to make the whole world Europe's frontier. With that expansion of Europe's place in the world, we return to the mid-sixteenth century, where our story begins.

THOMAS F. X. NOBLE

Europe in the Age of Religious War, 1555–1648

I n the early hours of a sultry summer morning—August 24, 1572—armed noblemen accompanied by the personal guard of the king of France hunted out about one hundred other nobles, asleep in their lodgings in and around the royal palace in Paris, and murdered them in cold blood. The attackers were Catholic, their victims were Protestant— but all were French nobles, many of them related to one another. The king and his counselors had planned the murders as a preemptive political strike because they feared that other Protestant noblemen were gathering an army outside of Paris. But the calculated strike became a general massacre when ordinary Parisians learned that their king had authorized the murders of Protestant leaders. Believing they were acting in the king's name, these Parisians, who were overwhelmingly Catholic, turned on their neighbors. About three thousand Protestants were murdered in Paris over the next three days.

This massacre came to be called the Saint Bartholomew's Day Massacre for the Catholic saint on whose feast day it fell. Though particularly horrible in its scope (indeed, thousands more people were murdered in the French provinces as word of events in Paris spread), the massacres were not unusual in the deadly combination of religious and political antagonisms they reflected. Throughout Europe ordinary people took religious conflict into their own hands as rulers, for their part, tried to enforce religious uniformity, or at least religious peace. Religious conflicts were by definition intractable political conflicts, since virtually every religious group felt that all others were heretics who must not be tolerated, and rulers of all stripes looked to religious authority and institutions to uphold their own power.

The Saint Bartholomew's
Day Massacre.

In addition, existing political tensions contributed to instability and violence, especially when reinforced by religious difference. Royal governments continued to consolidate authority, but resistance to royal power by provinces, nobles, or towns accustomed to independence now might have religious sanction. Tensions everywhere were also worsened by the rise of prices and unemployment as the sixteenth century wore on. Economic stress was heightened because changes in military technology and tactics made warfare itself more destructive than ever before.

A period of tension, even extraordinary violence, in political and social life, the late sixteenth and early seventeenth centuries were also distinguished by great creativity in some areas of cultural and intellectual life. The plays of Shakespeare, for example, mirrored the passions but also reflected on the tensions of the day and helped to analyze Europeans' circumstances with a new degree of sophistication.

SOCIETY AND THE STATE

Religious strife, warfare, and economic change disrupted the lives of whole communities as well as individuals in the late sixteenth and early seventeenth centuries. The sixteenth century, especially, saw profound economic transformation that, by the end of the century, altered power relations in cities, in the countryside, and in the relationship of both to central governments.

The most obvious economic change was a steady rise in prices, which resulted in the concentration of wealth in fewer hands. Economic change by itself, however, did not spawn all of this era's social and political change. States made war for religious and dynastic reasons more than for calculated economic advantage. Nevertheless, together, the movements of the economy and the policies of governments created notable shifts in centers of wealth and power.

Economic Transformation and the New Elites

Sixteenth-century observers attributed rising prices to the inflationary effects of the influx of precious metals from Spanish territories in the New World. Historians now believe that there were also European causes for this "price revolution." Steady population growth caused a relative shortage of goods, particularly food, and the result was a rise in prices. Both the amount and the effect of price changes were highly localized, depending on factors such as the structure of local economies and the success of harvests. Between 1550 and 1600, however, the price of grain may have risen between 50 and 100 percent, and sometimes more, in cities throughout Europe—including eastern Europe, the breadbasket for growing urban areas to the west. Where we have data about wages, we can estimate that wages lost between one-tenth and one-fourth of their value by the end of the century. The political and religious struggles of the era thus took place against a background of increasing want, and economic distress was often expressed in both political and religious terms.

These economic changes affected the wealthy as well as the poor. During this period, monarchs were making new accommodations with the hereditary aristocracy—with the Crown usually emerging stronger, if only through concessions to aristocrats' economic interests. Underlying this new symbiosis of monarchy and traditional warrior-nobles were the effects of economic changes that would eventually blur lines between these noble families and new elites and simplify power relationships within the state. Conditions in the countryside, where there were fewer resources to feed more mouths, grew less favorable. But at the same time more capital became available to wealthy urban or landholding families to invest in the countryside, by buying land outright on which to live like gentry or by making loans to desperate peasants. This capital came from profits from expanded production and trade and was also an effect of the scarcity of land as population and prices rose. Enterprising landholders raised ground rents wherever they could, or they converted land to the production of wool, grain, and other cash crops destined for distant markets.

As a result, a stratum of wealthy, educated, and socially ambitious "new gentry," as these families were called in England, began growing and solidifying. Many of the men of these families were royal officeholders, and they held on to their offices, confident of their wealth and the leisure it made possible. Where the practice existed, many bought titles outright or were granted nobility as a benefit of their offices. They often lent money to royal governments. The monumental expense of wars made becoming a lender to government, as well as to individuals, an attractive way to live off one's capital.

No one would have confused these up-and-coming families with warrior-aristocrats from old families, but the social distinctions between them are less important (to us) than what they had in common: legal privilege, the security of landownership, a cooperative relationship with the monarchy. Monarchs deliberately favored the new gentry as counterweights to independent aristocrats.

City governments also changed character as wealth accumulated in the hands of formerly commercial families. By the beginning of the seventeenth century, traditional guild control of government had been subverted in many places. Town councils became dominated by successive generations of privileged families, now more likely to live from landed than from commercial wealth. Towns became more closely tied to royal interests by means of the mutual interests of Crown and town elites. The long medieval tradition of towns serving as independent corporate bodies had come to an end.

Economic Change and the Common People

The growth of markets around Europe and in Spanish possessions overseas had a profound effect on urban producers in western Europe. Production of cloth on a large scale for export, for example, now required huge amounts of capital—much more than a typical guild craftsman could amass. In many regions, guild members lost political power in towns as the relative importance of their limited scale of production declined, and the guild structure itself began to break down. The decline in market size for traditional artisans meant that fewer and fewer apprentices and journeymen could expect to become master artisans. The masters began to treat apprentices virtually as wage laborers, at times letting them go when there was not enough work. The household mode of production, in which apprentices and journeymen had worked and lived side by side with the master's family, also began to break down, with profound economic, social, and political consequences.

Effects on women workers were particularly dramatic. One of the first reflections of the dire circumstances faced by artisans was an attempt to lessen competition at the expense of the artisans' own mothers, sisters, daughters, and sons. Increasingly, widows were forbidden to continue practicing their husband's trade, though they headed from 10 to 15 percent of households in many trades. Women had traditionally learned and practiced many trades but rarely followed the formal progress from apprenticeship to master status. A woman usually combined work of this kind with household production, with selling her products and those of her husband, and with bearing and nursing children. Outright exclusion of women from guild organization appears as early as the thirteenth century but now began regularly to appear in guild statutes. In addition, town governments tried to restrict women's participation in work such as selling in markets, which they had long dominated. Even midwives had to defend their practices, even though as part of housewifery women were expected to know about herbal remedies and practical medicine. (See the box, "A Woman Defends Her Right to Practice Healing.") Working women thus began to have difficulty supporting themselves if single or widowed and difficulty supporting their children. In the changing position of such women, we can see the distress of the entire stratum of society that they represent.

Many women worked in cloth production, for spinning was a life skill that women learned as a matter of course. Cloth production was changing, too; it became increasingly controlled by new investor-producers with large amounts of capital and access to distant markets. These entrepreneurs bought up large amounts of wool and hired it out to be cleaned, spun into thread, and woven into cloth by wage laborers in urban workshops or by pieceworkers in their homes. Thousands of women and men in the countryside helped to support themselves and families in this way.

Wealth in the countryside was also becoming more stratified, creating more families that could not adequately support themselves on the land. In western Europe, the most dramatic impact came from the investment in land by wealthy elites. Countless peasants lost their lands to these "rentiers," who lent them money and reclaimed the land when the money was not repaid. Other peasants were unable to rent land as rents rose, or they were unable to make a secure living because of the higher cost of land. To survive, some sought work

A Woman Defends Her Right to Practice Healing

In this document, Katharine Carberiner testifies to the city council of Munich that she does not deliberately compete with male doctors but has skills that might lead other women to choose her rather than male medical practitioners.

I use my feminine skills, given by the grace of God, only when someone entreats me earnestly, and never advertise myself, but only when someone has been left for lost. . . . I do whatever I can possibly do . . . using only simple and allowable means that should not be forbidden or proscribed in the least. Not one person who has come under my care has a complaint or grievance against me. If the doctors, apothecaries or barber-surgeons have claimed this, it is solely out of spite.

At all times, as is natural, women have more trust in other women to discover their se-crets, problems and illnesses, than they have in men—but perhaps this jealousy came from that. Undoubtedly as well, husbands who love and cherish their wives will seek any help and assistance they can, even that from women, if the wives have been given up (by the doctors) or otherwise come into great danger.

Because I know that I can help in my own small way, I will do all I can, even, as according to the Gospel, we should help pull an ox out of a well it has fallen into on Sunday.

Source: Merry Wiesner, "Women's Defense of Their Public Role," in Mary Beth Rose, ed., *Women in the Middle Ages and the Renaissance* (Syracuse: Syracuse University Press, 1986), p. 9.

---

as day laborers on the land of rich landlords or more prosperous farmers. But with the demise of so many opportunities for farming, there was not enough work. Many found their way to cities, where they swelled the ranks of the poor. Others, like some of their urban counterparts, coped by becoming part of the newly expanding network of cloth production, combining spinning and weaving with subsistence farming. However, one bad harvest might send them out on the roads begging or odd-jobbing; many did not long survive such a life.

In eastern Europe, peasants faced other dilemmas, for their lands had a different relationship to the wider European economy. The more densely urbanized western Europe, whose wealth controlled the patterns of trade, sought bulk goods, particularly grain, from eastern Germany, Poland, and Lithuania. Thus, there was an economic incentive for landowners in eastern Europe to bind peasants to the land just as the desire of their rulers for greater cooperation had granted the landlords more power. Serfdom now spread in eastern Europe when precisely the opposite conditions prevailed in the West.

Coping with Poverty and Violence

The common people of Europe did not submit passively either to economic difficulties or to the religious and political crises of their day. The townspeople of France and the Netherlands, for example, played a significant role in the establishment and defense of their "reformed" as well as Catholic religions. Whether Catholic or Protestant, common people took the initiative in attacking members of the other faith to rid their communities of them. At the community level, heretics were considered to be spiritual pollution that might provoke God's wrath. Thus, ordinary citizens believed that they had to eliminate heretics if the state failed to do so. Both elites and common people were responsible for the violence that sometimes occurred in the name of religion.

Ordinary people fought in wars from conviction but also from the need for self-defense. Indeed, although nobles remained military leaders, armies consisted mostly of infantry made up of common people, not mounted knights. It was ordinary people who defended the walls of towns, dug siege works, and manned artillery batteries. Women were part of armies, too. Much of the day-to-day work of finding food and firewood, cleaning guns, and endlessly repairing inadequate clothing was handled individually by women looking after their husbands and lovers among the troops.

Many men joined the armies and navies of their rulers because the military seemed a reasonable way of life, given their options. Landless farm hands, day laborers, and out-of-work artisans found the prospect of employment in the army attractive enough to outweigh the dangers of military life. Desertion was common, since joining up represented a choice, even if a choice among evils. Nothing more than the rumor that a soldier's home village was threatened might prompt a man to abandon his post. Battle-hardened troops could threaten their commanders not only with desertion but with mutiny. A mutiny of Spanish troops in 1574 was a well-organized affair, somewhat like a strike. Whole units of the army mutinied together and found ways to defend themselves while they negotiated with the Spanish command. Occasionally, mutinies were brutally suppressed; more often, they were successful and troops received some of their back wages.

Townspeople and countrypeople participated in riots and rebellions to protest their circumstances when the situation was particularly dire or when other means of action had failed. The devastation of civil war in France, for example, led to a number of peasant rebellions and urban uprisings. Former soldiers, prosperous farmers, or even noble landlords whose economic fortunes were tied to peasant profits might lead rural revolts. If they succeeded, it would be only to relieve a local problem, such as a local tax burden. Urban protests could begin spontaneously when new grievances worsened existing problems. In a town in central France in 1594, for example, the execution for thievery of a servant whose master was believed to be a thief became the occasion for a demonstration to protest the privilege of the well-to-do. In Naples, in 1585, food riots were provoked not

Food and Clothing Distributed by Government Officials In this rendering, a poor woman receives bread and a destitute man, clothing. Wealthy citizens' wills began to reflect the new definition of charity: Bequests to institutions increased and personal donations to the poor dwindled. *(The British Library)*

simply by a shortage of grain but by a government decision to raise the price of bread during the shortage. The property of the privileged was sometimes seized, and city leaders were sometimes killed, but these protests rarely generated lasting political change and were usually brutally quashed.

Governments at all levels tried to cope with the increasing problem of poverty by changing the administration and scale of poor relief. In both Catholic and Protestant Europe, caring for the poor became more institutionalized and systematic and more removed from religious impulses. In traditional Catholic doctrine, charity had been considered one of the many random ways by which an individual could merit grace and move toward eternal life. Such ideas were anathema to Protestant doctrine, but, interestingly, official Catholic practice concerning charity began to change early in the sixteenth century, before the pressure of Protestantism. Official Protestant attitudes toward charity, when they later came into being, closely resembled Catholic ones.

In the second half of the sixteenth century, public almshouses and poorhouses to distribute food or to care for orphans or the destitute sprang up in towns throughout Catholic and Protestant Europe. In certain ways, these institutions reflected an optimistic vision, drawn from humanism, of an ideal Christian community attentive to material want. But by the end of the century, the distribution of food was accompanied by attempts to distinguish "deserving" from "undeserving" poor, by an insistence that the poor be forced to work to receive their ration of food, and even by an effort to compel the poor to live in almshouses and poorhouses.

These efforts were not uniformly successful. Begging was outlawed by Catholic and Protestant city governments alike, but never thoroughly suppressed. Catholic religious orders and parishes often resisted efforts at rationalizing their charitable work imposed from above—even by Catholic governments. Nonetheless, the trend was clear. From viewing the poor as a fact of life and as an occasional lesson in Christian humility, European elites were beginning to view them collectively as a social problem and individual poor people as problems too, in need of collective control and institutional discipline. The establishment of centralized poor relief thus reflected a vision of Chris-

tian community in which the relationship between religious belief and community order, at least for elites, became increasingly direct.

The Hunt for Witches and the Illusion of Order

Between approximately 1550 and 1650, Europe saw a dramatic increase in the persecution of women and men for alleged witchcraft. Approximately one hundred thousand people were tried and about sixty thousand executed. The surge in witch-hunting was closely linked to the aftermath of the Protestant Reformation.

Certain kinds of witchcraft had long existed in Europe. So-called black magic of various kinds—one peasant casting a spell on another peasant's cow—had been common since the Middle Ages and continued to be a routine and favored means of coping with personal difficulty. What began to make black magic seem menacing to magistrates, judges, and other authorities were theories linking black magic to Devil worship. Catholic leaders and legal scholars first began to advance such theories in the fifteenth century. By the late sixteenth century, both Catholic and Protestant elites viewed a witch not only as someone who might cast harmful spells but also as a heretic. Persecution for witchcraft rose dramatically after the initial phases of the Reformation ended, reflecting a continuation of reforming zeal directed at the traditional forms of folk religion and magic.

As far as we can tell, no proof that an accused person ever attended a Devil-worshiping "black" Sabbath was ever produced in any witch trial. Nevertheless, authorities were certain that Devil worship occurred, so convinced were they that Satan was in their midst and that the folkways of common people were somehow threatening.

Contemporary legal procedures allowed the use of torture to extract confessions. Torture or the threat of torture led most of those accused of witchcraft to "confess." Probably willing to say what they thought their captors wanted to hear, many named accomplices or others who were also "witches." In this way, a single initial accusation could lead to dozens of prosecutions. In regions where procedures for appealing convictions and sentences were fragile or nonexistent, prosecutions were pursued with zeal. They were widespread, for example, in the small principalities and imperial cities of the Holy Roman Empire, which were virtually independent of all higher authority.

Prosecutions also numbered in the thousands in Switzerland, Poland, France, and Scotland. The majority—perhaps 80 percent—of those convicted and executed in all areas of Europe were women. Lacking legal, social, and political resources, women may have been more likely than men to use black magic for self-protection or advancement and hence were accused more often than men by their neighbors. Community fear and guilt may account for the fact that many of the accused women were poor. The marked increase in poverty during the late sixteenth and early seventeenth centuries made poor women particularly vulnerable to accusations of witchcraft. It was easier to find such a person menacing—and to accuse her of something—than to feel guilty because of her evident need. The modern stereotype that depicts the witch as an ugly old crone dates from this period.

Christian dogma and classically inspired humanistic writing portrayed women as morally weaker than men and thus as more susceptible to the Devil's enticements. Devil worship was described in sexual terms, and the prosecution of witches had a voyeuristic, sexual dimension. The bodies of accused witches were searched for the "Devil's mark"—a blemish thought to be the imprint of the Devil. Both Protestantism and Catholicism taught that sexual lust was evil. One theory is that women accused of being witches were victims of the guilt that elite men felt because of the latter's own sexual longings, which they believed were sinful and might be evidence of damnation. These men sought to lay blame elsewhere.

The witch-hunts virtually ended by the late seventeenth century, as intellectual energies shifted from religious to scientific thought. (See Chapter 17.) Reflecting religious fear, guilt, and class divisions, the witch-hunts are central to understanding European life in this period. They are both the last chapter in the history of the Reformation and a first chapter in the history of the modern state.

IMPERIAL SPAIN AND THE LIMITS OF POWER

To contemporary observers, no political fact of the late sixteenth century was more obvious than the ascendancy of Spain. Philip II (r. 1556–1598) even-tually ruled Portugal as well as Spain, plus the Netherlands, parts of Italy, and Spanish territories in the Americas (Map 15.1). Yet imperial Spain did not escape the political, social, and religious turmoil of the era. Explosive combinations of religious dissent and political disaffection led to revolt against Spain in the Netherlands. This conflict highlights the tensions of sixteenth-century political life: towns, provinces, and nobles trying to safeguard medieval liberties against efforts at greater centralization, with the added complications of economic strain and religious division. The revolt also demonstrated the material limits of royal power, since even with gold and silver from the American colonies pouring in, Philip could at times barely afford to keep armies in the field. As American resources dwindled in the seventeenth century, Philip's successors faced severe financial and political strains even in their Spanish homelands.

The Revolt of the Netherlands

Philip II's power stemmed in part from the far-flung territories he inherited from his father, the Habsburg Holy Roman emperor Charles V: Spain, the Low Countries (the Netherlands), the duchy of Milan, the kingdom of Naples, and the conquered lands in the Americas. (Control of Charles's Austrian lands had passed to his brother, Philip's uncle.) Treasure fleets bearing precious metals from the New World began to reach Spain regularly during Philip's reign. In addition, Spain now belonged to an expanding trading economy unlike any that had existed in Europe before. To supply its colonies, Spain needed timber and other shipbuilding materials from the hinterlands of the Baltic Sea. Grain from the Baltic fed the urban populations of Spain (where wool was the principal cash crop) and the Netherlands, while the Netherlands, in turn, was a source of finished goods, such as cloth. The major exchange point for all of these goods was the city of Antwerp in the Netherlands, the leading trading center of all of Europe.

Thus, Spain's expanding trading network necessitated tight links with the Netherlands, the real jewel among Philip's European possessions. These seventeen provinces (constituting mostly the modern nations of Belgium and the Netherlands) had been centers of trade and manufacture since the twelfth century and, in the fourteenth

Lands ruled by the Spanish Habsburgs

Lands ruled by the Austrian Habsburgs

Boundary of the Holy Roman Empire

Spanish military corridor ("Spanish Road")

Major battles

POLAND-LITHUANIA

HOLY ROMAN EMPIRE

THE NETHERLANDS

ENGLAND

FRANCE

SPAIN

PORTUGAL

NAVARRE

ARAGON

CASTILE

GRANADA

MILAN

PAPAL STATES

AFRICA

ATLANTIC OCEAN

North Sea

Baltic Sea

Mediterranean Sea

Constantinople

Lepanto

Malta

Rome

Naples

Venice

Florence

Genoa

Milan

Vienna

Augsburg

Antwerp

Gravelines

London

Paris

Madrid

Granada

Lisbon (1580)

Tunis

Algiers

Dniester

Danube

Vistula

Elbe

Rhine

Danube

Loire

Ebro

Tagus

400 Mi.

400 Km.

200

200

0

0

The City of Antwerp Antwerp, in the southern Netherlands, was the point of sale for Portuguese spices brought from around Africa, the selling and transshipping center for Baltic goods, including timber, fur, and grain, and the source for manufactured goods such as cloth. *(Musées royaux des Beaux-Arts de Belgique)*

and fifteenth centuries, had enjoyed political importance and a period of cultural innovation under the control of the dukes of Burgundy. By the time Philip inherited the provinces from his father, a sort of federal system of government had evolved to accommodate the various regional centers of power there. Each province had a representative assembly (Estates) that controlled taxation, but each also acknowledged a central administrative authority in the form of a governing council sitting in Brussels. Heading the principal council of state was a governor-general, typically, like Philip, a member of the Habsburg family.

Map 15.1 The Spanish Habsburgs and Europe Philip II's control of territories in northern Italy permitted the overland access of Spanish troops to the Netherlands and heightened the Spanish threat to France. Lands bordering the western Mediterranean made the sea a natural sphere of Spanish influence as well. Habsburg lands in central Europe were controlled after 1556 by Charles V's brother Ferdinand and his descendants.

Yet the revolt in the Netherlands that began early in Philip's reign clearly showed the limits to dynastic rule in such diverse territories (Map 15.2). Political power, here and elsewhere, was still highly decentralized, and Philip, like other rulers, could rule effectively only with the cooperation of local elites. Clumsy efforts to adjust this distribution of power in his favor caused Philip to push his subjects in the Netherlands into revolt.

Economic, political, and religious tensions began to strain the relationship between Philip and his subjects in the Netherlands early in his reign. Tensions arose partly over taxation and partly over Spanish insistence on maintaining tight control. Although taxes paid, in effect, to Spain were always resented, bad harvests and commercial disruptions occasioned by wars in the Baltic region in the 1560s depressed the Netherlands' economy and made it difficult for the provinces to afford higher taxes. When the Peace of Cateau-Cambrésis of 1559 brought an end to the long struggle over territory between the Habsburgs

Map 15.2 The Netherlands, 1559–1609 The seventeen provinces of the Netherlands were strikingly diverse politically, economically, and culturally. Like his father, Philip was, technically, the ruler of each province separately: He was count of Flanders, duke of Brabant, and so forth.

and the Valois kings of France, the people of the Netherlands had reason to hope for lower tax burdens and reduced levels of Spanish control.

Philip, born and raised in Spain, had little real familiarity with the densely populated, linguistically diverse Netherlands and never visited there after 1559. To assist the governor-general, his half-sister, Margaret of Parma, he left in place a council composed of ministers and secretaries who either were Spanish themselves or had close ties to the Spanish court. These arrangements affronted local nobles who had fought for Philip and his father before 1559 and who were accustomed to positions of influence in the council of state.

To economic and political tensions were added severe religious problems created by the

policies of Philip II. These policies addressed both heresy and ecclesiastical administration. Unlike his father, Philip directed the hunt for heretics not just at lower-class dissenters but also at well-to-do Calvinists—followers of the French Protestant religious reformer John Calvin—who now existed in increasing numbers. Punishment for heresy now included confiscation of family property as well as execution of the individual.

To ensure a high degree of religious control, Philip proposed in 1561 to add fourteen new bishoprics to the Netherlands' traditional four. Local nobles feared their family members would be passed over for appointment to these new church offices in favor of Spaniards or locals sympathetic to Spain. Moreover, each new bishopric was to have inquisitors to root out heretics. By 1565, municipal councils in the Netherlands routinely refused to enforce Philip's religious policies, believing that urban prosperity—as well as their personal security—depended on relative restraint in the prosecution of heresy. Leading nobles stopped enforcing the policies on their estates.

During the spring and summer of 1566, religious dissension in the Netherlands grew dramatically. Encouraged by greater tolerance, Protestants began to hold open-air meetings, and in many towns ordinary people began to embrace Protestantism for the first time. In a series of actions called the "iconoclastic fury," townsfolk stripped Catholic churches of the relics and statues deemed idolatrous by Calvinist doctrine. Reflecting the economic strain of these years, food riots also occurred. Both Spanish authorities and local elites feared the outbreak of general unrest. (See the box, "Elite Fears of Popular Religious Unrest in the Netherlands.")

By early 1567 Calvinist insurgents had seized two towns in the southern Netherlands by force of arms in hopes of stirring a general revolt that would secure freedom of worship. Nobles in various areas also supported a widening rebellion, for their own religious and political reasons. Margaret of Parma successfully quelled the uprisings by rallying city governments and loyal nobles, now alarmed for their own power and property. But she then learned that far away in Spain a decision had been made to send in the Spanish duke of Alba with an army of ten thousand men.

Alba arrived in August 1567 and, to bolster his own shaky standing at the Spanish court, acted more like a conqueror than a peacemaker. He bil-

Elite Fears of Popular Religious Unrest in the Netherlands

In 1566, Calvinists in the Netherlands, urged to action by their preachers, plundered Catholic churches and defied local authorities by holding large public worship services. In document (a), a government agent in a small city reports on the iconoclasm he has witnessed. In document (b), a member of Margaret of Parma's government, writing to a friend in Spain, describes his fears about the effects of the Calvinists' activities.

(a)

The audacity of the Calvinist preachers in this area has grown so great that in their sermons they admonish the people that it is not enough to remove all idolatry from their hearts; they must also remove it from their sight. Little by little, it seems, they are trying to impress upon their hearers the need to pillage the churches and abolish all images.

(b)

The town of Ypres, among others, is in turmoil on account of the daring of the populace inside and outside who go to the open-air services in the thousands, armed and defended as if they were going off to perform some great exploit of war. It is to be feared that the first blow will fall on the monasteries and clergy and that the fire, once lit, will spread, and that, since trade is beginning to cease on account of these troubles, several working folk—constrained by hunger—will join in, waiting for the opportunity to acquire a share of the property of the rich.

Source: Geoffrey Parker, *The Dutch Revolt* (London: Penguin, 1985), pp. 75–76.

leted troops in friendly cities, established new courts to try rebels, arrested thousands of people, executed about a thousand rebels (including Catholics as well as prominent Protestants), and imposed onerous taxes to support his own army. Thus, Alba repeated every mistake of Spanish policy that had triggered rebellion in the first place.

Margaret of Parma resigned in disgust and left the Netherlands. Protestants from rebellious towns escaped into exile and were joined by nobles who had been declared treasonous for minor lapses of loyalty. The most important of these was William of Nassau, prince of Orange (1533–1584), whose lands outside of the Netherlands, in France and the empire, lay out of Spanish reach and so could be used to finance continued warfare against Spain. Thus, a significant community with military capability began to grow in exile.

In 1572, ships of exiled Calvinist privateers known as the "Sea Beggars" captured some fifty towns in the northern provinces. The towns' impoverished inhabitants—eager to strike a blow at expensive Spanish rule—welcomed the exiles. Shortly thereafter, noble armies led by William of Orange invaded the southern provinces but were forced by Alba to withdraw when promised French help did not arrive. For the rest of the century, the northern provinces became increasingly Calvinist strongholds and were the center of opposition to the Spanish, who concentrated their efforts against rebellion in the wealthier southern provinces. Occasionally the French and English lent aid to the rebels.

The Spanish never had the resources to crush the rebellion. The war in the Netherlands exemplifies many of the tensions of the era—such as ones arising from aristocratic privilege, dynastic right, regionalism, and religion. The revolt was also a stage for the destructive and costly technology of warfare in this period. In an attempt to supply the

Netherlands with seasoned veterans and materiel from Spain and Spanish territories in Italy, the Spanish developed the "Spanish Road," an innovative string of supply depots where provisions could be gathered in advance of troops sent along the "Road" to the Netherlands (see Map 15.1).

Spanish supply efforts came partly in response to improved fortifications in the Netherlands' cities, some of which were equipped with new defensive works known as "bastions"; such cities could not be taken by storm but had to be besieged for long periods. Military campaigns in the Netherlands now consisted of grueling sieges, skirmishes in a city's surrounding area for control of villages' supplies, and occasional pitched battles between besiegers and forces attempting to break the siege. Vast numbers of men were required both for an effective besieging force and for garrisoning the fortresses that controlled farmlands and defended major towns. Inevitably, the army put a great strain on the countryside, and both soldiers and civilians suffered great privations. On occasion, Spanish troops reacted violently to difficult conditions and to delayed pay (American treasure dwindled badly between 1572 and 1578). In 1576, Spanish troops sacked the hitherto loyal southern city of Antwerp and massacred about eight thousand people. This event was remembered in the Netherlands as the "Spanish Fury."

Angered by the massacre, leaders in the southern provinces now raised money for citizen armies to protect themselves against the Spanish. In late 1576 the southern leaders concluded the Pacification of Ghent, an alliance with William of Orange and the northern rebels. The terms of the agreement called for nonbelligerence on religious grounds and cooperation to drive the Spanish out. This treaty might have initiated a self-governing United Netherlands were it not for old divisions and Spanish recovery.

The northern and southern provinces were increasingly divided by religion. When Calvinist artisans now seized control of several cities in the southern provinces, city leaders and nobles there grew frightened on political and religious grounds at the same time. Philip's new commander in the Netherlands, Margaret's son Alexander, duke of Parma, was skilled as both a negotiator and a soldier, and by 1578 had renewed shipments of American treasure to help him. He wooed the Catholic elites of the southern provinces back into

REVOLT OF THE NETHERLANDS	
1559	Peace of Cateau-Cambrésis
1561	Philip II attempts to place fourteen new bishoprics in the Netherlands
1564	Netherlands city councils and nobility ignore Philip's law against heresy
1566	Calvinist "iconoclastic fury" begins
1567	Duke of Alba arrives in the Netherlands; Margaret of Parma resigns her duties as governor-general
1572	"Second Revolt" of the Netherlands, led by William of Orange, begins
1573	Alba is relieved of his command
1576	Sack of Antwerp Pacification of Ghent
1579	Union of Utrecht
1609	Truce is declared between Spain and the Netherlands

loyalty to Philip, in return for promises to respect their provincial liberties and to safeguard their property from troops.

By 1579 the northern provinces concluded a defensive alliance, the Union of Utrecht, against the increasingly unified south. Parma could not cope with the geographic barrier of four rivers that bisect the Low Countries (see Map 15.2), and he faced declining resources as Spain diverted money to conflicts with England in 1588 and in France after 1589. In 1609 a truce was finally concluded between Spain and the northern provinces. This truce did not formally recognize the "United Provinces" as an independent entity, though in fact they were. The modern nations of Belgium and the Netherlands are the distant result of this truce.

The independent United Provinces (usually called, simply, the Netherlands) was a fragile state, an accident of warfare at first. But commercial prosperity had begun to emerge as its greatest strength. Much of the economic activity of Antwerp had shifted north to Amsterdam in the province of Holland because of fighting in the south and a naval

The Bastion Seen here in an example from an Italian fortress, the bastion was the triangular projection from the fortress wall. It enabled defenders to fire on the flanks of besieging forces; lower than medieval fortress walls and reinforced with earth, walls built in this manner were also less vulnerable to artillery blasts. *(Universitäts und Stadtbibliothek Cologne)*

blockade of Antwerp by rebel ships. Philip's policies had created a new enemy nation and had enriched it at his expense.

The Failure of the Invincible Armada

The political and economic importance of the Netherlands lured Spain into wider strategic involvement, most notably against England. England and Spain had long maintained cordial relations. They had a common foe in France and common economic interests. Philip's marriage to Mary Tudor, the Catholic queen of England (r. 1553–1558), had been a logical step in that relationship, though the opportunity to return England to Catholicism was an added inducement to maintaining close ties. Even after the accession of the Protestant queen Elizabeth (r. 1558-1603), Spanish-English relations initially remained cordial.

Relations started to sour, however, when Elizabeth began tolerating the use of English ports by the rebel Sea Beggars and authorizing English attacks on Spanish treasure fleets. In response, Spain supported Catholic resistance to Elizabeth within England, including a series of plots to replace Elizabeth on the throne with Mary, Queen of Scots. Greater Spanish success in the Netherlands, raids

by the Spanish and English on each other's shipping, and Elizabeth's execution of Mary in 1587 prompted Philip to order an invasion of England. A fleet (*armada*) of Spanish warships sailed in 1588.

"The enterprise of England," as the plan was called in Spain, represented an astounding logistical effort. The Spanish Armada was supposed to clear the English Channel of English ships in order to permit an invading force—troops under Parma in the Netherlands—to cross the Channel on barges. The fleet of about 130 ships also carried troops from Spain to supplement Parma's force, as well as large quantities of supplies for the invasion. The sheer number of ships required for the undertaking meant that some, inevitably, were slower supply ships, or naval vessels designed for the more protected waters of the Mediterranean. The fleet as a whole was slower and less maneuverable than the English force it faced. The English also had the advantage in arms, since they had better long-range artillery and better-trained gunners.

When the Armada entered the Channel on July 29, the English fleet fell in behind them, with the westerly wind and current in their favor. They could harass the Spanish with artillery from a distance without sustaining much damage themselves. The logistical problems of the Spanish plan, given the technologies of the day, then became apparent: Parma could not get his men readied on their barges quickly enough once the fleet's presence in the Channel had been confirmed by messenger. Nor could the fleet protect itself while waiting offshore, since no friendly harbor was available. On the night of August 7, the English launched eight fireships into the anchored Spanish fleet; at dawn on August 8, they attacked the disorganized enemy off Gravelines, and their advantage in arms was decisive (see Map 15.1).

The Battle at Gravelines was the first major gun battle by sailing ships and helped set the future course of naval warfare. For the Spanish, it was a disaster. Many ships were sunk at Gravelines. Many more sank in bad weather, or were forced into hostile harbors, as the Spanish rounded the northern tip of the British Isles and sailed for home along the west coast of Ireland. Fifteen thousand sailors and soldiers—half of all on board—died in battle or on the return journey. Less than half of Philip's great fleet made it back to Spain.

Successes at Home and Around the Mediterranean

Many of Philip's interests still centered on the Mediterranean, despite the new overseas empire and his preoccupation with the Netherlands. Spain and the kingdom of Naples had exchanged trade for centuries. Newer ties had been forged with the duchy of Milan and the city-state of Genoa, whose bankers were financiers to the Spanish monarchy. Charles V had tried to secure the western Mediterranean against the Turks and their client states along the African coast, but it was under Philip that the Turkish threat in the western Mediterranean receded.

The years of the greatest Turkish threat coincided with the beginning of the Netherlands' revolt. To Philip and his advisers, the Turks represented a potential internal threat to Spain as well. Philip thus inaugurated a new wave of persecution of his Muslim subjects, eventually provoking a major rebellion in Granada between 1568 and 1571. After this revolt was crushed, the Muslim inhabitants of Granada were forcibly exiled farther north in Spain. The Spanish allied temporarily with the papacy and Venice—both were concerned with the Turkish advances in the Mediter-

ranean—and their combined navies inflicted a massive defeat on the Turkish navy at Lepanto, off the coast of Greece, in October 1571 (see Map 15.1). The Turks remained a power in the eastern Mediterranean, but their ability to threaten Spain and Spanish possessions in the west was over.

Philip's powers in each of his Spanish kingdoms were circumscribed by the traditional privileges of towns, nobility, and clergy. In Aragon, for example, he could raise revenues only by appealing to local assemblies, the Cortes. In Castile, the arid kingdom in the center of the Iberian Peninsula, the king was able to levy taxes with greater ease but only because of concessions that allowed nobles undisputed authority over their peasants. Philip established his permanent capital, Madrid, and his principal residence, the Escorial, there. The Spanish Empire became more and more Castilian as the reign progressed, with royal advisers and counselors increasingly drawn only from the Castilian elite. Yet the rural economy of Castile was stunted by the dual oppression of landholders and royal tax collectors.

Philip made significant inroads into Aragonese independence by the end of his reign. Noble feuds and peasant rebellions had combined to create virtual anarchy in some areas of Aragon by the 1580s, and in 1591 Philip sent in veteran troops from the Netherlands campaigns to establish firmer royal control. Philip was successful in the long run in Aragon because he used adequate force but tempered it afterward with constitutional changes that were cleverly moderate. Finally, he cemented the peace by doing what he had failed to do in the Netherlands. He appeared in Aragon in person, in the words of a contemporary, "like a rainbow at the end of a storm."[1]

Philip also invaded and successfully annexed Portugal in 1580, thus completing the unification of the Iberian Peninsula. The annexation was ensured by armed force but had been preceded by careful negotiation to guarantee that Philip's claim to the throne—through his mother—would find some support within the country. This was old-fashioned dynastic politics at its best. When Philip died in 1598, he was old and ill, a man for whom daily life had become a painful burden. His Armada had been crushed; he had never quelled the Netherlands' revolt. Yet he had been more successful, by his own standards, in other regions that he ruled.

Spain in Decline

Spain steadily lost ground economically and strategically after the turn of the century. Imports of silver declined. The American mines were exhausted and the natives forced to work in them were decimated by European diseases and brutal treatment. Spain's economic health was further threatened by the very success of its colonies: Local industries in the Americas began to produce goods formerly obtained from Spain. The increasing presence of English, French, and Dutch shipping in the Americas provided colonists with rival sources for the goods they needed. Often, these competitors could offer their goods more cheaply than Spaniards could, for Spanish productivity was low and prices were high because of the inflationary effects of the influx of precious metals.

Spain renewed hostilities with the United Provinces in 1621, after the truce of 1609 had expired. Philip IV (r. 1621–1645) also aided his Habsburg cousins in the Thirty Years' War in the Holy Roman Empire (see page 571). Squeezed for troops and revenue for these commitments, other Spanish territories revolted. The uprisings reflected both economic distress and unresolved issues of regional autonomy. The government of Spain was Castilian, and Castile bore the brunt of the financial support of the state. The chief minister to Philip IV, Gaspar de Guzmán, Count Olivares (1587–1645), was an energetic Castilian aristocrat determined to distribute the burdens of government more equitably among the various regions of Spain. His policies provoked rebellions in Catalonia and Portugal.

In Catalonia, a province of the kingdom of Aragon, the revolt began as a popular uprising against the billeting of troops. At one point Catalan leaders invited French troops south to defend them and solemnly transferred their loyalty to the French king in the hope that he would respect their autonomy. Spain resumed control only in 1652, after years of military struggle and promises to respect Catalan liberties.

In Portugal, a war of independence began in 1640, also with a popular revolt. The Spanish government tried to restore order with troops under the command of a leading Portuguese prince, John, duke of Braganza. The duke, however, was the nearest living relative to the last king of Portugal, and he seized this opportunity to claim the

Philip II in 1583 Dressed in the austere black in fashion at the Spanish court, Philip holds a rosary and wears the Order of the Golden Fleece, an order of knighthood, around his neck. At age 56 Philip has outlived four wives and most of his children. *(Museo del Prado, Madrid)*

crown of Portugal for himself and lead a fight for independence. Although war dragged on until 1668, the Portuguese under John IV (r. 1640–1656) succeeded in winning independence from Spain.

As a result of these uprisings, Count Olivares resigned in disgrace in 1643. In 1647 there would also be upheaval in Spain's Italian possessions of Sicily and Naples. By midcentury, Spain had lost its position as the preeminent state in Europe.

RELIGIOUS AND POLITICAL CRISIS IN FRANCE AND ENGLAND

Civil war wracked France from 1562 until 1598. As in the Netherlands, the conflicts in France had religious and political origins as well as international implications, and political and religious questions became entangled in ways that made the conflicts almost impossible to resolve. Though a temporary resolution was achieved by 1598, religious division still existed, and conflict over the legitimate nature and extent of royal power remained. England, in contrast, was spared dramatic political and religious upheaval in the second half of the sixteenth century, in part because of the talents—and long life—of its ruler. But in the seventeenth century, constitutional and religious dissent began to reinforce each other in new and dramatic ways and threaten the stability of the realm.

The French Religious Wars

The king of France, Henry II (r. 1547–1559), had concluded the Peace of Cateau-Cambrésis with Philip II in 1559, ending the Habsburg-Valois Wars, but had died in July of that year from wounds suffered at a tournament held to celebrate the new treaty. His death was a political disaster. Great noble families vied for influence over his 15-year-old son, Francis II (r. 1559–1560). Two brothers of the house of Guise were related to the young king by marriage and succeeded in dominating him. But the Guises faced continual challenges from members of the Bourbon family, who claimed the right to influence the king because they were princes of royal blood and stood next in line to the throne after Henry II's sons.

The queen mother, Catherine de' Medici (1519–1589), worked carefully and intelligently to balance the nobles' interests. She gained greater authority when, in late 1560, the sickly Francis died and was succeeded by his brother, Charles IX—a 10-year-old for whom Catherine was officially the regent. But keeping the conflicts among the great courtiers from boiling over into civil war proved impossible.

In France, as elsewhere, noble conflict invariably had a violent component. Noble men went about armed and accompanied by armed entourages. Although they relied on patronage and army commands from the Crown, the Crown depended on their services. Provincial landholdings afforded enough resources to support private warfare, and the nobles assumed a right to wage it.

In addition, religious tension was rising throughout France. (Henry II had welcomed the 1559 treaty in part because he wanted to turn his attention to "heresy.") Public preaching by, and secret meetings of, Protestants (known as "Huguenots" in France) were causing unrest in towns. At court, members of the Bourbon family and other leading nobles had converted to Protestantism and worshiped openly in their rooms in the palace. In 1561 Catherine convened a national religious council, known as the Colloquy of Poissy, to reconcile the two faiths. When it failed, she decided that the only practical course was at least provisional religious toleration, so she issued a limited edict of toleration in the name of the king in January 1562.

The edict, however, led only to further unrest. Ignoring its restrictions, Protestants armed themselves, while townspeople of both faiths insulted and attacked one another at worship sites and religious festivals. Then in March 1562, at Vassy, the duke of Guise's men killed a few dozen Protestants gathered in worship near one of the duke's estates.

The killing at Vassy began the first of six civil wars because it brought together the military power of the nobility with the broader problem of religious division. In some ways, the initial conflict was decisive. The Protestant army lost the principal pitched battle of the war, near Dreux, west of Paris, in December. This defeat ultimately checked the growth of the Protestant movement. It reduced the appeal of the movement to nobles, and the limited rights granted to Protestants in the Crown's peace edict made it difficult for Protestant townspeople to worship, particularly in areas where they were not a majority. But if the Protestants were not powerful enough to win, neither could the Crown decisively beat them.

The turning point most obvious to contemporaries came a decade later. The Protestant faction was still well represented at court by the Bourbon princes and by the very able and influential nobleman Gaspard de Coligny, related to the Bourbons by marriage. Coligny pressed for a war against Spain in aid of Protestant rebels in the Netherlands. Alarmed by this pressure and by rumors of Protestant armies outside of Paris, Charles IX (r. 1560–1574) and his mother authorized royal guards to murder Coligny and other Protestant leaders on August 24, 1572—Saint Bartholomew's Day. Coligny's murder touched off a massacre of

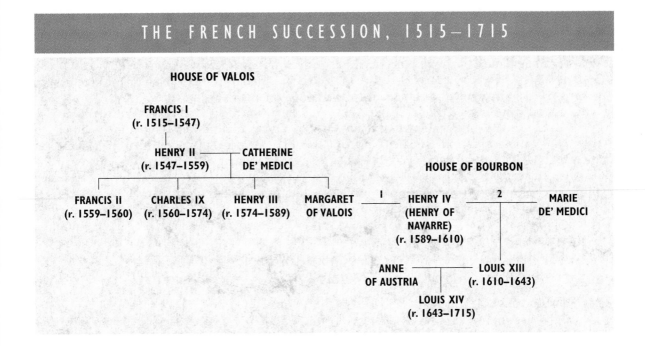

THE FRENCH SUCCESSION, 1515–1715

HOUSE OF VALOIS

FRANCIS I
(r. 1515–1547)

HENRY II ——— CATHERINE
(r. 1547–1559)   DE' MEDICI

HOUSE OF BOURBON

FRANCIS II   CHARLES IX   HENRY III   MARGARET   1   HENRY IV   2   MARIE
(r. 1559–1560)   (r. 1560–1574)   (r. 1574–1589)   OF VALOIS   (HENRY OF   DE' MEDICI
NAVARRE)
(r. 1589–1610)

ANNE ——— LOUIS XIII
OF AUSTRIA   (r. 1610–1643)

LOUIS XIV
(r. 1643–1715)

Protestants throughout Paris and, once news from Paris had spread, throughout the kingdom.

The Saint Bartholomew's Day Massacre revealed the degree to which religious differences had strained the fabric of community life. Neighbor murdered neighbor, in an effort to rid the community of heretical pollution; bodies of the dead, including Coligny's, were torn apart, mutilated. Gathered in the south of France, the remaining Huguenot forces vowed "never [to] trust those who have so often and so treacherously broken faith and the public peace."[2] Many Catholics also renounced reconciliation. When further war produced the inevitable truces and limited toleration, some noblemen formed a Catholic league to fight in place of the vacillating monarchy.

Another impetus to the breakdown of royal authority by the 1580s was the accession to the throne of Charles's brother, Henry III (r. 1574–1589), another king of limited abilities. Middle-aged, Henry had no children. The heir to his throne was the Protestant Henry of Navarre, and the assumption of the throne by a Protestant was unimaginable to the zealous Catholic faction at court and to thousands of ordinary Catholics besides. By the end of Henry III's reign, the king had almost no royal authority left to wield. He was forced to cooperate with first one of the warring parties and then with

another. In December 1588, he resorted to murdering two members of the Guise family who led the ultra-Catholic faction, and, in turn, he was murdered by a priest in early 1589.

Henry of Navarre, who became Henry IV (r. 1589–1610), had to fight for his throne. Facing him were Catholic armies now subsidized by Philip II of Spain, an extremist Catholic city government in Paris, a kingdom of subjects who were tired of war but mainly Catholic, and only meager support from Protestants abroad. Given these obstacles, Henry was able to force acceptance of his rule only after agreeing to return to Catholicism himself.

After his conversion in 1593, the wars continued for a time, but, after thirty years of civil war, many of his subjects realized that only rallying to the monarchy could save France from chaos. Catholic nobility and townspeople fought among themselves over the direction to take. The nobility favored acceptance of Henry IV and imposed its will on the citizens of Paris and other cities.

The civil wars had demonstrated the power of the warrior-nobility to disrupt the state. But now nobles grew increasingly disposed, for both psychological and practical reasons, to cooperate with the Crown. Service to a successful king could be a source of glory, and Henry was personally esteemed because he was a talented general and brave, gregarious, and charming. The civil war period thus proved to be an important phase in the continual accommodation of the nobility to the power of the state.

In April 1598 Henry granted toleration for the Huguenot minority in a royal edict proclaimed in the city of Nantes. The Edict of Nantes was primarily a repetition of provisions from the most generous edicts that had ended the various civil wars. Nobles were allowed to practice the Protestant faith on their estates; townspeople were granted more limited rights to worship in selected towns in each region. Protestants were guaranteed access to schools, hospitals, royal appointments, and separate judicial institutions to ensure fair treatment. They were also guaranteed rights of self-defense—specifically, the right to maintain garrisons in about two hundred towns. About half of these garrisons would be paid for by the Crown.

The problem was that the Edict of Nantes, like any royal edict, could be revoked by the king at any time. Moreover, the provision allowing Protestants to keep garrisoned towns reflected concessions to powerful nobles who could support their followers by paid garrison duty. These concessions also meant that living peacefully with religious diversity was not yet thought to be possible. Thus, although Henry IV successfully ended the French religious wars, the problem of religious and political division within France had not been solved.

The Consolidation of Royal Authority in France, 1610–1643

During Henry IV's reign, France recovered from the long years of civil war. Population and productivity began to grow; the Crown encouraged internal improvements to facilitate commerce. Henry's chief minister, Maximilien de Béthune, duke of Sully (1560–1641), increased royal revenue by nibbling away at traditional local self-government and control of taxation. He succeeded in creating a budget surplus and in extending mechanisms of centralized government.

Yet Henry's regime was stable only in comparison with the preceding years of civil war. The power of the great nobility had not been definitively broken. Several leading nobles plotted with foreign powers, including Spain, to influence French policy and gain materially themselves.

Moreover, the king had agreed to a provision, known as the *paulette* (named for the functionary who first administered it), that allowed royal officeholders not merely to own their offices but also to bequeath those offices to their heirs in return for the payment of an annual fee. It was, primarily, a financial expedient to raise revenue after decades of civil war. In addition, the paulette helped cement the loyalty of royal bureaucrats at a critical time, particularly that of the royal judges of the supreme law court, the Parlement of Paris, who had recently agreed to register the Edict of Nantes only under duress. However, that privileged position made royal officeholders largely immune from royal control since a position in the royal bureaucracy now became property, like the landed property of the traditional nobility.

A fanatical Catholic assassinated Henry IV in 1610. Henry's death left his son, Louis XIII (r. 1610–1643), only 9 years old, to face the challenges of governing as well as a return of religious conflict. Louis's mother, Marie de' Medici, acted ably as regent, but was temporarily disgraced when her unpopular leading minister was assassinated in 1617. This courtier was an Italian, and hence doubly resented for being a foreigner as well as for his crass ambition. His rise and fall was typical of the volatile court life of the period, as great aristocrats vied to control and profit from royal policies.

Soon after Louis took control of government from his mother, he faced a major rebellion by his Huguenot subjects in southwestern France. Huguenots felt threatened by the recent marriage of the king to a Spanish princess and by Louis's reintroduction of Catholic institutions in nearby Navarre (see Map 15.1). Louis's ancestors had themselves established Protestantism in this small kingdom bordering Spain, now united to the French crown. Certain Huguenot nobles, afraid that royal support of toleration was wavering, initiated fighting in 1621 as a show of force against the king.

These religious wars persisted, on and off, until 1629. They reflected not only the continuing power of great nobles to wield independent military might, but also the importance of fortifications in warfare: The Crown had difficulty successfully besieging even small fortress towns. The course of the wars also reflected the ascendancy of the western port city of La Rochelle—well-fortified, Protestant-controlled, and wealthy from mounting overseas and European trade. Not until the king took the city, after a siege lasting more than a year and costing thousands of lives, did the Protestants accept a peace on royal terms.

The Peace of Alais (1629) was a political triumph for the Crown because it broke the connection between religious dissent and political upheaval. The treaty reaffirmed the policy of religious toleration but rescinded the Protestants' military and political privileges. It thus deprived French Protestants of the means for further rebellion while reinforcing their dependence on the Crown for religious toleration. Most of the remaining great noble leaders began to convert to Catholicism.

The Peace of Alais was also a personal triumph for the king's leading minister, who crafted the treaty and who had directed the bloody siege that made it possible: Armand-Jean du Plessis (1585–1642), Cardinal Richelieu. From a provincial noble family, Richelieu had risen in the service of the queen mother. His enormous intelligence was apparent to everyone at court; he was admired and feared for his skill in the political game of seeking and bestowing patronage—a crucial skill in an age when elites received offices and honor through carefully cultivated links with the court. His control of many lucrative church offices gave him the resources to build up a large network of clients. He and the king—whose sensitive temperament Richelieu handled adeptly—formed a lasting partnership from this point on that had a decisive impact not only on French policy but also on the entire shape of the French state. (See the box, "Richelieu Supports the Authority of the State.")

Richelieu favored an aggressive foreign policy to counter what he believed still to be the greatest threat to the French crown: the Spanish Habsburgs. War had resumed between the Netherlands and Spain when their truce expired in 1621 (see page 561); since then, Richelieu had used his growing power to direct limited military campaigns against Spanish power in Italy. After 1630, with the king's full confidence, he superintended large-scale fighting against Spain in the Netherlands itself, as well as in Italy, and subsidized armies fighting the Spanish and Austrian Habsburgs in Germany.

Richelieu's policies were opposed by many people, who saw taxes double, then triple, in just a few years. Many courtiers and provincial elites had favored the tenuous peace with a fellow Catholic state and objected to alliances with German Protestants. They were alarmed by the increasing taxes and by the famine, disease, and, above all, the revolts that accompanied the peasants' distress. Their own power was also directly threatened by Richelieu's monopoly of royal patronage and by his creation of new mechanisms of government to manage his policies, which bypassed their offices. In 1632, for example, Richelieu created the office of *intendant*. Intendants had wide powers for defense and administration in the provinces that overrode the established bureaucracy.

By 1640 Richelieu's ambitious foreign policy seemed to be bearing fruit. The French had won territory along their northern and eastern borders by their successes against Habsburg forces. But when Richelieu and Louis XIII died within five months of each other, in December 1642 and May 1643, Richelieu's legacy was tested. Louis XIII was succeeded by his 5-year-old son, and the warrior-nobility as well as royal bureaucrats would dramatically challenge the Crown's new authority.

England: Precarious Stability, 1558–1603

England experienced no civil wars during the second half of the sixteenth century, but religious dissent challenged the stability of the monarchy. In Elizabeth I (r. 1558–1603), England—in stark contrast to France—possessed an able and long-lived ruler. Elizabeth was well educated in the humanistic tradition and was already an astute politician at the age of 25, when she acceded to the throne. Religious, political, and constitutional disputes existed in England as elsewhere, but they would not provoke violence on anything like the continental scale.

Elizabeth came to the throne at the death of her Catholic half-sister, Mary Tudor (r. 1553–1558), wife of Philip II. Elizabeth faced the urgent problem of reaching a policy of consensus in religious matters—a consensus that could embrace the two extremes of the Catholic-like doctrine and practice of Anglicanism, which had prevailed under her father, Henry VIII (r. 1509–1547), and Calvinist-inspired Protestantism, which had developed under her half-brother, Edward VI (r. 1547–1553). True Catholicism, such as Mary had tried to reimpose, was out of the question. The Roman church had never recognized Henry VIII's self-made di-

Richelieu Supports the Authority of the State

In this excerpt from his **Political Testament** *(assembled from his notes after his death by loyal secretaries), Richelieu justifies methods for ensuring obedience to the Crown. Notice his pessimistic view of human rationality; rewards (such as patronage) but also severity are both necessary to ensure obedience.*

It is a common but nevertheless true saying which has long been repeated by intelligent men that punishments and rewards are the two most important instruments of government in a realm. It is certain that whatever else one may do in governing states, one must be inflexible in punishing those who fail to obey, and religiously scrupulous in rewarding those who perform notable services. In other words, one would not govern badly if guided by this precept since most people can be held to their duty through either fear or hope. I rate punishments, I must say, higher than rewards, because if it were necessary to dispense with one of these, it would be better to give up the latter than the former. The good ought to be adhered to for its own sake, and in all justice no one should be rewarded for this. But there is no crime which does not violate those precepts men are obligated to obey, so that punishment to be expected for disobedience of this sort is therefore justified, and this obligation is so direct in many cases that to let the act go unpunished is to commit further error.

I speak here of things which injure the state and which have been premeditated, and not of those lesser offenses which result from chance or misfortune, toward which princes may and should often show indulgence. But while in matters of this sort it can be praise-worthy to pardon, it is a criminal omission not to punish breaches which open the door to licentious abandon. Both theologians and political experts agree that on special occasions it would be an error not to pardon certain individuals, but it would be inexcusable for those charged with public responsibilities to substitute indulgence for severe punishment. Experience teaches those who have had long practice in this world that men easily lose the memory of rewards and, when they are heaped with them, they expect even more, and become both ambitious and ungrateful at the same time. This teaches us to realize that punishments are a surer means of holding a person to his duty, since people are less likely to forget what has made an impression on their emotions. This is more persuasive for most men than reason, which has little power over many minds.

To be severe in dealing with private individuals who glory in disobeying the laws and orders of the state makes a good impression on the people, and one can commit no greater crime against the public interest than to be indulgent toward those who violate them. In thinking over the many cabals, factions, and plottings which have occurred in this realm in my time, I can recall none in which leniency induced any person with evil inclinations to rectify the error of his ways.

Source: Henry Bertram Hill, ed. and trans., *The Political Testament of Cardinal Richelieu* (Madison: University of Wisconsin Press, 1965), pp. 84–86.

vorce and thus regarded Elizabeth as a bastard with no right to the throne.

Most important to Elizabeth was a new Act of Supremacy (1559), intended to restore the monarch as head of the Church of England. Elizabeth and most of her ministers were willing to accept some room for maneuver between liturgical practice and personal belief for the sake of defeating the common enemy, Roman Catholicism. For example, a new prayer book, the *Book of Common Prayer,* incorporated, side by side, elements of both traditional and radical interpretations of

Elizabeth I: The Armada Portrait Both serene and resolute, Elizabeth is flanked by "before" and "after" glimpses of the Spanish fleet; her hand rests on the globe in a gesture of dominion that also memorializes the circumnavigation of the globe by her famous captain, Sir Francis Drake, some years before. *(By kind permission of Marquess of Tavistock and Trustees of Bedford Estate)*

communion. Church liturgy, clerical vestments, and, above all, the hierarchical structure of the clergy closely resembled Catholicism, however. Elizabeth firmly handled resistance to the Act of Supremacy. She simply arrested bishops and lords whose votes would have blocked its passage by Parliament.

The problem of religious dissent, however, was not definitively solved. Catholicism continued to be practiced. Loyal nobility and gentry in the north of England practiced it with discretion. But priests returning from exile beginning in the 1570s, most newly imbued with the proselytizing zeal of the Counter-Reformation (the Catholic response to the Protestant Reformation), practiced it more visibly. In the last twenty years of Elizabeth's reign, approximately 180 Catholics were executed for treason; two-thirds of them were priests. (By 1585, being a priest in itself was a crime.)

In the long run, however, the greater threat to the English crown came from growing tensions with the most radical Protestants in the realm, known (by their enemies initially) as Puritans. Puritanism was a broad movement for reform of church practice along familiar Protestant lines: emphasis on Bible reading, preaching, private scrutiny of conscience, and a de-emphasis on institutional ritual and clerical authority. Most Puritans had accepted Elizabeth's religious compromise for practical reasons but grew increasingly alienated by her insistence on clerical authority. A significant Presbyterian underground movement began to form among them. Presbyterians wanted to dismantle the episcopacy, the hierarchy of priests and bishops, and govern the church instead with councils, called "presbyterys," that included lay members of the congregation. Laws were passed late in the reign to enable the Crown more easily to prosecute, and even to force into exile, anyone who attended "nonconformist" (non-Anglican) services.

The greatest challenge Elizabeth faced from Puritans came in Parliament, where they were well represented by many literate gentry. Parliament met only when called by the monarch, and in theory could merely voice opinions and complaints; it could not initiate legislation or demand changes in royal policy. However, only Parliament could vote taxes, and, since its authority had, in effect, helped constitute royal authority by means of the Acts of Supremacy, Parliament's supposedly consultative role had been expanded by the monarchy itself. During Elizabeth's reign, Puritans used meetings of Parliament to press their cause of further religious reform. In 1586, they went so far as to introduce bills calling for an end to the episcopacy and the Anglican prayer book. Elizabeth had to resort to imprisoning one Puritan leader to end debate on the issue and on Parliament's right to address it.

Elizabeth's reign saw the beginnings of English expansion overseas, but great interest in overseas possessions lay in the future; Elizabeth, like all her forebears, felt her interests tightly linked to affairs on the European continent. Her prime interest lay in safeguarding the independence of the Netherlands. Philip II's policy in the Netherlands increasingly alarmed her, especially in view of France's weakness. She began to send small sums of money to the rebels and allowed their ships access to southern English ports, from which they could raid Spanish-held towns on the Netherlands' coast. In 1585, in the wake of the duke of Parma's successes against the rebellions, she committed troops to help the rebels.

Her decision was a reaction not only to the threat of a single continental power dominating the Netherlands but also to the threat of Catholicism. Spain had threatened her interests, and even her throne, in other ways. From 1579 to 1583, the Spanish had helped the Irish fight English domination and were involved in several plots to replace Elizabeth with her Catholic cousin, Mary, Queen of Scots. These threats occurred at the height of the return of Catholic exiles to England.

Eventually, in 1588, the English faced the Spanish Armada and the threat of invasion that it brought. The defeat of the Armada was by no means certain for the English. They did not know, for example, how poorly prepared Parma actually was to cross the Channel. Thus, in the wake of victory, a mythology quickly built that portrayed Spain as an aggressive Goliath confronting the tiny David of England. The victory over the Spanish fleet was quite rightly celebrated, for it ended any Catholic threat to Elizabeth's rule.

The success against the Armada has tended to overshadow other aims and outcomes of Elizabeth's foreign policy. In the case of Ireland, England was Goliath to Ireland's David. Since the twelfth century, an Anglo-Irish state dominated by

great princely families had been loosely supervised from England, but most of Ireland remained under the control of Gaelic chieftains. Just as Charles V and Philip II attempted to tighten their governing mechanisms in the Netherlands, so in England did Henry VIII's minister, Thomas Cromwell, streamline control of outlying areas such as Wales and Anglo-Ireland. Cromwell proposed that the whole of Ireland be brought under English control partly by the established mechanism of feudal ties: The Irish chieftains were to do homage as vassals to the king of England.

Under Elizabeth, this legalistic approach gave way to virtual conquest. Elizabeth's governor, Sir Henry Sidney, appointed in 1565, inaugurated a policy whereby Gaelic lords, by means of various technicalities, could be entirely dispossessed of their land. Any Englishman capable of raising a private force could help enforce these dispossessions and settle his conquered lands as he saw fit. This policy provoked stiff Irish resistance, which was viewed as rebellion and provided the excuse for further military action, more confiscations of land, and more new English settlers. Eventually, the Irish, with Spanish assistance, mounted a major rebellion, consciously Catholic and aimed against the "heretic" queen. The rebellion gave the English an excuse for brutal suppression and massive transfers of land to English control. The political domination of the Irish was complete with the defeat, in 1601, of the able Gaelic chieftain Hugh O'Neill, lord of Tyrone, who controlled most of the northern quarter of the island. Although the English were unable to impose their Protestantism on the conquered Irish, to Elizabeth and her English subjects the conquests in Ireland seemed as successful as the victory over the Spanish Armada.

The English enjoyed remarkable peace at home during Elizabeth's reign. However, her reign ended on a note of strain. The foreign involvements, particularly in Ireland, had been very expensive. Taxation granted by Parliament more than doubled during her reign, and local taxes further burdened the people. Price inflation caused by government spending, social problems caused by returned, unemployed soldiers, and a series of bad harvests heightened popular resentment against taxation. Despite her achievements, therefore, Elizabeth passed two potential problems on to her successors: unresolved religious tensions and financial instability. Elizabeth's successors would also find in Parliament an increasing focus of opposition to their policies.

Rising Tensions in England, 1603–1642

In 1603 Queen Elizabeth died and James VI of Scotland acceded to the English throne as James I (r. 1603–1625). Religious tensions between Anglicans and Puritans were temporarily quieted under James because of a plot, in 1605, by Catholic dissenters. The Gunpowder Plot, as it was called, was a conspiracy to blow up the palace housing both king and Parliament at Westminster. The attention of Protestants of all stripes once again became focused not on their differences but on their common enemy, Catholicism.

Financial problems were James's most pressing concern. Court life became more elaborate and an increasing drain on the monarchy's resources. James's own leanings toward extravagance were partly to blame for his financial problems, but so were pressures for patronage from elites. There were considerable debts left from the Irish conflicts and wars with Spain. Moreover, as the reign progressed, James was forced into further foreign involvement. His daughter and her husband, a German prince, were trying to defend their claim to rule Bohemia against the powerful Austrian Habsburgs (see page 573).

To raise revenue without Parliament's consent, James, like Elizabeth, relied on sources of revenue that the Crown had enjoyed since medieval times: customs duties granted to the monarch for life, wardship (the right to manage and liberally borrow from the estates of minor nobles), and the sale of monopolies, which conveyed the right to be sole agent for a particular kind of goods. James increased the number of monopolies sold and added other measures, such as the sale of Crown lands and of noble titles, to increase royal revenue.

These expanded financial expedients were resented: Merchants opposed monopolies' arbitrary restriction of production and trade; common people found that the prices of certain ordinary commodities, like soap, rose prohibitively. Resentments among the nobility were sharpened, and general criticism of the court heightened, by James's favoritism of certain courtiers and their families. The chief beneficiary of patronage and the most influential adviser to the king was George

Villiers (1592–1628), duke of Buckingham, a powerful but corrupt and inadequate first minister.

When James summoned Parliament for funds in 1621, Parliament used the occasion to protest court corruption and the king's financial expedients. The members impeached and removed from office two royal ministers. In 1624, still faced with expensive commitments to Protestants abroad and in failing health, James again called Parliament, which voted new taxes but also openly debated the king's foreign policy.

Under James's son, Charles I (r. 1625–1649), tensions between Crown and Parliament rose. One reason was the growing financial strain of foreign policy as well as the policies themselves. Retaining the unpopular duke of Buckingham as chief courtier and adviser, Charles declared war on Spain and pursued an indecisive but costly foreign policy in France in support of the Huguenot rebels there. Many wealthy merchants opposed this aggressive foreign policy, which disrupted trading relationships. In 1626, Parliament was dissolved without granting any monies in order to stifle its objections to royal policies. The Crown's reliance on unpopular financial expedients thus of necessity continued and reached a new level of coercion. In 1627, Charles imprisoned certain gentry who refused to lend money to the government.

Above all, Charles's religious policies were a source of controversy. Charles was personally inclined toward "high church" practices: an emphasis on ceremony and sacrament reminiscent of Catholic ritual. He also was a believer in Arminianism, a school of thought that justified the emphasis on sacrament and ritual by denying the Calvinist notion that God's grace cannot be earned. These emphases highlighted the authority of clerics instead of lay control over religion. Charles was intent on fashioning an official religion that would better reflect and justify royal claims to power but found himself on a collision course with gentry and aristocrats who leaned toward Puritanism.

Charles's views were supported by William Laud (1573–1645), archbishop of Canterbury from 1633 and thus leader of the Church of England. He tried to impose ritual changes in worship, spread Arminian ideas, and censor opposing views. He also challenged the redistribution of church property, which had occurred in the Reformation of the sixteenth century, and thereby alienated the gentry on economic as well as religious grounds.

Charles's style of rule worsened religious, political, and economic tensions. Cold and intensely private, he was not a man to build confidence or smooth over tensions with charm or dexterous political maneuvering. His court was ruled by formal protocol, and access to the king himself was highly restricted—a serious problem in an age when personal access to the monarch was the guarantee of political power.

Struggle over issues of revenue and religion dominated debate in the Parliament of 1628–1629, which Charles had called, once again, to get funds for his foreign policy. In 1628 the members of Parliament presented the king with a document called the Petition of Right, which protested his financial policies as well as arbitrary imprisonment. (Seventeen of Parliament's members had been imprisoned for refusing loans to the Crown.) Though couched conservatively as a restatement of customary practice, the petition was in fact a bold claim to a tradition of parliamentary participation in the government of the realm. It reflected Parliament's growing determination to check arbitrary royal actions. Charles dissolved the Parliament in March 1629, having decided that the money he might extract was not worth the risk.

For eleven years, Charles ruled without Parliament. When he was forced to call Parliament again, in 1640, not only were royal finances in desperate straits but political tension had risen markedly on many fronts. In the intervening eleven years, Archbishop Laud's religious policies had raised concern and opposition among a wide spectrum of elites, not just radical Puritans, as well as among ordinary citizens of London, where his clerical influence was greatest. Moreover, Charles had pressed collection of revenues far beyond traditional bounds. In 1634, for example, he revived annual collection of "ship money"—a medieval tax levied on coastal districts to help support the navy during war. England, however, was not at war, and the tax was levied not only on seaports but on inland areas, too. Resistance to the collection of various customs duties and taxes grew; some gentry refused outright to pay them.

In addition, Charles also faced a rebellion by his Scottish subjects, which had occasioned his now desperate need for money. Like Philip II in the Netherlands, Charles tried to rule in Scotland through a small council of men who did not represent the local elite. He also tried to force the Scots, most of whom practiced Presbyterianism, to adopt Anglican liturgy and ritual. In 1639, Charles had started a war against them but, lacking men and money, was forced to agree to a peace treaty. Intent on renewing the war, he was forced to summon Parliament to obtain funds.

Thus, in the spring of 1640, Charles faced Parliament further weakened by military failure. His political skills were far too limited for him to reestablish a workable relationship with Parliament under the circumstances; indeed, he compounded his own difficulties. Charles dissolved this body, which is now known as the "Short Parliament," after just three weeks, when members questioned the war with the Scots and other royal policies. More politically risky even than dissolving the Parliament at this juncture was the lack of respect Charles had shown the members: A number of them were harassed or arrested. Mistrust fo-

Criticism of Monopolies Holders of royally granted monopolies were bitterly resented by English consumers and tradespeople alike, as this contemporary print reveals. The greedy beast pictured here controls even ordinary commodities such as pins, soap, and butter. *(Courtesy of the Trustees of the British Museum)*

mented by the eleven years in which Charles had ruled without Parliament thus increased.

Another humiliating and decisive defeat at the hands of the Scots later in 1640 made summoning another Parliament imperative. Members of Parliament could now exploit the king's predicament. This Parliament is known as the "Long Parliament" because it sat from 1640 to 1653. Charles was forced to agree not to dissolve or adjourn Parliament without the members' own consent and to summon Parliament at least every three years. Parliament abolished many of his unorthodox and traditional sources of revenue and impeached and removed from office his leading ministers, including Archbishop Laud. The royal commander deemed responsible for the Scottish fiasco, Thomas Wentworth, earl of Strafford, was executed without trial in May 1641.

The execution of Strafford shocked many aristocrats in the House of Lords as well as some moderate members of the House of Commons. Meanwhile, Parliament began debating the perennially thorny religious question. A bare majority of members favored abolition of Anglican bishops as a first step in thoroughgoing religious reform. Working people in London, kept apprised of the issues by the regular publication of parliamentary debates, demonstrated in support of that majority. Moderate members of Parliament, in contrast, favored checking the king's power but not upsetting the Elizabethan religious compromise.

An event that unified public and parliamentary opinion at a crucial time—a revolt against English rule in Ireland in October 1641—temporarily eclipsed these divisions and once again focused suspicion on the king. The broad consensus of anti-Catholicism once again became the temporary driving force in politics. Few trusted the king with the troops necessary to quash the rebellion, however. It was even widely rumored that Charles would use Irish soldiers against his English subjects. Parliament demanded control of the army to put down the rebellion, and in November the Puritan majority introduced a document known as the "Grand Remonstrance," an appeal to the people and a long catalog of parliamentary grievances against the king. By a narrow margin it was passed, further setting public opinion in London against Charles. The king's remaining support in Parliament eroded in January 1642, when he attempted to arrest five leading members on charges of treason. The five escaped, but the attempt set the stage for wider violence. The king withdrew from London, unsure he could defend himself there, and began to raise an army. In mid-1642 the kingdom stood at the brink of civil war.

THE HOLY ROMAN EMPIRE AND THE THIRTY YEARS' WAR

The Holy Roman Empire enjoyed a period of comparative quiet after the Peace of Augsburg halted religious and political wars in 1555. By the early seventeenth century, however, fresh causes of instability brought about renewed fighting. Especially destabilizing was the drive by the Habsburgs, as emperors and territorial princes, to reverse the successes of Protestantism both in their own lands and in the empire at large and to consolidate their rule in their diverse personal territories.

In the Thirty Years' War (1618–1648), as it is now called, we can see the continuation of conflicts from the sixteenth century—religious tensions, regionalism versus centralizing forces, dynastic and strategic rivalries between rulers. The war was particularly destructive because of the size of the armies, the burden they imposed on civilian populations, and the degree to which army commanders evaded control by the states for which they fought. Some areas of the empire suffered catastrophic losses in population and productive capacity. As a result of the war, the empire was eclipsed as a political unit by the regional powers within it.

Peace Through Diversity, 1555–ca. 1618

Through most of the second half of the sixteenth century, the Holy Roman Empire enjoyed an uneasy peace. The Peace of Augsburg (1555) permitted rulers of the various states to impose either Lutheranism or Catholicism in their lands and, for a time, proved to be a workable enough solution to the problem of religious division. Complicating matters, however, was the rise of Calvinism, for which no provision had been necessary in 1555. A number of rulers adopted this newest religion, but the impact of their choices was felt more directly outside the empire than within it because they chose to support French Huguenots and the Dutch

THE THIRTY YEARS' WAR, 1618–1648

1618	Bohemian revolt against Habsburg rule Defenestration of Prague
1619	Ferdinand II is elected Holy Roman emperor
	Frederick, elector of the Palatinate, is elected king of Bohemia
1620	Catholic victory at Battle of White Mountain
1621	Truce between Spain and the Netherlands expires; war between Spain and the Netherlands begins
1626	Imperial forces defeat armies of Christian IV of Denmark
1629	Peace of Lübeck
1631	Swedes under Gustav Adolf defeat imperial forces at Breitenfeld
	Catholic forces sack Magdeburg
1632	Death of Gustav Adolf
1635	Peace of Prague
1643	French defeat Spanish in the Netherlands
1648	Peace of Westphalia

rebels but not to disturb the peace within the empire. For the most part, there was not a second wave of reforming zeal among the population.

The Habsburgs ruled over a diverse group of territories. Most lay within the boundaries of the empire, but many were not German (Map 15.3). Though largely contiguous, the territories comprised independent duchies and kingdoms, each with its own institutional structure. Habsburg lands included speakers of Italian, German, and Czech, as well as other languages. The non-German lands of Bohemia and Hungary had been distinct kingdoms since the High Middle Ages. Most of Hungary was now under Ottoman domination, but Bohemia, with its rich capital, Prague, was a wealthy center of population and culture in central Europe.

Unlike the Netherlands, these linguistically and culturally diverse lands were still governed by highly decentralized institutions. The Habsburg

family often divided rule of the various territories among themselves. For example, during the lifetime of Holy Roman Emperor Charles V, his brother Ferdinand (d. 1564) was more active than he in governing these family lands. At Ferdinand's death, as he wished, rule of the various provinces and kingdoms was split among his three sons. One member of the family was routinely elected Holy Roman emperor.

Moreover, the Habsburgs, unlike most of their contemporaries, made no attempt to impose religious uniformity in this period. Ferdinand was firmly Catholic but tolerant of diverse reform efforts within the church, including clerical marriage and allowing the laity to receive both wine and bread at communion. His son, Emperor Maximilian II (r. 1564–1576), granted limited rights of worship to Protestant subjects within his lands and kept his distance from policies pursued by Catholic rulers elsewhere—most notably, those of his cousin, Philip II, in the Netherlands. During Maximilian's reign, partly because of his positive leadership and partly because of a lack of persecution, a variety of faiths flourished side by side in Habsburg lands. In this tolerant atmosphere, education, printing, and humanistic intellectual life flourished.

But, given the course of events elsewhere in Europe, this late Renaissance was unlikely to last. The balance began to shift under Maximilian's son, Rudolf II (r. 1576–1612). Rudolf shared the religious style of his father and grandfather. He was an energetic patron of the arts and sponsored the work of scientists. Yet he was virtually a recluse at his court, pursuing an eccentric intellectual life, and he did not attend carefully to the routine problems of governing.

In any case, the religious balance began to shift on its own in the second half of the century in the wake of the appearance of resurgent Catholicism. Members of the Jesuit order began to appear in Habsburg lands in the reign of Maximilian. Tough-minded and well trained, they established Catholic schools and became confessors and preachers to the upper classes. Self-confident Catholicism emerged as one form of cultural identity among the German-speaking ruling classes and thus as a religious impetus to further political consolidation of all these Habsburg territories. Ferdinand II (r. 1619–1637) was raised in the atmosphere of reformed Catholicism. He was committed both to tighter rule and to uniformity in matters of relig-

Map 15.3 Territories of the Austrian Habsburgs In addition to the lands constituting modern Austria, Austrian Habsburg lands comprised the Tyrol (modern west Austria and northeast Italy), Carniola (modern Slovenia), part of Croatia, Bohemia (the core of the modern Czech Republic and southern Poland), and Hungary. Most of Hungary had been in Ottoman hands since the Battle of Mohács in 1527.

ion. Like the English under Elizabeth, Habsburg subjects had enjoyed a period of relative peace in political and religious matters. Now, as in England, the stage was set for conflict of both kinds.

The Thirty Years' War, 1618–1648

Both political and religious problems surfaced early in the seventeenth century. In one incident, in 1606, the aggressively Catholic prince of Bavaria seized an imperial free city in north central Germany, in the wake of religious in-fighting there—a city theoretically subject to no one but the emperor himself. Tensions between Catholic and Protestant states (and among Protestants, for Calvinists and Lutherans were not necessarily allies) were further heightened by a succession crisis. The childless emperor Rudolf II was aging, and factions of the Habsburg family sought allies among the German states to promote their various candidates for the imperial crown.

In 1618 a revolt against Habsburg rule in the kingdom of Bohemia touched off widespread warfare. Bohemia (the core of the modern Czech Republic) was populous and prosperous and had a large Protestant population. Rudolf II had used Prague, its bustling capital, as an imperial capital. Although Catholicism was reclaiming lost ground,

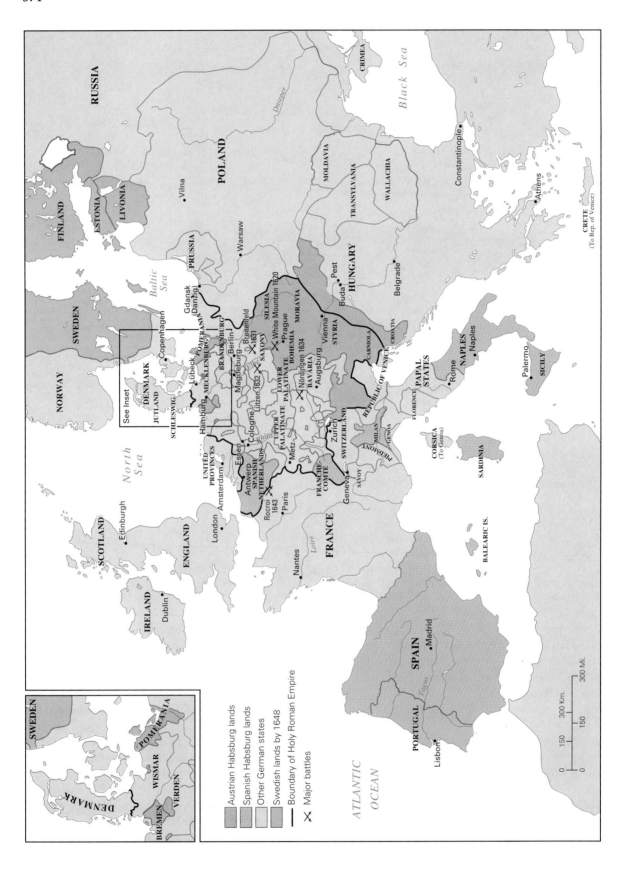

RUSSIA

FINLAND

ESTONIA

LIVONIA

NORWAY

SWEDEN

POLAND

• Vilna

• Warsaw

Baltic Sea

PRUSSIA

Gdansk (Danzig)

POMERANIA

Copenhagen •

Lübeck •

MECKLENBURG

DENMARK

JUTLAND

SCHLESWIG

Hamburg •

BRANDENBURG

Berlin •

Breitenfeld

× 1631

SAXONY

Magdeburg •

Lützen 1632 ×

SILESIA

White Mountain 1620 ×

Prague •

BOHEMIA

MORAVIA

Vienna •

STYRIA

Pest •

Buda •

HUNGARY

Belgrade •

MOLDAVIA

TRANSYLVANIA

WALLACHIA

CRIMEA

Black Sea

Constantinople •

Athens •

CRETE
(To Rep. of Venice)

North Sea

Cologne •

LOWER PALATINATE

Nördlingen 1634 ×

BAVARIA

Augsburg •

CARNIOLA

CROATIA

REPUBLIC OF VENICE

PAPAL STATES

Rome •

NAPLES

Naples •

Palermo •

SICILY

UNITED PROVINCES

Amsterdam •

Essen •

Antwerp •

SPANISH NETHERLANDS

Rocroi 1643 ×

London •

Paris •

UPPER PALATINATE

Metz •

Rhine

Zurich •

SWITZERLAND

Geneva •

FRANCHE COMTÉ

SAVOY

PIEDMONT

MILAN

GENOA

Florence •

CORSICA
(To Genoa)

SARDINIA

BALEARIC IS.

SCOTLAND

Edinburgh •

ENGLAND

IRELAND

Dublin •

Nantes •

Loire

FRANCE

ATLANTIC OCEAN

SPAIN

Madrid •

PORTUGAL

Lisbon •

Tagus

See Inset

300 Mi.

300 Km.

150

150

0

0

SWEDEN

POMERANIA

WISMAR

VERDEN

BREMEN

DENMARK

Austrian Habsburg lands

Spanish Habsburg lands

Other German states

Swedish lands by 1648

Boundary of Holy Roman Empire

× Major battles

Protestants had been confirmed in their rights to worship in the early seventeenth century both by Rudolf and by his younger brother, Matthias, who hoped to succeed Rudolf as king of Bohemia and as Holy Roman emperor. The crown of Bohemia was bestowed by election, so rival claimants to this wealthy throne needed the acquiescence of the ruling elites, both Protestant and Catholic, of the kingdom.

When Matthias did become king of Bohemia and Holy Roman emperor (r. 1612–1619), he reneged on his promise to the Protestants. The Habsburg succession to the Bohemian throne seemed secure, and concessions to Protestant elites seemed less necessary. As in the Netherlands, there was in Bohemia a delicate balance between regional integrity and Bohemia's expectation of sharing its ruler with other regions. As Philip II had done, Matthias appointed a council of regents that enforced unpopular policies, particularly with regard to religion. The right to build new Protestant churches was denied. Bohemian crown lands were given to the Catholic church.

On May 23, 1618, delegates to a Protestant assembly that had unsuccessfully petitioned Matthias to end these policies marched to the palace in Prague where the hated royal officials met. After a confrontation over their demands, the delegates "tried" the officials on the spot for treason and, literally, threw them out the window of the palace. The incident became known as the Defenestration of Prague (from the Latin, *fenestra*, "window"). (The officials' lives were saved only because they fell into a pile of manure.) The rebels proceeded to set up their own government.

The new Bohemian government deposed Matthias's successor as king, his Catholic cousin, Ferdinand, and elected a new king in 1619. Ferdinand, however, ruled as Holy Roman emperor until 1637. The direct challenge to Habsburg control in Bohemia had implications for the empire as a whole because the new king of Bohemia was a Protestant, Frederick, elector of the Palatinate. Frederick was a Calvinist prince. His territories in

west central Germany (called the Lower Palatinate and the Upper Palatinate) carried with them the right to be one of the seven electors who chose the emperor.

Encouraged by these events, Protestant subjects in other Habsburg lands asked for guarantees of freedom of worship like those enjoyed by Protestants in Bohemia. This new Protestant success seemed to threaten the religious balance of power in the empire. Other princes saw their chance to make political gains. Rival claimants to Habsburg rule in Hungary took up arms. The Protestant king of Denmark, Christian IV (r. 1588-1648), who was also duke of Holstein in northern Germany, sought to take advantage of the situation and conquer more German territory.

Foreign powers were also interested in these events. England practiced a pro-Protestant foreign policy, and the English king, James I, was Frederick's father-in-law. Spain's supply routes north from Italy to the Netherlands passed next to Frederick's lands in western Germany. France's first interest was its rivalry with Spain; thus, France kept its eye on the border principalities that were strategically important to Spain. In addition, it was in France's interest, much to the disgust of the devout Catholic faction at the French court, to keep Protestant as well as Catholic rulers in the empire strong enough to thwart Austrian Habsburg ambitions.

The revolt in Bohemia thus triggered a widespread war because it challenged Habsburg control in a direct and undeniable fashion and because other princes felt their interests to be involved. From the outset, the war was not only a conflict over the Habsburgs' power in their own lands but also a conflict over the balance of power in the empire and in Europe (Map 15.4).

By the fall of 1620 a Catholic army was closing in on Bohemia; the army was supported by the duke of Bavaria, who had been offered the Palatinate as a victory prize. On November 8, on a hillside west of Prague, the Catholic force faced a Bohemian army that had not garnered much concrete aid from Protestant allies. The resulting Battle of White Mountain was a complete Catholic victory.

Fighting then became more widespread. The truce between Spain and the Netherlands, established in 1609, expired in 1621, and the nearby Lower Palatinate, now in Catholic hands, offered a staging point for Spanish forces. At this point,

Map 15.4 Europe in the Thirty Years' War The Thirty Years' War was fought largely within the borders of the Holy Roman Empire. It was the result of conflicts within the empire as well as the meddling of neighbors for their own strategic advantage.

Christian IV, the Protestant king of Denmark, decided to seize more territory, both to give himself greater control over profitable German Baltic seaports and to defend himself against any Catholic attempt to seize northern German territory. Christian received little help from Protestant allies, however; the Dutch were busy with Spain, the English were still wary of continental entanglements, and Denmark's regional rivals, the Swedish, were uninterested in furthering Danish ambitions in the Baltic.

The confusing blend of politics and religion that motivated the Protestant rulers was also evident on the Catholic side. Imperial forces defeated Christian's armies in 1626. Alarmed at the possibility of greater imperial control in northern Germany, Catholic princes led by the duke of Bavaria arranged a truce that led to the Peace of Lübeck in 1629—and to Denmark's withdrawal from the fighting on relatively generous terms.

Christian's rival, Gustav Adolf, king of Sweden (r. 1611–1632), immediately assumed the role of Protestant champion. A brilliant and innovative military leader, Gustav Adolf hoped to gain territory along the Baltic seacoast, but personal aggrandizement also was one of his goals. His campaigns were capped by a victory over an imperial army at Breitenfeld in Saxony in 1631. The tide turned in the favor of imperial forces, however, after Gustav Adolf was killed at the Battle of Lützen in late 1632. A decisive imperial victory over a combined Swedish and German Protestant army, at Nördlingen in 1634, led to a general peace treaty favorable to the Catholics: the Peace of Prague (1635).

The Peace of Prague brought only a temporary peace, however, because French involvement increased, now that other anti-Habsburg forces had been eclipsed. France tried to seize imperial territory along its own eastern border and generously subsidized continued fighting within the empire by channeling monies to Protestant mercenaries there. Fighting dragged on. The Swedes reentered the war, hoping to obtain territory on the northern coast. In the south, rivals to the Habsburgs in Hungary tried to seize territory. By the end of the war, order had disintegrated so completely in the wake of the marauding armies that both staunchly Catholic rulers and firmly Protestant ones made alliances with religious enemies to safeguard their states.

A comprehensive peace treaty did not become possible until France withdrew its sponsorship of continued fighting. There were domestic reasons for France's withdrawal. Louis XIII (r. 1610–1643), the king of France, had died, leaving a minor child to rule and to face the burden of war debt. France wanted only a workable balance of power in the empire; more important to France was the continued rivalry with the Spanish Habsburgs for control of territory along France's eastern and northern borders and in Italy. A defeat by France in the Spanish Netherlands in 1643 had convinced Spain to concentrate on that rivalry too, and fighting between them continued until 1659.

The Effects of the War

The Thirty Years' War caused economic devastation and population decline in many parts of the empire and had long-term political consequences for the empire as a whole. One reason for the war's devastation was a further step in the application of firepower to warfare that increased both the size of armies and their deadly force in battle. This was the use of volley fire, the arrangement of foot soldiers in parallel lines so that one line of men could fire while another reloaded. This tactic, pioneered in the Netherlands around the turn of the century, was further refined by Gustav Adolf of Sweden. Gustav Adolf amassed large numbers of troops and increased the rate of fire so that a virtually continuous barrage was maintained; he also used maneuverable field artillery to protect the massed troops from cavalry charges.

Following Gustav Adolf's lead, armies of all the major states adopted these tactics. Despite these new offensive tactics, defensive tactics—such as holding fortresses—remained important, and pitched battles, such as at Nördlingen in 1634, still tended to be part of sieges. The costs in resources and human life of this kind of warfare reached unheard-of dimensions. Popular printed literature and court drama both condemned the seeming irrationality of the war.

Where fighting had been concentrated, such as in parts of Saxony, between a third and half of the inhabitants of rural villages and major towns may have disappeared. Many starved, were caught in the fighting, or were killed by marauding soldiers. The most notorious atrocity occurred

Gustav Adolf at the Battle of Lützen In this detail of Jan Asselyn's *Charge by the Swedish Cavalry*, the Swedish king (in the plumed hat with raised sword) leads a successful cavalry charge, a tactic he had helped to refine. Leading advancing infantry later in the battle, Gustav Adolf was shot and killed. *(Herzog Anton Ulrich—Museum Braunschweig)*

in the aftermath of the siege of Magdeburg in 1631. After the city surrendered to besieging Catholic forces, long-deprived soldiers ate and drank themselves into a frenzy, raped and killed indiscriminately, and set fires that destroyed the town (killing some of their own ranks in the process). Some victims of war migrated to other regions in search of peaceful conditions and work. Some joined the armies in order to survive. Others formed their own armed bands to fight off the soldiers or to steal back enough goods to live on.

Compounding these effects of war were the actions of armies hired by enterprising mercenary generals for whom loyalty to the princes who paid them took a back seat to personal advancement. They contracted to provide, supply, and lead troops and thus were more willing than the princes would have been to allow troops to live "economically" on plunder. All states and commanders strained to pay and supply their troops, but mercenary armies, and their generals, were especially difficult to control.

A series of treaties known as the Peace of Westphalia (1648) finally ended fighting in the empire. The treaties recognized Calvinism as a tolerated religion within the empire. The requirement that all subjects must follow their rulers' faith was retained, but some leeway was allowed for those who now found themselves under new rulers. The property of those who decided to move elsewhere for religious reasons was protected. In its recognition of religious plurality, the Peace of Westphalia effectively put an end to religious war in the empire. The rights of states, however, were still enforced over the desires of individuals.

In political matters, the treaties reflected some of the recent successes of the Swedish by granting them Baltic coast territory. France gained the important towns of Metz, Toul, and Verdun on its eastern border. Most of the major Catholic and Protestant rulers in the empire, such as the dukes of Bavaria and Saxony, extended their territories at the expense of smaller principalities and cities. The son of Frederick, king of Bohemia, was given the smaller of the two Palatine territories that his father had held. The Upper Palatinate—as well as the right to be a new elector of the emperor—was given to the powerful duke of Bavaria.

The most important political outcomes of the war were not explicitly mentioned in the peace treaties because no one needed to have them spelled out. One outcome was that the states within the empire would henceforth be virtually autonomous. From this point forward, each major state of the empire would conduct its own foreign policy; the Holy Roman Empire was no longer a meaningful political entity. Another outcome was that the Habsburgs, though weakened as emperors, were strengthened as rulers of their own hereditary lands on the eastern fringes of the empire. They moved their capital from Prague to Vienna, and the government of Habsburg lands gained in importance as administration of the empire waned.

SOCIETY AND CULTURE

Both imaginative literature and speculative writing, such as political theory, bear the stamp of their times. In the late sixteenth and early seventeenth centuries, political speculation often concerned questions of the legitimacy of rulers and of the relationship of political power to divine authority—urgent problems in an age when religious division threatened the very foundations of political order. The form as well as the content of thought reflected its context. Authors and rulers alike often relied on still-prevalent oral modes of communication. Indeed, some of the greatest literature of the period and some of the most effective political statements were presented as drama and not conveyed in print. Nevertheless, literacy continued to spread and led to greater opportunities for knowledge and reflection. The medium of print became increasingly important to political life. In the visual arts, the dramatic impulse was wedded to religious purposes to create works that conveyed both power and emotion.

Literacy and Literature

Traditional oral culture changed slowly under the impact of the spread of printing, education, and literacy. (See the feature, "Weighing the Evidence: Signatures," on pages 586–587.) Works of literature from the late sixteenth and early seventeenth century incorporate material from traditional folktales, consciously reflecting the coexistence of oral and literature culture. In *Don Quixote*, by Spain's Miguel de Cervantes (1547–1616), the title character and his companion, Sancho Panza, have a long discussion about the subject. The squire Panza

speaks in the style that was customary in oral culture—a rather roundabout and repetitive style, by our standards, that enabled the speaker and listener to remember what was said. Much of the richness of *Don Quixote* is due to the interweaving of prose styles and topical concerns from throughout Cervantes' culture—from the oral world of peasants to the refined world of court life. The detachment that enabled Cervantes to accomplish this rich portrayal came about from highly developed literacy and the awareness of language that literacy made possible.

The spread of education and literacy in the late sixteenth century had a dramatic impact on attitudes toward literature and on literature itself. The value of education—particularly of the continuing humanist recovery of ancient wisdom—was reflected in much literature of the period. Writers found in humanistic education a vision of what it meant to be cultivated and disciplined men of the world. This vision provided the beginnings of a new self-image for members of the warrior class.

Certain elite women who were able to secure a humanistic education were moved to reflect on their own situation in society. The French poet Louise Labé (1526–1566), writing in 1555, described the benefits of education for women but exaggerated its availability:

Since the time has come . . . when the severe laws of men no longer prevent women from applying themselves to the sciences and other disciplines, it seems to me that those of us who can should use this long-craved freedom to study and let men see how greatly they wronged us when depriving us of its honor and advantages. . . . Apart from the good name our sex will acquire thereby, we shall have caused men to devote more time and effort in the public good to virtuous studies.[3]

It is customary to regard the French author Michel de Montaigne (1533–1592) as the epitome of the reflective and—most important—*self*-reflective gentleman. Montaigne had trained for the law and became a judge in the Parlement of Bordeaux; he resigned from the court in 1570, however, and retired to his small chateau, where he wrote his *Essais* (from which we derive the word *essays*), a collection of short reflections that were revolutionary in both form and content. Montaigne invented writing in the form of a sketch, a "try" (the literal meaning of *essai*), which enabled him to combine self-reflection with formal analysis.

∽ ENCOUNTERS WITH THE WEST ∽

Montaigne Discusses Barbarity in the New World and the Old

In one of his most famous essays, Michel de Montaigne ironically compares the customs of Native Americans, about whom he has heard, with the customs of his own society.

They have their wars with [other] nations, to which they go quite naked, with no other arms than bows or wooden spears. . . . It is astonishing that firmness they show in their combats, which never end but in slaughter and bloodshed; for, as to routs and terror, they know nothing of either.

Each man brings back as his trophy the head of the enemy he has killed. . . . After they have treated their prisoners well for a long time with all the hospitality they can think of . . . they kill him with their swords. This done, they roast him and eat him in common and send some pieces to their absent friends.

I am not sorry that we notice the barbarous horror of such acts, but am heartily sorry that . . . we should be so blind to our own. I think there is more barbarity . . . in tearing by tortures and the rack a body still full of feeling, in roasting a man bit by bit, having him bitten and mangled by dogs (as we have not only read but seen within fresh memory . . . among neighbors and fellow citizens, and what is worse, on the pretext of piety and religion).

Three of these men (were brought to France) . . . and [someone] wanted to know what they had found most amazing. . . . They said that in the first place they thought it very strange that so many grown men, bearded, strong and armed who were around the king . . . should submit to obey a child. . . . Second (they have a way in their language of speaking of men as halves of one another), they had noticed that there were among us men full and gorged with all sorts of good things, and that their other halves were beggars at their doors, emaciated with hunger and poverty; and they thought it strange that these needy halves could endure such injustice.

Source: Donald M. Frame, trans., *The Complete Essays of Montaigne* (Stanford, Calif.: Stanford University Press, 1948), pp. 153, 155–159.

Montaigne's reflections ranged from the destructiveness of the French civil wars to the consequences of European exploration of the New World. Toward all of these events and circumstances, Montaigne was able to achieve an analytic detachment remarkable for his day. For example, he noted an irony in Europeans labeling New World peoples "savage," given Europeans' seemingly endless and wanton violence against those "savages" and against each other. (See the box, "Encounters with the West: Montaigne Discusses Barbarity in the New World and the Old.") He deflated pretensions to superiority in his own class of Frenchmen by noting "however high the chair, one is still sitting on one's own behind."

Montaigne's greatest achievement was the deep exploration of his own private moral and intellectual life, detached from any vocation or social role (though not detached, of course, from the leisure that his status made possible). Owing to the spread of printing and literacy, Montaigne had—in addition to his own effort and the resources of leisure—a virtually unparalleled opportunity to reflect on the world through reading the wide variety of printed texts available to him. For the first time, it was possible for the leisured lay reader to juxtapose different events, values, and cultures. Montaigne's writings thus reflect a distancing from his own society and a tolerance of others.

His essays also reveal a distancing from himself, and this distancing is another result of literacy—not simply the ability to read and write but the ability to put literacy to use so that one might enjoy long periods of solitude and reflection in the company of other solitary voices contained in books. Montaigne's works mark the beginning of what we know as the "invention" of private life, in which an individual is known more by internal character and personality traits than by social role and past behavior.

Dramatists, poets, and prose writers like Montaigne generally ask profound and in some ways timeless questions about the meaning of human experience; however, the kinds of questions thought important change as society changes. The works of the great English poet and playwright William Shakespeare (1564–1616) are still compelling to us because of the profundity of the questions he asked about love, honor, and political legitimacy, but he asked these questions in terms appropriate to his own day. One of his favorite themes—evident in *Hamlet* and *Macbeth*— is the legitimacy of rulers. He was at his most skilled, perhaps, when exploring the contradictions in values between the growing commercial world he saw around him and the older, seemingly more stable world of feudal society. Subtle political commentary distinguishes Shakespeare's later plays, written near and shortly after the death of Queen Elizabeth in 1603, when political and economic problems were becoming increasingly visible. Shakespeare explored not only the duties of rulers but also the rights of their subjects. In *Coriolanus*, he portrays commoners as poor but as neither ignorant nor wretched; they are in fact fully rational and capable of analyzing their situation—perhaps more capable, Shakespeare hints, than their ruler is. The play is safely set in ancient Rome, but the social and political tensions it depicts clearly referred to the Elizabethan present.

Shakespeare, Cervantes, and other writers of their day were also representatives of what were starting to be self-consciously distinct national literatures. The spread of humanism added a historical dimension to their awareness of their own languages and to their subject matter: their own society and its past. This kind of self-consciousness is evident in Shakespeare's play *Richard II*. The playwright depicts the kingdom of England, which King Richard is destroying, in terms that reflect the Elizabethan sense of England as a separate and self-contained nation:

This royal throne of kings, this sceptred isle,
This earth of majesty, this seat of Mars,
This other Eden, demi-paradise,
This fortress built by Nature for herself
Against infection and the hand of war,
This happy breed of men, this little world,
This precious stone set in the silver sea,
Which serves it in the office of a wall,
Or as [a] moat defensive to a house,
Against the envy of less happier lands;
This blessed plot, this earth, this realm, this England . . .
(*Richard II*, act 2, sc. 1, lines 40–50)[4]

The Great Age of Theater

Shakespeare's career was possible because his life coincided with the rise of professional theater. In the capitals of both England and Spain, professional theaters first opened in the 1570s. Some drama was produced at court or in aristocratic households, but most public theaters drew large and very mixed audiences, including the poorest city dwellers. Playwrights, including Shakespeare, often wrote in teams under great pressure to keep acting companies supplied with material. The best-known dramatist in Spain in this period, Lope de Vega (1562–1635), wrote more than fifteen hundred works with a wide range of topics. Although religious themes remained popular in Spanish theater, as an echo of medieval drama, most plays in England and Spain treated secular subjects and, as in *Coriolanus*, safely disguised political commentary.

Over time, theater became increasingly restricted to aristocratic circles. In England, Puritan criticism of the "immorality" of public performance drove actors and playwrights to seek royal patronage. The first professional theater to open in Paris, in 1629, as political and religious turmoil quieted, quickly became dependent on Cardinal Richelieu's patronage. Inevitably, as court patronage grew in importance, the wide range of subject matter treated in plays began to narrow to those of aristocratic concern, such as family honor and martial glory. These themes were depicted in the work of the Spaniard Pedro Calderón (1600–1681), who wrote for his enthusiastic patron, Philip IV, and in that of the Frenchman Pierre Corneille (1606–1684), whose great tragedy of aristocratic life, *Le Cid*, was one of the early successes of the seventeenth-century French theater.

That drama was one of the most important art forms of the late sixteenth and early seventeenth centuries is reflected in its impact on the development of music: The opera, which weds drama to music, was invented in Italy in the early seventeenth century. The first great work in this genre is generally acknowledged to be *Orfeo* (*Orpheus*, 1607) by Claudio Monteverdi (1567–1643). Opera, like drama, reflected the influence of humanism in its secular themes as well as a desire more precisely to emulate Greek drama, which had used both words and music. The practice of music itself changed under the dramatic impulse. Monteverdi was the first master of a new musical style known as monody, which emphasized the progression of chords. Monodic music was inherently dramatic, creating a sense of forward movement, expectation, and resolution.

Sovereignty in Ceremony, Image, and Word

Whether produced formally on a stage or in some less structured setting, drama was a favored method of communication in this era because people responded to and made extensive use of oral communication. Dramatic gesture and storytelling to get a message across were commonplace and were important components of politics.

What we might call "street drama" was an ordinary occurrence: When great noble governors entered major towns, such as when Margaret of Parma entered Brussels, a solemn yet ostentatious formal "entry" was often staged. The dignitary would ride into the town through its main gate, usually beneath a canopy made of luxurious cloth. The event might include staged tableaux in the town's streets, with costumed townspeople acting in brief symbolic dramas such as David and Goliath, and it might end in an elaborate banquet. A remnant of these proceedings survives today in the ceremony by which distinguished visitors are given "the keys to the city," which, in the sixteenth century, really were useful.

Royalty made deliberate and careful use of dramatic ceremony. Royal entries into towns took on an added weight, as did royal funerals and other occasions. These dramas reinforced political and constitutional assumptions in the minds of witnesses and participants. Thus, over time, we can see changes in the representations of royal power. In France, for example, the ritual entry of the king into Paris had originally stressed the participation of elites such as the leading guilds, judges, and administrators and had symbolized their active part in governing the city and the kingdom. But in the last half of the sixteenth century, the procession began to glorify the king alone.

The very fact that rulers experimented self-consciously with self-representation suggests that issues pertaining to the nature and extent of royal power were profoundly important and far from settled. Queen Elizabeth had the particular burden of assuming the throne in a period of great instability. Hence, she paid a great deal of attention to the image of herself that she fashioned in words and authorized to be fashioned in painting. Elizabeth styled herself variously as mother to her people and as a warrior-queen (drawing on ancient myths of Amazon women). She made artful use of the image of her virginity to buttress each of these images—as the wholly devoted, self-sacrificing mother (which, of course, had religious tradition behind it) or as an androgynous ruler, woman but doing the bodily work of man. (See the box, "Elizabeth I Addresses Her Troops.")

More formal speculation about constitutional matters also resulted from the tumult of the sixteenth and seventeenth centuries. The civil wars in France provided the impetus for energetic reconsideration of the principles and theories underlying royal government. The Huguenot party advanced an elaborate argument for the limitation of royal power, particularly after the Saint Bartholomew's Day Massacre. The best-known Huguenot tract (probably authored by the well-educated nobleman Philippe Duplessis-Mornay), *Defense of Liberty Against Tyrants* (1579), advanced the notion of a contract between the king and the people. Under the terms of this contract, obedience to the king was conditional, dependent on his acting for the common good—above all, maintaining and protecting God's true church.

Alternative theories enhancing royal authority were offered, principally in support of the Catholic position though also simply to buttress the beleaguered monarchy itself. The most famous of these appeared in *The Six Books of the Republic* (1576), by the legal scholar Jean Bodin (1530–1596). Bodin was a Catholic but offered a fundamentally secular perspective on the purposes and source of power

Elizabeth I Addresses Her Troops

The day after English ships dispersed the Spanish Armada in 1588, Elizabeth addressed a contingent of her troops. She used the opportunity to fashion an image of herself as a warrior above all but also as the beloved familiar of her people, unafraid of potential plots against her.

My loving people, we have been persuaded by some that are careful of our safety, to take heed how we commit ourselves to armed multitudes, for fear of treachery. But I assure you, I do not desire to live to distrust my faithful and loving people. Let tyrants fear. I have always so behaved myself that, under God, I have placed my chiefest strength in the loyal hearts and good will of my subjects; and therefore I am come amongst you, as you see, at this time, not for my reaction or disport, but being resolved, in the midst and heat of the battle, to live or die amongst you all, to lay down for my God, and for my kingdom, and for my people, my honor and my blood, even in the dust. I know I have the body of a weak and feeble woman, but I have the heart and the stomach of a king, and of a king of England too, and think foul scorn that Parma or Spain, or any prince of Europe should dare to invade the borders of my realm; to which, rather than any dishonor shall grow by me, I myself will take up arms, I myself will be your general, judge, and rewarder of every one of your virtues in the field.

Source: J. E. Neale, *Queen Elizabeth I* (New York: Anchor, 1957), pp. 308–309.

---

within a state. His special contribution was a vision of a truly sovereign monarch. Bodin offered theoretical understanding that is essential to states today and is the ground on which people can claim rights and protection from the state—namely, that there is a final sovereign authority. For Bodin that authority was the king. He recognized that in practice there were limitations to royal power, but it was the theoretical grounding for royal authority that interested Bodin.

French contract theory legitimized resistance to the Catholic monarchy but had to be abandoned when Henry IV granted toleration in 1598. In England, theoretical justification of resistance to Charles I was initially limited to invoking tradition and precedent; contract theory as well as other sweeping claims regarding subjects' rights would be more fully developed later in the century.

Bodin's theory of sovereignty, however, was immediately echoed in other theoretical works, most notably that of Hugo Grotius (1583–1645). A Dutch jurist and diplomat, Grotius developed the first principles of modern international law. He accepted the existence of sovereign states who owed no loyalty to higher authority (such as the papacy) and thus needed new principles to govern their interactions. His major work, *De Jure Belli ac Pacis (On the Law of War and Peace)* (1625), was written in response to the turmoil of the Thirty Years' War. Grotius argued that relations between states could be based on respect for treaties voluntarily reached between them. In perhaps his boldest move he argued that war must be justified and developed criteria to distinguish just wars.

Baroque Art and Architecture

Speculation about and celebration of power, as well as of dramatic emotion, also occurred in the visual arts—most notably in painting and architecture, in the style now known as "baroque." The word *baroque* comes from the Portuguese *barroco*, used to describe irregularly shaped pearls; the term as applied to the arts was initially derogatory, describing illogic and irregularity. Baroque architecture modified the precision, symmetry, and orderliness of Renaissance architecture to produce a sense of greater dynamism in space. Façades and

The Political Uses of Baroque Art This 1633 painting by Rubens was one of twenty-one commissioned by Marie de' Medici to celebrate her life and reign, after she was eclipsed as a power at her son's court. It commemorates the moment more than thirty years before when Henry IV first saw a likeness of Marie, his bride-to-be. The image is extravagant and fanciful by our standards, but also very engaging in its use of rich colors and flowing drapery, and in the beautifully executed figures of Jupiter and Juno, gazing down on Henry below them. *(Louvre/Giraudon/ Art Resource, NY)*

interiors were both massive and, through clever use of architectural and decorative components, suggestive of movement. Hence baroque churches, for example, were impressively grand and emotionally engaging at the same time. Baroque techniques were pioneered in Italy, first in church design, in the late sixteenth century and spread slowly, with many regional variations, especially throughout Catholic Europe, during the seventeenth century.

One of the primary purposes of baroque architecture and painting was to encourage piety that was emotionally involved but also capable of inspiring awe. Italian baroque painting made use of the realism developed in Renaissance art but added dynamism and emotional energy—such as by painting throngs of people or by using light to create direction and energy in the scene portrayed. Dramatic illusion was also a common device, such as painting a chapel ceiling with receding figures apparently ascending to heaven.

The most influential baroque painter in northern Europe was Peter Paul Rubens (1577–1640), a native of Flanders in the southern Netherlands.

His early career in Italy, from 1600 to 1608, was profoundly important both in shaping him as an artist and in establishing his secondary career as a diplomat, trusted by his princely patrons. Throughout his life, he undertook diplomatic missions, on behalf of the viceroys in the Spanish Netherlands, to Spain, France, and England, where he also gained artistic commissions. He simultaneously maintained a large studio in Antwerp where he could train students. Rubens's subject matter varied widely. It included church design and decoration as well as portraiture and landscapes. His technique was distinguished by the brilliant use of color and by the dynamic energy of his figures, often executed on a very large scale.

SUMMARY

The late sixteenth and early seventeenth centuries were an era of intense struggle over political and religious authority. Rulers everywhere, through a variety of expedients, tried to buttress and expand royal power. They were resisted by traditional centers of power, such as independent-minded nobles. But they were also resisted by the novel challenge of religious dissent, which empowered subjects both to claim a greater right to question authority and to risk more in their attempts to oppose it. In some areas of Europe, such as the Holy Roman Empire, the struggles reached some resolution. In other areas, such as England, decades of bloody conflict still lay ahead.

On the whole, these conflicts did not result in victories for ordinary people, since for the most part it was victorious elites who decided matters of religion and governance in their own interests. In addition, the difficult economic circumstances of these decades meant that working people, desperate for a secure livelihood, rioted or took up arms out of economic as well as religious concern.

Yet however grim the circumstances people faced, the technology of print and the spread of literacy helped spur speculative and creative works by providing the means for reflection and the audiences to receive it. Ironically, the increased importance of court life, although a cause of political strain, was also a source of patronage for art, literature, and drama. Some of the works we still value, such as Rubens's paintings, portray the splendor and power of court life. Other works, such as Shakespeare's plays, both reflect and re-flect on the tensions and contradictions in the society of the day: for example, the importance of the stability provided by royal authority and the dignity and wisdom of ordinary people, who had no claim to power at all.

NOTES

1. Quoted in A. W. Lovett, *Early Habsburg Spain, 1517–1598* (Oxford, England: Oxford University Press, 1986), p. 212.
2. Quoted in R. J. Knecht, *The French Wars of Religion, 1559–1598* (London: Longman, 1989), p. 109.
3. Quoted in Ann Rosalind Jones, "City Women and Their Audiences: Louise Labé and Veronica Franco," in Margaret W. Ferguson et al., *Rewriting the Renaissance: The Discourses of Sexual Difference in Early Modern Europe* (Chicago: University of Chicago Press, 1986), p. 307.
4. From *The Riverside Shakespeare*, 2d ed. (Boston: Houghton Mifflin, 1997), p. 855.

SUGGESTED READING

General Surveys

Bonney, Richard. *The European Dynastic States, 1494–1660.* 1991. A recent, rich survey of the period. Good on eastern as well as western Europe but written from an English point of view; thus, it does not consider England as part of Europe.

Elliott, J. H. *Europe Divided, 1559–1598.* 1968. An older but still reliable and readable survey by a leading scholar of Spanish history.

Hale, J. R. *War and Society in Renaissance Europe.* 1985. An analysis of war as a function of government and as a part of social, economic, and intellectual life through the sixteenth century.

Parker, Geoffrey. *The Military Revolution.* 1988; and Black, Jeremy. *A Military Revolution?* 1991. Two works that disagree about the nature and extent of the changes in military practices and their significance for military, political, and social history. Black tries to refute claims for a dramatic military "revolution."

Society and Economy

Braudel, Fernand. *The Perspective of the World.* Vol. 3, *Civilization and Capitalism, 15th to 18th Century.* Translated by S. Reynolds. 1984. A particularly useful volume by this celebrated author of economic history concerning overall patterns in the European and international economies.

Gutman, Myron P. *Toward the Modern Economy.* 1988. An account of the development of cloth production and the decline of guild manufacture through the early modern period.

Huppert, George. *After the Black Death: A Social History of Early Modern Europe.* 1986. A survey of developments in social and economic history throughout Europe from the fifteenth through the seventeenth centuries. A brief but very usable bibliography will guide further reading.

Jütte, Robert. *Poverty and Deviance in Early Modern Europe.* 1994. Discusses poverty, poor relief, and peasant rebellion.

Klaits, Joseph. *Servants of Satan.* 1985.

Levack, Brian P. *The Witch-Hunt in Early Modern Europe.* 1987. Two surveys of witch-hunting in the sixteenth and seventeenth centuries. Levack synthesizes the work of various historians with particular care; Klaits's work is more interpretive.

Wiesner, Merry. *Women and Gender in Early Modern Europe.* 1993. Discusses all aspects of women's experience, including their working lives.

Spain and the Dutch

Elliott, J. H. *Imperial Spain, 1469–1716.* 1963.

Lynch, John. *Spain, 1516–1598: From Nation-State to World Empire.* 1991. Two excellent surveys.

Parker, Geoffrey. *The Army of Flanders and the Spanish Road.* 1972. A detailed study of Spanish innovations in supplying its armies during the Netherlands' revolt.

———. *The Dutch Revolt.* 2d ed. 1985. The best survey of the revolt available in English.

Wedgewood, C. V. *William the Silent.* 1968. A sympathetic biography of the aristocratic leader of the Dutch revolt, which portrays him as a man ahead of his time in his acceptance of religious diversity. Useful for capturing the flavor of the period, though not for its interpretation.

France and England

Bercé, Yves-Marie. *The Birth of Absolutism: A History of France, 1598–1661.* 1992. A readable recent interpretation of the foundations of absolutism in France.

Diefendorf, Barbara. *Beneath the Cross: Catholics and Huguenots in Sixteenth-Century Paris.* 1991. Traces the intersection of political and religious conflict in the French capital during the religious wars. Excellent bibliography.

Hirst, Derek. *Authority and Conflict: England, 1603–1658.* 1986. A thorough study of political and social conditions in England.

Holt, Mack P. *The French Wars of Religion, 1562–1629.* 1995. An up-to-date synthesis that evaluates social and political context while not slighting the importance of religion.

Mattingly, Garrett. *The Armada.* 1959. A well-crafted and gripping narrative of the sailing of the Armada and all the interrelated events in France, the Netherlands, England, and Spain, told from a decidedly English perspective.

Smith, A. G. R. *The Emergence of a Nation-State: The Commonwealth of England, 1529–1660.* 1984. A good place to start through the immense bibliography on the Elizabethan period.

The Thirty Years' War and Its Aftermath

Evans, R. J. W. *The Making of the Hapsburg Monarchy.* 1979. A thorough survey of the rise of the Austrian Habsburg state from the breakup of Charles V's empire, emphasizing the importance of the ideology and institutions of Catholicism in shaping the identity and guaranteeing the coherence of the Habsburg state.

Parker, Geoffrey. *The Thirty Years' War.* 2d ed. 1987. A readable general history by one of the best-known military historians.

Literacy, Literature, and Political Theory

Church, William F. *Constitutional Thought in Sixteenth-Century France.* 1969. A survey of sixteenth-century political theory in France.

Eagleton, Terry. *William Shakespeare.* 1986. A brief and highly readable interpretation of Shakespeare that emphasizes the tensions in the plays caused by language and by ideas from the new world of bourgeois, commercial life.

Giesey, Ralph E. *The Royal Funeral Ceremony in Renaissance France.* 1960. One of the earliest studies of royal ceremony in the period.

Greenblatt, Stephen. *Renaissance Self-Fashioning.* 1979. An interpretation of sixteenth-century literature and culture that emphasizes the "invention" of interior self-reflection and self-awareness.

Houston, R. A. *Literacy in Early Modern Europe.* 1988. A general introduction to the issues of the spread of education and the impact of literacy in Europe.

Kamen, Henry. *The Rise of Toleration.* 1967. This older and rather optimistic study chronicles the slow emergence of secularism and toleration during and after the Reformation.

Kelley, Donald R. *The Beginnings of Ideology: Consciousness and Society in the French Reformation.* 1981. A study of political thought, including but not limited to formal theory, as inspired by the experience of the wars of religion.

Ong, Walter J. *Orality and Literacy: The Technologizing of the Word.* 1982. A synthesis of scholarship that concentrates on the psychological and cultural impact of literacy.

Patterson, Annabel. *Shakespeare and the Popular Voice.* 1989. An interpretation of Shakespeare's work that emphasizes his connection to the complex political and social milieu of his day.

Regosin, J. *The Matter of My Book: Montaigne's "Essais" as the Book of the Self.* 1977. One of the leading scholarly treatments of Montaigne's work.

Weighing the Evidence

SIGNATURES

Right now you are staring at words printed on the page of a book. We are so dependent on written communication that we cannot imagine functioning without these symbols. The often-heard warning "Don't believe everything you read" reflects our habit of trusting written information. But what might it be like if words were only fleeting events—spoken and heard in moments of personal interaction—and not things, objects gazed at in silence, easily saved and retrieved?

Let us consider what evidence we have about the spread of literacy in the sixteenth century. Historians have gained a rough idea about what portion of the population was literate in the sixteenth century by counting the signatures on representative samples of legal documents such as wills and marriage contracts. The ability to sign one's name is a fairly reliable indication of literacy in the sixteenth century because then, unlike today, writing was taught in schools only *after* reading was already mastered. For this reason, however, the *lack* of a signature may mask considerable reading ability, for no special significance was attached to learning to write one's name. Sixteenth-century documents are filled with signatures like those reproduced here: the scissors, for a tailor; the arrow, for a fletcher (arrow-maker). Both of the men who made these marks may well have been able to read.

Where documentation is dense, such as in towns, and where the evidence of signatures has been collected, we have profiles of the literacy rates of selected communities. Literacy rates varied widely according to the location of a particular community (remote ones had fewer literate inhabitants) and its economy (certain trades favored literacy; poverty generally worked against it). Overall, men were more literate than women, and western and northern Europeans were more literate than southern and eastern Europeans. In prosperous regions of western Europe, where literacy rates were highest, there was nearly 100 percent literacy, as one might predict, among bureaucrats, officials, and well-to-do townsmen. Among artisans, the rate neared 50 percent. Among peasants, it could be 10 percent or lower.

If we suppose these figures to be accurate, what can we conclude about the impact of literacy on people's lives? Our own reliance on literacy once led us to assume that people in the past would naturally use these skills if they knew how and that literate knowledge—gleaned from books—would quickly replace folk traditions and knowledge communicated orally. But the "signatures" of the tailor, the fletcher, and thousands of others imply that many Europeans lived with partial literacy. And we now realize that the spread of literacy only slowly changed Europeans' reliance on oral communication. Reading and writing supplemented but initially did not replace traditional ways of learning and communicating.

Aristocrats, for example, usually learned to read and write and occasionally were highly educated. But they learned their most valued skills, such as estate management and military expertise, from their older peers, rather as artisan children learned their skills through apprenticeship. Nobles kept copious written records about their landed property but often relied on memory instead of documents to settle disputes. At all levels of society, most reading was done in a group. It was integrated into the common entertainment of storytelling, illustrated in the drawing reproduced here. An evening's storytelling in a household or tavern might include reading aloud but was not fundamentally changed by the inclusion of reading.

Signatures from English Court Depositions *(Adapted from David Cressy,* Literacy and the Social Order *[Cambridge, England: Cambridge University Press, 1980], p. 60.)*

Tailor   Fletcher

Joseph Anton Koch: Shepherds Around the Fire *(Staatliche Kunstsammlungen Dresden/Kupferstich-Kabinett)*

There is evidence that people who could read still trusted written material less than, or at least no more than, spoken information. A literate peasant would consult a farmer's almanac, but more for entertainment than for information. His first-hand knowledge of the local climate, crops, and animal husbandry seemed more reliable to him—and was likely to be more reliable—than any text that a distant publisher might provide. Nobles frequently wrote brief letters to each other in which they said little other than "Please trust X, the bearer of this letter." The real message was imparted orally. It was face-to-face communication, built on a personal relationship, that was trusted.

Some of the most dramatic evidence of the persistence of oral culture is in the use of language that is preserved in informal documents such as long letters or the relatively rare memoir. Most people still relied on the repetitive phrasing that is common when language is wholly oral. Thus, even when they wrote words down, they were "thinking" without literacy.

Although we have learned that evidence of literacy does not mean that sixteenth-century people relied on reading and writing the way we do, we are just beginning to understand what their limited reliance on it really meant for their lives and their society. Access to literacy and the use of documents were tools of power and control. Our tailor might be at a disadvantage in a transaction if he could not read the document he signed. But unlike us, he did not need documents to establish his identity. And with virtually none of his past recorded in writing, he and other sixteenth-century people were free in ways that we are not.

Consider also the tenacity of oral communication. Let us set aside our assumption that written information is superior and try to imagine how powerful oral communication can be. Look carefully at the evidence supplied in the drawing of shepherds gathered around a fire. It dates from the late eighteenth century, when literacy was increasingly widespread and when the persistent oral culture of lower-class people was beginning to be derided in the way that illiteracy is derided today. The cultural gap between literate and illiterate is reflected here in the somewhat derisive representations of the subjects: They are made to seem uncouth. Yet still captured is something of the power of speech and of hearing. Words are events here, and speaker and listeners are active in their parts. The speaker gestures while his companions lean forward attentively to hear and perhaps to argue with him.

In an oral culture, information always is accompanied by sensory input: the sights, smells, and sounds of the person conveying it. And you always know your source. Is it any wonder that common people resisted the "authority" of book learning? ❧

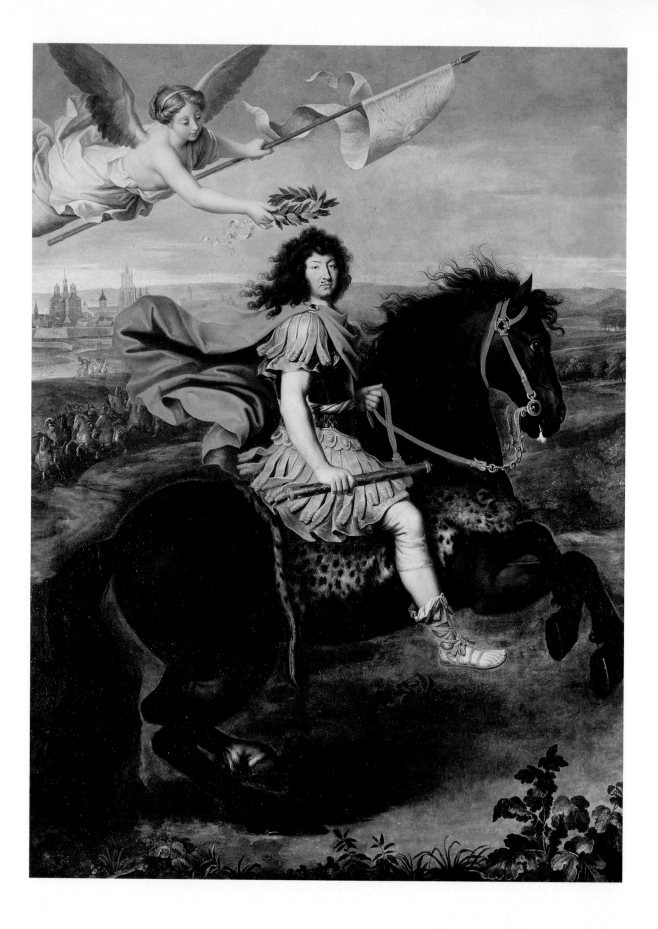

Europe in the Age of Louis XIV, ca. 1610–1715

Toward the end of his reign, the subjects of Louis XIV of France began to grumble that he had lived too long. In fact, he outlived his own son and grandson and was followed on the throne by a great-grandson when he died in 1715. In his prime, Louis symbolized the success of royal power in surmounting the challenges of warrior-nobles, in suppressing religious dissent, in tapping the wealth of the nation's population, and in waging war. A period of cultural brilliance early in his reign and the spectacle of an elaborate court life crowned his achievements. By the end of his reign, however, France was struggling under economic distress brought on by the many wars fought for his glory. Although Louis outlived his welcome, he was then, and is for us now, a symbol of the age that ended with his death.

In England, by contrast, the Crown was not as successful in overcoming political and religious challenges to its authority. Resistance to the king, led by Parliament, resulted in a revolutionary overturning of royal authority that was temporary but had long-term consequences. In central and eastern Europe, a period of state building in the aftermath of the Thirty Years' War led to the dominance in the region of Austria, Brandenburg-Prussia, and Russia. The power of these states derived, in part, from the economic relationship of their lands to the wider European economy.

The seventeenth century also witnessed a dynamic phase of European overseas expansion, following on the successes of the Portuguese and the Spanish in the fifteenth and sixteenth centuries. Eager migrants settled in the Americas in ever increasing numbers, while forced migrants— enslaved Africans—were transported by the thousands to work on the

The king in martial glory: Louis XIV in Roman armor, by the contemporary painter Charles Le Brun.

profitable plantations of European colonizers. Aristocrats, merchants, and peasants back in Europe jockeyed to take advantage of—or to mitigate the effects of—the local political and economic impact of Europe's expansion.

FRANCE IN THE AGE OF ABSOLUTISM

Absolutism describes the extraordinary concentration of power in royal hands achieved by the kings of France, most notably Louis XIV (r. 1643–1715), in the seventeenth century. Louis continued the expansion of state power begun by his father's minister, Cardinal Richelieu (see page 565). The extension of royal power, under Louis as well as his predecessor, was accelerated by the desire to sustain an expensive and aggressive foreign policy. The policy itself was a traditional one: fighting the familiar Habsburg enemy and seeking military glory more generally. Louis XIV's successes in these undertakings made him both envied and emulated by other rulers; the French court became a model of culture and refinement. But increased royal authority was not accepted without protest either by common French people or by elites.

The Last Challenge to Absolutism

Louis came to the throne as a 5-year-old child in 1643. Acting as his regent, his mother, Anne of Austria (1601–1666), had to defuse a serious challenge to royal authority during her son's minority. Together with her chief minister and personal friend, Cardinal Jules Mazarin (1602–1666), she faced opposition from royal bureaucrats and the traditional nobility as well as the common people.

Revolts against the concentration of power in royal hands and against high taxation that had prevailed under Louis's father began immediately. In one province, a group of armed peasants cornered the intendant and forced him to agree to lower taxes; elsewhere, provincial parlements tried to abolish special ranks of officials created by Richelieu. In 1648, after several more years of foreign war and of financial expedients to sustain it, the most serious revolt began, led by the Parlement and the other sovereign law courts in Paris.

The source of the Parlement's leverage over the monarchy was its traditional right to register laws and edicts, which amounted to a right of judicial review. Now, the Parlement, as the legitimate guardian of royal authority, attempted to extend this power by debating and even initiating government policy: The courts sitting together drew up a reform program abolishing most of the machinery of government established under Richelieu and calling for consent to future taxation. The citizens of Paris rose to defend the courts when royal troops were sent against them in October. In the countryside, the machinery of government, particularly tax collection, virtually ceased to function.

Mazarin was forced to accept the proposed reform of government, at least in theory. He also had to avert challenges by great nobles for control of the young king's council. Civil war waxed and waned around France from 1648 until 1653. The main combatants were conventionally ambitious great nobles, but reform-minded urban dwellers often had to make common cause with them, to benefit from their military power. Meanwhile, middling nobles in the region around Paris began to meet on their own to plan a thoroughgoing reform program and to prepare for a meeting of the Estates General to enact it.

These revolts, begun in 1648, were derided with the name "Fronde," which was a children's game of the time. However, the Fronde was a serious challenge to the legacy of royal government as it had developed under Richelieu. It ended without a noteworthy impact on the growth of royal power for several reasons. First, Mazarin methodically regained control of the kingdom through armed force and by making concessions to win the loyalty of individual aristocrats, always eager for the fruits of royal service. Meanwhile, the Parlement of Paris, as well as many citizens of the capital, welcomed a return to royal authority when civil war caused starvation as well as political unrest.

Moreover, the Parlement of Paris was a law court, not a representative assembly. Its legitimacy derived from its role as upholder of royal law, and it could not, over time, challenge the king on the pretext of upholding royal tradition in his name. Parlementaires tended to see the Estates General as a rival institution and helped quash the proposed meeting of an Estates General. Above all, they did not want reforms to include measures like the abolition of the paulette, a fee guaranteeing the hereditary right to royal office (see page 564), which were against their own self-interest.

Unlike in England, there was in France no single institutional focus for resistance to royal power. A strong-willed and able ruler, such as Louis XIV proved to be, could eclipse challenges to royal power, particularly when he satisfied the ambitions of aristocrats and those bureaucrats who profited from the expansion of royal authority.

France Under Louis XIV, 1661–1715

Louis XIV fully assumed control of government at Mazarin's death in 1661. It was a propitious moment. The Peace of the Pyrenees in 1659 had ended in France's favor the wars with Spain that had dragged on since the end of the Thirty Years' War. As part of the peace agreement, Louis married a Spanish princess, Maria Theresa. Louis had been called *le Dieudonné*, "the gift of God," when he was born in 1638, twenty years after his parents' marriage. He was physically attractive and extremely vigorous; he had been carefully and lovingly coached in his duties by Mazarin and by his mother, Queen Anne. Louis XIV proved a diligent king. He put in hours a day at a desk while sustaining the ceremonial life of the court with its elaborate hunts, balls, and other public events.

In the first ten years of his active reign, Louis achieved a degree of control over the mechanisms of government unparalleled in the history of monarchy in France or anywhere else in Europe. He did not invent any new bureaucratic devices but rather used existing ranks of officials in new ways that increased government efficiency and the centralization of control. He radically reduced the number of men in his High Council, the advisory body closest to the king, to include only three or four great ministers of state affairs. This intimate group, with Louis's active participation, handled all policymaking. The ministers of state, war, and finance were chosen exclusively from men of modest backgrounds whose training and experience fitted them for such positions. Jean-Baptiste Colbert (1619–1683), perhaps the greatest of them, served as minister of finance and of most domestic policy from 1665 until his death; he was from a merchant family and had served for years under Mazarin.

Several dozen other officials, picked from the ranks of up-and-coming lawyers and administrators, drew up laws and regulations and passed them to the intendants for execution at the provincial level. These officials at the center were often sent to the provinces as short-term intendants on special supervisory missions. The effect of this system was largely to bypass many entrenched provincial officials, particularly many responsible for tax collecting. The money saved by the more efficient collection of taxes enabled the government to streamline the bureaucracy: Dozens of the offices created to bring cash to the Crown were bought back by the Crown from their owners.

The system still relied on the bonds of patronage and personal service, however. Officials rose through the ranks by means of service to the great, and family connection and personal loyalty still were essential. Of the seventeen different men who were part of Louis XIV's High Council during his reign, five were members of the Colbert family, for example. In the provinces, important local families vied for minor posts, which at least provided prestige and some income.

Some of the benefits of centralized administration can be seen in certain achievements of the early years of Louis's regime. Colbert actively encouraged France's economic development. He reduced internal tolls and customs barriers, relics of medieval decentralization. He encouraged industry with state subsidies and protective tariffs. He set up state-sponsored trading companies—the two most important being the East India Company and the West India Company, established in 1664.

Mercantilism, the philosophy behind Colbert's efforts, stressed self-sufficiency in manufactured goods, tight control of trade to foster the domestic economy, and the absolute value of bullion. Capital for development—bullion—was presumed to be limited in quantity. Protectionist policies were believed necessary to guarantee a favorable balance of payments.

This static model of national wealth did not wholly fit the facts of growing international trade in the seventeenth century. Nevertheless, mercantilist philosophy was helpful to France. France became self-sufficient in the all-important production of woolen cloth, and French industry expanded notably in other sectors. Colbert's greatest success was the deliberate expansion of the navy and merchant marine. By 1677 the size of the navy had increased almost six times, to 144 ships. By the end of Louis XIV's reign, the French navy was virtually the equal of the English navy.

A general determination to manage national resources distinguished Louis's regime. Colbert and the other ministers began to develop the kind of planned government policymaking that we now take for granted. Partly by means of their itinerant supervisory officials, they tried to formulate and execute policy based on carefully collected information. How many men of military age were available? How abundant was the harvest? Answers to such questions enabled not only the formulation of sound economic policy but the deliberate management of production and services to achieve certain goals, such as the recruitment and supply of the king's vast armies.

Beginning in 1673, Louis tried to bring the religious life of the realm more fully under royal control by claiming for himself some of the church revenues and powers of appointment in France that still remained to the pope. Partly to bolster his position with the pope, he also began to attack the Huguenot community in France. He offered financial inducements for conversions to Catholicism, then quartered troops in Huguenots' households to force them to convert. In 1685 he declared that there was no longer any Protestant community, and he officially revoked the Edict of Nantes. A hundred thousand Protestant subjects who refused even nominal conversion to Catholicism chose to emigrate.

Despite the achievement of unprecedented centralized control, Louis's regime is poorly described by the term *absolutism*, which historians often apply to it. By modern standards, the power of the Crown was still greatly limited. Neither Louis nor his chief apologists claimed that he was all-powerful, in the sense of being above the law. Louis's foremost apologist, Bishop Jacques Bossuet (1627–1704), asserted that although the king was guided only by fear of God and his own reason in his application and interpretation of law, he was obligated to act within the law. The "divine right" of kingship, effectively claimed by Louis, did not mean unlimited power to rule; rather it meant that hereditary monarchy was the divinely ordained form of government, best suited to human needs.

Absolutism meant not iron-fisted control of the realm but rather the successful focusing of energy and loyalties on the Crown, in the absence of alternative institutions. The government functioned well in the opening decades of Louis's reign because his role as the focal point of power and loyalty was both logical, after the preceding years of

unrest, and skillfully exploited. Much of the glue holding together the absolutist state lay in informal mechanisms such as patronage and court life, as well as in the traditional hunt for military glory—all of which Louis amply supplied.

The Life of the Court

An observer comparing the way prominent noble families in the mid-sixteenth and mid-seventeenth centuries lived would have noticed striking differences. By the second half of the seventeenth century, most sovereigns or territorial princes had the power to crush revolts, and the heirs of the feudal nobility had to accommodate themselves to the increased power of the Crown. The nobility relinquished its former independence but retained economic and social supremacy and, as a consequence, considerable political clout. Nobles also developed new ways to safeguard their privilege by means of cultural distinctions. This process was particularly dramatic in France as a strong Crown won out over an independent and powerful nobility.

A sign of Louis's success in marshaling the loyalty of the aristocracy was the brilliant court life that his regime sustained. No longer able to wield independent political power, aristocrats lived at court whenever they could, where they could participate in the endless jostling for patronage and prestige—for commands in the royal army and for offices and honorific positions at court itself. Both women and men struggled to secure royal favor for themselves, their relations, and their clients. (See the box, "Politics and Ritual at the Court of Louis XIV.") In this environment, new codes of behavior were used to ensure their political and social distinctiveness. Elaborate rules of courtesy and etiquette regulated court life. Instead of safeguarding one's status with a code of honor backed up by force of arms, the seventeenth-century courtier relied on elegant ceremonial, precise etiquette, and clever conversation. (See the feature, "Weighing the Evidence: Table Manners," on pages 622–623.)

As literacy became more widespread, and the power of educated bureaucrats of humble origin became more obvious, more and more nobles from the traditional aristocracy began to use reading and writing as a means to think critically about their behavior—in the case of men, to reimagine them-

Politics and Ritual at the Court of Louis XIV

This document is from the memoirs of Louis de Rouvroy, duke of Saint-Simon (1675–1755), a favored courtier but one critical of Louis's power over the nobility. Notice his descriptions of court ceremony focusing on the most private moments of the king—an example of Louis's deliberate and exaggerated use of tradition, in this case of personal familiarity among warriors.

The frequent fetes, the . . . promenades at Versailles, the journeys, were means on which the king seized in order to distinguish or mortify courtiers, and thus render them more assiduous in pleasing him. He felt that of real favors he had not enough to bestow. . . . He therefore unceasingly invented all sorts of ideal ones, little preferences and petty distinctions, which answered his purpose as well.

He was exceedingly jealous of the attention paid him. . . . He looked to the right and to the left, not only upon rising but upon going to bed, at his meals, in passing through his apartments, or his gardens of Versailles . . . ; not one escaped him, not even those who hoped to remain unnoticed. He marked well all absences from court. . . .

At eight o'clock [every morning] the chief valet . . . woke the king. At the quarter [hour] the grand chamberlain was called, and those who had what was called the *grandes entrées*. The chamberlain or chief gentleman drew back the [bed] curtains and presented holy water from the vase. . . . The same officer gave [the king] his dressing gown; immediately after, other privileged courtiers entered, and then everybody, in time to find the king putting on his shoes and stockings. . . . Every other day we saw him shave himself; . . . he often spoke of [hunting] and sometimes said a word to somebody.

Source: Bayle St. John, trans., *The Memoirs of the Duke of Saint-Simon on the Reign of Louis XIV and the Regency*, 8th ed. (London: George Allen, 1913); quoted in Merry Wiesner et al., eds., *Discovering the Western Past*, 3d ed., vol. 2 (Boston: Houghton Mifflin, 1997), pp. 37–38.

selves as gentlemen rather than primarily as warriors. Noble women and men alike began to reflect on their new roles by means of writing—in letters, memoirs, and the first novels. A prominent theme of these works is the increasing necessity for a truly private life of affection and trust, with which to counterbalance the public façade necessary to an aspiring courtier. The most influential early French novel was *The Princess of Cleves* by Marie-Madeleine Pioche de la Vergne (1634–1693), best known by her title, Madame de Lafayette. Mme. de Lafayette's novel treats the particular difficulties faced by aristocratic women who, without military careers to buttress their honor, were more vulnerable than men to gossip and slander at court.

Louis XIV's court is usually associated with the palace he built at Versailles, southwest of Paris.

Some of the greatest talent of the day worked on the design and construction of Versailles from 1670 through the 1680s. It became a masterpiece of luxurious but restrained baroque styling—a model for royal and aristocratic palaces throughout Europe for the next one hundred years.

Before Louis's court settled in at Versailles, it traveled among the king's several chateaux in the countryside and in Paris, and in this period of the reign, court life was actually at its most creative and productive. These early years of Louis's personal reign were the heyday of French drama. The comedian Jean-Baptiste Poquelin, known as Molière (1622–1673), impressed the young Louis with his productions in the late 1650s and was rewarded with the use of a theater in the main royal palace in Paris. Like Shakespeare earlier in the

Louis at Versailles Louis XIV (center, on horseback) is pictured among a throng of courtiers at a grotto in the gardens of Versailles. The symbol of the sun appeared throughout the palace; the image of Louis as the "Sun King" further enchanced his authority. *(Château de Versailles/Art Resource, NY)*

century, Molière explored the social and political tensions of his day. He satirized the pretensions of the aristocracy, the social climbing of the bourgeoisie, the self-righteous piety of clerics. Some of his plays were banned from performance, but most not only were tolerated but were extremely popular with the elite audiences they mocked— their popularity is testimony to the confidence of Louis's regime in its early days.

Also popular at court were the tragedies of Jean Racine (1639–1699), who was for French theater what Shakespeare was to the English: the master of the poetic use of language. His plays, which treated familiar classical stories, focused on the emotional and psychological life of the characters and tended to stress the limits that fate places even on royal persons. The pessimism in Racine foreshadowed the less successful second half of Louis's reign.

Louis XIV and a Half-Century of War

Wars initiated by Louis XIV dominated the attention of most European states in the second half of the seventeenth century. Louis's wars sprang from traditional causes: the importance of the glory and dynastic aggrandizement of the king and the preoccupation of the aristocracy with military life.

But if Louis's wars were spurred by familiar concerns about territorial and economic advantage, they were more demanding on state resources than any previous wars.

In France and elsewhere, the size of armies and the need for greater state management of them grew markedly. The new offensive tactics developed during the Thirty Years' War (see page 576) changed the character of armies and hence the demands on governments to provide for them. A higher proportion of soldiers became gunners, and their effectiveness lay in how well they operated as a unit. Armies began to train seriously off the field of battle because drill and discipline were vital to success. The numbers of men on the battlefield increased somewhat, but the total numbers of men in arms supported by the state at any time increased dramatically once the organization to support them was in place. Late in the century, France kept about 400,000 men in arms when at war (which was most of the time).

Ironically, battles were not necessarily made more decisive by the great augmentation in army size. Most wars were still won by destroying enemy resources and by wearing down enemy forces. States that tended to matters off the battlefield such as recruitment and supply were most likely to be successful. Louis XIV's victories in the second half of the century are partly traceable to his regime's attention to such concerns.

Louis's first war reflected the continuing French preoccupation with Spanish power. The goal was territory along France's eastern border to add to the land recently gained by the Peace of Westphalia (1648) and the Peace of the Pyrenees (1659). Louis invoked rather dubious dynastic claims to demand, from Spain, lands in the Spanish Netherlands and the large independent county on France's eastern border called the Franche-Comté (Map 16.1).

War began in 1667. French troops first seized a wedge of territory in the Spanish Netherlands without difficulty and then, in early 1668, occupied the Franche-Comté. But the French retained only some towns in the Spanish Netherlands by the Treaty of Aix-la-Chapelle, which ended the brief conflict later that year. Louis had already begun to negotiate with the Austrian Habsburgs over the eventual division of Spanish Habsburg lands, for it seemed likely that the Spanish king, Charles II (r. 1665–1700), would die without heirs. So, for the moment, Louis was content to return the Franche-Comté, confident that he would get it back, and much more, in the future.

Louis's focus then shifted from Spain to a new enemy: the Dutch. The Dutch had been allied with France since the beginning of their existence as provinces in rebellion against Spain. The French now turned against the Dutch for reasons that reflect the growth of the international trading economy—specifically, the Dutch dominance of seaborne trade. The French at first tried to lessen the Dutch advantage in trade with tariff barriers against Dutch goods. But, after the easy victories of 1667–1668, Louis's generals urged action against the vulnerable Dutch lands. "It is impossible that his Majesty should tolerate any longer the insolence and arrogance of that nation," added the pragmatic Colbert in 1670.[1]

The Dutch War began in 1672, with Louis personally leading one of the largest armies ever fielded in Europe—perhaps 120,000 men. At the same time, the Dutch were challenged at sea by England. The English had fought the Dutch over these same issues, such as trade, in the 1650s; now Louis secretly sent the English king a pension to ensure his alliance with the French.

At first, the French were spectacularly successful against the tiny Dutch army. Louis, however, presumptuously overrode a plan to move decisively on Amsterdam so that he could preside at the solemn reinstatement of Catholic worship in one of the Dutch provincial cathedrals. The Dutch opened dikes and flooded the countryside to protect their capital, and what had begun as a French rout became a stalemate. Moreover, the Dutch were beating combined English and French forces at sea and were gathering allies who felt threatened by Louis's aggression. The French soon faced German and Austrian forces along their frontier, and, by 1674, the English had joined the alliance against France as well.

Nonetheless, the French managed to hold their own, and the Peace of Nijmegen, in 1678, gave the illusion of a French victory. Not only had the French met the challenge of an alliance against them, but Spain ceded them further border areas in the Spanish Netherlands as well as control of the Franche-Comté.

Ensconced at Versailles since 1682, Louis seemed to be at the height of his powers. Yet the Dutch War had in fact cost him more than he had gained. Meeting the alliance against him had meant

Map 16.1 Territorial Gains of Louis XIV, 1667–1715 Louis's wars, though enormously expensive for France, produced only modest gains of territory along France's eastern and northern frontiers.

fielding ever-increasing numbers of men—more than 200,000 in arms at one time. Internal reforms in government and finance ended under the pressure of paying for war, and old financial expedients of borrowing money and selling privileges were revived. Other government obligations, such as encouraging overseas trade, were neglected. Colbert's death in 1683 dramatically symbolized the end of an era of innovation in the French regime.

Louis's unforgiving Dutch opponent, William of Orange, king of England from 1689 to 1702, renewed former alliances against him. The war, now known as the Nine Years' War, or King William's War, was touched off late in 1688 by French aggression—an invasion of Germany to claim an in-

heritance there. In his ongoing dispute with the pope, Louis seized the papal territory of Avignon in southern France. Boldest of all, he helped the exiled Catholic claimant to the English crown mount an invasion to reclaim his throne.

A widespread war began with all the major powers—Spain, the Netherlands, England, Austria, the major German states—ranged against France. The French also carried the fighting abroad by seizing English territory in Canada. As with the Dutch War, the Nine Years' War was costly but had indecisive results on most fronts. And this time there was no illusion of victory for Louis. In the Treaty of Ryswick (1697), Louis had to give up most of the territories in Germany, the

Spanish Netherlands, and northern Spain that he managed to occupy by war's end. Avignon went back to the pope, and Louis gave up his contentious claim to papal revenues. The terrible burden of taxes to pay for the wars combined with crop failures in 1693 and 1694 caused widespread starvation in the countryside. French courtiers began to criticize Louis openly.

The final major war of Louis's reign, now called the War of Spanish Succession, broke out in 1702. In some ways it was a straightforward dynastic war in which France and its perennial Habsburg opponent had an equal interest. Both Louis and Holy Roman Emperor Leopold I (r. 1657–1705) hoped to claim for their heirs the throne of Spain, left open at the death in 1700 of the Spanish king, Charles II. A will of Charles II gave the throne to Louis's grandson, Philip of Anjou, who quickly proceeded to enter Spain and claim his new kingdom. War was made inevitable when Louis renounced one of the conditions of Charles's will by insisting that Philip's accession to the throne of Spain did not mean that he had abandoned his rights to the throne of France. This declaration was an act of sheer belligerence, for Philip was only third in line for the French throne. The Dutch and the English responded to the prospect of a Frenchman on the throne of Spain and the consequent disruption of the balance of power in Europe by joining the emperor in a formal Great Alliance in 1701. The Dutch and English also wanted to defend their colonial interests, since the French had already begun to profit from new trading opportunities with the Spanish colonies.

Again the French fought a major war on several fronts on land and at sea. Again the people of France felt the cost in crushing taxes worsened by harvest failures. Major revolts inside France forced Louis to divert troops from the war. For a time it seemed that the French would be soundly defeated, but they were saved by the superior organization of their forces and by dynastic accident: Unexpected deaths in the Habsburg family meant that the Austrian claimant to the Spanish throne suddenly was poised to inherit rule of Austria and the empire as well. The English, who were more afraid of a revival of unified Habsburg control of Spain and Austria than of French domination of Spain, began peace negotiations with France.

The Peace of Utrecht in 1713 resolved longstanding political conflicts and helped to set the agenda of European politics for the eighteenth century. Philip of Anjou became Philip V of Spain, but on the condition that the Spanish and French crowns would never be worn by the same monarch. To maintain the balance of power against French interests, the Spanish Netherlands and Spanish territories in Italy were ceded to Austria, which for many decades would be France's major continental rival. The Peace of Utrecht also marked the beginning of England's dominance of overseas trade and colonization. The French gave to England lands in Canada and the Caribbean and renounced any privileged relationship with Spanish colonies. England was allowed to control the highly profitable slave trade with Spanish colonies.

Louis XIV had added small amounts of strategically valuable territory along France's eastern border (see Map 16.1), and a Bourbon ruled in Spain. But the costs in human life and resources were great for the slim results achieved. Moreover, the army and navy had swallowed up capital for investment and trade; strategic opportunities overseas were lost, never to be regained. Louis's government had been innovative in its early years but remained constrained by traditional ways of imagining the interest of the state.

THE ENGLISH REVOLUTION

In England, unlike in France, a representative institution—Parliament—became an effective, permanent brake on royal authority. The process by which Parliament gained a secure role in governing the kingdom was neither easy nor peaceful, however. As we saw in Chapter 15, conflicts between the English crown and its subjects, focused in the Crown-Parliament conflict, concerned control over taxation and the direction of religious reform. Beginning in 1642, England was beset by civil war between royal and parliamentary forces. The king was eventually defeated and executed, and there followed a period when the monarchy was abolished altogether. The monarchy was restored in 1660, but Parliament retained a crucial role in governing the kingdom, a role that was confirmed when, in 1688, it again deposed a monarch whose fiscal and religious policies became unacceptable to its members.

Civil War and Revolution, 1642–1649

Fighting broke between Charles I and parliamentary armies in the late summer of 1642. The Long Parliament (see page 571) continued to represent a broad coalition of critics and opponents of the monarchy, ranging from aristocrats concerned primarily with the abuses of royal prerogative to radical Puritans eager for thorough religious reform and determined to defeat the king. Fighting was halfhearted, initially, and the tide of war at first favored Charles.

In 1643, however, the scope of the war broadened. Charles made peace with Irish rebels and brought Irish troops to England to help his cause. Parliament, in turn, sought military aid from the Scots in exchange for promises that Presbyterianism would become the religion of England. Meanwhile, Oliver Cromwell (1599–1658), a Puritan member of the Long Parliament and a cavalry officer, helped reorganize parliamentary forces in order to defeat the king's forces. The eleven-hundred-man cavalry trained by Cromwell and known as the "Ironsides" helped parliamentary and Scottish infantry defeat the king's troops at Marston Moor in July 1644. The victory made Cromwell famous.

Shortly afterward, Parliament reorganized its forces to create the New Model Army, rigorously trained like Cromwell's Ironsides. Sitting members of Parliament were barred from commanding troops, hence upper-class control of the army was reduced. This army played a decisive role not only in the war but also in the political settlement that followed the fighting.

The New Model Army won a convincing victory over royal forces at Naseby in 1645. In the spring of 1646, Charles surrendered to a Scottish army in the north. In January 1647, Parliament paid the Scots for their services in the war and took the king into custody. In the negotiations that followed, Charles tried to play his opponents off against each other, and, as he hoped, divisions among them widened.

Most members of Parliament were Presbyterians, Puritans who favored a strongly unified and controlled state church along Calvinist lines. They wanted peace with the king in return for acceptance of the new church structure and parliamentary control of standing militias for a specified pe-

riod. They did not favor expanding the right to vote or other dramatic constitutional or legal change. These men were increasingly alarmed by the rise of sectarian differences and the actual religious freedom that many ordinary people were claiming for themselves. With the weakening of royal authority and the disruption of civil war, censorship was relaxed and public preaching by ordinary women and men who felt a religious inspiration was becoming commonplace.

Above all, Presbyterian gentry in Parliament feared more radical groups in the army and in London that had supported them up to this point but favored more thoroughgoing reform. Most officers of the New Model Army, such as Cromwell, were Independents, Puritans who favored a decentralized church, a degree of religious toleration, and a wider sharing of political power among men of property, not just among the very wealthy gentry. In London, a well-organized artisans' movement known as the Levelers favored universal manhood suffrage, reform of law, and better access to education in addition to decentralized churches—in short, the separation of political power from wealth and virtual freedom of religion. Many of the rank and file of the army were deeply influenced by Leveler ideas.

In May 1647 the majority in Parliament voted to disband the New Model Army without first paying most of the soldiers' back wages and to offer terms to the king. This move provoked the first direct intervention by the army in politics. Representatives of the soldiers were chosen to present grievances to Parliament but, when this failed, the army seized the king and, in August, occupied Westminster, Parliament's meeting place. Independent and Leveler elements in the army debated the direction of possible reform to be imposed on Parliament. (See the box, "The Putney Debates.")

However, in November, Charles escaped from his captors and raised a new army among his erstwhile enemies, the Scots, who were also alarmed by the growing radicalism in England. Civil war began again early in 1648. Although it ended quickly with a victory by Cromwell and the New Model Army in August, the renewed war further hardened political divisions and enhanced the power of the army. The king was widely blamed for the renewed bloodshed, and the army did not

The Putney Debates

In October 1647, representatives of the Leveler movement in the army ranks confronted Independents—largely comprising the officer corps—in formally staged debates in a church at Putney, outside London. The debates reflected the importance of the army in deciding the shape of change. Reproduced here is one exchange between the Leveler representative, Thomas Rainsborough, advocating universal manhood suffrage, and Cromwell's fellow officer, Henry Ireton, who argues for a franchise more restricted to men of some means.

Rainsborough: . . . Really I think that the poorest he that is in England hath a life to live as the greatest he; and therefore truly, sir, I think it's clear, that every man that is to live under a government ought first by his own consent to put himself under that government; and I do think that the poorest man in England is not at all bound in a strict sense to that government that he hath not had a voice to put himself under; and I am confident that, when I have heard the reasons against it, that something will be said to answer those reasons, insomuch that I should doubt whether I was an Englishman or no, that should doubt of these things.

Ireton: That's this.

Give me leave to tell you, that if you make this the rule, I think you must fly for refuge to an absolute natural right, and you must deny all civil right; and I am sure it will come to that in the consequence. . . . I think that no person hath a right to an interest or share in the disposing of the affairs of the kingdom, and in determining or choosing those that shall determine what laws we shall be ruled by here, no person hath a right to this that hath not a permanent fixed interest in this kingdom, and those persons together are properly the represented of this kingdom, who taken together, and consequently are to make up the representers of this kingdom, are the representers, who taken together do comprehend whatsoever is of real or permanent interest in the kingdom, and I am sure there is otherwise (I cannot tell what), otherwise any man can say why a foreigner coming in amongst us, or as many as

will be coming in amongst us, or by force or otherwise settling themselves here, or at least by our permission having a being here, why they should not as well lay claim to it as any other. We talk of birthright. Truly birthright there is thus much claim: men may justly have by birthright, by their very being born in England, that we should not seclude them out of England. That we should not refuse to give them air and place and ground, and the freedom of the highways and other things, to live amongst us, not any man that is born here, though he in birth, or by his birth there come nothing at all that is part of the permanent interest of this kingdom to him. That I think is due to a man by birth. But that by a man's being born here he shall have a share in that power that shall dispose of the lands here, and of all things here, I do not think it a sufficient ground, but I am sure if we look upon that which is the utmost, within man's view, of what was originally the constitution of this kingdom, upon that which is most radical and fundamental, and which if you take away, there is no man hath any land, any goods, you take away any civil interest, and that is this: that those that choose the representers for the making of laws by which this state and kingdom are to be governed, are the persons who taken together, do comprehend the local interest of this kingdom; that is, the persons in whom all land lies, and those in corporations in whom all trading lies. This is the most fundamental constitution of this kingdom, and which if you do not allow, you allow none at all.

Source: G. E. Aylmer, ed., *The Levellers in the English Revolution* (Ithaca: Cornell University Press, 1975), pp. 100–101.

trust him to keep any agreement he might now sign. When Parliament, still dominated by Presbyterians, once again voted to negotiate with the king, army troops under a Colonel Thomas Pride prevented members who favored Presbyterianism or the king from attending sessions. The "Rump" Parliament that remained after "Pride's Purge" voted to try the king. Charles I was executed for "treason, tyranny and bloodshed" against his people on January 30, 1649.

The Interregnum, 1649–1660

A Commonwealth—a republic—was declared. Executive power resided in a council of state. Legislative power resided in a one-chamber Parliament, the Rump Parliament (the House of Lords was abolished). Declaring a republic proved far easier than running one, however. The execution of the king shocked most English and Scots people and alienated many elites from the new regime.

The legitimacy of the Commonwealth government would always be in question.

The tasks of making and implementing policy were made difficult by the narrow political base on which the government now rested. Excluded were the majority of the reformist gentry who had been purged from Parliament. Also excluded were the more radical Levelers; Leveler leaders in London were arrested when they published tracts critical of the new government. Within a few years, many disillusioned Levelers would join a new religious movement called the Society of Friends, or Quakers, which espoused complete religious autonomy. Quakers refused all oaths or service to the state, and they refused to acknowledge social rank.

Above all, the new government was vulnerable to the power of the army, which had created it. In 1649 and 1650 Cromwell led expeditions to Ireland and Scotland, partly for sheer revenge and partly to put down resistance to the new English government. In Ireland, Cromwell's forces acted with great ruthlessness. English control there was

Popular Preaching in England Many women took advantage of the collapse of royal authority to preach in public—a radical activity for women at the time. This print satirizes the Quakers, a religious movement that attracted many women. *(Mary Evans Picture Library)*

furthered by more dispossession of Irish land-holders, which also served to pay off the army's wages. Meanwhile, Parliament could not agree on systematic reforms, particularly the one reform Independents in the army insisted on: more broadly based elections for a new Parliament. Fresh from his victories in the north, Cromwell led his armies to London and dissolved Parliament in the spring of 1652.

In 1653 some army officers drew up the "Instrument of Government," England's first and only written constitution. It provided for an executive, the Lord Protector, and a Parliament to be based on somewhat wider male suffrage. Cromwell was the natural choice for Lord Protector, and whatever success the government of the Protectorate had was largely due to him.

Cromwell was an extremely able leader who was not averse to compromise. Although he had used the army against Parliament in 1648, he had worked hard to reconcile the Rump Parliament and the army before marching on London in 1652. He believed in a state church, but one that allowed for control, including choice of minister, by local congregations. He also believed in toleration for other Protestant sects, as well as for Catholics and Jews, as long as no one disturbed the peace.

As Lord Protector, Cromwell oversaw impressive reforms in law that testify to his belief in the limits of governing authority. For example, contrary to the practice of his day, he opposed capital punishment for petty crimes. The government of the Protectorate, however, accomplished little because Parliament remained internally divided and opposed to Cromwell's initiatives. Cromwell was challenged by radical republicans in Parliament who thought the Protectorate represented a step backward, away from republican government. In the population at large, there were still royalist sympathizers, and a royalist uprising in 1655 forced the temporary division of England into military districts administered by generals.

In the end, the Protectorate could not survive the strains over policy and the challenges to its legitimacy. When Cromwell died of a sudden illness in September 1658, the Protectorate did not long survive him. In February 1660, the decisive action of one army general seeking a solution to the chaos enabled all the surviving members of the Long Parliament to rejoin the Rump. The Parliament summarily dissolved itself and called for new elections.

Oliver Cromwell Cromwell had seen his family's income decline under the weight of Charles I's exactions. Elected to Parliament in 1628 and again in 1640, he also brought a long-standing religious zeal to his public life. His opposition to the "tyranny and usurpation" of the Anglican church hierarchy first prompted him to criticize royal government. *(In the collection of the Duke of Buccleuch and Queensberry KT)*

The newly elected Parliament recalled Charles II, son of Charles I, from exile abroad and restored the monarchy. The chaos and radicalism of the late civil war and interregnum—the period between reigns, as the years from 1649 to 1660 came to be called—now spawned a conservative reaction.

The Restoration, 1660–1685

Charles II (r. 1660–1685) claimed his throne at the age of 30. He had learned from his years of uncertain exile and from the fate of his father. He did not seek retribution but rather offered a general pardon to all but a few rebels (mostly those who had signed his father's death warrant), and he suggested to Parliament a relatively tolerant religious settlement that would include Anglicans as well as

Presbyterians. He was far more politically adept than his father and far more willing to compromise.

That the re-established royal government was not more tolerant than it turned out to be was not Charles's doing but Parliament's. During the 1660s, the "Cavalier" Parliament, named for royalists in the civil war, passed harsh laws aimed at religious dissenters. Anglican orthodoxy was reimposed, including the re-establishment of bishops and the Anglican *Book of Common Prayer*. All officeholders and clergy were required to swear oaths of obedience to the king and to the established church. As a result, hundreds of them were forced out of office. Holding nonconformist religious services became illegal, and Parliament passed a "five-mile" act to prevent dissenting ministers from traveling near their former congregations. Property laws were strengthened and the criminal codes made more severe.

The king's behavior began to mimic prerevolutionary royalist positions. Charles II began to flirt with Catholicism, and his brother and heir, James, openly converted. Charles promulgated a declaration of tolerance that would have included Catholics as well as nonconformist Protestants, but Parliament would not accept it. When Parliament moved to exclude the Catholic James from succession to the throne, Charles dissolved it. A subsequent Parliament, cowed by fears of a new civil war, backed down. By the end of his reign, Charles was financially independent of Parliament thanks to increased revenue from overseas trade and to secret subsidies from France, his recent ally against Dutch trading rivals.

Underneath this seeming return to a prerevolutionary status quo were conditions that reflected the legacy of the revolution that had cost Charles I his head. First, despite the harsh laws, to silence all dissent was not possible. After two decades of religious pluralism and broadly based political activity it was impossible to reimpose conformity; there were well-established communities of various sects and a self-confidence that bred vigorous resistance. Also, anti-Catholic feeling still united all Protestants. In 1678 Charles's secret treaties with the French became known, and rumors of a Catholic plot to murder Charles and reimpose Catholicism became widespread. No evidence of any plot was ever unearthed, though thirty-five people were executed for alleged participation. Parliament focused its attention on anti-Catholi-

cism, passing an act barring all but Anglicans from Parliament itself.

The clearest reflection of the regime's revolutionary background was the power of Parliament: It was able to assert its policies against the desires of the king. Nevertheless, financial independence and firm political tactics enabled Charles to retain a great deal of power. If he had been followed by an able successor, Parliament might have lost a good measure of its confidence and independence. But his brother James's reign and its aftermath further enhanced Parliament's power.

The Glorious Revolution, 1688

When James II (r. 1685–1689) succeeded Charles, Parliament's royalist leanings were at first evident. James was granted customs duties for life and was also given funds to suppress a rebellion by one of Charles's illegitimate sons. James did not try to impose Catholicism on England, but he did try to achieve toleration for Catholics in two declarations of indulgence in 1687 and 1688. His efforts were undermined by his heavy-handed tactics. When several leading Anglican bishops refused to read the declarations from their pulpits, he had them imprisoned and tried for seditious libel. The jury, however, acquitted them.

James also failed because of the coincidence of other events. In 1685, at the outset of James's reign, Louis XIV in France had revoked the Edict of Nantes. The possibility that subjects and monarchs in France and, by extension, elsewhere could be of different faiths seemed increasingly unlikely. Popular fears of James's Catholicism were thus heightened early in his reign, and his later declarations of tolerance, though benefiting Protestant dissenters, were viewed with suspicion. In 1688, not only were the Anglican bishops acquitted but the king's second wife, who was Catholic, gave birth to a son. The birth raised the specter of a Catholic succession.

In June 1688, to put pressure on James, leading members of Parliament invited William of Orange, husband of James's Protestant daughter, Mary, to come to England. William mounted an invasion that became a rout when James refused to defend his throne. James simply abandoned England and went to France. William called Parliament, which declared James to have abdicated and offered the throne to him and to Mary. James eventually invaded Ireland in 1690 with French support but was defeated by William at the Battle of Boyne that year.

The substitution of William (r. 1689–1702) and Mary (r. 1689–1694) for James, known as the "Glorious Revolution," was engineered by Parliament and confirmed its power. Parliament presented the new sovereigns with a Declaration of Rights upon their accession and, later that year, with a Bill of Rights that defended freedom of speech, called for frequent Parliaments, and required subsequent monarchs to be Protestant. The effectiveness of these documents was reinforced by Parliament's power of the purse. Parliament's role in the political process was ensured by William's interests in funding his ambitious military efforts, particularly to support the Netherlands' ongoing wars with France.

The issues that had faced the English since the beginning of the century were common to all European states: religious division and elite power, fiscal strains and resistance to taxation. Yet events in England had so far set it apart from the experience of other states in that the incremental assumption of authority by a well-established institution, Parliament, made challenge of the monarchy more legitimate and more effective. Political participation also developed more broadly in England than in other states. In the long run, the strength of Parliament would make easier the task of permanently broadening participation in government.

NEW POWERS IN CENTRAL AND EASTERN EUROPE

By the end of the seventeenth century, three states dominated central and eastern Europe: Austria, Brandenburg-Prussia, and Russia. After the Thirty Years' War, the Habsburgs' power as emperors waned, and their interest in the coherence of their own territories, which centered on Austria, grew. Brandenburg-Prussia, in northeastern Germany, grew to a position of power rivaling that of the Habsburg state. The rulers of Brandenburg-Prussia had gained lands in the Peace of Westphalia, and astute management transformed their relatively small and scattered holdings into one of the most powerful states in Europe. Russia's new stature in eastern Europe resulted in part from the weakness of its greatest rival, Poland, and the determination of one leader, Peter the Great, to as-

sume a major role in European affairs. Sweden controlled valuable Baltic territory through much of the century but by the end of the century was also eclipsed by Russia as a power in the region.

The development of and the competition among states in central and eastern Europe was closely linked to developments in western Europe. This was true politically and strategically as well as economically. One of the most important factors influencing the internal political development of these states was their relationship to the wider European economy: They were sources of grain and raw materials for the more densely urbanized west.

The Consolidation of Austria

The Thirty Years' War (see pages 571–577) weakened the Habsburgs as emperors but strengthened them in their own lands. The main Habsburg lands in 1648 were a collection of principalities comprising modern Austria, the kingdom of Hungary (largely in Turkish hands), and the kingdom of Bohemia (see Map 16.2). In 1713 the Peace of Utrecht ceded the Spanish Netherlands to Austria and renamed them the "Austrian Netherlands." Although language and ethnic differences prevented an absolutist state along French lines, Leopold I (r. 1657–1705) instituted political and institutional changes that enabled the Habsburg state to become one of the most powerful states in Europe through the eighteenth century.

Much of the coherence that already existed in Leopold's lands had been achieved by his predecessors in the wake of the Thirty Years' War. The lands of rebels in Bohemia had been confiscated and redistributed among loyal, mostly Austrian, families. In return for political and military support for the emperor, these families were given the right to exploit their newly acquired land and the peasants who worked it. The desire to recover population and productivity after the destruction of the Thirty Years' War gave landlords further incentive to curtail peasants' autonomy sharply, particularly in devastated Bohemia. Austrian landlords throughout the Habsburg domains provided grain and timber for the export market and grain and other foodstuffs for the Austrian armies, and elite families provided the army with officers. This political-economic arrangement provoked numerous serious peasant revolts, but the peasants were not able to force changes in a system that suited both the elites and the central authority.

Although Leopold had lost much influence within the empire itself, an imperial government made up of various councils, a war ministry, financial officials, and the like still functioned in his capital, Vienna. Leopold worked to extricate the government of his own lands from the apparatus of imperial institutions, which were staffed largely by Germans more loyal to imperial than to Habsburg interests. In addition, Leopold used the Catholic church as an institutional and ideological support for the Habsburg state.

Leopold's personal preoccupation was the re-establishment of zealous Catholicism throughout his territories. Acceptance of Catholicism became the litmus test of loyalty to the Habsburg regime,

Celebrating Habsburg Power Leopold I is depicted here trampling a Turkish soldier, wearing armor and a medieval order of knighthood around his neck—appropriate garb with which to represent a victory over "the Infidel." Compare this illustration with the painting of Louis XIV in Roman armor on page 588. *(Kunsthistorisches Museum, Vienna)*

and Protestantism vanished among elites. Leopold encouraged the work of Jesuit teachers and members of other Catholic orders. These men and women helped staff his government and administered religious life down to the most local levels.

Leopold's most dramatic success, as a Habsburg and as a religious leader, was his reconquest of the kingdom of Hungary from the Ottoman Empire. Since the mid-sixteenth century, the Habsburgs had controlled only a narrow strip of the kingdom. Preoccupied with countering Louis XIV's aggression, Leopold did not himself choose to begin a reconquest. His centralizing policies, however, alienated nobles and townspeople in the portion of Hungary he did control, as did his repression of Protestantism, which had flourished in Hungary. Hungarian nobles began a revolt, aided by the Turks, aiming for a reunited Hungary under Ottoman protection.

The Habsburgs emerged victorious in part because they received help from, among others, the talented Polish king, Jan Sobieski, whose own lands in Ukraine were threatened by the Turks. The Turks overreached their supply lines to besiege Vienna in 1683. After the siege failed, Habsburg armies slowly pressed east and south, recovering Buda, the capital of Hungary, in 1686 and Belgrade in 1688. The Danube basin lay once again in Christian hands.

Leopold gave land in the reclaimed kingdom to Austrian officers whom he believed were loyal to him. The traditions of Hungarian separatism, however, were strong, and the great magnates—whether they had defended the Habsburgs against Turkish encroachment or guarded the frontier for Turkish overlords—retained their independence. The peasantry, as elsewhere, suffered a decline in status as a result of the Crown's efforts to ensure the loyalty of elites. In the long run, Hungarian independence weakened the Habsburg state, but in the short run Leopold's victory over the Turks and the recovery of Hungary itself were momentous events, confirming the Habsburgs as the preeminent power in central Europe.

The Rise of Brandenburg-Prussia

Three German states, in addition to Austria, gained territory and stature after the Thirty Years' War: Bavaria, Saxony, and Brandenburg-Prussia. By the end of the seventeenth century, the strongest was

Brandenburg-Prussia, a conglomeration of small territories held, by dynastic accident, by the Hohenzollern family. The two principal territories were electoral Brandenburg, in northeastern Germany, with its capital, Berlin, and the duchy of Prussia, a fief of the Polish crown along the Baltic coast east of Poland proper (see Map 16.2). In addition there was a handful of small principalities near the Netherlands. The manipulation of resources and power that enabled these unpromising lands to become a powerful state was primarily the work of Frederick William, known as "the Great Elector" (r. 1640–1688).

Frederick William used the occasion of a war to effect a permanent change in the structure of government. He took advantage of a war between Poland and its rivals, Sweden and Russia (the First Great Northern War, described in the next section), to win independence for the duchy of Prussia from Polish overlordship. When his involvement in the war ended in 1657, he kept intact the general war commissariat, a combined civilian and military body that had efficiently directed the war effort; he thus bypassed traditional councils and representative bodies. He also used the standing army to force the payment of high taxes. Most significantly, he established a positive relationship with the *Junkers,* hereditary landholders, which assured him both revenue and loyalty. He agreed to allow the Junkers virtually total control of their own lands in return for their agreement to support his government—in short, to surrender their accustomed political independence.

Peasants and townspeople were taxed, but nobles were not. The freedom to control their estates led many nobles to invest in profitable agriculture for the export market. The peasants were serfs who received no benefits from the increased productivity of the land. Frederick William further enhanced his state's power by sponsoring state industries. These industries did not have to fear competition from urban producers because the towns had been frozen out of the political process and saddled with heavy taxes. Although an oppressive place for many Germans, Brandenburg-Prussia attracted many skilled refugees, such as Huguenot artisans fleeing Louis XIV.

Bavaria and Saxony, in contrast to Brandenburg-Prussia, had vibrant towns, largely free peasantries, and weaker aristocracies but were less powerful in international affairs. Power on the European stage depended on military force. Such power, whether in a large state like France or in a small one like Brandenburg-Prussia, usually came at the expense of the state's inhabitants.

Competition Around the Baltic: The Demise of the Polish State and the Zenith of Swedish Power

The rivers and port cities of the Baltic coast were conduits for the growing trade between the Baltic hinterland and the rest of Europe; tolls assessed on the passage of timber, grain, and naval stores were an important source of local income, and the commodities themselves brought profits to their producers. This trading system had profound social and political consequences for all of the states bordering the Baltic Sea in the seventeenth century.

First, it was a spur to war: Sweden and Denmark fought over control of the sea-lanes connecting the Baltic and North Seas. Sweden, Poland, and Russia fought for control of the eastern Baltic coastline in the sixteenth and seventeenth centuries. In the seventeenth century, Poland and Russia fought over grain- and timber-producing lands comprising modern Belarus, parts of modern Russia, and Ukraine. Second, profits from the production of grain for export in such volume reinforced the power of large landholders, particularly within Poland, where most of the grain was produced.

In 1600 a large portion of the Baltic hinterland lay under the control of Poland-Lithuania, a dual kingdom at the height of its power (Map 16.2). A marriage in 1386 had brought the duchy of Lithuania under a joint ruler with Poland; earlier in the fourteenth century, Lithuania had conquered Belarus and Ukraine. Poland-Lithuania commanded considerable resources, including the Vistula and Niemen Rivers and the ports of Gdansk and Riga on the Baltic coast. Like the neighboring Habsburg lands, it was a multi-ethnic state, particularly in the huge duchy of Lithuania, where Russian-speakers predominated. Poland was Catholic but had a large minority of Protestants and Jews. Owing to ties with Poland, Lithuanians themselves were mostly Catholic (and some were Protestant), but Russian-speakers were Orthodox. German-speaking families dominated trade in most coastal cities.

Internal strains and external challenges began to mount in Poland-Lithuania in the late sixteenth century. The economic power of Polish landlords

Map 16.2 New Powers in Central and Eastern Europe The balance of power in central and eastern Europe shifted with the strengthening of Austria, the rise of Brandenburg-Prussia, and the expansion of Russia at the expense of Poland and Sweden.

gave them considerable political clout; the king was forced to grant concessions that weakened urban freedoms and bound peasants to the nobles' estates. In 1572 the sudden death of the very able but childless king, Sigismund II (r. 1548–1572), only enhanced the nobles' power. Sigismund's successors would be elected, would have no voice in the succession, and would be closely supervised by noble counselors.

The spread of the Counter-Reformation, encouraged by the Crown, created tensions with both Protestant and Orthodox subjects in the diverse kingdom. In Ukraine, communities of Cossacks, nomadic farmer-warriors, grew as Polish and Lithuanian peasants fled harsh conditions to join them. The Cossacks had long been tolerated because they were a military buffer against the Ottoman Turks to the south, but now Polish landlords wanted to reincorporate the Cossacks into the profitable political-economic system that they controlled. Meanwhile, the Crown was involved in several wars. From 1609 to 1612 Polish armies tried but failed to impose a Polish king on the Russians during a dispute over the succession. While aiding Austria in the Thirty Years' War against the Turks, their common enemy, the Poles lost Livonia (modern Latvia) and other bits of northern territory to the aggressive Gustav Adolf of Sweden.

In 1648 the Polish crown faced revolt and invasion that it could not counter. The Cossacks, with the Crimean Tatars and their Ottoman overlords as allies, staged a major revolt, defeated Polish armies, and established an independent state. In 1654 the Cossacks transferred their allegiance to Moscow and became part of a Russian invasion of Poland that, by the next year, had engulfed much of the eastern half of the dual kingdom. At the same time, the Swedes seized central Poland and competed with the Russians for control elsewhere; the Swedes were helped by Polish and Lithuanian aristocrats acting like independent warlords.

Often called the First Great Northern War, this war is remembered in Poland as "the Deluge." Polish royal armies managed to recover much territory—most important, the western half of Ukraine. But the invasions and subsequent fighting were disastrous. The population of Poland may have declined by as much as 40 percent, and vital urban economies were in ruins. The Catholic identity of the Polish heartland had been a rallying point for resistance to the Protestant Swedes and the Ortho-

dox Russians, but the religious tolerance that had distinguished the Polish kingdom and had been mandated in its constitution was thereafter abandoned. In addition, much of its recovery of territory was only nominal. In parts of Lithuania inhabited by Russian-speaking peoples, the Russian presence during the wars had achieved local transfers of power from Lithuanian to Russian landlords loyal to Moscow.

The elective Polish crown passed in 1674 to the brilliant military commander Jan Sobieski (r. 1674–1696), known as "Vanquisher of the Turks" for his victory in raising the siege of Vienna. Given Poland's internal weakness, however, Sobieski's victories in the long run helped the Austrian and Russian rivals of the Turks more than they helped the Poles. His successor, Augustus II of Saxony (r. 1697–1704, 1709–1733), dragged Poland back into war, from which Russia would emerge the obvious winner in the power struggle in eastern Europe.

On the Baltic coast, however, Sweden remained the dominant power through most of the seventeenth century. Swedish efforts to control Baltic territory began in the sixteenth century, first to counter the power of its perennial rival, Denmark, in the western Baltic. It then competed with Poland to control Livonia, whose principal city, Riga, was an important trading center for goods from both Lithuania and Russia. By 1617, under Gustav Adolf, the Swedes gained the lands to the north surrounding the Gulf of Finland (the most direct outlet for Russian goods) and in 1621 displaced the Poles in Livonia itself. Swedish intervention in the Thirty Years' War came when imperial successes against Denmark both threatened the Baltic coast and created an opportunity to strike at Sweden's old enemy. The Treaty of Westphalia (1648) confirmed Sweden's earlier gains and added control of further coastal territory, mostly at Denmark's expense.

The port cities held by Sweden were indeed profitable but simply served to pay for the costly wars necessary to seize and defend them. All of these efforts to hold Baltic territory were driven by dynastic and strategic needs as much as economic rationales. The ruling dynasty struggled against Denmark's control of western Baltic territory in order to safeguard its independence from the Danes, who had ruled the combined kingdoms until 1523. Similarly, competition with Poland for the east Baltic was part of a dynastic struggle after

War for the Baltic Control of the Baltic littoral was hotly contested throughout the seventeenth century. While fighting in Poland during the First Great Northern War, the Swedes were attacked, in turn, by their longstanding rivals, the Danes. The Swedish king, Karl Gustav, marched his army over frozen sea lanes and beat the Danes at the Battle of Ifveros, depicted here, in the winter of 1658. *(National Museum of Stockholm)*

1592. Sigismund Vasa, son of the king of Sweden, had been elected king of Poland in 1587 but also inherited the Swedish throne in 1592. Other members of the ruling Swedish Vasa family fought him successfully to regain rule over Sweden and extricate Swedish interests from Poland's continental preoccupations. Sigismund ruled Poland until his death in 1632 but was replaced on the Swedish throne by an uncle in 1604.

The one permanent gain that Sweden realized from its aggression in the First Great Northern War was the renunciation of the Polish Vasa line to any claim to the Swedish crown. Owing to its earlier gains, Sweden remained the dominant power on the Baltic coast until the end of the century, when it was supplanted by the powerful Russian state.

The Expansion of Russia: From Ivan "the Terrible" Through Peter "the Great"

The Russian state expanded dramatically through the sixteenth century. Ivan IV (r. 1533–1584) was proclaimed "Tsar [Russian for "Caesar"] of All the Russias" in 1547. This act was the culmination of the accumulation of land and authority by the princes of Moscow through the late Middle Ages, when Moscow had vied for pre-eminence with other Russian principalities. Ivan IV's grandfather, Ivan III (r. 1462–1505), the first to use the title *tsar*, had absorbed neighboring Russian principalities and ended Moscow's subservience to Mongol overlords.

Ivan IV, also known as Ivan "the Terrible," was the first actually to be crowned tsar and routinely to use the title. His use of the title aptly reflected his imperial intentions, as he continued Moscow's push westward and, especially, eastward against the Mongol states of central Asia. Two of the three Mongol states to the east and south fell, and the Russians pushed eastward over the Ural Mountains to Siberia for the first time.

Within this expanding empire, Ivan IV ruled as an autocrat. Part of his authority stemmed from his own personality. He was willing—perhaps because of mental imbalance—to use ruthless methods, including the torture and murder of thousands of subjects, to enforce his will. The practice of gathering tribute for Mongol overlords had put many resources in the hands of Muscovite princes. Ivan IV was able to bypass noble participation and intensify the centralization of government by creating ranks of officials, known as the service gentry, loyal only to him. The name "the Terrible" comes from the Russian word *groznyi*, which is better translated as "awe-inspiring."

A period of disputed succession known as the Time of Troubles followed Ivan's death in 1584, not unlike similar crises in other European states, where jealous aristocrats vied for power during periods of royal weakness. In this case, aristocratic factions fought among themselves as well as against armies of Cossacks and other common people who disputed nobles' ambitions and wanted less oppressive government. Nonetheless, the foundations of the large and cohesive state laid by Ivan enabled Michael Romanov to rebuild autocratic government readily after being chosen tsar in 1613.

The Romanovs were an eminent aristocratic family related to Ivan's. Michael (r. 1613–1645) was chosen to rule by an assembly of aristocrats, gentry, and commoners who were more alarmed at the civil wars and recent Polish incursions than at the prospect of a return to strong tsarist rule. Michael was succeeded by his son, Alexis (r. 1645–1676), who presided over the extension of Russian control to Ukraine in 1654 and developed interest in further relationships with the West.

Shifting the balance of power in eastern Europe and the Baltic in Russia's favor was also the work of Alexis's son, Peter I, "the Great" (r. 1682–1725). Peter accomplished this by military successes against his enemies and by forcibly reorienting Russian government and society toward involvement with the rest of Europe.

Peter was almost literally larger than life. Nearly 7 feet tall, he towered over most of his contemporaries and had physical and mental energy to match his size. He set himself to learning trades and studied soldiering by rising in the ranks of the military like any common soldier. He traveled abroad to learn as much as he could about other states' economies and government. He wanted the revenue, manufacturing output, technology and trade, and, above all, the up-to-date army and navy that other rulers enjoyed. In short, Peter sought for Russia a more evolved state system because of the strength it would give him.

Peter initiated a bold and even brutal series of changes in Russian society upon his accession to power. Peasants already were bearing the brunt of taxation, but their tax burden worsened when they were assessed arbitrarily by head and not by output of the land. Peter noticed that European monarchs coexisted with a privileged but educated aristocracy and that a brilliant court life symbolized and reinforced the rulers' authority.

Peter the Great This portrait by a Dutch artist shows Peter in military dress according to European fashions of the day. *(Rijksmuseum-Stichting, Amsterdam)*

Peter the Great Changes Russia

Peter the Great's reforms included not only monumental building and a new relationship with elites but also practical changes in education, technology, and administration. Writing about a hundred years after the end of Peter's reign, the Russian historian Mikhail Pogodin (1800–1875) reflected on all the changes Peter had introduced, perhaps exaggerating only the respect Peter earned in foreign eyes in his lifetime.

Yes, Peter the Great did much for Russia. . . . One keeps adding and one cannot reach the sum. We cannot open our eyes, cannot make a move, cannot turn in any direction without encountering him everywhere, at home, in the streets, in church, in school, in court, in the regiment. . . .

We wake up. What day is it today? . . . Peter ordered us to count the years from the birth of Christ; Peter ordered us to count the months from January.

It is time to dress—our clothing is made according to the fashion established by Peter the First, our uniform according to his model. The cloth is woven in a factory which he created. . . .

Newspapers are brought in—Peter the Great introduced them.

You must buy different things—they all, from the silk neckerchief to the sole of your shoe, will remind you of Peter. . . . Some were ordered by him . . . or improved by him, carried on his ships, into his harbors, on his canals, on his roads.

Let us go to the university—the first secular school was founded by Peter the Great.

You decide to travel abroad—following [his] example; you will be received well—Peter the Great placed Russia among the European states and began to instill respect for her; and so on and so on.

Source: Nicholas V. Riasanovsky, *A History of Russia*, 2d ed. (London: Oxford University Press, 1969), pp. 266–267.

So he set out to refashion Russian society in what amounted to an enforced cultural revolution. (See the box, "Peter the Great Changes Russia.") He provoked a direct confrontation with Russia's traditional aristocracy over everything from education to matters of dress. He elevated numerous new families to the ranks of gentry and created an official ranking system for the nobility to encourage and reward service to his government.

Peter's effort to reorient his nation culturally, economically, and politically toward Europe was most apparent in the construction of the city of St. Petersburg on the Gulf of Finland, which provided access to the Baltic Sea (see Map 16.2). In stark contrast to Moscow, dominated by the medieval fortress of the Kremlin and churches in the traditional Russian style, St. Petersburg was a modern European city with wide avenues and palaces designed for a sophisticated court life.

But although Peter was highly intelligent, practical, and determined to create a more productive and better governed society, he was also cruel, ruthless, and authoritarian. The building of St. Petersburg cost staggering sums in money and in workers' lives. Peter's entire reform system was carried out autocratically; resistance was brutally suppressed. Victims of Peter's oppression included his son, Alexis, who died after torture while awaiting execution for questioning his father's policies.

Peter faced elite as well as populist rebellions against the exactions and the cultural changes of his regime. The most serious challenge, in 1707, was a revolt of Cossacks of the Don River region against the regime's tightened controls. The primary reason for the high cost of Peter's government to the Russian people was not the tsar's determination to increase his internal power but rather his ambition for territorial gain—hence Peter's emphasis on an improved, and costly, army and navy. Working side by side with workers and technicians, many of whom he had recruited while abroad, Peter created the Russian navy from scratch. At first, ships were built in the south to contest Turkish control of the Black Sea; later, they were built in the north to contest the Baltic. Peter also modernized the Russian army by employing tactics, training, and discipline he had observed in the West. He introduced military conscription. By 1709, Russia was able to manufacture most of the up-to-date firearms its army needed.

Russia waged war virtually throughout Peter's reign. Initially with some success, he struck at the Ottomans and their client state in the Crimea. Later phases of these conflicts brought reverses, however. Peter was spectacularly successful against his northern competitor, Sweden, for control of the weakened Polish state and the Baltic Sea. The conflicts between Sweden and Russia, known as the Second Great Northern War, raged from 1700 to 1709 and, in a less intense phase, lasted until 1721. By the Treaty of Nystadt in 1721, Russia gained the territory in the Gulf of Finland near St. Petersburg that it now has, plus Livonia and Estonia. These acquisitions gave Russia a secure window on the Baltic and, in combination with its gains of Lithuanian territory earlier in the century, made Russia the pre-eminent Baltic power at Sweden's and Poland's expense.

THE RISE OF OVERSEAS TRADE

By the beginning of the seventeenth century, competition from the Dutch, French, and English was disrupting the Spanish and Portuguese trading empires in Asia and the New World. During the seventeenth century, European trade and colonization expanded and changed dramatically. The Dutch not only became masters of the spice trade but led the expansion of that trade to include many other commodities. In the Americas, a new trading system linking Europe, Africa, and the New World came into being with the expansion of sugar and tobacco production. French and English colonists began settling in North America in increasing numbers. By the end of the century, trading and colonial outposts around the world figured regularly as bargaining chips in disagreements be-

tween European states. More importantly, overseas trade had a dramatic impact on life within Europe: on patterns of production and consumption, on social stratification, and the distribution of wealth.

The Growth of Trading Empires: The Success of the Dutch

By the end of the sixteenth century, the Dutch and the English were trying to make incursions into the Portuguese-controlled spice trade with areas of India, Ceylon, and the East Indies. Spain had annexed Portugal in 1580, but the drain on Spain's resources from its wars with the Dutch and French prevented Spain from adequately defending its enlarged trading empire in Asia. The Dutch and, to a lesser degree, the English rapidly supplanted Portuguese control of this lucrative trade (Map 16.3).

The Dutch were particularly well placed to be successful competitors in overseas trade. They already dominated seaborne trade within Europe, including the most important long-distance trade, which linked Spain and Portugal—with their wine and salt, as well as spices, hides, and gold from abroad—with the Baltic seacoast, where these products were sold for grain and timber produced in Germany, Poland-Lithuania, and Scandinavia. The geographic position of the Netherlands and the fact that the Dutch consumed more Baltic grain than any other area, because of their densely urbanized economy, help to explain their dominance of this trade. In addition, the Dutch had improved the design of their merchant ships to enhance their profits. By 1600 they were building the *fluitschip* (flyship) to transport cargo economically; it was a vessel with a long, flat hull and simple rigging and made from cheap materials.

The Dutch were successful in Asia because of institutional as well as technological innovations. In 1602 the Dutch East India Company was formed. The company combined the government management of trade, typical of the period, with both public and private investment. In the past, groups of investors had funded single voyages or small numbers of ships on a one-time basis. The formation of the Dutch East India Company created a permanent pool of capital to sustain trade. After 1612 investments in the company were negotiable as stock. The enlarged pool of capital meant the risks and delays of longer voyages

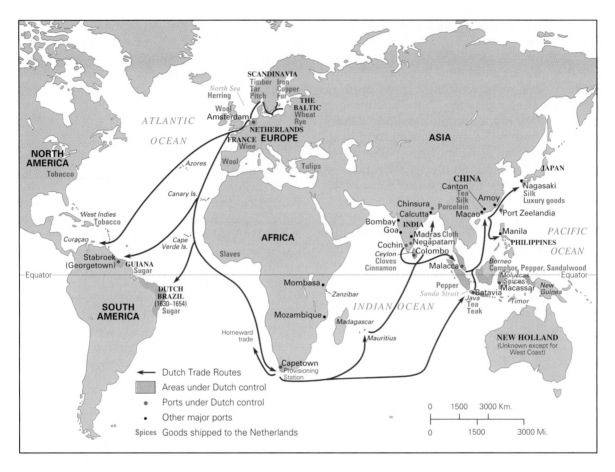

Map 16.3 Dutch Commerce in the Seventeenth Century The Dutch supplanted Portuguese control of trade with Asia and dominated seaborne trade within Europe.

could be spread among larger numbers of investors. In addition, more money was available for warehouses, docks, and ships. The English East India Company, founded in 1607, also supported trade, but more modestly. It had one-tenth the capital of the Dutch company and did not use the same system of permanent capital held as stock by investors until 1657. The Bank of Amsterdam, founded in 1609, became the depository for the bullion that flowed into the Netherlands with trade. The bank established currency-exchange rates and issued paper money and instruments of credit to facilitate commerce.

A dramatic expansion of trade with Asia resulted from the Dutch innovations, so much so that by 1650 the European market for spices was glutted, and traders' profits had begun to fall. To control the supply of spices, the Dutch seized some of the areas where they were produced.

Control of supply helped prop up prices, but these gains were somewhat offset by greater military and administrative costs.

The Dutch and English further responded to the oversupply of spices by diversifying their trade. The proportion of spices in cargoes from the East fell from about 70 percent at midcentury to just over 20 percent by the century's end. New consumer goods such as tea, coffee, silks, and cotton fabrics took their place. The demand of ordinary people for inexpensive yet serviceable Indian cottons grew steadily. Eventually, the Dutch and the English diversified their trade in Asia even more by entering the local carrying trade among Asian states. Doing so enabled them to make profits without purchasing goods, and it slowed the drain of hard currency from Europe—currency in increasingly short supply as silver mines in the Americas were worked out. (See the box, "En-

The Grain Market in Amsterdam Though the Dutch had spectacular success overseas in the seventeenth century, dominance of the carrying trade within Europe, particularly with the Baltic, remained a foundation of its prosperity. Grain exported from the Baltic was the single most important commodity traded in Amsterdam. *(British Library)*

counters with the West: Agents of the Dutch East India Company Confront Asian Powers.")

The "Golden Age" of the Netherlands

The prosperity occasioned by the Netherlands' "mother trade" within Europe and its burgeoning overseas commerce helped to foster social and political conditions unique within Europe. The concentration of trade and shipping sustained a large merchant oligarchy but also an extensive and prosperous artisanal sector. Disparities of wealth were smaller here than anywhere else in Europe. The shipbuilding and fishing trades, among others, supported large numbers of workers with a high standard of living for the age.

Political decentralization in the Netherlands persisted: Each of the seven provinces retained considerable autonomy. However, merchant oligarchs in the Estates of the province of Holland in fact constituted the government for the whole for long periods because of Holland's economic dominance. The head of government was the pensionary (executive secretary) of Holland's Estates. An Estates General existed but had no independent powers of taxation.

The only competition in the running of affairs came from the House of Orange, aristocratic leaders of the revolt against Spain (see pages 553–558). They exercised what control they had by means of the office of *stadholder*— a kind of military governorship—to which they were elected in individual provinces. Their principal interest was the traditional one of military glory and self-promotion. Therein lay a portion of their influence, for they continued to lead the defense of the Netherlands against Spanish attempts at reconquest until the Peace of Westphalia in 1648. Their power also came from the fact that they represented the only possible counterweight within the Netherlands to the dominance of Amsterdam merchant interests. Small towns dependent on land-based trade or rural areas dominated by farmers and gentry looked to the stadholders of the Orange family to defend their interests.

As elsewhere, religion was a source of political conflict. The stadholders and the leading families of Holland, known as regents, vied for control of the state church; the pensionaries and regents of Holland generally favored less rigid and austere Calvinism than the stadholders' faction. This view reflected the needs of the diverse mercantile com-

≈ **ENCOUNTERS WITH THE WEST** ≈

Agents of the Dutch East India Company Confront Asian Powers

This 1655 letter from a local agent of the Dutch East India Company to its board of directors (the "Seventeen") shows that the Dutch had to maintain good working relationships with local powers in Asia, in this case, with the king of Siam (modern Thailand). The letter discusses the Dutch blockade of Tennasserim, a major port under Siamese control, and the promises of help the Dutch, via their local agents, had made the king for some of his military ventures.

It appears that the merchant Hendrich Craijer Zalr had promised, so they [the Siamese] say, 20 ships, which was a very rash proceeding on his part, and thereupon they made the above-mentioned expedition, which they said, if our support did not appear, would be obliged to return unsuccessful and with shame and dishonor to the crown, as was actually the case. Moreover, it happened that a writing had come unexpectedly from the governor of Tennasserim that two Dutch ships had held the harbor there for 2 months, and had prevented the entrance and departure of foreign traders, which caused great annoyance in Siam, especially at Court, and embittered everyone against us. This gave the [English] Companies very favorable opportunity to blacken us and to make us odious to everyone, and to change the King's feeble opposition into open enmity, the more so since the news has from time to time been confirmed and assured, and no one there doubts it any longer.

Wherefore the resident Westerwolt, who was convinced of the contrary, since he would certainly have been informed before any such action was taken, finally found himself obliged to ask that certain persons, on the King's behalf and on his own, should be deputed and sent overland to Tennasserim, in order to discover on the spot the truth of the case, which request was granted by the King, and on our behalf the junior merchant, Hugo van Crujlenburgh was sent.

Meanwhile the aforementioned resident Westerwolt had on various occasions made complaint of the bad and unreasonable treatment received, . . . so that the resident was in very great embarrassment and did not know whether even his life was any longer safe. These questions were for the most part on the subject of the help asked for against Singgora, the Siamese professing to have gone to war with the Spanish on our account, and to have suffered much damage in the same, and that we now refused to assist his Majesty against the rebels with ships and men; whereas the beforementioned merchant, Hendrich Craijer, had definitely made him such promises.

Source: Records of the Relations Between Siam and Foreign Countries in the Seventeenth Century (Bangkok: Council of the Vajiranana National Library, 1916), vol. 2. Quoted in Alfred J. Andrea and James H. Overfield, *The Human Record: Sources of Global History*, 2d ed., vol. 2: *Since 1500* (Boston: Houghton Mifflin, 1994), pp. 134–135.

munities of Holland, where thousands of Jews as well as Catholics and various kinds of Protestants lived. Foreign policy also turned on Holland's desire for peace in order to foster commerce versus the stadholder's greater willingness to engage in warfare for territory and dynastic advantage.

These differences notwithstanding, Dutch commercial dominance involved them in costly wars throughout the second half of the century. Between 1657 and 1660 the Dutch defended Denmark against Swedish ambitions in order to safeguard the sea-lanes and port cities of the Baltic.

Other, more costly, conflicts arose simply because of rivalry with other states, notably England and France. Under Cromwell, the English attempted to close their ports to the Dutch carrying trade. In 1672 the English under Charles II allied with the French, assuming that together they could destroy Dutch power and perhaps even divide the Netherlands' territory between them. The Dutch navy, rebuilt since Cromwell's challenge, soon forced England out of the alliance.

Owing largely to the land war with France, the Estates in Holland lost control of policy to William of Nassau (d. 1702), prince of Orange after 1672. William drew the Netherlands into his family's long-standing close relationship with England. Like other members of his family before him, William had married into the English royal family: His wife was Mary, daughter of James II.

Ironically, after he and Mary assumed the English throne in 1689 (see page 602), Dutch commerce suffered more in alliance with England than in its previous rivalry. William used Dutch resources for the land war against Louis XIV and reserved for the English navy the fight at sea. Dutch maritime strength was being eclipsed by English seapower by the end of the century.

The Netherlands was controlled by a privileged few for most of the seventeenth century and was virtually a monarchy led from abroad by the end of the century. Nevertheless, the Netherlands appeared to contemporaries to be an astonishing exception to the normal structures of politics. In France and most other states in Europe, political life was dominated by a court where aristocrats and ministers mingled and conspired and an elaborate ritual of honor and deference glorified the king. The princes of Orange surrounded themselves with splendid trappings, but their court was not the sole focus of political life in the Netherlands. The portraits of the Dutch painter Rembrandt van Rijn (1606–1667) portray the austerity of the merchant oligarchs; theirs was a novel kind of power that could be symbolized with ostentatious simplicity.

Rembrandt: The Syndics of the Cloth Drapers' Guild (1662) In this painting, the last group portrait of his career, Rembrandt depicts the guild members with artful, stylized simplicity. It was Rembrandt's genius also to be able to convey a sense of personality and drama in such commissioned portraits. *(Rijksmuseum-Stichting, Amsterdam)*

The Growth of Atlantic Colonies and Commerce

In the seventeenth century, the Dutch, the English, and the French joined the Spanish as colonial and commercial powers in the Americas. The Spanish colonial empire, in theory a trading system closed to outsiders, was in fact vulnerable to incursion by other European traders. Spanish treasure fleets themselves were an attraction. In 1628, for example, a Dutch captain seized the entire fleet. But by then Spain's goals and those of its competitors had begun to shift; the limits of an economy based on the extraction of wealth rather than on the production of wealth became clear with the declining output of the Spanish silver mines during the 1620s. In response, the Spanish and their Dutch, French, and English competitors expanded the production of the cash crops of sugar and tobacco.

The European demand for sugar and tobacco, both addictive substances, grew steadily in the seventeenth century. The plantation system—the use of forced labor to work large tracts of land—had been developed on Mediterranean islands in the Middle Ages by European entrepreneurs who used slaves from the Black Sea region as well as local labor. Sugar production by this system was established on Atlantic Islands, using African labor, and then in the Americas by the Spanish and Portuguese. The French, English, and Dutch followed their lead and established sugar plantations on the Caribbean islands they held. Sugar production in the New World grew from about 20,000 tons in 1600 to about 200,000 tons by 1770.

While the Dutch were exploiting Portuguese weakness in the eastern spice trade, they were also seizing sugar regions in Brazil and replacing the Portuguese in slaving ports in Africa. The Portuguese were able to retake some of their Brazilian territory, but because the Dutch monopolized the carrying trade, they were able to become the official supplier of slaves to Spanish plantations in the New World and the chief supplier to most other regions. The Dutch were able to make handsome profits until the end of the seventeenth century, when they were supplanted by the British.

Aware of the great Spanish territorial advantage in the New World, and hoping for treasures such as the Spanish had found, the English, French, and Dutch were also ambitious to explore and settle North America. From the early six-teenth century, French, Dutch, English, and Portuguese seamen had fished and traded off New-foundland. By 1630, small French and Scottish settlements in Acadia (near modern Nova Scotia) and on the St. Lawrence River and English settlements in Newfoundland were established to systematically exploit the timber, fish, and fur of the north Atlantic coasts.

In England population growth and consequent unemployment, as well as religious discontent, created a large pool of potential colonists. The first of the English settlements to endure in what was to become the United States was established at Jamestown, named for James I, in Virginia in 1607. ("Virginia," named for Elizabeth I, the "virgin" queen, was an extremely vague designation for the Atlantic coast of North America and its hinterland.)

The Crown encouraged colonization, but a private company similar to the companies that financed long-distance trade was established actually to organize the enterprise. The directors of the Virginia Company were London businessmen. Investors and would-be colonists purchased shares. Shareholders among the colonists could participate in a colonial assembly, though the governor appointed by the company was the final authority.

The colonists arrived in Virginia with ambitious and optimistic instructions. They were to open mines, establish profitable cultivation, and search for sea routes to Asia. However, the colonists struggled at first merely to survive. (See the box, "The Disappointments of the Virginia Colony.") The indigenous peoples in Virginia, unlike those in Spanish-held territory, were not organized in urbanized, rigidly hierarchical societies that, after conquest, could provide the invaders with a labor force. Indeed, the native Americans in this region were quickly wiped out by European diseases. The introduction of tobacco as a cash crop a few years later saved the colonists economically—though the Virginia Company had already gone bankrupt and the Crown had assumed control of the colony. With the cultivation of tobacco, the Virginia colony, like the Caribbean islands, became dependent on forced, eventually slave, labor.

Among the Virginia colonists were impoverished men and women who came as servants indentured to those who had paid their passage. Colonies established to the north, in what was called "New England," also drew people from the

The Disappointments of the Virginia Colony

In this letter sent to the Virginia Company in 1608, Captain John Smith (1580–1631) explains some-what angrily that the colony cannot produce the profits that the investors were hoping for. He notes the folly of carrying boats west over the fall line of the Virginia rivers—where, it had been assumed, they might sight the Pacific Ocean as the Spaniards had done in Panama. He reports no sign of the colony of Sir Walter Raleigh, which vanished after settlement in North Carolina in 1587. He also notes the difficulties of extracting wealth and the difficulties of mere survival.

I have received your letter, wherein you write that . . . we feed you but with ifs and ands and hopes, and some few proofs . . . and that we must expressly follow your instructions sent by Captain Newport [the commander of the sup-ply ship], the charge of whose voyage . . . we cannot defray.

For the quartered boat to be borne by the soldiers over the falls, Newport had 120 of the best men. . . . If he had burned her to ashes, one might have carried her in a bag, but as she is, five hundred cannot, to a navigable place above the falls. And for him, at that time to find in the South Sea a mine of gold, or any of them sent by Sir Walter Raleigh, at our consultation I told them was as likely as the rest. . . . In their absence I followed the new begun works of pitch and tar, glass, [potash, and lumber], whereof some small quantities we have sent you. But if you rightly consider, what an infinite toil it is in Russia and [Sweden], where the woods are proper for naught else [and where] there be the help of both man and beast . . . yet thousands of those poor people can scarce get necessaries to live. . . .

From your ship we had not provision in victuals worth twenty pound, and we are more than two hundred to live upon this. . . . Though there be fish in the sea, fowls in the air, and beasts in the woods . . . they are so wild and we so weak and ignorant, we cannot much trouble them.

Source: Philip L. Barbour, ed., *The Complete Works of Captain John Smith (1580–1631),* vol. 2 (Chapel Hill: University of North Carolina Press, 1986), pp. 187–189.

margins of English society: Early settlers there were religious dissidents. The first to arrive were the Pilgrims, who arrived at New Plymouth (modern Massachusetts) in 1620. They were a community of religious separatists who had origi-nally immigrated to the Netherlands from Eng-land for freedom of conscience.

Following the Pilgrims came Puritans escap-ing escalating persecution under Charles I. The first, in 1629, settled under the auspices of another royally chartered company, the Massachusetts Bay Company. Among their number were many pros-perous Puritan merchants and landholders. Inde-pendence from investors in London allowed them an unprecedented degree of self-government once the Massachusetts Bay colony was established.

Nevertheless, the colonies in North America were disappointments to England because they generated much less wealth than expected. Ship-ping timber back to Europe proved too expensive, though New England timber did supply some of the Caribbean colonists' needs. The fur trade be-came less lucrative as English settlement pushed westward the native Americans who did most of the trapping and as French trappers to the north encroached on the trade. Certain colonists profited enormously from the tobacco economy, but the mother country did so only moderately because the demand in Europe for tobacco never grew as quickly as the demand for sugar.

The colonies' greatest strength, from the Eng-lish viewpoint, was that the settlements continued

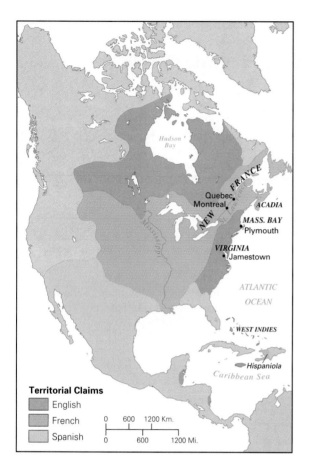

Map 16.4 British and French in North America, ca. 1700 By 1700 a veritable ring of French-claimed territory encircled the coastal colonies of England. English-claimed areas, however, were more densely settled and more economically viable.

to attract migrants. By 1640 Massachusetts had some 14,000 European inhabitants. Through most of the next century, the growth of colonial populations in North America would result in an English advantage over the French in control of territory. In the long run, however, the size of the colonial communities, their degree of routine political independence from the mother country, and their loose economic ties to England led them to seek independence.

The French began their settlement of North America at the same time as the English, in the same push to compensate for their mutual weakness vis-à-vis the Spanish (Map 16.4). The French efforts, however, had very different results, owing

partly to the sites of their settlements but mostly to the relationship between the mother country and the colonies. The French hold on territory was always tenuous because of the scant number of colonists from France. There seems to have been less economic impetus for colonization from France than from England. And, after the French crown took over the colonies, there was no religious impetus, for only Catholics were allowed to settle in New France. Moreover, control by the Crown forced a traditional hierarchical political organization on the French colonies. There was a royal governor, and large tracts of land were set aside for privileged investors. Thus, there was little in North America to tempt people of modest means who were seeking a better life.

The first successful French colony was established in Acadia in 1605. This settlement was an exception among the French efforts because it was founded by Huguenots, not by Catholics. A few years later, the intrepid explorer Samuel de Champlain (1567?–1635) navigated the St. Lawrence River and founded Quebec City. He convinced the royal government, emerging from its preoccupations with religious wars at home, to promote the development of the colony. French explorers went on to establish Montreal, farther inland on the St. Lawrence (1642), and to explore the Great Lakes and the Mississippi River basin (see Map 16.4).

Such investment as the French crown was able to attract went into profitable trade, mainly in furs, and not into the difficult business of colonization. French trappers and traders who ventured into wilderness areas were renowned for their hardiness and adaptability, but it was not their business to establish European-style communities. Quebec remained more of a trading station, dependent on shipments of food from France, than a growing urban community. Much of the energy of French colonization was expended by men and women of religious orders bringing their zeal to new frontiers. By the middle of the seventeenth century, all of New France had only about three thousand European inhabitants.

The seeming weakness of the French colonial effort in North America was not much noticed at the time. French and English fishermen, trappers, and traders competed intensely with each other, and there were outright battles between English and French settlements. But for both England and

France the major profits and strategic interests in the New World lay to the south, in the Caribbean. The Dutch experience in North America reveals the degree to which North America was of secondary importance, for all colonial powers, to the plantation profits farther south. In 1624 the Dutch founded a trading center, New Amsterdam, at the site of modern New York City. In 1674 they relinquished it to the English in return for recognition of the Dutch claims to sugar-producing Guiana (modern Suriname) in South America. Consequently, by far the largest group of migrants to European-held territories in the Americas were forced migrants: African men and women sold into slavery and transported across the Atlantic. A conservative estimate is that approximately 1,350,000 Africans were forcibly transported as slave labor to the New World during the seventeenth century.

The Beginning of the End of Traditional Society

Within Europe, the economic impact of overseas trade was profound. Merchants and investors in a few of Europe's largest cities reaped great profits. Mediterranean trading centers such as Venice and Genoa, once the heart of European trade, did not share in the profits generated by goods now being shipped to and from the New World. Atlantic ports such as Seville, through which most Spanish commerce with the New World flowed, and, above all, Amsterdam began to flourish. The population of Amsterdam increased from about 30,000 to 200,000 in the course of the seventeenth century.

All capital cities, however, not just seaports, grew substantially in the seventeenth century. Increasing numbers of government functionaries, courtiers and their hangers-on, and people involved in trade lived and worked in capital cities. These cities also grew indirectly from the demand such people generated for services and products, ranging from fashionable clothing to exotic foodstuffs. For the first time, cities employed vast numbers of country people. Perhaps as much as one-fifth of the population of England passed through London at one time or another, creating the mobile, volatile community so active in the English civil war and its aftermath.

The economy became more productive and flexible as it expanded, but social stratification in-

Marie de l'Incarnation, Colonial Settler Marie Guyart (1599–1672), as she was known in lay life, was an Ursuline nun who abandoned her own family in France to help found a convent and school for girls in Quebec, Canada. She welcomed both settlers' daughters and Native American girls to the school; she also learned several Amerindian languages during her life. (*Thomas Fisher Rare Book Library, University of Toronto*)

creased. Patterns of consumption in cities reflected the economic gulfs between residents. Most people could not afford to buy imported pepper or sugar. Poverty increased in cities, even in vibrant Amsterdam, because they attracted people fleeing rural unemployment. As growing central governments increased their tax burdens on peasants, many rural people were caught in a cycle of debt; they abandoned farming and made their way to cities.

Many such people on the margins of economic life were innovative in their efforts to survive, but they were increasingly vulnerable to both economic forces and state power. Thousands of rural people, particularly those close to thriving urban centers, supplemented their farm income by means of the putting-out system, or cottage industry. An entrepreneur loaned, or "put out," raw materials to rural workers, who processed them at home and returned a finished product to the entrepreneur. For example, the rural workers might receive wool to be spun and woven into cloth. The entrepreneur would pay the workers by the piece and then sell the finished product. In the long run, the putting-out system left workers open to economic vulnerability of a new, more modern, sort. A local harvest failure might still endanger them, and so might a foreign war or disaster at sea that affected the long-distance trade for their product.

Peasant rebellions occurred throughout the century as a result of depressed economic conditions and heavy taxation. Some of the revolts were extremely localized and involved limited direct action, such as seizing the tax collector's grain or stopping the movement of grain to the great cities. Urban demand for grain often caused severe shortages in rural areas in western Europe, despite the booming trade in grain with eastern Europe via the Baltic.

The typical peasant revolt in western Europe during the seventeenth century, however, was directed against escalating taxation. Tax rebellions often formed spontaneously, perhaps as tax officials passed through a village, but they were not mere chaotic gatherings of rabble. Countryfolk were accustomed to defending themselves as communities—against brigands and marauding soldiers, for example. Local gentry and even prosperous peasants might ordinarily fulfill the function of local constable or other lowly state office and generally be interested in maintaining order; yet they led such revolts from time to time, convinced that they represented the legitimate interests of the community against rapacious officials higher up. The scale of peasant violence meant that thousands of troops at times had to be diverted from a state's foreign wars; as a matter of routine, soldiers accompanied tax officials and enforced collection all over Europe. Thus, as the ambitions of rulers grew, so too did resistance of ordinary people to the exactions of the state.

SUMMARY

The beginning of the seventeenth century was marked by religious turmoil and by social and political upheaval. By the end of the century, the former had faded as a source of collective anxiety, and the latter was largely resolved. Nascent political configurations in the Low Countries, in the Holy Roman Empire, and on the frontiers of eastern Europe had evolved into new centers of power: the Netherlands, Brandenburg-Prussia, and the newly powerful Russia of Peter the Great. Most European states had moved from internal division—with independent provinces and aristocrats going their own way—to relative stability. This internal stability was both cause and consequence of rulers' desire to make war on an ever larger scale. By the end of the century, only those states able to field large armies were competitive on the European stage.

At the beginning of the century, overseas trade and colonization had been the near monopoly of Spain and Portugal; at the century's end, the English, French, and Dutch controlled much of the trade with Asia and were reaping many profits in the Americas. Beneath all these developments lay subtle but significant economic, social, and cultural shifts. One effect of the increased wealth generated by overseas trade and the increased power of governments to tax their subjects was a widening of the gulf between poor and rich. New styles of behavior and patterns of consumption highlighted differences between social classes. Long-term effects of overseas voyages on European attitudes, as well as fundamental change in viewing the world culminating in the development of modern science, would have revolutionary effects on Europeans and their cultures.

NOTES

1. Quoted in D. H. Pennington, *Europe in the Seventeenth Century*, 2d ed. (London: Longman, 1989), p. 508.

SUGGESTED READING

General Surveys

Howard, Michael. *War in European History*. 1976. A general study of warfare emphasizing the relationship between war making and state development.

Pennington, D. H. *Europe in the Seventeenth Century*. 2d ed. 1989; and Bonney, Richard. *The European Dynastic*

States, 1494–1660. 1991. Two general histories covering various portions of the century.

France

Beik, William. *Absolutism and Society in Seventeenth-Century France.* 1984. A case study focusing on a province in southern France but nevertheless an important interpretation of the nature and functioning of the absolutist state; has an extensive bibliography.

Collins, James B. *The State in Early Modern France.* 1995. An up-to-date synthesis by one of the leading scholars of French absolutism.

Goubert, Pierre. *The French Peasantry in the Seventeeth Century.* 1986.

———. *Louis XIV and Twenty Million Frenchmen.* 1970. Two works that consider political and social history from a broad analytic framework that includes long-term economic, demographic, and cultural data.

England

Aylmer, G. E. *Rebellion or Revolution? England from Civil War to Restoration.* 1987. A useful work that summarizes the important studies on each facet of the revolution; has an extensive bibliography.

Hill, Christopher. *A Century of Revolution, 1603–1714.* Rev. ed. 1980.

———. *The World Turned Upside Down.* 1972. The first work is a general history, the second an exploration of Levelers, Diggers, and other groups of lower-class participants in the English revolution.

Stone, Lawrence. *The Causes of the English Revolution, 1529–1642.* 1972. A brief and clear introduction.

Central and Eastern Europe

Bérenger, Jean. *A History of the Hapsburg Empire, 1273–1700.* 1990. A detailed and nuanced history of all the Habsburg domains and of the Habsburgs' relationship to Europe as a whole.

Kirby, David. *Northern Europe in the Early Modern Period, 1492–1772.* 1990.

Oakley, Stewart P. *War and Peace in the Baltic, 1560–1790.* 1992. Two excellent surveys of the Baltic region in the early modern period.

Riasanovsky, Nicolas V. *A History of Russia.* 2d ed. 1969. A reliable and readable survey of Russian history from medieval times; has an extensive bibliography of major works available in English.

Vierhaus, Rudolf. *Germany in the Age of Absolutism.* 1988. A concise survey of the development of German states from the end of the Thirty Years' War through the eighteenth century.

Wandycz, Piotr. *The Price of Freedom: A History of East Central Europe from the Middle Ages to the Present.* 1992.

A lively survey of the histories of Poland, Hungary, and Bohemia.

Early Modern Economy, Society, and Culture

Alpers, Svetlana. *The Art of Describing: Dutch Art in the Seventeenth Century.* 1983. An innovative approach to Dutch art, considering it in its social and broader cultural context.

Bercé, Yves-Marie. *Revolt and Revolution in Early Modern Europe.* Translated by Joseph Bergin. 1987.

———. *History of Peasant Revolts.* Translated by A. Whitmore. 1990. The first work is a general, comparative survey of revolts and revolutionary movements of all sorts across Europe between 1500 and 1800; the second is a more intensive study of French peasant movements.

Blum, Jerome. *Lord and Peasant in Russia.* 1961. A work that highlights the extension of serfdom in Russia fostered by Peter the Great and other tsars.

Boxer, C. R. *The Dutch Seaborne Empire.* 1965. The standard work detailing the development of the Dutch empire.

Curtin, Philip D. *The Rise and Fall of the Plantation Complex.* 1990. A good starting place for understanding the reasons behind and the significance of Europeans' establishment of plantation agriculture in the New World.

De Vries, Jan. *The Economy of Europe in an Age of Crisis, 1600–1750.* 1976. The single most important work on the development of the European economy in this period, integrating developments within and around Europe with the growth of overseas empires.

Parry, J. H. *The Establishment of European Hegemony, 1415–1715.* 1961. A brief introduction to the motives, means, and results of European expansion through the seventeenth century; somewhat dated in its overemphasis on the English in North America but nevertheless a useful overview.

Ritchie, Robert C. *Captain Kidd and the War Against the Pirates.* 1986. An interesting work on the communities of castoffs and adventurers that grew up in the Caribbean during European expansion and their place in the Atlantic economic and political worlds.

Sabean, David Warren. *Power in the Blood.* 1984. An innovative series of essays about life in German villages from the sixteenth through the eighteenth centuries; raises questions about the increasing efforts of the state to control village life and the resistance mounted by villagers to these efforts.

Wolf, Eric R. *Europe and the People Without History.* 1982. A survey of European contact with and conquest of peoples after 1400; includes extensive treatments of non-European societies and detailed explanation of the economic and political interests of the Europeans.

TABLE MANNERS

If you were to sit down in a fancy restaurant, order a juicy steak, and then eat it with your bare hands, other diners would undoubtedly stare and think what bad manners you have. It has not always been the case that table manners meant very much—were able to signal social status, for example. It was not always the case that table manners existed at all in the sense that we know them. How did they evolve? How did they come to have the importance that they do? And why should historians pay any attention to them?

Imagine that you have been invited to dinner at a noble estate in the year 1500. As you sit down, you notice that there are no knives, forks, and spoons at your place at the table, and no napkins either. A servant (a young girl from a neighboring village) sets a roast of meat in front of you and your fellow diners. The lords and ladies on either side of you hack off pieces of meat with the knives that they always carry with them, and then they eat the meat with their fingers. Hunks of bread on the table in front of them catch the dripping juices.

One hundred fifty years later, in 1650, dinner is a much more "civilized" meal. Notice the well-to-do women dining in this engraving by the French artist Abraham Bosse (1602–1676). The table setting, with tablecloths, napkins, plates, and silverware, is recognizable to us. The lady at the extreme right holds up her fork and napkin in a somewhat forced and obvious gesture. These diners have the utensils that we take for granted, but the artist does not take them for granted: They are intended to be noticed by Bosse's elite audience.

In the seventeenth century, aristocrats and gentry signaled their political and social privilege with behavior that distinguished them from the lower classes in ways their more powerful ancestors had felt no need for. Historians have called this the invention of civility. As we have seen, proper courtesy to one's superiors at court was considered essential. It marked the fact that rituals

of honor and deference were increasingly taking the place of armed conflict as the routine behavior of the upper classes. Also essential, however, were certain standards of physical privacy and delicacy. Something as seemingly trivial as the use of a fork became charged with symbolic significance. As the actual power of the aristocrats was circumscribed by the state, they found new expressions of status. Since the sixteenth century, new kinds of manners had been touted in handbooks, reflecting changes that already had occurred at Italian courts. During the seventeenth century, these practices became more widespread and opened up a gulf of behavior between upper and lower classes.

Some of the new behaviors concerned bodily privacy and discretion. A nobleman now used a handkerchief instead of his fingers or coat sleeve, and he did not urinate in public. The new "rules" about eating are particularly interesting. Why did eating with a fork seem refined and desirable to aristocrats trying to buttress their own self-image? As any 3-year-old knows, eating with a fork is remarkably inefficient.

Using a fork kept you at a distance—literal and symbolic—from the animal you were eating. Napkins wiped away all trace of bloody juices from your lips. Interestingly, as diners began to use utensils, other eating arrangements changed in parallel ways. Sideboards had been in use for a long time, but pieces of meat were now discreetly carved on the sideboard and presented to diners in individual portions. The carcass was brought to the sideboard cut into roasts instead of unmistakably whole, and it was often decorated—as it is today—to further disguise it.

The new aristocrat was increasingly separated from the world of brute physical force, both in daily life and on the battlefield. In warfare, brute force was no longer adequate. Training, discipline, and tactical knowledge were more important and heightened the significance of rank,

Table Manners of the Upper Class in the Seventeenth Century *(Courtesy of the Trustees of the British Museum)*

which separated officers from the vast numbers of common soldiers (see page 595). Aristocrats now lived in a privileged world where violence was no longer a fact of life. Their new behavior codes signaled their new invulnerability to others. Above all, they worked to transform a loss—of the independence that had gone hand in hand with a more violent life—into a gain: a privileged immunity to violence.

Specific manners became important, then, because they were symbols of power. The symbolic distance between the powerful and the humble was reinforced by other changes in habits and behavior. A sixteenth-century warrior customarily traveled on horseback and often went from place to place within a city on foot, attended by his ret-

inue. A seventeenth-century aristocrat was more likely to travel in a horsedrawn carriage. The presence of special commodities from abroad—such as sugar—in the seventeenth century created further possibilities for signaling status.

It is interesting to note that other personal habits still diverged dramatically from what we would consider acceptable today. Notice the large, stately bed in the same room as the dining table in Bosse's engraving. Interior space was still undifferentiated by our standards, and it was common for eating, talking, sleeping, and estate management all to go on in a single room. The grand bed is in the picture because, like the fork, it is a mark of status. Like virtually everything else, what is "proper" varies with historical circumstance. ✎

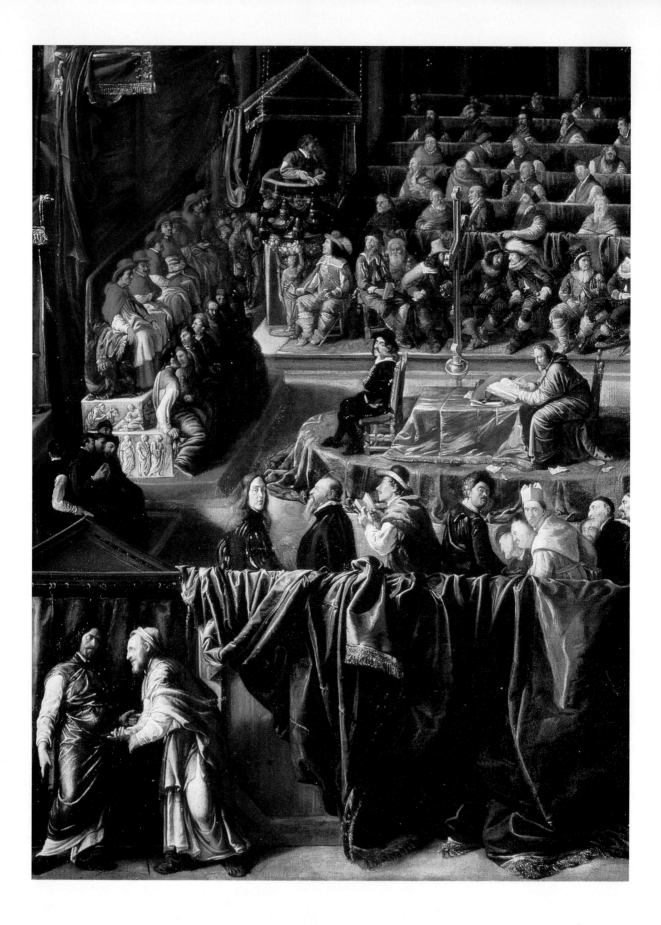

CHAPTER 17

A Revolution in World-View

As famous as the confrontation between the religious rebel Martin Luther and Holy Roman Emperor Charles V at Worms in 1521 is the confrontation between the astronomer Galileo and the judges of the papal inquisition that ended on June 22, 1633. On that day, Galileo knelt before the seven cardinals who represented the inquisition to renounce his errors and to receive his punishment. His "errors" included publishing scientific propositions that disagreed with views accepted by the church—particularly the view that the earth is stationary and does not spin on its axis and orbit the sun. As Galileo left the cardinals' presence, he is supposed to have muttered, "Eppur si muove" ("But it *does* move").

This seems a wonderful moment of historical drama, but we should be suspicious of it because it oversimplifies historical circumstances. The changes that we know as "the Reformation" and "the Scientific Revolution" were far more complex than the actions of a few individuals whose deeds now seem heroic and larger than life. Galileo, in fact, never made the defiant statement he is credited with.

Moreover, just as we cannot simply credit "heroes" with causing a revolution in scientific understanding, we cannot treat their new scientific views simply as truth finally overcoming ignorance and error. The history of scientific thought is not merely a history of discovery about the world; it is also a history of explanations of the world. From its beginnings the Scientific Revolution was a broad cultural movement. Copernicus, Galileo, and others contributed important new data to the pool of knowledge, but even more important was their collective contribution to a fundamentally

Trial of Galileo before
the inquisition, 1633.
(Anonymous, 17th century.)

new view of the universe and of the place of the earth and human beings in it.

By the end of the seventeenth century, a vision of an infinite but orderly cosmos appealing to human reason had largely replaced the medieval vision of a closed universe centered on earth and suffused with Christian purpose. Religion became an increasingly subordinate ally of science as confidence in an open-ended, experimental approach to knowledge came to be as strongly held as religious conviction. It is because of this larger shift in world-view, not because of particular scientific discoveries, that the seventeenth century may be labeled the era of the scientific *revolution.*

THE REVOLUTION IN ASTRONOMY

Because the Scientific Revolution was a revolution within science itself as well as a revolution in intellectual life more generally, we must seek its causes within the history of science as well as in the broader historical context. Many of the causes are familiar. They include the intellectual achievements of the Renaissance, the challenges that were posed by the discovery of the New World, the expansion of trade and production, the spread of literacy and access to books, and the increasing power of princes and monarchs.

The scientific origins of the seventeenth-century revolution in thought lie, for the most part, in developments in astronomy. Various advances in astronomy spurred dramatic intellectual transformation because of astronomy's role in the explanations of the world and of human life that had been devised by ancient and medieval scientists and philosophers. By the early part of the seventeenth century, fundamental astronomical tenets were successfully challenged. The consequence was the undermining of both the material explanation of the world (physics) and the philosophical explanation of the world (metaphysics) that had been standing for centuries.

The Inherited World-View and the Sixteenth-Century Context

Ancient and medieval astronomy accepted the perspective on the universe that unaided human senses support—namely, that the earth is at the center of the universe, and the celestial bodies ro-

tate around the earth. The intellectual and psychological journey from the notion of a closed world centered on the earth to an infinitely large universe of undifferentiated matter with no apparent place for humans was an immense process with complex causes.

The regular movements of heavenly bodies and the obvious importance of the sun for life on earth made astronomy a vital undertaking for both scientific and religious purposes in many ancient societies. Astronomers in ancient Greece carefully observed the heavens and learned to calculate and to predict the seemingly circular motion of the stars and the sun about the earth. The orbits of the planets were more difficult to explain, for the planets seemed to travel both east and west across the sky at various times and with no regularity that could be mathematically understood. Indeed, the very word *planet* comes from a Greek word meaning "wanderer."

We now know that all the planets simultaneously orbit the sun at different speeds and are at different distances from the sun. The relative positions of the planets thus constantly change; sometimes other planets are "ahead" of the earth and sometimes "behind." In the second century A.D. the Greek astronomer Ptolemy attempted to explain the planets' occasional "backward" motion by attributing it to "epicycles"—small circular orbits within the larger orbit. Ptolemy's mathematical explanations of the imagined epicycles were extremely complex, but neither Ptolemy nor medieval mathematicians and astronomers were ever able fully to account for planetary motion.

Ancient physics, most notably the work of Aristotle (384–322 B.C.), explained the fact that some objects (such as cannonballs) fall to earth but others (stars and planets) seem weightless relative to the earth by presuming that objects are made up of different sorts of matter. Aristotle thought that different kinds of matter had different inherent tendencies and properties. In this view, all earthbound matter (like cannonballs) falls because it is naturally attracted to earth—heaviness being a property of earthbound things.

In the Christian era, the Aristotelian explanation of the universe was infused with Christian meaning and purpose. The heavens were said to be made of different, pure matter because they were the abode of the angels. Both earth and the humans who inhabited it were changeable and

The Traditional Universe In this print from around 1600, heavenly bodies are depicted orbiting the earth in perfectly circular paths. In fact, the ancient astronomer Ptolemy believed that the planets followed complex orbits-within-orbits, known as *epicycles*, moving around the stationary earth. *(Hulton-Getty/Tony Stone Images)*

corruptible. Yet God had given human beings a unique and special place in the universe. The universe was thought to be literally a closed world with the stationary earth at the center. Revolving around the earth in circular orbits were the sun, the moon, the stars, and the planets. The motion of all lesser bodies was caused by the rotation of all the stars together in the crystal-like sphere in which they were embedded.

A few ancient astronomers theorized that the earth moved about the sun. Some medieval philosophers also adopted this heliocentric thesis (*helios* is the Greek word for "sun"), but it remained a minority view because it seemed to contradict both common sense and observed data. The sun and stars *appeared* to move around the earth with great regularity. Moreover, how could objects fall to earth if the earth was moving beneath them? Also, astronomers detected no difference in angles from which observers on earth viewed the stars at different times. Such differences would exist, they thought, if the earth changed positions by moving around the sun. It was inconceivable that the universe could be so large and the stars so distant that the earth's movement would produce no measurable change in the earth's position with respect to the stars.

Several conditions of intellectual life in the sixteenth century encouraged new work in astronomy and led to revision of the earth-centered world-view. The most important was the humanists' recovery of and commentary on ancient texts. Now able to work with new Greek versions of Ptolemy, mathematicians and astronomers noted that his explanations for the motions of the planets were imperfect and not simply inadequately transmitted, as they had long believed. Also, the discovery of the New World dramatically undercut the assumption that ancient knowledge was superior and specifically undermined Ptolemy's authority once again, for it disproved many of his assertions about geography.

The desire to explain heavenly motions better was still loaded with religious significance in the sixteenth century and was heightened by the immediate need for reform of the Julian calendar (named for Julius Caesar). Ancient observations of the movement of the sun, though remarkably accurate, could not measure the precise length of the solar year. By the sixteenth century, the cumulative error of this calendar had resulted in a change of ten days: The spring equinox fell on March 11 instead of March 21. An accurate and uniform system of dating was necessary for all rulers and their tax collectors and recordkeepers but was the particular project of the church, because the calculation of the date of Easter was at stake.

Impetus for new and better astronomical observations and calculations arose from other features of the intellectual and political landscape as well. Increasingly as the century went on, princely courts became important sources of patronage for and sites of scientific activity. Rulers eager to buttress their own power by symbolically linking it to dominion over nature sponsored investigations of the world, as Ferdinand and Isabella had so successfully done, and displayed the marvels of nature at their courts. Sponsoring scientific inquiry also yielded practical benefits: better mapping of the ruler's domains and better technology for mining, gunnery, and navigation.

Finally, schools of thought fashionable at the time, encouraged by the humanists' critique of Scholastic tradition, hinted at the possibilities of alternative physical and metaphysical systems. The first was Paracelsianism, named for the Swiss physician Philippus von Hohenheim (1493–1541), known as Paracelsus. Paracelsus offered an alternative to the theory, put forth by the ancient master, Galen (ca. 131–ca. 201), that the imbalance of bodily "humors" caused illness. He substituted a theory of chemical imbalance.

Neo-Platonism, the second school of thought, had a more systematic and far-reaching impact. Neo-Platonism, a revival primarily in Italian humanist circles of certain aspects of Plato's thought, contributed directly to innovation in science because it emphasized the abstract nature of true knowledge and thus encouraged mathematical investigation. This provided a spur to astronomical studies, which, since ancient times, had been concerned more with mathematical analysis of heavenly movements than with physical explanations for them. Also, like Paracelsianism, Neo-Platonism had a mystical dimension that encouraged creative speculation about the nature of matter and the organization of the universe. Neo-Platonists were particularly fascinated by the sun as a symbol of the one divine mind or soul at the heart of all creation.

The Copernican Challenge

Nicolaus Copernicus (1473–1543), son of a prosperous Polish merchant, pursued wide-ranging university studies in philosophy, law, astronomy, and mathematics—first in Cracow in Poland and then in Bologna and Padua in Italy. In Italy he was exposed to Neo-Platonic ideas. He took a degree in canon law in 1503 and became a cathedral canon in the city of Frauenburg in East Prussia (modern Poland), where he pursued his own interests in astronomy while carrying out administrative duties for the cathedral. When the pope asked Copernicus to assist with the reform of the Julian calendar, he replied that reform of the calendar required reform in astronomy. His major work, *De Revolutionibus Orbium Caelestium* (*On the Revolution of Heavenly Bodies,* 1543), was dedicated to the pope in the hopes that it would help with the task of calendar reform—as indeed it did. The Gregorian calendar, issued in 1582 during the pontificate of Gregory XIII (r. 1572–1585), was based on Copernicus's calculations.

Copernicus postulated that the earth and all the other planets orbit the sun. He did not assert that the earth does in fact move around the sun but offered the heliocentric system as a mathematical construct, useful for predicting the movements of planets, stars, and the sun. However, he walked a thin line between making claims for mathematical and physical reality. He had searched in ancient sources for thinkers who believed the earth did move. Other astronomers familiar with his work and reputation urged him to publish the results of his calculations. But not until 1542, twelve years after finishing the work, did he send *De Revolutionibus* to be published; he received a copy just before his death the next year. (See the box, "Copernicus's Preface to *On the Revolution of Heavenly Bodies*.")

Copernicus's colleagues were right: His work was immediately useful. Copernicus's schema

Copernicus's Preface to *On the Revolution of Heavenly Bodies*

In this dedicatory letter to the pope, Copernicus explains his desire to assist with calendar reform. Principally, however, he seeks to justify his novel conclusions. He not only cites ancient authority for the movement of the earth but also stresses the mathematical nature of the problem and of his solution.

To the Most Holy Lord, Pope Paul III

I may well presume, most Holy Father, that certain people, as soon as they hear that in this book about the Revolutions of the Spheres of the Universe I ascribe movement to the earthly globe, will cry out that, holding such views, I should at once be hissed off the stage. . . . How I came to dare to conceive such motion of the Earth, contrary to the received opinion of the Mathematicians and indeed contrary to the impression of the senses, is what your Holiness will rather expect to hear. So I should like your Holiness to know that I was induced to think of a method of computing the motions of the spheres by nothing else than the knowledge that the Mathematicians are inconsistent in these investigations. . . . Mathematicians are so unsure of the movements of the Sun and the Moon that they cannot even explain . . . the constant length of the seasonal year.

. . . I pondered long upon this uncertainty of mathematical tradition. I . . . read again the works of all the philosophers on whom I could lay a hand to seek out whether any of them had ever supposed that the motions of the spheres were other[wise]. I found first in Cicero that Hicetas [of Syracuse, fifth century B.C.] had realized that the earth moved. . . . Mathematics are for mathematicians, and they, if I be not wholly deceived, will hold that my labors contribute somewhat . . . to the Church. . . . For under Leo X, the question of correcting the ecclesiastical calendar was . . . left undecided.

Source: Thomas S. Kuhn, *The Copernican Revolution* (Cambridge, Mass.: Harvard University Press, 1985), pp. 137–143.

made possible a simpler explanation of all planetary motion. For example, he accounted for most backward motion without resorting to epicycles. But Copernicus still assumed that the planets traveled in circular orbits, so he retained some epicycles to account for the circular motion.

By positing the earth's movement around the sun but also retaining features of the old system, such as circular orbits, Copernicus faced burdens of explanation not faced by Ptolemy. In general, however, the Copernican account of planetary motion was simpler than the Ptolemaic account. It appealed to other astronomers of the age because it was useful and because it highlighted the harmony of heavenly motion, which remained a fundamental physical and metaphysical principle. Accessible only to other astronomers, Copernicus's work only slowly led to conceptual revolution, as astronomers worked with his calculations and assembled other evidence to support the heliocentric theory.

The most important reason that Copernican theory only gradually led to fundamental conceptual change was that Copernicus did not resolve the physical problems his theory raised. If Copernicus were right, the earth would have to be made of the same stuff as other planets. How, then, would Copernicus explain the motion of objects on earth—the fact that they fall to the earth—if it was not in their nature to fall toward the heavy, stationary earth? In Copernicus's system, the movement of the earth caused the *apparent* motion of the stars. But if the stars did not rotate in their crystalline sphere, what made all other heavenly bodies move?

Copernicus was not as troubled by these questions as we might expect him to be. Since ancient

MILESTONES OF THE SCIENTIFIC REVOLUTION

1543	Copernicus, *On the Revolution of Heavenly Bodies*
	Vesalius, *On the Fabric of the Human Body*
1576	Construction of Brahe's observatory begins
1591	Galileo's law of falling bodies
1609	Kepler's third law of motion
1610	Galileo, *The Starry Messenger*
1620	Bacon, *Novum Organum*
1628	Harvey, *On the Motion of the Heart*
1632	Galileo, *Dialogue on the Two Chief Systems of the World*
1637	Descartes, *Discourse on Method*
1660	Boyle, *New Experiments Physico-Mechanical*
1668	Cavendish, *Grounds of Natural Philosophy*
1687	Newton, *Principia*

times, mathematical astronomy—the science of measuring and predicting the movement of heavenly bodies—had been far more important than, and had proceeded independently of, physical explanations for observed motion. Nevertheless, as Copernicus's own efforts to buttress his notion that the earth moves reveal, his theories directly contradicted many of the supposed laws of motion. The usefulness of his theories to other astronomers meant that the contradictions between mathematical and physical models for the universe would have to be resolved. Copernicus himself might be best understood as the last Ptolemaic astronomer, working within inherited questions and with known tools. His work itself did not constitute a revolution, but it did initiate one.

The First Copernican Astronomers

In the first generation of astronomers after the publication of *De Revolutionibus* in 1543 we can see the effects of Copernicus's work. His impressive computations rapidly won converts among fellow astronomers. Several particularly gifted astronomers

continued to develop the Copernican system. Thus, by the second quarter of the seventeenth century, they and many others accepted the heliocentric theory as a reality and not just as a useful mathematical fiction. The three most important astronomers to build on Copernican assumptions, and on the work of each other, were the Dane Tycho Brahe (1546–1601), the German Johannes Kepler (1571–1630), and the Italian Galileo Galilei (1564–1642).

Like generations of observers before him, Tycho Brahe had been stirred by the majesty of the regular movements of heavenly bodies. After witnessing a partial eclipse of the sun, he abandoned a career in government and became an astronomer. Brahe was the first truly post-Ptolemaic astronomer because he was the first to improve on the data that the ancients and all subsequent astronomers had used. Ironically, *no* theory of planetary motion or mathematics to explain it could have reconciled the data that Copernicus had used: They were simply too inaccurate, based as they were on naked-eye observations, even when errors of translation and copying, accumulated over centuries, had been corrected.

In 1576 the king of Denmark showered Brahe with properties and pensions enabling him to build an observatory, Uraniborg, on an island near Copenhagen. At Uraniborg, Brahe improved on ancient observations with large and very finely calibrated instruments that permitted precise measurements of celestial movements by the naked eye. His attention to precision and frequency of observation produced results that were twice as accurate as any previous data had been.

As a result of his observations, Brahe agreed with Copernicus that the various planets did rotate around the sun, not around the earth. He still could not be persuaded that the earth itself moved, for none of his data supported such a notion. Brahe's lasting and crucial contribution was his astronomical data. They would become obsolete as soon as data from use of the telescope were accumulated about a century later. But in the meantime, they were used by Johannes Kepler to further develop Copernicus's model and arrive at a more accurate heliocentric theory.

Kepler was young enough to be exposed to Copernican ideas from the outset of his training, and he quickly recognized in Brahe's data the means of resolving the problems in Copernican analysis. Though trained in his native Germany,

Tycho Brahe's Observatory Brahe's fame was initially established by his observation and measurement of a new star in 1572, but his enduring contribution to astronomy was the meticulous collection of data by means of the instruments assembled at Uraniborg. (*The Fotomas Index*)

Kepler went to Prague, where Brahe spent the last years of his life after a quarrel with the Danish king, and became something of an apprentice to Brahe. After Brahe's death in 1601, Kepler kept his mentor's records of astronomical observation and continued to work at the imperial court as Rudolf II's court mathematician.

Kepler's contribution to the new astronomy, like that of Copernicus, was fundamentally mathematical. In it, we can see the stamp of the Neo-Platonic conviction about the purity of mathematical explanation. Kepler spent ten years working to apply Brahe's data to the most intricate of all the celestial motions—the movement of the planet Mars—as a key to explaining all planetary motion. Mars is close to the earth but farther from the sun than is the earth. This combination produces very puzzling and dramatic variations in the apparent movement of Mars to an earthly observer.

The result of Kepler's work was laws of planetary motion that, in the main, are still in use.

First, Kepler eliminated the need for epicycles by correctly asserting that planets follow elliptical and not circular orbits. Elliptical orbits could account, both mathematically and visually, for the motions of the planets when combined with Kepler's second law, which described the *rate* of a planet's motion around its orbital path. Kepler noted that the speed of a planet in its orbit slows proportionally as the planet's distance from the sun increases. A third law demonstrated that the distance of each planet from the sun and the time it takes each planet to orbit the sun are in a constant ratio.

Kepler's work was a breakthrough because it mathematically confirmed the Copernican helio-centric hypothesis. In so doing, the work directly challenged the ancient world-view, in which heavenly bodies constantly moved in circular orbits around a stationary earth. Hence, Kepler's laws invited speculation about the properties and motion of heavenly and terrestrial bodies alike. A new physics would be required to explain the novel motions that Kepler had posited. Kepler himself, in Neo-Platonic fashion, attributed planetary motion to the sun:

[The sun] is a fountain of light, rich in fruitful heat, most fair, limpid and pure . . . called king of the planets for his motion, heart of the world for his power. . . . Who would hesitate to confer the votes of the celestial motions on him who has been administering all other movements and changes by the benefit of the light which is entirely his possession?[1]

Galileo and the Triumph of Copernicanism

Galileo Galilei holds a pre-eminent position in the development of astronomy for several reasons. He provided compelling new evidence to support Copernican theory, and he contributed to the development of a new physics—or, more precisely, mechanics—that could account for the movement of bodies in new terms. Just as important, his efforts to publicize his findings and his condemnation by the church spurred popular debate about Copernican ideas in literate society and helped to determine the course science would take.

Born to a minor Florentine noble family, Galileo studied medicine and mathematics at the University of Pisa and became professor of mathematics there in 1589 at the age of 25. He had already completed important work on mechanics and within three years was given a chair at the University of Padua, where Copernicus had once studied. He continued work in mechanics during the 1590s but did not publish the results of his experiments until much later. Instead, he became famous for the results of his astronomical observations, which he began in 1609 and first published the next year. *Sidereus Nuncius* (*The Starry Messenger*, 1610) described in lay language the results of his scrutiny of the heavens with a telescope that he had built.

Galileo was the first person that we know who used a telescope to look at the sky. In *The Starry Messenger*, he documented sighting new (previously invisible) stars, another blow to the authority of ancient descriptions of the universe. He also noted craters and other "imperfections" on the surface of the moon as well as the existence of moons orbiting the planet Jupiter. Three years later he published his observations of sunspots in *Letters on Sunspots*. Sunspots are regions of relatively cool

gaseous material that appear as dark spots on the sun's surface. For Galileo the sunspots and the craters of the moon constituted proof that the heavens were not perfect and changeless but rather were like the supposedly "corrupt" and changeable earth. His telescopic observations also provided further support for Copernican heliocentrism because they revealed that each heavenly body rotated on its axis: Sunspots, for example, could be tracked across the visible surface of the sun as the sun rotated.

Galileo's principal contribution to mechanics lay in his working out of an early theory of inertia. As a result of a number of experiments with falling bodies (balls rolling on carefully constructed inclines—not free-falling objects that, according to myth, he dropped from the Leaning Tower of Pisa), Galileo ventured a new view of what is "natural" to bodies. Galileo's view was that uniform motion is as natural as a state of rest. In the ancient and medieval universe, all motion needed a cause, and all motion could be explained in terms of purpose. "I hold," Galileo countered, "that there exists nothing in external bodies . . . but size, shape, quantity and motion."[2] Galileo retained the old assumption that motion was somehow naturally circular. Nevertheless, his theory was a crucial step in explaining motion according to new principles and in fashioning a world-view that accepted a mechanical universe devoid of metaphysical purpose. These theories were published only toward the end of his life. His astronomical theories were more influential at the time.

Galileo's works were widely read, and his work became common currency in the scientific societies already flourishing in his lifetime and in courtly circles where science was encouraged. In 1610 Galileo became court mathematician to Cosimo de' Medici, the grand duke of Tuscany (r. 1609–1620), as a result of the fame brought by *The Starry Messenger*. Soon after his arrival, however, rumors that "Galileists" were openly promulgating heliocentrism led to an investigation and, in 1616, the official condemnation of Copernicus's works by the inquisition in Rome. This condemnation allowed room for maneuver. After meeting personally with the pope, Galileo was assured that he could continue to use Copernican theory, but only as a theory.

In 1632 Galileo issued a bold response to that limitation. *Dialogue on the Two Chief Systems of*

Galileo Confronts the Church

His work increasingly under attack after the publication of **Letters on Sunspots** *(1613), Galileo defended himself by criticizing the claim that biblical authority could decide matters of astronomy. This dangerous line of argument not only argued for a separation of theology and science but also presumed to evaluate the work of theologians and even offered an interpretation of biblical passages. In this document, from a 1615 essay couched as a letter to his patron Christina of Lorraine, Galileo broaches these ideas.*

But I do not feel obliged to believe that . . . God who has endowed us with senses, reason and intellect has intended to forgo their use and by some other means to give us knowledge which we can attain by them. . . . This must be especially true in those sciences of which but the faintest trace . . . is to be found in the Bible. Of astronomy, for instance, so little is found that none of the planets except Venus are so much as mentioned. . . .

Now, if the Holy Spirit has purposely neglected to teach us propositions of this sort as irrelevant to the highest goal (that is, to our salvation), how can anyone affirm that it is obligatory to take sides on them, and that one belief is required by faith, while another side is erroneous? . . . I would assert here something that was heard from [a respected cleric]: . . . "the intention of the Holy Ghost is to teach us how to go to heaven, not how heaven goes."

Moreover, we are unable to affirm that all interpreters of the Bible speak with divine inspiration, for if that were so there would exist no differences between them about the sense of a given passage. Hence [it would be wise] not to permit anyone to usurp scriptural texts and force them in some way to maintain any physical conclusion to be true, when at some future time the senses . . . may show the contrary. Who . . . will set bounds to human ingenuity? Who will assert that everything in the universe capable of being perceived is already . . . known?

Source: Stillman Drake, *The Discoveries and Opinions of Galileo* (New York: Doubleday, 1957), pp. 183–187.

the World was perhaps the most important single source for the popularization of Copernican theory. The work consists of a dialogue among three characters supposedly debating the merits of Copernican theory. Simplicio, the character representing the old world-view, was, as his name suggests, an example of ignorance, not wisdom. In this work, Galileo expresses his supreme confidence—bordering on arrogance—in his own powers and in human power generally to use the senses and reason to understand the physical world.

By publishing the *Dialogue*, Galileo was defying the papal ban on advocating Copernicanism. In an earlier work, *Letter to the Grand Duchess Christina* (1615), Galileo had also been impolitic. In the *Letter*, he had trespassed on the church's authority to interpret the Scriptures. (See the box, "Galileo Confronts the Church.") He was tried for heresy and forced to condemn his "errors" in 1633, though Pope Urban VIII (r. 1623–1644) intervened to give him the light sentence of house arrest at his villa in Tuscany. There, until his death in 1642, Galileo continued his investigations of mechanics.

THE SCIENTIFIC REVOLUTION GENERALIZED

Galileo's work found such a willing audience because Galileo, like Kepler and Brahe, was not working alone. Dozens of other scientists were working energetically on old problems from the fresh perspective offered by the breakthroughs in astronomy. Some were analyzing the nature of matter, now that it was supposed that all matter in the universe was somehow the same despite its varying appearances. Many of these thinkers addressed the metaphysical issues that their investigations inevitably raised.

The Promise of the New Science

No less a man than Francis Bacon (1561–1626), lord chancellor of England during the reign of James I, wrote a utopian essay extolling the benefits of science for a peaceful society and for human happiness. In *New Atlantis,* published one year after his death, Bacon argued that science would produce "things of use and practice for man's life."[3] In *New Atlantis* and in *Novum Organum* (1620), Bacon revealed his faith in science by advocating patient, systematic observation and experimentation to accumulate knowledge about the world. He argued that the proper method of investigation "derives axioms from . . . particulars, rising by gradual and unbroken ascent, so that it arrives at the most general axioms of all. This is the true way but untried."[4]

Bacon himself did not undertake experiments, though his widely read works were influential in encouraging both the empirical method (relying on observation and experimentation) and inductive reasoning (deriving general principles from particular facts). Indeed, Bacon was a visionary. Given the early date of his writings, it might even seem difficult to account for his enthusiasm and confidence. In fact, Bacon's writings reflect the widespread interest and confidence in science within his elite milieu, an interest actively encouraged by the state. In another of his writings he argued that a successful state should concentrate on effective "rule in religion *and nature,* as well as civil administration."[5]

Bacon's writing reflected the fact that an interest in exploring nature's secrets and exercising "dominion over nature" had become an indispensable part of princely rule. Princely courts were the main source of financial support for science and a primary site of scientific work during Bacon's lifetime. Part of the impetus for this development had come from the civic humanism of the Italian Renaissance, which had celebrated the state and service to it and had provided models both for educated rulers and for cultivated courtiers. The specific turning of the rulers' attention to science

and to its benefits for the state also reflected the scope of princely resources and ambitions: the desire of rulers for technical expertise in armaments, fortification, building projects in general, navigation, and mapmaking. (See the feature, "Weighing the Evidence: Modern Maps," on pages 654–655.)

The promise of the New World and the drive for overseas trade and exploration especially encouraged princely support of scientific investigation. A renowned patron of geographic investigation, from mapmaking to navigation, was Henry, prince of Wales (d. 1612), son of James I. Prince Henry patronized technical experts such as experienced gunners and seamen as well as those with broader and more theoretical expertise. One geographer at his court worked on the vital problem of calculating longitude, sketched the moon after reading and emulating Galileo's work with the telescope, and—in a spirit of empiricism often associated with Bacon—compiled information about the new territory Virginia, including the first dictionary of any Native American language.

Science was an ideological as well as a practical tool for power. Most courts housed collections of marvels, specimens of exotic plants and animals, and mechanical contrivances. These demonstrated the ruler's interest in investigation of the world—his or her status, in other words, as an educated person. These collections and the work of court experts also enhanced the ruler's reputation as a patron and the image of the ruler's power. Galileo was playing off such expectations when he named some of his newly discovered bodies "Medician Stars."

Exploring the secrets of nature became a tool for rulers and an honorable activity for scholars and courtiers. By the beginning of the seventeenth century, private salons and academies where investigators might meet on their own were another major site of scientific investigation. These, too, had their roots in the humanist culture of Italy, where circles of scholars without university affiliations had formed. They were an important alternative to princely patronage, since a ruler's funds might wax and wane according to his or her other commitments. Also, private organizations could avoid the hierarchical distinctions that were inevitable at court.

The earliest academy dedicated to scientific study was the Accadèmia Segreta (Secret Academy) founded in Naples in the 1540s. The members pur-

A Collection of Naturalia Displays of exotica, such as these specimens in Naples, symbolized the ruler's authority by suggesting his or her power over nature. *(From Ferrante Imperato, Dell' Historia Naturale [Naples, 1599]. By permission of the Houghton Library, Harvard University)*

sued experiments together, in order, in the words of one member, "to make a true anatomy of the things and operations of nature itself."[6] During the remainder of the sixteenth century and on into the seventeenth, such academies sprang up in many cities. The most celebrated was the Accadèmia dei Lincei, founded in Rome by an aristocrat in 1603. Its most famous member, Galileo, joined in 1611. The name "Lincei," from *lynx*, was chosen because of the legendary keen sight of that animal, an appropriate mascot for "searchers of secrets."

Galileo's notoriety and the importance of his discoveries forced acceptance or rejection of Copernicanism on all communities. Throughout the seventeenth century, specific investigation of natural phenomena would continue in increasingly sophisticated institutional settings. The flowering of scientific thought in the seventeenth century occurred because of the specific innovations in astronomy and the general spread of scientific investigation that had been achieved by the end of Bacon's life.

Scientific Thought in France: Descartes and a New Cosmology

Philosophers, mathematicians, and educated elites engaged in lively debate and practical investigation throughout Europe in the first half of the seventeenth century, but in France questions about cosmic order were being posed at a time of political disorder. The years following the religious wars

René Descartes had been given the best of traditional educations. From the Jesuits he had learned not only scholastic logic and rhetoric but also, perhaps for purposes of debate, Galileo's new discoveries. *(Royal Museum of Fine Arts, Copenhagen)*

saw the murder of Henry IV, another regency, and further civil war in the 1620s (see pages 564–565). In this environment, questions about order in the universe and the possibilities of human knowledge took on particular urgency. It is not surprising that a Frenchman, René Descartes (1596–1650), created the first fully articulated alternative world-view.

Descartes's work emerged in dialogue with a circle of other French thinkers. His work became more influential among philosophers and lay people than the work of some of his equally talented contemporaries because of its thoroughness and rigor, grounded in Descartes's mathematical expertise, and because of his graceful, readable French. His system was fully presented in his *Discours de la méthode* (*Discourse on Method*, 1637). This work was intended to be the centerpiece of a series of scien-

tific treatises, including works on optics and geometry. Descartes described some of his intellectual crises in *Meditations* (1641).

Descartes accepted Galileo's conclusion that the heavens and the earth are made of the same elements. In his theorizing about the composition of matter, he drew on ancient atomic models that previously had not been generally accepted. His theory that all matter is made up of identical bits, which he named "corpuscles," is a forerunner of modern atomic and quantum theories. Descartes believed that all the different appearances and behaviors of matter (for example, why stone is always hard and water is always wet) could be explained solely by the size, shape, and motion of these "corpuscles." Descartes's was an extremely mechanistic explanation of the universe. It nevertheless permitted new, more specific observations and hypotheses and greater understanding of inertia. For example, because he reimagined the universe as being filled with "corpuscles" free to move in any direction, "natural" motion no longer seemed either circular (Galileo's idea) or toward the center of the earth (Aristotle's idea). The new understanding of motion would be crucial to Isaac Newton's formulations later in the century.

In his various works, Descartes depicts and then firmly resolves the crisis of confidence that the new discoveries about the universe had produced. The collapse of the old explanations about the world made Descartes and other investigators doubt not only what they knew but also their capacity to know anything at all. Their physical senses—which denied that the earth moved, for example—had been proved untrustworthy. Descartes's solution was to re-envision the human rational capacity, the mind, as completely distinct from the world—that is, as distinct from the human body—and the betraying sense data it offers. In a leap of faith, Descartes presumed that he could count on the fact that God would not have given humans a mind if that mind were to betray them. For Descartes, God became the guarantor of human reasoning capacity, and humans, in Descartes's view, were distinguished by that capacity. This is the significance of his famous claim "I think, therefore I am."

Descartes thus achieved a resolution of the terrifying doubt about the world, a resolution that exalted the role of the human knower. The Cartesian universe was one of mechanical motion, not purpose or mystical meaning, and the Cartesian human being was pre-eminently a mind that could apprehend that universe. In what came to be known as "Cartesian dualism," Descartes was proposing that humans are detached from the world yet at the same time can be objective observers of the world.

Important implications followed from Descartes's ambitious view of human reason. One was the emphasis on deductive reasoning (a process of reasoning in which the conclusion follows necessarily from the stated premises), which naturally followed from his philosophical rejection of sense data. In actuality, Descartes did rely on sense data; he did experiments and urged his readers to keep careful records of their thoughts, observations, and conclusions. But, like the mathematician he was, he urged that science "[keep] the right order for one thing to be deduced from that which precedes it."[7] In the short run, Descartes's embrace of absolute certainty proved very useful to the advancement of knowledge because with a positive sense of purpose—even within the limits of deductive reasoning—natural philosophers could tolerate enormous uncertainty and speculate fruitfully about specific problems.

Descartes's vision of the enhanced position of the individual knower, and of the power of the knower's reason, was attractive to philosophers. (Galileo's self-confidence comes to mind.) His views were also attractive to educated lay people who sought in science an affirmation of their own status in the world, which could now be expressed in terms of intellectual power and power over nature, rather than only as political power. Descartes was careful not to advocate the "madness" of applying reason to changing the state. The state alone had made humans civilized, he maintained; and although he and other thinkers had to rebuild knowledge of the universe from its foundations, he believed it was "unreasonable for an individual to conceive the plan of reforming a state by changing everything from the foundations."[8]

Similar possibilities for human perception were being suggested in other areas of creative endeavor. Renaissance painters, who utilized the principles of linear perspective, presented views of the world as detached still life—more distant and distinct than the world ever was in real life. A similar detachment was evident in the memoirs and essays of writers such as Michel de Montaigne (1533–1592; see page 578). Descartes's view of rationality, however, was the most radical detachment of all, for Descartes claimed objectivity for his perspective.

Though much of Cartesian physics would be surpassed by Newton at the end of the century, Descartes's assumption about the objectivity of the observer would become an enduring part of scientific practice. The sense of detachment from the world also fostered a belief in humans' ability to control nature. In our own time, we have become aware of the possible limits of our ability to control nature, as well as the arbitrariness of Descartes's distinction of mind and body. In Descartes's day, the most radical aspect of his thought was the reduction of God from being an active presence in the world to the position of guarantor of knowledge. Later generations of scientists would be fearful of Descartes's system because it seemed to encourage "atheism." In fact, a profound faith in God was necessary for Descartes's creativity in imagining his new world system—but the system did work without God. Although Descartes would have been surprised and offended by charges of atheism, he knew that his work would antagonize the church. He had moved to the Netherlands to study in 1628, and his *Discourse* was first published there.

A contemporary of Descartes, Blaise Pascal (1623–1662), drew attention in his writings and in his life to the limits of scientific knowledge. Son of a royal official, Pascal was perhaps the most brilliant mind of his generation. A mathematician like Descartes, he stressed the importance of mathematical representations of phenomena, built one of the first calculating machines, and invented probability theory. He also carried out experiments to investigate air pressure, the behavior of liquids, and the existence of vacuums.

Pascal's career alternated between periods of intense scientific work and religious retreat. Today he is well known for his writings that defended Jansenism, an austere strain of Catholicism, and explored the human soul and psyche. His *Pensées* (*Thoughts,* 1657) consists of the published fragments of his defense of Christian faith, which remained unfinished at the time of his early death. Pascal's appeal for generations after him may lie in his assumption that matters of faith and of feeling must also be open to investigation. His most famous statement, "The heart has its reasons which the reason knows not," can be read as a statement of the limits of the Cartesian world-view.

Science and Revolution in England

The new science had adherents and practitioners throughout Europe by 1650. Dutch scientists in the commercial milieu of the Netherlands, for example, had the freedom to pursue practical and experimental interests. The Dutch investigator Christiaan Huygens (1629–1695) worked on a great variety of problems, including air pressure and optics. He invented and patented the pendulum clock in 1657, the first device accurately to measure small units of time, essential for a variety of measurements.

England, however, because of the political revolution that occurred there, offered a unique environment for the development of science in the middle of the century. Religious and political struggle in England took place at a time when scientific questions were also to the fore. Thus, differing positions on science became part and parcel of differing positions on Puritanism, church hierarchy, and royal power. Scientific investigation and speculation were spurred by the urgency of religious and political agendas. Scientific, along with political and religious, debate was generally encouraged by the collapse of censorship beginning in the 1640s.

In the 1640s natural philosophers with Puritan leanings were encouraged in their investigations by dreams that science, of the practical Baconian sort, could be the means by which the perfection of life on earth could be brought about and the end of history, the reign of the saints preceding the return of Christ, accelerated. Their concerns ranged from improved production of gunpowder (for the armies fighting against Charles I) to surveying and mapmaking. Perhaps the best-known member of this group was Robert Boyle (1627–1691). In his career we can trace the evolution of English science through the second half of the seventeenth century.

Boyle and his colleagues were theoretically eclectic, drawing on Cartesian mechanics and even Paracelsian chemical theories. They attacked the university system, still under the sway of Aristotelianism, and proposed widespread reform of education. They were forced to moderate many of their positions, however, as the English revolution

proceeded. Radical groups such as the Levelers used Hermeticism and the related Paracelsianism as part of their political and religious tenets. The ancient doctrine of Hermeticism, revived since the Renaissance, claimed that matter is universally imbued with divine (or magical) spirit. The Levelers and others believed that each person was capable of a godly life and divine knowledge without the coercive hierarchy of officials of church and state.

Boyle and his colleagues responded to these challenges. They gained institutional power, accepting positions at Oxford and Cambridge. They formed the core of the Royal Society of London, which they persuaded Charles II to recognize and charter on his accession to the throne in 1660. They worked to articulate a theoretical position that combined the orderliness of mechanism, a continued divine presence in the world, and a Baconian emphasis on scientific progress. This unwieldy set of notions was attractive to the educated elite of their day who wanted the certainties of science without losing all of the authoritarian aspects of the old Christian world-view.

Their most creative contribution, both to their own cause and to the advancement of science, was their emphasis on and refinement of experimental philosophy and practice. In 1660, Boyle published *New Experiments Physico-Mechanical*. The work described the results of his experiments with an air pump that he had designed, and it laid out general rules for experimental procedure. Descartes had accounted for motion by postulating that "corpuscles" of matter act on each other, thereby eliminating the possibility of a vacuum in nature. Recent experiments on air pressure suggested otherwise, however, and Boyle tried to confirm their findings with his air pump.

Boyle's efforts to demonstrate that a vacuum could exist—by evacuating a sealed chamber with his pump—were not successes by modern standards because they could not readily be replicated. Boyle tied the validity of experimental results to the agreement of witnesses to the experiment—a problematic solution, for only investigators sympathetic to his hypothesis and convinced of his credibility usually witnessed the results. In response to a Cambridge scholar who criticized his interpretation of one of his experiments, Boyle replied that he could not understand his critic's objections, ". . . the experiment having been tried both before our whole society [the Royal Society of London], and very critically, by its royal founder, his majesty himself."[9] Rather than debate differing interpretations, Boyle chose to fall back on the authority and prestige of the participants themselves. In English science in the mid-seventeenth century, the various aspects of the modern scientific profession—the agreement on principles, the acceptance of experimental procedures, and the authority of practitioners—were all being worked out simultaneously.

The Newtonian Synthesis: The Copernican Revolution Completed

The Copernican revolution reached its high point with the work of the Englishman Isaac Newton (1642–1724), who was born the year Galileo died. Newton completed the new explanation for motion in the heavens and on earth that Copernicus's work had initiated and that Kepler, Galileo, and others had sought. In Newton's career, we can see how different was the climate for science by the second half of the seventeenth century. When Newton entered Cambridge University as a student in 1661, Copernicanism was studied, the benefits of scientific investigation were debated, and much attention was focused on the problems of Descartes's explanations of matter.

Like all the other natural philosophers before him, Newton was as concerned by questions of metaphysics as by physics. In the 1680s, he devoted himself primarily to the study of church history, theology, and alchemy. As a student at Cambridge he was strongly influenced by the work of a group of Neo-Platonists who were critical of Cartesian dualism, which posited God as a cause of all matter and motion but removed God as an explanation for the behavior of matter. Their concerns were both religious and scientific. As Newton says in some of his early writing while a student, "However we cast about we find almost no other reason for atheism than this [Cartesian] notion of bodies having . . . a complete, absolute and independent reality."[10] He reflected his mentors' concern to harmonize science with a securely Christian world-view following the "excesses" of the English revolution. Meanwhile, they were all uncertain how to account for motion in a world filled with matter, as Descartes had posited. The experiments of Robert Boyle in creating a vacuum shed further doubt on Descartes's schema.

Newton combined his scientific skepticism and his religious certainty to posit the existence of gravity—a mysterious force that accounts for the movement of heavenly bodies. Others had speculated about the existence of gravity, but Newton's extraordinary contribution was the mathematical computation of the laws of gravity and planetary motion, which he combined with a fully developed concept of inertia. The concept of inertia as so far elaborated by Galileo, Descartes, and others suggested the need for the concept of gravity. Otherwise, if a planet was "pushed" (say, in Kepler's view, by the "motive force" of the sun), it would

Isaac Newton Pictured here about fifteen years after the publication of the *Principia*, Newton was also one of the developers of calculus. The cumbersome mathematics he still relied on in the *Principia*, however, has led one scholar to ponder: "What manner of man he was who could use as a weapon what we can scarcely lift as a burden."[11] *(National Portrait Gallery, London)*

continue along that course forever unless "pulled back" by something else.

In 1687 Newton published *Philosophia Naturalis Principia Mathematica* (*Mathematical Principles of Natural Philosophy*). In this mathematical treatise—so intricate that it was inaccessible to lay people, even those able to read Latin—Newton lays out his laws of motion and expresses them as mathematical theorems that can be used to test future observations of moving bodies. Then he demonstrates that these laws also apply to the solar system, confirming the data already gathered about the planets and even predicting the existence of an as-yet-unseen planet. His supreme achievement was his law of gravitation, with which he could predict the discovery of the invisible planet. This law states that every body, indeed every bit of matter, in the universe exerts over every other body an attractive force proportional to the product of their masses and inversely proportional to the square of the distance between them. Newton not only accounted for motion but definitively united heaven and earth in a single scheme and created a convincing picture of an orderly nature.

Neither Newton nor anyone else claimed that his theorems resolved all questions about motion and matter. Exactly what gravity is and how it operates were not clear, as they still are not. Newton himself was troubled by his lack of understanding of gravity except in mathematical terms. He couched the *Principia* as a mathematical treatise rather than as a general treatise in philosophy because he felt he could make no systematic claims, as did Descartes, since the problem of gravity had not been solved. After its publication, he experienced periods of severe depression, leading to a nervous breakdown in 1693.

Newton's laws of motion are still taught because they still adequately account for most problems of motion. The fact that so fundamental a principle as gravity remains unexplained in no way diminishes Newton's achievement but is clear evidence about the nature of scientific understanding: Science provides explanatory schemas that account for many—but not all—observed phenomena. When a scientific explanation ceases to account satisfactorily for enough data, it collapses of its own weight. No schema explains everything, and each schema contains open doorways that lead to further discovery and blind alleys that lead to mistaken impressions. Newton, for example, also studied alchemy during his most productive years. He assumed that the spiritual forces that somehow accounted for gravity would mysteriously work on metals so that they might "quickly pass into gold."[12]

Other Branches of Science

The innovations in astronomy that led to the new mechanistic view of the behavior of matter did not automatically spill over to other branches of science. Developments in astronomy were very specific to that field; innovation came at the hands of skilled practitioners after the ancient and medieval inheritance had been fully assimilated and its errors made undeniable. Other branches of science followed their own paths, though all were strongly influenced by the mechanistic world-view.

In chemistry, the mechanistic assumption that all matter was composed of small, equivalent parts was crucial to understanding the properties and behavior of compounds (combinations of elements). But knowledge of these small units of matter was not yet detailed enough to be of much use in advancing chemistry conceptually. Nevertheless, the flawed conceptual schema did not hold back all chemical discovery and development. Lack of understanding of gases, and of the specific elements that make them up, for example, did not prevent the development and improvement of gunpowder. Indeed, unlike the innovations in astronomy, eventual conceptual innovation in chemistry and biology owed a great deal to the results of experiment and the slow accumulation of data.

A conceptual leap forward was made in biology in the sixteenth and seventeenth centuries. Because biological knowledge was mostly a byproduct of the practice of medicine, biological studies had been and remained very practical and experimental. But the discovery of *On Anatomical Procedures*, a treatise by Galen, encouraged dissection and other practical research. Andreas Vesalius (1514–1564), in particular, made important advances by following Galen's exhortation to anatomical research. Born in Brussels, Vesalius studied at the nearby University of Louvain, and then at Padua, where he was appointed professor of surgery. He ended his career as physician to Emperor Charles V and his son, Philip II of Spain. In his teaching at Padua he embodied newly discovered Galenic precepts by doing dissections himself rather than giving the work to technicians. In 1543 he published versions of his lectures as an illustrated compendium of anatomy, *De Humani Corporis Fabrica* (*On the Fabric of the Human Body*). The results of his dissections of human corpses, revealed in this work, demonstrated a number of errors in Galen's knowledge of human anatomy, much of which had been derived from dissection of animals. Neither Vesalius nor his immediate successors, however, questioned overall Galenic theory about the functioning of the human body, any more than Copernicus had utterly rejected Aristotelian physics.

The slow movement from new observation to changed explanation is clearly illustrated in the career of the Englishman William Harvey (1578–1657). Much like Vesalius, Harvey was educated first in his own land and then at Padua, where he benefited from the tradition of anatomical research. He also had a career as a practicing physician in London and at the courts of James I and Charles I.

Harvey postulated the circulation of the blood—postulated rather than discovered because, owing to the technology of the day, he could not observe the tiny capillaries where the movement of arterial blood into the veins occurs. After conducting on animals vivisectional experiments that revealed the actual functioning of the heart and lungs, he reasoned that circulation must occur. He carefully described his experiments and his conclusions in *Exercitatio Anatomica de Motu Cordis et Sanguinis in Animalibus* (1628), usually shortened to *De Motu Cordis* (*On the Motion of the Heart*).

Harvey's work challenged Galenic anatomy and, like Copernicus's discoveries, created new burdens of explanation. According to Galenic theory, the heart and the lungs helped each other to function. The heart sent nourishment to the lungs through the pulmonary artery, and the lungs provided raw material for the "vital spirit," which the heart gave to the blood to produce and sustain life. The lungs also helped the heart to sustain its "heat." Like "vital spirit," "heat" was considered necessary to living organisms. It was understood to be an innate property of organs, just as "heavi-

ness," in traditional physics, was considered to be an innate property of earthbound objects. One chamber of the heart was supposedly reserved for the cleansing of waste products from venous blood—which was thought to be entirely separate from the "nourishing" blood pumped out by the heart.

From his observations, Harvey came to think of the heart in terms consonant with the new mechanistic notions about nature: as a pump to circulate the blood. But to Harvey the heart was never only that. Harvey did not leap to a new conceptualization of the body's function. Rather, he adjusted but did not abandon Galenic theories, for example, concerning how "heat" and "vital spirit" were made. The lungs had been thought to "ventilate" the heart by providing air to maintain "heat" (like bellows on a fire) and by drawing off heat to cool the heart as necessary. In light of his discovery of the pulmonary transit (that all of the blood is pumped through the lungs and back through the heart), Harvey suggested that the lungs carried out some of these functions for the blood, helping it to concoct the "vital spirit." Only in this context could the heart be thought of as a machine, circulating this life-giving material around the body.

Harvey's explanation of bodily functions in light of his new knowledge thus did not constitute a rupture with Galenic tradition. But by the end of his life, Harvey's own adjustments of Galenic theory were suggesting new conceptual possibilities. His work inspired additional research in physiology, chemistry, and physics. Robert Boyle's efforts to understand vacuums can be traced in part to questions Harvey raised about the function of the lungs and the properties of air.

SCIENCE AND SOCIETY

Scientists wrestled with questions about God, human capacity, and the possibilities of understanding the world every bit as intently as they attempted to find new explanations for the behavior of matter and the motion of the heavens. Eventually, the profound implications of the new scientific posture would affect thought and behavior throughout society. Once people no longer thought of the universe in hierarchical terms, questioning the hierarchical organization of society became easier. Once all matter was thought of as equal, thinking of all people as equal became easier. Once people questioned the authority of traditional knowledge about the universe, the way was clear for them to begin to question traditional views of the state and social order.

Such profound changes of perspective happened gradually. In the short term, Louis XIV and other rulers actually welcomed the new science for its practical value, and the practice of science remained wedded to religion. The advances in science did lead to revolutionary cultural change; but, until the end of the seventeenth century, traditional institutions and ideologies circumscribed this change.

The Rise of Scientific Professionalism

Institutions both old and new supported the new science developing in the sixteenth and seventeenth centuries. Some universities were the setting for scientific breakthroughs, but court patronage, a well-established institution, also sponsored scientific activity. The development of the Accadèmia dei Lincei (see page 635), to which Galileo belonged, and other academies was a step toward modern professional societies of scholars, although these new organizations depended on patronage.

In both England and France, royally sponsored scientific societies were founded in the third quarter of the century. The Royal Society of London, inaugurated in 1660, received royal recognition but no money and remained an informal institution sponsoring amateur scientific interests as well as specialized independent research. The Académie Royale des Sciences in France, established in 1666 by Jean-Baptiste Colbert, Louis XIV's minister of finance (see page 591), sponsored research and supported chosen scientists with pensions. These associations were extensions to science of traditional kinds of royal recognition and patronage. Thus, the French Académie was well funded but tightly controlled by the government of Louis XIV, and the Royal Society of London received little of Charles II's precious resources or his scarce political capital.

One important role of academies and patrons was to support the publication of scientific work.

The Accadèmia dei Lincei published two of Galileo's best-known works. The Royal Society of London published its fellows' work in *Philosophical Transactions of the Royal Society,* beginning in 1665.

The practice of seventeenth-century science took place in so many diverse institutions—academies, universities, royal courts—that neither *science* nor *scientist* was rigorously defined. Science as a discipline was not yet detached from broad metaphysical questions. Boyle, Newton, Pascal, and Descartes all concerned themselves with questions of religion, and all thought of themselves not as scientists but, like their medieval forebears, as natural philosophers. These natural philosophers were among the elite who met in aristocratic salons to discuss literature, politics, or science with equal ease and interest. Nevertheless, the beginning of the narrowing of the practice of science to a tightly defined, truly professional community is evident. Robert Boyle and his fellow advocates of experimentalism, for example, claimed that their procedures alone constituted true science.

The importance of court life and patronage to the new science had at first enabled women to be actively involved. Women ran important salons in France, aristocratic women everywhere were important sources of patronage for scientists, and women themselves were scientists, combining, as did men, science with other pursuits.

Noblewomen and daughters of gentry families had access to education in their homes, and a number of such women were active scientists—astronomers, mathematicians, and botanists. The astronomer Maria Cunitz (1610–1664), from Silesia (a Habsburg-controlled province, now in modern Poland), learned six languages with the support and encouragement of her father, who was a medical doctor. Later, she published a useful simplification of some of Kepler's mathematical calculations. Women from artisanal families might also receive useful training at home. Such was the case of the German entomologist Maria Sibylla Merian (1647–1717). Merian learned the techniques of illustration in the workshop of her father, an artist in Frankfurt. Later, she used her artistic training and her refined powers of observation to study and record the lives of insects and plants.

Margaret Cavendish, duchess of Newcastle (1623–1673), wrote several major philosophical

Maria Merian, Entomologist Merian's scientific drawings of insect life in Europe and South America (where she traveled with her daughter) were widely used and reproduced until the nineteenth century. Eleven insect and six plant species, which she discovered and recorded, are named for her. *(Oeffentliche Kunstsammlung Basel)*

works, including *Grounds of Natural Philosophy* (1668). She was a Cartesian but was influenced by Neo-Platonism. She believed matter to have "intelligence" and thus disagreed with Cartesian dualism, but she criticized English philosophers with whom she agreed on some matters because, like Descartes, she distrusted sense knowledge as a guide to philosophy.

Women were proposed as members of and were accepted in Italian academies regularly but they were excluded from formal membership in the academies in London and Paris, though they could use the academies' facilities and received prizes from the societies for their work. One reason for the exclusion of women was the limited amount of patronage available: Coveted positions automatically went to men. Moreover, the hierarchical distinction signified by gender made the ex-

clusion of women a useful way to define the academies as special and privileged.

Margaret Cavendish was aware of the degree to which her participation in scientific life depended on informal networks and on the resources available to her because of her aristocratic status. (See the box, "Margaret Cavendish Challenges Male Scientists.") Women scientists from more modest backgrounds, without Cavendish's resources, had to fight for the right to employment as public institutions gained importance as settings for the pursuit of science. The German astronomer Maria Winkelman (1670–1720), for example, tried to succeed her late husband in an official position in the Berlin Academy of Sciences in 1710. She had worked as her husband's unofficial partner during his tenure as astronomer to the academy and now sought to continue her work to support her four children. The academy would not extend an official position to Winkelman after her husband's death, however, despite her experience and accomplishments (she had discovered a new comet, for example, in 1702). The secretary of the academy stated:

That she be kept on in an official capacity to work on the calendar or to continue with observations simply will not do. Already during her husband's lifetime the society was burdened with ridicule because its calendar was prepared by a woman. If she were now to be kept on in such a capacity, mouths would gape even wider.[13]

Winkelman worked in private observatories, but was able to return to the Berlin Academy only as the unofficial assistant to her own son, whose training she herself had supervised.

Margaret Cavendish Challenges Male Scientists

In her preface to her earliest scientific work, **The Philosophical and Physical Opinions (1655),** *Cavendish addresses scholars at Oxford and Cambridge universities with deceptive humility. She implies that the seeming limitations of women's abilities are in fact the consequence of their exclusion from education and from participation in affairs.*

Most Famously Learned,

I here present to you this philosophical work, not that I can hope wise school-men and industrious laborious students should value it for any worth, but to receive it without scorn, for the good encouragement of our sex, lest in time we should grow irrational as idiots, by the dejectedness of our spirits, through the careless neglects and despisements of the masculine sex to the female, thinking it impossible we should have either learning or understanding, wit or judgment, as if we had not rational souls as well as men, and we out of a custom of dejectedness think so too, which makes us quit all industry towards profitable knowledge, being imployed only in low and petty imployments which take away not only our abilities towards arts but higher capacities in speculations, so that we are become like worms, that only live in the dull earth of ignorance, winding ourselves sometimes out by the help of some refreshing rain of good education, which seldom is given us, for we are kept like birds in cages, to hop up and down in our houses . . . ; thus by an opinion, which I hope is but an erroneous one in men, we are shut out of all power and authority by reason we are never employed either in civil or martial affairs, our counsels are despised and laughed at and the best of our actions are trodden down with scorn, by the over-weening conceit men have of themselves and through a despisement of us.

Source: Moira Ferguson, ed., *First Feminists: British Women Writers, 1578–1799* (Bloomington and New York: Indiana University Press and The Feminist Press, 1985), pp. 85–86.

The New Science and the Needs of the State

The new natural philosophy had implications for traditional notions about the state. The new worldview that all matter was alike and answerable to discernible natural laws gradually undermined political systems resting on a belief in the inherent inequality of persons and on royal prerogative. By the middle of the eighteenth century, a fully formed alternative political philosophy would argue for more "rational" government in keeping with the rational, natural order of things. But the change came slowly, and while it was coming, the state of Louis XIV and other rulers found much to admire and make use of in the new science.

New technological possibilities were very attractive to governments and members of ruling elites. Experiments with vacuum pumps had important applications in the mining industry. The astronomy professor at Gresham College in London was required to teach navigation, and other professors at Gresham worked with naval architects to improve the design of ships.

Governments also sponsored purely scientific research. The French Académie des Sciences sponsored the construction of an astronomical observatory in Paris. A naval expedition to Cayenne, in French Guiana, led to refinements of the pendulum clock but had as its main purpose progressive observations of the sun to permit the calculation of the earth's distance from the sun.

The sponsorship of pure science is evidence of both the adaptability of institutions and the complexity of change. Members of the elite, such as

Colbert in France, saw the opportunity not only for practical advances but also for prestige and, most important, confirmation of the orderliness of nature. It is hard to overestimate the psychological impact and intellectual power of this fundamental tenet of the new science—namely, that nature is an inanimate machine that reflects God's design not through its purposes but simply by its orderliness. Human beings could now hope to dominate nature in ways not possible before. Dominion, order, control—these were the goals of ambitious and powerful rulers in the seventeenth century.

Thus, in the short run, the new science supported a vision of order that was very pleasing to a monarch of absolutist pretensions. Louis XIV, among others, energetically sponsored scientific investigation by the Académie des Sciences and reaped the benefits in improved ships, increasingly skillful military engineers, and new and improved industrial products.

Religion and the New Science

Because of Galileo's trial, the Catholic church is often seen as an opponent of scientific thought, and science and religion are often seen as antagonists. But this view is an oversimplification. Indeed, scientific thought remained closely tied to religion during the seventeenth century. Both religion and the Catholic church as an institution were involved with scientific advancement from the time of Copernicus. Copernicus himself was a cleric, as

Science and Royal Power This painting memorializes the founding of the French Académie des Sciences and the building of the royal observatory in Paris. This celebration of the institutions' openings reveals Louis XIV's belief in their importance, both symbolic and practical. *(Château de Versailles/Laurie Platt Winfrey, Inc.)*

were many philosophers and scientists active in the early seventeenth century. This is not surprising, for most research in the sciences to this point had occurred within universities sponsored and staffed by members of religious orders.

Moreover, religious and metaphysical concerns were central to the work of virtually every scientist. The entire Cartesian edifice of reasoning about the world, for example, was founded on Descartes's certainty about God. God's gift of the capacity to reason was the only certainty that Descartes claimed. Copernicus, Kepler, and other investigators perceived God's purpose in the mathematical regularity of nature. In addition, traditional Christian views of the operations and purpose of the universe were evident in the work of all scientists from Copernicus to Newton—from Galileo's acceptance of perfect circular motion to Newton's theological writings.

It is true that the new astronomy and mechanics challenged specific tenets of faith and the Catholic church's role in shaping and controlling matters of knowledge and faith. Adjusting to a new view of nature in which God was less imminently and obviously represented was not easy for the church, for several reasons. First of all, the church itself mirrored the hierarchy of the old view of the universe in its own hierarchy of believers, priests, bishops, popes, and saints. Moreover, in its sponsorship of institutions of higher learning, the church was the repository of the old view. In the inevitable scientific disagreements spawned by the new theories and discoveries, the church was both theoretically and literally invested in the old view.

Nevertheless, the church's condemnation of Galileo shocked many clerics, including a number of whom were scientists themselves, as well as three of Galileo's judges, who voted for leniency at his trial. Over the course of the centuries, several apparent conflicts between scientific arguments and sacred teachings had been resolved with great intelligence and flexibility. Many scientists who were also clerics continued to study and teach the new science when they could; for example, Copernicanism was taught by Catholic missionaries abroad. (See the box, "Encounters with the West: Jesuits and Astronomy in China.")

The rigid response of the church hierarchy to Galileo's challenge must be seen in the context of the Protestant Reformation, which, in the minds of the pope and others, had demonstrated the need for a firm response to any challenge. Galileo seemed threatening because he was well known, wrote for a wide audience, and, like the Protestants, presumed on the church's right to interpret the Scriptures.

The condemnation of Galileo had a chilling effect on scientific investigators in most Catholic regions of Europe. They could and did continue their research, but many could publish results only by smuggling manuscripts to Protestant lands. Descartes, as we have seen, left France for the more tolerant Netherlands, where his *Discourse on Method* was first published; he also sojourned at the Swedish court at the invitation of Queen Christina. Many of the most important empirical and theoretical innovations in science occurred in Protestant regions after the middle of the seventeenth century.

Protestant leaders, however, at first were not receptive to Copernican ideas because they defied scriptural authority as well as common sense. In 1549 one of Martin Luther's associates wrote:

The eyes are witnesses that the heavens revolve in the space of twenty-four hours. But certain men, either from love of novelty or to make a display of ingenuity, have concluded that the earth moves. . . . Now it is want of honesty and decency to assert such notions publicly and the example is pernicious. It is part of a good mind to accept the truth as revealed by God and to acquiesce in it.[14]

Protestant thinkers were also as troubled as Catholics by the metaphysical problems that the new theories seemed to raise. In 1611, one year after the publication of Galileo's *Starry Messenger*, the English poet John Donne (1573–1631) reflected in "An Anatomie of the World" on the confusion about human capacities and social relationships that Copernican astronomy caused:

[The] new Philosophy calls all in doubt,
The Element of fire is quite put out;
The Sun is lost, and th'earth, and no man's wit
Can well direct him where to look for it.

. . . .

Tis all in pieces, all coherence gone;
All just supply, and all Relation:
Prince, Subject, Father, Son, are things forgot,
For every man alone thinks he hath got
To be a Phoenix, and that then can be
None of that kinde, of which he is, but he.[15]

∼ ENCOUNTERS WITH THE WEST ∼

Jesuits and Astronomy in China

The Italian Matteo Ricci (1552–1610) was one of the first of a series of Jesuit missionaries to establish himself at the imperial court in China. He was appreciative as well as critical of Chinese science, but his remarks are more interesting to us because they reveal that Ricci himself regarded expertise in mathematics and astronomy as worthy of esteem. Ricci's own scientific knowledge was crucial to his acceptance at court; Jesuit missionaries who followed Ricci in the seventeenth century found their scientific expertise equally valued, and several openly taught Copernican theory there.

The Chinese have not only made considerable progress in moral philosophy but in astronomy and in many branches of mathematics as well. At one time they were quite proficient in arithmetic and geometry, but in the study and teaching of these branches of learning they labored with more or less confusion. They divide the heavens into constellations in a manner somewhat different from that which we employ. Their count of the stars outnumbers the calculations of our astronomers by fully four hundred, because they include in it many of the fainter stars which are not always visible. And yet with all this, the Chinese astronomers take no pains whatever to reduce the phenomena of celestial bodies to the discipline of mathematics. Much of their time is spent in determining the moment of eclipses and the mass of the planets and the stars, but here, too, their deductions are spoiled by innumerable errors. Finally they center their whole attention on that phase of astronomy which our scientists term astrology, which may be accounted for the fact that they believe that everything happening on this terrestrial globe of ours depends upon the stars.

Some knowledge of the science of mathematics was given to the Chinese by the Saracens [Mongols], who penetrated into their country from the West, but very little of this knowledge was based upon definite mathematical proofs. What the Saracens left them, for the most part, consisted of certain tables of rules by which the Chinese regulated their calendar and to which they reduced their calculations of planets and the movements of the heavenly bodies in general. The founder of the family which at present regulates the study of astrology prohibited anyone from indulging in the study of this science unless he were chosen for it by hereditary right. The prohibition was founded upon fear, lest he who should acquire a knowledge of the stars might become capable of disrupting the order of the empire and seek an opportunity to do so.

Source: Louis J. Gallagher, trans., *China in the Sixteenth Century: The Journals of Matthew Ricci: 1583–1610* (New York: Random House, 1953), pp. 30–31.

The dilemma of accounting in religious terms for the ideas of Copernicus and Descartes became more urgent for Protestants as the ideas acquired an anti-Catholic status after the trial of Galileo in 1633, and as they became common scientific currency by about 1640. The development of the new science in the mid-seventeenth century coincided with religious and political upheavals throughout Europe. Religious, political, and scientific view-points became inextricably mixed. A religious certainty about divine force that could account for the motion of bodies in a vacuum enabled Newton to develop his theories on motion and gravity. In short, religion did not merely remain in the scientists' panoply of explanations; it remained a fundamental building block of scientific thought, in the same way that it remained central to most scientists' lives.

The Mechanistic World Order and Human Affairs at the End of the Seventeenth Century

Traditional institutions and ideologies checked the potential effects of the new science for a time, but by the middle of the seventeenth century, political theory was beginning to show the impact of the mechanistic world-view. Political philosophers viewed neither the world nor human society as an organic whole in which each part was distinguished in nature and function from the rest. Thomas Hobbes, John Locke, and others reimagined the bonds that link citizens to each other and to their rulers.

Because of the political turmoil in England, Thomas Hobbes (1588–1679) spent much of his productive life on the Continent. After the beginnings of the parliamentary rebellion, he joined a group of royalist émigrés in France. He met Galileo and lived for extended periods in Paris, in contact with the circle of French thinkers that included Descartes. Like Descartes, he theorized about the nature and behavior of matter; he published a treatise on his views in 1655.

Hobbes is best known today for *Leviathan* (1651), his treatise on political philosophy. *Leviathan* applies to the world of human beings Hobbes's mostly Cartesian view of nature as composed of "self-motivated" atomlike structures. Hobbes viewed people as mechanistically as he viewed the rest of nature. In his view, people were made up of appetites of various sorts—the same kind of innate forces that drove all matter. The ideal state, concluded Hobbes, is one in which a strong sovereign controls the disorder that inevitably arises from the clash of desires. Unlike the medieval philosophers, Hobbes did not draw analogies between the state and the human body (the king as head, judges and magistrates as arms, and so forth). Instead, Hobbes compared the state to a machine that "ran" by means of laws and was kept in good working order by a skilled technician—the ruler.

Hobbes's pessimism about human behavior and his insistence on the need for order imposed from above reflect, like the work of Descartes, a concern for order in the wake of political turmoil. This concern was one reason he was welcomed into the community of French philosophers, who were naturally comfortable with royalty as a powerful guarantor of order. But Hobbes's work, like theirs, was a radical departure because it envisions citizens as potentially equal and constrained neither by morality nor by natural obedience to authority.

Another Englishman, John Locke (1632–1704), offered an entirely different vision of natural equality among people and of social order. Locke's major works, *Essay on Human Understanding* (1690) and *Two Treatises on Government* (1690), reflect the experimentalism of Robert Boyle, the systematizing rationality of Descartes, and other strands of the new scientific thought. In the *Essay*, Locke offers a view of human knowledge that is more pragmatic and utilitarian than the rigorous mathematical model of certainty used by many other philosophers. He argues that human knowledge is largely the product of experience. He agrees with Descartes that reason orders and explains human experience. But he thinks that reason does not necessarily perceive reality as it really is but rather perceives reality in a limited way that is nevertheless useful. Unlike Descartes, Locke thinks there are limits to what human reason can achieve, but Locke offers a more optimistic vision of the possible uses of human reason. Whereas Descartes was interested in mentally ordering and understanding the world, Locke was interested in humans' functioning in the world.

Locke's treatises on government reflect his notion of knowledge based on experience as well as his particular experiences as a member of elite circles in the aftermath of the English revolution. A trained physician, he served as personal physician and general political assistant to Anthony Ashley Cooper (1621–1683), Lord Shaftsbury, one of the members of Parliament most opposed to Charles II's pretensions to absolutist government. When James II acceded to the throne in 1685, Locke remained in the Netherlands, where he had fled to avoid prosecution for treason. He became an adviser to William of Orange and returned to England with William and Mary in 1688. Locke's view of the principles of good government, then, came to reflect the pro-parliamentary stance of his political milieu.

Unlike Hobbes, Locke argues that people are capable of restraint and mutual respect in their pursuit of self-interest. The state arises from a contract that individuals freely enter into to protect themselves, their property, and their happiness

Locke's View of the Purpose of Government

In this passage from the second of his treatises on government, Locke describes men as naturally free and willing to enter into communities only for the protection of property. Notice how Locke justifies private property as "natural" by linking it to an individual's labor.

Men being . . . by nature all free, equal, and independent, no one can be put out of this estate and subjected to the political power of another without his own consent. The only way whereby any one divests himself of his natural liberty and puts on the bonds of civil society is by agreeing with other men to join and unite into a community for their comfortable, safe, and peaceable living amongst one another, in a secure enjoyment of their properties and a greater security against any that are not of it. This any number of men may do, because it injures not the freedom of the rest; they are left as they were in the liberty of the state of nature. When any number of men have so consented to make one community or government, they are thereby presently incorporated and make one body politic wherein the majority have a right to act and conclude the rest. . . . And thus that which begins and acutally constitutes any political society is nothing but the consent of any number of freemen capable of a majority to unite and incorporate into such a society. And this is that, and that only, which did or could give beginning to any lawful government in the world.

If man in the state of nature be so free . . . , and if he be absolute lord of his own person and possessions, equal to the greatest, and

subject to nobody, why will he part with his freedom, why will he give up his empire and subject himself to the dominion and control of any other power?

The great and chief end, therefore, of men's uniting into commonwealths and putting themselves under government is the preservation of their property. . . . Though the earth and all inferior creatures be common to all men, yet every man has a property in his own person; this nobody has any right to but himself. The labor of his body and the work of his hands, we may say, are properly his. Whatsoever then he removes out of the state that nature has provided and left it in, he has mixed his labor with, and joined to it something that is his own, and thereby makes it his property. It being by him removed from the common state nature has placed it in, it has by this labor something annexed to it that excludes the common right of other men. For this labor being the unquestionable property of the laborer, no man but he can have a right to what that is once joined to, at least where there is enough and as good left in common for others. . . . As much land as a man tills, plants, improves, cultivates, and can use the product of, so much is his property. He by his labor does, as it were, enclose it from the common.

Source: Second Treatise, in John Locke, *Two Treatises of Civil Government* (London: G. Routledge & Sons, 1884).

from possible aggression by others. They can invest the executive and legislative authority to carry out this protection in monarchy or any other governing institution, though Locke believed the English Parliament was the best available model. Because sovereignty resides with the people who enter into the contract, rebellion against abuse of power is justified. Thus, Locke frees people from

arbitrary bonds of authority to the state and to each other.

Locke's experience as a member of the elite of his society is apparent in his emphasis on private property, which he considers one of the fundamental human rights. (See the box, "Locke's View of the Purpose of Government.") Indeed, there is no place in his political vision for serious disagree-

Science Gains an Audience This illustration from Bernard de Fontenelle's major work popularized the new science. It reveals the audience for which the work was intended. A gentleman, sitting with a lady in a formal garden, gestures to a depiction of the solar system as it was now understood; the lady is presumed to understand and to be interested in the information. *(By permission of Houghton Library, Harvard University)*

ment about the nature of property. Locke even found a justification for slavery. He also did not consider women to be political beings in the same way as men. The family, he felt, was a separate domain from the state, not bound by the same contractual obligations.

Locke's dismissal of women from the realm of politics and of questions of power and justice from the family was not an accident. The ability of Locke and many other seventeenth-century thinkers to imagine a new physical or political order was constrained by the prevailing view of gender as a "nat-

ural" principle of order and hierarchy. Gender distinctions are in the main socially ascribed roles that are easily misinterpreted as "natural" differences between women and men. Although Margaret Cavendish (see the box on page 645) and other women disputed the validity of such distinctions, men frequently used them. Locke's use of gender as an arbitrary organizing principle gave his bold new political vision a claim to being "natural." The use of gender-specific vocabulary to describe nature itself had the effect of making the new objective attitude toward the world seem "natural."

Works by seventeenth-century scientists are filled with references to nature as a woman who must be "conquered," "subdued," or "penetrated."

Traditional gender distinctions limited and buttressed most facets of political thought, but in other areas, the fact of uncertainty and the need for tolerance was embraced. Another of Locke's influential works was the impassioned *Letter on Toleration* (1689). In it he argues that religious belief is fundamentally private and that only the most basic Christian principles need be accepted by everyone. Others went further than Locke by entirely removing traditional religion as a fundamental guarantor of morality and order. Fostering this climate of religious skepticism were religious pluralism in England and the irrationality of religious intolerance—demonstrated by Louis XIV's persecution of Protestants.

Pierre Bayle (1647–1706), a Frenchman of Protestant origins, argued that morality can be wholly detached from traditional religion. Bayle cited as an example of morality the philosopher Baruch Spinoza (1632–1677). Spinoza believed the state to have a moral purpose and human happiness to have spiritual roots. Yet he was not a Christian at all but a Dutch Jew who had been ejected from his local synagogue for supposed atheism. One need hardly be a Christian of any sort in order to be a moral being, Bayle concluded.

Bayle's skepticism toward traditional knowledge was more wide ranging than his views on religion. His best-known work, *Dictionnaire historique et critique* (*Historical and Critical Dictionary*, 1702), was a compendium of observations about and criticisms of virtually every thinker whose works were known at the time, including recent and lionized figures such as Descartes and Newton. Bayle was the first systematic skeptic, and he relentlessly exposed errors and shortcomings in all received knowledge. His works were very popular with elite lay readers.

Bayle's fellow countryman Bernard de Fontenelle (1657–1757), secretary to the Académie des Sciences from 1699 to 1741, was the greatest popularizer of the new science of his time. His *Entretiens sur la Pluralités des Mondes* (*Conversations on the Plurality of Worlds*, 1686) was, as the title implies, an informally presented description of the infinite universe of matter. It went through numerous editions and translations. As secretary to the Académie, Fontenelle continued his work as popularizer by publishing descriptions of the work of the Académie's scientists. He died one month short of his hundredth birthday. At his death in 1757 it was said that "the Philosophic spirit, today so much in evidence, owes its beginnings to Monsieur de Fontenelle."[16]

SUMMARY

Fontenelle is a fitting figure with whom to end a discussion of the Scientific Revolution because he represents, and worked to accomplish, the transference of the new natural philosophy into political and social philosophy—a movement we know as the "Enlightenment." The Scientific Revolution began, as innovation in scientific thinking often does, with a specific research problem whose answer led in unexpected directions. Copernicus's response to traditional astronomical problems led to scientific and philosophical innovation because of his solution and because of the context into which it was received.

Other scientists, following Copernicus, built on his theories, culminating in the work of Galileo, who supported Copernican theory with additional data and widely published his findings. The Frenchman Descartes was the first to fashion a systematic explanation for the operations of nature to replace the medieval view. The political and intellectual climate in England, meanwhile, encouraged the development of experimental science and inductive reasoning. Isaac Newton provided new theories to explain the behavior of matter and expressed them in mathematical terms that could apply to either the earth or the cosmos; with his work, traditional astronomy and physics were overturned.

Rulers made use of the new science for the practical results it offered despite the ideological challenge it presented to their power. By the end of the seventeenth century, the hierarchical Christian world-view grounded in the old science was being challenged on many fronts. A fully articulated secular world-view would be the product of the Enlightenment.

NOTES

1. Quoted in Thomas S. Kuhn, *The Copernican Revolution* (Cambridge, Mass.: Harvard University Press, 1985), p. 131.
2. Quoted in Margaret C. Jacob, *The Cultural Meaning of the Scientific Revolution* (Philadelphia: Temple, 1988), p. 18.
3. Quoted ibid., p. 33.
4. Quoted in Alan G. R. Smith, *Science and Society in the Sixteenth and Seventeenth Centuries* (New York: Science History Publications, 1972), p. 72.
5. Quoted in Jacob, *Cultural Meaning*, p. 32 (emphasis added).
6. Quoted in Bruce T. Moran, ed., *Patronage and Institutions: Science, Technology and Medicine at the European Court* (Rochester: The Boyden Press, 1991), p. 43.
7. Quoted in Jacob, *Cultural Meaning*, p. 59.
8. Quoted ibid., p. 58.
9. Quoted in Steven Shapin, *A Social History of Truth* (Chicago: University of Chicago Press, 1994), p. 298.
10. Quoted in Jacob, *Cultural Meaning*, p. 89.
11. Quoted in Smith, *Science and Society*, p. 130.
12. Quoted in Jacob, *Cultural Meaning*, p. 25.
13. Quoted in Londa Schiebinger, *The Mind Has No Sex?* (Cambridge, Mass.: Harvard University Press, 1989), p. 92.
14. Quoted in Kuhn, *The Copernican Revolution*, p. 191.
15. *Complete Poetry and Selected Prose of John Donne*, ed. John Hayward (Bloomsbury, England: Nonesuch Press, 1929), p. 365; quoted in Kuhn, *The Copernican Revolution*, p. 194.
16. Quoted in Paul Edwards, ed., *The Encyclopedia of Philosophy*, vol. 3 (New York: Macmillan, 1967), p. 209.

SUGGESTED READING

General Surveys

Debus, Allen G. *Man and Nature in the Renaissance*. 1978. A survey of developments in science and medicine during the two centuries leading up to the seventeenth-century revolution; its special contribution stems from Debus's emphasis on Paracelsianism and alchemy.

Hall, A. Rupert. *The Revolution in Science, 1500–1800*. 1983. A thorough introduction to all scientific disciplines that de-emphasizes the larger context of scientific development but explains many of the innovations in detail.

Kearney, Hugh. *Science and Change*. 1971. A readable general introduction to the Scientific Revolution.

Kuhn, Thomas. *The Copernican Revolution*. 1985. A readable treatment of the revolution in astronomy that also lucidly explains the Aristotelian world-view; important for setting Copernicus's work in the context of the history of astronomy; the first thing to read to understand the Copernican revolution.

———. *The Structure of Scientific Revolutions*. 1970. A path-breaking work that argues that all scientific schemas are systems of explanation and that science progresses by shifting from one general paradigm to another, not from error to "truth."

Lindberg, D. C., and R. S. Westman. *Reappraisals of the Scientific Revolution*. 1990. Essays re-evaluating classic interpretations of the Scientific Revolution. Includes a rich bibliography.

Mandrou, Robert. *From Humanism to Science*. 1978. A general intellectual history of the period 1450–1650 that sets the Scientific Revolution in the context of broader intellectual, social, and economic currents.

Merchant, Carolyn. *The Death of Nature: Women, Ecology and the Scientific Revolution*. 1980. An important corrective interpretation that focuses on the changing definition of nature—particularly how nature became something to be dominated and consumed—and the way in which this definition reinforced negative cultural views of women.

Thomas, Keith. *Religion and the Decline of Magic*. 1971. An exploration of the changing character of religious belief and "superstitious" practice; finds roots outside of science for changing, increasingly secular world-views.

Westfall, Richard S. *The Construction of Modern Science: Mechanisms and Mechanics*. 1977. A general treatment of the Scientific Revolution that emphasizes and explains the mechanistic world-view.

Individual Scientists

Bordo, Susan R. *The Flight to Objectivity: Essays on Cartesianism and Culture*. 1987. A collection that studies Descartes's work as a metaphysical and psychological crisis and discusses implications of Cartesian mind-body dualism.

Cohen, I. Bernard. *The Newtonian Revolution*. 1987. A brief introduction to Newton and the meaning of his discoveries; a good place to start on Newton.

Drake, Stillman. *Galileo at Work: His Scientific Biography*. 1978. A detailed chronological study that reveals Galileo's character and illuminates his scientific achievements.

Frank, Robert G., Jr. *Harvey and the Oxford Physiologists*. 1980. An explanation of Harvey's work in the context of traditional Galenic medicine and a discussion of the community of scholars who accepted and built on Harvey's innovations.

Redondi, Pietro. *Galileo Heretic*. 1987. A careful account of Galileo's confrontation with the church.

(continued on page 656)

MODERN MAPS

We take for granted that contemporary maps will provide accurate representations of geography and present information in standardized ways we can easily read. But how did these standards of clarity and accuracy come about?

Modern mapping was developed during the Scientific Revolution. Like most of the changes we have labeled the "Scientific Revolution," changes in mapping were the result of several influences: innovations in Renaissance art, knowledge gleaned from voyages of exploration, the impact of new astronomical discoveries, and the interest and support of princely patrons.

Let us look at Christopher Saxton's map of Somerset, a county in England. This map was printed in 1579 in one of the first atlases ever published. We might be struck by how different this map appears from contemporary maps; many of its features seem decorative or even quaint. Ships, not drawn to scale, ride at anchor or sail off the coast. Towns are represented not by dots of various sizes but by miniature town buildings. Relief

in the landscape is depicted with hills drawn, like the town buildings, from a side view inconsistent with the aerial perspective of the map as a whole. The large royal coat of arms that occupies the upper left quadrant of the map seems the most antiquated and irrelevant feature.

But is it irrelevant? Let us try to appreciate what a striking and powerful image this map must have been for its original viewers. Because the features are represented in ways that we consider decorative, it is easy for us to overlook the fact that this map illustrates a revolutionary method of depicting space. Saxton provides an aerial view of an entire county, with all locales arrayed in accurate spatial relationship to one another. This accurate rendering of space was, first, the result of the discovery of linear perspective by Renaissance artists. This discovery enabled space to be imagined from the perspective of a distanced observer. Saxton's maps—and the few others published at about the same time—represented the first time Europeans could take "visual possession" of the land they

Map of the County of Somerset, England, 1579
(British Library)

Map of the French Coastline, 1693 (*Bibliothèque Nationale*)

lived in, in the way we now take for granted whenever we buy a road map.*

Precise measurement of land forms—the location of hills in this map, for example—still relied on the established craft of systematic surveying. And here is where the royal coat of arms enters the picture, literally. Saxton's surveying and the production of his atlas were sponsored by the government of Queen Elizabeth. Thus, just as this map enabled contemporary observers to envision for the first time, in its entirety, the land they lived in, it simultaneously marked royal power over that land.

Now let us look at a 1693 map of the coastline of France. We immediately note that most decorative elements are gone: No ships sail the abundant seas, for example. The figure of a compass marks the Paris meridian—the site of the city, we are shown, has been precisely determined by means of its longitude and latitude. More accurate calculation of longitude had been made possible by the work of Kepler and Galileo, whose mapping of heavenly bodies provided known points in the night sky from which to calculate the longitude of the observer's position on earth. (Calculation of latitude had always been easier, since it involved

only determining the angle of the sun above the horizon, but it was also improved by better instrumentation in the seventeenth century.) After 1650, French cartographers, among others, systematically collected astronomical observations from around the world more precisely to map all known lands.

This map superimposes a corrected view of the coastline of France over an older rendering. The power of this coastline map, then, lies in the way it dramatically advertises the progress of mapmaking itself. Royal power remains connected to scientific effort: The title reads, "Map of France, corrected by order of the King by the observations of Messieurs of the Academy of Sciences."

Thus, both of these maps glorify royal power: one by linking it with a dramatically new visualization of the land it ruled, the other by presenting royalty as a patron and guarantor of knowledge. But in the second map, royal identity is no longer pictured along with the land it claims. Instead, the king is mentioned discreetly, in what is coming to be a standardized label.

Like all innovations of the Scientific Revolution, those in mapmaking had unintended consequences. Claims to royal power articulated on maps lost their force when placed next to the information the maps conveyed; royal power had many practical and ideological uses for the new science but, in the end, would be undermined by the world-view the new science made possible. ❧

*Richard Helgerson, "The Land Speaks: Cartography, Chorography, and Subversion in Renaissance England," *Representations* 16 (Fall 1986): 51. This discussion of Saxton's map and the evolution of mapmaking is drawn from Helgerson and from Norman J. W. Thrower, *Maps and Civilization* (Chicago: University of Chicago Press, 1996), chaps. 5 and 6.

Shapin, Steven, and Simon Schaffer. *Leviathan and the Air-Pump*. 1985. One of the most important studies of seventeenth-century science: traces the conflict between Cartesian science, as represented by Hobbes, and experimental science, in the work of Boyle; and shows the relationship of Hobbes and Boyle to their respective contexts as well as some of the political, cultural, and philosophical implications of each school of thought.

Thoren, Victor E. *The Lord of Uraniborg: A Biography of Tycho Brahe*. 1990. An up-to-date study of the life and work of the Danish astronomer.

Political, Social, and Cultural Contexts for Science

Biagioli, Mario. *Galileo, Courtier*. 1993. A new study that stresses the power of patronage relations to shape scientific process.

Hunter, Michael. *Science and Society in Restoration England*. 1981. A study that sets English science in its political and cultural contexts; critical of Webster's classic study (see below).

Jacob, Margaret C. *The Cultural Meaning of the Scientific Revolution*. 1988. An account that moves from the Scientific Revolution through the industrial transformation of the nineteenth century, sketching the relationship of developments in science, metaphysics, and technology to the political and social history of the various eras.

———. *The Newtonians and the English Revolution*. 1976. A work that links the development of Newtonian science to its political and social context and examines the simultaneous evolution of religion that could accept the new science yet maintain traditional perspectives.

Moran, Bruce T., ed. *Patronage and Institutions: Science, Technology and Medicine at the European Court*. 1991. A work that looks at royal courts as shaping and sustaining institutions for science from the early sixteenth century onward.

Schiebinger, Londa. *The Mind Has No Sex?* 1989. An examination of the participation of women in the practice of science and an explanation of how science began to reflect the exclusion of women in its values and objects of study—above all, in its claims about scientific "facts" about women themselves.

Webster, Charles. *The Great Instauration*. 1975. A classic study that links the development of the modern scientific attitude to the Puritan revolution in England.

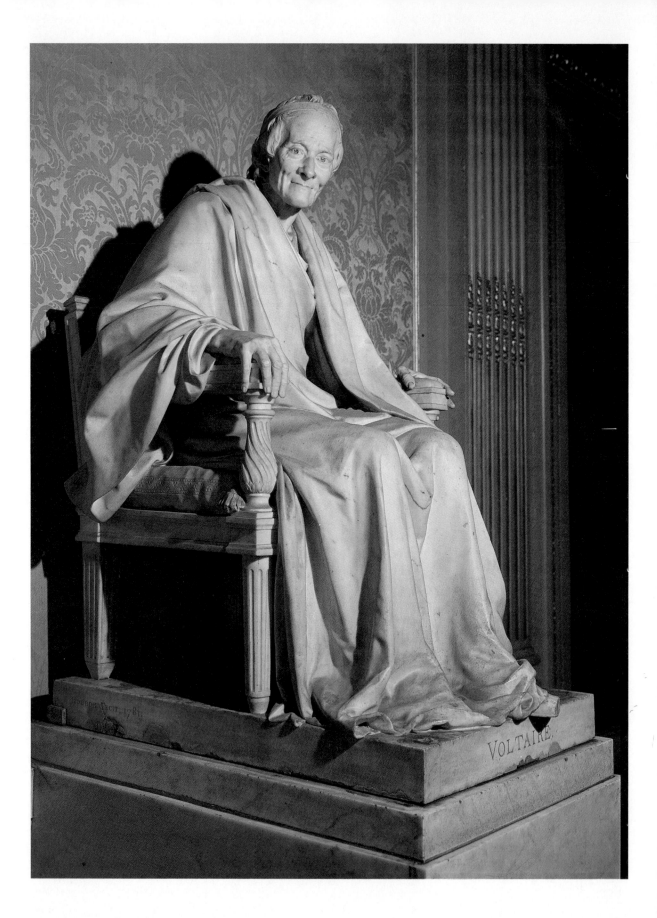

CHAPTER 18

Europe on the Threshold of Modernity, ca. 1715–1789

A customer in one of the growing number of cafés in Paris on February 10, 1778, might have wondered if the king himself was entering the city, such was the commotion as Parisians turned out to welcome a former resident. Now 84, this old man had journeyed to the city to preside at the opening of his latest play, but everyone realized that this most likely would be his last visit, and he was given a hero's welcome. The king himself would not receive the visitor, but literary and political elites clamored to be admitted to audiences with him. Benjamin Franklin brought his grandson to receive the old man's blessing. Though he was treated like royalty, the man was not a ruler, but a political thinker and writer: the philosopher Voltaire.

A prolific writer, critic, and reformer in his own country of France, Voltaire was lionized by elites everywhere, including the rulers of several European states. Voltaire is an apt symbol for the age not only because of his personal influence, but also because he was simply the best known of dozens of thinkers and writers who made up the philosophical movement we know as the Enlightenment. The Enlightenment constituted a revolution in political philosophy, but it was also much more: The era witnessed the emergence of an informed body of public opinion, critical of the prevailing political system, that existed outside the corridors of power. The relationship between governments and the governed had begun to change: Subjects of monarchs were becoming citizens of nations.

Frederick the Great of Prussia, Catherine the Great of Russia, and other rulers self-consciously tried to use Enlightenment precepts to guide

Voltaire, by Houdon.
In the foyer of the
Théâtre Français, Paris.

their efforts at governing. They had mixed success, however. Powerful interests opposed their efforts at reform, and their own hereditary and autocratic power was incompatible with Enlightenment perspectives. Elites still sure of their power, as well as the traditional interests of states, dominated eighteenth-century politics.

Nevertheless, profound changes in economic, social, and political life began in this period. Economic growth spurred population growth, which in turn stimulated industry and trade. The increasing economic and strategic importance of overseas colonies made them important focal points of international conflict. The dramatic political and social changes that began as the century closed had their roots in the intellectual, economic, and social ferment of eighteenth-century life.

THE ENLIGHTENMENT

One of Isaac Newton's countrymen wrote the following epitaph for the English scientist:

Nature and Nature's Laws lay hid in Night.
God said, "Let Newton be," and all was Light.

The most important works of Enlightenment philosophy reflected the intellectual confidence that Newton's work generated. The poet's assertion that "all was Light," however, requires scrutiny.

The phrase evokes the determination and confidence of an intellectual elite that felt it held a new key to truth. In this sense, the Enlightenment was nothing less than the transfer into general philosophy, particularly political and social thought, of the intellectual revolution that had already taken place within the physical sciences. But, like the Scientific Revolution, the Enlightenment was not only sweeping in its impact but specific in its content. In this so-called Age of Reason, *reason* had specific meanings, and philosophers' speculations had particular goals.

Enlightenment philosophy occurred in the context of increasingly widespread publications and new opportunities in literary societies, clubs, and salons for the exchange of views. This context shaped the outline of Enlightenment thought, which was for the most part an elite set of preoccupations. It also determined the radicalism of the Enlightenment, by helping to ensure that an entire

level of society would share in attitudes that were fundamentally critical of that society.

Voltaire and the Enlightenment

The Enlightenment was not so much a body of thought as it was an intellectual and social movement. Originating in France, it consisted, first, of the application to political and social thought of the confidence in the intelligibility of natural law that theoretical science had recently achieved. Enlightenment thinkers combined confidence in the intelligibility of the world and its laws with confidence in the human capacity to discern and work in concert with those laws. The former confidence was Newton's legacy; the latter was the legacy of Descartes and Locke. The most dramatic effect of confidence was the desacralizing of social and political bonds—a new belief that society can be grounded on rational foundations to be determined by humans, not arbitrary foundations determined by God.

A wide range of thinkers participated in the Enlightenment; in France, they were known as *philosophes,* a term meaning not a formal philosopher but rather a thinker and critic. To most philosophes, the main agenda was clear. For too long, humans had been mired in ignorance. Rather than regarding themselves as thinkers, they thought of themselves as sinners. Arbitrary laws and institutions oppressed them. Lack of proper education and the tyranny of the church condemned them to ignorance. French thinkers singled out the Catholic church as the archenemy because of its opposition to their positive views of human nature and because it controlled much education and was still a force in political life.

The following passage from Voltaire's *Dictionnaire philosophique* (*Philosophical Dictionary,* 1764) is typical of his work in its casual format and biting wit and is also typical of the venomous Enlightenment view of the church. The dictionary entry for "authority" is not about authority in general but focuses on the arbitrary authority of the church:

A hundred times [you clerics] have been spoken to of the insolent absurdity with which you condemned Galileo, and I shall speak to you for the hundred and first. . . . I desire that there be engraved on the door of your holy office: Here seven cardinals assisted by minor brethren had the master of thought of Italy thrown into prison at the age of seventy, made him fast on bread and water, because he instructed the human race.

The life of Voltaire (1694–1778), the most famous of the philosophes, spanned the century. Born François-Marie Arouet to a middle-class family, he took the pen name Voltaire in 1718, after one of his early plays was a critical success. He was educated by the Jesuits, whom he despised but admired for their teaching methods. He produced a vast array of written work: plays, epic poems, novelettes—some of which have explicit philosophical or political content—as well as philosophical tracts. Voltaire moved in courtly circles. Mockery of the regent, the duke of Orléans, led to a year's imprisonment in 1717, and an exchange of insults with a leading courtier some years later led to enforced exile in Great Britain for two years.

After returning from Britain, Voltaire published his first major philosophical work. *Lettres philosophiques* (*Philosophical Letters*, 1734) revealed the influence of his British sojourn and helped to popularize Newton's achievement. The empirical tradition in British philosophy profoundly influenced Voltaire. To his confidence in the laws governing nature he added cautious confidence in humans' attempts to establish truth. From Locke's work (see pages 649–651) he drew confidence in human educability tempered by awareness of the finite nature of the human mind. These elements gave Voltaire's philosophy both its passionate conviction and its practicality.

Voltaire portrayed Great Britain as a more rational society than France. He was particularly impressed with the religious and intellectual toleration evident there. The British government had a more workable set of institutions and the economy was less crippled by the remnants of feudal privilege, and education was not in the hands of the church. (See the box, "Voltaire on Britain's Commercial Success.")

After the publication of his audacious *Lettres*, Voltaire was again forced into exile from Paris, and he resided for some years in the country home of a woman with whom he shared a remarkable intellectual and emotional relationship: Emilie, marquise du Châtelet (1706–1749). Châtelet was a mathematician and a scientist. She set to work on a French translation of Newton's *Principia* while Voltaire worked at his accustomed variety of writing, which also included a commen-

Etablissement de la nouvelle Philosophie. Notre Berceau fut un Caffé.

Café Society The caption under this contemporary illustration reads: "Establishment of the new philosophy; our cradle was the café." Cafés were one of the new settings where literate elites could discuss the new philosophy and explore its implications for social and political life. (*Carnavalet Museum, Paris*)

tary on Newton's work. Because of Châtelet's tutelage, Voltaire became more knowledgeable about the sciences and more serious in his efforts to apply scientific rationality to human affairs. He was devastated by her sudden death in 1749.

Shortly afterward, he accepted the invitation of the king of Prussia, Frederick II, to visit Berlin. His stay was stormy and brief because of disagreements with other court philosophers. He resided

Voltaire on Britain's Commercial Success

In this excerpt from Philosophical Letters, *Voltaire compares British trade and seapower with the commercial activities of the German and French elites, who scorn trade in order to engage in aristocratic pretentiousness and court politics. Voltaire's admiration for England and his penchant for criticizing irrationalities of all sorts are evident, as is his famed wit. Wit and irony were important tools, enabling Voltaire to advance trenchant criticism when seeming only to poke fun.*

Commerce, which has brought wealth to the citizenry of England, has helped to make them free, and freedom has developed commerce in its turn. By means of it the nation has grown great; it is commerce that little by little has strengthened the naval forces that make the English the masters of the seas. . . . Posterity may learn with some surprise that a little island with nothing of its own but a bit of lead, tin . . . and coarse wool became, by means of its commerce, powerful enough to send three fleets at one time to three different ends of the earth.

All this makes the English merchant justly proud; moreover, the younger brother of a peer of the realm does not scorn to enter into trade. . . . [In Germany], they are unable to imagine how [an aristocrat could enter trade since they have] as many as thirty Highnesses of the same name, with nothing to show for it but pride and a coat of arms.

In France anybody who wants to can [act the part of marquis] and whoever arrives in Paris with money to spend and a [plausible name] may indulge in such phrases as "a man of my rank and quality" and with sovereign eye look down upon a wholesaler. . . . Yet I don't know which is the more useful to a state, a well-powdered lord who knows precisely what time the king gets up in the morning . . . and who gives himself airs of grandeur while playing the role of slave in a minister's antechamber, or a great merchant who enriches his country.

Source: Ernest Dilworth, trans. and ed., *Voltaire: Philosophical Letters* (New York: Bobbs-Merrill, 1961), pp. 39–40.

for a time in Geneva, until his criticisms of the city's moral codes forced yet another exile on him. He spent most of the last twenty years of his life at his estates on the Franco-Swiss border, where he could be relatively free from interference by any government. These were productive years. He produced his best-known satirical novelette, *Candide,* in 1758. It criticized aristocratic privilege and the power of clerics as well as the naiveté of philosophers who took "natural law" to mean that the world was already operating as it should.

Voltaire's belief that one must struggle to overturn the accumulated habits of centuries is also reflected in his political activity. Voltaire became involved in several celebrated legal cases in which individuals were pitted against the authority of the church, which was still backed by the authority of the state. The most famous case was that of Jean Calas (1698–1762), a Protestant from southern France who was accused of murdering his son, allegedly to prevent him from converting to Catholicism. Calas maintained his innocence until his execution in 1762. Voltaire saw in this case the worst aspects of religious prejudice and injustice and worked tirelessly to establish Calas's innocence as a matter of principle and so that his family could inherit his property. In pursuit of justice in these cases and in criticism of his archenemy the church, Voltaire added a stream of straightforward political pamphlets to his literary output. He also worked closer to home, initiating agricultural reform on his estates and working to improve the status of peasants in the vicinity.

Voltaire died in Paris in May 1778, shortly after his triumphal return there. By then, he was no longer leader of the Enlightenment in strictly intellectual terms. Thinkers and writers more radical than he had earned prominence during his long life and had dismissed some of his beliefs, such as the notion that reform could be introduced by a monarch. But Voltaire had provided a crucial stimulus to French thought with his *Lettres philosophiques*. His importance lies also in his embodiment of the critical spirit of eighteenth-century rationalism: its confidence, its increasingly practical bent, its wit and sophistication. Until the end of his life, Voltaire remained a bridge between the increasingly diverse body of Enlightenment thought and the literate elite audience.

The Variety of Enlightenment Thought

Differences among philosophes grew as the century progressed. In the matter of religion, for example, there was virtual unanimity of opposition to the Catholic church among French thinkers, but no unanimity about God. Voltaire was a theist—believing firmly in God, creator of the universe, but not a specifically Christian God. To some later thinkers, God was irrelevant—the creator of the world, but a world that ran continuously according to established laws. Some philosophes were atheists, arguing that a universe that ran according to discoverable laws needs no higher purpose and no divine presence to explain, run, or justify it. In Protestant areas of Europe, in contrast to France, Enlightenment thought was often less hostile to Christianity.

Questions about social and political order, as well as about human rationality itself, were also pondered. Charles de Secondat (1689–1755), baron of Montesquieu, a French judge and legal philosopher, combined the belief that human institutions must be rational with Locke's assumption of human educability. Montesquieu's treatise *De L'Esprit des lois* (*The Spirit of the Laws*, 1748) was published in twenty-two printings within two years. In it Montesquieu maintained that laws were not meant to be arbitrary rules but derived naturally from human society: The more evolved a society was, the

MAJOR WORKS OF THE ENLIGHTENMENT

1721	Montesquieu, *Persian Letters*
1734	Voltaire, *Philosophical Letters*
1748	Montesquieu, *The Spirit of the Laws* Hume, *Essay Concerning Human Understanding*
1758	Voltaire, *Candide*
1751–65	Diderot, *The Encyclopedia*
1762	Rousseau, *The Social Contract*
1764	Voltaire, *Philosophical Dictionary*
1776	Smith, *The Wealth of Nations*
1784	Kant, *What Is Enlightenment?*
1792	Wollstonecraft, *A Vindication of the Rights of Woman*
1795	Condorcet, *The Progress of the Human Mind*

more liberal were its laws. This notion provided a sense of the progress possible within society and government and deflated Europeans' pretensions in regard to other societies, for a variety of laws could equally be "rational" given differing conditions. Montesquieu is perhaps best known to Americans as the advocate of the separation of legislative, executive, and judicial powers that later became enshrined in the American Constitution. To Montesquieu, this scheme seemed to parallel in human government the balance of forces observable in nature and seemed best to guarantee liberty.

The "laws" of economic life were also investigated. In France, economic thinkers known as *physiocrats* proposed ending what they regarded as artificial control over land use in order to free productive capacity and permit the flow of produce to market. Their target was traditional forms of land tenure, including collective control of village lands by peasants and seigneurial rights over land and peasant labor by landlords. The freeing of restrictions on agriculture, manufacture, and trade was proposed by the Scotsman Adam Smith in his treatise *An Inquiry into the Nature and Causes of the Wealth of Nations* (1776).

Smith (1723–1790), a professor at the University of Glasgow, is best known in modern times as the originator of "laissez-faire" economics: the assumption that an economy will regulate itself without interference by government and, of more concern to Smith, without the monopolies and other economic privileges common in his day. Smith's schema for economic growth was not merely a rigid application to economics of faith in natural law. His ideas grew out of an optimistic view of human nature and human rationality that was heavily indebted to Locke. Humans, Smith believed, have drives and passions that they can direct and govern by means of reason and inherent sympathy for one another. Thus, Smith said, in seeking their own achievement and well-being, they are often "led by an invisible hand" to simultaneously benefit society as a whole.

Throughout the century, philosophers of various stripes disagreed about the nature and the limits of human reason. Smith's countryman and friend David Hume (1711–1776) was perhaps the most radical in his critique of the human capacity for knowing. He was the archskeptic, taking Locke's view of the limitations on pure reason to the point of doubting the efficacy of sense data. His major work in which he expounded these views, *Essay Concerning Human Understanding* (1748), led to important innovations later in the century in the work of the German philosopher Immanuel Kant but were, at the time, almost contrary to the prevailing spirit of confidence in empirical knowledge. Hume himself separated this work from his other efforts in moral, political, and economic philosophy, which were more in tune with the prevailing views of the day.

Mainstream confidence in empirical knowledge and in the intelligibility of the world is evident in the production of the *Encyclopédie* (*Encyclopedia*), a seventeen-volume compendium of knowledge, criticism, and philosophy assembled by leading philosophes in France and published there between 1751 and 1765. The volumes were designed to contain state-of-the-art knowledge about arts, sciences, technology, and philosophy. The guiding philosophy of the project, set forth by its chief editor, Denis Diderot (1713–1784), was a belief in the advance of human happiness through the advance of knowledge. The *Encyclopédie* was a kind of history of the advance of knowledge as

Diderot's Encyclopedia This illustration of typesetting at a newspaper printshop is one of many depicting industry and technology of the day in the multivolume *Encyclopedia*. Newspapers increased in size, number, and frequency of publication during the course of the eighteenth century. *(Division of Rare & Manuscript Collections, Cornell University Library)*

well as a compendium of known achievements. It was revolutionary in that it not only intrigued and inspired intellectuals but assisted thousands of government officials and professionals. Catherine the Great, empress of Russia, remarked in a letter that she consulted its pages to find guidance concerning one of her reform schemes.

The encyclopedia project illustrates the political context of Enlightenment thought as well as its philosophical premises. The Catholic church placed the work on the Index of prohibited books, and the French government might have barred its publication but for the fact that the official who would have made the decision was drawn to Enlightenment thinking. Many other officials, however, worked to suppress it. By the late 1750s, losses in wars overseas had made French officials highly sensitive to political challenges of any kind. Thus, like Voltaire, the major contributors to the *Encyclopédie* were lionized by certain segments of the elite and persecuted by others in their official functions.

The *Encyclopédie* reflects the complexities and limitations of Enlightenment thought on another score—the position of women. One might expect that the Enlightenment penchant for challenging received knowledge and traditional social and political hierarchies would lead to revised views of women's abilities and rights. Indeed, some contributors blamed women's inequality with men not on any deficiencies in women but rather on the customs and laws that had kept women from education and the development of their abilities. However, other contributors blamed women, and not society, for the inequality women suffered, or they argued that women had talents that fit them only for the domestic sphere.

Both positions were represented in Enlightenment thought as a whole. The assumption of the natural equality of all people provided a powerful ground for arguing the equality of women with men. Some thinkers, such as Mary Astell (1666–1731), challenged Locke's separation of family life from the public world of free, contractual relationships. (See the box, "An English Feminist Criticizes Unenlightened Views of Women.") Most advocated increased education for women, if only to make them more fit to raise enlightened children. By 1800 the most radical thinkers were advocating full citizenship rights for women and equal rights to property along with enhanced education.

The best-known proponent of those views was an English woman, Mary Wollstonecraft (1759–1797), who authored *A Vindication of the Rights of Woman* (1792). She assumed that most elite women would devote themselves to domestic duties, but she argued that without the responsibilities of citizenship, the leavening of education, and economic independence, women could be neither fully formed individuals nor worthy of their duties. Working women, she concluded, needed these rights simply to survive.

A more limited view of women's capacities was one element in the influential work of Jean-Jacques Rousseau (1712–1778). Like Locke, Rousseau could conceive of the free individual only as male, and he grounded his critique of the old order and his novel political ideas in an arbitrary division of gender roles. Rousseau's view of women was linked to a critique of the artificiality of elite, cosmopolitan society in which Enlightenment thought was then flourishing and in which aristocratic women were fully involved. Rousseau believed in the educability of men but was as concerned with issues of character and emotional life as with knowledge. Society—particularly the artificial courtly society—was corrupting. The true citizen had to cultivate virtue and sensibility, not manners, taste, or refinement. Rousseau designated women as guarantors of the "natural" virtues of children and as nurturers of the emotional life and character of men—but not as fully formed beings in their own right.

Rousseau's emphasis on the education and virtue of citizens was the underpinning of his larger political vision, set forth in *Du Contrat social* (*The Social Contract*, 1762). He imagined an egalitarian republic—possible particularly in small states such as his native Geneva—in which men would consent to be governed because the government would determine and act in accordance with the "general will" of the citizens. The "general will" was not majority opinion but rather what each citizen *would* want if he were fully informed and were acting in accordance with his highest nature. The "general will" became apparent whenever the citizens met as a body and made collective decisions, and it could be imposed on all inhabitants. (See the box, "Rousseau Discusses the Benefits of Submitting to the General Will.") This was a breathtaking vision of direct democracy—but one with ominous possibilities, for Rousseau

An English Feminist Criticizes Unenlightened Views of Women

Both male and female writers criticized the failure of some Enlightenment thinkers to view ideas about women with the same skepticism and rationalism that they brought to other subjects. One of the earliest was the Englishwoman Mary Astell (1666–1731). In this excerpt from **Some Reflections on Marriage (1700),** *Astell criticizes, in an ironic tone, negative assessments of women's capacities, Locke's separation of the public and private spheres, and the denial to women of the rights that men enjoy in public life.*

'Tis true, through want of learning, and that of superior genius which men, as men, lay claim to, she [the author] was ignorant of the natural inferiority of our sex, which our masters lay down as self-evident and fundamental truth. She saw nothing in the reason of things to make this either a principle or a conclusion, but much to the contrary.

If they mean that some men are superior to some women, this is no great discovery; had they turned the tables, they might have seen that some women are superior to some men. . . .

Again, if absolute sovereignty be not necessary in a state, how comes it to be so in a fam-
ily? Or if in a family why not in a state, since no reason can be alleged for the one that will not hold more strongly for the other? If the authority of the husband, so far as it extends, is sacred and inalienable, why not that of the prince? The domestic sovereign is without dispute elected and the stipulations and contract are mutual; is it not then partial in men to the last degree to contend for and practice that arbitrary dominion in their families which they abhor and exclaim against in the state? For if arbitrary power is evil in itself, and an improper method of governing rational and free agents, it ought not to be practiced anywhere.

Source: Moira Ferguson, ed., *First Feminists* (Bloomington: Indiana University Press, 1985), pp. 191–193.

---

rejected the institutional brakes on state authority proposed by Locke and Montesquieu. Also, the demands of citizenship in such a political order, in contrast to simple obedience under a monarchy, necessitated, for Rousseau, the subordination of women's lives to those of male citizens.

Rousseau's emphasis on the private emotional life anticipates the romanticism of the early nineteenth century. It also reflects Rousseau's own experience as the son of a humble family, always sensing himself an outcast in the brilliant world of Parisian salons. He had a love-hate relationship with this life, remaining attached to several aristocratic women patrons even as he decried their influence. His own personal life did not match his prescriptions for others. He completely neglected to give his own four children the nurturing and education that he argued were vital; indeed, he

abandoned all of them to a foundling home. He was nevertheless influential as a critic of an elite society still dominated by status, patronage, and privilege. Rousseau's work reflects to an extreme degree the tensions in Enlightenment thought generally: It was part of elite culture as well as its principal critic.

The Growth of Public Opinion

It is impossible to understand the significance of the Enlightenment without an analysis of how it was a part of public life. Most of the philosophes were of modest origin. They influenced the privileged elite of their day because of the social and political environment in which their ideas were elaborated. Indeed, the clearest distinguishing feature of the Enlightenment may be the creation of

Rousseau Discusses the Benefits of Submitting to the General Will

In this excerpt from his **Social Contract**, *Rousseau describes the relationship of individuals to the general will. Notice the wider-ranging benefits Rousseau believes men will enjoy in society as he envisions it; Rousseau is clearly interested in intellectual, moral, and emotional well-being.*

I assume that men reach a point where the obstacles to their preservation in a state of nature prove greater than the strength that each man has to preserve himself in that state. Beyond this point, the primitive condition cannot endure, for then the human race will perish if it does not change its mode of existence. . . .

"How to find a form of association which will defend the person and goods of each member with the collective force of all, and under which each individual, while uniting himself with the others, obeys no one but himself, and remains as free as before." This is the fundamental problem to which the social contract holds the solution. . . .

The passing from the state of nature to the civil society produces a remarkable change in man; it puts justice as a rule of conduct in the place of instinct, and gives his actions the moral quality they previously lacked. . . . And although in civil society man surrenders some of the advantages that belong to the state of nature, he gains in return far greater ones; his faculties are so exercised and developed, his mind is so enlarged, his sentiments so ennobled, and his whole spirit so elevated that . . . he should constantly bless the happy hour that lifted him for ever from the state of nature and from a stupid, limited animal made a creature of intelligence and a man. . . .

For every individual as a man may have a private will contrary to, or different from, the general will that he has as a citizen. His private interest may speak with a very different voice from that of the public interest; his absolute and naturally independent existence may make him regard what he owes to the common cause as a gratuitous contribution, the loss of which would be less painful for others than the payment is onerous for him; and fancying that the artificial person which constitutes the state is a mere fictitious entity (since it is not a man), he might seek to enjoy the rights of a citizen without doing the duties of a subject. The growth of this kind of injustice would bring about the ruin of the body politic.

Hence, in order that the social pact shall not be an empty formula, it is tacitly implied in that commitment—which alone can give force to all others—that whoever refuses to obey the general will shall be constrained to do so by the whole body, which means nothing other than that he shall be forced to be free; for this is the necessary condition which, by giving each citizen to the nation, secures him against all personal dependence, it is the condition which shapes both the design and the working of the political machine, and which alone bestows justice on civil contracts—without it, such contracts would be absurd, tyrannical and liable to the grossest abuse.

Source: Jean-Jacques Rousseau, *The Social Contract*, trans. Maurice Cranston (London: Penguin Books, 1968), pp. 59–60, 63–65.

an informed body of public opinion that stood apart from court society.

Increased literacy and access to books and other print media are an important part of the story. Perhaps more important, the kinds of reading that people favored began to change. We know from inventories made of people's belongings at the time of their death (required for inheritance laws) that books in the homes of ordinary people were no longer just traditional works such as devotional literature. Ordinary people now read secular and contemporary philosophical works. As the availability of such works increased, reading itself evolved from a reverential encounter with traditional material to a critical encounter with new material. Solitary reading for reflection and pleasure became more widespread.

Habits of reading and responding to written material changed not only because there were increased opportunities to read but also because there were changes in the social environment. In the eighteenth century, forerunners of the modern lending libraries made their debut. In Paris, for a fee, one could join a *salle de lecture* (literally, a "reading room") where the latest works were available to any member. Booksellers, whose numbers increased dramatically, found ways to meet readers' demands for inexpensive access to reading matter. One might pay for the right to read a book in the bookshop itself. In short, new venues encouraged people to see themselves not just as readers but as members of a reading public.

Among the most famous and most important of these venues were the Parisian salons, where Voltaire and others read their works in progress aloud and discussed them. Several Parisian women—mostly wealthy, but of modest social status—invited courtiers, bureaucrats, and intellectuals to meet in their homes at regular times each week. The *salonnières* (salon leaders) themselves read widely in order to facilitate the exchange of ideas among their guests. This mediating function was crucial to the success and the importance of the salons. Manners and polite conversation had been a defining feature of aristocratic life since the seventeenth century, but they had largely been means of displaying status and safeguarding honor. The leadership of the salonnières and the protected environment they provided away from court life enabled a further evolution of "polite society" to occur: Anyone with appropriate manners could participate in conversation as an equal. The assumption of equality, in turn, enabled conversation to turn away from maintaining the status quo to questioning it.

The influence of salons was extended by the wide networks of correspondence salonnières maintained. Perhaps the most famous salonnière in her day, Marie-Thérèse Geoffrin (1699–1777) corresponded with Catherine the Great, the reform-minded empress of Russia, as well as with philosophes outside of Paris and with interested would-be participants in her salon. The ambas-

sador of Naples regularly attended her salon before returning to his native city, from which he exchanged weekly letters with her. He reflected on the importance of salon leaders like Geoffrin when he wrote from Naples, lamenting,

[our gatherings here] are getting farther away from the character and tone of those of France, despite all [our] efforts. . . . There is no way to make Naples resemble Paris unless we find a woman to guide us, organize us, *Geoffrinise* us.[1]

Various clubs, local academies, and learned and secret societies copied some features of the salons of Paris. Hardly any municipality was without a private society that functioned both as a forum for political and philosophical discussion and as an elite social club. Here mingled doctors, lawyers, local officials—some of whom enjoyed the fruits of the political system in offices and patronage. In Scotland, universities were flourishing centers of Enlightenment thought, but political clubs in Glasgow and Edinburgh enriched debate and the development of ideas.

Ideas circulated beyond the membership of even the many far-flung clubs by means of print. Newsletters reporting the goings-on at salons in Paris were produced by some participants. Regularly published periodicals in Great Britain, France, and Italy also served as important means for the dissemination of enlightened opinion in the form of reviews, essays, and published correspondence. Some of these journals had been in existence since the second half of the seventeenth century, when they had begun as a means to circulate the new scientific work. Now, subscribers included Americans anxious to keep up with intellectual life in Europe. Europeans who could not afford the annual subscriptions could peruse the journals in the newly available reading rooms and libraries. In addition to newsletters and journals, newspapers, which were regularly published even in small cities throughout western and central Europe, circulated ideas.

In all these arenas, Enlightenment ideas became the encouragement for and the legitimation of a type of far-reaching political debate that had never before existed, except possibly in England during the seventeenth century. Understanding the Enlightenment involves understanding the milieu in which these ideas were received. The first and greatest impact of the Enlightenment,

The Growth of the Book Trade Book ownership dramatically increased in the eighteenth century, and a wide range of secular works—from racy novelettes to philosophical tracts— was available in print. In this rendering of a bookshop, shipments of books have arrived from around Europe. Notice the artist's optimism in the great variety of persons, from the peasant with a scythe to a white-robed cleric, who are drawn to the shop by "Minerva" (the Roman goddess of wisdom). *(Musée des Beaux-Arts de Dijon)*

particularly in France, was not the creation of a program for political or social change but the creation of a culture of politics that could generate change.

Art in the Age of Reason

The Enlightenment reverberated throughout all aspects of cultural life. Just as the market for books and the reading public expanded, so did the audience for works of art in the growing leisured urban circles of Paris and other great cities. The modern cultured public—a public of concertgoers and art-gallery enthusiasts—began to make its first appearance. The brilliant and sophisticated courts around Europe continued to sponsor composers, musicians, and painters by providing both patronage and audiences. Yet some performances of concerts and operas began to take place in theaters and halls outside the courts and were more accessible to the public.

Beginning in 1737, one section of the Louvre palace in Paris was devoted annually to public exhibitions of painting and sculpture (though by royally sponsored and approved artists). In both France and Britain, public discussion of art began to take place in published reviews and criticisms: The role of art critic was born. Works of art were also sold by public means, such as auctions. As works became more available by such means, demand grew and production increased.

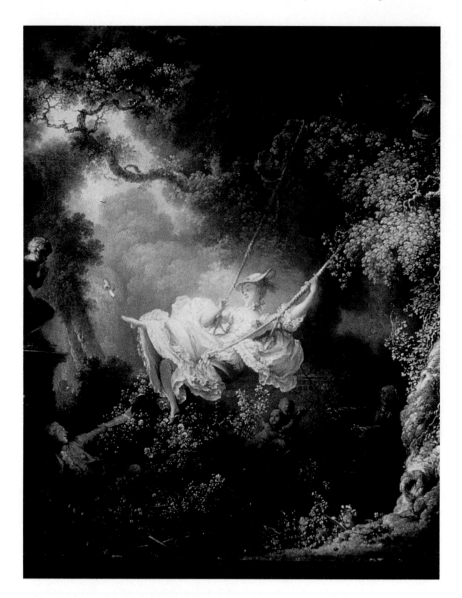

The Cult of Sensibility in Art
This painting, *The Swing*, by the Frenchman Fragonard, depicts a moment of playful and sensuous intimacy. This style of painting was an elaboration of baroque style known as *rococo*. It began to be considered too excessive and lighthearted and was replaced by the more serious neoclassical style as the century wore on. *(Wallace Collection/Bridgeman Art Library/Art Resource, NY)*

In subject matter and style these various art forms exhibited greater variety than works in preceding centuries had shown. We can nevertheless discern certain patterns and tendencies in both the content and the form of eighteenth-century European art. Late baroque painters contributed to an exploration of private life and emotion sometimes called the "cult of sensibility." Frequently, they depicted private scenes of upper-class life, especially moments of intimate conversation or flirtation.

The cult of sensibility was fostered by literature as well. The private life of emotion was nurtured by increased literacy, greater access to books, and the need to retreat from the elaborate artifice of court life. The novel became an increasingly important genre as a means of exploring human problems and relationships. In English literature the novels of Samuel Richardson (1689–1761)—*Pamela* (1740) and *Clarissa* (1747–1748)—explored personal psychology and passion. Rousseau followed Richardson's lead in structuring his own novels *La Nouvelle Héloïse* (1761) and *Emile* (1762). The cult of sensibility was not mere entertainment; it also carried the political and philosophical message that honest emotion was a "natural" virtue and that courtly manners, by contrast, were irrational and degrading. The enormous popularity of Rousseau's novels, for example, came from the fact that their intense emotional appeal was simultaneously felt to be uplifting.

A revival of classical subjects and styles after the middle of the century evoked what were thought to be the pure and timeless values of classical heroes. This revival revealed the influence of Enlightenment thought by assuming the educability of its audience by means of example. Classical revival architecture illustrated a belief in order, symmetry, and proportion. Americans are familiar with its evocations because it has been the architecture of their republic, but even churches were built in this style in eighteenth-century Europe. The classical movement in music reflected both the cult of sensibility and the classicizing styles in the visual arts. Embodied in the works of Austrians Franz Josef Haydn (1732–1809) and Wolfgang Amadeus Mozart (1756–1791), this movement saw the clarification of musical structures, such as the modern sonata and symphony, and enabled melody to take center stage.

Another trend in art and literature was a fascination with nature and with the seemingly "natural" in human culture—less "developed" or more historically distant societies. One of the most popular printed works in the middle of the century was the supposed translation of the poems of Ossian, a third-century Scots Highland poet. Early English, German, Norse, and other folktales were "discovered" (in some cases invented) and published. Many of these went through several editions during the century.

The fact that folk life, other cultures, and untamed nature itself began to be celebrated just when they were being more definitively conquered is very revealing. (See the feature, "Weighing the Evidence: Gardens," on pages 694–695.) The early poetry of Scotland, for example, was celebrated just as the Scottish Highlands were being punished and pacified by the English because of the clans' support for a rival claimant to the English throne. Once purged of any threat, the exotic image of another culture (even the folk culture of one's own society) could be a source of imagination and create a sense of distance from which to measure one's own sophistication. Thus, both ancient and exotic subjects reinforced a sense of dominance and control.

EUROPEAN RULERS AND EUROPEAN SOCIETY

Mindful of the lessons to be learned from the revolution in England and the achievements of Louis XIV, European rulers in the eighteenth century continued their efforts to govern with greater effectiveness. Some, like the rulers of Prussia and Russia, were encouraged in their efforts by Enlightenment ideas that stressed the need for reforms in law, economy, and government. In the main they, like Voltaire, believed that monarchs could be agents for change. In Austria, significant reforms, including the abolition of serfdom, were made. The changes were uneven, however, and at times owed as much to traditional efforts at better government as to enlightened persuasion.

In all cases, rulers' efforts to govern more effectively meant continual readjustments in relationships with traditional elites. Whether or not elites could formally participate in the governing process by means of established institutions such as the English Parliament, royal governments everywhere were still dependent on their participation. Enlightened monarchs were changing their view of themselves and their image from the diligent but self-aggrandizing image of Louis XIV to that of servant of the state. In this way, monarchs actually undermined the dynastic claim to rule by refounding it on a utilitarian basis. The state was increasingly seen as separate from the ruler.

France During the Enlightenment

It is one of the seeming paradoxes of the era of the Enlightenment that critical thought about society and politics flourished in France, an autocratic state with institutionally privileged elites. Yet in France there was a well-educated elite, a tradition of scientific inquiry, and a legacy of cultured court life that, since the early days of Louis XIV, had become the model for all Europe (see pages 592–594). French was the international intellectual language, and France was the most fertile center of elite cultural life. Both Adam Smith and David Hume, for example, spent portions of their careers in Paris and were welcomed into the salons. In fact, the French capital was an environment that encouraged debate and dissent precisely because of the juxtaposition of the new intellectual climate with the difficulties the French state was facing and the institutional rigidities of its political system—a system that excluded many talented and productive members of the elite from its privileged circles.

In the last decades of the reign of Louis XIV (d. 1715), many thoughtful French people criticized the direction the French state was taking. They began to question the point of foreign wars that yielded ever diminishing returns. The intoxicating blend of stability, effective government, national interest, and the personal glory of the monarch began to dissolve.

Louis XIV was followed on the throne by his 5-year-old great-grandson, Louis XV (r. 1715–1774). During the regency, nobles clamored for the establishment of councils so that they could become more active partners in government. Likewise, the supreme law courts, the parlements, reclaimed the right of remonstrance—the right to object to royal edicts and thus to exercise some control over the enactment of law. Throughout Louis XV's reign, his administration often locked horns with the parlements, particularly as royal ministers coped with France's financial crises. Louis XIV had exhausted the nation financially—in need of more money and of new and more reliable ways to get money. During Louis XV's reign the pressures of further wars intensified the need for wholesale reform.

Louis XV's government continued some of the rationalizing policies of Louis XIV by which relics of the decentralized medieval economy were abolished. Roads were improved and more and more internal customs barriers eliminated. The Crown did not challenge the Catholic church's privileged status or property, which would have been welcomed by many elites. Nor was Louis XV able, for most of his reign, to undercut the power of the parlements in order to reform the fiscal system.

By the late 1760s, the weight of government debt from foreign wars finally forced the king into action. He threw his support behind the reforming schemes of his chancellor, Nicolas de Maupeou. Maupeou dissolved the parlements early in 1771 and created new law courts whose judges would not enjoy independent power.

Public opinion was split over this conflict between the monarch and the parlements. A number of ministers under Louis XV and his successor, Louis XVI (r. 1774–1792), shared Enlightenment views of the efficiency of creating economic change from the top and the rationality of doing away with privileges such as the exemption of the nobility from taxation. However, the role of consultative bodies and the separation of powers beloved of Montesquieu, himself a parlementaire, were much prized, and the parlements were the only institutions that could legitimately check monarchical powers. Ordinary property holders, such as provincial nobles, who had little in common with privileged officeholders, might nevertheless see the parlementaires' privileges as the best guarantor of their own.

Further hampering reform efforts was the character of the king himself. Louis XV displayed none of the kingly qualities of his great-grandfather. He was not pleasant or affable, and he was lazy. By the end of his reign, he was roundly despised. He did not give the "rationality" of royal government a good name.

Not surprisingly, from about the middle of the century, enlightened public opinion, nurtured in salons and other new settings, began proposing a variety of ways to enhance representation, consultation, and reform. There were calls to revive the moribund Estates General, the cumbersome representative assembly last called in 1614, as well as for the establishment of new councils or local, decentralized representative assemblies. The workability of these proposals is less important than the simple fact that they were made.

The Crown lost control of reform in 1774, when Louis XV died. His grandson, Louis XVI, well meaning but insecure, allowed the complete restoration of the parlements. Further reform efforts, sponsored by the king and several talented ministers, came to naught because of parlementary opposition. The French crown had lost the chance to reform royal government from above. By the time an Estates General was finally called in the wake of further financial problems in 1788, the enlightened elites' habit of carrying on political analysis and criticism of government outside the actual corridors of power had given rise to a volatile situation.

Monarchy and Constitutional Government in Great Britain

After the deaths of William (d. 1702) and Mary (d. 1694), the British crown passed to Mary's sister, Anne (r. 1702–1714), and then to a collateral line descended from Elizabeth (d. 1662), sister of the beheaded Charles I. Elizabeth had married Frederick, elector of the Palatinate (and had reigned with him briefly in Bohemia at the outset of the Thirty Years' War; see page 575), and her descendants were Germans, now electors of Hanover. The new British sovereign in 1714, who reigned as George I (r. 1714–1727), was both a foreigner and a man of mediocre abilities. Moreover, his claim to the throne was immediately contested by Catholic descendants of James II, who attempted to depose him in 1715, and later his son, George II (r. 1727–1760), in 1745.

This second attempt to depose the Hanoverian kings in 1745 was more nearly successful. The son of the Stuart claimant to the throne, Charles (known in legend as Bonnie Prince Charlie), landed on the west coast of Scotland, with French assistance, and marched south into England with surprising ease. Most of the British army, and George II himself, was on the continent, fighting in the War of Austrian Succession (see page 682).

Scotland had been formally united with England in 1707 (hence the term *Great Britain* after that time), and Charles found some support among Scots dissatisfied with the economic and political results of that union.

But the vast majority of Britons did not want the civil war that Charles's challenge inevitably meant, especially on behalf of a Catholic pretender who relied on support from Britain's great commercial and political rival, France. Landholders and merchants in lowland Scotland and northern England gathered militia to oppose Charles until regular army units returned from abroad. Charles's army, made up mostly of poor Highland clansmen, was destroyed at the Battle of Culloden in April 1746. Charles fled back to France, and the British government used the failed uprising as justification for the brutal and forceful integration of the still-remote Highlands into the British state.

Traditional practices, from wearing tartans to carrying the accustomed personal daggers and

The Destruction of the Highlanders Although English rulers had previously attacked individual clans, Highland culture maintained its independence until the uprising of 1745. For the first time, clansmen were decisively beaten in battle by British troops, who used the tactics of volley fire and disciplined bayonet charge. *(The Royal Collection © 1993 Her Majesty Queen Elizabeth II)*

even playing bagpipes, were forbidden. Control of land was redistributed to break the social and economic bonds of clan society. Thousands of Highlanders died at the battle itself, in prisons or deportation ships, or by deliberate extermination by British troops in the aftermath of the battle.

Despite this serious challenge to the new dynasty and the brutal response it occasioned, the British state, overall, enjoyed a period of relative stability as well as innovation in the eighteenth century. The events of the seventeenth century had reaffirmed both the need for a strong monarchy and the role of Parliament in defending elite interests. The power of Parliament had recently been reinforced by the Act of Settlement, by which the Protestant heir to Queen Anne had been chosen in 1701. By excluding the Catholic Stuarts from the throne and establishing the line of succession, this document reasserted that Parliament determined the legitimacy of the monarchy. In addition, the act claimed greater parliamentary authority over foreign and domestic policy in the wake of the bellicose William's rule (see pages 602–603).

Noteworthy in the eighteenth century were the ways in which cooperation evolved between monarchy and Parliament as Parliament became a more sophisticated and secure institution. Political parties—that is, distinct groups within the elite favoring certain foreign and domestic policies—came into existence. Two groups, the Whigs and the Tories, had begun to form during the reign of Charles II (d. 1685). The Whigs (named derisively by their opponents with a Scottish term for horse thieves) had opposed Charles's pro-French policies and his efforts to tolerate Catholicism and had wholly opposed his brother and successor, James II. Initially, the Whigs favored an aggressive foreign policy against continental opponents, particularly France. The Tories (also derisively named— for Irish cattle rustlers) tended to be staunch Anglicans uninterested in Protestant anti-Catholic agitation. They tended to have a conservative view of their own role, favoring isolationism in foreign affairs and an attitude of deference toward monarchical authority. Whigs generally represented the interests of the great aristocrats or wealthy merchants or gentry. Tories tended to represent the interests of provincial gentry and the traditional concerns of landholding and local administration.

The Whigs were the dominant influence in government through most of the century to 1770. William and Mary as well as Queen Anne favored Whig religious and foreign policy interests. The loyalty of many Tories was called into question by their support for a Stuart, not Hanoverian, succession at Anne's death in 1714. The long Whig dominance of government was also ensured by the talents of Robert Walpole, a member of Parliament who functioned virtually as a prime minister from 1722 to 1742.

Walpole (1676–1745) was from a minor gentry family and was brought into government in 1714 with other Whig ministers in George I's new regime. An extremely talented politician, he took advantage of the mistakes of other ministers over the years and, in 1722, became both the first lord of the treasury and chancellor of the exchequer. There was not yet any official post or title of "prime minister," but the great contribution of Walpole's tenure was to create that office in fact, if not officially. He chose to maintain peace abroad where he could and thus presided over a period of recovery and relative prosperity that enhanced the stability of government.

Initially, Walpole was helped in his role as go-between for king and Parliament by George I's own limitations. The king rarely attended meetings of his own council of ministers and, in any case, was hampered by his limited command of English. Gradually, the Privy Council of the king became something resembling a modern Cabinet dominated by a prime minister. By the end of the century the notions of "loyal opposition" to the Crown within Parliament and parliamentary responsibility for policy had taken root.

In some respects, the maturation of political life in Parliament resembled the lively political debates in the salons of Paris. In both cases, political life was being legitimized on a new basis. In England, however, that legitimation was enshrined in a legislative institution, which made it especially effective and resilient.

Parliament was not yet in any sense representative of the British population, however. Because of strict property qualifications, only about 200,000 adult men could vote. In addition, representation was very uneven, heavily favoring traditional landed wealth. Some constituencies with only a few dozen voters sent members to Parliament.

Many of these "pocket boroughs" were under the control of (in the pockets of) powerful local families who could intimidate the local electorate, particularly in the absence of secret ballots.

Movements for reform of representation in Parliament began in the late 1760s as professionals, such as doctors and lawyers, with movable (as opposed to landed) property and merchants in booming but underrepresented cities began to demand the vote. As the burden of taxation grew—the result of the recently concluded Seven Years' War (see page 682)—these groups felt increasingly deprived of representation. Indeed, many felt kinship and sympathy with the American colonists who opposed increased taxation by the British government on these same grounds and began a revolt in 1775.

However, the reform movement faltered over the issue of religion. In 1780, a tentative effort by Parliament to extend some civil rights to British Catholics provoked rioting in London (known as the Gordon Riots, after one of the leaders). The riots lasted for eight days and claimed three hundred lives. Pressure for parliamentary reform had been building as Britain met with reversals in its war against the American rebels, but this specter of a popular movement out of control temporarily ended the drive for reform.

"Enlightened" Monarchy

Arbitrary monarchical power might seem antithetical to Enlightenment thought, which stressed the reasonableness of human beings and their capacity to discern and act in accord with natural law. Yet monarchy seemed an ideal instrument of reform to Voltaire and to many of his contemporaries. The work of curtailing the influence of the church, reforming legal codes, and eliminating barriers to economic activity might be done more efficiently by a powerful monarch than by other means then available, particularly because there was great confidence in the power of education to transform an individual (in this case, a ruler) and in the accessibility of the principles of reason. Historians have labeled a number of rulers of this era "enlightened despots" because of the arbitrary nature of their power and the enlightened or reformist uses to which they put it.

"Enlightened despotism" aptly describes certain developments in the Scandinavian kingdoms in the late eighteenth century. In Denmark, the Crown had governed without significant challenge from the landholding nobility since the mid-seventeenth century. The nobility, however, like its counterparts in eastern Europe, had guaranteed its supremacy by means of ironclad domination of the peasantry. In 1784, a reform-minded group of nobles, led by the young Crown Prince Frederick (governing on behalf of his mentally ill father), began to apply Enlightenment remedies to the kingdom's economic problems. The reformers encouraged freer trade and sought, above all, to improve agriculture by improving the status of the peasantry. With improved legal status and with land reform, which enabled some peasants to own the land they worked for the first time, agricultural productivity in Denmark rose dramatically. These reforms constitute some of the clearest achievements of any of the "enlightened" rulers.

In Sweden, in 1772, Gustav III (r. 1771–1796) staged a coup with army support that overturned the dominance of the Swedish parliament, the Riksdag. In contrast to Denmark, Sweden had a relatively unbroken tradition of noble involvement in government, stemming in part from its marginal economy and the consequent interest of the nobility in participation in the Crown's aggressive foreign policy. Since Sweden's eclipse as a major power after the Great Northern War (see pages 607–608), factions of the Riksdag, not unlike the rudimentary political parties in Great Britain, had fought over the reins of government. After reasserting his control, Gustav III began an ambitious program of reform of the government. Bureaucrats more loyal to parliamentary patrons than to the Crown were replaced, restrictions on trade in grain and other economic controls were liberalized, the legal system was rationalized, the death penalty was strictly limited, and legal torture was abolished.

Despite his abilities (and his charm), Gustav III suffered the consequences of the contradictory position of advancing reform by autocratic means in a kingdom with a strong tradition of representative government. Gustav eventually tried to deflect the criticisms of the nobility by reviving grandiose—but completely untenable—schemes for the reconquest of Baltic territory. However, in

Frederick the Great is pictured here returning from military maneuvers. Frederick's self-imposed work as king included arduous travel throughout his domains to check on local conditions and monitor local governments. *(Staatliches Schlösser und Gärten, Potsdam-Sans Souci)*

1796 he was mortally wounded by an assassin hired by disgruntled nobles.

Another claimant to the title "enlightened" monarch was Frederick II of Prussia (r. 1740–1786), "the Great." Much of the time, Frederick resided in his imperial electorate of Brandenburg, near his capital, Berlin. His scattered states, which he extended by seizing new lands, are referred to as "Prussia," rather than as "Brandenburg-Prussia," because members of his family were now kings of Prussia thanks to their ambitions and the weakness of the Polish state of which Prussia had once been a dependent duchy. In many ways, the Prussian state *was* its military victories, for Frederick's bold moves and the policies of his father, grandfather, and great-grandfather committed the state's resources to a military presence of dramatic proportions. Prussia was on the European stage only due to the degree of that commitment.

The institutions that constituted the state and linked the various provinces under one administration were dominated by the needs of the mili-

tary. Frederick II's father, Frederick William (r. 1713–1740), had added an efficient provincial recruiting system to the state's central institutions, which he also further consolidated. But in many other respects, the Prussian state was in its infancy. There was no tradition of political participation—even by elites—and little chance of cultivating any. Nor was there any political or social room for maneuver at the lower part of the social scale. The rulers of Prussia had long ago acceded to the aristocracy's demand for tighter control over peasant labor on their own lands in return for their support of the monarchy. The rulers relied on nobles for local administration and army commands. Thus, there was a stark limit to the kinds of social, judicial, or political reforms that Frederick could personally hope to carry out.

Frederick tried to introduce improved agricultural methods and simultaneously to improve the condition of peasants, but he met stiff resistance from noble landholders. He did succeed in abolishing serfdom in some regions. He tried to stimulate the economy by sponsoring state industries and trading monopolies, but there were not enough resources or initiative from the tightly controlled merchant communities to create much economic expansion. Simplifying and codifying the inherited jumble of local laws was a goal of every ruler. A law code published in 1794, after Frederick's death, was partly the product of his efforts.

Frederick's views of the role of Enlightenment thought reflect the limitations of his situation. One doesn't have to lead a frontal assault on prejudices consecrated by time, he thought; instead, one must be tolerant of superstition because it will always have a hold on the masses. Perhaps his most distinctive "enlightened" characteristic was the seriousness with which he took his task as ruler. He was energetic and disciplined to a fault. In his book *Anti-Machiavel* (1741) he argued that a ruler has a moral obligation to work for the betterment of the state. He styled himself as the "first servant" or steward of the state. However superficial this claim may appear, in his energy and diligence he compares favorably to Louis XV of France, who, having a much more wealthy and flexible society to work with, did much less.

Describing Frederick as "enlightened," however, masks the degree to which his activities reflected as much the traditional goals of security and prosperity as the impetus of "enlightened" thinking. Indeed, some of the most thoroughgoing administrative, legal, and economic reforms were accomplished in rival Austria entirely within such a traditional framework, during the reign of Maria Theresa (r. 1740–1780), the daughter of Emperor Charles VI (r. 1711–1740).

Maria Theresa was a remarkable ruler in her diligence and determination. She overcame difficulties that surrounded her accession, survived the near dismemberment of Austrian territories in the wars that marked her reign, and embarked on an energetic reform program to shore up the weaknesses in the state that the conflicts had revealed. The Austrian monarchy was still a highly decentralized state. Maria Theresa worked to streamline and centralize administration, finances, and defense. She created new centralized governing councils and, above all, reformed the assessment and collection of taxes so that the Crown could better tap the wealth of its subjects. She established new courts of justice and limited the exploitation of serfs by landlords. In general, she

presided over an effort to bypass many of the provincial and privatized controls on government still in the hands of great nobility. She accomplished all of this without being in any way "enlightened." For example, she had a traditional fear of freedom of the press and insisted on orthodoxy in religious matters.

Her son, Joseph, is an interesting contrast. Self-consciously "enlightened," Joseph II (r. 1780–1790) carried out a variety of reforms that his mother had not attempted, including freedom of the press and limited freedom of religion. Some of his reforms were particularly dramatic, such as drastic curtailment of the death penalty and encouragement of widespread literacy. Like Frederick the Great, Joseph regarded himself as a servant of the state. During his ten-year reign, the political climate in Vienna began to resemble that in Paris, London, and other capitals where political life was no longer confined to court life.

Many of Joseph's reforms, however, were simply extensions of his mother's. For example, he extended further legal protection to peasants and eventually abolished serfdom in all Habsburg lands. And in some ways he was less successful than Maria Theresa had been. Though persuaded of the benefits of enlightened government, he was by temperament an inflexible autocrat, whose methods antagonized many of his most powerful subjects. In the name of "rational" administration, he tried to extend Austrian institutions to the kingdom of Hungary—including the use of the German language for official business. He also tried to bypass the authority of the representative Estates in the Austrian Netherlands in order to achieve some of his aims. In this action reminiscent of his ancestor Philip II of Spain, Joseph II revealed that the curious blend of "enlightenment" and traditional absolutism was not greater than the sum of its parts. Joseph's policies provoked simmering opposition and open revolt in a number of his lands, and some of his reforms were repealed even before his death.

Catherine the Great and the Empire of Russia

Another ruler with a claim to the title "enlightened despot" was Catherine, empress of Russia (r. 1762–1796). Catherine was one of the ablest rulers in the eighteenth century and perhaps

Catherine the Great Catherine was a German princess who had been brought to Russia to marry another German, Peter of Holstein-Gottorp, who was being groomed as heir to the Russian throne. There had been several Russian monarchs of mixed Russian and German parentage since the time of Peter the Great's deliberate interest in and ties with other European states. *(The Luton Hoo Foundation)*

the single most able of all the rulers of imperial Russia. She combined intelligence with vision, diligence, and skill in handling people and choosing advisers. Her intelligence and political acumen were obvious early in her life in Russia simply from the fact that she survived at court. In 1745 she had been brought to Russia from her native Germany to marry the heir to the Russian throne. She was brutally treated by her husband, Tsar Peter III. In the summer of 1762, Catherine engineered a coup against him. Peter was overthrown and killed, and Catherine ruled alone as empress for most of the rest of the century.

Catherine the Great, as she came to be called, was the true heir of Peter the Great in her abilities,

policies, and ambitions. Under Catherine, Russia committed itself to general European affairs in addition to its traditional territorial ambitions. In situations involving the major European powers, Russia tended to ally with Britain (with which it had important trading connections, including the provision of timber for British shipbuilding) and with Austria (against their common nemesis, Turkey), and against France, Poland, and Prussia. In 1768, Catherine initiated a war against the Turks from which Russia gained much of the Crimean coast. She also continued Peter's efforts to dominate the weakened Poland. She was aided by Frederick the Great, who proposed the deliberate partitioning of Poland to satisfy his own territorial

Map 18.1 The Partition of Poland and the Expansion of Russia Catherine the Great acquired modern Lithuania, Belarus, and Ukraine, which had once constituted the duchy of Lithuania, part of the multi-ethnic Polish kingdom.

ambitions as well as those of Russia and Austria, with which he competed. In 1772, portions of Poland were gobbled up in the first of three successive "grabs" of territory (Map 18.1). Warsaw itself eventually landed in Prussian hands, but Catherine gained all of Belarus, Ukraine, and modern Lithuania—which had constituted the duchy of Lithuania. Thus, like any successful ruler of her age, Catherine counted territorial aggrandizement among her chief achievements.

Nevertheless, Catherine also counted herself a sincere follower of the Enlightenment. While young, she had received an education that bore the strong stamp of the Enlightenment. Like Frederick, she attempted to take an active role in the intellectual community, corresponding with Voltaire over the course of many years and acting as patron to Diderot. One of Catherine's boldest political moves was the secularization of church lands. Although Peter the Great had extended government control of the church, he had not touched church lands. Catherine also licensed private publishing houses and permitted a burgeoning periodical press. The number of books published in Russia tripled during her reign. This enriched cultural life was one of the principal causes of the flowering of Russian literature that began in the early nineteenth century.

The stamp of the Enlightenment on Catherine's policies is also clearly visible in her attempts at legal reform. In 1767 she convened a legislative commission and provided it with a guiding document, the *Instruction*, which she had authored. The commission was remarkable because it included representatives of all classes, including peasants, and provided a place for the airing of general grievances. Catherine hoped for a general codification of law as well as reforms such as the abolition of torture and capital punishment—reforms that made the *Instruction* radical enough to be banned from publication in other countries. She did not propose changing the legal status of serfs, however, and class differences made the commission unworkable in the end. Most legal reforms were accomplished piecemeal and favored the interests of landed gentry. Property rights were clarified and strengthened, and judicial procedures were streamlined but constructed to include legal privileges for the gentry.

Like the Austrian rulers, Catherine undertook far-reaching administrative reform to create more effective local units of government. Here again, political imperatives were fundamental, and reforms in local government strengthened the hand of the gentry. The legal subjection of peasants in serfdom was also extended as a matter of state policy to help win the allegiance of landholders in newly acquired areas—such as Ukrainian territory gained in the partition of Poland. Gentry in general and court favorites in particular, on whom the stability of her government depended, were rewarded with estates and serfs to work them.

In Russia as in Prussia and Austria, decline of the peasantry occurred because the monarch wanted to win the allegiance of the elites who lived from their labor. The cooperation of elites was particularly valued by Catherine because the Russian state was in a formative stage in another sense as well. It was trying to incorporate new peoples, such as the Tatars in the Crimea, and to manage its relationship with border peoples such

as the Cossacks. Catherine's reign was marked by one of the most massive and best-organized peasant rebellions of the century. Occurring in 1773, the rebellion expressed the grievances of the thousands of peasants who joined its ranks and called for the abolition of serfdom. The revolt took its name, however, from its Cossack leader, Emelian Pugachev (d. 1775), and reflected the dissatisfaction with the Russian government of this semiautonomous people.

The dramatic dilemmas faced by Catherine illustrate both the promise and the costs of state formation throughout Europe. State consolidation permitted the imposition of internal peace, of coordinated economic policy, of reform of justice, but it came at the price of greater—in some cases much greater—control and coercion of the population. Thus, we can see from the alternative perspective of Russia the importance of the political sphere that was opening up in France and was being consolidated in England. It was in that environment, rather than in Russia, that the Enlightenment philosophy could find most fertile ground.

STATES IN CONFLICT

In the eighteenth century a new constellation of states emerged to dominate politics on the Continent. Along with the traditional powers of England, France, and Austria were Prussia in central Europe and Russia to the east (see Map 18.1). Certain characteristics common to all these states account for their dominance. None is more crucial than their various abilities to field effective armies. Traditional territorial ambitions accounted for many wars in the eighteenth century, but the increasing significance of overseas trade and colonization was the most important source of conflict between England and France.

A Century of Warfare: Circumstances and Rationales

The large and small states of Europe continued to make war on each other for both strategic and dynastic reasons. The expense of war, the number of powerful states involved, and the complexities of their interests meant that wars were preceded and carried out with complex systems of alliances and were followed by the adjustments of many borders and the changing control of many bits of territory. We can distinguish certain consistent interests of the major states, however, and some of the circumstances within which all of the states acted.

States fought over territory that had obvious economic and strategic value. A fight over the Baltic coastline, for example, absorbed Sweden and Russia early in the century (see pages 605–608). Often these conflicts were carried out in arbitrary ways that revealed the dynastic view of territory that still existed. Although rational and defensible "national" borders were important, collecting isolated bits of territory was also still the norm. The wars between European powers thus became extremely complex strategically. France, for example, might choose to strike a blow against Austria by invading an Italian state in order to use the conquered Italian territory as a bargaining chip in eventual negotiations.

Dynastic claims were not merely strategic ploys but also major causes of war. Indeed, the fundamental instability caused by hereditary rule accounts for many of the major wars of the eighteenth century. The century opened with the War of Spanish Succession, and later the succession of the Austrian Habsburgs would be the cause of a major continental war.

The state of military technology, tactics, and organization also shaped the outcomes of conflicts. In the eighteenth century, weapons and tactics became increasingly refined. More reliable muskets were used. A bayonet that could slip over a musket barrel without blocking the muzzle was invented. Coordinated use of bayonets required even more assured drill of troops than volley fire alone to ensure disciplined action in the face of enemy fire and charges. Artillery and cavalry forces were also subjected to greater standardization of training and discipline in action. Increased discipline of forces meant that commanders could exercise meaningful control over a battle for the first time, but such battles were not necessarily decisive, especially when waged against a comparable force.

One sure result of the new equipment and tactics was that war became a more expensive proposition than ever before and an ever greater burden on a state's resources and administration. It became increasingly difficult for small states such as

Sweden to compete with the forces that others could mount. Small and relatively poor states, such as Prussia, that did support large forces did so by means of an extraordinary bending of civil society to the economic and social needs of the army. In Prussia, twice as many people were in the armed forces, proportionally, as in other states, and a staggering 80 percent of meager state revenue went to support the army.

Most states introduced some form of conscription in the eighteenth century. In all regions, the very poor often volunteered for army service to improve their lives. However, conscription of peasants, throughout Europe but particularly in Prussia and Russia, imposed a significant burden on peasant communities and a sacrifice of productive members to the state. Governments everywhere supplemented volunteers and conscripts with mercenaries and even criminals, as necessary, to fill the ranks without tapping the wealthier elements of the community. Thus, common soldiers were increasingly seen not as members of society but as its rejects. Said Frederick II, "Useful hardworking people should [not be conscripted but rather] be guarded as the apple of one's eye," and a French war minister agreed that armies had to consist of the "scum of people and of all those for whom society has no use."[2] Brutality became an accepted tool for governments to use to manage such groups of men. From the eighteenth century, the army increasingly became an instrument of social control used to manage and make use of individuals who otherwise would have had no role in society.

But the costs of maintaining these forces had other outcomes as well. Wars could still be won or lost not on the battlefield but on the supply line. Incentive still existed to bleed civilian populations and to exploit the countryside. Moreover, when supply lines were disrupted and soldiers not equipped or fed, the armies of a major power could be vulnerable to the small and "unmodernized" armies of lesser states. Finally, neither good generalship nor the discipline of soldiers could be guaranteed, yet both were crucial to success. Culloden, in 1746 (see page 673), was the first battle in which the British army was able decisively to defeat the fierce charge and hand-to-hand fighting of Highland clansmen by holding its position and using disciplined volley fire. Warfare became increasingly professional but was still an uncertain business with unpredictable results.

The Power of Austria and Prussia

Major continental wars had a marked impact on the balance of power among states in western and central Europe. The first of these, now known as the War of Austrian Succession, began in 1740. Emperor Charles VI died that year without a male heir, and his daughter, Maria Theresa, succeeded him. Charles VI had worked to shore up his daughter's position as his heir by means of an act called the Pragmatic Sanction, first issued in 1713. He had negotiated carefully to persuade allies and potential opponents to accept it. The question was not whether a woman could rule, for many women had ruled and did rule other states. However, a new ruler about whom there was any doubt—a woman, child, or any distant relative—opened the door for rival dynastic claims. In 1740, Frederick II of Prussia took advantage of Habsburg vulnerability by invading the wealthy Habsburg province of Silesia (see Map 18.1), to which he had a hereditary claim of sorts.

Maria Theresa proved a much more tenacious opponent than Frederick had anticipated. In the end, he was lucky to be able to hold onto Silesia, which was at some distance from Maria Theresa's other territories. Although Austrian forces were never able to dislodge Frederick, they did best most of the forces ranged against them by their perpetual opponent, France, and by other German states allied with Frederick. In a preliminary peace signed in 1745, Frederick was confirmed in possession of Silesia, but the throne of the Holy Roman Empire was returned to the Habsburgs—given to Maria Theresa's husband, who reigned as Francis (Franz) I (r. 1745–1765). A final treaty in 1748 ended all the fighting that had continued since 1745, mostly by France on the Continent and simultaneous fighting by France and Britain overseas.

The gainers were Prussia and Austria. Austria came out ahead because its succession had not been disrupted and its lands had not been dismembered. Prussia, because of the annexation of Silesia and the psychological imprint of victory, emerged as a power of virtually equal rank to the Habsburgs in Germany. Frederick II was now well placed to make further territorial gains.

Not surprisingly, the power of Prussia provoked the outbreak of the next major war. Indeed, the unprecedented threat that Austria now felt from Prussia caused a veritable revolution in alliances across Europe. So great in Austrian minds was the change in the balance of power that Austria was willing to ally with France, its traditional enemy, in order to isolate Prussia. In the years before what would later be known as the Seven Years' War (1756–1763), Austrian officials began to approach France to propose a mutual defensive alliance—a move that became known as the Diplomatic Revolution. Sweden and Russia, with territory to gain at Prussia's expense, joined the alliance system. Sweden wanted to regain territory along the Baltic Sea, and Russia coveted East Prussia, which bordered Russian territory.

Frederick initiated hostilities in 1756, hoping, among other outcomes, to prevent consolidation of the new alliances. Instead, he found that he had started a war against overwhelming odds. What saved him was limited English aid. The English, engaged with France in the overseas conflict known as the French and Indian War, wanted France to be heavily committed on the Continent. Also helpful to Frederick was Russia's withdrawal from the alliance against him when a new ruler took the throne there in 1762. Prussia managed to emerge intact—though strained economically and demographically.

The results of the war confirmed Prussia and Austria as the two states of European rank in German-speaking Europe. Their rivalry would dominate German history until the late nineteenth century. The war also demonstrated how fragile even successful states could be and revealed something about what it took for them to be successful. Military victory and the reputation that went with it—even at great cost—could allow a ruler a place on the European stage. The nearness of Prussia's escape also revealed that fortune had a great deal to do with the rise of this state.

The Atlantic World: Trade, Colonization, Competition

The importance of international trade and colonial possessions to the states of western Europe grew dramatically in the eighteenth century. Between 1715 and 1785, Britain's trade with North America rose from 19 to 34 percent of its total trade, and its trade with Asia and Africa rose from 7 to 19 percent of the total. By the end of the century, more than half of all British trade was carried on outside of Europe; for France, the figure was more than a third.

European commercial and colonial energies were concentrated in the Atlantic world in the eighteenth century, because there the profits were greatest. The population of British North America grew from about 250,000 in 1700 to about 1.7 million by 1760. The densely settled New England colonies provided a market for manufactured goods from the mother country, though they produced little by way of raw materials or bulk goods on which traders could make a profit. The colonies of Maryland and Virginia produced tobacco, the Carolinas rice and indigo (a dyestuff). England reexported all three throughout Europe at considerable profit.

The French in New France, numbering only 56,000 in 1740, were vastly outnumbered by the British colonists. Nevertheless, the French successfully expanded their control of territory in Canada. Settlements sprang up between the outposts of Montreal and Quebec on the St. Lawrence River. Despite resistance, the French extended their fur trapping—the source of most of the profits that New France generated—west and north along the Great Lakes, consolidating their hold as they went by building forts. They penetrated as far as the modern Canadian province of Manitoba, where they cut into the British trade run out of Hudson Bay to the north. The French also contested the mouth of the St. Lawrence River and the Gulf of St. Lawrence with the British. The British held Nova Scotia and Newfoundland, the French held parts of Cape Breton Island, and both states fished the surrounding waters.

The commercial importance of all of these holdings, as well as those in Asia, was dwarfed by the European states' Caribbean possessions, however. The British held Jamaica and Barbados; the French, Guadeloupe and Martinique; the Spanish, Cuba and San Domingo; and the Dutch, a few small islands. Sugar produced by slave labor was the major source of profits, along with other cash crops such as coffee, indigo, and cochineal (another dyestuff). The concentration of shipping to this region indicates the region's importance.

Tobbaco Label This shipping label for American-grown tobacco fancifully depicts slaves enjoying a smoke. *(The Granger Collection, New York)*

By the 1760s, the British China trade occupied seven or eight ships. In the 1730s, British trade with Jamaica alone drew three hundred ships. The tiny Dutch possession of Guiana on the South American coast required twice as many visits by Dutch ships as the Dutch East India Company sent into Asia.

The economic dependence of the colonies on slave labor meant that the colonies were tied to their home countries not with a two-way commercial exchange but with a three-way "triangle" trade (Map 18.2). Certain European manufactures were shipped to western ports in Africa, where they were traded for slaves. The enslaved Africans were then transported to South America, the Caribbean, or North America, where planters bought and paid for them with profits from their sugar and tobacco plantations. (See the box, "Encounters with the West: An African Recalls the Horrors of the Slave Ship.") Sugar and tobacco

684

Great Britain
France
Portugal
Spain
Netherlands

LOUISIANA

MEXICO

NEW FRANCE
QUEBEC

HUDSON
Bay

NEWFOUNDLAND
(To Gr. Br., 1713)

NOVA SCOTIA
(ACADIA)
(To Gr. Br., 1713)

GREAT
BRITAIN

NETH.

FLORIDA

Tobacco

Furs

Colonial products

FRANCE

Silver

Manufactured goods

CUBA

Sugar

PORTUGAL SPAIN

JAMAICA

Porto
Bello

HISPANIOLA

ATLANTIC OCEAN

CANARY IS.
(Spain)

GUADELOUPE
(Fr.)

MARTINIQUE
(Fr.)

NEW GRANADA

BARBADOS
(Gr. Br.)

DUTCH
GUIANA

FRENCH
GUIANA

AFRICA

CAPE VERDE IS.
(Port.)

Cape
Verde

Amazon

PERU

Sugar

European forts and trading stations

BRAZIL

Slaves

ANGOLA

~ ENCOUNTERS WITH THE WEST ~

An African Recalls the Horrors of the Slave Ship

Olaudah Equiano (ca. 1750–1797) was one of the few Africans sold into slavery in the Americas to leave a written record of his experiences. An Ibo from the Niger region, he first experienced slavery as a boy when kidnapped from his village by other Africans. But nothing prepared him for the brutality of the Europeans who bought and shipped him to Barbados, in the British West Indies. He eventually regained his freedom and received an education.

The first object which saluted my eyes when I arrived on the [African] coast was the sea and a slaveship . . . waiting for its cargo. . . . When I was carried on board I was immediately handled, and tossed up, to see if I were sound, by some of the crew. . . . I was soon put down under the decks, and there I received such a salutation in the nostrils as I had never experienced in my life; so that, with the loathsomeness of the stench . . . I became so sick and low that I was not able to eat. . . . I now wished for the last friend, death, to relieve me; but soon, to my grief, two of the white men offered me eatables; and, on my refusing to eat, one of them held me fast by the hands and laid me across, I think, the windlass, and tied my feet while the other flogged me severely.

One day, when we had a smooth sea and a moderate wind, two of my wearied countrymen, who were chained together, preferring death to such a life of misery, somehow made through the nettings and jumped into the sea; immediately another dejected fellow who [was ill and so not in irons] followed their example. . . . Two of the wretches were drowned, but they got the other and afterwards flogged him unmercifully for thus attempting to prefer death to slavery. In this manner we continued to undergo more hardships than I can now relate. Many a time we were near suffocation for want of fresh air. . . . This, and the stench of the necessary tubs, carried off many.

Source: Philip D. Curtin, *Africa Remembered* (Madison: University of Wisconsin Press, 1967), pp. 92–96.

were then shipped back to the mother country to be re-exported at great profit throughout Europe. A variety of smaller exchanges also took place. For example, timber from British North America was traded in the Caribbean for sugar or its byproducts, molasses and rum. Individual planters in the colonies were not the only ones whose fortunes and status depended on these networks. Merchants in cities such as Bordeaux in France and

Map 18.2 The Atlantic Economy, ca. 1750 The "triangle trade" linked Europe, Africa, and European colonies in the Americas. The most important component of this trade for Europe was the profitable plantation agriculture that depended on enslaved Africans for labor.

Liverpool in England were also heavily invested in the slave trade and the re-export business.

The proximity and growth of French and British settlements in North America ensured conflict (see Map 18.3). The Caribbean and the coasts of Central and South America were strategic flashpoints as well. At the beginning of the eighteenth century, several substantial islands remained unclaimed by any power. The British were making incursions along the coastline claimed by Spain and were trying to break into the monopoly of trade between Spain and Spain's vast possessions in the region. Public opinion in both Britain and France became increasingly sensitive to colonial issues. For the first time, tensions abroad would fuel major conflicts between two European states.

Great Britain and France: Wars Overseas

In the eighteenth century, England became the dominant naval power in Europe. Its navy protected its far-flung trading networks, its merchant fleet, and the coast of England itself. England had strategic interests on the Continent as well, however. England's interest lay in promoting a variety of powers on the Continent, none of which (or no combination of which) posed too great a threat to England, to its coastline, or to its widespread trading system. From across the Channel, the French appeared a particular threat. They assembled a fleet on more than one occasion and actually dispatched one fleet to aid the cause of the Stuart claimants to the British throne (see page 673).

A second, dynastic consideration in continental affairs was the electorate of Hanover, the large principality in western Germany that was the native territory of the Hanoverian kings of England. Early in the century especially, the interests of this German territory were of importance to the Hanoverian kings and were a significant factor in British foreign policy. Unable to field a large army, given their maritime interests, the British sought protection for Hanover in alliances and subsidies for allies' armies on the Continent. The money for these ventures came from the profits on trade.

After the death of Louis XIV in 1715, England's energies centered on colonial rivalries with France, its greatest competitor overseas. There were three major phases of conflict between England and France in colonial regions. The first two were concurrent with the major land wars in Europe: the War of Austrian Succession (1740–1748) and the Seven Years' War (1756–1763). The third phase coincided with the rebellion of British colonies in North America—the American Revolution—beginning in the 1770s. France was inevitably more committed to affairs on the Continent than were the British. The French were able to hold their own successfully in both arenas during the 1740s, but by 1763, though pre-eminent on the Continent, they had lost many of their colonial possessions to the English.

In the 1740s, France was heavily involved in the War of Austrian Succession while Britain vied with Spain for certain Caribbean territories. Both France and England also tested each other's strength in scattered colonial fighting, which began in 1744 and produced a few well-balanced gains and losses. Their conquests were traded when peace was made in 1748.

Tension was renewed almost immediately at many of the strategic points in North America. French and British naval forces harassed each

French Fort Builders in North America
The French, whose settlements in North America were sparsely populated, tried to secure the vast territories they claimed with a series of strategically placed forts. The imagined fortifications in this contemporary engraving, which probably mocks the French effort, were far too elaborate for American conditions, where simple wooden palisades were the rule. (*Colonial Williamsburg Foundation*)

other's shipping in the Gulf of St. Lawrence. The French reinforced their encirclement of British colonies with more forts along the Great Lakes and the Ohio River. When British troops (at one point led by the colonial commander George Washington) attempted to strike at these forts, beginning in 1754, open fighting between the French and the English began.

In India, meanwhile, both the French and the British attempted to strengthen their commercial footholds by making military and political alliances with local Indian rulers. The disintegration of the Mogul Empire facilitated this move, heightening competition among Indian rulers, and sparked a new level of ambition on the part of the European powers in their struggle with each other. A British attack on a French convoy provoked a declaration of war by France in May 1756, three months before fighting in the Seven Years' War broke out in Europe. For the first time, a major war between European nations had started and would be fought in their empires, signifying a profound change in the relation of these nations to the world.

The French had already committed themselves to an alliance with Austria and were increasingly involved on the Continent after Frederick II initiated war there in August 1756. Slowly, the drain of sustaining war both on the Continent and abroad began to tell, and Britain scored major victories against French forces after an initial period of balanced successes and failures. The French lost a number of fortresses on the Mississippi and Ohio Rivers and on the Great Lakes and, finally, also lost the interior of Canada with the fall of Quebec and of Montreal in 1759 and 1760, respectively (Map 18.3).

In the Caribbean, the British seized Guadeloupe, the main French sugar-producing island. Superior resources in India enabled the British to take several French outposts there, including Pondicherry, the most important. The cost of involvement on so many fronts meant that French troops were short of money and supplies. They were particularly vulnerable to both supply and personnel shortages—especially in North America—not only because they were weaker than the British at sea but also because the territory they had occupied and fortified remained sparsely settled and dependent on the mother country for food.

By the terms of the Peace of Paris in 1763, France regained Guadeloupe. In India, France re-

tained many of its trading stations but lost its political and military clout. British power in India was dramatically enhanced not only by French losses but also by victories over Indian rulers who had allied with the French. In the interior Britain now controlled lands that had never before been under the control of any European power; British political rule in India, as opposed to merely a mercantile presence, began at this time. The British now also held Canada. They emerged as the preeminent world power among European states.

ECONOMIC EXPANSION AND SOCIAL CHANGE

The eighteenth century was an era of dramatic change, though that change was not always apparent to those who lived through it. The intellectual and cultural ferment of the Enlightenment laid the groundwork for domestic political changes to come, just as British victories in the Seven Years' War shifted the balance of power abroad. More subtle and potentially more profound changes were occurring in the European countryside, however: Population, production, and consumption were beginning to grow beyond the bounds that all preceding generations had lived within and taken for granted.

More Food and More People

Throughout European history, there had been a delicate balance between available food and numbers of people to feed. Population growth had accompanied increases in the amount of land under cultivation. From time to time, however, population growth surpassed the ability of the land to produce food, and people became malnourished and prey to disease. In 1348 the epidemic outbreak of bubonic plague known as the Black Death struck just such a vulnerable population in decline.

There were few ways to increase the productivity of land. Peasants safeguarded its fertility by alternately cultivating some portions while letting others lie fallow or using them as pasture. Manure provided fertilizer, but during the winter months livestock could not be kept alive in large numbers. Limited food for livestock meant limited fertilizer, which in turn meant limited production of food for both humans and animals.

Map 18.3 British Gains in North America The British colonies on the Atlantic coast were effective staging posts for the armies that ousted the French from North America by 1763. However, taxes imposed on the colonies to pay the costs of the Seven Years' War helped spark revolt—the American Revolution—a decade later.

After devastating decline in the fourteenth century, the European population experienced a prolonged recovery, and in the eighteenth century the balance that had previously been reached began to be exceeded for the first time. Infant mortality remained as high as ever. No less privileged a person than Queen Anne of England outlived every one of the seventeen children she bore, and all but one of them died in infancy. Population growth occurred because of a decline in the death rate for adults and a simultaneous increase in the birthrate in some areas owing to earlier marriages.

Adults began to live longer partly because of a decline in the incidence of the plague. However, the primary reason adults were living longer, despite the presence of various epidemic diseases, was that they were better nourished and thus bet-

ter able to resist disease. More and different kinds of food began to be produced. The increase in the food supply also meant that more new families could be started.

Food production increased because of the introduction of new crops and other changes in agricultural practices. The cumulative effect of these changes was so dramatic that historians have called them an "agricultural revolution." The new crops included fodder, such as clover, legumes, and turnips, which did not deplete the soil and could be fed to livestock over the winter. The greater availability of animal manure, in turn, boosted grain production. The potato, introduced from the Americas in the sixteenth century, is nutrient-dense and can feed more people per acre than can grain. In certain areas, farming families produced potatoes to feed themselves while they grew grain to be sold and shipped elsewhere.

More food being produced meant more food available for purchase. The opportunity to buy food freed up land and labor. A family that could purchase food might decide to convert its farm into a dairy farm. In such a case, many families might be supported from a piece of land that had supported only one family when used for traditional agriculture. Over a generation or two, a number of children might share the inheritance of what had previously been a single farm, yet each could make a living from his or her share, and population could grow as it had not done before.

Farmers had known about and experimented with many of the crops used for fodder for centuries. However, the widespread planting of these crops, as well as other changes, was long in coming and happened in scattered areas. A farmer had to have control over land in order to institute change. In the traditional open-field system, peasants had split up all the land in each community so that each family might have a piece of each field. Making dramatic changes was hard when an entire community had to act together. Most important, changing agriculture required capital for seed and fertilizer and for the greater number of people and animals needed to cultivate the new crops. Only prosperous farmers had spare capital. Few were inclined to take risks with the production of food and trust the workings of the market. The bad condition of roads alone was reason enough not to rely on distant markets.

Yet where both decent roads and growing urban markets existed, some farmers—even entire villages working together—were willing to produce for urban populations. Capital cities, like London and Amsterdam, and trading centers such as Glasgow and Bordeaux were booming. These growing cities demanded not only grain but also specialized produce such as dairy products and fruits and vegetables. Thus, farmers had an incentive to make changes such as to dairy farming. Urbanization and improved transportation networks also encouraged agriculture because human waste produced by city dwellers—known as "night soil"—could be collected and distributed in the surrounding agricultural regions to further increase soil fertility. By the late eighteenth century, pockets of intensive, diversified agriculture existed in England, northern France, the Rhineland

in Germany, the Po Valley in Italy, and Catalonia in Spain.

In other areas, changes in agriculture were often accompanied by a shift in power in the countryside. Wealthy landlords began to invest in change in order to reap the profits of producing for the new markets. Where the traditional authority of the village to regulate agriculture was weak, peasants were vulnerable. In England, a combination of weak village structure and the attraction of urban markets created a climate that encouraged landlords to treat land speculatively. To make their holdings more profitable, they raised the rents that farmers paid. They changed cultivation patterns on the land that they controlled directly. They appropriated the village common lands, a process known as "enclosure," and used them for cash crops such as sheep (raised for their wool) or beef cattle. Among other ramifications, the clans of Scotland completely disintegrated as meaningful social units as markets for beef, wool, and other Highland commodities drew chieftains' resources and turned what remained of their traditional relationships with dependent clansmen into exploitative commercial ones.

Thus, although the agricultural revolution increased the food supply to sustain more people in Europe generally, it did not create general prosperity. The growth of population did not mean that most people were better off. Indeed, many rural people were driven off the land or made destitute by the loss of the resources of common lands. Peasants in eastern Europe produced grain for export to the growing urban centers in western Europe, but usually by traditional methods. In both eastern and western Europe, the power and profits of landlords were a major force in structuring the rural economy.

The Growth of Industry

Agricultural changes fostered change in other areas of economic and social life. As more food was grown with less labor, that labor was freed to do other productive work. If there was enough work to be had making other products that people needed, then the nonagricultural population could continue to grow. If population grew, more and more consumers would be born, and the demand for more goods would help continue the cycle of population growth, changes in production, and economic expansion. This is precisely what happened in the eighteenth century. A combination of forces increased the numbers of people who worked at producing a few essential materials and products (Map 18.4).

There was a dramatic expansion in the putting-out system, also known as cottage industry, in the eighteenth century, for reasons that were closely related to the changes in the agricultural economy (see page 620). All agricultural work was seasonal, demanding intensive effort and many hands at certain times but not at others. The labor demands of the new crops meant that an even larger number of people might periodically need nonfarm work in order to make ends meet. Rural poverty, whether as a result of traditional or new agricultural methods, made manufacturing work in the home attractive to more people.

Overseas trade stimulated the expansion of production by spurring the demand in Europe's colonies for cloth and other finished products and increasing the demand at home for manufactured items, such as nails to build the ships on which trade depended. The production of cloth expanded also because heightened demand led to changes in the way cloth was made. Wool was increasingly combined with other fibers to make less expensive fabrics. By the end of the century wholly cotton fabrics were being made cheaply in Europe from cotton grown in America by slave labor.

Steady innovation in production played an important part in the expansion of production because it meant that products were being aimed at a broad market. In the Middle Ages, weavers produced a luxury-quality cloth, and their profits came not from demand, which was relatively low, but from the high price that consumers paid. In the eighteenth century, cloth production became a spur to a transformed industrial economy because cheaper kinds of cloth were made for mass consumption. Producing more became important, and innovations that promoted productivity were soon introduced.

A crucial innovation was increased mechanization. The invention of machines to spin thread in the late eighteenth century brought a marked increase in the rate of production and profound changes to the lives of rural workers who had been juggling agricultural and textile work according to season and need. The selected areas of England, France, and the Low Countries where the new technologies were introduced stood, by the end of the century, on the verge of a massive industrial transformation that would have dramatic social consequences.

Control and Resistance

The economic changes of the century produced both resistance and adaptation by ordinary people and, at times, direct action by state authorities. Sometimes ordinary people coped in ways that revealed their desperation. In many cities, numbers of abandoned children rose greatly because urban families, particularly recent immigrants from the countryside, could not support their offspring. The major cities of Europe put increasing resources into police forces and city lighting schemes. Charitable institutions run by cities, churches, and central governments expanded. By 1789, for example, there were more than two thousand *hôpitaux*—poorhouses for the destitute and ill—in France. The poor received food and shelter but were forced to work for the city or to live in poorhouses against their will. Men were sometimes taken out of poorhouses and forced to become soldiers.

Resistance and adaptation were particularly visible wherever the needs of common people conflicted with the states' desire for order and for revenue. The states' desire for order and revenue on the high seas, for example, led to the suppression of piracy. Piracy had been a way of life for hundreds of Europeans and colonial settlers since the sixteenth century. From the earliest days of exploration, European rulers had authorized men known as privateers to commit acts of war against specific targets; the Crown took little risk and was spared the cost of arming the ships but shared in the plunder. True piracy—outright robbery on the high seas—was illegal, but in practice the difference between piracy and privateering was often small. As governments' and merchants' desire for regular trade began to outweigh that for the irregular profits of plunder, and as national navies developed in the late seventeenth century, a concerted effort to eliminate piracy began.

Life on the seas became an increasingly vital part of west European economic life in the eighteenth century, and it began to resemble life on land in the amount of compulsion it included. English-speaking seamen alone numbered about thirty thousand around the middle of the eighteenth

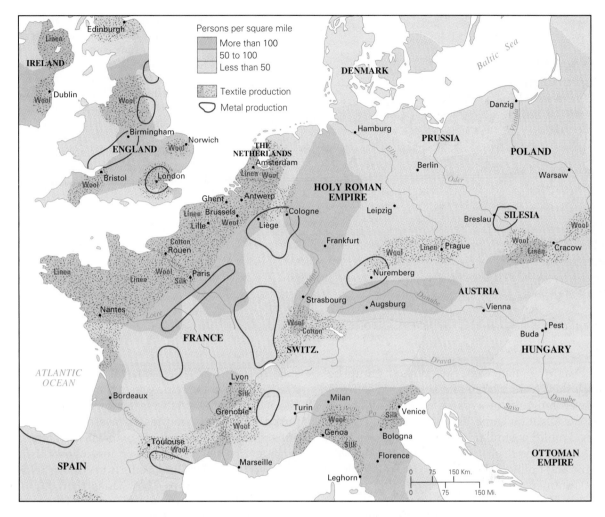

Map 18.4 Population and Production in Eighteenth-Century Europe The growth of cottage industry helped to support a growing population. With changes in agriculture, more land-poor workers were available in the countryside to accept work as spinners, knitters, and weavers.

century. Sailors in port were always vulnerable to forcible enlistment in the navy by impressment gangs, particularly during wartime. A drowsy sailor sleeping off a night of celebrating with new-gotten wages could wake up to find himself aboard a navy ship. Press gangs operated throughout England and not just in major ports, for authorities were as interested in controlling "vagrancy" as in staffing the navy. Merchant captains occasionally filled their crews by such means, particularly when sailing unpopular routes.

Like soldiers in the growing eighteenth-century armies, sailors in the merchant marine as well as the navy could be subjected to brutal disci-

pline and appalling conditions. Merchant seamen attempted to improve their lot by trying to regulate their relationship with ships' captains. Contracts for pay on merchant ships were becoming more regularized, and seamen often negotiated their terms very carefully, including, for example, details about how rations were to be allotted. Sailors might even take bold collective action aboard ship. The English-language term for a collective job action, *strike*, comes from the sailing expression "to strike sail," meaning to lower the sails so that they cannot fill with wind. Its use dates from the eighteenth century, from "strikes" of sailors protesting unfair conditions.

An Idle Apprentice Is Sent to Sea, 1747 In one of a series of moralizing engravings by William Hogarth, the lazy apprentice, Tom, is sent away to a life at sea. The experienced seamen in the boat introduce him to some of its terrors: On the left dangles a cat-o'-nine-tails, and on the distant promontory is a gallows, where pirates and rebels meet their fate. *(From the Collections of Lauinger Library, Georgetown University)*

Seafaring men were an unusual group because they were a large and somewhat self-conscious community of workers for wages. Not until industrialization came into full swing a century later would a similar group of workers exist within Europe itself (see Chapter 21). But economic and political protest by ordinary people on the Continent also showed interesting parallel changes, even though strike activity itself would await the large wage labor force of industrialization. Peasant revolts in the past had ranged from small-scale actions against local tax officials to massive uprisings suppressed by an army. The immediate goals of the rebels were usually practical. They aimed not to eliminate taxation altogether but to limit its extent or to protest the collection of a particularly burdensome tax. The political rationale behind such actions was not a hope that the system could be eliminated but rather a hope that it could be adjusted to operate more fairly. Where there was a revolutionary vision, it was usually a utopian one—a political system with no kings, landlords, taxes, or state of any kind.

Peasant revolts continued to be commonplace and to follow those patterns in the eighteenth century. They were also driven by the localized unemployment caused by agricultural reforms or by objections to press gangs. In certain cases, however, peasants, like sailors, began to confront the state in new ways. Peasants often attacked not state power but the remnants of the various powers over them wielded by landlords, including forced labor and compulsory use of landlords' mills. They also increasingly marshaled whatever legal devices they could to keep control over their land and thwart landlords' efforts to enclose fields and cultivate cash crops. This change, though subtle, was important because it signaled an effort to bring permanent structural change to economic and legal relationships and was not simply a temporary redress of grievances. (See the box, "The Condition of Serfs in Russia.")

Both the old and the new approaches to resisting authority are evident in the Pugachev rebellion of 1773, during the reign of Catherine in Russia (see page 677). The movement began among the Ural Cossacks but eventually included thousands of people with traditional grievances against the regime: Cossacks resisting absorption by the state, miners and other poor workers, peasants, and rebellious dissidents. The rebels thus represented a mixture of traditional grievances and acted under the rubric of "tsarist" legitimacy. Pugachev, in fact, proclaimed himself the legitimate tsar and set up a quasi-imperial court. The rebels' demands were utopian—the elimination of all landlords, all state officials, and all taxation. Less idealistic and more modern were their de-

The Condition of Serfs in Russia

Generally, the condition of agricultural workers was worst in eastern Europe, where political and economic forces kept them bound in serfdom. In A Journey from St. Petersburg to Moscow *(1790), the reform-minded nobleman Alexander Radishchev (1749–1802) describes an encounter with a serf who, like most serfs, was forced to work the lord's lands at the expense of his own.*

A few steps from the road I saw a peasant plowing a field. It was now Sunday, [about midday]. The ploughing peasant, of course, belonged to a landed proprietor, who would not let him pay a commutation tax. The peasant was plowing very carefully. The field . . . was not part of the master's land. He turned the plow with astonishing ease.

"God help you," I said, walking up to the ploughman, who, without stopping, was finishing the furrow he had started. . . . "Have you no time to work during the week, then, and can you not have any rest on Sundays, in the hottest part of the day, at that?"

"In a week, sir, there are six days, and we go six times a week to work on the master's field; in the evening, if the weather is good, we haul to the master's house the hay that is left in the woods. . . . God grant that it rains this evening. If you have peasants of your own, sir, they are praying for the same thing."

"But how do you manage to get food enough [for your family] if you have only the holidays free?"

"Not only the holidays, the nights are ours too."

"Do you work the same way for your master?"

"No, sir, it would be a sin to work the same way. On his fields there are a hundred hands for one mouth, while I have two for seven mouths: you can figure it out for yourself."

Source: Alexander Radishchev, *A Journey from St. Petersburg to Moscow,* trans. Leo Wiener, ed. Roderick Page Thaler (Cambridge, Mass.: Harvard University Press, 1958); quoted in Robert and Elborg Forster, eds., *European Society in the Eighteenth Century* (New York: Harper and Row, 1969), pp. 136–139.

---

mands to end serfdom and their attempts to set up an alternative administration in the areas they controlled. They also tried to form a creditable army—inevitably the weak spot of popular uprisings.

SUMMARY

It is important not to exaggerate the degree to which circumstances of life changed in the eighteenth century. The economy was expanding and the population growing beyond previous limits, and the system of production was being restructured. But these changes happened incrementally over many decades and were not recognized for the fundamental changes they were.

Most of the long-familiar material constraints were still in place. Roads, on which much commerce depended, were generally impassable in bad weather. Shipping was relatively dependable and economical—but only relatively. Military life likewise reflected traditional constraints. Despite technological changes and developments of the administrative and economic resources of the state to equip, train, and enforce discipline, the conduct of war was still hampered by problems of transport and supply that would have been familiar to warriors two centuries before.

Similarly, though some rulers were inspired by precepts of the Enlightenment, all were guided by traditional concerns of dynastic aggrandizement and strategic advantage. One new dimension of relations between states was the importance of conflict over colonies abroad, but the full economic and strategic impact of British colonial gains would not be felt until the next century.

The most visible change would happen first in politics, where goals and expectations
(continued on page 696)

GARDENS

What is a garden? We first think of intensely cultivated flower gardens, such as the famous Rose Garden at the White House. We usually don't think of the yards around houses as gardens, yet that is what they are. The landscaping around most ordinary American homes derives from English landscape gardening of the eighteenth century and after—a fact that is reflected in the British custom of calling the "yards" around their homes "gardens." Like most of the art forms that we see habitually, the garden, reproduced in the American backyard, is difficult to analyze or even to think of as an art form. Like the buildings they surround, however, gardens have much to tell us about human habits and values. Let us examine their eighteenth-century ancestors for evidence of contemporaries' attitudes toward nature and their relationship with it.

Look at the two English-style gardens illustrated here. The first is next to the Governor's Mansion in Williamsburg, the capital of the English colony of Virginia. Construction of this garden began at the end of the seventeenth century; the photograph shows the restored gardens that tourists may visit today. The second garden, from the private estate of West Wycombe in England, looks very different—much more like a natural landscape. The engraving reproduced here dates from the 1770s. The two gardens represent distinct epochs in the development of the garden, hence the differences between them. However, each of these gardens in its own way celebrates human domination of nature.

This symbolic domination of nature is more obvious to us in the Williamsburg garden. The lawns and hedges are trimmed in precise geometrical shapes and are laid out, with the walkways, in straight lines. This "palace garden" was a small English variant of the classical garden developed in France—most spectacularly at Versailles Palace—and then imitated throughout Europe during the seventeenth century. At Versailles, the garden is so vast that at many points all of nature visible to the eye is nature disciplined by humans.

We can think of such gardens as pieces of architecture, because that is how they were originally conceived: The design originated in the enclosed courtyard gardens of the homes of classical antiquity. The straight lines and squared shapes of these gardens mimic the buildings they are at-

The Governor's Mansion and Formal Gardens at Williamsburg, Virginia *(© Robert Llewellyn)*

Landscape Garden at West Wycombe, England (*Courtesy of the Trustees of the British Museum*)

tached to. In fact, these seventeenth- and eighteenth-century gardens were usually laid out as an extension of the building itself. Notice the wide staircase that descends from the central axis of the Governor's Mansion into the central walkway of the garden. Other architectural details, such as the benches positioned at the ends of various walkways, add to the sense of the garden as an exterior room. Elsewhere, this sense was enhanced by the construction of devices such as grottoes, such as that at Versailles. The garden symbolizes the taming of nature into a pleasing vision of order and regularity.

The later, eighteenth-century garden represents even greater confidence in the human relationship with nature, although it does not appear to do so at first glance. The extensive gardens at first seem to be nature itself plus a few added details, such as the statuary, and a few improvements, such as the grass kept trim by the workers in the foreground. Our familiarity with such landscapes—in our own suburban yards—keeps us from immediately perceiving how contrived such a landscape is. Nature, however, does not intersperse dense stands of trees or clumps of shrubbery with green expanses of lawns. Nor does nature conveniently leave portions of a hillside bare of trees to provide a view of the water from the palatial house, to the left on the hill. Note also that the waterfall cascading over rocks and statuary flows from an artificial lake, neatly bordered by a path.

This kind of garden reflects Enlightenment optimism about humans' ability to understand and work with nature. Such gardens were asym-

metrical: Paths were usually curved, and lakes and ponds were irregularly shaped, as they would be in nature. Trees and shrubs were allowed to maintain their natural form. Nevertheless, this landscaping conveys a powerful message of order. Humans cannot bend or distort nature to their own ends, but they can live in harmony with it as they manage it and enjoy its beneficence. People were freed from regarding nature as hostile and needing to be fought. In this garden, one lives with nature but improves upon it. The workers cutting the grass do not detract from the engraving but rather make the scene more compelling.

This brand of landscape gardening appeared in English colonies across the Atlantic by the end of the eighteenth century. One of the best examples is at Monticello, Thomas Jefferson's Virginia estate, first designed in the 1770s and constructed and improved over the remainder of Jefferson's life (1743–1826). If you tour Monticello, you will notice a curving garden path bordered by flowers in season, with mature trees scattered here and there. Jefferson, we know, planned every inch of this largely random-looking outdoor space, just as he planned the regimented fruit and vegetable garden that borders it. The older classical style of the Williamsburg garden is partly explained by its earlier date and also because this more aggressively controlling style lasted longer in the American colonies than in Europe, perhaps because "nature" seemed more wild and still more formidable in the New World. You might wish to consider the curious blend of "nature" and order that is evident in the landscapes we create and live with today. ✒

nurtured by Enlightenment philosophy clashed with the rigid structure of the French state and triggered the French Revolution. The Enlightenment was not simply an intellectual movement that criticized society. It also encompassed the public and private settings where "enlightened" opinion flourished. The revolutionary potential of Enlightenment thought came from belief in its rationality and from the fact that it was both critical of its society and fashionable to practice.

NOTES

1. Quoted in M. S. Anderson, *Europe in the Eighteenth Century, 1713–1783*, 3d ed. (London: Longman, 1987), pp. 218–219.
2. Dena Goodman, *The Republic of Letters: A Cultural History of the French Enlightenment* (Ithaca: Cornell University Press, 1994), p. 89.

SUGGESTED READING

General Surveys

Anderson, M. S. *Europe in the Eighteenth Century, 1713–1783.* 3d ed. 1987.
Doyle, William. *The Old European Order, 1660–1800.* 1978.
Treasure, Geoffrey. *The Making of Modern Europe, 1648–1780.* 1985. Three general histories covering political, social, economic, and cultural developments; each has an extensive bibliography.

The Enlightenment

Chartier, Roger. *The Cultural Uses of Print in Early Modern France.* 1987. A discussion of changes in reading habits and in the uses of printed materials throughout the eighteenth century in France.
Darnton, Robert. *The Literary Underground of the Old Regime.* 1982. One of several important works by Darnton on the social history of print culture.
Gay, Peter. *The Enlightenment: An Interpretation.* 2 vols. 1966–1969. A detailed study of Enlightenment thought by one of its foremost modern interpreters.
———. *Voltaire's Politics.* 1959. A lively introduction to Voltaire's career as a political and social reformer.
Goodman, Dena. *The Republic of Letters: A Cultural History of the French Enlightenment.* 1994. Indispensable for understanding the social context of the enlightenment and the role of women.
Hampson, Norman. *The Enlightenment.* 1968. A useful general survey.
Hazard, Paul. *The European Mind.* 1935. An older but still useful interpretation that depicts a European intellectual crisis between 1680 and 1715.

State Building and Warfare

Carsten, F. L. *The Origins of Prussia.* 1982. An introduction to the growth of the Prussian state in the seventeenth and eighteenth centuries.
Colley, Linda. *Britons: Forging the Nation, 1707–1837.* 1992. A history of the British that emphasizes the interrelationships of political, social, and cultural history.
Devine, T. M. *Clanship to Crofters' War: The Social Transformation of the Scottish Highlands.* 1994. A brief and readable study that follows the destruction and transformation of Highland culture from the Late Middle Ages to the nineteenth century.
Ford, Franklin. *Robe and Sword.* 1953. A path-breaking though controversial study of the consolidation of aristocratic power in France in the eighteenth century.
Gagliardo, John. *Enlightened Despotism.* 1968. A general introduction to the concept and to the rulers of the era.
Hubatsch, Walter. *Frederick the Great.* 1981. A recent biography that illuminates Frederick's system of government.
Kennedy, Paul. *The Rise and Fall of British Naval Mastery.* 1976. The authoritative work on the rise of British seapower from the sixteenth century to modern times.
Madariaga, Isobel de. *Russia in the Age of Catherine the Great.* 1981. The best recent biography of Catherine.
See also the works by Evans, Howard, Parker, Riasanovsky, and Vierhaus cited in Chapters 15 and 16.

Early Modern Economy and Society

Cipolla, Carlo. *Before the Industrial Revolution.* 1976. The most comprehensive single treatment of the development of the European economy and technology through this period.
De Vries, Jan. *The Economy of Europe in an Age of Crisis, 1600–1750.* 1976. Essential reading for understanding the changes in Europe's economy and in its trade and colonial relationships throughout the world.
Gullickson, Gay. *Spinners and Weavers of Auffay.* 1986.
Gutman, Myron P. *Toward the Modern Economy.* 1988. Two works that focus on specific communities in western Europe and thus provide compelling, detailed analyses of the changes in the European economy in the seventeenth and eighteenth centuries.
Hufton, Olwen. *The Poor of Eighteenth-Century Paris.* 1974. An analysis of the lives of the poor and the responses of the state.
Laslett, Peter. *The World We Have Lost.* 1965. An innovative study of premodern society and culture, emphasizing the differences in habits and values that separate our society from preindustrial times.
Parry, J. H. *Trade and Dominion: The European Overseas Empires in the Eighteenth Century.* 1971. A reliable survey of developments.

CHAPTER 19

Revolutionary Europe, 1789–1815

O ne day in early July 1792, a troop of national guardsmen from the city of Marseille in southern France marched into Paris, singing as they came:

Allons enfants de la patrie,	(Come, children of the nation)
Le jour de gloire est arrivé	(The day of glory is at hand)
Contre nous de la tyrannie	(Against us is raised)
L'étendard sanglant est levé!	(The bloody standard of tyranny!)

Their song quickly became famous as the "Marseillaise," and three years later was officially declared the French national anthem. This choice is appropriate, for the French Revolution, which was unfolding that July, profoundly shaped the growth and character of modern France.

Today the Revolution is considered the initiation of modern European as well as modern French history. The "Marseillaise" had been composed some months earlier by a French army captain in Alsace, where French troops were facing Austrian and German forces. Events in France reverberated throughout Europe because the overthrow of absolute monarchy threatened other monarchs. Revolutionary fervor on the part of ordinary soldiers compensated for inexperience, and France's armies unexpectedly bested many of their opponents. By the late 1790s the armies of France would be led in outright conquest of other European states by one of the most talented generals in European history: Napoleon Bonaparte. What he brought to the continental European nations that his armies eventually conquered was a fascinating amalgam of imperial aggression and revolutionary fervor. Europe was transformed both by the changing balance of power and by the spread of revolutionary ideas.

Léon Cogniet, *The National Guard of Paris leaves to join the army in September 1792* (detail).

Understanding the French Revolution means understanding not only how it began but also the complicated course it took and why, together with the significance of those events. Part of the Revolution's importance lay in the power of symbols, such as the "Marseillaise," to challenge an old political order and to legitimate a new one. Challenges to the power of the king were not new, but the Revolution overthrew his right to rule at all. The notion that the people constituted the nation, were responsible as citizens, and had some right to representation in government replaced a system of government by inherited privilege. Louis XVI was transformed from the divinely appointed father of his people to an enemy of the people, worthy only of execution. But on the day in 1792 the men from Marseille marched into Paris, none of this was clear.

BACKGROUND TO REVOLUTION

"I am a citizen of the world," wrote John Paul Jones, a captain of the fledgling United States Navy, in 1778. He was writing to a Scottish aristocrat, apologizing for the conduct of men under his command who had raided the lord's estate while conducting coastal raids against the British Isles during the American Revolution. Jones (1747–1792) himself was a Scotsman, who had begun a life at sea as a boy. He was one of the thousands of cosmopolitan Europeans who were familiar with European cultures on both sides of the Atlantic. As a sailor, Jones literally knew his way around the Atlantic world. He was a "citizen of the world" in another sense as well. When the Scotsman, Lord Selkirk, wrote back to Jones, he expressed surprise that his home had been raided because he was sympathetic to the American colonists. Like Jones, he said, he was a man of "liberal sentiments."[1] Both Jones and Lord Selkirk felt they belonged to an international society of gentlemen who recognized certain principles regarding just and rational government that grew out of the Enlightenment.

In the Atlantic world of the late eighteenth century, both practical links of property and trade and shared ideals about "liberty" were important shaping forces. The strategic interests of the great European powers were also always involved. Thus, when the American colonists actively re-

sisted British rule and then in 1776 declared their independence from Britain, there were many consequences: British trading interests were challenged, French appetites for gains at British expense were whetted, and illusive notions of "liberty" seemed more plausible and desirable. The victory of the American colonies in 1783, followed by the creation of the United States Constitution in 1787, further heightened the appeal of liberal ideas elsewhere. There were attempts at liberal reform in several states, including Ireland, the Netherlands, and Poland. However, the American Revolution had the most direct impact on later events in France because the French had been directly involved in the American effort.

Revolutionary Movements Around Europe

While the British government was facing the revolt of the American colonies, it also confronted trouble closer to home. The war against the American colonies was not firmly supported by Britons. Like many Americans, many Britons had divided loyalties, and many others were convinced that the war was being mismanaged. The prosecution of the war against the American colonies proceeded amid calls for reform of the ministerial government. In this setting, a reform movement in Ireland began to spring up in 1779. The reformers demanded greater autonomy from Britain. Like the Americans, Irish elites felt like disadvantaged junior partners in the British Empire. They chafed over British policies that favored British imperial interests over those of the Irish ruling class: for example, the exclusion of Irish ports from much trade in favor of English and Scottish ports and the granting of political rights to Irish Catholics so that they might fight in Britain's overseas armies.

Protestant Irish landlords, threatened by such policies, expressed their opposition not only in parliamentary but also in military ways. Following the example of the American rebels, middle- and upper-class Anglo-Irish set up a system of locally sponsored voluntary militia to resist British troops if necessary. The Volunteer Movement was undercut when greater parliamentary autonomy for Ireland was granted in 1782, following the repeal of many restrictions on Irish commerce. Unlike the Americans, the Irish elites faced an internal challenge to their own authority—the Catholic population whom they had for centuries dominated. That challenge forced them to reach an accommodation with the British government.

Meanwhile, a political crisis with constitutional overtones was also brewing in the Netherlands. Tensions between the aristocratic stadtholders of the House of Orange and the merchant oligarchies of the major cities deepened during the American Revolution, because the Dutch were then engaged in a commercial war against the British, to whom the stadtholder was supposed to be sympathetic. The conflict ceased to be wholly traditional for two reasons. First, the representatives of the various cities, calling themselves the Dutch "Patriot" party, defended their position in the name of the traditional balance of powers within the Netherlands as well as with wider claims to "liberty," like those of the American revolutionaries. Second, the challenge to traditional political arrangements widened when middling urban dwellers, long disenfranchised by these oligarchies, demanded "liberty," too—that is, political enfranchisement within the cities—and briefly took over the Patriot movement. Just as many Irish rebels accepted the concessions of 1782, many "Patriot" oligarchs in the Netherlands did nothing to resist an invasion in 1787 that restored the power of the stadtholder, the prince of Orange, and thereby ended the challenge to their own control of urban government.

Both the Irish "volunteers" and the Dutch "Patriots," though members of very limited movements, echoed the American rebels in practical and ideological ways. Both were influenced by the economic and political consequences of Britain's relationship with its colonies. Both were inspired by the success of the American rebels and their thoroughgoing claims for political self-determination.

Desire for political reform flared in Poland as well during this period. Reform along lines suggested by Enlightenment precepts was accepted as a necessity by Polish leaders after the first partition of Poland in 1772 had left the remnant state without some of its wealthiest territories (see Map 18.1 on page 679). Beginning in 1788, however, reforming gentry in the *sejm* (representative assembly) went further; they established a commission to write a constitution, following the American example. The resulting document, known as the May 3 (1791) Constitution, was the first codified constitution in Europe; it was read and admired by George Washington.

The Constitution established a constitutional monarchy in which representatives of major towns as well as gentry and nobility could sit as deputies. The *liberum veto*, which had allowed great magnates to obstruct royal authority at will, was abolished. However, Catherine the Great, empress of Russia, would not tolerate a constitutional government in place so close to her own autocratic regime; she ordered an invasion of Poland in 1792. The unsuccessful defense of Poland was led by a veteran of the American Revolution, Tadeusz Kościuszko (1746–1817). The second, more extensive partition of Poland followed, to be followed in turn in 1794 by a widespread insurrection against Russian rule, again led by Kościuszko. The uprising was mercilessly suppressed by an alliance of Russian and Prussian troops. Unlike the Americans from whom they drew inspiration, the Poles' constitutional experiment was doomed by the power of its neighbor.

The American Revolution and the Kingdom of France

As one of Britain's greatest commercial and political rivals, France naturally was drawn into Britain's struggle with its North American colonies. The consequences for France were momentous for two reasons. First, the cost of French aid for the American rebels was so great that it helped accelerate a financial crisis in the French monarchy. Second, French involvement directly exposed many French aristocrats and common soldiers to the "enlightened" international community to which John Paul Jones felt he belonged, though the absolute monarchy of France turned a cold shoulder toward "liberal" ideas.

Rivalry with Great Britain gave France a special relationship with the American colonies and their fight for independence. In the Seven Years' War (1756–1763), the French had lost many of their colonial settlements and trading outposts to the English (see page 687). Stung by this outcome, certain courtiers and ministers pressed for an aggressive colonial policy that would regain for France some of the riches in trade that Britain was threatening to monopolize. The American Revolution seemed to offer the perfect opportunity. The French extended covert aid to the Americans from the very beginning of the conflict in 1775. After the first major defeat of British troops by the

Americans—at the Battle of Saratoga in 1777—France formally recognized the independent United States and established an alliance with them. The French then committed troops as well as monetary support for American forces. John Paul Jones's most famous ship, the *Bonhomme Richard*, was purchased and outfitted in France at French government expense, as were many other American naval vessels during the war. French support was decisive. In 1781 the French fleet kept reinforcements from reaching the British force besieged at Yorktown by George Washington. The American victory at Yorktown effectively ended the war; the colonies' independence was formally recognized by the Treaty of Paris in 1783.

The effect on France of the alliance with the American colonies was complicated. Aid for the Americans saddled France with a debt of about 1 million *livres* (pounds), which represented as much as one-quarter of the total debt that the French government was trying to service. A less tangible impact of the American Revolution was also important. About nine thousand French soldiers, sailors, and aristocrats participated in the war. The best known is the Marquis de Lafayette, who became an aide to George Washington and helped to command American troops. For many humble men, the war was simply employment. For others, it was a quest of sorts. For them, the promise of the Enlightenment—belief in the rationality of men, natural rights, and natural laws by which society should be organized—was brought to life in America.

Exposure to the American conflict occurred at the French court, too. Beginning in 1775, a permanent American mission to Versailles lobbied hard for aid and later managed the flow of that assistance. The chief emissary of the Americans was Benjamin Franklin (1706–1790), a philosophe by French standards, whose writings and scientific experiments were already known to French elites. His talents—among them, a skillful exploitation of a simple, Quaker-like demeanor—succeeded in promoting the idealization of America at the French court.

The United States Constitution and the various state constitutions and the debates surrounding them were all published in Paris and were much discussed in salons and at court, where lively debate about reform of French institutions had been going on for decades. America became the prototype of what Enlightenment philosophy

said was possible. It was hailed as the place where the irrationalities of inherited privilege did not prevail. A British observer, Arthur Young (1741–1820), believed that "the American revolution has laid the foundation of another in France, if [the French] government does not take care of itself."[2]

By the mid-1780s there was no longer a question of whether the French regime would experience reform but rather what form the reform would take. The royal government was almost bankrupt. A significant minority of the politically active elite was convinced of the fundamental irrationality of France's system of government. Nevertheless, the cataclysmic proportions that the French Revolution eventually reached raise questions about why less drastic change did not happen. A dissatisfied elite and a financial crisis—even with the encouragement of a successful revolt elsewhere—do not necessarily lead to revolution. Why did the French government—the *Ancien Régime*, or "Old Regime," as it became known after the Revolution—not take care of itself?

The Crisis of the Old Regime

The Old Regime was brought to the point of crisis in the late 1780s by three factors: (1) an antiquated system for collecting revenue, as well as old and recent debts; (2) institutional constraints on the monarchy that defended privileged interests; and (3) elite public opinion that envisioned thoroughgoing reform and pushed the monarchy in that direction. Another factor was the ineptitude of the king, Louis XVI (r. 1774–1793).

Louis came to the throne in 1774, a year before the American Revolution began. He was a kind, well-meaning man better suited to carry out the finite responsibilities of a petty bureaucrat than to be king. The queen, the Austrian Marie Antoinette (1755–1793), was unpopular. She was regarded with suspicion by those for whom the alliance with Austria had never felt natural. She, too, was politically inept, unable to negotiate the complexities of court life, and widely rumored to be selfishly wasteful of royal resources despite the realm's financial crises.

The fiscal crisis of the monarchy had been a long time in the making and was an outgrowth of the system in which the greatest wealth was protected by traditional privileges. At the top of the social and political pyramid were the nobles, a legal grouping that included warriors and royal officials. In France, nobility conferred exemption from much taxation. Thus, the royal government could not directly tax its wealthiest subjects.

This situation existed throughout much of Europe, a legacy of the individual contractual relationships that had formed the political and economic framework of medieval Europe. Unique to France, however, was the strength of the institutions that defended this system. Of particular importance were the royal law courts, the parlements, which claimed a right of judicial review over royal edicts. All the Parlementaires—well-educated lawyers and judges—were noble and loudly defended the traditional privileges of all nobles. Louis XV (d. 1774), near the end of his life, had successfully undermined the power of the parlements by a bold series of moves. Louis XVI, immediately after coming to the throne, buckled under pressure and restored the parlements to full power.

Deficit financing had been a way of life for the monarchy for centuries. After early efforts at reform, Louis XIV (d. 1715) had reverted to common fund-raising expedients such as selling offices, which only added to the weight of privileged investment in the old order. England had established a national bank to free its government from the problem, but the comparable French effort early in the century had been undercapitalized and had failed. Late in the 1780s, under Louis XVI, one-fourth of the annual operating expenses of the government was borrowed, and half of all government expenditure went to paying interest on its debt.

Short-term economic crises added to the cumulative problem of government finance. During Louis's reign there were several years of disastrously poor harvests, and throughout the reign there was a downturn in the economy. The weakness of the economy proved to be a crucial component in the failure of overall reform.

The king employed able finance ministers who tried to institute fundamental reforms, such as replacing the tangle of taxes with a simpler system in which all would pay and eliminating local tariffs, which were stifling commerce. The parlements and many courtiers and aristocrats, as well as ordinary people, resisted these policies. Ordinary people did not trust the "free market" (free from traditional trade controls) for grain; most feared that speculators would buy up the grain supply and people would starve. Trying

Criticism of Marie Antoinette In a satirical engraving from 1787, the queen toasts the dismissal of a reforming minister. She wears a famous diamond necklace that had caused scandal and widespread criticism of the monarchy two years before; it was a gift from a cardinal with whom the queen was wrongly accused of having an affair. *(Musée Carnavalet/Jean-Loup Charmet)*

to implement such reforms in a time of grain shortage almost guaranteed their failure. Moreover, many supported the parlements out of self-interest and because they were the only institution capable of standing up to the monarchy. Yet not all members of the elite joined the parlements in opposing reform. The imprint of "enlightened" public opinion shaped in salons and literary societies was apparent in the thinking of some aristocrats, who believed that the government and the economic system as a whole needed reform and debated the nature and extent of reform needed.

In 1787 the king called an "Assembly of Notables"—an ad hoc group of elites—to support him in facing down the parlements and proceeding with some reforms. He found little support even among men known to be sympathetic to reform. Some did not support particular reforms, and many were reluctant to allow the monarchy free rein. Others, reflecting the influence of the American Revolution, maintained that a "constitutional" body such as the Estates General, which had not been called since 1614, needed to make these decisions.

Ironically, nobles and clergy who were opposed to reform supported the call for the Estates General, for they assumed that they could control its deliberations. The three Estates met and voted separately by "order"—clergy (First Estate), nobles (Second Estate), and commoners (Third Estate). It was thus assumed that the votes of the clergy and nobles would nullify whatever the Third Estate might propose.

In 1788 popular resistance to reform in the streets of Paris and mounting pressure from his courtiers and bureaucrats induced Louis to summon the Estates General. On Louis's orders, deputies to the Estates General were elected by intermediate assemblies chosen by wide male suffrage. Louis assumed there was widespread loyalty to the monarchy in the provinces, and he wished to tap into it by means of this voting. Louis also agreed that the Third Estate should have twice as many deputies as the other two Estates, but he did not authorize voting by head rather than by order, which would have brought about the dominance of the Third Estate. Nevertheless, he hoped that the specter of drastic proposals put forth by the Third Estate would frighten the aristocrats and clergy into accepting some of his reforms.

Louis faced a critical situation when the Estates General convened in May 1789. As ever, he faced immediate financial crisis. He also faced a constitutional crisis. There was already a sense of legitimacy about the Estates General, about the role of the Third Estate, and about the authority of the Third Estate to enact change. Political pamphlets abounded arguing that the Third Estate deserved enhanced power because it carried the mandate of the people. The most important of them was *What Is the Third Estate?* (1789) by Joseph Emmanuel Sieyès (1748–1836), a church official from the diocese of Chartres. The sympathies of Abbé Sieyès, as he was known, were with the Third Estate: His career had suffered because he was not noble. Sieyès argued that the Third Estate represented the nation because it did not reflect special privilege.

Among the deputies of the first two Estates—clergy and nobility—were men, like the Marquis de Lafayette (1757–1834), who were sympathetic to reform. More important, however, the elections had returned to the Third Estate a large majority of deputies who reflected the most radical political thought possible for men of their standing. Most were lawyers and other professionals who were functionaries in the government but, like Sieyès, of low social rank. They frequented provincial academies, salons, and political societies. They were convinced of their viewpoints and determined on reform and had little stake in the system as it was. When this group convened and met with resistance from the First and Second Estates and from Louis himself, they seized the reins of government and a revolution began.

1789: The Revolution Begins

The three Estates met at Versailles, but the opening of the Estates General was celebrated first in Paris with a solemn procession and religious services attended by all the participants—the last public ritual of the Old Regime. The three Estates marched separately—the clergy arrayed in magnificent vestments, the nobles decked out in furs and velvet, the "commoners" dressed in simple black, bringing up the rear. Neither this staged portrayal of social distinctions, nor the spectacularly presented king and queen, nor the religious symbolism that linked monarchy to divine order could conceal the political conflicts.

As soon as the three Estates began to meet, the conflicts surfaced. The ineptness of the Crown was immediately clear. On the first day of the meetings, Louis and his ministers failed to introduce a program of reforms for the deputies to consider. This failure raised doubt about the monarchy's commitment to reform. More important, it allowed the political initiative to pass to the Third Estate. The deputies challenged the Crown's insistence that the three Estates meet and vote separately. Deputies to the Third Estate refused to be certified (that is, to have their credentials officially recognized) as members of only the Third Estate rather than as members of the Estates General as a whole.

For six weeks the Estates General was unable to meet officially, and the king did nothing to break the impasse. During this interlude, the determination of the deputies of the Third Estate strengthened. More and more deputies were won over to the notion that the three Estates should meet together and that the reform process must begin in the most systematic way: France must have a written constitution.

By the middle of June, more than thirty reformist members of the clergy were sitting jointly with the Third Estate, which had invited all deputies from all three Estates to meet and be certified together. On June 17 the Third Estate simply declared itself the National Assembly of France. At first, the king did nothing, but when the deputies arrived to meet on the morning of June 20, they discovered they had been locked out of the hall. Undaunted, they assembled instead in a nearby indoor tennis court and produced the document that has come to be known as the "Tennis Court Oath." It was a collective pledge to meet until a written constitution had been achieved. Only one deputy refused to support it. Sure of their mandate, the deputies had assumed the reins of government.

The king continued to handle the situation with both ill-timed self-assertion and attempts at compromise. As more and more deputies from the First and Second Estates joined the National Assembly, Louis "ordered" the remaining loyal deputies to join it, too. Simultaneously, however, he ordered troops to come to Paris. He feared disorder in the wake of the recent disturbances throughout France and believed that any challenge to the legitimacy of arbitrary monarchical authority would be disastrous.

The Tennis Court Oath It was raining on June 20 when the deputies found themselves barred from their meeting hall and sought shelter in the royal tennis court. Their defiance created one of the turning points of the Revolution; the significance was recognized several years later by this painting's artist. *(Photographie Bulloz)*

Storming the Bastille The crowd was convinced that the Bastille held political prisoners as well as a large supply of arms. In fact, it held neither. Thousands of Parisians—including artisans and shopkeepers and not merely desperate rabble— surrounded the fortress and forced the garrison to surrender. *(Photographie Bulloz)*

This appeal for armed assistance stirred unrest in the capital. Paris, with a population of about 600,000 in 1789, was one of the largest cities in Europe. There were thousands of workers in all trades plus thousands more—perhaps one-tenth of the inhabitants—jobless recent immigrants from the countryside. Paris was the political nerve center of the nation; it was the site of the publishing industry, salons, the homes of Parlementaires and royal ministers. The city was both extremely volatile and extremely important to the stability of royal power. The king's call for troops aroused Parisians' suspicions. Some assumed that there was a plot afoot to

starve Paris and destroy the National Assembly. Already they considered the Assembly to be a guarantor of acceptable government.

It took little—the announcement of the dismissal of a reformist finance minister—for Paris to erupt in demonstrations and looting. Crowds besieged City Hall and the royal armory, where they seized thousands of weapons. A popular militia formed as citizens armed themselves. Armed crowds assailed other sites of royal authority, including the huge fortified prison, the Bastille, on the morning of July 14. The Bastille now held only a handful of petty criminals, but it still remained a

Declaration of the Rights of Man and the Citizen

Each of the articles of the 1789 Declaration was a response to some feature of Old Regime society or law that was now deemed unacceptable.

Preamble: The representatives of the French people, organized as a National Assembly, believing that the ignorance, neglect, or contempt of the rights of man are the sole cause of public calamities and the corruption of governments, have determined to set forth in a solemn declaration the natural, inalienable, and sacred rights of man. . . .

(1) Men are born and remain free and equal in rights. Social distinctions may be founded only upon the general good.

(2) The aim of all political association is the preservation of the natural and imprescriptible rights of man. These rights are liberty, property, security, and resistance to oppression.

(3) The principle of all sovereignty resides essentially in the nation. No body or individual may exercise any authority which does not proceed directly from the nation.

(6) Law is the expression of the general will. Every citizen has the right to participate personally, or through his representative, in its formation. It must be the same for all. . . . All citizens, being equal in the eyes of the law, are equally eligible to all dignities and to all public positions and occupations, according to their abilities, and without distinction except that of their virtues and talents.

(11) The free communication of ideas and opinions is one of the most precious rights of man. . . .

(13) A common contribution is essential for the maintenance of the public forces and for the cost of administration. This should be equitably distributed among all the citizens in proportion to their means.

Source: James Harvey Robinson, *Readings in European History* (Boston: Ginn, 1906), pp. 409–411.

potent symbol of royal power and, it was assumed, held large supplies of arms. Like the troops at the armory, the garrison at the Bastille had not been given firm orders to fire on the crowds if necessary. After leading a hesitant defense, the garrison commander decided to surrender after citizens managed to secure cannon and drag them to face the prison. Most of the garrison were allowed to go free, although several officers, including the commander, were murdered by the crowd.

The citizens' victory was a great embarrassment to royal authority. The king immediately had to embrace the popular movement. He came to Paris and in front of crowds at City Hall donned the red and blue cockade worn by the militia and ordinary folk as a badge of resolve and defiance. This symbolic action signaled the legitimation of politics based on new principles.

Encouraged by events in Paris, inhabitants of cities and towns around France staged similar uprisings. In many, the machinery of royal government completely broke down. City councils, officials, and even Parlementaires were thrown out of office. Popular militias took control of the streets. There was a simultaneous wave of uprisings in rural areas. Most of them were the result of food shortages, but their timing added momentum to the more strictly political protests in urban areas. These events forced the members of the National Assembly to work energetically on the constitution and to pass legislation to satisfy popular protests against economic and political privileges.

On August 4 the Assembly issued a set of decrees abolishing the remnants of powers that landlords had enjoyed since the Middle Ages, including the right to compel peasants to labor for them and the bondage of serfdom itself. Although largely symbolic, because serfdom and forced labor had been eliminated in much of France, these changes represented a dramatic inroad into the property rights of the elite as they had been traditionally construed. They were hailed as the "end of feudalism." A blow was also struck at established religion by abolishing the tithe. At the end of August, the Assembly issued a Declaration of the Rights of Man and the Citizen. It was a bold assertion of principles condemning the old order. (See the box, "Declaration of the Rights of Man and the Citizen.")

In September, the deputies debated the king's role in a new constitutional government. Deputies known as "monarchists" favored a government rather like England's, with a two-house legislature, including an upper house representing the hereditary aristocracy and a royal right to veto legislation. More radical deputies favored a single legislative chamber and no veto power for the king. After deliberation, the Assembly reached a compromise. The king was given a three-year suspensive veto—the power to suspend legislation for the sitting of two legislatures. This was still a formidable amount of power but a drastic limitation of the king's formerly absolute sovereignty.

Again, Louis resorted to troops. This time, he called them directly to Versailles, where the Assembly sat. News of the troops' arrival provoked outrage, which heightened with the threat of another grain shortage. Women in street markets in Paris, early on the morning of October 5, noticed food shortages and took immediate collective action. "We want bread!" they shouted at the steps of City Hall. Women often led protests over bread shortages, because they procured food for their families. This protest, however, went far beyond the ordinary. A crowd of thousands gathered and decided to go all the way to Versailles, accompanied by the popular militia (now called the "National Guard"), to petition the king directly for sustenance.

At Versailles, they presented a delegation to the National Assembly, and a joint delegation of the women and deputies was dispatched to see the king. Some of the women fell at the feet of the king with their tales of hardship, convinced that the "father of the people" would alleviate their suffering. He did order stored grain supplies distributed in Paris, and he also agreed to accept the

Women's March on Versailles The Parisian marketwomen marched the twelve miles to Versailles, some provisioning themselves with tools, stolen firearms, and horses as they left the capital. *(Jean-Loup Charmet)*

A Young Woman Recounts the March to Versailles

In the months after the women's march of October 1789, the municipal council in Paris, suspicious of such popular action, questioned some of the participants. These depositions present problems as historical sources because the witnesses' words were not recorded verbatim and, in any case, each witness would have been very careful in her testimony. The following document comes from the questioning of a 20-year-old Marie-Rose Barré, a lace worker.

[Marie-Rose Barré] . . . [d]eposes that on October 5 last, at about eight o'clock in the morning, going to take back some work, she was stopped at the Pont Notre Dame by about a hundred women who told her that it was necessary for her to go with them to Versailles to ask for bread there. Not being able to resist this great number of women, she decided to go with them. At the hamlet at the Point-du-Jour, two young men, unknown to her, who were on foot and going their way, told them that they were running a great risk, that there were cannon mounted at the bridge at Saint-Cloud. This did not prevent them from continuing on their way. . . . The two young men of whom she spoke met them near Viroflay and told them that they had escaped at Saint-Cloud but that at Versailles they would be fired on. But they continued on their way. At Versailles they found the King's Guards lined up in three ranks before the palace. A gentleman dressed in the uniform of the King's Guard . . . came to ask them what they wanted of the King, recommending peaceful behavior on their part. They answered that they were coming to ask him for bread. This gentleman was absent for a few minutes and then returned to take four of them

to introduce them to the King. The deponent was one of the four. . . .

They spoke first to M. de Saint-Priest, and then to His Majesty, whom they asked for bread. His Majesty answered them that he was suffering at least as much as they were, to see them lacking it, and that so far as he was able he had taken care to prevent them from experiencing a dearth. Upon the King's response, they begged him to be so good as to arrange escorts for the flour transports intended for the provisioning of Paris, because according to what they had been told at the bridge in Sèvres by the two young men of whom she spoke earlier, only two wagons out of seventy intended for Paris actually arrived there. The King promised them to have the flour escorted and said that if it depended on him, they would have bread then and there. They took leave of His Majesty and were led, by a gentleman in a blue uniform with red piping, into the apartments and courts of the palace to the ranks of the Flanders regiment, to which they called out, "Vive Le Roi!" It was then about nine o'clock. After this, they retired into a house on Rue Satory and went to bed in a stable.

Source: Philip Dawson, ed., *The French Revolution* (Englewood Cliffs, N.J.: Prentice-Hall, Inc., 1967), pp. 66–67.

constitutional role that the Assembly had voted for him. (See the box, "A Young Woman Recounts the March to Versailles.")

The march ended on an odd note as the National Guard replaced much of the royal guard around the person of the king. That night the National Guard saved the king's life when members of the crowd broke into the palace and managed to kill two members of the royal guard still in atten-

dance outside the queen's chamber. The king agreed to return to Paris, so that he could reassure the people. But the procession back to the city was a curious one. The entire royal family was escorted by militia and city people, and the severed heads of the killed guardsmen were carried on pikes.

The king was now in the hands of his people. Already, dramatic change had occurred as a result of a complex dynamic among the three Estates, the

Crown, and the people of Paris. The king was still assumed to be the fatherly guardian of his people's well-being; but his powers were now limited, and his authority was badly shaken. The Assembly had begun to govern in the name of the "nation" and, so far, had the support of the people.

THE FRENCH REVOLUTIONS

The French Revolution was a complicated affair. It was a series of changes, in a sense a series of revolutions, driven not by one group of people but by several groups. Even among elites convinced of the need for reform there was a wide range of opinion. The people of Paris continued to be an important force for change. Country people also became active, primarily in resisting changes forced on them by the central government.

All of the wrangling within France was complicated by foreign reaction. Managing foreign war soon became a routine burden for the fragile revolutionary governments. In addition, there were the continuing problems that had precipitated the Revolution in the first place: the indebtedness of the government, economic difficulties, and recurrent shortages of grain. Finally, the Revolution itself was an issue in that momentum for further change was created once the traditional arrangements of royal government had been altered.

The First Phase Completed, 1789–1791

At the end of 1789, Paris was in ferment, but for a time the forward progress of change blunted the threat of disastrous divisions between king and Assembly and between either of those and the people of Paris. The capital continued to be the center of lively political debate. Salons continued to meet; academies and private societies proliferated. Deputies to the Assembly swelled the ranks of these societies or helped to found new ones. Several would be important throughout the Revolution—particularly the Jacobin Club, named for the monastic order whose buildings the members used as a meeting hall.

These clubs represented a wide range of revolutionary opinion. Some, in which ordinary Parisians were well represented, focused on economic policies that would directly benefit common people. Women were active in a few of the more

radical groups. Monarchists dominated other clubs. At first similar to the salons and debating societies of the Enlightenment era, the clubs increasingly became both sites of political action and sources of political pressure on the government. A bevy of popular newspapers also contributed to the vigorous political life in the capital.

The broad front of revolutionary consensus began to break apart as the Assembly forged ahead with decisions about the constitution and with policies necessary to remedy France's still-desperate financial situation. The largest portion of the untapped wealth of the nation lay with the Catholic church, an obvious target for anticlerical reformers. The deputies did not propose to dismantle the church, but they did make sweeping changes. They kept church buildings intact and retained the clergy as salaried officials of the state. They abolished all monasteries and pensioned the monks and nuns to permit them to continue as nurses and teachers where possible. The Assembly seized most of the vast properties of the church and declared them national property (*biens nationaux*) to be sold for revenue.

Economic and political problems ensued. Revenue was needed faster than the property could be inventoried and sold, so government bonds (*assignats*) were issued against the eventual sale of church properties. Unfortunately, in the cash-strapped economy, the bonds were treated like money, their value became inflated, and the government never realized the hoped-for profits. A greater problem was the political divisiveness generated by the restructuring of the church. Many members of the lower clergy, living as they did near ordinary citizens, were among the most reform-minded of the deputies. These clergy were willing to go along with many changes, but the required oath of loyalty to the state challenged clerical identity and seemed overly intrusive.

The Civil Constitution of the Clergy, as these measures were called, was passed by the Assembly in July 1790 because the clerical deputies opposing it were outvoted. More than half of the clergy did take the oath of loyalty. Those who refused, concentrated among the higher clergy, were in theory thrown out of their offices. A year later (April 1791) the pope declared that clergy who had taken the oath were suspended from their offices. Antirevolutionary sentiment grew among thousands of French people, particularly among rural people, to whom the church was still important. This religious opposition helped to undermine the legitimacy of the new government.

Meanwhile, the Assembly proceeded with administrative and judicial reform. The deputies abolished the medieval provinces as administrative districts and replaced them with uniform *départements* (departments). They declared that local officials would be elected—a revolutionary dispersal of power that had previously belonged to the king.

As work on the constitution drew to a close in the spring of 1791, the king decided that he had had enough. Royal authority and government had been virtually dismantled. Louis had always lived in splendid isolation in Versailles, but he now was a virtual prisoner in the Tuileries Palace in the very heart of Paris. Afraid for himself and his family, he and a few loyal aides worked out a plan to flee France. The king and the members of his immediate family set out incognito on June 20, 1791. However, the royal party missed a rendezvous with a troop escort and was stopped along the way—and recognized—in the town of Varennes, near the eastern border of the kingdom.

Louis and his family were returned to Paris and now lived under lightly disguised house arrest. The circumstances of his flight were quickly discovered. He had intended to invade France with Austrian troops if necessary. He and the queen had sent money abroad ahead of themselves. He had left behind a document condemning the constitution. Thus, in July 1791, just as the Assembly was completing its proposal for a constitutional monarchy, the constitution it had created began to seem unworkable because the king was not trustworthy.

Editorials and popular demonstrations against the monarchy echoed these sentiments. In an incident known as the Massacre of the Champ (Field) de Mars, government troops led by Lafayette charged citizens gathered in a public demonstration organized by certain clubs against the monarchy. The government of the National Assembly fired on the demonstrators, and about fifty men and women died. This incident both reflected and heightened tensions between moderate reformers satisfied with the constitutional monarchy, such as Lafayette, and those, including increasing numbers of Parisian citizens, who were openly republican and hoping to eliminate the monarchy.

THE FRENCH REVOLUTION, 1789–1791

May 5, 1789	Meeting of Estates General
June 17, 1789	Third Estate declares itself the National Assembly
June 20, 1789	Tennis Court Oath
July–August 1789	Storming of the Bastille (July 14); abolition of feudalism (August 4); Declaration of the Rights of Man and of the Citizen (August 27)
October 5–6, 1789	Women's march on Versailles; Louis XVI's return to Paris
July 1790	Civil Constitution of the Clergy
June 1791	Louis XVI attempts to flee Paris; is captured and returned
September 1791	New constitution is implemented; Girondins dominate newly formed Legislative Assembly

On September 14 the king swore to uphold the constitution. He had no choice. The event became an occasion for celebration, but the tension between the interests of the Parisians and the provisions of the new constitution could not be glossed over. Though a liberal document for its day, the constitution reflected the views of the elite deputies who had created it. The right to vote, based on a minimal property qualification, was given to about half of all adult men. However, these men only chose electors, for whom the property qualifications were higher. The electors in turn chose deputies to national bodies and also local officials. Although in theory any eligible voter could be an elected deputy or official, the fact that elite electors voted candidates into office reduced the likelihood that ordinary citizens would be national deputies or local officials. The Declaration

Declaration of the Rights of Woman

Authored in 1791 by Olympe de Gouges (1748?–1793), a butcher's daughter from southwestern France, this document and its author's career reflect the complexity of political life during the Revolution. Gouges's advocacy of women's rights represents the extension to women of the broad-based challenge to tradition that the Revolution embodied. Gouges dedicates the Declaration to the queen, drawing on the tradition of aristocratic patronage. Ironically, given Article 10, Gouges died on the scaffold for her revolutionary sympathies.

Man, Are you capable of being just? It is a woman who poses the question; you will not deprive her of that right at least. Tell me, what gives you sovereign empire to oppress my sex? . . . Bizarre, blind, bloated with science and degenerated—in a century of enlightenment and wisdom—into the crassest ignorance, he wants to command as a despot a sex which is in full possession of its intellectual faculties; he pretends to enjoy the Revolution and to claim his rights to equality in order to say nothing more about it.

(1) Woman is born free and lives equal to man in her rights. Social distinctions can be based only on the common utility.

(2) The purpose of any political association is the conservation of the natural and imprescriptible rights of woman and man; these rights are liberty, property, security, and especially resistance to oppression.

(4) Liberty and justice consist of restoring all that belongs to others; thus, the only limits on the exercise of the natural rights of woman are perpetual male tyranny; these limits are to be reformed by the laws of nature and reason.

(10) No one is to be disquieted for his very basic opinions; woman has the right to mount the scaffold; she must equally have the right to mount the rostrum. . . .

Source: Darlene Gay Levy, Harriet Branson Applewhite, and Mary Durham Johnson, *Women in Revolutionary Paris, 1789–1795* (Urbana: University of Illinois Press, 1979), pp. 87–91.

of Rights that accompanied the constitution reflected a fear of the masses that had not existed when the Declaration of the Rights of Man and the Citizen was promulgated in 1789. Freedom of the press and freedom of assembly, for example, were not fully guaranteed.

Further, no political rights were accorded to women. Educated women had joined Parisian clubs such as the Cercle sociale (Social Circle), where opinion favored extending rights to women. Through such clubs, these women had tried to influence the National Assembly. But the Assembly granted neither political rights nor legal equality to women, nor did it pass other laws beneficial to women such as legalizing divorce or mandating female education. The prevailing view of women

among deputies seemed to reflect those of the Enlightenment philosophe Rousseau, who imagined women's competence to be entirely circumscribed within the family. A Declaration of the Rights of Woman was drafted by a woman named Olympe de Gouges to draw attention to the treatment of women in the constitution. (See the box, "Declaration of the Rights of Woman.")

Very soon after the constitution was implemented, the fragility of the new system became clear. The National Assembly declared that its members could not serve in the first assembly to be elected under the constitution. Thus, the members of the newly elected Legislative Assembly, which began to meet in October 1791, lacked any of the cohesiveness that would have come from collective experience. Also, unlike the previous National Assembly, they did not represent a broad range of opinion but were mostly republicans.

In fact, the Legislative Assembly was dominated by republican members of the Jacobin Club. They were known as Girondins, after the region in southwestern France from which many of the club's leaders came. The policies of these new deputies and continued pressure from the ordinary citizens of Paris would cause the constitutional monarchy to collapse in less than a year.

The Second Revolution and Foreign War, 1791–1793

An additional pressure on the new regime soon arose: a threat from outside France and a war to counter the threat. Antirevolutionary aristocratic émigrés, including the king's brothers, had taken refuge in nearby German states and were planning to invade France. The emperor and other German rulers did little actively to aid the émigrés. Austria and Prussia, however, in the Declaration of Pilnitz of August 1791, declared, as a concession to the émigrés, that they would intervene if necessary to support the monarchy in France.

The threat of invasion, when coupled with distrust of the royal family, seemed more real to the revolutionaries in Paris than it actually was. Many deputies actively wanted war. They assumed that the outcome would be a French defeat, which would lead to a popular uprising that would rid them, at last, of the monarchy. In April 1792, under pressure from the Assembly, Louis XVI declared war against Austria. From this point, foreign war would be an ongoing factor in France's revolution—not only because of the threat of foreign invasion but also because of deliberate decisions to take war abroad in order to safeguard the revolution at home.

At first, the war was a disaster for France. The army had not been reorganized into an effective fighting force after the loss of many aristocratic officers and the addition of newly self-aware citizens. On one occasion, troops insisted on putting an officer's command to a vote. The French lost early battles in the Austrian Netherlands, but the Austrians did not press their advantage and invade France because they were preoccupied with problems in eastern Europe.

THE FRENCH REVOLUTION, 1792–1793

April 1792	France declares war on Austria
August 10, 1792	Storming of the Tuileries; Louis XVI arrested
September 21, 1792	National Convention declares France a republic
January 21, 1793	Louis XVI is guillotined

Louis XVI in 1792 The king, though a kindly man, had neither the character nor the convictions necessary to refashion royal authority symbolically as the Revolution proceeded. When Parisian crowds forced him to wear the "liberty cap," the monarchy was close to collapse. (*Metropolitan Museum of Art, The Elisha Whittelsey Collection, The Elisha Whittelsey Fund, 1962*)

The defeats heightened criticism of the monarchy and pressure for dramatic change. Under the direction of the Girondins, the Legislative Assembly began to press for the deportation of priests who had been leading demonstrations against the government. The Assembly abolished the personal guard of the king and ordered provincial national guardsmen, including those from Marseille, to come to Paris. The king's resistance to these measures, as well as fears of acute grain shortages owing to a poor harvest and the needs of the armies, created further unrest. Crowds staged dramatic marches near the king's palace, physically confronted him, and forced him to don the "liberty cap," a symbol of republicanism. The king's authority and prestige were now thoroughly undermined.

By July 1792, tensions had become acute. The grain shortage was severe, Austrian and Prussian troops committed to saving the royal family were threatening to invade, and, most important, the populace was better organized and more determined than ever before. In each of the forty-eight "sections"—administrative wards—of Paris a miniature popular assembly thrashed out all the events and issues of the day just as deputies in the nationwide Legislative Assembly did. Derisively called *sans-culottes*, "without knee pants," because they could not afford elite fashions, the ordinary Parisians in the section assemblies included shopkeepers, artisans, and laborers. Their political organization enhanced their influence with the Assembly, the clubs, and the newspapers in the capital. By late July most sections of the city had approved a petition calling for the exile of the king, the election of new city officials, the exemption of the poor from taxation, and other radical measures.

10 August 1792 One of the turning points of the Revolution is captured by the contemporary painter François Gérard. The Parisian crowds have just successfully stormed the Tuileries Palace and now confront members of the Legislative Assembly. Notice the sympathetic portrayal of the people, accomplished in part by the inclusion of figures of children. The royal family, having just taken refuge in the Assembly's meeting hall, is visible behind the grille. *(Louvre © R.M.N.)*

In August they took matters into their own hands. On the night of August 9, after careful preparations, the section assemblies sent representatives who constituted themselves as a new city government with the aim of "saving the state." They then proceeded with an organized assault on the Tuileries Palace, where the royal family was living. In the bloody confrontation, hundreds of royal guards and citizens died. After briefly taking refuge in the Legislative Assembly itself, the king and his family were imprisoned in one of the fortified towers in the city, under guard of the popularly controlled city government.

The storming of the Tuileries inaugurated the second major phase of the Revolution: the establishment of republican government in place of the monarchy. The people of Paris now physically dominated the Legislative Assembly. Some deputies had fled. Those who remained agreed under pressure to dissolve the Assembly and make way for another body to be elected by universal manhood suffrage. On September 20, that assembly—known as the National Convention—began to meet. The next day, the Convention declared the end of the monarchy and began to work on a constitution for the new republic.

Coincidentally, on the same day French forces won their first real victory over the allied Austrian and Prussian forces that had attempted to invade France. Though not a decisive battle, it was a profound psychological victory. A citizen army had defeated the professional force of a ruling prince. The victory bolstered the republican government and encouraged it to put more energy into the wars. Indeed, maintaining armies in the field became increasingly a factor in the delicate equilibrium of revolutionary government. The new republican regime let it be known that its armies were not merely for self-defense but for the liberation of all peoples in the "name of the French Nation."

The Convention faced the divisive issue of what to do with the king. Louis had not done anything truly treasonous, but some of the king's correspondence, discovered after the storming of the Tuileries, provided the pretext for charges of treason. The Convention held a trial for him, lasting from December 11, 1792, through January 15, 1793. He was found guilty of treason by an overwhelming vote (683 to 39), reflecting the fact that the republican government would not compromise with monarchy. Less certain was the sentence:

THE FRENCH REVOLUTION, 1793–1794

February 1793	France declares war on Britain, Spain, and the Netherlands
June 1793	Radical Jacobins purge Girondins from the Convention
July 1793	Robespierre assumes leadership of Committee of Public Safety
July 1793–July 1794	Reign of Terror
July 1794	Robespierre is guillotined

Louis was condemned to death by a narrow majority, 387 to 334.

The consequences for the king were immediate. On January 21, 1793, Louis mounted the scaffold in a public square near the Tuileries and was beheaded. The execution split the ranks of the Convention and soon resulted in the breakdown of the institution itself.

The Faltering Republic and the Terror, 1793–1794

In February 1793, the republic was at war with virtually every state in Europe, except the Scandinavian kingdoms and Russia. Moreover, the regime faced massive and widespread counter-revolutionary uprisings within France. Vigilance against internal as well as external enemies seemed necessary. Nevertheless, for a time, the republican government functioned adequately. In May 1793, for example, it passed the first Law of the Maximum, which tried to fix the price of grain and ensure adequate supplies of bread flour, so that urban people could afford their staple food.

The Convention established an executive body, the Committee of Public Safety. In theory, this executive council was answerable to the Convention as a whole. As the months passed, however, it acted with greater and greater autonomy not only to institute various policies but also to

Robespierre Justifies the Terror

In this excerpt from a speech before the Convention in December 1793, Robespierre justifies the revolutionary government's need to act in an extraconstitutional manner. He echoes Rousseau's notion of a highly abstract sense of the public good. He also warns against challenges to the Revolution within France posed by foreign powers.

The defenders of the Republic must adopt Caesar's maxim, for they believe that "nothing has been done so long as anything remains to be done." Enough dangers still face us to engage all our efforts. It has not fully extended the valor of our Republican soldiers to conquer a few Englishmen and a few traitors. A task no less important, and one more difficult, now awaits us: to sustain an energy sufficient to defeat the constant intrigues of all the enemies of our freedom and to bring to a triumphant realization the principles that must be the cornerstone of public welfare. . . . Revolution is the war waged by liberty against its enemies; a constitution . . . crowns the edifice of freedom once victory has been won and the nation is at peace. . . . The principal concern of a constitutional government is civil liberty; that of a revolutionary government, public liberty. [A] revolutionary government is obliged to defend the state itself against the factions that assail it

from every quarter. To good citizens revolutionary government owes the full protection of the state; to the enemies of the people it owes only death.

Is a revolutionary government the less just and the less legitimate because it must be more vigorous in its actions and freer in its movement than ordinary government? . . . It also has its rules, all based on justice and public order. . . . It has nothing in common with arbitrary rule; it is public interest which governs it and not the whims of private individuals.

Thanks to five years of treason and tyranny, thanks to our credulity and lack of foresight . . . Austria and England, Russia, Prussia, and Italy had time to set up in our country a secret government to challenge the authority of our own. . . . We shall strike terror, not in the hearts of patriots, but in the haunts of foreign brigands.

Source: George Rudé, ed., *Robespierre* (Englewood Cliffs, N.J.: Prentice-Hall, 1967), pp. 58–63.

eradicate internal and external enemies. The broadly based republican government represented by the Convention began to disintegrate.

The first major narrowing of control came in June 1793. Pushed by the Parisian sections, a group of extreme Jacobins purged the Girondin deputies from the Convention and arrested many of them. The Girondins were republicans who favored an activist government in the people's behalf, but they were less radical than the Jacobins, less insistent on central control of the Revolution, and less willing to share power with the citizens of Paris. After the purge, the Convention still met, but most authority was held by the Committee of Public Safety.

New uprisings against the regime began. Added to counterrevolutionary revolts by peasants and aristocrats were new revolts by Girondin sympathizers. As resistance to the government mounted and the foreign threat continued, a dramatic event in Paris led the Committee of Public Safety officially to adopt a policy of political repression. A well-known figure of the Revolution, Jean Paul Marat (1743–1793), publisher of a radical republican newspaper very popular with ordinary Parisians, was murdered on July 13 by Charlotte Corday (1768–1793), a young aristocratic woman who had asked to meet with him. Shortly afterward, a long-time member of the Jacobin Club, Maximilien Robespierre (1758–1794), joined the

A Citizen of Paris Suffers Under the Terror

The apparatus of the Terror meant that ordinary citizens could be arrested for the slightest of-fense. Here, a woman describes her arrest, which led to months of grim imprisonment. (She was eventually released only because she persuaded the authorities that she was pregnant.)

For a long time I have had to feed the members of my household on bread and cheese and . . . tired of complaints from my husband and my boys, I was compelled to go wait in line to get something to eat. For three days I had been go-ing to the same market without being able to get anything, despite the fact that I waited [all day]. After the distribution of butter on the twenty-second, . . . a citizen came over to me and said I was in a very delicate condition [and I answered] "You can't be delicate and be on your legs for so long . . ." He replied that I needed to drink milk. I answered that I had men in my house and couldn't nourish them on milk [and that] if he . . . was sensitive to the dif-ficulty of obtaining food, he would not vex me so, and that he was an imbecile and wanted to play despot, and no one had that right.

I was arrested [on the spot and] was led to the Revolutionary Committee [of the section] where I was called a counterrevolutionary and was told I was asking for the guillotine because I told them I preferred death to being treated ignominiously. . . . I was asked if I knew whom I had called a despot . . . and I was told that he was the commander of the post. I said he was more [a commander] beneath his own roof than anyone, given that he was there to main-tain order and not to provoke bad feelings. For [these] answers, I was told that I had done three times more than was needed to get the guillotine and that I would be explaining my-self before the Revolutionary Tribunal.

Source: Darlene Gay Levy, Harriet Branson Applewhite, and Mary Durham Johnson, *Women in Revolutionary Paris, 1789–1795* (Urbana: University of Illinois Press, 1979), pp. 267–268.

Committee and called for "Terror"—the systematic repression of internal enemies. He was not alone in his views. Radicals in the section assemblies of Paris led demonstrations to pressure the govern-ment into making Terror the order of the day.

Robespierre himself embodied all the contra-diction of the policy of Terror. He was an austere, almost prim, man who lived very modestly—a model, of sorts, of the virtuous, disinterested citi-zen. The policies followed by the government dur-ing the year of his greatest influence, from July 1793 to July 1794, included generous, rational, and humane policies to benefit ordinary citizens as well as the policy of official Terror. (See the box, "Robespierre Justifies the Terror.")

Terror meant the use of intimidation to silence dissent. Since the previous autumn, the guillotine had been at work against identified enemies of the regime, but now a more energetic apparatus of terror was instituted. A Law of Suspects was passed that allowed citizens to be arrested simply on vague suspicion of counterrevolutionary sym-pathies. (See the box, "A Citizen of Paris Suffers Under the Terror.") Revolutionary tribunals and an oversight committee made arbitrary arrests and rendered summary judgment. In October a steady stream of executions began, beginning with the queen, imprisoned since the storming of the Tuileries the year before. The imprisoned Girondin deputies followed, and then the process continued relentlessly. In Paris there were about 2600 executions from 1793 to 1794.

Around France, approximately 14,000 execu-tions were the result of verdicts from revolution-ary tribunals. Another 10,000 to 12,000 people died in prison. Ten thousand or more were killed,

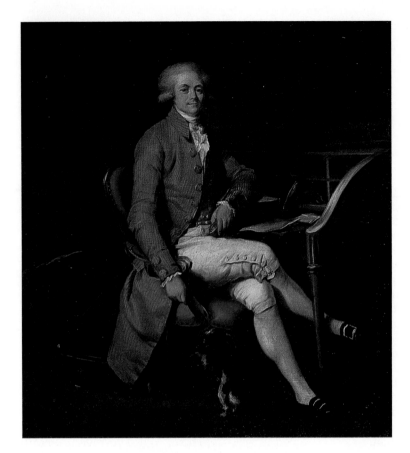

Robespierre the Incorruptible A lawyer who had often championed the poor, Robespierre was elected to the Estates General in 1789 and was a consistent advocate of republican government from the beginning of the Revolution. His unswerving loyalty to his political principles earned him the nickname "the Incorruptible." *(Musée des Beaux-Arts, Lille)*

usually by summary execution, after the defeat of counterrevolutionary uprisings. For example, 2000 people were summarily executed in Lyon when a Girondin revolt collapsed there in October. The repression in Paris, however, was unique because of the city's role in the nation's political life. The aim of the repression was not merely to stifle active resistance; it was also to stifle simple dissent. The victims in Paris included not merely aristocrats or former deputies but also sans-culottes. The radical Jacobins wanted to seize control of the Revolution from the Parisian citizens who had helped them to power.

The Terror notwithstanding, the government of the Committee of Public Safety was effective in providing direction for the nation at a critical time. It instituted the first mass conscription of citizens into the army (*levée en masse*), and an effective popular army came into existence. In the autumn of 1793, this army won impressive victories. Accomplishments in domestic policy included an extended Law of the Maximum (September 1793) that applied to necessary commodities other than

bread. Extensive plans were made for a system of free and universal primary education. Slavery in the French colonies was abolished in February 1794. Divorce, first legalized in 1792, was made easier for women to obtain.

In the name of "reason," traditional rituals and rhythms of life were changed. One reform of long-term significance was the introduction of the metric system of weights and measures. Although people continued to use the old, familiar measures for a very long time, the change was eventually accomplished, leading the way for change throughout Europe. Equally "rational" but not as successful was the elimination of the traditional calendar. The traditional days, weeks, and months were replaced by forty-day months and *decadi* (ten-day weeks with one day of rest). All saints' days and Christian holidays were eliminated. The years had already been changed—Year I had been declared with the founding of the republic in the autumn of 1792.

Churches were rededicated as "temples of reason." Believing that outright atheism left people with no basis for personal or national morality, Robespierre sought instead to promote a cult of the Supreme Being. The public festivals organized around either principle were solemn civic ceremonies intended to ritualize and legitimize the new political order. These and other innovations of the regime were not necessarily welcomed. The French people generally resented the elimination of the traditional calendar. In the countryside, there were massive peasant uprisings over loss of poor relief, community life, and familiar ritual.

Divorce law and economic regulation were a boon, especially to urban women, but women's participation in sectional assemblies and in all organized political activity—which had been energetic and widespread—was banned in October 1793. The particular target of the regime was the Society of Revolutionary Republican Women, a powerful club representing the interests of female sans-culottes. By banning women from political life, the regime helped to ground its legitimacy, since the seemingly "natural" exclusion of women might make the new system of government appear part of the "natural" order. (See the feature, "Weighing the Evidence: Political Symbols," on pages 734–735.) Elimination of women's clubs and women's participation in section assemblies also eliminated a source of popular power, from which the regime was now trying to distance itself.

The Committee and the Convention were divided over religious and other policies, but the main policy differences concerned economic matters: how far to go to assist the poor, the unemployed, and the landless. Several of the temperate critics of Robespierre and his allies were guillotined because they differed with them on policy and on the continuing need for the Terror itself. Their deaths helped to precipitate the end of the Terror because Robespierre's power base shrank so much that it had no further legitimacy.

Deputies to the Convention finally dared to move against Robespierre in July 1794. French armies had scored a major victory over Austrian troops on June 26, so there was no longer any need for the emergency status that the Terror had thrived on. In late July (the month of Thermidor, according to the revolutionary calendar), the Convention voted to arrest Robespierre, the head of the Revolutionary Tribunal in Paris, and their closest associates and allies in the city government. On July 28 and 29, Robespierre and the others—

about a hundred in all—were guillotined, and the Terror ended.

Thermidorian Reaction and the Directory, 1794–1799

After the death of Robespierre, the Convention reclaimed many of the executive powers that the Committee of Public Safety had seized. The Convention dismantled the apparatus of the Terror, repealed the Law of Suspects, and forced the revolutionary tribunals to adopt ordinary legal procedures. The Convention also passed into law some initiatives, such as expanded public education, that had been proposed in the preceding year but not enacted. This phase of the Revolution that followed the Terror is called the "Thermidorian Reaction" because it began in the revolutionary month of Thermidor (July 19–August 17).

The stability of the government, however, was threatened from the outset. Counterrevolutionary uprisings in western France during the autumn of 1794 were joined by landings of émigré troops the following June. These challenges were put down. There were also popular uprisings against the Terror throughout France. Officials of the previous regime were lynched, and pro-revolutionary groups were massacred by their fellow citizens.

The people of Paris tried to retain influence with the new government. With the apparatus of Terror dismantled, the Convention was unable to enforce controls on the supply and price of bread. Thus, economic difficulties and a hard winter produced famine by the spring of 1795. In May crowds marched on the Convention, chanting "Bread and the Constitution of '93," referring to the republican constitution drafted by the Convention but never implemented because of the Terror. The demonstrations were met with force and were dispersed.

Fearful of a renewed, popularly supported Terror, or even of desperate popular support for a royalist uprising, the Convention drafted a new constitution that limited popular participation, as had the first constitution of 1791. The new plan allowed fairly widespread (but not universal) male suffrage, but only for electors, who would choose deputies for the two houses of the legislature. The property qualifications for being an elector were very high, so all but elite citizens were effectively disenfranchised.

THE FRENCH REVOLUTION, 1794–1799

August 1794	Thermidorian reaction begins
October 1795	Directory is established
November 1799	Napoleon seizes power

In the fall of 1795, as the Convention was preparing to dissolve so that new elections might proceed, a final popular uprising shook Paris. The Convention anticipated the trouble, and when a crowd of twenty thousand or more converged on the Tuileries Palace, the officer in charge ordered his troops to fire. Parisian crowds never again seriously threatened the government, although living conditions worsened as food prices soared. The army officer who issued the command to fire was Napoleon Bonaparte.

A new government began under the provisions of the new constitution. It was called the Directory for the executive council of five men chosen by the upper house of the new legislature. To avoid the concentration of authority that had produced the Terror, the members of the Convention had tried to enshrine separation of powers in the new system. However, because of unsettled conditions throughout France, the governments under the Directory were never stable and never free from attempted coups and extraconstitutional maneuvering.

The most spectacular challenge, the Conspiracy of Equals, was led by extreme Jacobins who wanted to restore popular government and aggressive economic and social policy on behalf of the common people. The conspiracy ended with arrests and executions in 1797. When elections in 1797 and 1798 returned many royalist as well as Jacobin deputies, the Directory resorted to force to forestall challenges to its authority: Many deputies were arrested, sent into exile, or denied seats.

By 1799, conditions had once again reached a critical juncture. France was again at war with a coalition of states and was faring badly in the fighting. The demands of the war effort, together with other economic woes, brought the government again to the brink of bankruptcy. The government seemed to be losing control of the countryside; there were continued royalist uprisings and local political vendettas as well as outright banditry.

Members of the Directory had often turned to sympathetic army commanders to carry out the arrests and purge of the legislature. They now invited General Napoleon Bonaparte to help them form a government that they could more strictly control. Two members of the Directory plotted with Napoleon and his brother, Louis Bonaparte, to seize power on November 9, 1799.

THE NAPOLEONIC ERA

Napoleon Bonaparte (1769–1821) was the kind of person who gives rise to myths. He was talented, daring, and ruthless. He was also charming and charismatic. His audacity, determination, and personal magnetism enabled him to profit from the political instability and confusion in France and ensconce himself in power. Once in power, he stabilized the political scene by enshrining in law the more conservative gains of the Revolution. He also used his power and his abilities as a general to continue wars of conquest against France's neighbors.

Napoleon's troops, in effect, exported the Revolution when they conquered most of Europe. Law codes were reformed, governing elites were opened to talent, and public works were undertaken in most states under French control. Yet French conquest also meant domination, pure and simple, and involvement in France's rivalry with Britain. The Napoleonic era left Europe an ambiguous legacy—war and its complex aftermath yet also revolution and encouragement to further change.

Napoleon: From Soldier to Emperor, 1799–1804

Napoleon was from Corsica, a Mediterranean island that had passed from Genoese to French control in the eighteenth century. The second son of a large gentry family, he was educated at military academies in France, and he married the politically well-connected widow Joséphine de Beauharnais (1763–1814), whose aristocratic husband had been a victim of the Terror.

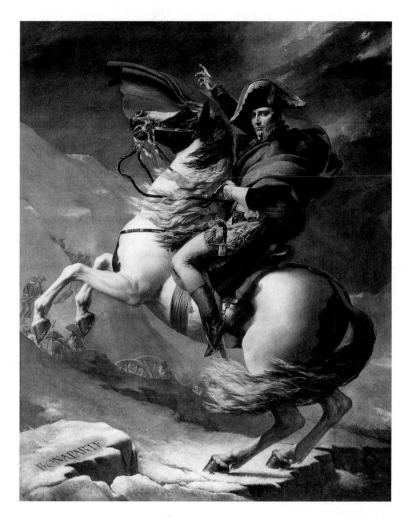

Napoleon Crossing the Great St. Bernard This stirring portrait by the great neoclassical painter Jacques-Louis David memorializes Napoleon's 1796 crossing of the Alps before his victorious Italian campaign, as a general under the Directory. The painting depicts the moment heroically rather than realistically (Napoleon wisely crossed the Alps on a sure-footed mule, not a stallion), in part because it was executed in 1801–1802. Napoleon, as First Consul, wanted images of himself that would justify his increasingly ambitious claims to power. *(Louvre © R.M.N.)*

Napoleon steered a careful course through the political turmoil of the Revolution. By 1799, however, he was well known and popular because of his military victories. He demonstrated his reliability and ruthlessness in 1795 when he ordered troops guarding the Convention to fire on the Parisian crowd, but his greatest victories had been against France's foreign opponents. In 1796 and 1797 he had conquered all of northern Italy, forcing Austria to relinquish that territory as well as to cede control of the Austrian Netherlands, which revolutionary armies had seized in 1795. He then commanded an invasion of Egypt in an attempt to strike at British influence and trade connections in the eastern Mediterranean. The Egyptian campaign failed in its goals, but individual spectacular victories during the campaign ensured Napoleon's military reputation. In addition, Napoleon had demonstrated his widening ambitions. He had taken leading scientists and skilled administrators with him to Egypt in order to export the seeming benefits of French civilization as well as to buttress military victory with more lasting military authority.

Napoleon's partners in the new government after the November coup in 1799 soon learned of his great political ambition and skill. In theory, the new system was to be a streamlined version of the Directory: Napoleon was to be first among equals in a three-man executive—First Consul, according to borrowed Roman terminology. But Napoleon soon asserted his primacy among them and began not only to dominate executive functions but also to bypass the authority of the various legislative bodies in the new regime.

Napoleon was careful to avoid heavy-handed displays of power. He cleverly sought ratification of each stage of his assumption of power through national plebiscites (national referendums in which all eligible voters could vote for or against proposals)—one plebiscite for a new constitution in 1800 and another when he claimed consulship for life in 1802. Perhaps most important to the success of his increasingly authoritarian regime was his effort to include, among his ministers, advisers, and bureaucrats, men of many political stripes—Jacobins, reforming liberals, even former Old Regime bureaucrats. He welcomed many exiles back to France, including all but the most ardent royalists. He thus stabilized his regime by healing some of the rifts among ruling elites.

Napoleon combined toleration with ruthlessness, however. Between 1800 and 1804 he imprisoned, executed, or exiled dozens of individuals for alleged Jacobin agitation or royalist sympathies. His final gesture to intimidate royalist opposition came in 1804 when he kidnapped and coldly murdered a Bourbon prince who had been in exile in Germany.

By the terms of the Treaty of Amiens in 1802, Napoleon made peace with Britain, France's one remaining enemy. The fragile and short-lived peace only papered over the two countries' commercial and strategic rivalries, but it gave Napoleon breathing room to establish his rule more securely in France. One of the most important steps had been accomplished a year earlier by means of the Concordat of 1801. The aim of this treaty with the pope was to solve the problem of church-state relations that for years had caused antirevolutionary rebellions. The agreement allowed for the resumption of Catholic worship and the continued support of the clergy by the state, but also accepted the more dramatic changes accomplished by the Revolution. Church lands that had been sold were guaranteed to their new owners. Protestant churches were also allowed and their clergy was paid, although Catholicism was recognized as the "religion of the majority of Frenchmen." Later, Napoleon granted new rights to Jews also. Nonetheless, the Concordat removed one of the most important grounds for counterrevolutionary upheaval in the countryside and undermined royalist resistance to the new regime from abroad.

The law code that Napoleon established in 1804 was much like his accommodation with the church in its limited acceptance of revolutionary gains. His Civil Code reflected the revolutionary legacy in its guarantee of equality before the law and its requirement for the taxation of all social classes; it also enshrined modern forms of property ownership and civil contracts.

But neither the code nor Napoleon's political regime fostered individual rights, especially for women. Women lost all of the rights they had gained during the Revolution. Fathers' control over their families was enhanced. Divorce was no longer permitted except in rare instances. Women lost all property rights when they married, and they generally faced legal domination by fathers and husbands.

Napoleon helped to put the regime on better financial footing by establishing a national bank. The Bank of France, modeled on the Bank of England, provided capital for investment and could help the state manage its money and return to a system of hard coinage. Napoleon also further streamlined and centralized the administrative system, set up by the first wave of revolutionaries in 1789, by establishing the office of prefect to govern the départements. All prefects and their subordinates were appointed by Napoleon.

Some of these legal and administrative changes occurred after the final political coup that Napoleon undertook—declaring himself emperor. This was a bold move, but Napoleon approached it dexterously. For example, long before he declared himself emperor, Napoleon had begun to sponsor an active court life appropriate to imperial pretensions. The empire was proclaimed in May 1804 with the approval of the Senate; it was also approved by another plebiscite. Members of Napoleon's family were given princely status, and a number of his favorites received various titles and honors. The titles brought no legal privilege but signaled social and political distinctions of great importance. Old nobles were allowed to use their titles on this basis.

Many members of the elite, whatever their persuasions, tolerated Napoleon's claims to power because he safeguarded a number of revolutionary gains and reconfirmed their own status. War soon resumed against political and economic enemies—principally Britain, Austria, and Russia—and, for a time, Napoleon's success in the field continued. Because military success was central to the political purpose and self-esteem of elites, Napoleon's early successes as emperor further enhanced his power.

Conquering Europe, 1805–1810

Napoleon maintained relatively peaceful relations with other nations while he consolidated power at home, but the truces did not last. Tensions with the British quickly re-escalated when Britain resumed aggression against French shipping in 1803, and Napoleon countered by seizing Hanover, the ancestral German home of the English king. Then Napoleon seized several Italian territories and extended his influence in other German states. By 1805, all the states of Europe were threatened. Austria was alarmed by his power in Italy. England was at war on the high seas with Spain and the Netherlands, which Napoleon had forced to enter the fray. Napoleon began to gather a large French force on the northern coast of France, with which he could invade England.

The British fleet, commanded by Horatio Nelson (1758–1805), intercepted the combined French and Spanish fleets that were to have been the invasion flotilla and inflicted a devastating defeat off Cape Trafalgar in southern Spain (see Map 19.1) on October 21, 1805. The victory ensured British mastery of the seas and, in the long run, contributed to Napoleon's defeat. In the short run, the defeat at Trafalgar paled for the French beside Napoleon's impressive victories on land. Even as the French admirals were preparing for battle, Napoleon had abandoned the plans to invade England and in August had begun to march his army east through Germany.

In December 1805, after some preliminary, small-scale victories, Napoleon's army confronted a Russian force near Austerlitz, which is north of Vienna (see Map 19.1). Tsar Alexander I (r. 1801–1825) led his own troops into a battle that he ought to have avoided. Austrian reinforcements could not reach him in time, and French armies shattered the Russian force. The Battle of Austerlitz was Napoleon's most spectacular victory. Austria sued for peace. In further battles in 1806, French forces defeated Prussia as well as Russian armies once again.

Prussia was virtually dismembered by the subsequent Treaty of Tilsit (1807), but Napoleon tried to work out terms to make Russia into a contented ally. His hold on central Europe would not be secure with a hostile Russia, nor would the anti-British economic system that he envisioned—the Continental System (see page 725)—be workable without Russian participation.

French forces were still trying to prevail in Spain, which had been a client state since its defeat by revolutionary armies in 1795 but was resisting outright rule by a French-imposed king. In 1808, however, Napoleon turned his attention to a more fully subduing Austria. Napoleon won the Battle of Wagram in July 1809 but did not totally defeat Austria. Like Russia, Austria accepted French political and economic hegemony in a sort of alliance. By 1810 Napoleon had transformed most of Europe into allied or dependent states (see Map 19.1). The only exceptions were Britain and the parts of Spain and Portugal that continued to resist France with British help.

The states least affected by French hegemony were its reluctant allies: Austria, Russia, and the Scandinavian countries. Denmark had allied with France in 1807 only for help in fending off British naval supremacy in the Baltic. Sweden had reluctantly made peace in 1810 after losing control of Finland to Napoleon's ally, Russia. Sweden only minimally participated in the Continental System. At the other extreme were territories that had been incorporated into France. These included the Austrian Netherlands, territory along the Rhineland, and territories in Italy that bordered France. These regions were occupied by French troops and were treated as though they were départements of France itself.

In most other regions, some form of French-controlled government was in place, usually headed by a member of Napoleon's family. In both northern Italy and, initially, the Netherlands, where "sister" republics had been established after French conquests under the Directory, Napoleon imposed monarchies. Rulers were also imposed in the kingdom of Naples and in Spain. Western German states of the Holy Roman Empire that had allied with Napoleon against Austria were organized into the Confederation of the Rhine, with Napoleon as its "Protector." After a thousand years, the Holy Roman Empire ceased to exist. Two further states were created, largely out of the defeated Prussia's territory: the kingdom of Westphalia in western Germany and the duchy of Warsaw in the east (see Map 19.1).

Napoleon's domination of these various regions had complex, and at times contradictory,

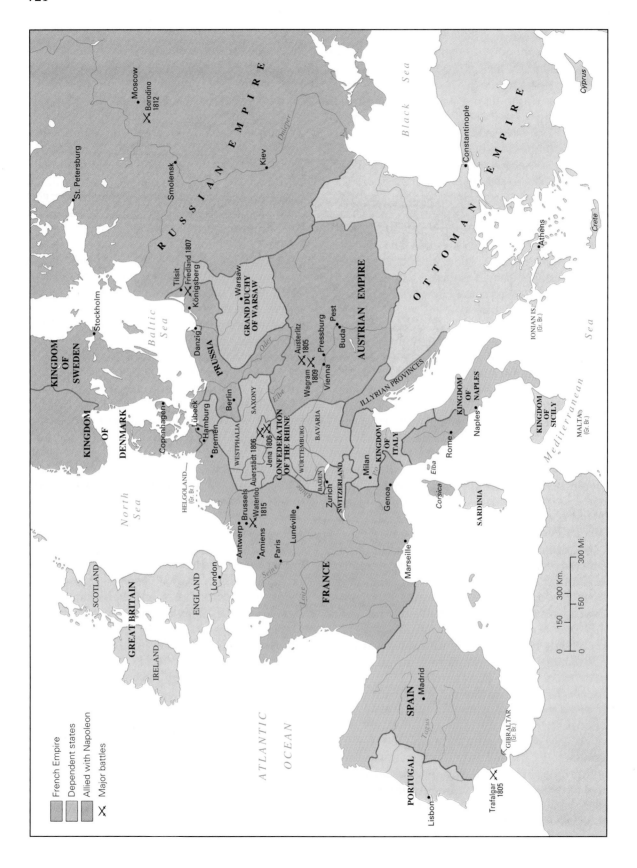

Moscow
Borodino
1812

St. Petersburg

RUSSIAN EMPIRE

Smolensk

Kiev

Dnieper

Black Sea

OTTOMAN EMPIRE

Constantinople

Cyprus

Athens

Crete

KINGDOM
OF
SWEDEN

Stockholm

*Baltic
Sea*

Tilsit
Friedland 1807
Königsberg

Warsaw

GRAND DUCHY
OF WARSAW

AUSTRIAN EMPIRE

Pest
Buda
Pressburg

IONIAN IS.
(Gr. Br.)

Sea

Danzig

Oder

Austerlitz
1805

PRUSSIA

Wagram
1809
Vienna

ILLYRIAN PROVINCES

KINGDOM
OF
DENMARK

Copenhagen

Lübeck
Hamburg
Bremen

Berlin

SAXONY

Elbe

Jena 1806
Auerstädt 1806

WESTPHALIA

KINGDOM
OF
NAPLES

Naples

KINGDOM
OF
SICILY

MALTA
(Gr. Br.)

CONFEDERATION
OF THE RHINE

WÜRTTEMBURG

BAVARIA

KINGDOM
OF
ITALY

Milan

Rome

Mediterranean

HELGOLAND
(Gr. Br.)

*North
Sea*

BADEN

Zurich

SWITZERLAND

Po

Genoa

Elba

Corsica

Waterloo
1815

Brussels

Antwerp

Amiens
Paris

Lunéville

Rhine

Seine

FRANCE

Loire

Marseille

SARDINIA

SCOTLAND

GREAT BRITAIN

IRELAND

ENGLAND

London

*ATLANTIC
OCEAN*

300 Mi.

300 Km.

150

150

0   0

GIBRALTAR
(Gr. Br.)

SPAIN

Madrid

Tagus

PORTUGAL

Lisbon

Trafalgar
1805

French Empire
Dependent states
Allied with Napoleon
Major battles

consequences. On the one hand, Napoleonic armies literally exported the French Revolution, in that French domination brought with it political and economic reform akin to that of the early phases of the Revolution, now enshrined in the Napoleonic Civil Code. Equality before the law was decreed following the French example; this meant the end of noble exemption from taxation in the many areas, like France, where it existed. In general, the complex snarl of medieval taxes and tolls was replaced with straightforward property taxes from which no one was exempt. As a consequence, tax revenues rose dramatically—by 50 percent in the kingdom of Italy, for example. Serfdom and forced labor were also abolished, as they had been in France in August 1789.

In most Catholic regions, the church was subjected to the terms of the Concordat of 1801. The tithe was abolished, church property seized and sold, and religious orders dissolved. Though Catholicism remained the state-supported religion in these areas, Protestantism was tolerated and Jews were granted rights of citizenship. Secular education, at least for males, was encouraged.

On the other hand, Napoleon would countenance only those aspects of France's revolutionary legacy that he tolerated in France itself. Just as he had suppressed any meaningful participatory government in France, so too did he suppress it in conquered regions. This came as a blow in states like the Netherlands, which had experienced its own democratizing "Patriot" movement and which had enjoyed republican self-government after invasion by French armies during the Revolution itself. Throughout the Napoleonic Empire, many of the benefits of streamlined administration and taxation were offset by the drain of continual warfare; deficits rose three- and fourfold, despite increased revenues. In addition, one of the inevitable costs of empire was political compromise to secure allies. In the duchy of Warsaw, reconstituted from lands Prussia had seized in the eighteenth century, Napoleon tampered little with either noble privileges or the power of the church. And, throughout Europe, Napoleon randomly al-

Map 19.1 Napoleonic Europe, ca. 1810 France dominated continental Europe after Napoleon's victories. Though French control would collapse quickly after defeats in Russia and Spain in 1812, the effects of French domination were more long-lasting.

lotted lands to reward his greatest generals and ministers, thereby exempting those lands from taxation and control by his own bureaucracy.

If true self-government was not allowed, a broad segment of the elite in all regions was nevertheless won over to cooperation with Napoleon by being welcomed into his bureaucracy or into the large multinational army, called the Grande Armée. Their loyalty was cemented when they bought confiscated church lands.

The impact of Napoleon's Continental System was equally mixed. Under this system, the Continent was in theory closed to all British shipping and British goods. The effects were widespread but uneven, and smuggling to evade controls on British goods became a major enterprise. Regions heavily involved in trade with Britain or its colonies or dependent on British shipping suffered in the new system, as did overseas trade in general when Britain gained dominance of the seas after Trafalgar. Peasants and landlords in many regions that produced grain for export suffered, and some cities dependent on overseas trade experienced catastrophic decline. However, the closing of the Continent to British trade, combined with increases in demand resulting from the need to supply Napoleon's armies, spurred the development of continental industries, at least in the short run. This industrial growth, enhanced by the improvement of roads, canals, and the like, formed the basis for further industrial development.

Defeat and Abdication, 1812–1815

Whatever its achievements, Napoleon's empire was ultimately precarious because of the hostility of Austria and Russia, as well as the belligerence of Britain. Austria resented losing the former Austrian Netherlands and lands in northern Italy to the French. Russia was a particularly weak link in the chain of alliances and subject states because Russian landowners and merchants were angered when their vital trade in timber for the British navy was interrupted and when supplies of luxury goods, brought in British ships, began to dwindle. A century of close alliances with German ruling houses made alliance with a French ruler extremely difficult politically for Tsar Alexander I.

It was Napoleon, however, who ended the alliance by provoking a breach with Russia. He suddenly backed away from an arrangement to marry one of Alexander's younger sisters and accepted the Austrian princess Marie Louise instead. (He had reluctantly divorced Joséphine in 1809 because their marriage had not produced an heir.) In addition, he seized lands along the German Baltic seacoast belonging to a member of Alexander's family. When Alexander threatened rupture of the alliance if the lands were not returned, Napoleon mounted an invasion. Advisers warned him about the magnitude of the task he seemed so eager to undertake—particularly about the preparations needed for winter fighting in Russia—but their warnings went unheard.

Napoleon's previous military successes had stemmed from a combination of strategic innovations and audacity. Napoleon divided his forces into independent corps. Each corps included infantry, cavalry, and artillery. Organized in these workable units, his armies could travel quickly by several separate routes and converge in massive force to face the enemy. Numbers were important to success, but so were discipline, control of troop movements, and determination to follow up initial gains. Leadership on the battlefield came from a loyal and talented officer corps that Napoleon had fashioned by welcoming returning aristocrats and favoring rising new talent. The final ingredient in the success formula was the high morale of French troops under Napoleon. Napoleon's English nemesis, Arthur Wellesley (1769–1852), duke of Wellington, once remarked that Napoleon's presence on a battlefield was worth forty thousand men.

The campaign against Russia began in June 1812. It was a spectacular failure. Napoleon had gathered a force of about 700,000 men—about half from France and half from allied states—a force twice as large as Russia's. The strategy of quickly moving independent corps and assembling massive forces could not be implemented because simply assembling so many men along the border was already the equivalent of gathering them for battle. Also, sustaining them thereafter was beyond the capacity of the supply system, which had always been Napoleon's weakness. Bold victories had often enabled Napoleon's troops to live off the countryside while they waited for supplies to catch up with them. But when the enemy attacked supply lines, when the distances traveled were very great, when the countryside was impoverished, or when battles were not decisive, Napoleon's ambitious strategies proved unworkable. In varying degrees, these conditions prevailed in Russia.

By the time the French faced the Russians in the principal battle of the Russian campaign—at Borodino, west of Moscow (see Map 19.1)—the Grande Armée had been on the march for two and a half months and stood at less than half its original strength. After the indecisive but bloody battle, the French occupied and pillaged Moscow but found scarcely enough food and supplies to sustain them. When Napoleon finally led his troops out of Moscow late in October, after an uncharacteristic period of indecisiveness, the fate of the French forces was all but sealed. The army marched south to reach the warmer and better-provisioned Ukraine but was turned back by Russian forces. The French then retreated north and west out of Russia, the way they had come. French soldiers who had not died in battle died of exposure or starvation or were killed by Russian peasants when they wandered away from their units. Of the original 700,000 French and allied troops, fewer than 100,000 made it out of Russia.

Napoleon left his army before it was fully out of Russia. A coup attempt in Paris prompted him to return to his governing duties before the French people realized the extent of the disaster in Russia. The collapse of his reign had begun, spurred by a coincidental defeat in Spain. Since 1808, Spain had been largely under French domination, with Napoleon's brother, Joseph, as king. A rebel Cortes (assembly), however, continued to meet in territory that the French did not control, and British troops were never expelled from the Iberian Peninsula. In 1812, as Napoleon was beginning his move against Russia, the collapse of French control accelerated. By the time Napoleon got back to Paris at the turn of the new year, Joseph had been expelled from Spain, and an Anglo-Spanish force led by the duke of Wellington was poised to invade France.

Napoleon's most able generals rallied what remained of his troops and held off Prussian and Russian forces in the east until he returned from France in April 1813 with a new army of raw recruits. Napoleon lost his last chance to stave off a coalition of all major powers against him when he refused an Austrian offer of peace for the return of conquered Austrian territories. With Britain willing to subsidize the allied armies, Tsar Alexander determined to destroy Napoleon, and the Austrians now anxious to share the spoils, Napoleon's empire

The French Army Flees Russia Napoleon's engineers built bridges for a night crossing of the Berezina River (in Belarus), which blocked the French retreat. The remainder of the army was saved from annihilation, but as in the rest of the Russian campaign, the cost was high: wagons and provisions, as well as thousands of wounded soldiers, were abandoned on the Russian side. Many of the engineers died of exposure. *(Musée de l'Armée)*

began to crumble. Napoleon's forces were crushed in a massive "Battle of Nations" near Leipzig in October, during which some of his troops from German satellite states deserted him on the battlefield. The allies were able to invade France and forced Napoleon to abdicate on April 6, 1814.

Napoleon was exiled to the island of Elba, off France's Mediterranean coast, but was still treated somewhat royally. He was installed as the island's ruler and was given an income drawn on the French treasury. Meanwhile, however, the restored French king was having his own troubles. Louis XVIII (r. 1814–1824) was the brother of the executed Louis XVI; he took the number eighteen out of respect for Louis XVI's son, who had died in prison in 1795. He had been out of the country and out of touch with its circumstances since the

beginning of the Revolution. In addition to the delicate task of establishing his own legitimacy, he faced enormous practical problems, including pensioning off thousands of soldiers now unemployed and still loyal to Napoleon.

Napoleon, bored and almost penniless on his island kingdom (the promised French pension never materialized), took advantage of the circumstances and returned surreptitiously to France on February 26, 1815. His small band of attendants was joined by the soldiers sent by the king to prevent him from advancing to Paris. Louis XVIII abandoned Paris to the returned emperor.

Napoleon's triumphant return lasted only one hundred days, however. Though many soldiers welcomed his return, many members of the elite were reluctant to throw in their lot with Napoleon again. Many ordinary French citizens had also become disenchanted with him since the defeat in Russia, and with the high costs, in conscription and taxation, of raising new armies. In any case, Napoleon's reappearance galvanized the divided allies, who had been haggling over a peace settlement, into unity. Napoleon tried to strike first, but he lost against English and Prussian troops in his first major battle, at Waterloo (in modern Belgium; see Map 19.1) on June 18, 1815. When Napoleon reached Paris after the defeat, he discovered the government in the hands of an ad hoc committee that included the Marquis de Lafayette. Under pressure, he abdicated once again. He was exiled to the tiny, remote island of St. Helena in the South Atlantic, from which escape would be impossible. He died there in 1821.

THE IMPACT OF REVOLUTION ON FRANCE AND THE WORLD

The process of change in France between 1789 and 1815 was so complex that it is easy to overlook the overall impact of the Revolution. Superficially, the changes seemed to come full circle—with first Louis XVI on the throne, then Napoleon as emperor, and then Louis XVIII on the throne. Even though the monarchy was restored, however, the Revolution changed the fundamental premises of political life in France and served to catalyze challenges to the existing order elsewhere.

The Significance of Revolution in France

The French monarchy was restored in 1815, but the Revolution had discredited absolute monarchy in theory and practice. The restored constitutional monarchy governed with only a small group of representatives of the elite, but their participation slowly widened during the nineteenth century. An important legacy of the Revolution was thus new principles on which to base a government: the right of "the people," however narrowly defined, to participate in government and to enjoy due process of law.

There was fundamental disagreement, however, about which people were worthy of inclusion in the political process and the degree to which the government might govern in their interests. There was a significant philosophical differ-

ence between many republicans and the reformers who had supported the Revolution in its initial stages. The latter argued for access to government only by the politically sophisticated elite and for the freeing of the economy from traditional constraints. The more inclusive view and the more activist posture regarding the appropriate role of government would be reinstated by revolutionary action later in the nineteenth century (see Chapter 20). Neither notion included a vision of women as citizens coequal with men.

Other legacies of the Revolution and the Napoleonic era included a centralized political system. The nation was divided into départements rather than provinces. For the first time, a single code of law applied to all French people. Most officials—from département administrators to city mayors—were appointed by the central government until the late twentieth century. The conscientious attention of the government, at various stages of the Revolution, to advances for France generally reflects the positive side of this centralization. The government sponsored national scientific societies, a national library and archives, and a system of teachers' colleges and universities. Particularly under Napoleon, there was a spate of canal- and road-building.

Napoleon's legacy, like that of the Revolution itself, was mixed. His self-serving reconciliation of aristocratic pretensions with the opening of careers to men of talent helped to ensure the long-term success of revolutionary principles from which the elite as a whole profited. His reconciliation of the state with the Catholic church helped to stabilize his regime and to ensure some revolutionary gains. The restored monarchy could not renege on these gains. But Napoleon could not eliminate the antirevolutionary bent of the church as a whole, and the church continued to be a reactionary force in France. The Napoleonic Code was a uniform system of law for the nation. But although it guaranteed equality under the law for men, it enshrined political and legal inferiority for women.

Whatever the concrete gains of the Revolution and Napoleon's rule, Napoleon's overthrow of constitutional principles worsened the problem of political instability. Napoleon's return to power in 1815, though brief, was nevertheless important. It reflects the degree to which his power was always rooted in military adventurism and in the loyalty of soldiers and officers. His bravado suggests the importance of personal qualities to the success of an authoritarian regime. But the swiftness of his collapse suggests that although the empire under Napoleon may have seemed an enduring solution to the political instability of the late 1790s, its legitimacy and security were as uncertain as the legitimacy and security of the revolutionary governments.

Although Louis XVIII acknowledged the principle of constitutionalism at the end of the Revolution, it rested on fragile footing. Indeed, the fragility of new political systems was one of the most profound lessons of the Revolution. There was division over policies, but even greater division over legitimacy—that is, the acceptance by a significant portion of the politically active citizenry of a particular system or of a particular government's right to rule.

Politics, the Revolution revealed, takes place in part on a symbolic level. What is acceptable and what is legitimate are expressed not only in words but also symbolically. The symbols are effective because they link a specific political system to a broader, fundamental system of values. The religious symbolism used by the monarchy, for example, linked royal government to divine order. Similarly, the public cults of reason and of the Supreme Being that Robespierre promoted during the Terror were attempts to link patriotism and support of the government to universal principles. Other, more limited, symbols were constantly in use: the red and blue cockades that supporters of the National Assembly put in their caps; the "liberty cap" that Louis XVI donned on one occasion; various representations of the abstract notion of "Liberty" in newspapers and journals widely available at the time.

Before the Revolution started, there was a significant shift in notions about political legitimacy. The deputies who declared themselves to be the National Assembly in June 1789 already believed that they had a right to do so. In their view, they represented "the nation," and their voice had legitimacy for that reason. The shift reflects not the innate power of ideas but the power of ideas in context. The deputies brought to Versailles not only their individual convictions that "reason" should be applied to the political system but also their experience in social settings where those ideas were well received. In their salons, clubs, and literary societies, they had experienced the fa-

miliarity, trust, and sense of community that are essential to effective political action.

The deputies' attempt to transplant their sense of community into national politics was not wholly successful. Factions, competing interests, and clashes of personality can be fatal to an insecure system. The National Assembly had scarcely inaugurated a secure system when its deputies undermined its workability by making themselves ineligible to hold office under the new constitution. The king also actively undermined the system because he disagreed with it in principle. The British parliamentary system, by comparison, though every bit as elitist as the narrowest of the representative systems during the French Revolution, had a long history as a workable institution for lords, commoners, and rulers. This shared experience was an important counterweight to differences over fundamental issues, so that Parliament as an institution both survived political crises and helped solve them.

The Revolution thus left a powerful yet ambiguous legacy for France. Politics was established on a new footing, yet still lacking were the practical means to achieve the promise inherent in the new principles.

The Impact of the Revolution Overseas

Throughout Europe and overseas, the Revolution left a powerful and complex legacy. French conquests in Europe were the least enduring of the dramatic changes of the revolutionary era. Nevertheless, French domination had certain lasting effects: Elites were exposed to modern bureaucratic management, and equality under the law transformed social and political relationships. Although national self-determination had an enemy in Napoleon, the breaking down of ancient political divisions provided important practical grounding for later cooperation among elites in nationalist movements. In Napoleon's kingdom of Italy, for example, a tax collector from Florence for the first time worked side by side with one from Milan. The example of the Revolution also helped inspire the uprising against Russian domination of Poland in 1794 (see page 701). This insurrection included not only educated elites, such as its leader Kościuszko, but also artisans and peasants; indeed, Catherine the Great was appalled when the rebels hanged members of a Russian-supported puppet government and vowed to crush the Polish "Jacobins."

European colonies overseas felt the impact of the Revolution and subsequent European wars in several ways. The British tried to take advantage of Napoleon's preoccupation with continental affairs by seizing French colonies and the colonies of the French-dominated Dutch. They were largely successful. In 1806 they seized the Dutch colony of Capetown—crucial for support of trade around Africa—as well as French bases along the African coast. In 1811 they grabbed the island of Java. In the Americas, French sugar colonies in the Caribbean were particularly vulnerable to English seapower. The British readily seized Martinique, Guadeloupe, and other islands while Napoleon was executing his brilliant victories on the Continent after 1805. The sugar island of Haiti was an exception to this pattern of French losses because British aggression there occurred in the context of a local revolution.

In Haiti the Revolution itself, and not merely the strategic moves of great powers, had an impact. The National Assembly in Paris delayed abolishing slavery in French colonies, despite the moral appeal of such a move, because of pressure from the white planters on Haiti and out of fear that the financially strapped French government would lose some of its profitable sugar trade. But the example of revolutionary daring in Paris and confusion about ruling authority that occurred as the Assembly and the king wrangled invited challenges to authority in the colonies.

Many white planters hoped to seize the opportunity the Revolution provided to gain political and economic independence from France. White planter rule in Haiti was challenged, in turn, by wealthy people of mixed European and African descent and then by a full-fledged slave rebellion, beginning in 1791. (See the box, "Encounters with the West: A Planter's Wife on the Haitian Slave Revolt.") Britain sent aid to the rebels when it went to war against the French revolutionary government in 1793. Only when the republic was declared in Paris and the Convention abolished slavery did the Haitian rebels abandon alliances with France's enemies and attempt to govern in concert with the mother country.

France, however, never regained control of Haiti. Led by a former slave, François Dominique Toussaint-Louverture (1743–1803), the new gov-

ernment of Haiti tried to run its own affairs, though without formally declaring independence from France. Napoleon, early in his rule, decided to tighten control of the profitable colonies by reinstituting slavery and ousting the independent government of Haiti. In 1802 French forces fought their way onto the island. They captured Toussaint-Louverture, who died shortly thereafter in prison. But in 1803 they were forced to leave by another rebellion prompted by the threat of renewed slavery.

The French Revolution and Napoleonic rule had a great impact on Spanish colonies in the Americas also, and for many of the same reasons as in Haiti. The confusion of authority in Spain enabled some Spanish colonies to govern themselves independently in all but name. Like the British North American colonies, the Spanish colonies wanted freedom from the closed economic ties the mother country tried to impose.

The liberal ideas that had helped spawn the French Revolution spurred moves toward independence in Spanish America. There were also echoes of radical republican ideology in some of the events in Spanish America. For example, participants in two major rebellions in Mexico espoused the end of slavery and generally championed the interests of the poor against local and Spanish elites. The leaders of these self-declared revolutions were executed (in 1811 and 1815), and their movements were crushed by local elites in alliance with Spanish troops. The efforts of local elites to become self-governing—the attempted liberal revolutions—were little more successful. Only Argentina and Paraguay broke away from Spain at this time. But as in Europe, a legacy remained of both limited and more radical revolutionary activity.

The View from Britain

Today the city of Paris is dotted with public monuments that celebrate Napoleon's victories. One of the main train stations is the Gare (Station) d'Austerlitz. A column in a city square, crowned with a statue of Napoleon, was made from the metal of enemy cannon captured at Austerlitz.

In London, another set of events and another hero is celebrated. In Trafalgar Square stands a statue of Lord Nelson, the British naval commander whose fleet destroyed a combined French and

∼ ENCOUNTERS WITH THE WEST ∼

A Planter's Wife on the Haitian Slave Revolt

The following are excerpts from two letters of Madame de Rouvray, a wealthy planter's wife living in the French colony of Saint-Domingue (the western half of the island of Hispaniola), to her married daughter in France. The decree of May 15, 1791, that Madame de Rouvray mentions in her first letter granted civil rights to free persons of mixed race. The decree affected only a few hundred persons on Saint-Domingue (many of whom themselves owned slaves), but white planters feared any breach in the barriers between the races. Tensions between white planters, on the one hand, and mulattos and modest white settlers who favored revolutionary changes, on the other, enabled the well-organized slave rebellion to be dramatically successful. It began in late August 1791 and is the backdrop to Madame de Rouvray's second letter. Madame de Rouvray and her husband fled the island—renamed Haiti, the Native American term for Hispaniola, after the revolt—for the United States in 1793.

July 30, 1791 I am writing to you from Cap [a city on the island] where I came to find out what the general mood is here. . . . All the deputies who make up the general assembly [of the colony] left here the day before yesterday to gather at Léogane [another city]. If they conduct themselves wisely their first action should be to send emissaries to all the powers who have colonies with slaves in order to tell them of the decree [of May 15] and of the consequences that will follow from it, and ask for help from them in case it happens that the National Assembly actually abolishes slavery too, which they will surely do. After their decree of May 15, one cannot doubt that that is their plan. And you understand that all the powers who have slave colonies have a common interest in opposing such a crazy plan because the contagion of liberty will soon infect their colonies too, especially in nearby Jamaica. It is said that [the English] will send a ship and troops [which] would be wonderful for us. Your father thinks it won't be long before the English take control here.

September 4, 1791 If news of the horrors that have happened here since the 23rd of last month have reached you, you must have been very worried. Luckily, we are all safe. We can't say whether our fortunes are also safe because we are still at war with the slaves who revolted [and] who have slaughtered and torched much of the countryside hereabouts. . . . All of this will gravely damage our revenues for this year and for the future, because how can we stay in a country where slaves have raised their hands against their masters? . . . You have no idea, my dear, of the state of this colony; it would make you tremble. Don't breathe a word of this to anyone but your father is determined, once the rebels have been defeated, to take refuge in Havanna.

Source: M. E. McIntosh and B. C. Weber, *Une Correspondance familiale au temps des troubles de Saint-Domingue* (Paris: Société de l'Histoire des Colonies Françaises et Librairie Larose, 1959), pp. 22–23, 26–28. Trans. by Kristen B. Neuschel.

Spanish fleet in 1805. Horatio Nelson was a brilliant tactician, whose innovations in maneuvering ships in the battle line resulted in stunning victories at Trafalgar and, in 1798, at the Nile Delta, which limited French ambitions in Egypt and the eastern Mediterranean.

Trafalgar looms large in British history in part because Nelson was mortally wounded during the battle. More significant, the battle ensured British mastery of the seas, which then forced Napoleon into economic policies that strained French ties to France's allies and satellites. Virtually

The Funeral of Lord Nelson, January 8, 1806 Nelson had been mortally wounded on the deck of his flagship at the Battle of Trafalgar in October. Rather than being buried at sea, as was the custom, his body was returned to London for an impressive state funeral, commemorated here in a contemporary engraving. *(National Maritime Museum, London)*

unchallenged seapower enabled the British to seize colonies formerly ruled by France and its allies.

Britain's seizure of French possessions expanded British trading networks overseas. The struggles against Napoleon also enhanced British trading networks and strategic dominance closer to home, particularly in the Mediterranean. As long as the British had been involved in trade with India, the Mediterranean had been important for economic and strategic reasons: It marked the end of the land route for trade from the Indian Ocean. Especially after Napoleon's aggression in Egypt, the British redoubled their efforts to control important strategic outposts in the Mediterranean, such as ports in southern Italy and on the island of Malta.

Since the late eighteenth century, the British had steadily made other gains abroad. In 1783, Britain had lost control of thirteen of its North American colonies; however, it had more successfully resolved the Irish rebellions. Similarly, in the Caribbean, British planter families, like Irish elites, were willing to accept tighter rule from the mother country in return for greater security against their subject population. In regions of India, the East India Company was increasing its political domination, and hence its economic stranglehold on Indian manufacture and trade.

The British economy would expand dramatically in the nineteenth century as industrial production expanded. The roots for that expansion were laid in this period in the countryside of Britain, where changes in agriculture and in production were occurring. These roots were also laid in Britain's overseas possessions by the profits made there and also, increasingly, by the control of sources of raw materials, notably raw cotton raised in India. The export of Indian cotton expanded significantly during the revolutionary period as part of an expanding trading system that included China, the source of tea.

However, economic expansion was not the sole motive for British aggression. In fact, economic expansion was often the product of increased British control of particular regions or sea-lanes, and the reasons for it were as much strategic as economic. Not every conquest had direct economic payoffs, but British elites were sure that strategic domination was a desirable step, wherever it could be managed. One Scottish landholder, writing in the opening years of the nineteenth century, spoke for many when he said that Britain needed an empire to ensure its greatness and that an empire of the sea was an effective counterweight to Napoleon's empire on land. Much as the French were at that moment exporting features of their own political system, the British, he said, could export their constitution wherever they conquered territory.

Thus, England and France were in fact engaged in similar phases of expansion in this period. In both, the desire for power and profit drove policy. In each, myths about heroes and about the supposed benefits of domination masked the state's self-interest. In both, the effects of conquest would become a fundamental shaping force in the nineteenth century.

SUMMARY

The French Revolution was a watershed in European history because it successfully challenged the principles of hereditary rule and political privilege by which all European states had hitherto been governed. The Revolution began when a financial crisis forced the monarchy to confront the desire for political reform by a segment of the French elite. Political philosophy emerging from the Enlightenment and the example of the American Revolution moved the French reformers to action. In its initial phase, the French Revolution established the principle of constitutional government and ended many of the traditional political privileges of the Old Regime.

The Revolution moved in more radical directions because of the intransigence of the king, the threat of foreign invasion, and the actions of republican legislators and Parisian citizens. Its most radical phase, the Terror, produced the most effective legislation for ordinary citizens but also the worst violence of the Revolution. A period of unstable conservative rule that followed the Terror ended when Napoleon seized power.

Though Napoleonic rule enshrined some of the gains of the Revolution, it also subjected France and most of Europe to the great costs of wars of conquest. After Napoleon, the French

monarchy was restored but forced to accept many limitations on its power as a result of the Revolution. Indeed, hereditary rule and traditional social hierarchies remained in place in much of Europe, but they would not be secure in the future. The legacy of revolutionary change would prove impossible to contain in France or anywhere else.

NOTES

1. Quoted in Samuel Eliot Morison, *John Paul Jones: A Sailor's Biography* (Boston: Little, Brown, 1959), pp. 149–154.
2. Quoted in Owen Connelly, *The French Revolution and Napoleonic Era* (New York: Holt, Rinehart and Winston, 1979), p. 32.

SUGGESTED READING

General Surveys

Connelly, Owen. *French Revolution/Napoleonic Era.* 1979. A clear and readable survey that devotes equal time to the Revolution and to Napoleon.

Sutherland, D. M. G. *France, 1789–1815.* 1986. A dense and detailed treatment, with extensive bibliography, that emphasizes the revolutionary over the Napoleonic period.

Thompson, John. *The French Revolution.* 1951. A classic liberal interpretation of the Revolution, useful for its clarity and detail.

Recent Interpretations of the Revolution

Baker, Keith Michael, ed. *The French Revolution and the Creation of Modern Political Culture.* 1987. A collection of essays by diverse scholars emphasizing the Revolution as a period of change in political culture.

Furet, François. *Interpreting the French Revolution.* 1981. The major work by the outstanding French scholar of the Revolution of the current generation, written in reaction to liberal and Marxist interpretations.

Hufton, Olwen. *Women and the Limits of Citizenship in the French Revolution.* 1992. A series of essays by the leading scholar on the history of women in the Revolution.

Hunt, Lynn. *The Family Romance of the French Revolution.* 1992. A study of political ideology and symbolic politics emphasizing the vast cultural consequences of killing the king and queen.

———. *Politics, Culture and Class in the French Revolution.* 1984. A survey and assessment of other interpretations of the Revolution, emphasizing the role of symbols and symbolic politics.

Kennedy, Emmet. *A Cultural History of the French Revolution.* 1989. An ambitious interpretation of the Revolution as a period of cultural change.

(continued on page 736)

POLITICAL SYMBOLS

During the French Revolution, thousands of illustrations in support of various revolutionary (or counterrevolutionary) ideas were reproduced on posters, on handbills, and in pamphlets. Some satirized their subjects, such as Marie Antoinette, or celebrated revolutionary milestones, such as the fall of the Bastille. The etching here of the woman armed with a pike, dating from 1792, falls into this category. Other pictures, such as the representation from 1795 of Liberty as a young woman wearing

An Armed Citizen, ca. 1792 *(Bibliothèque Nationale, Cabinet des estampes)*

the liberty cap, symbolized or reinforced various revolutionary ideals.*

Political images like these are an invaluable though problematic source for historians. Let us examine these two images of women and consider how French people during the Revolution might have responded to them. To understand what they meant to contemporaries, we must know something about the other images that these would have been compared to. We must also view the images in the context of the events of the Revolution itself. Immediately, then, we are presented with an interpretive agenda. How ordinary and acceptable was this image of an armed woman? If women were not citizens coequal with men, how could a woman be a symbol of liberty? What, in short, do these political images reveal about the spectrum of political life in their society?

The woman holding the pike stares determinedly at the viewer. Many details confirm what the caption announces: This is a French woman who has become free. In her hat she wears one of the symbols of revolutionary nationhood: the tricolor cockade. The badge around her waist celebrates a defining moment for the revolutionary nation: the fall of the Bastille. Her pike itself is inscribed with the words "Liberty or death!"

The woman appears to be serving not merely as a symbol of free women. She comes close to being the generic image of a free citizen, willing and able to fight for liberty—an astonishing symbolic possibility in a time when women were not yet treated equally under the law or granted the same

*This discussion draws on the work of Joan Landes, "Representing the Body Politic: The Paradox of Gender in the Graphic Politics of the French Revolution," and Darlene Gay Levy and Harriet B. Applewhite, "Women and Militant Citizenship in Revolutionary Paris," in Sara E. Melzer and Leslie W. Rabine, eds., *Rebel Daughters: Women and the French Revolution* (New York: Oxford University Press, 1992), pp. 15–37, 79–101.

political rights as the men of their class. Other images prevalent at the time echo this possibility. Many contemporary representations of the women's march on Versailles in 1789 (see page 708) show women carrying arms, active in advancing the Revolution. By the time this image was created (most likely in 1792), many other demonstrations and violent confrontations by ordinary people had resulted in the creation of dozens of popular prints and engravings that showed women acting in the same ways as men.

Repeatedly during 1792, women proposed to the revolutionary government that they be granted the right to bear arms. Their request was denied, but it was not dismissed out of hand. There was debate, and the issue was in effect tabled. Nevertheless, women's actions in the Revolution had created at least the possibility of envisaging citizenship with a female face.

The image of liberty from 1795 does not reflect the actions of women but rather represents their exclusion from political participation. It is one of a number of images of Liberty that portray this ideal as a passive, innocent woman, here garbed in ancient dress, surrounded by a glow that in the past had been reserved for saints. Liberty here is envisaged as a pure and lofty goal, symbolized as a pure young woman.

Late in 1793, during the Terror, women were excluded from formal participation in politics with the disbanding of women's organizations. Nor did they gain political rights under the Directory, which re-established some of the limited gains of the first phase of the Revolution. The justification offered for their exclusion in 1793 was borrowed from Rousseau: It is contrary to nature for women to be in public life (see page 665). Women "belong" in the private world of the family, where they will nurture male citizens. Women embody ideal qualities such as patience and self-sacrifice; they are not fully formed beings capable of action in their own right.

"Liberty" as a Young Woman, ca. 1795 (*S. P. Avery Collection, Miriam and Ira D. Wallach Division of Art, Prints, and Photographs, The New York Public Library, Astor, Lenox, and Tilden Foundations*)

Such notions made it easy to use images of women to embody ideals for public purposes. A woman could represent Liberty precisely because actual women were not able to be political players.

The two images shown here thus demonstrate that political symbols can have varying relationships to "reality." The pike-bearing citizen is the more "real." Her image reflects the way actual women acted, and it represents a way of thinking about politics that became possible for the first time because of their actions. The other woman reflects not the attributes of actual women but an ideal type spawned by the use of arbitrary gender distinctions to legitimize political power. In these images we can see modern political life taking shape: the sophistication of its symbolic language, the importance of abstract ideas such as liberty and nationhood—as well as the grounding of much political life in rigid distinctions between public and private, male and female. ✑

Landes, Joan. *Women and the Public Sphere in the Age of the French Revolution.* 1988. An analysis of the uses of gender ideology to fashion the new political world of the revolutionaries.

Manceron, Claude. *The Age of the French Revolution.* 1986. An innovative, multivolume study of the experience of the Revolution, beginning in the 1770s, told by means of biographical vignettes.

Origins and Preconditions of the Revolution

Censer, Jack, and Jeremy D. Popkin. *Press and Politics in Pre-Revolutionary France.* 1987. A work that is helpful in understanding the context of opposition to the monarchy before the outbreak of the Revolution.

Chartier, Roger. *The Cultural Origins of the French Revolution.* 1991. An interpretation of intellectual and cultural life in the eighteenth century with a view to explaining its revolutionary results; has a good bibliography.

Lefebvre, Georges. *The Coming of the French Revolution.* Translated by R. R. Palmer. 1947. The greatest of several works by this French historian; a readable Marxist interpretation that remains useful.

Palmer, R. R. *The Age of Democratic Revolution.* 2 vols. 1959. A study of the American and European revolutionary movements and their reciprocal influences; detailed, erudite, but immensely readable.

The Phases of Revolution, 1789–1791

Godeschot, J. *The Taking of the Bastille, July 14, 1789.* 1970. An explanation of the circumstances and significance of the seizure of the Bastille.

Rudé, George. *The Crowd in the French Revolution.* 1959. A classic Marxist assessment of the importance of common people to the progress of the Revolution.

Tackett, Timothy. *Priest and Paris in Eighteenth-Century France.* 1977. A study of rural Catholic life before the Revolution and after the impact of the Civil Constitution of the Clergy.

The Phases of Revolution, 1791–1794

Jordan, D. P. *The King's Trial.* 1979. A thorough and readable study of Louis XVI's trial and its importance.

Palmer, R. R. *Twelve Who Ruled.* 1941. A study of the principal figures of the Terror by one of the greatest American historians of the French Revolution.

Patrick, A. *The Men of the First French Republic.* 1972. A study of the Girondins—their identity and their coherence as a political faction.

Soboul, Albert. *The Sans-Culottes.* 1972. A study of the workers of Paris who were active in the Revolution, by Georges Lefebvre's successor as the foremost Marxist historian of the Revolution.

The Phases of Revolution, 1795–1799

Barton, H. Arnold. *Scandinavia in the Revolutionary Era, 1760–1815.* 1986. Treats the Scandinavian countries' response to and involvement in revolutionary movements and the Napoleonic wars.

James, C. L. R. *The Black Jacobins.* 1938. The classic study of the Haitian revolution in the context of events in Europe.

Sydenham, M. *The First French Republic, 1792–1804.* 1974. A useful survey of the relatively neglected phases of the Revolution.

Napoleon and Napoleonic Europe

Bayly, C. A. *Imperial Meridian.* 1989. A new study of the developing British Empire in the context of both European and world affairs; has an extensive bibliography.

Connelly, Owen. *Blundering to Glory: The Campaigns of Napoleon.* 1992. A new assessment of Napoleon's military achievements by an expert on Napoleonic warfare.

Lyons, Martyn. *Napoleon Bonaparte and the Legacy of the French Revolution.* 1994. A clear, readable, and up-to-date synthesis of scholarship on Napoleon.

Markham, Felix. *Napoleon.* 1963. The best biography in English of Napoleon.

Restoration, Reform, and Revolution, 1814–1848

I n 1791 in the midst of revolution the comte de Provence had fled his homeland, disguised as a foreign merchant. Shunted from country to country he lived in exile, depending upon subsidies of foreign courts. Since the revolutionaries had beheaded his brother, Louis XVI, and a nephew had died in captivity, when he returned to France after twenty-three years abroad, he did so as king of France, Louis XVIII (r. 1814–1824).

With Louis's return to French soil in April 1814, the Bourbons were restored. In many other states, too, with the fall of Napoleon, monarchy and aristocracy attempted to reassert, to "restore," their authority. Historians often call the period from 1814 to 1832 in Europe the "restoration." Yet the old world could not be entirely re-created—from the beginning efforts to restore it were challenged by forces that had appeared during the revolutionary years.

The Great Powers tried to re-establish as much of the old European state system as possible. The international arrangements of the victorious powers—Austria, Great Britain, Prussia, and Russia—were soon shaken by outbreaks of nationalist fervor. Nationalists aimed either to create larger political units, as in Italy and Germany, or to win independence from foreign rule, as in Greece.

Domestically, the attempt to set the clock back was of limited success. The conservatism of European rulers and their opposition to change were at odds with the new dynamism of European society. Between 1800 and 1850, Europe's population increased by nearly 50 percent, from around 190 million to 280 million. Population growth and the development of

Celebrating the revolution of 1848 in Vienna. Anton Ziegler, *The Barricade at Michaelerplatz on the Evening of 26th May* (1848).

739

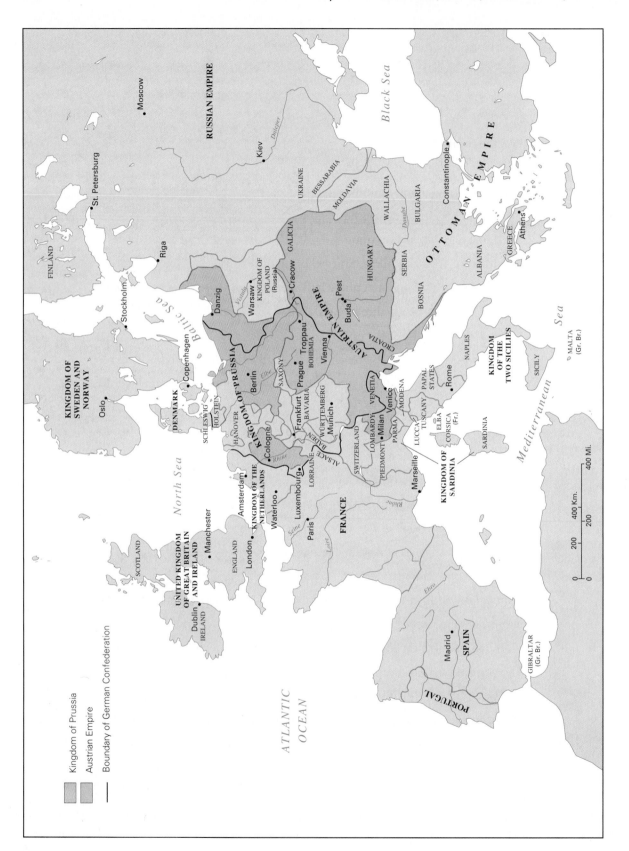

industry created large cities where there had been small towns or rural areas. Factory manufacturing was on the rise, promising to reshape class structures and the lives of workers. Romanticism, liberalism, and other systems of thought were redefining the relationship of the individual to society.

European statesmen in 1814 consciously tried to forestall revolution, but in less than a generation they were challenged by waves of protest and violence, most notably in the revolutions of 1848. Revolutionaries did not win all their goals, and in many cases the forces of order crushed them. Yet major intellectual, social, and political changes had occurred by midcentury.

THE SEARCH FOR STABILITY: THE CONGRESS OF VIENNA

The defeat of Napoleon put an end to French dominance in Europe. In September 1814 the victorious Great Powers—Austria, Great Britain, Prussia, and Russia—convened an international conference in Vienna to negotiate the terms of peace. The victors sought to draw territorial boundaries advantageous to themselves and to provide long-term stability on the European continent.

Although many small powers attended the Congress of Vienna, their role was reduced to ratifying the large states' decisions. Having faced a powerful France, which had mobilized popular forces with revolutionary principles, the victors decided to erect an international system that would remove such threats. One method was to restore the European order that had existed before the French Revolution. Thus, following principles of "legitimacy and compensation," they redrew the map of Europe (Map 20.1). Rulers who had been overthrown were restored to their thrones. As we have seen, the eldest surviving brother of Louis XVI of France became King Louis XVIII. In Spain, Ferdinand VII was restored to the throne from which Napoleon had toppled him and his father. The restoration, however, was not so complete as its proponents claimed. Since the French Revolution, certain new realities had to be recognized. For example, Napoleon had consolidated the German and Italian states; the process was acknowledged in the former with the creation of a loose German Confederation.

Negotiations at the Congress of Vienna strengthened the territories bordering France, enlarged Prussia, created the kingdom of Piedmont-Sardinia, joined Belgium to Holland, and provided the victors with spoils and compensation for territories bartered away. Russia's reward for its contribution to the war effort was most of Poland and all of Finland, which had belonged to Sweden. Sweden's king was compensated for the loss of Finland by being permitted to rule in a joint union over Norway, formerly under the Danish crown. Denmark was thus punished for adhering to the Napoleonic alliance longer than the victorious Great Powers thought was appropriate. Austria received Venetia and Lombardy in northern Italy to compensate for the loss of Belgium and the loss of parts of Poland to Russia and to strengthen its position in general. Prussia was also allowed annexations in compensation for giving up parts of Poland. England acquired a number of colonies and naval outposts. Thus, even as they proclaimed their loyalty to the prerevolutionary past, conservative statesmen changed the map of Europe.

The leading personality at the Congress of Vienna was the Austrian foreign minister, Prince Clemens von Metternich (1773–1859), who presided over the meetings. An aristocrat in exile from the Rhineland, which had been annexed by revolutionary France, he had gone into the service of the Habsburg empire and risen to become its highest official. Personal charm, tact, and representation of a state that for the time being was satisfied with its territories made Metternich seem a disinterested statesman. His influence at the Congress was great.

Made wary by their long war against France, the four powers of the Quadruple Alliance—Austria, Great Britain, Prussia, and Russia—had pledged before the Congress of Vienna to cooperate to prevent any future French aggression. They also planned to meet periodically to resolve all European issues, creating what was known as the "Concert of Europe." Yet at Vienna the wily French foreign minister, Count Charles Talleyrand (1754–1838), was able to insinuate himself into the councils of the Great Powers. The desire of Russia and Prussia for sizable territorial gains alarmed both

Map 20.1 Europe in 1815 The map of Europe was redrawn at the Congress of Vienna.

Metternich The consummate statesman and aristocrat, Metternich tried to quell revolution at home and abroad. Some called his era the Metternichean age. *(The Royal Collection © 1993 Her Majesty Queen Elizabeth II)*

Austria and Great Britain, and France joined them in limiting Russian and Prussian ambitions. At Talleyrand's insistence, France was counted as one of the five Great Powers.

The Concert of Europe, including France, continued to function, and met several times to try to resolve subsequent crises. Underlying the states' cooperation was the principle of a common European destiny.

IDEOLOGICAL CONFRONTATIONS

The international and domestic political system established in 1815 was modified by a series of challenges, even revolts, culminating in revolutions throughout Europe in 1848. The order established in 1815 was inspired by conservatism. Its challengers advocated competing ideologies: romanticism, nationalism, liberalism, and socialism.

Conservatism

The architects of the restoration justified their policies with doctrines based on the ideology of conservatism, emphasizing the need to preserve the existing order. As a coherent movement, conservatism sprang up during and after the French Revolution to resist the forces of change. When the old order faced serious challenges in the late eighteenth and early nineteenth centuries, an ideology justifying traditional authority emerged. Before the American and French Revolutions, the existing political institutions appeared to be permanent.

Edmund Burke (1729–1797), a British statesman and political theorist, launched one of the first intellectual assaults on the French Revolution. The revolutionary National Assembly had asserted that ancient prerogatives were superseded by the rights of man and principles of human equality based on appeals to natural law. In *Reflections on the Revolution in France* (1790), Burke said that such claims were abstract and dangerous and that the belief in human equality undermined the social order. Government should be anchored in tradition, he argued. No matter how poorly the French monarchy and its institutions had served the nation, they should be preserved; their very longevity proved their usefulness. Burke's writings were widely read and influential on the Continent.

In the English-speaking world, one of the most popular writers, Hannah More (1745–1833), who with her four sisters ran a prosperous school, saw piety as a rampart against rebellion. In a series of moral tracts entitled *Cheap Repository Tracts*, she advocated the acceptance of the existing order and the solace of religious faith. Costing but a penny, the tracts were often handed out by the rich together with alms or food to the poor. More was the first writer in history to sell over a million copies; within three years the sales doubled. Conservative values thus spread to a very large audience in both Britain and the United States, where one of her works appeared in thirty editions.

A more extreme version of conservatism was the counterrevolutionary or ultra-royalist ideology. Unlike Burke, who was willing to tolerate some change, counterrevolutionaries wanted to restore society to its prerevolutionary condition. The most extreme counterrevolutionaries were those with personal experience of the upheavals of the Revolution. Count Joseph de Maistre (1753–1821), a

Savoyard (from the Franco-Italian border region) nobleman whose estates were occupied by the invading French, described monarchy as a God-given form of government in his *Considerations on France* in 1796. Any attempt to abolish or even limit it was a violation of divine law. According to de Maistre and his fellow reactionaries, the authority of church and state was necessary to prevent human beings from falling into evil ways. De Maistre advocated stern government control, including the generous use of the death penalty, to keep people loyal to throne and altar.

In Germany the influential thought of Georg Wilhelm Friedrich Hegel (1770–1831), philosophy professor at the University of Berlin, was interpreted by many of his disciples as a defense of the conservative order re-established by the restoration. In Hegel's view, history was propelled from one stage to another by the "world spirit" incarnate in the dominant power. Just as Rome had fulfilled divine plans by dominating the ancient world, so Napoleon, when he entered Jena in 1806, was hailed by Hegel as a "world soul." The emperor's fall, however, convinced Hegel that the true world soul was incarnate in the victorious allies, particularly Prussia. The state, Hegel said, showed "the march of God in the world"; the existing power, reactionary and authoritarian, was divinely ordained.

Conservatism was also influenced by romanticism, with its glorification of the past, taste for pageantry, and belief in the organic unity of society. But by no means were all conservatives romantics. Metternich, for instance, saw his work as the attempt of an enlightened mind to restore the world that had been undermined by the emotional turmoil of the French Revolution. (See the box, "Metternich's Cure for Europe.")

Romanticism

The long-lived romantic movement emerged in the 1760s as a rebellion against rationalism and persisted until the 1840s. It was primarily a movement in the arts. Writers, painters, composers, and others consciously rebelled against the Enlightenment and its values (see pages 660–671). In contrast to the philosophes with their emphasis on reason, romantics praised emotion and feeling. Jean-Jacques Rousseau's strong appeal to sentiment was taken up by the German writer Johann Wolfgang von Goethe (1749–1832), who declared that "Feeling is everything." Goethe's *Sorrows of Young Werther* (1774), the most widely read book of the era—Napoleon had a copy by his bedside—depicted the passions of the hero, who, depressed by unrequited love, kills himself. Many readers dressed in "Werther clothes"—tight black pants, blue vest, and an open yellow shirt—and in some cases emulated the tragic hero by committing suicide.

Whereas the Enlightenment had studied nature for the principles that it could impart, romantics worshiped nature for its inherent beauty. The German composer Ludwig van Beethoven (1770–1827) wrote his *Pastoral* Symphony in praise of nature. The English poets William Wordsworth (1770–1850) and Samuel Taylor Coleridge (1772–1834) treated untamed wilderness as a particular subject of wonder. Fellow Englishman Joseph Turner (1775–1851) displayed the raw passions of the sea in his paintings *Fire at Sea* (1834) and *Snowstorm, Steamboat off a Harbour's Mouth* (1842). To paint the latter, Turner is said to have tied himself to a ship's mast and braved a snowstorm for four hours.

In pursuit of the authentic and the ancient, and in pursuit of feeling rather than rationality, many romantics rediscovered religion. In some areas of Europe, popular religion had anticipated the artists' and intellectuals' romantic sensibilities. France experienced a revival of Catholicism. In the German states, pietism, which emerged in the seventeenth and eighteenth centuries, stressed the personal relationship of the individual to God, unimpeded by formal theology or religious authorities. The influence of pietism, with its emphasis on feeling and emotion, spread throughout central Europe in schools and churches.

In England emotionalism in religion expressed itself in the popularity of Methodism. Founded in the 1730s by the English preacher John Wesley (1703–1791), this movement emphasized salvation by faith. Appealing especially to the poor and desperate, Methodism by the 1790s had gained 70,000 members, and within a generation it quadrupled its flock.

The classicism of the Enlightenment had required an audience well versed in the traditional texts. Since the mid-eighteenth century, however, the reading public had grown to include people without access to elite culture. Appeals to emotion and sentiment were congenial to these new

Metternich's Cure for Europe

Metternich, Austria's foreign minister from 1809 to 1848, had an impact beyond his empire's borders, providing much of the leadership of the reactionary regimes of Europe between 1815 and 1848. In this secret letter to Russia's Tsar Alexander I, Metternich analyzed the current ailments of Europe and saw their cure in firm support for king and church.

Kings have to calculate the chances of their very existence in the immediate future; passions are let loose, and league together to overthrow everything which society respects as the basis of its existence; religion, public morality, laws, customs, rights, and duties all are attacked, confounded, overthrown, or called in question. . . .

Having now thrown a rapid glance over the first causes of the present state of society, it is necessary to point out in a more particular manner the evil which threatens to deprive it, at one blow, of the real blessings, the fruits of genuine civilisation, and to disturb it in the midst of its enjoyments. This evil may be described in one word—presumption; the natural effect of the rapid progression of the human mind towards the perfecting of so many things. This it is which at the present day leads so many individuals astray, for it has become an almost universal sentiment. . . .

The Governments, having lost their balance, are frightened, intimidated, and thrown into confusion, by the cries of the intermediary class of society, which, placed between the Kings and their subjects, breaks the sceptre of the monarch, and usurps the cry of the people. . . .

We are convinced that society can no longer be saved without strong and vigorous resolutions on the part of the Governments. . . . By this course the monarchs will fulfill the duties imposed upon them by Him who, by entrusting them with power, has charged them to watch over the maintenance of justice, and the rights of all, to avoid the paths of error and tread firmly in the way of truth. . . .

. . . [L]et the Governments govern. . . . Let them not encourage by their attitude or actions the suspicion of being favourable or indifferent to error: let them not allow it to be believed that experience has lost its rights to make way for experiments which at the least are dangerous.

Source: Metternich to Emperor Alexander, Troppau, December 15, 1820, in Prince Richard Metternich, ed., *Memoirs of Prince Metternich, 1815–1829,* vol. 3, trans. Mrs. Alexander Napier (New York: Scribner & Sons, 1881), pp. 455, 458–459, 468–470, 474.

---

audiences, and a new interest developed in folklore and rustic life. But where an earlier era had mythologized country life, the romantic in loving detail painted its realistic charms.

The philosophes had decried the Middle Ages, but romantics celebrated the medieval period. Sir Walter Scott (1771–1832) in Scotland and Victor Hugo (1802–1885) in France celebrated chivalry and the age of faith in such popular works as *Ivanhoe* (1819) and *The Hunchback of Notre Dame* (1831). Painters frequently had as their theme Gothic buildings or ruins. Architects imitated the Gothic style in both private and public buildings.

The romantics sought displacement not only in time but also in place. The exotic had great appeal to them. Recently conquered Algeria in North Africa provided exotic scenes for French painters, among them Eugène Delacroix (1798–1863) and Jean Ingrès (1780–1867). Senegal in West Africa, recovered by the French from the British in 1815, offered the setting for Théodore Géricault's powerful *Raft of the "Medusa."* (See the feature, "Weighing the Evidence: *Raft of the 'Medusa,'*" on pages 772–773.)

After the French Revolution, nobles and monarchs ceased sponsoring art on a grand scale and were expected to conduct their lives soberly. Cut

Turner: Snowstorm, Steamboat Off a Harbour's Mouth Completed in 1842, this painting powerfully displays one of the romantics' prime subjects—the force of raw nature. Although the steamship is one of the new wonders of human inventiveness, it is insignificant in the face of the storm. *(The Clore Collection, Tate Gallery, London/ Art Resource, NY)*

off from royal patronage, artists had to depend on members of the new middle classes to buy paintings and books and attend plays and musical performances. Earning a livelihood had often been difficult for artists in the past, but now it became even more so. Forced to live marginally, they cultivated the image of the artist as a bohemian—a gypsy. In their lifestyles and their work, they deliberately rejected the conventions of society. The romantic period gave rise to the notion of the starving genius, alienated from society, loyal only to art.

Romanticism exalted mythical figures as the embodiment of human energy and passion. In the dramatic poem *Faust*, Goethe retold the legend of a man who sold his soul to the devil in exchange for worldly success. In the poetic drama *Prometheus*

Unbound, the English romantic poet Percy Bysshe Shelley (1792–1822) celebrated Prometheus, who stole fire from the gods and gave it to human beings. In much the same spirit, many romantics exalted Napoleon, who had overthrown kings and states. Delacroix, who witnessed the July Revolution of 1830 in Paris, celebrated the heroism and passion of the revolutionaries in his huge canvas, *Liberty Leading the People* (1830).

Romantics often challenged existing power relations, including the relation of the sexes. The French writer Amandine-Aurore Dupin (1804–1876), better known by her pen name, George Sand, spoke for the emancipation of women from the close supervision of their husbands, fathers, and brothers. In her personal life, Sand practiced the freedom she preached, dressing like a man, smoking cigars, and openly pursuing affairs with the writer Prosper Mérimée (1803–1870), the poet Alfred de Musset (1810–1857), and the composer Frédéric Chopin (1810–1849). The English writer Mary Ann Evans (1819–1892), like George Sand, adopted a male pseudonym, George Eliot. She conducted her life in a nonconformist manner, living with a married man. The adoption of male pen names by both writers attests to the hostility that intellectual women still faced.

Romantics of many stripes declared their determination to overthrow the smug present and create a new world. Victor Hugo called for "no more rules, no more models" to constrain the human imagination. Romantic painters and musicians consciously turned their backs on the classical tradition in both subject matter and style. Old methods were discarded for new ones. The English poet George Gordon, Lord Byron (1788–1824), declared war on kings, on established religion, and on the international order; a nationalist as well as a romantic, he died while fighting for the independence of Greece.

Nationalism

The ideology of nationalism emerged in, and partly shaped, this era. Nationalism is the belief that people derive their identity from their nation and owe their nation their primary loyalty. A list of criteria for nationhood is likely to include a common language, religion, and political authority, as well as common traditions and shared historic experiences. Some nineteenth-century nationalists found any one of those criteria sufficient. Others insisted that all of them had to be present before a group could consider itself a nation.

In an era that saw the undermining of traditional religious values, nationalism offered a new locus of faith. To people who experienced the social turmoil brought about by the erosion of the old order, nationalism held out the promise of a new community. Nationalism became an ideal espoused as strongly as religion. The Italian nationalist Giuseppe Mazzini (1805–1872) declared that nationalism was "a faith and mission" ordained by God. The religious intensity of nationalism helps explain its widespread appeal.

Many forces shaped nationalism. Its earliest manifestation, cultural nationalism, had its origins in Rousseau's ideas of the organic nature of a people (see pages 665–666). Johann Gottfried Herder (1744–1833), Rousseau's German disciple, elaborated on Rousseau's ideas, declaring that every people has a "national spirit." To explore the unique nature of this spirit, intellectuals all over Europe began collecting folk poems, songs, and tales. In an effort to document the spirit of the German people, the Grimm brothers, Jacob (1785–1863) and Wilhelm (1786–1859), collected fairy tales and published them between 1812 and 1818; among the better known are "Little Red Riding Hood" and "Snow White."

Political nationalism, born in the era of the French Revolution, injected urgency and passion into the new ideology. In the 1770s, French aristocrats resisted attempts by the French monarchy to impose taxes, claiming that they embodied the rights of "the nation" and could not be taxed without its consent. Thus, the concept of nation was given general currency. When revolutionary France was attacked by neighboring countries, which were ruled by kings and dukes, the Legislative Assembly called on the French people to rise and save the nation. The realm of the king of France had become the French nation.

In reaction to the French threat, intellectuals in Germany and Italy embraced the spirit of nationalism. In Germany the philosopher Johann Gottlieb Fichte (1762–1814) delivered his series of *Addresses to the German Nation* after the Prussian defeat at Jena, calling on all Germans to rise up against Napoleon. He argued that Germans were endowed with a special genius that had to be safeguarded for the well-being of all humankind. In Italy, the writer Vittorio Alfieri (1749–1803) challenged France's claim to the right to lead the peoples of Europe. That right, Alfieri insisted, properly belonged to Italians, the descendants and heirs of ancient Rome.

Culture could also be invoked for the purpose of throwing off a foreign yoke and shaping a newly independent state. In the 1810s, as part of a campaign to free Greece from the Turks, Greek intellectuals reissued the classics of ancient Greek literature in "purified" language, ridding Greek of developments in popular speech that spanned two millennia, to make the language resemble more closely its classical antecedent. These intellectuals wanted to remind their fellow Greeks that they were the sons and daughters of Hellas.

For the most part, however, early-nineteenth-century nationalism was generous and cosmopolitan in its outlook—excepting the French Revolution and the Napoleonic era. Herder and Mazzini believed that each of Europe's peoples was destined to achieve nationhood and that the nations of Europe would then live peacefully side by side. The members of dedicated nationalist groups like Young Germany and Young Italy were also members of Young Europe. Many nationalists in the 1830s and 1840s were also committed to the ideal of a "Europe of free peoples." Victor Hugo even envisioned a "European republic" with its own parliament.

It is important to remember, however, that although many intellectuals found nationalism attractive, in the first half of the nineteenth century most people were likely to feel local and regional affinities more than national loyalties. Only as the result of several decades of propaganda by nationalists and governments was the ideology to win wide support, and only then did it become natural for Europeans to think of dying for their nation.

Liberalism

Liberalism was a direct descendant of the Enlightenment's critique of eighteenth-century absolutism. Nineteenth-century liberals believed that individual freedom was best safeguarded by the reduction of government powers to a minimum. They wanted to impose constitutional limits on government, to establish the rule of law, to sweep away all restrictions on individual enterprise—specifically, state regulation of the economy—and to ensure a voice in government for men of property and education. Liberalism was influenced by romanticism, with its emphasis on individual freedom and the imperative of the human personality to develop to its full potential. Liberalism was also affected by nationalism, especially in multinational autocratic states like Austria, Russia, and the Ottoman Empire, in which free institutions could be established only if political independence were wrested from, respectively, Vienna, St. Petersburg, and Constantinople.

Liberalism was both an economic and a political theory. In 1776 Adam Smith (1723–1790), the influential Scottish economist, published *An Inquiry into the Nature and Causes of the Wealth of Nations*, a systematic study of the economic knowledge of his era. Smith advocated freeing national economies from the fetters of the state. (See the box, "Adam Smith Describes the Workings of the Market Economy.") Under the mercantilist system, prevalent throughout Europe until about 1800, the state regulated the prices and conditions of manufacture (see page 591). Smith argued for letting the free forces of the marketplace shape economic decisions. He was the founder of the classical school of economics; this school rested on the belief that economics was subject to basic unalterable laws, which could be discerned and applied in the same fashion as natural laws. Chief among them, in Smith's view, was the idea that economic self-interest was compatible with and even advantageous to the general interest. He argued that entrepreneurs who lower prices will sell more goods, thus increasing their own profits and providing the community with affordable goods. In this way, an individual's drive for profit benefits society as a whole. The economy is driven as if "by an invisible hand." This competitive drive for profits, Smith predicted, would expand the "wealth of nations." In France, advocates of nonintervention by government in the economy were called supporters of *laissez faire* (to leave alone, to let run on its own). Adam Smith was the most widely read and influential proponent of this policy.

Wages and employment were also seen as subject to the laws of supply and demand. Thomas Malthus (1766–1834), an Anglican minister, published in 1798 *An Essay on the Principle of Population*. Malthus posited that if employers paid their workers higher salaries, workers would be able to afford to marry earlier and have more children, thus glutting the labor market and driving wages down. He wanted wages to be kept at subsistence level. Workers, Malthus suggested, are "themselves the cause of their own poverty."

The third giant among the classical economists was the retired English stockbroker David Ricardo (1772–1823), who set forth his ideas in *Principles of Political Economy* (1817). Ricardo saw the capitalist system as typified by what he called the "iron law of wages." Capitalists' major expenses were wages, and to be competitive they had to keep depressing wages. According to the school of classical economics, the economy is driven by laws, and intervention of any sort will only worsen the situation.

Adam Smith Describes the Workings of the Market Economy

In **An Inquiry into the Nature and Causes of the Wealth of Nations,** *Adam Smith stressed how the economy can expand and society as a whole benefit if all participants try to maximize their own interests. Among the various economic activities, trade and specialization particularly contribute to the well-being of both society and the individual. Characterized by a mixture of theory and down-to-earth examples, his writings remain a pleasure to read.*

In almost every other race of animals each individual, when it is grown up to maturity, is entirely independent, and in its state has occasion for the assistance of no other living creature. But man has almost constant occasion for the help of his brethren, and it is in vain for him to expect it from their benevolence only. He will be more likely to prevail, if he can interest their self-love in his favour, and shew them that it is for their advantage to do for him what he requires of them. Whoever offers to another a bargain of any kind, proposes to do this. Give me that which I want, and you shall have this which you want, is the meaning of every such offer; and it is in this manner that we obtain from one another the far greater part of those good offices which we stand in need of. It is not from the benevolence of the butcher, the brewer, or the baker, that we expect our dinner, but from their regard to their own interest. We address ourselves, not to their humanity, but to their self-love, and never talk to them of our own necessities, but of their advantages. Nobody but a beggar chooses to depend chiefly upon the benevolence of his fellow-citizens. . . .

So it is this same trucking [trading] disposition which originally gives occasion to the division of labour. In a tribe of hunters or shepherds a particular person makes bows and arrows, for example, with more readiness and dexterity than any other. He frequently exchanges them for cattle or venison with his companions; and he finds at last that he can in this manner get more cattle and venison, than if he himself went to the field to catch them. From a regard to his own interest, therefore, the making of bows and arrows grows to be his chief business, and he becomes a sort of armourer. Another excels in making the frames and covers of their little huts or moveable houses. He is accustomed to be of use in this way to his neighbours, who reward him in the same manner with cattle and with venison, till at last he finds it in his interest to dedicate himself entirely to this employment, and to become a sort of house-carpenter. In the same manner a third becomes a smith or a brazier, a fourth a tanner or dresser of hides of skin, the principal part of the clothing of savages. And thus the certainty of being able to exchange all that surplus part of the produce of his own labour, which is over and above his own consumption, for such parts of the produce of other men's labour as he may have occasion for, encourages every man to apply himself to a particular occupation. . . .

Source: Adam Smith, *Inquiry into the Nature and Causes of the Wealth of Nations* (London: W. Strahan, 1776), pp. 17–18.

Liberals in the political realm argued that political power must be limited to prevent despotism. Enlightened eighteenth-century monarchs had declared that the purpose of their rule was to promote the public good. In even more ringing terms, the French Revolution had proclaimed that the purpose of government is to ensure the happiness of humankind. As Thomas Jefferson (1743–1826), another child of the Enlightenment, asserted in the Declaration of Independence (1776), among the "unalienable rights" of individuals are "life, liberty, and the pursuit of happiness." The purpose of government is to safeguard and promote those rights.

The Enlightenment had posited natural law as the basis of government. French liberals in the nineteenth century continued to see human liberty as founded on natural law but their English counterparts were less theoretical in outlook. Jeremy Bentham (1748–1832) argued that the purpose of government is to provide "the greatest happiness of the greatest number" and that governments should be judged on that basis. Bentham and his disciples believed that the test of government is its usefulness; they were known as "utilitarians."

Democracy was implicit in Bentham's philosophy: The greatest number could ensure its own happiness only by voting for its rulers. John Stuart Mill (1803–1873), a disciple of Bentham, was the foremost proponent of liberalism, seeing it as ensuring the development of a free society. Individuals could best develop their talents if they were not hampered by the interference of the state. In his essay *On Liberty*, one of the fundamental documents of nineteenth-century liberalism, Mill argued for the free circulation of ideas—even false ideas. For in the free marketplace of ideas, false ideas will be defeated in open debate and truth will be vindicated. Mill also asserted that a free society should be free for all its members. Influenced by Harriet Taylor (1807–1856), who was to become his wife, he penned *On the Subjection of Women* (1861). Women should vote and have access to equal educational opportunities as well as to the professions. Such equality not only would be just but also would have the advantage of "doubling the mass of mental faculties available for the higher service of humanity." Mill, the foremost male proponent of women's rights in his generation, helped win a broader audience for the principle of equality between the sexes.

Despite Mill's influence, many liberals, especially in the early nineteenth century, feared the masses and therefore vigorously opposed democracy. The French liberal Benjamin Constant (1767–1836) denounced democracy as "the vulgarization of despotism"; the vote, he declared, should be reserved for the well-off and educated. When less fortunate Frenchmen denounced the property requirements that prevented them from voting, the liberal statesman François Guizot (1787–1874) smugly replied, "Get rich."

If unsympathetic to extending suffrage to the lower classes, the bourgeoisie championed liberalism, which justified its right to participate in governance. Economic liberalism was also congenial to merchants and manufacturers who wished to produce wealth without state interference.

In the second half of the century, however, many people came to believe that the laws of the marketplace could not be allowed to operate without intervention. Even Mill grew to accept that to protect workers and consumers, some controls on market forces were needed. In politics, however, the basic tenets of the liberal credo—the sanctity of human rights, freedom of speech and freedom to organize, the rule of law and equality before the law, and the abolition of torture—eventually became so widely accepted that even conservative and socialist opponents of liberalism accepted them as fundamental rights.

Socialism

The notion that human happiness can best be assured by the common ownership of property had been suggested in earlier times by individuals as different as the Greek philosopher Plato (427?–347 B.C.) and Sir Thomas More (1478–1535), English author of *Utopia*. Troubled by the condition of the working classes, thinkers in Britain and France came to espouse theories that, beginning in the 1820s, were called "socialist." Socialists believed that the "social" ownership of property, unlike private ownership, would benefit society as a whole. During the first half of the nineteenth century, most workers, even in industrializing England, were artisans. It was in a later era that socialism would address the issues raised by industry.

In 1796, during the French Revolution, Gracchus Babeuf (1760–1797), a minor civil servant, participated in the Conspiracy of Equals (see page 720). The Revolution, however haltingly, had proclaimed political equality for its citizens, but it had failed to bring economic equality. Babeuf decided to resort to revolution to bring about a "communist" society—a society in which all property would be owned in common and private property would be abolished. Work would be provided for everyone; medical services and education would be free to all. Babeuf's plot was discovered, and he was guillotined, but his theories and example of conspiratorial revolutionary action would influence later socialists.

Several other important French thinkers made contributions to European socialism. Curiously, a French aristocrat, Henri de Saint-Simon (1760–1825), emphasized the need "to ameliorate as promptly and as quickly as possible the moral and physical existence of the most numerous class." The proper role for the state, Saint-Simon declared, was to ensure the welfare of the masses. The course of history, he suggested, was in the direction of expertise. No longer could people rule on the basis of their birth. Rather, Europe should come to be governed by a council of artists and scientists who would oversee the economy and ensure that everyone enjoyed a minimum level of well-being.

Young intellectuals who gravitated to Saint-Simonism took on the master's faith in the capacity of technology to transform society. They became the dynamic entrepreneurs and engineers who in the 1850s would build up the French banking, investment, and rail systems. Still later, Saint-Simonism would inspire technocracy, the notion that social problems can be resolved by the application of technology.

Another vital contribution to socialist thought came from thinkers who tried to imagine an ideal world. They were later derisively dismissed as dreamers, as builders of utopias, fantasy worlds (the Greek word *utopia* means "no place"). Their schemes varied, but they shared the view that property should be owned in common and used for the common good. They also believed that society should rest on principles of cooperation rather than competitive individualism.

One of the earliest and most notable utopians was the Welsh mill-owner Robert Owen (1771–1859). In New Lanark, Scotland, beginning in 1800 he ran an economically successful cotton mill. He also provided generously for his workers, including guaranteeing them a job and a decent education for their children. In his writings Owen suggested the establishment of self-governing communes owning the means of production. Essentials would be distributed to all members according to their needs. Owen's ideas for the new society included equal rights for women.

Owen received little support from fellow manufacturers and political leaders. In 1824 he established in New Harmony, Indiana, an ideal new society that was to be a model for others. Within four years of its founding, New Harmony ran into economic difficulty and was torn by internal dissension. Disheartened, Owen abandoned the community and returned to Britain.

Another influential contributor to early socialist theory was the Frenchman Charles Fourier (1772–1837). A clerk and salesman, Fourier wrote out in great detail his vision of the ideal future society. It would consist of cooperative organizations called "phalanxes," each with 1600 inhabitants who would live in harmony with nature and with one another. Everyone would be assured gainful employment. Work would be made enjoyable by rotating jobs and by sharing pleasurable and unpleasurable tasks. Cooperative communes often faced the issue of who would carry out the unpleasant tasks. Fourier thought that because children enjoy playing with dirt, they should be put in charge of picking up garbage.

Fourier's belief in equality of the sexes gave him an important female following. In Belgium, the activist Zoé Gatti de Gamond (1806–1854) co-founded a phalanx for women. She believed that if women could be assured of economic well-being, other rights would follow. Inspired also by Fourier, Flora Tristan (1801–1844) was an effective advocate for workers' rights. In her book *Union Ouvrière (Workers' Union)*, she suggested that all workers should contribute to establish a "Worker's Palace" in every town. In the palace, the sick and disabled would have shelter and the workers' children could be given a free education. Crossing France on foot, she spread the word of workers' solidarity and self-help.

There were other approaches. The French socialist journalist Louis Blanc (1811–1882) saw in democracy the means of bringing into existence a socialist state. By securing the vote, the common people could win control over the state and have it serve their needs. The state could be induced to buy up banks, insurance companies, and railway systems and set up a commercial and retail chain that would provide jobs for workers and offer goods and services at prices unaffected by the search for profits. Once the workers controlled the state by the ballot, the state in turn would establish social workshops where the workers were responsible for production and supervision of business matters. Society should be established in such a way that it would be possible to "Let each produce according to his aptitudes and strength; let each consume according to his need."

Blanc's contemporary Louis Blanqui (1805–1882) suggested a more violent mode of action. He advocated seizure of the state by a small, dedicated band of men who were devoted to the welfare of the working class and who would install communism, for the equality of all. Blanqui was a perpetual conspirator, confined to state prisons for much of his long life. His ideas strengthened the notion of class warfare, and his own life served as a symbol of this struggle. The thought and example of Blanqui and the other socialists would play a major role in shaping the thinking of the most important socialist of the nineteenth century, Karl Marx (see pages 802–805).

RESTORATION AND REFORM

Despite the new ideologies that emerged to challenge the existing order, efforts at restoration appeared successful until at least 1830. Indeed in central and eastern Europe, from the German states to Russia and the Ottoman Empire, the political systems established in 1815 would persist virtually unchanged until midcentury. In western Europe, however, important transformations would occur by the 1830s as reaction gave way to reform. Then in 1848, widespread revolutions would break out on much of the Continent. The language of liberalism and nationalism and even the newer idiom of socialism would be heard on the barricades, in popular assemblies, and in parliamentary halls.

France

The most dramatic restoration was that of the Bourbons in France. The restoration turned the clock back, not to 1789 but closer to 1791, when the country had briefly enjoyed a constitutional monarchy, and it went beyond that in maintaining the Napoleonic Code with its provisions of legal equality.

Louis XVIII granted France a charter. Liberals considered such a grant ominous, for what the king gave he could presumably also revoke. Yet the charter had many reassuring provisions. Political and religious liberties and legal equality were confirmed. The new constitution provided for a parliament with an elected lower house, the Chamber of Deputies, and an appointed upper house, the Chamber of Peers. Although suffrage to the Chamber of Deputies was limited to a small elite of men with landed property—100,000 voters, about 0.2 percent—it was a concession to representative government that had not existed in the Old Regime (see pages 702–704). Louis XVIII stands out among European rulers because he realized that it would be necessary to compromise on the principles of popular sovereignty proclaimed by the French Revolution. His intention was to "popularize the monarchy" and "royalize the nation." However, the exiled noblemen who returned with him thwarted this worthy goal. Opposed to new ideas, they were determined to restore all their old privileges and prerogatives.

In an effort to win over the people who had benefited from the sale of confiscated church and aristocratic property, Louis's charter guaranteed the ownership of property acquired during the Revolution. But the returned émigrés and spokesmen of the church challenged these terms, demanding the return of their lost properties. Returning aristocrats also reclaimed their previous positions in the army and administration from men identified with the revolutionary and Napoleonic regimes.

The most extreme reactionaries strengthened their position when liberals were blamed for the assassination in 1820 of the Duc de Berry (1778–1820), second in line to the throne. The press was fettered; suffrage, already limited, was further restricted, and a new law allowed the government to imprison without trial anyone suspected of conspiracy.

When Louis was succeeded by his ultra-reactionary brother, Charles X (r. 1824–1830), the reactionaries came into their own. The new king encouraged passage of an indemnity bill to pay the émigrés for property lost during the Revolution and Napoleon's regime. Bourgeois and lower-class taxpayers were outraged. Many of them resented the increased power granted the clergy and were shocked by the introduction of the death penalty for acts deemed sacrilegious. Charles X's dissolution of the National Guard, one of the bastions of the middle class, further alienated the bourgeoisie.

Frustration mounted with an economic downturn in 1827, marked by poor harvests and increased unemployment in the cities. Liberal

Louis XVIII as Military Leader The French king, returned to his throne by France's foreign enemies, had no military glory attached to his reign. But in 1823 France successfully invaded Spain, helping its reactionary king quell a liberal revolt. This painting celebrates the return of the victorious French troops. *(Château de Versailles/Laurie Platt Winfrey, Inc.)*

parliamentary majorities refused to accept the reactionary ministers the king appointed. On July 26, 1830, after the humiliating defeat of his party at the polls, the king issued a set of decrees suspending freedom of the press, dissolving the Chamber of Deputies, and stiffening property qualifications for voters in subsequent elections. The king appeared to be engineering a coup against the existing political system.

The first to protest were the Parisian journalists and typesetters, directly threatened by the censorship laws. On July 28, others joined the protest and began erecting barricades across many streets. After killing several hundred protesters, the king's forces lost control over the city. The uprising, known as "the three glorious days," drove the king into exile.

Alarmed by the crowds' clamor for a republic, the liberal opposition—consisting of some of the leading newspaper editors and liberal deputies—quickly drafted the duke of Orléans, Louis Philippe (1773–1850), known for his liberal opinions, to occupy the throne. The idea of a republic frightened the middle classes because it evoked memories of the Terror. A liberal constitutional monarchy was more in tune with their goals. They were better organized than the republicans and prevailed on the Chamber of Deputies to invite Louis Philippe to accept the throne.

Louis Philippe proclaimed himself "King of the French," thus acknowledging that he reigned at the behest of the people. Freedom of the press was reinstated, suffrage was extended to twice as many voters as before, 200,000 men. The July

Monarchy, named after the month in which it was established by revolution, legitimated itself by celebrating the great Revolution of 1789. Louis Philippe commissioned huge canvasses celebrating great moments of the Revolution, and on the site where the Bastille had been razed in 1789, the government erected a large column with the names of the victims of the July 1830 revolution, thus suggesting a continuity between those who had fought tyranny in 1789 and 1830.

Identification with the Revolution appeared to legitimate the regime, but could also subvert it. Fearful that the cult of revolution would encourage violence against the new monarchy, the regime censored artistic production, promoting only works that celebrated the period from 1789 to 1791, when the revolutionaries had attempted to found a constitutional monarchy. Now that the revolution of 1830 had established a constitutional monarchy, the regime was suggesting, any further uprisings were illegitimate.

But the July Monarchy was challenged from many quarters. As time passed, more people were nostalgic for the republic that had existed under the Revolution. Republicanism, the belief that France should have a republic rather than a monarchy, spread. The lackluster foreign policy of the July Monarchy made some long for the glories of the Napoleonic era. Shortly after the revolution of 1830, another downturn in the economy led to further unemployment. Then came an epidemic of cholera that affected most of Europe. Also contributing to the unsettled atmosphere was labor agitation. In the silk-producing city of Lyon, for instance, artisans who were exasperated by their worsening prospects staged bloody uprisings in 1831 and 1834. In the countryside there were rumors of mass arson. In the face of unrest, the monarchy often resorted to censorship and other forces of repression. Parliament became essentially a rubber stamp. The most advanced liberals demanded that suffrage be broadened, but the government was unyielding. Foreign visitors coming from more authoritarian societies were impressed by France's apparently liberal institutions (see the box, "Encounters with the West: A Moroccan Description of the French Freedom of the Press"), but many French liberals saw the regime as a travesty of the hopes and promises it had represented on coming to power in 1830. In-

augurated by revolution, in a few years it would face revolution.

Great Britain

In comparison to the rest of Europe, Great Britain enjoyed considerable constitutional guarantees and a parliamentary regime. Yet liberals and radicals found their government retrograde and repressive. Traumatized by the French Revolution, the ruling class clung to the past, certain that advocates for change were Jacobins in disguise. Change seemed to invite revolution.

Social unrest beset Britain as it faced serious economic dislocation. The arrival of peace in 1815 led to a sudden drop in government expenditures, the return into the economy of several hundred thousand men who had been away at war, financial disarray, and a drop in prices. There was much discontent among the poor and the middle classes, who were incensed by the clear economic advantages that the landed classes, dominating Parliament, had secured for themselves in 1815 in passing the Corn Law. This legislation imposed high tariffs on imported "corn"—that is, various forms of grain. It thus shielded the domestic market from international competition and allowed landowners to reap huge profits at the expense of consumers. All these issues were cause for demonstrations, petitions, protest marches, and other challenges to the authorities.

In August 1819, sixty thousand people gathered in St. Peter's Fields in Manchester to demand universal suffrage for men and women alike, an annual Parliament, and other democratic reforms. The crowd was peaceful and unarmed, but when a speaker whom the government considered a rabble-rouser took to the podium, mounted soldiers charged, attempting to arrest him. In the ensuing melee, eleven people were killed and four hundred wounded. The British public was shocked by this use of violence against peaceful demonstrators. Parliament responded in autumn 1819 by passing the Six Acts, which outlawed freedom of assembly and effectively imposed censorship.

While continuing conservative policies, the government began to embrace change in the 1820s. The provisions that prevented Catholics from holding any government position and from serving in Parliament were removed in 1829. In

≈ **ENCOUNTERS WITH THE WEST** ≈

A Moroccan Description of the French Freedom of the Press

In 1845–1846 a Moroccan diplomatic mission visited Paris; the ambassador's secretary, Muham-
mad as-Saffar (d. 1881), wrote an account of this visit. He was struck by many aspects of French
society, and in the following passage he described France's press.

The people of Paris, like all the French—indeed, like all of [Europe]—are eager to know the latest news and events that are taking place in other parts [of the world]. For this purpose they have the gazette. [In] these papers . . . they write all the news that has reached them that day about events in their own country and in other lands both near and far.

This is the way it is done. The owner of a newspaper dispatches his people to collect everything they see or hear in the way of important events or unusual happenings. Among the places where they collect the news are the two Chambers, the Great and the Small, where they come together to make their laws. When the members of the Chamber meet to deliberate, the men of the gazette sit nearby and write down everything that is said, for all debating and ratifying of laws is matter for the gazette and is known to everyone. No one can prevent them from doing this. . . .

. . . [I]f someone has an idea about a subject but he is not a member of the press, he may write about it in the gazette and make it known to others, so that the leaders of opinion learn about it. If the idea is worthy they may follow it, and if its author was out of favor it may bring him recognition.

No person in France is prohibited from expressing his opinion or from writing it and printing it, on condition that he does not violate the law. . . .

In the newspapers they write rejoinders to the men of the two Chambers about the laws they are making. If their Sultan demands gifts from the notables or goes against the law in any way, they write about that too, saying that he is a tyrant and in the wrong. He cannot confront them or cause them harm. Also, if someone behaves out of the ordinary, they write about that too, making it common knowledge among people of every rank. If his deeds were admirable, they praise and delight in him, lauding his example; but if he behaved badly, they revile him to discourage the like.

Moreover, if someone is being oppressed by another, they write about that too, so that everyone will know the story from both sides just as it happened, until it is decided in court. One can also read in it what their courts have decided.

Source: Susan Gilson Miller, ed. and trans., *Disorienting Encounters—Travels of a Moroccan Scholar in France in 1845–1846. The Voyage of Muhammad as-Saffar* (Berkeley: University of California Press, 1992), pp. 150–153.

other ways as well, a more just order was introduced. The number of crimes punishable by death was reduced to just one, homicide. Prison reforms were made. Sir Robert Peel (1788–1850), heir to a manufacturing fortune and an enthusiastic reader of Bentham's works, was the driving force behind many of these reforms. He became home secretary (with duties including internal security) in 1828, and the following year he organized an efficient London police force, known ever after as "bobbies" in his honor, to control crime and contain popular protests.

The major political problem facing Britain in the early nineteenth century was the composition of Parliament. It did not reflect the dramatic population shifts that had occurred since the seventeenth century. Industrialization had transformed mere villages into major cities—Manchester, Birmingham, Leeds, Sheffield—but those cities had no representation in Parliament. Localities that had lost population, however, were still represented. In districts known as "pocket boroughs," single individuals owned the right to a seat in Parliament. In districts known as "the rotten boroughs," a handful of voters elected a representative.

News of the July 1830 revolution in Paris encouraged liberals to push for reform and made some conservatives reluctant to oppose reform for fear of suffering the same fate as the hapless Charles X. In 1831 the liberal Whig government of Earl Grey (1764–1845), a hereditary peer who nevertheless was well attuned to the demands of the middle classes, introduced a reform bill abolishing or reducing representation for sparsely populated areas while granting representation for the populous and unrepresented cities. The bill also widened the franchise by lowering property qualifications to include many middle-class men. Following a prolonged, bitter political battle between the government and middle classes on one side and aristocracy on the other, the House of Lords finally passed what came to be known as the "Great Reform Bill of 1832."

The reform was not particularly radical. Only the upper layers of the middle class were enfranchised, or one of seven adult males. The old franchise had not excluded women from the vote, but the new law did so. Yet despite its shortcomings, the reform demonstrated the willingness of the political leaders to acknowledge the increasing economic importance of manufacturing. Parliament became a more representative forum whose composition better reflected the shift of economic power from agricultural landowners to the industrial and commercial classes. The bill passed as a result of nationwide agitation; its passage revealed the ability of the political system to bring about reform peacefully.

Parliament justified the population's newfound faith in its efficacy by undertaking several more reforms. The Poor Law of 1834 had a mixed impact. The new law denied aid to the able-bodied, no matter how destitute, offering them only the option of entering workhouses, where prison-like conditions deterred all but the most desperate. This measure of the bill was severe, but another of its features potentially improved the lot of

"Peterloo" Massacre In August 1819 at St. Peter's Fields in Manchester, a crowd demanding parliamentary reform was charged by government troops, leading to bloodshed. Many English people derided the event and called it "Peterloo." (*Public Record Office*)

the poor. Previous poor laws had provided supplements to very low salaries, thus making it unnecessary for employers to pay workers a living wage; such measures depressed wages. The law of 1834 abolished this provision and may have played some role in raising wages. Though harsh toward the poor, the Poor Law was an acknowledgment of a national responsibility for the underprivileged. The following year Parliament passed the Municipal Corporation Act, which provided for more representative municipal councils with increased decision-making powers in local affairs.

A series of colonial reforms also showed a willingness to adapt to changing circumstances. In Britain opposition to slavery had been voiced since the 1780s. (See the box, "A Plea to Abolish Slavery in the British Colonies.") Slavery, the very opposite of human freedom, was an affront to liberal principles. Moreover, its persistence threatened the

A Plea to Abolish Slavery in the British Colonies

Among the causes that British reformers embraced was the abolition of slavery. The slave trade had been abolished in 1807; one more step was left—ending in the colonies the institution of slavery itself. In this petition to Parliament in 1823, the Society for the Mitigation and Gradual Abolition of Slavery Throughout the British Dominions explained the harsh and immoral nature of the institution. Under the pressure of this type of agitation, Parliament in 1833 abolished slavery in the British Empire.

In the colonies of Great Britain there are at this moment upwards of 800,000 human beings in a state of degrading personal slavery.

These unhappy persons, whether young or old, male or female, are the absolute property of their master, who may sell or transfer them at his pleasure, and who may also regulate according to his discretion (within certain limits) the measure of their labour, their food, and their punishment.

Many of the slaves are (and all may be) branded like cattle, by means of a hot iron, on the shoulder or other conspicuous part of the body, with the initials of their master's name; and thus bear about them in indelible characters the proof of their debased and servile state. . . .

It can hardly be alleged that any man can have a right to obtain his fellow creatures in a state so miserable and degrading as has been described. And the absence of such right will be still more apparent, if we consider how these slaves were originally obtained. They, or their parents, were the victims of the Slave Trade. They were obtained, not by lawful means, or under any colourable pretext, but by the most undisguised rapine, and the most atrocious fraud. Torn from their homes and from every dear relation in life, barbarously manacled, driven like herds of cattle to the sea-shore, crowded into the potential holds of slave-ships, they were transported to our colonies and there sold in bondage. . . .

The Government and Legislature of this country have on various occasions, and in the most solemn and unequivocal terms denounced the Slave Trade as immoral, inhuman, and unjust; but the legal perpetuation of that state of slavery, which has been produced by it, is surely, in its principle, no less immoral, inhuman and unjust, than the trade itself. . . .

Source: Reprinted in *Circular Letters of the Society for the Mitigation and Gradual Abolition of Slavery Throughout the British Dominions* (April 1823).

empire—in 1831, 60,000 slaves rebelled in Jamaica. Parliament took heed of the call for change and in 1833 abolished slavery in the British Empire.

In addition, the British began to review their imperial administration. Their control over Canada had been challenged in an uprising in 1837; London sent out a fact-finding mission headed by Lord Durham (1806–1848). As a result of the *Durham Report,* the British government promulgated self-government for Canada in 1839 and 1841; eventually all the British colonies with a majority of white settlers were given similar rights of self-rule.

Reforms solidified Britain's influence overseas. In Canada they reduced opposition to British rule.

The antislavery campaign led to the extension of British power into Africa. Having abolished the slave trade in 1807, the British worked to compel other nations to end the trade. With the largest navy in the world, Britain was well equipped to patrol the coast of West Africa, trying to suppress the traffic in humans and hinder its colonial rivals from benefiting from the trade. Needing bases for these patrols, the British established a number of minor settlements in West Africa, becoming the predominant European power along the coast. Although unimportant when acquired, these possessions foreshadowed the increasing European intrusion into African affairs.

Parliament's reforming zeal stimulated support for Chartism, a movement intended to transform Britain from essentially an oligarchy—rule by a few—into a democracy. In 1838 political radicals with working-class support drew up a "people's charter" calling for universal male suffrage, equal electoral districts, salaries and the abolition of property qualifications for members of Parliament, the secret ballot, and annual general elections. By giving workers the vote, Chartists hoped to end the dominance of narrow upper classes in Parliament and ensure an improvement in the workers' lot. Chartism won wide support among men and women in the working class, sparking demonstrations and petition drives of unprecedented size. Women participated to a larger extent than in any other political movement of the day, founding over a hundred female Chartist organizations. Some Chartists, especially female members, asked for women's suffrage; but this demand failed to gain overall adherence from the membership.

Winning mass support during particularly hard economic years, Chartism lost followers during a temporary economic upswing. The movement also fell under the sway of advocates of violence, who scared off many artisans and potential middle-class supporters. It lost credibility too by criticizing British institutions for being unresponsive to the needs of the working class, whereas in fact Parliament introduced a number of significant reforms. Lacking popular support, Chartism failed as a political movement; yet it drew public attention to an integrated democratic program whose main provisions (except for yearly elections) would be adopted piecemeal over the next half-century.

In 1839 urban businessmen founded the Anti–Corn Law League for the purpose of abolishing the Corn Law of 1815, which was increasing the price of grain. The Corn Law was unpopular with manufacturers, who knew that low food prices would allow them to pay low wages. It was also unpopular with workers, who wanted bread at a price they could afford. The anti–Corn Law movement proved more effective than Chartism because it had the support of the middle classes. Parliament, alarmed by the threat of famine due to the poor harvest of 1845, repealed the Corn Law in 1846.

In the end, repeal did not affect the price of grain. Nevertheless, repeal of the Corn Law was a milestone in British history, demonstrating the extent to which organized groups could bring about economic and social reform by putting pressure on Parliament. It also underscored what the Great Reform Act of 1832 had already revealed: Political and economic power was shifting away from the landed gentry to the urban industrial classes, and the British political system responded more flexibly to this change than did the political systems of the Continent. When revolution broke out on the Continent, it did not cross the English Channel.

Spain

The term *liberal* was first coined in Spain, where the fate of liberals prefigured what would happen elsewhere in continental Europe. In 1812 a national parliament, the Cortes, elected during the Napoleonic occupation, issued a democratic constitution that provided for universal manhood suffrage and a unicameral legislature with control over government policy. Supporters and admirers of the constitution in Spain and elsewhere were known as "liberals," or friends of liberty.

The Bourbon king Ferdinand VII (r. 1808, 1814–1833) was overthrown by Napoleon and replaced by the French emperor's brother, Joseph Bonaparte (r. 1808–1813). In 1814 Ferdinand returned to power, promising to respect the 1812 constitution. But Ferdinand was by temperament hostile to the new order, and he was a believer in the divine right of kings. He had no real intention of abiding by the constitution of 1812, a document drawn up by the educated middle classes and reflecting their anticlericalism and desire for power. Ferdinand drew his support from the aristocracy and from segments of the general population still loyal to the call of throne and altar. Liberals were arrested or driven into exile.

Ferdinand's plan to restore Spain to its earlier prominence included a reassertion of control over its American colonies. The Spanish dominions had grown restless in the eighteenth century, for they had witnessed the advent of an independent United States and the French occupation of Spain itself. The dominions refused to recognize the Napoleonic regime in Madrid and became increasingly self-reliant. Their attitude did not change when French control of Spain ended. Ferdinand refused to compromise with the overseas territories. Instead, he gathered an army to subdue them. Some liberal junior officers, declaring the army's

EUROPEAN REVOLUTIONS, 1820–1831

January 1820	Spain
July 1820	Naples
August 1820	Portugal
March 1821	Piedmont; Greece
December 1825	Russia
July 1830	France
August 1830	Belgium
September 1830	Brunswick; Saxony; Hesse-Cassel
November 1830	Poland
February 1831	Revolt in Piedmont, Modena, and Parma; revolt in Papal States

loyalty to the constitution of 1812, won support from the rank and file, who balked at going overseas. This military mutiny coincided with a sympathetic provincial uprising to produce the "revolution of 1820," the first major assault on the European order established in 1815 at the Congress of Vienna. Ferdinand appealed to the European powers for help. France intervened on his behalf and crushed the uprising.

Ferdinand restored his reactionary regime but could not regain Spain's American colonies. The British, sympathetic to the cause of Latin American independence and eager for commercial access to the region, opposed reconquest, and their naval dominance of the seas rendered Britain's opposition effective. The United States, meanwhile, had recognized the independence of the Latin American republics and wished to see their independence maintained. In 1823 President James Monroe issued the statement known as the Monroe Doctrine, proclaiming U.S. opposition to any European colonization or intervention in the affairs of independent republics in the Americas. The United States had no military power to back this proclamation, but the British navy effectively enforced it. By 1825 all Spain's colonies on the mainland in Central and South America had won their freedom.

The newly independent states patterned their regimes on models of Spanish liberalism; all of them had constitutions, separation of powers, and guaranteed human rights. Brazil, the Portuguese empire in the Americas, was a monarchy for most of the rest of the nineteenth century, as was Mexico for a short time, but all the other states became republics, opting for what was then an unusual form of government. Although most of the Latin regimes eventually became despotic, lip service continued to be paid to liberal values.

Upon Ferdinand's death in 1833, Spain was torn by competing claims to the succession. A civil war between liberal and conservative factions led to extreme cruelty on both sides. The moderates and liberals won, but the military gained the upper hand in governing. A Cortes and what appeared to be constitutional government were established, but real power lay in the hands of the army, representing a small oligarchy of the business and landowning classes. Several successive officers served as dictators of the country, replacing each other in a series of coups. One of them, General Ramón Narváez (1799–1868), brutally ran the country from 1844 to 1851. When he was on his deathbed, he was asked whether he forgave his enemies. He answered, "I have no enemies. I have shot them all!"

Austria and the German States

The Austrian empire's far-flung territories seemed to its Habsburg rulers to require a firm hand (see Map 20.1). Liberalism, which challenged imperial power, could not be countenanced. Nor, in this multinational empire, could nationalism be tolerated. The emperor, Francis I (r. 1806–1835), was opposed to any change; his motto was "Rule and change nothing." Prince Metternich, Francis's chief minister, viewed the French Revolution of 1789 and its aftermath as a disaster and believed his task was to hold the line against the threat of revolution. Quick to interpret protests or the desire for change as a threat to the fundamental order, Metternich established a network of secret police and informers to spy on the imperial subjects and keep them in check.

In most of the German states, the political order was authoritarian and inflexible. The states of Baden and Württemberg in the west and Bavaria in the south had been granted constitutions by their rulers, although effective power remained in the hands of the ruling houses. The king of Prussia had repeatedly promised a constitution, but none had materialized. A central, representative Diet would not meet until 1847. Prussia was ruled by an alliance of the king and the *Junkers,* the landowning aristocrats who staffed the officer corps and the bureaucracy. Both the officer corps and the bureaucracy were efficient enough to serve as models for the rest of Europe. Where Prussia lagged by liberal standards was in its political institutions.

Throughout the German states, the urban middle classes, intellectuals, journalists, university professors, and students were frustrated with the existing system. They were disappointed by the lack of free institutions and the failure of the patriotic wars against Napoleon to create a united Germany. University students formed *Burschenschaften,* or brotherhoods, whose slogan was "Honor, Liberty, Fatherland." Metternich imposed a policy of reaction on the German Confederation and had it adopt the Carlsbad Decrees in July 1819, establishing close supervision over the universities, censorship of the press, and dissolution of the youth groups. Wholesale persecution of liberals and nationalists followed. The Prussian king dismissed his more enlightened officials.

The outbreak of revolution in Paris in 1830 inspired further political agitation. The authoritarian ruler of the state of Brunswick was forced to resign. Under pressure, his successor and the rulers of Saxony, Hanover, and Hesse-Cassel promulgated new constitutions. Mounting opposition to local despots and agitation for national unity led to the prosecution of outspoken liberals. Many associated with the nationalist "Young Germany" movement fled abroad, particularly to Paris.

Renewed nationalist agitation swept the German states in the 1840s. In response to possible French ambitions on the Rhine during a diplomatic crisis in 1840, there was a mass outpouring of patriotic sentiment. Two patriotic songs were penned: "The Watch on the Rhine" and "Deutschland, Deutschland über alles" ("Germany, Germany above all"), the latter becoming Germany's national anthem half a century later. German rulers, who in the past had been reluctant to support the national idea, now attempted to co-opt it. In Bavaria King Ludwig II built the Walhalla, named after the hall where fallen heroes gather in

Germanic lore; Ludwig's Walhalla was to be a "sacred monument" to German unity adorned with statues of famous Germans. The Cologne Cathedral, unfinished in its construction, became a symbol of German enthusiasm; from all over Germany donations came in to finish it. Inaugurating the rebuilding, Prussia's King William Frederick IV (r. 1840–1861) declared it "the spirit of German unity and strength." These events suggested a broadening base for nationhood, which potentially could replace the existing system of a fragmented Germany.

Italy

Austria exercised considerable power over Italy through its possession of Italian territory. Some lands had been acquired in the eighteenth century; some, like Lombardy and Venetia, were acquired in 1815 (see Map 20.1). Austria had dynastic ties to several ruling houses in the central part of the peninsula and political alliances with others, including the papacy. The only ruling house free of Austrian ties—and hence eventually looked to by nationalists as a possible rallying point for the independence of the peninsula—was the Savoy dynasty of Piedmont-Sardinia.

Italy consisted of eight political states, and it was in Austria's interest to maintain disunity. Many Italian rulers—notably the papacy, the kingdom of Naples, and the central Italian duchies—imposed repressive policies, knowing that they could count on Austrian assistance in case of a popular uprising. Metternich's interventions to crush liberal rebellions generated hatred of Austria among Italian liberals and nationalists.

Political reaction in the Italian states cannot be wholly blamed on Austria, however. Piedmont, which was free of Austrian influence, nevertheless embraced restoration. When the royal house of Savoy returned to power in 1815, it nullified all laws passed during Napoleon's reign and banned from government service all officials who had served the French. The Jesuits were put in charge of education and censorship.

Throughout Italy, there was resistance to the restoration. Liberal journalists favored a constitutional system. The Carbonari (literally, "charcoal burners," suggestive of men of simple occupations), a nationalist conspiratorial group that had been formed to fight the French occupation, after

1815 targeted the restoration regimes. In March 1821, liberal-minded young army officers in Piedmont, inspired by recent events in Spain, proclaimed their support of a constitution and their desire to evict Austria from Italy. The movement, essentially military, did not win much popular support. With the help of Austria, Piedmontese loyal to the monarch Charles Felix (r. 1821–1831) crushed the uprising.

A decade later, catalyzed by the July revolution in Paris, the same forces came to the fore. An uprising broke out in Piedmont, then spread to the Papal States and Modena. The revolt was aimed at the authoritarian rulers of the various Italian states, but it was also in support of a united Italy. Led by intellectuals and some members of the middle classes, the uprisings lacked a popular base and were fragmented by the participants' primary loyalties to their individual states and cities. The Austrians promptly crushed hopes for the liberty and unity of Italy.

Russia

By far the most autocratic of the European states was tsarist Russia. Since 1801 it had been ruled by Alexander I (r. 1801–1825). An enigmatic character whose domestic policy vacillated between liberalism and reaction and whose foreign policy wavered between brutal power politics and apparently selfless idealism, Alexander puzzled his contemporaries. When the Congress of Vienna gave additional Polish lands to the tsar, he demonstrated his liberalism to the world (and curried favor with his new subjects) by granting Poland a liberal constitution. But he offered no such constitution to his own people. He and his council discussed terms for the abolition of serfdom in 1803 and again in 1812, but like so many of his plans this one was not implemented. Although he earnestly desired freedom for the serfs, the tsar was unwilling to impose any policy detrimental to the interests and privileges of the landed gentry.

Toward the end of his rule, Alexander became increasingly authoritarian and repressive, probably in response to growing opposition. Western liberal ideas, including constitutionalism, were adopted by Russian military officers who had served in western Europe, by Russian Freemasons who had corresponded with Masonic lodges in western Europe, and by Russian intellectuals who read Western liberal political tracts. These groups formed secret societies with varying programs. Some envisioned Russia as a republic, others as a constitutional monarchy, but all shared a commitment to the abolition of serfdom and the establishment of a freer society.

Alexander died in December 1825, leaving ambiguous which of his brothers would succeed him. Taking advantage of the confusion, the military conspirators declared in favor of the older brother, Constantine, in the belief that he favored a constitutional government. The younger brother, Nicholas, claimed to be the legal heir. The St. Petersburg garrison rallied to the conspirators' cause. The officers, taking their cue from the Spanish uprising of 1820, believed that the military could bring about change on its own in a country in which popular participation in governance was unknown.

The "Decembrist uprising," as it is known, quickly failed. The military revolt in the Russian capital was badly coordinated with uprisings planned in the countryside, and Nicholas moved quickly to crush the rebellion. He had the leaders executed, sent to Siberia, or sent into exile. In spite of its tragic end, throughout the nineteenth century the Decembrist uprising served as an inspiration to Russians resisting tsarist oppression.

Coming to the throne after crushing a revolt, Nicholas I (r. 1825–1855) was obsessed with the danger of revolution and determined to suppress all challenges to his authority. The declared goal of his rule was to uphold "orthodoxy, autocracy, and nationality." Nicholas created a stern, centralized bureaucracy to control all facets of Russian life. He originated the modern Russian secret police called the "Third Section"; it was above the law—a state within the state. Believing in the divine right of monarchs, Nicholas refused to accept limits to his imperial powers. The tsar supported the primacy of the Russian Orthodox church within Russian society; the church in turn upheld the powers of the state. Nicholas also used nationalism to strengthen the state, glorifying the country's past and trying to Russify non-Russian peoples, especially the Poles, by imposing the Russian language on them.

Russia's single most overwhelming problem was serfdom. Economically, serfdom had little to recommend it; free labor was far more efficient.

Moreover, public safety was threatened by the serfs' dissatisfaction with their lot. During Nicholas's thirty-year reign there were over six hundred peasant uprisings, half of them quelled by the military. Nicholas understood that serfdom had to be abolished for Russia's own good, but he could envision no clear alternative to it. Emancipation, he believed, would only sow further disorder. Except for a few minor reforms, he did nothing. Nicholas's death, followed by Russia's defeat in the Crimean War (see page 812), eventually brought to an end the institution that had held nearly half of the Russian people in bondage.

The Ottoman Empire

In its sheer mass, the Ottoman Empire continued to be a world empire. It extended over three continents. In Africa it ran across the whole North African coast. In Europe it stretched from Dalmatia (on the Adriatic coast) to Constantinople. In Asia it extended from Mesopotamia (present-day Iraq) to Anatolia (present-day Turkey). But it was an empire in decline, seriously challenged from within by nationalist movements and from outside by foreign threats.

The Ottoman bureaucracy, once the mainstay of the government, had fallen into decay. In the past, officials had been recruited and advanced by merit; now lacking funds, Constantinople sold government offices. Tax collectors ruthlessly squeezed the peasantry. The Janissaries, formerly an elite military force, by the eighteenth century had become an undisciplined band that menaced the peoples of the Ottoman Empire—especially those located at great distances from the close control of the capital. The reform-minded Sultan Selim III (r. 1789–1807) sought to curb the army, but he was killed by rebellious Janissaries, who forced the new ruler, Mahmud II (r. 1808–1839), to retract most of the previous improvements. The worst features of the declining empire were restored.

Most of the Ottoman Empire was inhabited by Muslims, but in the Balkans Christians were in the majority. Ottoman officials usually treated Christians no differently from their Muslim neighbors. But the Christian subject people found in their religion a means of collectively resisting a harsh and at times capricious rule. Some Christian peoples in the Balkans looked back nostalgically to earlier eras—the Greeks to when they had formed a great

Nicholas I, Emperor of Russia Acceding to the throne at the same time as the Decembrist uprising, Nicholas was haunted by the danger of revolution and ran a repressive regime. *(The Fotomas Index)*

civilization or the Serbs to when they had lived under Serb rule. The ideas of nationalism and liberty that triggered changes in western Europe also stirred the peoples of the Balkans.

The Serbs were the first people to revolt successfully against Ottoman rule. A poor, mountainous region, Serbia suffered greatly from the rapaciousness of the Janissaries. In protest a revolt broke out in 1804. At first the Ottomans were able to quell the uprising, but in 1815 they had to recognize one of its leaders, Milosh Obrenovich (r. 1815–1839), as governor and allow the formation of a national assembly. In 1830, under pressure from Russia, which took an interest in fellow Slavs and members of the Orthodox faith, Constantinople recognized Milosh as hereditary ruler over an autonomous Serbia.

The Greeks' struggle led to complete independence from Ottoman rule. Greeks served as administrators throughout the Ottoman lands and, as merchants and seafarers, traveled widely throughout the Mediterranean world and beyond. They had encountered the ideas of the French Revolution; wanting to revive their own homeland, they formed a conspiratorial group, the *Philike Hetairia* (Society of Friends), which was dedicated to restoring Greek independence.

Greek peasants were not particularly interested in politics, but they were hostile to the Turks, who had accumulated vast landholdings at their expense. This in part motivated Greek peasants to join the anti-Turkish revolt that began in 1821. Greeks killed large numbers of defenseless Turks in the Morea, in the Peloponnesus. The Turkish authorities hanged the Greek patriarch in Constantinople and massacred or sold into slavery the population of the Aegean island of Chios. The war continued fitfully. By 1827 the Ottomans, aided by their vassal Mehemet Ali (1769–1849) of Egypt, controlled most of the Balkan peninsula. The rest of Europe, excited by the idea of an independent Greece restored to its past greatness, widely supported the Greek movement for freedom. The Great Powers intervened in 1827, sending their navies to intercept supplies intended for the Ottoman forces. At Navarino Bay, in the southwest of the Peloponnesus, the Ottoman navy fired on the allies, who returned fire and sank the Turkish ships. With the destruction of Ottoman power, the independence of Greece was ensured. In 1830 an international agreement spelled out Greek independence.

In the 1820s and 1830s, local agitation and several Russian military interventions weakened Ottoman control over Wallachia and Moldavia (future Romania). Constantinople lost its right to name the governors of the provinces. It had to reduce its fortifications there, and from 1828 to 1834 Russian troops occupied the provinces.

Losing influence in the Balkans, the Ottoman Empire was also challenged elsewhere. In Egypt, Mehemet Ali modernized his army and used it to wrest Syria away in 1831. He threatened to march against his overlord, the sultan. Britain and Russia, concerned lest the Ottoman Empire collapse and thus threaten the region's balance of power, intervened on the empire's behalf. Constantinople won back Syria but in 1841 had to acknowledge Mehemet Ali as the hereditary ruler of Egypt. The survival of the Ottoman Empire was beginning to depend on the goodwill of the Great Powers.

THE REVOLUTIONS OF 1848

From France in the west to Poland in the east, at least fifty separate revolts and uprisings shook the Continent in 1848, the most extensive outbreak of popular violence in nineteenth-century Europe (Map 20.2). The revolt had an impact far beyond Europe's borders. Brazilians, inspired by the example of the European revolutions, rose up against their government. In Bogota, Colombia, church bells rang to celebrate the announcement of a republic in France. And as a result of the Parisian revolution, slaves in French colonies were emancipated.

Roots of Rebellion

At no time since 1800 had so many Europeans been involved in collective action. There were many reasons for this outbreak of discontent. In the countryside, such changes in access to land as land enclosure (see page 689) frustrated peasants. Although in the past many had enjoyed free access to village commons, these were coming increasingly under private control, or there was competition for their use; formerly a peasant might have grazed his sheep in the commons, but now his two or three competed with herds of sometimes hundreds of sheep, owned by a rich farmer. Also, the poor once had relatively free access to forests to forage for firewood, but the limitation of this right now led to frequent conflicts in the countryside.

Points of friction were made worse by growing populations that put pressure on available resources. In the urban environment there was a crisis in the handicrafts industry, which dominated city economies. Urban artisans were being undercut by the putting-out system or cottage industry (see page 690), in which capitalists had goods produced in the countryside by cottagers—part-time artisans who supported themselves partly through agriculture and were thus willing to work for lower wages. Crises in the crafts hurt the journeymen who wanted to be masters; they had to serve far longer apprenticeships and in many cases could never expect promotion. Where the guild system still existed, it was in decline, unable

Map 20.2 Major Revolutions and Reforms, 1848–1849 In no other year had as many revolts broken out simultaneously; in many cases the revolutions led to reforms and new constitutions.

to protect the economic interests of artisans anxious about their future.

These developing concerns came to a crisis point as a result of the economic depression of 1845–1846. In 1845 there was a crop disaster, including the spread of potato blight, destroying the basic food of the poor in northern Europe. Wheat and rye production also plummeted. Food prices doubled from what they had been in the early 1840s. An industrial downturn accompanied these agricultural disasters, creating massive unemployment. Municipal and national governments seemed unable to deal with the crowding, disease, and unsanitary conditions that were worsening tensions running high in the cities, the sites of national governments. People were ready to heed

those who called for the overthrow of the existing regimes. The established political and administrative elites were disoriented and found they could not count on their traditional sources of support. Revolts were triggered by discontent, but also by the hope for change.

France

Once again the spark for revolution was ignited in Paris and spread from there to the rest of the Continent. Economic crisis had a severe impact in the French capital. In some occupations as many as half the people were out of work. The price of bread had shot up to over one franc a pound, which meant that the entire salary of the average male worker—a franc a day—would not even buy enough bread to sustain him. Thousands of workers were willing to pour into the streets to protest the government's seeming indifference to their desperation.

Meanwhile, liberals were agitating for the expansion of suffrage. When political meetings were forbidden in 1847, they resorted to banquets featuring long-winded toasts indistinguishable from political speeches. Such a banquet was scheduled for Paris on February 22, 1848, to celebrate the birthday of George Washington—an icon to French liberals. When the government banned the meeting, mass demonstrations by students and workers broke out. Unlike the British with their professional urban police, the French had no forces trained in crowd control. The government called in the military, whose tactics were more appropriate to engaging an enemy army than to containing civilian demonstrators. On February 23, soldiers guarding the Ministry of Foreign Affairs panicked and shot into a crowd; fifty-two people died.

Word spread that the government was shooting at the people. To protect themselves, residents of the traditionally revolutionary neighborhoods near the Bastille square erected barricades. On February 24, police and army posts were attacked, and the royal palace was surrounded. The National Guard, a civilian force recruited from the artisans and the middle class and charged with restoring order, had become sympathetic to the protesters and refused to fight the populace. Louis Philippe resigned as king and fled for London under the pseudonym "Mr. Smith." The royalists were clearly discredited.

The abruptness of the king's resignation left the opposition in disarray. The protesters shared one goal, the extension of suffrage, but otherwise diverged sharply. Liberals accepted the monarchy but were offended by its corruption, manipulation of elections, and restrictive suffrage. More radical elements favored a democratic republic. Socialists' prime goal was a government that would ensure social justice.

The new regime, hastily organized under the pressure of a mob invasion of the Chamber of Deputies, lacked uniformity in its makeup or ideas. The provisional government consisted of well-known liberal opponents of the July Monarchy such as the poet Alphonse de Lamartine (1790–1869) and the journalist Alexandre Ledru-

Rollin (1807–1874). Under pressure from the radicals, socialist journalist Louis Blanc (see page 750) and a worker known only as Albert joined the government. At first, the liberal supporters of constitutional democracy and the radical republicans committed to economic justice for the underprivileged cooperated with each other. Under the strain of events, however, the coalition fell apart by late spring.

Bowing to pressure from the poor and unemployed of Paris, who resorted to demonstrations and occupied City Hall, the government established national workshops and a commission headed by Louis Blanc to study the problems of the poor. The national workshops were not a substitute for the capitalist order, as Louis Blanc had intended, but were a stopgap measure to enable the unemployed to earn a livelihood. They nevertheless represented the most ambitious plan that any French government had yet undertaken to combat the misery of the poor.

The new republic was quick to institute other reforms. It abolished slavery in the colonies and the death penalty for political crimes. Imprisonment for debt ceased, and the workday was limited to ten hours in Paris, eleven hours in the départements. The most radical move was the adoption of universal male suffrage. Men in 1789 had identified citizenship as a distinctly male prerogative, and they continued to do so.

In the general euphoria over human liberties, women asserted their rights. A new woman's newspaper, *La Voix des Femmes* (*The Voice of Women*), argued for equal pay, political rights, and educational opportunities. Many of the militants took their cue from the women who had fought for their rights in 1789 (see page 708). Women's political clubs flourished in the capital as well as in Lyon and lesser provincial towns. (See the box: "A Revolutionary of 1848 Calls for Women's Political Rights.") When women's political clubs petitioned for the vote, the revolutionary government abolished them. In light of women's active role at the barricades that had toppled the monarchy, this was a bitter disappointment.

The first universal-manhood elections took place in April. The results were surprising. Nearly everyone expected enfranchisement of the poor and uneducated to bring about the election of radicals and outsiders. Most of France's population, however, consisted of rural peasants. Although

Revolutionary Women In this cartoon, entitled "The Divorced Women," Daumier ridicules women who fought for their rights in the revolution of 1848. They are seen as divorced, deprived of male companionship, and probably therefore crazed. This kind of depiction was one of many ways in which women were discouraged from participating in politics. *(Jean-Loup Charmet)*

there were some radical peasants, particularly in the south, most peasants distrusted the radicalism of the capital and resented the tax increases needed to support social programs. At the polls, peasants tended to vote for their social superiors: the local landowner, notary, or lawyer. Even Paris elected mostly moderate deputies. The new National Assembly elected by popular vote did not look much different from that of the July Monarchy. Most members were landowners and lawyers; among the new deputies, there were only seventeen workers and no peasants.

The government was soon at loggerheads with the radical workers in Paris. Under conservative pressure, the Assembly in May disbanded the national workshops, which were expensive to run and—though they provided a livelihood for more than half of working-class males—were accomplishing little construction of buildings, roads, and the like. At the news of the closings, people who depended on the workshops rose up in despair. After days of fighting in which 1500 were killed and 12,000 arrested, government forces regained control of the city. Passionate feelings on both sides led to savagery: Corpses were mutilated, and severed heads were paraded through the streets. Both the liberal Alexis de Tocqueville and the socialist Karl Marx called the June uprisings class warfare between the poor and the rich.

The defeat of the insurgents revealed that universal suffrage had enabled the government to mobilize moderate public opinion against radicalism in Paris. The advent of railroads had allowed the government to muster military support from outside the city. Thereafter, it would be far more difficult for radical Parisian crowds to dictate policies to the rest of the country.

People had entered into the revolution in February with confidence, but the June uprisings transformed the situation. The propertied classes, feeling menaced by the poor, looked to the authorities for security. Of the several candidates for

A Revolutionary of 1848 Calls for Women's Political Rights

Jeanne Deroin was a French advocate of women's suffrage who served as editor of the newspaper representing women, L'opinion des femmes, *during the revolution of 1848. Frustrated that women were denied a role in the political process, she tried to run for parliament in 1849. In an election poster and in correspondence with a socialist paper, which although socially radical was opposed to female suffrage, Deroin proclaimed the rights of women.*

I present myself for your votes, out of devotion to the consecration of a great principle: the civil and political equality of the sexes.

It is in the name of justice that I appeal to the sovereign people against negating the great principles that are the foundation for the future of our society.

If using your right, you call upon women to take part in the work of the Legislative Assembly, you will consecrate our republican dogmas in all their integrity: Liberty, Equality, Fraternity for all women as well as for all men.

A Legislative Assembly composed entirely of men is incompetent to make the laws that rule a society of men and women, as an assembly composed entirely of privileged people to debate the interests of workers, or an assembly of capitalists to sustain the honor of the country. . . .

It is precisely because woman is equal to man, and yet not identical to him, that she should take part in the work of social reform and incorporate in it those necessary elements that are lacking in man, so that the work can be complete.

Liberty for woman, as well as for man, is the right to utilize and to develop one's faculties freely.

Life's unity can be considered to be in three parts: individual life, family life, and social life; this is a complete life. To refuse woman the right to live the social life is to commit a crime against humanity.

. . . this is a holy and legitimate protest against the errors of the old society and against a clear violation of our sacred principles of liberty, equality, and fraternity.

Source: Election poster to the Electors of the Department of Seine, *L'opinion des femmes,* April 10, 1849; *La Démocratie pacifique,* April 13, 1849. Trans. K. Offen. Reprinted in Susan Groag Bell and Karen M. Offen, eds., *Women, the Family, and Freedom: The Debate in Documents,* vol. I (Stanford: Stanford University Press, 1983), pp. 280–281.

president in 1848, Louis Napoleon (1808–1873), a nephew of Napoleon Bonaparte, appealed to the largest cross section of the population. The bourgeoisie was attracted by the promise of authority and order. Peasants disillusioned by the tax policies of the republic remained loyal to the memory of Napoleonic glory. Workers embittered by the government's repression of the June uprisings were impressed by Louis Napoleon's vaguely socialistic program.

Louis Napoleon received nearly three times as many votes as all his opponents combined. His government was conservative, composed of men

of the old order. Three years later, Louis Napoleon dissolved the National Assembly by force and established a personal dictatorship. In 1852 he declared himself Emperor Napoleon III.

Austria

In Austria, news of the overthrow of Louis Philippe and of agitation in the German states prompted demonstrations and petitions calling for a constitution and the dismissal of Metternich, the symbol of the reactionary order. In the face of growing opposition, Metternich resigned, and the army withdrew from Vienna, which appeared to have fallen under the control of students and workers. On March 15, 1848, the imperial court, surrounded by crowds of students and workers, announced its willingness to issue a constitution. Even more important was the decision to abolish serfdom. There had been fear of a serf uprising, but the relatively generous terms of the emancipation mollified the peasantry.

The promised constitution was issued, but it was drafted by the emperor rather than by representatives of the people. It was probably acceptable to the male middle classes because it enfranchised them, but students and workers who favored popular sovereignty opposed it. Mass demonstrations and an invasion of the prime minister's office prompted the court to leave Vienna for Innsbruck on May 17.

The government also faced revolts in the non-German parts of the empire: in Italy, Hungary, the Czech lands, and Croatia. In March Vienna acquiesced to Hungary's demands; from that point on, Hungary was joined to the Austrian Empire by personal union to the emperor. Constitutional government was then established in Hungary, but participation in the political process was limited to Magyars, who were the single largest ethnic group but who made up only 40 percent of the population. The other peoples of Hungary—Romanians, Slovaks, Croats, and Slovenes—preferred the more distant rule of German Vienna to Magyar authority.

Many nationalities rallied to the Austrian Empire in 1848 for their own reasons—fear of falling under German rule in Bohemia, fear of Magyar rule in Hungary, fear of Polish rule in Galicia (the Austrian part of Poland)—and the empire survived. There was no solidarity among the various nationalities that rose up against Vienna's rule. The empire had been able to practice a policy of divide and rule, yet the dangers nationalism posed to its survival were also revealed.

The revolution in Austria and its possessions was suppressed as soon as the court was able to gather an army and send it against the rebels. Prague was bombarded into submission in June and Vienna in November 1848. By the following August, Austria had crushed the rebellious Hungarians with the help of Russia and suspended the liberal constitution it had previously granted. A reactionary regime under Prince Felix von Schwarzenberg (1800–1852) re-established absolutist rule over the empire.

Italy

In the years before 1848, the Italian peninsula was in the grip of economic hardship and social unrest; nationalists and liberals hoped somehow to see their program of a united and free Italy implemented. The election in 1846 of Pius IX (r. 1846–1878) was seen as a harbinger of change. The pope was not only a religious leader but also secular ruler of the Papal States. Pius appeared to be a liberal and a supporter of Italian unification. In January 1848, revolution forced the king of Sicily to grant a constitution to his subjects. The Sicilian revolution was the first to erupt in Europe, but it was news of the Paris uprising in February that stimulated revolutions elsewhere in Italy.

Italians under Austrian rule revolted, forcing the Austrians to evacuate their Italian possessions. The middle classes, though eager to be free of Austrian rule, saw working-class radicals as a threat. They believed that annexation to nearby Piedmont would provide security from both Austria and the lower classes. The king of Piedmont, Charles Albert (r. 1831–1849), reluctantly decided to unite Italy under his throne if doing so would prevent the spread of radicalism to his kingdom. On March 24, 1848, he declared war on Austria but was defeated in July and had to sue for an armistice.

The pope had expressed sympathy for Italian unification but provided no support for the cause. Republicans, disappointed by the pope's abandonment of the national cause and a liberal program, forced the pope to flee. In January 1849 they declared the Roman Republic. Hope ran high that it would become the capital of a united republican Italy. Giuseppe Mazzini was to be a member of the governing triumvirate.

In Piedmont, meanwhile, Charles Albert's desire to bring the radical movement under control by defeating the Austrians tempted him to declare war on Austria once again, in March 1849. The outcome for Piedmont was even worse than it had been a year earlier. Within six days its army was defeated. Humiliated, Charles Albert resigned his throne to his son, Victor Emmanuel II (r. 1849–1878).

The Austrians quickly reconquered their lost provinces and helped restore their puppet governments to power. Louis Napoleon, the newly elected president of France, eager to curry favor with Catholic voters, sent French troops to Rome, restoring the pope to power in July 1849. Nevertheless, profound liberal and even revolutionary ideas—constitutional government, universal suffrage, abolition of the remnants of the Old Regime—had been expressed and in some cases implemented, though briefly. Most reforms were rescinded, but Piedmont's liberal constitution, the *Statuto,* implemented in 1848, was retained and later became the constitution of a united Italy.

The German States

News of the February uprising in Paris also acted as a catalyst for change in the German states. In response to large public demonstrations in the grand duchy of Baden in southwestern Germany, the duke—reluctant to suffer the same fate as Louis Philippe—dismissed his conservative prime minister and installed in March 1848 a government sympathetic to the aspirations of middle-class liberals. The forces of change seemed irresistible. As the king of Württemberg observed, "I cannot mount on horseback against ideas." The wisest course appeared to be compromise. He and many of his fellow dukes and princes changed their governments, dismissing their cabinets and instituting constitutions. Bavaria's King Ludwig I (r. 1825–1848), who had scandalized the court by his public liaison with an exotic dancer, found himself without supporters when public demonstrations broke out. The only German monarch to lose his throne, he abdicated in favor of his son.

Up to this point Prussia was conspicuous for being untouched by the revolutionary wave. But when news of Metternich's fall reached Berlin on March 16, middle-class liberals and artisans demonstrated for reforms. To appease his subjects, King Frederick William IV appointed a liberal Rhenish businessman to head a new government. Representative government was introduced, and suffrage was extended, though it was still restricted to men of property. Government, no longer the exclusive preserve of the aristocracy, was opened to men from the liberal professions and the business classes.

The revolutionary outbreaks in the German states in 1848 were triggered by dissatisfaction with local economic and political conditions, not by agitation for German unification. But once the revolutions had taken hold, preoccupying the two largest states, Prussia and Austria—which both opposed unification lest it undermine their power—the question of a single Germany quickly came to the fore. In March 1848, a self-appointed national committee invited five hundred prominent German liberals to convene in Frankfurt to begin the process of national unification. In addition to fulfilling a long-standing liberal dream, a united nation would consolidate the liberal victory over absolutism.

The gathering called for suffrage based on property qualifications. The poor and the artisan classes were thus excluded from the political process and alienated from the evolving new order. The vast majority of those elected to the first all-German National Assembly in 1848 came from the liberal professions; one quarter were lawyers, only four were artisans, and one was a peasant. The liberals rejoiced that they controlled the new parliament, but it was unrepresentative and lacked broad popular support.

The first all-German elected legislature met in May 1848 in Frankfurt to pursue the unification of Germany. It faced the thorny issue of the shape of this new Germany: which regions should be included and which excluded? The most ambitious plan envisioned a *Grossdeutschland,* or large Germany, consisting of all the members of the German Confederation, including the German-speaking parts of Austria and the Germanized western parts of Bohemia. Such a solution would include many non-Germans, including Poles, Czechs, and Danes. The proponents of *Kleindeutschland,* or small Germany, which would exclude Austria and its possessions, saw their solution as a more likely scenario for national unity, although it would exclude many Germans. They succeeded in the end, largely because the reassertion of Austrian imperial power in the fall of 1848 made the areas under Vienna's control ineligible for inclusion.

The Frankfurt assembly formed a provisional government in June 1848. The individual states, however, including Prussia and Austria, did not recognize the assembly's authority, so it was utterly powerless. The minister of war could not raise any soldiers, and the minister of finance could not impose taxes. The United States, enthusiastic about a new republic consciously modeled

Constitutional Government in Denmark On March 21, 1848, 15,000 Danes, inspired by the example of Paris, marched on the palace to demand constitutional rights. Unlike in the French capital, however, this event was peaceful and led to the establishment of constitutional government. This painting honors the new parliament that came into being after the liberal constitution was adopted in 1849. *(Statens Museum for Kunst, Copenhagen)*

on its own, was one of the few nations to accept an ambassador from the all-German government.

The parliament also lacked the power to transfer authority from the individual states to itself. It might have succeeded if it had called for a national uprising against the princes, but the liberals in Frankfurt were loath to do so. They distrusted the populace and feared working-class opposition. Force was still in the hands of the traditional authorities. At one point, when the parliament was invaded by radicals, it survived only by calling on Prussia to restore order. Its longevity apparently depended on how long the king of Prussia would tolerate it.

By the fall of 1848, a royalist reaction had begun to take shape in Prussia. In October, facing a workers' uprising triggered by economic despair, the king brought soldiers into Berlin, declared a state of siege, and dissolved the Prussian assembly. The Prussian reassertion of royal power, though partial, was a signal for other German rulers in late 1848 to dismiss their liberal ministers.

The moment for liberalism and national unification to triumph had passed by the time the Frankfurt assembly drew up a constitution in the spring of 1849. Having opted for the *Kleindeutsch* solution, the parliament offered the throne to Frederick William IV, king of Prussia. Although the king was not a liberal, he ruled the largest state within the designated empire. If power had to be used to promote and protect German unity, he possessed it in the form of the Prussian army. But Frederick William feared that accepting the throne would lead to war with Austria. Believing in the principle of monarchy, he also did not want an office offered by representatives of the people.

Lacking an alternative plan in case their offer was refused, most members of the Frankfurt assembly went home. A rump parliament and a series of uprisings in favor of German unity were crushed by the Prussian army.

So German unification failed. Liberalism was unable to bring about German unity; other means would be required to do so.

SUMMARY

The revolutions of 1848 released many of the forces for change that had been gathering strength since 1815. In spite of the Congress of Vienna's effort to restore the old order after Napoleon's fall, the generation after 1815 established a new order. The ideas of change that had powered the French Revolution of 1789 continued to shape an era that claimed to be rolling history back to prerevolutionary times. Liberalism contested authoritarianism.

Reform-minded regimes in Europe improved the lives of people in colonies overseas, abolishing slavery in British and then French colonies and providing self-rule for Canada. Some states even turned away from monarchy and experimented with republicanism, a form of government that until then many had thought fit only for small states. All of the Latin American colonies except Mexico became republics on gaining independence from Spain. In Europe during 1848–1849 the French, German, Hungarian, and Roman republics were proclaimed. These experiments suggested new modes of political organization that were to become common in the following century.

The generation after 1815 experienced revolutions frequently and broadly. These uprisings usually failed, and the forces of order were able to recapture power. Yet the status quo was altered. In many cases absolutist rulers had to grant constitutions and accept ministers who were not their choice. Even though most of these arrangements were temporary, they established an important precedent. If unusual in the first half, constitutions became the norm in the second half of the century.

Nationalism arose in these years. The desire for national independence and unity was voiced in Italy, Germany, Hungary, Poland, and the land of the Czechs. The Spanish colonies in freeing themselves from Madrid's rule employed a nationalist discourse borrowed from Europe. Europe

in the second half of the century was to contend with the forces of nationalism that first appeared after 1814.

The middle classes found their position strengthened after 1848. They did not dominate the political system, but their influence was increasing with the growth of entrepreneurship. Middle-class professionals were recruited into the civil services of states determined to streamline their operation in order to withstand revolution more effectively. Revolutionary fervor waned after 1848, but the current of economic and social change continued to transform Europe.

SUGGESTED READING

General Surveys

Hobsbawm, E. J. *The Age of Revolution, 1789–1848.* 1962. A compellingly argued book that describes the era as being dominated by two simultaneous revolutions, the French Revolution and the industrial transformation.

Johnson, Paul. *The Birth of the Modern World Society, 1815–1830.* 1991. A weighty but readable book providing a panoramic view of the era. Particularly strong in providing biographical sketches of some of the major figures of the time.

Langer, William L. *Europe in Social Upheaval, 1832–1852.* 1969. Provides a strong emphasis on the social aspects of these years.

Kissinger, Henry. *A World Restored.* 1957. A study by a future U.S. secretary of state who emphasizes the efforts of diplomats to build an international order resistant to revolution.

Nicolson, Harold. *The Congress of Vienna.* 1946. An account by a prominent British diplomat who provides colorful sketches of the diplomats at Vienna.

Palmer, Alan. *Metternich.* 1972. The best one-volume life in English of the dominant statesman of the era.

Ideological Confrontations

Anderson, Benedict. *Imagined Communities.* 1983. A noted anthropologist underscores the extent to which a nation is an "imagined community."

Carlisle, Robert B. *The Proffered Crown: Saint-Simonianism and the Doctrine of Hope.* 1987. A work that shows the originality of Saint-Simonian thought and its continuity after the founder's death.

Grana, Cesar. *Bohemian vs. Bourgeois: French Society and the Man of Letters in the Nineteenth Century.* 1964. A consideration of the intellectual origins of the notion of artist as rebel.

Harrison, J. F. C. *Quest for the New Moral World: Robert Owen and the Owenites in Britain and America.* 1969. A good biography that views the movement as affected by contemporary religious notions of a coming millennium.

Kedourie, Elie. *Nationalism*. 1960. An account that describes the German romantics as developers of modern nationalism and creators of an essentially pernicious force.

Porter, Roy, and Mikulas Teich, eds. *Romanticism in National Context*. 1988. An up-to-date series of essays on romanticism in different national settings.

Restoration and Reform

Brock, Michael. *The Great Reform Act*. 1973. An account that emphasizes the sense of crisis on the eve of the Great Reform Act.

Bushnell, David, and Neill Macaulay. *The Emergence of Latin America in the Nineteenth Century*. 1988. A brief but suggestive synthesis.

Church, Clive. *Europe in 1830: Revolution and Political Change*. 1983. A view of the end of the restoration period, punctured by the revolutions of 1830, from a European-wide perspective.

Collingham, H. A. C. *The July Monarchy: A Political History of France*. 1988. An account of the divisions in France that continued in spite of the new king's well-meaning efforts.

Jardin, André, and André-Jean Tudesq. *Restoration and Reaction, 1815–1848*. 1988. A general survey of France.

Jones, Gareth Stedman. *The Languages of Class: Studies in English Working-Class History, 1832–1982*. 1983. A work that considers Chartism a movement of the politically disenfranchised seeking a voice within the political system.

Kann, Robert A. *A History of the Habsburg Empire, 1526–1918*. 1977. Examines the problems of maintaining the multinational empire.

Kirmmse, Bruce H. *Kierkegaard in Golden Age Denmark*. 1990. A rich survey of Danish society and politics in the first half of the nineteenth century.

Lincoln, W. Bruce. *Nicholas I: Emperor and Autocrat of All the Russias*. 1978. A biography of the tsar, revealing the ruler's dedication to preserve the autocratic regime and its values.

More, Charles. *The Industrial Age: Economy and Society in Britain, 1750–1985*. 1989. A survey of British economic and social history.

Pinkney, David H. *The French Revolution of 1830*. 1972. The standard work on the subject.

Sheehan, James J. *German History, 1770–1866*. 1989. A survey of the variety and contrast of the German experience.

Sked, Alan. *The Decline and Fall of the Habsburg Empire, 1815–1918*. 1989. A brief, clear study stressing the very real threat the revolutions of 1848 posed to imperial survival.

Woodward, Sir Llewellyn. *The Age of Reform, 1815–1870*. 2d ed. 1962. A strong political narrative of British history.

Woolf, Stuart Joseph. *A History of Italy, 1700–1860*. 1979. A consideration of the problems of political divisions in Italian life.

The Revolutions of 1848

Agulhon, Maurice. *The Republican Experiment*. 1983. A work that stresses how the splits between different political groups made it difficult for revolutionary goals to succeed.

Ginsborg, P. *Daniele Manin and the Venetian Revolution of 1848–1849*. 1979. An account portraying a heroic opponent of Habsburg rule as a representative of the local bourgeoisie.

Price, Roger. *The French Second Republic: A Social History*. 1972. An account suggesting that divisions in French society produced the revolution of 1848 and that local elites asserting their interests caused its demise.

————. *The Revolutions of 1848*. 1989. A general history of the European revolutions describing them as the result of discontent with an economic and political system out of tune with the needs and desires of most peoples.

Sheehan, James J. *German Liberalism in the Nineteenth Century*. 1978. The standard work revealing the difficulties that German liberals faced as early as the first half of the nineteenth century.

Snell, John L. *The Democratic Movement in Germany, 1789–1914*. 1976. A long and detailed work emphasizing the development of a democratic and liberal movement over more than a century.

Sperber, Jonathan. *The European Revolutions, 1848–1851*. 1994. The best up-to-date synthesis, which includes some new emphases, such as the role of rural and religious discontent in shaping the revolts.

Stadelmann, Rudolf. *Social and Political History of the German 1848 Revolution*. 1975. An account in which both the outbreak and the unraveling of the 1848 revolution are attributed to social and political forces.

RAFT OF THE "MEDUSA"

In September 1816 the French were shocked at the news of the disaster that had befallen the government ship, *Méduse* (Medusa), as it headed for Senegal in West Africa the previous July. Including the ship's crew, 400 passengers had boarded the vessel.

The captain of the ship was a nobleman, Duroys de Chaumareys, whom the restoration government had appointed solely on the basis of his family and political connections. Inexperienced as a seaman, the captain clumsily ran his ship aground on the Mauritanian coast, off West Africa, on July 2. The *Medusa* had only six lifeboats capable of carrying a total of 250 people; for the rest of the passengers a raft was rigged with planks, beams, and ropes. The captain and his officers forcefully took over the lifeboats, abandoning 150 passengers, including one woman, to the less secure raft. With no navigational tools and insufficient food and water, the passengers of the raft were at the mercy of stormy seas and a brutal sun. Anger at officers for having abandoned them led seamen on the raft to murder some of their superiors. By the third day, driven by thirst and hunger, some passengers ate their dead companions— killed by exposure or drowned by huge waves. On the sixth day, the strongest among the survivors, fearing that their rations were dwindling, banded together and murdered the weaker ones. On the thirteenth day, the French brig *Argus* spotted the raft and rescued fifteen survivors. Five died soon after, leaving only ten survivors out of the raft's original 150 passengers.

Although the government tried to suppress information about the event, the French press exposed the incompetence and cowardice of Captain de Chaumareys. The event was understood to reflect the weakness of the regime that had appointed him. The selfish act of the captain and his fellow officers suggested the narrow class interest of the restoration government, favoring aristocracy at the cost of the common people.

The French painter Théodore Géricault (1791–1824) befriended the ship surgeon Henri Savigny,

772

one of the lucky ten who survived the harrowing experience on the raft of the *Medusa*. In addition to press reports, Géricault thus had a direct eyewitness account of the event. The painter shared Savigny's sense of outrage against the government for having appointed the incompetent captain and for having treated the survivors callously—at one point arresting Savigny for publicizing the tragedy. The light prison sentence imposed on the captain was another source of grievance.

Since 1815 the French government had sought to bring distinction to itself by displaying art in salon expositions. That of 1819 was intended to be larger, more glorious than any previous one. Among its paintings was Géricault's huge canvas—the largest in that year's exposition— measuring 16 feet high by 24 feet wide, innocently titled *Scene of Shipwreck*. Carelessly, the regime had wanted to gain glory for itself by exhibiting this impressive artwork, while at the same time keeping hidden its real subject. But the stratagem failed; everyone recognized the painting to be the *Raft of the "Medusa"* and an attack on the Bourbon regime.

The painting, reproduced here, depicts the moment the survivors have spotted the frigate, the *Argus*, barely visible in the horizon. Notice the figure of an African standing at the fore of the raft, waving a red-and-white cloth to attract the ship's attention. In this painting the nobility and symbol of hope the African symbolizes is an attack on the slave trade, which Britain had abolished but which France was still engaged in. And so by including the African, the painting is implicitly criticizing the restoration regime for sanctioning commerce in humans. Just as the *Argus* is coming to the rescue of the shipwrecked, the painting appears to suggest, so Africans will see the day when their enslavement will be ended.

Historians often regard the *Raft of the "Medusa"* as the most important painting of French romanticism, and it includes nearly all the major themes of the movement. By locating the scene off the coast of Africa, Géricault incorporates an element of ex-

Géricault: Raft of the "Medusa" *(Erich Lessing/Art Resource, NY)*

oticism. Nature—cruel and unforgiving—is central to the scene, reflected in the turbulent sea, dark clouds, and imperiled raft. The canvas includes an extraordinary range of passions: Observe, for example, the inconsolable grief of the figure at the bottom left, a father cradling the dead body of his son. Other figures express despair and terror, and still others limitless hope. The painting evokes the dark passions humans are capable of. Although it does not show the scenes of insanity, murder, and cannibalism that the survivors had witnessed, they undoubtedly came to the mind of the viewers, who were familiar with the tragic events. The painting was a powerful indictment of Enlightenment faith in humans as creatures of reason and balance.

Romantic artists wanted to engage the passions of those viewing, reading, or hearing their works. *Raft of the "Medusa"* purposely stages the events in the foreground in order to pull viewers into the picture and make them participants in the drama; they thus share in the alternating feelings of terror and hope that swept the raft.

The fate of the painting and the artist followed a romantic script. When Géricault started the painting, he intended it as an indictment of the restoration government. He poured energy into it in an effort to take his mind off a disastrous love affair, and as his work proceeded he came to see the painting as an allegory of larger human passions and concerns. Yet when it was displayed, much to his disappointment, the painting was mainly understood in political terms. Disillusioned by this reaction, Géricault thereafter painted no major works. He grew sickly, rarely bestirred himself, and died of bone tuberculosis in 1824, aged 33. He illustrated the romantics' view of a heroic life—the genius who performs a major feat and then dies young, before realizing his potential. To the romantics, human intent and effort often appeared thwarted by larger forces. This painting, originally meant to criticize the regime, was after Géricault's death purchased by the restoration government and hung in France's national museum, the Louvre. ✒

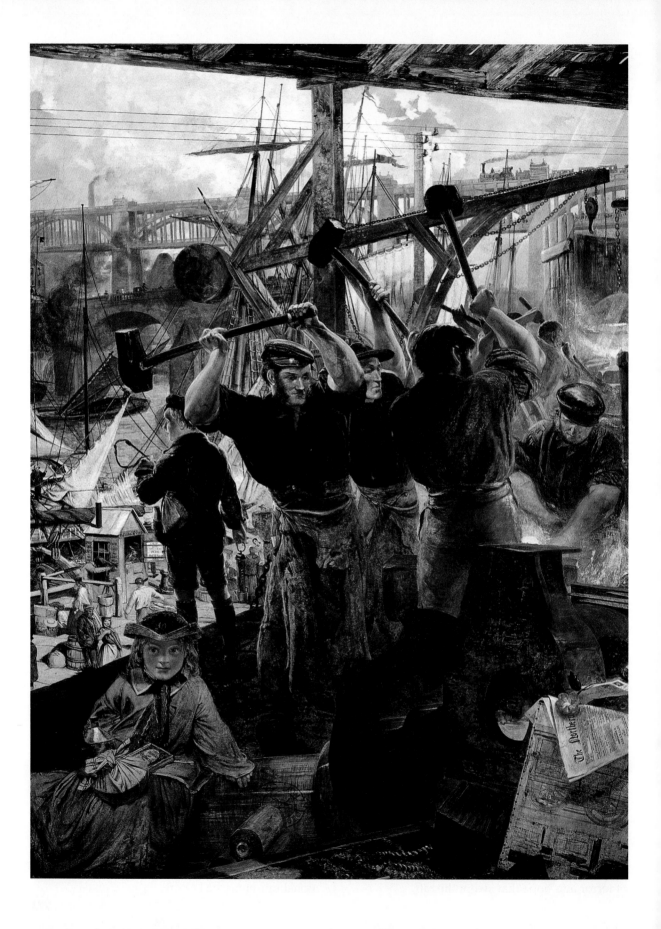

The Industrial Transformation of Europe

A s his country was swept by economic and technological changes, the eighteenth-century English writer Samuel Johnson (1709–1784) remarked, "The age is running mad after innovation. All the business of the world is to be done in a new way." A generation later, in the 1830s, the French socialist Louis Blanqui (see page 751), struck by the dramatic transformations across the Channel, proposed a descriptive term for them, suggesting that just as France had experienced a political revolution, so Britain was undergoing an "industrial revolution." Eventually, that expression entered the general vocabulary to describe the advances in production that occurred first in England and were dominating most of western Europe by the end of the nineteenth century. Many economic historians now emphasize how gradual and cumulative the changes were and question the appropriateness of the term. Indeed, it seems best to discuss the changes not as an industrial revolution but as a continuous process of economic transformation.

Industrial development left its mark on just about every sphere of human activity. Scientific and rational methods altered production. Economic activity became increasingly specialized. The unit of production changed from the family to a larger and less personal group. Significant numbers of workers left farming to enter mining and manufacturing, and major portions of the population moved from a rural to an urban environment. Machines replaced or supplemented manual labor.[1]

The economic changes physically transformed Europe. Greater levels of production were achieved and more wealth was created than ever before. Factory chimneys belched soot into the air. Miners in search

The Nineteenth Century, Iron and Coal (detail), by William Bell Scott.

of coal, iron ore, and other minerals cut deep gashes into the earth. Cities, spurred by industrialization, grew quickly, and Europe became increasingly urban.

Industrialization simultaneously created unprecedented advancement and opportunity as well as unprecedented hardships and social problems. Different groups tried various strategies to strike a balance between the positive and negative effects. Many entrepreneurs and their sympathizers stood for liberal principles based on classical economics. Workers, with a growing sense of solidarity, struggled for their common interests. Out of the socialist ideologies of the early nineteenth century, Karl Marx forged a militant ideology to address the needs of the industrial working class.

SETTING THE STAGE FOR INDUSTRIALIZATION

No one can say with certainty which conditions were necessary for the industrialization of Europe. Nevertheless, we do know why industrialization did not spread widely to the rest of the world in the nineteenth century. A certain combination of conditions—geographic, cultural, economic, demographic—helped make industrialization possible in Europe.

Why Europe?

A fortunate set of circumstances seems to explain why Europe was the stage for industrial development. Since the Middle Ages, political transformations in western Europe reduced risk and uncertainty while encouraging productive investment. With the development of legal due process, rich merchants did not run the risk of having their wealth confiscated—as they did, for instance, in the Ottoman Empire. The unfolding of state power in Europe reduced the frequency of brigandage—still common in many parts of the world—and thus encouraged trade. Discrepancies in risk are apparent in the differences in interest rates on borrowing money in the eighteenth century: 3 percent in England, 36 percent in China.

In Europe, disparities of wealth, though serious, were less extreme than in other parts of the world; thus, there was a better market for goods. At the time western Europe industrialized, the average yearly income per person was equivalent to $500—more than the amount in many non-Western societies even today. And nearly half of the population was literate, again a very high proportion compared to non-Western societies.

Although population grew in Europe during the eighteenth century (see page 687), late marriages and limited family sizes kept its rise in check; hence European society was rarely overwhelmed by the pressures of population. In India and China, by contrast, population growth was so dramatic that society had to be fully engaged to feed the people and could not be readily mobilized for other production.

Europe enjoyed a measure of cultural, political, and social diversity unknown elsewhere. Challenges to dominant religious and political powers had brought some religious diversity—a rarity outside the West, where large territories tended to be dominated by a single ruler and faith. Diversity encouraged a culture that tolerated and eventually promoted innovation. Competitiveness drove states to try to catch up with each other. Governments actively encouraged industries and commerce to enrich a country and make it more powerful than its neighbors. None of these factors alone explains why industrialization occurred, but their combination seems to have facilitated the process when it did occur.[2]

The industrialization of Europe radically transformed power relationships between the industrial West and nonindustrial Africa, Asia, and South America. By 1900 the latter were overwhelmed by the economic and military power of the former. Within Europe, power shifted to the nations that were most industrial. Britain was the first to industrialize, and it was the dominant political power throughout the nineteenth century. Britain was widely admired and seen not only as an economic model but also as a political and cultural one. As France had been the dominant power in the eighteenth century, so Britain dominated the nineteenth, a stellar accomplishment for a small island nation.

Transformations Accompanying Industrialization

A number of transformations preceded or accompanied and helped define the industrializing era. Changes in commerce, agriculture, transportation,

~ ENCOUNTERS WITH THE WEST ~

A Persian Discovers the British Rail System

In 1836 a delegation of three Persian princes visited England. Traveling widely, they had the opportunity to meet important Englishmen and to inspect and experience some of the new technological advances, including the railroad. One of the princes, Najaf-Kuli Mirza, wrote down his observations. In this entry on the new British rail system, he attempts to describe its workings to fellow Persians.

All the wonderful arts which require strong power are carried on by means of steam, which has rendered immense profits and advantages. The English then began to think of steam coaches, which are especially applicable to their country, because it is small, but contains an enormous population. Therefore, in order to do away with the necessity for horses, and that the land which is sown with horse-corn [rye] should be cultivated with wheat, so as to cause it to become much more plentiful (as it is the most important article of food), and that England might thereby support a much greater population, they have with their ingenious skill invented this miraculous wonder, so as to have railroads from the capital to all parts of the kingdom.

Thus, by geometrical wisdom, they have made roads of iron, and where it was necessary these roads are elevated on arches. The roads on which the coaches are placed and fixed are made of iron bars. The coach is so fixed that no air or wind can do it any harm and twenty or thirty coaches may be fixed to the first in the train, and these one after the other.

All that seems to draw these coaches is a box of iron, in which they put water to boil, as in a fire-place; underneath this iron box is like an urn, and from it rises the steam which gives the wonderful force: when the steam rises up, the wheels take their motion, the coach spreads its wings, and the travellers become like birds. In this way these coaches go the incredible distance of forty miles an hour.

We actually travelled in this coach, and we found it very agreeable, and it does not give more but even less motion than horses; whenever we came to the sight of a distant place, in a second we passed it. The little steam engine possesses the power of eighteen horses.

Source: Najaf-Kuli Mirza, *Journal of a Residence in England and of a Journey to and from Syria* II (London, 1839, Reprinted, Farnborough, England: Gregg International Publishers, 1971), pp. 11–12.

and behavior of the population, if not always creating the preconditions of industrial development, were at least the major stimuli making them possible.

Changes in agriculture increased the productivity of the land. Farmers more frequently used fertilizer and improved the rotation of their crops, easing the exhaustion of the soil. New, more efficient plows enabled them to cultivate more land than ever before. In the eighteenth century, new crops that provided high yields even in poor soil were introduced into Europe: maize (corn) and potatoes from the Americas (see page 688). The wealth created by agriculture allowed for investment in industry and for expenditures on infrastructure, such as roads and canal systems, useful to industry. A wealthier landed class could purchase manufactured goods such as iron plows and even machine-woven textiles, thus providing an impetus for industry. Most important, the new crops and the more efficient cultivation of traditional ones increased the capacity to feed a growing population and freed many people to go to the city and work in the industries.

In the seventeenth and eighteenth centuries, European trade had increased significantly, enriching businessmen and making them aware of the fortunes to be made by marketing goods that were in demand not just locally but even far away. A new dynamic ethos took hold of businessmen eager to venture into untried fields of economic endeavor.

Population grew during the years of the industrial transformation. It was significant enough to promote industrialization, yet not so large as to put a brake on economic expansion. The first spurt in population growth occurred in the mid-eighteenth century, before the effects of industrialization could be widely felt. Thereafter the population of Europe increased dramatically throughout the industrial era: from 1750 to 1850 it grew by 100 percent.

The growth was largely due to a lowering of the death rate. Infant mortality had been very high from diseases such as smallpox and tuberculosis. Although none of these diseases had been medically conquered, improved standards of living after 1750, such as greater food intake, enabled children to better resist killer diseases. Better employment opportunities led to earlier marriages and thus higher fertility. Most of the population increase occurred in the countryside. This growing group of people supplied the labor force for the new industries and provided the large surge in consumers of various industrial goods.

In the countryside industrialization was foreshadowed by a form of production that had developed beginning in the seventeenth century—the putting-out system or cottage industry (see page 690). During the winter and at other slack times, peasants took in handwork such as spinning, weaving, or dyeing. Often they were marginal agriculturists, who on a part-time basis were able to augment their incomes. Entrepreneurs discovered that some individuals were better than others at specific tasks. Rather than have one household process the wool through all the steps of production until it was a finished piece, the entrepreneur would buy wool from one family, then take it to another to spin, a third to dye, a fourth to weave, and so on.

Some historians believe that this form of production, also called *protoindustrialization,* laid the basis for industrial manufacture. Like the latter it depended on specialization and supplied goods to a market beyond the producers' needs. In some ar-

eas, for instance, Flanders and northern Italy, protoindustry was followed by industrial manufacture; in other regions, such as western France, it became a substitute for industry. In still other areas, like Catalonia and the Ruhr region of western Germany, industry flourished without the previous development of cottage industries. Although cottage industry was an important contributor to industrialization in some regions, it did not play a role in every case.

A less ambiguous prerequisite for industry was a good transportation network. Transportation improved significantly in the eighteenth century. Better roads were built; coaches and carriages were constructed to travel faster and carry larger loads. Government and private companies built canals linking rivers to each other or to lakes. Road- and canal-building were important preconditions for industrialization, hastening and cheapening transportation and making possible the movement of raw materials to manufacture and from there to market without too great an increase in the price of the finished good. In Great Britain these transformations occurred simultaneously with industrialization; on the Continent they were actual precursors to economic change.

In Britain, industrialization preceded rail-building; yet once railroad expansion occurred, beginning in the 1830s, the order for iron rails, steam engines, and wagons sustained and advanced industrial growth. (See the box, "Encounters with the West: A Persian Discovers the British Rail System," on page 777.) On the Continent rail-building promoted industrialization, notably in Germany and later in Italy.

INDUSTRIALIZATION AND EUROPEAN PRODUCTION

Several important technological advances powered European industry, and breakthroughs in one field often led to breakthroughs in others. The first two industries to be affected by major technological breakthroughs were textiles and iron. New forms of energy drove the machinery; novel forms of directing labor and organizing management further enhanced production. At first limited to the British Isles, industry spread to the Continent, a development that occurred unevenly in various regions and at different times.

Advances in the Cotton Industry

A series of inventions in the eighteenth century led the way to the mass manufacture of textiles. One of the earliest was the flying shuttle, introduced in Britain in 1733 by John Kay (1704–1764). It accelerated the weaving process to such an extent that it increased the demand for thread. This need was met in the 1760s by James Hargreaves (d. 1778), who invented the spinning jenny, a device that spun thread from wool or cotton. Improved spinning machines, such as the "mule" of Samuel Crompton (1753–1827), made the spinning jenny increasingly efficient, and by 1812 one spinner could produce as much yarn as two hundred had made before the invention of the jenny. In 1769

Richard Arkwright (1732–1792), a barber and wigmaker, invented the water frame. This huge spinning machine drove two pairs of rollers, moving at different speeds. It was installed in a single establishment with three hundred employees, forming the first modern factory. The frame was originally powered by horses or by a waterfall, but in 1777 Arkwright had James Watt construct a steam engine to operate it. With these innovations, cotton manufacturing increased 130-fold between 1770 and 1841.

In the past, finished cloth had been soaked in buttermilk and spread out in the meadows to be bleached by the sun. That method was hardly practical for the unprecedented quantities of cloth rolling out of the factories. The introduction of

British Cotton Manufacture Machines simultaneously performed various functions. The carding machine (front left) separated cotton fibers, readying them for spinning. The roving machine (front right) wound the cotton onto spools. The drawing machine (rear left) wove patterns into the cloth. Rich in machines, this factory needed relatively few employees; most were women and children. *(The Granger Collection, New York)*

MAJOR INVENTIONS OF THE INDUSTRIAL TRANSFORMATION

1708	Use of coke in blast furnaces by Abraham Darby
1712	Steam-operated water pump by Thomas Newcomen
1733	Flying shuttle by John Kay
1764	Spinning jenny by James Hargreaves
1769	Water frame by Richard Arkwright
	Improved steam engine by James Watt
1776	Steam engine–operated machinery by James Watt
1779	The "mule" by Samuel Crompton
1784	Chlorine gas as a textile bleach by Claude Berthollet
1793	Cotton gin by Eli Whitney

sulfuric acid solved the problem. It was a far more economical bleach than buttermilk and sunlight, and it could be produced in commercial quantities. It in turn was replaced in the 1790s when the Frenchman C. L. Berthollet (1748–1822) discovered the bleaching powers of chlorine gas. Entrepreneurs or artisans made many of the other industrial inventions, but the breakthroughs in bleaching demonstrated that more and more, industry would be fueled by advances in scientific knowledge and training.

The cotton-manufacturing industry in Great Britain represented another important departure. For the first time in history a staple industry was based on a natural resource that was not domestically provided. Grown mainly in the U.S. South, cotton was transformed into cloth in Britain.

Manufactured cotton was comfortable to wear and easy to wash and became so cheap that it competed effectively with all handmade textiles. The popularity of cotton may have improved public health as well, for it enabled people to own several changes of clothing and keep them clean. Everyone was eager to buy British cottons. The higher demand for raw material put pressure on cotton growers in the U.S. South, who opened up new land.

In 1793, the American Eli Whitney (1765–1825) invented the cotton gin, a device that mechanically removed the seeds from cotton. The cotton gin meant that more cotton could be processed and thus more could be grown. It heightened the profitability of the United States's southern plantation economy, and that situation increased the attractiveness of slave labor. The second half of the eighteenth century marked the height of the slave trade. Between 1750 and 1800 approximately 3 million Africans were forcibly transported to the New World.

The cotton industry in Britain is an example of how local manufacturing may produce a ripple effect across the oceans. Among those benefiting overseas were American farmers, cotton traders, and merchants, as well as consumers of English cotton cloth around the world. Elsewhere, people were adversely affected—in Africa, where slaving raids increased, and in India, where local spinners were driven out of business.

In ways beneficial and not, people were interconnected by the cotton trade; later other products would also link the economies of various nations and peoples. No longer, as in preindustrial trade, were all goods locally made, nor did the consumer meet producers and buy from them. Increasingly, specialization became the norm. Those best fit performed a particular function efficiently and productively. The results were high production and low price for the finished product.

Iron, Steam, and Factories

Charcoal had traditionally fueled the smelting of iron. Britain, however, ran out of wood before other European countries did and needed an alternative source of fuel. There was plenty of coal, but it contained impurities, particularly sulfur, which contaminated the materials with which it came into contact. In 1708, Abraham Darby (1677–1717), an English ironmaster, discovered that coal in a blast furnace could smelt iron without these attending complications. His discovery triggered the iron industry's use of coal. In 1777, the introduction of a steam engine to operate the blast furnace considerably increased efficiency. In 1783, a steam engine was used to drive a forge hammer to shape the iron; three years later, steam-driven rollers rolled the iron into sheets. With these innovations, the output of the English iron industry doubled between 1788 and 1796 and again in the following eight years.

The greater supply of iron stimulated other changes. Relatively cheap and durable iron machines replaced wooden machines, which wore out rapidly. The new machines fueled further advances. Improvements in manufacturing methods and techniques led to the production of ever larger amounts of goods, usually at lower prices. Industrial change started with cotton but was continued and sustained by breakthroughs in the use of iron and coal.

Before the age of industry, the basic sources of power were humans, animals, wind, and water. Humans and animals were limited in their capacity to drive the large mills needed to grind corn or operate a sawmill. Wind was unreliable because it was not constant. Water-driven mills depended on the seasons—streams dried up in the summer and froze in the winter. And water mills could be placed only where there was a waterfall. Clearly what was needed was a power source that was constant and that could be located just about anywhere. The steam engine, invented and improved on in Britain, met that need and stoked the island's industrial growth. As late as the 1860s more than half of the energy needs of manufacturing in Great Britain and the United States were still supplied by people, animals, and wind- and water-operated machines. But the steam engine was clearly the wave of the future.

The steam engine was first used to pump out coal mines. As mining shafts were dug ever deeper, water in the mines became an increasing hindrance. In 1712 Thomas Newcomen (1663–1729) invented a steam-operated water pump. Its use spread rapidly. The first steam engine in the Americas was a Newcomen engine installed in New Jersey in 1753. James Watt (1736–1819) improved on the Newcomen engine considerably, making it twice as efficient in energy output. Eventually he made it capable of converting the reciprocating motion of the piston to rotary motion. This breakthrough enabled the steam engine to power a variety of machines. Thus, mills that had been powered by water or wind could be operated by steam engines. Further changes improved Watt's engines—most notably, the invention of the powerful and energy-efficient high-pressure steam engine. The use of steam engines spread in Britain, to the Continent, and to the United States.

Newcomen Engine Thomas Newcomen, an iron-monger, produced the first successful operating steam engine in 1712. Steam was introduced into a cylinder that was then cooled, creating a partial vacuum. The pressure of the atmosphere forced the piston down, pulling down one end of the beam, creating a pumping stroke. The engine could make as many as fourteen pumping strokes a minute. (*The Fotomas Index*)

The steam engine centralized the workplace. With the machine as a central power source, it became practical and commonplace to organize work in a central factory. The location of a factory where it was most convenient eliminated the expense of transporting raw materials to be worked on at a power source such as a waterfall. The central factory also reinforced work discipline. These factories were large, austere edifices inspired sometimes by military architecture and therefore resembling barracks. With the introduction of blast furnaces and other heat-producing manufacturing methods, the tall factory chimney became a common sight on the industrial landscape.

Factories ranged in size from small food-manufacturing operations to large textile mills. In the first half of the nineteenth century, the average number of employees in both English and French textile mills was between 200 and 300. Some plants were big, but by 1850 the small workshop, worked by the owner and his relatives or by a handful of employees, was still the most common site of manufacturing in Britain.

British production became truly industrial only after 1850. For decades industry coexisted with the artisan trades and other nonindustrial occupations, and indeed in a number of cases it aided their growth. Cheap industrially manufactured thread allowed handweaving to survive. Skilled craftsmen made by hand many of the machines and boilers used in factories. Income from the new industries created a wealthy middle class, which consumed more handmade goods and employed a great number of domestic servants; except for agriculture, domestic service was the single largest field of employment for women. By 1850 factory labor did not yet dominate the economy of western Europe, but it had become clear that the mechanized factory had overwhelming advantages and that it would be increasingly difficult for handmade products to compete.

The steam engine powered a dramatic growth in production. It increased the force of blast furnaces and the mechanical power of machinery used to forge iron and to produce equipment for spinning and weaving. In Britain cotton production grew 200-fold between 1740 and 1840, more than 400-fold between 1840 and 1860. Assisted by machines, workers were enormously more productive than when they depended on hand-operated tools. In 1700 spinning 100 pounds of cotton took 50,000 worker-hours; by 1825, it took only 135—a 370-fold increase in productivity capacity per worker.

Inventions and Entrepreneurs

The industrial age was triggered by inventions, and it was sustained by the continued flow of new ones. In the decade 1700–1709, 22 patents were issued in Britain; between 1840 and 1849, 4581 had been issued. Something revolutionary was occurring. People were seeing in their lifetime sizable growth in productivity, both in the factory and on the farm. Rather than cling to traditional methods, many entrepreneurs consciously and persistently challenged tradition and attempted to find new ways of improving production. In this age of invention, invention was prized as never before.

Most of the early industrialists belonged to merchant families. In Britain, very few were landed noblemen, industrial workers, or artisans. However, in the iron industry, it was not uncommon for metalworkers to build up a modest iron mill and then enlarge it. That was also the case with potters. Josiah Wedgwood (1730–1795), who pioneered the industrial manufacturing of china, came from a long line of artisan potters and is a good example of a self-made man. The thirteenth child of a potter, who died when Josiah was 9 years old, he went to work for his brother as an apprentice and gradually established himself on his own. Richard Arkwright was a barber before his invention of the water frame brought him a knighthood and a personal fortune of half a million pounds. Many entrepreneurs began as farmers, then became involved in the putting-out system, and then graduated to industrial manufacture. A disproportionate number of the early manufacturers were university educated, a fact suggesting that even in the early stages of industry, scientific knowledge was valuable. In fact, the self-made man was more the exception than the rule. Most entrepreneurs came from relatively privileged backgrounds.

Entrepreneurs such as Arkwright and Watt pioneered innovations and became famous, but most who advanced the cause of industrial production were not particularly inventive. They just replicated methods of production that had proved profitable to others. Truly successful entrepreneurs, however, seemed to share one attribute: They were driven by a nearly insatiable appetite for innovation, work, and profit. Near the mid-nineteenth century mark, one of the most successful French textile tycoons advised his son, "One seeks by means of imagination, by means of effort, to surpass one's neighbor; therefore, work, work, always work."

Entrepreneurs took the financial risk of investing in new types of enterprises. Most entrepreneurs by themselves or with a partner ran a single plant, but even in the early stages, some ran several plants. In 1788, Richard Arkwright and his partners ran eight mills. Some enterprises were vertically integrated, controlling production at the various stages. The Peels in Britain owned enterprises ranging from spinning to printing and even banking. The entrepreneurs' dynamism and boldness fostered the growth of the British industrial system, making the small nation the "workshop of the world."

Britain's Lead in Industrial Innovation

Britain led the way industrially for many reasons. It was the first European country to have a standard currency, tax, and tariff system. It enjoyed the most emancipated labor. Although Britain was by no means an egalitarian society, it accommodated some movement between the classes. Ideas and experiments were readily communicated among entrepreneurs, workers, and scientists. Although other countries had scientific societies, several societies in Britain brought together theoreticians and practical businessmen—for example, the Lunar Society in Birmingham and the Literary and Philosophical Society in Manchester.

Britain was far more open to dissent than were other European countries at the time. The lack of conformity was reflected in religion, and also in a willingness to try new methods of production. In fact, the two often went together. A large proportion of British entrepreneurs were Quakers or belonged to one of the dissenting (non-Anglican) religious groups—for instance, the ironmaking Darby family, the engineer of the steam engine James Watt, and the inventor of the "mule" Samuel Crompton. Perhaps they were accustomed to questioning authority and treading new paths. They were also well educated and, as a result of common religious bonds, inclined to provide mutual aid, including financial support.

England had gained an increasing share of international trade since the seventeenth century. This trade provided capital for investment in industrial plants. The world trade network also ensured that Britain had a market beyond its borders, and because aggregate demand was relatively high, mass manufacture was feasible. The international network built up by trade also enabled Britain to import raw materials for its industry, the most important of which was cotton.

Earlier than its competitors, Britain had a national banking system that could provide capital to industries in areas where it was needed. In addition to numerous London banks lending mainly in the capital, there were by 1810 six hundred pro-

Map 21.1 The Industrial Transformation in England, ca. 1850 Industry developed in the areas rich in coal and iron fields. Important cities sprang up nearby and were linked to each other by a growing rail network.

vincial banks. The banking system reflected the growth of the economy as much as it contributed to it. Banking could flourish because Britons had wide experience in trade, had accumulated considerable amounts of wealth, and had found a constant demand for credit.

Geographically, Britain was also fortunate. Coal and iron were located close to each other (Map 21.1). A relatively narrow island, Britain has easy access to the sea—no part of the country is more than 70 miles from a seacoast. This was a strategic advantage, for water was by far the cheapest means of transportation. Compared to the Continent, Britain had few tolls, and goods could move around easily.

On the whole, British workers were better off than their continental counterparts. They were more skilled, earned higher wages, and had discretionary income to spend on the manufactured goods now for sale. But because their wages were higher than wages on the Continent, there was an incentive for British business owners to find labor-saving devices and reduce the number of workers needed for production.

Population growth in Great Britain—in part the result of industrial growth—increased by 8 percent in each decade from 1750 to 1800. This swelling population expanded the market for goods. The most rapid growth occurred in the countryside, causing a steady movement of people from rural to urban areas. The presence of this work force was another contributing factor in Britain's readiness for change.

The timing of the industrial transformation in Britain was also influenced by plentiful harvests in the years 1715–1750, creating low food prices and thus making possible low industrial wages. The demand for industrial goods was reasonably high. Farmers with good earnings could afford to order the new iron manufactured plows. It is likely that the income from farming helped bring about changes associated with industrialization, such as population growth, improvements to the transportation system, and the growing availability of capital for investment. Thus, each change triggered more change, and the cumulative effect was staggering (see Map 21.1).

The Spread of Industry to the Continent

The ideas and methods that were changing industry in Britain spread to the Continent by direct contact and emulation. Visitors came to Britain, studied local methods of production, and returned home to set up blast furnaces and spinning works inspired by British design. The German engineer August Börsig (1804–1854), after studying steam engines in Britain, built the first German steam engine in 1825 and the first German locomotive in 1842. Some visitors even resorted to industrial espionage, smuggling blueprints of machines out of Britain. Although a British law forbade local artisans from emigrating, some did leave, including entrepreneurs who helped set up industrial plants in France and Belgium. By the 1820s British technicians were all over Europe—in Belgium, France, Germany, and as far east as Austria.

Belgium was the first country on the Continent to industrialize, perhaps because, like Britain, Belgium had iron and coal in proximity (Map 21.2). Belgium also had a long tradition of working cloth and iron and could readily adapt new methods to increase production of both. Belgium's location on the route between Britain and Germany fostered the development of railroads. And rail-building facilitated industrialization not only by providing fast and cheap transportation but also by stimulating the iron industry. In 1840, there were 200 miles of rail in Belgium; twenty years later, there were 1200 miles. Belgium was more densely equipped with railroads than any European country. The Belgian government encouraged industrial modernization by building railroads and investing in the shipping industry. In the early years it kept tariffs high to protect nascent industries; later it negotiated free-trade agreements providing expanded markets for its manufacturers.

In the eighteenth century France seemed a more likely candidate for economic growth than Britain. France's overseas trade was growing faster than Britain's. In 1780, France's industrial output was greater than Britain's, though production per person was less. In the nineteenth century, however, while Britain's industry boomed and it became the workshop of the world, France lagged behind. Why?

Historians have suggested several reasons. The war and revolutions of the late eighteenth century were certainly contributing factors. They slowed economic growth and cut France off from the flow of information and new techniques from Britain. Moreover, in the 1790s, when the French peasants pressured for legislation to ease their situation, the revolutionaries responded positively. Thus, the misery of the peasantry was somewhat relieved, and peasants were comfortable enough to feel no urgency to leave the land and provide the kind of cheap and ready labor that Britain had. Further, the Napoleonic Code of 1804 abolished primogeniture, so that when a peasant died, his younger sons were not forced off the land.

Population figures suggest another reason for France's relatively low economic growth. Between 1800 and 1914, the population of France grew at half the average rate of the rest of the Continent. In Britain during this period, much of the labor that left the land and worked the factories and mills came from the rural population explosion;

Map 21.2 Continental Industrialization, ca. 1850 Despite the fact that industry had begun on the Continent by the mid-nineteenth century, it was still sparse there, as was the rail network.

but no such phenomenon occurred in the French countryside, and thus the labor force in France was not as available for industrial growth.

Traditionally France had produced high-quality luxury goods, and French entrepreneurs who sought to emulate British accomplishments faced serious difficulties. Iron and coal in France were not close together (see Map 21.2). Labor was still quite cheap; there was no incentive to invest in labor-saving machines, because goods still could be manufactured inexpensively by hand. Soon, however, French manufacturers found themselves facing British competition. By being the first to industrialize, the British had the advantage of being able to manufacture goods and to corner markets efficiently and relatively cheaply. The French were

the first to feel the negative effects of being an industrial latecomer.

Although France's growth rate was lower than that of its neighbors, the French economy experienced slow but nearly constant growth throughout the nineteenth century. When population is taken into account, the French did better than Great Britain and only slightly less well than Germany. From 1810 to 1850, both the production of coal and the consumption of raw cotton quintupled. In 1830 France had 130 steam-driven machines; by 1852 it had 16,000. In ceramics, glass, porcelain, and paper manufacturing, France was a pioneer. Most French manufacturing, however, remained small; the typical firm had a handful of employees. Production by artisans, rather than by mass industrial production, continued longer there than in Britain or Germany.

The invasions of Germany by Napoleon caused considerable destruction, but they also brought some positive economic benefits. The example of the French Revolution led to important socioeconomic changes. Restrictive guilds declined. The French occupiers suppressed the small German states with their many tariffs and taxes, established a single unified legal system—which survived even after 1815—and introduced a single standard of measurement based on the metric system.

Government in Germany played an important role in the adoption of improved methods of manufacturing. The Prussian state, eager for industrial development, sent an official to Britain to observe the puddling process (the method by which iron is freed of carbon) and bring that know-how back to Prussia. The Prussian government promoted in-

dustrial growth by investing in a transportation network to carry raw materials for processing and finished goods to their markets. To spur both trade and industrial growth, Prussia took the lead in creating a customs union, the Zollverein, which abolished tariffs among its members. By 1834 a German market embracing eighteen German states with a population of 23 million had been created.

German industrial growth accelerated dramatically in the 1850s. Massive expenditures on railways created a large demand for metal, which pressured German manufacturers to enlarge their plant capacities and increase efficiency. Germany was not yet politically unified, but the German middle classes saw economic growth as the means by which their country could win a prominent place among Europe's nation-states. Germany's growth was phenomenal. It successfully emulated Britain, overtook France, and toward the end of

The Börsig Ironworks in the 1840s August Börsig, an artisan, founded these ironworks in Berlin. The factory expanded to meet the needs of the burgeoning German rail system. By the time of Börsig's death in 1854, his factory had built five hundred locomotives. *(Bildarchiv Preussischer Kulturbesitz)*

the nineteenth century served as a pioneer in the electrical engineering and chemical industries. If France experienced the disadvantages of being a latecomer, Germany reaped the benefits of that situation. The Germans were able to avoid costly and inefficient early experimentation and adapt the latest methods; moreover, Germany entered fields that Britain had neglected.

Even by the end of the century, however, progress remained slow in many areas of Europe. As long as Russia retained serfdom (until 1861), it would lack the mobile labor force needed for industrial growth. And until late in the century, the ruling Russian aristocracy hesitated to adopt an economic system in which wealth was not based on land. In Austria, Bohemia was the only important industrial center; otherwise, Austria was heavily agrarian (see Map 21.2).

The impoverished southern Mediterranean countries experienced little economic growth. With mostly poor soil, their agriculture yielded only a meager surplus. Spain, lacking coal and access to other energy sources, could not easily diversify its economic base. There was some industry in Catalonia, especially around Barcelona, but it was limited in scope and did not have much impact on the rest of the country. The Italian peninsula was still industrially underdeveloped in the middle of the nineteenth century. There were modest advances, but growth was too slow to have a measurable positive impact on the Italian economy. In 1871, 61 percent of the population of Italy was still agrarian.

Although by midcentury only a few European nations had experienced industrialization to any great extent, many more would do so by the end of the century, pressured by severe competition from their more advanced neighbors (Figure 21.1). The potential threat was political and military as well as economic, for the industrialized nations represented military might and superiority. As compared to the rest of the world, the European continent in the nineteenth century had acquired a distinct material culture that was increasingly based on machine manufacture or recognized to be in the process of becoming so. The possession of "skillful industry," one Victorian writer exulted, was "ever a proof of superior civilization." Although only some regions of Europe were industrialized, many Europeans came to view their continent as obviously "superior," while the

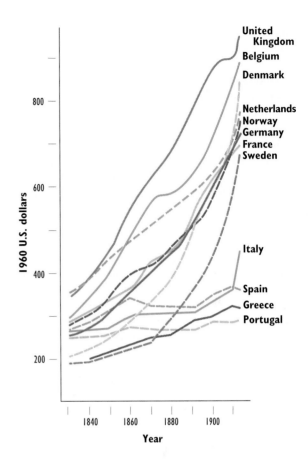

Figure 21.1 The Increase in Gross National Product per Capita in Principal European Countries, 1830–1913
The countries that industrialized rapidly—such as the United Kingdom in particular, and also Belgium, France, and Germany—experienced dramatic increase in per capita income during the nineteenth century. Other countries such as Greece and Portugal economically trailed the industrial leaders, and per capita income remained essentially flat. (*Source:* Norman J. G. Pounds, *An Historical Geography of Europe, 1800–1914* [New York: Cambridge University Press, 1985], p. 32. Used by permission of Cambridge University Press.)

other continents were in comparison deemed to be "inferior."

THE TRANSFORMATION OF EUROPE AND ITS ENVIRONMENT

Industry changed the traditional methods of agriculture, commerce, trade, and manufacture. It also transformed people's lives, individually and collectively. It altered how they made a livelihood, where and how they lived, and how they thought of themselves. Industry's need of people with specialized skills created new occupations. Because industry required specialization, the range of occupations that people adopted expanded dramatically.

The advent of industry transformed the way society functioned. Until the eighteenth century, the basis of influence and power was hereditary privilege, which meant aristocratic birth and land. The aristocracy did not disappear overnight. In the late eighteenth century, however, it was challenged by a rising class of people whose wealth was self-made and whose influence was based on economic contributions to society rather than on bloodlines. Increased social mobility opened opportunities even for some workers. Industrialization transformed both the social and the natural environment. Cities grew dramatically as a result of industrialization, and Europeans faced urban problems and the pollution of their air and water.

Urbanization and Its Discontents

A sociologist at the end of the nineteenth century observed, "The most remarkable social phenomenon of the present century is the concentration of population in cities."[3] The number and size of cities grew as never before. The major impetus for urban growth was the concentration of industry in cities and the resulting need of large numbers of urban workers and their families for goods and services (Map 21.3).

Industrialization was not the only stimulus. France provides many examples of urban growth with little industry. Increased commercial, trading, and administrative functions led to the growth of cities such as Toulouse, Bordeaux, and Nancy. Neither Holland, Italy, nor Switzerland experienced much industrial development in the first half of the nineteenth century, yet their cities grew. In general, however, industry transformed people from rural to urban inhabitants. People wanted to live near their work, and as industries concentrated in cities, so did populations.

Urban growth in some places was dramatic. In the entire eighteenth century, London grew by only 200,000; but in the first half of the nineteenth century, it grew by 1.4 million, more than doubling its size. Liverpool and Manchester experienced similar growth in the same period. Census figures show that by 1851 Britain was a predominantly urban society, the first country to have as many people living in cities as in the countryside. For Germany that date was 1891, and for France it was 1931. Although the proportion of people who were urban varied from place to place, the trend was clear and has continued.

In some cases factories were built in the countryside at a distance from towns, and as they prospered, cities grew up around them. The steelworks in Le Creusot, France, followed that pattern. In 1846 Le Creusot had 6000 inhabitants; in 1860, 16,000; by 1875, 25,000. In other cases industry gave rise to dramatic growth in once-modest towns—for instance, the west German town of Essen. In 1850 Essen had 9000 inhabitants; by 1900 its population had increased 30-fold. Occasionally, industry actually led to people leaving a city, when manufacturers located on the outskirts of urban areas or when subcontracting expanded the work of people involved in the putting-out system. But such an outward flow was unusual.

As the pace of industry governed in part urban growth, it was fueled in turn by urbanization. Large cities provided convenient markets for goods and a labor pool for manufacturing. The concentration of people encouraged the exchange of ideas. A large city was likely to have scientific societies and laboratories in which engineers and scientists could discuss new ideas and new inventions that would encourage industrial production. After midcentury, industrialization was driven more and more by scientific and technological breakthroughs made in urban environments.

Cities pulled in people from near and far. Usually, the larger the city, the stronger its ability to attract migrants from great distances. The medium-sized French town of Saint-Etienne drew migrants from the nearby mountains, while Paris drew from the entire country. Industrial centers attracted people from beyond the nation's borders. The Irish arrived in large numbers to work in the factories in Lancashire, Belgians came for mine work in northern France, and Poles sought employment in the Ruhr in western Germany. Industrial activity stimulated the growth of world trade and shipping across the seas, taking merchant sailors far from home. Africans and Asians inhabited port cities such as Amsterdam, Marseille, and Liverpool. Many large cities were marked by heterogeneous populations, which included people

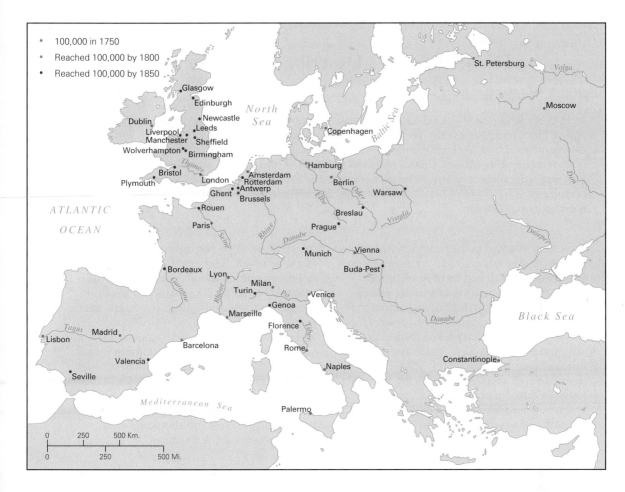

Map 21.3 Cities Reaching Population Level of 100,000 by 1750, 1800, and 1850 In 1750 the largest cities owed their existence to factors other than industry, but thereafter the development of industry often determined the growth of cities. England, the leading industrial nation, contained many of the largest cities. (*Source:* Data from Tertius Chandler, *Four Thousand Years of Urban Growth: An Historical Census* [Lewistown, N.Y.: St. David's University Press, 1987], pp. 22–24.)

with different native languages, religions, and national origins, as well as, in some cases, people of different races.

With the growth of cities came a multitude of urban ills. In the first half of the nineteenth century, mortality rates were higher in the cities than in the countryside. In the 1840s Britain as a whole had a death rate of 22 per thousand, but Liverpool averaged 39.2 and Manchester 33.1. In France national mortality rates were around 22 per thousand, but in some French cities the rate was as high as 35 per thousand. There was a dramatic social inequality in the face of death. Including the high child mortality rate, the average age at death for members of gentry families in Liverpool in 1842 was 35; for members of laborers's families it was 15. In 1800 boys living in urban slums were 8 inches shorter than their more fortunate contemporaries.

The rapid growth of the cities caught local authorities unprepared, and in the early stages of industrialization city life was particularly severe for the poor. Urban slums developed. The most notorious London slum was St. Giles, which became a tourist attraction because of its squalor. (See the box, "Friedrich Engels Describes an Urban Slum.") In many cities, large numbers of people were crammed into small areas. The houses were built back to back on small lots and had insufficient

Friedrich Engels Describes an Urban Slum

In 1845 the young socialist Friedrich Engels, who later became Karl Marx's literary partner, pub-
lished **The Condition of the Working Class in England.** *Having lived in England in 1842–1844,*
Engels on his return to Germany provided a lively description of the hardships facing the English
industrial working classes. Critics then and later noted that Engels, motivated by socialist zeal,
at times exaggerated the misery he encountered. His description of the urban slum, however, was
corroborated by many of his contemporaries. In this selection he describes St. Giles, one of the
worst slums of London.

St. Giles is situated in the most densely-popu-
lated part of London. . . . It is a confused conglomeration of tall houses of three or four
stories. The narrow, dirty streets are just as
crowded as the main thoroughfares, but in St.
Giles one sees only members of the working
classes. The houses are packed from cellar to
attic and they are as dirty inside as outside. No
human being would willingly inhabit such
dens. Yet even worse conditions are to be
found in the houses which lie off the main road
down narrow alleys leading to the courts.
These dwellings are approached by covered
passages between the houses. The extent to
which these filthy passages are falling into decay beggars all description. There is hardly an
unbroken windowpane to be seen, the walls
are crumbling, the door posts and window
frames are loose and rotten. The doors, where
they exist, are made of old boards nailed together. Indeed in this nest of thieves doors are
superfluous, because there is nothing worth
stealing. Piles of refuse and ashes lie all over
the place and the slops thrown out into the
street collect in pools which emit a foul stench.
Here live the poorest of the poor. Here the
worst-paid workers rub shoulders with
thieves, rogues and prostitutes.

Source: Friedrich Engels, *The Condition of the Working Class in England,* trans. and ed. W. O. Henderson and W. H.
Chaloner (Stanford, Calif.: Stanford University Press, 1968), pp. 33–34.

lighting and ventilation. Overcrowding was the
norm. One study of a working-class parish in central London in midcentury showed three-quarters
of the families living in single rooms. On one particular street, between twelve and twenty people
were sleeping in each room. In Preston in 1842,
2400 persons slept three to a bed. The proximity of
buildings blocked out sunlight. In the 1840s from
12 to 20 percent of people in Manchester and Liverpool were living in cellars.

Sanitation was rudimentary or nonexistent. A
single privy in a courtyard was likely to serve
dozens of tenants—in some notorious cases in
Britain and France, a few hundred. Waste from the
privy might drain through open sewers to a nearby
river, which was likely to be the local source of
drinking water. Or the privy might be connected to
a cesspool from which wastewater would seep and

contaminate nearby wells. Some tenants lacked
toilets and relieved themselves in the street. In the
1830s people living in the poorest sections of Glasgow stored human waste in heaps along their
houses and sold it as manure.

In the cities water was scarce and dirty. Piped
water was reserved for the rich. The poor had to
supply themselves from public fountains or wells
and were often obliged to carry water a considerable distance. In Birmingham in the middle of the
century, out of 40,000 houses only one-fifth had
running water. French cities were usually worse;
some of the major ones had only about two gallons of public water available per person a day.

In manufacturing towns factory chimneys
spewed soot, and everything was covered with
dirt and grime. Smoke and fog created the famous
London fog, which not only reduced visibility but

St. Giles The most notorious London slum was St. Giles, whose human squalor made it a tourist attraction. *(From Thomas Beames,* The Rookeries of London. *Courtesy Harvard University Library)*

posed serious health risks. City streets were littered with refuse; rotting corpses of dogs and horses were common. In 1858 the stench from sewage and other rot was so severe that the British House of Commons was forced to suspend its sessions.

At midcentury the city fathers of Marseille described the center of their city as "covered with old, narrow houses that are in ruins, where air and light hardly reach, [and] infected sewers spread epidemics." It is not surprising that cholera, a highly infectious disease transmitted through contaminated water, swept the city and other European urban centers. In the 1830s one of the first epidemics of modern times struck Europe, killing 100,000 in France, 50,000 in Britain, and 238,000 in Russia. The cholera epidemic of 1854 killed 150,000 Frenchmen. Typhoid fever, also an acute infectious disease, hit mostly the poor but did not spare the privileged. Queen Victoria of Great Britain nearly died of it, and her husband, Prince Albert, did.

For most of its denizens, the city provided a crowded and squalid environment. Only in the second half of the nineteenth century would any attempts be made to bring order to the chaos of urban life.

The Working Classes and Their Lot

In 1842 a middle-class observer traveling in industrial Lancashire noted that around the mills and factories there had developed a "population [that] like the system to which it belongs is NEW . . . hourly increasing in breadth and strength."[4] A French countess, using the pen name Daniel Stern, wrote in her memoirs of France in the 1830s and 1840s of the emergence of "a class apart, as if it were a nation within the nation," working in factories and mines, called "by a new name: the industrial proletariat."[5]

As industry advanced and spread, more and more people depended on it for a livelihood. In the putting-out system, when there was an agricultural downturn, a cottager could spend more time on hand labor, and when there was a slack in demand for hand labor, the cottager could devote more time to the land. But people living in industrial cities were totally dependent on manufacturing. And neither skilled nor unskilled workers were assured of regular employment: Any downturn in the economy translated into layoffs or loss of jobs.

In addition, the introduction of new industries often devastated laborers in older forms of production. The mechanization of cotton production reduced the earning power of weavers in England and in Flanders, for instance. The production of linen was mechanized in Belgium by the 1840s, but cotton production was so much cheaper that in order to price their wares competitively, linen producers drastically reduced their workers' wages.

Most factory work was dirty and laborious, in grim plants with heavy machinery. Sixteen-hour days were common. Child labor was widespread. Because there were no safety provisions, the workers were prone to accidents—especially new workers unaccustomed to work routines, or experienced workers untrained on new machines. Few factory owners protected their workers against dangerous substances or circumstances. Mercury used in hat manufacturing gradually poisoned the hatmakers and often led to dementia. There were sound reasons to speak of "mad hatters." Lead used in paints and pottery also had a devastating impact on workers' health. Metal grinding caused serious health problems. In Sheffield in 1842, three-quarters of the cutlery workers had lung disease by the age of 40. In the 1840s the British military rejected four of ten rural volunteers because of some health deficiency; in the industrializing cities the rate of rejection was 90 percent. In the industrial area of Saint-Etienne in France from 1836 to 1847, the average life expectancy of a farmer was 59 years, but that of a miner was 37 years.

Usually physically lighter than boys and often underfed, young girls were faced with heavy labor that undermined their health. In 1842, 18-year-old Ann Eggley, a mineworker since the age of 7, hauled carriages loaded with ore weighing 800 pounds, for twelve hours a day. She testified to a parliamentary commission that she was so tired from her work that when she came home she often fell asleep before even going to bed. Isabel Wilson, another mineworker, testified that she had given birth to ten children and had suffered five miscarriages. These women—overworked, exhausted, vulnerable to disease, and especially endangered by complications from giving birth—faced premature death. The mortality rate for adult women during the era of industrial transformation was slightly higher than that for men. This situation changed only toward the end of the nineteenth century, and today women outlive men.

Did industrialization improve the workers' lot? Perhaps the question is best answered by an-other question: What would the workers have done without industrial employment? A population explosion meant that many did not have enough land to make a living, and more efficient farming methods lessened the need for farm hands. It is not clear that these workers could have made a living if they had remained in the country.

Until the mid-nineteenth century, information on workers' income and expenses is incomplete. The best evidence comes from Britain, where an average family needed at least 21 shillings a week to escape from poverty. Skilled workers, who were in demand, might earn as much as 30 shillings a week, but most workers were unskilled. In Manchester in the mid-1830s, workmen producing coarse calicoes earned only between 6 and 8 shillings a week. And although a healthy, skilled male worker might earn 30 shillings, if he became less productive because of illness or old age, his wages fell. Thus, if women and children did not always need to work to help the family meet its minimum needs, at some point they usually did have to pitch in. Women who were the main breadwinners almost never received wages high enough to meet a family's total needs.

Incomes were so low that workers normally spent between two-thirds and three-fourths of their budget on food. Those who lived in rural areas might raise chickens or pigs or have a plot of potatoes. Bread was the largest single item consumed, varying between one and two pounds a day per person. In Britain and Germany people also ate a lot of potatoes. A little bacon or other meat gave flavor to the soup in which people dipped their bread or potatoes, but meat was rarely consumed as a main course. Because men were the chief breadwinners and tended to have the most strenuous occupation, they received the choice piece of meat and the largest amount of food. Women and children ate what was left.

Nevertheless, from the beginning, industrialization did increase wealth. "Optimist" historians argue that some of the new wealth trickled down to the lower levels of society. "Pessimist" historians say that a downward flow did not necessarily occur. Statistics suggest that by the 1840s workers' lives in Britain did improve. Their real income rose by 40 percent between 1800 and 1850. In part this advance was due to an increase in the numbers of skilled workers, who were paid more than their unskilled counterparts. And if factory workers' wages took time to improve, they were usually higher than wages in the handicrafts; in Lille, in northern France, in the 1830s women in spinning mills received wages one-quarter to one-half higher than those of lacemakers, whose work was done by hand.

Factory workers benefited not only from increased earnings but from the relatively low prices of many basic goods. In London, the price of 4 pounds of household bread fell from 15 pennies at the beginning of the nineteenth century to 8½ pennies in the 1830s. As the cost of cloth declined, there was a marked improvement in the dress of working-class people. On the Continent, the lot of workers improved a little later than in Britain, but the process followed the same pattern. In Germany workers' wages did not increase appreciably between 1800 and 1829, but by 1850 they had increased by 25 percent and by 1870 by another 50 percent. (See the feature, "Weighing the Evidence: Workers' Wages," on pages 808–809.)

Industrialization and the Family

Industrialization dramatically changed the character of the working-class family and household. Job segregation reserved the best-paying jobs for men; positions as foremen and the running of machinery such as the jenny were reserved for men. Especially in the textile industries, factory owners employed children and women in the lowliest positions. They were thought to be more pliable than men, and their wages were considerably lower. Women generally received from 30 to 50 percent of men's wages, children from 5 to 25 percent. In 1839 Thomas Heath, a weaver in Spitalfields, a London neighborhood, earned 15 shillings a week, his wife but 3 shillings.

Factory work often undermined the ability of women to take care of their children. As farmers or cottagers, women had been able simultaneously to work and to supervise their children; the factory, however, often separated mothers from their children. Many children were given heavy burdens at an early age, and it was not uncommon for an older child, sometimes only 5 or 6 years old, to be entrusted with the care of his or her sibling. Suzanne Monnier, the daughter of a French worker, described in her memoirs how her mother on giving birth had the 9-year-old Suzanne kiss her new sister

and then told her, "This is not a sister I am giving you, but a daughter."

Other workers resorted to more dangerous methods of child care. They might send a newborn to a "babyfarm," to individuals in the countryside who were paid to take care of the child. Very often these babies were neglected, and their mortality rate was extremely high. In many cases, babyfarming was no more than a camouflaged form of infanticide. Mothers who kept their children but were obliged to leave them unwatched at home during factory hours sometimes pacified the children by drugging them with mixtures of opium, readily available from the local druggist.

Working-class women carried a heavy burden in the family. In addition to sometimes working outside the home, they were responsible for running the household, managing the family income, and taking care of the children, providing most of the nurture and supervision they required. Because of the many demands on married women, their employment pattern often was affected by the life cycle. Young women might work before marriage, or before giving birth, then stay home until the children were older, and then return to work. Factory work had a harsh impact on women's lives, but it should be remembered that relatively few women were in the wage market— by 1850 only about a quarter in both Britain and France. And of that quarter few worked in factories; far more were in agriculture, crafts industries (which still flourished despite poor working conditions), and domestic service, with many of these women working part-time while their children were small.

Some sectors of industry had a large proportion of women in them—for instance, textiles. Other sectors, such as the metal and mining industries, were heavily male-dominated. In Belgium, however, women represented 15 percent of miners.

The textile industry found employment for children once they were over the age of 5 or 6. Their size made them useful for certain jobs, such as reaching under machines to pick up loose cotton. Because of their small hands they were also hired as "doffers," taking bobbins off frames and replacing them. Elizabeth Bentley began work as a doffer in 1815 at the age of 6. At the age of 23, when she testified before a parliamentary commission, she was "considerably deformed . . . in consequence of this labor." (See the box, "The

The Young Girl in the Factory

Reformers in Parliament, among them Michael Sadler, denounced the appalling conditions in the factories. Sadler was appointed to head a commission to hold hearings; workers appeared before it giving vivid descriptions of their lot. Public and parliamentary outrage at the conditions revealed by these hearings led to the Factory Act of 1833. Among the witnesses was Elizabeth Bentley, a 23-year-old weaving machine operative, who gave the following testimony.

What age are you?—23 . . .

What time did you begin to work in a factory?—When I was 6 years old. . . .

What were your hours of labor? . . . —From 5 in the morning till 9 at night, when they were thronged.

For how long have you worked that excessive length of time?—For about half a year.

What were your usual hours of labor when they were not so thronged?—From 6 in the morning till 7 at night.

What time was allowed for your meals?—40 minutes at noon. . . .

Your labor is very excessive?—Yes, you have not time for anything.

Suppose you flagged a little, or were too late, what would they do?—Strap us. . . .

Girls as well as boys?—Yes.

Severely?—Yes.

Could you eat your food well in that factory? —No, indeed, I had not much to eat, and the little I had I could not eat it, my appetite was so poor, and being covered with dust; and it was no use taking it home, I could not eat it . . . .

Did you live far from the mill?—Yes, two miles.

Had you a clock?—No, we had not. . . .

Were you generally there in time?—Yes; my mother has been up at four o'clock in the morning and at two o'clock; the colliers used to go to their work at about three or four o'clock, and when she heard them stirring she has got up out of her warm bed, and gone out and asked them the time; and I have sometimes been at Hunslet Car at 2 o'clock when it was steaming down with rain, and we have had to stay till the mill was opened [at 5 A.M.].

Source: Great Britain, *Sessional Papers, House of Commons,* Hearing of June 4, 1832, vol. XV (1831–1832), pp. 195–197.

Young Girl in the Factory.") Child labor certainly did not start with the industrial transformation; it had always existed. What was new was the harsh industrial discipline imposed on the children.

Although children were common in British textile industries, overall less than 10 percent of working children were in industry. Most were in agriculture or the service sector. In the early stages of industrialization, children were primarily employed in textile mills to pick up waste and repair broken threads. As technological advances reduced both problems, the need for children lessened.

Improved technology and the growth of industries other than textiles increased the employment of adult men. In iron and later steel plants, physical strength was essential. Despite the higher labor costs that resulted when men were employed, managers had no choice but to hire them. However, in France, where textiles were still the predominant product after the turn of the nineteenth century, women made up two-thirds of the work force as late as 1906.

In some cases, industrialization meant a transformation in the authority structure of workers' households, undermining the influence of the male as head of the household. A woman could make a living independent of her spouse, and children at a reasonably early age could emancipate themselves from their parents and make a go of it working in a factory or a mine. These options were not possible in agriculture or in the putting-out system. As in the putting-out system, however, often whole families were hired as a group to perform a specific function. Contemporaries sometimes denounced industry for dissolving family bonds, but the family remained an effective work unit.

If not participating in the wage market, wives and children contributed in other ways to the household budget—by making clothes, raising a pig, tending a potato patch, and performing daily household chores. Grandparents often moved from the country to live with the family and take care of children. A study of Verviers, an industrial city in eastern Belgium, showed that at mid-nineteenth century a sizable number of children over the age of 20 continued to live with their parents and to contribute to the financial well-being of the family unit. (See the feature, "Weighing the Evidence: Workers' Wages," on pages 808–809.) In the steel-manufacturing city of Solingen in western Germany, a cutlery worker known as Fritz B., the subject of a sociological study in 1851, lived with his wife and four children. All were contributing either in cash or in labor to the family's well-being. When industrial workers married, they often settled with their spouses on the same street or in the same neighborhood where their parents lived. Although industry had the potential to undermine traditional family structures, the historical evidence is that the family adjusted and survived the challenges posed by the new economic system.

The Land, the Water, and the Air

Industrialization seriously challenged as well the environment, transforming the surface of the earth, the water, and the air. To run the new machinery, coal was mined in increasing amounts (Table 21.1). Iron and other minerals were also in great demand. The exploitation of coal ushered in the modern age of energy use, in which massive amounts of nonrenewable resources are consumed.

To extract coal and other minerals, miners dug deep tunnels. Millions of tons of earth, rock, and other debris were removed from underground.

Table 21.1 Coal Production in Industrializing Nations

	Millions of tons	Kilograms per inhabitant
1700	4	26
1750	7	16
1800	16	76
1830	30	120
1860	129	390

Source: Based on B. R. Mitchell, "Statistical Appendix, 1700–1914," in Carlo Cippola, ed., *The Fontana Economic History of Europe,* vol. 4 (London: Collins, 1973), pp. 747, 770; and Norman J. G. Pounds, *An Historical Geography of Europe, 1500–1840* (New York: Cambridge University Press, 1979), pp. 268–269.

This material, plus slag and other waste from the factories, was heaped up in mounds that at times covered acres of land, creating new geological formations. In one district in England in 1870, a million cubic yards of soda waste occupied 50 acres.

With axes and saws people cut down trees, depleting forests to supply the wood needed to build shafts for coal, iron, and tin mines, or to make the charcoal necessary for glassmaking. Between 1750 and 1900, industrial and agricultural needs led to the clearing of 50 percent of all the forests ever cleared. Many of Europe's major forests disappeared or were seriously diminished. Deforestation in turn sped up soil erosion.

Industry changed the physical environment in which people lived. Forests, lakes, rivers, and air—as well as people themselves—showed the harmful effects of industry. Centrifugal pumps drained large marshes in the Fenland in eastern England. A contemporary lamented, "The wind which, in the autumn of 1851 was curling the blue water of the lake, in the autumn of 1853 was blowing in the same place over fields of yellow corn." Factories dumped waste ash into rivers, changing their channels and making them considerably shallower. Because of pollution from industrial and human waste, by 1850 no fish could survive in the lower Thames River. Smoke and soot darkened the skies, intensifying the fog over London and other cities. Foul odors from factories could be detected at several miles' distance. Not merely

Manchester, England, 1851 A small, unimportant town of 20,000 in the 1750s, Manchester—as a result of industrialization—had 400,000 inhabitants in 1850. In this 1851 painting, the polluted industrial city is contrasted with its idealized rural suburb. *(The Royal Collection © 1993 Her Majesty Queen Elizabeth II)*

unpleasant, various air pollutants caused cancer and lung disease.

RESPONSES TO INDUSTRIALIZATION

People in the new industrial classes living at subsistence levels were disquieting evidence of the impact of industrialization. What should be done about the working classes—or for them? These new classes developed their own sense of a common interest and fate. The result was a resounding cry for political and social democracy that began in the first half of the nineteenth century and became increasingly insistent. Many solutions were proffered. The proposals became powerful ideologies shaping the nineteenth and twentieth centuries, not only in Europe but also in most of the world.

Economic Liberalism

The classical economists of the late eighteenth and early nineteenth centuries (see page 747) argued in favor of laissez faire, the policy of nonintervention by the government in the economy. The laws of supply and demand, they contended, if allowed to operate unhindered, would provide for the well-being of both the individual and society. Their arguments formed the basis of what is known as "economic liberalism."

The classical economists' theories had a large audience. Popularizers spread the gospel of free enterprise, teaching the advantages of the capitalist system while justifying the conditions of the wealthy. They were particularly prevalent in Britain. Among them, Samuel Smiles (1812–1904) was widely read. Originally a physician, Smiles turned to popular education and in 1859 published *Self-Help*, one of the most influential books of the nineteenth century. In *Self-Help* he argued that the remedy for poverty lay in the hands of poor people themselves. If they lived thrifty, industrious lives, the good life would come to them. The improvement of the human condition was dependent not on society but on the character of the individual. Smiles's works sold a quarter million copies in Britain by the end of the century and were translated into many languages.

Building on earlier liberals' advocacy of laissez-faire policies, others more directly and even more uncompromisingly argued against any government action to improve the condition of the working classes. The British social theorist Herbert Spencer (1820–1903) took to extremes the lessons of classical economics. Although he lived on inherited money, he unabashedly asserted that wealth reflected innate virtue and poverty indicated innate vice. According to Spencer, the state should guarantee the right of everyone to pursue freedom as long as the pursuit did not infringe on others. In *Social Statics* (1851), Spencer opposed relief for the poor on the grounds that it unfairly deprived some—the rich—of their property. He also argued that schooling was outside the authority of the state.

Applying to human society Charles Darwin's principle of "natural selection" (see page 865), Spencer was a Social Darwinist. In 1864 he coined the expression "survival of the fittest." Society, he believed, should be established in such a way that the strongest and most resourceful would survive. The weak, poor, and improvident were not worthy of survival, and if the state helped them survive—such as by providing education—it would only perpetuate the unfit. Spencer's harsh doctrine was widely acclaimed.

Many of those who basically favored laissez-faire policies criticized some aspects of the market economy, however. In France in the first half of the nineteenth century, commentators on the factory system, including industrialists, expressed fear that factory work would undermine the stability of family life and hence of society itself. Philanthropic intervention, they hoped, would resolve the problems they had identified.

Even some of the British classical economists doubted the wisdom of allowing the market economy to operate entirely without regulation and of trusting it to provide for human happiness.

The Scottish economist Adam Smith (1723–1790) warned that the market tended to form monopolies, and he suggested that government intervene to prevent this situation. According to Smith, not all human needs could be provided by the marketplace; the government needed to supply education, road systems, and an equitable system of justice. The liberal thinker and government reformer Jeremy Bentham (1748–1832) was fearful of an overly intrusive government but also saw government as a possible force for good, to ensure the greatest happiness for the greatest number. Edwin Chadwick (1800–1895) advocated government intervention to ensure public sanitation and care for the poor; as a government official he worked to implement these twin goals.

John Stuart Mill (1806–1873), the leading British economic and political thinker at midcentury, in the first edition of his *Principles of Political Economy* (1848), voiced strong support for laissez-faire economics. The individual if left alone could carry on economic functions better than the government, Mill insisted. In subsequent editions, however, he remarked that the state had an obligation to intervene in the face of human misery. There were also many human needs that the free market could not address satisfactorily. Once wealth was produced, he noted, its distribution was subject to traditions and to decisions made by those in power. Thus, presumably, wealth could be shared by society as a whole. Toward the end of his life, Mill seemed to be leaning toward socialism.

The liberal economists' views on the virtues of laissez-faire policy gradually changed. In the face of unsanitary urban conditions, child labor, and other alarming results of industrialization, the state in many countries around midcentury began to intervene in areas of concern that would have been unthinkable a half-century earlier.

The Growth of Working-Class Solidarity

Hardest hit by economic changes, workers sought to improve their conditions by organizing and articulating their needs. In the preindustrial economy, artisans and craftsmen lived in an accepted hierarchy with prescribed rules. They began by serving for a certain number of years as apprentices to a master, next became journeymen, and finally with hard work and good fortune became masters of their trade. As tradesmen with common interests, they tended to band together into brotherhoods, promising one another help and trying to improve their working conditions.

With industrialization, guilds declined. Unlike the skilled handicrafts that required years of apprenticeship, much of industrial production did not require lengthy periods of training. The system of dependence between apprentice and master became irrelevant. Guilds trying to protect their members often resisted new technologies and came to be seen as a hindrance to economic development. Liberals viewed guilds as constraints on trade and the free flow of labor. In France, the revolutionaries abolished the guilds and all workers' coalitions. In Britain, Parliament throughout the eighteenth century passed various acts against "combinations" by workmen.

While guilds faded in importance, the solidarity and language born of the guild continued to shape workers' attitudes throughout much of the nineteenth century. New experiences also reinforced the sense of belonging to a group and sharing common aspirations.

Cultural forces fostered workers' sense of solidarity. The common language of religion and shared religious practice united workers, and many religious groups were born as a result. Religious sects flourished in an environment of despair punctuated by hopes of deliverance. Some historians believe that the growth of Methodism in England in the 1790s (see page 743) was a response to economic conditions. Emphasis on equality before God fueled the sense of injustice in a world where some were privileged and living in luxury while others were condemned to work along with their children for a pittance. Joanna, a self-proclaimed prophet active in the 1810s in England, announced both salvation and the coming of a new world of material well-being. In France, workers believed the new society would come about by their martyrdom; like Jesus, the workers would suffer, and from their suffering would emerge a new, better society. Ideas of social justice were linked in the countryside with religious broadsides speaking of "Jesus the worker." Religious themes and language continued to be important in labor organization for many years.

Other cultural and social factors created bonds among workers. Housing was increasingly segregated. Workers lived in low-rent areas—in slums in the center of cities or in outlying areas near the factories. Thus, urban workers lived close together, in similar conditions of squalor and hardship. Entrepreneurs who built factories or established mineworks in the countryside had to provide housing in order to attract and retain workers. Although this housing was sometimes better than the quarters of urban workers, it nevertheless reinforced the workers' solidarity and sense of commonality.

Workers grew close by spending their leisure time together, drinking in pubs, attending theaters and new forms of popular entertainment such as the circus, or watching traditional blood sports like boxing or cockfights. Popular sports emerged in the 1880s. In sports such as soccer, which developed in England at this time, both players and fans were drawn overwhelmingly from the working class.

Social institutions also encouraged class unity. In the eighteenth century both husband and wife were usually in the same craft. By 1900 it became more common for workers to marry across their crafts, thereby strengthening the sense of solidarity that encompassed the working classes as a whole.

Faced with the uncertainties of unemployment and job-related accidents, in addition to disease and other natural catastrophes, workers formed so-called friendly societies in which they pooled their resources to provide mutual aid. These societies, descendants of benefit organizations of the Middle Ages and Renaissance, combined business activity with feasts, drinking bouts, and other social functions.

Friendly societies had existed as early as the seventeenth century, but they became increasingly popular and important after industrialization. Their strength in a region often reflected the degree to which the area was industrialized. First started to provide aid for workers in a particular trade, they soon included members in several crafts. They federated into national organizations, so that a worker who moved to a new town could continue membership in the new locale. Connected by common membership in friendly societies, workers expressed a feeling of group solidarity beyond their individual occupations. Though far from accomplished, a working class was in the making.

Leisure Activity for the Working Poor Some harsh forms of entertainment turned up in the industrial period. Scores of working-class spectators came to see the celebrated dog "Billy" kill a hundred rats at one time at the Westminster Pit in London in 1822. *(The British Library)*

Collective Action

Militant and in some cases violent action strengthened workers' solidarity. In politics, workers expressed common grievances, and some of their disappointments in the political arena underscored their common situation.

In the face of hardships, artisans organized for collective action. In 1811–1812 British hand weavers, faced with competition from mechanized looms, organized in groups claiming to be led by a mythical General Ned Ludd. In the name of economic justice and to protect their livelihood, the "Luddites," as the general's followers were called, smashed machines or threatened to do so. To bring the Luddite riots under control, twelve thousand troops were dispatched, and in January 1813, British authorities executed ten people for Luddism. Similarly, in Saxony in eastern Germany in the 1830s and 1840s, weavers went on machine-

crushing campaigns. These movements revealed the militance of labor and its willingness to resort to violence.

In Lyon, France, in 1831 and 1834, workers led uprisings demanding fair wages for piecework. Angered when the silk merchants lowered the amount they would pay, the workers marched in the streets bearing banners proclaiming "Live Working or Die Fighting." Troops were brought in to restore order to the riot-torn city. Although conditions of the silk trade had been the immediate impetus for the uprising, the workers appealed for help to their fellow workers in other trades.

Labor agitation in much of Europe increased in the 1840s; a major strike wave involving twenty thousand workers broke out in Paris in 1840. In the summer of 1842, an industrial downturn in England led to massive unemployment and rioting. During summer of 1844 in Silesia, in eastern Prussia, linen handloom weavers desperate because of worsening conditions brought on by competition from machine-made cotton fabrics, attacked the homes of the wealthy. In 1855 in Barcelona, the government tried to dissolve unions, and fifty thousand workers went on strike carrying banners that warned "Association or Death."

Many of the friendly societies struggled to improve their members' working conditions, acting very much as labor unions would. They organized strikes and provided support to members while they were on strike. Unions were illegal in Britain until 1825, in Prussia until 1859, and in France until the 1860s. The advantages offered by unions were well understood. As a French workers' paper declared in 1847, "If workers came together and organized . . . nothing would be able to stop them." An organized force could threaten to withhold labor if the employer did not grant decent wages and acceptable conditions. Unions made workers a countervailing force to the factory owners.

Discipline in the factory was often severe. (See the box, "The New Discipline of the Factory System.") Workers had to conform to rigid rules not only in the workplace but also away from it. Workers in some factories were forbidden to read certain newspapers, had to attend religious services, and could marry only with the owners' permission. Workers resisted these attempts at control and resented employers' intrusiveness. They wanted freedom from outside regulation, and unions provided a means to ensure that freedom.

The process of unionization was difficult. By 1850 many countries had passed laws supporting employers against the workers. Censorship and the use of force against organized strikes were not uncommon. Population growth made it difficult for workers to withhold labor lest they be replaced by others only too willing to take their place. Foreign workers—for example, the Irish who streamed into England and the Belgians and Italians who streamed into France—were often desperate for work and not well informed about local conditions.

In many countries, workers formed unions before unions were legalized. Most were centered around a single craft or a single industry. In Britain, however, there were early attempts to organize unions on a national basis. In 1834 Welsh

socialist Robert Owen (1771–1858) helped launch the Grand National Consolidated Trades Union. The organization's goal was to use the principles of cooperation to unite all of labor against the capitalist system. Internal strife and government repression kept this organization from succeeding. Not until 1860 was a federal structure created for the British unions—the Trade Union Congress.

In Germany in 1848 the General Workers' Brotherhood was founded. Its first members were people from many walks of life, but gradually its membership included workers only. Most of the members were craftsmen and artisans: skilled workers such as cigar makers, book printers, typesetters. The year after its founding, the General Workers' Brotherhood had 15,000 members and 170 locals. After 1859, when labor unions were legalized, they grew significantly.

The composition of union membership evolved over time. Because labor unions originated in the crafts tradition, the earliest members were skilled craftsmen who organized to protect their livelihood from the challenge that industrialization posed. These craftsmen were usually literate and long-time residents of their communities. They provided the labor movement with much of its leadership and organization. Skilled craft workers played a strong role in developing a sense of class consciousness. The language and institutions that they had developed over decades and sometimes over centuries became the common heritage of workers in general.

Workers looked to political action as the means to improve their situation. In the 1830s and 1840s English workers agitated for the right to vote; they saw voting as a way to put themselves on equal footing with the privileged and to win better conditions. The failure to win the vote in 1832 with the passage of the Great Reform Bill disappointed many workers, and they heavily backed the Chartist movement of the 1840s (see page 757). Symptomatically, Chartism won its greatest support in the industrial areas.

In France urban laborers who had played an important part in the various stages of the Revolution continued to shape political events. In July 1830 workers helped topple the Bourbon monarchy and bring Louis Philippe (r. 1830–1848) to the throne. They insisted that their labor had created the wealth of the nation and that their self-sacri-

The New Discipline of the Factory System

The new factories regimented the work force and were likely to impose stiff penalties for infractions of the rules. This document lists some of the regulations of the Berlin Foundry and Engineering Works of the Royal Overseas Trading Company of 1844.

The normal working day begins at all seasons at 6 A.M. precisely and ends, after the usual break of half an hour for breakfast, an hour for dinner, and half an hour for tea, at 7 P.M., and it shall be strictly observed.

Five minutes before the beginning of the stated hours of work until their actual commencement, a bell shall ring and indicate that every worker employed in the concern has to proceed to his place of work, in order to start as soon as the bell stops.

The doorkeeper shall lock the door punctually at 6 A.M., 8:30 A.M., 1 P.M., and 4:30 P.M.

Workers arriving 2 minutes late shall lose half an hour's wages; whoever is more than 2 minutes late may not start work until after the next break, or at least shall lose his wages until then.

Repeated irregular arrival at work shall lead to dismissal. This shall also apply to those who are found idling by an official or overseer, and refuse to obey their order to resume work. . . .

All conversation with fellow-workers is prohibited. . . .

Smoking in the workshops or in the yard is prohibited during working-hours; anyone caught smoking shall be fined five silver groschen for the sick fund.

Natural functions must be performed at the appropriate places. . . .

It goes without saying that all overseers and officials of the firm shall be obeyed without question, and shall be treated with due deference. Disobedience will be punished by dismissal.

Immediate dismissal shall also be the fate of anyone found drunk in any of the workshops. . . .

The gatekeeper and the watchman, as well as every official, are entitled to search the baskets, parcels, aprons, etc. of the women and children who are taking the dinners into the works, on their departure, as well as search any worker suspected of stealing any article whatever. . . .

A free copy of these rules is handed to every workman, but whoever loses it and requires a new one, or cannot produce it on leaving, shall be fined 2½ silver groschen.

Source: S. Pollard and C. Holmes, eds., *Documents of European Economic History*, vol. 1 (New York: St. Martin's Press, 1968), pp. 534–536.

---

fice had brought in a freer government. Workers were disappointed by their failure to win political representation under the July Monarchy, and their sense of betrayal strengthened their class solidarity vis-à-vis the wealthy, privileged upper classes.

Politically, workers played a major role in the European revolutions of 1848. They demonstrated and helped bring down the July Monarchy in France. In Germany and Austria, they participated as organized groups in the initial successful upris-

ings against the established orders. Workers also influenced the course of the revolutions. However vague their ideas, European workers showed that their organizations were legitimate representatives of the people and that the lot of the worker should be the concern of government. In general, workers upheld the ideal of a moral economy—one in which all who labored got a just wage and a minimum level of well-being was assured to all.

The working classes were never a monolithic group. They consisted of people with varying skills, responsibilities, and incomes. (See the feature, "Weighing the Evidence: Workers' Wages," on pages 808–809.) Craftsmen with valuable skills were the segment that employers most respected and favored in pay and in working conditions. In contrast, unskilled workers were poorly paid, harshly treated, and often given only temporary work. Many skilled workers looked with contempt on the unskilled.

If both sexes worked side by side, there was little solidarity between them. Men worried that women were undermining their earning power by accepting lower wages. They often excluded women from their unions. They even went on strike to force employers to discharge women. An exception to this practice was Belgium, where labor organizations were remarkably receptive to female members.

Nor was there solidarity across nationalities. Foreign workers were heartily despised. British workers were hostile to their Irish colleagues, the French to the Belgians and Italians in their midst. The hostility often led to fisticuffs. In London anti-Irish riots were common.

Thus, many forces fostered dissension among the working classes in the nineteenth century, and unity among workers was far from achieved. Nevertheless, various experiences, including the spread of industry, broadened and deepened workers' sense of a common fate and goal.

The middle classes came to believe that all workers formed a single class. By the mid-nineteenth century, they had developed a clear fear of workers, not only as individuals but as a group, as a class. It was not unusual for members of the elite to refer to workers as "the swinish multitude" or, as the title of a popular English book put it, *The Great Unwashed* (1868). In France reference was alternately made to "the dangerous classes" and "the laboring classes." Not just workers but even the privileged seemed to see relations between the groups as a form of class war.

Marx and Marxism

Socialism provided a powerful language for the expression of working-class interests. Many of the workers who were enfranchised in the latter part of the century joined political parties espousing this doctrine. As we have seen, socialism existed before Karl Marx came on the scene. Henri de Saint-Simon and Charles Fourier in France, and Robert Owen in Great Britain, were the foremost prophets of socialism (see page 750). Marx drew on their theories and gave them a very special twist, and in the end his became the dominant form of socialism.

Karl Marx (1818–1883), the son of a lawyer, grew up in the Rhineland, in western Germany, an industrializing area that was particularly open to political ideas and agitation. The Rhineland had been influenced by the ideas of the French Revolution and was primed for political radicalism. As a young man Marx studied philosophy at the University of Berlin and joined a group known as the "Young Hegelians," self-declared disciples of the idealist philosopher G. W. F. Hegel (1770–1831) (see page 743). Marx showed an early interest in political liberty and socialism. In 1842–1843 he edited a newspaper that spoke out for freedom and democracy in Germany. The following year in Paris, he met several of the French socialist writers. Even as a young man, he was perceived by his contemporaries as bright but unyielding in his determination.

Because of his radical journalism, he was exiled from the Rhineland and lived briefly in Paris, then Brussels. In 1849 he settled in London, where he lived for the rest of his life, dedicated to establishing his ideas on what he viewed as scientific bases. Deriving a modest income from writing for the *New York Daily Tribune* and from funds provided by his friend and collaborator Friedrich Engels (1820–1895), Marx was never able to provide well for his family, which constantly lived on the edge of poverty. Of the six children born to the Marx household, three died in infancy.

In 1848 Marx and Engels published the *Communist Manifesto*. (See the box, "The *Communist Manifesto*.") A pamphlet written for the Communist League, a group of Germans living in exile, the manifesto was an appeal to the working classes of the world. The league deliberately called itself "Communist" rather than "Socialist." Communism was a radical program, bent on changing property relations by violence; socialism was associated with more peaceful means of transformation. The pamphlet was too late and too obscure to influence the revolutions of 1848. However, it laid out Marx's basic ideas, calling on the proletariat to rise—"You have nothing to lose but your chains"—and create a society that would end the exploitation of man by man.

A number of political and polemical works flowed from Marx's pen, but most of them remained unpublished during his lifetime. The first volume of his major work, *Capital,* was published in 1867; subsequent volumes appeared posthumously. Marxism, the body of Marx's thought, is complex and sometimes contradictory. It is written in an obscure style, difficult to penetrate. But certain basic concepts resound throughout and were embraced by Marx's followers.

Marx agreed with Hegel and many of his contemporaries that human history has a goal. Hegel believed that the goal was the realization of the world spirit. Marx believed that it was the abolition of capitalism, the victory of the proletariat, the disappearance of the state, and the ultimate liberation of all humankind.

Whereas Hegel thought that ideas govern the world, Marx insisted that material conditions determine it. Hegel said that truth evolves by a "dialectic method": A person states a proposition and then states its opposite; from the clash of the two emerges a synthesis that leads to a higher truth. Marx called his philosophy "dialectic materialism." Following Hegel, he posited a world of change but said that it was embedded in material conditions, not in a clash of ideas. Ideas, to Marx, were but a reflection of the material world.

Marx grouped human beings into classes based on their relationship to factories and machines—the means of production. Capitalists were one class, because they owned the means of production. Workers were a separate class—the proletariat—because they did not own any of the means of production and their income came only from their own hands. Because these two classes had different relationships to the means of production, they had different—in fact, antagonistic—interests and were destined (Marx believed) to engage in a class struggle.

Some of Marx's contemporaries lamented the increasing hostility between workers and capitalists. Marx, however, saw the conflict as necessary to advance human history, and he sought to validate his thesis by the study of the past. In the Mid-

Karl Marx Through his writings and agitation, Marx transformed the socialism of his day and created an ideology that helped shape the nineteenth and twentieth centuries. *(Corbis-Bettmann)*

dle Ages, he pointed out, the feudal class dominated society but eventually lost the struggle to the commercial classes. Now, in turn, the capitalists were destined to be overwhelmed by the rising proletariat.

In the study of history and economics, Marx found not only justification for but irrefutable proof of the "scientific" basis of his ideas. Capitalism was itself creating the forces that would supplant it. The large industrial plants necessitated an ever greater work force with a growing sense of class interest. The inherently competitive nature of capitalism would inevitably drive an increasing number of enterprises out of business, and there would emerge a form of monopoly capitalism, abusive of both consumers and workers. As a result of ever more savage competition, more businesses would fail, and consequently more workers would become unemployed. Angered and frustrated by their lot, workers would overthrow the system that had abused them for so long: "The

The *Communist Manifesto*

The **Communist Manifesto** *provides a preview of the major themes that would inform Marx and Engels's later writings: the concept of class formation and class antagonism, the privileged role of the proletariat, and the inevitability of the proletariat's success.*

The history of all hitherto existing society is the history of class struggles.

Freeman and slave, patrician and plebeian, lord and serf, guild-master and journeyman, in a word, oppressor and oppressed, stood in constant opposition to one another, carried on an uninterrupted, now hidden, now open fight, that each time ended, either in a revolutionary reconstitution of society at large, or in the common ruin of the contending classes. . . .

In ancient Rome we have patricians, knights, plebeians, slaves; in the Middle Ages, feudal lords, vassals, guild-masters, journeymen, apprentices, serfs; in almost all of these classes, again, subordinate gradations.

The modern bourgeois society that has sprouted from the ruins of feudal society, has not done away with class antagonisms. It has but established new classes, new conditions of oppression, new forms of struggle in place of the old ones. . . .

Society as a whole is more and more splitting up into two great hostile camps, into two great classes directly facing each other: Bourgeoisie and Proletariat. . . .

With the development of industry the proletariat not only increases in number; it becomes concentrated in greater masses, its strength grows and it feels that strength more. . . . the collisions between individual workmen and individual bourgeois take more and more the character of collisions between two classes. . . .

Of all the classes that stand face to face with the bourgeoisie today, the proletariat alone is a really revolutionary class. The other classes decay and finally disappear in the face of modern industry; the proletariat is its special and essential product.

All previous historical movements were movements of minorities. The proletarian movement is the self-conscious, independent movement of the immense majority. The proletariat, the stratum of our present society, cannot stir, cannot raise itself up, without the whole superincumbent strata of official society being sprung into the air. . . .

. . . The development of modern industry, therefore, cuts from under its feet the very foundation on which the bourgeoisie produces and appropriates products. What the bourgeoisie therefore produces, above all, are its own grave-diggers. Its fall and the victory of the proletariat are equally inevitable.

Source: Karl Marx and Friedrich Engels, *Communist Manifesto* (1848; reprint, New York: International Publishers, 1948), pp. 9, 17, 20–21.

knell of private property has sounded. The expropriators will be expropriated." The proletariat would take power and to solidify its rule would temporarily exercise the "dictatorship of the proletariat." Once that had taken place, the state would wither away. With the coming to power of the proletariat, the history of class war would end and the ideal society would prevail. Ironically,

Marx, who spent his life writing about the nature and history of social change, envisaged a time when change would cease, when history, as it were, would stop.

Many protested the evils of industrialism but Marx described economic change in dramatic terms as a necessary stage for humankind to traverse on its way to liberation. The suffering of the workers was not in vain; rather, it was a necessary process, part of the drama that would finally lead to human emancipation. Unlike some of the utopians who deplored industrialism, Marx accepted it and saw it as part of the path that history was fated to take.

Marx's study of economics and history proved to him that the coming of socialism was not only desirable—as the utopians had thought—but inevitable. The laws of history dictated that capitalism would collapse, having created within itself the means of its own destruction—namely, the rising proletariat. By proclaiming his brand of socialism as scientific, Marx gave it the aura it needed to become the faith for millions of people. For to declare ideas scientific in the nineteenth century, when science was held in such high esteem, was a promising way of gaining a popular following for them.

SUMMARY

Its industrial transformation altered the face of Europe. The process, which started around 1750 in parts of England, spread by 1850 to other states of Europe. Material and cultural factors combined with a number of fortuitous circumstances explain why industrial production originated in England. The proximity of coal and iron, the relative ease of domestic transportation, a culture open to innovation and entrepreneurship, and the existence of an already relatively dynamic economy help explain why Britain was the first nation to industrialize.

Economies based on industry changed power relations within Europe and altered the relationship of Europe to the rest of the world. As a result of the transformation in its economy Britain became in the nineteenth century the most powerful nation in Europe and achieved worldwide influence. Although Europe was industrialized only in certain areas, many Europeans came to think of their continent as economically and technologically superior to the rest of the world. Being industrial became synonymous for many with Europe's identity.

Industry changed the nature of work for large numbers of Europeans. Machines replaced human energy in the workplace. By the application of science and technology, manufacturing productivity increased significantly. A decreasing number of people worked in agriculture, and more entered manufacturing. Population patterns changed; cities grew dramatically, and for the first time European cities had over a million inhabitants.

The massing of workers in factories and urban areas called attention to their misery and also to their potential power. Eager to improve their lives and working conditions, workers began to express their solidarity. They organized into groups that were more broadly based and therefore more powerful than workers' groups of the past. As workers began to think of themselves as a group, the dominant groups within society began to perceive them as such.

Confronted by the realities of industrialization, many people changed their intellectual convictions. It was obvious that the laissez-faire system could not meet many workers' needs. Classical liberal economists revised their orthodoxy; the state became more interventionist, trying to remove some of the worst abuses.

Drawing on earlier strands of socialism, Karl Marx articulated this ideology in a new and compelling way. Marxism gave a powerful voice to the new proletarian class that industrialization had created, and it was to cast a shadow far into the next century.

NOTES

1. Phyllis Deane, *The First Industrial Revolution* (Cambridge, England: Cambridge University Press, 1965), p. 1.
2. These ideas are provocatively developed by E. L. Jones, *The European Miracle: Environments, Economies and Geopolitics of Europe and Asia* (Cambridge, England: Cambridge University Press, 1981).
3. Adna Ferrin Weber, *The Growth of Cities in the Nineteenth Century: A Study in Statistics* (New York: Macmillan, 1899; Ithaca, N.Y.: Cornell University Press, 1963), p. 1.
4. W. Cooke Taylor, *Notes of a Tour in the Manufacturing Districts of Lancashire, in a Series of Letters to His Grace the Archbishop of Dublin* (London, 1842), pp. 4–6, quoted in E. P. Thompson, *The Making of the English Working Class* (New York: Vintage, 1963), p. 191.
5. Marie de Flavigny d'Agoult [Daniel Stern], *Histoire de la Révolution de 1848*, 2d ed., vol. 1 (Paris, 1862), p. 7, quoted in Theodore S. Hamerow, *The Birth of a New Europe: State and Society in the Nineteenth Century* (Chapel Hill: University of North Carolina Press, 1983), pp. 206–207.

SUGGESTED READING

General Surveys

Jones, E. L. *The European Miracle.* 1981. A broad comparative work considering the forces leading to the industrialization of the West.

Landes, David S. *Prometheus Unbound.* 1969. A standard work emphasizing technological and cultural factors as explanations for industry.

Mokyr, Joel. *The Lever of Riches: Technological Creativity and Economic Progress.* 1990. A work that provides a comparative study of Western and Chinese technology, emphasizing cultural elements as explanations for the industrialization of the West.

Industrialization of Britain

Brown, Richard. *Society and Economy in Modern Britain, 1700–1850.* 1991. A work pointing out that British development was gradual, varied regionally, and was unequally spread.

Mathias, Peter. *The First Industrial Nation: An Economic History of Britain, 1700–1914.* 1969. A consideration of the unique combination of factors that explain Britain's pioneering role as an industrializer.

O'Brien, Patrick K., and Roland Quinault, eds. *The Industrial Revolution and British Society.* 1993. A broad set of essays on the origins and impact of industry on British society.

The Spread of Industry to the Continent

Gullickson, Gay L. *Spinners and Weavers of Auffay: Rural Industry and the Sexual Division of Labor in a French Village, 1750–1850.* 1986. A very fine study of the long-term subsistence of rural industry in a rural environment.

Milward, A., and S. B. Saul. *The Development of the Economies of Continental Europe.* 1977. An examination of the relationship between the availability of capital, labor, and technology and the speed of industrial development.

Pollard, Sidney. *Peaceful Conquest.* 1981. A reminder that although industrialization started in England, it occurred not throughout the whole country but only in specific regions; likewise when industry spread to the Continent, it spread only to specific regions.

Pounds, Norman J. G. *An Historical Geography of Europe, 1800–1914.* 1985. A consideration of the impact of geographic factors in shaping industry and how industry changed the physical face of Europe.

Sylla, Richard, and Gianni Toniolo, eds. *Patterns of European Industrialization.* 1991. A volume describing the patterns of industrialization in a comparative perspective.

The Industrial Transformation of Society

Alter, George. *Family and the Female Life Course: The Women of Verviers, Belgium, 1849–80.* 1988. A reminder that women were usually not continuously in the industrial work force but entered and exited according to family needs.

Anderson, Michael S. *Family Structure in Nineteenth Century Lancashire.* 1971. A study of the industrial town of Preston, revealing a family system far more resilient than the system usually described by contemporaries.

Brimblecombe, Peter. *The Big Smoke: A History of Air Pollution in London Since Medieval Times.* 1987. An account of the causes of pollution and the attempts to control it.

Chinn, Carl. *Poverty Amidst Prosperity: The Urban Poor in England, 1834–1914.* 1995. Concentrates on the harsher aspects of industrialization.

Hilden, Patricia P. *Women, Work, and Politics: Belgium, 1830–1914.* 1993. Reveals the unique experience of women in the industrial work force in the first continental country to industrialize.

Hohenberg, Paul M., and Lynn Hollen Lees. *The Making of Urban Europe, 1000–1950.* 1985. A good general introduction to the impact of industry on urbanization, emphasizing less the pathology of cities and more their resilience.

Hopkins, Eric. *Birmingham: The First Manufacturing Town in the World, 1760–1840.* 1989. An account that emphasizes the extent to which the city and its industry depended on manufacture by hand rather than by machine.

Lawton, Richard, and Robert Lee. *Urban Population Development in Western Europe from the Late Eighteenth to the Early Twentieth Century.* 1989. A country-by-country study of urban growth.

Nardinelli, Clark. *Child Labor and the Industrial Revolution.* 1990. A work that represents child labor as less harsh than some contemporaries claimed and as a rational adjustment to existing economic conditions.

Ponting, Clive. *A Green History of the World.* 1991. A work that includes some remarks on the impact of early industry on the European environment.

Tilly, Louise, and Joan Scott. *Women, Work and Family.* 1978. A description of the family wage economy in which all members contributed to the economy of the family, especially in the early stages of industrialization.

Turner, B. L., et al. *The Earth as Transformed by Human Action: Global and Regional Changes in the Biosphere over the Past 300 Years.* 1990. A work that includes some information on the nineteenth-century impact of industry on the environment.

Responses to Industrialization

Furet, François. *Marx and the French Revolution.* 1988. A consideration of the impact of the French Revolution on Marx.

Himmelfarb, Gertrude. *The Idea of Poverty: England in the Early Industrial Age.* 1983. A work that describes the image of the poor among Victorian middle-class observers.

Kelly, Alfred, ed. *The German Worker: Working-Class Autobiographies from the Age of Industrialization.* 1987. A collection of workers' accounts of their lives.

Kolakowski, Leszek. *Main Currents of Marxism,* vol. 1, *The Founders.* 1978. A work that traces the intellectual background of Marx's thought and the nature of the original synthesis he created.

Lynch, Katherine A. *Family, Class, and Ideology in Early Industrial France: Social Policy and the Working-Class Family, 1825–1848.* 1988. A study of social concerns in France over the corrosive impact of industry on working-class families.

Maynes, Mary Jo. *Taking the Hard Road.* 1995. An analysis of French and German workers' experiences during industrialization.

Mazlish, Bruce. *The Meaning of Karl Marx.* 1984. An easy-to-read introduction to the man and his thought, emphasizing the shaping of both by the era in which Marx lived.

Moss, Bernard H. *The Origins of the French Labor Movement, 1830–1914: The Socialism of Skilled Workers.* 1976. A work that traces the origins of labor militancy among artisans.

Sewell, William H., Jr. *Work and Revolution in France: The Language of Labor from the Old Regime to 1848.* 1980. An account that stresses continuity in the development of the French working class from the time of the Old Regime to the mid-nineteenth century.

Thompson, E. P. *The Making of the English Working Class.* 1963. A work that emphasizes cultural factors that encouraged the development of working-class consciousness in England.

Traugott, Mark, ed. *The French Worker: Autobiographies from the Early Industrial Era.* 1993. A collection of telling excerpts from workers' recollections.

WORKERS' WAGES

In 1869 the Chamber of Commerce of Verviers, a town in eastern Belgium, published a report on workers' wages. In the seventeenth century, Verviers, located on the Vesdre River, had become a major producer of woolens. The river provided water for power, for washing the cloth, and for carrying away industrial waste. Thus, the site was ideal for finishing textiles, and the merchants of Verviers drew upon the labor of spinners and weavers in the surrounding farm areas. With a population of 4500 in the mid-seventeenth century, Verviers had 10,000 inhabitants by the end of the eighteenth.

Two local entrepreneurs brought the Englishman John Cockerill to town. In 1802 he set up the first spinning machine on the Continent and in 1816 the first steam engine in Belgium. Thirty years later, Verviers boasted forty factories and the population had increased to 23,000.

Industrialization transformed the people's lives in many ways. The table of wages reveals the existence of a variegated, hierarchical work force with clear, separate functions and specified salaries. It indicates the uneven ways in which people benefited from industry, depending on their skills, age, and gender.

For example, this list allows us to compare the wages of industrial workers and artisans. Industry made it difficult for the artisans to survive; unable to compete with machine manufacture, many had to give up their trade or tighten their belts to make ends meet. The new machine age, however, created an increased demand for the services of some artisans. Early in the nineteenth century the new machines eliminated hand spinning, for example, but inexpensive yarn at first increased the demand for handloom weavers. Notice that handloom weavers ("hand weavers" in the table) were relatively well paid in 1836. This is due to the uneven introduction of mechanical production. Weaving of high-quality woolens proved to be more difficult to mechanize than cotton goods. Power looms did not become common in Verviers until the 1860s, and we see the relative wages of hand-

loom weavers decline in 1869. Joiners and ironsmiths not only did the work they had traditionally done but found new opportunities building and repairing machines. The ironsmiths, joiners, and carpenters of Verviers were all paid better than other workers.

We may note several things about the impact of industry on the labor force. Notice the specialized descriptions of occupations in the textile industry. Among the factory workers we find some significant wage discrepancies. Compare, for example, the wages of the nonspecialized laborer to the wages of the other industrial workers.

Changes in technology, productivity, labor supply, and market demand for certain goods increased the relative wages of workers. Thus the relative wages of jobs changed between 1836 and 1869. Notice that a wool washer in 1869 was making 174 percent more than a wool washer made in 1836, but in the same period the wages paid to a warper had increased by 300 percent.

Let us next consider women in the labor force. Notice that the list is divided into "male occupations," "female occupations," and finally "children's occupation." Work is divided according to gender and age. Look at the list of women's industrial occupations. The absence of spinning female occupations in this list is significant. Spinning had been a female occupation since antiquity, but the spinning machines in Verviers were tended by men. Notice how little differentiation is evident; far fewer industrial occupations are listed for women than for men. Also look at the wages. Women's wages were all equally depressed, with the one exception of menders' wages, hovering in 1836 around .7 francs but climbing by 1869 to 2.25 francs, an increase of over 300 percent. Among men's occupations the spread of salaries was far greater. In 1869 the highest-paid women (menders) received 40 percent more than the lowest-paid women in 1836 (scourers), but the highest-paid men (ironsmiths) received 138 percent more than the lowest-paid men (wool washers) in 1836. By 1869 the wage gap had somewhat dimin-

Wage Differentials in Verviers, Belgium, 1836–1869

		Wages (francs per day)				
		1836	1846	1856	1863	1869
Male Occupations	Ironsmith*	1.73	2.25	2.50	3.00	3.87
	Carpenter*	1.90	2.25	2.65	2.87	3.50
	Dyer	1.40	1.46	1.60	2.60	3.37
	Spinner	1.80	1.90	2.90	3.12	3.40
	Carder	1.47	1.75	2.30	3.25	3.30
	Tanner*	1.83	2.00	2.25	3.00	3.25
	Warper	0.80	0.95	1.57	1.65	3.25
	Hand weaver*	1.97	1.70	2.85	3.00	3.00
	Joiner*	1.98	2.00	2.25	2.75	3.00
	Tenterer	—	1.25	1.40	2.34	3.00
	Presser	1.47	1.78	1.78	2.15	3.00
	Machine weaver	—	—	—	—	2.75
	Comber	0.84	1.27	1.50	1.75	2.65
	Fuller	1.40	1.50	1.75	2.30	2.67
	Laborer	—	1.25	1.50	1.87	2.50
	Wool washer	1.15	1.25	1.40	1.75	2.25
Female Occupations	Mender	0.73	0.80	1.10	1.40	2.25
	Wool sorter	0.98	1.08	1.70	1.85	2.00
	Gigger	0.75	0.80	0.80	1.25	2.00
	Burler	0.77	1.00	1.20	1.70	1.80
	Seamstress*	0.73	0.80	1.10	1.40	—
	Scourer	0.70	0.75	0.85	1.35	1.62
Children's Occupation	Piecener	—	0.70	0.90	1.10	1.60

*Artisans. (Those not starred were industrial workers.)

Source: Chamber of Commerce of Verviers, *Rapport général sur la situation du commerce et de l'industrie en 1868* (Verviers, 1869), p. 69; repr. in George Alter, *Family and the Female Life Course—The Women of Verviers, Belgium, 1849–1880* (Madison: University of Wisconsin Press, 1988), p. 103. Used by permission.

ished for both men and women, but it was still far larger for men (72 percent) than for women (28 percent).

Some male artisans consistently received wages higher than the wages of many machine operators—consider the wages of carpenters, for example. But notice the one female artisan occupation: seamstress. Although a seamstress was probably quite skilled, she was paid no more than the women in the factories. Special crafts, still prized for some men, were not given much monetary value when practiced by women.

Note the wage differences overall between male and female workers. In 1836 the average female worker received wages equivalent to 53.2 percent of the average male worker's wages. By 1869, there was some improvement: The difference had declined by 11 percentage points; still, women earned 64 percent of men's pay.

The table lists only one occupation for children: piecener. Small and nimble, children were paid to fix broken threads. They worked in many other capacities as well. Some were paid wages by their employers; others helped their parents in a factory or workshop. The wages of some adults probably included compensation for their children's labor.

We can learn much from a statistical table such as this about the impact of industrialization on the labor force. Some workers benefited, and others were harmed by the adoption of industry; over time workers experienced changes in their circumstances. If statistical tables are informative on such issues, they also have their limits. They do not tell us how workers interpreted and understood their experience. As workers suffered daily hardships, they had to try to make sense of their changing world. ✧

CHAPTER 22

New Powers and New Tensions, 1850–1880

I n 1866 when Prince Charles, a member of the Prussian royal family, was offered the throne of Romania, he reportedly had to look at a map to locate his future kingdom. His puzzlement was partly understandable, for a united Romania had existed for only five years. The prince and his contemporaries in the generation after 1848 witnessed the emergence of several new nation-states. And as the map of Europe changed, a much enlarged and more powerful United States also emerged.

The changing political scenery was accompanied by the development of new political institutions. To meet the demand for popular participation in government so dramatically expressed in 1848, every European state, except the Ottoman and Russian Empires, found it necessary to have a parliament. Rare before midcentury, such institutions became common thereafter. No longer was the demand for popular participation seen as a threat to the existing political and social order. In fact, popular participation, or the appearance of it, gave the existing order a legitimacy it had not enjoyed since the French Revolution. Nationalism flourished during this period, emerging as a decisive force in European affairs and in the United States, where it promoted territorial expansion and a determination to preserve the Union.

These political transformations occurred in an era of unprecedented economic growth and prosperity, touched off by the discovery of gold in California in 1848. The increased supply of gold allowed for the expansion of credit, which led to the founding of new banks and mass investments in growing industries. The iron output of Britain, France, and Germany tripled in the years between 1850 and 1880. During this same period the

William I is proclaimed ruler of the German Empire at Versailles, 1871.

standard of living of every class rose significantly in industrializing nations. The middle classes expanded dramatically, while the elites sought to reestablish their power in new ways.

In the first half of the century, international relations had been dominated by the congress system, in which representatives of the major European states met periodically to preserve the balance of power. This order disappeared in the second half of the century, as political leaders pursued the narrow interests of their state. Instead of negotiation, brute military force—or the threat of its use—was employed to resolve international conflict. The new age was dominated not by ideals but by force, announced Prussian chancellor Otto von Bismarck, the main practitioner of what became known as *Realpolitik,* a policy in which war became a regular instrument of statecraft.

Crimean War This photograph shows the interior of the Sevastapol fortress after it had been battered into surrender. The Crimean War was the first conflict to be documented by photographers. *(Courtesy of the Board of Trustees of the Victoria & Albert Museum)*

THE CHANGING SCOPE OF INTERNATIONAL RELATIONS

The Crimean War and its aftermath shaped European international relations for several decades. Rising mutual suspicion led nations to act in their own self-interest and ignore the concerns of the other major players in the international system.

The Crimean War as a Turning Point, 1854–1856

The Crimean War had many causes. Principally, however, it was ignited by the decision of French and British statesmen to contain Russian power in the Balkans and keep it from encroaching on the weakening Ottoman Empire. Russian claims to have the right to intervene on behalf of Ottoman Christians had led to war between the two states in October 1853. The defeat of the Ottoman navy at Sinope in November left the Ottoman Empire defenseless.

British and French statesmen had considerable interest in the conflict. Britain had long feared that the collapse of the Ottoman Empire would lead Russia to seek territorial gains in the Mediterranean. Such a move would challenge Britain's supremacy. An explosion of public sentiment against Russia also obliged the British government to take an aggressive stance. Meanwhile, the French emperor, Napoleon III, viewed defeat of Russia as a way to eclipse one of the states most dedicated to preserving the existing European borders. He wanted to undermine existing power relations, hoping that a new order would lead to increased French power and influence. Napoleon also imagined that fighting side by side with Britain could lay the foundation for Anglo-French friendship. And so England and France rushed to defend the Ottoman Empire and declared war on Russia in March 1854.

The war was poorly fought on all sides. Leadership was woefully inadequate, and there were five times more casualties from disease than from enemy fire. The Russians had a standing army of a million but never managed to use more than a fraction of that number due largely to poor communications and supply systems. In Britain, failures in military supplies and leadership were denounced in the press and in Parliament. For the first time the press played an active role in report-

Florence Nightingale in the Crimean War

Florence Nightingale used her influential family connections to win an appointment to the Crimean battlefield. Once there, she organized nursing for the wounded and was able to secure additional personnel and medical supplies for her hospital. In this letter, Nightingale describes the plight of the wounded in an army lacking sufficient supplies.

We have no room for corpses in the wards. The Surgeons pass on to the next, an excision of the shoulder-joint—beautifully performed and going on well—ball lodged just in the head of the joint, and fracture starred all round. The next poor fellow has two stumps for arms—and the next has lost an arm and leg. As for the balls, they go in where they like, and do as much harm as they can in passing. That is the only rule they have. The next case has one eye put out, and paralysis of the iris of the other. He can neither see nor understand. But all who can walk come into us for Tobacco, but I tell them that we have not a bit to put into our own mouths. Not a sponge, nor a rag of linen, not anything have I left. Everything is gone to make slings and stump pillows and shirts. These poor fellows have not had a clean shirt nor been washed for two months before they came here, and the state in which they arrive from the transport is literally *crawling*. I hope in a few days we shall establish a little cleanliness. But we have not a basin nor a towel nor a bit of soap nor a broom—I have ordered 300 scrubbing brushes. But one half the Barrack is so sadly out of repair that it is impossible to use a drop of water on the stone floors, which are all laid upon rotten wood, and would give our men fever in no time. . . .

I am getting a screen now for the Amputations, for when one poor fellow, who is to be amputated tomorrow, sees his comrade today die under the knife it makes impression—and diminishes his chance. But, anyway, among these exhausted frames the mortality of the operations is frightful.

Source: Letter to Dr. William Bowman, November 14, 1854, in Sue M. Goldie, ed., *"I Have Done My Duty": Florence Nightingale in the Crimean War, 1854–56* (Iowa City: University of Iowa Press, 1987), pp. 37–38.

ing war, and photography brought to readers at home the gruesome realities of battle.

One of the few heroic figures to emerge from this conflict was Florence Nightingale (1820–1910), who organized a nursing service to care for the British sick and wounded. Later, her wartime experience allowed her to pioneer nursing as a professional calling. (See the box, "Florence Nightingale in the Crimean War.")

The war ended in December 1855 when Russia surrendered the fortified port of Sevastopol after a long, bitter siege. The Russians were reluctant to admit defeat, but the threat of Austrian entry into the war on the side of the Western allies convinced them to sue for peace.

The Crimean War killed three-quarters of a million people—more than any European war be-tween the end of the Napoleonic Wars and World War I. The slowness with which each side mobilized, the lack of planning and foresight in staging battles, the large number of fatalities from causes other than enemy fire—all were reminiscent of hostilities from earlier eras. It was a particularly futile, senseless war whose most important consequence was political, for it unleashed dramatic new changes in the international order.

The Congress of Paris and Its Aftermath

The former combatants met in Paris in February 1856 to work out a peace treaty: Their decisions—which pleased no one—shaped relations among European states for the next half-century. Russian statesmen were especially discontented. The Congress of Paris forbade Russia from having a fleet in the Black Sea and forced it to withdraw from Moldavia and Wallachia, where it had enjoyed the right of intervention since the 1830s. Tsar Nicholas I had expected Austrian assistance in the war in return for his help in crushing the Hungarian rebellion in 1849. Instead, Austria's leaders had not only withheld aid but even threatened to join the Western alliance, and Russian officials denounced Austrian "betrayal." Nor did French leaders feel their nation had benefited. Although holding the congress in Paris flattered the emperor's pride, no other clear advantages emerged for France. The north Italian state of Piedmont, which had joined the allies, gained from the congress only a vague statement on the unsatisfactory nature of the existing situation in Italy. Prussia was invited to attend the congress only as an afterthought and hence also felt slighted.

Although the war seemed to have sustained the integrity of the Ottoman Empire, the peace settlement weakened it indirectly by dictating reforms in the treatment of its Christian populations. These reforms impaired the empire's ability to repress growing national movements and opened the door to the possibility of independent Balkan states. British political leaders, galled by the heavy sacrifices of the war, moved toward isolationism in foreign policy. Austrian policymakers, who hoped to gain the aid of Britain and France in preserving the Habsburg empire, found them hostile instead, thereby encouraging the forces undermining it. At the time the peace treaty was signed, few people foresaw the enormous results that would flow from it.

In the past the congress system had tried to ensure that no major power was dissatisfied enough to subvert the existing distribution of power, but the Crimean War and the peace treaty markedly changed that situation. For example, in the first half of the century the international order had been upheld in part by the cooperation of the rulers of the conservative Eastern powers: Russia, Austria, and Prussia. Now these powers were rivals, and their competition contributed to growing instability in the international system. By and large, the decisions reached in Paris were either disregarded or unilaterally revised. This new international climate also allowed the emergence of new states without international sanction.

ITALIAN UNIFICATION

In the words of Prince von Metternich of Austria, Italy at midcentury was nothing but a "geographic expression." The revolution of 1848 (see page 767) had revealed an interest in national unification, but the attempt had failed. Yet within a dozen years what many believed to be impossible would come to pass. Idealists like Giuseppe Mazzini (1805–1872) had preached that Italy would be unified by its people, who would rise and establish a free republic. Instead, it was unified by royalty, by war, and by the help of a foreign state. Although ideals were not absent from the process of unification, cynical manipulation and scheming also came into play.

After the failed 1848 revolution, various Italian rulers resorted to repression. In Modena, the Habsburg duke Francis V jailed liberals, closed the universities, and personally caned passersby who did not tip their hat to him. In the Papal States, men were imprisoned for "appearing inclined to novelty." Pope Pius IX, who first had appeared sympathetic to Italian unification, opposed it as soon as he realized it was attainable only by war against Catholic Austria. Italian nationalists viewed him as a traitor as he became a firm opponent of both liberalism and nationalism. In Naples, the government was so weak it established its authority by working with organized crime. In Parma, the duke was assassinated in 1854—to the relief of his people—and the uprising that accompanied this desperate act was suppressed by three thousand Austrian troops sent in by the duke's ally, the Habsburgs.

Compared to this dismal record, the kingdom of Piedmont in northern Italy appeared stable and successful. It was the only Italian state that kept the liberal constitution it had adopted during the 1848 revolution, and it welcomed political refugees from other Italian states. Economically, it was a beacon to the rest of Italy, establishing modern banks and laying half the rail lines on the peninsula.

Since the late eighteenth century, some Italians had called for a *risorgimento*, a political and cultural renewal of Italy. By the mid-nineteenth century the idea was actively supported by a small, elite group of the educated middle class, urban property owners, and members of the professional classes, who were open to nationalist arguments. For merchants, industrialists, and professionals, a unified state would provide a larger stage on which to pursue their ambitions. Members of these groups founded the National Society, a grassroots unification movement. This organization now looked to Piedmont to lead the peninsula toward national unity.

Cavour Plots Unification

The statesman who was to catapult Piedmont into a position of leadership in the dramatic events leading to Italian unification was Count Camillo di Cavour (1810–1861). The son of a Piedmontese nobleman and high government official, he grew up speaking French, the language of the court and of formal education in Piedmont, and mastered Italian only as an adult. Cosmopolitan in his interests, Cavour knew more about Britain and France than about Italy. He was sympathetic to the aspirations of the middle class and saw in Britain and France models of what Italy ought to become, a liberal and economically advanced society.

Short, fat, and near-sighted, Cavour hardly cut a heroic figure. Yet he was ambitious, hard-working, and driven to succeed. In 1850 he joined the government of Piedmont. Two years later he was appointed prime minister. He shared the general enthusiasm of the middle classes for an Italian nation, but his vision probably did not include the entire Italian peninsula, only its north and center, which then could dominate the rest of the peninsula in a loose federation. One fateful lesson he had learned from the failures of 1848 was that foreign help, especially French assistance, would be necessary to expel the Austrians from the peninsula.

When the Crimean War broke out in 1854, Cavour steered Piedmont to the allied side, hoping to advance his cause. He sent twenty thousand troops to the Crimea, one-tenth of whom died. This act gained him a seat at the Congress of Paris, where his presence boosted the kingdom's prestige—and where he and Napoleon III had an opportunity to meet and size up each other.

Napoleon III favored the cause of Italian liberation from Austrian rule and some form of unification of the peninsula. Austria had been France's traditional opponent; destroying Austria's power in Italy might strengthen France. Thus the French emperor and the Piedmontese prime minister, both desirous of changing the map of Europe,

each for his own reasons, secretly met in July 1858 at Plombières, a French spa, to discuss how Italian unity could be achieved. They agreed that Piedmont would stir up trouble in one of Austria's Italian territories in an effort to goad the Austrians into war. France would help the Piedmontese expel Austria from the peninsula, and the new Piedmont, doubled in size, would become part of a confederation under the papacy. In exchange, the French emperor demanded the cession of Nice and Savoy. (See the box, "Cavour and Napoleon III Plot War.")

This demand presented difficulties: Savoy was the heartland of the Piedmont kingdom, the area from which the royal house came; and the city of Nice was clearly Italian in nationality. France's other demand was that the king of Piedmont, who represented the House of Savoy, the oldest reigning house in Europe, allow his 15-year-old daughter to marry the emperor's 38-year-old dissipated cousin. To accept these terms seemed a betrayal of national honor and conventional morality. But such scruples gave way to political ambition, and Cavour assented.

War between Austria and Piedmont began in April 1859. By June the combined Piedmontese and French forces had routed the Austrians at Magenta and Solferino (Map 22.1). The bloodiness of these battles impressed contemporaries: The color magenta was named after the color of the blood flowing on the battlefield, and when a Swiss humanitarian, Henri Dunant (1828–1901), organized emergency services for both French and Austrians wounded at Solferino, he proposed the founding of voluntary relief societies in every nation, called the Red Cross.

Instead of pressing on after these two military victories, Napoleon III decided to end the fighting. Several developments motivated his decision. First, he was truly shocked by the bloodshed he had witnessed, and he was alarmed by the Prussian mobilization on the Rhine on behalf of Austria. Second, his plans for Italy threatened to develop in unforeseen directions. To the south of Piedmont, popular revolts in August and September had broken out against local rulers. Each side fearing victory by the other, both revolutionaries and the local officials appealed for annexation to Piedmont, which resulted in a larger independent state than Napoleon III had anticipated. These factors led Napoleon to sign an armistice with the

Cavour and Napoleon III Plot War

In July 1858 Cavour and Napoleon III met at Plombières in France to plot war against Austria with the intention of evicting it from Italy. Italy's borders were to be reorganized, giving Piedmont additional territory, and France was to receive compensation for its assistance. On July 24, Cavour outlined the contents of the agreement in a letter to the king of Piedmont, a cynical display of realpolitik.

. . . [T]ogether we began to go through the Italian States, in search of those grounds for war which were so difficult to find. After we had traveled the whole length of the peninsula without success, we came almost unawares upon Massa and Carrara, and there discovered what we had been trying so hard to find. When I had given the Emperor an exact description of that unfortunate country, of which he already had a pretty clear idea anyway, we agreed on getting in a petition from the inhabitants to Your Majesty asking for his protection and even requesting the annexation of these Duchies to Sardinia. Your Majesty would not accept the proposed surrender, but would support the cause of these oppressed populations by addressing a haughty and menacing note to the Duke of Modena. The Duke, confident of Austrian support, would reply in an impertinent manner. Thereupon, Your Majesty would occupy Massa, and the war would begin. . . .

What would be the aim of the war?

The Emperor freely agreed that the Austrians must be driven out of Italy altogether, leaving them not an inch of land this side of the Alps and the Isonzo. . . .

After we had settled the future fate of Italy, the Emperor asked me what France would get, and if Your Majesty would cede Savoy and the County of Nice.

Source: Cavour to Victor Emmanuel, July 24, 1858, in David Thomson, ed., *France: Empire and Republic, 1850–1940* (New York: Harper, 1968), pp. 322–324.

Austrians, allowing Austria to keep part of Lombardy and all of Venetia and to participate in an Italian Confederation. Cavour was outraged by Napoleon's betrayal of their agreement and resigned as prime minister; he returned to office, however, in January 1860.

Unification Achieved, 1860

The overthrow of the Austrian-backed rulers in Parma, Modena, and Tuscany led these areas in 1859 to vote in plebiscites to join Piedmont. Farther south, in central Italy, agitation against the papal misrule also inclined those regions toward the more enlightened Piedmont.

Cavour had envisioned no more than a united northern Italy. Unexpected events in the south, however, dramatically changed that vision. The centuries-old misgovernment of Naples led to an uprising, further abetted by the revolutionary firebrand Giuseppe Garibaldi (1807–1882), a rival of Cavour who favored unification and won a large popular following. In May 1860, with but a thousand poorly armed, red-shirted followers, he set sail for Sicily to help the island rise up against its Bourbon ruler. Winning that struggle, Garibaldi's forces crossed to the mainland. Victory followed victory, and enthusiasm for Garibaldi grew. His army swelled to 57,000 men, and he won the entire kingdom of Naples.

Threatened by the advance of Garibaldi's power and fearing its reach into the Papal States, Cavour sent his army into the area in September 1860. This action, a brutal attack on a weak state that had not harmed Piedmont, was viewed by many Catholics as aggression against the spiritual head of their church. However, as Cavour explained to his parliament, political necessity required it. The inter-

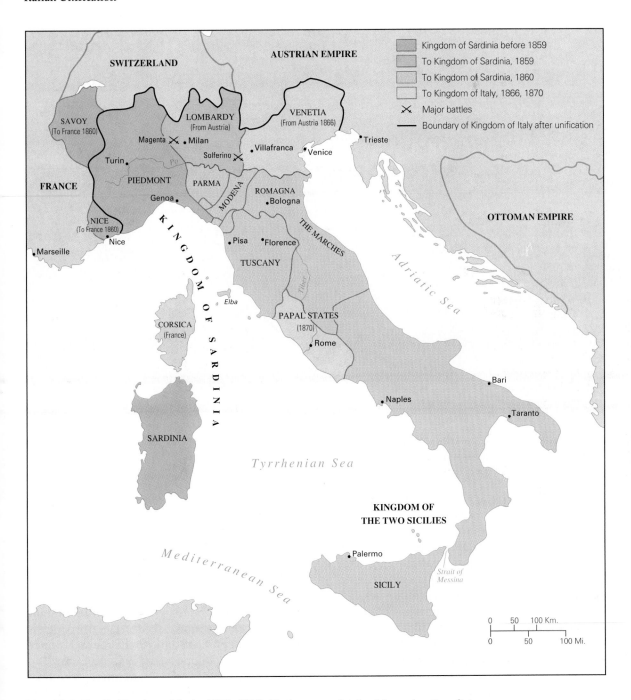

Map 22.1 The Unification of Italy, 1859–1870 Piedmontese leadership and nationalist fervor united Italy.

ests of the state of Piedmont and the about-to-be-born Italy superseded traditional morality.

Although Garibaldi was a republican, he was convinced that Italy could best achieve unity under the king of Piedmont, and he willingly submit-

ted the southern part of Italy, which he controlled, to the king, Victor Emmanuel II (r. 1849–1878). Thus by November 1860, Italy lay united under Piedmontese rule (see Map 22.1). The territories that came under Piedmontese control affirmed

Garibaldi Leading His "Red Shirts" to Victory over the Neapolitan Army, May 1860
Garibaldi's successful conquests in the south and Cavour's in the north opened the way
for Italian unification. *(Museo di Risorgimento, Milan/Scala/Art Resource, NY)*

their desire to be part of the new Italy in plebiscites based on universal male suffrage. By huge majorities, the populations voted affirmatively. Undoubtedly there was pressure from the occupying army and from the upper classes, who marched the people dependent on them—workers, employees, tenant farmers—to the polls. Voting was not secret, and fraud was widespread. But in an age drawn to democracy, the plebiscite gave legitimacy to the new state and won sympathy from liberally inclined states abroad.

Still to be joined to the new state were Austrian-held Venetia in the northeast and Rome and its environs, held by the pope with the support of a French garrison. But within a decade, a propitious international situation enabled the fledgling country to acquire both key areas. After Austria was defeated in the Austro-Prussian War in 1866, Venetia was ceded to Italy. Then the Franco-Prussian War forced the French to evacuate Rome, which they had occupied since 1849. Rome was joined to Italy

and became its capital in 1870. With that event, unification was complete (see Map 22.1).

The Problems of Unified Italy

National unity had been achieved, but it was frail. The nation was divided between the modernizing north and the traditional south. The uprisings in the south that had led to its inclusion in a united Italy were motivated more by hatred of the Bourbons than by fervor for national union. And once the union occurred, the north behaved like a conquering state—sending its officials to the south, raising taxes, and imposing its laws. In 1861 an uprising of disbanded Neapolitan soldiers and brigands broke out. To crush the revolt, half the Italian army was sent south; the civil war lasted five years and produced more casualties than the entire effort of unification.

Other major divisions remained. In 1861 only 2.5 percent of the population spoke the national language, Florentine Italian. The economy also remained divided. The north was far more industrialized than the rural south. In the south, child mortality was higher, life expectancy was lower, and illiteracy reached the 90 percent mark. The two regions seemed to belong to two different nations.

Piedmont imposed strong central control, resolutely refusing a federal system of government, which many Italians in an earlier era had hoped for. This choice reflected the determination of Piedmont to project its power onto the rest of the peninsula, as well as fear that any other form of government might lead to disintegration of the new state. The United States, with a federal system of government, was wracked by secessionism leading in early 1861 to the Civil War (see page 831). Piedmont wanted to save the new Italian state from such a fate.

Piedmont imposed its constitution on unified Italy. This constitution limited suffrage to men of property and education, less than 2 percent of the population. Further, although parliamentarism was enshrined in the constitution, Cavour's maneuvering as prime minister had kept governments from being answerable to the parliament. Shifting majorities meant that the government could cajole and bribe the opposition, transforming previous foes into supporters. This system of manipulation, known as *trasformismo,* characterized Italian government for decades. However, although Italian parliamentarism was far from complete, a liberal state recognizing legal equality and freedom of association had been established, providing more freedom for its citizens than the peninsula had seen for centuries.

The new Italian state was weakened by the hostility the Catholic church directed against it. In the process of unifying Italy, Piedmont had seized the Papal States and finally in 1870 annexed Rome, leaving the pope to administer only a few square blocks around the papal palace, the Vatican. The popes considered themselves prisoners of the new Italian state and denounced it and all those supporting it, including those participating in elections. Thus the new state was contested by many Catholics, who refused to recognize it for decades, thwarting its claim to legitimacy.

In 1870 Italy, with its 27 million people, was the sixth-most-populated European nation. It was too small to be a great power and too large to accept being a small state. Italian statesmen found it difficult to define their country's role in international politics, and they lacked a firm consensus on Italy's future.

GERMAN UNIFICATION

Like Italy, Germany began as a collection of polities, first loosely united in the Holy Roman Empire and then, after 1815, equally loosely organized in the German Confederation. As did Piedmont in Italy, Prussia, the most powerful German state, led the unification movement. And just as Italy had in Cavour a strong leader who imposed his will, so did German unification have a ruthless and cunning leader: Otto von Bismarck, prime minister of Prussia.

In 1848 German unification under Prussian leadership had appeared likely, but the process ended quickly when the king of Prussia refused to accept a throne offered by an elected assembly. When national unity was ultimately achieved, it was not as a result of popular decision but by the use of military force and the imposition of Prussian absolutism over the whole country.

The Rise of Bismarck

Austria under Metternich had always treated Prussia as a privileged junior partner. After Metternich's fall in 1848, however, rivalry erupted between the two German states. Each tried to use for its own aggrandizement the desire for national unity that had become manifest during the revolution of 1848.

In March 1850, Prussia invited various German rulers to a meeting in Erfurt to consider possible unification under its sponsorship. Austria, which had been excluded, insisted that the "Erfurt Union" be dissolved and that Prussia remain in the German Confederation. Austrian leaders backed their demands with the threat of war; at a meeting in Olmütz in November, Prussia had to scuttle the Erfurt Union and accept Austrian leadership in Germany. The Prussians dubbed this event the "humiliation of Olmütz," and many were determined to regain the advantage in Germany. At that time, however, the Prussian military was not strong enough to challenge Austria. But this situation changed under the new Prussian king, William I (r. 1861–1888), who was committed to expanding the size and effectiveness of the army. He wanted to reduce the reserve army, increase the professional army, and expand the training period from two to three years. These measures needed parliamentary approval, but the parliament, which was dominated by the liberals, opposed the increased costs.

When the parliament refused to accept the king's proposals, he dissolved it. It was immediately re-elected, with an even stronger liberal majority. The issue was not purely military, but rather one of who should govern the country—the king or the elected representatives. To get his way, the king appointed Otto von Bismarck as prime minister to implement his program of reforms.

Bismarck was a Junker, a Prussian aristocrat known for his reactionary views, who had opposed the liberal movement in 1848. As Prussian emissary to the German Confederation, he had challenged Austrian primacy. Devoted to his monarch, Bismarck smarted at the humiliation of Olmütz and sought to heighten Prussian power in Germany and throughout Europe. He faced down the parliament, telling the Budget Commission in 1862, "The position of Prussia in Germany will be decided not by its liberalism but by its power . . . not through speeches and majority decisions are the great questions of the day decided—that was the mistake of 1848–49—but by 'iron and blood.'"[1]

Bismarck tried to win over the liberals by suggesting that with military force at its disposal, Prussia could lead German unification. But the liberals resisted, and the Parliament voted against the military reforms. Ignoring the elected assembly, Bismarck decided to carry out the military measures anyway and to collect the taxes that would make them possible. The citizens acquiesced and organized no resistance.

Several factors explain why Bismarck prevailed. The liberals who opposed him represented the business and professional classes who had received the vote as a result of the 1848 revolution. They had not implemented effective political or social programs, and they did not enjoy mass support. Had they wished to mobilize large segments of the population on behalf of their principles, they could not have done so.

Neither the Prussian king nor Bismarck's fellow aristocrats were nationalists. They believed in a strong Prussia, but they feared that a united Germany would dilute Prussian power and influence.

German unification had been part of the liberals' program, not the conservatives'.

German liberals were faced with a dilemma: Did they value nationhood or the principles of liberty more? Fellow liberals elsewhere lived in existing nation-states, where statehood had preceded the development of liberalism. Even in Italy, the liberals had been faced by a less harsh dilemma, for unification was led by the liberal state of Piedmont. That was not the case in Germany, where the natural leader, Prussia, had a long tradition of militarism and authoritarianism. To be effective in opposition to Bismarck, German liberals would have had to join with the working classes, but they feared them and held themselves aloof from such an alliance.

Bismarck's genius was to exploit a growing desire for German unification. During the Franco-Austrian War of 1859, which launched Italian unification, Germans had feared that the French would cross the Rhine River; only a strong, united Germany could give its inhabitants security. Professional and cultural organizations now often extended beyond a single state and were all German, for instance, the German Commercial Association, the Congress of German Jurists, and the German Sharpshooters League. Many individual German states, each calculating possible political gains, launched proposals for unification in the 1860s. Although it had yet to find much resonance among the lower classes, the idea of a united Germany was gaining a wider audience.

Prussian Wars and German Unity

Having established the supremacy of royal power in Prussia, Bismarck was ready to enlarge Prussia's role in Germany at the expense of Austria. The provocation was a crisis over Schleswig-Holstein (Map 22.2). These two provinces, ethnically and linguistically German (except for northern Schleswig), were ruled by Denmark. Historically and by previous treaty agreements Schleswig and Holstein were legally inseparable. When in 1863 the Danish king, contrary to earlier treaty obligations, attempted to connect Schleswig more closely to the Crown, Holstein, with a mainly German population, felt threatened. Although the latter was under Danish rule, it was also a member of the German Confederation, and it called on the Confederation for protection.

Map 22.2 The Unification of Germany A series of military victories made it possible for Prussia to unite Germany under its domain.

Acting on behalf of the Confederation, Prussia and Austria intervened, sending troops that won a quick, cheap victory. Prussia occupied Schleswig, and Austria took Holstein.

Joint military action in no way united Prussia and Austria, who continued to be bitter rivals for domination of Germany. Bismarck believed war was the only means to win this contest, and conflicts over the administration of Schleswig and Holstein served as a pretext. With no declaration of war, Prussia attacked Austrian-administered Holstein in June 1866 and defeated the Austrian

GERMAN UNIFICATION

1862	Bismarck appointed prime minister of Prussia
January 1864	Austria and Prussia attack Denmark and occupy Schleswig and Holstein
June 1866	Austro-Prussian War
July 3, 1866	Prussia wins Battle of Sadowa
1867	The North German Confederation
March–July 1870	Crisis over Hohenzollern candidacy for Spanish throne
July 13, 1870	Interview at Ems and publication of Ems dispatch
July 19, 1870	France declares war on Prussia
September 1, 1870	Prussia victorious at Battle of Sedan
January 18, 1871	The German Empire declared in the Hall of Mirrors in Versailles

army at Sadowa (Königgratz) on July 3. Austria sued for peace.

Prussia annexed its smaller neighbors who had supported Austria, thus creating a contiguous state linking Prussia with the Rhineland. This enlarged Prussia intended to dominate the newly formed North German Confederation, comprising all the states north of the Main River. Henceforth Austria was excluded from German affairs.

The triumph of Sadowa transformed Bismarck into a popular hero. Elections held on the day of the battle returned a conservative pro-Bismarck majority to the Prussian parliament. The legislature, including a large number of liberals mesmerized by the military victory, voted retroactively to legalize the illegal taxes that had been levied since 1862 for the purpose of upgrading the military. Enthusiastic at the prospect that Prussia might now successfully lead German unity, these liberals readily compromised their principles. They rational-

ized that national unity ought to be gained first, with liberal constitutional institutions secured later. They proved to be wrong.

The unification of Germany, like that of Italy, was facilitated by a favorable international situation. The Crimean War had estranged Russia from Austria. In 1850 Austrian resistance to Prussian attempts to lead Germany had been backed by Russia, but by the time the Austro-Prussian War broke out in 1866, Austria stood alone. Although it would have been opportune for France to intervene on the Austrian side, the French emperor was indecisive and in the end did nothing. He also had been lulled into security by vague Prussian promises of support for French plans to annex Luxembourg. Once the war was won, however, Bismarck reneged on these promises, and France was left with the problem of a strong, enlarged Prussia on its eastern border, which threatened France's position as a Great Power. British statesmen likewise did not intervene in the unification process. Disillusioned by the results of the Crimean War, they were in an isolationist mood. Moreover, Britain's government was sympathetic to the rise of a fellow Protestant power.

Bismarck hoped that the southern German states would eventually merge with the North German Confederation. For the time being, he allowed them to remain outside the new body, but he obliged them to sign a military treaty with Prussia. Economically, they continued to be dependent as a result of the *Zollverein* (the customs union). Many southerners favored unity, especially business people who saw in it the hope of an improved economy. And German nationalists, north and south, sought the realization of a decades-long dream.

The Franco-Prussian War and Unification, 1870–1871

French leaders, however, were determined to prevent German unity. They feared the loss of influence in the southern German states that had traditionally been France's allies. Moreover, since the mid-seventeenth century, French security had been linked to a weak and divided Germany.

Both Berlin and Paris anticipated war. And war came soon enough, precipitated by a crisis over the Spanish succession. In 1868, a military coup had overthrown the Spanish queen Isabella, and the new authorities offered the throne to a

The Battle of Sadowa, July 3, 1866 In this important battle, the Prussians defeated Austria, eclipsing it as a German power. Now the road to Prussian supremacy in Germany lay open. *(Giraudon/Art Resource, NY)*

Catholic member of the Hohenzollerns, the reigning Prussian monarch's family. The French viewed this candidacy as an unacceptable expansion of Prussian power and influence. Fearing a two-front war with Prussia in the east and Spain in the south, they insisted the Hohenzollerns refuse the proffered throne. As passions heated, Bismarck was elated at the prospect of war. But the Prussian king was not. On July 12, 1870, he withdrew the young prince's candidacy, removing the cause for war. Bismarck was bitterly disappointed.

Not content with the prestige they won with this diplomatic victory, the French pushed their luck further. On July 13 the French ambassador met the king of Prussia at Ems and demanded guarantees that no Hohenzollern would ever again be a candidate to the Spanish throne. Unable to provide any more concessions without a serious loss of prestige, the Prussian king refused the French demand.

William telegraphed an account of his meeting to Bismarck. The chancellor was heartened by the opportunity this message provided. He edited what became known as the Ems dispatch, making the exchange between king and ambassador seem more curt than it actually had been; then he re-

leased it to the press. As he hoped, the French interpreted the account as a deliberate snub to their ambassador. Faced by a flood of emotional demands for redress of the imagined slight to French national honor, Napoleon III declared war on July 15.

The Prussians led a well-planned campaign. An army of 384,000 Prussians was rushed by rail to confront a force of 270,000 Frenchmen. The French had the advantage of better rifles, but the Prussians were equipped with heavier guns, which at a distance could pulverize French positions. Within a few weeks, Prussia won a decisive victory at Sedan, taking the French emperor prisoner on September 2. The French continued the struggle, despite difficult odds. Infuriated by the continuation of the war, the Prussians resorted to extreme measures, even targeting civilians. They took hostages and burned down whole villages, and they laid siege to Paris, starving and bombarding its beleaguered population.

Throughout Germany the outbreak of the war was met with general enthusiasm for the Prussian cause. Exploiting this popular feeling, Bismarck called on the other German states to accept the unification of Germany under the Prussian king. Reluctant princes, such as the king of Bavaria, were bought off with bribes. On January 18, 1871, the German princes met in the hall of mirrors of the Versailles palace, symbol of past French greatness, and acclaimed William I as German emperor (see Map 22.2).

In May 1871 the Treaty of Frankfurt established the peace terms. France was forced to give up the provinces of Alsace and Lorraine and to pay a heavy indemnity of five billion francs. These harsh terms embittered the French, leading many to desire revenge and establishing a formidable barrier to future relations between France and Germany.

The Character of the New Germany

German unity had been forged by a series of wars—against Denmark in 1864, Austria in 1866, and France in 1870—and lacked the popular democratic base that had been present in Italy. Because the military had been instrumental in the formation of the new German state, it remained dominant in the new society that followed. Italian unity had been sanctioned by plebiscites and a vote by an elected assembly accepting the popular verdict. The founding act of the new German state was the meeting of the German rulers on the soil of a defeated neighbor. Thus the rulers placed themselves above elected assemblies and popular sanction. (See the box, "Bismarck Considers the Dynastic Role in German Unification.")

The constitution of the new Germany was remarkably democratic on the surface, however. It provided for an upper, appointed house, the Bundesrat, representing the individual German states, and a lower house, the Reichstag, which was elected by universal manhood suffrage. The latter seemed a surprising concession from Bismarck, the authoritarian aristocrat. But he knew the liberals lacked mass support and gambled that, with appropriate appeals, he would be able to create majorities that could be manipulated for his purposes.

The dominant state in the new Germany was, of course, Prussia, which also had two-thirds of its population. Within the Bundesrat, Prussia had 17 of the 43 seats and could block any legislation it opposed with the aid of only a few other states. The king of Prussia occupied the post of emperor, and the chancellor and other cabinet members were responsible not to parliament but to him. He alone could make foreign policy and war, com-

mand the army, and interpret the constitution. The authoritarianism of Prussia had been projected onto all of Germany.

The emergence of a strong, united Germany disrupted the European balance of power. In February 1871 the British political leader Benjamin Disraeli observed that the unification of Germany was "a greater political event than the French revolution of last century. . . . There is not a diplomatic tradition which has not been swept away. You have a new world. . . . The balance of power has been entirely destroyed."[2] Germany had become the dominant power on the Continent.

PRECARIOUS SUPRANATIONAL EMPIRES

In an age of nationalism that saw two new nation-states emerge—Italy and Germany—those European states that were multinational found themselves in a precarious position. The Habsburg and Ottoman Empires of central and eastern Europe consisted of numerous peoples speaking different languages, holding different religious beliefs, and having different historical traditions. In the past such multinational states had been quite normal in Europe, but in the nineteenth century they became increasingly anomalous. The peoples living under the authority of Vienna and Constantinople became more and more restive. Facing this severe challenge, the Austrian and Ottoman Empires attempted to strengthen themselves by restructuring their institutions.

The Dual Monarchy in Austria-Hungary

Austrian statesmen sensed the vulnerability of their empire. By 1860 they had lost much of their Italian possessions; they met with resistance in Hungary from the Magyars, a powerful minority still resentful they had not won independence in 1848; and they faced the bitter struggle for German supremacy with Prussia. To give his government credibility, in February 1861, Emperor Francis Joseph (r. 1848–1916) issued what were known as the February Patents, which liberalized the government, guaranteed civil liberties, and provided local self-government and an elected parliament.

The need to concentrate on safeguarding the remaining territories was clear. By 1866 the Austrian Habsburgs were no longer a German or Ital-

Bismarck Considers the Dynastic Role in German Unification

After leaving office in 1890, Bismarck wrote his **Memoirs.** *In this selection he examines the efforts of the various states in promoting national unification. He denounces many of them for having resisted this movement but emphasizes the importance of Prussia's role. The rulers, rather than the German people, he insists, formed the new united Germany. And only monarchy can guarantee national unity.*

Never, not even in Frankfurt [in 1848] did I doubt the key to German politics was to be found in princes and dynasties, not in publicists, whether in parliament and the press, or on the barricades. The opinion of the cultivated public as uttered in parliament and the press might promote and sustain the determination of the dynasties, but perhaps provoked their resistance more frequently than it urged them forward in the direction of national unity. ... The Prussian dynasty might anticipate that the hegemony in the future German empire would eventually fall to it, with an increase of consideration and power. It could foresee its own advantage....

The Gordian knot of German circumstances ... could only be cut by the sword: it came to this, that the King of Prussia, conscious or unconscious, and with him the Prussian army, must be gained for the national cause, whether from the "Borussian" [Prussian]

point of view one regarded the hegemony of Prussia or from the national point of view the unification of Germany as the main object; both aims were co-extensive. So much was clear to me. ...

In order that German patriotism should be active and effective, it needs as a rule to hang on the peg of dependence upon a dynasty; independent of dynasty it rarely comes to the rising point, though in theory it daily does so in parliament, in the press, in public meeting. ... The German's love of Fatherland has need of a prince on whom it can concentrate its attachment. ...

The preponderance of dynastic attachment, and the use of a dynasty as the indispensable cement to hold together a definite portion of the nation calling itself by the name of the dynasty, is a specific peculiarity of the German empire.

Source: Otto von Bismarck, *The Man and the Statesman*, trans. A. J. Butler (London: Smith Elder & Co., 1898), vol. 1, pp. 318–321, 323–324.

ian power (Venetia had been handed over to a united Italy). The strongest challenge to Habsburg rule came from Hungary, where the Magyars insisted on self-rule, a claim based on age-old historic rights and Vienna's initial acceptance of autonomy in 1848. Since Magyar cooperation was crucial for the well-being of the Habsburg empire, the government entered into lengthy negotiations with Magyar leaders in 1867. The outcome was a compromise that created a new structure for the empire that lasted until 1918. The agreement divided the Habsburg holdings into Austria in the west and Hungary in the east (Map 22.3). Each was

independent, but they were linked by the person of the emperor of Austria, Francis Joseph, who was also king of Hungary. Hungary had full internal autonomy and participated jointly in imperial affairs—state finance, defense, and foreign relations. The new state created by the compromise was known as the dual monarchy of Austria-Hungary.

The emperor of the new state of Austria-Hungary had come to the throne as an 18-year-old in that year of crisis, 1848. Francis Joseph was a well-meaning monarch who took his duties seriously. His upbringing was German, he lived in German-speaking Vienna, and he headed an

RUSSIA

TRANSYLVANIA

ROMANIA

GALICIA

Danube

OTTOMAN   EMPIRE

Carpatho-Ukrainians (Ruthenians)

Serbs and Croats

Slovaks

Slovenes

Habsburg Monarchy boundaries

Germans

Hungarians

Italians

Romanians

Poles

Czechs

POLAND

Tisza

Budapest

HUNGARY

SERBIA

SILESIA

MORAVIA

Danube

Vienna

BOSNIA
Sarajevo

CROATIA-SLAVONIA

ILLYRIA

Prague

BOHEMIA

AUSTRIA

SALZBURG

CARINTHIA

Adriatic Sea

100 Mi.

100 Km.

50

50

0

0

GERMAN
STATES

BAVARIA

TYROL

VENETIA

ITALIAN
STATES

SWITZERLAND

LOMBARDY

Po

army and a bureaucracy that was mostly German, but Francis Joseph was markedly cosmopolitan. He spoke several of his subjects' languages and thought of himself as the emperor of all his peoples. In both halves of the empire, he was a much-loved, regal figure who provided a visible symbol of the state. He lacked imagination, however, and did little more than try to conserve a disintegrating empire coping with the modern forces of liberalism and nationalism.

The compromise confirmed Magyar dominance in Hungary. Although numerically a minority, Magyars controlled the Hungarian parliament, the army, the bureaucracy, and other state institutions. They opposed self-rule by the Croats, Serbs, Slovaks, Romanians, and others in the kingdom and attempted a policy of Magyarization—teaching only Magyar in the schools, conducting all government business in Magyar, and giving access to government positions only to those fully assimilated in Magyar culture. This arrangement created frustrations and resistance among the various nationalities under their rule.

The terms of the compromise also gave the Hungarians a voice in imperial foreign policy. Magyars feared that Slavic groups outside the empire, who planned to form independent states or had already done so, would inspire fellow Slavs in Austria-Hungary to revolt. To prevent that, the Hungarians favored an expansionist foreign policy in the Balkans, which the monarchy gladly embraced (see Map 22.3). Having lost its influence in Germany, Austria-Hungary found in the Balkans an area in which to assert itself. The policy was fraught with risks and, by bringing more discontented Slavs into the empire, led to hostility with other states.

The Ailing Ottoman Empire

At midcentury the Ottoman Empire was still one of the largest European powers, but it faced unrest within its borders and threats by the expansionist designs of its neighbors. The ailing empire was commonly referred to as "the sick man of Eu-

Map 22.3 Austria-Hungary in 1878 A multinational state, the Austro-Hungarian Empire acquired Bosnia in 1878, bringing more dissatisfied peoples under its rule. Tensions in the Balkans would lead to the outbreak of war in 1914.

rope." Over the next twenty-five years, the empire shed some of its territory and modernized its government, but nothing could save it from decline in the face of nationalist uprisings in its Balkan possessions.

As early as the 1840s, the Ottoman Empire had begun various reform movements to bring more security to its subjects. Known as the *Tanzimat*, these changes were initiated by Sultan Abdul Mejid (r. 1839–1861), with the help of his able prime minister, Reshid Mustafa Pasha (1800–1858). Reshid had served as the Ottoman ambassador in London and Paris and was familiar with Western institutions, which he admired and wished to emulate. The reforms tightened control over the Janissaries, the traditional military elite that had become a marauding force in the countryside. They also introduced security of property, equality of taxation, and equality before the law regardless of religion. Government officials—who previously had been free to collect taxes arbitrarily, sending the required amount to the central government and keeping the rest—were given fixed salaries and subjected to regular inspections.

These reforms were strengthened after the Crimean War by further imperial edicts. Contacts with the West encouraged Turks to think of transforming their empire into a more modern, Westernized state. Many young intellectuals were impatient with the rate of change, however, and critical of the sultan. Unable freely to express their opinions at home, some went into exile in the late 1860s to Paris and London. Their hosts called them the "Young Turks," an expression that became synonymous with the desire for change and improvement.

Alarmed by challenges to its rule, the central government began to turn away from reform, and in 1871 the sultan decided to assert his personal rule. His inability successfully to wage war and hold onto the empire led to dissatisfaction, and in the spring of 1876 rioters demanded and won the establishment of constitutional government. Within less than a year, however, the new sultan, Abdul Hamid II (r. 1876–1909), dismissed the constitutional government and reverted to personal rule.

Part of the administration's problem was financial. The Crimean War had forced the empire to borrow money abroad. The easy terms of foreign credit lured the sultan into taking out huge loans to finance extravagant projects. By 1875 more than half the annual income of the empire went to pay the interest on the debt. In spite of a drought and famine, the authorities raised taxes, fostering discontent within the realm.

Opposition to the government increased, fueled by nationalist fervor. The empire tolerated religious diversity and did not persecute people because of their religion. But the central administration had lost control over its provincial officials, who were often corrupt and tyrannical. In particular, much of the Balkan region was isolated from any benign control Constantinople might have wished to exercise. Christians, the majority population in the Balkans, blamed their suffering on Islamic rule, and many were inspired by the 1821

Nationalistic Uprising in Bulgaria In this 1879 lithograph, Bulgaria is depicted in the form of a maiden—protected by the Russian eagle, breaking her chains, and winning liberty from the Ottoman Empire. (*St. Cyril and Methodius National Library, Sofia*)

Greek war of independence and the revolutions of 1848 to seek their own independence.

The Romanians, for example, who lived mainly in the adjoining provinces of Moldavia in the north and Wallachia in the south, began to express nationalist sentiments in the late eighteenth century. These sentiments were nurtured by Western-educated students, who claimed for their countrymen illustrious descent from Roman settlers of antiquity. News of revolution in Paris in 1848 helped trigger a revolt in both provinces demanding unification and independence. This uprising was quickly crushed by the Turks.

The 1856 Peace of Paris removed Russia's right of protection over Moldavia and Wallachia and provided for a referendum to determine their future. Forbidden by international agreement from uniting, the two provinces chose a local nobleman, Alexander Cuza (r. 1859–1866), as ruler of each territory. Thus they were separate legally but united under one ruler. In 1861, the Ottoman Empire under pressure from the Romanians recognized the union of the two principalities in the single, autonomous state of Romania, and in 1878, at the Congress of Berlin, full independence was granted. Thus, in less than a quarter-century, two provinces of the Ottoman Empire merged and gained full sovereignty.

The path to independence was much more violent for the Bulgars. Influenced by neighboring Serbia and encouraged by the Russians, revolutionary committees spread propaganda and agitated against Ottoman rule. An uprising in Bulgaria broke out in May 1876. The Christian rebels attacked not only symbols of Ottoman authority but also peaceable Turks living in their midst. The imperial army, aided by local Turk volunteers, quickly re-established Ottoman authority. Incensed by the massacre of fellow Muslims, the volunteers resorted to mass killing, looting, and burning of Christian villages. The "Bulgarian horrors" shocked Europe and made the continuation of Turkish rule unacceptable.

The Bulgar crisis was resolved by the Balkan wars of 1876–1878, which were provoked by the uprising of the westernmost Ottoman provinces of Bosnia and Herzegovina. Since many of the inhabitants of these two provinces were Serbs, they had the sympathy of Serbia, which believed it could unify the southern Slavs. Together with the neighboring mountain state of Montenegro, Serbia declared war on the Ottoman Empire. They were savagely defeated by the Turks.

Russia, which saw itself as the protector of the Slavic peoples, reacted to the Bulgarian horrors by also declaring war on the empire, in April 1877. At first progress was slow, then the Russians broke through the Turkish lines and forced the sultan to sue for peace. The resulting Treaty of San Stefano, signed in March 1878, excluded the Ottoman Empire from Europe and created a huge, independent Bulgaria as essentially a Russian satellite.

The British, Austrians, and French were shocked at the extent to which the San Stefano treaty favored Russia. Under their pressure, the European powers met in Berlin in 1878 to reconsider the treaty. The Congress of Berlin reduced the size of the Bulgarian territory, allowing the rest to revert to Constantinople. Bosnia and Herzegovina were removed from Ottoman rule and put under that of Austria-Hungary (see Map 24.4 on page 911). Constantinople was forced to acknowledge the legal independence of Serbia, Montenegro, and Romania and the autonomy of Bulgaria. The British insisted on being given nearby Cyprus to administer, an outpost from which they might prevent further challenges to the existing balance of power.

Thus Turkey was plundered, not only by its enemies but also by powers that had intervened on its behalf. When France complained that it received no compensation, it was given the chance to grab Tunisia, another land under Ottoman rule. Russia, which had signed an alliance with Romania and promised to respect its territorial integrity, ignored its obligations and took southern Bessarabia from its ally. The work of the congress reflected the power politics that now characterized international affairs. Statesmen shamelessly used force against both foe and friend for the aggrandizement of their own state. Neither morality nor international law restrained ambition.

THE EMERGENCE OF A POWERFUL UNITED STATES, 1840–1880

Across the seas a new power emerged in these years, the United States. It enlarged its territories, strengthened its national government, and broadened its democracy by including a large category of people previously excluded from the political process—African Americans. But these achievements came at the expense of the bloodiest conflict in all of American history, the Civil War.

Territorial Expansion and Slavery

In the first few years of its existence, the United States was confined to the thirteen colonies, but in the nineteenth century it gained much territory through westward expansion (Map 22.4). In 1803 President Thomas Jefferson, negotiating with the French, secured the Louisiana Purchase, which nearly doubled the size of the United States. In 1819 most of Florida was acquired from Spain. Some Americans looked even farther, moving into Mexican-held territories in the southwest and British-held territories in the Pacific Northwest. The United States, some began to insist, was destined to occupy the whole North American continent from coast to coast; expansion would fulfill what was often called America's Manifest Destiny.

The U.S. government used the settlements of American citizens in Mexican- and British-held territories as pretexts for expansion. In 1845 Congress voted to annex Texas, which had gained independence from Mexico in 1836. Threats of war against Britain, if it did not hand over the Oregon territory, led the British government to abandon its claims to this region by treaty in 1846. Declaring war on Mexico in the same year, the United States won California and the southwest in 1848. Territorial growth in the 1840s increased the size of the country by about 60 percent. The Gadsden Purchase in 1853 rounded off the American gains. The United States now spanned the continent from the Atlantic to the Pacific.

The nature of the U.S. federal government was transformed in these years: From being a weak institution exercising authority only in a limited number of domains, the government in Washington, D.C., became a powerful authority. This change represented the only practical resolution of regional disagreements that threatened to tear the country apart in the mid-nineteenth century.

Beginning in the 1820s the United States saw serious sectional clashes between east and west as well as north and south. The latter were more important. Many issues divided the two regions, notably a conflict between the industrial interests of the North and the agrarian interests of the South. What particularly sharpened this divide, however,

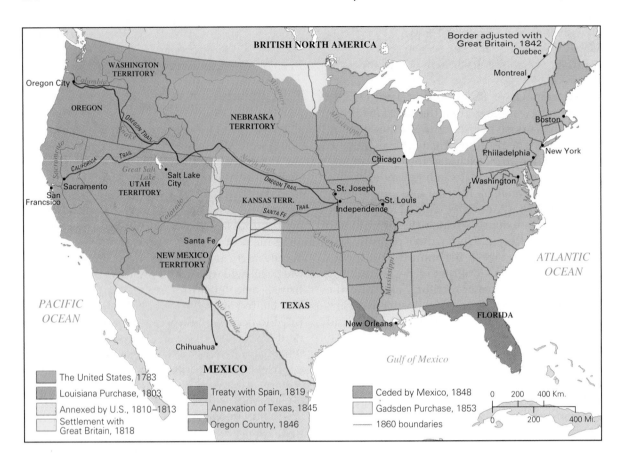

Map 22.4 U.S. Expansion Through 1853 In eight short years, from 1845 to 1853, the United States increased its territorial size by a third. The principle of Manifest Destiny appeared to be fulfilled, as the United States now stretched from the Atlantic to the Pacific.

was the issue of slavery. As the United States annexed new territories, the question of whether they would be slave or free divided the North and South, the North opposing the spread of the "peculiar institution," and much of the South, fearing isolation, favoring its spread. Southerners believed that if the new areas were closed to slavery, the institution would weaken in the South and eventually disappear. They would then be unable to withstand the political and economic pressure of an economically richer and more populous North, unsympathetic to slavery.

The issue of slavery was passionately debated for decades. Some Americans wanted slavery abolished throughout the United States; if that could not be done, some of the most committed abolitionists, especially in New England, advocated the secession of free states from the Union. On the other side, southerners threatened that if their

way of life—meaning a society based upon slavery—were not assured, then the South would secede. The threat of secession was lightly and frequently made by partisans of various causes for many decades. Commitment to national unity was weak and underdeveloped.

The election in November 1860 of the Illinois Republican Abraham Lincoln (1809–1865) as president appeared to the South as a final blow. Lincoln opposed the spread of slavery beyond its existing borders and hence appeared to threaten the future of slavery. Within a few weeks, the South reacted to Lincoln's election.

Beginning in December 1860 a number of southern state legislatures voted to secede from the Union, forming in February 1861 the Confederate States of America. The South saw its cause as being one of states' rights, claiming that the people of each state had the right to determine their destiny, free from what they viewed as the tyranny of the national government. Southern states seized federal funds and property, and in April 1861 the Confederates bombarded federally held Fort Sumter. Lincoln, inaugurated in March 1861, was determined to preserve the Union and to put down the insurrection. A calamitous civil war (1861–1865) had begun.

Civil War and National Unity

The North had many advantages over the South. It was nearly three times more populous than the South, it had a strong industrial base that could supply an endless stream of manufactured weapons, and it had a more extensive rail system allowing for better transport of men and materiel to the front. Although there were a number of important military engagements between the two parties, the North essentially strangled the South, which toward the end of the war was short of men, money, and supplies.

During both the war and its aftermath, the government took measures that centralized power in the United States, changing the nation from a loose federation of states to a more centrally governed entity. As one historian has noted, the United States changed from "they" to "it." The federal government intruded into areas of life from which it had before been absent. Slaves, previously considered property, were declared by Lincoln to be free with the Emancipation Proclamation in 1863. In fighting the war, the Union imposed conscription, enrolling every young able-bodied male in the army. A federal income tax was instituted, and with the National Banking Act of 1863, state banks were driven out of business and replaced by a uniform national banking system. The federal government provided massive subsidies for a national railroad system, and with the Morrill Land Grant College Act of 1862, it created a national system of state universities. Lincoln established the National Academy of Sciences to advise him on scientific matters. The word *national* came into increasing use. Senator John Sherman of Ohio declared during the war that "the policy of this country ought to be to make everything national as far as possible."

The principle of state sovereignty, which the Southern states had espoused and which the North had tried to accommodate before the war,

now lay defeated. The North occupied the South in an attempt to "reconstruct" it. Reconstruction included efforts to root out the Confederate leadership and to ensure full civil and political rights for the newly emancipated African Americans. The government also embarked on a short-lived campaign to provide freed slaves with enough land to ensure them of a livelihood—another example of federal authority at work. When the occupation of all the South ended in 1877, the supremacy of the national government over states was clearly established.

The Frontiers of Democracy

One of the major transformations in the United States that began in the 1820s and culminated in the 1860s was the inclusion of an ever greater number of people in the political process. By the late 1820s, under the impact of popular pressure, states abandoned restrictions on voting, and most adult white males received the vote. Symbolic of this new "age of the common man" was the election of Andrew Jackson as U.S. president in 1828. All his predecessors had been men of education and property—some were even described as "Virginia aristocrats"—but Jackson represented himself as a self-made man, a rugged frontiersman. State legislatures had in the past elected members to the presidential Electoral College, but in response to public calls for change, state legislatures altered the system so that Electoral College members were selected by direct popular vote.

National presidential campaigns became rough-and-tumble affairs, with emotional appeals to the public. Scurrilous attacks, many untrue, were mounted against opponents. In 1828, for instance, during President John Quincy Adams's re-election campaign, his opponents charged him with corruption, although once he was defeated, they admitted he had been one of the nation's most honest officeholders. Campaigns began to revolve around easily grasped symbols, and when William Henry Harrison ran for president in 1840 he was depicted as a simple frontiersman. His supporters wore log-cabin badges, sang log-cabin songs, and carried log-cabin replicas on floats in parades. Such paraphernalia became a common sight in American elections. If some contemporary observers, such as the Frenchman Alexis de Tocqueville (1805–1859), were disappointed at the

Bingham: The Verdict of the People In George Caleb Bingham's 1855 painting set in the American West, voters await election results. Unlike in Europe, where religious and property barriers to suffrage continued throughout the nineteenth century, many U.S. states had universal white male suffrage by the 1820s. *(From the Art Collection of NationsBank)*

lack of a thoughtful and deliberate process in choosing political leaders, they thought democracy was nowhere in the world as fully developed as in the United States, where it foreshadowed the future of other societies.

When Abraham Lincoln was elected U.S. president in 1860, nobody of his social standing occupied an equivalent position in Europe. At the news of his assassination in 1865, workmen and artisans, seeing in the dead president a kindred spirit, stood for hours in line outside the U.S. legation in London and the consul general's office in Lyon (France) to sign a book of condolence to express their sorrow. It was also a form of tribute to a nation that had elected a backwoodsman, born in a log cabin, to its highest office.

The frontiers of democracy appeared to have widened after the Civil War when amendments to the U. S. Constitution granted African Americans full equality with whites. Slavery was forbidden throughout the United States, and regardless of "race, color, or previous condition of servitude," all Americans were declared to be citizens and guaranteed the exercise of their rights. During the first few years of Reconstruction, whites who had supported the Confederacy were deprived of the right to vote, and African Americans represented a voting bloc in the South. As a result, for the first time the United States saw the election of a black governor as well as several lieutenant-governors, senators, congressmen, postmasters, and innumerable county and town officials who were black. After the end of military occupation of the south, however, local white power reasserted itself and the rights of African Americans were sharply curtailed. Yet, compared to the situation before the Civil War, African Americans had advanced significantly. They were no longer slaves but citizens, they were free to move where they wanted, and in some places they were able to participate in the political process.

By 1880 the United States not only had seen four decades of territorial expansion but had been transformed by the ordeal of the Civil War, which brought about the extension of federal authority and—however hesitatingly—of the rights of citi-

~ ENCOUNTERS WITH THE WEST ~

A Japanese View of the British Parliament

In 1862 the Japanese government sent its first diplomatic mission to Europe. Accompanying the delegation was its young translator, Fukuzawa Yukichi (1835–1901). Intrigued by what he saw and eager to interest his fellow Japanese in the West, Fukuzawa published several books. In fact, all books about the West in Japan came to be known as "Fukuzawa-bon." Toward the end of his life in his **Autobiography** *he described how, while in London, he had tried to understand the workings of the British Parliament.*

Of political situations at that time, I tried to learn as much as I could from various persons that I met in London . . . though it was often difficult to understand things clearly as I was as yet unfamiliar with the history of Europe. . . . A perplexing institution was representative government. When I asked a gentleman what the "election law" was and what kind of an institution the Parliament really was, he simply replied with a smile, meaning I suppose that no intelligent person was expected to ask such questions. But these were the things most difficult of all for me to understand. In this connection, I learned that there were different political parties—the Liberal and the Conservative—who were always "fighting" against each other in the government.

For some time it was beyond my comprehension to understand what they were "fighting" for, and what was meant, anyway, by "fighting" in peace time. "This man and that man are 'enemies' in the House," they would tell me. But these "enemies" were to be seen at the same table, eating and drinking with each other. I felt as if I could not make much out of this. It took me a long time, with some tedious thinking, before I could gather a general notion of these separate mysterious facts. In some of the more complicated matters, I might achieve an understanding five or ten days after they were explained to me. But all in all, I learned much from this initial tour of Europe.

Source: The Autobiography of Fukuzawa Yukichi, trans. Eiichi Kiyooka (Tokyo: Hokuseida Press, 1948), pp. 138, 143–144.

zenship to new groups. A large, powerful democracy had arisen in the North American continent.

STABILITY IN VICTORIAN BRITAIN

The mid-nineteenth century was a period of exceptional wealth and security for Britain as the population as a whole began to share in the economic benefits of industrialization. Britain enjoyed both social and political peace. The political system was not challenged as it had been in the generation after the Napoleonic wars. A self-assured, even smug, elite—merchants, industrialists, and landowners—developed a political system reflecting liberal values.

Parliamentary Government

Although suffrage was still very restricted, the parliamentary system became firmly established, with a government clearly responsible to the electorate. The importance of Parliament was symbolized by the new building in which it met, finished in 1850 on the site of previous parliamentary buildings but of a splendor and size that was unprecedented. The form of government developed in its halls after midcentury represented a model that aroused the curiosity and envy of much of the world. (See the box, "Encounters with the West: A Japanese View of the British Parliament.") Parliament consisted of an upper, hereditary House of Lords and a lower, elected House of Commons.

Increasingly, the royal cabinet became answerable to Parliament.

In the twenty years after 1846, five different parties vied for power. Depending on the issue, parties and factions coalesced to support particular policies. After 1867, however, a clear two-party system emerged: Liberal and Conservative (Tory), both with strong leadership. This development gave the electorate a distinct choice. The Conservatives were wedded to preserving traditional institutions and practices, while the Liberals tended to be open to change.

Gladstone, Disraeli, and the Two-Party System

Heading these parties were two strong-minded individuals who dominated British political life for over a generation: William E. Gladstone (1809–1898), a Liberal, and Benjamin Disraeli (1804–1881), a Conservative. Gladstone came from an industrial family and married into the aristocracy; Disraeli was the son of a Jewish man of letters who had converted to Christianity. His father's conversion made possible his career—before the 1850s Jews were barred from Parliament. Prior to heading their parties, Gladstone and Disraeli both served in important cabinet positions. They were master debaters; Parliament and the press hung on their every word. Each was capable of making speeches lasting five hours or more and of conducting debates that kept the house in session until 4 A.M. The rivalry between the two men thrilled the nation and made politics a popular pastime.

The Conservatives' electoral base came from the landed classes, Anglicans, and from England, rather than the rest of the United Kingdom. The Liberals' base came from the middle classes, Christian groups other than the Church of England, and from Scotland and Wales. In the House of Commons both parties had a large number of members from the landed aristocracy, but increasingly cabinet members were chosen for political competence rather than family background. Aristocratic birth was no longer a requirement for reaching the pinnacle of power, as Gladstone and Disraeli so clearly illustrated.

The competition for power between the Liberals and Conservatives led to an extension of suffrage in 1867. The Second Reform Bill lowered property qualifications, extending the vote from 1.4 to 2.5 million electors out of a population of 22 million, and gave new urban areas better representation by equalizing the electoral districts. Although some in Parliament feared that these changes would lead to the masses capturing political power—"a leap into the dark," one member called it—in fact no radical change ensued. Extending the vote to clerks, artisans, and other skilled workers made them feel more a part of society, and thus bolstered the existing system. John Stuart Mill, then a member of Parliament, championed the cause of women's suffrage, but he had few allies and that effort failed.

As the extension of voting rights increased the electorate, parties became larger and stronger. Strong party systems meant a clear alternation of power between the Liberals and the Conservatives. With an obvious majority and minority party, the monarch could no longer play favorites in choosing a prime minister. The leader of the majority party had to be asked to form a government. Thus, even though Queen Victoria (r. 1837–1901) detested Gladstone, she had to ask him to form governments when the Liberals won parliamentary elections. (See the feature, "Weighing the Evidence: An Engraving of the British Royal Family," on pages 842–843.)

The creation of a mass electorate also meant that politicians had to make clear appeals to the public and its interests. In the past, oratory had been limited to the halls of Parliament, but after the electoral reforms, it occurred in the public arena as well. Public election campaigns became part of the political scene in England. The democratic "American" style of campaigning appealed to the common man. Also borrowed from across the seas was the "Australian ballot"—the secret ballot—adopted in 1872. This protected lower-class voters from intimidation by their employers, landowners, or other social superiors. In 1874 the first two working-class members of Parliament were elected, sitting as Liberals. Although their victory represented a very modest gain for workers' representation, it presaged the increasingly democratic turn England was to take.

FRANCE: FROM EMPIRE TO REPUBLIC

Unlike Britain, which gradually tranformed into a parliamentary democracy, France took a more tumultuous path. Revolutions and war overthrew existing political systems and inaugurated new ones. Each time the French seemed to have democracy within reach, the opportunity slipped away. At the same time, authoritarianism was equally elusive.

The People's Emperor, Napoleon III

The constitution of the Second French Republic provided for a single four-year presidential term. Frustrated by this limitation of power, Louis Napoleon by a coup d'état extended his presidency to a ten-year term in 1851. The following year, he called for a plebiscite to confirm him as Napoleon III (r. 1852–1870), emperor of the French. Both of these moves were resisted in the countryside, particularly in the south, but the resistance was put down by massive repression.

In the rest of the country, huge majorities of voters endorsed first the prolonged presidency and then the imperial title. The new emperor seemed different from his predecessors. He believed in the principle of popular sovereignty (he maintained universal male suffrage, introduced in 1848), he did not pretend to reign by divine grace, and he repeatedly tested his right to rule by an appeal to the popular vote. He seemed to combine order and authority with the promises of the Revolution—equality before the law, careers open to talent, and the abolition of hereditary rights.

The mid-nineteenth century was a period of prosperity for most Frenchmen, including urban workers and peasants. Louis Napoleon, in his youth the author of a book on pauperism, introduced government measures congenial to labor. On the one hand, workers were required to keep a booklet in which their conduct was to be recorded by their employers; on the other hand, they were granted limited rights to organize strikes, and labor unions were virtually legalized. The emperor expressed his desire to improve the workers' lot, and the government initiated a few concrete measures, such as providing some public housing. Although slum clearance during the rebuilding of Paris drove many from their homes to the outskirts of the city, it did provide healthier towns for those who stayed behind, and the ambitious urban projects provided work for many (see page 858). Other public works projects, such as ports, roads, railroads, and monumental public buildings, also created jobs. Railroads in France in-

Disraeli and Gladstone: Victorian Political Rivals This 1868 cartoon from *Punch* magazine captures the politians' personalities. Disraeli was known as vain and theatrical, while Gladstone was dour and moralistic. *(Mary Evans Picture Library)*

creased tenfold and provided the means for peasants to market their harvests more widely. If some peasants had initially opposed Louis Napoleon, most supported him once he was in power. Not only were they a cautious group, preferring stable authority, but they saw in the emperor—the heir to the great Napoleon—an incarnation of national glory.

Not all the French supported the emperor; many republicans could not forget that he had usurped the constitution of 1848. In protest, some had gone into exile, including the poet Victor Hugo. Trying to win over the opposition, Napoleon made some concessions in 1860, easing censorship and making his government more accountable to the parliament. Instead of winning him new support, however, this liberalization allowed the expression of mounting opposition. A coordinated republican opposition rebuked the economic policies of the empire, notably the decision to sign a free-trade treaty with England. Although this policy helped the wine and silk exporters, it left iron and textile manufacturers unprotected. Businessmen in these fields rallied their workers against the imperial regime.

A number of other issues—notably, widespread hostility to the influence of the Catholic church and the desire for more extensive freedoms of expression and assembly—also helped forge a republican alliance of the middle classes and workers. This alliance was particularly powerful in the large cities and in some southern regions notorious for their opposition to central government control. Republicanism was better organized than in earlier years and had a more explicit program, and its proponents were now better prepared to take over the government, if the opportunity arose.

By 1869 the regime, which declared itself a "liberal empire," had fully evolved into a constitutional monarchy, responsible to the Legislative Corps, the lower house of the parliament. In a plebiscite in May 1870, Frenchmen supported the liberal empire by a vote of five to one. It might have endured, but two months later Napoleon III rashly declared war against Prussia over the imagined slight to French national honor precipitated by the Ems dispatch (see page 823). Defeat brought down the empire. In September, at news of the emperor's capture, the republican opposition in the Legislative Corps declared a republic. It continued the war but had to sign an armistice in January 1871.

The leader of the new government was an old prime minister of Louis Philippe, Adolphe Thiers (1797–1877). To sign a definite peace, the provisional government held elections. The liberals, known as republicans since they favored a republic, were identified with continuing the war; the conservatives, mostly royalists, favored peace. Mainly because of their position on this issue, the royalists won a majority from a country discouraged by defeat.

The Paris Commune, 1871

The new regime had no time to establish itself before an uprising in the spring of 1871 shook France, while reminding the rest of Europe of revolutionary

dangers. The uprising was called the Paris Commune, a name that harked back to 1792–1794, when the Paris crowds had dictated to the government. The Commune insisted on its right to home rule. It was greeted by both radicals and conservatives as a workers' revolt that sought to establish a workers' government. Marx described it as the "bold champion of the emancipation of labor."

Although labor discontent played a role in the Paris Commune, other forces also contributed to its outbreak. Primarily the uprising was triggered by the Prussian siege of Paris during the Franco-Prussian war. Paris had become radicalized during the siege: The rich had evacuated the city, leaving a power vacuum quickly filled by the lower classes. Parisians suffered much because of the siege, and angered at the lack of recognition for their economic needs and their courage in withstanding the Prussians, they rose up against the new French government. Under their pressure, the Commune, composed largely of artisans, began governing the city.

In March 1871 the Commune declared itself free to carry out policies without hindrance from the central government in Versailles. The government sent forces to crush the Commune, and they massacred 25,000 people, arrested 40,000, and deported several thousand more. Although the savagery of this repression indicated that the Commune was viewed as unacceptably radical, it was, in fact, quite moderate. It sought free universal education, a fairer taxation system, a minimum wage, and disestablishment of the official Catholic church.

Nonetheless, the crushing of the Paris Commune and some of its sister communes in southern France, which were also asserting local autonomy, signified the increasing power of the centralized state. The emerging modern state had the strength to squelch popular revolts that in the past had seriously threatened regimes. Western Europe would not again witness a popular uprising of this magnitude.

Creation of the Third Republic, 1871–1875

Despite its brutality, the crushing of the Commune by Thiers's new government reassured many Frenchmen. "The Republic will be conservative, or it will not be," declared Thiers. The question now at hand was what form the new government would

Manet: The Barricade In detail from this 1871 painting, Edouard Manet catches a scene from the Paris Commune of 1871. With barricades, the communards are trying to protect themselves from the onslaught of government troops. Although fewer than a thousand government soldiers died, over 25,000 communards were killed. *(Reproduced by courtesy of the Board of Directors of the Budapest Museum of Fine Arts)*

take. The monarchist majority was split between those favoring a restoration to the throne of the Bourbon heir, the grandson of Charles X, and those favoring the Orléanist heir, grandson of Louis Philippe. Partisans of both sides finally compromised on an offer of the throne to the elderly and childless Bourbon pretender. However, he insisted he would become king only if the *tricouleur*—the flag of the Revolution, which long since had become a cherished national symbol—were discarded and replaced by the white flag of the house of Bourbon. The monarchists realized their project was unfeasible; their plan was thus scuttled and France remained a republic. The republic, as Thiers put it, "is the regime which divides us the least."

By 1875 the parliament had approved a set of basic laws that became the constitution of the Third Republic. Ironically, a monarchist parliament had created a liberal, democratic parliamentary regime. The parliament was to consist of two chambers: the Chamber of Deputies, elected by universal male suffrage, and the Senate, chosen indirectly by local officials. The two houses sitting jointly elected the president, who was to occupy essentially a ceremonial role as chief of state. The head of government—the premier—and his cabinet were responsible to the parliament. A century after the French Revolution, the republican system of government in France was firmly launched.

RUSSIA AND THE GREAT REFORMS

By the 1840s concern about the archaic nature and structure of Russian government was mounting. Many officials lamented the tendency of a timid bureaucracy to lie and mislead the public. Defeat in the Crimean War widened the critique of Russian institutions. Calls for *glasnost*—greater openess—became the leading motif in the great reforms of the 1860s.

The Abolition of Serfdom, 1861

The chief problem that needed resolution was serfdom. Educated opinion had long denounced serfdom as immoral, but this was not the principal reason for its abolition. Serfdom was abolished because it presented clear political disadvantages in both the domestic and international domains. The new tsar, Alexander II (r. 1855–1881), feared that if the abolition of serfdom was not mandated from above, it would occur from below—by a violent serf rebellion that would sweep away everything in its path, including the autocracy itself.

Serfdom was also linked to Russia's place in the world. Defeat in the Crimean War suggested that if Russia depended for its defense upon a soldiery of serfs rather than free men, it would be unable to survive in an increasingly competitive international situation. The Russian army would be more powerful if it consisted of soldiers with a stake in their society rather than men committed to lifetime servitude. In addition, the victorious Western states had won in part because their industrial might translated into more and better guns, ammunition, and transportation. Industrial progress required a mobile labor force, not one tied to the soil by serfdom. For many educated Russians, the defeat in the Crimea revealed general Russian backwardness. To catch up with the West, Russia needed to rid itself of its timeworn institutions, particularly serfdom.

In April 1861, the tsar issued a decree freeing the serfs. (See the box, "The Tsar Demands the Freeing of the Serfs.") It was a radical measure to emancipate 22 million people from a system that allowed them to be bought and sold, separated from their families, and treated in the cruelest ways imaginable. Emancipation represented a compromise with the gentry, which had reluctantly agreed to liberate its serfs but insisted on compensation. As a result, the newly liberated peasants had to reimburse the government with mortgage payments lasting fifty years. The peasants received some land, but its value was vastly overrated and its quantity insufficient for peasant families. To make ends meet, the freed peasants continued working for their former masters.

The mortgage payments and taxes imposed on the peasants by the central government were handled by the local commune, the *mir*. The mir determined how the land was to be used, and it paid collectively for the mortgage and taxes on the land. As a consequence, the commune was reluctant for the peasants to leave the land, and they could do so only with its permission. Freed from serfdom, the peasants still suffered many constraints. In fact, the emancipation declaration was accompanied by massive peasant uprisings that had to be put down by force.

The tsar and his advisers feared the large mass of uneducated peasants as a potential source of anarchy and rebellion. Thus they depended on the mir to preserve control even though the commune system had some inherent economic disadvantages. Increased productivity benefited the commune as much as the individual peasant; hence there was little incentive for land improvement, and yield remained low.

Reforms in Russian Institutions

Alexander was called the "tsar emancipator" by his contemporaries, but he was wedded to the principles of autocracy. His aim in abolishing serfdom and introducing other reforms was to modernize and strengthen Russia and stabilize his divinely mandated rule. Like most Russians, Alexander believed that only the firm hand of autocracy could hold together a large, ethnically diverse country. The peasant uprisings that accompanied emancipation only confirmed these beliefs.

Clearly, however, the sudden freedom of 22 million illiterate peasants threatened to overwhelm existing institutions, and some changes had to be made. Although he surrendered no powers, Alexander did promulgate a number of reforms, altering the government and the judicial and military systems so they could more effectively deal with all the changes in Russian society.

Government reform had paramount importance. Between about 1800 and 1850, the Russian population had increased from 36 to 59 million, and it had become more and more difficult to administer this vast country. Overcentralized, with a poorly trained civil service, the government was unable to cope effectively with the problems of its people. Emancipation of the serfs greatly exacerbated this situation; an enormous number of people, freed

The Tsar Demands the Freeing of the Serfs

In January 1861, Tsar Alexander II addressed the Council of State, an advisory body that he had asked four years earlier to prepare a draft law emancipating the serfs. After this forceful speech, a workable proposal emerged and was implemented six weeks later.

The matter of the liberation of the serfs, which has been submitted for the consideration of the State Council, I consider to be a vital question for Russia, upon which will depend the development of her strength and power. . . . [T]his matter cannot be postponed . . . I repeat—and this is my absolute will—that this matter should be finished right away.

. . . [Y]ou will assure yourselves that all that can be done for the protection of the interests of the nobility has been done . . . but I ask you only not to forget that the basis of the whole work must be the improvement of the life of the peasants—an improvement not in words alone or on paper but in actual fact. . . .

My predecessors felt all the evils of serfdom and continually endeavored, if not to destroy it completely, to work toward the grad-ual limitation of the arbitrary power of the estate owners.

Already in 1856, before the coronation, while in Moscow I called the attention of the leaders of the nobility of the Moscow guberniia to the necessity for them to occupy themselves with improving the life of the serfs, adding that serfdom could not continue forever and that it would therefore be better if the transformation took place from above rather than from below. . . .

I have the right to demand one thing from you: that you, putting aside all personal interests, act not like estate owners but like imperial statesmen invested with my trust. Approaching this important matter I have not concealed from myself all those difficulties that awaited us and I do not conceal them now.

Source: Speech of January 28, 1861, in George Vernadsky et al., eds., *A Sourcebook for Russian History from Early Times to 1917*, vol. 3. Copyright © 1972. Reprinted by permission of the publisher, Yale University Press.

from their owners' control, were abruptly in need of services. Thus in 1864 a law was passed providing for local governments, or *zemstvos*, at the village and regional level, giving Russians the authority and the opportunity to use initiative in local matters.

The zemstvos were largely controlled by the gentry and not particularly democratic. They were forbidden to debate political issues, and their decisions could be overridden or ignored by local officials appointed by the tsar. Some hoped that zemstvos could become the basis for self-government at the national level and looked for the creation of an all-Russian zemstvo, but such hopes were firmly squelched by the tsar, who jealously insisted on undivided and undiminished absolutism. Nonetheless, the zemstvos were an attempt to modernize an overburdened central government.

The tsar also created an independent judiciary that ensured equality before the law, public jury trials, and uniform sentences. Russian political leaders recognized that public confidence in the judiciary was a prerequisite for the development of commerce and industry. Businessmen would no longer fear arbitrary intervention by capricious officials and could develop enterprises in greater security.

In addition, censorship of the press was abolished. Under the previous tsar, Nicholas, all ideas that did not conform to government policy were censored. Such censorship prevented the central government from being well informed about public opinion or about the effects of its policies on the country. Under Alexander, openness in the press was viewed as a remedy for corruption and misuse of power. People could be punished only for specific violations after publication, and they would face trial in an independent court.

Reform also extended to the Russian army. Its structure and methods became more Western. Military service, previously limited to peasants, became the obligation of all Russians. All men submitted to a lottery, and those with an "unlucky" number entered the service. In an effort to make military service more attractive, however, the length of service was drastically cut and corporal punishment was abolished. Access to the officer corps was to be by merit rather than by social connection. The Ministry of War also improved the system of reserves, enabling Russia to mobilize a larger army with more modern weapons in case of war.

Although the tsarist regime remained autocratic and repressive, it did institute several key reforms. A new page had been turned in Russian history.

SUMMARY

Novel configurations of power appeared on the West's chessboard in the period from about 1850 to 1880 as new or enlarged states were created through warfare or the threat of force. Liberal nationalists in the early nineteenth century had believed that Europe would be freer and more peaceful if each people had a separate nation, but they were now proved wrong. The Crimean War and its aftermath replaced the congress system, which had sought a balance of power among partners, with a system of rival states in pursuit of their own self-interest. The international order was severely shaken as Italy and Germany emerged from the center of Europe and Romania and Bulgaria were carved out of the Ottoman Empire in the east.

Both new and existing states faced a choice between federalism and centralized rule. In the process of unification, Italy and Germany could have opted for a loose federal union, but both Piedmont and Prussia chose central control. And the crushing of the Paris Commune spelled the doom of those who wanted a France of decentralized self-governing units. Strong, centralized governments increasingly became the norm. That was also the case across the ocean in the United States, where North and South fought a bloody civil war over the issues of slavery and state sovereignty,

and the victorious federal government imposed its will on the rebellious states.

To achieve legitimacy, however, governments had to appear to be enjoying the consent of their peoples. Hence all European rulers except those of the Ottoman and Russian Empires found it necessary to have a parliament. France and Britain became increasingly democratic in these years, answerable to a growing electorate. In other states parliaments had only limited powers, but once they were in place, it could be argued—and was—that more power should be shifted toward them and that they should be chosen by an expanded electorate. In the United States whites already enjoyed freer and more open institutions than existed anywhere else, and the post–Civil War era marked a further enlargement of political participation when African Americans were granted the rights of citizenship.

Two major changes that liberals in 1848 had agitated for had become reality: freer political institutions and the organization of nation-states. Although neither of these was fully implemented everywhere, both appeared to have been successfully established. Many Europeans could easily believe they were living in an age of optimism.

NOTES

1. Quoted in Otto Pflanze, *Bismarck and the Development of Germany*, vol. 1 (Princeton: Princeton University Press, 1990), p. 184.
2. Quoted in William Flavelle Monypenny and George Earle Buckle, *The Life of Benjamin Disraeli: Earl of Beaconsfield*, vol. 2 (London: John Murray, 1929), pp. 473–474.

SUGGESTED READING

International Relations

Goldfrank, David M. *The Origins of the Crimean War.* 1994. Blames the Russian Tsar Nicholas I for irresponsibly launching the war.

Pearton, Maurice. *The Knowledgeable State: Diplomacy, War and Technology since 1830.* 1982. Emphasizes the contribution of breakthroughs in science, technology, and social organization to military matters.

Rich, Norman. *Why the Crimean War? A Cautionary Tale.* 1985. Argues that the war was caused by the Western powers' decision to eliminate the Russian threat to the Ottoman Empire.

Italian Unification

Coppa, Frank J. *The Wars of Italian Independence.* 1992. Views Italian unification within an international context.

Grew, Raymond. *A Sterner Plan for Italian Unity.* 1963. Studies the role of the National Society in advancing the cause of unification.

Hearder, H. *Italy in the Age of the Risorgimento, 1790–1870.* 1983. Considers regional differences in the peninsula and analyzes the debates among various protagonists of the risorgimento.

Smith, Dennis Mack. *Cavour and Garibaldi, 1860.* 1954. Contrasts the heroic, but sometimes naive, Garibaldi with the master manipulator, Cavour.

———. *The Making of Italy, 1796–1870.* 1968. Considers the long-term forces leading to Italian unity.

———. *Cavour.* 1985. Debunks the notion that the Italian statesman was a liberal nationalist who carried out a carefully planned strategy to unite the peninsula.

Woolf, Stuart. *A History of Italy, 1700–1860.* 1979. Provides a long-term view of the place of unification in Italian history.

German Unification

Carr, William. *The Wars of German Unification.* 1991. A careful examination of the three wars that led to unification.

Hamerow, Theodore S. *The Social Foundations of German Unification, 1858–1871,* 2 vols. 1969 and 1972. Reveals the essentially middle-class support for the program of German unification.

Howard, Michael. *The Franco-Prussian War: The German Invasion of France, 1870–71.* 1961. Reveals some of the more "modern" aspects of the war, including a willingness to target civilians.

Pflanze, Otto. *Bismarck and the Development of Germany. I: The Period of Unification, 1815–1871.* 1990. Emphasizes Bismarck's flexibility and ability to improvise to accomplish long-range goals.

Sheehan, James. *German Liberalism in the Nineteenth Century.* 1978. Emphasizes the environment that conditioned the shaping of liberalism in a country that unified late and had to deal with a fast-emerging working class.

The Ottoman and Habsburg Empires

Jelavich, Charles and Barbara. *The Establishment of the Balkan National States, 1804–1920.* 1977. Traces the emergence of independent states from the Ottoman Empire.

Shaw, Stanford J. *History of the Ottoman Empire and Modern Turkey. II: Reform, Revolution and Republic: The Rise of Modern Turkey, 1808–1975.* 1977. Emphasizes the success of reform in the Ottoman Empire and sees its decline as essentially due to foreign aggression.

Sked, Alan. *The Decline and Fall of the Habsburg Empire, 1815–1918.* 1989. Provides a revisionist interpretation, concentrating on the strengths of the empire.

The United States, 1840–1880

Bensel, Richard Franklin. *Yankee Leviathan: The Origins of Central State Authority in America, 1859–1877.* 1990. Emphasizes the extent to which the Civil War led to centralization of government in the United States.

Smith, Page. *The Nation Comes of Age: A People's History,* vol. 4. 1981. Describes the development of the United States from 1828 to 1860, in an account marked by vivid prose and strong narrative.

———. *Trial by Fire: A People's History,* vol. 5. 1982. Equally strong in analysis and narrative, it covers the Civil War and Reconstruction.

Victorian Britain

Blake, Robert. *Disraeli.* 1966. The authoritative biography of the Victorian statesman who helped shape the British parliamentary system.

Evans, Eric J. *The Forging of the Modern State: Early Industrial Britain, 1783–1870.* 1983. Considers the development of political parties for the period covered in this chapter.

Wilson, A. N. *Eminent Victorians.* 1990. Has a chapter devoted to Gladstone that emphasizes his idealism and devotion to great causes.

France, from Empire to Republic

Greenberg, Louis. *Sisters of Liberty: Marseilles, Lyon, Paris, and the Reaction to a Centralized State, 1868–1871.* 1971. Reminds us that the Commune did not break out only in Paris but also in several provincial French cities and insists that local self-government was at least as important a goal to the Communards as their social program.

Smith, William H. C. *Napoleon III.* 1972. Provides a sympathetic view of Napoleon III as a staunch believer in popular sovereignty who was devoted to the welfare of his people.

Williams, Roger L. *The French Revolution of 1870–1871.* 1969. Describes the Commune as the continuation of the French revolutionary tradition.

Russia and the Great Reforms

Kolchin, Peter. *Unfree Labor: American Slavery and Russian Serfdom.* 1987. The most recent study of Russian serfdom, of particular interest to American readers.

Lincoln, W. Bruce. "The Problem of Glasnost in Mid-Nineteenth-Century Russian Politics." *European Historical Quarterly,* 11 (April 1981): 171–188. Considers the origins of the concept in the Russian bureaucracy.

———. *In the Vanguard of Reform.* 1982. Argues that the great reforms originated in the 1840s.

———. *Great Reforms.* 1990. Shows the reforms to be part of a general program of modernization.

AN ENGRAVING OF THE BRITISH ROYAL FAMILY

Why were Queen Victoria and her family depicted in the manner shown in this popular engraving? The illustration might well have been of an upper-middle-class family. Note the family's attire. The queen is soberly dressed; her husband, Prince Albert, is wearing a dark business suit; the children are simply dressed. The image extends from the royal family to the rest of England, depicted as a simple farm, some cottages, and a grouping of common people. Notice the crown hovering over this idyllic scene. Victoria's reign was the longest of any British monarch; the manner in which she conducted herself, and her subjects' image of her, shaped the monarchy and people's expectations of it.

Illustrations of this type familiarized the British with their monarch. Surrounded by her husband and children, the queen seemed to have an endearing common touch. In the past representations of the monarchy had suggested power and intimidation. The aura of the close-knit, nuclear royal family, akin to the families of the queen's middle-class subjects, suggested a serenity that was reassuring to those subjects.

Victoria cultivated the image of herself as contented mother, but in reality she resented much about motherhood. She complained of the extent to which her pregnancies interfered with her daily routines, preventing her from traveling and being as much with her beloved Albert as she would have liked; she described childbearing as an "annoyance" that made her feel "so pinned down—one's wings clipped." She also refused to romanticize birthing, seeing it as an animal-like act, reducing a woman to "a cow or a dog." Biology put women in an inauspicious position; "I think our sex a most unenviable one," she lamented. And Victoria continued viewing the children, once they were no longer babies, as a burden, describing them as "an awful plague and anxiety for which they show one so little gratitude very often!" But such views were expressed strictly privately, and the public never suspected Victoria's ambivalence toward her role as mother.

Whatever her complaints about children, Victoria's family life was in strong contrast to that of her predecessors, projecting a new image of the monarchy. Her grandfather George III (r. 1760–1820) had bouts of insanity. Her uncle George IV (r. 1820–1830) was a notorious philanderer. George IV and his brothers, the Duke of Clarence (later to be William IV [r. 1830–1837]) and the Duke of Kent (Victoria's father), were bigamists. They fathered a large brood of illegitimate children and were involved in numerous public scandals.

The character of Victoria's three predecessors and of the various other men in line to the throne had strengthened opposition to the monarchy. Public outrage at their excesses had led to a call for the abolition of the institution. When the 18-year-old Victoria came to the throne, it would have been difficult to imagine that she would on her death leave the monarchy considerably strengthened.

The image of Victoria shown here intentionally contrasts her reign to the reigns of her predecessors. Victoria is surrounded by four of her children (eventually she would have nine). Her predecessors had died leaving no legitimate direct heirs and thus endangering the regular succession to the throne. The engraving announces that the royal line is assured. English people wary of a female ruler can find solace in knowing that Victoria would be succeeded by one of her sons. Later, Victoria's children and their progeny would intermarry with the rest of Europe's royalty, and by the end of her reign most of Europe's crowned heads would be related to one another.

Although Victoria's uncles and father were wastrels and bankrupts, the queen and her husband lived frugally by royal standards and conducted an exemplary family life. Under the wise administration of Prince Albert, royal wealth increased; he carefully administered various royal estates and investments. Instead of being subject to various debtors, the British royal house became one of the wealthiest landowners in Great Britain, achieving financial independence and winning social prestige. Among the large landowning mag-

THY CHOICEST GIFTS IN STORE   ON HER BE PLEASED   TO POUR

GOD SAVE THE QUEEN.

Illustration from *A Book of English Song*

nates of Britain, the royal house became the most prominent.

The model royal family appealed to the growing middle class of Victorian society. Consider how the simple terms in which the monarch is depicted here and in many other illustrations reflect the increasingly democratic spirit of the era. The ruler and her family appear in a common scene. Victoria is queen, but she also is a mother and wife. There is no sign here of pomp and ceremony.

Given the disrepute into which the monarchy had fallen and the rise of republican sentiment, the coming to the throne of a woman in 1837 may have substantially lessened antimonarchical sentiment. The last woman to rule England had been one of its greatest monarchs, Elizabeth I (r. 1558–1603), who had provided stability and brought glory to her kingdom. There also happened to be a certain gallantry toward a young, seemingly frail woman coming to the throne. Also, because of her gender Victoria was seen as less of a threat to constitutional liberties.

Under Victoria's rule Britain completed the process of becoming a constitutional monarchy. Although Victoria's predecessors had been openly partisan, the queen cultivated the image of being above party, a symbol of national unity and the state. Fellow monarchs in central and eastern Europe exercised greater power, but after World War I they were toppled. In Britain, monarchy in its constitutional form endured. Victoria established a pattern of public and private behavior by which members of subsequent generations of the British royal family were to be judged. ✦

The Age of Optimism, 1850–1880

The first department store in Paris, which served as a model for others in France and abroad, "Bon Marché" (the "good buy") opened its doors in the 1850s. The store bought goods in mass quantities and thus could sell them at low prices. Constructed of glass and iron, Bon Marché represented the new, modern age. It combined under one roof a large range of products that previously had been available only in separate specialty shops—a time-saving device in an increasingly harried age. The store also had a large catalog sales department for customers too busy or distant to shop in person. Filled with toys, bed linens, furniture, crystal, and other items, the department store was a symbol of the new opulence of the middle classes.

This new type of store would not have been possible in an earlier age. It serves as a summary of the various technological and social changes experienced by the more prosperous regions of the West as industrialization advanced in the second half of the nineteenth century. Industrial innovation had lowered the price of glass and steel, so that these new, huge commercial emporiums could be built at reasonable cost. Railroads brought customers from outside the city and trams and omnibuses from within it. The penny press provided advertising for the department store, which in turn supported the emergence of this new medium. The expansion of the postal system facilitated catalog sales and the mailing of goods to customers. And the higher incomes available to many people allowed them to purchase more than just the necessities. A phenomenon began that became predominant in the West a century later—the consumer society.

Felix Valloton,
Le bon marché.

As industrialization spread throughout western Europe, rising productivity brought greater wealth to many social groups and nations. This wealth not only led to more consumer spending but also contributed to a change in attitudes. The late nineteenth century was an era shaped to a large extent by the growing middle classes, who were filled with optimism and convinced they were living in an age of progress. The successful application of science and technology to social problems gave many men and women confidence in the human ability to improve the world. People controlled their environment to a degree never before possible. On farms they increased the fertility of the soil; to the burgeoning cities they brought greater order. Scientists used new methods to study and combat disease. Public authorities founded schools, trained teachers, and reduced illiteracy. Transportation and communication rapidly improved.

In fact, not all of society benefited from the fruits of progress. The new wealth was far from equally shared. Eastern and southern Europe changed little, and even in the western part a large group of the population still lived in great misery. If some cities carried out ambitious programs of urban renewal, others continued to neglect slums. Public sanitation programs did not affect the majority of Europeans who lived in rural areas. Despite spectacular advances in science, much of the population maintained a traditional belief in divine intervention. Many intellectuals strongly denounced the materialism and smugness of the age, stressing the meanness and ignorance that lay just beneath the surface.

Still, the tone of the age was set by the ascendant middle classes in western Europe, which embraced change and believed that the era was heading toward even more remarkable improvements. Their optimism was all the greater because the ultimate effects of the social and technological changes taking place in Europe were not yet known: The major processes discussed in this chapter occurred in the generation living between 1850 and 1880, but many were as yet incomplete by 1880.

INDUSTRIAL GROWTH AND ACCELERATION

Beginning in the 1850s, western Europe experienced an unprecedented level of economic expansion. Manufacturers created new products and employed new sources of energy. An enlarged banking system provided more abundant credit to fund the expansion. Scientific research was systematically employed to improve methods of manufacture. A revolution in transportation speedily delivered goods and services to distant places. For many Europeans, daily life was profoundly changed by technological innovations.

The "Second Industrial Revolution," 1850–1914

The interrelated cluster of economic changes that began in the generation after 1850 is often called the "second industrial revolution." It was characterized by a significant speedup in production and by the introduction of new materials such as mass-produced steel, synthetic dyes, and aluminum. Manufacturers replaced the traditional steam engine with stronger steam-powered turbines or with machines powered by new forms of energy—petroleum and electricity.

The invention of new products and methods of manufacture spurred this industrial expansion. The second half of the nineteenth century has often been called the "age of steel." Up to then, steel production had been limited by the expense involved in its manufacture, but in 1856, Sir Henry Bessemer (1813–1898) discovered a much cheaper method, which produced in twenty minutes the same amount of steel previously produced in twenty-four hours. Ten years later, William Siemens (1823–1883) in England and Pierre Martin (1824–1915) in France developed an even better technique of steel production, the open-hearth process. The Thomas-Gilchrist method, invented in 1878, made possible the use of phosphor-laden iron ore, which previously had been economically unfeasible.

The results were dramatic. In Great Britain, steel production increased fourfold, and the price of steel fell by more than 50 percent between the early 1870s and the following decade. Greater steel production made possible the expansion of the rail system, the creation of a steamship fleet, and an explosive growth in the building industry. No longer was steel a rare alloy used only for the finest swords and knives; it became the material that defined the age.

Significant changes in the supply of credit further stimulated economic expansion. Discovery of gold in California and Australia led to the inflow of huge amounts of the precious metal to Europe, expanding the supply of money and credit. This led to the establishment of the modern banking system.

Each advance made possible additional changes. Increased wealth and credit accelerated further expansion of industrial plants and the financing of an ambitious infrastructure of roads, railroads, and steamships, which in turn boosted trade. Between 1800 and 1840, the value of world trade had doubled. In the twenty years following 1850, it increased by 260 percent.

By the 1880s important scientific discoveries fueled industrial improvements. Electricity began to be more widely used, replacing coal as a source of energy. Synthetic dyes revolutionized the textile industry, as did alkali in the manufacture of soap and glass. Dynamite, invented by the Swedish chemist Alfred Nobel (1833–1896) in the 1860s, made it possible to level hills and blast tunnels through mountains, facilitating construction. Five years after Nobel's death, his will established a prestigious prize named after its donor, to honor significant contributions to science and peace.

Transportation and Communications

The rail system grew dramatically in the middle decades of the nineteenth century. When the English engineer Robert Stephenson (1803–1859) demonstrated the feasibility of the steam locomotive, the "Rocket," in 1829, it ran on a track that was one-and-a-half miles long. By 1880 the total European railroad mileage was 102,000 (Map 23.1). In 1888 the "Orient Express" line opened, linking Constantinople to Vienna and thus to the rest of Europe. Distance was conquered by speed as well: By midcentury trains ran 50 miles per hour, ten times as fast as when they were invented. The cost of rail transport steadily decreased, allowing for its greater use. Between 1850 and 1880 in Germany, the number of rail passengers increased tenfold and the volume of goods eightyfold. In France and Great Britain, the increases were nearly as impressive.

Ocean transportation also changed dramatically. In 1869 the French built the Suez Canal

IMPROVEMENTS IN COMMUNICATIONS AND TRANSPORTATION

1820s	The omnibus is introduced in France
1829	Robert Stephenson runs the "Rocket"
1833	Invention of the telegraph
1840	Introduction of the penny stamp
1850s	Clipper ships
	Invention of the tramway
1863	Building of underground railroad in London
1865	Transoceanic telegraph cable installed
1869	Opening of Suez Canal
1875	Alexander Graham Bell invents the telephone

across Egyptian territory, linking the Mediterranean to the Red Sea and the Indian Ocean. It reduced by 40 percent the journey between London and Bombay. More efficient ships were developed; by midcentury the clipper ship could cross the Atlantic in fourteen days. Steamships were also built, although they did not dominate ocean traffic until the 1890s. By 1880 European shipping carried nearly three times the cargo it had thirty years earlier.

The optimism born of conquering vast distance was reflected in a popular novel by the French writer Jules Verne (1828–1905), *Around the World in Eighty Days* (1873). The hero, Phineas Fogg, traveled by balloon, llama, and ostrich, as well as by the modern steam locomotive and steamship to accomplish in eighty days a feat that, only thirty years earlier, would have taken at least eleven months. Such was the impact of the steamship, locomotive, and the Suez Canal.

Along with the new speed, advances in refrigeration changed food transport. Formerly, refrigeration could be achieved only with natural ice, cut from frozen ponds and lakes, but this changed in the 1870s with the introduction of mechanical ice-making machines. By the 1880s dairy products and meat were being transported vast distances by rail and even across the seas by ship. Thanks to

— Railroads in 1850
— Railroads added by 1880

North Sea

Baltic Sea

ATLANTIC OCEAN

Stockholm

Edinburgh
Belfast
Newcastle
Dublin
Liverpool
Manchester
Birmingham
Bristol
London

Copenhagen
Danzig
Hamburg
Amsterdam
Berlin
Brussels
Warsaw
Frankfurt
Paris
Prague
Cracow
Lyon
Zürich
Bern
Vienna
Turin
Milan
Madrid
Rome

Mediterranean Sea

0   200   400 Km.
0   200   400 Mi.

Map 23.1 European Rails, 1850 and 1880 During the mid-nineteenth century, European states built railroads at an increasing rate, creating a dense network by the 1880s. (*Adapted from Norman J. G. Pounds*, An Historical Geography of Europe, 1800–1914 *[New York: Cambridge University Press, 1985].*)

these advances, the surplus food of the Americas and Australia, rich in grasslands, could offer Europe a cheaper and far more varied diet.

Regular postal service was also a child of the new era of improved transportation. In 1840 Britain instituted a postage system based on standard rates. Replacing the earlier practice in which the recipient paid for the delivery of a letter, the British system enabled the sender to buy a stamp—priced at the low rate of one penny—and drop the letter

into a mailbox. It was collected, transported speedily by the new railroads, and delivered. The efficiency and low cost of mail led to a massive increase in its use. In Great Britain the number of letters mailed in a year increased from 7 per person per year in 1840 to 32 by 1880.

The post combined with transoceanic telegraphs and the invention of the telephone to transform the world of information. In the late 1830s the telegraph was invented, and by 1864,

The Suez Canal Opened in 1869, the canal significantly shortened the voyage by ship from Europe to East Asia. The Suez Canal exemplified the speeding up of transportation and communication in the second half of the nineteenth century. *(AKG London)*

80,000 miles of telegraph wire were laid on the European continent. By 1865 transoceanic cables connected the Americas to Europe. Suddenly news from distant parts of the globe—of earthquakes, revolutions, or the outbreak of war—could reach Europe within minutes. In 1875 American inventor Alexander Graham Bell (1847–1922) invented a machine capable of transmitting the human voice by electrical impulses; in 1879 the first telephones were installed in Germany; two years later they appeared in France.

The speedy linking of distant places called attention to the need to standardize time. Up to now, countries typically had innumerable time zones; each town established its time according to the location of the sun. Railroad traffic made these quaint differences a source of annoyance to travelers and railroad officials, and it became imperative to have a standard time for each nation. The electric telegraph made it possible to set that time to the second.

CHANGING CONDITIONS AMONG SOCIAL GROUPS

Industrial advances transformed the traditional structure of European society. Fewer people worked the land; more worked in industry. The social and political influence of the landed aristocracy waned as wealth became far less dependent on ownership of land. To varying degrees, this influence now had to be shared with the growing middle classes. Generally, life for both industrial and farm workers improved in this period. However, there were great disparities; many people continued to suffer from profound deprivation.

The Declining Aristocracy

Always a small, exclusive group, the European aristocracy in the nineteenth century represented less than 1 percent of the population. There were regional variations; in Bavaria and Bohemia, nobles accounted for less than one-tenth of 1 percent of the population, while in Hungary they represented 5 percent. Many of those of noble birth were quite poor and economically indistinguishable from their non-noble neighbors. Others owned vast estates and were fabulously wealthy. The duke of Sutherland in Britain and the Esterhazy family in Hungary owned over one million acres, Count Orloff in Russia half that amount.

Some ennoblements were of recent origin. In England, most titles were less than a hundred years old, having originally been conferred on individuals in recognition of service to the state, the arts, or the economy. In France both Napoleons had ennobled persons they wished to honor. In Germany, Bismarck ennobled the Jewish banker Gerson Bleichröder (1822–1893) for helping finance the wars of the Prussian state and for relieving the German chancellor of personal financial worries by making profitable investments for him.

Distinctions between aristocrats and members of the upper middle class became increasingly blurred; noble families in financial straits often married their children to the offspring of wealthy merchants. And many nobles who previously had shunned manufacture participated in the new economy by becoming industrialists and bankers. Idle members of the nobility were now somewhat rare. Although many aristocrats still enjoyed a lavish lifestyle, others had the habits of successful business people.

Despite the theories of egalitarianism sweeping Europe in the aftermath of the French Revolution and the rapidly changing social structure engendered by industrialization, the power of the aristocracy did not disappear. In Prussia, some of the wealthiest industrialists came from the highest aristocracy—among them Prince Henckel von Donnersmarck and the duke of Utjest. The heavily aristocratic officer corps played an important role in running the Prussian state and unified Germany. In France about 20 to 25 percent of officers and many diplomats were aristocrats. In Britain officers, diplomats, and high-ranking civil servants were usually of noble birth. In Austria and Russia, aristocratic origin was the norm for government service.

Nonetheless, nobles no longer asserted privileges based exclusively on birth. In most European states, such a claim had become an anachronism.

The Expanding Middle Classes

Up to the eighteenth century, society had been divided by legally separate orders based on birth. In the nineteenth century, it became more customary to classify people by their economic function. The "middle class" belonged neither to the nobility nor to the peasantry nor to the industrial working class. It included such people as wealthy manufacturers, country physicians, and bank tellers. Given this diversity, it has become common to use the plural and think of all these people as forming the "middle classes." Another term frequently used to describe these people is *bourgeois*, which originated in the twelfth and thirteenth centuries when a new wealthy class based on urban occupations—whose members were called burghers, or bourgeois—emerged.

The nineteenth century has often been described as "the bourgeois century." Although such a label may be too broad, after the midcentury mark it is appropriate enough to use as a shorthand term to describe the dominance of the bourgeois elites. This situation was especially prevalent in western Europe, where the middle classes helped fashion much of society.

The middle classes expanded dramatically in the wake of industrialization. More trade and manufacture meant more entrepreneurs and managers, while the increasingly complex society called for more engineers, lawyers, accountants, and bankers. New standards of comfort and health demanded more merchants and doctors. Urban improvements in the generation after 1850 created a need for architects and contractors, among other professionals.

The middle and lower levels of middle-class society grew most rapidly as business, the professions, and government administration created more jobs. In the 1870s about 10 percent of urban working-class people reached lower-middle-class status by becoming storekeepers, lower civil servants, clerks, or salespeople. Faster growth occurred for white-collar workers than for their blue-collar counterparts. As industries matured, the increasing use of machinery and better industrial organization meant that fewer additional laborers and more clerks and bureaucrats were needed. Large import-export businesses, insurance companies, and department stores provided opportunities of this kind. So did the expansion of government services. In the second half of the nineteenth century, France increased its teacher corps by 80,000 and hired 50,000 more postal employees. In Britain the size of the postal staff grew by six times and the teaching corps by two-and-one-half times between 1851 and 1891.

The social impact of job growth was great. The men and women staffing these new positions often came from modest backgrounds. For the son or daughter of peasants to become village postmaster, schoolteacher, or clerk in a major firm signified social ascension, however modest. And for the family, such a position, even more than income, meant joining the lower stratum of the middle classes. Accessibility to its ranks was certainly one of the strengths of the bourgeoisie. It was an ever growing group whose promise of social respectability and material comfort exercised a compelling force of attraction over the lower classes. In midcentury Britain the middle classes represented 15 percent of the population; by 1881, 25 percent. Elsewhere, the proportion was lower, but it was growing in number and strength as the economy expanded.

A widening subgroup of the middle classes consisted of members of the professions, those whose prestige rested on the claim of exclusive expertise in a particular field. In the early nineteenth century, requirements for exercising a profession varied, depending on the country. In France and Prussia, for example, government regulation stipulated the necessary qualifications to practice medicine; in England anyone might practice it. As the professions attempted to create a monopoly for themselves and eliminate rivals, they established more standards. Medical doctors, for instance, began requiring specialized education to distinguish themselves from herbalists, midwives, bonesetters, healers, and other rivals, and they insisted on their exclusive right to exercise their profession.

Although the professionalization of medicine did not create better doctors immediately, as the science of medicine taught at universities improved, so did the preparation and expertise of doctors. Similarly, in other professions, such as law, architecture, and engineering, common standards and requirements encouraged professional practice. By midcentury either professional associations or the state itself accredited members of the professions. Women had limited access to these professions; typically their opportunities were confined to lower teaching positions. After the Crimean War, as a result of Florence Nightingale's efforts (see page 813), nursing became an increasingly popular profession for women.

The growing role of the state in society led to bureaucratic expansion. More and more, civil servants were selected by merit rather than through patronage. By the eighteenth century, Prussia had instituted a civil service examination system. After the Revolution, France instituted educational requirements for certain government corps, and by the 1880s it established civil service exams for the rest of government service. Beginning in 1870, Britain introduced the civil service examination and eliminated patronage.

Middle-Class Lifestyles

The standard of living of the growing middle classes varied considerably, from the wealthy entrepreneur who bought a château, or built one, to the bourgeois who dwelled in a modest apartment. But they all lived in new standards of comfort. Their homes had running water, upholstered furniture, and enough space to provide separate sleeping and living quarters. They had several changes of clothing and consumed a varied diet that included meat and dairy products, sugar, coffee, and tea. They read books and subscribed to newspapers and journals. Having at least one servant was a requisite for anyone who wished to be counted among the middle classes in the mid-nineteenth century.

By 1900 servants were still common among bourgeois households, but they were fewer in proportion to the population as a whole. In 1861 in Barmen, Germany (present-day Wuppertal), 16 percent of the population consisted of domestics; by 1911 the figure was 2.5 percent. As service industries developed, the need for servants decreased. With the growth of cab services, for instance, a family could dispense with a coachman and stable boy. And many families went without servants. Toward the end of the century, domestics' wages rose as competing forms of employment vied for their service, and only the upper layers of the bourgeoisie still employed domestic help.

In some areas suburban living became fashionable. The wealthy lived in large, imposing houses; the less well-off lived in smaller houses with a garden for privacy and quiet. Some owned two homes—one in the city and one in the countryside, providing respite from the rushed urban environment.

For further relief from the crowded cities, visits to resorts became popular. Throughout Europe, resort towns sprang up, devoted principally to the amusement of the well-off. It became fashionable to "take the waters"—bathing in hot springs and drinking the mineral waters thought to have special attributes—and gamble in resorts such as Baden-Baden in Germany and Vichy in France. For the first time, tourism became big business. Thomas Cook (1808–1892), an Englishman, organized tours to the Crystal Palace exhibition of 1851. (See the feature, "Weighing the Evidence: The Crystal Palace," on pages 876–877.) Discovering the large market for travel tours, he began running tours in England and on the Continent. In the eighteenth century the European tour had been a custom of the aristocracy, but now many members of the middle classes demanded this experience as well. Beginning in 1835, a German publisher, Karl Baedeker (1801–1859), issued a tourist guide to the Rhine, followed by guidebooks to various European countries and the Middle East. The Baedeker guides were eagerly purchased and provided the pattern for the multitude of guidebooks that followed.

New wealth and leisure time led as well to more hotels, restaurants, and cafés. In 1869 Paris had 20,000 cafés and 4000 hotels and lodging houses; the largest hotel had 700 well-appointed rooms. Vienna's National Hotel, with 300 rooms, had steam heat, spring water on every floor, and an icehouse providing cool drinks. For the traveler's convenience, many hotels, such as the monumental Charing Cross Hotel in London, were located next to train stations. At home or away, the bourgeois valued comfort.

The middle classes shared certain attitudes about the conduct of their lives. They believed their successes were due not to birth but to talent and effort. They wanted to be judged by their merits, and they expected their members to abide by strict moral principles. Their lives were supposed to be disciplined, especially with regard to sex and drink. The age was called "Victorian" because the middle classes in Britain saw in the queen who reigned for two-thirds of the century a reflection of their own values. (See the feature, "Weighing the Evidence: An Engraving of the British Royal Family," on pages 842–843.) "Victorian morality," preached but not always practiced, was often viewed as hypocritical by social critics. Yet as the middle classes came to dominate society, their values became the social norms. Public drunkenness was discouraged, and anti-alcoholic movements vigorously campaigned against drinking. Public festivals were regulated, making them more respectable and less rowdy. In several countries, societies for the protection of animals agitated against blood sports such as cock-and-bull fights.

In spite of their differences in education, wealth, and social standing, most of the bourgeoisie resembled one another in dress, habits of speech, and deportment. Bourgeois men dressed somberly, in dark colors, avoiding any outward signs of luxury. Their clothing fit closely and eschewed decoration—an adjustment to the machine age, where elaborate dress hampered activity. It also reflected a conscious attempt to emphasize the frugal and achievement-oriented attitudes of the bourgeoisie in contrast to what was seen as the frivolous nobility.

Bourgeois conventions regarding women's dress were less reserved. Extravagant amounts of colorful cloth used to fashion huge, beribboned hoop dresses reflected the newfound wealth of the middle classes and confirmed their view of women as ornaments whose lives were to be limited to the home and made easier by servants. This era was dominated by domesticity, by the ideal of the home. The wife was to provide her family with

Advice on Running the Middle-Class Household

In 1861 Isabella Mary Mayson Beeton, a London housewife, published **Mrs. Beeton's Book of Household Management,** *which in Britain was outsold only by the Bible. Her popular book provided British middle-class women with advice on running their households and reflected their values concerning discipline, frugality, and cleanliness.*

As with the commander of an army, or the leader of an enterprise, so is it with the mistress of a house. Her spirit will be seen through the whole establishment; and just in proportion as she performs her duties intelligently and thoroughly, so will her domestics follow in her path. Of all those acquirements, which more particularly belong to the feminine character, there are none which take a higher rank, in our estimation, than such as enter into a knowledge of household duties; for on these are perpetually dependent the happiness, comfort, and well-being of a family. . . .

Early rising is one of the most essential qualities which enter into good Household Management, as it is not only the parent of health, but of innumerable other advantages. Indeed, when a mistress is an early riser, it is almost certain that her house will be orderly and well-managed. . . .

Cleanliness is indispensable to health, and must be studied both in regard to the person and the house, and all that it contains. . . .

Frugality and economy are home virtues, without which no household can prosper. . . .

Charity and benevolence are duties which a mistress owes to herself as well as to her fellow-creatures; and there is scarcely any income so small, but something may be spared from it. . . . Great advantages may result from visits paid the poor, for there being, unfortunately, much ignorance, generally amongst them with respect to all household knowledge, there will be opportunities for advising and instructing them in a pleasant and unobtrusive manner, in cleanliness, industry, cookery, and good management. . . .

A housekeeping account-book should invariably be kept, and kept punctually and precisely. . . .

. . . The treatment of servants is of the highest possible moment as well to the mistress as to the domestics themselves. On the head of the house the latter will naturally fix their attention; and if they perceive that the mistress's conduct is regulated by high and correct principles, they will not fail to respect her. If, also a benevolent desire is shown to promote their comfort, at the same time that a steady performance of their duty is exacted, then their respect will not be unmingled with affection, and they will be more solicitous to continue to deserve her favour.

Source: Isabella Mary Mayson Beeton, *Mrs. Beeton's Book of Household Management* (London: S. O. Beeton, 1861), pp. 1–6.

a shelter from the storms of daily life. (See the box, "Advice on Running the Middle-Class Household.") While the man was out in the secular world earning a living and advancing his career, the bourgeois woman was to run her household. She decorated the house, changed curtains with the seasons and the styles, supervised the servants, kept the accounts, oversaw the children's homework and religious education, and involved herself in charitable works. In the decades around midcentury, the assumption that there were two separate spheres—one male and public, the other female and private—reached its height.

In spite of the relatively passive role assigned to women, many bourgeois women were very active. Some took up philanthropic causes, helping

Josephine Grey Butler An important Victorian reformer, Butler agitated for several causes, most notably abolition of the Contagious Diseases Act. This act empowered the police to arrest any woman it suspected of prostitution and to force her to be examined for venereal disease. Largely as a result of Butler's efforts, this act was repealed in 1886. *(Fawcett Library/Mary Evans Picture Library)*

the sick and the poor. In England, Josephine Grey Butler (1828–1906), a member of a family of reformers, fought for the spread of education to impoverished women. She also waged a fierce battle against prostitution. Many bourgeois women helped their husbands or fathers in the office, the business, or the writing of scientific treatises. Others achieved success on their own terms, running their own businesses, writing, painting, teaching. Some took advantage of the very impediments placed in their way. Rosa Bonheur (1822–1899), who because of her gender was not allowed to attend sketching sessions of nudes at her art school, concentrated on painting animals and became the best-known painter of domestic animals in the nineteenth century.

The expectation that middle-class women would be married and taken care of by their husbands led to the provision of inferior education for girls and young women. Even bright and intellectually curious young girls could not receive as good an education as their brothers, nor as a consequence pursue as interesting a career—a situation that had prevailed for centuries. Proponents of women's rights protested against this situation, insisting on equal access to education and the professions. Slowly, secondary and university education was made available to young women. In Europe the first university to admit women was the University of Zurich in Switzerland in 1865. Although British universities admitted women, the University of London did not grant them degrees until after 1878, and the most prestigious British institutions, Oxford and Cambridge, did not grant degrees to women until after World War I. In spite of discriminatory laws, harassment by male students, and initial obstruction by professional and accrediting groups, a few female doctors and lawyers practiced in England by the 1870s and on the Continent in the following decades.

Women more easily penetrated lower levels of middle-class occupations. Expanding school systems, civil services, and businesses provided new employment opportunities for women. By the 1890s, two-thirds of primary school teachers in England and half the post office staff in France were women; by 1914 nearly half a million women worked as shop assistants in England. Some new technologies created jobs that were heavily feminized, such as the positions of typist and telephone operator.

The Workers' Lot

The increased prosperity and greater productivity of the period gradually improved the conditions of both female and male workers in the generation after 1850. Their wages and standard of living rose, and they enjoyed more job security. In Britain the earning power of the average worker rose by one-third between 1850 and 1875.

For the first time, workers were able to put money aside to tide them over in hard times. By 1870 two million Frenchmen had savings accounts. By the 1860s, one million people in England subscribed to post office savings accounts established especially for those of limited means.

The workers' increased income permitted a better diet. In France the average number of calories consumed per adult male increased by one-third between 1840 and 1890. In Britain, between 1844 and 1876, per capita consumption of tea tripled, and that of sugar quadrupled. The quality of food as well as the amount also improved; people consumed more meat, fish, eggs, and dairy products.

Legislation gradually reduced the length of the workweek. The British workweek, typically 73 hours in the 1840s, was reduced to 56 hours in 1874. In France it was reduced to 10 hours a day, in Germany to 11. But these improvements were accompanied by an increased emphasis on efficiency at the workplace. Fewer informal breaks were allowed as industrialists insisted on greater worker productivity. New machines increased the tempo of work, frequently leading to accidents and exhaustion.

As workers had more time and more money, their leisure patterns changed. Some leisure activities that previously had been limited to the upper classes became available to workers. The introduction of rail connections to resort towns such as Brighton in England or Trouville and Dieppe in France enabled workers to visit such places. New music and dance halls, popular theaters, and other forms of public entertainment sprang up to claim workers' increased spending money.

Although most workers believed their lot had improved, they were also aware that a vast gulf remained between them and the middle and upper classes. In the 1880s in the northern French industrial city of Lille, the combined estate of 20,000 workers equaled that of an average industrialist. In Paris the gluttonous rich ate multicourse meals; the leftover scraps from their plates found a ready market among the poor, who bought them for a few centimes from specialized vendors. Life expectancies still varied dramatically according to income; in Bordeaux in 1853 the life expectancy of a male bourgeois was twenty years greater than that of a male laborer.

The disparity between rich and poor was especially striking in the case of domestics. Most servants were female, and they led tiring and restricted lives under close supervision of their

Ladies' Bicycling Fashion This new mode of transportation suggested possibilities for female emancipation. Free, on her bicycle, the young woman is contrasted with a man, who rides only a tricycle. *(From Karin Helm (ed.),* Rosinen aus der Gartenlaube *[Gutersloh: Signum Verlag, n.d.]. Reproduced with permission.)*

employers. Their hours were overly long: A six-and-one-half-day week was not uncommon. Housed in either the basement or the attic, servants experienced extremes of cold, heat, and humidity. Sometimes they were subjected to physical or sexual abuse by the master of the house, his sons, or the head of the domestic staff. And yet, for impoverished rural women with little chance of finding better work, domestic service was a risky but often necessary option. It provided free housing, food, and clothing and allowed the servant to save an annual sum equivalent to an amount between one-third and one-half of a worker's yearly wages. These savings often served as a dowry and allowed the young woman to make an advantageous match. Two out of five female wage earners in England were in domestic employ in 1851.

Although a few members of the working class managed to enter the lower levels of the middle classes, most remained mired in the same profession as their grandparents. Poverty was still pervasive. In the 1880s about one-third of Londoners were living at or below the subsistence level. Industrial and urban diseases, such as tuberculosis, were common among workers. Compared to the healthier, better-fed, and better-housed middle classes, the workers continued living in shabby and limited circumstances.

The Transformation of the Countryside

Before the nineteenth century, the countryside had hardly changed at all, but beginning at midcentury it was radically transformed. Especially in western Europe, an increasing number of people left the land. In 1850, 20 percent of the population of Britain were agricultural workers; by 1881 only 11 percent were. The decrease of the agricultural population led in many places to labor shortages and therefore higher wages for farm hands.

Agriculture became increasingly efficient, and the food supply grew significantly. More land was put under the plow. Sweden's acreage more than doubled, Italy's grew by more than one-half, Germany's and Hungary's by more than one-third. In Italy and Denmark, land was reclaimed from marshes, in Holland from the North Sea. Not only was more land cultivated but the yield per acre increased. In 1760 an agricultural worker in England could feed himself and one other person; by 1841 he could feed himself and 2.7 others. The population of Europe nearly doubled in the years between 1800 and 1880, and yet it was nourished better than ever before.

Higher yields were due to an increased use of manure, augmented in the 1870s by saltpeter imported from Chile and, beginning in the 1880s, by chemical fertilizers manufactured in Europe. Innovations in tools also improved productivity. The

Steam-Powered Thresher This image shows the thresher being operated in the French countryside in 1860. It would be decades before this kind of technology became a common sight in Europe, but it was a harbinger of the change coming to the rural world. *(Bibliothèque Nationale)*

sickle, which required the laborer to crouch to cut grass or wheat, was replaced by the long-handled scythe, which allowed the field hand to stand and use the full weight of the body to swing the instrument through the grain. This new method increased efficiency fourfold. And in the 1850s steam-driven threshing machinery was introduced in some parts of western Europe. Organizational techniques borrowed from industrial labor, including specialization and the insistence on regularity in the workplace, also contributed to greater productivity on the land.

Improved roads and dramatically expanded rail lines enabled farmers to extend their markets. No longer did they need to produce only for the local area; they could depend on a national market and beyond for customers. In Brittany, in western France, a rail line to Paris led to a boom in dairy farming. The demand for agricultural products rose, and so did the price on many items, thus improving the lot of the farmer.

While the prices of farm products rose, those of industrial products fell, allowing farmers to purchase machinery to work the land and items providing personal convenience such as cast-iron stoves. Owners of medium and large farms did particularly well. For the first time, many had credit available to them, and some of the vagaries of farming were buffered by the availability of fire and weather insurance.

Life in the countryside became less insular. Not only did rail lines connect farms to cities, but national school systems brought teachers into the villages. Local dialects and in some cases even distinct languages that peasants had spoken for generations were replaced by a standardized national language. Local provincial costumes became less common as styles adopted in the cities spread to the countryside via consumer catalogs. The farm girls who went to the cities as maids to work in middle-class homes returned to their villages with urban and middle-class ideals. The military draft brought the young men of the village into contact with urban folk and further spread urban values to the countryside.

Even so, the rural world remained very distinct from urban society. Many of the forces seen as contributing to modernity exacerbated rural conditions. The expansion of manufacturing in cities contributed to the decline of cottage industry in rural areas, where agricultural workers had relied on the putting-out system to provide supplementary income; thus farm workers were idle during slack seasons, and rural unemployment grew. In many cases railroads bringing goods made elsewhere wiped out some of the local markets on which these cottage industries had depended. The steamship lowered the cost of transporting freight, including grain from distant Canada and Argentina, which often undersold wheat grown in Europe. The resultant crisis, worsened by a rural population explosion, led to the emigration of millions, who left the land for towns and cities or even migrated across the seas to the Americas and Australia (see pages 897–898). Although this process was painful for large segments of the rural population, the result was that for those who were able to remain on the land, the situation eventually improved.

These trends had a striking effect in the rural areas of western Europe. Eastern Europe, in contrast, was hardly touched by them. In Russia agriculture remained backward; the average yield per acre in 1880 was one-quarter that of Great Britain. The land sheltered a large surplus population that was underemployed and contributed little to the rural economy. In the Balkans, most peasants were landless and heavily indebted.

URBAN PROBLEMS AND SOLUTIONS

By 1851 the majority of English people lived in cities; by 1891 the majority of Germans did as well. To cope with urban growth and its attendant problems—epidemics, crowding, traffic jams—cities developed public health measures and introduced planning and rebuilding programs. They adapted the new technologies to provide such urban amenities as streetlights, public transportation, water and sewer systems, and police forces. Cities gradually became safer and more pleasant places to live, although for a long time city dwellers continued to suffer high mortality rates.

City Planning and Urban Renovation

Most of Europe's cities had begun as medieval walled cities and had grown haphazardly into major industrial centers. Their narrow, crooked streets

Pissarro: L' avenue de l' Opéra, Sunlight, Winter Morning Camille Pissarro, one of the leading impressionists, portrayed the broad new avenue designed by Baron Haussmann. The avenue leads to the new opera, in background, also planned during the Second Empire. (*Musée Saint-Denis, Reims/Giraudon/Art Resource, NY*)

could not accommodate the increased trade and daily movement of goods and people, and traffic snarls were common. City officials began to recognize that broad, straight avenues would resolve the traffic problem and also bring sunlight and fresh air into the narrow and perpetually dank lanes and alleys. In the 1820s, London saw the first ambitious street-widening initiative. On Regency Street, old hovels were torn down and replaced with fancy new houses; the poor were usually displaced. Later projects followed this pattern.

The most extensive program of urban rebuilding took place in midcentury Paris. Over a period of eighteen years, Napoleon III and his aide, Baron Georges Haussmann (1809–1891), transformed Paris from a dirty medieval city to a beautiful modern one (Map 23.2). Broad, straight avenues were carved through what had been dingy slums. The avenues were lined with trees and graced with elegant houses. Enhancing the city were public monuments and buildings, such as the new opera house. The tremendous costs of this ambitious

Map 23.2 Haussmann's Paris, 1850–1870 During the reign of Napoleon III, Baron Georges Haussmann reshaped the city of Paris, replacing its narrow medieval streets with a system of broad avenues and public parks and encircling the city with a railway.

scheme kept the city of Paris in debt for decades. (See the box, "Haussmann Justifies the Rebuilding of Paris.") In addition, the slum-removal program drove tens of thousands of the poorest Parisians to the outskirts of the city, leading to greater social segregation than had previously existed.

Haussmann's extensive work in Paris served as a model for other cities, and although none was rebuilt as extensively, many underwent significant improvements. The cities of Europe began to display an expansive grace and sense of order, supporting the belief of the middle classes that theirs was an age of progress.

The Introduction of Public Services

Beginning at midcentury, government at the central and local level helped make cities more livable by

Haussmann Justifies the Rebuilding of Paris

Baron Georges Haussmann, whom Napoleon III had appointed to rebuild Paris, explained in his **Memoirs** *(published in 1890) what he had accomplished and why. Haussmann also justified the important role the central government played in the capital's transformation.*

The present generation does not know what this part [the center] of Paris was like, before its complete transformation between 1852 and 1854.

It ignores that the first section of Rue Rivoli, along the Tuileries Gardens, ended abruptly. . . . beyond was an unspeakably foul neighborhood, consisting of squalid houses. . . . the Place de la Colonnade was obstructed by wretched constructions and was connected to other neighborhoods which were equally obstructed and impassable to traffic. . . .

. . . This last named street was so narrow that the rotten front of a house which in vain was trying to topple over could not do so for it was leaning on the house across.

And what a population lived there!

Those who had not explored the Paris of that time in all directions would not have an idea of what it was like. . . . the narrow, crooked streets were nearly impenetrable to traffic, dirty, stinking, unhealthy. . . .

. . . Our widening of streets gave old and new neighborhoods air, light, green space and flowers—in a word everything needed to improve public health and to be pleasant to the eye. . . .

The splendor of this city reflects on the whole country; the well-being of its population is meaningful to nearly all families in France. . . . If Paris is a great city, the center of commercial and industrial activities, as well as specialized production, and the site of prodigious consumption and constant trade, it is the capital of a mighty Empire, the governmental seat of a glorious sovereign. . . . the world capital of letters, the sciences and the arts. . . .

The State must directly and constantly intervene in the city's affairs, for it contributes to its splendor, by the palaces and public buildings which it constructs, by its financial contribution to certain public services such as the police, the upkeep of the streets, street lighting, water services and public transportation. . . .

Source: Baron Georges Haussmann, *Mémoires,* 2d ed., vol. 2 (Paris: Victor-Havard, 1890), pp. 26–28, 197–198, 203. Trans. by William Cohen.

---

legislating sanitary reforms and providing public transportation and lighting. Medical practitioners in the 1820s had observed that disease and higher mortality were related to dirt and lack of clean air, water, and sunshine. Since diseases spreading from the poorer quarters of town threatened the rich and powerful, there was a general interest in improving public health by clearing slums, broadening streets, and supplying clean air and water to the cities.

Reform began in England, where the lawyer and civil servant Edwin Chadwick (1800–1895) drafted important plans for reform that became

the basis for legislation. The Public Health Bill of 1848 established national standards for urban sanitation and required cities to regulate the installation of sewers and the disposal of refuse. The 1875 Health Act required cities to maintain certain basic health standards such as water and drainage. Armed with these laws, cities and towns took the initiative: Birmingham cleared fifty acres of slums in the 1870s, for example.

London was also a leader in supplying public water, a service later adopted by Paris and many other cities. Berlin had a municipal water system in 1850, but it took several decades before clean water was available in every household. As late as the 1870s, Berlin's sewage was carried in open pipes. In Paris, which typically led France in innovations, 60 percent of the houses had running water in 1882. The French capital did not have a unitary sewer system until the 1890s, however.

As running water in the home became a standard rather than a luxury, bathing became more common. The English upper classes had learned the habit of daily baths from their colonial experience in India; on the Continent it was not the custom until about the third quarter of the nineteenth century. French artist Edgar Degas (1834–1917) frequently painted bath scenes portraying the new European habit.

All these changes had a direct impact on the lives of city dwellers. Life became healthier, more comfortable, and more orderly. Between the 1840s and 1880, London's death rate fell from 26 per thousand to 20 per thousand. In Paris for the same period the decline was from 29.3 to 23.7 per thousand. There was a more immediate decline in the incidence of diseases associated with filthy living conditions. Improved water supplies provided a cleaner environment and reduced the prevalence of water-borne diseases such as cholera and typhoid.

Other improvements also contributed to a better quality of life. With the introduction of urban transportation, city dwellers no longer had to live within walking distance of their work. Early public transportation was seen in the French omnibus service of the 1820s—a system of horse-drawn carriages available to the public on fixed routes. Other cities followed—Hamburg in 1843, Berlin in 1846. In the 1850s the tram was introduced. A carriage drawn on a rail line, it could pull larger loads of passengers faster than the omnibus. Because of the many rail stations in London and the difficulty of getting from one station to another in time to make a connection, London built an underground railway in 1863, the predecessor of the subway system. The bicycle also became a serious means of transportation for some city dwellers. By the mid-1880s, there were nearly 100,000 bicycles in Great Britain, and a decade later, 375,000 in France.

Improvements in public transportation enabled workers to move out of the inner city into the less dense and less expensive suburbs. This trend in turn led to a decrease in urban population

Public Transportation in Berlin A few years after this photograph was taken, horses were dispensed with, as trams were electrified and buses were motorized. *(Landesbildstelle, Berlin)*

density and eventually helped make the city a healthier place to live.

Gaslights also improved city life, making it easier and safer to move around at night. (Prior to gaslights, city dwellers depended mainly on moonlight or, rarely, expensive and time-consuming oil lamps for street lighting.) In 1813 London was the first city to be illuminated by gas; Berlin followed in 1816. By 1860, 250 German towns had some form of street illumination. The first gaslights appeared in Paris in the 1820s, and by 1844 the city had 65,000 gas lamps. Electrical lights were introduced in Paris in 1875, although they were not common until the end of the century.

Cities also significantly expanded police forces to impose order, to control criminal activity, and to discourage behavior deemed undesirable, such as dumping garbage on the street, relieving oneself in public, or singing loud, raucous songs late at night. In 1850 London was the best-policed city in Europe with a 5000-man force. Paris had around 3000 policemen. These numbers continued to increase: By 1870 the French capital had 6000 policemen and London about 8000.

SOCIAL AND POLITICAL INITIATIVES

New institutions and groups emerged to tackle the unequal wealth and critical urban problems that followed in the wake of economic growth. The state intervened in the economy in new ways. Private charitable groups sprang up. And socialist parties, exclusively dedicated to improving the lot of the worker, gained in numbers and strength.

State Intervention in Welfare

The difficult conditions industry imposed on workers led to debates in several countries about the need for the state to protect the workers. The growing militancy of organized labor also forced the established authority to consider ways to meet the workers' needs. While some rejected government intervention in the free operation of market forces, others argued that the laws of supply and demand had caused the exploitation of many who ought to have been protected—especially very young children and pregnant women.

To right some of these abuses, the Scottish philanthropist Robert Owen (1771–1858) agitated in Parliament for the first effective British factory act, which passed in 1819. This act forbade labor for children under the age of 9 and limited the workday of children over that age to twelve hours a day. Then, beginning in 1833, a series of factory acts further limited the work hours of children and women in factories and mines and funded inspections to enforce these laws. French laws for the protection of children were passed as early as 1841, but government funding for their enforcement was not approved until 1874. Confronted with a declining birthrate and the need to strengthen itself against rival Germany, France further limited the work hours of children and women in a series of laws between 1892 and 1905. In addition, workmen's compensation became law in 1898.

In Prussia an 1839 law prohibited factory work for children under the age of 9 and established the precedent for state intervention in the rest of Germany. Ten years later, legislation was passed to create a social security system to which workers and their employers were required to contribute. Beginning in the 1840s, Prussia limited a city's right to refuse welfare support to its poor. Laws passed in the 1890s protected workers from harsh conditions and limited the hours of women. In much of Europe, however, the state did little to improve the welfare of the working class. In eastern Europe, where industry was still in its infancy, there was no protection of workers.

Fear of social upheaval and the rising strength of socialist political parties prompted some governments to act. In France moderate bourgeois liberals attempted to defuse class war by advocating "Solidarism," insisting on the responsibility of each class and individual for its fellow citizens. In newly unified Germany, the government wanted to show workers the benefits they could gain from the state so they would abandon the growing Socialist party and back the kaiser's government. It embarked on a deliberate program to tame the workers and win their support for the existing political and economic institutions. Thus, in the 1880s the new German government provided a comprehensive welfare plan that included health insurance and old-age pensions. Although local governments in many European states had provided welfare services in various forms, Germany was the first to recognize a national responsibility, and German social programs became models for the rest of Europe.

In addition to the welfare initiatives by state and city governments, middle and upper classes worked to better the workers' lot. Concern among these groups and individuals arose from a mixture of pity for workers' conditions, religious teachings about their responsibilities for the less fortunate, and fear of the consequences of unrelieved misery. In Paris, for example, three thousand private charitable organizations were founded between 1840 and 1900; their combined outlay in aid equaled the public charity available. In London the sum of £6 million—more than the total budget of many European states—was employed on behalf of the poor in 1890.

Women participated heavily in volunteer charity work. By the end of the nineteenth century, as many as half a million English women contributed their time to provide charity to the less fortunate. In Sweden by the 1880s, women had founded refuges for the destitute, old-age homes, a children's hospital, an asylum for the mentally handicapped, and various societies to promote female industry. In Spain a number of religious orders devoted to providing free education to the poor flourished in the 1880s.

In Catholic and Protestant countries, the Christian churches traditionally had identified with the rights of employers and seemed to ignore the lot of the workers. However, a number of Christians, lay and clerical, began to emphasize the need to address social issues. In Germany, Bishop Wilhelm Von Ketteler (1811–1877) preached the need for the well-off to take responsibility for the less privileged. His message was taken up in France, Italy, and Spain among what became known as "social Catholics." In England, Protestants' concern for the poor was evidenced by the founding of the Salvation Army in 1878. Religious groups also hoped they could win converts among the less privileged by demonstrating concern for their plight.

Increasingly, states, municipalities, volunteer groups, and churches accepted responsibility for the well-being of others. This trend marked the beginning of an evolution that would eventually spread in scope and lead to the welfare state in much of twentieth-century Europe.

Educational and Cultural Opportunities

At the beginning of the nineteenth century, governments took little responsibility for providing education. The upper classes educated their children with private tutors, parents from more modest economic groups taught their children what they knew, and the poor attended the few schools—usually one-room schools—provided by charitable and religious groups. In England the education of the masses became a national responsibility after the Second Reform Bill of 1867. This legislation extended the vote to the artisan classes and prompted a movement to ensure that the new voters were educated. In 1870 the English government began to provide significant subsidies for education, to set educational standards, and to establish a national inspection system to enforce them. England and France initiated mandatory primary school education in the 1880s. In Britain, one million children attended school in 1865; by 1880 more than three million attended.

Public education included not only reading, writing, and arithmetic but other skills as well. By insisting on punctuality and obliging students to carry out repetitive skills such as copying letters, words, or sentences, schools encouraged people to fit into the emerging industrial society. Obedience and the respect for authority learned at school shaped the soldiers and factory workers of the future. And regardless of political inclination, each regime took advantage of its control of the educational system to inculcate in the young the love of country and of its form of government.

Secondary education was, on the whole, available only to the privileged few in the upper middle classes. It confirmed their social status and won them access to the universities and the professions. To a very small number from the lower middle classes, secondary school attendance provided the means to ascend socially. The lower middle class was sparsely represented in universities, and the children of workers and peasants were totally absent.

Public education spread from the schools to other institutions, which made culture available to the masses in new ways. Between 1840 and 1880, the number of large libraries in Europe increased from 40 to 500, and by the late 1870s England had over 66 public lending libraries. The French national public library, the Bibliothèque Nationale, was established in Paris in the 1860s. This iron-and-glass building, radical for its time, was an impressive monument to the desire to make reading available to an expanded public. Many provincial cities, as well as the glittering capitals of Europe, were endowed with new libraries. Less grandiose, but probably more important for mostly rural populations, were the traveling libraries.

Museums and art galleries, which in the previous century had been open to only a select few, gradually became accessible to the general public. The first museum to open to the public was the Louvre in Paris after the French Revolution. The rest of Europe lagged behind in making the cultural heritage available to the masses. The British Museum restricted entrance to the wealthy and the well connected, for there was widespread fear of the possible destruction that the "vulgar classes" might cause if they were allowed to visit. But the sedate manner in which the crowds behaved during the Crystal Palace exposition reassured British authorities, and finally in 1879 the museum was opened daily to the general public. (See the feature, "Weighing the Evidence: The Crystal Palace," on pages 876–877.)

CULTURE IN AN AGE OF OPTIMISM

The improving economic and material conditions of the second half of the nineteenth century buoyed European thinkers. Many believed that men and women were becoming more enlightened, and they expressed faith in humankind's ability to transform the world with new scientific and technological breakthroughs. The world seemed knowable and perfectible. This faith advanced secularism while it undermined the certainties of traditional religion. The arts reflected these new values, emphasizing realism and science—as well as an underlying foreboding of the dark side of this "age of optimism."

Darwin and the Doctrine of Evolution

By midcentury most thinkers accepted the notion of change and transformation of society—and by analogy of the natural environment. The French thinker Auguste Comte (1798–1857) championed

the notion that human progress proceeded by developmental stages. Human progress was a law of nature leading men and women irresistibly to the final and highest stage of development, the positive—or scientific—stage. Widely read throughout Europe and Latin America, Comte's writings helped gird the era's faith in science, and the very progress science made seemed to confirm its precepts. Comte's philosophy, known as *positivism,* dominated the era. While the romantics had emphasized feeling, positivists upheld the significance of the measurable, the palpable, that which could be scientifically understood. Their methods, they were confident, would assure the continued progress of humanity. Science had proved that the world was evolving to ever higher forms.

In the field of geology, the Englishman Charles Lyell (1797–1875) maintained that the earth was far older than the biblical story of Genesis suggested. He argued that its geological formations—the mountains, valleys, and seas—had been subject to natural forces that, over hundreds of thousands, even millions, of years, had transformed them. Most educated people accepted his theory, which led many to wonder if it might also be true that the animal kingdom had evolved gradually over long periods of time.

Although evolution in the biological realm had been suggested as early as the end of the eighteenth century, Charles Darwin (1809–1882) was the first to offer a plausible explanation of the process. As the naturalist on an official British scientific expedition in the 1830s, he had visited the Galápagos Islands off the coast of South America. On these islands he found species similar to but different from those on the mainland and even different from one another. Could they be the result of separate creation? Or was it more likely that in varying environments they had adapted differently? Darwin theorized that closely related species compete for food and living space. In this struggle, those in each species that are better adapted to the environment have the advantage over the others and are hence more likely to survive. These surviving members of the species, Darwin claimed, pass on their desirable adaptive traits to their offspring, while the others die off. Darwin described this continuous process as a "struggle for existence," in which only the fittest endure. He called the mechanism that explained the evolution and development of new species "natural selection," a process that was imperceptible but continuous. (See the box, "Darwin's Basic Laws of Evolution.")

Darwin's theory of the inevitability of evolution in nature echoed the era's confidence in change and its conviction that the present represented a more developed stage of the past. His work was seen as confirming the notion that societies—like species—were preordained to evolve toward progressively higher stages. Darwin at first avoided the question of whether human beings, too, were affected by the laws of evolution. To do so would be to question humanity's uniqueness, its separation from the rest of creation by its possession (in the Christian view) of a soul. But in *Descent of Man* (1871), Darwin did confront this issue, clearly stating his belief that humanity, too, was subject to these natural laws. The recognition that human beings were members of the animal kingdom like other species disturbed him, and the admission, he wrote, "is like confessing a murder." Nonetheless, for Darwin scientific evidence took precedence over all other considerations.

Many Christians were shocked by these assertions, and some denounced the new scientific findings. Some argued that science and faith belonged to two different worlds. Others claimed that there was no reason that God could not have created the world through natural forces. In the long run, however, Darwinism seemed to undermine the certainties of religious orthodoxies by showing their incompatibility with scientific discovery.

Physics, Chemistry, and Medicine

Dramatic scientific breakthroughs occurred in the nineteenth century, confirming the prevalent belief that human beings could understand and control nature. In physics, laws regarding electricity and magnetism were articulated by Michael Faraday (1791–1867) and James Clerk Maxwell (1831–1879) in the 1830s and 1850s, respectively. Their work established the field of electrical science. In the 1840s, Hermann von Helmholtz (1821–1894) in Germany and James Joule (1818–1889) in Great Britain defined the nature of energy in the laws of thermodynamics. In chemistry, new elements were discovered almost every year, and individual findings contributed to the under-

Darwin as an Ape This was one of many cartoons suggesting that if Darwin's theories on evolution were correct, then the great scientist must be descended from apes. (*From* The Hornet, *March 22, 1871*)

standing of larger patterns. In 1869 Russian chemist Dmitri Mendeleev (1834–1907) developed the periodic table, in which the elements are arranged by their atomic weight. He left blank spaces for elements still unknown but that he predicted would be discovered. Within ten years, three of these elements were discovered, affirming the belief that science is not only knowledge that can be experimentally tested but also knowledge that can have predictive value. Such triumphs further enhanced science's prestige.

Prolific research yielded discoveries in one field of knowledge that could be transferred to another. For example, chemists produced new dyes, enabling biologists to color slides of microorganisms and better study their evolution. Scientific breakthroughs also led to technical achievements that had industrial uses; for instance, inventions in

Darwin's Basic Laws of Evolution

In On the Origin of Species by Means of Natural Selection *(1859) Darwin explained his theories of evolution. Writing in an age of vast transformations, he could imagine the mutability of all nature, including species, over time. And, like his contemporaries, he could imagine that evolution would lead to improvement, to increasing "perfection" of various species.*

A religious man, who lost much of his faith as a result of his scientific work, he was anxious to reassure Christians that evolution could be seen as part of the divine plan.

Nothing at first can appear more difficult to believe than that the more complex organs and instincts have been perfected, not by means superior to, though analogous with, human reason, but by the accumulation of innumerable slight variations, each good for the individual possessor. Nevertheless, this difficulty, though appearing to our imagination insuperably great, cannot be considered real if we admit the following propositions, namely, that all parts of the organisation and instincts offer, at least, individual differences—that there is a struggle for existence leading to the preservation of profitable deviations of structure or instinct—and, lastly, that gradations in the state of perfection of each organ may have existed, each good of its kind. The truth of these propositions cannot, I think, be disputed. . . .

As geology plainly proclaims that each land has undergone great physical changes, we might have expected to find that organic beings have varied under nature, in the same way as they have varied under domestication. And if there has been any variability under nature, it would be an unaccountable fact if natural selection had not come into play. . . .

There is grandeur in this view of life, with its several powers, having been originally breathed by the Creator into a few forms or into one; and that, whilst this planet has gone cycling on according to the fixed law of gravity, from so simple a beginning endless forms most beautiful and most wonderful have been, and are being evolved.

Source: Charles Darwin, *On the Origin of Species by Means of Natural Selection*, 6th ed., vol. 2 (1872; reprint, New York: Appleton, 1923), pp. 267–268, 279, 305–306.

chemistry led to the development of the first artificial fertilizers in 1842 and to synthetic dyes in the 1850s.

Science also became increasingly specialized. In the eighteenth century, the scientist had been a learned amateur practicing a hobby. In the nineteenth century, as the state and industry became more involved in promoting scientific research, the scientist became a professional, employed by a university, a hospital, or some other institution. New theories and discoveries were disseminated by scientific journals and by meetings of scientific associations and congresses.

Internationally, scientific cooperation became common, but science also promoted international rivalry. The nationalism of the late nineteenth century spurred on scientific competition. When cholera broke out in Egypt in 1883, a French and a German team of scientists rushed to the area to discover its cause. The German team led by Robert Koch (1843–1910) uncovered the cholera bacillus as the source; on returning to his homeland he was feted as a national hero who had vindicated German superiority in science.

Around the midcentury mark, a number of important breakthroughs occurred in medicine.

Before the development of anesthesia, surgical intervention had been nearly impossible. With only alcohol to dull the patient's pain, even the swiftest surgeons could perform only modest surgical procedures. In the 1840s, however, the introduction of ether and then chloroform allowed people to undergo more extensive surgery. It also was used to quiet pain in more routine procedures such as childbirth; Queen Victoria asked for chloroform when giving birth.

Increasingly, the experimental method in science was applied to medicine, and as a result physicians became concerned not simply with treating diseases but with discovering their origins. Louis Pasteur (1822–1895) achieved notable breakthroughs when he discovered that microbes, small organisms invisible to the naked eye, cause various diseases. Pasteur found that heating milk to a certain temperature kills disease-carrying organisms. This process, called *pasteurization,* reduced the incidence of certain diseases that were particularly harmful to children. Pasteur initiated other advances as well in the prevention of disease. Vaccination against smallpox had started in England in the eighteenth century, but Pasteur invented vaccines for other diseases and was able to explain the process by which the body, inoculated with a weak form of bacilli, developed antibodies that successfully overcame more serious infections.

In England the surgeon John Lister (1827–1912) developed an effective disinfectant, carbolic acid, to kill the germs that caused gangrene and other infections in surgical patients. Eventually, midwives and doctors began to reduce the incidence of the puerperal fever that killed so many women after childbirth by washing their hands and sterilizing their instruments. Lister's development of germ-free procedures transformed the science of surgery. By reducing the patient's risk, more ambitious surgery could be attempted. The first surgical kidney removal took place in 1876; the first successful brain surgery in modern times was performed three years later.

The increasingly scientific base of medicine and its visible success in combating disease improved its reputation. The medical profession began to control access to its ranks by establishing powerful professional associations—for example, the British Medical Association (1832) and the German Medical Association (1872). In addition, medical journals also emerged to spread scientific knowledge.

Science was fashionable. In 1869 Empress Eugénie in France had Louis Pasteur come to tea, draw blood from her finger, and examine it under a microscope, all to the astonishment of her guests. Some frogs, brought in for experimentation, escaped down palace corridors. The spectacle of science as the chic entertainment of an empress was a reminder of the increasing authority it commanded in the later nineteenth century.

Birth of the Social Sciences

The scientific method, so dramatically effective in uncovering the mysteries of nature, was also applied to the human enterprise. Just as the secrets of nature were unlocked, the workings of society, it was thought, could be understood in a scientific manner.

No field in the human sciences flourished as much in the nineteenth century as history. In an era undergoing vast transformations, many people became interested in change over time. They were eager to employ the methods of the scientist to explore their past. The father of modern historical writing is the German Leopold von Ranke (1795–1886). Departing from the tradition of earlier historians, who explained the past as the ongoing fulfillment of an overarching purpose—divine will, the liberation of humanity, or some other goal—Ranke insisted that the role of the historian was to "show how things actually were." Like a scientist, the historian must be objective and dispassionate. By viewing humankind of all eras and environments on their own terms, and not those of others, historians could arrive at a better understanding of humanity.

This perspective transformed the study of history into a discipline with recognizable common standards of evidence. Historians studied and interpreted original (or "primary") sources; they collected and published their findings; they founded professional organizations and published major journals.

Other social sciences also developed in this period. Anthropology, the comparative study of people in different societies, had been the subject of speculative literature for hundreds of years. Increased contacts with non-European societies in the nineteenth century as a result of dramatically increased trade, exploration, and missionary activities stimulated anthropological curiosity. In 1844 the Society of Ethnology was founded in Paris, followed by the Anthropological Society (1859). London, Berlin, and Vienna quickly followed suit, establishing similar societies in the 1860s. Consisting of medical doctors, biologists, and travelers, these societies speculated on the causes of the perceived differences among human races. The Paris Anthropological Society was dominated by the medical doctor Paul Broca (1824–1880) and other physicians, who saw in biological structure the explanation for differences among human groups, thus giving apparent "scientific" backing to the era's racism. They used their findings to demonstrate that non-Europeans were condemned to an existence inferior to the white races.

In Britain, the main anthropological theorist was Edward Tylor (1832–1917), the son of a brass manufacturer. Through his travels, Tylor came into contact with non-European peoples, who aroused his curiosity. Strongly influenced by the evolutionary doctrines of his day, Tylor believed that the various societies of humankind were subject to discoverable scientific laws. Just as if one could travel back in time, one would find humankind increasingly unsophisticated, so Tylor posited, the farther one became distanced from Europe, the more primitive humankind became. The contemporary African was at a level of development similar to that of Europeans in an earlier era.

Tylor was not technically a racist, since he argued that the conditions of non-Europeans were not due to biology but rather were a function of their institutions. Like racists, however, evolutionists believed in the superiority of the European over other races. Anthropology gave scientific sanction to the idea of a single European people, sharing either a similar biological structure or a common stage of social development, which distinguished them from non-Europeans.

Anthropology gradually gained recognition and legitimacy as a profession. In 1872 in France, Broca founded a journal emphasizing physical anthropology. In 1876 he founded a school of anthropology with six chaired professors. In Britain in 1884, Tylor—who was so closely identified with anthropology it was called "Mr Tylor's science"—was appointed to the first university chair in anthropology in his country.

Sociology is a term originally coined by Auguste Comte. A number of ambitious thinkers, among them the English "social philosopher" Herbert Spencer (see page 797), had considered how individuals are affected by the society in which they live. In the 1840s various social reformers published detailed statistical investigations revealing relationships between, for instance, income and disease and death rates. A few decades later, the theoretical principles underlying sociology were spelled out. Among the first to do so was Emile Durkheim (1858–1917), who insisted that sociology was a verifiable science. He occupied the first chair of sociology at a French university in 1887. A few years later he founded a journal of sociology and gathered around him a coterie of disciples who ensured the success of sociology as a professionalized discipline.

Whereas in the past, history, anthropology, and sociology were the purview of amateurs, now professional historians, anthropologists, and sociologists were engaged full-time in research and teaching at universities or research institutes. The professionalization that had occurred in medicine and physics also transformed the social sciences. Professionalization and specialization led to significant advances in several disciplines, but it also led to the fragmentation and compartmentalization of knowledge. People of broad learning and expertise became far less common.

The Challenge to Religion

The scientific claims of the era seemed to clash with the traditions of religion. A number of scientists, including Darwin himself, found their Christian faith undermined by theories on evolution. Although most Europeans continued to be strongly influenced by traditional religious beliefs, they appeared less confident than in earlier eras.

After the revolutions of 1848, religion was seen as a bulwark of order. In France, Napoleon III gave the Catholic church new powers in education, and the bourgeoisie flocked to worship. In Spain, moderates who had been anticlerical began to support the church, and in 1851 they signed a concordat declaring Roman Catholicism "the only religion of the Spanish nation." In Austria in 1855, the state surrendered to the bishops full control over the clergy, the seminaries, and the administration of marriage laws.

In 1848 the papacy had been nearly overthrown by revolution, and in 1860 it lost most of its domains to Italy. Thus Pope Pius IX became a sworn enemy of liberalism, and in 1864, in the *Syllabus of Errors*, he condemned a long list of what he perceived to be modern errors, among them "progress," "liberalism," and "modern civilization." To establish full control over the clergy and believers, the Lateran Council in 1870 issued the controversial doctrine of infallibility, declaring that the pope, when speaking officially on faith and morals, was infallible. This doctrine became a target of anticlerical opinion.

The political alliance the Catholic church struck with reactionary forces meant that when new political groups came to power they moved against the church. In Italy, since the church had discouraged national unification, conflict raged between the church and the new state. In Germany, Catholics had either held on to their regional loyalties or favored unification under Austrian auspices. When Protestant Prussia unified Germany, Chancellor Bismarck viewed the Catholics with suspicion as unpatriotic and started a campaign against them, the *Kulturkampf* ("cultural struggle").

In France the republicans, who finally won the upper hand over monarchists in 1879, bitterly resented the church's support of the monarchist party. They were also strongly influenced by Comte's ideas of positivism, believing that France would not be a free country until the power of the church was diminished and its nonscientific or antiscientific disposition was overcome. The republican regime reduced the role of the church in education as well as some other clerical privileges.

Greater religious tolerance, or perhaps indifference to religion in general, led to more acceptance of religious diversity. In 1854 and 1871 England opened university admission and teaching posts at all universities to non-Anglicans. Anti-Catholicism, at times a popular and virulent movement, declined in the 1870s. In France, too, the position of religious minorities improved. Some of the highest officials of the Second Empire were Protestants, as were some early leaders of the Third Republic and some important business leaders and scientists.

Legal emancipation of Jews, started in France in 1791, subsequently spread to the rest of the Continent. England removed restrictions on Jews when the House of Commons, in 1858, and the House of Lords the following decade allowed Jews to hold a parliamentary seat. In the 1860s Germany and Austria-Hungary granted Jews the rights of citizenship. Social discrimination continued, however, and Jews were not accepted as social equals in most of European society. Although some Jews occupied high office in France and Italy, in Germany and Austria-Hungary they had to convert before they could aspire to such position. In other fields, access was easier. Some of the major banking houses were founded by Jews—the Rothschilds in France, Britain, and Germany, and the Warburgs in Germany, for instance.

In the expanding economy of western Europe, where the condition of most people was improving, the enhanced opportunity of a previously despised minority aroused relatively little attention. In other parts of Europe, Jews were not so fortunate. When they seized economic opportunities in eastern Europe and moved into commerce, industry, and the professions, they were resented. Rashes of violence against them, called *pogroms,* broke out in Bucharest, capital of Romania, in 1866 and in the Russian seaport of Odessa in 1871. Although economic rivalries may have fueled this anti-Semitism, they do not completely explain it. In most cases anti-Jewish sentiment occurred in the areas of Europe least exposed to liberal ideas of human equality and human rights.

The emphasis on science and reason transformed religion in the nineteenth century, but, as the continued anti-Semitism showed, it by no means always led to increased tolerance or weakened religious fervor. On the contrary, in certain cases religiosity grew. French people reported frequent sightings of the Virgin Mary. A shepherdess in 1858 claimed to have seen and spoken with her at Lourdes, which became an especially important shrine whose waters were reputed to heal the lame and the sick. In 1872 construction of a rail line allowed 100,000 people a year to visit the town.

Church attendance continued to be high, especially in rural areas. In England villagers usually attended church, many twice or more each Sunday. Children dutifully attended Sunday schools. Advances in printing made it possible to distribute large quantities of inexpensive religious tracts to a sizable and avid readership. The faithful eagerly engaged in proselytizing, sending large numbers of missionaries to all corners of the globe.

Art in the Age of Material Change

The new era of technology, science, and faith in progress was reflected in the arts. Some artists optimistically believed they could more accurately depict reality by adopting the methods of the scientist, cooly describing their subject. A minority, however, were disillusioned by the materialism of the age and warned against its loss of values.

Photography had a direct impact on painting. Various experiments in the late eighteenth century, plus the inventions of the Frenchman Louis Daguerre (1789–1851), made the camera relatively usable by the 1830s. It was still a large, cumbersome object, however, until the dry plate and miniature camera were introduced in the 1870s. Twenty years later, with the invention of celluloid film, it came into wide use—the best-known mass-produced camera being the Kodak camera invented by the American George Eastman (1854–1932). Unlike paintings and portraits, photography was accessible to the public. And photographic services were in high demand; by the 1860s, 30,000 people in Paris made a living from photography and allied fields. Many Europeans became amateur photographers—Queen Victoria and Prince Albert had a darkroom at Windsor Castle.

The ability of photography to depict a scene with exactitude had a significant impact on art. On the one hand, it encouraged many artists to be true to reality, to reproduce on the canvas a visual image akin to that of a photograph. On the other hand, other artists felt that such realism was now no longer necessary in their sphere. However, the great majority of the public, which now had wide access to museum exhibitions, was accustomed to photographic accuracy and desired art that was accessible and understandable. Realistic works of art met this need, at least superficially.

Discarding myths and symbols, many artists described the world as it actually was or appeared to them—a world without illusions, everyday life in all its grimness. The realist painter Gustave Courbet (1819–1877) proclaimed himself "without ideals and without religion." His fellow Frenchman, Jean-François Millet (1814–1875), held a similar opinion. Instead of romanticizing peasants in the manner of earlier artists, he painted the harsh physical conditions under which they labored. In England the pre-Raphaelites took as their model the painters of Renaissance Italy prior to Raphael, who presumably had depicted the realistic simplicity of nature. In painting historical scenes, these artists emphasized meticulous research of the landscape, architecture, fauna, and costumes of their subjects. To paint the Dead Sea in *The Scapegoat,* English artist Holman Hunt (1827–1910) traveled all the way to Palestine to guarantee accurate portrayal of the site.

In the past, artists had been concerned about composition and perspective. But under the influence of photography, they began to paint incomplete, off-center pictures. *Orchestra of the Paris Opera* by French artist Edgar Degas looks as if it has been cropped, with only half of a musician showing on each edge and the top half of the ballet dancers missing.

On April 15, 1874, six French artists—Edgar Degas (1834–1917), Claude Monet (1840–1926), Camille Pissarro (1830–1903), Auguste Renoir (1840–1919), Alfred Sisley (1839–1899), and Berthe Morisot (1841–1895)—opened an exhibition in Paris that a critic disparagingly called "impressionist," after the title of one of Monet's paintings, *Impression: Sunrise.* The impressionists were influenced by new theories of physics that claimed images were transmitted to the brain as small light particles that the brain then reconstituted. The impressionists wanted their paintings to capture what things looked like before they had been "distorted" by the brain. In their search for realism, impressionist painters ceased painting in their studios and increasingly went outdoors to paint objects exactly as they looked when light hit them at a certain angle. Monet, for example, emphasized outdoor painting and the need for spontaneity—for reproducing subjects without the preconception of how they had been depicted in earlier work, and seeking to show exactly how the colors and shapes hit the eye. Monet was particularly interested in painting several views of the same object to underscore that there was no single correct depiction of a subject but that it depended on viewpoint, weather, and time of day.

Courbet: The Stone Breakers This realistic 1849 painting depicts the rough existence of manual laborers. The bleakness of the subject matter and the style in which it was carried out characterized much of the realistic school of art. *(Staatliche Kunstsammlungen, Dresden/The Bridgeman Art Library, London)*

The school of realism also influenced literature, especially the novel. In realist novels, life was not glorified or infused with mythical elements; the stark existence of daily life was seen as a suitable subject. Charles Dickens (1812–1870), who came from a poor background and had personally experienced the inhumanity of the London underworld, wrote novels depicting the lot of the poor with humor and sympathy. The appalling social conditions he described helped educate his large middle-class audience on the state of the poor. He also provided numerous examples of individuals who by hard work were able to rise above their circumstances. In fact, the income from Dickens' many novels provided him with a comfortable income; by the pen he was able to join the middle class himself.

Another realist, the French novelist Gustave Flaubert (1821–1880), consciously debunked the romanticism of his elders. His famous novel, *Madame Bovary*, describes middle-class life as bleak, boring, and meaningless. The heroine seeks to escape the narrow confines of provincial life by adulterous and disastrous affairs.

Emile Zola (1840–1902), another Frenchman, belonged to the naturalist school of literature. The writer, he declared, should be like a surgeon or chemist, providing a scientific cause and record of human behavior; his work, in Zola's words, is similar to "the analysis that surgeons make on cadavers." (See the box, "Emile Zola on the Novelist as Scientist.") In his Rougon-Macquart series, which describes in detail the experience of several generations of a family, Zola's major theme is the impact of environment and heredity on his characters' lives of degradation and vice. His characters seem locked in a Darwinian struggle for survival; some are doomed by the laws of biology to succeed and others to succumb.

Emile Zola on the Novelist as Scientist

Emile Zola believed that the novelist should act like a scientist, experimenting with characters' reactions to differing circumstances in order to determine the laws that govern thought and emotion. Zola wanted to be the literary equivalent of the great French scientist, Claude Bernard (1813–1878), one of the founders of experimental science. The title of this essay, "The Experimental Novel," published in 1880, echoes the title of Bernard's Introduction to Experimental Medicine *(1865).*

Here you have scientific progress. In the last century, a more exact application of the experimental method creates chemistry and physics which free themselves from the irrational and the supernatural. Profound studies lead to the discovery that there are established laws; phenomena are mastered. Then a fresh step is taken. Living bodies, in which the vitalists still admitted a mysterious influence, are in their turn reduced to the general mechanism of matter.

Science proves that the conditions of life of all phenomena are the same in matter and in living bodies; hence, physiology gradually acquires the same certitude as chemistry and physics. But will we stop at that? Evidently not.

When we have proved that the body of man is a machine, which we shall one day be able to take to pieces and put together again at the experimenter's will, then it will be time to pass on to the sentimental and intellectual activities of man. This means that we should enter a realm which, until now, belonged wholly to philosophy and literature; it will be the decisive victory of science over the hypotheses of philosophers and writers. We already have experimental chemistry and physics; we are going to have experimental physiology; and then, later, we shall have the experimental novel. This is a necessary progression, and one whose end can easily be foreseen today. Everything is related, one had to start from the determinism of matter to arrive at the determinism of living bodies. . . . The same determinism must rule the stones in the roadway and the brains of man. . . .

It follows that science already enters our domain—the domain of writers like us, who are at the moment the students of man in his private and social activities. By our observations, by our experiments, we carry forward the work of the physiologist who had continued that of physicists and chemists.

Source: Eugen Weber, ed. and trans., *Paths to the Present* (New York: Dodd, Mead & Co., 1960), p. 170.

The Russian novelist Leo Tolstoy (1828–1910) brought a new perspective to the historical novel in *War and Peace*. Instead of a heroic approach to battle, he showed the individual caught in forces beyond his control. Small and insignificant events, rather than major ones, seem to govern human destiny. Another Russian novelist often associated with the realist school, Feodor Dostoyevsky (1821–1881), aimed to portray realistically the psychological dimensions of his characters in novels such as *Crime and Punishment* (1866), *The Idiot* (1868), and *The Brothers Karamazov* (1879–1880).

Although material progress was generally celebrated in this era, a number of intellectuals reacted against it. They were alarmed by the prospect of the popular masses achieving political power by winning the vote and by mass production and consumption. They denounced the smug and the self-satisfied, who saw happiness in acquisition and consumption. Some condemned the age in severe terms. Dostoyevsky denounced the materialism and egotism of the West, describing its civilization as driven by "trade, shipping, markets, factories." In Britain—the nation that seemed to embody

---

∾ ENCOUNTERS WITH THE WEST ∾

A Chinese Official's Views of European Material Progress

Educated in European universities, Ku Hung-Ming rose to become a high official in the Chinese court. His essays were penned under the impact of the European military intervention in China during the Boxer Rebellion in 1900. Ku denounced European notions of superiority over Asia, arguing that material progress was an inappropriate measure of a civilization.

In order to estimate the value of a civilisation, it seems to me, the question we must finally ask is not what great cities, what magnificent houses, what fine roads it has built and is able to build; what beautiful and comfortable furniture, what clever and useful implements, tools and instruments it has made and is able to make; no, not even what institutions, what arts and sciences it has invested: the question we must ask, in order to estimate the value of a civilisation,—is, *what type of humanity, what kind of men and women it has been able to produce.* In fact, the man and woman,—the type of human beings—which a civilisation produces, it is this which shows the essence, the personality, so to speak, the soul of that civilisation. Now if the men and women of a civilisation show the essence, the personality and soul of that civilisation, the language which the men and women in that civilisation speak, shows the essence, the personality, the soul of the men and women of that civilisation. . . .

To Europeans, and especially to unthinking practical Englishmen, who are accustomed to take what modern political economists call "the standard of living" as the test of the moral culture of or civilisation of a people, the actual life of the Chinese and of the people of the East at the present day, will no doubt appear very sordid and undesirable. But the standard of living by itself is not a proper test of the civilisation of a people. The standard of living in America at the present day, is, I believe, much higher than it is in Germany. But although the son of an American millionaire, who regards the simple and comparatively low standard of living among the professors of a German University, may doubt the value of the education in such a University, yet no educated man, I believe, who has travelled in both countries, will admit that the Germans are a less civilised people than the Americans.

Source: Ku Hung-Ming, *The Spirit of the Chinese People,* 2d ed. (Beijing: Commercial Press, 1922), pp. 1, 144–145.

---

progress—the historian Thomas Carlyle (1795–1881) denounced his age as one not of progress but of selfishness. Parliamentarianism he saw as a sham, and he called for a strong leader to save the nation from endless palavers and compromises. Unlike most of his contemporaries, who saw in material plenty a sign of progress, Carlyle saw the era as one of decline, bereft of spiritual values.

Another Englishman, John Ruskin (1819–1900), looked back to the Middle Ages as an ideal era in human history. People then did not produce with machines, but exercised a fine sense of craftsmanship. People then supposedly had a better sense of community and labored for the common good. Ruskin was one of the founders of the arts and crafts movement, which emphasized the need to produce goods for daily use with an eye for beauty and originality. "Industry without art is brutality," Ruskin warned.

In France republicans saw in the ostentation of the Second Empire a sign of depravity and decline. Defeat in war in 1870 and the outbreak of the Commune furthered a mood of pessimism among many intellectuals. Flaubert detested his own age, seeing it as petty and mean. The characters in Zola's Rougon-Macquart novels are constantly headed downward in mental faculties, social position, and morality. And some abroad were also unimpressed. (See the box, "Encounters with the West: A Chinese Official's Views of European Material Progress.")

Thus, all was not optimistic in this age of optimism. If many people celebrated what they viewed as an age of progress, others claimed that under the outer trappings of material comfort lay a frightening ignorance of aesthetic, moral, and spiritual values.

SUMMARY

During the second half of the nineteenth century, advances in industry created for many westerners an era of material plenty, providing more riches and comforts to a larger population than ever before. It was a self-confident age that believed in progress and anticipated further improvements in its material and intellectual environment.

Economic changes transformed the class structure of many European countries, and middle-class values and tastes defined the second half of the century. The new wealth and technologies led to improvements in both the countryside and the cities; in both, life became more comfortable and safer. Governments provided new services such as public education, cultural facilities, and expanded welfare services.

The material changes in society were reflected in intellectual currents. Change and evolution were embraced as an explanation for the origin of species. A new confidence in scientific research led to many scientific and technological breakthroughs. Novelists and painters aimed to dissect as scientists the world around them, creating realism in the arts. Some intellectuals, however, revolted against a certain crass self-satisfaction that imbued the bourgeoisie, and they criticized an age that worshiped industry and materialism.

Progress, as Europeans were to learn in a later era, was two-edged: The very forces that improved life for many also threatened it. The same breakthroughs in chemistry that led to the development of artificial fertilizers also provided more powerful military explosives. The expansion of education and reduction of illiteracy meant an end to ignorance but also the creation of a public that could more easily absorb messages of hate against a rival nation or against religious or ethnic minorities at home. Material progress and well-being continued, but there were new forces in the shadows that would ultimately undermine the comforts, self-assurance, and peace of this age.

SUGGESTED READING

General Surveys

Hearder, Harry. *Europe in the Nineteenth Century, 1830–1880*. 2d ed. 1988. A broad survey of this period.

Hobsbawm, Eric J. *The Age of Capital, 1848–1875*. 1979. Particularly strong on social and economic developments.

Rich, Norman. *The Age of Nationalism and Reform, 1850–1890*. 1970. Emphasizes the growing confidence in human progress in these years.

Economic Growth

Milward, A. S., and S. B. Saul. *The Development of the Economies of Continental Europe, 1850–1914*. 1977. Has good chapters on economic developments in the second half of the nineteenth century.

Ville, Simon P. *Transport and the Development of the European Economy, 1750–1918*. 1990. Describes the importance of transportation in the modernization of Europe.

Social Change

Blum, Jerome. *The End of the Old Order in Rural Europe*. 1978. A broad, comparative study of the position of the peasantry in nineteenth-century Europe.

Cocks, Geoffrey, and Konrad H. Jarausch, eds. *German Professions, 1800–1950*. 1990. Describes the relationship between the professions and the state.

Geison, Gerald L., ed. *Professions and the French State, 1700–1900*. 1984. Considers the development of the various professions in France.

Grew, Raymond, and Patrick J. Harrigan. *School, State and Society—The Growth of Elementary Schooling in Nineteenth-Century France*. 1991. Reveals the constantly growing demand for education throughout the nineteenth century and the spread of formal schooling to the whole country.

Hurt, J. S. *Elementary Schooling and the Working Classes, 1860–1918*. 1979. Studies the impact of compulsory education on the British working class.

Mayer, Arno. *The Persistence of the Old Regime—Europe to the Great War*. 1981. Argues for the persistence of the aristocracy throughout the nineteenth century.

Pilbeam, Pamela. *The Middle Classes in Europe, 1789–1914*. 1990. Reviews the formation and values of the bourgeoisie in four continental European nations.

Thompson, F. M. L. *The Rise of Respectable Society—A Social History of Victorian Britain, 1830–1910*. 1988. Depicts considerable social mobility and well-being in Britain in the second half of the nineteenth century.

Weber, Eugen. *Peasants into Frenchmen: The Modernization of Rural France, 1870–1914*. 1976. A lively description of the process by which the French peasantry was modernized.

Women's Experience

Adams, Carole Elizabeth. *Women Clerks in Wilhelmine Germany*. 1988. Provides a history of female store employees.

Holcombe, Lee. *Victorian Ladies at Work*. 1973. Considers the various forms of employment open to middle-class Victorian women.

Peterson, M. Jeanne. *Family, Love, and Work in the Lives of Victorian Gentlewomen*. 1989. Offers a revisionist examination of the view that women were passive in the Victorian era.

Prochaska, F. K. *Women and Philanthropy in Nineteenth-Century England*. 1980. Reveals the important role women played in charity work throughout the century.

Robertson, Priscilla. *An Experience of Women and Change in Nineteenth-Century Europe*. 1982. Describes the private lives of bourgeois women in the nineteenth century, emphasizing the differing cultural traditions of various nations.

Smith, Bonnie G. *Ladies of the Leisure Class—The Bourgeoises of Northern France in the Nineteenth Century*. 1981. Emphasizes the separate world of domesticity bourgeois women created and maintained.

Urban Development

Briggs, Asa. *Victorian Things*. 1989. Provides an amusing and instructive history of the various new objects that became part of consumer culture.

Lees, Andrew. *Cities Perceived: Urban Society in European and American Thought, 1820–1940*. 1985. Depicts how various writers in Europe and the United States perceived their cities.

Miller, Michael B. *The Bon Marché—Bourgeois Culture and the Department Store, 1869–1920*. 1981. Views the first and largest department store in Paris as both manifestation and promoter of bourgeois culture.

Olsen, Donald J. *The City as a Work of Art—London, Paris, Vienna*. 1986. Compares and contrasts how these cities evolved in the nineteenth century.

Pinkney, David. *Napoleon III and the Rebuilding of Paris*. 1958. The standard work on the urban renewal of Paris.

Science and Medicine

Bowler, Peter J. *Evolution—The History of an Idea*. Rev. ed. 1989. Written by a scientist, who examines the history and development of the concept while evaluating the scientific merit of the debates.

Burrow, J. W. *Evolution and Society: A Study in Victorian Social Theory*. 1966. Considers the impact of the evolutionary paradigm in the social sciences.

Chadwick, Owen. *The Secularization of the European Mind in the Nineteenth Century*. 1973. Considers the rise and spread of secular attitudes at the cost of religion.

Desmond, Adrian, and James Moore. *Darwin*. 1991. A lengthy and interesting biography of the great scientist.

Youngson, A. J. *The Scientific Revolution in Victorian Medicine*. 1979. A record of innovation in British medicine.

Art

Clark, T. J. *Image of the People: Gustave Courbet and the 1848 Revolution*. 1973. Explores the impact of the sociopolitical environment on Courbet's paintings and the audience's reactions to them.

Pool, Phoebe. *Impressionism*. 1985. Studies the origins, accomplishments, and legacies of impressionism.

Weisberg, Gabriel P., ed. *The European Realist Tradition*. 1982. A multinational study revealing the pervasiveness of realism in European art.

THE CRYSTAL PALACE

No construction summarized the aspirations and achievements of the mid-nineteenth century as well as the Crystal Palace, erected in London in 1851 to house the "Great Exhibition of the Works of Industry of all Nations." Presided over by Prince Albert, consort to Queen Victoria, the exhibition was the first of many international expositions proudly displaying the new world of invention and plenty.

The building, a major technological feat, was a product of the new age. Observe that the building is mainly made of two materials that as a result of industrialization could now be produced cheaply—steel and glass. They also could be produced rapidly, shortening the time between the design of the building and its erection. The structure was put up within six months; the secret of its speedy construction was that it consisted of standard interchangeable parts: 3300 iron columns, 2300 girders, and 293,655 glass panes.

The designer of the building was Joseph Paxton (1801–1856); his plan perhaps predictably resembled one of the greenhouses he had designed at the estate where he started his gardening career. Paxton's life and career exemplified the opportunities that at least some people could seize in an era of expanding wealth and possibilities. The son of a farmer, Paxton did not have even an elementary education. He took employ as a gardener and then became estate manager; investments in railways made him a wealthy man. Having already designed and constructed a number of important buildings—among them the duke of Devonshire's iron and glass conservatory at Chatsworth—he accepted the invitation to plan the exposition hall. His ingenious project provided for a light and airy structure with the added advantage, unlike some competing designs, of easy removal at the end of the exposition, planned to last only six months. The iron and glass structure provided a model for much industrial architecture in the nineteenth century, including the Victoria railroad station in

London, department stores like the Bon Marché in Paris (see pages 844–845), and public libraries such as France's National Library.

The Crystal Palace was immense, 1848 feet long and 450 feet wide, or more than four times the size of a football field. Not wanting to cut down some elm trees on the planned site, the organizing committee decided to make the building tall enough to enclose them; it was 66 feet high, rising to 108 feet at the arched ceilings of its transepts. It was built to accommodate tens of thousands of people at once; in fact during peak attendance 110,000 men, women, and children fit inside the building at the same time. Just before the building was to open, sparrows invaded it and no stratagem seemed capable of dislodging them. Queen Victoria decided to call on the duke of Wellington, victor at Waterloo (see page 728), for advice. After a moment's reflection, he suggested, "Try sparrow-hawks, Ma'am." And that worked.

The "Great Exhibition of the Works of Industry of all Nations" displayed 100,000 objects from 14,000 exhibitors, half from Great Britain and its empire and the other half from foreign nations. Note the panels indicating the nation of origin of various booths—next to the Indian booth are the Persian and Russian ones. The Crystal Palace was a celebration of plenty and of a new form of globalism made possible by improved communications, transport, and imperialism. Never before had so many objects from so many different parts of the world been brought together in one place. The exposition represented a triumph of industry, wealth, and power.

Among the objects the Crystal Palace proudly displayed were some of the newest products of the industrial age—turbine engines and sophisticated printing presses. It celebrated ingenuity and inventions, some useful, others merely novel, such as the bed that could wake up sleepers at a predetermined time by dumping them on the floor. Luxuries available to the newly prosperous

The Crystal Palace
(Courtesy of the Trustees of the British Museum)

were also shown: elaborate vases, overstuffed furniture, grand pianos, reproductions—from the sublime to the garish—of various paintings and statuary from ancient and modern times. Many exhibitors showed consumer goods produced by artisans, such as glycerine soap, perfume, lace, porcelain, and glass.

Britain, with the most far-flung empire in the first half of the century, displayed an array of objects bound to strike visitors as exotic. A birch-bark canoe from Canada able to hold twenty people and a stuffed Indian elephant carrying a silk canopied seat reflected the rich diversity of the world's largest empire.

The exposition was the first in Great Britain intended for the masses; depending on the day, the entrance fee was as low as one shilling, thus accessible to the working classes. During the six months it was open the exposition attracted six million visitors, a feat possible only because of the development of railroads, which provided rapid and cheap access to nearly all Britons; without trains, only Londoners would have been able to attend. Members of the elite had voiced some apprehension about how the "public" would behave, fearing it might be rowdy and harm the objects on display. The crowd's collective good behavior was, however, reassuring and led to the opening of museums to the general public.

Most visitors to the Crystal Palace in 1851 left with a great sense of pride in their contemporaries' accomplishments, but there were also reasons for unease. Some noticed the crass materialism. Charles Dickens complained, "There's too much." The exposition included a number of cannon by the Prussian arms manufacturer Alfred Krupp, a grim reminder that industry was capable of producing instruments of death at record levels. Many of the exotic objects came from Europe's overseas possessions—an empire acquired and maintained by force. If the exposition showed Britain's global ascendancy, it also revealed that that ascendancy was ensured not only by Britain's economic prowess but also by its domination of other peoples.

The Crystal Palace was scheduled for demolition after the exposition ended its successful run in October 1851, but Joseph Paxton was able to save his creation by having it moved to Sydenham Hill near London. Rebuilt, the structure was even larger, and over the years a number of buildings such as an aquarium were added to it. A visible celebration of a great age of optimism, the Crystal Palace burned down at a time when prospects for the future appeared far less promising—in 1936, when Great Britain was mired in a worldwide economic depression and had to face an increasingly menacing Germany. ❧

877

CHAPTER 24

Escalating Tensions, 1880–1914

In the spring of 1914, U.S. President Woodrow Wilson, concerned over the growing international crisis, sent his aide, Colonel Edward House, to Europe. The colonel toured several capitals—Berlin, Paris, and London—and on May 29, 1914, he reported, "The situation is extraordinary. It is militarism run stark mad. Unless some one . . . can bring about a different understanding there is one day to be an awful cataclysm."[1] This prediction was far more accurate than the author could have imagined; nine weeks later Europe was at war. And in less than three years even the United States was swept into what became a world war.

Colonel House could imagine war breaking out in 1914, yet the preceding years in Europe had on the whole been peaceful and prosperous. Contemporaries often characterized the generation before the war as "la belle époque"—the beautiful era. A growing economy provided expanding opportunities for many. The arts flourished and were celebrated. Parliamentary government continued to spread, and more nations seemed to be adapting to democracy as suffrage was extended. Yet hand in hand with these trends of apparent progress came troubling new tendencies. Several developments in the generation before 1914 undermined and threatened all the accomplishments of these years.

In many societies, governing became more complex as populations increased. The population of Europe jumped from 330 million in 1880 to 460 million by 1914. A larger population coupled with extended suffrage meant that more people participated in the political system, but it became harder to find consensus. The example of democracy in some countries led to frustration in the autocratic ones at their failure to move toward freer

Arnold Bocklin,
The War (1896).

institutions. In the same way that prosperity and economic growth aroused resentment in those who did not share in the benefits, some groups were frustrated by their exclusion from the political system.

Intellectuals revolted against what they viewed as the smug self-assuredness of earlier years. They no longer felt certain that the world was knowable, stable, subject to comprehension and, ultimately, mastery by rational human beings. Some jettisoned rationality, imagining that they had made strides in sophistication by glorifying emotion, irrationality, and, in some cases, violence. The works of painters and writers seemed to anticipate the impending destruction of world order.

The anxieties and tensions that beset many Europeans took a variety of forms. Ethnic minorities became the target of hatreds. Overseas, non-Europeans were forcibly put under white domination as European states embarked on a race for empire throughout the world. On the European continent, states increasingly felt insecure, worried that they would be subject to attack. They established standing armies, shifted alliances, drafted war plans, and, ultimately, went to war.

FROM OPTIMISM TO ANXIETY: POLITICS AND CULTURE

Many of the beliefs and institutions that had seemed so solid in the "age of optimism" found themselves under attack in the next generation. Forces hostile to liberalism became increasingly vocal. In the arts and philosophy, the earlier confidence was replaced by doubt, relativism, and a desire to flee the routines of everyday life.

The Erosion of the Liberal Consensus

In 1850 liberalism appeared to be the ascendant ideology, and liberals assumed that with the passage of time more and more people would be won over to their world-view. By 1900, however, toward the end of the century, liberalism faced serious challenges. Principles eroded within the liberal camp, and in addition, various ideas and movements—some new, some rooted in the past—served to erode the liberal consensus. Prominent among these were socialism, anarchism, a new political right, racism, and anti-Semitism.

The undermining of the liberal consensus began among liberals themselves, who, in the face of changing circumstances, retreated from some of their basic tenets. For example, one of the principal emphases of liberalism had always been free trade. But under the pressure of economic competition, liberals supported tariffs at home and created closed markets for the mother country overseas in the empire.

Historically, liberals had typically stood for an expansion of civil liberties, yet several groups were denied their rights. Power remained an exclusively male domain, and liberal males saw nothing wrong or inconsistent in continuing to deny women both the vote and free access to education and professional advancement. In the face of labor agitation, many liberals no longer unconditionally supported civil liberties and favored instead the violent crushing of strikes.

Similarly, liberals had always upheld the sanctity of private property, but under the pressure of events, they abandoned this principle as an absolute goal. To ensure workers' safety, they placed limits on employers by passing legislation on working conditions. In some countries, they supported progressive income taxes, which many perceived as a serious invasion of private property. When it became clear that a free market was unable to meet many human needs, welfare programs were instituted in several countries. These reforms were intended to strengthen the state by winning support from the masses. But because they reflected the liberals' willingness to breach fundamental principles, these measures also revealed the apparent inability of liberal ideology to deal with the problems of the day.

The Growth of Socialism and Anarchism

Among the groups challenging the power and liberal ideology of the middle classes were the socialist parties, both Marxist and non-Marxist, whose goal was to win the support of workers by espousing their cause. Socialists varied in their notions of how their goals should be achieved; some thought they could be achieved gradually and peacefully; others were dedicated to a violent overthrow of capitalist society.

In Britain, where the Liberal party was more open to the needs of workers than in other European states, a separate socialist party, the Independent Labour party, was established relatively late, in 1893. It was not until the 1920s that this party gained any particular electoral success. More influential in the late nineteenth century was the Fabian Society, founded in 1884. The Fabians criticized the capitalist system as inefficient, wasteful, and unjust. They believed that by gradual, democratic means, factories and land could be transferred from the private sector to the state, which would employ them for the benefit of society as a whole. Socialism was a desirable system that would replace capitalism because it was more efficient and more just. It would come into being not through class war but through enlightened ideas. This gradualist approach became the hallmark of British socialism.

In Germany there were two socialist parties in the 1860s. The first, founded in 1863 by Ferdinand Lassalle (1825–1864), viewed universal suffrage as the means of assuring the workers' well-being. A competing party, formed in 1868 and influenced by Marx, called for a workers' revolution. In 1875 the two socialist parties united around a common program.

Unification did not prevent the German Social Democratic party from a bitter debate soon to be echoed in all European socialist parties. A German socialist leader, Eduard Bernstein (1850–1932), who had visited England and had soaked up the influence of the Fabians, argued in a book with the telling English title *Evolutionary Socialism* (1898) that Marx had been wrong to suggest that capitalism necessarily led to the increasing wretchedness of the working class. The capitalist economy had in fact expanded and been able to provide for steadily improved conditions. Workers would not need to seize power by some cataclysmic act. Rather, by piecemeal democratic action they could win more power and legislate on behalf of their interests. Since he argued for a revision of Marxist theory, Bernstein was labeled a "revisionist."

Opposing Bernstein in this great debate was the party theoretician Karl Kautsky (1854–1938). Although Kautsky agreed that in material terms the workers' lot had not worsened, he insisted that workers were worse off in political terms, as their rights were abridged and their hopes of having a voice in government grew fainter. In Germany, he argued, workers could come to power only if they first overthrew autocracy. A violent revolution would thus be necessary to institute socialism.

Although the party officially rejected revisionism and seemed to embrace the doctrine of a violent proletarian revolution, it in fact practiced the former. The German Social Democratic party had become a part of established society, with its newspapers, party bureaucracy, and headquarters; it had gained a vested interest in society and was not ready to overthrow it. Nevertheless, it continued to espouse a militant ideology of class war.

Similarly ambiguous developments occurred in neighboring France. One of Marx's French disciples, Jules Guesde (1845–1922), founded a socialist party with a strong working-class membership devoted to carrying on a workers' revolution. Opposing his brand of socialism was Jean Jaurès (1859–1914), an idealistic schoolteacher who saw socialism as an ethical system. Unlike the Marxists, he did not regard the advent of socialism as inevitable but rather as desirable to bring about a more equitable and just society. Jaurès believed that socialism could be achieved in cooperation with the more enlightened members of the middle

Jean Jaurès The leader of the French Socialist party, Jean Jaurès, addresses a meeting in 1913. A charismatic figure, he was one of France's greatest orators. *(Roger-Viollet)*

classes, and he abhorred the vocabulary of class warfare so frequently voiced by Guesde. In 1905 the socialist parties led by Guesde and Jaurès merged, and Jaurès became virtual party leader. Although Jaurès' brand of gradual democratic socialism influenced the daily functioning of the newly unified party, the French Socialist party formally continued to adhere to Guesde's doctrines of revolution and class war. In 1914, on the eve of the outbreak of war, a nationalist, incensed by Jaurès' call on his government to avoid war, assassinated him.

Another movement that sought to liberate the downtrodden was anarchism, which proclaimed that humans could be free only when the state had been abolished. According to anarchist theory, in a stateless society people would naturally join together in communes and share the fruits of their labor. Some anarchists believed their goal could be reached by educating people, but others were more impatient and hoped to speed up the process by making direct attacks on existing authority. The Russian nobleman Michael Bakunin (1814–1876), frustrated at the authoritarianism of his homeland, became a lifelong anarchist. He challenged tsarism at home and participated in the 1848 revolutions throughout Europe. He viewed all governments as repressive and declared war on them: "The passion for destruction is also a creative passion." His ideas were particularly influential in Italy, Spain, and parts of France, especially among the artisan classes.

Many anarchists of this period wanted to bring about the new society by "propaganda of the deed." An attack on the bastions of power, these anarchists believed, could bring about the dissolution of the state. They formed secret terrorist organizations that assassinated heads of state or those close to them. Between 1894 and 1901, the president of France, the prime minister of Spain, the empress of Austria, the king of Italy, and the president of the United States were killed by anarchists. These murders fixed the popular image of anarchism as a violence-prone ideology. More important, such manifestations of the "propaganda of the deed" produced no particular improvement in the lives of the working-class people, on whose behalf these campaigns were supposedly launched.

Without accepting the anarchists' methods, some in the labor movement shared their hostility toward parliamentary institutions. A working-class program, labor activists argued, could be implemented only by a pure workers' movement, such as unionization. Workers should eschew the political arena and concentrate on direct workers' action. According to this line of thought, known as *syndicalism* (after the French word for unions), workers should amass their power in unions, and at the right moment carry out a general strike, crippling capitalist society and bringing it down. Syndicalism was particularly popular in Mediterranean countries, where its more militant form, *anarchosyndicalism*, radicalized labor and made a sizable number of workers hostile to parliamentarism.

European socialism also attempted to have an international presence. In 1864 Marx had participated in the founding of the International Workers' Association, which fell prey to internal dissension and dissolved after a few years. Known as the First International, it was followed by a more robust organization, the Second International, in 1889. The International met yearly and debated issues of concern to socialists in general, including the worsening relations among European states. As early as 1893 the International called on European states to resolve their conflicts by mandatory arbitration.

In 1907, sensing impending war, the International called on the workers to strike and refuse military service in case of international conflict. The International saw itself as a bulwark of peace; it did not realize that once war broke out, Europeans, including socialists, would be swept up in nationalist fervor and would willingly go to war. Although most socialists advocated peace at home and abroad, many had contributed to a militant discourse by emphasizing class war.

The New Right, Racism, and Anti-Semitism

The traditional opponents of liberalism on the political right were the conservatives, wedded to preserving the existing order. Beginning in the 1880s, however, a "new right" emerged that was populist and demagogic. Although conservatives had been wary of nationalism, the new right embraced it. Alienated by industry, democracy, and social egalitarianism, many in this new right rejected doctrines of human equality and embraced racist ideologies.

Racist thinking was common in the nineteenth century. Many Europeans believed human races were not only different physiologically but also—as a result of these biological variations—differently endowed in intelligence and other qualities (see page 868). Europeans were often ethnocentric, convinced they were the epitome of humankind while members of other races belonged to lesser groups. In midcentury the Frenchman Arthur de Gobineau (1816–1882) published his *Essay on the Inequality of Human Races,* declaring that race "dominates all other problems and is the key to it." Biologists and early anthropologists made similar statements, thus giving racism a scientific aura. Throughout the second half of the nineteenth century, race was thought to be the principal explanation for the differences that were discovered among human groupings. Some races were relegated to near subhuman levels. For example, the British anatomist Robert Knox (1798–1862) declared that the Africans lacked the "grand qualities which distinguish man from animal."

These racist ideas helped fuel anti-Semitism. For centuries Jews had been the object of suspicion and bigotry. Originally, the basis of the prejudice was religious. As early as the Middle Ages, however, the argument emerged that "Jewish blood" was different. And with the popularization of pseudoscientific racist thinking in the nineteenth century, Jews were commonly viewed as a separate, inferior race, unworthy of the same rights as the majority of the population.

Historically, Christians had relegated the Jews in their midst to marginal positions. In the Middle Ages, when land was the basis of wealth and prestige, Jews had been confined to such urban trades as cattle trading and moneylending. They incurred high risks by lending money: They often were not paid back and faced unsympathetic courts when they tried to collect their due. To counteract these risks, Jewish moneylenders charged high interest rates that gave them the unpopular reputation as usurers.

The emancipation of the Jews, which began in France with the Revolution and spread to Germany and Austria by the 1860s, provided them opportunities they had not had before, and some members of society found it hard to adjust to the prominence a few Jews gained. Because their increased prominence and success occurred concur-

rently with the wrenching social transformations brought by industrialization and urbanization, anti-Semites pointed to the Jews as the perpetrators of these unsettling changes.

Many people perceived Jews as prototypical of the new capitalist class. Although most Jews were of modest means, resentment of the rich often was aimed at Jews. Earlier in the century, many anti-Semites were socialists, speaking on behalf of the working class. Later they came from among the petty bourgeois, small shopkeepers and artisans, who felt threatened by economic change.

Political movements based on anti-Semitism were founded in the 1880s. They depicted Jews as dangerous and wicked and called for their exclusion from the political arena and from certain professions. In some cases they suggested that Jews be expelled from the state. The mayor of Vienna, Karl Lueger (1844–1928), was elected on an anti-Semitic platform. In Berlin the emperor's chaplain, Adolf Stöcker (1835–1909), founded an anti-Semitic party, hoping to make political inroads among the working-class supporters of socialism. In France Edouard Drumont (1844–1917) published one of the best-sellers of the second half of the nineteenth century, *Jewish France,* in which he attributed all the nation's misfortunes to the Jews.

In Russia organized pogroms, or mass attacks, on Jews killed two thousand in the 1880s and one thousand in 1905, frightening two million Jews into exile, mostly to the United States. Russian Jews lived under social as well as legal disabilities; condemned to second-class citizenship, they won full emancipation only with the Bolshevik Revolution of 1917.

In the face of growing hostility, some Jews speculated that they would be safe only in their own nation. The Austrian Jewish journalist Theodore Herzl (1860–1904), outraged by the Dreyfus affair in France, in which a Jewish officer was imprisoned on trumped-up charges of treason (see page 901), founded the Zionist movement. He advocated establishing a Jewish state in the Jews' ancient homeland of Israel. In the beginning, the Zionist movement won a following only in eastern Europe, where the Jews were particularly ill-treated, but by 1948, it led to the founding of the state of Israel.

Various manifestations of anti-Semitism revealed the vulnerability of the principle of toleration, one of the basic ideas of liberalism. It became eminently clear that racism, with its penchant for irrationality and violence, could easily be aroused.

Irrationality and Uncertainty

In contrast to the confidence in reason and science that prevailed at midcentury, the era starting in the 1880s wrestled with the issues of irrationality and uncertainty—in philosophy, in science, in the arts, even in religion. The positivism of the earlier era had emphasized surface reality but neglected inner meaning and ignored the emotive and intuitive aspects of life. By the 1890s a neoromantic mood, emphasizing emotion and feeling, stirred major intellectual movements.

The intellectuals who matured in the 1890s, and thus are known as "the generation of 1890," stressed the extent to which irrational forces guide human beings and their relation to one another. Nonetheless, they remained strongly affected by the positivists, adopting their scientific methods to study irrationality and hoping to find ways to make human beings more rational. Following this group came those intellectuals who matured around 1905, known as the "generation of 1905." Like their seniors, they believed human beings were irrational and the world was unknowable, but they did not express any regret at this condition. Rather, they glorified it.

The intellectual trends of the 1890s are exemplified in the work of the Austro-Hungarian Sigmund Freud (1856–1939), who founded psychoanalysis, a method of treating psychic disorders by exploring the unconscious. Freud believed that people were motivated not only by observed reality but also by their unconscious feelings and emotions. Whereas earlier physicians had described the mental condition of hysteria as a physical ailment, Freud saw its roots as psychological, the result of unresolved inner conflicts. Although Freud's work was influenced by rational methods, he stressed that irrational forces played a significant role in human behavior. Reflecting the concerns of his contemporaries, Freud hoped that understanding these forces would make people more rational.

In philosophy, the tension between reason and emotion was expressed in the work of the German philosopher Friedrich Nietzsche (1844–1900), who proclaimed that rationality had led humankind into a meaningless abyss. Reason would not resolve human problems, nor would any preconceived ideas. "God is dead," Nietzsche declared. With no God, humankind was free of all outside constraints, free to overthrow all conventions. Nietzsche admonished his readers to challenge existing institutions and accepted truths and create new ones. However, he realized that such nihilism offered great temptations to inflict unspeakable horrors. According to Nietzsche, only a "superman" could resist these temptations. Nietzsche's call for restraint reflected a hesitation to embrace the full implications of his philosophy. Unfortunately, his warnings were not always heeded. Nietzsche's ideas spread throughout Europe by the turn of the century and were reflected not only in philosophy but also in art and literature.

In contrast to Nietzsche, the French philosopher Henri Bergson (1859–1940) reflected the values of the generation of 1905. He argued that science—and indeed life—must be interpreted not rationally but intuitively. "Science," Bergson declared, "can teach us nothing of the truth; it can only serve as a rule of action." Meaningful truths could best be understood emotively, such as the truth of religion, literature, and art. (See the box, "The Limits of Intellect.")

The scientists of this period seemed to underscore the philosophers' conclusions. In 1905, Albert Einstein (1879–1955) proposed the theory of relativity, which undermined the certainties of Newtonian physics. Einstein's theory demonstrated that time and space are not absolute but exist relative to the observer. Much of the research in atomic theory also revealed variations and unexplained phenomena. For example, the work of German physicist Max Planck (1858–1947) in quantum theory showed that energy was not absorbed or emitted continuously, as previously assumed, but rather emitted discontinuously. Some scientists no longer shared the self-confidence that their colleagues had maintained half a century earlier, finding it increasingly difficult to believe in ultimate certainties.

In the arts, the idea of being *avant-garde*— French for "at the forefront"—took hold among creative people. Breaking the taboos of society and the conventions of one's craft seemed to be signs of artistic creativity. Artistic movements pro-

The Limits of Intellect

In Creative Evolution *(1907), a widely heralded work that influenced a whole generation of European intellectuals, the French philosopher Henri Bergson spearheaded the revolt against intellectualism, arguing that intuition was a far better guide.*

We see that the intellect, so skillful in dealing with the inert, is awkward the moment it touches the living. Whether it wants to treat the life of the body or the life of the mind, it proceeds with the rigor, the stiffness and the brutality of an instrument not designed for such use. . . . *The intellect is characterized by a natural inability to comprehend life.* . . .

Instinct, on the contrary, is molded on the very form of life. While intelligence treats everything mechanically, instinct proceeds, so to speak, organically. If the consciousness that slumbers in it should awake, if it were wound up into knowledge instead of being wound off into action, if we could ask and it could reply, it would give up to us the most intimate secrets of life. For it only carries out further the work by which life organizes matter—so that we cannot say, as has often been shown, where organization ends and where instinct begins. . . .

Our eye perceives the features of the living being, merely as assembled, not as mutually organized. The intention of life, the simple movement that runs through the lines, that binds them together and gives them significance, escapes it. This intention is just what the artist tries to regain, in placing himself back within the object by a kind of sympathy, in breaking down, by an effort of intuition, the barrier that space puts up between him and his model. It is true that this aesthetic intuition, like external perception, only attains the individual. But we can conceive an inquiry turned in the same direction as art, which would take life in *general* for its object, just as physical science, in following to the end the direction pointed out by external perception, prolongs the individual facts into general laws. . . .

. . . A complete and perfect humanity would be that in which these two forms of conscious activity [intuition and intellect] should attain their full development. . . . Intuition . . . is a lamp almost extinguished, which only glimmers now and then, for a few moments at most. But it glimmers wherever a vital interest is at stake. On our personality, on our liberty, on the place we occupy in the whole of nature, on our origin and perhaps also on our destiny, it throws a light feeble and vacillating, but which none the less pierces the darkness of the night in which the intellect leaves us.

Source: Henri Bergson, *Creative Evolution,* trans. Arthur Mitchell (New York: Holt Rinehart & Winston, 1911), pp. 165, 177, 267–268.

---

claimed idiosyncratic manifestos and constantly called for the rejection of existing forms of expression and the creation of new ones. The symbolists in France and Italy, the expressionists in Germany, the futurists in Italy, and the secessionists in Austria all reflected the sense that they were living through a fractured period.

In protest against the mass culture of their day, artists focused on images that were different and unique. Unlike earlier art, which had a clear message, the art of this era did not. Many artists no longer believed their role was to portray or spread ideals; rather, they tended to be introspective and even self-absorbed. The public at large found it difficult to decipher the meaning of the new art, but a number of patrons confirmed the avant-garde artists' talent and insight.

Unlike the realists who preceded them, artists in the 1890s surrendered to neoromanticism, trying to investigate and express inner forces. As French

Munch: The Scream Painted in 1893, this work reflects the fear and horror that some intellectuals experienced at the end of the nineteenth century. *(Edvard Munch,* The Scream, *1893. Tempera and oil pastel on cardboard. 91 × 73.5 cm. Photo: J. Lathion, Nasjonalgalleriet, Oslo. Copyright Munch Museum, Oslo, 1993)*

painter Paul Gauguin (1848–1903) noted, the purpose of painting was to communicate not how things looked but the emotions they conveyed. The Russian Wassily Kandinsky (1866–1944) asked viewers of his art to "look at the picture as a graphic representation of a mood and not as a representation of objects." Artists appeared to be examining the hidden anxieties of society. The Frenchman Gustave Moreau (1826–1898) displayed monsters, creations of nightmare, byproducts of the unconscious. The Austrian artist Egon Schiele (1890–1918) and the Norwegian painter Edvard Munch (1863–1944) emphasized scenes of violence, fear, and sheer horror.

Religion, too, felt the effects of these intellectual trends. Although large numbers of people still held traditional religious beliefs and followed traditional practices, indifference to organized religion spread. In urban areas of western Europe,

church attendance declined; as these regions urbanized, they became increasingly secular. But with the decline of traditional Christian practices, various forms of mysticism became more widespread. Some people were attracted to Eastern religions like Buddhism and Hinduism and to other mystical beliefs. These attitudes may have reflected a loss of faith in Western culture itself. As the century came to an end, a number of intellectuals argued that their culture, like the century, was destined for decline.

THE NEW IMPERIALISM

The age of empire building that started in Europe in the sixteenth century seemed to have ended by 1750. Then, in the 1880s, the European states launched a new era of expansionism and conquered an unprecedented amount of territory. In only twenty-five years, Europeans seized 10 million square miles and subjugated 500 million people—one half of the world's non-European population. European expansion was also manifest in a massive movement of people; between 1870 and 1914, 55 million Europeans moved overseas, mainly to Australia, the United States, Canada, and Argentina.

This era of ambitious conquest is often called the "new imperialism" to differentiate it from the earlier stage of empire building. Whereas the earlier imperialism focused on the Americas, nineteenth-century imperialism centered on Africa and Asia. And unlike the earlier period, the new imperialism occurred in an age of mass participation in politics and was accompanied by expressions of popular enthusiasm.

Economic and Social Motives

The hope of profit overseas was crucial in the dynamic of the new imperialism. When the English explorer Henry Stanley (1841–1904) returned from Africa in the late 1870s, he told the Manchester Chamber of Commerce, "There are forty million people beyond the gateway of Congo, and the cotton spinners of Manchester are waiting to clothe them." However, many Europeans had unrealistic notions of the potential markets that might be available to them. French explorers and statesmen spoke of a western Sudan inhabited by "two hundred million" people—a sixtyfold exaggeration of the real situation. Nonetheless, such illusions of huge markets were instrumental in stirring an interest in empire.

Certain economic anxieties beset European states, and colonization seemed to resolve them. An economic downturn in 1873 had led to a decade-long depression, and many political leaders worried about the economic and social repercussions of this economic crisis. Colonies, it was believed, would provide eager markets for European goods that would stimulate production at home. "Colonial policy is the daughter of industrial policy," declared French Prime Minister Jules Ferry (1832–1893). In the face of rising tariff walls, European nations sought to establish colonies that would provide reliable markets.

However, there is considerable evidence that colonies did not represent large markets for the mother countries. In 1914, France's colonies represented only 12 percent of its foreign trade. Great Britain's trade with its colonies represented one-third of its foreign trade, but most of that was with the settlement colonies and not those acquired through direct conquest. As for Germany, colonial trade represented less than 1 percent of its exports. Even when protective tariffs were imposed in colonies, monopoly of trade was by no means secured. Despite tariffs in Indochina, French exports represented only 40 percent of goods entering the Asian colony in 1914. And despite rising tariffs, France, Germany, and Great Britain continued as one another's main customers, rather than rely on their colonies.

Although export to the colonies proved to be economically unprofitable, many people agreed with those who contended that the colonies would turn out to be profitable in the long run. Though the colonies were not necessary to the capitalist system—as Marxist critics argued—the belief in colonial profitability was certainly present.

Some proponents of empire, known as social imperialists, argued that possession of an empire could resolve social as well as economic issues. It would give employment to the working classes and thus keep them satisfied with their lot. Joseph Chamberlain (1836–1914), a former mayor of Birmingham and British colonial secretary between 1895 and 1903, was a vigorous proponent of empire, asserting that its loss meant "half at least of our population would be starved." His fellow imperialist Cecil Rhodes (1853–1902) claimed that Britain's empire was saving the country "from a murderous civil war." In Belgium King Leopold II (r. 1865–1909) believed that the political strife between Catholics and liberals in his state could be overcome by territorial aquisition overseas.

An empire could be an outlet for a variety of domestic frustrations, especially for those nations concerned about overpopulation. German and Italian imperialists often argued that their nations needed colonies to settle their multiplying poor. Once the overseas territories were acquired, however, few found them attractive for settlement.

Nationalistic Motives

To a large extent, empire building was triggered by the desire to assert national power. At the end of the nineteenth century, two major powers emerged, Russia and the United States. Compared to them, western European nations seemed small and insignificant, and many of their leaders believed that to compete effectively on the world stage they needed to become large territorial entities. Empires would enable them to achieve that goal.

The British Empire, with India as its crown jewel, constituted the largest, most powerful, and apparently wealthiest of all the European domains. It was the envy of Europe. Although the real source of Britain's wealth and power was the country's industrial economy, many people believed possession of a vast empire explained Britain's success. And so the British example stimulated other nations to carve out empires.

Once the European states entered the fray, they excited mutual suspicion and fear. When the French appeared to be expanding in West Africa in the 1890s, the British, afraid they would be cut off

from the trade of the Niger Valley, aggressively conquered huge tracts of land that previously had been ignored. And the French had begun their conquests believing that they needed to reach the Niger before the British did (see Map 24.1). Thus the scramble for Africa was triggered by European rivalries, by fear of missing an opportunity that would never return. Similarly in Asia, Britain annexed Burma in 1885 under the impression that France was about to annex it. And France expanded in Indochina in the 1880s and 1890s for fear the British would beat them to the punch (see Map 24.2).

France, defeated by Prussia in 1870, found in its colonies proof that it was still a Great Power. Germany and Italy, which formed their national identities relatively late, cast a jealous eye on the British and French empires and decided that if they were to be counted as Great Powers, they too

Queen Victoria Proclaimed Empress of India In 1877 British officials in the Indian capital, Delhi, conducted a *Durbar,* a large public festival, at which Victoria was declared empress of India. The new title was intended to impress Indians and the rest of the world with Britain's resolve to hold on to India permanently. (*The Illustrated London News Picture Library*)

would need overseas colonies. King Leopold II of Belgium spun out various plans to acquire colonies to compensate for his nation's small size. And Britain, anxious at the emergence of rival economic and political powers in the late nineteenth century, found in its colonies a guarantee for the future. Even colonies with no current value might come to possess some in the future; a British prime minister in the 1890s declared colonial acquisition important "in order to peg out claims for posterity."

In the race for colonies, worldwide strategic concerns stimulated expansion. Because the Suez Canal ensured the route to India, the British established a protectorate over Egypt in 1882. And then, in 1900, fearing that a rival power might threaten their position by encroaching on the Nile, they established control over the Nile Valley all the way south to Uganda. Russian expansion southward into central Asia toward Afghanistan was intended to avert a British takeover of this area, while the British movement northwestward to Afghanistan had the opposite intention—to prevent Russia from encroaching on India. The "great game" played by Russia and Britain in central Asia lasted the entire nineteenth century, ending only in 1907.

The strategic imperative also applied to areas contiguous to an acquired territory, which were viewed as vital for the protection of the original colony. European statesmen decided that these adjoining regions must not fall to rival powers or become staging areas for attacks by the local peoples on the colonial power. Such concerns help explain why France, after conquering Algeria in 1830, turned on Tunisia in 1881 and Morocco in 1911, and why Britain, wanting to safeguard its position in India, forcibly annexed Burma in 1885. In the second half of the nineteenth century, Russia steadily pushed southward and eastward, annexing much of central Asia and portions of China, creating a vast contiguous territory reaching to the Pacific (see Map 24.2).

Much of this expansion was due to the desire to control the often turbulent frontiers of newly acquired areas. Once these frontiers had been brought under control, there were, of course, again new frontiers that had to be subdued. As the Russian foreign minister said of such an incentive for expansion, "The chief difficulty is to know where to stop." The imperial powers rarely did.

The bitter rivalry among the Great Powers helps explain the division of the globe, but it also protected some regions from falling under European domination. In an effort to contain their rivalry in southeast Asia, Britain and France established Siam (Thailand) as a buffer state. China's sovereignty was seriously violated when Russia took large chunks of territory as it moved southward and eastward, and the Western powers seized "treaty ports" and insisted on the right of their merchants and missionaries to move freely. Yet most of China survived because the European powers held one another's ambitions in check. No state alone could conquer all of China; none would allow another to do so either.

Given all the arguments Europeans marshalled in favor of imperialism, one might assume that far-flung lands were acquired as a result of a policy determination in the capitals of Europe. However, that was not always the case. The local situation and "the man on the spot," the European official dispatched overseas, often determined the pace and direction of empire building. In 1883 British Prime Minister Gladstone sent General Charles Gordon (1833–1885) to the Sudan to supervise the withdrawal of British troops who had only temporarily entered the country. Gordon disregarded orders and tried to overthrow the local political and religious leader, the Mahdi, who counterattacked, laid siege to Khartoum, entered the city, and killed Gordon. In the face of public outrage over the killing, the British annexed the Sudan.

A parallel incident in Indochina also highlighted how disobedient officials, hungry for action, created unexpected opportunities for colonial annexation. In 1883 France dispatched Commander Henri Rivière (1827–1883) to the southern part of Vietnam, already under French authority. Exceeding his orders, Rivière marched northward and he and his troops were massacred. When news reached Paris, the National Assembly unanimously voted an expedition of 20,000 men, who more than avenged the hapless commander. They brought northern Vietnam under French control.

Other Ideological Motives

In addition to the search for profit and nationalistic pride, a strong sense of mission was used to rationalize imperialism. Because Europeans were endowed with technological and scientific know-how, many imperialists believed it was Europe's duty to develop Africa and Asia for the benefit of colonizer and colonized. Railroads, telegraphs, hospitals, and schools would transform colonial peoples by opening them to what were seen as the beneficent influences of Europe. If necessary, these changes would be realized by force.

Influenced by Darwin and his theory of the struggle for survival, many argued that just as competition among species existed in nature, so did groups of humans struggle for survival. Dubbed "Social Darwinists," these thinkers envisioned a world of fierce competition. They believed that the most serious struggle was among the races; and in this struggle the white race was destined to succeed, the nonwhites to succumb.

At the same time that Europeans were making substantial material progress as a result of industrialization, their wide-scale expansion overseas brought them into contact with Africans and Asians who had not created an industrial economy. They assumed that the dramatic disparity between their own material culture and that of colonial peoples was proof of their own innate superiority. Africans and Asians were seen as primitive, inferior peoples, still in their evolutionary "infancy." (See the feature, "Weighing the Evidence: The Layout of the British Museum," on pages 914–915.)

Social Darwinists claimed that the law of nature dictated the eclipse of weaker races and the victory of the stronger and presumably better race. Lord Salisbury (1830–1903), the British prime minister, declared that the nations of the world could be divided between "the living and the dying," the former replacing the latter. Others believed that the white man had an obligation to dominate and lead the "lesser breeds" to a "higher stage." The British bard of imperialism, Rudyard Kipling (1865–1936), celebrated this view in his poem "White Man's Burden" (1899):

Take up the White Man's burden—
Send forth the best ye breed—
Go bind your sons to exile
To serve your captives' need. . . .

Each nation was certain that providence had chosen it for a colonial mission. Cecil Rhodes declared that he thought God wanted him to "paint as much of the map of Africa British as possible." His superior, Secretary of Colonies Chamberlain,

exulted that "the British race is the greatest governing race the world has ever seen." France, its leaders announced, had a civilizing mission to fulfill in the world; Ferry, its prime minister, declared it the duty of his country "to civilize the inferior races." Although European states were colonial rivals, they also believed they were engaged in a joint mission overseas. Empire building underscored the belief in a common European destiny, as opposed to the ascribed savagery and backwardness of non-Europeans.

Pointing to historic antecedents, imperialists colored their activities with a hue of heroism. Many Europeans took satisfaction in the idea that their country performed feats akin to those of ancient Rome or the Crusaders, spreading "civilization" to far-flung empires. Colonial literature celebrated white men of action who, by their heroism, conquered and administered what had been large kingdoms or empires in Africa and Asia. Novelists like Kipling emphasized the superiority and heroism of white men over perfidious, cowardly "natives."

Missionary groups also were motivated by strong ideals favoring expansion. David Livingstone (1813–1873), a missionary doctor who had explored central and East Africa in the 1850s, had come across slave caravans and other practices that he found shocking. If the area were opened to commerce, he proclaimed, then Christianity and civilization would follow. His *Travels* and posthumous *Last Journals* were widely read by the British public, and they seemed to suggest that Africa would be vastly improved if it were "opened" to European contact. Missionaries were gripped by the notion of millions of "heathens" in Africa and Asia, and they welcomed European expansion to ensure the spread of Christianity.

Missionaries also unwittingly created conditions that invited European intervention. Often they went to lands that were inhospitable and even hostile. In societies where the indigenous religion sanctioned existing social and political structures, local leaders perceived European missionaries who preached a different religion as a threat. The execution of French missionaries in Vietnam in 1851 and 1852 led to reprisals by the French navy; Emperor Napoleon III saw this action as a convenient way to win support from Catholics at home. The killing of missionaries in China also brought intervention by Europe. In addition to demanding in 1860 the right of missionaries to travel freely in China, the European powers also demanded the right of traders to move about freely and forced the Chinese government to cede to them treaty ports. In 1886 the murder of British missionaries in the kingdom of Buganda, in East Africa, fixed British interest on the area and eventually led to its conquest. In Madagascar, competition between British Protestant and French Catholic missionaries for influence over the Malagasy queen precipitated French military intervention and conquest in 1896.

Colonial acquisitions triggered public support for further expansion of the empire—support that was expressed by the founding of various colonial societies. Britain's Primrose League, which supported empire as well as other patriotic goals, had one million members. In Germany, the German Colonial Society, founded in 1888, had 43,000 members by 1914. The French and Italian groups were limited in size but had influential contacts with policymakers. Colonial societies generally drew their membership from the professional middle classes, who were quite open to nationalist arguments—civil servants, professors, and journalists. These societies produced a steady stream of propaganda favoring empire building.

Much of the literature celebrating empire building described it in manly terms. European men were seen as proving their virility by going overseas, conquering, and running empires. Women were to stay home; if later they came overseas, it was as helpmates to male colonial officials. A few women heroically explored distant lands; Englishwoman Mary Kingsley (1862–1900) went on two exploration trips into Africa. (See the box, "Mary Kingsley on Africans and British Imperialism.") Her books were popular and focused British interest on overseas territories, but they in no way shook the established view that empire was a manly enterprise.

Conquest, Administration, and Westernization

Industrialization gave Europeans the means to conquer overseas territories. They manufactured rapid-fire weapons and had steam-driven gunboats and ocean-going vessels, effectively projecting power overseas. Telegraphic communications tied the whole world into a single network, allowing Europeans to gather information and coordinate military and political decision making. Such advantages made Europeans virtually invincible in a colonial conflict. One remarkable exception was the defeat of the Italians in Adowa in 1896, when the Italians faced an Ethiopian force that was not only superior in numbers but better armed.

Conquest was often brutal. In September 1898, British-led forces at the Battle of Omdurman slaughtered 20,000 Sudanese. From 1904 to 1908, an uprising in southwest Africa against German rule led to the killing of an estimated 60,000 of the Herero people; the German general, who had expressly given an order to exterminate the whole population, was awarded a medal by William II.

In many colonies resistance continued long after conquest had officially been declared. Continuous skirmishes, in some cases full-scale wars, were fought. Britain annexed Burma in 1886, but it then faced popular rebellion for five years. In Indochina, the French were confronted with the "Scholars' Revolt," led by mandarins who refused the protectorate; it took twenty years to defeat the uprising. In West Africa, France declared the Ivory Coast to be a French possession in the 1890s; it was 1916 before the whole territory was "pacified" (Map 24.1).

Colonial governments could be brutally insensitive to the needs of the indigenous peoples. (See the box, "Encounters with the West: Chief Montshiwa Petitions Queen Victoria.") To save money, France in the 1890s put large tracts of land in the French Congo under the administration of private rubber companies, which systematically and brutally coerced the local people to collect rubber. When the scandal broke in Paris, the concessionary companies were abolished and the French state re-established its control.

The most notorious example of exploitation, terror, and mass killings was connected with the Belgian Congo. Leopold II of Belgium had acquired it as a personal empire and mercilessly exploited it and its people. An international chorus of condemnation finally forced the king to surrender his empire and put it under the administration of the Belgian government, which abolished some of the worst features of Leopold's rule.

Brutal and exploitive, imperialism spread Western technologies, institutions, and values. By 1914 Great Britain had built 40,000 miles of rail in India—nearly twice as much as in Britain. In India

Mary Kingsley on Africans and British Imperialism

Mary Kingsley belonged to a small but hardy group of women who, despite the Victorian ideal of the woman as homebody, went exploring overseas. In two separate expeditions she visited the western part of Africa. Her observations of Africans represent a mixture of views: If she believes that Africans are different from Europeans, and even inferior in some aspects, she also sees them as excelling in other fields. Kingsley bases her views on differences of culture, rather than of biology. She suggests that because Africans are less developed than Europeans, Britain has a special duty and obligation to them.

I openly and honestly own I sincerely detest touching on this race question. For one thing, Science has not finished with it; for another, it belongs to a group of enormous magnitude, upon which I have no opinion, but merely feelings, and those of a nature which I am informed by superior people would barely be a credit to a cave man of the paleolithic period. . . . I am often cornered for the detail view, whether I can reconcile my admiration for Africans with my statement that they are a different kind of human being to white men. Naturally I can, to my own satisfaction, just as I can admire an oak tree or a palm; but it is an uncommonly difficult thing to explain. All that I can say is, that when I come back from a spell in Africa, the thing that makes me proud of being one of the English is not the manners of customs up here, certainly not the houses or the climate; but it is the thing embodied in a great railway engine. I once came home on a ship with an Englishman who had been in South West Africa, for seven unbroken years; he was sane and in his right mind. But no sooner did we get ashore at Liverpool, than he rushed at and threw his arms round a postman, to that official's embarrassment and surprise. Well, that is how I feel about the first magnifi-

cent bit of machinery I come across: it is the manifestation of the superiority of my race.

In philosophic moments I call superiority difference, from a feeling that it is not mine to judge the grade in these things. Careful scientific study has enforced on me, as it has on other students, the recognition that the African mind naturally approaches all things from a spiritual point of view. . . . [H]is mind works along the line that things happen because of the action of spirit upon spirit. . . . We think along the line that things happen from action of matter upon matter. . . . This steady sticking to the material side of things, I think, has given our race its dominion over matter; the want of it has caused the African to be notably behind us in this. . . .

This seems to me simply to lay upon us English for the sake of our honour that we keep clean hands and a cool head, and be careful of Justice; to do this we must know what there is we wish to wipe out of the African, and what there is we wish to put in, and so we must not content ourselves by relying materially on our superior wealth and power, and morally on catch phrases. All we need to look to is justice.

Source: Mary H. Kingsley, *West African Studies* (London: Macmillan, 1899), pp. 329–331.

and Egypt, the British erected hydraulic systems that irrigated previously arid lands. Colonials built cities often modeled on the European grid system. In some cases they were graced with large, tree-lined avenues, and some neighborhoods were equipped with running water and modern sanita-

tion. Schools, patterned after those in Europe, taught the imperial language and spread Western

Map 24.1 Africa in 1914 European powers in the late nineteenth century conquered most of Africa. Only Liberia and Ethiopia were left unoccupied by 1914.

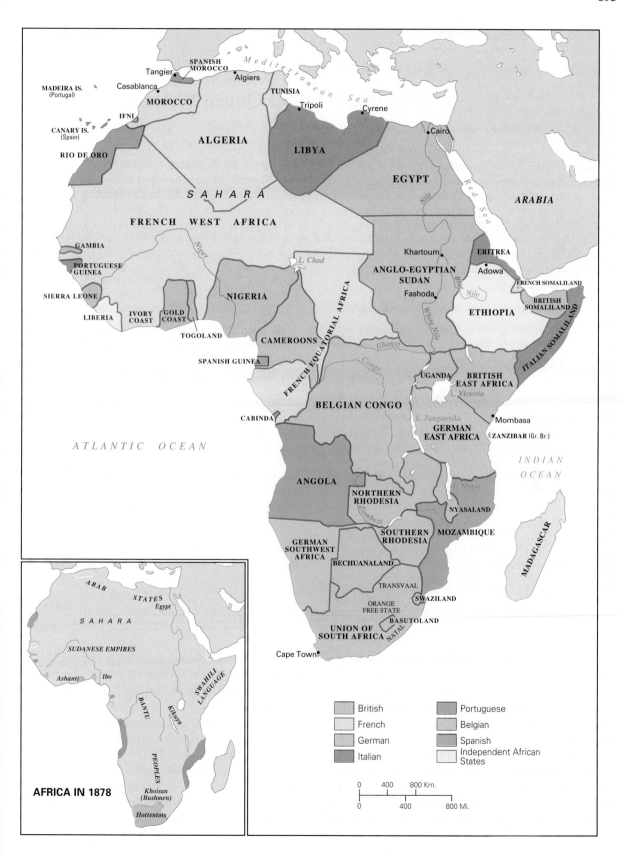

MADEIRA IS.
(Portugal)

Tangier
Casablanca
SPANISH MOROCCO
Algiers
TUNISIA
Tripoli
Cyrene
Cairo

CANARY IS.
(Spain)

IFNI

MOROCCO

RIO DE ORO

ALGERIA

S A H A R A

LIBYA

EGYPT

Nile

Red Sea

ARABIA

FRENCH WEST AFRICA

Niger

GAMBIA
PORTUGUESE GUINEA
SIERRA LEONE
LIBERIA
IVORY COAST
GOLD COAST
TOGOLAND

L. Chad

NIGERIA

CAMEROONS

SPANISH GUINEA

FRENCH EQUATORIAL AFRICA

Ubangi

Congo

CABINDA

Khartoum

ANGLO-EGYPTIAN SUDAN

Fashoda

Blue Nile

White Nile

ERITREA

Adowa

FRENCH SOMALILAND

BRITISH SOMALILAND

ETHIOPIA

ITALIAN SOMALILAND

BELGIAN CONGO

UGANDA

BRITISH EAST AFRICA

L. Victoria

L. Tanganyika

Mombasa

GERMAN EAST AFRICA

ZANZIBAR (Gr. Br.)

ATLANTIC OCEAN

INDIAN OCEAN

ANGOLA

NORTHERN RHODESIA

L. Nyasa

NYASALAND

Zambezi

SOUTHERN RHODESIA

MOZAMBIQUE

GERMAN SOUTHWEST AFRICA

BECHUANALAND

TRANSVAAL

SWAZILAND

ORANGE FREE STATE

BASUTOLAND

NATAL

MADAGASCAR

UNION OF SOUTH AFRICA

Cape Town

AFRICA IN 1878

ARAB STATES
Egypt
SAHARA
SUDANESE EMPIRES
Ashanti *Ibo*
BANTU *Kikuyu*
SWAHILI LANGUAGE
PEOPLES
Khoisan (Bushmen)
Hottentots

British		Portuguese
French		Belgian
German		Spanish
Italian		Independent African States

0   400   800 Km.

0   400   800 Mi.

∼ ENCOUNTERS WITH THE WEST ∼

Chief Montshiwa Petitions Queen Victoria

In 1885 Bechuanaland in southern Africa became a British protectorate. The Bechuana leaders saw British protection as a means to prevent takeover by the Boers, Dutch-speaking white settlers who were aggressively expanding in South Africa. The British were cavalier about their responsibilities, however, and a few years later allowed the British South Africa Company, a particularly exploitive enterprise, to take control of Bechuanaland. In protest, Chief Montshiwa (1815–1896), a major chief of the Baralong people, petitioned Queen Victoria for redress. His petition was supported by missionary lobbying, and most of Bechuana was saved from the clutches of the company.

Mafeking, 16 August, 1895

To the Queen of England and Her Ministers:

We send greetings and pray that you are all living nicely. You will know us; we are not strangers. We have been your children since 1885.

Your Government has been good, and under it we have received much blessing, prosperity, and peace. . . .

We Baralong are very astonished because we hear that the Queen's Government wants to give away our country in the Protectorate to the Chartered Company; we mean the B[ritish] S[outh] A[frica] Company.

Our land there is a good land, our fathers lived in it and buried in it, and we keep all our cattle in it. What will we do if you give our land away? My people are increasing very fast and are filling the land.

We keep all the laws of the great Queen; we have fought for her; we have always been the friends of her people; we are not idle; we build houses; we plough many gardens; we sow. . . .

Why are you tired of ruling us? Why do you want to throw us away? We do not fight against your laws. We keep them and are living nicely.

Our words are No: No. The Queen's Government must not give my people's land in the Protectorate to the Chartered Company. . . .

Peace to you all, we greet you;
Please send a good word back.

I am etc,

Montshiwa

Source: S. M. Molema, *Montshiwa, 1815–1896* (Cape Town: G. Struik, 1966), pp. 181–182.

---

ideas and scientific knowledge—though only to a small percentage of the local population.

Colonial rulers imposed laws and practices modeled after those of the home country. In India the colonial administration prided itself on safeguarding the condition of Indian women by, for instance, abolishing in 1829 the tradition of "suttee" whereby widows were burned on their husband's pyre. At times, however, European models reduced the rights of indigenous women. In Hindu law a wife could leave her husband, but

British law introduced into India the right of a husband to force his wife to return to him. In Kerala, in the southern part of the subcontinent, inheritance and descent were matrilineal; the British tried to legislate this tradition out of existence since it disturbed their notion of the proper relationship between the sexes.

The European empire builders created political units that had never existed before. Although there had been many efforts in the past to join the whole Indian subcontinent under a single author-

Victoria Terminus, Bombay Europeans' tendency to transfer values and institutions to their colonies included the export of architectural style. Various traditional European architectural styles, mainly the neo-Gothic that was so popular in nineteenth-century England, shaped this edifice, completed in 1888. *(The British Library, Oriental and India Office Collections)*

ity, the British were the first to accomplish this feat (Map 24.2). Through a common administration, rail network, and trade, Britain gave Indians the sense of a common condition, leading in 1885 to the founding of the India Congress party. Initially this party demanded reforms within the British colonial system; eventually it became the major nationalist group. The Congress party platform included the demand for constitutional government, representative assemblies, and the rule of law—concepts all based on Western theory and practice.

The transformations that Europeans wrought confirmed their sense of themselves as agents of progress, building a new and better world. Europeans arrogantly believed they knew what was best for other people; and they accepted force as a means of dealing with others. Such attitudes may have colored the increasingly caustic relations between European states.

The ties of empire affected metropolitan cultures. The Hindi word for bandit became the Eng-

lish word *thug;* the Hindi number five, denoting the five ingredients necessary for a particular drink, became *punch.* Scenes from the colonial world often were the themes of European art, such as Paul Gauguin's paintings of Tahiti and advertising posters for products as different as soap and whiskey. After the turn of the century Pablo Picasso's cubism reflected his growing familiarity with African art. In running the largest empire in the world, the British emphasized the need to develop masculine virtues; they cultivated competitive sports and stern schooling, which, they believed, would develop "character" and leadership. To administer their overseas colonies, Europeans developed sophisticated means of gathering and managing information that benefited metropolitan societies. A growing number of people from the colonies also came to live in European cities. By 1900 some former colonists, despite various forms of discrimination, had become full participants in the life of their host country; two East Indians won election to the British Parliament in the 1890s.

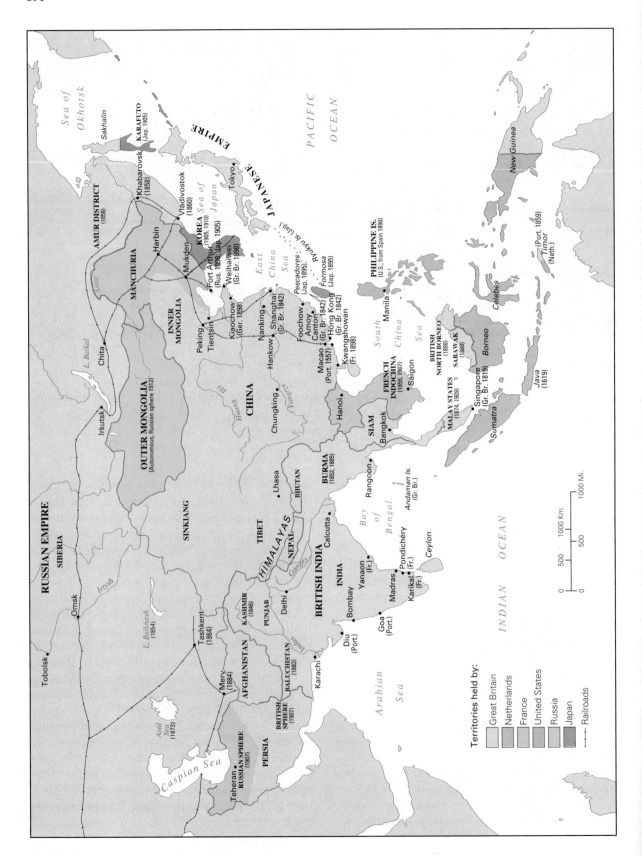

Sea of Okhotsk

KARAFUTO (Jap. 1905)

Sakhalin

JAPANESE EMPIRE

Khabarovsk (1858)

AMUR DISTRICT (1858)

Vladivostok (1860)

MANCHURIA

Harbin

Sea of Japan

Tokyo

PACIFIC OCEAN

New Guinea

(Port. 1859)
Timor (Neth.)

KOREA (1905, 1910)

Mukden

Port Arthur (Rus. 1898, 1910)

Weihaiwei (Gr. Br. 1898)

East China Sea

Ryūkyū Is. (Jap.)

Formosa (Jap. 1895)

Pescadores (Jap. 1895)

PHILIPPINE IS. (U.S. from Spain 1898)

Manila

Celebes

RUSSIAN EMPIRE

SIBERIA

L. Baikal

Chita

Irkutsk

INNER MONGOLIA

OUTER MONGOLIA (Autonomous, Russian sphere 1912)

Peking
Tientsin

Kiaochow (Ger. 1898)

Huang Ho

Nanking

Shanghai (Gr. Br. 1842)

Hankow

Yangtze

Foochow
Amoy (Gr. Br. 1842)
Canton (Gr. Br. 1842)

Macao (Port. 1557)

Hong Kong (Gr. Br. 1842)

Kwangshowan (Fr. 1898)

South China Sea

BRITISH NORTH BORNEO (1888)

SARAWAK (1888)

Borneo

CHINA

Chungking

SINKIANG

FRENCH INDOCHINA (1859, 1907)

Hanoi

Saigon

MALAY STATES (1874, 1909)

Singapore (Gr. Br. 1819)

Sumatra

Java (1619)

Omsk

Tobolsk

Irtysh

L. Balkhash (1854)

Tashkent (1864)

Merv (1884)

Aral Sea (1873)

AFGHANISTAN

BRITISH SPHERE (1907)

RUSSIAN SPHERE (1907)

PERSIA

Teheran

Caspian Sea

BALUCHISTAN (1883)

KASHMIR (1846)

PUNJAB

Delhi

Indus

Karachi

Diu (Port.)

HIMALAYAS

TIBET

Lhasa

NEPAL

BHUTAN

Ganges

BRITISH INDIA

INDIA

BURMA (1852, 1885)

Rangoon

SIAM

Bangkok

Calcutta

Bombay

Goa (Port.)

Madras

Yanaon (Fr.)

Pondichéry (Fr.)

Karikal (Fr.)

Ceylon

Bay of Bengal

Andaman Is. (Gr. Br.)

Arabian Sea

INDIAN OCEAN

Territories held by:

Great Britain
Netherlands
France
United States
Russia
Japan
Railroads

1000 Mi.

1000 Km.
500

500

0
0

Overseas Migrations and the Spread of European Values

The nineteenth century saw a phenomenal expansion in European overseas migrations, adding to Europe's impact on other societies (Map 24.3). Europeans had always migrated. They left villages for towns, or in the case of migrant farm laborers, traveled from village to village as the seasons changed and different crops needed to be harvested. With the expansion of European power abroad beginning in the sixteenth century, Europeans migrated overseas; between the sixteenth and eighteenth centuries around six million people left Europe. These numbers pale in significance, however, in the nineteenth century. Between 1870 and 1914, 55 million Europeans left the Continent for the New World, Australia, and New Zealand.

As with the new imperialism migration was male dominated. As many as three-quarters of all immigrants to the United States were young males, and even though Brazil recruited whole families, the majority of immigrants were also male. There were, however, some notable exceptions to these rules; during some decades women dominated Irish immigration to the United States, arriving as domestics.

Changing social and technological forces account for migrations. Economic crises and overpopulation in rural Europe (see page 857) led many men and women to look overseas for new opportunities; they either settled there or labored as migrant workers to save money, which when brought home could pay the mortgage or buy more land for a family whose holdings were too small to sustain it. Advances in technology such as the steamship introduced cheap and rapid communications with other continents. A trans-Atlantic ticket did not cost much, and in many cases employers in the Americas advanced the price of a ticket in efforts to recruit labor. The trip was relatively short—a crossing from Liverpool to New York took no more than two weeks. If in the past people had trekked for weeks from their village to the city in search of work, they could now in the same amount of time reach New York or Buenos Aires. And unlike overseas migrants of the seventeenth and eighteenth centuries, those of the nineteenth century could envision the move as temporary. In fact, of the 34 million migrants to the Americas, about a third returned to Europe. Many were truly seasonal workers, known as swallows in Italy, who every year went back and forth between Europe and the Americas.

Increased literacy, inexpensive printing, and the ease of correspondence with the outside world spread what was called "America fever." Many immigrants wrote back to their native villages; between 1900 and 1906 three million letters were sent to eastern Europe from the United States. Correspondence to relatives and friends boasted of the material advantages of life in the New World. A Swede who had settled in the United States wrote home, "And I can tell you that here we do not live frugally but here one has egg pancake and canned fish and fresh fish and fruits of all kinds, so it is different from you who have to sit and hold herring bones." Such letters, often reprinted in local newspapers or gathered in pamphlets, unleashed mass waves of migration.

Certain European groups migrated to specific areas. Scandinavians settled in the upper Midwest of the United States, Italians in Argentina, Germans in Paraguay, Britons in South Africa, Portuguese in Brazil, each group leaving its imprint on its adopted land. The upper Midwest was known as "the great desert," but Scandinavians used farm techniques from their homelands to cultivate these dry lands. German Mennonites settled in Kansas and brought with them a strain of wheat that became the basis of the state's prosperity. Immigrants also put their imprint on urban sites. Durban in South Africa looks like an English city, and some towns in Paraguay resemble Alpine villages of southern Germany. The Germans who came to Milwaukee, Wisconsin, made it a city of beer and strong socialist convictions.

Emigration scattered peoples and extended cultures overseas. By 1914 nearly half of all the Irish and the Portuguese lived outside Europe. The settlers consumed many European goods and in turn produced for the European market, increasing the centrality of Europe in the world market. The migrations across the globe were an added force to that of imperial conquest, further

Map 24.2 Asia in 1914 China, Siam (Thailand), and a portion of Persia were the only parts of Asia still independent after the great powers, including the United States and Japan, subjugated the Continent to alien rule.

Map 24.3 European Migrations, 1820–1910 Throughout the nineteenth century, millions of Europeans left home for overseas; most headed for the United States. *(Source:* Reproduced from *The Times Atlas of World History,* 3d ed., by kind permission of Times Books. Some data from Eric Hobsbawm, *The Age of Empire, 1875–1914* [New York: Pantheon, 1987].)

putting Europe's imprint on peoples and societies abroad.

THE DEMOCRATIC POWERS

By the end of the nineteenth century, most of Europe's political systems floundered in crisis. The major powers with democratic institutions—Great Britain, France, and Italy—confronted volatile public opinion and had difficulty winning broad consensus for their policies. They struggled with new challenges emerging from an expanded electorate that was at times frustrated by the failure of the system to resolve its demands. Turning away from the democratic precept to resolve differences through the ballot and legislation, many people—both in government and out—were willing to resort to extraparliamentary means, including violence, to see their interests prevail.

Petersen: Emigrants Preparing to Depart Edward Petersen's 1890 painting depicts Danish emigrants readying to leave their homeland. Between 1860 and 1914, 300,000 people emigrated from the small country of Denmark, most of them to the United States. *(Courtesy of the Aarhus Kunstmuseum. Reproduced with permission of Thomas, Poul, and Ole Hein Pedersen, Aarhus.)*

Great Britain

In Great Britain the Reform Bill of 1884 transformed the political landscape by doubling suffrage to five million—giving the vote to two of every three adult males. The appeal of this enlarged electorate tempted politicians to make demagogic promises, which were often broken later to the frustration of their constituents. It was also more difficult to establish compromise in a Parliament that no longer consisted of a fairly limited class of people with common interests and values. The British political system was faced with issues it was unable to resolve peacefully, and it was obliged—uncharacteristically—to resort to force or the threat of force.

As in earlier periods, Ireland proved to be a persistent problem. The political consciousness of the Irish had risen considerably, and they seethed

under alien rule. In an attempt to quell Irish opposition in 1886, Prime Minister Gladstone proposed autonomy, or "home rule," for Ireland. There were many objections to such a plan, the most serious being that if Ireland, a predominately Catholic country, ruled itself, the local Protestant majority in Ulster, the northeast part of the island, would be overwhelmed and likely to fall under Catholic control. "Home rule is Rome rule," chanted the supporters of Ulster Protestantism. Among Gladstone's own Liberals, many opposed changing the existing relationship between England and its possession. They seceded from the Liberals and formed the Unionist party, which, in coalition with the Conservatives, ruled the country from 1886 to 1905. When the Liberals returned to power in 1906, they again proposed home rule. In 1911, the House of Commons passed a home-rule bill, but it was obstructed in the House of Lords and was not slated to go into effect until September 1914.

In the process of debating the Irish issue, many segments of British society showed they were willing to resort to extralegal and even violent means. Fearing Catholic domination, Protestants in northern Ireland armed themselves, determined to resist home rule. In the rest of Ireland, Catholic groups armed, too, insisting on the unity of the island; they were ready to fight for home rule for the whole of Ireland. The Conservative party in Britain, which opposed home rule, called on Ulster to revolt. British officers threatened to resign their commissions, rather than fight Ulster. The behavior of the Conservatives and the army indicated a breakdown of order and authority, a disregard for tradition by two of its bulwarks. Only the outbreak of world war in 1914 delayed a showdown over Ireland, and then for only a few years.

Once back in power in 1906, the Liberals committed themselves to a vast array of social reforms but were frustrated by the difficulty of getting their program through the House of Lords. The feisty Liberal chancellor of the Exchequer, David Lloyd George (1863–1945), expressed his outrage that the will of the people was being thwarted by a handful of magnates in the House of Lords, sitting there not by election but by hereditary right.

The Liberals' social reform program included old-age pensions. To finance them, Lloyd George proposed raising income taxes and death duties and levying a tax on landed wealth. A bill with these measures easily passed the House of Commons in 1909 but was stymied in the upper chamber, where many members were prominent landowners. The House of Lords technically had the power to amend or reject a bill passed by Commons, but for nearly 250 years it had been understood that it did not have the right to reject a money bill. Nonetheless, motivated by economic self-interest and personal spite against the Liberals, a majority in the House of Lords disregarded convention and voted against the bill. This decision created a major constitutional crisis.

The Liberal government wanted not only to pass its bill but to reduce the power of the House of Lords. In 1911 it sponsored a bill, quickly passed by the House of Commons, to limit the House of Lords to a suspensive veto. This would mean that a bill defeated in the House of Lords

could be prevented from going into effect for only a predetermined period—in this case, two years. The House of Lords refused at first to pass such a law. But at the request of the government, the king threatened to appoint four hundred new lords. Reluctantly, the House of Lords passed the bill.

During the debate over the bill, Conservatives—the representatives of British traditionalism and the upholders of decorum—resorted to brawling and refused to let the prime minister speak. It was the first time in British parliamentary history that such an act of defiance had occurred. The British Parliament, considered the model for supporters of free institutions, had shown itself unable to resolve issues in a reasoned manner.

Violence also appeared in another unlikely place: the women's suffrage movement. Most liberal males, when speaking of the need to extend human liberty, had excluded the female gender. Toward the end of the nineteenth century, that, too, was challenged. Women began to organize into groups devoted to winning the vote but had little initial success. In 1903 Emmeline Pankhurst (1858–1928) and her two daughters founded the Women's Social and Political Union, whose goal was immediate suffrage.

Angered and frustrated by their lack of progress, the suffragists (often referred to by contemporaries as "suffragettes"), led by the Pankhursts, began in 1906 a more militant program of protest—disturbing proceedings in Parliament, breaking windows at the prime minister's residence, slashing canvases at the National Gallery, burning down empty houses, dropping acid into mailboxes, and throwing bombs. There were even threats on the lives of the prime minister and the king. Suffragists who were arrested often engaged in hunger strikes. Fearing they would die, the authorities force-fed the women. Female protesters were also physically attacked by male thugs. (See the box, "Pankhurst on Women's Rights.") That women would resort to violence, and that men in and outside of the government would resort to force against them, seemed to show how widespread the cult of force had become.

France

The Third Republic, founded in 1870 after France's humiliating military defeat at the hands

A Suffragist Attempts to Chain Herself to the Gates of Buckingham Palace, 1914 In their effort to win the vote, women resorted to public protests and the police often violently intervened. *(Popperfoto/Archive Photos)*

of the Prussians, also continued to face an ongoing series of crises. Challenged by enemies on the political left and right who continually called for the abolition of democracy, the regime found itself buffeted from all sides.

The French government itself contributed to an unstable political situation by its lack of strong leadership. The need to build coalitions among the several parties in the parliament rewarded those politicians who had moderate programs and were flexible. Thus there was little premium on firm ideas and commitments, and the prime minister was often more a conciliator than a leader. Further, lackluster leadership appealed to republicans, who continued to fear that a popular leader might—as Louis Napoleon had in 1851—exploit his support to make himself dictator.

The regime seemed to lurch from scandal to scandal. The most notorious was the Dreyfus affair. In October 1894, Captain Alfred Dreyfus (1859–1935) of the French army was arrested and charged with passing military secrets to the German embassy. Dreyfus seems to have attracted suspicion because he was the only Jewish officer on the general staff. The evidence was flimsy—a letter written in a handwriting that some thought resembled that of Dreyfus, although other experts testified it was not that of the young officer.

This letter, and materials that later turned out to be forged, led the French army to court-martial Dreyfus and sentence him to life imprisonment on Devil's Island off the coast of South America. By March 1896, the general staff had evidence that it was another officer, Major Esterhazy, who was actually the spy. But to reopen the case would be to admit the army had made an error, and the general staff refused to do so.

By late 1897, when the apparent miscarriage of justice became widely known, French society split over "the affair." The political left, including many intellectuals, argued for reopening the case. For them it was crucial that justice be carried out.

Pankhurst on Women's Rights

In 1908 the suffragists, led by Emmeline Pankhurst, issued a handbill calling on the people of London to "rush" Parliament and win the vote for women. The legal authorities interpreted their action as a violation of the peace, and several suffragists, including Pankhurst, were put on trial. They put up a spirited defense, in which Pankhurst movingly explained her motives for leading the suffragist cause.

I want you to realise how we women feel; because we are women, because we are not men, we need some legitimate influence to bear upon our law-makers.

Now, we have tried every way. We have presented larger petitions than were ever presented for any other reform, we have succeeded in holding greater public meetings than men have ever had for any reform, in spite of the difficulty which women have in throwing off their natural diffidence, that desire to escape publicity which we have inherited from generations of our foremothers; we have broken through that. We have faced hostile mobs at street corners, because we were told that we could not have that representation for our taxes which men have won unless we converted the whole of the country to our side. Because we have done this, we have been misrepresented, we have been ridiculed, we have had contempt poured upon us. The ignorant mob at the street corner has been incited to offer us violence, which we have faced unarmed and unprotected by the safeguards which Cabinet Ministers have. We know that we need the protection of the vote even more than men have needed it. . . .

We believe that if we get the vote it will mean better conditions for our unfortunate sisters. We know what the condition of the woman worker is . . . and we have been driven to the conclusion that only through legislation can any improvement be effected, and that that legislation can never be effected until we have the same power as men have to bring pressure to bear upon our representatives and upon Governments to give us the necessary legislation. . . .

I should never be here if I had the same kind of power that the very meanest and commonest of men have—the same power that the wife-beater has, the same power that the drunkard has. I should never be here if I had that power, and I speak for all the women who have come before you and other magistrates. . . .

If you had power to send us to prison, not for six months, but for six years, for sixteen years, or for the whole of our lives, the Government must not think that they can stop this agitation. It will go on. . . .

We are here not because we are law-breakers; we are here in our efforts to become lawmakers.

Source: F. W. Pethick Lawrence, ed. *The Trial of the Suffragette Leaders* (London: The Women's Press, 1909), pp. 21–24.

The army and its supporters, right-wing politicians, royalists, and Catholics, argued that the decision should not be changed. As the bulwark against internal and foreign threats, the army should be above challenge, and the fate of a single man—guilty or innocent—was immaterial.

The affair unleashed a swirl of controversy and rioting, which led the government to order a retrial in 1899. But the court again found Dreyfus guilty—this time with "extenuating circumstances" and the recommendation that he be pardoned. Finally, in 1906, Dreyfus was fully exonerated. He ended his days as a general in the army that had subjected him to so much suffering.

The strong encouragement Catholics gave to those who supported the original verdict confirmed the republicans' belief that the church was a menace to the regime. The Radical party, the staunchest backers of Dreyfus, won the elections in 1898. Despite its title, the Radical party favored moderate social reforms. It was uncompromising, however, in its anticlericalism, determined to wreak vengeance on Catholics and end the influence of the church once and for all. In 1905 the parliament passed a law separating church and state, thus ending the privileged position the Catholic church had enjoyed. Violent language and physical confrontations on both sides accompanied this separation. Catholics trying to prevent state officials from entering churches to take required inventories sometimes resorted to force, using weapons or, in one case, a bear chained to the church. Armed soldiers broke down church doors and dragged monks away.

Labor problems also triggered repeated confrontations with the government. Increased labor militancy produced long, drawn-out strikes, which in 1904 alone led to the loss of four million workdays. There was agitation in the countryside, too, particularly in 1907 in the Midi, the south of France. This region suffered from a crisis in the wine industry caused by disease, competition from cheap foreign wines, and fraud. More important, the region witnessed increased rural proletarianization as population grew and larger landholdings were concentrated under smaller numbers of owners. Rural militancy led to revolt in 1907. Troops were sent in, killing dozens and winning for the Radical government the title "government of assassins."

Italy

The third major power in Europe to adopt parliamentary government also had grave problems. Although unification took place in 1860, Italy found genuine unity elusive; the country was plagued by regionalism, social strife, and an unrepresentative political system. As in the past, the south especially challenged the central government. Assertive regionalism, brigandage, and poverty made the areas resistant to most government programs.

The parliamentary system established in 1860 was far from democratic. Property qualifications limited suffrage to less than 3 percent of the population. And as a result of the persistence of tras-

formismo—the practice by which government corrupted and co-opted the opposition—electoral choice was short-circuited.

Between 1870 and 1890 the Italian government introduced some important reforms, but it was difficult to improve the general standard of living for a people undergoing rapid population growth. In the fifty years after unification, population increased from 25 to 35 million, and the country had limited resources to deal with such growth. In the south, a few wealthy landowners held large latifundia, or private estates, while the majority of the peasants were landless and forced to work the land for minimum wages. In the north, industrialization had started, but the region was not rich in coal or iron. To be competitive, industry paid very low wages, and the workers lived in abject misery.

Conditions on the land and in the factory led to widespread protests, followed by stern government repression. In 1893 a Sicilian labor movement won the adherence of 300,000 members, who seized land and attacked government offices. The government responded with massive force and declared martial law. In 1896, with unrest spreading throughout the peninsula, the government placed half of the provinces under military rule. A cycle of violence and counterviolence gripped the nation. In May 1898 labor protests against government repression in the northern industrial city of Milan led to brutal retaliation. In this general atmosphere of violence, an anarchist killed King Umberto I on July 29, 1900.

After the turn of the century, a new prime minister, Giovanni Giolitti (1842–1928), tried to bring an end to the upheaval. He used government force more sparingly and showed a spirit of cooperation toward the workers. Seeking to broaden his popularity by an appeal to nationalist fervor, Giolitti launched an attack on Libya in 1911, wresting it from the ailing Ottoman Empire. The territory was arid and bereft of economic promise, but its conquest was championed as a test of national virility and the foundation of national greatness. The imperialists proudly proclaimed force the arbiter of the nation's future.

Domestically, the nation also returned to force. A wave of workers' discontent seized the nation again, and in June 1914 a national strike led to rioting and seizure of power in many municipalities, including Bologna. In the Romagna, an

William II The German emperor liked to be viewed in a heroic and military posture. His crippled left hand is turned away from the viewer. *(Landesbildstelle, Berlin)*

independent workers' republic was proclaimed. It took 100,000 government troops ten days to restore order. The workers' restlessness and the apparent difficulty of keeping them under control led some nationalist right-wing extremists to form "volunteers for the defense of order," anticipating the vigilante thugs who were to make up the early bands of Italian fascism.

THE AUTOCRACIES

Four major autocracies dominated central and eastern Europe: Germany, Austria-Hungary, the Ottoman Empire, and Russia. If the democracies were faced with difficulties in these years, the autocracies faced even more severe challenges. Although many groups in the parliamentary regimes grew impatient at the slowness of change, theoretically at least they could believe that someday their goals would be realized. Not so in the autocracies. The severity of autocratic rule varied

from state to state, ranging from the absolutism of the Ottoman Empire to the semiparliamentary regime of Germany, but the ruler had the final political say in all of them. Resistance to the autocracies included broad popular challenges to the German imperial system, the reduction of Austria-Hungary into a nearly ungovernable empire, and revolution in the Russian and Ottoman Empires.

Germany

Although Germany had a parliament, the government was answerable to the kaiser, not the people's electoral representatives. And in the late nineteenth century, Prussia, the most reactionary part of the country, continued to dominate.

To rule effectively, Chancellor Otto von Bismarck maneuvered and intrigued to quell opposition. In the face of socialist growth, he used an attempt to assassinate the emperor as the excuse to ban the Socialist party in 1879. He succeeded in simultaneously winning over conservative agrarian and liberal industrial interests by supporting tariffs on both imported foodstuffs and industrial goods. He also turned against the Catholics, who were lukewarm toward Protestant Prussia, persecuting them and their institutions. These measures, however, did not prevent the growth of the Socialist and Catholic Center parties.

Unfortunately for Bismarck, whose tenure in office depended on the goodwill of the emperor, William I died in 1888, to be succeeded first by his son Frederick, who ruled only a few months, and then by his grandson, William II (r. 1888–1918). The young Kaiser William intended to rule as well as reign, but he was ill fit to govern. Convinced of his own infallibility, he bothered to learn very little. Born with a crippled hand, William seemed to want to compensate for this infirmity by appearing forceful, even brutal. He hated any hints of limitation to his powers, announcing, "There is only one ruler in the Reich and I am he. I tolerate no other." A restless individual, William changed uniforms eight times daily and traveled ceaselessly among his seventy-five castles and palaces. Dismayed by Bismarck's proposals of reprisals against the Socialists and the chancellor's unwillingness to take on a clearly pro-Austrian and anti-Russian foreign policy, the kaiser dismissed him. But he also did so to rid himself of a formidable, intimidating individual.

The emperor was determined to make Germany a world power whose foreign policy would have a global impact. He wanted Germany to have colonies, a navy, and major influence among the Great Powers. This policy, *Weltpolitik,* or "world politics," greatly troubled Germany's neighbors, partly because they were already worried by a new, assertive power in central Europe and partly because German moves were accompanied by the kaiser's bombastic threats. Within Germany, however, *Weltpolitik* won support. Steel manufacturers and shipbuilders received lucrative contracts; workers seemed assured of employment.

Although the nationalist appeals impressed many Germans, the nation could not be easily managed. The emperor's autocratic style was challenged, and his behavior was increasingly viewed as irresponsible. In the elections of 1912, one-third of all Germans voted for the Socialist party. Thus the largest single party in the Reichstag was at least rhetorically committed to the downfall of the capitalist system and autocracy. Labor militancy also reached new heights. In 1912, one million workers—a record number—went on strike. More and more Germans pressed for a parliamentary system with a government accountable to the people's elected representatives.

The emperor could not tolerate criticism of his behavior. He had come to Bismarck's conclusions and frequently talked about using the military to crush socialists and the parliament. These thoughts were echoed in the officer corps and in government circles. To some observers it seemed likely that the days of German autocracy were numbered—or that there would be a violent confrontation between the army and the people.

Austria-Hungary

The neighboring Austro-Hungarian Empire also continued to face a series of crises. In an age of intense nationalism, a multinational empire was an anomaly, as the Emperor Francis Joseph (r. 1848–1916) himself acknowledged. Although the relationship between the two parts of the empire was regulated by the agreement of 1867 (see page 825), the agreement did not prevent conflict between Austria and Hungary, particularly over control of their joint army. The insistence on separate Hungarian interests had developed to such a degree that, had it not been for the outbreak of the world war, Hungary probably would have broken loose from the dual monarchy.

In the Hungarian half of the empire, the Magyars found it increasingly difficult to maintain control. Other nationalities opposed Magyarization—the imposition of the Magyar language and institutions—and insisted on the right to use their own languages in the schools and administration. The Hungarian government resorted to censorship and jailings to silence nationalist leaders. In the Austrian half of the empire, the treatment of nationalities was less harsh, but the government was equally strife-ridden.

There were no easy solutions to the many conflicts that the empire faced. Since much of the national agitation was led by middle-class intellectuals, the Habsburg government introduced universal male suffrage in 1907 in an effort to undercut their influence. However, the result was an empire even more difficult to govern. It became nearly impossible to find a workable majority within a parliament that included thirty ethnically based political parties.

The virulence of debate based on nationality and class divisions grew to unprecedented extremes. Within the parliament, deputies threw inkwells at each other, rang sleigh bells, and sounded bugles. Parliament ceased to be relevant. By 1914 it had been dissolved and so had several regional assemblies. Austria was being ruled by decree. Emperor Francis Joseph feared the empire would not survive him.

The Ottoman Empire

In the generation before 1914, no political system in Europe suffered from so advanced a case of dissolution as the Ottoman Empire, undermined by both secessionist movements within its own borders and aggression from other European powers. Sultan Abdul Hamid II (r. 1876–1909) ruled the country as a despot and authorized mass carnage against those who contested his rule, earning him the title of the "Great Assassin."

Young, Western-educated Turks—the "Young Turks"—dismayed at one-man rule and the continuing loss of territory and influence, overthrew Abdul Hamid in a coup in July 1908. They set up a government responsible to an elected parliament. The Young Turks hoped to stem the loss of territory by establishing firmer central control, but their efforts had the opposite effect. The various nationalities of the empire resented the attempts at "Turkification," the imposition of Turkish education and administration. Renewed agitation broke out in Macedonia, Albania, and among the Armenians. The government carried out severely repressive measures to end the unrest, killing thousands of Armenians.

For foreign powers, the moment seemed propitious to plunder the weakened empire. In 1911 Italy occupied Libya, an Ottoman province. Greece, Bulgaria, and Serbia—impatient to enlarge their territory—formed an alliance, the Balkan League, which in 1912 prosecuted a successful war against the empire. Albania became independent, and Macedonia was partitioned among members of the league. Thus the empire lost most of its European possessions, except for the capital, Constantinople, and a narrow strip of surrounding land.

Russia

Through the Great Reforms of the 1860s, the Russian autocracy had attempted to resolve many of the problems facing its empire and people. But the reforms and the major social changes of the period unleashed new forces, making it even more difficult for the tsars to rule.

The needs of a modernizing country led to an increase in the number of universities and students. However, the newly educated Russian youths began almost instantly an ardent, sustained critique of autocracy. In the absence of a large group upholding liberal, advanced ideas, university students and graduates, who came to be known as the intelligentsia, saw it as their mission to transform Russia. In the 1870s, university youths by the thousands organized a populist movement, hoping to bring change to the countryside.

These youthful idealists intended to educate the peasants and make them more politically aware. But they met with suspicion from the peasantry and repression by the government. Large numbers of populists were arrested and put on trial. Frustrated at the difficulty of bringing about change from below by transforming the people, disaffected young radicals formed the People's Will, which turned to murdering public officials to hasten the day of revolution.

Although the regime intensified repression, it also sought to broaden its public support. In 1881 Tsar Alexander II decided to create an advisory committee that some thought would eventually lead to a parliamentary form of government. In March 1881, as he was about to sign the decree establishing this committee, the tsar was assassinated by members of the People's Will.

The new ruler, Tsar Alexander III (r. 1881–1894), who had witnessed the assassination, blamed his father's leniency for his death. By contrast, he was determined to uphold autocracy firmly. He sought to weaken his father's reforms, reducing local self-rule in the process.

When Alexander's son, Nicholas II (r. 1894–1917), succeeded his father on the throne in 1894, he declared he would be as autocratic as his father. However, he lacked the methodical, consistent temperament such a pledge required. A pleasant man, he wanted to be liked, and he lacked the forcefulness to establish a coherent policy for his troubled country.

Since the Great Reforms, serious problems had accumulated that threatened the stability of the regime. In the countryside the situation worsened steadily as the population exploded and pressure on the land increased. The provisions that had accompanied the freeing of the serfs left considerable discontent. The peasants were not free to come and go as they pleased; they had to have the permission of the village council. Agriculture remained inefficient, far inferior to that of western Europe; hence the allotted land was insufficient to feed the peasants, creating a constant demand for more land.

The attempted modernization of Russia had changed it more dramatically and rapidly than any other central or eastern European state. In the 1890s the minister of finance, Sergei Witte (1849–1915), launched an ambitious railroad-expansion program, which triggered a broader program of industrial development. Although Russia remained largely agrarian, pockets of industrial growth were created. Some factories and mining concerns were unusually large, with as many as six thousand employees. When workers grew incensed at their condition and insistent on winning the same rights and protection that existed in western Europe, they engaged in massive strikes that crippled industry.

A Conspiratorial Revolutionary Party

The Russian Socialist party was racked by internal debates over the direction and means by which a socialist revolution could be created. The majority favored a broad-based Socialist party, but in his 1902 essay, "What Is to Be Done?" Lenin explained why revolution in Russia could succeed only if it were led by a cadre of professional revolutionaries, organized into a tightly knit conspiratorial group.

We must have a committee of professional *revolutionaries* . . . irrespective of whether they are students or working men. I assert: 1) That no movement can be durable without a stable organization of leaders to maintain continuity; 2) that the more widely the masses are drawn into the struggle and form the basis of the movement, the more necessary it is to have such an organization and the more stable it must be— otherwise it is much easier for demagogues to sidetrack the more backward sections of the masses; 3) that the organization must consist chiefly of persons engaged in revolution as a profession; 4) that in a country with a despotic government, the more we *restrict* the membership of this organization to persons who are engaged in revolution as a profession and who have been professionally trained in the art of combating the political police, the more difficult will it be to catch the organization; and

5) the *wider* will be the circle of men and women of the working class or of other classes of society able to join the movement and perform active work in it. . . .

It is . . . argued against us that the views on organization here expounded contradict the "principles of democracy."

Ponder a little over the real meaning of the high-sounding phrase . . . and you will realize that "broad democracy" in party organization, amidst the gloom of autocracy and the domination of the gendarmes, is nothing more than a *useless and harmful toy*. It is a useless toy, because as a matter of fact, no revolutionary organization has ever practiced *broad* democracy, nor could it, however much it desired to do so.

The only serious organizational principle the active workers of our movement can accept is: Strict secrecy, strict selection of members and the training of professional revolutionists.

Source: Lenin, "What Is to Be Done?" *Collected Works*, vol. 4 (New York: International Publishers, 1929), pp. 198–199, 210–213.

Political dissatisfaction with the autocracy grew. Members of the expanding middle classes began to clamor that, like their contemporaries in western Europe, they should be given the opportunity to participate in governance. Increasingly, aristocrats also demanded a right to political participation.

Various revolutionary groups committed to socialism continued to flourish. The heirs to the populists were the Social Revolutionaries, who emerged as a political force in the 1890s. They believed that the peasants would bring socialism to Russia. In 1898 the Russian Social Democratic

party was founded; a Marxist party, it promoted the industrial working class as the harbinger of socialism. In 1903 that party split between the Mensheviks and the Bolsheviks. The Mensheviks insisted that Russia had to go through the stages of history Marx had predicted—to witness the full development of capitalism and its subsequent collapse before socialism could come to power. The Bolsheviks, a minority group, were led by Vladimir Lenin (1870–1924), a zealous revolutionary and Marxist. Rather than wait for historic forces to undermine capitalism, he insisted that a revolutionary cadre could seize power on behalf

Workers' Demonstration in Moscow, 1905 In 1905 workers as well as peasants protested
against the Russian autocracy. To bring the revolution under control, Nicholas II was
obliged to grant several concessions. *(Novosti)*

of the working class. Lenin favored a small, disciplined, conspiratorial party, like the People's Will,
while the Mensheviks favored a more open, democratic party. (See the box, "A Conspiratorial
Revolutionary Party," on page 907.)

At the turn of the century these groups were
still quite small and played a limited role in the
mounting opposition to tsarism. But popular opposition soon grew in the face of Russian military ineptness in the war against Japan, which had broken
out in February 1904 in a dispute over control of
northern Korea. Antagonism to the tsarist regime
escalated as a result of social tensions, heightened
by an economic slowdown.

Beginning in January 1905, a series of demonstrations, strikes, and other acts of collective violence began. Together, they were dubbed "the revolution of 1905." One Sunday in January 1905,
400,000 workers seeking redress of their griev-

ances gathered in front of the tsar's palace. Rather
than hear their protests, officials ordered soldiers
to fire on them, resulting in 150 deaths and hundreds more wounded. "Bloody Sunday" angered
the populace. The tsar, instead of being viewed as
an understanding, paternal authority, had become
the murderer of his people. Unrest spread to most
of the country. As reports reached Russia of more
defeats in the war with Japan, the regime's prestige was further undermined. By September 1905,
Russia had to sue for peace and admit defeat.
Challenged in the capital, where independent
workers' councils called soviets had sprung up,
the government also lost control over the countryside, the site of widespread peasant uprisings.

Fearing for his regime, Nicholas hoped to split
the forces challenging tsarism by meeting the demands for parliamentary government and granting
major constitutional and civil liberties, including

freedom of religion, speech, assembly, and association. At the end of October, the tsar established an elective assembly, the Duma, with restricted male suffrage and limited political power. It was far from the Western-style parliament that Russian liberals had desired, but it quickly became the arena for criticism of autocracy. Anxious to create a more pliant instrument, the tsar suspended the assembly, changing its electoral base and its rules of operations. Even many conservatives were disillusioned with the tsar's backtracking and his breach of the promise he had made in 1905 to establish constitutionalism and parliamentarism.

A new prime minister, Peter Stolypin (1862–1911), tried to win support for the regime by a series of reforms, including improvement in the lot of the peasantry: The government reduced the peasants' financial obligations; the power of the commune was weakened; and local self-rule was extended to the peasants. But these changes did little to alleviate a worsening relationship between population and land. Between emancipation and 1914 the peasant population grew by 50 percent, but it acquired only ten percent more land. Rural poverty was widespread; in 1891 famine broke out in 20 provinces, killing a quarter of a million people. Rural discontent was widespread.

Labor unrest also mounted among industrial workers. In 1912 there were 725,000 strikers, but by the first half of 1914 there were twice that number. When the French president visited St. Petersburg on the eve of the outbreak of the war, barricades were rising in the workers' neighborhoods.

THE COMING WAR

Instability and upheaval characterized international relations in the years between 1880 and 1914. But the outbreak of war was not inevitable. Good common sense dictated against it, and some intelligent people predicted that in the new modern era, war had become so destructive that it was unthinkable. Finally, no European state wanted a war, although the Great Powers carried on policies that brought them to its brink.

Power Alignments

Germany enjoyed an unchallenged position in the international order of the 1870s and 1880s.

It was united in an alliance with the two other eastern conservative states—Russia and Austria-Hungary—in the Three Emperors' League, formed in 1873 and renewed by treaty in 1884. And it was part of the Triple Alliance with Austria and Italy. France was isolated, without allies. Britain, with little interest in continental affairs, appeared to be enjoying a "splendid isolation."

However, Germany's alliance system was not free from problems. Two of its allies, Austria-Hungary and Russia, were at loggerheads over control of the Balkans. How could Germany be the friend of both? To reassure the Russian government, wary of apparent German preference for Austria, Bismarck signed the Reinsurance Treaty in 1887, assuring Russia that Germany would not honor its alliance with Austria if the latter attacked Russia. After Bismarck's resignation in 1890, Emperor William allowed the Reinsurance Treaty to lapse. Alarmed, the Russians turned to France and, in January 1894, signed the Franco-Russian Alliance, by which each side pledged to help the other in case either was attacked by Germany.

The Great Powers on the Continent were now divided into two alliances, the Triple Alliance and the Franco-Russian Alliance. Britain formally belonged to neither. But if it favored any side, it would be the German-led alliance. Britain's strongest competitors in the 1880s and 1890s were France and Russia. Both rivaled Britain for influence in Asia, while France challenged Britain for control of Africa.

However, distrust of Germany, increasingly seen as a dangerous neighbor, led Britain and France to resolve their difficulties overseas. In 1904 Britain and France signed an understanding, or entente, resolving their rivalries in Egypt; and in 1907, Great Britain and Russia regulated their competition for influence in Persia (present-day Iran) with the Anglo-Russian Entente. Now Europe was loosely divided into two groups: the Triple Alliance of Germany, Austria-Hungary, and Italy, and the Triple Entente of Great Britain, France, and Russia.

The Momentum for War

Only through a series of crises did these alignments solidify to the point where their members were willing to go to war to save them. France's attempts to take over Morocco twice led to conflict with

MAJOR DIPLOMATIC ALLIANCES AND AGREEMENTS

1873	Three Emperors' League (Germany, Austria-Hungary, and Russia)
1879	Alliance between Germany and Austria
1882	Triple Alliance (Germany, Austria, and Italy)
1884	Renewal of Three Emperors' League
1887	Reinsurance Treaty (Germany and Russia)
1894	Franco-Russian Alliance
1904	Anglo-French Entente
1907	Anglo-Russian Entente

Germany. In 1905 Germany insisted that an international conference discuss the issue and deny France this kingdom adjacent to its colony of Algeria. In 1911, when France grabbed Morocco anyway, Germany accepted the situation only after extorting compensation from the French, who deeply resented what they viewed as German bullying.

Britain also began to view Germany as a serious international menace. Over the years, Britain had developed a navy equal to none. An island nation, dependent on international trade for its economic survival, Britain saw its navy as a necessity. Wishing to challenge Britain's supremacy on the seas, however, Germany began building its own navy in the 1890s.

The heightened international rivalry forced the European states to increase their arms expenditures, which added in turn to their sense of insecurity. The British had felt safe with a huge navy that none could equal. In 1906 they introduced a new class of ships with the launching of the *Dreadnought*. Powered by steam turbines, it was faster than any other ship; heavily armored, it could not be sunk easily; and its ten 12-inch guns made it a menace on the seas. The British thought Germany could not build equivalent ships, but it did, wiping out British supremacy—older British ships could easily be sunk by German dreadnoughts. No longer able to depend on its past supremacy, Britain was feeling less secure than at any time since the Napoleonic Wars, and it continued an expensive and feverish naval race with Germany.

In Germany the changing military capacity of Russia created great anxieties. When Japan defeated the tsarist empire in 1905, the Russian military was revealed to be inferior and was thought of as a lumbering giant, slow to mobilize in case of war. As a result Germany was not particularly afraid of its eastern neighbor. But stung by its humiliation in 1905, Russia quickly rebuilt its army and planned to establish an extensive rail network in the west. Russia thus had a greater military capacity than ever. To many in Germany, their country appeared encircled by a hostile Russia in the east and an equally unfriendly France in the west. Germany became genuinely worried, and beginning in 1912 many in the military and within the government started thinking about a preventive war. If war was inevitable, it should, many Germans argued, occur before Russia became even stronger. Fear of the future military balance made some of the highest policymakers see the crisis that broke out in the summer of 1914 as an opportunity to go to war and throttle Russia.

Many political leaders viewed the escalating arms race as a form of madness. Between 1904 and 1913 French and Russian arms expenditures increased by 80 percent; that of Germany by 120 percent; Austria-Hungary by 50 percent; and Italy by 100 percent. British Foreign Secretary Sir Edward Grey (1862–1933) warned that if the arms race continued, "it will submerge civilization." But no way was found to stop it.

On the whole warfare was not feared. Except for short victorious colonial wars, the Western powers had not experienced a major conflict since the Crimean War. Russia had successfully warred against the Ottoman Empire in 1876. Its war against Japan in 1905 had been a calamity, but it could imagine that this was a nonreplicable disaster. Most policymakers believed that the next war would be short. The wars that had so dramatically changed the borders of European states in the second half of the nineteenth century, notably the Austro-Prussian War of 1866 and the Franco-Prussian War of 1870, had been decided within a few short weeks. Few imagined that the war, if it came, would be so brutal and lengthy. And therefore many of Europe's leaders did not dread war enough to make a major effort to prevent or avoid it.

It was the territorial rivalry between Austria and Russia that triggered international disaster. For decades there had been growing enmity between the two empires for control over the Balkans (Map 24.4). In 1903, following a bloody military coup that killed the king and queen of Serbia, a pro-Russian party took control of the Serbian government. It spread anti-Austrian propaganda and sought to unify under its banner the Slavs living in the Balkans, including those under Austrian rule. As a result, many Austrian officials were convinced that the survival of the Austro-Hungarian Empire required that Serbia be destroyed. Talk of an attack on Serbia filled the Austrian court in 1914.

On June 28, 1914, the heir to the Habsburg throne, Archduke Francis Ferdinand, visited Sarajevo in Austrian-ruled Bosnia. A young Bosnian-Serb nationalist, hostile to Austrian rule, who had been trained and armed by a Serb terrorist group called the Black Hand, assassinated the archduke and his wife.

The assassination of the heir to the throne provided Austria with an ideal pretext for military action. The German kaiser, fearing that failure to support Vienna would lead to Austrian collapse and a Germany bereft of any allies, urged Austria to attack Serbia. On July 23, Austria issued an ultimatum to Serbia, deliberately worded in such a way as to be unacceptable. When Serbia refused the ultimatum, Austria declared war on July 28.

Perceived self-interest motivated each state's behavior in the ensuing crisis. Although in the past Russia had failed to protect Serbia, now it was determined to help. Russia's status as a great power demanded that it not allow its client state to be humiliated, much less obliterated. In the past the French government had acted as a brake on Russian ambitions in the Balkans. On the very eve of the war in 1914 France counseled restraint, but it did not withhold its aid; increasingly after 1911, France feared isolation in the face of what it perceived as growing German aggressiveness. Its only ally on the continent was Russia. To remain a great power, France needed to preserve its friendship with Russia and help it maintain its own great power status.

Germany could not allow Austria, its only ally, to be destroyed. Its leaders may also have seen the crisis as a propitious moment to begin a war that was going to occur sooner or later any-

Map 24.4 The Balkans in 1914 By 1914 the Ottoman Empire was much diminished, containing virtually none of Europe. Political boundaries did not follow nationality lines. Serbia was committed to unite all Serbs at the expense of the Austro-Hungarian Empire.

way. Before the entente powers, especially Russia, became stronger, it appeared to be a good moment to strike. As the German prime minister put it, his country was about to take "a leap in the dark," and he declared war on Russia. Assuming that France would come to the aid of Russia, Germany invaded France through Belgium. The British, concerned by the threat to their ally France, and outraged by the violation of Belgian neutrality to which all the great powers had been signatories since 1839, declared war on Germany. Events had hurtled forward between the Austrian declaration of war on Serbia on July 28 and the British decision on August 4. Europe was at war. Eventually so would be much of the world.

SUMMARY

On the surface, the years from 1880 to 1914 seemed comfortable. More people than ever before enjoyed material advantages and an improved standard of living. Literacy spread. Death rates went down; life expectancy rose. But a revolution of rising expectations had been created, and people grew more demanding, insisting in sometimes violent ways on their political and economic rights. Although mass movements such as socialism and the women's suffragist movement generally made use of peaceful means in their campaigns to change society, some of their members advocated and employed force. Anarchism appeared to stalk Europe. And in turn, states did not hesitate to use force in efforts to quell various protest movements, even resorting to martial law.

Reflecting these trends, intellectuals like Freud and Bergson and artists like Munch and Moreau suggested that there was a hidden, irrational dimension of life beneath surface appearances. Behind the façade of security and conformity lay many disturbing impulses such as racism, anti-Semitism, and the desire to suppress the emerging democracies by violent means and replace them with dictatorships.

In their relations with Africa and Asia, Europeans to an unprecedented degree resorted to force, conquering most of the African and much of the Asian continents. The new empires were intended to benefit Europe by providing it with new sources of wealth, trade, and the trappings of power. Increasingly, Europeans found it natural to regard themselves as belonging to a master race, destined to dominate the world.

Although most Europeans were confident and optimistic about their future, such self-assuredness was not universally shared. Intellectuals spoke of decadence and decline. Statesmen, worried about the future of their countries and anxious to avoid the threat of decline, resorted to extreme measures such as empire building overseas and armed competition in Europe. Among European thinkers and statesmen, force had become widely accepted as the means to an end, and some leaders—notably those of Austria-Hungary and Germany—favored war over negotiation in July 1914.

The major powers—except Britain, confident in its naval dominance—built up large standing armies with millions of men and much modern equipment. Europe's network of alliances led inexorably to the larger conflict. If there were some leaders who feared war, more dreaded the consequences of not fighting, believing that war would save their regimes from the internal and external challenges they faced. Few could foresee the dire consequences of such a choice.

NOTES

1. Charles Seymour, ed. *The Intimate Papers of Colonel House,* vol. 1 (Boston: Houghton Mifflin, 1926), p. 249.

SUGGESTED READING

General Surveys

Gilbert, Felix. *The End of the European Era, 1890 to the Present.* 1979. Sees the years from 1890 to 1914 as helping to shape the rest of the twentieth century.

Hobsbawm, Eric. *The Age of Empire, 1875–1914.* 1987. A fine survey, emphasizing social change, by a leading British historian.

Romein, Jan. *The Watershed of Two Eras—Europe in 1900.* 1978. A long and at times challenging study of the generation straddling the turn of the century.

Politics and Culture

Gay, Peter. *Freud—A Life for Our Time.* 1988. An admiring study by a prominent historian and trained psychoanalyst.

Geary, Dick. *European Labor Protest, 1848–1939.* 1981. A brief, clearly written work that emphasizes the deradicalization of labor.

Hughes, H. Stuart. *Consciousness and Society: The Reorientation of European Social Thought, 1890–1930.* 1979. A classic on changes in European social thought.

Joll, James. *The Second International, 1889–1914.* 1955. A brief, well-written history of the successes and failures of the international socialist organization.

Katz, Jacob. *From Prejudice to Destruction, 1700–1933.* 1980. A survey of two centuries of European anti-Semitism.

Schorske, Carl E. *Fin de Siècle Vienna—Politics and Culture.* 1980. A critically acclaimed work on the arts and social and political thought in the Habsburg capital at the turn of the century.

Teich, Mikulas, and Roy Porter, eds. *Fin de Siècle and Its Legacy.* 1990. A collection of critical essays summarizing the cultural trends at the end of the century.

European Migration and Imperialism

Baumgart, Winfried. *Imperialism—The Idea and Reality of British and French Colonial Expansion, 1880–1914.* 1989.

A comparative study, emphasizing the political aspects of imperialism.

Betts, Raymond F. *The False Dawn—European Imperialism in the Nineteenth Century.* 1975. An elegantly written survey by one of the most authoritative historians of the subject.

Davis, Lance E., and Huttenback, Robert A. *Mammon and the Pursuit of Empire.* 1988. A careful statistical study that shows British imperialism overall not to have been a profitable venture.

Headrick, Daniel R. *The Tentacles of Progress—Technology Transfer in the Age of Imperialism, 1850–1940.* 1988. Considers the extent and limits of technology transfer from the West to its empire.

Hoerder, Dirk, and Leslie Page Moch, eds. *European Migrants—Global and Local Perspectives.* 1996. A collection of up-to-date articles on migrations of Europeans within their continent and overseas.

Pakenham, Thomas. *The Scramble for Africa.* 1991. A long but colorful narrative of the European conquest of Africa, emphasizing personalities.

Strobel, Margaret. *European Women and the Second British Empire.* 1991. Considers the role of women in the formation of the British Empire.

The Democratic Powers

Brédin, Jean-Denis. *The Affair: The Case of Alfred Dreyfus.* 1986. The most authoritative account, written by a prominent French lawyer, covers both the details of the affair and its context.

Clark, Martin. *Modern Italy, 1872–1982.* 1984. Contains some fine chapters on the decades before the war, emphasizing the difficulties of governing a society as divided and diverse as Italy.

Feuchtwanger, E. J. *Democracy and Empire, Britain, 1865–1914.* 1985. While describing the challenges to the existing order, emphasizes the resilience of British institutions.

Harrison, J. F. C. *Late Victorian Britain, 1875–1901.* 1990. Considers how different social classes experienced the social and economic transformations of the era.

Levine, Philippa. *Victorian Feminism.* 1987. Shows that Victorian women were involved in several campaigns for their rights, including the suffragist movement.

Mayeur, Jean-Marie, and Madeleine Réberioux. *The Third Republic—From Its Origins to the Great War, 1871–1914.* 1987. The most up-to-date survey of France in these years, emphasizing the emergence of republican government and the challenges it faced.

Thayer, John A. *Italy and the Great War, Politics and Culture, 1870–1915.* 1964. Surveys Italy's political and cultural life in these years.

Townshend, Charles. *Political Violence in Ireland.* 1983. Concentrates on violence in Ireland since 1848, stressing its social and economic origins.

The Autocracies

Bridge, F. R. *The Habsburg Monarchy among the Great Powers, 1815–1918.* 1990. Contrary to most works on the Habsburg empire, praises Austrian leaders for preserving the empire as long as they did.

Kohut, Thomas A. *Wilhelm II and the Germans—A Study in Leadership.* 1991. A psychohistorical study, analyzing the German emperor's youth and unsatisfactory relations with his parents.

Lieven, Dominic. *Russia's Rulers under the Old Regime.* 1989. Presents a study of Russia's aristocracy and its attitudes toward most public issues in the nineteenth century.

Rogger, Hans. *Russia in the Age of Modernization, 1881–1917.* 1983. Concentrates on Russian institutions in the generation prior to the revolution.

Origins of World War I

Joll, James. *The Origins of the First World War.* 1984. A clear, concise, readable history emphasizing strategic interests and nationalist passions leading to the outbreak of the war.

Kennedy, Paul. *The Rise and Fall of the Great Powers, 1500 to 2000.* 1987. Masterfully summarizes the factors that led to the shifting fates of the Great Powers.

Massie, Robert K. *Dreadnought—Britain, Germany and the Coming of the Great War.* 1991. A very long but lively discussion of Anglo-German affairs in the generation leading up to the war. The author emphasizes the leading personalities involved.

Wilson, Keith, ed. *Decisions for War, 1914.* 1995. A collection of articles, based on the most recent scholarship, highlighting the actions of the major and some minor powers in the crises of July 1914.

THE LAYOUT OF THE BRITISH MUSEUM

The British Museum was founded in the mid-eighteenth century when the government acquired some private collections. The museum increased the size of its collections, largely through donations, bringing in objects from around the world. In its early years the museum was located in a converted private mansion; then in 1847, to house its growing collection, the museum moved into a monumental building with a neoclassical façade. Until the 1830s public access was limited to the upper classes, mainly the learned. By the mid-nineteenth century, however, a million people a year were visiting the museum. Displays of materials gathered from non-European cultures drew particularly large audiences.

Consider how the exhibits reflected British imperialism. In the first half of the nineteenth century, objects from Oceania, reflecting British activities in the Pacific, were acquired. African materials became more plentiful with the British conquest of much of Africa after the 1880s; the British military expedition to Nigeria in 1897 led to the acquisition of the fabulous Benin bronzes.

While imperial adventures were shaping the museum collection, the museum in turn was supporting imperialism. Museum officials declared that increased knowledge about regions overseas would fuel enthusiasm for the imperial venture and make the British people better fit to rule their new subjects.

The manner in which the British Museum displayed some of its possessions reflected the intellectual currents of the times. In the late eighteenth and early nineteenth centuries the museum grouped its non-European objects with "natural history"; non-Europeans were associated with nature, with the beasts of the earth. Running out of space, the museum moved the natural history collection to a separate Natural Museum in South Kensington, and in the 1880s ethnography, the branch of anthropology devoted to human cultures, constituted a separate collection.

The late-nineteenth-century plan of the upper floor of the museum shown here reflects the racial views of imperial Britain. After climbing the stairs from the ground floor, we start at the room labeled 1, the Anglo-Saxon Room, which celebrates England's early history. Then comes the Waddesdon Bequest Room, which houses various artifacts of ancient and medieval English and European history (the room is named after the Rothschild mansion where the collection was previously housed). Next we arrive at the Medieval Room itself. Using the route most visitors would then take, we come to the Asiatic Saloon, filled with pottery, porcelain, and other works of art from Japan, China, Persia, and India.

What is the significance of this juxtaposition of rooms? The British and other Europeans had developed an ethnocentric view of the human races, believing that the white race was by far superior to all others. This belief seemed confirmed by the material accomplishments of Europeans, especially impressive in the nineteenth century. Of the non-Europeans, Asians had won the grudging respect of the British and other Europeans. China, with its thousands of years of recorded history and sophisticated government structures, was one of several Asian societies that impressed them. Because many African societies lacked a written culture and had government and religious systems dramatically different from the Europeans', the British and other Europeans often considered Africans ignorant and primitive.

Biologists, anthropologists, and others speculating about the human races offered two different explanations for racial variations. These hypotheses competed with each other for public acceptance. According to the first, biology determined the level of civilization of each people. According to the second, different peoples were at different levels of development. In this view, Europeans were most developed, Africans least; but eventually Asians and Africans would progress and reach a level akin to that of Europeans. In the meantime non-Europeans illustrated European life at earlier stages of development.

It is interesting that the Asiatic Saloon, with its swords, shields, and other elaborate Asian objects, was next to the Medieval Room. The position-

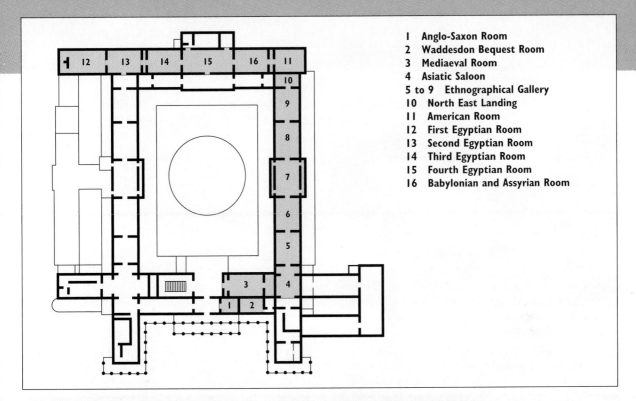

Plan of the Upper Floor of the British Museum, ca. 1880 *(Based on map in Henry C. Shelley,*
The British Museum: Its History and Treasures [Boston: L. C. Page, 1911], pp. 274–275.)

ing invites consideration that some nineteenth-century Asian societies were at a level of development akin to medieval England.

An empty corridor separated this part of the museum from the Ethnographic Gallery, giving visitors the sense that what they would view was separate from medieval England and selected Asian societies. The Ethnographic Gallery displayed objects from Asia, Oceania, Africa, and the Americas. They tended to be objects of daily life such as household wares, weapons, and clothing. The stress was on their simplicity and primitiveness—presumably reflections of the primitive culture of their makers. The objects were not differentiated chronologically; pre-Columbian artifacts from the Americas were displayed beside modern African crafts. Ethnographic items were seldom dated, implying that the peoples who created them did not develop and had no history. The museum guidebook invited nineteenth-century viewers to consider how close the development of these peoples was to that of the earliest Europeans.

After passing through the Ethnographic Gallery, a visitor would arrive at the North East Landing and then enter the American Room. It con-tained items from Eskimos, native Americans, and other peoples whom Victorians considered "primitives," but it also included artifacts from the Aztecs and Incas, whom the British considered to have been highly developed.

The Aztec and Inca collections abutted the room devoted to two ancient civilizations with monumental architecture, the Babylonian and Assyrian Room. Next came four Egyptian rooms. In the nineteenth century the greatness of ancient Egyptian culture was recognized. The British Museum allotted ancient Egypt ample space far removed from what were seen as the "primitive" peoples represented in the Ethnographic Gallery.

In 1972 the ethnographic collection was moved out of the British Museum and now constitutes a separate Museum of Mankind. With the loss of empire and the decline of confidence in the superiority of the white race, the old uses for the objects collected overseas had become obsolete.* ✂

*I am grateful to Thomas Prasch, Washburn University, for his help and advice and for making available to me two of his unpublished papers on this subject.

CHAPTER 25

War and Revolution, 1914–1919

As the European powers prepared for a military showdown, an Egyptian-Sudanese intellectual, Mohammed Ali Duse (1867–1944), contemplated the long-term consequences this war might have—both for the Europeans themselves and for the millions in the non-Western world caught up in the European orbit: "We can only watch and pray. Unarmed, undisciplined, disunited, we cannot strike a blow; we can only await the event. But whatever that may be, all the combatants, the conquerers and the conquered alike, will be exhausted by the struggle, and will require years for their recovery, and during that time much may be done. Watch and wait! It may be that the non-European races will profit by the European disaster. God's ways are mysterious."[1]

Duse was right. The fighting that began in August 1914 would become the first "world war"—a dramatic turning point in world history and the beginning of the end of European hegemony. The geographic reach of the war was unprecedented, especially after the intervention of the Ottoman Empire spread the war to the Middle East. But also because of the European colonial networks, the war directly involved non-Europeans, from Chinese to sub-Saharan Africans, in combat or support roles. Although the old colonialism continued into the postwar era, the war nourished the forces that would later overthrow it.

In Europe the overwhelming majority initially welcomed the war, but the eventual consequences for Europeans—from emperors to ordinary people—were often cataclysmic, most dramatically in the countries that met defeat. Long-standing empires and dynasties fell apart, so the political and territorial map had to be fundamentally redrawn after the war was over.

Paul Nash,
The Menin Road.

Coming after a century of relative peace and apparent progress, the war had an enduring impact partly because of the way it was fought, the experience it entailed; much about that experience was so new that it could scarcely have been imagined before 1914. A far wider and more destructive war would follow within a generation, but it was World War I, known to contemporaries as "the Great War," that shattered the old European order, with its comfortable assumptions of superiority, rationality, and progress. After this war, neither Westerners nor non-Westerners could still believe in the privileged place of Western civilization in quite the same way.

The war proved such a turning point because the fighting, which had been expected to produce a quick result, instead bogged down in a stalemate during the fall of 1914. By the time it finally ended, in November 1918, the war had strained the whole fabric of life, affecting everything from economic organization to literary vocabulary, from journalistic techniques to the role of women. And because of these unforeseen strains, the war ended up producing effects unrelated to its causes. Most notably, the difficulties of war led to a communist revolution in Russia that had an incalculable impact on the subsequent history of the twentieth century. So whereas the war solved some of the problems that had caused it, it introduced significant new problems and left much unresolved.

THE UNFORESEEN STALEMATE, 1914–1917

When the war began in August 1914, enthusiasm and high morale, based on expectations of quick victory, marked both sides. But fighting on the crucial western front led to a stalemate by the end of 1914, and the particularly brutal encounters of 1916 made it clear that this was not the sort of war most had expected at its start. By early 1917 the difficulties of the war experience brought to the surface underlying questions about what it was all for—and whether it was worth the price.

August 1914: The Domestic and Military Setting

Although some, like Helmuth von Moltke (1848–1916), chief of the German general staff, worried

that this would prove a long, destructive war testing the very fabric of Western civilization, the outbreak of fighting early in August produced a wave of euphoria and a remarkable degree of domestic unity. To many, war came almost as a relief; at last, the issues that had produced tension and intermittent crisis for the past decade would find a definitive solution. Especially among educated young people, this settling of accounts seemed to offer the prospect of renewal, even a kind of redemption, for themselves and their societies. The war promised an escape from the stiflingly respectable bourgeois world and, in response to the common danger, an end to the petty bickering and divisiveness of everyday politics.

An unexpected display of patriotism from the socialist left reinforced the sense of domestic unity and the high morale that went with it. Defying their long-standing rhetoric about international proletarian solidarity, members of the socialist parties of the Second International rallied to their respective national war efforts almost everywhere in Europe. To socialists and workers, national defense against a more backward aggressor seemed essential to the eventual creation of socialism. French socialists had to defend France's democratic republic against autocratic and militaristic Germany; German socialists had to defend German institutions, and the strong socialist organizations that had proven possible within them, against repressive tsarist Russia. The German Socialists' vote for war credits in the Reichstag on August 4 dramatically symbolized the failure of the Second International to prevent working-class involvement in a European war.

In France, the government had planned, as a precaution, to arrest roughly one thousand trade union and socialist leaders in the event of war, but no such arrests seemed necessary when the war began. Instead, the order of the day was "Sacred Union," which even entailed Socialist participation in the new government of national defense. Germany enjoyed a comparable "Fortress Truce," including an agreement to suspend labor conflict during the war, although here no Socialist was invited to join the war cabinet.

The high spirits of August were possible because so few Europeans could foresee what they were getting into. It would be "business as usual" as the British government put it—no shortages, no rationing, no massive government intervention.

There was little inkling of the total mobilization to come or of the eventual costs of the war.

Before the war began, the forces of the Triple Entente outnumbered those of Germany and Austria-Hungary. Russia had an army of over 1 million men, the largest in Europe, and France had 700,000. Britain, which did not introduce conscription until 1916, had about 250,000. Germany led the Central Powers with 850,000; Austria-Hungary contributed 450,000. Though outnumbered, the Central Powers had potential advantages in equipment, coordination, and speed over their more dispersed adversaries. Thus, the outcome was hardly a foregone conclusion in August 1914.

After the fighting began, a second tier of belligerents intervened one by one, expanding the war's scope and complicating the strategic alternatives. In November 1914 the Ottoman Empire, fearful of Russia, joined the Central Powers, thereby extending the war along the Russo-Turkish border and on to Mesopotamia and the approaches to the Suez Canal in the Middle East. For Arabs disaffected with Ottoman Turkish rule, the war presented an opportunity to take up arms—with the active support of Britain and France. Italy, after dickering with both sides, committed itself to join the Entente with the Treaty of London of April 1915. This secret agreement specified the territorial compensation Italy was to receive in the event of Entente victory—primarily the Italian-speaking areas still within Austria-Hungary. In September 1915 Bulgaria entered the war on the side of the Central Powers, seeking territorial advantages at the expense of Serbia, which had defeated Bulgaria in the Second Balkan War in 1913. In much the same way, Romania intervened on the side of the Entente, in August 1916, hoping to gain Transylvania, then part of Hungary.

Thus the war was fought on a variety of fronts (Map 25.1). This fact, combined with uncertainties about the role of sea power, led to ongoing debate among military decision makers about strategic priorities. Because of the antagonism that the prewar German naval buildup had caused, some expected that Britain and Germany would quickly be drawn into a decisive naval battle. Britain promptly instituted an effective naval blockade on imports to Germany, but the great showdown on the seas never materialized. Even the most significant naval encounter between them, the Battle of

No Trenches in Sight Spirits were high early in August 1914, as soldiers like these in Paris marched off to war. None foresaw what fighting this war would be like. None grasped the long-term impact the war would have. *(Archives Larousse-Giraudon)*

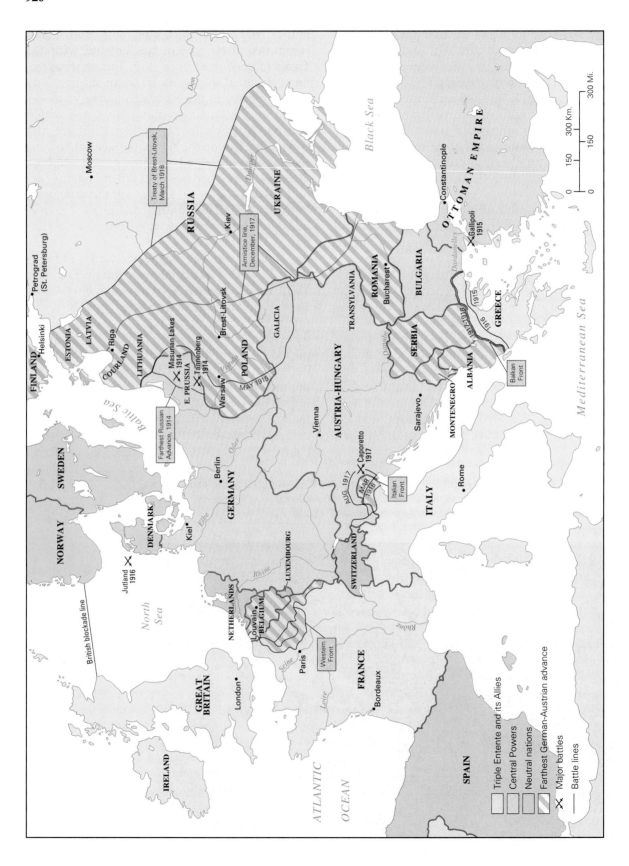

Jutland in 1916, was indecisive. Despite the naval rivalry of the prewar years, World War I proved fundamentally a land war.

Germany faced not only the long-anticipated two-front war against Russia in the east and France and Britain in the west; it also had to look to the southeast, given the precarious situation of its ally Austria-Hungary, fighting Serbia and Russia, then also Italy and eventually Romania as well. On the eastern front, Germany managed decisive victories during 1917 and 1918, forcing first Russia, then Romania, to seek a separate peace. But it was the western front that proved decisive.

Into the Nightmare, 1914

With the lessons of the wars of German unification in mind, both sides had planned for a short war based on rapid offensives, a war of movement. According to the Schlieffen Plan, drafted in 1905, Germany would concentrate first on France, devoting but one-eighth of its forces to containing the Russians, who were bound to need longer to mobilize. After taking just six weeks to knock France out of the war, Germany would then concentrate on Russia. French strategy, crafted by General Joseph Joffre (1852–1931), similarly relied on rapid offensives. The boys would be home by Christmas—or so it was thought.

Although German troops encountered more opposition than expected from the formerly neutral Belgians, they moved rapidly through Belgium into northern France during August. By the first week of September they had reached the Marne River, threatening Paris and forcing the French government to retreat south to Bordeaux. But French and British troops under Joffre counterattacked September 6–10, forcing the Germans to fall back and begin digging in along the Aisne River. By holding off the German offensive at this first Battle of the Marne, the Entente had undercut the Schlieffen Plan—and with it, it turned out, any chance of a rapid victory by either side.

Map 25.1 Major Fronts of World War I Although World War I included engagements in East Asia and the Middle East, it was essentially a European conflict, encompassing fighting on a number of fronts. A vast territory was contested in the east, but on the western front, which proved decisive, fighting was concentrated in a relatively small area.

During the rest of the fall of 1914, each side tried—unsuccessfully—to outflank the other. When, by the end of November, active fighting ceased for the winter, a military front of about three hundred miles had been established, all the way from Switzerland to the coast of the North Sea in Belgium (Map 25.2). And this line failed to shift more than ten miles in either direction over the next three years. So the result of the first six weeks of fighting on the western front was not gallant victory by either side but a grim and unforeseen stalemate.

Virtually from the start, the war took a destructive turn that few had predicted. In northern France in September 1914, the Germans fired on the cathedral at Reims, severely damaging the roof and nave, because they believed—apparently correctly—that the French were using one of the cathedral's towers as an observation post. If this could happen, at the very outset, to one of the great Gothic monuments in Europe, who could say what else this war might bring?

The two sides were forced to settle into a war of attrition relying on an elaborate network of defensive trenches. Although separated by as much as five miles in some places, enemy trenches were sometimes within shouting distance, so there was occasionally banter back and forth, even attempts to entertain the other side. But the trenches quickly became almost unimaginably grim—filthy, ridden with rats and lice, noisy and smoky from artillery fire, and foul-smelling, partly from the odor of decaying bodies.

As defensive instruments, however, the trenches proved quite effective, especially because each side quickly learned to take advantage of barbed wire, mines, and especially machine guns to defend its positions. A mass of barbed wire, 3 to 5 feet high and 30 yards wide, guarded a typical trench. The machine gun had been developed before the war as an offensive weapon; few foresaw the decided advantage it would give the defense. But with machine guns, it proved possible to defend trenches even against massive assaults—and to impose heavy casualties on the attackers.

In 1916 the tank was introduced as an antidote to the machine gun, but, as skeptics had warned, tanks proved too ungainly and unreliable to be widely effective. Although the French used them to advantage in the decisive Allied offensive in 1918, tanks were not crucial to the outcome of the war.

Map 25.2 Stalemate and Decision on the Western Front On the western front, in
northern France and Belgium, trench warfare developed and the most famous battles of
the war were fought. Notable sites included Verdun, Passchendaele, and the Marne and
Somme Rivers.

Though the defensive trenches had formidable
advantages, neither side could give up the vision
of a decisive offensive to break through on the
western front. Thus the troops were periodically
called on to go "over the top" and then across "no
man's land" to assault the enemy trenches. Again
and again, however, such offensives proved futile,
producing incredibly heavy casualties: "Whole
regiments gambled away eternity for ten yards
of wasteland."[2]

For the soldiers on the western front the war
became a nightmarish experience in a hellish landscape. Bombardment by new, heavier forms of
artillery not only threatened the enemy more
directly but devastated the terrain in the war zone
with craters, which then became muddy, turning
the landscape into a near swamp. (See the box,
"Into the Trenches.") Beginning early in 1915, tear
gas, chlorine gas, and finally mustard gas found
use on both sides. Although the development of

gas masks significantly reduced the impact of this
menacing new chemical warfare, the threat of poison gas added another nightmarish element to the
experience of those who fought the war.

The notions of patriotism, comradeship, duty,
and glory that had been prevalent in 1914 gradually dissolved as those in the trenches experienced
the unforeseen horrors of warfare on the western
front. A French soldier, questioning his own reactions after battle in 1916, responded with sarcasm
and irony: "What sublime emotion inspires you at
the moment of assault? I thought of nothing other
than dragging my feet out of the mud encasing
them. What did you feel after surviving the attack? I grumbled because I would have to remain
several days more without *pinard* [wine]. Is not
one's first act to kneel down and thank God? No.
One relieves oneself."[3]

Although the Germans had been denied their
quick victory in the west, by the end of 1914 they

Trench Warfare Grim though they were, the trenches proved effective for defensive purposes. Here a British soldier guards a trench at Ovillers, on the Somme, in July 1916. *(Trustees of the Imperial War Museum)*

occupied much of Belgium and almost one-tenth of France, including major industrial areas and mines producing most of France's coal and iron. On the eastern front, as well, the Germans won some substantial advantages in 1914—but not a decisive victory.

The first season of fighting in the east suggested that the pattern there would not be trench warfare but rapid movement across a vast but thinly held front. When the fighting began in August, the Russians came more quickly than anticipated, confronting an outnumbered German force in a menacing, if reckless, invasion of East Prussia. But by mid-September German forces under General Paul von Hindenburg (1847–1934) and his chief of staff General Erich Ludendorff (1865–1937) repelled the Russian advance, taking a huge number of prisoners and seriously demoralizing the Russians.

As a result of their victory in East Prussia, Hindenburg and Ludendorff emerged as heroes, and they would play major roles in German public life thereafter. Hindenburg, the senior partner, became chief of staff of the entire German army in August 1916, but the able and energetic Ludendorff remained at his side. Ludendorff proved to be the key figure as this powerful duo gradually assumed undisputed control of the whole German war effort, both military and domestic.

Seeking a Breakthrough, 1915–1917

After the campaigns of 1915 proved inconclusive, German leaders decided to concentrate in 1916 on a massive offensive against the great French fortress at Verdun, intending to inflict a definitive defeat on France. To assault the fortress, the Germans gathered 1220 pieces of artillery for attack along an 8-mile front. Included were thirteen "Big Bertha" siege guns, weapons so large that nine tractors were required to position each of them; a crane was necessary to insert the shell, which weighed over a ton. The level of heavy artillery firepower that the Germans applied at Verdun was unprecedented in the history of warfare.

German forces attacked on February 21, taking the outer defenses of the fortress, and appeared poised for victory. The tide turned, however, when General Philippe Pétain (1856–1951) assumed control of the French defense at Verdun.

Into the Trenches

As the initial offensives on the western front turned into stalemate, ordinary soldiers on both sides began to experience unprecedented forms of warfare in an eerie new landscape. Writing home to his family from France in November 1914, a young German soldier, Fritz Franke (1892–1915), sought to convey what this new war was like. He was killed six months later.

Yesterday we didn't feel sure that a single one of us would come through alive. You can't possibly picture to yourselves what such a battlefield looks like. It is impossible to describe it, and even now, when it is a day behind us, I myself can hardly believe that such bestial barbarity and unspeakable suffering are possible. Every foot of ground contested; every hundred yards another trench; and everywhere bodies—rows of them! All the trees shot to pieces; the whole ground churned up a yard deep by the heaviest shells; dead animals; houses and churches so utterly destroyed by shellfire that they can never be of the least use again. And every troop that advances in support must pass through a mile of this chaos, through this gigantic burial ground and the reek of corpses.

In this way we advanced on Tuesday, marching for three hours, a silent column, in the moonlight, toward the Front and into a trench as Reserve, two to three hundred yards from the English, close behind our own infantry.

There we lay the whole day, a yard and a half to two yards below the level of the ground, crouching in the narrow trench on a thin layer of straw, in an overpowering din which never ceased all day or the greater part of the night—the whole ground trembling and shaking! There is every variety of sound—whistling, whining, ringing, crashing, rolling . . . [ellipses in the original] the beastly things pitch right above one and burst and the fragments buzz in all directions, and the only question one asks is: "Why doesn't one get me?" Often the things land within a hand's breath and one just looks on. One gets so hardened to it that at the most one ducks one's head a little if a great, big naval-gun shell comes a bit too near and its grey-green stink is a bit too thick. Otherwise one soon just lies there and thinks of other things. . . .

One just lives from one hour to the next. For instance, if one starts to prepare some food, one never knows if one may'nt have to leave it behind within an hour. . . .

. . . Above all one acquires a knowledge of human nature! We all live so naturally and unconventionally here, every one according to his own instincts. That brings much that is good and much that is ugly to the surface.

Source: A. F. Wedd, ed., *German Students' War Letters,* translated and arranged from the original edition of Dr. Philipp Witkop (London: Methuen, 1929), pp. 123–125.

Pétain had the patience and skill necessary to organize supply for a long and difficult siege. Furthermore, he proved able, through considerate treatment, to inspire affection and confidence among his men. By mid-July the French army had repelled the German offensive, although only in December did the French retake the outer defenses of the fortress. The French had held firm in what would prove the war's longest, most trying battle—one that killed 600,000 men on both sides. For the French the Battle of Verdun would remain the epitome of the horrors of World War I.

Meanwhile, early in July 1916, the British led a major attack at the Somme River that was similarly bloody—and that affected Britain much as Verdun affected France. On the first day alone the British suffered 60,000 casualties, including 21,000 killed. Fighting continued into the fall, but the offensive proved futile in the end. One-third of those involved, or over 1 million soldiers, ended up dead, missing, or wounded.

Dominated by the devastating battles at Verdun and the Somme, the campaigns of 1916 marked the decisive end to the high spirits of the summer of 1914. Both sides suffered huge losses—and apparently for nothing. By the end of 1916, the front had shifted only a few miles from its location at the beginning of the year.

In light of the frustrating outcome so far, the French turned to new military leadership, replacing Joffre with Robert Nivelle (1856–1924), who promptly sought to prove himself with a new offensive during the spring of 1917. Persisting even as it became clear that this effort had no chance of success, Nivelle provoked increasing resistance among French soldiers, some of whom were simply refusing to follow orders by the end of May.

With the French war effort in danger of collapse, the French government replaced Nivelle with General Pétain, the hero of the defense of Verdun and the obvious person to restore morale. Pétain managed to re-establish discipline by adopting a conciliatory approach—improving food and rest, visiting the troops in the field, listening, offering encouragement, urging patience, even dealing relatively mercifully with most of the resisters themselves. To be sure, many of the soldiers who had participated in this near-mutiny were court-martialed, and over 3400 were convicted. But of the 554 sentenced to death, only 49 were actually executed.

After the failure of the Nivelle offensive, the initiative fell to the British under General Douglas Haig (1861–1928), who was convinced, despite skepticism in the British cabinet, that Nivelle's offensive had failed simply because of tactical mistakes. Beginning near Ypres in Belgium on July 31, 1917, and continuing until November, the British attacked, but, as before, the effort yielded only minimal territorial gains—about fifty square miles—at a horrifying cost, including 240,000 British casualties. Known as the Battle of Passchendaele, the British offensive of 1917 ranks with the Battles of Verdun and the Somme as the bloodiest of the war.

1917 as a Turning Point

Meanwhile, the Germans, feeling that the Russians could not hold out much longer, decided to

Paul von Hindenburg and Erich Ludendorff The talents of Hindenburg (left) and Ludendorff meshed effectively to carry them from success on the eastern front in 1914 to a predominant role in the German war effort. They are shown here at a reception in honor of Hindenburg's seventieth birthday in October 1917. (*AKG London*)

concentrate on the eastern front in 1917 in an effort to knock Russia out of the war at last. This intensified German military pressure helped spark revolution in Russia, and in December 1917 Russia's new revolutionary regime asked for a separate peace. The defeat of Russia freed the Germans at last to concentrate on the west, but by this time France and Britain had a new ally.

On April 6, 1917, the United States entered the war on the side of the Entente, in response to Germany's controversial use of submarines. Germany lacked sufficient strength in surface ships to respond to Britain's naval blockade, whether by attacking the British fleet directly or by mounting a comparable blockade of the British Isles. So the Germans decided to use submarines to interfere with shipping to Britain. Submarines, however, were too vulnerable to be able to surface and confiscate goods, so the Germans had to settle for sinking suspect ships with torpedoes. In February 1915 they declared the waters around the British Isles to be a war zone and served notice that they would torpedo not only enemy ships but also neutral ships carrying goods to Britain.

The German response was harsh, but so was the British blockade, which violated a number of earlier international agreements about the rights of neutral shipping and the scope of wartime blockades. The British had agreed that only military goods such as munitions and certain raw materials, not such everyday goods as food and clothing, were to be subject to confiscation. Yet in blockading Germany, the British refused to make this distinction, prompting the sarcastic German quip that Britannia not only rules the waves, but waives the rules.[4]

In May 1915 a German sub torpedoed the *Lusitania,* a British passenger liner, killing almost 1200 people and producing widespread indignation. Partly because 128 of those killed were Americans, U.S. President Woodrow Wilson issued a severe warning, which contributed to the German decision in September 1915 to pull back from unrestricted submarine warfare. But in this war of attrition, the flow of supplies became ever more critical. As German suffering under the British blockade increased, pressure steadily mounted within Germany to put the subs back into action.

The issue provoked bitter debate among German leaders. Chancellor Theobald von Bethmann-Hollweg and the civilian authorities opposed resumption out of fear it would provoke the United States to enter the war. But Ludendorff and the military finally prevailed, partly with the argument that even if the United States did intervene, U.S. troops could not get to Europe in sufficient numbers, and in sufficient haste, to have a major impact. Germany announced the resumption of unrestricted submarine warfare on January 31, 1917, and the United States responded with a declaration of war on April 6.

Many on both sides doubted that U.S. intervention would make a decisive difference; most assumed that it would take at least a year for the American presence to materialize in force—an assessment that proved accurate. Still, the entry of the United States gave the Entente at least the promise of more fighting power. And the United States seemed capable of renewing the sense of purpose on the Entente side, showing that the war had a meaning that could justify the unexpected costs and sacrifice.

THE EXPERIENCE OF TOTAL WAR

As the war dragged on, the distinction between the military and civilian spheres blurred. Suffering increased on the home front, and unprecedented governmental mobilization of society proved necessary to wage war on the scale that had come to be required. Because it became "total" in this way, the war affected not simply international relations and the power balance but also culture, society, and the patterns of everyday life.

Hardship on the Home Front

The war meant food shortages, and thus malnutrition, for ordinary people in the belligerent countries, although Britain and France, with their more favorable geographic positions, suffered considerably less than others. Germany was especially vulnerable and promptly began suffering under the British naval blockade. With military needs taking priority, the Germans encountered shortages of the chemical fertilizers, farm machinery, and draft animals necessary for agricultural production. The government began rationing bread, meat, and fats during 1915. The increasing scarcity of foodstuffs produced sharp increases in diseases like rickets and tuberculosis and in infant and childhood mortality rates in wartime Germany.

The need to pay for the war produced economic dislocations as well. Government borrowing covered some of the cost for the short term, but to cover the rest, governments all over Europe found it more palatable to inflate the currency, by printing more money, than to raise taxes. The notion that the enemy would be made to pay once victory had been won seemed to justify this decision. But this way of financing the war meant rising prices and severe erosion of purchasing power for ordinary people all over Europe. In both France and Germany, the labor truce of 1914 gave way to increasing strike activity during 1916.

With an especially severe winter in 1916–1917 adding to the misery, there were serious instances of domestic disorder, including strikes and food riots, in many parts of Europe during 1917. In Italy, major strikes developed in Turin and other cities over wages and access to foodstuffs. The revolution that overthrew the tsarist autocracy in Russia that same year began with comparable protests over wartime food shortages.

The strains of war even fanned the flames in Ireland, where an uneasy truce over the home-rule controversy accompanied the British decision for war in 1914. Partly because of German efforts to stir up domestic trouble for Britain, unrest built up again in Ireland, culminating in the Easter Rebellion in Dublin in 1916. The brutality with which British forces crushed the uprising intensified demands for full independence—precisely what Britain would be forced to yield to the Irish Republic shortly after the war.

Moreover, new technologies made civilians ever less immune to wartime violence. Most dramatically, an entirely new aspect of war-making, bombing from aircraft, directly assaulted civilians. Although bombing began with an immediate military aim—to destroy industrial targets or to provide tactical support for other military units—it quickly became clear that night bombing, especially, might demoralize civilian populations. As early as 1915, German airplanes were bombing English cities, provoking British retaliation against cities in the German Ruhr and Rhineland areas. These raids had little effect on the course of the war, but they showed that new technologies could make warfare more destructive even for civilians.

Domestic Mobilization

Once it became clear, by the end of 1914, that the war would not be over quickly, leaders on both sides began to realize that the outcome would not be determined on the battlefield alone. Victory required mobilizing all of the nation's resources and energies. So World War I became a total war, involving the whole society, not just the military.

The British naval blockade on Germany, which made no distinction between military and nonmilitary goods, was a stratagem characteristic of total war. The blockade would not affect Germany's immediate strength on the battlefield, but it could damage Germany's long-term war-making capac-

ity. And the blockade did prove significant, partly because Germany had not made effective economic preparations—including stockpiling—for this long war of attrition.

In peacetime, Germany had depended on imports of food, fats, oils, and chemicals, including the nitrates needed for ammunition. With the onset of war, these commodities were immediately in short supply, as was labor. Thus Germany seemed to need stringent economic coordination and control. By the end of 1916, the country had developed a militarized economy, with all aspects of economic life coordinated for the war effort. Under the supervision of the military, state agencies, big business, and the trade unions were brought into close collaboration. The new system included rationing, price controls, and compulsory labor arbitration, as well as a national service law enabling the military to channel workers into jobs deemed vital to the war effort.

Forced to provide for an unexpectedly long war, the Germans did not hesitate to exploit the economy of occupied Belgium, requisitioning foodstuffs even to the point of causing starvation among the Belgians themselves. They forced 62,000 Belgians to work in German factories under conditions of virtual slave labor. Although this practice was stopped in February 1917, by then nearly a thousand Belgian workers had died in German labor camps.

The most influential feature of Germany's war economy was the Kriegsrohstoffabteilung (KRA), or war raw materials office, established under the authority of the War Ministry to provide the materials essential to the war effort. Led initially by the able Jewish industrialist Walther Rathenau (1867–1922), this agency came to symbolize the unprecedented coordination of the German economy for war. Recognizing as early as the fall of 1914 that Germany lacked the raw materials for a long war, Rathenau devised an imaginative program that included the development of synthetic substitute products and the creation of new mixed (private and government) companies to allocate raw materials. The KRA's effort was remarkably successful—a model for later economic planning and coordination.

Although Germany presented the most dramatic example of domestic coordination, the same pattern was evident everywhere, even in France, with its economic individualism and distrust of an

Domestic Mobilization and the Role of Women

Early in 1917, the British writer Gilbert Stone published a remarkable collection of statements intended to illuminate the new experiences that British women were encountering in the workplace. The following passage by Naomi Loughnan, a well-to-do woman who worked in a munitions factory, makes it clear that the new work experience during the war opened the way to new questions about both gender and class.

Engineering mankind is possessed of the unshakable opinion that no woman can have the mechanical sense. If one of us asks humbly why such and such an alteration is not made to prevent this or that drawback to a machine, she is told, with a superior smile, that a man has worked her machine before her for years, and that therefore if there were any improvement possible it would have been made. As long as we do exactly as we are told and do not attempt to use our brains, we give entire satisfaction, and are treated as nice, good children. Any swerving from the easy path prepared for us by our males arouses the most scathing contempt in their manly bosoms. . . . Women have, however, proved that their entry into the munitions world has increased the output. Employers who forget things personal in their patriotic desire for large results are enthusiastic over the success of women in the shops. But their workmen have to be handled with the utmost tenderness and caution lest they should actually imagine it was being suggested that women could do their work equally well, given equal conditions of training—at least where muscle is not the driving force. This undercurrent of jealousy rises to the surface rather often, but as a general rule the men behave with much kindness, and are ready to help with muscle and ad-

vice whenever called upon. If eyes are very bright and hair inclined to curl, the muscle and advice do not even wait for a call.

The coming of the mixed classes of women into the factory is slowly but surely having an educative effect upon the men. "Language" is almost unconsciously becoming subdued. There are fiery exceptions who make our hair stand up on end under our close-fitting caps, but a sharp rebuke or a look of horror will often bring to book the most truculent. . . . It is grievous to hear the girls also swearing and using disgusting language. Shoulder to shoulder with the children of the slums, the upper classes are having their eyes pried open at last to the awful conditions among which their sisters have dwelt. Foul language, immorality, and many other evils are but the natural outcome of overcrowding and bitter poverty. If some of us, still blind and ignorant of our responsibilities, shrink horrified and repelled from the rougher set, the compliment is returned with open derision and ribald laughter. . . . On the other hand, attempts at friendliness from the more understanding are treated with the utmost suspicion, though once that suspicion is overcome and friendship is established, it is unshakable.

Source: Naomi Loughnan, "Munition Work," in Gilbert Stone, ed., *Women War Workers: Accounts Contributed by Representative Workers of the Work Done by Women in the More Important Branches of War Employment* (New York: Thomas Y. Crowell, [1917]), pp. 35–38.

interventionist state. In Britain, the central figure proved to be David Lloyd George (1863–1945), appointed to the newly created post of minister of munitions in 1915. During his year in that office, ninety-five new factories opened, soon overcoming the shortage of guns and ammunition that had

impeded the British war effort until then. In fact, types of ammunition that had formerly taken a year to manufacture were now being produced in weeks, even days. His performance as munitions minister made Lloyd George seem the one person who could organize Britain for victory. Succeeding

Herbert Asquith as prime minister in December 1916, he would direct the British war effort to its victorious conclusion.

Accelerating Socioeconomic Change

Everywhere the war effort quickened the long-term socioeconomic change associated with industrialization. Guaranteed government orders for war materiel fueled industrial expansion. In France, the Paris region now became a center of heavy industrial production for the first time. The needs of war spawned new technologies—advances in food processing and medical treatment, for example—that would carry over into peacetime.

With so many men needed for military service, women were called on to assume new economic roles—running farms in France, for example, or working in the new munitions factories in Britain. (See the box, "Domestic Mobilization and the Role of Women.") During the course of the war, the number of women employed in Britain rose from 3.25 million to 5 million. In Italy, 200,000 women had war-related jobs by 1917. Women also played indispensable roles at the front, especially in nursing units.

The expanded opportunities of wartime intensified the debate over the sociopolitical role of women that the movement for women's suffrage had stimulated. The outbreak of war led some antiwar feminists to argue that women would be better able than men to prevent wars, which were essentially masculine undertakings. Women should have full access to public life, not because they could be expected to respond as men did but because they had a distinctive—and valuable—role to play. At the same time, by giving women jobs and the opportunity to do many of the same things men had done, the war undermined the stereotypes that had long justified restrictions on women's political roles and life choices.

For many women, doing a difficult job well, serving their country in this emergency situation, afforded a new sense of accomplishment, as well as a new taste of independence. Freed from male domination, women were now much more likely to have their own residences, to go out in public on their own, eating in restaurants, even smoking and drinking. Yet while many seized new opportunities and learned new skills, women frequently had to combine paid employment with housework and child rearing, and those who left home—to serve in nursing units, for example—often felt guilty about neglecting traditional family roles.

Propaganda and the "Mobilization of Enthusiasm"

Because the domestic front was crucial to sustaining a long war of attrition, it became ever more important to shore up civilian morale as the war dragged on. The result was the "mobilization of enthusiasm"—the conscious manipulation of collective passions by national governments on

Mobilizing Women Responding to appeals like this, women quickly become prominent in the munitions industry in Britain as elsewhere. The chance to perform valued public roles during the wartime emergency proved a watershed for many women. *(Trustees of the Imperial War Museum)*

an unprecedented scale. Everywhere there was extensive censorship, even of soldiers' letters from the front. Because of concerns about civilian morale, the French press carried no news of the Battle of Verdun, with the horrifying number of casualties it involved. In addition, systematic propaganda included not only patriotic themes but also attempts to discredit the enemy, even through outright falsification of the news. British anti-German propaganda helped draw the United States into the war in 1917.

At the outset of the war, the brutal behavior of the German armies in Belgium made it easy for the French and the British to discredit the Germans. Having expected to pass through neutral Belgium unopposed, the Germans were infuriated by the Belgian resistance they encountered. At Louvain late in August 1914 they responded to alleged Belgian sniping by shooting a number of hostages and setting the town on fire, destroying the famous old library at the university. This noto-

rious episode led the London *Times* to characterize the Germans as "Huns," a reference to the Mongolian tribe that began invading Europe in the fourth century. Stories about German soldiers eating Belgian babies began to circulate.

In October 1914 ninety-three important German intellectuals, artists, and scientists signed a manifesto, addressed to "the World of Culture," justifying Germany's conduct in Belgium and larger purposes in the war. To a point, such gestures stemmed from expected forms of patriotism, but as passions heated up, major intellectuals on both sides—from the German theologian Adolf von Harnack (1851–1930) to the French philosopher Henri Bergson (1859–1941)—began denigrating the culture of the enemy and claiming a monopoly of virtue for their own side.

This unprecedented propaganda combined with the unexpected destruction and loss of life to give the war an increasingly catastrophic aura. This was no mere adjustment in the traditional

Devastation at Louvain Unexpected destruction at the outset of the war fanned the flames of hatred and changed the stakes of the conflict. Located in the path of the first German advance, the Belgian city of Louvain was particularly hard hit. *(Trustees of the Imperial War Museum)*

balance of power; so great were the strains of war, in fact, that the sense of common involvement in a single civilization, or a single European state system based on an accepted set of rules, began to weaken. Some came to believe that real peace with an adversary so evil, so different, was simply not possible. Thus, there must be no compromise, but rather total victory, no matter what the cost.

At the same time, however, war-weariness produced a countervailing tendency to seek a "white peace," a peace without victory for either side. Both sets of impulses were at work as Europeans began debating war aims in earnest in 1917, at a time when dramatic events were changing the war's meaning for contemporaries. The most significant was the Russian Revolution, which developed from wartime difficulties and which then fundamentally affected the nature of the war.

TWO REVOLUTIONS IN RUSSIA: MARCH AND NOVEMBER 1917

Strained by war, the old European order finally cracked in Russia in 1917. Revolution against the tsarist autocracy seemed first to lay the foundations for parliamentary democracy. But by the end of the year, the Bolsheviks, the smallest and most extreme of Russia's major socialist parties, had taken power, an outcome that was hardly conceivable when the revolution began.

The Wartime Crisis of the Russian Autocracy

The Russian army performed better than many had expected during the first year of the war, and as late as June 1916, it was strong enough for a successful offensive against Austria-Hungary. Russia had industrialized sufficiently by 1914 to sustain a modern war, at least for a while, and the country's war production increased significantly by 1916. But Russia suffered from problems of leadership and organization—in transportation, for example—that made it less prepared for a long war than the other belligerents. Even early in 1915, perhaps a fourth of Russia's newly conscripted troops were sent to the front without weapons, instructed to pick up rifles and supplies from the dead.

As problems mounted, Tsar Nicholas II (1868–1918) assumed personal command of the army in August 1915, but his absence from the capital only accelerated the deterioration in government and deepened the bitter divisions within the ruling clique. With the tsar away, the illiterate but charismatic Siberian monk Grigori Rasputin (c. 1872–1916) emerged as the key political power within the circle of the German-born Empress Alexandra (1872–1918). He won her confidence because of his alleged ability to control the bleeding of her hemophiliac son, Alexis, the heir to the throne. Led by Rasputin, those around the empress made a shambles of the state administration. Many educated Russians, appalled at what was happening, assumed—incorrectly—that pro-German elements at court were responsible for the eclipse of the tsar and the resulting government chaos. Asked one Duma deputy of the government's performance, "Is this stupidity, or is it treason?"

Finally, late in December 1916, Rasputin was assassinated by aristocrats seeking to save the autocracy from these apparently pro-German influences. This act indicated how desperate the situation was becoming, but it made no decisive difference.

By the end of 1916, the immediate difficulties of war had combined with the strains of rapid wartime industrialization to produce a revolutionary situation in Russia. The country's urban population had increased rapidly, and now, partly because of transport problems, the cities faced severe food shortages. Strikes and demonstrations spread from Petrograd (the former St. Petersburg) to other cities during the first two months of 1917. In March renewed demonstrations in Petrograd, spearheaded by women protesting the lack of bread and coal, led to revolution.

The March Revolution and the Fate of the Provisional Government

At first, the agitation that began in Petrograd on March 8, 1917, appeared to be just another bread riot. Even when it turned into a wave of strikes, the revolutionary parties expected it to be crushed by the government troops stationed at the Petrograd garrison. But when called out to help the police break up the demonstrations, the soldiers generally avoided firing at the strikers. Within days, they were sharing weapons and ammunition with the workers; the garrison was going over to what was now becoming a revolution.

Late in the afternoon of March 12, leaders of the strike committees, delegates elected by factory workers, and representatives of the socialist parties formed a soviet, or council, following the example of the revolution of 1905, when such soviets had first appeared. Regiments of the Petrograd garrison also began electing representatives, soon to be admitted to the Petrograd Soviet, which officially became the Council of Workers' and Soldiers' Deputies. This soviet was now the ruling power in the Russian capital. It had been elected and was genuinely representative—though of a limited constituency of workers and soldiers. Following the lead of Petrograd, Russians elsewhere promptly began forming soviets, so that over 350 local units were represented when the first All-Russian Council of Soviets met in Petrograd in April. The overwhelming majority of their representatives were Mensheviks and Socialist Revolutionaries; only about one-sixth were Bolsheviks.

On March 14 a committee of the Duma, recognizing that the tsar's authority had been lost for good, persuaded Nicholas to abdicate, then formed a new provisional government. Particularly because it derived from the Duma elected in 1907, under extremely limited suffrage, this government was supposed to be temporary, to pave the way for an elected constituent assembly, which would establish fully legitimate governmental institutions.

Considering the strains in the autocratic system that had produced the revolution of 1905 after the Russo-Japanese War, it was hardly surprising that the system would shatter now, in light of this far more trying war and the resulting disarray within the tsarist government. Russia had apparently experienced, at last, the bourgeois political revolution necessary to develop a Western-style parliamentary democracy. Even from an orthodox Marxist perspective, this was the revolution to expect, and Marxists could only help consolidate bourgeois democracy. The longer-term pursuit of socialism could take place within that new political framework. These, however, were anything but orthodox times, and the March revolution proved only the beginning.

Although the fall of the tsarist order produced widespread relief, Russia's new leaders faced difficult questions about priorities. Many, both inside and outside Russia, believed that the revolution's immediate purpose was to revitalize the Russian war effort. Yet war-weariness was widespread,

and there were pressures to get on with domestic political change. Moreover, the provisional government had to operate with the potentially more radical Petrograd Soviet, the keystone of the network of soviets across the country, looking over its shoulder.

At first the Petrograd Soviet was perfectly willing to give the provisional government a chance to govern. In this bourgeois revolution, it was not up to socialists and workers to take responsibility by participating directly in government, though they could offer support, especially against any attempt at counterrevolution. Even among the Bolsheviks, there was widespread support for conciliation and at least short-term acceptance of the new government. Although the Bolshevik leader, Vladimir Lenin, took a different tack, he was in exile in Switzerland and could not yet make his will prevail.

Given its chance by the Petrograd Soviet, the provisional government took important steps toward Western-style liberal democracy, establishing universal suffrage, civil liberties, autonomy for ethnic minorities, and labor legislation, including provision for an eight-hour workday. But the government failed in two key areas, fostering discontents that the Bolsheviks soon exploited. First, the new government persisted in fighting the war. Second, it dragged its feet on agrarian reform.

The provisional government's determination to renew the war effort stemmed from genuine concern about Russia's obligations to its allies, about the country's national honor and position among the great powers. Moreover, the long-standing goal of Russian diplomacy—an outlet to the Mediterranean Sea through the Dardanelles Strait—seemed within reach if a revitalized Russia could continue the war, contributing to an Allied victory. The educated, well-to-do Russians who led the new government expected that ordinary citizens, now free, would fight with renewed enthusiasm, like the armies that had grown from the French Revolution over a century before. These leaders failed to grasp how desperate the situation of ordinary people had become.

The March revolution grew from unrest in the cities, but in the aftermath the peasantry moved into action as well, seizing land, sometimes burning the houses of their landlords. By midsummer, a full-scale peasant war seemed to be in the offing in the countryside, and calls for radical agrarian

Lenin as Leader Although he was in exile during much of 1917, Lenin's leadership was crucial to the Bolshevik success in Russia. He is shown here addressing a May Day rally in Red Square, Moscow, on May 1, 1919. *(ITAR-TASS/Sovfoto)*

reform became increasingly insistent. Partly from expediency, partly from genuine concern for social justice, the provisional government promised a major redistribution of land, but it insisted that the reform be carried out legally—not by the present provisional government, but by a duly elected constituent assembly.

Calling for elections would thus seem to have been the first priority. The new political leaders kept putting it off, however, waiting for the situation to cool before giving up power to a newly elected assembly. But the situation did not allow the luxury of playing for time. As unrest grew in the countryside, the authority of the provisional government diminished and the soviets gained in stature. But what role were the soviets to play?

The Bolsheviks Come to Power

In the immediate aftermath of the March revolution, the Bolsheviks had not seemed to differ substantially from their rivals within the socialist movement, at least on matters of most immediate

concern—the war, land reform, and the character of the revolution itself. But the situation began to change in April when Lenin returned from exile in Switzerland, thanks partly to the help with transportation that the German military provided. The Germans assumed—correctly, it turned out—that the Bolsheviks would help undermine the Russian war effort. Largely through the force of Lenin's leadership, the Bolsheviks soon assumed the initiative.

Lenin (1870–1924), born Vladimir Ilich Ulianov, came from a comfortable upper-middle-class family and was university-educated and trained as a lawyer. But after an older brother was executed in 1887 for participating in a plot against the tsar's life, Lenin followed him into revolutionary activity. He was arrested for the first time in 1895, then exiled to Siberia. After his release in 1900, he made his way to western Europe, and there he remained, except for a brief return to Russia during the revolution of 1905, until the renewal of revolution in 1917.

The Bolshevik party was identified with Lenin from its beginning in 1903, when it emerged from the schism in Russian Marxist socialism. Because of his emphases, Bolshevism came to mean discipline, organization, and a special leadership role for a revolutionary vanguard. Lenin proved effective because he was a stern and somewhat forbidding figure, disciplined, fiercely intelligent, sometimes ruthless. As a Bolshevik colleague put it, Lenin was "the one indisputable leader . . . a man of iron will, inexhaustible energy, combining a fanatical faith in the movement, in the cause, with an equal faith in himself."[5]

Still, when Lenin began taking the initiative in 1917, his reading of the situation astonished even many Bolsheviks. He held that the revolution was about to pass from the present bourgeois-democratic stage to a socialist phase, involving dictatorship of the proletariat in the form of government by the soviets. It was time, then, for active opposition to the provisional government, and this meant both criticism of the war, as fundamentally imperialist, and calls for the distribution of land from the large estates to the peasants. This latter measure had long been identified with the Socialist Revolutionaries; most Bolsheviks had envisioned collectivization and nationalization instead.

But what Lenin envisioned was anything but "socialism in one country," with embattled, relatively backward Russia trying to create a socialist order on its own. Rather, a Bolshevik-led revolution in Russia would provide the spark to ignite the proletarian revolution smoldering elsewhere in Europe, especially in Germany. Although some remained skeptical, Lenin's strategic vision promptly won acceptance among most of his fellow Bolsheviks.

In April 1917 moderate socialists still had majority support in the soviets, so the Bolsheviks sought to build gradually, postponing any decisive test of strength. But events escaped the control of the Bolshevik leadership in mid-July when impatient workers, largely Bolshevik in sympathy, took to the streets of Petrograd on their own. The Petrograd Soviet refused to support the uprising, and the provisional government had no difficulty getting military units to put it down, killing two hundred in the process. Though the uprising had developed spontaneously, Bolshevik leaders felt compelled to offer public support, and this gave the government an excuse to crack down on the Bolshevik leadership in the aftermath. Lenin managed to escape to Finland as a number of his colleagues suffered arrest and imprisonment.

With the Bolsheviks on the defensive, counterrevolutionary elements in the Russian military decided to seize the initiative with a march on Petrograd in September. In resisting this attempted coup, the provisional government, now under the young, charismatic Socialist Revolutionary Alexander Kerensky (1881–1970), had to rely on whomever could offer help, including the Bolsheviks. Bolshevik propaganda led the soldiers under the command of the counterrevolutionaries to refuse to fight against the upholders of the revolution in Petrograd. Within days, the Bolsheviks won their first clear-cut majority in the Petrograd Soviet, then shortly gained majorities in most of the other soviets as well.

During the fall of 1917, the situation became increasingly volatile, eluding control by anyone. People looted food from shops; peasants seized land, sometimes murdering their landlords. Desertions and the murder of officers increased within the Russian military.

With the Bolsheviks at last the dominant power in the soviets, and with the government's control diminishing, Lenin, from his hideout in Finland, began urging the Bolshevik central committee to prepare for armed insurrection. Although some found this step unnecessarily risky, the majority accepted Lenin's argument that the provisional government would continue dragging its feet, inadvertently giving right-wing officer leagues time for another counterrevolutionary coup.

Because Lenin himself remained in hiding, the task of organizing the seizure of power fell to Leon Trotsky (1870–1940), who skillfully modified Lenin's aggressive strategy. Lenin wanted the Bolsheviks to rise in their own name, in opposition to the provisional government, but Trotsky linked the insurrection to the cause of the soviets and played up its defensive character, against the ongoing danger of a counterrevolutionary coup. With the political center at an impasse, the only alternative to such a coup seemed to be a Bolshevik initiative to preserve the Petrograd Soviet, by now the sole viable institutional embodiment of the revolution and its promise. Trotsky's interpretation led people who wanted simply to defend the Soviet to support the Bolsheviks' initiative.

During the night of November 9, armed Bolsheviks and regular army regiments occupied key points in Petrograd, including railroad stations, post offices, telephone exchanges, power stations, and the national bank. Able to muster only token resistance, the provisional government collapsed. Kerensky escaped by morning and mounted what quickly proved a futile effort to rally troops at the front for a counterattack against the Bolsheviks. In contrast to the March revolution, which had taken about a week, the Bolsheviks took over the capital, overthrowing the Kerensky government, literally overnight, and almost without bloodshed. A wave of popular euphoria followed. But though the Bolsheviks had taken Petrograd, they would need three more years and a civil war to extend their control across the whole Russian Empire. (See the box, "The Bolsheviks in Power, November 1917.")

However, the revolution's immediate prospects, and the wider impact it might have, were bound up with the course of the war. Would the Bolshevik Revolution in Russia prove the spark for revolution elsewhere in war-weary Europe, as Lenin anticipated? If not, could a Bolshevik regime survive in Russia on its own?

The Russian Revolution and the War

Having stood for peace throughout the revolution, the Bolsheviks promptly moved to get Russia out of the war, agreeing to an armistice with Germany in December 1917. They hoped that Russia's withdrawal would speed the collapse of the war effort on all sides and that this, in turn, would intensify the movement toward revolution elsewhere in Europe. The Russian Revolution, they believed, was but a chapter in a larger story, proceeding from war to wider revolution. As Lenin noted to Trotsky, "If it were necessary for us to go under to assure the success of the German revolution, we should have to do it. The German revolution is vastly more important than ours." Indeed, said Lenin to the Communist party congress of March 1918, "It is an absolute truth that we will go under without the German revolution."[6]

Still, the Bolsheviks did not have to wait passively for events elsewhere to unfold. They could help spark wider revolution by demonstrating the imperialist basis of the war. After assuming control in November, they published the tsarist government's secret documents concerning the war— the treaties and understandings specifying how the spoils were to be divided in the event of victory. In doing so, the Bolsheviks hoped to show ordinary people elsewhere that this had been, all along, a war on behalf of capitalist interests. This Bolshevik initiative added fuel to the controversy already developing in all the belligerent countries over the war's purpose and significance.

THE NEW WAR AND THE ENTENTE VICTORY, 1917–1918

Because the stakes of the war changed during 1917, the outcome, once the war finally ended in November 1918, included consequences that Europeans could not have foreseen in 1914. Thus German defeat brought revolution against the monarchy and the beginning of a new democracy. Thus grandiose new visions competed to shape the postwar world.

The Debate over War Aims

The French and British governments publicly welcomed the March revolution in Russia, partly because they expected Russia's military performance to improve under new leadership, but also because the change of regime seemed to have highly favorable psychological implications. With Russia no longer an autocracy, the war could be portrayed—and experienced—as a crusade for democracy. At the same time, the March revolution could only sow confusion among the many Germans who had understood their own war effort as a matter of self-defense against reactionary Russia. But the November revolution required a deeper reconsideration for all the belligerents.

Entente war aims agreements, like the secret Treaty of London that brought Italy into the war in 1915, had remained secret until the Bolsheviks published the tsarist documents. Products of old-style diplomacy, those agreements had been made by a restricted foreign policy elite within the governing circles of each country; not only the general public but also the elected parliaments were generally not aware of what they contained. The debate over war aims that developed in 1917 thus became a debate over decision making as well, stimulating calls for greater popular involvement, which seemed sure to diminish the possibility of such wars in the future. In addition, there were exhortations for all the parties in the present war to renounce annexations and settle for a white peace.

The Bolsheviks in Power, November 1917

John Reed (1887–1920), an American journalist and communist leader from Portland, Oregon, was in Russia during the fall of 1917, when the second revolution began. His enthusiastic first-hand account, which drew the praise of Lenin himself, conveys the drama and excitement of the revolution. In the following passage, Reed provides a sense of the combination of emergency, improvisation, and revolutionary enthusiasm that marked the Bolsheviks' first days in power.

Having settled the question of power, the Bolsheviki turned their attention to problems of practical administration. First of all the city, the country, the Army must be fed. Bands of sailors and Red Guards scoured the warehouses, the railway terminals, even the barges in the canals, unearthing and confiscating thousands of *poods* [a *pood* is thirty-six pounds] of food held by private speculators. Emissaries were sent to the provinces, where with the assistance of the Land Committees they seized the storehouses of the great grain dealers. Expeditions of sailors, heavily armed, were sent out in groups of five thousand to the South, to Siberia, with roving commissions to capture cities still held by the White Guards, establish order and *get food* [italics in the original]. . . .

Towards the end of November occurred the "wine-pogrom"—looting of the wine cellars—beginning with the plundering of the Winter Palace vaults. For days there were drunken soldiers on the streets. In all this was evident the hand of the counterrevolutionists, who distributed among the regiments plans showing the location of the stores of liquor. The Commissars of Smolny began by pleading and arguing, which did not stop the growing disorder, followed by pitched battles between soldiers and Red Guards. Finally the Military Revolutionary Committee sent out companies of sailors with machine-guns, who fired mercilessly upon the rioters, killing many; and by executive order the wine cellars were invaded by Committees with hatchets, who smashed the bottles—or blew them up with dynamite.

. . . In all quarters of the city small elective Revolutionary Tribunals were set up by the workers and soldiers to deal with petty crime. . . .

Alert and suspicious, the working class of the city constituted itself a vast spy system, through the servants prying into bourgeois households, and reporting all information to the Military Revolutionary Committee, which struck with an iron hand, unceasing. In this way was discovered the Monarchist plot led by a former Duma-member Purishkevich and a group of nobles and officers, who had planned an officers' uprising. . . .

Still the strike of the Ministries went on, still the sabotage of the old officials, the stoppage of normal economic life. Behind Smolny was only the will of the vast, unorganized popular masses; and with them the Council of People's Commissars dealt, directing revolutionary mass action against its enemies. In eloquent proclamations, couched in simple words and spread over Russia, Lenin explained the Revolution, urged the people to take the power into their own hands, by force to break down the resistance of the propertied classes, by force to take over the institutions of Government. Revolutionary order. Revolutionary discipline! Strict accounting and control! No strikes! No loafing!

Source: John Reed, *Ten Days That Shook the World* (London: Penguin, 1977), pp. 244–246.

It was time to call the whole thing off and bring the soldiers home.

Seeking to counter such sentiments, especially the Russian contention that the war was not worth continuing, the idealistic U.S. president, Woodrow Wilson (1856–1924), insisted on the great potential significance of an Allied victory. First in his State of the Union speech of January 1918, and in several declarations thereafter, Wilson developed the "Fourteen Points" that he proposed should guide the new international order. (See the box, "A Meaning to the War: Wilson's Fourteen Points.") Notable among them were open diplomacy, free trade, reduced armaments, self-determination, a league of nations, and a recasting of the colonial system, recognizing that the indigenous populations had rights equal to those of the colonizers.

Lenin and Wilson, then, offered radically different interpretations of the war, with radically different implications for present priorities. Yet they had something in common compared to the old diplomacy. Together, they seemed to represent a whole new approach to international relations—and the possibility of a more peaceful world. Thus, they found an eager audience among the war-weary peoples of Europe.

Despite the unforeseen strains of the war, Sacred Union in France did not weaken substantially until April 1917, with General Nivelle's disastrous offensive. But then, as near-mutiny began to develop within the army, rank-and-file pressures forced Socialist leaders to demand clarification, then revision, of French war aims. Suddenly French government leaders found themselves under considerable pressure to endorse the notion that the war had idealistic and democratic purposes. Growing doubts about the government's goals threatened to turn into active opposition to the war.

The same pressures were at work in Germany, where antiwar sentiment grew within the Social Democratic party (SPD), finally leading the antiwar faction to split off and form the Independent Socialist party (USPD) in April 1917. A large-scale debate on war aims, linked to considerations of domestic political reform, developed in the Reichstag by the summer of 1917, culminating in the Reichstag war aims resolution of July 19. Affirming that Germany's purposes were solely defensive, the measure passed by a solid 60 percent majority. Germany too seemed open to a white peace.

But just as the dramatic events of 1917 interjected important new pressures for moderation and peace, pressures in the opposite direction also mounted as the war dragged on. The old European order seemed to have changed irrevocably; this war might prove only the beginning of a new era of intense international competition, in which the old rules would no longer apply. War aims grew more grandiose as it began to seem that this

WORLD WAR I AND ITS AFTERMATH

August 1914	Fighting begins
September 1914	French forces hold off the German assault at the Marne
August–September 1914	German victories over the Russians in the Battles of Tannenberg and Masurian Lakes
May 1915	Italy declares war on Austria-Hungary
February–December 1916	Battle of Verdun
May 1916	Naval Battle of Jutland
July–November 1916	Battle of the Somme
January 1917	Germans resume unrestricted submarine warfare
March 1917	First Russian revolution: fall of the tsar
April 1917	U.S. declaration of war
July 1917	German Reichstag war-aims resolution
November 1917	Second Russian revolution: the Bolsheviks take power
March 1918	Treaty of Brest-Litovsk between Germany and Russia
March–July 1918	Germany's last western offensive
July 1918	Second Battle of the Marne
July–November 1918	French-led counter-offensive
November 1918	Armistice: fighting ends
January 1919	Peace congress convenes at Paris
June 1919	Victors impose Treaty of Versailles on Germany

war offered a precious opportunity to secure advantages for the more contentious world that would follow, and that would surely entail further war before long.

A Meaning to the War: Wilson's Fourteen Points

After the United States entered the war in April 1917, President Woodrow Wilson sought to play down conventional national interests and to emphasize wider, more idealistic purposes. His key statement proved to be his 1918 State of the Union address, during which he offered his famous Fourteen Points.

It will be our wish and purpose that the processes of peace, when they are begun, shall be absolutely open and that they shall involve and permit henceforth no secret understandings of any kind. The day of conquest and aggrandizement is gone by; so is also the day of secret covenants entered into in the interest of particular governments and likely at some unlooked-for moment to upset the peace of the world. . . .

. . . What we demand in this war, therefore, is nothing peculiar to ourselves. It is that the world be made fit and safe to live in; and particularly that it be made safe for every peace-loving nation which, like our own, wishes to live its own life, determine its own institutions, be assured of justice and fair dealing by the other peoples of the world as against force and selfish aggression. All the peoples of the world are in effect partners in this interest; and for our own part we see very clearly that unless justice be done to others it will not be done to us. The program of the world's peace, therefore, is our program; and that program, the only possible program, as we see it, is this:

I. Open covenants of peace, openly arrived at, after which there shall be no private international understandings of any kind but diplomacy shall proceed always frankly and in public view. . . .

IV. Adequate guarantees given and taken that national armaments will be reduced to the lowest point consistent with domestic safety.

V. A free, open-minded, and absolutely impartial adjustment of all colonial claims, based upon a strict observance of the principle that in determining all such questions of sovereignty the interests of the populations concerned must have equal weight with the equitable claims of the government whose title is to be determined. . . .

XII. The Turkish portions of the present Ottoman Empire should be assured a secure sovereignty, but the other nationalities which are now under Turkish rule should be assured an undoubted security of life and an absolutely unmolested opportunity of autonomous development. . . .

XIII. An independent Polish state should be erected which should include the territories inhabited by indisputably Polish populations, which should be assured a free and secure access to the sea, and whose political and economic independence and territorial integrity should be guaranteed by international covenant.

XIV. A general association of nations must be formed under specific covenants for the purpose of affording mutual guarantees of political independence and territorial integrity to great and small states alike. . . .

Source: The Public Papers of Woodrow Wilson, V. War and Peace: Presidential Messages, Addresses, and Public Papers (1917–1924) (New York: Harper & Brothers, 1927; New York: Kraus Reprint, 1970), vol. 1, pp. 158–161.

The shape of the present war convinced top German officials that Germany's geography and dependence on imports made it especially vulnerable in a long war. The purpose of the war for Germany increasingly seemed the conquest of the means to fight the next war on a more favorable footing. Responding in February 1918 to calls for a white peace, General Ludendorff stressed that "if Germany makes peace without profit, it has lost the war." Germany, insisted Ludendorff, must win the military and economic basis for future security—to "enable us to contemplate confidently some future defensive war."[7]

Many in German government circles felt that Germany had to win control of the Belgian coast to achieve the parity with Britain necessary for peace. German security seemed to require a more favorable situation in eastern Europe as well, including control over Russian Poland and over Lithuania and Courland (western Latvia) on the Baltic Sea.

When, in response to the Russian request for an armistice, Germany was able to establish the terms of peace with Russia, it became clear how radically annexationist Germany's war aims had become. The outcome of negotiations at Brest-Litovsk early in 1918 was a dictated peace that Russia finally had no choice but to accept. Germany was to annex 27 percent of Russia's European territory, including the agriculturally valuable Ukraine, 40 percent of its population, and 75 percent of its iron and coal. All the German Reichstag parties, except the Socialists, accepted the terms of the treaty, which, in fact, produced a new wave of enthusiasm for a victorious peace after the disillusionment that had led to the Reichstag war aims resolution of July 1917.

France, less vulnerable geographically than Germany, tended to be more modest. But news of the terms the Germans had imposed at Brest-Litovsk inflamed the French, supporting the notion that France must push on to definitive victory in order to secure substantial advantages against an ongoing German menace.

The Renewal of the French War Effort

The domestic division in France that followed the failure of Nivelle's offensive reached its peak during the fall of 1917. In November, with pressures for a white peace intensifying and France's ability to continue fighting in doubt, President Raymond Poincaré called on Georges Clemenceau (1841–1929) to lead a new government. The 76-year-old Clemenceau was already known as a "hawk"; his appointment portended a stepped-up prosecution of the war, using whatever measures were necessary to achieve a decisive victory. And his message was simple as he appeared before the Chamber of Deputies on November 20, 1917: "If you ask me about my war aims, I reply: my aim is to be victorious." For the remainder of the war, France was under the virtual dictatorship of Clemenceau and his cabinet.

Clemenceau moved decisively on both the domestic and military levels. By cracking down on the antiwar movement—imprisoning antiwar leaders, suppressing defeatist newspapers—he produced an undeniable stiffening of morale. Choosing a new commander of all Allied forces in the west, Clemenceau bypassed Pétain and picked General Ferdinand Foch (1851–1929). From Clemenceau's perspective, Pétain was too passive, even defeatist. After some initial friction, Clemenceau let Foch have his way on the military level, and the two proved an effective leadership combination.

The German Gamble, 1918

As the campaign of 1918 began, Germany seemed in a relatively favorable military position: Russia had been knocked out at last, and American troops were yet to arrive. Moderates in Germany wanted to take advantage of the situation to work out a compromise peace while there was still a chance. But the military leadership persuaded Emperor William II that Germany could still win a definitive victory on the western front if it struck quickly, before U.S. help became significant. Germany would be out of reserves by summer, so the alternative to decisive victory in the west would be total German defeat.

The German gamble almost succeeded. From March to June 1918, German forces seized the initiative with four months of sustained and effective attacks. By May 30 they had again reached the Marne, where they had been held in 1914, and again Paris, only 37 miles away, had to be evacuated (see Map 25.2). Even as late as mid-July, Ludendorff remained confident of victory, but by mid-August it was becoming clear that Germany lacked the manpower to exploit the successes of the first several months of 1918.

Those successes had caused mutual suspicion between the French and the British at first, but under Foch's leadership the Western allies eventually managed fuller and more effective coordination. By mid-1918 American involvement was also becoming a factor. On June 4, over a year after the U.S. declaration of war, American troops went into action for the first time, bolstering French forces along the Marne. Even this was a small operation, in which the Americans' performance was amateurish when compared to that of their battle-seasoned allies. But as the Allied counterattack proceeded, 250,000 U.S. troops were arriving per month, considerably boosting Allied morale and battlefield strength.

Germany lost the initiative for good during the second Battle of the Marne, which began on July 15 with yet another German attack. Foch commenced a sustained counterattack on July 18, using tanks to good advantage, and never lost the initiative thereafter. By early August the whole western front began to roll back. With astonishing suddenness, the outcome was no longer in doubt, although most expected the war to drag on into 1919. Few realized how desperate Germany's situation had become.

Military Defeat and Political Change in Germany

By late September it was clear to Ludendorff that his armies could not stop the Allied advance, so he informed the government on September 29 that to avoid invasion, Germany had to seek an immediate armistice. Hoping to secure favorable peace terms and to make the parliamentary politicians take responsibility for the defeat, Hindenburg and Ludendorff asked that a government based on greater popular support be formed. A leading moderate, Prince Max von Baden (1867–1929), became chancellor, and the Reichstag again became significant after its eclipse during the virtual dictatorship of the military. Prince Max promptly replaced Ludendorff with General Wilhelm Groener (1867–1939), who seemed more democratic in orientation. By now it was clear that ending the war could not be separated from the push for political change in Germany.

After securing a written request for an armistice from Hindenburg, Prince Max sent a peace note to President Wilson early in October, asking for an armistice based on Wilson's Fourteen Points. During the month that followed, Prince Max engineered a series of measures, passed by the Reichstag and approved by the emperor, that reformed the constitution, abolishing the three-class voting system in Prussia and making the chancellor responsible to the Reichstag. At last Germany had a constitutional monarchy. But President Wilson encouraged speculation that Germany could expect better peace terms if William II

were to abdicate and Germany were to become a republic. If the emperor, and even the monarchy itself, could not survive, was Germany to become a parliamentary democracy on the Western model, or was there to be more radical change, perhaps inspired by the Russian example?

A radical outcome seemed a real possibility during late 1918 and early 1919. As negotiations for an armistice proceeded in October, the continuing war effort produced instances of mutiny in the navy and breaches of discipline in the army. By early November workers' and soldiers' councils were being formed all over the country, just as in Russia the year before. In Munich, on November 7, antiwar socialists led an uprising of workers and soldiers that expelled the king of Bavaria and proclaimed a new Bavarian republic, which sought its own peace negotiations with the Allies. In Berlin on November 9, thousands of workers took to the streets to demand immediate peace, and the authorities could not muster enough reliable military force to move against them.

The senior army leadership grew concerned that the collapse of governmental authority would undermine the ability of army officers even to march their troops home. So Hindenburg and Groener persuaded the emperor to abdicate. Having lost the support of the army, William II accepted the inevitable and left for exile in the Netherlands.

With the German right, including the military, in disarray, and with even the centrist parties discredited by their support for what had become an annexationist war, the initiative passed to the socialists. They, at least, had been in the forefront of the movement for peace. But the socialists had divided in 1917, mostly over the question of response to the war. To many leftist socialists, the fact that the reformist mainstream of the SPD had supported the war for so long had discredited the party irrevocably. The most militant of these leftist socialists, led by Karl Liebknecht (1871–1919) and Rosa Luxemburg (1870–1919), envisioned using the workers' and soldiers' councils as the basis for a full-scale revolution, more or less on the Bolshevik model.

The SPD, on the other hand, clung to its reformist heritage and insisted on working within parliamentary institutions. A Bolshevik-style revolution was neither appropriate nor necessary under the circumstances Germany faced. Partly to head off the extreme left, SPD moderates proclaimed a parliamentary republic on November 9, just hours before the revolutionaries proclaimed a soviet-style republic. The next day the soldiers' and workers' councils in Berlin elected a provisional executive committee, to be led by the moderate socialist Friedrich Ebert (1871–1925). As the new republic sought to consolidate itself, the radical leftists continued to promote further revolution. So the end of the war meant for Germany a leap into an unfamiliar democratic republic, which had to establish itself in conditions not only of military defeat and economic hardship but also of incipient revolution on the extreme left.

Birth from military defeat was especially disabling for this new republic because the German people were so little prepared for the defeat when it came. The vigorous censorship had kept the public from any grasp of Germany's real situation as the war sped to conclusion. Thus the request for an armistice early in October came as a shock. At no time during the war had Germany been invaded from the west, and by mid-1918 the German army had seemed on the brink of victory. It appeared inconceivable that Germany had lost a military decision, plain and simple. Thus the "stab in the back" myth, the notion that political intrigue and revolution at home had undermined the German military effort, developed to explain what otherwise seemed an inexplicable defeat. This notion would prove a heavy burden for Germany's new democracy to bear.

THE OUTCOME AND THE IMPACT

After the armistice officially ended the fighting on November 11, 1918, those responsible for a formal peace settlement faced unprecedented challenges. The war's casualties included the Habsburg and Ottoman Empires, as well as the Hohenzollern and Romanov dynasties, so the peacemakers had to deal not just with defeated adversaries but with a changed political and territorial order in much of Europe and beyond. And the volatile sociopolitical situation in the wake of war and revolution inevitably colored their deliberations.

To make peace was to restore order, though necessarily on a new basis. But the disintegration of the old order had produced a sense of vulnerability hard to overcome. The number of casualties,

the advent of terrifying new weapons, the destruction of famous monuments—all gave the war an apocalyptic aura that heightened its psychological impact. After all that had happened since August 1914, it was not clear what a restoration of peace and order would require.

The Costs of War

Raw casualty figures do not begin to convey the war's human toll, but they afford some sense of the magnitude of the catastrophe that had befallen Europe and much of the world. Estimates differ, but it is generally agreed that from 10 to 13 million military men lost their lives, with another 20 million wounded. In addition, between 7 and 10 million civilians died as a result of the war and its hardships. In the defeated countries, especially, food shortages and the resulting malnutrition continued well after the end of the fighting. Adding to the devastation in 1918 was a pandemic of influenza that killed 20 million people worldwide.

Germany suffered the highest number of military casualties, but France suffered the most in proportional terms. Two million Germans were killed, with another 4 million wounded. Military deaths per capita for France were roughly 15 percent higher than for Germany—and twice as severe as for Britain. Of 8 million Frenchmen mobilized, over 5 million were killed or wounded. Roughly 1.5 million French soldiers, or 10 percent of the active male population, were killed—and this in a country already concerned about demographic decline. The other belligerents suffered less, but still in great numbers. Among the military personnel killed were 2 million Russians, 500,000 Italians, and 114,000 Americans.

Especially in light of all the assumptions about European superiority and progress, this unprecedented bloodletting deeply affected the European self-image. It was the worst loss of life Europe had suffered since the Black Death of the fourteenth century. Although World War II would be far more destructive, its psychological impact was in some ways less, for the illusions had been shattered by World War I. (See the feature, "Weighing the Evidence: The Poetry of World War I," on pages 954–955.)

Economic costs were heavy as well. In addition to the privations suffered during the years of war, Europeans found themselves reeling from inflation and saddled with debt, especially to the United States, once the war was over. Although the immediate transition to a peacetime economy did not prove as difficult as many had feared, the war and its aftermath produced an economic disequilibrium that lingered, helping to produce a worldwide depression by the end of the 1920s.

The Search for Peace in a Revolutionary Era

The war had begun because of an unmanageable nationality problem in Austria-Hungary, and it led not simply to military defeat for Austria-Hungary but to the breakup of the Habsburg system. Thus, in east-central Europe, the end of the war brought bright hopes for self-determination to peoples like the Czechs, Slovaks, Poles, Serbs, and Croats. Even before the peacemakers began deliberating in January 1919, some of these ethnic groups had begun creating a new order on their own. For example, a popular movement of Czechs and Slovaks established a Czechoslovak republic on October 29, 1918, and a new Yugoslavia and an independent Hungary similarly emerged from indigenous movements. Some of these new nations were amalgams of different ethnic groups that found cooperation advantageous now, but that might disagree in the future. Moreover, many of these countries lacked traditions of self-government, and they had reason to feud among themselves. With the Habsburg system no longer imposing one form of stability, a power vacuum seemed likely in this potentially volatile part of Europe.

The triumph of a revolutionary regime in Russia immeasurably complicated the situation, because in the unsettled conditions of the former Habsburg territories, as in Germany, the revolution seemed poised to spread in the wake of defeat—precisely according to the script the Russian revolutionaries were reading to the world. Still a precarious minority within Russia in 1918, the Bolsheviks continued to bank on immediate revolution elsewhere in Europe until 1920. Shortly after taking power, they had rechristened themselves "Communists," partly to jettison the provincial Russian term *bolshevik,* but especially to underline their departure from the old reformist socialists of the Second International. Communism meant revolution along Russian

lines. The Russian Communists influenced revolutionaries elsewhere both by force of example and by actively seeking to spread the revolution.

Outside Russia, the greatest communist success in the wake of the war was in Hungary, where a communist regime under Béla Kun (1885–1937) governed Budapest and other parts of the country from March to August 1919, before it was put down by Allied-sponsored forces from Romania. At about the same time, separatist communist republics lasted for months in the Slovak part of Czechoslovakia and in the important German state of Bavaria. Even in Italy, which had shared in the victory, Socialists infatuated with the Bolshevik example claimed that the labor unrest of 1919–1920 was the beginning of full-scale revolution.

Fears that the Russian Revolution might spread fueled foreign intervention in Russia beginning in June 1918, when 24,000 French and British troops entered the country. As long as the war with Germany lasted, military concerns helped justify this course, but after the armistice of November 1918, the intervention became overtly anticommunist. A series of thrusts, involving troops from fourteen countries at one time or another, struck at Russia from diverse points on its huge border. That effort aided the counterrevolutionary Whites, especially members of the old elites dispossessed by the Bolsheviks, who challenged the communist control of the Russian Empire in what became a brutal civil war during 1918–1920. There was never a coordinated strategy between the Whites and the foreign troops, but foreign intervention was intended to help topple the new regime and undercut its effort to export revolution.

The fourth of the major prewar regimes to disappear with defeat was the Turkish Ottoman Empire, which had controlled much of the Middle East in 1914. The Arab revolt against the Turks that developed in the Arabian peninsula in 1916 did not achieve its major military aims, though it endured, causing some disruption to the Turkish war effort. Its success was due partly to the collaboration of a young British officer, T. E. Lawrence (1888–1935), who proved an effective military leader and an impassioned advocate of the Arab cause. The support that Britain, especially, had offered the Arabs suggested that independence, perhaps even a single Arab kingdom, might follow from a defeat of the Ottoman Empire.

But British policy toward the Arabs was uncertain and contradictory. Concerned about the Suez Canal, the British government sought to tighten its control in Egypt by declaring it a protectorate in 1914, causing increased anti-British sentiment. The secret Sykes-Picot Agreement of May 1916, named for the British and French diplomats who negotiated it, projected a division of the Ottoman territories of the Middle East into colonial spheres of influence. France would control Syria and Lebanon, while Britain would rule Palestine and Mesopotamia, or present-day Iraq.

Potentially complicating the situation in the region was Zionism, the movement to win a Jewish state in Palestine. Led by Chaim Weizmann (1874–1952), a remarkable Russian-born British chemist, the Zionists reached an important milestone when British foreign secretary Arthur Balfour (1848–1930) cautiously announced, in the Balfour Declaration of November 1917, that the British government "looked with favor" on the prospect of a "Jewish home" in Palestine. At this point, British leaders sympathetic to Zionism saw no conflict in embracing the cause of the Arabs against the Ottoman Turks at the same time; indeed, Arabs and Jews, each seeking self-determination, could be expected to collaborate.

In the heat of war, the British, especially, established their policy for the former Ottoman territories of the Middle East without careful study. Thus, they made promises and agreements that were not entirely compatible. After the war, the victors' effort to install a new order in the Middle East would create fresh conflicts.

The Peace Settlement

The peace conference took place in Paris, beginning in January 1919. Its labors led to five separate treaties, with each of the five defeated states, known collectively as the Paris peace settlement. The first and most significant was the Treaty of Versailles with Germany, signed in the Hall of Mirrors of the Versailles Palace on June 28, 1919. But treaties were also worked out, in turn, with Austria, Bulgaria, Hungary, and finally Turkey, in August 1920.

This was to be a dictated, not a negotiated, peace. Germany and its allies were excluded, as was renegade Russia. The passions unleashed by the long war had dissolved the possibility of a

more conciliatory outcome, a genuinely negotiated peace. Having won the war, France, Britain, the United States, and Italy were to call the shots on their own, with the future of Europe and much of the world in the balance. However, spokesmen for many groups—from Slovaks and Croats to Arabs, Jews, and pan-Africanists—were in Paris as well, seeking a hearing for their respective causes. For example, both the Arab Prince Faisal (1885–1933), who would later become king of Iraq, and Colonel T. E. Lawrence were there to plead for an independent Arab kingdom. (See the box, "Encounters with the West: Prince Faisal at the Peace Conference.") The African American leader W. E. B. DuBois (1898–1963), who took his Ph.D. at Harvard in 1895, led a major pan-African congress in Paris concurrently with the peace conference.

The fundamental challenge for the peacemakers was to reconcile the conflicting visions of the postwar world that had emerged by the end of the war. U.S. President Wilson represented the promise of a new order that could give this terrible war a lasting meaning. As he toured parts of Europe en route to the peace conference, Wilson was greeted as a hero. Clemenceau, in contrast, was a hard-liner concerned with French security and dismissive of the new diplomacy. Since becoming prime minister in 1917, he had stressed that only a permanent preponderance of French military power over Germany, and not some utopian league of nations, could guarantee a lasting peace. The negotiations at Paris centered on this fundamental difference between Wilson and Clemenceau. Although Britain's Lloyd George took a hard line on certain issues, he also sought to mediate, helping engineer the somewhat awkward compromise that resulted. When, after the peace conference, he encountered criticism for the outcome, Lloyd George replied, "I think I did as well as might be expected, seated as I was between Jesus Christ and Napoleon Bonaparte."[8]

In Article 231 of the final treaty, the peacemakers sought to establish a moral basis for their treatment of Germany by assigning responsibility for the war to Germany and its allies. On this basis, the Germans would be made to pay reparations to reimburse the victors for the costs of the war. The determination to make Germany pay for what had become a fabulously expensive war was one of the factors militating against a compromise peace by 1917. Thus the peacemakers found it essential to fix a reparations responsibility, although the amount

~ **ENCOUNTERS WITH THE WEST** ~

Prince Faisal at the Peace Conference

With the war nearing its end in October 1918, British authorities, in line with provisions of the Sykes-Picot agreement, permitted Faisal ibn-Husayn (1885–1933) to set up a provisional Arab state, with its capital at Damascus. As head of a delegation from this area to the Paris Peace Conference, Faisal claimed to speak for all Arab Asia, but some in the Arabian peninsula challenged his claim. In the memorandum of January 1919 that follows, he outlined the Arab position, mixing pride and assertiveness with a recognition that the Arabs would continue to need the support and help of Western powers. After the peace was concluded, Faisal found himself caught up in British and French rivalries as he was installed as king first of Syria, then of Iraq, but his efforts were central to the eventual achievement of Arab independence in the Middle East.

We believe that our ideal of Arab unity in Asia is justified beyond need of argument. If argument is required, we would point to the general principles accepted by the Allies when the United States joined them, to our splendid past, to the tenacity with which our race has for 600 years resisted Turkish attempts to absorb us, and, in a lesser degree, to what we tried our best to do in this war as one of the Allies. . . .

The various provinces of Arab Asia—Syria, Irak, Jezireh, Hedjaz, Nejd, Yemen—are very different economically and socially, and it is impossible to constrain them into one frame of government.

We believe that Syria, an agricultural and industrial area thickly peopled with sedentary classes, is sufficiently advanced politically to manage her own internal affairs. We feel also that foreign technical advice and help will be a most valuable factor in our national growth. We are willing to pay for this help in cash; we cannot sacrifice for it any part of the freedom we have just won for ourselves by force of arms.

. . . The world wishes to exploit Mesopotamia rapidly, and we therefore believe that the system of government there will have to be buttressed by the men and material resources of a great foreign Power. We ask, however, that the Government be Arab, in principle and spirit, the selective rather than the elective

principle being necessarily followed in the neglected districts, until time makes the broader basis possible. . . .

In Palestine the enormous majority of the people are Arabs. The Jews are very close to the Arabs in blood, and there is no conflict of character between the two races. In principles we are absolutely at one. Nevertheless, the Arabs cannot risk assuming the responsibility of holding level the scales in the clash of races and religions that have, in this one province, so often involved the world in difficulties. They would wish for the effective super-position of a great trustee, so long as a representative local administration commended itself by actively promoting the material prosperity of the country. . . .

In our opinion, if our independence be conceded and our local competence established, the natural influences of race, language, and interest will soon draw us together into one people; but for this the Great Powers will have to ensure us open internal frontiers, common railways and telegraphs, and uniform systems of education. To achieve this they must lay aside the thought of individual profits, and of their old jealousies. In a word, we ask you not to force your whole civilisation upon us, but to help us to pick out what serves us from your experience. In return we can offer you little but gratitude.

Source: J. C. Hurewitz, *Diplomacy in the Near and Middle East: A Documentary Record: 1914–1956* (Princeton, N.J.: D. Van Nostrand, 1956), vol. 2, pp. 38–39.

An Arab in Paris Prince Faisal (foreground) attended the Paris Peace Conference, where he lobbied for the creation of an independent Arab kingdom from part of the former Ottoman Turkish holdings in the Middle East. Among his supporters was the British Officer T. E. Lawrence (middle row, second from the right), on his way to legend as "Lawrence of Arabia." *(Trustees of the Imperial War Museum)*

that Germany was to pay was not established until 1921.

In addition, Germany was forced to dismantle much of its military apparatus. For example, the army was to be limited to 100,000 men, all of whom would be volunteers. The treaty severely restricted the size of the German navy as well, and Germany was forbidden to manufacture or possess military aircraft, submarines, tanks, heavy artillery, or poison gas.

France took back Alsace and Lorraine, the provinces it had lost to Germany in 1871 (Map 25.3). But for France, the crucial security provision of the 1919 peace settlement was the treatment of the adjacent Rhineland section of Germany itself. For fifteen years Allied troops were to occupy the west bank of the Rhine River in Germany—the usual military occupation of a defeated adversary. But this would only be temporary. The long-term advantage for France was to be the permanent demilitarization of all German territory west of the Rhine and a strip of 50 kilometers along its east bank. Germany was to maintain no troops on this part of its own soil, so in the event of hostilities French forces could march unopposed into this economically vital area of Germany.

French interests also helped shape the settlement in east-central Europe. Wilsonian principles called for self-determination, but in this area of great ethnic complexity, ethnic differences were not readily sorted out geographically. Was it best to countenance proliferation and fragmentation of ethnic groups, or to foster consolidation in an effort to build larger states, which might have a better chance of maintaining their independence and succeeding economically?

Worrying little about the problematic principle of self-determination, the French approached the situation in east-central Europe in terms of their own strategic concerns. So that Germany would again face potential enemies from both east and west, the French envisioned building a network of allies starting with the new Poland, created from Polish territories formerly in the German, Russian, and Austro-Hungarian Empires. That network might come to include Czechoslovakia, Yugoslavia, and Romania as well. These states would be weak enough to remain under French influence but, taken together, strong enough to replace Russia as a force against Germany. Yet to maximize the strength of these countries often required combining more than one nationality grouping within

Boundaries of German, Russian, and Austro-Hungarian empires in 1914

Areas lost by Austro-Hungarian Empire

Areas lost by Russian Empire

Areas lost by German Empire

Areas lost by Bulgaria

Areas lost by Ottoman Empire

Demilitarized Zones

Boundaries of 1926

Areas controlled under mandates from the League of Nations, 1920

North Sea

NORWAY

Oslo

SWEDEN

Helsinki

Stockholm

FINLAND

Baltic Sea

Tallinn

ESTONIA

Leningrad (St. Petersburg)

GREAT BRITAIN

DENMARK

Copenhagen

Riga LATVIA

Memel

Volga

NETHERLANDS

Amsterdam

GERMANY

Berlin

Danzig

POLISH CORRIDOR

EAST PRUSSIA

LITHUANIA

Vilnius

RUSSIAN EMPIRE

(Became Union of Soviet Socialist Republics, 1922)

Ural

Brussels

BELGIUM

RUHR

Cologne

Weimar

Frankfurt

Elbe

Oder

Vistula

POLAND

Warsaw

Paris

LUX.

FRANCE

Rhine

Strasbourg

Prague

CZECHOSLOVAKIA

GALICIA

Kiev

Don

Dnieper

LORRAINE

ALSACE

Geneva

Seine

Loire

Bern

SWITZ.

Locarno

Milan

Rhône

S. TYROL

Vienna

AUSTRIA

Budapest

HUNGARY

BESSARABIA

Caspian Sea

Genoa

Po

Venice

Trieste

Rapallo

Zagreb

CROATIA

Belgrade

ROMANIA

Bucharest

Danube

Black Sea

ITALY

Corsica

Rome

YUGOSLAVIA

SERBIA

MONTENEGRO

(To Yugoslavia 1921)

BULGARIA

Sofia

Batum

Kars

Baku

Sardinia

Naples

ALBANIA

Istanbul

(Constantinople)

Ankara

TURKEY

Tabriz

PERSIA (IRAN)

GREECE

Izmir

(Smyrna)

Athens

Sicily

Crete

Annexed by Turkey 1939

Aleppo

SYRIA

(French Mandate)

Tigris

Euphrates

Baghdad

PERSIA (IRAN)

TUNISIA

(French)

Mediterranean Sea

Cyprus

(Gr. Br.)

Beirut

Damascus

IRAQ

(MESOPOTAMIA)

(British Mandate)

Kut el Amara

PALESTINE

(British Mandate)

Jerusalem

Amman

TRANSJORDAN

(British Mandate)

Basra

KUWAIT

(Gr. Br.)

NEUTRAL ZONES

Suez Canal

Cairo

LIBYA

(Italian)

EGYPT

(Independent 1922)

Nile

Red Sea

NEJD

(SAUDI ARABIA)

Riyadh

Medina

0   200   400 Km.

0   200   400 Mi.

The Victors and the Peace In June 1919 the leaders of the major victorious powers exude confidence after signing with Germany the Treaty of Versailles, the most important of the five treaties that resulted from the Paris Peace Conference. From the left are David Lloyd George of Britain, Georges Clemenceau of France, and Woodrow Wilson of the United States. *(Corbis-Bettmann)*

them; some of those national groups were more numerous and advantaged than others.

The new Czechoslovakia was not only an amalgam of Czechs and Slovaks but also included numerous Germans and Magyars. Indeed, Germans, mostly from the old Bohemia, made up 22 percent of the population of Czechoslovakia. Yugoslavia was even more complex, encompassing not only Serbs and Croats, but also Slovenes, Macedonians, Albanians, and other minorities.

Map 25.3 The Impact of the War: The Territorial Settlement in Europe and the Middle East The defeat of Russia, Austria-Hungary, Germany, and Ottoman Turkey opened the way to major changes in the map of east-central Europe and the Middle East. A number of new nations emerged in east-central Europe, while in the Arab world the end of Ottoman rule meant not independence but new roles for European powers.

But French policymakers were so determined to foster a strong Czechoslovakia and Yugoslavia that they ordered the French police to force the spokesmen for Slovak and Croat separatism to leave Paris as the conference deliberated.

Partly as a result of French priorities, Poland, Czechoslovakia, Yugoslavia, and Romania ended up as large as possible, either by the fusion of ethnic groups or by the incorporation of minorities that, on ethnic grounds, belonged with neighboring states. Austria, Hungary, and Bulgaria, on the other hand, found themselves diminished (Map 25.4). What remained of Austria, the German part of the old Habsburg empire, was prohibited from choosing to join Germany, an obvious violation of the Wilsonian principle of self-determination.

Concern to contain and weaken communist Russia was also at work in the settlement in east-central Europe. A band of states in east-central

Map 25.4 Ethnicity in East-Central Europe, 1919
Ethnic diversity made it hard to create homogeneous nation-states in east-central Europe. The new states that emerged after World War I mixed ethnic groups, and ethnic tensions would contribute to future problems.

Europe, led by France, could serve not only as a check to Germany but also as a shield against the Russian threat. Romania's aggrandizement came partly at the expense of the Russian Empire, as did the creation of the new Poland. Finland, Latvia, Estonia, and Lithuania, all part of the Russian Empire for over a century, now became independent states (see Map 25.3).

The overall territorial settlement cost Germany almost 15 percent of its prewar territory, including major iron- and coal-producing regions, as well as about 10 percent of its prewar population. But the great bitterness that developed in

Germany over the terms of the peace stemmed above all from a sense of betrayal. In requesting an armistice, German authorities had appealed to Wilson, whose emphasis had not been on war guilt and reparations. He seemed to be saying that the whole prewar international system, not one side or the other, had been to blame for the current conflict. In 1919, however, the peacemakers treated Germany as the guilty party, so for Germans the terms of the peace greatly intensified the sting of defeat.

Wilson had been forced to compromise with French interests in dealing with east-central Europe, but he achieved a potentially significant success in exchange—the establishment of a League of Nations, embodying the widespread hope for a new international order. According to the League covenant worked out by April, disputes among member states were no longer to be settled by war but by mechanisms established by the League. Other members were to participate in sanctions, from economic blockade to military action, against a member that went to war in violation of League provisions.

How could Wilsonian hopes for a new international order be squared with the imperialist system, which seemed utterly at odds with the ideal of self-determination? As Mohammed Ali Duse had anticipated in 1914, the war had sown the seeds of dramatic change in those areas of the world subject to European colonial rule. Elites among the colonial peoples tended to support the war efforts of their imperial rulers, but often in the hope of winning greater autonomy or even independence. The Indian leader Mohandas Gandhi (1869–1948), who had been educated in the West and admitted to the English bar in 1889, actively supported the British war effort, even helping recruit Indians to fight on the British side. But his aim was to speed Indian independence, and he led demonstrations that embarrassed the British during the war. (See the box, "Encounters with the West: Gandhi on Nonviolence," on page 1001.) And though most educated Indians, after over a century of British rule and Western influence, rallied to the British side, the war unleashed expectations and demands that led the British, in 1917, to promise home rule for India.

Colonial peoples participated directly in the war on both sides. In sub-Saharan Africa, for example, German-led Africans fought—and fought well—against Africans under British or French command. France brought colonial subjects from West and North Africa into front-line service during the war. But this experience expanded political consciousness—and raised expectations—among the peoples subject to European imperialism.

Duse's *African Times and Orient Review* found reason for optimism in March 1917: "[A] Franco-British success will mean a greater freedom of the peoples we represent than they have previously experienced. The once despised black man is coming to the front in the battle for freedom, and the freedom which he helps to win for the white man, must also be meted out to him when the day of reckoning arrives. In helping the British Empire and the French Republic in the hour of need you are helping yourselves to a freedom that cannot be denied to you."[9] The same line of thinking led China and Siam (now Thailand) to associate with the Allied side in 1917, in an effort to win international stature and thereby eventually to regain their lost sovereignty. China sent 200,000 people to work in France to help ease France's wartime labor shortage.

At the peace conference, spokesmen for the non-Western world tended to be moderate in their demands. Even DuBois, who was often more radical, called simply for colonial peoples to be given a voice in colonial governments. And the victors, prodded by Wilson, made some concessions.

German colonies and Ottoman territories were not simply taken over by the victors, in the old-fashioned way, but fell under the authority of the League, which then assigned them as mandates to one of the victorious powers, which was to report back to the League annually. There were various classes of mandates, based on how prepared for sovereignty the area was taken to be. In devising this system, the Western powers formally recognized for the first time that non-Western peoples under Western influence had rights and interests of their own and that, in principle, they were progressing toward independence.

Still, the mandate approach to the colonial question was a halting departure at best. Although Britain granted considerable sovereignty to Iraq in 1932, the victorious powers generally operated as before, assimilating the new territories into their existing systems of colonial possessions. After the hopes raised in the Arab world during the war, this outcome produced a sense of betrayal among Arab leaders, who had expected complete independence. Continuing Arab unrest provoked, most notably, a revolt against the French presence in Syria, put down only at heavy expense to the French during the mid-1920s.

The Chinese felt similarly betrayed. Despite China's contribution to the Allied war effort, the victors acquiesced in special rights for Japan in China, causing a renewed sense of humiliation among Chinese elites and provoking a wave of popular demonstrations and a boycott of Japanese goods. In this instance, Western leaders were allowing a non-Western power, Japan, access to the imperial club, but they were hardly departing from imperialism. For Chinese, Arabs, and others, the West appeared hypocritical. Those whose political consciousness had been raised by the war came to believe not only that colonialism should end, but that the colonial peoples would themselves have to take the lead in ending it.

The incongruities of the postwar settlement prompted Marshal Foch to proclaim, "This is not peace. It is an armistice for twenty years."[10] The most basic question was whether the three principal victors had the resolve, and the capacity, to preserve the new order they had solidified at Paris. Debate over the American role promptly developed in the United States as President Wilson sought Senate ratification of the peace treaty, which entailed U.S. membership in the League of Nations as well as commitments to France and Britain. Wilson's opponents worried especially that League membership would compromise U.S. sovereignty. Although it was not clear, at this point, how significant the departure from the old international system was to be, other nations proved more willing to ratify the treaty and join the League. U.S. reluctance stemmed especially from the isolationist backlash that developed as Americans increasingly questioned whether the United States had been wise to become involved, for the first time, in a war in Europe. Late in 1919, at the height of the debate, Wilson suffered a disabling stroke. The Senate then refused to ratify the peace treaty, thereby keeping the United States out of the League of Nations. By 1920 the United States seemed to be pulling back from the leadership role it had been poised to play in 1918.

American hesitation stemmed partly from the doubts about the wisdom of the peace settlement that quickly developed in both Britain and the United States. During the peace conference, a member of the British delegation, the economist

Beckmann: The Night In this painting from 1918–1919, the German expressionist Max Beckmann (1884–1950) drew on medieval art and a complex personal symbolism to convey the violence, insecurity, and hardship that surrounded Germany's defeat in 1918. *(Kunstsammlung Nordrhein-Westfalen)*

John Maynard Keynes (1883–1946), resigned to write *The Economic Consequences of the Peace* (1920), which helped undermine confidence in the whole settlement. Keynes charged that the shortsighted, vindictive policy of the French, by crippling Germany with a punishing reparations burden, threatened the European economy and thus the peace of Europe over the long term. For some, then, the challenge was not to enforce the Versailles treaty but to revise it. This lack of consensus about the legitimacy of the peace made it especially hard to predict what the longer-term outcome of the war would be.

SUMMARY

By destroying the Habsburg empire and the imperial regime in Germany, World War I seemed to have solved the immediate problems that caused it. More generally, the war accelerated processes, involving everything from technological development to women's suffrage, that many deemed progressive.

Yet the war also produced new tensions and revealed possibilities that seemed considerably less benign. Despite all the hopes for a peaceful new order, the novel forms of warfare introduced during World War I portended a dangerous and even terrifying new era. A generation later, to be sure, the advent of the nuclear age occasioned a measure of terror hardly imaginable earlier, but the experience of World War I was the turning point, the end of an earlier innocence. Thanks to modern technology, which had been central to the West's confident belief in progress, Europeans had now experienced machine-gun fire, poison gas attacks, and the terror-bombing of civilians from airplanes.

The war touched virtually everyone, but it marked for life those who knew the nightmarish experience of the trenches. At first, traditional notions of glory, heroism, and patriotic duty combined with images of fellowship and regeneration to enable the soldiers to make a certain sense of their wartime experience. But as the war dragged on, such sentiments gradually eroded, giving way to resignation and cynicism. (See the feature, "Weighing the Evidence: The Poetry of World War I," on pages 954–955.)

After the war was over, many of those who had fought it felt a sense of ironic betrayal; their prewar upbringing, the values and assumptions they had inherited, had not equipped them to make sense of what they had lived through. But the quest for meaning continued, and beginning in the late 1920s a wave of writings about the war appeared. Many were memoirs, such as *Goodbye to All That* by the English writer Robert Graves (1895–1985) and *Testament of Youth* by Vera Brittain (1893–1970), who had served as a British army nurse at the front. The most famous exploration of the war was the antiwar novel *All Quiet on the Western Front* (1929) by German writer Erich Maria Remarque (1898–1970), which sold 2.5 million copies in twenty-five languages in its first eighteen months in print.

Although Remarque had seen front-line action, his novel said more about the growing feeling of disillusionment after the war than it did about the actual experience of those in the trenches. By the end of the 1920s an element of myth-making was creeping into these efforts to give meaning to the war experience. Still, there was something undeniably genuine in the laments of loss of innocence, in the sense of belonging to a "lost generation," that marked much of this writing. Not only were many friends dead or maimed for life, but all the sacrifices seemed to have been largely in vain, a sentiment that fueled determination to avoid another war in the future.

What followed from the war, most fundamentally, was a new sense that Western civilization was neither as secure nor as superior as it had seemed. The celebrated French poet Paul Valéry (1871–1945), speaking at Oxford shortly after the war, observed that "we modern civilizations have learned to recognize that we are mortal like the others. We had heard . . . of whole worlds vanished, of empires foundered. . . . Elam, Nineveh, Babylon were

vague and splendid names; the total ruin of these worlds, for us, meant as little as did their existence. But France, England, Russia . . . these names, too, are splendid. . . . And now we see that the abyss of history is deep enough to bury all the world. We feel that a civilization is as fragile as a life."[11] Valéry went on to warn that the coming transition to peace would be even more difficult and disorienting than the war itself. So traumatic might be the convulsion that Europe might lose its leadership and be shown up for what it was in fact—a pathetically small corner of the world, a mere cape on the Asiatic landmass. Astounding words for a European, yet even Valéry, for all his foresight, could not anticipate what Europe would go through in the decades to follow.

NOTES

1. From *African Times and Orient Review,* August 4, 1914; quoted in Imanuel Geiss, *The Pan-African Movement,* translated by Ann Keep (London: Methuen & Co., 1974), pp. 229–230.

2. Thus wrote the German poet Ivan Goll in 1917; quoted in Modris Eksteins, *Rites of Spring: The Great War and the Birth of the Modern Age* (Boston: Houghton Mifflin, 1989), p. 144.

3. The remarks of Raymond Joubert, as quoted in John Ellis, *Eye-Deep in Hell: Trench Warfare in World War I* (Baltimore: Johns Hopkins University Press, 1989), p. 104.

4. Brian Bond, *War and Society in Europe, 1870–1970* (New York: Oxford University Press, 1986), p. 114.

5. By A. N. Potresov, as quoted in Richard Pipes, *The Russian Revolution* (New York: Random House, Vintage, 1991), p. 348.

6. Both statements are quoted in Koppel S. Pinson, *Modern Germany: Its History and Civilization,* 2d ed. (New York: Macmillan, 1966), p. 337.

7. Quoted in Arno J. Mayer, *Political Origins of the New Diplomacy, 1917–18* (New York: Random House, Vintage, 1970), p. 135.

8. Quoted in Walter Arnstein, *Britain Yesterday and Today: 1830 to the Present,* 6th ed. (Lexington, Mass.: D. C. Heath, 1992), p. 266.

9. Unsigned editorial, *African Times and Orient Review,* March 1917; quoted in Geiss, *The Pan-African Movement,* p. 479, n. 2.

10. Quoted in P. M. H. Bell, *The Origins of the Second World War* (London and New York: Longman, 1986), p. 14.

11. Paul Valéry, *Variety,* 1st series (New York: Harcourt, Brace, 1938), pp. 3–4.

SUGGESTED READING

General Surveys

Ferro, Marc. *The Great War, 1914–1918*. 1973. Combines a narrative of events with a feel for the war experience, based on the expectations and perceptions of those involved.

King, Jere Clemens, ed. *The First World War*. 1972. A superior documentary history, with selections on an array of topics, from military operations to trench life, from diplomacy and peacemaking to the role of women in the war.

Robbins, Keith. *The First World War*. 1985. An accessible, balanced, and comprehensive treatment, covering everything from military operations to the domestic impact of the war.

Winter, J. M. *The Experience of World War I*. 1989. An ideal introductory work that proceeds via concentric circles from politicians to generals to soldiers to civilians, then to the war's longer-term effects.

Fighting the War

Ellis, John. *Eye-Deep in Hell: Trench Warfare in World War I*. 1989. A compelling account of life and death in the trenches, covering topics from trench construction to eating, drinking, and sex. Includes striking photographs.

Hough, Richard. *The Great War at Sea, 1914–1918*. 1983. A survey of naval operations, featuring the British navy. Includes photographs.

Kennett, Lee. *The First Air War, 1914–1918*. 1991. A vivid account of the new flying machines, those who flew them, and their diverse wartime roles, from reconnaissance to combat.

Leed, Eric J. *No Man's Land: Combat and Identity in World War I*. 1979. A pioneering study of the experience of World War I, exploring its challenge to masculine identity.

War and Society

Becker, Jean-Jacques. *The Great War and the French People*. 1985. Landmark study of the relationship between battlefield fortunes and wider public responses as France bore the brunt of the fighting during World War I.

Bond, Brian. *War and Society in Europe, 1870–1970*. 1986. Lucid, well-balanced survey of the relationship between war and society, with particular attention to the two world wars.

Brayborn, Gail, and Penny Summerfield. *Out of the Cage: Women's Experiences in Two World Wars*. 1987. Comparative study of the impact of the two world wars on women, relying especially on direct testimony. Considers not only the workplace but also everyday experience, from home life and health to courtship and marriage.

Higonnet, Margaret Randolph, et al., eds. *Behind the Lines: Gender and the Two World Wars*. 1987. Varied essays on the role of women during the two world wars, concerned especially with the impact of war on gender definition.

Horne, John N. *Labour at War: France and Britain, 1914–1918*. 1991. A sophisticated study exploring the impact of wartime challenges on the evolution of the organized labor movement, with a useful comparative dimension.

Kocka, Jürgen. *Facing Total War: German Society, 1914–1918*. 1984. Using concepts of class and monopoly capitalism in a flexible way, a leading German historian analyzes the impact of the war on German society.

Marwick, Arthur. *The Deluge: British Society and the First World War*. 1970. A lively account by a leading British social historian, conveying what it was like to live in Britain during the war and tracing the enduring impact of wartime social changes.

Winter, Jay, and Jean-Louis Robert, eds. *Capital Cities at War: Paris, London, and Berlin, 1914–1919*. 1997. Assessing the war's impact on the lives of ordinary city dwellers, this collection of scholarly essays ranges from purchasing power to food supply to public health. Concludes with an effective synthesis by the editors.

The Russian Revolution

Fitzpatrick, Sheila. *The Russian Revolution, 1917–1932*, 2d ed. 1994. An ideal introductory work that places the events of 1917 in the sweep of Russian history.

Pipes, Richard. *The Russian Revolution*. 1991. A detailed, comprehensive study, critical of the Bolshevik takeover as a mere coup, as opposed to a genuinely revolutionary transformation. Argues that a tendency toward terror followed from the nature of the revolution itself.

Service, Robert. *Lenin: A Political Life*, 3 vols. 1985, 1991, 1995. Landmark, readable biography that does justice both to Lenin's ruthlessness and to the visionary purpose that made him one of the decisive actors of the twentieth century. The third volume, covering the years from 1918 until Lenin's death in 1924, takes advantage of newly available Russian sources.

Ulam, Adam B. *The Bolsheviks: The Intellectual, Personal and Political History of the Triumph of Communism in Russia*. 1968. Well-known study focusing on Lenin and his central role in shaping the strategy that brought the Bolsheviks to power.

Von Laue, Theodore H. *Why Lenin? Why Stalin? Why Gorbachev? The Rise and Fall of the Soviet System*, 3d ed. 1993. A widely used survey. Accents the larger context of international preoccupations and power relations that helped shape the revolution and the system that developed from it.

War Aims, Diplomacy, and Peacemaking

Fromkin, David. *A Peace to End All Peace: The Fall of the Ottoman Empire and the Creation of the Modern Middle East.* 1989. Detailed but gripping account of the role of the war and the peace process in transforming the lands of the Ottoman Empire.

Mayer, Arno J. *The Politics and Diplomacy of Peacemaking: Containment and Counterrevolution at Versailles, 1918–1919.* 1967. Emphasizes the impact of domestic political concerns and fears of spreading revolution on thinking about the end of the war and the aims of the peace.

———. *Political Origins of the New Diplomacy, 1917–18.* 1970; first pub. 1959. Influential account of the war-aims debate; analyzes the competing efforts of Wilson and Lenin to redefine the meaning of the war.

Nicolson, Harold. *Peacemaking 1919.* 1965. A classic account, critical of the treaty, by a junior member of the British delegation.

Rowland, Peter. *David Lloyd George: A Biography.* 1975. Lively, balanced—one of the best one-volume treatments of Lloyd George, including his role as a wartime leader and a major architect of the peace.

Sharp, Alan. *The Versailles Settlement: Peacemaking in Paris, 1919.* 1991. A brief, clear, and balanced overview that seeks to do justice to the magnitude of the task the peacemakers faced.

Memory and Cultural Impact

Eksteins, Modris. *Rites of Spring: The Great War and the Birth of the Modern Age.* 1989. Original and provocative exploration of the relationship between culture and the war experience. Good on the difference between the actual experience of the war and the memory fabricated after the fact.

Ellis, John. *The Social History of the Machine Gun.* 1986. A pioneering exploration of the wider impact of the new technologies that came of age during World War I.

Fussell, Paul. *The Great War and Modern Memory.* 1975. Widely admired study of the attempts to forge the new language, through literature, necessary to make sense of the British war experience.

Hanna, Martha. *The Mobilization of Intellect: French Scholars and Writers During the Great War.* 1996. Challenges the widespread notion that World War I galvanized a unified assault of French intellectuals against German culture. Traces the ongoing divisions in the French intellectual community during the war.

Mosse, George L. *Fallen Soldiers: Reshaping the Memory of the World Wars.* 1990. Shows how the encounter with mass death in World War I led to new ways of sanctifying and justifying war.

Winter, J. R. *Sites of Memory, Sites of Mourning.* 1995. Using an effective comparative approach, a leading authority argues that Europeans relied on relatively traditional means of making sense of the bloodletting of World War I.

Wohl, Robert. *The Generation of 1914.* 1979. Probes the common features in the experience of educated young people in France, Britain, Germany, Italy, and Spain.

———. *A Passion for Wings: Aviation and the Western Imagination, 1908–1918.* 1994. Engaging, handsomely illustrated exploration of the cultural impact of flight in the context of the rapid technological change surrounding World War I.

THE POETRY OF WORLD WAR I

We don't normally think of poetry and war together, and World War I, with its unexpected brutality and hardship, may seem the least poetic of wars. Yet even during the war, soldiers like the Englishmen Rupert Brooke (1887–1915) and Wilfred Owen (1893–1918) sought to shape their experiences into poetic imagery. What does such poetry tell us about what the war meant to those who fought it? How has poetic testimony affected our understanding of the place of World War I in the Western experience?

In Brooke's wartime poetry what strikes us first is his gratitude that his generation had come of age at this dramatic historical moment:

Now, God be thanked Who has matched us with His hour,
  And caught our youth, and wakened us from sleeping

But why would a young man like Brooke welcome war? He seemed to envision release, deliverance— but from what?

ANTHEM FOR DOOMED YOUTH

What passing-bells for these who die as cattle?
  —Only the monstrous anger of the guns.
  Only the stuttering rifles' rapid rattle
Can patter out their hasty orisons.
No mockeries now for them; no prayers nor bells;
  Nor any voice of mourning save the choirs,—
The shrill, demented choirs of wailing shells;
  And bugles calling for them from sad shires.

What candles may be held to speed them all?
  Not in the hands of boys but in their eyes
Shall shine the holy glimmers of goodbyes.
  The pallor of girls' brows shall be their pall;
Their flowers the tenderness of patient minds,
And each slow dusk a drawing-down of blinds.

Wilfred Owen

When the war broke out, Brooke promptly volunteered, even pulling strings to get into a combat unit. Seeing action for the first time, in Belgium in October 1914, he was excited by the intensity of battle and pleased by his own calm self-control. Back in England for further training shortly thereafter, he wrote several sonnets, including "Peace," the one reproduced here, expressing his feelings about the war. But he died of blood poisoning on the way to battle in April 1915—without ever fully experiencing trench warfare.

Although most of the young Englishmen who took up arms with such enthusiasm in 1914 assumed that their country was in the right, that Germany was at fault, they did not worry much about the purposes of the war or the larger historical impact it might have. Brooke understood that the war would not accomplish all that was claimed for it, but he was grateful for the personal experience it made possible. Somehow it meant "peace," as the title of his sonnet suggests, and even cleanliness:

To turn, as swimmers into cleanness leaping,
Glad from a world grown old and cold and weary

Brooke's sense of deliverance responded to personal frustrations, yet he spoke for others of his generation who also were finding it difficult to assume a place in adult society at that particular time. Though they came from educated, upper-middle-class families, they were contemptuous of the routines and compromises of the respectable, everyday world to which they were expected to adjust. Thus Brooke welcomed the chance to

Leave the sick hearts that honour could not move,
And half-men, and their dirty songs and dreary

Yet those of Brooke's generation were equally troubled by their own uncertainty about values and commitments—to marriage, career, a place in society. Thanks to the overwhelming, inescapable reality of the war, values that had seemed empty— honor, country, duty, fellowship—now seemed

PEACE

Now, God be thanked Who has matched us with His hour,
  And caught our youth, and wakened us from sleeping,
With hand made sure, clear eye, and sharpened power,
  To turn, as swimmers into cleanness leaping,
Glad from a world grown old and cold and weary,
  Leave the sick hearts that honour could not move,
And half-men, and their dirty songs and dreary,
  And all the little emptiness of love!

Oh! we, who have known shame, we have found release there,
  Where there's no ill, no grief, but sleep has mending.
    Naught broken save this body, lost but breath;
Nothing to shake the laughing heart's long peace there
  But only agony, and that has ending;
    And the worst friend and enemy is but Death.

Rupert Brooke

Rupert Brooke (1887–1915)
(Mansell/ Time Inc.)

meaningful after all. To his surprise and relief, Brooke found that he himself was capable of courage, commitment, and sacrifice. With its promise of cleanliness and renewal, the war was worth even its highest price, which was merely death.

Unlike Brooke, Wilfred Owen hated the war from the start. He was quickly struck by its sheer ugliness, as manifested in the landscape, the noise, the language of the soldiers themselves. Yet he served with distinction, was decorated for bravery, and was killed by machine-gun fire just one week before the armistice in November 1918.

Owen, then, experienced the reality of World War I in a way that Brooke did not. The sonnet here, "Anthem for Doomed Youth," was written during September and October 1917, after the war had come to entail a terrible bloodletting. Thus Owen sought to shape sentiments very different from Brooke's—a sense of waste, of loss, of incongruity between suffering endured and results achieved. Whereas Brooke had brushed aside the possibility of death, Owen saw death as relentless, carrying off a generation of innocent youth, dying like cattle.

In a sense, even the dignity of death had become a casualty of the war. Thus Owen mixed funeral images with the new horror that this war had brought forth: The only mourning was "The shrill, demented choirs of wailing shells." Mock-

ing the ongoing effort to sweeten the reality of death at the front through reference to nobility and sacrifice, Owen drowned out his initial suggestion of bells with the new and awful sounds of machine-gun fire:

—Only the monstrous anger of the guns.
Only the stuttering rifles' rapid rattle

Quite apart from its military and political outcome, World War I has assumed a particular place in our collective memory, thanks partly to those like Brooke and Owen who managed to frame their wartime experiences in the memorable language of poetry. At first, Brooke's poetry helped to justify the alarming slaughter to those who began questioning the war's purpose as it claimed the lives of their sons. Yet by now we find it hard to grasp the ideals that inspired his poetic testimony, for they were in one sense consumed by the war and the era of violence that it began. We still live in the world that emerged from that war, so Owen, with his cynicism and sense of tragedy, is far more our contemporary. Brooke may still reveal for us something of the innocence that was lost, but it is especially through Owen's way of conveying the tragedy, the sense of betrayal and lost innocence, that World War I has continued to haunt the memory of Western civilization.

CHAPTER 26

The Illusion of Stability, 1919–1930

I n 1925 Josephine Baker (1906–1975), a black entertainer from St. Louis, moved from the chorus lines of New York to Paris, where she quickly became a singing and dancing sensation. Also a favorite in Germany, she was the most famous of the African American entertainers who took the cultural capitals of Europe by storm during the 1920s. After the disillusioning experience of war, many Europeans found a valuable infusion of vitality in Baker's jazz music, exotic costumes, and "savage," uninhibited dancing.

The attraction to African Americans as primitive and savage, vital and sensual, reflected a good deal of racial stereotyping, and black performers like Baker sometimes played to these stereotypes. But there really was something fresh and uninhibited about American culture, especially its African American variant. African American entertainers in Europe had great fun ironically subverting racial stereotypes even as they played to them. And many realized they could enjoy opportunities in parts of Europe that were still denied them in the United States. Baker herself was a woman of great sophistication who became a French citizen in 1937, participated in progressive causes, and was decorated for her secret intelligence work in the anti-Nazi resistance during World War II.

The prominence of African Americans in European popular culture during the 1920s was part of a wider infatuation with things American as Europeans reached out to embrace the new. America was exciting because it seemed at once primitive and modern. Lacking the cultural baggage of Europe, Americans could help revitalize Europe and point the way to modernity at the same time. With so many old conventions shattered

Kees van Dongen,
Au cabaret nègre (detail).

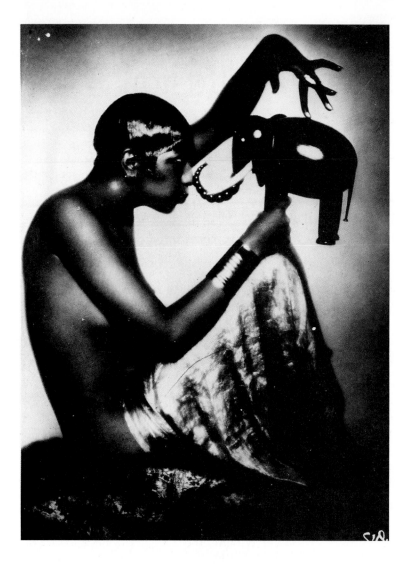

The Sensational Josephine Baker A native of St. Louis, the African American Josephine Baker moved to Paris in 1925 and quickly created a sensation in both France and Germany as a cabaret dancer and singer. Playing on the European association of Africa with the wild and uninhibited, she featured unusual poses and exotic costumes. *(Hulton-Getty/Tony Stone Images)*

by the war, the ideal of being "modern" became widespread among Europeans, affecting everything from sex education to furniture design. "Modern" meant no-nonsense efficiency, mass production, and a vital popular culture, expressed in jazz, movies, sport, and even advertising.

Although the new infatuation with America made clear the depth of the change at work in European culture and society, Europeans themselves had pioneered modernism in many areas of the arts and sciences. During the 1920s, Paris held its own as an international cultural center, nurturing innovative artistic movements like surrealism, which drew on Freudian psychoanalysis, and hosting a decorative arts exhibition in 1925 that produced art deco, the sleek, "modernistic" style that helped give the decade its distinctive flavor. And in the unsettled conditions of postwar Germany, Berlin emerged to rival Paris for cultural leadership during what Germans called "the Golden Twenties." Innovations ranged from avant-garde drama to a sophisticated cabaret scene with a prominent homosexual dimension.

But there was something dizzying, even unnerving, in the eager embrace of the new during the 1920s. Whereas many European cultural observers saw, in the vogue of black American entertainers like Josephine Baker, the revitalization needed to overcome European decadence and loss of confidence, others saw the African American influence as a symptom of that decadence. It could only undermine further the best of European civilization.

More generally, insecurity lurked beneath the quest for novelty and vitality during the 1920s. After the disruption of World War I, many wanted simply to return to normal. But so much had been changed in the crucible of war that the prewar European order was gone forever. And so attempts to find new bases of order, in everything from architecture to classical music to the international economy, were central to the decade.

Although the immediate disruptions of wartime carried over to 1923, a more hopeful era of relative prosperity and international conciliation followed, continuing until 1929. It seemed, briefly, that European civilization had managed to quell the disorder unleashed by the war. The new communist regime in the Soviet Union remained a potentially disruptive force, but it suspended its effort to lead a wider revolution. In Germany, where the new democracy got off to a rocky start, political stability seemed on its way by the later 1920s, as Germany gradually patched things up with the war's victors. Still, the victors' decreasing willingness to enforce the harsh and punitive peace, though helpful in one sense, could be destabilizing in another. And disillusionment at Western hypocrisy led colonial elites to question colonial rule more aggressively, which contributed, in turn, to serious if sporadic outbreaks of anticolonialist activity.

In Italy, the democracy that had emerged in the nineteenth century gave way to the first regime to call itself fascist, and some of the new democracies in east-central Europe did not survive the decade. Even in the more established democracies of Britain and France, tensions came close to the surface. When the Great Depression began at the end of the decade, serious sociopolitical strains became evident throughout most of the Western world. The restabilization of the 1920s proved only an illusion.

THE WEST AND THE WORLD AFTER THE GREAT WAR

Before 1914, the great powers had been the European powers, who had apportioned much of the non-Western world in imperial networks. But the war and the peace had weakened—and to some extent discredited—the belligerent countries of Europe, who now found themselves saddled with foreign debts and unbalanced economies. Though the United States had pulled back from a direct political role in Europe, it became far more active in world affairs, helping to engineer major conferences on arms limitation and international economic relations during the 1920s. But in crucial respects the shape of the postwar international order still depended on Europeans. Six European countries—Britain, France, the Netherlands, Belgium, Italy, and Portugal—had significant colonial possessions at a time when colonialism was under strain. And colonial concerns continued to affect the balance of power in Europe, where it fell to the two major victors in the war, France and Britain, to enforce the controversial peace settlement.

The Erosion of European Power

Emerging from the war as the principal power in East Asia was a non-Western country, Japan, whose claims to the German bases in the region and to special rights in China were formally recognized by the other victors at the Paris Peace Conference. With the Washington treaty of 1922, Japan won naval parity with Britain and the United States in the East Asian region. The Western nations were recognizing Japan as a peer, a great power—even a threat. Aspects of the Washington agreements were intended to block Japanese expansion in East Asia. If a new international system was to emerge, it would not be centered in Europe to the extent the old one had been.

The European colonial presence was as strong as ever, but after the slaughter of the war and the hypocrisy of the peace, Europeans could no longer claim to embody civilization with the same arrogance. But if the old Europe lost prestige, President Wilson's ideals of self-determination and democracy were greeted enthusiastically outside the West—in China, for example. At the same time, the Russian revolutionary model appealed to those in the colonial world seeking to understand the mainsprings of Western imperialism—and the means of overcoming colonial rule. To some Chinese intellectuals by the early 1920s, Leninism was attractive because it showed the scope for mass mobilization by a revolutionary vanguard.

Non-Western elites were learning to pick and choose from among the elements of the Western tradition. During the war and continuing into the 1920s, ever greater numbers of colonial subjects went to western Europe, often for education. Paris was a favored destination, partly because France made some genuine effort to assimilate colonial peoples. In one sense, those educated in Paris and elsewhere in the West were subject to Westernization, but that did not have to mean accepting Western rule. In fact, Western political education led many not only to question colonialism but to ask new questions about their own traditions—and how they might serve the quest for a postcolonial order.

By the 1920s, a generation of anticolonialist, nationalist intellectuals was emerging to lead the non-Western world. Some were more radical than others, but now began variations on themes that would be heard for decades—decades of struggle for independence, cultural confidence, and national self-respect. In response to imperial rule, the challenge was to learn from the West and to modernize, but without simply copying the West and losing one's own distinctive cultural identity. It was imperative to sift through tradition, asking what needed to be changed and what was worth preserving. The pioneering Chinese nationalist Sun Yixien (Sun Yat-sen, 1866–1925) was typical in recognizing the need to adopt the science and technology of the West. But China, he insisted, could do so in its own way, without sacrificing the distinctiveness of its cultural and political traditions. (See the box, "Encounters with the West: Sun Yixien on Chinese Nationalism.")

Britain had been the greatest imperial power, and as an island nation, it still emphasized its navy and its empire even after playing a major role on the Continent during World War I. But this meant Britain was especially vulnerable to the growing anticolonial sentiment. Although the British were comparatively sensitive and flexible in handling colonial pressures, they seem, in retrospect, to have faced a losing battle. Yet that battle drew British attention and energy away from the problems of Europe after the war and the peace settlement.

In light of the strong Indian support for the British war effort, in 1917 the British government promised to extend the scope for Indian involvement in the colonial administration in India. Growing expectations as the war was ending provoked episodes of violence against the British, whose troops retaliated brutally in April 1919, firing indiscriminately into an unarmed crowd. This Amritsar Massacre helped galvanize India's independence movement, even though the British,

seeking conciliation in the aftermath, extended self-rule by entrusting certain less essential government services to Indians. Another milestone was reached in 1921, when Mohandas Gandhi, the British-educated leader of the Indian independence movement, shed his European clothes in favor of simple Indian attire. But it was on the basis of Western egalitarianism, not some indigenous value, that he demanded political rights for the "untouchables," the lowest group in India's longstanding caste system.

In Egypt anticolonialist violence led to a full-scale anti-British insurrection in 1919. After the rebellion was suppressed by British troops, British authorities offered to grant moderate concessions in Egypt, as in India. Tensions remained, however, for Egyptian nationalists demanded more substantial concessions. Finally, in 1922, the British granted Egypt formal independence, to be followed over the next few years by representative government and universal suffrage under a constitutional monarchy. But Britain retained a predominant influence in Egypt until a nationalist revolution in 1952.

At the same time, nationalism was growing among West Africans studying in England. Even before the war, demands for representation in colonial government had been raised in the African press, and such demands were stepped up after the war. In March 1919 Western-educated Africans in the Gold Coast asked the British governor to establish representative institutions so that Africans could at least be consulted. The West African National Congress, formed in 1920, concentrated on the same demands. The British agreed to new constitutions for Nigeria in 1923 and the Gold Coast in 1925 that took significant steps in that direction. They also agreed to build more schools, though they tended to promote practical education, including African languages and agriculture, whereas the African leaders wanted room for the Western classics that "made gentlemen." Such differences in priorities indicate the complexities of the relationships at work between colonial rulers and the emerging elites among the colonized peoples.

Enforcing the Versailles Settlement

The strains that followed World War I were evident not only in the colonies but in Europe. It was up to France and Britain to make sure the new

≈ **ENCOUNTERS WITH THE WEST** ≈

Sun Yixien on Chinese Nationalism

Sun Yixien (Sun Yat-sen), widely regarded as the father of modern China, founded the Guomindang (Kuomintang), the Chinese nationalist movement, in 1912. Educated by Western missionaries in China, he lived in the United States for extended periods and came to admire the West in important respects. But he insisted that China, to make the best use of what the West offered, had to reconnect with its own unique traditions. Variations on this argument would be heard for decades as the rest of the world sought to come to terms with the apparently more advanced West. The following passages are from an influential series of lectures that Sun Yixien presented in China in the early 1920s.

What is the standing of our nation in the world? In comparison with other nations we have the greatest population and the oldest culture, of four thousand years' duration. We ought to be advancing in line with the nations of Europe and America. But the Chinese people have only family and clan groups; there is no national spirit. Consequently, in spite of four hundred million people gathered together in one China, we are in fact but a sheet of loose sand. We are the poorest and weakest state in the world, occupying the lowest position in international affairs; the rest of mankind is the carving knife and the serving dish, while we are the fish and the meat. Our position now is extremely perilous; if we do not earnestly promote nationalism and weld together our four hundred millions into a strong nation, we face a tragedy—the loss of our country and the destruction of our race. To ward off this danger, we must espouse Nationalism and employ the national spirit to save the country. . . .

But even if we succeed in reviving our ancient morality, learning, and powers, we will still not be able, in this modern world, to advance China to a first place among the nations. . . . [W]e will still need to learn the strong points of Europe and America before we can progress at an equal rate with them. Unless we do study the best from foreign countries, we will go backward. With our own fine foundation of knowledge and our age-long culture,

with our own native intelligence besides, we should be able to acquire all the best things from abroad. The strongest point of the West is its science. . . .

As soon as we learn Western machinery we can use it anytime, anywhere; electric lights, for example, can be installed and used in any kind of Chinese house. But Western social customs and sentiments are different from ours in innumerable points; if, without regard to customs and popular feelings in China, we try to apply Western methods of social control as we would Western machinery—in a hard and fast way—we shall be making a serious mistake. . . .

. . . For the governmental machinery of the United States and France still has many defects, and does not satisfy the desires of the people nor give them a complete measure of happiness. So we in our proposed reconstruction must not think that if we imitate the West of to-day we shall reach the last stage of progress and be perfectly contented. . . .

Only in recent times has Western culture advanced beyond ours, and the passion for this new civilization has stimulated our revolution. Now that the revolution is a reality, we naturally desire to see China excel the West and build up the newest and most progressive state in the world. We certainly possess the qualifications necessary to reach this ideal, but we must not merely imitate the democratic systems of the West.

Source: Sun Yat-sen, *San Min Chu I: The Three Principles of the People* (Taipei, Taiwan: China Cultural Service, 1953), pp. 5, 46, 109–113, 136, 138–139.

international order worked, but it was not clear that either had the will and the resources to do so. Cooperation between them was essential, yet sometimes their differences—in geography, in values, and in perceptions—seemed to doom them to work at cross-purposes.

France was unquestionably the dominant power on the European continent after World War I, and until well into the 1930s it boasted the strongest army in the world. Yet even in the early 1920s there was something artificial about France's strength—thus the shrillness and the defensiveness that marked French thinking and French policy. To be sure, France seized the initiative and offered strong leadership at first, but contradictions, and resignation, gradually came to the fore.

In light of Germany's stronger demographic and industrial base, France's long-term security seemed to require certain measures to tip the scales in its favor. By imposing German disarmament and the demilitarization of the Rhineland, the Versailles treaty gave France immediate military advantages. Yet each of these measures was in some ways limited. How long could they be maintained, once the passions of war had died down and Germany no longer seemed such a threat? France had hoped for British help in enforcing the treaty, but during the 1920s, as after other major European wars, Britain pulled back from the Continent to concentrate on its empire.

At first, France felt confident enough to take strong steps even without British support. In response to German foot-dragging in paying reparations, Prime Minister Raymond Poincaré decided to get tough in January 1923. Declaring the Germans in default, he sent French troops at the head of an international force to occupy the Ruhr industrial area and force German compliance. But the move backfired. The costs of this military intervention more than offset the increase in reparations that France received, so the French government had to raise taxes to pay for the venture. Moreover, the move alienated the British, whose lack of support bordered on active hostility.

Quite apart from their imperial concerns, the British wanted to avoid getting dragged into the uncertain situation in east-central Europe, where vital national interests did not seem to be at stake. Yet the French, to replace their earlier link with Russia, promptly developed an alliance system with several of the new or expanded states of the region, including Poland, Czechoslovakia, Romania, and Yugoslavia. France's ties to east-central Europe made the British especially wary of definitive agreements with the French.

Even when western Europe was at issue, Britain was reluctant to become closely allied with France, which seemed unnecessarily vindictive and bellicose. Indeed, the Versailles treaty increasingly seemed counterproductive to the British, who placed great store in the League of Nations and in the international arms reduction effort prominent by the later 1920s. So France found itself with ever less support from its wartime allies as it sought to enforce the peace settlement. The Ruhr occupation of 1923 proved the last time the French dared to go it alone.

From that point on, France lost the advantages it had gained by defeating Germany, and its veneer of self-confidence gradually peeled away to reveal defensiveness and resignation. The defensive mentality found physical embodiment in the Maginot Line, a system of fortifications on the country's eastern border. Remembering the defensive warfare of World War I, and determined to preclude the sort of invasion France had suffered in 1914, Marshal Pétain and the military convinced France's political leaders to adopt a defensive strategy based on a fortified line. The Maginot system was conceived in 1925, begun in 1929, and reached at least preliminary completion in 1935, when it extended along France's border with Germany from Switzerland to the Ardennes Forest at the border with Belgium.

Although this defensive system had some military justification, it was not consistent with the other major strands of French military and diplomatic policy, especially the alliances with several of the states between Germany and Russia in east-central Europe. If France emphasized defense behind an impregnable system of forts, what good were French security guarantees to such new allies as Poland and Czechoslovakia? French efforts to avoid another war by adopting a defensive strategy were not consistent with the role that France set out to play in Europe after its victory in 1918.

Still, the situation remained fluid during the 1920s. In France, as in Britain, national elections in 1924 produced a victory for the moderate left, ending a period of conservative nationalist dominance since the war. In each country, international relations was a major issue in the elections, and the

Cracks in Western Imperialism There was no return to normal in the areas subject to European imperial control after World War I. Here, in Cairo in 1919, British-led troops attempt to control rioting Egyptian nationalists protesting the banishment of a major nationalist leader. Such pressure continued, forcing the British not only to permit the leader to return but to allow Egypt greater autonomy. *(Hulton-Getty/Tony Stone Images)*

outcome forecast a more conciliatory tack, especially in relations with Germany. If democracy was taking root in the land of its old enemy, then perhaps France's fears about German aggressiveness and the European power balance were misplaced.

TOWARD MASS SOCIETY

As many had feared, the problems of readjustment to peace caused wild economic swings in the first few years after the war. The downturns were relatively short, however, and by the later 1920s, Europe was enjoying renewed prosperity. Common involvement in the war had blurred class lines and accelerated the trend toward what contemporaries began to call "mass society." As the new prosperity spread the fruits of industrialization more widely, ordinary people increasingly set

the cultural tone, partly through new mass media like film and radio. To some, the advent of mass society portended a welcome revitalization of culture and a more authentic kind of democracy, while others saw only a debasement of cultural standards and a susceptibility to populist demagoguery. But though the contours of mass society now became evident, social change did not keep up with the promise of—and the requirements for—democratic politics.

The war was supposed to have paved the way for democracy, and the fall of the monarchies in Russia, Germany, and Austria-Hungary seemed especially to create opportunities. But where democracy was new, as in Poland and Germany, it often led a tortured existence and soon gave way to more authoritarian forms of government. Even in France and Britain, where victory in the war seemed to have confirmed democratic values and institutions, the new strains and missed opportunities of the 1920s stand out in retrospect. In Italy, hopes for democratic renewal gradually receded as a new regime, hostile to parliamentary democracy, triumphed by the middle of the decade. So despite the aspirations that had surrounded the end of the war, the decade that followed did not see the consolidation of the political democracy that optimistic observers had assumed would correspond with the emerging mass society.

Economic Readjustment and the New Prosperity

In their effort to return to normal, governments were quick to dismantle wartime planning and control mechanisms. But the needs of war had stimulated innovations that helped fuel the renewed economic growth of the 1920s. The civilian air industry, for example, developed rapidly during the decade by taking advantage of wartime work on aviation for military purposes. More generally, newer industries such as chemicals, electricity, and advanced machinery led the way to a new prosperity in the 1920s, which significantly altered patterns of life in the more industrialized parts of the West. The automobile, a luxury plaything for the wealthy before the war, began to be mass-produced in western Europe. In France, which had pioneered automotive manufacture, the production of automobiles shot up dramatically, from 40,000 in 1920 to 254,000 in 1929.

But the heady pace masked problems that lay beneath the relative prosperity of the 1920s, even in victorious Britain and France. If new industries prospered, old ones declined in the face of new technologies and stronger foreign competition. In Britain, the industries responsible for Britain's earlier industrial pre-eminence—textiles, coal, shipbuilding, and iron and steel—were now having trouble competing. Rather than investing in new technologies, companies in these older industries sought to survive by demanding government protection and by imposing lower wages and longer hours on their workers. At the same time, however, British labor unions resisted the mechanization necessary to make these older industries more competitive.

Rather than realistically assessing Britain's prospects in the more competitive international economy, British leaders sought to return to the prewar situation, based on the gold standard, with London the world's financial center. For many Britons, the government's announcement in 1925 that the British pound was again freely convertible to gold at 1914 exchange rates was the long-awaited indication that normality had returned at last. Yet the return to 1914 exchange rates overvalued the pound relative to the U.S. dollar, making British goods more expensive on export markets and making it still more difficult for aging British industries to compete. Further, Britain no longer had the capital to act as the world's banker. By trying to do so, Britain became all the more vulnerable when the international economy reached a crisis in 1929.

If the structural decline of older industries was clearest in Britain, inflation and its psychological impact was most prominent in Germany and France. By the summer of 1923, Germany's response to the French occupation of the Ruhr had transformed an already serious inflationary problem, stemming from wartime deficit spending, into one of the great hyperinflations in history. At its height, when it took 4.2 trillion marks to equal a dollar, Germans were forced to take wheelbarrows of paper money to buy ordinary grocery items. Simply printing the necessary currency was a severe strain for the government. By the end of 1923, the government managed to stabilize prices through currency reform and drastically reduced government spending—a combination that elicited greater cooperation from the victors. But the rampant inflation, and the readjustment necessary to control it, wiped out the life savings of ordinary people while profiting speculators and those in debt, including some large industrialists. This inequity left scars that remained even as Germany enjoyed a measure of prosperity in the years that followed.

Inflation was less dramatic in France, but it affected French perceptions and priorities in significant ways between the two world wars. For over a century, from the Napoleonic era to the outbreak of war in 1914, the value of the French franc had remained stable. But the war started France on an inflationary cycle that shattered the security of its many small savers—those, like teachers and shopkeepers, who had been the backbone of the Third Republic. To repay war debts and rebuild war-damaged industries, the French government continued to run budget deficits, and thereby cause inflation, even after 1918. Runaway inflation threatened during 1925 and 1926, but the franc was finally restabilized in 1928, though at only about one-fifth its prewar value.

On the international level, war debts and reparations strained the financial system, creating problems with the financing of trade. But in the course of the 1920s, experts made adjustments that seemed to be returning the international exchange system to equilibrium. Only in retrospect, after the international capitalist system fell into crisis late in 1929, did it become clear how potent those strains were—and how inadequate the efforts at readjustment.

Work, Leisure, and the New Popular Culture

The wartime spur to industrialization produced a large increase in the industrial labor force all over Europe, and a good deal of labor unrest accompanied the transition to peacetime. Some of that agitation challenged factory discipline and authority relationships. Seeking to re-establish authority on a new basis for the competitive postwar world, business leaders and publicists fostered a new cult of efficiency and productivity, partly by adapting Taylorism and Fordism, influential American ideas about mass production. On the basis of his "time-and-motion" studies of factory labor, Frederick W. Taylor (1856–1915) argued that breaking down assembly line production into small, repetitive tasks was the key to maximizing worker efficiency. In contrast, Henry Ford (1863–1947) linked the gospel of mass production to mass consumption. In exchange for accepting the discipline of the assembly line, the workers should be paid well enough to be able to buy the products they produced—even automobiles. Sharing in the prosperity that mass production made possible, factory workers would be loyal to the companies that employed them. Not all Europeans, however, welcomed the new ideas from America. In the new cult of efficiency and mass production, some saw an unwelcome sameness and a debasement of cultural standards. (See the box, "Doubts About Mass Society.")

In light of the major role women had played in the wartime labor force, the demand for women's suffrage proved irresistible in Britain, Germany, and much of Europe, though not yet in France or Italy. In Britain, where the call for women's suffrage had earlier met with controversy (see page 902), the right to vote was readily conceded in 1918, partly because women no longer seemed a threat to the political system. Once given the vote, British women simply flowed into the existing parties, dissolving earlier hopes—and fears—that a specifically feminist political agenda would follow from women's suffrage.

Although female employment remained higher than before the war, many women were willing to return home, yielding their jobs to the returning soldiers. The need to replace the men killed in the war lent renewed force to the traditional notion that women served society, and fulfilled themselves, by marrying and rearing families. This notion was symptomatic of the widespread desire to return to normal after the disruptions of the war years.

Still, the spirit of innovation brought into the public arena subjects with significant implications for gender roles—subjects largely taboo before the war. The desire to be "modern" produced a more open, unsentimental, even scientific discussion of sexuality and reproduction. Theodore Hendrik van de Velde's *Ideal Marriage* (1927) sold widely throughout the Western world for decades. Though van de Velde assumed male leadership in the sexual relationship, his study furthered the growing sense that sexual fulfillment was important to a healthy marriage—and required techniques that could be learned and discussed.

The new "rationalization of sexuality" fed demands that governments provide access to sex counseling, birth control, and even abortion as they assumed ever greater responsibilities for promoting social health. This direction was especially prominent in Germany, although German innovators learned from experiments in the new Soviet Union and from the birth control movement that Margaret Sanger (1883–1966) was spearheading in the United States. The more open and tolerant attitude toward sexuality fostered the development of a gay subculture, prominent in the vibrant cabaret scene that emerged in Berlin during the 1920s.

Innovation affected many reaches of everyday life. Mass consumption was the reverse side of the mass production that created the new prosperity of the 1920s. As it became possible to mass-produce

Doubts About Mass Society

The writer Stefan Zweig (1881–1942) was born in Vienna and traveled widely in America, Asia, and Europe. In an article for a Berlin newspaper in 1925, he expressed misgivings about the new sociocultural tendencies prominent after the war—tendencies that he, like many of his contemporaries, identified with Americanization. His thinking combined hyperbole with an acute sense that something valuable was being lost.

Everything is becoming more uniform in its outward manifestations, everything leveled into a uniform cultural schema. The characteristic habits of individual peoples are being worn away, native dress giving way to uniforms, customs becoming international. Countries seem increasingly to have slipped simultaneously into each other; people's activity and vitality follows a single schema; cities grow increasingly similar in appearance. Paris has been three-quarters Americanized, Vienna Budapested: more and more the fine aroma of the particular in cultures is evaporating, their colorful foliage being stripped with ever-increasing speed, rendering the steel-grey pistons of mechanical operation, of the modern world machine, visible beneath the cracked veneer. . . .

Two or three decades ago dance was still specific to nations and to the personal inclinations of the individual. One waltzed in Vienna, danced the csardas in Hungary, the bolero in Spain, all to the tune of countless different rhythms and melodies in which both the genius of an artist and the spirit of the nation took obvious form. Today millions of people, from Capetown to Stockholm, from Buenos Aires to Calcutta, dance the same dance to the same short-winded, impersonal melodies. . . .

A second example is fashion. Never before has such a striking uniformity developed in all countries as during our age. . . . New York decrees short hair for women: within a month, as if cut by the same scythe, 50 or 100 million female manes fall to the floor. . . .

A third example: cinema. Once again utter simultaneity in all countries and languages, the cultivation of the same performance, the same taste (or lack of it) in masses by the hundreds of millions. . . .

A fourth example is radio. All of these inventions have a single meaning: simultaneity. Londoners, Parisians, and Viennese listen at the same second to the same thing, and the supernatural proportions of this simultaneity, of this uniformity, are intoxicating. There is an intoxication, a stimulus for the masses, in all of these new technological miracles, and simultaneously an enormous sobriety of the soul, a dangerous seduction of the individual into passivity. Here too, as in dance, fashion, and the cinema, the individual acquiesces to a herdlike taste that is everywhere the same. . . .

America is the source of that terrible wave of uniformity. . . . From the other side of our world, from Russia, the same will to monotony presses ominously in a different form: the will to the compartmentalization of the individual, to uniformity in world views, the same dreadful will to monotony. Europe remains the last bulwark of individualism and, perhaps, of the overly taut cramp of peoples—our vigorous nationalism, despite all its senselessness, represents to some extent a fevered, unconscious rebellion, a last, desperate effort to defend ourselves against leveling. But precisely that cramped form of resistance betrays our weakness. . . .

. . . [I]n all of these new means for mechanizing humanity there is an enormous power that is not to be overcome. For they all fulfill the highest ideal of the average: to offer amusement without demanding exertion. . . . Autonomy in the conduct of one's life and even in the enjoyment of life has by now become a goal for so few people that most no longer feel how they are becoming particles, atoms in the wash of a gigantic power.

Source: Anton Kaes, Martin Jay, and Edward Dimendberg, eds., *The Weimar Republic Sourcebook* (Berkeley and Los Angeles: University of California Press, 1994), pp. 397–400.

the products of the second industrial transformation, more people could afford automobiles, electrical gadgets like the radio and phonograph, and clothing of synthetic fabrics, developed through innovations in chemistry. First came rayon, produced in small quantities since 1891 but mass-produced beginning in the 1920s. Its advent was of particular symbolic importance; in this new artificial form, silk, which had long been one of the trappings of wealth, was now within the means of ordinary people.

With the eight-hour day increasingly the norm, growing attention was devoted to leisure as a positive source of human fulfillment—for everyone, not just the wealthy. Ordinary people began to have the time, and the means, to take vacations. European beach resorts grew crowded. An explosion of interest in soccer among Europeans paralleled the growth of baseball and football in the United States. Huge stadiums were built across Europe.

The growth of leisure was linked to the development of mass media and mass culture. During the early 1920s radio became a commercial venture, reaching a mass audience in Europe, as in the United States. Although movies had begun to emerge as vehicles of popular entertainment even before the war, they came into their own during the 1920s, when the names of film stars became household words for the first time.

The rapid development of film showed that new, more accessible media could nurture extraordinary innovation. Germany led the way with such films as *The Cabinet of Dr. Caligari* (1920), *Metropolis* (1927), and *The Blue Angel* (1930), but the Russian Sergei Eisenstein (1898–1948) became perhaps the most admired film maker of the era with *Potemkin* (1925), his brilliant portrayal of the Russian revolution of 1905. In some spheres, however, America was beginning to outdo both Paris and Berlin. Marlene Dietrich (1901–1992), famous as Lola Lola in *The Blue Angel*, was among a number of German film celebrities who went to Hollywood.

Exploiting the new popular fascination with air travel, the American Charles Lindbergh (1902–1974) captured the European imagination in 1927 with the first solo flight across the Atlantic. Lindbergh's feat epitomized the affirmative side of the decade—the sense that there were new worlds to conquer and that there still were heroes, despite the ironies of the war and the ambiguities of the peace.

Weimar Cinema This poster advertises Fritz Lang's film *Metropolis*, which explored the dehumanization and exploitation of the modern city. (*Schulz-Neudamm,* Metropolis, *1926. Lithograph, 83"× 36½". The Museum of Modern Art, New York. Gift of Universum Film Aktiengesellschaft.*)

Society and Politics in the Victorious Democracies

France and Britain seemed the best positioned of the major European countries to take advantage of renewed peace and stability to confront the sociopolitical challenges of the postwar era. And during the 1920s, each seemed to return to normal. But was normal good enough, in light of the rupture of the war and the challenges of the emerging mass society?

Victory in the Great War seemed to belie France's prewar concerns about decadence and decline. In the immediate aftermath of the war, French leaders were confident in dealing with radical labor unrest and aggressive in translating the battlefield victory into a dominant position on the European continent. But despite the victorious outcome, the war itself, with its tremendous loss of French lives, had produced a widespread conviction that France could not withstand another such challenge. The renewed confidence thus proved hollow.

Although some in prewar France had worried about falling behind rapidly industrializing Germany, the victory seemed to have vindicated France's more cautious, balanced economy, with its blend of industry and agriculture. Thus, the prewar mistrust of rapid industrial development continued. Rather than foster a program of economic modernization that might have afforded the basis for genuine security, the French pulled back even from the measure of state responsibility for the economy that had developed during the war.

To be sure, in France, as elsewhere, the 1920s were a decade of relative prosperity. Led by the oil and electricity industries, the economy grew at an annual rate of 4.6 percent between 1923 and 1929, double the prewar rate. Industrial production by 1929 was 40 percent higher than it had been in 1913. But, with the exception of Britain, other Western economies grew more rapidly during the 1920s, and the opportunity that growth afforded to modernize the French economy was not seized. Although government grants helped reconstruct almost eight thousand factories, most were simply rebuilt as they were before the war. Moreover, the working class benefited little from the relative prosperity of the 1920s. Housing remained poor, wages failed to keep up with inflation, and France continued to lag other countries in social legislation.

The British political system remained stable between the wars, although it opened up in one significant sense as the Labour party supplanted the Liberals to become the dominant alternative to the Conservatives by the early 1920s. The Labour party even got a brief taste of power when Ramsay MacDonald (1866–1937) formed Britain's first Labour government in January 1924. The coming of Labour to power wrought a significant expansion of the governmental elite to incorporate those, like MacDonald himself, with genuinely working-class backgrounds.

The rise of Labour was striking, but it was the Conservative leader, Stanley Baldwin (1867–1947), who set the tone for British politics between the wars in three stints as prime minister during the years from 1923 to 1937. Although the wealthy son of a steel manufacturer, Baldwin deliberately departed from the old aristocratic style of British conservative politics. More down-to-earth and pragmatic than his predecessors, he was the first British prime minister to use radio effectively, and he made an effort to foster good relations with the workers. Yet Baldwin's era was one of growing social tension.

With exports declining, unemployment remained high in Britain throughout the interwar period, never falling below 10 percent. The coal industry, though still the country's largest employer, had become a particular trouble spot in the British economy. As coal exports declined, British mine owners became ever more aggressive in their dealings with labor, finally, in 1926, insisting on a longer workday and a wage cut of 13 percent to restore competitiveness. The result was a coal miners' strike in May that promptly turned into a general strike, involving almost all of organized labor—about 4 million workers—in the most notable display of trade-union solidarity Britain had ever seen. For nine days the British economy stood at a virtual standstill. But threats of arrest and a growing public backlash forced the union leadership to back down, accepting a compromise. The miners continued the strike on their own, but they finally returned to work six months later at considerably lower wages.

Although for somewhat different reasons, Britain and France both failed during the 1920s to take advantage of what would soon seem, in retrospect, to have been a precious opportunity to adjust their economies, to heal social wounds, and thereby to create a deeper consensus and a more meaningful democracy. The lost opportunity would mean growing social tensions once the relative prosperity of the decade had ended.

Democracy Aborted

In east-central Europe, new democracies seemed to take root after the war, but except in Czechoslovakia and Finland the practice of parliamentary government did not match the promise of the immediate postwar period. Democracy seemed divisive and ineffective, so one country after another adopted a more authoritarian alternative during the 1920s and early 1930s.

Poland offers the most dramatic example. Although its democratic constitution of 1921 established a cabinet responsible to a parliamentary majority, the parliament fragmented into numerous parties so that instability proved endemic from the start. Indeed, Poland had fourteen different ministries from November 1918 to May 1926, when a coup d'état led by Marshal Josef Pilsudski replaced parliamentary government with an authoritarian regime stressing national unity. This suppression of democracy came as a relief to many Poles—and was even welcomed by the trade unions. After Pilsudski's death in 1935, a group of colonels ruled Poland until the country was invaded by Nazi Germany in 1939.

Democracy proved hard to manage in east-central Europe partly because of special economic difficulties resulting from the breakup of the Habsburg system. New national borders meant new economic barriers, disrupting long-standing economic relationships. Centers of relative industrial strength like Vienna and Budapest found themselves cut off from their traditional markets and sources of raw materials. In what was now Poland, Silesians had long been oriented toward Germany, Galicians toward Vienna, and those in eastern Poland toward Russia; the creation of the Polish nation-state was not in itself sufficient to form a cohesive economic unit.

The countries of east-central Europe remained overwhelmingly agrarian, and this, too, proved unconducive to democracy. Land reform that accompanied the transition to democracy made small properties the norm in much of the region. But these units were often too small to be efficient, so agricultural output actually decreased after land was redistributed, most dramatically in Romania and Yugoslavia. When agricultural prices declined by the late 1920s, many of those peasants had no choice but to sell out to larger landowners. What had seemed a progressive and democratic reform thus failed to provide a stable agrarian smallholder base for democracy.

THE WEIMAR REPUBLIC IN GERMANY: A CANDLE BURNING AT BOTH ENDS

The trial of democracy in Poland and elsewhere in east-central Europe was important, but the venue for the most significant test was Germany, a large, dynamic, culturally sophisticated country where democracy had never taken firm root. With the Weimar Republic of 1918–1933, Germany experienced full-fledged parliamentary democracy for the first time, but this democracy had great difficulty establishing its legitimacy, and it reached an impasse when confronted with economic depression by 1930. As a result, the Nazi leader Adolf Hitler (1889–1945) got a chance to govern early in 1933. He immediately began creating a new regime, the Third Reich, intended as the antithesis of Weimar democracy.

Because its failure led to Nazism, the Weimar Republic has been much scrutinized. What might its leaders have done differently to produce a more viable democracy at this point in German history? Are the republic's immediate problems enough to explain its failure, or was some longer-term German aversion to democratic institutions crucial as well?

Germany's Cautious Revolution, 1919–1920

The Weimar Republic had two strikes against it virtually from the outset: It was born of national defeat, and it was forced to take responsibility for the harsh and dictated Treaty of Versailles in 1919. During its first years, moreover, the regime encountered severe economic dislocation, culminating in the hyperinflation of 1923, as well as ideological polarization that threatened to tear the country apart.

Although Germany had strong military and authoritarian traditions, the initial threat to the new democracy came not from the right, disoriented and discredited, but from the left, stimulated by the Russian example. Those seeking further revolution, and those who feared it, could easily equate the proclamation of a German republic in November 1918 with the first revolution in Russia; as in Russia, the new, more democratic order could prove a mere prelude to communist revolution.

Spearheaded by Karl Liebknecht and Rosa Luxemburg in Berlin, revolutionary unrest reached its peak in Germany during December 1918 and January 1919. But even after Liebknecht and Luxemburg were captured and murdered in January, there remained a serious chance of further revolution through May 1919, and communist revolutionary agitation continued to flare up until the end of 1923.

As it turned out, there was no further revolution, partly because the parallel between Germany and Russia carried only so far. The new German government had made peace, whereas the leaders of the provisional government in Russia had sought to continue the war. Furthermore, those who ended up controlling the councils that sprang up in Germany during the fall of 1918 favored political democracy, not communist revolution, and therefore they supported the provisional government.

Even so, the revolutionary minority constituted a credible threat. And the new government made repression of the extreme left a priority—even if it meant leaving in place some of the institutions and personnel of the old imperial system. In November 1918, at the birth of the new republic, the moderate socialist leader Friedrich Ebert had agreed with General Groener to preserve the old imperial officer corps to help prevent further revolution. But when the regular army, weakened by war and defeat, proved unable to control radical agitation in Berlin in December, it seemed the republic would have to take extraordinary measures to defend itself from the revolutionary left. With the support of Ebert and Groener, Gustav Noske (1868–1946), the minister of national defense, began to organize "Free Corps," irregular volunteer paramilitary groups to be used against the revolutionaries. Noske, who was a socialist, but one long supportive of the military, noted that "somebody will have to be the bloodhound—I won't shirk the responsibility."[1]

During the first five months of 1919, the government unleashed the Free Corps to crush leftist movements all over Germany, often with wanton brutality. In relying on right-wing paramilitary groups, the republic's leaders were playing with fire, but the immediate threat at this point came from the left. In 1920, however, the government faced a right-wing coup attempt, the Kapp Putsch. The army declined to defend the republic, but the government managed to survive thanks largely to a general strike by leftist workers. The republic's early leaders had to juggle both extremes because, as one of them put it, the Weimar Republic was "a candle burning at both ends."

Though sporadic street fighting by paramilitary groups continued, the republic survived its traumatic birth and by 1924 had achieved an uneasy stability. But Germany's postwar revolution had remained confined to the political level. There was no program to break up the cartels, with their concentrations of economic power. Even on the level of government personnel, continuity was more striking than change. There was no effort to build a loyal republican army, and no attempt to purge the bureaucracy and the judiciary of antidemocratic elements from the old imperial order. When right-wing extremists assassinated prominent leaders, such as the Jewish industrialist Walther Rathenau in 1922, the courts often proved unwilling to prosecute those responsible. In general, those who ran the new government day-to-day were often skeptical of democracy, even hostile to the new regime.

In light of the republic's eventual failure, the willingness of its early leaders to leave intact so much from the old order has made them easy targets for criticism. It can be argued, however, that the course they followed—heading off the extreme left, reassuring the established elites, and playing for time—was the republic's best chance of success. The new regime might establish its legitimacy by inertia, much like the Third Republic in France, which had similarly been born of defeat. Even lacking the sentimental fervor that had earlier surrounded democratic ideals, Germans might gradually become "republicans of reason," recognizing that this regime was the lesser of evils, that it could be a framework for prosperity and renewed German prominence in international affairs. In the event of an early crisis, however, a republic consolidating itself in this cautious way would be likely to find fewer active defenders than active opponents.

Elections in January 1919 produced a constituent assembly that convened in Weimar, seat of what seemed the best traditions of German culture, to draft a democratic constitution. The elections took place before the peace conference had produced the widely detested Treaty of Versailles. When the first regular parliamentary elections finally were held in June 1920, the three moderate parties that had led the new government and been forced to accept the treaty now suffered a major defeat, dropping from 76 to 47 percent of the seats. Those were the parties most committed to democratic institutions, but they were never again to achieve a parliamentary majority. The 1920 elections, like many of those that followed, revealed a lack of consensus and a tendency toward polarization and extremism in the German electorate.

The lack of consensus produced a multiparty system and a fragmented Reichstag. Indeed, no single party ever won an absolute majority during the Weimar years, so government was always by inherently unstable party coalition. Not only was the Weimar party system fragmented and complex, but it encompassed a wide ideological array, including extremes both of left and right that were interested not in consolidating but in sabotaging or at best exploiting the new democratic institutions. Polarization to the left favored the Communists, who constantly criticized the more moderate Socialists for supporting the republic. To the right, the situation was more complex. On the extreme right, the National Socialists, or Nazis, were noisy and often violent, but they did not attract much electoral support until 1930. More damaging to parliamentary democracy for most of the Weimar period was the right-wing Nationalist party (DNVP), which played on nationalist resentments and fears of socialism and offered only the most tenuous support for democratic institutions.

Gustav Stresemann and the Scope for Gradual Consolidation, 1920–1929

Still, all was not necessarily lost for the republic when the three moderate, pro-Weimar parties were defeated in 1920. Germans who were unsupportive or hostile at first might be gradually won over. After the death of President Ebert in 1925, Paul von Hindenburg, the emperor's field mar-

shal, was elected president. Depending on the circumstances, having a conservative military leader from the old order in this role could be advantageous, or damaging, for the future of democracy. As long as there remained scope for consolidation, Hindenburg's presidency suggested to skeptics that the new regime was legitimate and a worthy object of German patriotism. But when crisis came by 1930, Hindenburg was quick to give up on parliamentary government—with devastating results.

The individual who best exemplified the possibility of winning converts to the Weimar Republic in the early 1920s was Gustav Stresemann (1878–1929), the leader of the German People's Party (DVP), a conservative but relatively flexible party that offered at least the possibility of broadening the republic's base of support. As chancellor, and especially as foreign minister, Stresemann proved the republic's leading statesman.

Stresemann was conservative in background and instinct. Early in 1918, for example, he was among the many to applaud the annexationist treaty of Brest-Litovsk, and he was sufficiently frustrated with the new republic by 1920 tacitly to support a coup attempt, the Kapp Putsch. But the volatility that marked German politics in 1920 convinced Stresemann that the alternative to the new republic would not be the conservative monarchy he preferred in principle, but increasing polarization leading to the triumph of the extreme left. Moreover, it had become clear by 1920 that the new democratic republic was not likely to be revolutionary on the socioeconomic level. It made sense, then, to work actively to make the new regime succeed; the alternative could be much worse. Within the framework that the new republic afforded, Germany could pursue its international aims, negotiating modifications of the Versailles treaty and returning to great power status. So although Stresemann was never emotionally attached to democratic ideals, he came to accept the republic and did his best to make it work.

Stresemann became chancellor in August 1923, when inflation was raging out of control. Within months his government had Germany back on its feet, exporting more and again growing economically. Stresemann managed to surmount the inflationary crisis partly because the other powers were becoming more conciliatory. By November 1923 even the French agreed that an

Hopes for Peace Foreign ministers Aristide Briand (left) of France and Gustav Stresemann of Germany spearheaded the improved international relations that bred optimism during the later 1920s. (*Corbis-Bettmann*)

international commission should review the reparations question, specifying realistic amounts based on Germany's ability to pay. During the summer of 1924, a commission led by the American financier Charles G. Dawes produced the Dawes Plan, which remained in force until 1929. The plan worked well by pinpointing revenue sources, lowering payments, providing loans, and securing the stability of the German currency.

At the same time, Stresemann understood that better relations with the victors, starting with France, had to be a priority if Germany was not only to overcome the present crisis but also to return to the councils of the great powers. French foreign minister Aristide Briand (1862–1932) shared Stresemann's desire for improved relations, and together they engineered the new, more conciliatory spirit in international relations evident by 1924. Its most substantial fruit was the Locarno Agreement of October 1925. France and Germany accepted the postwar border between the two countries, which meant that Germany gave up any claim to Alsace-Lorraine. France, for

its part, renounced the sort of direct military intervention in Germany that it had attempted with the Ruhr invasion of 1923 and agreed to begin withdrawing troops from the Rhineland ahead of schedule. On the other hand, Germany freely accepted France's key advantage, the demilitarization of the Rhineland, and Britain and Italy now explicitly guaranteed the measure.

By acquiescing in the status quo in the west, Stresemann was freeing Germany to concentrate on eastern Europe, where he envisioned gradual but substantial revision in the territorial settlement that had resulted from the war. Especially with the creation of Poland, that settlement had come partly at Germany's expense. Stresemann, then, was pursuing German interests, not subordinating them to some larger European vision. But he was willing to compromise and, for the most part, to play by the rules as he did so.

With the Locarno treaty, the victors accepted Germany as a diplomatic equal for the first time since the war. Germany's return to good graces culminated in its entry into the League of Nations in 1926, further evidence of conciliation that was widely welcomed. Indeed, Stresemann and Briand were joint winners of the Nobel Peace Prize for 1926.

Still, Stresemann had already discovered that even successes in dealing with Germany's former enemies could prove costly to him and his party in the volatile German political climate. Beginning in 1924 the German Nationalist party continually exploited German resentments by criticizing Stresemann's compromises with the victors of 1918—in accepting the Dawes Plan, for example. Stresemann concluded that he could overcome this domestic political volatility only by completing the revision of the Versailles treaty as quickly as possible. But his negotiations continued to agitate the German electorate.

With the expiration of the Dawes Plan in 1929, the Young Plan, conceived by American businessman Owen D. Young, removed Allied controls over the German economy and specified that Germany pay reparations until 1988. The annual amount was less than Germany had been paying, so it was expected that this plan constituted a permanent, and reasonable, settlement. Nevertheless, the Young Plan produced considerable resentment in Germany, leading, yet again, to political gains on the right.

The political controversy that surrounded Stresemann, a German conservative pursuing conventional national interests, indicates how volatile the German political situation remained, even with the improved economic and diplomatic climate of the later 1920s. Still, Stresemann's diplomatic successes were considerable, and his death in October 1929, at the age of 51, was a severe blow to the republic.

The End of the Weimar Republic, 1929–1933

Although Weimar Germany was considerably better off in 1929 than it had been in 1923, the political consensus remained weak, the political party system remained fragmented, and unstable coalition government remained the rule. The onset of the economic depression by the end of 1929 produced problems that Germany's fragile new democracy proved unable to handle. The pivotal issue was unemployment insurance, which became a tremendous financial burden for the government as unemployment grew. As it happened, a Socialist chancellor, Hermann Müller (1876–1931), was leading the government when the Depression began, and as the crisis deepened, his party demanded increases in insurance coverage. When the Socialists failed to convince their coalition partners, the Müller government resigned in March 1930. That proved to be the end of normal parliamentary government in Weimar Germany.

By this point conservatives, including military leaders close to President Hindenburg, sensed the chance to replace the fragmented parliamentary system with a more authoritarian government that would attack the economic crisis head on. Upon the advice of these advisers, Hindenburg called on Heinrich Brüning (1885–1970), leader of the moderate, Catholic Center party, to replace Müller as chancellor. Brüning promptly proposed to the Reichstag a hard-nosed, deflationary economic program intended to stimulate exports by lowering prices. Like most of the German middle classes, Brüning feared inflation, disliked unemployment insurance, and believed that Germany could not afford public works projects to pump up demand—the obvious alternative to his deflationary policy.

Though able, upright, and sincere in his economic program, Brüning did not understand the risky political game in which he had become enmeshed. His program encountered opposition not only from socialists but also from conservatives, eager to undermine the republic altogether. As a result, Brüning could get no parliamentary majority. Rather than resigning or seeking a compromise, he invoked Article 48, the emergency provision of the Weimar constitution, which enabled him to govern under presidential decree.

When this expedient provoked strenuous protests, Brüning decided to dissolve the Reichstag and schedule new elections for September 1930. At this point there was still some chance that a more conciliatory tack would have enabled the chancellor to build a new parliamentary majority—and save parliamentary government. The Socialists were seeking to be more cooperative in the face of the deepening economic crisis and the prospect of new parliamentary elections, which, under these difficult circumstances, seemed to invite trouble. However, Brüning persisted, believing the electorate would vindicate him.

In fact, the outcome of the 1930 elections was disastrous—for Brüning, and ultimately for Germany as well. While two of the democratic, pro-Weimar parties lost heavily, the two extremes proved the big winners. The Communists gained 23 seats, for a total of 77 deputies in the Reichstag; the National Socialists did even better, climbing from the 12 seats they had garnered in 1928 to 107.

Brüning continued to govern, still relying on President Hindenburg and Article 48 rather than majority support in the Reichstag. His efforts climaxed in December 1931 with a series of deflationary measures that raised taxes and decreased government spending, even for unemployment benefits. But the impact on the economy was disappointing. Meanwhile, the growth of the political extremes helped fuel an intensification of the political violence and streetfighting that had bedeviled the Weimar Republic from the beginning. As scuffles between Nazis and Communists sometimes approached pitched battles, the inability of the government to keep order further damaged the prestige of the republic.

In May 1932 Hindenburg's advisers finally persuaded him to dump Brüning in favor of an antidemocratic conservative. By this point the republic was a mere shell covering the backroom manipulation and dealing in Hindenburg's circle. The results of the elections that followed in July 1932 proved the republic's death knell. The Nazis won 37.3 percent of the vote (230 seats), and the Communists 14.3 percent (89 seats). Together, the two extremes controlled a majority of the seats in the Reichstag, and each refused to work in coalition with any of the mainstream parties. Although he resisted for months, Hindenburg found it difficult not to give Adolf Hitler, as the leader of the largest party in the Reichstag, a chance to govern. He finally called upon Hitler to form a government in January 1933.

It became clear virtually at once that the outcome of the Weimar crisis was a dramatic change of regime, the triumph of Hitler and Nazism. But though the Nazis had always wanted to destroy the Weimar Republic, they were not directly responsible for overthrowing it. The Weimar Republic failed on its own—or collapsed from within—largely because the Germans disagreed fundamentally about problems and priorities after the war. The new democracy produced unstable government based on multiparty coalitions and encountered virtual paralysis by 1930, when Germany faced the crisis of the Depression.

During the brief and tortured history of the Weimar Republic, there were twenty different cabinets, lasting an average of eight and a half months each. The experience of instability, divisiveness, and finally paralysis reinforced the perception, long prominent in Germany, that parliamentary democracy was petty, divisive, and ineffective. By 1932, the majority of the German electorate had simply lost confidence in the institutions of parliamentary democracy. Even those who voted for the Nazis were not clear what they might be getting instead, but, in light of economic depression and political impasse, it seemed time to try something else.

It was also crucial that elements from Germany's traditional antidemocratic elites were eager to exploit the economic crisis and the political impasse to get rid of the democratic republic altogether. Even as the Socialists became more conciliatory in an effort to find a compromise, those around Hindenburg pushed toward an authoritarian alternative. They were not seeking what proved the outcome—a monopoly of power for Hitler and the Nazis. Indeed, they finally tried working with Hitler in 1933 only as a last resort. But they were quick to begin undercutting a democracy that they had never really embraced in the first place.

COMMUNISM, FASCISM, AND THE NEW POLITICAL SPECTRUM

The Weimar Republic encountered crisis by 1930 partly because of the strength of the new extremes of left and right that had emerged directly from World War I. In making their revolution in 1917, the Bolsheviks had expected to spark a series of revolutions elsewhere. The postwar period began in the context of hopes for—and fears of—further revolution all over Europe. The Russian communists initially enjoyed extraordinary prestige on the European left; but as the nature of Leninist communism became clearer, some Marxists grew skeptical or hostile, and so the Russian model eventually produced a damaging split in international socialism. By the end of the 1920s revolution elsewhere was nowhere in sight, and it seemed that, for the foreseeable future, the communist regime in Russia would have to go it alone.

By then, a new and unexpected political movement had developed in Italy, expanding the political spectrum in a different direction. This was fascism, which brought Benito Mussolini to power in 1922. Emerging directly from the war, the fascism movement was violent—and thus disturbing. The term *fascism* derived from the ancient Roman *fasces,* a bundle of rods surrounding an ax that guards carried at state occasions as a symbol of power and unity. Stressing national solidarity and discipline, the fascists were hostile not only to liberal individualism and multiparty parliamentary democracy, but also to Marxist socialism, with its emphasis on class struggle and the special role of the working class. Largely because of its hostility to Marxism, fascism is generally placed on the "right" of the political spectrum. But though conservatives sought to exploit it, fascism was not merely conservative. It claimed to be a third way—a new, specifically modern alternative to both liberal democracy and Marxist communism, based on values that the war had brought to the fore.

With its claim to offer a modern political alternative, Italian fascism quickly attracted the attention of those in other countries who were disillusioned with parliamentary politics and hostile to the Marxist left. And just as fascism was anti-Marxist, the communists eventually made struggle against fascism their top priority. The interplay of communism and fascism, as new political experiments, proved central to the whole interwar period.

Consolidating Communist Power in Russia, 1917–1921

Even after leading the revolution that toppled the provisional government in November 1917, the Bolsheviks could not claim majority support in Russia. When the long-delayed elections to select a constituent assembly were finally held a few weeks after the revolution, the Bolsheviks ended up with fewer than one-quarter of the seats, while the Socialist Revolutionaries won a clear majority. But over the next three years the Communists, as the Bolsheviks renamed themselves, gradually consolidated their power, establishing a centralized and nondemocratic communist regime. Power lay not with the soviets, and not with some coalition of socialist parties, but solely with the Communist party. The Communists also established centralized control of the economy, subjecting workers to more rigorous discipline.

During its first years, the new communist regime encountered a genuine emergency that seemed to require a monopoly of power. For over two years the communist "Reds" had to fight a brutal civil war against counter revolutionary "Whites," people who had been dispossessed by the revolution or who had grown disillusioned with the Communist party. The Whites drew support from foreign intervention and from separatist sentiment, as several of the non-Russian nationalities of the old Russian Empire sought to defect, freeing themselves from Russian and communist control.

The counterrevolutionary assault seriously threatened the young communist regime and the territorial basis of the state it had inherited from the Russian Empire. In the final analysis, however, the Whites proved unable to rally much popular support. Peasants feared, plausibly enough, that a White victory would mean a restoration of the old order, including the return of their newly won lands to their former landlords. By the end of active fighting in November 1920, the communist regime had not only survived but regained most of the territory it had lost early in the civil war (Map 26.1).

The need to launch the new communist regime in this way, fighting counterrevolutionaries sup-

ported by foreign troops, inevitably affected Communist perceptions and priorities. Separatist sentiment might continue to feed counterrevolutionary efforts, so the new regime exerted careful control over the non-Russian nationalities. Ukraine, for example, had been the base for anticommunist activity as an independent republic under Menshevik leadership beginning in 1918, so in retaking the area in 1920 the Communists sought to bury all hopes for Ukrainian self-determination.

Even after the end of active fighting, the communist government had trouble re-establishing control over Georgia, Azerbaijan, and Russian Armenia in light of the strong separatist sentiment in those areas. Thus, when the Union of Soviet Socialist Republics (U.S.S.R.) was organized in December 1922, it was only nominally a federation of autonomous republics; strong centralization from the Communists' new capital in Moscow was the rule from the start.

Although they had to concentrate on the civil war from 1918 to late 1920, the Russian communists founded the Third, or Communist, International—commonly known as the Comintern—in March 1919, to make clear their break with the seemingly discredited strategies of the Second International. Through the Comintern, the Russian communists expected to translate their success in Russia into leadership of the international socialist movement. At the same time, however, many old-line Marxists elsewhere found it hard to swallow the notion that the leadership of European socialism had passed to the Bolshevik leaders of backward Russia. (See the box, "A Marxist Critique of Communism.")

From its founding in March 1919 until the spring of 1920, as a wave of leftist political agitation and labor unrest swept Europe, the Comintern actively promoted the wider revolution that Lenin had originally envisioned. Seeking to win mass support, the organization accented leftist solidarity and reached out to the rank and file in the labor unions. By the spring of 1920, however, it seemed clear that further revolution was not imminent. Thus, Comintern leaders began concentrating on improving organization and discipline for a more protracted revolutionary struggle.

The Russians felt that poor organization and planning had undermined the wider revolutionary possibility in Europe during 1919 and 1920. The Comintern would therefore cut through all

the revolutionary romanticism and rhetoric to show the others what the Leninist strategy, or communism, meant in fact. The Russians themselves would have to call the shots, because what communism meant, above all, was tight organization and discipline.

The second Comintern congress, during the summer of 1920, devised twenty-one points, or conditions, to be fulfilled by a socialist party seeking affiliation with the Comintern. Most notably, any such party had to accept the Comintern's authority, to adopt a centralized organization, and to purge its reformists. The result of the Comintern's aggressive claim to leadership was a lasting schism in the European socialist movement by early 1921, for the Comintern attracted some, but not all, of the members of the existing socialist parties. All over the world those parties split between "communists," who chose to affiliate with the Comintern, and "socialists," who rejected Comintern leadership. These socialists still claimed to be Marxists, but they were not Leninists; they rejected the Russian Bolshevik strategy for taking political power.

At first, many European socialists had difficulty assessing the Comintern objectively. The Russian communists enjoyed great prestige because they had made a real revolution, while elsewhere socialists had talked and compromised, even getting swept up in wartime patriotism. When, for example, the French socialist party considered the matter at its national congress in December 1920, about 70 percent of the delegates opted for the Comintern and the twenty-one points, while a minority walked out to form a new socialist party. But as the implications of Comintern membership became clearer over the next few years, the balance shifted to favor the social-

Tatlin: Monument to the Third International Vladimir Tatlin created this model for a monument to the Third International, or Comintern, during 1919 and 1920. He envisioned a revolving structure, made of glass and iron, and twice as tall as the later Empire State Building. Although the monument was never built, Tatlin's bold, dynamic form symbolized the utopian aspirations of the early years of the communist experiment in Russia. (*David King Collection*)

Map 26.1 Foreign Intervention and Civil War in Revolutionary Russia, 1918–1920 By mid-1918 the new communist regime was under attack from many sides, by both foreign troops and anticommunist Russians. Bolshevik-held territory shrank during 1919, but over the next year the Red Army managed to regain much of what had been lost and to secure the new communist state. Anton Deniken, Alexander Kolchak, and Nicholas Yudenich commanded the most significant counter-revolutionary forces. (*Source:* Adapted from *The Times Atlas of World History,* 3d ed., by kind permission of Times Books.)

ists. Membership in the French Communist party, which stood at 131,000 in 1921, declined to 28,000 by 1932.

Late in 1923 the Comintern finally concluded that revolution elsewhere could not be expected any time soon. The immediate enemy was not capitalism or the bourgeoisie, but the socialists, the communists' rivals for working-class support. The communists' incessant criticism of the socialists, whom they eventually dubbed "social fascists," demoralized and weakened the European left, especially in the face of the growing threat of fascism.

A Marxist Critique of Communism

Karl Kautsky (1854–1938) was the leading spokesman for orthodox Marxism within the German Social Democratic party, the most influential Marxist party in the world during the era of the Second International. Thus it is striking that he harshly criticized Leninist Bolshevism, or communism, as a heretical departure that could lead only to disaster. Kautsky's Terrorism and Communism, *written in 1919, was central to a volley of charges and counter-charges that pitted him first against Lenin, then against Trotsky.*

The hereditary sin of Bolshevism has been its suppression of democracy through a form of government, namely, the dictatorship, which has no meaning unless it represents the unlimited and despotic power, either of one single person, or of a small organization intimately bound together. . . . It is easy to begin a dictatorship as it is to begin war, if one has the State power under control. But when once such steps have been taken, it is as difficult at will to stop the one as the other. . . .

. . . [W]herever Socialism does not appear to be possible on a democratic basis, and where the majority of the population rejects it, its time has not yet fully come. Bolshevism, on the other hand, argues that Socialism can only be introduced by being forced on a majority by a minority. . . . The Bolsheviks are prepared, in order to maintain their position, to make all sorts of possible concessions to bureaucracy, to militarism, and to capitalism, whereas any concession to democracy seems to them to be sheer suicide. And yet that alone offers any

possibility . . . of leading Russia along paths of economic progress and prosperous development towards some higher form of existence. . . .

. . . [S]ince the rise of the Soviet Republic, a new wedge has been driven through the Socialist ranks of Germany by Bolshevik propaganda, which has demanded that our Party should relinquish the essential claims of democracy. . . .

. . . It was only after long and bitter struggle that the proletariat succeeded in acquiring universal and equal suffrage—a perfectly well-known fact, which, however, all communists and their friends seem to have completely forgotten. Democracy, with its universal equal suffrage, is the method to transform the class-struggle out of a hand-to-hand fight into a battle of intelligence, in which one particular class can triumph only if it is intellectually and morally on a level with its opponent. Democracy is the one and only method through which the higher form of life can be realised. . . .

Source: Karl Kautsky, *Terrorism and Communism: A Contribution to the Natural History of Revolution* (Westport, Conn.: Hyperion Press, 1973), pp. 217–218, 220–222, 226, 229, 231.

From Lenin to Stalin, 1921–1929

Although it managed to win the civil war, the communist regime was clearly in crisis by the beginning of 1921, partly because of "war communism," the rough-and-ready controlled economy that the war effort seemed to make necessary. With industrial production only about one-fifth the 1913 total, there were strikes in the factories, and peasants

were resisting further requisitions of grain. Finally, in March 1921, sailors at the Kronstadt naval base mutinied, suffering considerable loss of life as governmental control was re-established.

With the very survival of the revolution in question, Lenin replaced war communism with the New Economic Policy, or NEP, in March 1921. Although transport, banking, heavy industry, and wholesale commerce remained under state control, the NEP restored considerable scope for private enterprise, especially in the retail sector and in agriculture. The economy quickly began to revive and by 1927 was producing at prewar levels.

But what about the longer term? If revolution elsewhere was no longer on the immediate horizon, could the Soviet Union—relatively backward economically and scarred by over a decade of upheaval—build a genuinely socialist order on its own? Certain measures were obvious: The new regime engineered rapid improvements in literacy, for example. But the Marxist understanding of historical progress required industrialization, and so debate focused on industrial development—the scope for it under Soviet conditions and its relationship to the creation of socialism.

This debate about priorities became bound up with questions about the leadership of the new regime. Lenin suffered the first of a series of strokes in May 1922 and then died in January 1924, setting off a struggle among his possible succes-sors. Leon Trotsky, a powerful thinker and architect of the Red Army, was by most measures Lenin's heir apparent. Although he favored tighter economic controls to speed industrial development, Trotsky insisted that the Soviet Union should continue to concentrate on spreading the revolution to other countries.

In contrast, Nikolai Bukharin wanted to concentrate on the gradual development of the Soviet Union, based on a more open and conciliatory strategy than Trotsky envisioned. The way to promote industrialization was not by tightening controls, squeezing a surplus from agricultural producers, as Trotsky proposed, but by allowing those producers to profit, thereby building up purchasing power. By the time of his death early in 1924, Lenin had apparently begun thinking along the same lines. And he had come to have considerable misgivings about the man who would win this struggle for direction within the fragile new Soviet regime.

Rivals for the Soviet Leadership In July 1926 in Moscow, Soviet leaders carry the coffin of Feliks Dzerzhinsky, the first head of the secret police. Among them are Trotsky (with glasses, center left), Stalin (right foreground), and Bukharin (with mustache, at far right), rivals for the Soviet leadership after Lenin's death. The winner, Stalin, would eventually have his two competitors killed. *(David King Collection)*

The victory of Joseph Stalin (1879–1953), born Josef Djugashvili into a lower-class family in Georgia, in the Caucasian region, proved crucial to twentieth-century history—and decisive for the fate of Soviet communism. From the position of party secretary that he had assumed in 1922, he established his control within the Soviet system by 1929. Though he lacked Trotsky's charisma and knew little of economics, Stalin proved a master of backstage political maneuvering, playing his rivals against each other and accusing his critics of lack of faith in the Soviet working class. He first outmaneuvered Trotsky and his allies, removing them from positions of power, and finally forcing Trotsky himself into exile in 1929. Bitterly critical of Stalin to the end, Trotsky was finally murdered by Stalin's agents in Mexico in 1940. Stalin's victory over those like Bukharin was more gradual, but ultimately just as decisive.

The key was the policy of crash industrialization, favoring heavy industry and based on forced agricultural collectivization, that Stalin had put in place by 1929. In embarking on this program, he played up the great historical drama surrounding the Soviet experiment, with its almost incredible targets and goals. Suggestions by some that the pace could not be maintained only proved grist for Stalin's mill: "No, comrades," he told a workers' conference early in 1931, "the tempo must not be reduced. On the contrary, we must increase it as much as is within our powers and capabilities. . . . To slow the tempo would mean falling behind. And those who fall behind get beaten. . . . Do you want our socialist fatherland to be beaten and to lose its independence? . . . We are fifty or a hundred years behind the advanced countries. We must make good this distance in ten years. Either we do this or they will crush us."[2]

Stalin's program of rapid industrialization called forth an attempt to mobilize and control society without precedent in Western history. Although the economic sphere was crucial, this mobilization affected the whole shape of the regime—including, for example, cultural and artistic policy. During the 1920s, the possibility of building a new socialist society in the Soviet Union had attracted a number of modernist artists, who assumed that artistic innovation went hand in hand with the radical socioeconomic transformation the communists were seeking to engineer. These artists wanted to make art more socially useful and more central to the lives of ordinary people. With Soviet cultural officials welcoming their experiments, such Soviet artists as Vladimir Tatlin (1885–1956) and Kasimir Malevich (1878–1935) developed striking new cultural forms between 1919 and 1929.

But in 1929 Soviet officials began mobilizing the cultural realm to serve the grandiose task of building socialism in one country. No longer welcoming experiment and innovation, they demanded "socialist realism," which portrayed the achievements of the ongoing Soviet revolution in an inspiring, heroic light. Modernism, in contrast, they denounced as decadent and counterrevolutionary.

In retrospect, it is clear that a Stalinist revolution within the Soviet regime began in 1929, but where it was to lead was by no means certain—not even to Stalin himself. Still, the Soviet Union was pulling back, going its own way, by the end of the 1920s. For the foreseeable future, the presence of a revolutionary regime in the old Russia would apparently be less disruptive for the rest of Europe than it had first appeared.

The Crisis of Liberal Italy and the Creation of Fascism, 1919–1925

Fascism emerged directly from the Italian experience of World War I, which proved especially controversial because the Italians could have avoided it altogether. No one attacked Italy in 1914, and the country could have received significant territorial benefits just by remaining neutral. Yet it seemed to many, including leading intellectuals and educated young people, that Italy could not stand idly by in a European war, especially one involving Austria-Hungary, which still controlled significant Italian-speaking areas. To participate in this major war would be the test of Italy's maturity as a nation. In May 1915, Italy finally intervened on the side of the Triple Entente. The government's decision stemmed not from vague visions of renewal but from the commitment of tangible territorial gains, primarily at the expense of Austria-Hungary, that France and Britain made to Italy with the secret Treaty of London in April.

Despite the near collapse of the Italian armies in October 1917, Italy lasted out the war and contributed to the victory over Austria-Hungary. Supporters of the war felt that this success could lead to a thoroughgoing renewal of Italian public life. Yet many Italians had been skeptical of claims for the war from the outset, and the fact that it proved so much more difficult than expected hardly won them over. To Socialists, Catholics, and those loyal to the long-time liberal political leader Giovanni Giolitti, intervention itself had been a tragic mistake. Thus, despite Italy's participation in the victory, division over the war's significance immensely complicated the Italian political situation after the war was over.

The situation became even more volatile when Italy did not manage all the gains expected at the Paris Peace Conference. Italy got most of what it had been promised in the Treaty of London, but appetites increased with the dissolution of the Austro-Hungarian Empire. To some Italians, the disappointing outcome of the peace conference simply confirmed that the war had been a mistake, its benefits not worth the costs. But others were outraged at what seemed a denigration of the Italian contribution by France, Britain, and the United States. Thus the outcome fanned resentment not only of Italy's allies but also of the country's political leaders, who seemed too weak to deliver on what they had promised.

Italy's established leaders also failed at the task of renewing the country's political system in light of the war experience. The last gasp of the old liberal politics was Giovanni Giolitti, who returned for a final stint as prime minister in 1920, at the age of 78. But Giolitti, who had been adept at piecing together parliamentary majorities before the war, found the situation much less manageable now. In 1919, in a spirit of democratic reform, Italy had adopted proportional representation to replace the old system of small, single-member constituencies. The new system meant a greater premium on mass parties and party discipline at the expense of the one-to-one bargaining at which Giolitti had excelled. But the new mass politics quickly reached an impasse—partly because of the stance of the Italian Socialist party.

In contrast to the French and German parties, the Italian Socialists had never supported the war, and they did not accept the notion that the war experience could yield political renewal in the aftermath. So rather than reaching out to discontented war veterans, Socialist leaders talked of imitating the Bolshevik Revolution. During 1919 and 1920, the Italian situation seemed at least potentially revolutionary. A wave of quasi-revolutionary labor unrest included several national strikes and finally a series of factory occupations during September 1920. But despite their revolutionary rhetoric, Italian Socialist leaders did not understand what Leninism involved in practice, and they did not carry out the planning and organization that might have made an Italian revolution possible.

The established political system was at an impasse, and the Socialist party seemed at once too inflexible and too romantic to lead some sort of radical transformation. It was in this context that fascism emerged, claiming to offer a third way. It was bound to oppose the Socialists and the socialist working class because of conflict over the meaning of the war and the kind of transformation Italy needed. And this antisocialist posture made fascism open to exploitation by reactionary interests. By early 1921 landowners in northern and central Italy were footing the bill as bands of young fascists drove around the countryside in trucks, beating up workers and burning down socialist meeting halls. But fascist spokesmen claimed to offer something other than mere reaction, a new politics that would prove better than Marxist socialism at pursuing the long-term interests of the working class.

At the same time, important sectors of Italian industry, which had grown rapidly thanks to government orders during the war, looked with apprehension toward the more competitive international economy that loomed now that the war was over. With its relative lack of capital and raw materials, Italy seemed to face an especially difficult situation. Nationalist thinkers and business spokesmen questioned the capacity of the present parliamentary system to provide the vigorous leadership that Italy needed. Prone to short-term bickering and partisanship, ordinary politicians lacked both the vision to pursue Italy's long-term international economic interests and the will to impose the necessary discipline on the domestic level. Thus, the government had been relatively weak in responding to the labor unrest of 1919 and 1920. (See the box, "Toward Fascism: Alfredo Rocco on the Weakness of the Liberal Democratic State.")

In postwar Italy, then, there was widespread discontent with established forms of politics, but those discontented were socially disparate, and their aims were not entirely compatible. Some had

Toward Fascism: Alfredo Rocco on the Weakness of the Liberal Democratic State

As Italy's minister of justice from 1925 to 1932, the Italian legal scholar Alfredo Rocco (1875–1935) spearheaded the construction of the new fascist state. Speaking in November 1920, he revealed why he would seek to replace parliamentary democracy with a new, stronger form of government. Rocco was troubled, most immediately, by the apparent weakness of the liberal state in the face of strikes by unions, or syndicates, of public-service employees. But the deeper problem he saw was liberal individualism, linked to shortsighted pursuit of personal advantage.

There is a crisis within the state; day by day, the state is dissolving into a mass of small particles, parties, associations, groups and syndicates that are binding it in chains and paralysing and stifling its activity: one by one, with increasing speed, the state is losing its attributes of sovereignty. . . . The conflict of interests between groups and classes is now being settled by the use of private force alone. . . . The state stands by impassively watching these conflicts which involve countless violations of public and private rights. This neutrality which, in liberal doctrine, was intended to allow free play for economic law in the clash of interests between the classes is now being interpreted as allowing the state to abandon its essential function of guardian of public order and agent of justice. . . .

. . . The eighteenth-century reaction against the state . . . came to a head politically in the explosion of the French Revolution. . . . From that time onwards, the claims of individualism knew no bounds. The masses of individuals wanted to govern the state and govern it in accordance with their own individual interests.

The state, a living organism with a continuous existence over the centuries that extends beyond successive generations and as such the guardian of the immanent historical interests of the species, was turned into a monopoly to serve the individual interests of each separate generation. . . .

Now there can be no doubt that one of the most serious consequences of liberal agnosticism was the emergence of syndicalism, a syndicalism that was at once violent, subversive, and opposed to the state.

. . . The state must return to its traditions, interrupted by the triumph of liberal ideology, and treat the modern syndicates exactly as it treated the medieval corporations. It must absorb them and make them part of the state. . . . On the one hand, syndicates must be recognized as essential and on the other they must be placed firmly beneath the control of the state. . . . But above all, it is necessary to change them from aggressive bodies defending particular interests into a means of collaboration to achieve common aims.

Source: Adrian Lyttelton, ed., *Italian Fascisms from Pareto to Gentile* (New York: Harper & Row, Harper Torchbooks, 1975), pp. 269, 273–275, 278–280.

been socialists before the war, others nationalists hostile to socialism. While some envisioned a more intense kind of mass politics, others thought the masses already had too much power. Still, these discontented groups agreed on the need for an alternative to both conventional parliamentary politics and conventional Marxist socialism. It was

widely felt that the germs of that alternative could be found in the Italian war experience.

The one person who seemed able to translate these discontents and aspirations into a new political force was the one-time socialist, Benito Mussolini (1883–1945). Mussolini came from the Romagna region of central Italy, his father a

Benito Mussolini The founder of fascism is shown with other fascist leaders in 1922, as he becomes prime minister of Italy. Standing at Mussolini's right (with beard) is Italo Balbo, later a pioneering aviator and fascist Italy's air force minister. *(Corbis-Bettmann)*

blacksmith and a socialist, his mother a teacher. Moderately well educated, Mussolini taught French for a time, but he demonstrated such talent in socialist journalism that he became editor of the Socialist party's national newspaper, *Avanti!*, in 1912, when only 29 years old. At that point many saw him as the fresh face needed to revitalize Italian socialism.

His concern with renewal had made Mussolini an unorthodox socialist even before 1914, and when the European war broke out, he was prominent among those on the Italian left who began to call for Italian intervention. The fact that socialists in France, Germany, and elsewhere had immediately rallied to their respective national war efforts caused him to reconsider the old socialism, based on international proletarian solidarity. But the Socialist party refused to follow his call for intervention, remaining neutralist and aloof, so Mussolini found himself cut off from his earlier constituency.

Through his new newspaper, *Il popolo d'Italia (The People of Italy),* however, Mussolini promptly emerged as a leading advocate of Italian participation in the war. He saw military service once Italy intervened, and after the war he sought to rally those who aspired to translate the war experience into a new form of politics. But after founding the *fasci di combattimento* in March 1919, Mussolini became embroiled in periodic disputes with important sectors of his movement, especially as fascism gathered force in violent reaction against the socialist labor movement by 1921. Although young fascist militants wanted to replace the established parliamentary system with a wholly new political order, Mussolini seemed ever more prone to use fascism simply as his personal instrument as he jockeyed for power within the existing system. When his maneuvering finally won him the prime minister's post in October 1922, it was not at all clear that a change of regime, or a one-party dictatorship, was in the offing.

At that point, Mussolini, like most Italians, emphasized normalization and legality. Fascism had apparently been absorbed within the political system, perhaps to provide an infusion of youthful vitality after the war. With Mussolini as prime minister, there would be changes, but not revolutionary changes. Government would become more vigorous and efficient; the swollen Italian bureaucracy would be streamlined; the trains would run on time. But those who had envisioned more sweeping change were frustrated that nothing more had come of fascism than this.

In June 1924 the murder of Giacomo Matteotti (1885–1924), a moderate socialist parliamentary deputy, sparked a crisis that forced fascism to begin replacing the existing political system with a regime of its own. Shortly after a speech denouncing fascist violence, Matteotti was killed by fascist thugs. A great public outcry followed, and the key question for Italians in the months that followed concerned the responsibility of the government—and especially Mussolini himself—for the crime. Many of those from the establishment who had tolerated Mussolini as the man who could keep order now deserted him. A growing chorus called for his resignation.

Mussolini sought at first to be conciliatory and reassuring, but more radical fascists saw the crisis as a precious opportunity for fascism to end the compromise with the old order and to commit itself to creating a whole new political system. The crisis came to a head on December 31, 1924, when thirty-three militants called on Mussolini to demand that he make up his mind. The way out of the crisis was not to delimit the scope of fascism but to expand it. And Mussolini himself would have to accept responsibility for the fascist revolution, including its violent excesses. He was not an ordinary prime minister but the leader of fascism, *Il Duce*, and in that role he would have to implement the fascist revolution.

Finally at a crossroads, Mussolini committed himself to a more radical course when he addressed the Chamber of Deputies a few days later, on January 3, 1925. Defiantly claiming the "full political, moral, and historical responsibility for all that has happened," including "all the acts of violence," he promised to accelerate the transformation that he claimed to have initiated with his agitation for intervention in 1914 and 1915.[3] And now began the creation of a new fascist state, although the compromises continued and the direction was never as clear as committed fascists desired.

Innovation and Compromise in Fascist Italy, 1925–1930

Early in 1925, the fascist government began to undermine the existing liberal system by imprisoning or exiling opposition leaders and outlawing the other parties and the nonfascist labor unions. But fascism was not seeking simply a conventional monopoly of political power; the new fascist state was to be totalitarian, all-encompassing, limitless in its reach. Under the old liberal regime, the fascists charged, the state had been too weak to promote the national interest, and the society had been too fragmented to enable the Italian nation to achieve its potential. So Mussolini's regime expanded the state's sovereignty and mobilized the society to create a deeper sense of national identity and solidarity among Italians. Thus, for example, a new system of labor judges settled labor disputes, replacing the right to strike. And the Fascist party fostered new forms of participation in organizations it devised for youth, for women, for leisure-time activities, and the like.

The centerpiece of the new fascist state was corporativism, which entailed mobilizing people as producers, through organization of the workplace. Groupings based on occupation, or economic function, were gradually to replace parliament as the basis for political participation and decision making. Beginning in 1926, corporativist institutions were established in stages until a Chamber of Fasces and Corporations at last replaced the old Chamber of Deputies in 1939.

It was especially through this corporative state that the fascists claimed to be fulfilling their grandiose mission and providing the world with a third way beyond both outmoded democracy and misguided communism. The practice of corporativism during the 1930s never lived up to such rhetoric, but the effort to devise new forms of political participation and decision making, as an alternative to parliamentary democracy, was central to fascism's self-understanding and its quest for legitimacy. And that effort attracted much attention abroad, especially with the Great Depression of the 1930s.

Despite the commitment to a new regime, however, fascism continued to compromise with pre-existing elites and institutions. The accommodation was especially evident in the arrangements with the Catholic church that Mussolini worked out in 1929, formally ending the dispute between the church and the new Italian state that had resulted from national unification in the nineteenth century. With the Concordat and the Lateran Pact, Mussolini restored the sovereignty of the Vatican and conceded to the church autonomy in education and supremacy in marriage law. This settlement of an old and thorny dispute afforded Mussolini a good deal of prestige abroad, as well as among nonfascist Italians. At the same time, the compromise seemed to imply a kind of endorsement of Mussolini's government on the part of the church and the establishment in Italy.

But such a compromise with a traditional institution displeased many fascists, who complained that it undermined the totalitarian aspirations of fascism to give this powerful, nonfascist institution an autonomous role in Italian public life. Such complaints led to a partial crackdown on Catholic youth organizations in 1931, as Mussolini continued trying to juggle traditionalist compromise and revolutionary pretension.

By the end of the 1920s, then, it remained unclear whether Italian fascism was a form of revolution or a form of restoration. It could be violent and disruptive, dictatorial and repressive, but Mussolini seemed dynamic and creative. Fascism featured corporativist reconstruction during the later 1920s, but it might move in other directions, especially if a new international configuration should tempt its restless leader. Though its ultimate direction remained unclear, fascism attracted those discontented with liberal democracy and Marxist socialism all over Europe. It was thus a major source of the volatility and ideological polarization that marked the postwar European political order.

THE SEARCH FOR MEANING IN A DISORDERED WORLD

For all its vitality, the new culture of the 1920s had something brittle about it; the frenetic pace masked a deeper sense that things had started to come apart and might well get worse. The feeling of release and excitement combined with an anxious longing for stability, for a return to order. The war had accelerated the long-term "moderniza-

EVENTS OF THE 1920s	
March 1919	Founding of the Italian fascist movement
November 1920	End of fighting in the Russian civil war
October 1922	Mussolini becomes Italian prime minister
January 1923	French-led occupation of the Ruhr
January 1924	First Labour government in Britain
	Death of Lenin
August 1924	Acceptance of the Dawes Plan on German reparations
October 1925	Locarno Agreement
May 1926	Pilsudski's coup d'état in Poland
	Beginning of general strike in Britain
August 1929	Acceptance of the Young Plan on German reparations
October 1929	Death of Stresemann

tion" process toward large industries, cities, and bureaucracies, and toward mass politics, society, and culture. That process was positive, even liberating, in certain respects, but it was also disruptive and disturbing. Thus the emphases of intellectuals and artists differed dramatically in the 1920s.

Anxiety, Alienation, and Disillusionment

Concern about the dangers of the emerging mass civilization was especially clear in the *Revolt of the Masses* (1930), by the influential Spanish thinker José Ortega y Gasset (1883–1955). Ortega concluded that contemporary experience showed that ordinary people were intolerant and illiberal, incapable of creating standards, and content with the least common denominator. Communism and fascism indicated the violent, intolerant, and ultimately barbaric quality of the new mass age. But Ortega found the same tendencies in American-style democracy. Much of Europe seemed to be moving toward the mass politics and culture of the United States, but, as far as Ortega was concerned, that was a symptom of the deeper problem, not a solution.

Concern with cultural decline was part of a wider pessimism about the condition of the West, which stood in stark contrast to the belief in progress, and the attendant confidence in Western superiority, that had been essential to Western self-understanding before 1914. The German thinker Oswald Spengler (1880–1936) made concern with decline almost fashionable with his bestseller of the immediate postwar years, *The Decline of the West* (1918), which offered a cyclical theory purporting to explain how spirituality and creativity were giving way to a materialistic mass-based culture in the West.

To Sigmund Freud, the eruption of violence and hatred during the war and after indicated a deep, instinctual problem in the human makeup. In his gloomy essay *Civilization and Its Discontents* (1930), he suggested that the progress of civilization entails the bottling up of aggressive instincts, which are directed inward as guilt, or left to erupt in violent outbursts. This notion raised fundamental questions not only about the scope for progress but also about the plausibility of the Wilsonian ideals that had surrounded the end of the war. Perhaps, with civilization growing more complex, the Great War had been only the beginning of a new era of hatred and violence.

The sense that there is something incomprehensible, even nightmarish, about modern civilization, with its ever more complex bureaucracies, technologies, and cities, found vivid expression in the works of the Czech Jewish writer Franz Kafka (1883–1924), most notably in the novels *The Trial* and *The Castle*, published posthumously in the mid-1920s. In a world that claimed to be increasingly rational, Kafka's individual is the lonely, fragile plaything of forces utterly beyond reason, comprehension, and control. In such a world, the quest for law, or meaning, or God is futile, ridiculous.

Especially in the unsettled conditions of Weimar Germany, the anxiety of the 1920s tended to take extreme forms, from irrational activism to a preoccupation with death. There was a striking increase in suicides among students, even before the Depression. Youthful alienation prompted the novelist Jakob Wassermann (1873–1934) to caution German young people in 1932 that not all action is good simply because it is action, that feeling is not always better than reason and discipline, and that youth is not in itself a badge of superiority.

Recasting the Tradition

Expressions of disillusionment revealed something about human experience in the unsettled new world, but they were sometimes morbid and self-indulgent. Other cultural leaders sought to be more positive; the challenge was not to give vent to new anxieties but to find antidotes to them. One direction was to recast traditional categories—in the arts, in religion, in politics—to make them relevant to contemporary experience. Although not all were optimistic about human prospects, an array of figures found such a renewal of tradition to be the best hope for responding to the disarray of the postwar world.

Even modernist artists sought to consolidate earlier gains, to pull things back together after the headlong experiment of the years before 1914. In music, composers as different as Igor Stravinsky (1882–1971) and Paul Hindemith (1895–1963) adapted earlier styles, although often in a somewhat ironic spirit, as they sought to weave new means of expression into familiar forms. The overall tendency toward neoclassicism during the period was an effort to give musical composition a renewed basis of order.

One of the most striking responses to the anxieties of this increasingly secular age was a wave of neo-orthodox religious thinking, most prominent in Protestants like the Swiss theologian Karl Barth (1886–1968). In his *Epistle to the Romans* (1919), Barth reacted against the liberal theology, the attempt to marry religious categories to secular progress, that had become prominent by the later nineteenth century. The war, especially, had seemed to shatter the liberal notion that the hand of God was at work in history, and Barth emphasized the radical cleft between God and this, the human world of history, sunken in sin. Recalling the accents of Augustine and Luther, he portrayed humanity as utterly lost, capable only of a difficult relationship with God, through faith, grace, and revelation.

With democracy faring poorly in parts of Europe, and with fascism and communism claiming to offer superior alternatives, some sought to make new sense of the democratic tradition. In Italy, Benedetto Croce (1866–1952) agreed with critics that the old justifications for liberal democracy, based on natural law or utilitarianism, were deeply inadequate, but he also became one of Europe's most influential antifascists. He insisted that the most significant innovations in modern thought show us why democratic values, institutions, and practices are still appropriate. We human beings are free, creative agents of a history that we make as best we can, without quite understanding what will result from what we do. Humility, tolerance, and equal access to political participation are essential to the process whereby the world is endlessly remade.

The new political challenges also stimulated fresh thinking within the Marxist tradition. By showing that Marxism could encompass consciousness as well as economic relationships, the Hungarian Georg Lukács (1885–1971) invited a far more sophisticated Marxist analysis of capitalist culture than had been possible before. Lukács accented the progressive role of realistic fiction and attacked the disordered fictional world of Kafka, which seemed to abandon all hope for human understanding of the forces of history. Though more eclectic, the Institute for Social Research, founded in Frankfurt, Germany, in 1923, gave rise to an influential tradition of criticism of capitalist civilization in what came to be known as the Frankfurt School. These innovations helped give the Marxist tradition a new lease on life in the West, even as it was developing in unforeseen ways in the Soviet Union.

The Search for a New Tradition

While some sought renewal from within the tradition, others insisted that a more radical break was needed—but also that the elements for a viable new cultural tradition were available.

Reflecting on the situation of women writers in 1928, the British novelist Virginia Woolf (1882–1941) showed how women in the past had suffered from the absence of a tradition of writing by women. By the 1920s, women had made important strides, but Woolf suggested that further advance required a more self-conscious effort by women to develop their own tradition. Most basically, women needed greater financial independence so that they could have the time for scholarship, the leisure of cultivated conversation, and the privacy of "a room of one's own." Woolf also envisioned a new sort of historical inquiry, focusing on how ordinary women lived their lives, that could show contemporary women where they have come from—and thus deepen their sense of who they are. (See the box, "Tradition and Women: The Conditions of Independence.")

A very different effort to establish a new tradition developed in Paris in the early 1920s as the poet André Breton (1896–1966) spearheaded the surrealist movement in literature and the visual arts. Surrealism grew directly from Dada, an artistic movement that had emerged in neutral Zurich and elsewhere during the war. Radically hostile to the war, Dada artists developed shocking, sometimes nihilistic forms to deal with a reality that now seemed senseless and out of control. Some made collages from gutter trash; others indulged in nonsense or relied on chance. By the early 1920s, however, the surrealists felt it was time to create a new and deeper basis of order after the willful disordering of Dada. Having learned from Sigmund Freud about the subconscious, they sought to adapt Dada's novel techniques—especially the use of chance—to gain access to the subconscious, which they believed contains a deeper truth, without the overlay of logic, reason, and conscious control.

But other artists, seeking to embrace the modern industrial world in a more positive spirit, found surrealism merely escapist. Among them was Walter Gropius (1883–1969), a pioneering modernist architect and leader of an influential German art school, the Bauhaus, during the 1920s. (See the feature, "Weighing the Evidence: Modern Design," on pages 992–993.) Gropius held that it was possible to establish new forms of culture, even a new tradition, that could be affirmative and reassuring in the face of the postwar cultural disarray. Rather than putting up familiar neoclassical or neo-Gothic buildings, "feigning a culture that has long since disappeared," we must face up to the kind of civilization we have become—industrial, technological, efficient, urban, democratic, mass-based. If we pick and choose from among the elements of our new machine-based civilization, we can again have a culture that works, an "integrated pattern for living."[4]

Tradition and Women: The Conditions of Independence

Speaking in 1928 about the situation of women writers, the British novelist Virginia Woolf raised questions that were relevant to all women seeking the opportunity to realize their potential. Indeed, her reflections about the value of difference, and the need for particular traditions, inspired those seeking equal opportunity for decades to come. And her question about why we know so little about women's lives in the past helped stimulate later historians to ask precisely the questions she envisioned about the experience of ordinary people.

Woman . . . pervades poetry from cover to cover; she is all but absent from history. . . .

Occasionally an individual woman is mentioned, an Elizabeth, or a Mary; a queen or a great lady. But by no possible means could middle-class women with nothing but brains and character at their command have taken part in any one of the great movements which, brought together, constitute the historian's view of the past. . . . What one wants . . . is a mass of information; at what age did she marry; how many children had she as a rule; what was her house like; had she a room to herself; did she do the cooking; would she be likely to have a servant? All these facts lie somewhere, presumably, in parish registers and account books; the life of the average Elizabethan woman must be scattered about somewhere, could one collect it and make a book of it. It would be ambitious beyond my daring, I thought, looking about the shelves for books that were not there, to suggest to the students of those famous colleges that they should rewrite history, though I own that it often seems a little queer as it is, unreal, lop-sided. . . .

But whatever effect discouragement and criticism had upon their writing—and I believe they had a very great effect—that was unimportant compared with the other difficulty which faced them (I was still considering those early nineteenth-century novelists) when they came to set their thoughts on paper—that is that they had no tradition behind them, or one so short and partial that it was of little help. For we think back through our mothers if we are women. It is useless to go to the great men writers for help, however much one may go to them for pleasure. . . .

. . . [W]omen have sat indoors all these millions of years, so that by this time the very walls are permeated by their creative force, which has, indeed, so overcharged the capacity of bricks and mortar that it must needs harness itself to pens and brushes and business and politics. But this creative power differs greatly from the creative power of men. And one must conclude that it would be a thousand pities if it were hindered or wasted, for it was won by centuries of the most drastic discipline, and there is nothing to take its place. It would be a thousand pities if women wrote like men, or lived like men, or looked like men. . . . Ought not education to bring out and fortify the differences rather than the similarities?

Source: Virginia Woolf, *A Room of One's Own* (San Diego: Harcourt Brace Jovanovich, Harvest/HBJ, 1989), pp. 43–45, 76, 87–88.

This "constructive," promodern impulse was particularly prominent in Germany, but it could be found all over—in the modernists of the Russian Revolution, in the French painter Fernand Léger (1881–1955), in the Swiss architect Le Corbusier (1887–1965). Whereas many of their contemporaries were at best ambivalent about the masses, these artists sought to bring high art and mass society together in the interests of both. And they welcomed the new patterns of life that seemed to be emerging in the new world of mass production and fast-paced cities.

Léger: Three Women With their sleekly impersonal forms, Fernand Léger's paintings suggested that human beings could fit comfortably into the mass machine age that was emerging. This work dates from 1921. (*Léger, Fernand,* Three Women [Le grand dejeuner], *1921. Oil on canvas, 6'¼" × 8'3". The Museum of Modern Art, New York. Mrs. Simon Guggenheim Fund.*)

SUMMARY

The 1920s proved a contradictory period of vitality and despair, pacifism and violence, restabilization and instability. The era began with bright hopes for democracy, yet the outcome of the democratic experiment in east-central Europe was disappointing. In Germany as well, the new democratic republic remained on the defensive, then failed to weather the economic depression that began in 1929. Even Italy, heir by the 1920s to a respectable tradition of democracy, gave rise to the troubling new phenomenon of fascism. A hopeful new spirit of international conciliation drew France and Germany closer together by the end of 1925, but France and Britain seemed to draw further apart as the British, preoccupied with colonial concerns, distanced themselves from politics on the Continent.

Despite tensions and doubts, however, in early 1929 restabilization seemed to have taken hold in Europe. Even Germany, Italy, and the Soviet Union, the most volatile and potentially disruptive of the major countries, seemed to be settling down. Still, it would all come apart over the next decade, leading to political extremism and another major war. In light of that outcome, the successes, even the vitality, of the 1920s appear superficial, and the unrecognized tensions stand out. When the decade is taken on its own terms, it is clear that the vitality, the renewed prosperity, and the diplomatic goodwill were all real, but so were the unresolved problems that made the 1920s a prelude to the more difficult 1930s, when the notion that Europe had returned to normal came to seem but a fairy tale.

NOTES

1. Quoted in Robert G. L. Waite, *Vanguard of Nazism: The Free Corps Movement in Postwar Germany, 1918–1923* (New York: W. W. Norton, 1969), pp. 14–15.
2. Quoted in Martin McCauley, *The Soviet Union Since 1917* (London and New York: Longman, 1981), pp. 72–73.
3. Benito Mussolini, speech to the Italian Chamber of Deputies, January 3, 1925, from Charles F. Delzell, ed., *Mediterranean Fascism, 1919–1945* (New York: Harper & Row, 1970), pp. 59–60.
4. Walter Gropius, *Scope of Total Architecture* (New York: Collier Books, 1962), pp. 15, 67.

SUGGESTED READING

General Surveys

Ansprenger, Franz. *The Dissolution of the Colonial Empires.* 1989. Covers the whole decolonization process but is stronger than most surveys on the impact of World War I and the events of the interwar period.

Kitchen, Martin. *Europe Between the Wars: A Political History.* 1988. A clear narrative of international and domestic political developments from a leftist perspective.

Sontag, Raymond J. *A Broken World, 1919–1939.* 1971. Comprehensive survey by a master historian. Concerned especially with domestic politics and international relations but includes developments in science and the arts.

Political Restoration

Carsten, F. L. *Revolution in Central Europe, 1918–1919.* 1972. A straightforward study emphasizing Germany, Austria, and Hungary. Accents the failure to overcome conservative forces and to lay the foundations for successful democracy.

Maier, Charles S. *Recasting Bourgeois Europe: Stabilization in France, Germany, and Italy in the Decade After World War I.* 1975. An important but somewhat difficult study showing how European elites sought new bases of stability, especially through new authority relationships in industry, during the 1920s.

Marquand, David. *Ramsay MacDonald.* 1977. Thorough and balanced account of the controversial career of Britain's first Labour prime minister.

Trachtenberg, Marc. *Reparation in World Politics: France and European Economic Diplomacy, 1916–1923.* 1980. A detailed but readable study questioning the widespread view that France imposed an unreasonable reparations burden on Germany after World War I.

The Soviet Union

Fitzpatrick, Sheila, Alexander Rabinowitch, and Richard Stites, eds. *Russia in the Era of NEP: Explorations in Soviet Society and Culture.* 1991. Illuminating scholarly essays accenting the ambiguities of the transitional 1920s, when class identity, economic activity, and gender roles had been radically disrupted but had not yet settled into the forms that, in the 1930s, came to characterize the Soviet experiment.

Lewin, M[oshe]. *Russian Peasants and Soviet Power: A Study of Collectivization.* 1975. A pioneering account of the process leading to the decision for forced collectivization by 1929.

———. *The Making of the Soviet System: Essays in the Social History of Interwar Russia.* 1985. Essays by a leading social historian. Especially strong on agriculture and the peasantry.

Stites, Richard. *Revolutionary Dreams: Utopian Visions and Experimental Life in the Russian Revolution.* 1989. A vivid account of the utopian aspirations that gave the new communist regime emotional force from 1917 to 1930.

Tucker, Robert C. *Stalin as Revolutionary, 1879–1929: A Study in History and Personality.* 1973. A pioneering account of Stalin's early years and rise to power, probing the sources of the elements of character and personality that helped shape his subsequent rule.

Fascism in Italy

De Grand, Alexander. *Italian Fascism: Its Origins and Development,* 2d ed. 1989. An accessible overview, providing a good sense of the heterogeneity of both the purposes and the policies of Italian fascism.

Forgacs, David, ed. *Rethinking Italian Fascism: Capitalism, Populism and Culture.* 1986. An important collection of essays, reflecting critical rethinking of conventional approaches and interpretations.

Gentile, Emilio. *The Sacralization of Politics in Fascist Italy.* 1996. Engaging account of the rituals, symbols, and myths that, in Italy during the 1920s, fed the first overtly totalitarian experiment.

Lyttelton, Adrian. *The Seizure of Power,* 2d ed. 1988. Based on pioneering archival research, this book offers a detailed dissection of the complex process through which the fascist movement took control of Italy.

Mack Smith, Denis. *Mussolini: A Biography.* 1983. A lively, critical account, and one of the most important biographies of Mussolini in English.

Sarti, Roland. *Fascism and the Industrial Leadership in Italy, 1919–1940: A Study in the Expansion of Private Power Under Fascism.* 1971. Carefully researched study demonstrating the cat-and-mouse relationship between the fascist regime and big business.

Segré, Claudio. *Italo Balbo: A Fascist Life*. 1987. A readable biography of one of the most colorful of Mussolini's lieutenants.

Tannenbaum, Edward. *The Fascist Experience: Italian Society and Culture, 1922–1945*. 1972. A comprehensive study of life in fascist Italy.

Weimar Germany

Diehl, James M. *Paramilitary Politics in Weimar Germany*. 1977. Probing account of the rise and normalization of political violence, showing how it helped undermine the Weimar Republic.

Gay, Peter. *Weimar Culture: The Outsider as Insider*. 1970. An influential study providing a good sense of the conflicting impulses—the embrace of modernity, the nostalgia for wholeness, the sense of foreboding—that made German culture so intense and vital during the 1920s.

Herf, Jeffrey. *Reactionary Modernism: Technology, Culture, and Politics in Weimar and the Third Reich*. 1984. Influential study showing how antimodern and technocratic themes could be fused in the special circumstances of interwar Germany.

Kolb, Eberhard. *The Weimar Republic*. 1988. Provides a good overall survey, then pinpoints the recent trends in research and the questions at issue among historians of the period.

Mommsen, Hans. *The Rise and Fall of Weimar Democracy*. 1996. A detailed political history identifying the social tensions that the democratic political process proved unable to handle.

Peukert, Detlev. *The Weimar Republic: The Crisis of Classical Modernity*. 1992. Accessible interpretive study, accenting the strains stemming from the rapid modernization of the 1920s. Stresses the loss of political legitimacy even before the onset of Depression.

Schrader, Bärbel, and Jürgen Schebera. *The "Golden" Twenties: Art and Literature in the Weimar Republic*. 1988. A superbly illustrated study that gives a good sense of complexity and contradiction of German culture in the 1920s.

Stern, Fritz. *The Politics of Cultural Despair: A Study in the Rise of the Germanic Ideology*. 1961. A classic work focusing on three thinkers of the German radical right; shows how their resentment of the modernization process fed antidemocratic sentiment in Germany.

Turner, Jr., Henry Ashby. *Stresemann and the Politics of the Weimar Republic*. 1963. A well-balanced study of the most important German statesman of the Weimar period.

Willett, John. *Art and Politics in the Weimar Period: The New Sobriety, 1917–1933*. 1978. A lively, complex study that plays up the effort of German cultural innovators to make art constructive by combining it with work, production, and everyday life.

Social Change and Gender Relations

Grossmann, Atina. *Reforming Sex: The German Movement for Birth Control and Abortion Reform, 1920-1950*. 1995. Innovative study tracing German debate and policy across three distinct political regimes.

Kent, Susan Kingsley. *Making Peace: The Reconstruction of Gender in Interwar Britain*. 1993. Concise and accessible work examining the use of traditionalist representations of gender roles in response to the anxieties unleashed in Britain by the war.

Nolan, Mary. *Visions of Modernity: American Business in the Modernization of Germany*. 1994. Examines the ambiguous impact of Americanism on Germany in the 1920s, when the United States seemed to stand both for economic success based on mass production and for an impersonal, alienating mass culture.

Pedersen, Susan. *Family, Dependence, and the Origins of the Welfare State: Britain and France, 1914–1945*. 1993. An effective comparative study showing how concerns about gender roles and family relations helped shape discussion and policy as government assumed greater responsibility for social welfare. Detailed but readable, a landmark in the new gender history.

Roberts, Mary Louise. *Civilization Without Sexes: Reconstructing Gender in Postwar France, 1917-1927*. 1994. Sophisticated study arguing that the anxieties accompanying dislocation and change in France after World War I were brought to the level of ordinary people through gender categories, which even came to shape the understanding and experience of change itself.

MODERN DESIGN

Led by Walter Gropius, the Bauhaus of Weimar Germany became the most influential art school of the twentieth century. As the incubator of modern architecture and design, it helped determine what the "modern world" would look like. And it did so consciously, believing it could help us embrace as our own the unnerving new world of machines, mass production, and rapid transit. But many, especially in the unsettled conditions of Weimar Germany, found the Bauhaus style alienating and threatening. Bauhaus artists seemed to foster all that was negative in the emerging world of industry and technology, impersonal cities, and large bureaucracies. When the Nazis came to power in 1933, they promptly closed the Bauhaus down.

Things made by the Bauhaus, from chairs to housing projects, still look "modern"—but why? How do they symbolize or manifest modernity? Do these new forms lead us to affirm the modern world, or are they alienating and repelling?

We note first that the Bauhaus stressed clean lines, simple and precise forms. In designing the chair shown here, Marcel Breuer tried to eliminate

Marcel Breuer, Chair, Tubular Steel and Black Fabric, 1925–1926 *(Bauhaus Archiv, Berlin)*

everything extraneous to the function of the chair as an object to sit in. The Bauhaus's own building, illustrated here, has none of the classical or Gothic ornament—the columns and pediments, the gargoyles and pointed arches—that had long seemed essential to architecture. Notice the extensive use of glass and steel. Bauhaus architects sought to use the new materials and construction techniques that industrialization made possible. On the one hand, Bauhaus design seems coolly impersonal, on the other utilitarian and functional.

In evaluating these pioneering modern forms, we must ask what the Bauhaus architects and designers were reacting against. In the nineteenth century, historical revivals dominated architecture, but by the 1920s such historical references seemed irrelevant, even dishonest. Why should banks look like Greek temples? Why should modern universities copy Gothic guild halls? According to the Bauhaus, it was time we faced up to the fact that the industrial age has cut us off from the old tradition. At first, the experience of disruption may be troubling, but we can develop an honest, satisfying, distinctively modern style based on the possibilities and patterns of the industrial world itself.

If the modern world is one of mass culture and mass society, perhaps even the best artists need to rethink the purpose of what they do. Students at the Bauhaus were taught that art was no longer something to be venerated in a museum or acquired by a cultivated and wealthy elite. Rather, art was to be socially useful. No longer was there to be a rigid distinction between art objects and utilitarian objects. Bauhaus artists placed great emphasis on the design of ordinary things for everyday use, from textiles to chairs to desk lamps. No longer was art to express the personality of the artist. Reacting against the romantic cult of individual self-expression, the Bauhaus stressed teamwork and impersonal design. Moreover, by using new materials, mass production, and even prefabrication, artists could play a newly democratic role—in designing, for example, housing projects that would give ordinary working people more light and fresh air than older urban buildings provided. Projects like the one shown here, built for employees of the Siemens electrical company, could be constructed affordably because they stressed the efficient use of materials and avoided irrelevant ornamentation.

Mass production, efficiency, and the purging of ornaments, however, did not have to undermine beauty. According to the Bauhaus, beauty in the modern world is to be found in clarity, in economy of means, in sleekly impersonal precision. From the Bauhaus perspective, Breuer's chair and the Siemens housing project are beautiful because they are efficient and functional.

Others, however, found the impersonal art of the Bauhaus to be cold and materialistic. Some, including the Nazis, labeled it "international" and "Bolshevik" as well. As far as such critics were concerned, the Bauhaus was simply giving in to the tyranny of the machine.

The cultural historian Peter Gay has argued that "what Gropius taught, and what most Germans did not want to learn, was . . . that . . . the cure for the ills of modernity is more, and the right kind of modernity."* Surely it is true that many Germans were particularly nostalgic and resistant to change during the 1920s. But perhaps the Bauhaus was too quick to assume that in the modern world we have no choice but to start over; perhaps it underestimated the need for continuity with our cultural traditions.

The kind of thinking nurtured at the Bauhaus led to the urban renewal and freeway projects that, by the end of the 1960s, had radically altered the face of many American cities, destroying much that had connected the present with the past. We continue to wrestle with what tradition means in the face of modernity and change, but

*Peter Gay, *Weimar Culture: The Outsider as Insider* (New York: Harper & Row, 1970), p. 101.

The Bauhaus Building, Dessau, 1925–1926 *(Vanni/Art Resource, NY)*

Housing Complex for Siemens Company Employees, Berlin, 1929 *(Bauhaus Archiv, Berlin)*

we are now less likely to assume that we can do without the old, the visible embodiments of a living tradition.

In the aftermath of World War I, however, Walter Gropius and his colleagues at the Bauhaus thought it would be healthier and more honest to make a clean break with the past. They set out with missionary fervor to derive a wholly new tradition from the modern industrial world. And controversial though they were, their designs were instrumental in giving "modern" its characteristic look. ❧

The Tortured Decade, 1930–1939

"They shall not pass," proclaimed the charismatic Spanish communist Dolores Ibarruri (1895–1989), whose impassioned speeches and radio broadcasts helped inspire the heroic defense of Madrid during the civil war that gripped Spain, and captured the attention of the world, during the later 1930s. Known as La Pasionaria—the passion flower—Ibarruri became a living legend for her role in defending the new Spanish republic, formed in 1931, against the nationalist forces seeking to overthrow it. But the Republican side lost, and she spent 38 years in exile before returning to Spain in 1977, after the end of the military dictatorship that had resulted from the Spanish civil war.

In her effort to rally the Republican side, Ibarruri stressed the political power of women, and indeed women were prominent in the citizen militias defending Madrid and other Spanish cities. Women fought for the Spanish republic in part because it seemed to open new opportunities for them, especially as it became more radical by 1936. But just as some women welcomed the new direction, others became politically active on the opposing Nationalist side—to support the church, to combat divorce, to defend separate spheres for women as the guardians of private life and family values.

The ideological polarization that characterized the Spanish civil war reflected the expanding reach of politics in the 1930s, whenthe advent of economic depression and the challenge from new governmental systems immeasurably complicated the European situation. The intricate mechanisms used to realign the international economy after World War I had seemed effective for most of the 1920s, but by 1929, they were beginning

"¡No pasarán!" ("they shall not pass"): Defending the democratic republic during the Spanish civil war.

to backfire, helping to trigger the Great Depression. During the early 1930s the economic crisis intensified sociopolitical strains all over the Western world and even beyond, intensifying anti-Western feeling and creating further opportunities for anticolonialists. In Germany, the Depression helped undermine the Weimar Republic and gave a major impetus to Nazism. The rise to power of the Nazi leader, Adolf Hitler, intensified the ideological polarization in Europe, and his policies produced a series of diplomatic crises that eventually led to a new European war.

German Nazism paralleled Italian fascism in its hostility to both parliamentary democracy and Marxist socialism, in its willingness to use violence, and in its reliance on a single charismatic leader. But Nazism emphasized racism and anti-Semitism in a way that Italian fascism did not, and it more radically transformed its society.

At about the same time, the direction of Stalin's communist regime in the Soviet Union seemed to converge, in some ways, with these new fascist regimes—especially with German Nazism. So though they expressed widely different aims, Stalinism and Nazism are sometimes lumped together as instances of totalitarianism. Both apparently sought total government control over all aspects of society, and in both secret police agencies came to play significant roles. But by the later 1930s the Soviet Union under Stalin experienced a form of police terror that not even Nazi Germany could match. Thus, although "totalitarianism" has become central to twentieth-century political language, it proves a tricky concept indeed, and whether it is correct to group Stalinist communism with Nazism remains controversial.

However they are to be classified, fascism, Nazism, and communism seemed able to sidestep—or surmount—the ills of the Depression, and they stood opposed to the parliamentary democracy that had established roots in Britain, France, Scandinavia, and elsewhere. Such liberal democracy had long seemed the direction of progressive political change, but in the face of the political and economic challenges of the 1930s the democratic movement appeared to lose its momentum. The defeat, by early 1939, of the democratic republic in Spain by the authoritarian Nationalists seemed to exemplify the political direction of the decade.

THE GREAT DEPRESSION

Although the stock market crash of October 1929 in the United States helped usher in the world economic crisis of the early 1930s, it had this effect only because the new international economic order after World War I was extremely fragile. By October 1929, in fact, production was already declining in all the major Western countries except France.

The economies of Germany and the states of east-central Europe remained particularly vulnerable after World War I, and in the increasingly interdependent economic world, their weaknesses magnified problems that started elsewhere. The crash of the U.S. stock market led to a restriction of credit in central Europe, which triggered a more general contraction in production and trade. Facing cruel dilemmas, policymakers proved unable to master the situation for the first few years of the crisis. The consequences—both human and political—were profound.

Sources of the Economic Contraction

Certain economic sectors, especially coal mining and agriculture, were already suffering severe problems by the mid-1920s, well before the stock market crash of 1929. British coal exports fell partly because oil and hydroelectricity were rapidly developing as alternatives. Unemployment in Britain was never less than 10 percent even in the best of times between the wars. In agriculture high prices worldwide during the war produced oversupply, which, in turn, led to a sharp drop in prices once the war was over. During the later 1920s, bumper harvests of grain and rice in many parts of the world renewed the downward pressure on prices. The result of low agricultural prices was a diminished demand for industrial goods, which impeded growth in the world economy.

Throughout the 1920s, finance ministers and central bankers had difficulty juggling the economic imbalances created by the war, centering on war debts to the United States and German reparations obligations to France, Britain, and Belgium. The strains in the system finally caught up with policymakers by 1929, when an international restriction of credit forced an end to the international economic cooperation that had been attempted in the past decade.

Unemployment in Britain
The Depression hit Britain hard—and its effects continued to be felt throughout the 1930s. These unemployed shipyard workers from Jarrow, in northeastern England, are marching to London in 1936 to present a protest petition. *(Hulton-Getty/Tony Stone Images)*

The shaky postwar economic system depended on U.S. bank loans to Germany, funneled partly by international agreements but also drawn by high interest rates. By 1928, however, U.S. investors were rapidly withdrawing their capital from Germany in search of the higher returns that could be made in the booming U.S. stock market. This tightened credit in Germany. And then the crash of the overpriced U.S. market in October 1929 deepened the problem by forcing suddenly strapped American investors to pull still more of their funds out of Germany. This process continued over the next two years, weakening the major banks in Germany and the other countries of central Europe, which were closely tied to the German economy. In May 1931 the bankruptcy of Vienna's most powerful bank, the Credit-Anstalt, made it clear that a crisis of potentially catastrophic proportions was in progress.

Despite attempts at adjustment on the international level, fears of bank failure or currency devaluation led to runs on the banks and currencies of Germany and east-central Europe. To maintain the value of the domestic currency in world markets, and thereby to resist the withdrawal of capital, government policymakers raised interest rates. This measure was not sufficient to stem the capital flight, but by restricting credit still more, it further dampened domestic economic activity.

Finally, the Germans seemed to have no choice but to freeze foreign assets—that is, to cease allowing conversion of assets held in German marks to other currencies. In this atmosphere, investors seeking the safest place for their capital tried to cash in currency for gold—or for British pounds, which could then be converted to gold. This flight to gold, however, soon put such pressure on the British currency that Britain was forced to devalue the pound and sever it from the gold standard in September 1931. This proved the definitive end of the worldwide system of economic exchange based on the gold standard that had gradually crystallized during the nineteenth century.

The absence of a single standard of exchange, combined with various currency restrictions, made foreign trade more difficult and uncertain, thereby diminishing it further. So did the scramble for tariff protection that proved a widespread response to the developing crisis. Crucial was the U.S. Smoot-Hawley Tariff Act of June 1930, which raised taxes on imports by 50 to 100 percent, forcing other nations to take comparable steps. Even Britain, long a bastion of free trade, adopted a peacetime tariff for the first time in nearly a century with the Import Duties Act of 1932, which imposed a 10 percent tax on most imports.

The decline of trade spread depression throughout the world economic system. By 1933 most major European countries were able to export no more than two-thirds, and in some cases as little as one-third, of the amount they had sold in 1929. At the same time, losses from international bank failures contracted credit and purchasing power and furthered the downward spiral, until by 1932 the European economies had shrunk to a little over half their 1929 size. This was the astonishing outcome of the short-lived prosperity of the 1920s.

Consequences and Responses

The Depression was essentially a radical contraction in economic activity; with less being produced and sold, demand for labor declined sharply. In Germany, industrial production by early 1933 was only half what it had been in 1929, and roughly 6 million Germans, or one-third of the labor force, were unemployed.

Although its timing and severity varied, the Depression profoundly affected the lives of ordinary people throughout the Western world and beyond. Unemployment produced widespread malnutrition, which led, in turn, to sharp increases in such diseases as tuberculosis, scarlet fever, and rickets. The decline in employment opportunities helped produce a backlash against the ideal of "the new woman," working outside the home, which had been a prominent aspect of the new freedom of the 1920s in Germany and elsewhere. (See the box, "Retreating from 'the New Woman.'") Even those men and women who hung on to jobs suffered from growing insecurity. In his aptly titled *Little Man, What Now?* (1932), the German novelist Hans Fallada (1893–1947) explored the effects of the Depression on members of the lower middle class—store clerks, shopowners, civil servants. Such people were first resentful, then resigned, as their dreams of security, of "order and cleanliness," fell apart.

During the first years of the Depression, central bankers everywhere sought to balance budgets in order to reassure investors and stabilize the currency. With economies contracting and tax revenues declining, the only way to balance the budget was to reduce sharply government spending. In addition, governments responded to the decline in exports by forcing wages down, seeking to enhance competitiveness abroad. But by cutting

purchasing power at home, both these measures reinforced the contraction in economic activity.

Economic policymakers based their responses on the "classical" economic model that had developed from the ideas of Adam Smith in the eighteenth century (see pages 747–748). According to this model, a benign "invisible hand" ensured that a free-market price for labor, for capital, and for goods and services would produce an ongoing tendency to economic equilibrium. A downward turn in the business cycle was a normal and necessary adjustment; government interference would only upset this self-adjusting mechanism.

By 1932, however, it was clear that the conventional response was not working, and governments began seeking more actively to stimulate the economy. Strategies varied widely. In the United States, Franklin D. Roosevelt (1882–1945) defeated the incumbent president, Herbert Hoover, in 1932 with the promise of a New Deal—a commitment to increase government spending to restore purchasing power. In fascist Italy, a state agency created to infuse capital into failing companies proved a reasonably effective basis for collaboration between government and business. In Germany, economics minister Hjalmar Schacht (1877–1970) mounted an energetic assault on the economic problem after Hitler came to power in 1933. Government measures sealed off the German mark from international fluctuations, stimulated public spending, partly on rearmament, and kept wages low. By 1935 Germany was back to full employment. This success added tremendously to Hitler's popularity.

High unemployment in Norway, Sweden, and Denmark helped social democrats win power in all three of these Scandinavian countries by the mid-1930s. The new left-leaning governments responded to the economic crisis not by a frontal assault on capitalism but by pioneering the "welfare state," providing such benefits as health care, unemployment insurance, and family allowances. To pay for the new welfare safety net, the Scandinavian countries adopted a high level of progressive taxation and pared military expenditures to a minimum. The turn to a welfare state in Scandinavia eased the immediate human costs of the Depression and helped restore production by stimulating demand. At the same time, the Scandinavian model attracted much admiration as a "third way"

Retreating from "the New Woman"

By the 1930s the ideal of "the new woman" was fading, partly because, with jobs scarce, women felt pressured to concentrate on home and family. But some women had already begun to question the ideal after encountering the disillusioning side of the new freedom, the "modernity," of the 1920s. In an essay entitled "Back to the Good Old Days?" published in Germany in January 1933, just as Hitler was coming to power, the leftist psychologist Alice Rühle-Gerstel (1894–1943) sought to make sense of the changes at work.

It began with a slight uneasiness; with a feeling that something was not right, was no longer right. About two or three years ago. Just at the time, incidentally, when the world crisis was first making itself known with the same slight, uneasy feeling. Gradually a few timid women's emancipationists retreated into the ranks of the opponents of women's emancipation, into the ranks of those who had always—already in 1870, already in 1920—said "that's as far as it can go" with the so-called liberation of women. It began, that is, as women began to cut an entirely new figure. A new economic figure who went out into public economic life as an independent worker or wage-earner entering the free market that had up until then been free only for men. A new political figure who appeared in the parties and parliaments, at demonstrations and gatherings. A new physical figure who not only cut her hair and shortened her skirts but began to emancipate herself altogether from the physical limitations of being female. Finally, a new intellectual-psychological figure who fought her way out of the fog of sentimental ideologies and strove toward a clear, objective knowledge of the world and the self.

This new figure never became average, never became the mass female. There was no time for that. Until today this new figure has remained a pioneer, the standard-bearer—no, the female standard-bearer—of something that had yet to develop. But before she could evolve into a type and expand into an average, she once again ran up against barriers. Her old womanly fate—motherhood, love, family—trailed after her into the spheres of the new womanliness, which immediately presented itself as a new objectivity. And she therefore found herself not liberated, as she had naively assumed, but now doubly bound: conflicts between work and marriage now appeared, between uninhibited drives and inhibited mores, conflicts between the public and private aspects of her life, which could not be synthesized. . . .

The emancipated woman, having emerged from the muddy pond (or, if you will, the clear lake) of her previous state, found herself on a bleak shore, surrounded here and there by skyscrapers that blocked her view. She simply noted: I have less time than my mother had; I have less money, less joy, less hope, less consolation. And thus did she too, with quiet disillusion defiantly concealed, begin her cautious return to the ranks of the backward-looking.

. . . [T]he ideology of the new womanliness hangs in the present vacuum, flat as yesterday's balloon.

Source: Anton Kaes, Martin Jay, and Edward Dimendberg, eds., *The Weimar Republic Sourcebook* (Berkeley and Los Angeles: University of California Press, 1994), pp. 218–219.

between free-market capitalism and the various dictatorial extremes.

In the other European democracies the Depression proved more intractable. Although Britain saw some recovery by the mid-1930s, it was especially the rearmament of the later 1930s, financed by borrowing, or deficit spending, that got the British economy growing again. France, less dependent on international trade, experienced the consequences of the world crisis only gradually. But by the early

∼ ENCOUNTERS WITH THE WEST ∼

Gandhi on Nonviolence

Mohandas Gandhi, a successful English-educated lawyer, emerged as a major force in the move-
ment for Indian independence just after World War I. Calling first for a strategy of noncoopera-
tion with the British colonial overlords, Gandhi gradually developed a philosophy of nonviolent
civil disobedience, which won widespread sympathy for the cause of Indian independence. The fol-
lowing excerpts from articles published in 1935 and 1939—years notable for outbreaks of violence
elsewhere—explain the significance of nonviolence to Gandhi's overall strategy.

Non-violence to be a creed has to be all-perva-
sive. I cannot be non-violent about one activity
of mine and violent about others. That would
be a policy, not a life-force. That being so, I
cannot be indifferent about the war that Italy is
now waging against Abyssinia. . . . India had
an unbroken tradition of non-violence from
times immemorial. But at no time in her ancient history, as far as I know it, has it had
complete non-violence in action pervading the
whole land. Nevertheless, it is my unshakeable
belief that her destiny is to deliver the message
of non-violence to mankind. . . .

. . . India as a nation is not non-violent in
the full sense of the term. . . . Her non-violence
is that of the weak. . . . She lacks the ability to
offer physical resistance. She has no consciousness of strength. She is conscious only of her
weakness. If she were otherwise, there would
be no communal problems, nor political. If she
were non-violent in the consciousness of her
strength, Englishmen would lose their role of
distrustful conquerors. We may talk politically
as we like and often legitimately blame the
English rulers. But if we, as Indians, could but
for a moment visualize ourselves as a strong
people disdaining to strike, we should cease to
fear Englishmen whether as soldiers, traders
or administrators, and they to distrust us.
Therefore if we became truly non-violent we
should carry Englishmen with us in all we
might do. In other words, we being millions
would be the greatest moral force in the world,
and Italy would listen to our friendly word. . . .

. . . [W]hen society is deliberately constructed in accordance with the law of non-
violence, its structure will be different in material particulars from what it is today. But I can-

not say in advance what the government based
wholly on non-violence will be like.

What is happening today is disregard of
the law of non-violence and enthronement of
violence as if it were an eternal law. The democracies, therefore, that we see at work in
England, America and France are only so called,
because they are no less based on violence
than Nazi Germany, Fascist Italy or even Soviet Russia. The only difference is that the violence of the last three is much better organized
than that of the three democratic powers. Nevertheless we see today a mad race for outdoing
one another in the matter of armaments. And
if when the clash comes, as it is bound to come
one day, the democracies win, they will do so
only because they will have the backing of their
peoples who imagine that they have a voice in
their own government whereas in the other
three cases the peoples might rebel against their
own dictatorships.

Holding the view that without the recognition of non-violence on a national scale there
is no such thing as a constitutional or democratic government, I devote my energy to the
propagation of non-violence as the law of our
life—individual, social, political, national and
international. I fancy that I have seen the light,
though dimly. I write cautiously, for I do not
profess to know the whole of the Law. If I
know the successes of my experiments, I know
also my failures. But the successes are enough
to fill me with undying hope.

I have often said that if one takes care of
the means, the end will take care of itself. Non-
violence is the means, the end for every nation
is complete independence.

Source: Raghavan Iyer, ed., *The Essential Writings of Mahatma Gandhi* (Delhi: Oxford University Press, 1991), pp.
245–247, 262–263.

1930s, France, too, was suffering its effects, which lingered to the end of the decade, helping to poison the political atmosphere.

The Depression also had a major impact on the non-Western world and its relations with the West. The radical restriction of international trade meant a sharp decline in demand for the basic commodities that colonial and other regions exported to the industrialized West. The value of Latin American exports declined by half. With foreign exchange scarce, Latin Americans had to curtail imports and to intensify their efforts to industrialize on their own. This enterprise required a greater role for the state—and often entailed political change in an authoritarian direction.

In colonial nations, strains from the Depression further undermined the prestige of the liberal capitalist West, already shaken by World War I, and fed nationalist, anti-Western sentiments. In India, the increase in misery among rural villagers spread the movement for national independence from urban elites to the rural masses. In this context Mohandas Gandhi, who had become known by 1920 for advocating noncooperation with the British, became the first Indian leader to win a mass following throughout the Indian subcontinent. Encouraging villagers to boycott British goods, Gandhi accented simplicity, self-reliance, and an overall strategy of nonviolent civil disobedience based on Indian traditions. (See the box, "Encounters with the West: Gandhi on Nonviolence.")

In Japan, the strains of the Great Depression helped produce precisely the turn to imperialist violence that Gandhi sought to counter. Densely populated yet lacking raw materials, Japan was particularly dependent on international trade and thus reacted strongly as increasing tariffs elsewhere cut sharply into Japanese exports. Led by young army officers who were already eager for their country to embrace a less subservient form of Westernization, Japan turned to aggressive imperialism, seeking to justify its course by claiming to spearhead a wider struggle to free East Asia from Western imperialism. Attacking in 1931, Japanese forces quickly reduced Manchuria to a puppet state, but the Japanese met stubborn resistance when they began seeking to extend this conquest to the rest of China in 1937.

Japanese pressure indirectly furthered the rise of the Chinese communist movement, led by Mao Zedong (1893–1976). Securing a base in the Yanan district in 1936, Mao began seeking to apply Marxism-Leninism to China through land reform and other measures to link the communist elite to the Chinese peasantry. Mao was notable among those adapting Western ideas to build an indigenous movement that would at once overcome Western imperialism and create an alternative to Western liberal capitalism.

The Depression, and the halting responses of the democracies in dealing with it, enhanced the prestige of the new regimes in the Soviet Union, Italy, and Germany, which appeared either to have avoided the economic crisis or to be dealing with it more creatively. Capitalism seemed to be on trial—and so, increasingly, did parliamentary democracy.

THE STALINIST REVOLUTION IN THE SOVIET UNION

Seeking to build "socialism in one country," Joseph Stalin led the Soviet Union during the 1930s through one of the most astounding transformations the world had ever seen. It mixed change and achievement with brutality and terror in bizarre and often tragic ways. The resulting governmental system, which gave Stalin unprecedented power, proved crucial to the outcome of the great experiment that began with the Russian Revolution of 1917. But whether the fateful turn of the 1930s had been implicit in the Leninist revolutionary model all along, or stemmed mostly from unforeseen circumstances and Stalin's idiosyncratic personality, remains uncertain.

Crash Industrialization and Forced Collectivization, 1929–1933

Stalin's strategy entailed rapid industrialization accompanied by compulsory collectivization in agriculture. By forcing peasants into large, government-controlled farms, political leaders could control agricultural pricing and distribution. On that basis, the government could squeeze a surplus from agriculture to be sold abroad, earning money to buy the equipment needed to build factories, dams, and power plants.

Beginning in 1930, the peasants were forcibly herded into collectives. So unpopular was this measure that many peasants killed their livestock or smashed their farm implements rather than let

The Struggle for Socialism
The effort to create a socialist society in the Soviet Union required that Communist party activists educate the peasants in rural areas. As a result of the Stalinist strategy chosen by 1930, this process included touting the new collective farms and denouncing those peasants who had prospered in the relatively liberal economic climate after 1923. Here, a party activist (in dark shirt) leads a meeting of a rural committee in the Chuvash Republic of Russia during the early years of collectivization. *(Endeavour Group UK)*

them be collectivized. During the first two months of 1930, as many as 14 million head of cattle were slaughtered, resulting in an orgy of meat eating and a shortage of draft animals. In 1928, there had been 60 million cattle in the Soviet Union; by 1934 there were only 33.5 million.

Collectivization served, as intended, to squeeze from the peasantry the resources needed to finance industrialization. But it was carried out with extreme brutality. What was being squeezed was not merely a surplus—the state's extractions cut into subsistence. So while Soviet agricultural exports went up in the years after 1930, large numbers of peasants starved to death. The great famine that developed during 1932–1933 resulted in between 5 and 6 million deaths, over half of them in Ukraine. This "terror-famine" went unrecorded in the Soviet press. (See the box, "Carrying out the Stalinist Revolution.")

By 1937 almost all Soviet agriculture took place on collective farms—or on state farms set up in areas not previously under agriculture. However, restrictions on private plots and livestock ownership were eased slightly after 1933, and partly as a result agriculture rebounded and living standards began to rise. By the late 1930s, moreover, significant increases in industrial output had

established solid foundations in heavy industry, including the bases for military production.

Soviet propaganda, including art in the official socialist realist style, glorified the achievements of the new Soviet industrial and agricultural workers. "Stakhanovism," named for a coal miner who had heroically exceeded his production quota, became the term for the prodigious economic achievements that the regime came to expect as it proclaimed the superiority of the communist system. Indeed, the fact that in the Soviet Union state management seemed to produce results while much of the world languished in depression helps explain the prestige that communism developed among intellectuals, in both the Western and non-Western worlds.

But, whatever its successes, this forced development program created many inefficiencies and entailed tremendous human costs. The Soviet Union could probably have done at least as well, with much less suffering, through other strategies of industrial development. Moreover, Stalin's program departed from certain socialist principles—egalitarianism in wages, for example—that the regime had taken very seriously during the late 1920s. By 1931, bureaucratic managers, concerned simply with maximizing output, were openly fa-

Carrying out the Stalinist Revolution

Lev Kopelev (b. 1912), who came from a middle-class Jewish family, was an enthusiastic Communist as a young man. Believing the Soviet Communist party embodied the progressive movement of history, he eagerly assisted in the forced collectivization drive of the early 1930s, which caused such suffering and death in his native Ukraine. But after World War II he became critical of Soviet communism, and he was finally exiled from the Soviet Union in 1980.

Our great goal was the universal triumph of Communism, and for the sake of that goal everything was permissible. . . . And to hesitate or doubt about all this was to give in to "intellectual squeamishness" and "stupid liberalism," the attributes of people who "could not see the forest for the trees."

. . . . I saw what "total collectivization" meant—how . . . mercilessly they stripped the peasants in the winter of 1932–33. I took part in this myself, scouring the countryside, searching for hidden grain, testing the earth with an iron rod for loose spots that might lead to buried grain. With the others, I emptied out the old folks' storage chests, stopping my ears to the children's crying and the women's wails. For I was convinced that I was accomplishing the great and necessary transformation of the countryside; that in the days to come the people who lived there would be better off for it; that their distress and suffering were a result of their own ignorance or the machinations of the class enemy; that those who sent me—and I myself—knew better than the peasants how they should live, what they should sow and when they should plow.

In the terrible spring of 1933 I saw people dying from hunger. I saw women and children with distended bellies, turning blue, still breathing but with vacant, lifeless eyes. . . .

Nor did I lose my faith. As before, I believed because I wanted to believe. Thus from time immemorial men have believed when possessed by a desire to serve powers and values above and beyond humanity. . . .

That was how we thought and acted—we, the fanatical disciples of the all-saving ideals of communism. When we saw the base and cruel acts that were committed in the name of our exalted notions of good, and when we ourselves took part in those actions, what we feared most was to lose our heads, fall into doubt or heresy and forfeit our unbounded faith. . . .

. . . The concepts of conscience, honor, humaneness we dismissed as idealistic prejudices, "intellectual" or "bourgeois," and, hence, perverse.

Source: Lev Kopelev, *No Jail for Thought* (London: Secker & Warburg, 1977), pp. 11–13.

voring workers in certain industries. To ensure labor discipline, new labor laws established harsh punishments for absenteeism or tardiness and severely limited the freedom of workers to change jobs. There was no collective bargaining and no right to strike.

From Opposition to Terror, 1932–1938

Stalin's radical course, with its brutality and uncertain economic justification, quickly provoked opposition. During the summer of 1932, a group centered around M. N. Ryutin (1890–1937) circulated among party leaders a two-hundred-page tract calling for a retreat from Stalin's economic program and a return to democracy within the party. It advocated readmitting those who had been expelled—including Stalin's archenemy, Leon Trotsky. Moreover, the document strongly condemned Stalin personally, describing him as "the evil genius of the Russian Revolution, who, motivated by a personal desire for power and revenge, brought the Revolution to the verge of ruin."[1]

Stalin promptly had Ryutin and his associates expelled from the party, then arrested and imprisoned. But especially as the international situation grew menacing during the 1930s, Stalin became ever more preoccupied with the scope for further opposition. Both Germany and Japan exhibited expansionist aims that might threaten Soviet territories. Trotsky from exile might work with foreign agents and Soviet dissidents to sabotage the Soviet development effort.

In 1934 the assassination of Sergei Kirov (1888–1934), party leader of Leningrad (the former Petrograd), gave Stalin an excuse to intensify the crackdown against actual and potential opponents. Though not conclusive, the evidence suggests that Stalin was himself responsible for killing Kirov, a popular moderate who seemed a plausible rival. In any case, the event served Stalin's interests by creating a sense of emergency justifying extraordinary measures. The eventual result was a series of bizarre show trials, deadly purges, and, ultimately, a kind of terror, with no one safe from arrest by the secret police.

Between 1936 and 1938, famed Bolshevik veterans like Nikolai Bukharin and major functionaries like Genrikh Yagoda (1891–1938), who had just been removed as chief of the secret police, confessed to a series of sensational trumped-up charges: that they had been behind the assassination of Kirov, that they would have killed Stalin if given the chance, that they constituted an "anti-Soviet, Trotskyite center," spying for Germany and Japan and preparing to sabotage Soviet industry in the event of war.

The authorities extracted these confessions partly through torture, partly through threats to the families of the accused. But some, at least, offered false confessions because they believed they were serving the revolution in doing so. All along, the revolution had required a willingness to compromise one's personal scruples, including concerns about personal honor and dignity. Even though they were false, these confessions could help the communist regime ward off the genuine dangers it faced. So in confessing, the accused would be serving the long-term cause, which they believed to be bigger than Stalin and the issues of the moment. What some could not see—or admit—was that the triumph of Stalinism was fatally compromising the original revolutionary vision.

Almost all the accused, including Bukharin and others who had been central to the revolution, were convicted and executed. Soviet authorities did not dare risk public trial for the few who refused, even in the face of torture, to play their assigned roles and confess. Among them was Ryutin, who was shot in secret early in 1937.

But the show trials were very public, surrounded by great propaganda. And the unending talk of foreign intrigues, assassination plots, and "wrecking"—all intended to undo the heroic achievements of the Soviet Union—shaped the perceptions of the Soviet people. There seemed a vast conspiracy at work, responsible, among other things, for the shortages and economic misfortunes that had accompanied the crash industrialization program.

Meanwhile, a purge of the army in 1937 wiped out its top ranks, with 35,000 officers—half the entire officer corps—shot or imprisoned in response to unfounded charges of spying and treason. The Communist party underwent several purges, culminating in the great purge of 1937 and 1938. Of the roughly two thousand delegates to the 1934 congress of the Communist party, over half were shot during the next few years. In particular, the purge of the party got rid of the remaining "old Bolsheviks," those who had been involved in the revolution in 1917 and who thus retained a certain independence. By 1939, Stalin loyalists constituted the entire party leadership.

Although it centered on the party, the purge process touched virtually everyone as the net widened by 1938. Everybody knew someone who had been implicated, so everyone felt some measure of vulnerability to arrest, which would be followed by execution or exile to forced-labor camps. Moreover, there was a random, arbitrary quality to the purges, so there was no way to be sure what was punishable or who was "guilty." Ordinary people were thus tempted to denounce others, if only to demonstrate their own loyalty and conscientiousness.

The final toll was staggering. Of the approximately 160 million people in the Soviet Union, something like 8.5 million were arrested during 1937 and 1938, and of these perhaps 1 million were executed by shooting. Half the total membership of the Communist party—1.2 million people—was arrested; of these, 600,000 were executed, and the vast majority of the rest died in forced-labor camps. Altogether, the several purges resulted in approximately 8 million deaths. The death toll from all of Stalin's peacetime policies between

1929 and 1939, including the forced collectivizations, was perhaps 20 million. Even Hitler and the Nazi regime did not match this appalling total.

Communism and Stalinism

This fateful turn in the development of the communist regime in the Soviet Union proved to be one of the pivotal events of modern history. Some insist that Stalin was pursuing a deliberate, coordinated policy, seeking to create an all-encompassing system of control. Others argue that though Stalin's ultimate responsibility is undeniable, he was simply responding on an improvised basis to a situation that became chaotic as the communists tried to carry through a revolution in a backward country.

Virtually from the beginning of its power, the Communist party had attracted careerists and opportunists, and thus there were bitter differences among party leaders over party membership. Was membership to be limited to a trained professional elite, which would need to purge the party of opportunists periodically, or was the party to be a mass-based vehicle for socialist education? The concern to root out potential opponents during the 1930s gave various factions an opportunity to have it out with their enemies. Stalin sometimes held back before lending his support to one side or the other. But even if the chain of events did not stem from a coherent policy, Stalin took advantage of it and, by 1939, had crushed all actual or potential opposition. In a sense, the outcome was the triumph of Stalin over the Communist party, which had held on to the original Bolshevik ideal of collective leadership by a revolutionary vanguard.

Obviously Stalinism was one possible outcome of Leninist communism, but was it the logical, even the inevitable, outcome? Leninism had accented centralized authority and the scope for human will to force events, so it may have created a framework in which Stalinism was likely to develop. Yet Stalin's personal idiosyncrasies and growing paranoia seem to have been crucial for the Soviet system to develop as it did by the end of the 1930s.

Stalin had won his position from within the Communist party, based on his backroom political skill, not his popular appeal. Although a special aura came to surround him by the end of the 1930s, he remained essentially the chief bureaucrat, referring to the surviving fragments of the Marxist-Leninist blueprint as he oversaw the process of revolutionary implementation. So even as Stalin monopolized power, his style of leadership remained decidedly different from that of Mussolini and Hitler, who based their power on personal charisma and a direct relationship with the people.

HITLER AND NAZISM IN GERMANY

Beset with problems from the start, the Weimar Republic lay gravely wounded by 1932. Various antidemocratic groups competed to replace it. The winner was the Nazi movement, led by Adolf Hitler, who became chancellor in January 1933. Nazism took inspiration from Italian fascism, but Hitler's regime proved far more dynamic—and more troubling—than Mussolini's.

To understand where Nazism came from, it is necessary to distinguish among the motives and purposes that nourished it. For example, the substantial voting support the Nazis gained by 1932 was essential in giving Hitler a chance to govern. But to understand why so many Germans voted for the Nazis is not to understand why Hitler ended up using power as he did. Nor can we explain Nazism simply by invoking power and opportunism, because the most troubling aspects of Nazism, from personal dictatorship to the extermination of the Jews, stemmed from a wider vision of the world, radiating from Hitler himself.

Nazism was not conventionally revolutionary, in the sense of mounting a frontal challenge to the existing socioeconomic order. Some of its themes were traditionalist and even antimodernizing. But in the final analysis Nazism was anything but conservative. Indeed, it constituted a direct assault on what had long been held as the best of the Western tradition.

The Rise of Nazism, 1919–1933

The National Socialist German Workers' party (NSDAP), or Nazism, emerged from the turbulent situation of Munich just after the war. A center of leftist agitation, the city also became a hotbed of the radical right, nurturing a number of new nationalist, militantly anticommunist political groups. One of them, a workers' party founded

Early Nazism Although Nazism did poorly in national elections before the Depression, the movement attracted a loyal and militant membership, in which young people were especially numerous. Here young Nazis parade with banners in 1923. *(© Harlingue-Viollet)*

under the aegis of the right-wing Thule Society early in 1919, attracted the attention of Adolf Hitler, who soon gave it his personal stamp.

Adolf Hitler (1889–1945) had been born not German but Austrian, the son of a lower government official. As a young man he had gone to Vienna, hoping to become an artist, but he failed to gain admission to the Viennese Academy of Fine Arts. By 1913 he had become a German nationalist hostile to the multinational Habsburg empire, and he immigrated to Germany to escape service in the Austrian army. He was not opposed to military service per se, however, and when war broke out in 1914, he immediately volunteered for service in the German army.

Corporal Hitler experienced firsthand the fighting at the front and, as a courier, performed bravely and effectively. Indeed, he was in a field hospital being treated for gas poisoning when the war ended. Although his fellow soldiers considered him quirky and introverted, Hitler found the war experience crucial; it was during the war, he said later, that he "found himself."

Following his release from the hospital, Hitler worked for the army in routine surveillance of extremist groups in Munich. In this role he joined the infant German Workers' party late in 1919. When his first political speech at a rally in February 1920 proved a resounding success, Hitler began to believe he could play a special political role. From this point, he gradually developed the confidence to lead a new nationalist, anticommunist, and anti-Weimar movement.

But Hitler jumped the gun in November 1923 when, with Erich Ludendorff at his side, he led the Beer Hall Putsch in Munich, an abortive attempt to launch a march on Berlin to overthrow the Republic. On trial after this effort failed, Hitler gained greater national visibility as he denounced the Versailles treaty and the Weimar government. Still, *Mein Kampf* (My Battle), the political tract that he wrote while in prison during 1924, sold poorly. To most, Hitler was simply a right-wing rabble-rouser whose views were not worth taking seriously.

His failure in 1923 convinced Hitler that he should exploit the existing political system, but not challenge it directly, in his quest for power on the national level. Yet Hitler did not view the NSDAP as just another political party, playing by the same rules as the others within the Weimar system. Thus, most notably, the Nazi party maintained a paramilitary arm, the *Sturmabteilung* (SA), which provoked a good deal of antileftist street violence.

By 1928, the Nazis were still peripheral to national politics, attracting only 2.6 percent of the vote in the Reichstag elections of that year. However, in the elections of September 1930, the first since the onset of the Depression, they increased their share dramatically to 18.3 percent of the vote. When elections were held again in July 1932, their vote exploded to 37.3 percent, enough to make them the largest party in the Reichstag.

Both the Nazis and the Communists gained electoral support as unemployment grew, but the Germans voting for the Nazis were not simply those most threatened economically. Nor did the Nazi party appeal primarily to the uneducated or socially marginal. Rather, the party served as a focus of opposition for those now alienated from the

Weimar Republic itself. Although the Nazis did relatively poorly among Catholics and industrial workers, they put together a broad, fairly diverse base of electoral support, ranging from artisans and small shopkeepers to university students and civil servants. Still, that support was shallow. The Nazi vote in 1932 was largely a protest vote, reflecting the hope that Nazism, or Hitler himself, portended something new and more effective. Although Nazism was clearly anticommunist, anti-Weimar, and anti-Versailles, its positive program remained vague.

As the crisis of the Weimar Republic deepened in 1932, conservative fears of a Marxist outcome played into Hitler's hands. By May 1932, when Heinrich Brüning's government fell, President Hindenburg was relying heavily on a narrow circle of advisers who wanted to take advantage of the Nazis' mass support for conservative purposes. Two of those advisers, Franz von Papen (1878–1969) and General Kurt von Schleicher (1882–1934), each got a chance to govern, but neither succeeded. By January 1933, each had grown hostile to the other, and Papen lined up a new coalition that he proposed to Hindenburg to replace Schleicher's government. Hitler would be chancellor, Papen himself vice chancellor, and Alfred Hugenberg (1865–1951), the leader of the Nationalist party, finance minister. For months, Hindenburg had resisted giving Hitler a chance to govern. But he felt this combination might work to establish a parliamentary majority, box out the left, and contain Nazism. So Hindenburg turned to Hitler, who became chancellor at last on January 30, 1933.

The Consolidation of Hitler's Power, 1933–1934

When Hitler became chancellor, it was not obvious that a change of regime was beginning. Like his predecessors, he could govern only with the president's approval, and governmental institutions like the army, the judiciary, and the diplomatic corps, though hardly bastions of democracy, were not in the hands of committed Nazis. But although an element of caution and cultivated ambiguity remained, a revolution quickly began, creating a new regime, the Third Reich.

On February 23, just weeks after Hitler became chancellor, a fire engulfed the Reichstag building in Berlin. It was set by a young Dutch communist acting on his own, but it seemed to suggest that a communist uprising was imminent. This sense of emergency afforded the new Hitler government an excuse to restrict civil liberties and imprison leftist leaders, including the entire Communist parliamentary delegation. Even in this atmosphere of crisis the Nazis could not win a majority in the Reichstag elections of March 5. But support from the Nationalists and the Center party enabled the Nazis to win Reichstag approval for an enabling act granting Hitler the power to make laws on his own for the next four years, bypassing both the Reichstag and the president.

Although the Weimar Republic was never formally abolished, the laws that followed fundamentally altered government, politics, and public life in Germany. The other parties were either outlawed or persuaded to dissolve so that in July 1933 the Nazi party was declared the only legal party. When President Hindenburg died in August 1934, the offices of chancellor and president were merged, and Germany had just one leader, Adolf Hitler, with unprecedented power in his hands. Members of the German armed forces now swore loyalty to him personally.

During this period of power consolidation, Hitler acted decisively but carefully, generally accenting normalization. To be sure, his methods occasionally gave conservatives pause. In an especially dramatic episode, the "blood purge" of June 30, 1934, he had several hundred people murdered. Although Hitler used the occasion to settle a number of old scores, the purge was directed against the SA, led by Ernst Röhm (1887–1934). Because Röhm and the SA had had pretensions of controlling the army, his removal seemed evidence that Hitler was taming the radical elements in his own movement. In fact, however, this purge led to the ascendancy of the Schutzstaffel, or SS, the select Nazi elite, led by Heinrich Himmler (1900–1945). Linked to the Gestapo, the secret police apparatus, the SS became the institutional basis for the most troubling aspects of Nazism. The blood purge proved a step to radical measures barely conceivable in 1934.

Hitler's World-View

In achieving the chancellorship and in expanding his power thereafter, Hitler showed himself an

Hitler's World-View: Nature, Race, and Struggle

Hitler outlined his beliefs and aims in **Mein Kampf,** *which he wrote while in prison in 1924. The following passages reveal the racism, the anti-Semitism, and the emphasis on nature and struggle that formed the core of his world-view.*

No more than Nature desires the mating of weaker with stronger individuals, even less does she desire the blending of a higher with a lower race, since, if she did, her whole work of higher breeding, over perhaps hundreds of thousands of years, might be ruined with one blow.

Historical experience . . . shows with terrifying clarity that in every mingling of Aryan blood with that of lower peoples the result was the end of the cultured people. . . .

Here, of course, we encounter the objection of the modern pacifist, as truly Jewish in its effrontery as it is stupid! "Man's rôle is to overcome Nature!"

. . . [T]his planet once moved through the ether for millions of years without human beings and it can do so again some day if men forget that they owe their higher existence, not to the ideas of a few crazy ideologists, but to the knowledge and ruthless application of Nature's stern and rigid laws. . . .

In the Jewish people the will to self-sacrifice does not go beyond the individual's naked instinct of self-preservation. . . .

If the Jews were alone in the world, they would stifle in filth and offal; they would try to get ahead of one another in hate-filled struggle and exterminate one another. . . .

Source: Adolf Hitler, *Mein Kampf* (Boston: Houghton Mifflin, Sentry, 1943), pp. 286–289, 299, 301–302.

adept politician, but he was hardly a mere opportunist, seeking to amass power for its own sake. Power was only the instrument for the grandiose transformation he believed necessary.

Hitler acted on the basis of a world-view that coalesced by about 1924—and that remained extremely important to him. (See the box, "Hitler's World-View: Nature, Race, and Struggle.") This is not to say that he was an original thinker or that his ideas were true—or even plausible. But he sought to make systematic sense of things, and the most disturbing features of his political activity stemmed directly from the resulting world-view. His most committed followers shared certain of his ideas, although fanatical loyalty to Hitler himself was more important for some of them. The central components of Hitler's thinking—geopolitics, biological racism, anti-Semitism, and Social Darwinism—were by no means specifically German. They could be found all over the Western world by the early twentieth century.

Geopolitics claimed to offer a scientific understanding of world power relationships based on geographic determinism. In his writings of the 1920s, Hitler warned that Germany faced imminent decline unless it confronted its geopolitical limitations. To remain fully sovereign in the emerging new era of global superpowers like the United States, Germany would have to act quickly to expand its territory. Otherwise it would end up like Switzerland or the Netherlands.

For decades German imperialists had argued about whether Germany was better advised to seek overseas colonies or to expand its reach in Europe. As Hitler saw it, Germany's failure to make a clear choice had led to its defeat in World War I. Now choice was imperative, and current geopolitical thinking seemed to indicate the direction for expansion. Far-flung empires relying on naval support were said to be in decline. The future lay with land-based states—unified, geographically contiguous, with the space necessary for self-sufficiency. By expanding eastward, into Poland and the western part of the Soviet Union, including Ukraine especially, Germany could conquer the living space, or *Lebensraum*, necessary for agricultural-industrial balance—and ultimately for self-sufficiency.

Though limited and mechanistic, this geopolitical way of thinking is at least comprehensible, in light of the German vulnerabilities that had surfaced during the war. The other three strands of Hitler's world-view were much less plausible, though each had become prominent during the second half of the nineteenth century. Biological racism insisted that built-in racial characteristics determine what is most important about any individual. Anti-Semitism went beyond racism in claiming that Jews play a special and negative role. The fact that the Jews were dispersed and often landless indicated that they were different—and parasitical. Finally, Social Darwinism, especially in its German incarnation, accented the positive role of struggle—not among individuals, as in a prominent American strand, but among racial groups.

The dominant current of racist thinking labeled the "Aryans" as healthy, creative, superior. Originally the Sanskrit term for "noble," Aryan came to indicate the ancient language assumed to have been the common source of the modern Indo-European languages. An Aryan was simply a speaker of one of those languages. By the late nineteenth century, however, the term had become supremely ill defined. In much racist thinking, Germanic peoples were somehow especially Aryan, but race mixing had produced impurity—and thus degeneration. Success in struggle with the other races was the ultimate measure of vitality, the only proof of racial superiority for the future.

Hitler brought these themes together by emphasizing that humanity is not special, but simply part of nature, subject to the same laws of struggle and selection as the other animal species. Humanitarian ideals are thus dangerous illusions. As he put it to a group of officer cadets in 1944:

Nature is always teaching us . . . that she is governed by the principle of selection: that victory is to the strong and that the weak must go to the wall. She teaches us that what may seem cruel to us, because it affects us personally or because we have been brought up in ignorance of her laws, is nevertheless often essential if a higher way of life is to be attained. Nature . . . knows nothing of the notion of humanitarianism, which signifies that the weak must at all costs be protected and preserved even at the expense of the strong.

Nature does not see in weakness any extenuating reasons . . . on the contrary, weakness calls for condemnation.[2]

To Hitler, the Jews were not simply another of the races involved in this endless struggle. Rather, as landless parasites, they had played a special historical role, embodying the principles—from humanitarianism to class struggle—that were antithetical to the healthy natural struggle among unified racial groups. "Jewishness" was bound up with the negative, critical intellect that dared suggest things ought to be not natural but just, even that it was up to human beings to change the world and make it just. The Jews were the virus keeping the community from a healthy natural footing. Marxist communism, embodying divisive class struggle as well as utopian humanitarian ideals, was fundamentally Jewish.

The central features of Nazism in practice, from personal dictatorship to the extermination of the Jews, followed from Hitler's view of the world. First, the racial community must organize itself politically for this ceaseless struggle. Individuals are but instruments for the success of the racial community. Parliamentary democracy, reflecting short-term individual interests, fostered selfish materialism and division, thereby weakening that community. The political order must rest instead on a charismatic leader, united with the whole people through bonds of common blood.

Nazi Aims and German Society

Although Hitler's world-view provided the underlying momentum for the Nazi regime, it did not specify a consistent program that could be implemented all at once. Moreover, the regime sometimes found it necessary to adopt short-term expedients that conflicted with its long-term aims. Thus it was possible for Germans living under Nazi rule in the 1930s to embrace aspects of Nazism in practice without seeing where it was all leading.

Hitler's special leadership function was based on a charismatic relationship with the German people, a nonrational bond resting on common race. But to create a genuine racial community, or *Volksgemeinschaft*, it was necessary to unify society and instill Nazi values, thereby making the individual feel part of the whole—and ultimately an instrument to serve the whole. This entailed more or less forced participation in an array of Nazi organizations, from women's groups to the Hitler Youth, from the Labor Front to the Strength Through Joy leisure-time organization.

Common participation meant shared experiences such as weekend hikes and the weekly one-dish meal. Even the most ordinary, once-private activities took on a public or political dimension. Moreover, the Nazis devised unprecedented ways to stage-manage public life, using rituals like the Hitler salute, symbols like the swastika, new media like radio and film, and carefully orchestrated party rallies—all in an effort to foster this sense of belonging. (See the feature, "Weighing the Evidence: Film as Propaganda," on pages 1028–1029.)

Hitler and Children Adolf Hitler was often portrayed as the friend of children. This photograph accompanied a story for an elementary school reader that described how Hitler, told it was this young girl's birthday, picked her from a crowd of well-wishers to treat her "to cake and strawberries with thick, sweet cream." *(From* Jugend um Hitler, *Heinrich Hoffman © "Zeitgeschichte" Verlag und Vertriebs-Gesellschaft Berlin. Reproduced with permission. Photo courtesy Wiener Library, London)*

Did the Nazis succeed in drawing ordinary Germans into their orbit? The matter remains sensitive and difficult. Hitler's regime enjoyed considerable popular support, but even after Hitler was well entrenched in power, most Germans did not grasp the regime's deeper dynamic. Certainly some welcomed the sense of unity, the feeling of belonging and participation, especially after what had seemed the alienation and divisiveness of the Weimar years. Moreover, Hitler himself was immensely popular, partly because of his personal charisma, partly because his apparently decisive leadership was a welcome departure from the near paralysis of the Weimar parliamentary system. But most important, before the coming of war in 1939, he seemed to go from success to success, surmounting the Depression and repudiating the major terms of the hated Versailles treaty.

The skillful work of Hitler's propaganda minister, Joseph Goebbels (1897–1945), played on these successes to create a "Hitler myth," which made Hitler seem at once heroic and a man of the people, even the embodiment of healthy German ideals against the excesses and corruptions of the Nazi party. This myth became central to the Nazi regime, but it merely provided a façade behind which the real Hitler could pursue deeper, longer-term aims. These aims were not publicized directly, because the German people did not seem ready for them. In this sense, then, support for Hitler and his regime was broad but shallow during the 1930s.

Moreover, resistance increased as the regime became more intrusive. Youth gangs actively opposed the official Hitler Youth organization as it became more overbearing and militaristic by the late 1930s. But people resisted especially by minimizing their involvement with the regime, retreating into the private realm, in response to the Nazi attempt to make everything public.

Did such people feel constantly under threat of the Gestapo, the secret police? In principle, the Gestapo could interpret the will of the *Führer*, or leader, and decide whether any individual citizen was "guilty" or not. And the Gestapo was not concerned about due process; on occasion it simply bypassed the regular court system. But the Gestapo did not terrorize Germans at random. Its victims were generally members of specific groups, people suspected of active opposition, or people who protected those the Gestapo had targeted. It did not become as intrusive as its Soviet counterpart, the

NKVD, became during the height of the Stalinist terror in the late 1930s.

Moreover, changes and contradictions in Nazi goals allowed considerable space for personal choices. For example, the Nazis claimed to embrace traditional family values. During the 1920s they had emphasized the woman's role as wife and mother and deplored the ongoing emancipation of women. Once Hitler came to power, concerns about unemployment reinforced these views. During the summer of 1933, Hitler's government began offering interest-free loans to help couples set up house if the woman agreed to leave the labor force. Moreover, efforts to increase the German birthrate reinforced the emphasis on child rearing in Nazi women's organizations. Nonetheless, the size of the family continued to decrease in Germany as elsewhere in the industrialized world during the 1930s.

And beginning in 1936, when rapid rearmament began to produce labor shortages, the regime did an about-face and began seeking to attract women back to the workplace, especially into jobs central to military preparation. These efforts were not notably successful, and by 1940 the military was calling for conscription of women into war industries.

Further, the Nazis valued the family only insofar as it was congruent with the "health" of the racial community, so efforts to promote that health also compromised traditional family values. The regime regulated marriage and sought actively to eliminate the "unhealthy," those deemed unfit. Just months after coming to power in 1933, Hitler brushed aside the objections of Vice Chancellor Franz von Papen, a Catholic, and engineered a law mandating the compulsory sterilization of persons suffering from certain allegedly hereditary diseases. Medical personnel sterilized some 400,000, the vast majority of them "Aryan" Germans, during the Nazi years.

Hitler's regime also began immediately to single out the Jews, although Nazi Jewish policy remained an improvised hodgepodge prior to World War II. Within weeks after Hitler became chancellor in 1933, new restrictions limited Jewish participation in the civil service, in the professions, and in German cultural life—and quickly drew censure from the League of Nations. The Nuremberg Laws, announced at a party rally in 1935, included prohibition of sexual relations and marriage between Jews and non-Jewish Germans. Beginning in 1938, the Jews had to carry special identification cards and to add "Sarah" or "Israel" to their given names.

Although Hitler and other Nazi leaders claimed periodically to be seeking a definitive solution to Germany's "Jewish problem," this led during the 1930s only to sporadic attempts to force German Jews to emigrate. About 11 percent, or 60,000, of Germany's 550,000 Jews emigrated during 1933 and 1934, and perhaps 25 percent had gotten out by 1938. The fact that the regime stripped emigrating Jews of their assets made emigration more difficult, because other countries were unwilling to take in substantial numbers of penniless Jews.

On November 9, 1938, using the assassination of a German diplomat in Paris as a pretext, the Nazis staged the Kristallnacht (Crystal Night) pogrom, during which almost all the synagogues in Germany and about seven thousand Jewish-owned stores were destroyed. Between 30,000 and 50,000 relatively prosperous Jews were arrested and forced to emigrate after their property was confiscated. Although the German public had generally acquiesced in the earlier restrictions on Jews, this pogrom with its wanton violation of private property shocked many Germans.

Concentration camps—supplementary detention centers—had become a feature of the Nazi regime virtually at once, but prior to 1938 they were used primarily to hold political prisoners. As part of the Crystal Night pogrom, about 35,000 Jews were rounded up and sent to the camps, but most were soon released as long as they could document their intention to emigrate. When World War II began in 1939, the total camp population was about 25,000. The systematic physical extermination of the Jews began only during the war, in newly constructed death camps in Poland.

However, the killing of others deemed superfluous or threatening to the racial community began earlier, with the so-called euthanasia program initiated under volunteer medical teams in 1939. Its aim was to eliminate chronic mental patients, the incurably ill, and people with severe physical handicaps. Those subject to such treatment were primarily ethnic Germans, not Jews or foreigners. Although the regime did all it could to make it appear the victims had died naturally, a public outcry developed, especially among relatives and church leaders. Thus the program had to be discontinued in 1941, but by then it had claimed 100,000 lives.

The euthanasia program was based on the sense, fundamental to radical Nazism, that readiness for war was the real norm for society. In war, societies send individuals to their deaths and, on the battlefield, make difficult distinctions among the wounded, letting some die in order to save those most likely to survive and return to battle. Struggle necessitates selection, which requires overcoming humanitarian scruples—the notion that "weakness" calls for special societal protection. Thus it was desirable to kill even ethnic Germans who were deemed unfit, as "life unworthy of life."

Preparation for war was the core of Nazism in practice. The conquest of living space in the east would make possible a more advantageous

agricultural-industrial balance, thereby providing not only the self-sufficiency necessary for sovereignty but also the land-rootedness necessary for racial health. Such a war of conquest would strike not only the Slavic peoples of the region but also communism, centered in the Soviet Union.

The point of domestic reorganization was to marshal the community's energies and resources for this war. Because business interests generally seemed congruent with Nazi purposes, Nazi aims did not appear to require some revolutionary assault on business elites or the capitalist economy. But the Nazis had their own road to travel, and beginning in 1936 they proved quite prepared to bend the economy, and to coordinate big business, to serve their longer-term aims of war-making.

The Nazi drive toward war during the 1930s transformed international relations in Europe. The other European powers sought to understand

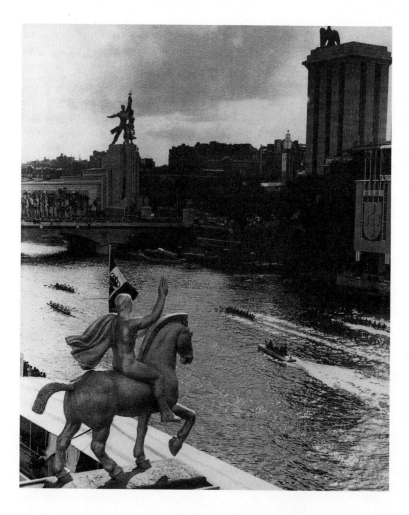

Ideological Confrontation At a major international exhibition in Paris in 1937, the new antidemocratic political regimes of the interwar period made bold propaganda statements. With a sculpture from fascist Italy's pavilion in the foreground, we look across the Seine River to a classic representation of the ideological warfare of the 1930s: the Soviet Pavilion, on the left, facing the German pavilion, on the right. (*Wide World Photos*)

Hitler's Germany in terms of the increasingly polarized political context of the period. Before considering the fortunes of Hitler's foreign policy, we must consider fascism as a wider phenomenon—and the efforts of the democracies, on the one hand, and the Soviet Union, on the other, to come to terms with it.

FASCIST CHALLENGE AND ANTIFASCIST RESPONSE

Communism, fascism, and Nazism departed from the parliamentary democracy that had been the West's political norm. Each seemed subject to violence and excess, yet each had features that some found attractive. In the difficult socioeconomic circumstances of the 1930s, the very presence of these new political systems caused polarization all over Europe.

Yet communists and adherents of the various forms of fascism were bitterly hostile to each other, and beginning in 1934 communists sought to join with anyone who would work with them to defend democracy against further fascist assaults. This effort led to new antifascist coalition governments in Spain and France. In each case, however, the Depression restricted maneuvering room, and these governments ended up furthering the polarization they were seeking to avoid. By mid-1940 democracy had fallen in Spain, after a brutal civil war, and even in France, in the wake of military defeat. Ideological polarization had weakened and then undermined democracy in much of Europe.

The Reorientation of Fascist Italy

Mussolini's regime in Italy continued to seek, through corporativism, to involve people in political decision making based on their roles in the national economy (see page 984). But though corporativist institutions were gradually constructed, with great rhetorical fanfare, fascism became bogged down in compromise with prefascist elites and institutions by the mid-1930s. Italian businessmen, cautious and suspicious of Mussolini, sought to maintain their autonomy against the fascist effort to subordinate business to the political sphere. And generally they succeeded. The corporative institutions never developed into genuine vehicles of mass participation through the workplace—if anything, in fact, they served simply to regiment the working class. Mussolini offered assurances that, despite the necessary compromises, fascism's corporativist revolution was continuing, but those seeking a corporative state were sharply critical of the inadequacies of the new system.

Mussolini was never merely the instrument of the established Italian elites, but neither was he a consistent ideologue like Hitler, forcing his regime in a certain direction. By the early 1930s, he sometimes seemed satisfied with his cult of power as he juggled the various contending forces in fascist Italy. But he was increasingly frustrated by the limitations he had encountered on the domestic level. On the international level, however, the new context after Hitler came to power offered him some welcome space for maneuver. So as the fascist revolution in Italy faltered, Mussolini began concentrating on foreign policy.

Though Italy, like Germany, remained dissatisfied with the territorial status quo, it was not obvious that fascist Italy and Nazi Germany had to end up in the same camp. For one thing, Italy was anxious to preserve an independent Austria as a buffer with Germany, whereas there was considerable sentiment among Germans and Austrians for the unification of the two countries. Such a greater Germany might then threaten the gains Italy had won at the peace conference at the expense of Austria. When, in 1934, Germany seemed poised to absorb Austria, Mussolini helped stiffen the resistance of Austria's leaders and played a part in forcing Hitler to back down. Mussolini even warned that Nazism, with its racist orientation, posed a significant threat to the best of European civilization.

As it began to appear that France and Britain might have to work with the Soviet Union to check Hitler's Germany, French and British conservatives pushed for good relations with Mussolini's Italy to provide ideological balance. So Italy was well positioned to play off both sides as Hitler began shaking things up on the international level after 1933. In 1935, just after Hitler announced significant rearmament measures, unilaterally repudiating provisions of the Versailles treaty for the first time, Mussolini hosted a meeting with the French and British prime ministers at Stresa, in northern Italy. In a move clearly intended to contain Germany, the three powers agreed to resist "any unilateral repudiation of treaties which may endanger the peace of Europe."

However, Mussolini was already preparing to extend Italy's possessions in East Africa to encompass Ethiopia (formerly called Abyssinia), assuming that the French and British, who needed his support against Hitler, would not offer significant opposition. Ethiopia had become a League of Nations member in 1923—sponsored by Italy, but opposed by Britain and France because it still practiced slavery. After a border incident in December 1934, Italian troops invaded in October 1935, prompting the League to announce sanctions against Italy.

These sanctions were applied haphazardly, largely because France and Britain wanted to avoid irreparable damage to their longer-term relations with Italy. In any case, the sanctions did not deter Mussolini, whose forces prevailed through the use of aircraft and poison gas by May 1936. But they did make Italy receptive to German overtures in the aftermath of its victory. And the victory made Mussolini more restless. Rather than seeking to play again the enviable role of European balancer, he began sending Italian troops and materiel to aid the antidemocratic Nationalists in the Spanish civil war, thereby further alienating democratic opinion elsewhere.

Conservatives in Britain and France continued to push for accommodation with Italy, hoping to revive the "Stresa Front" against Hitler. Some even defended Italian imperialism in East Africa. But Italy continued its drift toward Germany. Late in 1936 Mussolini spoke of a new Rome-Berlin axis for the first time. During 1937 and 1938 he and Hitler exchanged visits. Finally, in May 1939, Italy joined Germany in an open-ended military alliance, the Pact of Steel, but Mussolini made it clear that Italy could not be ready for a major European war before 1943.

To cement this developing relationship, fascist Italy adopted anti-Semitic racial laws modeled on Germany's, even though Italian fascism had not originally been anti-Semitic and indeed had attracted Jewish Italians to its membership in about the same proportion as non-Jews. Although the imperial venture in Ethiopia had been popular among the Italian people, the increasing subservience to Nazi Germany displeased even many committed fascists. Such opposition helped keep Mussolini from immediate intervention when war broke out in September 1939.

But in the wake of stunning Nazi successes by May 1940, Italy finally intervened, expecting to gain territorial advantage at the expense of France at relatively low cost. Mussolini was not expecting a long war, for which he knew Italy was unprepared. But a long and difficult war was forthcoming, and in July 1943 the poor Italian performance led not only to military defeat but to the fall of Mussolini and the collapse of the fascist regime.

Fascism and the Popular Front Response

The influence of Hitler's regime extended far beyond fascist Italy. With its apparent dynamism and success, Nazi Germany stimulated interest in fascism among those elsewhere who were disaffected with democracy and hostile to communism. But the line between fascism and conservative authoritarianism blurred in the volatile political climate of the 1930s. To some, any retreat from democracy appeared a step toward fascism.

In east-central Europe, political distinctions became especially problematic. Movements like the Arrow Cross in Hungary and the Legion of the Archangel Michael in Romania modeled themselves on the Italian and German prototypes, but they never achieved political power. Those who controlled the antidemocratic governments in Hungary and Romania, as in Poland, Bulgaria, and Yugoslavia, were authoritarian traditionalist, not really fascist. Still, many government leaders welcomed the closer economic ties with Germany that Hitler's economics minister, Hjalmar Schacht, engineered. The difference between authoritarianism and fascism remained clearest in Austria, where Catholic conservatives undermined democracy during 1933 and 1934. They were actively hostile to the growing pro-Nazi agitation in Austria, partly because they wanted to keep Austria independent.

In France various nationalist, anticommunist, and anti-Semitic leagues gathered momentum during the early 1930s. They covered a spectrum from monarchism to outspoken profascism, but together they constituted at least a potential threat to French democracy. In February 1934, right-wing demonstrations against the Chamber of Deputies provoked a bloody clash with police and forced a change of ministry. As it began to seem that even France might be vulnerable to fascism, those from the center and left of the political spectrum began to think about working together to keep fascism from spreading further. The Communists, especially, took the initiative by promoting "popular fronts" of all those seeking to save democracy from fascism.

This was a dramatic change in strategy for international communism. Even as Hitler was closing in on the German chancellorship in the early 1930s, German Communists, following Comintern policy, continued to attack their socialist rivals rather than seek a unified response to Nazism. From the communist perspective, fascism represented the crisis phase of monopoly capitalism, so a Nazi government would actually be useful to strip away the democratic façade hiding class oppression in Germany. But when the new Hitler government promptly outlawed the German Communist party and arrested all the Communists it could find, and when the demonstrations in Paris in February 1934 made it seem that even France might "go fascist," the Comintern abruptly changed direction. The threat of fascism was so pressing that the Communists had to begin actively promoting electoral alliances and governing coalitions with Socialists and even liberal democrats to resist its further spread. From 1934 until 1939, Communists everywhere consistently pursued this "popular front" strategy.

But by the mid-1930s it was becoming ever harder to be sure what was fascist, what was dangerous, what might lead where. As fears intensified, perceptions became as important as realities. Popular front governments, intended to preserve democracy against what appeared to be fascism, could seem, to conservatives, to be leaning too far to the left. Ideological polarization made democracy extraordinarily difficult. The archetypal example proved to be Spain, where a tragedy of classical proportions was played out.

From Democracy to Civil War in Spain, 1931–1939

Spain became a center of attention in the 1930s, when its promising new parliamentary democracy, launched in 1931, led to civil war in 1936 and the triumph of a repressive authoritarian regime

THE DIPLOMATIC REVOLUTION OF THE 1930s	
January 1933	Hitler becomes German chancellor
October 1933	Germany withdraws from the League of Nations
March 1935	Hitler announces rearmament in defiance of the Versailles treaty
April 1935	Britain, France, and Italy meet at Stresa
October 1935	Italy invades Ethiopia
March 1936	Remilitarization of the Rhineland
July 1936	Beginning of the Spanish civil war
March 1938	The Anschluss: Germany absorbs Austria
September 1938	Munich conference ends Sudetenland crisis
March 1939	Dismemberment of Czechoslovakia
August 1939	Nazi-Soviet nonaggression pact
September 1, 1939	German invasion of Poland
September 3, 1939	Britain and France declare war on Germany

in 1939. The country's earlier effort at constitutional monarchy had fizzled by 1923, when King Alfonso XIII (1886–1941) supported a new military dictatorship. But growing opposition led first to the resignation of the dictator in 1930 and then, in April 1931, to the end of the monarchy and the proclamation of a republic. The elections for a constituent assembly that followed in June produced a solid victory for a coalition of liberal democrats and Socialists, as well as considerable hope and expectation.

The optimism began to break down first because the leaders of the new republic dragged their feet on land reform, which seemed necessary especially in southern Spain, where large estates

Map 27.1 The Spanish Civil War, 1936–1939 The Nationalist insurgents quickly took over most of northern and eastern Spain in 1936 and then gradually expanded their territory. The fall of Madrid early in 1939 marked the end of fighting. The revolutionary effort of 1936–1937 within the Republican zone was centered in Barcelona. (*Source:* Adapted from *The Times Atlas of World History,* 3d ed., by kind permission of Times Books.)

worked by landless day laborers remained the rule. A significant agrarian reform law was passed in 1932, but the new government was slow to implement it. Feeling betrayed, Socialists and agricultural workers became increasingly radical, producing growing upheaval in the countryside. Radicalism on the left made it harder for the moderates to govern and, at the same time, stimulated conservatives to become more politically active.

A conservative, or right-wing, coalition (the CEDA) under José Maria Gil Robles (1898–1980) grew in strength, becoming the largest party in parliament with the first regular elections, held in November 1933. In light of its parliamentary strength, the CEDA had a plausible claim to a government role, but it was kept from participation in government until October 1934. It seemed to the left, in the ideologically charged atmosphere of the time, that the growing role of the CEDA was

a prelude to fascism. To let the CEDA into the government would be to hand the republic over to its enemies.

A strong Catholic from the traditional Spanish right, Gil Robles refused to endorse the democratic republic as a form of government, but he and the CEDA were willing to work within it. So the Spanish left may have been too quick to see the CEDA as fascist—and to react when the CEDA finally got its government role. However, Mussolini and Hitler had each come to power more or less legally, from within parliamentary institutions. The German left has been criticized for its passive response to the advent of Hitler; the Spanish left wanted to avoid the same mistake.

Thus, during the fall of 1934 the left responded to the opening of the government to the CEDA with quasi-revolutionary uprisings in Catalonia and Asturias, where a miners' commune was put down only after two weeks of heavy fighting. In the aftermath, the right-leaning government of 1935 began undoing some of the reforms of the left-leaning government of 1931–1933, though still legally, within the framework of the parliamentary republic.

In February 1936 a popular front coalition to ward off fascism won a narrow electoral victory, sufficient for an absolute majority in parliament. As would be true in France a few months later, electoral victory produced popular expectations that went well beyond the essentially defensive purposes of the popular front. Hoping to win back the leftist rank and file and head off what seemed a dangerous attempt at revolution, the new popular front government began to implement a progressive program, now including the land reform that had been promised but not implemented earlier. But it was too late to undercut the growing radicalization of the masses.

A wave of land seizures began in March, followed by a quasi-insurrectionary strike movement, the most extensive in Spanish history, which took on a clearly revolutionary character during June and July. To many, the government's inability to keep order had become the immediate issue. By the early summer of 1936, leaders of the democratic republic had become isolated between the extremes of left and right, each preparing an extralegal solution.

Finally, in mid-July, several army officers initiated a military uprising intended as a coup to seize power. Soon led by General Francisco Franco (1892–1975), these Nationalist insurgents took control of substantial parts of Spain, but elsewhere they failed to overcome the resistance of the Republican Loyalists, those determined to defend the republic. So the result was not the intended military takeover but a brutal civil war (Map 27.1). The substantial Italian fascist and Nazi German intervention on the Nationalist side by the end of 1936 intensified the war's ideological ramifications. At the same time, the remarkable, often heroic resistance of the Loyalists captured the imagination of the world. Indeed, 40,000 volunteers came from abroad to fight to preserve the Spanish republic.

It proved a war of stunning brutality on both sides. Loyalist anticlericalism led to the murder of twelve bishops and perhaps one-eighth of the parish clergy in Spain. On the other side, the German bombing of the Basque town of Guernica on a crowded market day in April 1937, represented

Picasso: Guernica Created for the Spanish pavilion at the famed 1937 Paris Exhibition, Picasso's painting conveyed horror and outrage in response to the German bombing of Guernica on a crowded market day in 1937, during the Spanish civil war. Picasso's stark, elemental imagery helped define this era of violence and suffering for the generations that followed. *(Pablo Picasso,* Guernica *[1937, May–early June]. Oil on canvas. © SPADEM, Paris/ARS, New York)*

unforgettably in Pablo Picasso's painting, came to symbolize the violence and suffering of the whole era.

Republican Loyalists assumed that Franco and the Nationalists represented another instance of fascism. In fact, however, Franco was no fascist, but rather a traditional military man whose leadership role did not rest on personal charisma. He was an authoritarian emphasizing discipline, order, and Spain's Catholic traditions.

Still, in their effort to rally support during the civil war, Franco's forces found it expedient to take advantage of the appeal of the Falange, a genuinely fascist movement that had emerged under the leadership of the charismatic young José Antonio Primo de Rivera (1903–1936). Although extremely weak at the time of the election in February 1936, the Falange grew rapidly in opposition to the leftist radicalism that followed the popular front victory. As street fighting between left and right intensified that spring, the republic arrested José Antonio, as he was called, and thus he was in prison when the civil war began.

José Antonio decided his best hope was alliance with the military. Although he was contemptuous of their shortsighted conservatism, he felt their very absence of ideas, "their abysmal political mediocrity," afforded an opening for the Falange to provide direction, a genuine alternative. But it worked out the other way. In November 1936, José Antonio was tried and executed for conspiring to overthrow the republic, and the Nationalists promptly began using the trappings of the Falange, including the memory of José Antonio, to increase their popular appeal.

Meanwhile, the Republicans had to fight a civil war while dealing with continuing revolution in their own ranks. Developing especially in Catalonia from the uprisings of 1936, that revolution was not communist but anarchist and syndicalist in orientation. The Communists, true to popular front principles, insisted that this was no time for such "infantile leftist" revolutionary experiments. What mattered, throughout the Republican zone, was the factory discipline necessary to produce essential war materiel. So the Communists, under Stalin's orders, were instrumental in putting down the anarchist revolution in Catalonia in June 1937.

Under these extraordinary circumstances, the Communists, at first a distinct minority on the Spanish left, gradually gained the ascendancy on the Republican side, partly because they were disciplined and effective, partly because the assistance the Soviets offered enhanced their prestige. When all was said and done, however, this single-minded prosecution of the civil war did not prove enough to defeat the military insurgency, despite the considerable heroism on the Loyalist side. The war ended with the fall of Madrid to the Nationalists in March 1939. General Franco's authoritarian regime governed Spain until his death in 1975.

In Spain, as in Weimar Germany, the initial lack of consensus in a new republic made parliamentary democracy difficult, and the wider ideological framework magnified the difficulties. With the political boiling point so low, the left and the right each viewed the other in extreme terms and assumed that extraordinary responses to the other were necessary. Thus the tendency of the left to view even conservatives operating within a parliamentary framework as "fascist." And each side was relatively quick to give up on a democratic republic that seemed to be tilting too far in the other direction.

France in the Era of the Popular Front

In France, as in Spain, concern to arrest the spread of fascism led to a popular front coalition, here including Socialists, Communists, and Radicals, that governed the country from 1936 to 1938. Although it did not lead to civil war, the popular front was central to the French experience of the 1930s, producing polarization and resignation, and undermining confidence in the Third Republic.

Beginning in 1934, the French Communists took the initiative in approaching first the Socialists, then the Radicals, to develop a popular front coalition against fascism. In reaching out to the Radicals, the Communists stressed French patriotism and made no demand for significant economic reforms. Stalin gave this effort a major push in 1935 when, in a stunning change in the communist line, he stressed the legitimacy of national defense and explicitly approved of French rearmament.

In the elections of April and May 1936, the popular front won a sizable majority in the Chamber of Deputies, putting the Socialists' leader, Léon Blum (1872–1950), in line to become France's first socialist prime minister. The Communists pledged full support of the new Blum government but, to avoid fanning fears, they did not participate directly. However, despite the popular front's moderate and essentially defensive aims, the situation quickly began to polarize after the elections.

Fearing that the new Blum government would be forced to devalue the French currency, thereby diminishing the value of assets denominated in francs, French investors immediately began moving their capital abroad. At the same time, the popular front victory produced a wave of enthusiasm among workers that escaped the control of popular front leaders and culminated late in May in a spontaneous strike movement, the largest France had ever seen. By June 4 it had spread to all major industries nationwide. Although the workers' demands—for collective bargaining, a forty-hour week, and paid vacations—were not extraordinary, the movement involved sit-down strikes as well as the normal walk-out form and thus seemed quasi-revolutionary in character. The major trade union confederation, the Communists, and most Socialists, including Blum himself, saw the strikes as a danger to the popular front, with its more modest aims of defending the republic, and eagerly pursued a settlement.

That settlement, the Matignon Agreement of June 8, 1936, was a major victory for the French working class. Having been genuinely frightened by the strikes, and now reassured that the popular front government would at least uphold the law, French industrialists were willing to make significant concessions. So the workers got collective bargaining, elected shop stewards, and wage increases as a direct result of Matignon, then a forty-hour week and paid vacations in a reform package promptly passed by parliament.

In the enthusiasm of the summer of 1936, there were other reforms as well, but after that the popular front was forced onto the defensive. Two problems undermined its energy and cohesion: the noncooperation of French business and the Spanish civil war. The cautious response of Blum, the Socialist prime minister, is striking in each case, but he faced a situation with little maneuvering room in 1936.

From the outset Blum stressed that he had no mandate for revolution, and as France's first Socialist prime minister, he felt it essential to prove that a Socialist could govern responsibly. Thus, Blum did not respond energetically to the capital flight, even though it produced serious currency

Léon Blum The French Socialist leader appears in an enthusiastic moment after the popular front victory in 1936. He was about to become France's first socialist prime minister, but in that role he encountered one dilemma after another. By 1938, the high spirits of 1936 had dissolved. *(Archives Ringart)*

and budgetary difficulties. Instead of devaluing the franc or imposing exchange controls, he simply tried to persuade French capital holders to repatriate their assets. When this proved unsuccessful, he finally was forced to devalue in September 1936, but with only limited results. Perhaps, as critics suggest, he should have acted more aggressively to overhaul the French banking and credit system, but Blum shied away from any such drastic measures, both to prove he could be responsible and to avoid antagonizing business.

Blum was also uncertain as he faced the dilemmas surrounding the Spanish civil war. The key question was whether the French government should help the beleaguered Spanish republic, at least by sending supplies. Although he initially favored such help, Blum changed his mind under pressure from three sides. The Conservative government of Stanley Baldwin in Britain was against it. So was the French right; some even suggested that French intervention would provoke civil war in France as well. Moreover, the Radicals in his own coalition were generally opposed to helping the Spanish republic, so intervention would jeopardize the popular front itself. Thus, rather than help supply the Spanish republic, Blum promoted a nonintervention agreement among the major powers, including Italy and Germany. Many Socialists and Communists within the popular front disliked Blum's nonintervention policy, however, especially as it became clear that Mussolini and Hitler were violating the nonintervention agreement. As Blum stuck to nonintervention, the moral force of the popular front dissolved.

Blum's first government lasted about a year. He got a brief second chance in 1938, but by then the popular front was simply disintegrating. A new government under the Radical Edouard Daladier (1884–1970), still nominally a creature of the popular front, began dismantling some of the key gains of 1936, even attacking the forty-hour week. Citing productivity and national security concerns, Daladier adopted pro-business policies and succeeded in attracting capital back to France.

Daladier's policies produced a serious rift with Blum, however, and a sense of betrayal among the workers, who watched the gains they had won in 1936 gradually slip away. At the same time, businessmen and conservatives began blaming the workers' gains—like the five-day week—for slowing French rearmament. Rather than work shifts, the argument went, the workers insisted on a "double Sunday," or two-day weekend, so the provision for a five-day week cut into the production necessary for rearmament. Although such charges were not entirely fair, they indicated how poisoned the atmosphere in France had become in the wake of the popular front.

As France began to face the possibility of a new war, the popular front was widely blamed for French weakness. When war came at last, resignation and division were prevalent, in contrast with the patriotic unity and high spirits of 1914. It was partly for that reason that France was so easily defeated by Germany in 1940. And partly for the same reason, when France fell the democratic Third Republic fell with it, and the country opted for an authoritarian alternative.

THE COMING OF WORLD WAR II, 1935–1939

Still under the long shadow of World War I, most Western leaders were determined to preserve the peace during the two ensuing decades. But the peace settlement that had followed the war created new problems, many of which remained when Hitler came to power in 1933 despite promising adjustments during the 1920s. And Hitler had consistently trumpeted his intention to overturn that settlement. What scope was there for peaceful revision? Could Hitler be stopped by threat of war?

Restoring German Sovereignty, 1935–1936

During his first years in power, through 1936, Hitler could be understood as merely restoring German sovereignty, revising a postwar settlement that had been misconceived in the first place. However uncouth and abrasive he might seem, it was hard to find a basis for opposing him. Yet in commencing German rearmament in 1935, and especially in remilitarizing the Rhineland in March 1936, Hitler fundamentally reversed the power balance established in France's favor at the peace conference.

France's special advantage had been the demilitarization of the entire German territory west of the Rhine River and a 50-kilometer strip on the east bank. The measure had been reaffirmed at Locarno in 1925, now with Germany's free agreement, and it was guaranteed by Britain and Italy. Yet on a Saturday morning in March 1936, that advantage disappeared as German troops moved into the forbidden area. The French and British acquiesced, uncertain of what else to do. After all, Hitler was only restoring Germany to full sovereignty.

But Hitler was not likely to stop there. As a result of the war and the peace, three new countries—Austria, Czechoslovakia, and Poland—bordered Germany (see Map 27.2). In each, the peace settlement had left trouble spots involving the status of ethnic Germans; in each the status quo was open to question.

Austria, Czechoslovakia, and Appeasement

As early as 1934, Hitler had moved to encompass his homeland, Austria, but strenuous opposition from Italy led him to back down. The developing understanding with Italy by 1936 enabled Hitler to focus again on Austria—initiating the second, more radical phase of his prewar foreign policy. On a pretext in March 1938, German troops moved into Austria, which was promptly incorporated into Germany. This time Mussolini was willing to acquiesce, and Hitler was genuinely grateful.

The Treaty of Versailles had explicitly prohibited this *Anschluss,* or unity with Germany, though that prohibition violated the principle of self-determination. It was widely believed in the West that most Austrians favored unity with Germany—and this perception was no doubt correct. The Anschluss could be justified as revising a misconceived aspect of the peace settlement.

Czechoslovakia presented quite a different situation. Although it had preserved democratic institutions, the country suffered from nationality problems. It included restive minorities of Slovaks, Magyars, Ruthenians, Poles, and—concentrated especially in the Sudetenland, along the German and Austrian borders—about 3.25 million Germans. After having been part of the dominant nationality in the old Habsburg empire, those Germans were frustrated with their minority status in the new Czechoslovakia, especially because they seemed to suffer disproportionately from the Depression. Hitler's agents actively stirred up their resentments.

Leading the West's response, when Hitler began making an issue of Czechoslovakia, was Neville Chamberlain (1869–1940), who followed Stanley Baldwin as Britain's prime minister and foreign minister in May 1937. An intelligent, vigorous, and public-spirited man from the progressive wing of the Conservative party, Chamberlain has long been derided as the architect of the "appeasement" of Hitler at the Munich conference of 1938, which settled the crisis over Czechoslovakia. Trumpeted as the key to peace, the Munich agreement proved but a step to the war that broke out less than a year later. Yet though it failed, Chamberlain's policy of appeasement stemmed not from cowardice or mere drift and certainly not from some unspoken pro-Nazi sentiment.

Rather than let events spin out of control, as seemed to have happened in 1914, Chamberlain sought to master the difficult international situation through creative bargaining. The excesses of Hitler's policy resulted from the mistakes of

Versailles; redo the settlement on a more realistic basis, and Germany would behave responsibly. The key, Chamberlain felt, was to pinpoint the sources of Germany's frustrations and, as he put it, "to remove the danger spots one by one."

Moreover, in Britain as elsewhere, there were some who saw Hitler's resurgent Germany as a bulwark against communism, which might spread into east-central Europe—especially in the event of another war. Indeed, the victor in another war might well be the revolutionary left. To prevent such an outcome was worth a few concessions to Hitler.

Although the Czechs, led by Eduard Beneš (1884–1948), made some attempt to liberalize their nationality policy, by April 1938 they were becoming ever less sympathetic to Sudeten German demands for autonomy, especially because a threat of German intervention seemed to accompany them. Tensions between Czechoslovakia and Germany mounted, and by late September 1938 war

The Illusion of Peace Neville Chamberlain, returning home to Britain from Munich to a hero's welcome, waves the peace declaration that was supposed to have brought "peace in our time." This was late September 1938. Less than a year later, Europe was again at war. *(Hulton-Getty/Tony Stone Images)*

Toward Appeasement: The Longing for Peace

Late in September 1938, the crisis that developed over Germany's demands on Czechoslovakia produced an emotional roller coaster for Europeans. Central to the continuing effort to preserve the peace was the British prime minister, Neville Chamberlain, who flew to Germany twice to meet with Hitler before the crisis reached its climax. At first, Chamberlain thought he had found a formula for peace, but then Hitler upped his demands. Thus, Chamberlain's tone was somber when he addressed the British people by radio shortly after his second trip, on September 27, at what proved the height of the crisis.

First of all I must say something to those who have written to my wife or myself in these last weeks to tell us of their gratitude for my efforts and to assure us of their prayers for my success. Most of these letters have come from women— mothers or sisters of our own countrymen. But there are countless others besides—from France, from Belgium, from Italy, even from Germany, and it has been heartbreaking to read of the growing anxiety they reveal. . . .

If I felt my responsibility heavy before, to read such letters has made it seem almost overwhelming. How horrible, fantastic, incredible it is that we should be digging trenches and trying on gas masks here because of a quarrel in a far-away country between people of whom we know nothing. It seems still more impossible that a quarrel which has already been settled in principle should be the subject of war.

I can well understand the reasons why the Czech Government have felt unable to accept the terms which have been put before them in the German memorandum. Yet I believe after my talks with Herr Hitler that, if only time

were allowed, it ought to be possible for the arrangements for transferring the territory that the Czech government has agreed to give to Germany to be settled by agreement under conditions which would assure fair treatment to the population concerned. . . .

However much we may sympathise with a small nation confronted by a big and powerful neighbor, we cannot in all circumstances undertake to involve the whole British Empire in war simply on her account. If we have to fight it must be on larger issues than that. . . . [I]f I were convinced that any nation had made up its mind to dominate the world by fear of its force, I should feel that it must be resisted. . . . but war is a fearful thing, and we must be very clear, before we embark on it, that it is really the great issues that are at stake. . . .

For the present I ask you to await as calmly as you can the events of the next few days. As long as war has not begun, there is always hope that it may be prevented, and you know that I am going to work for peace to the last moment. Good night.

Source: Neville Chamberlain, *In Search of Peace: Speeches (1937–1938)* (London: Hutchinson, 1939), pp. 274–276.

appeared imminent, despite Chamberlain's efforts to mediate. (See the box, "Toward Appeasement: The Longing for Peace.") Both the French and the British began mobilizing, with French troops manning the Maginot Line for the first time.

A 1924 treaty bound France to come to the aid of Czechoslovakia in the event of aggression. Moreover, the Soviet Union, according to a treaty of 1935, was bound to assist Czechoslovakia if the French did so. And throughout the crisis, the Soviets pushed for a strong stand in defense of Czecho

slovakia against German aggression. For both ideological and military reasons, however, the British and French were not anxious for a war on the side of the Soviet Union. The value of the Soviet military was uncertain, at best, at a time when the Soviet officer corps had just been purged.

By September, Hitler seemed eager to smash the Czechs by force, but when Mussolini proposed a four-power conference, he was persuaded to talk again. At Munich late in September, Britain, France, Italy, and Germany settled the matter, with Czechoslovakia—and the Soviet Union—excluded. Determined not to risk war over what seemed Czech intransigence, the British ended up agreeing to what Hitler had wanted all along—not merely autonomy for the Sudeten Germans but German annexation of the Sudetenland.

The Munich agreement specified that all Sudeten areas with German majorities be transferred to Germany; plebiscites were to be held in areas with large German minorities, and Hitler pledged to respect the sovereignty of the newly diminished Czechoslovak state. Chamberlain and his French counterpart, Edouard Daladier, each returned home to a hero's welcome, having transformed what had seemed certain war to, in Chamberlain's memorable phrase, "peace in our time."

Rather than settle the nationality questions bedeviling Czechoslovakia, the Munich agreement only provoked further unrest. First, disputed areas with large Polish and Hungarian populations fell to Poland and Hungary, respectively. Each proved eager to exploit the new weakness of Czechoslovakia. Then unrest stemming from Slovak separatism afforded a pretext for Germany to send troops into Prague in March 1939. The Slovak areas were spun off as a separate nation, while the Czech areas became the Protectorate of Bohemia and Moravia. Less than six months after the Munich conference, most of what had been Czechoslovakia had landed firmly within the Nazi orbit (Map 27.2). It was no longer possible to justify Hitler's actions as seeking to unite all Germans in one state.

Poland, the Nazi-Soviet Pact, and the Coming of War

With Poland, the German grievance was still more serious, for the new Polish state had been created partly at German expense. Especially galling to Germans was the Polish corridor, which cut off East Prussia from the bulk of Germany in order to give Poland access to the sea. The city of Danzig, historically Polish (Gdansk) but part of Germany before World War I, was left a "free city," supervised by the League of Nations.

Disillusioned by Hitler's dismemberment of Czechoslovakia, and angered by the Germans' menacing rhetoric regarding Poland, Chamberlain announced in the House of Commons on March 31, 1939, that Britain and France would intervene militarily in the event of a threat to Poland's independence. Chamberlain was not only abandoning the policy of appeasement; he was making a clear commitment to the Continent, of the sort that British governments had resisted since 1919. He could do so partly because Britain was rapidly rearming; by early 1940, in fact, Britain was spending nearly as large a share of its national income on the military as Germany was.

Chamberlain's assertive statement was not enough to deter Hitler, who seems to have been determined to settle the Polish question by force. Hitler continued, however, to stress how limited and reasonable German aims were in an effort to localize the conflict. Germany simply wanted Danzig and German transit across the corridor; it was the Polish stance that was rigid and unreasonable. Hitler seems to have believed that Polish intransigence would alienate the British and French, undercutting their support. And as the crisis developed by mid-1939, doubts were increasingly expressed, on all sides, that the British and French were really prepared to aid Poland militarily—that they had the will "to die for Danzig."

Although they had been lukewarm to Soviet proposals for a military alliance, Britain and France began to negotiate with the Soviet Union more seriously during the spring and summer of 1939. But doubts about the value of a Soviet alliance continued to gnaw at Western leaders. For one thing, Soviet troops could gain access to Germany only by moving through Poland or Romania, neither of which was willing to grant passage. Poland and Romania each had territory gained at the expense of Russia in the postwar settlement, so the British and French, suspicious of Soviet designs on both, were reluctant to insist that Soviet troops be allowed to pass through them.

Even as negotiations between the Soviet Union and the democracies seemed to continue, the Soviet Union came to its own agreement with Nazi Germany on August 22, 1939, in a pact that astonished the world. Each of them had been denouncing the other, and although Hitler had explored the possibility of Soviet neutrality in May, serious negotiations began only that August, when the Soviets got the clear signal that a German invasion of Poland was inevitable. It now appeared that no Soviet alliance with Britain and France could prevent war. Under these circumstances, a nonaggression pact with Germany

International boundaries, 1936
Germany in 1933
Remilitarized in 1936
Annexed in 1938
Satellite states, March 1939
Conquered by Germany in September 1939

Annexed by Soviet Union in September 1939

Map 27.2 The Expansion of Nazi Germany, 1936–1939 Especially with the remilitarization of the Rhineland in 1936, Hitler's Germany began moving, step by step, to alter the European power balance. In September 1939 the Soviet Union also began annexing territory, capitalizing on its agreement with Germany the month before.

seemed better to serve Soviet interests than a problematic war on the side of Britain and France. So the Soviets agreed with the Germans that each would remain neutral in the event that either became involved in a war with some other nation.

The Soviet flip-flop stemmed partly from disillusionment with the British and French response to the accelerating threat of Nazism. The democracies seemed no more trustworthy, and potentially no less hostile, than Nazi Germany. Moreover, a secret protocol to the Nazi-Soviet Pact apportioned major areas of east-central Europe between the Soviet Union and Germany. Thus the Soviets soon regained much of what they had lost after

World War I, when Poland, Finland, and other states had been created or aggrandized with territories that had been part of the Russian Empire.

The Nazi-Soviet Pact seemed to give Hitler the free hand he wanted in Poland. With the dramatic change in alignment, the democracies were surely much less likely to intervene. But Chamberlain, again determined to avoid the hesitations of 1914, publicly reaffirmed the British guarantee to Poland on August 25. Britain would indeed intervene in the event of a German attack. And after Hitler ordered the German invasion of Poland on September 1, the British and French responded with a declaration of war on September 3.

With each step on the path to war, Hitler had vacillated between apparent reasonableness and wanton aggressiveness. Sometimes he accented the plausibility of his demands in light of problems with the postwar settlement; sometimes he seemed to be actively seeking war. Even in invading Poland, he may still have been hoping to localize hostilities. But he was certainly willing to risk a more general European war, and the deepest thrust of his policy was toward a war of conquest—first against Poland, but ultimately against the Soviet Union. War was essential to the Nazi vision, and only when the assault on Poland became a full-scale war did the underlying purposes of Nazism become clear.

SUMMARY

The 1930s made a cruel mockery of the hopes for restabilization that had followed World War I. The Depression and the challenges from new political regimes called both capitalism and democracy into question. Hitler's Germany, especially, presented an unprecedented challenge to the European order, but the leading democracies, Britain and France, were slow to respond. Eagerness to avoid another war affected their reactions, as did the ideological polarization of the decade. Led by Britain, the democracies began unequivocally to resist the Nazi challenge only in 1939.

The most important new political systems of the interwar period—Italian fascism, German Nazism, and Stalinist communism—were dictatorial and hostile to liberal democracy, but they were not merely authoritarian in the old-fashioned, predemocratic sense. They were clearly novel, and they had some features in common. Their common direction is often summed up as *totalitarian*, a useful though problematic term. In each of the three regimes, the sovereignty of the state was to become all-encompassing, breaking down the distinction between public and private—thus Mussolini's boast that there was "nothing outside the state" in fascist Italy, and the proclamation of Robert Ley, head of the Nazi Labor Front, that "the private citizen has ceased to exist."

The common totalitarian direction is important, but it glosses over differences, especially in origins and purposes, that are at least as important. Racism and anti-Semitism, fundamental to radical Nazism, were not central to Italian fascism, which sought to respond to the apparent inadequacies of parliamentary democracy by constructing a new "corporative state." Though it never lived up to the rhetoric, Italian fascist corporativism produced a web of institutions that Nazi Germany did not duplicate.

In practice, Nazism and Stalinism were far more extreme than Italian fascism, so comparison of these two regimes is crucial to any attempt to understand the troubling political experience of the 1930s. Again, whatever the convergence in practice, the difference in origins and purposes must not be forgotten.

Twisted though it became, the Marxist vision of human liberation, based on long-standing Western values, was still manifest in the ongoing Soviet revolution during the 1930s. Committed communists believed that extreme measures were necessary if they were to carry out, in the difficult conditions the Soviet Union faced, a transformation that would eventually benefit all humanity. Nazism never claimed a comparably universal aim. Indeed, with its emphasis on racial determinism and natural struggle, Hitler's world-view was the antithesis of the humanistic tradition that found in Marxism one coherent, if extreme, manifestation. More generally, Hitler's radical Nazism was fundamentally antithetical to basic Western values, which emphasized the worth of human life and the dignity of every individual.

But whatever the differences in values and intentions, the final reckoning must rest on the results. Stalin's way of implementing the Marxist revolution made individual human lives expendable, just as they were for Hitler. The outcome of both Stalinism and Nazism was mass murder on a horrifying scale.

It was symptomatic that Hitler and Stalin came together with the cynical nonaggression pact of August 1939, the immediate prelude to war. Yet the underlying difference between the two became paramount in the life-and-death struggle that began in 1941, when Hitler betrayed Stalin and invaded the Soviet Union. If he could realize his long-standing aim of conquering the Soviet Union, Hitler could eradicate communism and provide Germany with essential living space at the same time. The four-year battle between Nazi Germany and the Soviet Union would be decisive to World War II, which proved the awful culmination of the destructiveness unleashed in the 1930s.

NOTES

1. Quoted in Robert Conquest, *The Great Terror: A Reassessment* (New York: Oxford University Press, 1990), p. 24.
2. Quoted in Helmut Krausnick et al., *Anatomy of the SS State* (New York: Walker, 1968), p. 13.

SUGGESTED READING

The Great Depression

Eichengreen, Barry. *Golden Fetters: The Gold Standard and the Great Depression, 1919–1939.* 1992. Accents the role of the gold standard both in intensifying the destabilizing process that led to the Depression and in limiting the responses of policymakers.

James, Harold. *The German Slump: Politics and Economics, 1924–1936.* 1986. Weaves economics and politics to explain the Depression in Germany and the economic recovery after Hitler came to power in 1933.

Kindleberger, Charles. *The World in Depression, 1929–1939.* Revised and enlarged ed. 1986. An important revisionist work arguing that the Depression stemmed from difficulties in the international exchange system rather than from problems and responses in the United States.

Skidelsky, Robert. *Politicians in the Slump: The Labour Government of 1929–1931.* 1967. Searching analysis of the inability of Britain's Labour government to respond effectively to the mass unemployment of the first years of the Depression.

Stalinism and the Soviet Union

Conquest, Robert. *The Harvest of Sorrow: Soviet Collectivization and the Terror-Famine.* 1986. Dramatic, pioneering account of the deportation and forced collec-

tivization of peasants that proved the cornerstone of the Stalinist revolution of 1929–1933.

———. *The Great Terror: A Reassessment.* 1990. Updated edition of an influential work first published in 1968. Offers a gripping account of the Stalinist purges of the 1930s, emphasizing Stalin's personal responsibility.

Fitzpatrick, Sheila. *Stalin's Peasants: Resistance and Survival in the Russian Village after Collectivization.* 1994. Probing study of the peasant response to the forced collectivization that inaugurated Stalin's rule in the Soviet Union.

Getty, J. Arch. *Origins of the Great Purges: The Soviet Communist Party Reconsidered, 1933–1938.* 1985. Challenges the notion that the purges, show trials, and terror of the 1930s were parts of a single totalitarian system orchestrated by Stalin. Argues that they were ad hoc responses to disparate pressures.

Rosenberg, William G., and Lewis H. Siegelbaum, eds. *Social Dimensions of Soviet Industrialization.* 1993. Important series of essays showing the impact of the crash industrialization program of the 1930s on the experience of ordinary people, from peasants to industrial workers to those responsible for factory discipline.

Thurston, Robert W. *Life and Terror in Stalin's Russia, 1934–1941.* 1996. Challenges the conventional understanding based on notions of terror and totalitarianism. Seeks to penetrate to the level of ordinary people and everyday life to understand the successes of the Stalinist regime during the pivotal 1930s.

Tucker, Robert C. *Stalin in Power: The Revolution from Above, 1928–1941.* 1990. The second volume of the author's acclaimed study of Stalin, but stands on its own. Provides a superb account of the crash industrialization and forced collectivization that led to the Stalinist regime.

Hitler and Nazism

Bessel, Richard, ed. *Life in the Third Reich.* 1987. Essays on the connections between the Nazi regime and German society. An ideal introductory work.

Bracher, Karl Dietrich. *The German Dictatorship: The Origins, Structure, and Effects of National Socialism.* 1970. A comprehensive synthesis by a major German authority.

Fest, Joachim C. *The Face of the Third Reich: Portraits of the Nazi Leadership.* 1970. Perceptive collective biography of the major Nazi hierarchs, highlighting common personal weaknesses.

Fischer, Klaus P. *Nazi Germany: A New History.* 1995. Comprehensive, well researched, and carefully balanced, this is perhaps the best one-volume treatment of Nazism in English.

Jaeckel, Eberhard. *Hitler's World View: A Blueprint for Power.* 1981. Influential account of the combination of racism, anti-Semitism, and Social Darwinism that structured Hitler's thinking—and ultimately the aspirations of the Nazi regime.

Kershaw, Ian. *The "Hitler Myth": Image and Reality in the Third Reich.* 1987. Explores the often contradictory image of Hitler created in Nazi propaganda.

———. *The Nazi Dictatorship: Problems and Perspectives of Interpretation.* 3rd ed. 1993. Excellent historiographical account of the major issues and recent controversies concerning the Nazi regime in practice.

Koonz, Claudia. *Mothers in the Fatherland: Women, the Family, and Nazi Politics.* 1987. Influential and accessible study of women in Nazism, accenting the active roles of women in implementing Nazism on the grassroots level in welfare, education, and leisure activities, while ultimately stressing the subordination of women within the wider Nazi universe.

Noakes, J[eremy], and G[eoffrey] Pridham, eds. *Nazism: A History in Documents and Eyewitness Accounts, 1919–1945.* 2 vols. 1990. An invaluable collection of documents on all aspects of Nazism, usefully arranged with running commentary by the editors.

Peukert, Detlev J. K. *Inside Nazi Germany: Conformity, Opposition, and Racism in Everyday Life.* 1987. Among the best of recent efforts to understand Nazi Germany by depicting how Nazism affected the everyday lives of ordinary people.

Stephenson, Jill. *Women in Nazi Society.* 1975. Pioneering work on what Nazism meant for women's status and opportunities. Shows that by the late 1930s, German women were neither better nor worse off than women elsewhere in the West.

Comparative Approaches to the Dictatorships

Bessel, Richard, ed. *Fascist Italy and Nazi Germany: Comparisons and Contrasts.* 1996. A well-selected series of essays by major experts on fascism.

Bullock, Alan. *Hitler and Stalin: Parallel Lives.* 1992. A lengthy yet gripping comparative account by a master of the biographical approach to history.

Griffin, Roger. *The Nature of Fascism.* 1991. Sophisticated but accessible effort to identify the core of aspirations, stemming especially from the new situation created by the war and the Russian Revolution, that led to the fascist movements of the interwar period.

Laqueur, Walter. *Fascism: Past, Present, Future.* 1996. Wide-ranging interpretative account, devoting much attention to recent "neofascism," including comparisons with religious extremism.

Payne, Stanley G. *A History of Fascism, 1914–1945.* 1995. A comprehensive account by a leading historian of twentieth-century Europe. Includes historical and

interpretive sections, as well as an epilogue on the scope for neofascism.

France and Spain

Carr, Raymond. *The Spanish Tragedy: The Civil War in Perspective.* 1977. An accessible account, blending narrative with analysis and commentary. Particularly useful on the politics of the Nationalist zone.

Colton, Joel. *Leon Blum: Humanist in Politics.* 1987. First pub. 1966. Sympathetic but carefully balanced biography, featuring dilemmas stemming from Blum's background as a socialist intellectual.

Fraser, Ronald. *Blood of Spain: An Oral History of the Spanish Civil War.* 1986. Based on interviews with participants, this book provides a running history of the war and the revolutionary efforts that accompanied it.

Jackson, Julian. *The Popular Front in France: Defending Democracy, 1934–38.* 1988. Combines narrative with thematic chapters on the most controversial issues surrounding the popular front experience.

Payne, Stanley. *The Spanish Revolution.* 1970. Focuses on the disintegration of the second Spanish republic and the coming of the civil war.

Weber, Eugen. *The Hollow Years: France in the 1930s.* 1994. Lively account of French life and manners during a decade that led to humiliation and defeat.

Diplomacy and the Coming of War

Bell, P. M. H. *The Origins of the Second World War in Europe.* 1986. A well-organized and nicely balanced survey.

Cameron, Donald Watt. *How War Came: The Immediate Origins of the Second World War, 1938–1939.* 1989. Detailed but readable narrative account, based on thorough research.

Overy, R. J., and Andrew Wheatcroft. *The Road to War.* 1989. Without questioning Hitler's ruthlessness and ultimate responsibility, the authors challenge standard views of the causes of World War II by recreating the particular situations and perspectives of each country.

Weinberg, Gerhard L. *The Foreign Policy of Hitler's Germany.* Vol. 1, *Diplomatic Revolution in Europe, 1933–1936,* and Vol. 2, *Starting World War II, 1937–1939.* 1970, 1980. Comprehensive study focusing on the key decisions and those who made them. Emphasizes Hitler's aims and German initiatives in the process that led to war.

FILM AS PROPAGANDA

One of the extraordinary pieces of evidence from the Nazi period is *Triumph of the Will*, a documentary film on the sixth Nazi party rally, which took place September 4–10, 1934, in the historic city of Nuremberg, by this time the official site for such party rallies. Directed by a talented young woman, Leni Riefenstahl (b. 1902), *Triumph of the Will* has long been recognized as one of the most compelling propaganda films ever made. What can we learn from this film about how the Nazis understood and used propaganda? What was the Nazi regime trying to convey in sponsoring the film, with the particular images it contained?

A sense of the scope for political propaganda was one of the defining features of the Nazi movement virtually from its inception. In his quest for power Hitler allotted an especially significant role to his future propaganda minister, Joseph Goebbels. Both Hitler and Goebbels saw that new media and carefully orchestrated events might be used to shape the political views of masses of people.

The Nazi party held the first of what would become annual conventions in Nuremberg in 1927. From the start, these meetings were rallies of

As seen in *Triumph of the Will*, the Leader . . .

the faithful, intended to give the Nazi movement a sense of cohesion and common purpose; but they increasingly became carefully staged propaganda spectacles, with banners and searchlights, parades and speeches. When, by 1934, the regime had completed the task of immediate power consolidation, it seemed time to seize the potential of the film medium to carry the spectacle beyond those present in Nuremberg. The intention to make a film thus influenced the staging of the 1934 rally. Film would transform the six-day event into a single potent work of art.

When Hitler came to power, Goebbels, as propaganda minister, assumed control of the German film industry, and he was particularly jealous of his prerogatives in this sphere. If there was to be a film of one of the Nuremberg rallies, he assumed that he would be in charge. So he objected strenuously when Hitler decided that Riefenstahl, who was not even a party member, should film the 1934 rally.

Already popular as an actress, Riefenstahl had established her own film-making company in 1931, before she turned 30. Her first film won the admiration of Hitler, who sought her out and eventually proposed that she direct the film of the party rally. Although she was an artist with no special interest in politics, Riefenstahl, like many Germans, believed at this point that Hitler might be able to revive Germany's fortunes. So despite considerable reluctance, she bowed to Hitler's persistence and agreed to do the film—though only after she was guaranteed final control over editing. Her relations with Goebbels remained strained, but Hitler continued to support her as she made *Triumph of the Will*.

Riefenstahl developed the 107-minute film by editing sixty-one hours of footage that covered everything from Hitler's arrival and motorcade to the closing parades and speeches. As depicted on film, the party rally does not convey an overt ideological message. We hear Hitler not attacking Jews or glorifying conquest but simply trumpeting German renewal. What strikes us in Riefenstahl's portrayal are the unity and epic monumentality that

. . . and the Disciplined, Tightly Knit Community of Followers *(Both photos from the Museum of Modern Art/Film Stills Archive)*

Nazism had apparently brought to Germany thanks to Hitler's leadership.

The film opens as Hitler emerges from dramatic cloud formations to arrive by airplane, descending from the sky like a god. He appears throughout the film as an almost superhuman figure, even, as in the shot shown here, as inspired, possessed, uncanny. Above all, he is a creator who shapes reality by blending will and art, forging masses of anonymous individuals into one people, one racial community, ready for anything. Those individuals seem, from one perspective, to lose their individuality in a monolithic mass, as in the shot of the parade grounds. But their sense of involvement in grandiose purposes charges them emotionally, even gives them a kind of ecstasy. The symbols, the massed banners, the ritualistic show of conformity, all strengthened this sense of participation in the new people's community. But unity and community were not ends in themselves; the film exalted military values and depicted a disciplined society organized for war.

Triumph of the Will extended participation in the spectacle to those who were not actually present in Nuremberg. The film chiseled the sprawl-ing event into a work of art, so seeing the film was in some ways more effective than being there. The Nazis looked for every means possible to involve the whole society in ritualistic spectacles that could promote a sense of belonging and unity. In addition to film, they made effective use of radio, even subsidizing the purchase of radio sets, or "people's receivers." Such new media were to help ordinary Germans feel a more meaningful kind of belonging than possible under the democracy of the Weimar Republic. But this was only an emotional involvement, not the active participation of free citizens invited to make rational choices.

Triumph of the Will had its premiere in March 1935, with Hitler in the audience. It won several prizes in Germany and abroad but enjoyed only mixed success with the German public, especially outside the large cities. For some, it was altogether too artistic, and the Nazi regime did not use it widely for overt propaganda purposes. Still, the Nazis commissioned no other film about Hitler, for *Triumph of the Will* captured the way he wanted to be seen. Indeed, Hitler praised the film as an "incomparable glorification of the power and beauty of our Movement." ✦

CHAPTER 28

The Era of the Second World War, 1939–1949

"The effects could well be called unprecedented, magnificent, beautiful, stupendous and terrifying. No man-made phenomenon of such tremendous power had ever occurred before. . . . Thirty seconds after the explosion came first, the air blast pressing hard against the people and things, to be followed almost immediately by the strong, sustained, awesome roar which warned of doomsday and made us feel that we puny things were blasphemous to dare tamper with the forces heretofore reserved to The Almighty."[1]

So wrote Brigadier General Thomas F. Farrell, who had just witnessed the birth of the atomic age. On July 16, 1945, watching from a control shelter 10,000 yards away, Farrell had seen the first explosion of an atomic bomb at a remote, top-secret U.S. government testing ground near Alamogordo, New Mexico. Such a weapon had been little more than a theoretical possibility when World War II began, and it required a remarkable concentration of effort, centered first in Britain, then in the United States, to make possible the awesome spectacle that confronted General Farrell. Exceeding most expectations, the test revealed a weapon of unprecedented power and destructiveness.

Within weeks, the United States dropped two other atomic bombs—first on Hiroshima, then on Nagasaki—to force the surrender of Japan. Thus ended the Second World War, the conflict that had begun six long years earlier with the German invasion of Poland. The atomic bomb was the awesome final step in an escalation of violence that made World War II the most destructive in history. In using the atomic bomb, the Americans not only ended the war but assured that a new set of anxieties would accompany the return to peace.

A new war,
a new age.

World War II proved more destructive than World War I, and more truly global in scope, partly because it grew from its European beginnings to encompass Japan late in 1941. In World War I, Japan had played only a secondary role, on the side of Britain. But now, allied with Germany and Italy, Japan was aggressively seeking an empire in East Asia and the Pacific. Japan's far greater involvement in World War II brought the full brunt of the war to that region and dramatically changed the geography and strategy of the war. Moreover, because the war expanded as it did, it profoundly affected the place of Western civilization in the world, speeding the dissolution of the Western colonial empires. Yet the Japanese dared to become fully involved in the war, attacking the United States late in 1941, only because of the outcome in Europe to that point. And ultimately it was the European theater that proved decisive.

The ironic outcome of the Second World War was a new cold war between the United States and the Soviet Union, allies in the victorious struggle against Germany, Italy, and Japan. Of the European states, only the Soviet Union emerged from the war with more territory and more power, thrust into a world role that would have been inconceivable just a few years before. But the wartime success of the United States had been even more dramatic, and the Americans were determined not to repeat what now seemed their mistaken return to isolationism in the aftermath of World War I. By the end of the 1940s, the United States and the Soviet Union had divided Europe into competing spheres of influence. Indeed, the competition between these two superpowers almost immediately became global in scope, creating a bipolar world. And the cold war between them was especially terrifying because, seeking military advantage, they raced to stockpile ever more destructive nuclear weapons. Thus the threat of nuclear annihilation helped define the cold war era.

World War II led to the defeat of the Axis powers—first Italy, then Germany, and finally Japan—and in this sense resolved the conflicts that had caused it. But the experience of this particular war changed the world forever. Before finally meeting defeat, the Nazis were sufficiently successful to begin implementing their "new order" in Europe, especially in the territories they conquered to the east of Germany. As part of this effort, in what has become known as the Holocaust, they began systematically murdering Jews in extermination camps, eventually killing as many as 6 million. The most destructive of the camps was at Auschwitz, in Poland. Often paired after the war, Auschwitz and Hiroshima came to stand for the incredible new forms of death and destruction that the war had spawned—and that continued to haunt the world long after it had ended, posing new questions about the meaning of Western civilization.

THE VICTORY OF NAZI GERMANY, 1939–1941

Instead of the enthusiasm evident in 1914, the German invasion of Poland on September 1, 1939, produced a grim sense of foreboding, even in Germany. Well-publicized incidents like the German bombing of civilians during the Spanish civil war and the Italian use of poison gas in Ethiopia suggested that the frightening new technologies introduced in World War I would now be used on a far greater scale, making the new conflict a much uglier war, more directly involving civilians.

Still, as in 1914, there were hopes that this war could be localized and brief—that it would not become a "world war." Hitler did not expect a protracted war with Britain. In light of the Nazi-Soviet Pact (see page 1023), war between Germany and the Soviet Union seemed unlikely. And isolationist sentiment in the United States made U.S. intervention doubtful.

Rather than a long war, Hitler and the Germans envisioned a *Blitzkrieg,* or "lightning war." At first events seemed to confirm German expectations. When Poland fell after just over a month, Hitler publicly offered peace to Britain and France, seriously thinking that might be the end of it. The British and French refused to call off the war, but from 1939 through 1941 the Nazis won victory after victory, establishing the foundation for their new order in Europe.

Initial Conquests and "Phony War"

The Polish army was large enough to have given the Germans a serious battle. But in adapting the technological innovations of World War I, Germany had developed a new military strategy based on rapid mobility. This Blitzkrieg strategy employed swift, highly concentrated offensives based on mobile tanks covered with concentrated air support, including dive-bombers that struck just ahead of the tanks. In Poland this strategy proved decisive. The French could offer only token help, and the last Polish unit surrendered on October 2, barely a month after the fighting had begun. The speed of the German victory stunned the world.

Meanwhile, the Soviets began cashing in on the pact they had made with Nazi Germany a few weeks before. It offered a precious opportunity to undo provisions of the World War I settlement that had significantly diminished the western territories of the former Russian Empire, thereby damaging the interests and defenses of the new Soviet state. On September 17, with the German victory in Poland assured, Stalin sent Soviet forces into Poland. Soon Poland was again divided between Germany and Russia, as it had been before 1914. Stalin looked next to the Baltic states of Estonia, Latvia, and Lithuania, which had been part of the Russian Empire before World War I. The Nazi-Soviet agreement had assigned Lithuania to the German orbit, but the Germans agreed to let the Soviets have it in exchange for an additional slice of Poland. Initially let off with treaties of mutual assistance, Estonia, Latvia, and Lithuania were incorporated as republics within the Soviet Union during the summer of 1940.

When Finland proved less pliable, the Soviets invaded in November 1939. In the ensuing "Winter War," the Finns held out bravely, and only by taking heavy casualties did the Soviets manage to prevail by March 1940. These difficulties seemed to confirm suspicions that Stalin's purge during the mid-1930s had substantially weakened the Soviet army. Still, by midsummer 1940 the Soviet Union had regained much of the territory it had lost during the upheavals surrounding the revolution of 1917.

In the West, little happened during the strained winter of 1939–1940, known as the "Phony War." Then, on April 9, 1940, the Germans attacked Norway and Denmark in a surprise move to preempt a British and French scheme to cut off the major route for the shipment of Swedish iron ore to Germany. Denmark fell almost at once, while the staunch resistance in Norway was effectively broken by the end of April. The stage was set for the German assault on France.

The Fall of France, 1940

The war in the West began in earnest on May 10, 1940, when the Germans attacked France and the Low Countries. They launched their assault on France through the Ardennes Forest, above the northern end of the Maginot Line—terrain so difficult the French had discounted the possibility of an enemy strike there (see page 962). As in 1914, northern France quickly became the focus of a major war pitting French forces and their British allies against invading Germans. But this time, in startling contrast to World War I, the Battle of France was over in less than six weeks, a humiliating defeat for the French. What had happened?

The problem for the French was not lack of men and materiel, but strategy: how men and materiel were used. For example, Germany had no more than a slight numerical advantage in tanks. But in France, as in Poland, Germany took advantage of mobile tanks and dive-bombers to mount rapid, highly concentrated offensives. Germany achieved the essential breakthrough partly because the French command underestimated the speed with which the German army could move through Belgium.

French strategy, in contrast, was based on lessons learned during World War I. Anticipating another long, defensive war, France dispersed its tanks among infantry units along a broad front. Once the German tank column broke through the French lines, it quickly cut through northern France toward the North Sea. France's poor showing convinced the British that rather than commit troops and planes to a hopeless battle in France, they should get out and regroup for a longer global war. Finally, 200,000 British troops—as well as 130,000 French—escaped German encirclement and capture through a difficult evacuation at Dunkirk early in June (see Map 28.1).

By mid-June, barely five weeks after the fighting began, France had been thoroughly defeated. As the French military collapsed, the French cabinet resigned, to be replaced by a new government under Marshal Philippe Pétain, who had led the successful French effort in the Battle of Verdun during World War I. Pétain's government first asked for an armistice and then engineered a change of regime. The French parliament voted by an overwhelming majority to give Pétain exceptional powers, including the power to draw up a new constitution. So ended the parliamentary democracy of the Third Republic, which seemed responsible for France's weakness. The republic gave way to the more authoritarian Vichy regime, named after the resort city to which the government retreated as the Germans moved into Paris. The end of the fighting in France resulted in a kind of antidemocratic revolution, but one in which the French people, stunned by military defeat, at first acquiesced.

According to the armistice agreement, the French government was not only to cease hostilities but also to collaborate with the victorious Germans. French resistance began immediately, however. In a radio broadcast from London on June 18, Charles de Gaulle (1890–1970), the youngest general in the French army, called on French forces to rally to him to continue the fight against Nazi Germany. The military forces stationed in the French colonies, as well as the French troops that had been evacuated at Dunkirk, could form the nucleus of a new French army. Under the circumstances of military defeat and political change, de Gaulle's appeal seemed quixotic at best, and most French colonies went along with what seemed the legitimate French government at Vichy. For the new Vichy government, de Gaulle was a traitor. Yet a new Free French force grew from de Gaulle's remarkable appeal, and its subsequent role in the war helped overcome the humiliation of France's quick defeat in 1940.

What next for Hitler and the Germans, who seemed virtually invincible after their conquest of France? Ultimately decisive would be the assault on the Soviet Union in June 1941, but two chains of events after the Battle of France influenced the timing of the assault—perhaps in crucial ways. Britain proved a more implacable foe, and Italy a more burdensome friend, than Hitler had expected.

Winston Churchill and the Battle of Britain

With the defeat of France, Hitler seems to have expected that Britain, now apparently vulnerable to German invasion, would come to terms. But the British, having none of it, found a new spokesman and leader in Winston Churchill (1874–1965), who had replaced Neville Chamberlain as prime minister when the German invasion of western Europe began on May 10. Although Churchill had been prominent in British public life for years, his career to this point had not been noteworthy

for either judgment or success. He was obstinate, difficult, something of a curmudgeon. Yet he rose to the wartime challenge, becoming one of the notable leaders of the modern era. In speeches to the House of Commons during the remainder of 1940, he uttered perhaps the most memorable words of the war as he sought to dramatize the situation and inspire his nation. Some Britons, hoping for a negotiated settlement with Germany as the Battle of France ended, objected to Churchill's rhetoric, but his dogged promise of "blood, toil, tears, and sweat" helped rally the British people, so that later he could say, without exaggeration, that "this was their finest hour."

After the fall of France, Britain moved to full mobilization for a protracted war. Churchill consolidated economic policy under a small committee that promptly gave Britain the most thoroughly coordinated war economy of all the belligerents. Between 1940 and 1942, Britain outstripped Germany in the production of tanks, aircraft, and machine guns. In 1941 Britain adopted a National Service Act that subjected men aged 18 to 50 and women aged 20 to 30 to military or civilian war service. The upper age limits were subsequently raised to meet the demand for labor. Almost 70 percent of the 3 million people added to the British work force during the war were women.

Britain, then, intended to continue the fight even after France fell. Hitler weighed his options and decided to attack. In light of British naval superiority, he hoped to rely on aerial bombardment to knock the British out of the war without an actual invasion. The ensuing Battle of Britain culminated in the nightly bombing of London from September 7 through November 2, 1940, killing 15,000 and destroying thousands of buildings. But the British held. Ordinary people holed up in cellars and subway stations, while the fighter planes of the Royal Air Force fought back effectively, inflicting heavy losses against German aircraft over Britain.

Although the bombing continued into 1941, the British had withstood the worst the Germans could deliver, and Hitler began looking to the east, his ultimate objective all along. In December 1940 he ordered preparations for Operation Barbarossa, the assault on the Soviet Union. Rather than continuing the attack on Britain directly, Germany would use submarines to cut off shipping—and thus the supplies the British needed for a long war. Once Germany had defeated the Soviet

British Resistance At the height of the German bombing of Britain in 1940, Winston Churchill surveys the damage in London. *(Hulton-Getty/Tony Stone Images)*

Union, it would enjoy the geopolitical basis for world power, while Britain, as an island nation relying on a dispersed empire, would sooner or later be forced to come to terms.

Italian Intervention and the Spread of the War

Lacking sufficient domestic support, and unready for a major war, Mussolini could only look on as the war began in 1939. But as the Battle of France neared its end, it seemed safe for Italy to intervene, sharing in the spoils of what appeared certain victory. Thus in June 1940 Italy entered the war, expecting to secure territorial advantages in the Mediterranean, starting with Corsica, Nice, and Tunisia at the expense of France. Italy also hoped eventually to supplant Britain in the region—and even to take the Suez Canal.

Although Hitler and Mussolini got along remarkably well, their relationship was sensitive. When Hitler seemed to be proceeding without Italy during the first year of the war, Mussolini grew determined to show his independence and finally, in October 1940, ordered Italian forces to attack Greece. But the Greeks mounted a strong resistance, thanks partly to the help of British forces from North Africa.

Meanwhile, Germany had established its hegemony in much of east-central Europe without military force, often by exploiting grievances over the outcome of the peace conference in 1919. In November 1940 Romania and Hungary joined the Axis camp, and Bulgaria followed a few months later. But in March 1941, just after Yugoslavia had similarly committed to the Axis, a coup overthrew the pro-Axis government in Yugoslavia, and the new Yugoslav government prepared to aid the Allies.

By this point Hitler had decided it was expedient to push into the Balkans with German troops, both to reinforce the Italians and to consolidate Axis control of the area. As the war's geographic extent expanded, its stakes increased, yet the Germans continued to meet every challenge. By the end of May 1941 they had taken Yugoslavia and Greece (Map 28.1).

At the same time, the war was spreading to North Africa and the Middle East because of European colonial ties. The native peoples of the area sought to take advantage of the conflict among the Europeans to pursue their own independence. Iraq

SOVIET UNION

Baku•

Siege of Stalingrad,
Aug. 21, 1942–Jan. 31 1943

Stalingrad•

Russian front, Nov. 1942

Russian front,
Dec. 1941

Moscow•

•Tula
Smolensk•

Russian front, Spring 1944

Siege of Leningrad,
Sept. 1941–Jan. 1944

Leningrad•

Kiev•

UKRAINE

Black
Sea

Yalta•

TURKEY

SYRIA

PALESTINE
(Br. Mandate)

TRANS-
JORDAN
(Br. Mandate)

Ankara•

Suez
Canal

CYPRUS

Cairo•

Nile

EGYPT

El Alamein,
Summer 1942

Mediterranean
Sea

LIBYA

Crete

FINLAND

Helsinki•

Riga•

Pinsk•

Russian front, Feb. 1945

Warsaw•
Posen•

Cracow•

SLOVAKIA

HUNGARY

Budapest•

Bucharest•

ROMANIA

Danube

BULGARIA

Sofia•

SERBIA

YUGOSLAVIA

ALBANIA

GREECE

Athens•

Baltic
Sea

SWEDEN

Stockholm•

Vistula

Berlin•

GERMANY

Vienna•

CROATIA

Italian front,
Feb. 1945

ITALY

Monte Cassino,
May 1944

Salerno,
Sept. 1943

Sicily,
July 1943

Sicily

MALTA
(Gr. Br.)

NORWAY

Oslo•

DENMARK

Copenhagen•

Elbe

Danube

SWITZERLAND

Po

Bologna•

Rome•

Allies invade
Sicily and Italy,
July–Sept. 1943

Rommel defeated
in Tunisia, Axis
troops evacuated,
May 1943

TUNISIA

German surrender:
Reims, May 7, 1945
Berlin, May 8, 1945

Rhine Crossing,
March 7, 1945

Rhine

Dnieper

Don

Volga

NETHERLANDS

Dunkirk•

BELGIUM

Battle of
the Bulge,
Dec. 1944

Western front, Feb. 1945

Paris•

FRANCE

VICHY FRANCE
(occupied Nov. 1942)

Vichy•

Allies land in Provence,
Aug. 15, 1944

North
Sea

Battle of Britain,
Fall 1940

GREAT
BRITAIN

London•

NORTHERN
IRELAND

IRELAND

Invasion of Normandy,
June 6, 1944

Axis troops occupy
Vichy France,
Nov. 10 and 11, 1942

Ebro

SPAIN

Madrid•

PORTUGAL

Lisbon•

GIBRALTAR (Gr. Br.)

SP. MOROCCO

ALGERIA
(Vichy France)

FRENCH
MOROCCO

Casablanca,
Nov. 1942

ATLANTIC
OCEAN

Hitler's Greater Germany
Allied with Germany
Occupied by Germany and its allies
Grand Alliance
Neutral nations
Major battles

400 Mi.

400 Km.

200

200

0

0

and Syria became involved as Germans operating from Syria, administered by Vichy France, aided anti-British Arab nationalists in Iraq. But most important proved to be North Africa, where Libya, an Italian colony since 1912, lay adjacent to Egypt, where the British presence remained strong.

In September 1940 the Italian army drove 65 miles into Egypt, initiating almost three years of fighting across the North African desert. A British counteroffensive from December 1940 to February 1941 drove the Italians back 340 miles into Libya, prompting Germany to send some of its forces from the Balkans into North Africa. Under General Erwin Rommel (1891–1944), the famous "Desert Fox," Axis forces won remarkable successes in North Africa from February to May 1941. But successful though they had been by this point, the German forays into the Balkans and North Africa had delayed the crucial attack on the Soviet Union.

THE ASSAULT ON THE SOVIET UNION AND THE NAZI NEW ORDER

In ordering preparations for Operation Barbarossa in December 1940, Hitler decided to risk attacking the Soviet Union before knocking Britain out of the war. Then he invaded the Balkans and North Africa in what may have been an unnecessary diversion. In retrospect, it is easy to pinpoint that combination as his fatal mistake. But in light of the Soviet purges of the 1930s and the poor performance of the Soviet army in 1939 and 1940, Hitler had reason to believe the Soviet Union would crack relatively easily. Western military experts had come to similar conclusions, estimating that German forces would need but six weeks to take Moscow. And if Germany were to defeat the Soviet Union with another Blitzkrieg, it could gain control of the oil and other resources required for a longer war against Britain and, if necessary, the United States.

Map 28.1 World War II: European Theaters Much of Europe saw fighting during World War II, although different fronts were important at different times. What proved decisive was the fighting that ensued in the vast expanse of the Soviet Union after the Germans invaded in June 1941.

Forgive Me, Comrade . . . On June 23, 1941, the day after Nazi Germany attacked the Soviet Union, the London *Daily Mail* published this cartoon depicting Hitler's betrayal of his 1939 pact with Stalin. (Daily Mail, *London, 23 June 1941. Reprinted with permission*)

So the Nazi assault on the Soviet Union was not ill considered. Ultimately, however, it failed, and its failure was the decisive fact of World War II. Although supplies from its new Allies—Britain and eventually the United States—helped the Soviet forces to prevail, the most important factor was the unexpected strength of the Soviet military effort.

Before they were defeated, the Germans penetrated well into the Soviet Union, reaching the apex of their power in 1942. German conquests by that point enabled Hitler to begin constructing the new European order he had dreamed of. Although in western Europe the Nazis generally sought the collaboration of local leaders, in Poland and the Soviet Union the new order meant brutal subjugation of local populations. Now, and only now, did

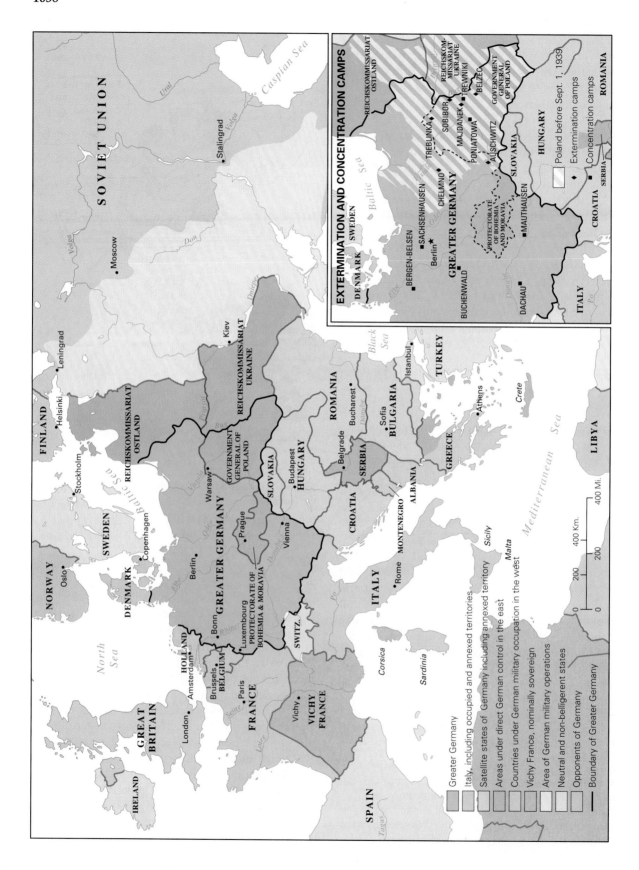

EXTERMINATION AND CONCENTRATION CAMPS

Poland before Sept. 1, 1939
♦ Extermination camps
■ Concentration camps

REICHSKOMMISSARIAT OSTLAND
REICHSKOMMISSARIAT UKRAINE
GOVERNMENT GENERAL OF POLAND
GREATER GERMANY
PROTECTORATE OF BOHEMIA AND MORAVIA
HUNGARY
SLOVAKIA
ROMANIA
CROATIA
SERBIA
ITALY
DENMARK
SWEDEN

TREBLINKA
SOBIBOR
MAJDANEK
BELZEC
PONIATOWA
AUSCHWITZ
CHELMNO
SACHSENHAUSEN
Berlin
BERGEN-BELSEN
BUCHENWALD
MAUTHAUSEN
DACHAU

Caspian Sea
Ural
Volga
Don
Dnieper
Stalingrad
Moscow
Leningrad

SOVIET UNION

FINLAND
Helsinki
SWEDEN
Stockholm
NORWAY
Oslo
Copenhagen
DENMARK

Baltic Sea
North Sea
IRELAND
GREAT BRITAIN
London
HOLLAND
Amsterdam
BELGIUM
Brussels
Luxembourg
FRANCE
Paris
VICHY FRANCE
Vichy
SWITZ.

REICHSKOMMISSARIAT OSTLAND
REICHSKOMMISSARIAT UKRAINE
Kiev
Warsaw
GOVERNMENT GENERAL OF POLAND
GREATER GERMANY
Berlin
Bonn
PROTECTORATE OF BOHEMIA & MORAVIA
Prague
Vienna
SLOVAKIA
HUNGARY
Budapest

Vistula
Oder
Elbe
Rhine
Seine
Loire
Bug
Pripet
Danube

Black Sea
ROMANIA
Bucharest
BULGARIA
Sofia
SERBIA
Belgrade
CROATIA
MONTENEGRO
ALBANIA
GREECE
Athens
Crete

TURKEY
Istanbul

ITALY
Rome
Po
Sardinia
Corsica
Sicily
Malta

Mediterranean Sea
LIBYA

SPAIN

Greater Germany
Italy, including occupied and annexed territories
Satellite states of Germany including annexed territory
Areas under direct German control in the east
Countries under German military occupation in the west
Vichy France, nominally sovereign
Area of German military operations
Neutral and non-belligerent states
Opponents of Germany
Boundary of Greater Germany

0   200   400 Km.
0   200   400 Mi.

the Nazis begin physically exterminating the Jews of Europe in specially constructed death camps.

An Ambiguous Outcome, 1941–1942

Attacking the Soviet Union on June 22, 1941, German forces achieved notable successes during the first month of fighting, partly because Stalin was so unprepared for this German betrayal. Ignoring warnings of an impending German assault, he had continued to live up to his end of the 1939 bargain with Hitler, even supplying the Germans with oil and grain. After the attack, Russia's defenses were at first totally disorganized, and by late November, German forces were within 20 miles of Moscow.

But the Germans were ill equipped for Russian weather, and as an early and severe winter descended, the German offensive bogged down. In December, the Soviets mounted a formidable surprise counterattack near Moscow. The German Blitzkrieg, which had seemed a sure thing in July, had failed; Germany might still prevail, but a different strategy would be required.

Although their initial assault had stalled, the Germans still had the advantage. German forces failed to take the key city of Leningrad in 1941, but they cut it off by blockade and, until early 1944, kept it under siege with relentless bombing and shelling. And during the summer of 1942, they mounted another offensive, moving more deeply into the Soviet Union than before, reaching Stalingrad in November. But this proved the deepest penetration of German forces—and the zenith of Nazi power in Europe.

Hitler's New Order

By the summer of 1942, Nazi Germany dominated the European continent as no power ever had be-

Map 28.2 The Nazi New Order in Europe, 1942
At the zenith of its power in 1942, Nazi Germany controlled much of Europe. Concerned most immediately with winning the war, the Nazis sought to coordinate the economies of their satellite states and conquered territories. But they also began establishing what was supposed to be an enduring new order in eastern Europe. The inset shows the location of the major Nazi concentration camps and of the six extermination camps the Nazis constructed in what had been Poland.

fore (Map 28.2). German military successes allowed the Nazi regime to begin building a new order in the territories under German domination. Satellite states in Slovakia and Croatia, and client governments in Romania and Hungary, owed their existence to Nazi Germany and readily adapted themselves to the Nazi system. Elsewhere in the Nazi orbit, some countries proved eager collaborators; others did their best to resist; still others were given no opportunity to collaborate but were ruthlessly subjugated instead.

The Nazis' immediate aim was simply to exploit the conquered territories to serve the continuing war effort. Precisely as envisioned, access to the resources of so much of Europe made Germany considerably less vulnerable to naval blockade than it had been during World War I. France proved a particularly valuable source of raw materials; by 1943, for example, 75 percent of French iron ore went to German factories.

But the deeper purposes of the war were also clear in the way the Nazis treated the territories under their control, especially in the difference between east and west. In western Europe, there was plenty of brutality, but Nazi victory still led to something like conventional military occupation. The Germans tried to enlist the cooperation of local authorities in countries like Denmark, the Netherlands, and France, though with mixed results. And though the Nazis exploited the economy of France, for example, it never became clear what role France might play in Europe after a Nazi victory. However, in Poland and later in the conquered parts of the Soviet Union, there was no pretense of cooperation, and it at once became clear what the Nazi order would entail.

After the conquest of Poland, the Germans annexed the western part of the country outright and promptly executed, jailed, or expelled members of the Polish elite—professionals, journalists, business leaders, and priests. The Nazis prohibited the Poles from entering the professions and restricted even their right to marry. All the Polish schools and most of the churches were simply closed.

In the rest of Poland, administered by a German governor-general, Nazi policy was slightly less brutal at first. Most churches remained open, and Poles were allowed to practice the professions, but the Nazis closed most schools above the fourth grade, as well as libraries, theaters, and museums as they sought to root out every expression of Polish culture. Whether the Poles in this area were to be exterminated, enslaved, or shipped off to Siberia was much debated, but the decision was postponed—to be made after the victory. (See the box, "Toward the Nazi New Order.")

With the conquest of Poland, Nazi leaders proclaimed that a new era of monumental resettlement in eastern Europe had begun for Germany. By mid-1941, 200,000 Germans, carefully selected for their racial characteristics, had been resettled—primarily on farms—in the part of Poland annexed to Germany. Many were ethnic Germans who had been living outside Germany. During the fall of 1942, the select Nazi elite, the Schutzstaffel (SS), under the leadership of Heinrich Himmler, began to arrest and expel peasants from the rest of Poland to make way for further German resettlement. By 1943 perhaps one million Germans had been moved into what had been Poland.

After the assault on the Soviet Union, Hitler made it clear that eastern Europe as far as the Ural Mountains was to be opened for German settlement. War veterans were to be given priority, partly because the German settlers would have to be tough to resist the Slavs, who would be concentrated east of the Urals. To prepare for German colonization, Himmler told SS leaders that Germany would have to exterminate 30 million Slavs in the Soviet Union. After the German invasion, the SS promptly began executing prisoners of war, as well as any Soviet leaders they could find. However, the Nazis expected that several generations would be required for the resettlement of European Russia, and here, in contrast to Poland, the program barely got started during the war years.

The Holocaust

Conquest of the east also gave the Nazis the opportunity for a more radical solution to the "Jewish problem" than they had attempted before. Under the cover of war, they began exterminating the Jews within their orbit. Thus began the process, and the experience, that has come to be known as the Holocaust.

When and why this policy was chosen remains controversial. Although prewar Nazi rhetoric occasionally suggested the possibility of actual physical destruction, the Nazi goal of a "final solution to the Jewish problem" seemed to mean simply forced emigration. The conquest of Poland, with a

Jewish population of 3 million, gave the Nazis control over a far greater number of Jews than ever before. In 1940, as part of their effort to create a new order, the Nazis began confining Polish Jews to ghettos set up in Warsaw and five other cities. No one knew what was to become of these Jews at first. Himmler and the SS were making tentative plans to develop, after the Nazi victory, a kind of superghetto for perhaps 4 million Jews on the island of Madagascar, at that point still a French colony. However, as the Polish ghettos grew more crowded and difficult to manage, Nazi officials in Poland began pressing for a more definitive policy.

In 1940 Hitler seemed to endorse the Madagascar plan, but he cultivated ambiguity on the operational level—and he left no paper trail. So the precise chain of events that led to a more radical approach will no doubt remain uncertain. The evidence suggests, however, that Hitler ordered the physical extermination of the Jews in the spring of 1941, before the German assault on the Soviet Union in June. By the fall, the Nazis were actively impeding further Jewish emigration from the occupied territories. And they were sending large numbers of German and Austrian Jews to the ghettos in Poland.

With the invasion of the Soviet Union, special SS "intervention squads" were assigned to get rid of Jews and Communist party officials. By late November, the Nazis had killed 136,000 Jews, most by shooting, in the invaded Soviet territories. But as it became obvious that mass shooting was impractical, Nazi leaders sought a more systematic and impersonal method of mass extermination. Late in July 1941, Reinhard Heydrich of the SS began developing a detailed plan, which he explained in January 1942 at a conference of high-ranking officials at Wannsee, a suburb of Berlin. The conference had been postponed from November, and by now the Nazis were already implementing Heydrich's plan for the extermination of the Jews.

The Nazis took advantage of the methods, and especially the deadly Zyklon-B gas, that had proven effective during the euthanasia campaign of 1939 through 1941 in Germany (see page 1011). By March 1942 they had constructed several large extermination camps with gas chambers and crematoria, intended to kill Jews and dispose of their bodies as quickly and efficiently as possible. And now they began the full-scale mass killing, target-

Toward the Nazi New Order

After Nazi Germany conquered much of Poland in 1939, the SS assumed major responsibility for creating a new Nazi order in the conquered territories. In a memorandum dated May 15, 1940, and endorsed by Hitler, the SS leader Heinrich Himmler offered "some thoughts on the treatment of the alien population in the east." The passages that follow make clear the racist basis of Nazi wartime policy.

In our treatment of the foreign ethnic groups in the east we must . . . fish out the racially valuable people from this mishmash, take them to Germany and assimilate them there.

. . . The non-German population of the eastern territories must not receive any education higher than that of elementary school with four forms. The objective of this elementary school must simply be to teach: simple arithmetic up to 500 at the most, how to write one's name, and to teach that it is God's commandment to be obedient to the Germans and to be honest, hard-working, and well-behaved. I consider it unnecessary to teach reading.

There must be no schools at all in the east apart from this type of school. Parents who wish to provide their children with a better education both in the elementary school and later in a secondary school, must make an application to the higher SS and Police Leader. . . . If we recognize such a child as being of our blood then the parents will be informed that the child will be placed in a school in Germany and will remain in Germany indefinitely. . . .

The parents of these children of good blood will be given the choice of either giving up their child . . . or they would have to agree to go to Germany and become loyal citizens there. . . .

Apart from the examination of the petitions which parents put forward for a better education, all 6–10 year olds will be sifted each year to sort out those with valuable blood and those with worthless blood. Those who are selected as valuable will be treated in the same way as the children who are admitted on the basis of the approval of the parents' petition.

. . . [T]he moment the children and parents arrive in Germany they should not be treated in school and life as outcasts but—after changing their names and despite being treated with vigilance—should be integrated into German life on the basis of trust. The children must not be made to feel rejected; for, after all, we believe in our own blood, which through the mistakes of German history has flowed into a foreign nation, and are convinced that our ideology and ideals will find an echo in the souls of these children which are racially identical to our own. . . . Abusive expressions such as "Polack" or "Ukrainian" and such like must be out of the question. . . .

After these measures have been systematically implemented during the next ten years, the population of the General Government will inevitably consist of an inferior remnant. . . . This population will be available as a leaderless laboring class and provide Germany with migrant and seasonal labor for special work projects (road-building, quarries, construction); even then they will get more to eat and have more from life than under Polish rule. . . .

Source: J. Noakes and G. Pridham, *Nazism: A History in Documents and Eyewitness Accounts, 1919–1945,* vol. 2 (New York: Schocken, 1990), pp. 932–934.

ing first the Polish Jews who had already been confined to ghettos. Once the apparatus for mass extermination had been constructed, the ghettos became mere way stations on the journey to the death camps. The Nazis brutally suppressed attempts at resistance, like the Warsaw ghetto uprising of April and May 1943.

During the course of the war the Nazis constructed six full-scale death camps, although not all were operating at peak capacity at the same time. All six were located in what had been Poland (see inset, Map 28.2). Horrifying though they were, the concentration camps in Germany, such as Dachau, Buchenwald, and Bergen-Belsen, were not extermination camps, although many Jews died in them late in the war.

The largest of the six death camps was the Auschwitz-Birkenau complex, which became the principal extermination center in 1943. The Nazis shipped Jews from all over Europe to Auschwitz, which was killing about 12,000 people a day at the peak of its operation in 1944. Auschwitz was one of two extermination camps that included affili-

Children at Auschwitz Images from the Nazi camps haunted the decades that followed the Second World War. The Auschwitz-Birkenau complex proved the largest and most destructive of the camps that the Nazis created specifically for mass killing. The overwhelming majority of those sent to these camps were Jews, most of whom were killed by gassing shortly after their arrival. Those deemed fit for work might be spared, at least for a while, but children were typically killed at once. *(Hulton-Getty/Tony Stone Images)*

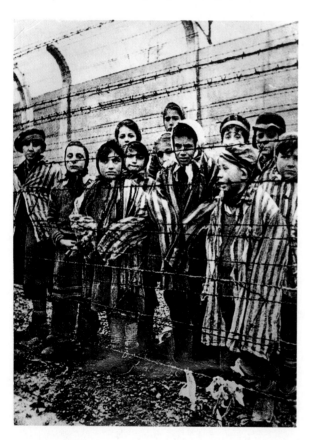

ated slave-labor factories, in which Jews most able to work were literally worked to death. Among the companies profiting from the arrangement were two of Germany's best-known, Krupp and IG Farben.

The Jews typically arrived at one of the camps crammed into cattle cars on special trains. Camp personnel, generally SS medical doctors, subjected new arrivals to "selection," picking some for labor assignments and sending the others, including most women and children, to the gas chambers. Camp personnel made every effort to deceive the Jews who were about to be killed, to lead them to believe they were to be showered and deloused. Even in camps without forced-labor factories, Jews were compelled to do much of the dirty work of the extermination operation. But under the brutal conditions of the camps, those initially assigned to work inevitably weakened; most were then deemed unfit and put to death.

The Nazis took every precaution to hide what was going on in the death camps. The SS personnel involved were sworn to silence. Himmler insisted that if secrecy was to be maintained, the operation would have to be quick—and total, to include women and children, "so that no Jews will remain to take revenge on our sons and grandsons." Indeed, Himmler constantly sought to accelerate the process, even though it required labor and transport facilities desperately needed for the war effort.

Himmler and the other major SS officials, such as Rudolf Höss, the commandant at Auschwitz, or Adolf Eichmann, who organized the transport of the Jews to the camps, cannot be understood simply as sadists who enjoyed humiliating their victims. Rather, they took satisfaction in doing what they believed was their duty without flinching, without signs of weakness. Addressing a group of SS members in 1943, Himmler portrayed the extermination of the Jews as a difficult "historical task" that they, the Nazi elite, must do for their racial community: "Most of you know what it means to see a hundred corpses piled up, or five hundred, or a thousand. To have gone through this and—except for cases of human weakness— to have remained decent, that has made us tough. This is an unwritten, never to be written, page of glory in our history."[2]

However, as Himmler's casual reference to "cases of human weakness" suggests, some among the SS camp guards failed to live up to this image and indulged in wanton cruelty, humiliating their helpless victims. For some, the extermination process became the occasion to act out sadistic fantasies. But though this dimension is surely horrifying, the bureaucratic, factory-like nature of the extermination process is in some ways more troubling.

Despite the overriding emphasis on secrecy, reports of the genocide reached the West almost immediately in 1942. Especially at first, however, most tended to discount them as wartime propaganda of the sort many had believed during World War I, when stories about Germans eating Belgian babies had circulated. Skepticism about extermination reports was easier because there were a few concentration camps, like Theresienstadt in the former Czechoslovakia, that housed Jews who had been selected for special treatment. These camps were not used for extermination and were not secret; the Red Cross was even allowed to inspect Theresienstadt several times. Those outside, and the German people as well, were led to believe that all the Jews were being interned, for the duration of the war, in camps like these, much as Japanese-Americans were being interned in camps in the western United States at the same time. But even as the evidence grew, Allied governments, citing military priorities, refused pleas from Jewish leaders in 1944 to bomb the rail line into Auschwitz.

The Nazis' policy of actually murdering persons deemed undesirable or superfluous did not start with, and was not limited to, the Jews. First came the euthanasia program in Germany, and the war afforded the Nazis the chance to do away with an array of other "undesirables," from communists and homosexuals to Gypsies and Poles. So the most radical and appalling aspect of Nazism did not stem from anti-Semitism alone. This must not be forgotten, but neither must the fact that the Jews constituted by far the largest group of victims—perhaps 5.7 to 6 million, almost two-thirds of the Jews in Europe. (See the feature, "Weighing the Evidence: Holocaust Testimony," on pages 1070–1071.)

Collaboration and Resistance

In rounding up Jews for extermination, and in establishing their new order in Europe, the Nazis found willing collaborators among some of the countries within their orbit. Croatia, the most pro-Nazi of the satellite states, was eager to round up Jews and Gypsies, as well as to attack Serbs, on its own. Romania, too, was happy to deliver foreign-born Jews to the Germans, though it dragged its feet when the Germans began demanding acculturated Romanian Jews.

But degrees of collaboration varied widely across Europe. In Denmark, Norway, and the Netherlands, the Nazis thought racial kinship would matter, but they never found sufficient support to make possible genuinely independent collaborationist governments. In Denmark and the Netherlands, governments put up a façade of cooperation but still managed to foster resistance. Denmark did especially well at resisting the German effort to round up Jews, as did Italy and Bulgaria.

Vichy France was somewhere in the middle, and thus it has remained particularly controversial. When the Vichy regime was launched during the summer of 1940, there was widespread support for Marshal Pétain, its 84-year-old chief of state. Pétain promised to maximize French sovereignty and shield his people from the worst aspects of Nazi occupation. At the same time, the Vichy government claimed to be implementing its own "national revolution," returning France to authority, discipline, and tradition after the shambles of the Third Republic. Vichy's revolution was anti-Semitic and hostile to the left, so it seemed compatible, up to a point, with Nazism. And at first Germany seemed likely to win the war. Thus, Pétain's second-in-command, Pierre Laval (1883–1945), was willing to collaborate actively with the Nazis. The Vichy regime ended up doing much of the Nazis' dirty work for them—rounding up workers for forced shipment to German factories, hunting down members of the anti-German resistance, and picking up Jews to be sent to the Nazi extermination camps.

After the war, Pétain, Laval, and others were found guilty of treason by the new French government. Because of his advanced age, Pétain was merely imprisoned, while Laval and others were executed. But the shame of Vichy collaboration continued to haunt the French, deepening the humiliation of the defeat in 1940.

Though the Nazis found some willing collaborators, the great majority of those living under German occupation came to despise the Nazis as their brutality became ever clearer. Nazi rule meant pillage; it meant rounding up workers for forced labor in Germany; it meant randomly killing hostages in reprisal for resistance activity. In one extreme case, the Germans destroyed the Czech village of Lidice, killing all its inhabitants, in retaliation for the assassination of SS security chief Reinhard Heydrich.

Clandestine movements of resistance to the occupying Nazi forces gradually developed all over Europe. In western Europe, resistance was especially prominent in France and, beginning in 1943, northern Italy, which was subjected to German occupation after the Allies defeated Mussolini's regime. But the anti-German resistance was strongest in Yugoslavia, Poland, and the occupied portions of the Soviet Union, where full-scale guerrilla war against the Germans and their collaborators produced the highest civilian casualties of World War II. The Polish resistance achieved some notable successes in sabotaging roads and railroads, although it met disastrous defeat when it sought to tackle the Germans head-on in Warsaw in 1944.

The role of the resistance proved most significant in Yugoslavia, where the Croatian Marxist Josip Broz, taking the pseudonym Tito (1892–1980), forged the opponents of the Axis powers into a broadly based guerrilla army. Its initial foe was the inflated Croatian state that the Germans, early in 1941, carved from Yugoslavia and entrusted to the pro-Axis Croatian separatist movement, the Ustashe. But Tito's forces soon came up against a rival resistance movement, led by Serb officers, that tended to be pro-Serb, monarchist, and anticommunist. By 1943 Tito led 250,000 men and women in what had become a brutal civil war, one that deepened ethnic divisions and left a legacy of bitterness. Tito's forces prevailed, enabling him to create a communist-led government in Yugoslavia late in the war.

In France and Italy as well, communists played a leading role in the wartime resistance movements. As a result, the Communist party in each country overcame the disarray that followed from the Nazi-Soviet Pact of 1939 and after the war enjoyed a level of prestige that would have been unthinkable earlier.

In the French case, there could have been conflict between the indigenous resistance, with its significant communist component, and the Free French under Charles de Gaulle, operating outside France until August 1944. But it is striking how well they were able to work together. Still, de Gaulle took pains to cement his own leadership in the overall struggle. Among the measures to this end, he decreed women's suffrage for France, partly because women were playing a major role in the resistance. After the liberation of France in 1944, he sought to control a potentially volatile situation by disarming the resistance as quickly as possible.

The western European resistance movements are easily romanticized, their extent and importance overstated. Compared to regular troops, resistance forces were poorly trained, equipped, and disciplined. In France, fewer than 30 percent of the nearly 400,000 active resisters had firearms in 1944. But though the Allies never tried to use them in a systematic way, the resistance movements made at least some military contribution, especially through sabotage. And they boosted national self-esteem for the longer term, helping countries humiliated by defeat and occupation make a fresh start after the war.

Toward the Soviet Triumph

The import of what happened elsewhere in Europe depended on the outcome of the main event, the German invasion of the Soviet Union. Although the German Sixth Army, numbering almost 300,000 men, reached Stalingrad by late 1942, the Germans could not achieve a knockout. (See the box, "Stalingrad: The Diary of a German Soldier.") The Soviets managed to defend the city in what was arguably the pivotal military engagement of World War II. While some Soviet troops fought street by street, house by house, others counterattacked, encircling the attacking German force. Hitler refused a strategic retreat, but his doggedness backfired. By the end of January 1943, the Soviets had captured what remained of the German force, about 100,000 men, very few of whom survived to return to Germany. Perhaps 240,000 German soldiers died in the Battle of Stalingrad or as prisoners afterward. But the price to the Soviets for their victory was far greater: A million Soviet soldiers and civilians died at Stalingrad.

Although the Germans resumed the offensive on several fronts during the summer of 1943, the Soviets won the tank battle of Kursk-Orel in July, and from then on Soviet troops relentlessly moved

Stalingrad: The Diary of a German Soldier

The following excerpts from the diary of a soldier named Wilhelm Hoffman reveal the changing German mood during 1942, as the Nazis penetrated deeply into the Soviet Union, then met disastrous defeat at Stalingrad. The writer himself did not survive the battle; his closing curse was his last diary entry.

July 29. The company commander says the Russian troops are completely broken, and cannot hold out any longer. To reach the Volga and take Stalingrad is not so difficult for us. The Führer knows where the Russians' weak point is. Victory is not far away. . . .

August 2. . . . What great spaces the Soviets occupy, what rich fields there are to be had here after the war's over!

August 17. The last few days our regiment has been in battle all the time. . . . The heat and the constant fighting are utterly exhausting. But we are all ready to advance quickly to the Volga. . . .

September 26. Our regiment is involved in constant heavy fighting. After the [grain storage] elevator was taken the Russians continued to defend themselves just as stubbornly. You don't see them at all, they have established themselves in houses and cellars and are firing on all sides, including from our rear—barbarians, they use gangster methods. . . .

October 14. It has been fantastic since morning: our aeroplanes and artillery have been hammering the Russian positions for hours on end; everything in sight is being blotted from the face of the earth. . . .

October 22. Our regiment has failed to break into the factory. We have lost many men;

every time you move you have to jump over bodies. . . . Who would have thought three months ago that instead of the joy of victory we would have to endure such sacrifice and torture, the end of which is nowhere in sight? . . .

The soldiers are calling Stalingrad the mass grave of the [German army]. . . .

October 27. Our troops have captured the whole of the Barrikady factory, but we cannot break through to the Volga. The Russians are not men, but some kind of cast-iron creatures; they never get tired and are not afraid of fire. We are absolutely exhausted; our regiment now has barely the strength of a company. . . .

November 21. The Russians have gone over to the offensive along the whole front. . . . So, there it is—the Volga, victory and soon home to our families! We shall obviously be seeing them next in the other world.

December 14. Everybody is racked with hunger. Frozen potatoes are the best meal, but to get them out of the ice-covered ground under fire from Russian bullets is not so easy.

December 26. . . . The soldiers look like corpses or lunatics, looking for something to put in their mouths. They no longer take cover from Russian shells; they haven't the strength to walk, run away and hide. A curse on this war!

Source: Vasili I. Chuikov, *The Battle for Stalingrad* (New York: Holt, Rinehart and Winston, 1964), pp. 248–254.

west, forcing the Germans to retreat. By February 1944 Soviet troops had pushed the Germans back to the Polish border, and the outcome of the war was no longer in doubt (see Map 28.1).

The Soviet victory in what proved the decisive front of World War II was incredible, in light of the upheavals of the 1930s and the low esteem in which most held the Soviet military in 1941. Portraying

the struggle as "the Great Patriotic War" for national defense, Stalin managed to rally the Soviet peoples as the Germans attacked. Rather than emphasize communist themes, he recalled the heroic defenses mounted against invaders in tsarist times, including the resistance to Napoleon in 1812. But though the Soviets ultimately prevailed, the cost in death, destruction, and suffering was almost unimaginable. For example, by the time Soviet forces finally broke the siege of Leningrad in January 1944, a million people in the city had died, most from starvation, freezing, or disease.

The invading Germans gained access to major areas of Soviet industry and oil supply, and by the end of 1941 the country's industrial output had been cut in half. Yet the Soviet Union was able to weather this blow and go on to triumph. Help from the outside contributed a little, but only 5 to 15 percent of Soviet supplies came from the West. Between 1939 and 1941, Soviet leaders had begun building a new industrial base east of the Urals. And when the Germans invaded in 1941, the plant and equipment of 1500 enterprises were dismantled and shipped by rail for reassembly farther east, out of reach of German attack. Then, beginning in 1942, thousands of brand-new factories were constructed in eastern regions as well.

Moreover, the earlier purges of the armed forces proved to have done less long-term damage than outside observers had expected. If anything, the removal of so many in the top ranks of the military hierarchy made it easier for talented young officers like Georgi Zhukov (1896–1974), who would become the country's top military commander, to move quickly into major leadership positions.

When the United States entered the war in December 1941, the Soviets were fighting for survival. They immediately began pressuring the United States and Britain to open another front in Europe, preferably by landing in northern France, where an Allied assault could be expected to have the greatest impact. But the Allies did not invade northern France and open a major second front until June 1944. By then the Soviets had turned the tide in Europe on their own.

A GLOBAL WAR, 1941–1944

European colonial links spread the war almost at once, most dramatically to North Africa but also to East Asia and the Pacific. The Soviet Union also had interests in Asia and the Pacific, where it had long bumped up against the Japanese. During the 1930s, the United States, too, had become involved in friction with Japan. By 1941 President Franklin Roosevelt was openly favoring the anti-Axis cause, though it took a surprise attack by the Japanese in December 1941 finally to bring the United States into the war.

Japan and the Origins of the Pacific War

As a densely populated island nation lacking the raw materials essential for industry, Japan had been especially concerned about foreign trade and spheres of economic influence as it modernized after 1868. By the interwar period, the Japanese had become unusually reliant on exports of textiles and other products. During the Depression of the 1930s, when countries all over the world adopted protectionist policies, Japan suffered from increasing tariffs against its exports. This situation tilted the balance in Japanese ruling circles from free-trade proponents to those who favored a military-imperialist solution.

To gain economic hegemony by force, Japan could choose either of two directions. The northern strategy, concentrating on China, would risk Soviet opposition as well as strong local resistance. The southern strategy, focusing on southeast Asia and the East Indies, would encounter the imperial presence of Britain, France, the Netherlands, and the United States.

Japan opted for the northern strategy in 1931, when it took control of Manchuria, in northeastern China. But the Japanese attempt to conquer the rest of China, beginning in 1937, led only to an impasse by 1940. Japanese aggression in China drew the increasing hostility of the United States, a strong supporter of the Chinese nationalist leader Chiang Kai-shek (1887–1975), as well as the active opposition of the Soviet Union. Clashes with Soviet troops along the border between Mongolia and Manchuria led to significant defeats for the Japanese in 1938 and 1939. The combination of China and the Soviet Union seemed more than Japan could handle.

By 1941, however, Germany's victories in Europe had seriously weakened Britain, France, and the Netherlands, the major European colonial powers in southeast Asia and the East Indies. This seemed a precious opportunity for Japan to shift to a southern strategy. To keep the Soviets at bay, Japan agreed to a neutrality pact with the Soviet Union in April 1941. Rather than worry about China and the areas of dispute with the Soviet Union, the Japanese would seek control of south-

THE ERA OF WORLD WAR II

September 1, 1939	Germany invades Poland	**June 6, 1944**	D-Day: Allied landings in Normandy
May 10, 1940	Germany attacks the Netherlands, Belgium, and France	**February 1945**	Yalta conference
		April 30, 1945	Suicide of Adolf Hitler
June 22, 1941	Germany attacks the Soviet Union	**May 7–8, 1945**	German surrender
August 1941	Churchill and Roosevelt agree to the Atlantic Charter	**June 1945**	Founding of the United Nations
December 7, 1941	Japanese attack on Pearl Harbor	**July–August 1945**	Potsdam conference
		August 6, 1945	U.S. atomic bombing of Hiroshima
January 1942	Wannsee conference; Nazi plan for the extermination of the Jews	**August 14, 1945**	Japanese surrender
		March 1947	Truman Doctrine speech
August 1942–February 1943	Battle of Stalingrad	**August 1947**	India becomes independent
November 1942	Allied landings in North Africa	**May 1948**	Founding of Israel
January 1943	Casablanca conference	**June 1948–May 1949**	Berlin Blockade and airlift
April–May 1943	Warsaw Ghetto revolt	**August 1949**	First Soviet atomic bomb
July 1943	Soviet victory in Battle of Kursk-Orel	**September 1949**	Founding of the Federal Republic in West Germany
July 1943	Allied landings in Sicily; fall of Mussolini; Italy asks for an armistice	**October 1949**	Founding of the People's Republic of China
November 1943	Teheran conference		

east Asia, a region rich in such raw materials as oil, rubber, and tin—precisely what Japan lacked.

Japan had already joined with Nazi Germany and fascist Italy in an anticommunist agreement in 1936. In September 1940, the three agreed to a formal military alliance. For the Germans, alliance with Japan was useful to help discourage U.S. intervention in the European war. Japan, for its part, could expect the major share of the spoils of the European empires in Asia. However, diplomatic and military coordination between Germany and Japan remained minimal.

The United States began imposing embargoes on certain exports to Japan in 1938, in response to the Japanese aggression in China. After Japan had assumed control of Indochina, nominally held by Vichy France, by the summer of 1941, the United

States imposed total sanctions, and the British and Dutch followed, forcing Japan to begin rapidly drawing down its oil reserves. Conquest of the oil fields of the Dutch East Indies now seemed a matter of life and death to the Japanese.

These economic sanctions brought home how vulnerable Japan was and heightened its determination to press forward aggressively now, when its likely enemies were weakened or distracted. But the Japanese did not expect to achieve a definitive victory over the United States in a long, drawn-out war. Rather, Japanese policymakers anticipated, first, that their initial successes would enable them to grab the resources to sustain a longer war if necessary, and, second, that Germany would defeat Britain, leading the United States to accept a compromise peace allowing the Japanese what they wanted—a secure sphere of economic hegemony in southeast Asia.

Some Japanese leaders—diplomats, business-men, naval officers, and even the emperor and some of his circle—were dismayed by the prospect of war with the United States. But as the influence of the military grew during the 1930s, it became ever more difficult for those opposing Japan's new imperialist direction to make themselves heard. By 1941, a conformist confidence in victory was de-manded, and dissenters dared not speak out for fear of being labeled traitors.

The Japanese finally provoked a showdown on December 7, 1941, with a surprise attack on Pearl Harbor, a U.S. naval base in Hawaii. The next day, Japanese forces seized Hong Kong and Malaya, both British colonies, and Wake Island and the Philippines, both under U.S. control. The United States promptly declared war; in response, Hitler kept an earlier promise to Japan and de-clared war on the United States. World War II was now unprecedented in its geographic scope (see Map 28.3).

Much like their German counterparts, Japan-ese forces got off to a remarkably good start. By the summer of 1942, Japan had taken Thailand, the Dutch East Indies, the Philippines, and the Malay Peninsula. Having won much of what it had been seeking, it began devising the Greater East Asia Co-Prosperity Sphere, its own new order in the conquered territories. (See the box, "Encounters with the West: Japan's 'Pan-Asian' Mission.")

The United States in Europe and the Pacific

During the first years of the war in Europe, the United States under President Franklin Roosevelt had not been a disinterested bystander. At this point the United States did not have armed forces commensurate with its economic strength; in 1940, in fact, its army was smaller than the Belgian army. But the United States could be a supplier in the short term, and, if it chose to intervene, a major player over the longer term. With the Lend-Lease Act of March 1941, intended to provide war ma-teriel without the economic dislocations of World War I, the United States lined up on the side of Britain against the Axis powers. In August 1941, a meeting between Churchill and Roosevelt aboard a cruiser off the coast of Newfoundland produced the Atlantic Charter, the first tentative agreement

about the aims and ideals that were to guide the anti-Axis war effort. The Americans extended lend-lease to the Soviet Union the next month.

But though President Roosevelt was deeply committed to the anti-Axis cause, isolationist sen-timent remained strong in the United States. It took the Japanese attack on Pearl Harbor in De-cember to bring the United States into the war as an active belligerent. By May 1942 the United States had joined with Britain and the Soviet Union in a formal military alliance against the Axis powers.

The two democracies had joined with Stalin's Soviet Union in a marriage of expediency, and mutual suspicions marked the relationship from the start. Initially, Britain and the United States feared that the Soviet Union might even seek a separate peace, as Russia had in World War I. The Soviets, for their part, worried that these new-found allies, with their long-standing anticommu-nism, might hold back from full commitment, or even seek to undermine the Soviet Union.

In response to pressure from Stalin, Britain and the United States agreed to open a second front in Europe as soon as possible. But the Nazis dominated the Continent, so opening such a front required landing troops from the outside. It proved far more difficult to mount an effective as-sault on Europe than either Churchill or Roosevelt anticipated in 1942. The resulting delays furthered Stalin's suspicions that his allies were only too ea-ger to have the Soviets do the bulk of the fighting against Nazi Germany—and weaken themselves in the process.

The United States agreed with its new allies to give priority to the war in Europe. But because it had to respond to the direct Japanese assault in the Pacific, the United States was not prepared to act militarily in Europe right away. However, it quickly played a major role in supplying the British with the ships needed to overcome Ger-man submarines, which seriously threatened ship-ping to Britain by 1942.

In the Pacific theater, in contrast, it was imme-diately clear that the United States would bear the brunt of the fighting against Japan. Although the Japanese went from one success to another during the first months of the war, they lacked the long-term resources to exploit their initial victories. In May 1942 the Battle of Coral Sea—off New Guinea, north of Australia—ended in a stalemate, stopping

✑ ENCOUNTERS WITH THE WEST ✑

Japan's "Pan-Asian" Mission

With the coming of war against the Western powers in 1941, the Japanese could claim to be free-ing Asians from Western imperialism and establishing a new economic order in East Asia and the Pacific. This selection from an essay entitled "Our Present War and Its Cultural Signifi-cance," written just after the bombing of Pearl Harbor by the well-known author Nagayo Yoshio (1888–1961), accents Japan's anti-Western mission in the region. Yoshio understood, especially from his country's recent experience in China, that Asians might find Japanese hegemony just as oppressive as Western domination. Although it served Japan's own economic interests and was often applied brutally, Japanese "Pan-Asianism" helped fuel the reaction against Western impe-rialism in Asia and the Pacific, with lasting results after the war.

Whenever Japan has faced a powerful enemy it has been the *yamato damashii* [Japanese na-tional spirit] which provided the basis of our courage. Now that we can talk in retrospect of the Sino-Japanese War, I am afraid our national spirit has not been given a proper chance to be aroused, due to the deplorable fact that we had to fight with China, our sister nation, with no foreseeable conclusion to look forward to. . . . While desperately fighting with a country which we made our enemy only reluctantly we were trying to find out a principle, an ethic based upon a new view of the world, which would justify our course of action. . . . The China incident was not only insufficient to ful-fill this goal but also met with insurmountable obstacles. Consequently, time and opportunity ripened to declare war against the United States and England. . . .

. . . We would have nothing to say for our-selves if we were merely to follow the exam-ples of the imperialistic and capitalistic ex-ploitation of Greater East-Asia by Europe and the United States. . . .

. . . It is true that the science of war is one manifestation of a nation's culture. But from this time on we have to realize the increasing responsibility on our part if we are to deserve the respect of the people of East-Asian coun-tries as their leaders, in the sphere of culture in general (not only the mere fusion and continu-ance of Western and Oriental cultures but some-thing surpassing and elevating them while making the most out of them) such as the for-mation of national character, refinement, intel-lect, training to become a world citizen, etc. . . .

The sense of awe and respect with which the Orientals have held the white race, espe-cially the Anglo-Saxons, for three hundred years is deep-rooted almost beyond our imagi-nation. It is our task to realize this fact and deal this servility at its root, find out why the white people became the objects of such rever-ence. It goes without saying that we cannot conclude simplemindedly that their shrewd-ness is the cause. Also we have to be very care-ful not to impose the *hakko ichiu* [the gathering of the whole world under one roof] spirit arbi-trarily upon the Asians. If we make this kind of mistake we might antagonize those who could have become our compatriots and thus might also blaspheme our Imperial rule. . . .

To sum up, we have finally witnessed the dawn of a new principle which we had been searching for over ten years. . . . [T]he phrase "Greater East-Asian Coprosperity Sphere" is no longer a mere abstract idea.

Source: William H. McNeill and Mitsuko Iriye, eds., *Modern Asia and Africa* (New York: Oxford University Press, 1971), pp. 232–236.

the string of impressive Japanese successes. Then in June, the United States defeated the Japanese navy for the first time in the Battle of Midway, northwest of Hawaii. After the United States stopped at-tempted Japanese advances in the Solomon Islands and New Guinea early in 1943, U.S. forces began steadily advancing across the islands of the Pacific toward Japan (Map 28.3).

Map 28.3 The War in East Asia and the Pacific After a series of conquests in 1941 and 1942, the Japanese were forced gradually to fall back before U.S. forces. When the war abruptly ended in August 1945, however, the Japanese still controlled much of the territory they had conquered.

The Search for a Second Front in Europe

As the Soviet army fought the Germans in the Soviet Union, the United States and Britain tried to determine how they could help tip the scales in Europe, now an almost impregnable German fortress. Stalin kept urging a direct assault across the English Channel, which, if successful, would have the greatest immediate impact. Churchill, however, advocated attacking the underbelly of the Axis empire by way of the Mediterranean, which would first require winning control of North Africa. And it was that strategy that the Allies tried first, starting in 1942.

In North Africa the initial Italian assault on Egypt in 1940 led to eighteen months of attack and counterattack across the desert. But after Axis forces under Rommel pushed 570 miles east by

June 1942, the British held at El Alamein, in Egypt, and then began a counterattack that forced the Axis troops to begin what proved a definitive retreat. In November, as this British counterattack proceeded, American and additional British forces landed at several points on the coasts of Morocco and Algeria, weakly defended by Vichy France. Joined by Free French troops, they, too, steadily advanced, squeezing Rommel's Axis forces, until, by May 1943, the Allies had won control of North Africa (see Map 28.1).

But North Africa was valuable for the Allies only as a staging ground for an attempt to penetrate Europe from the south. Meeting at the Moroccan city of Casablanca in January 1943, Churchill and Roosevelt agreed that British and American forces would proceed from North Africa to Sicily and on up through Italy. The Soviets, still pushing for an invasion across the English Channel into France, objected that the Germans could easily block Allied advance through the long, mountainous Italian peninsula.

Crossing from North Africa, Allied troops landed in Sicily in July 1943, leading to the arrest of Mussolini and the collapse of the fascist regime. Supported by King Victor Emmanuel III, the Italian military commander, Pietro Badoglio, formed a new government to seek an armistice. Meanwhile, Allied forces moved on to the Italian mainland, but the Germans quickly occupied much of Italy in response. They even managed a daring rescue of Mussolini and promptly re-established him as puppet leader of a new rump republic in northern Italy, now under German control. Just as the Soviets had warned, the Germans sought to block the Italian peninsula, and it was only nine months later, in June 1944, that the Allies reached Rome. So Churchill's strategy of assaulting Europe from the south proved less than decisive.

Only when Churchill, Roosevelt, and Stalin met for the first time, at Teheran, Iran, in November 1943, did they agree that the next step would be to invade western Europe from Britain. Preparations had been underway since early 1942. Finally, Allied troops crossed the English Channel to make an amphibious landing on the beaches of Normandy, in northern France, on June 6, 1944, known to history as D-Day.

The success of the D-Day invasion opened a major second front in Europe at last. Now American-led forces from the west and Soviet forces from the east worked systematically toward Germany. The one substantial German counterattack in the west, the Battle of the Bulge in December 1944, slowed the Allies' advance, but on March 7, 1945, Allied troops crossed the Rhine River (see Map 28.1).

By June 1944, when Allied forces landed at Normandy, Soviet forces had already crossed the 1939 border with Poland as they moved steadily westward. But in August the Soviets stopped before reaching Warsaw, and the major Soviet thrust began cutting south, through Romania, which surrendered in August, and on into the Danube valley in Hungary and Yugoslavia during the fall. The Soviets resumed their advance westward through Poland and toward Germany only in January 1945.

Now, with the defeat of Germany simply a matter of time, Allied concern shifted to the postwar order. Churchill, especially, worried about the implications of the Soviet advances in east-central Europe and the Balkans. As a supplement to the D-Day landings, he wanted to strike from Italy through Yugoslavia into east-central Europe. But the Americans resisted; Churchill's priorities, they felt, reflected old-fashioned concerns over spheres of influence that were no longer appropriate. So the Allies concentrated instead on a secondary landing in southern France in August 1944. This assault, in which Free French forces were prominent, led quickly to the liberation of Paris. But because the Allies made both their landings in France, and not in southeastern Europe, the Western democracies were involved only in the liberation of western Europe. It was the Soviets who drove the Germans from east-central Europe and the Balkans. This fact, and the resulting geographic distribution of military strength, fundamentally affected the postwar order in Europe.

THE SHAPE OF THE ALLIED VICTORY, 1944–1945

The leaders of the Soviet Union, Britain, and the United States sought to mold that postwar order at two notable conferences in 1945. They brought different aspirations for the postwar world, but they also had to face the hard military realities that had resulted from the fighting so far: Each had armies in certain places, but not in others.

D-Day, 1944 Allied forces land at Normandy, early in the morning of June 6, 1944, at last opening a major second front in Europe. *(National Archives, Washington)*

Those military realities led to the informal division of Europe into spheres of influence among the victors.

The most serious question the Allies faced concerned Germany, which would soon be forced to surrender unconditionally. Germany was widely held responsible for the two world wars, as well as for Nazism with all its atrocities—including the concentration and extermination camps, discovered with shock and horror by the advancing Allied armies in 1945. How should Germany be treated?

In the Pacific theater, as in Europe, the way the war ended had major implications for the postwar world. The United States decided to use the atomic bomb, forcing Japan to surrender in a matter of days. The suddenness of the ending helped determine the fate of the European empires in Asia.

Yalta: Shaping the Postwar World

When Stalin, Roosevelt, and Churchill met at Yalta, a Soviet Black Sea resort, in February 1945, Allied victory was assured, and the three leaders accomplished a great deal. Yet the Yalta conference has long been surrounded by controversy. Western critics have charged that the concessions made there to Stalin consigned east-central Europe to communist domination and opened the way to the dangerous cold war of the next forty years. At the time, however, the anticipation of victory produced a relatively cooperative spirit among the Allies. Thus, they firmed up plans for military occupation of Germany in separate zones, for joint occupation of Berlin, and for an Allied Control Council, composed of the military commanders-in-chief, which would make policy for all of Germany by unanimous agreement.

Each of the Allies had special concerns, but each got much of what it was seeking at Yalta. Roosevelt was eager for Soviet help against Japan as soon as possible, and he won Soviet commitment to an agreement tentatively worked out earlier. In exchange for territorial concessions in Asia and the Pacific, Stalin agreed to declare war on Japan within three months of the German surrender.

Churchill, meanwhile, worried about the future of Europe in light of the American intention, which Roosevelt announced at Yalta, to maintain occupation troops in Europe for only two years after the war. To help balance Soviet power on the Continent, Churchill felt it essential to restore France as a great power. To this end, he urged that France be granted a share in the occupation of Germany and a permanent seat on the Security Council of the proposed new international organization, the United Nations (see page 1061). Roosevelt agreed, even though he had little use for

Charles de Gaulle or what he viewed as the pretensions of the French.

It seemed to the Americans that both Britain and the Soviet Union remained too wedded to traditional conceptions of national interest as they sought to shape the postwar world. Hence, one of Roosevelt's major priorities was to secure British and Soviet commitment to the United Nations before the three allies began to disagree over particular issues. He won that commitment at Yalta, but only by giving in to Churchill on the sensitive matter of British colonies.

Because anti-imperial sentiment had worked to Japan's advantage in Asia, the United States had pestered Britain on the colonial issue since early in the war. Roosevelt had even asked Churchill in 1941 about British intentions in India. So prickly was Churchill that he proclaimed in 1942, "I have not become the King's First Minister in order to preside over the liquidation of the

The Big Three at Yalta With victory over Nazi Germany assured, Churchill, Roosevelt, and Stalin were in reasonably good spirits when they met at Yalta, a Black Sea resort in the Soviet Union, in February 1945. Important sources of friction among them were evident at the meeting, but the differences that led to the cold war did not seem paramount at this point. The Yalta conference proved to be the last meeting of the three leaders. *(F.D.R. Library)*

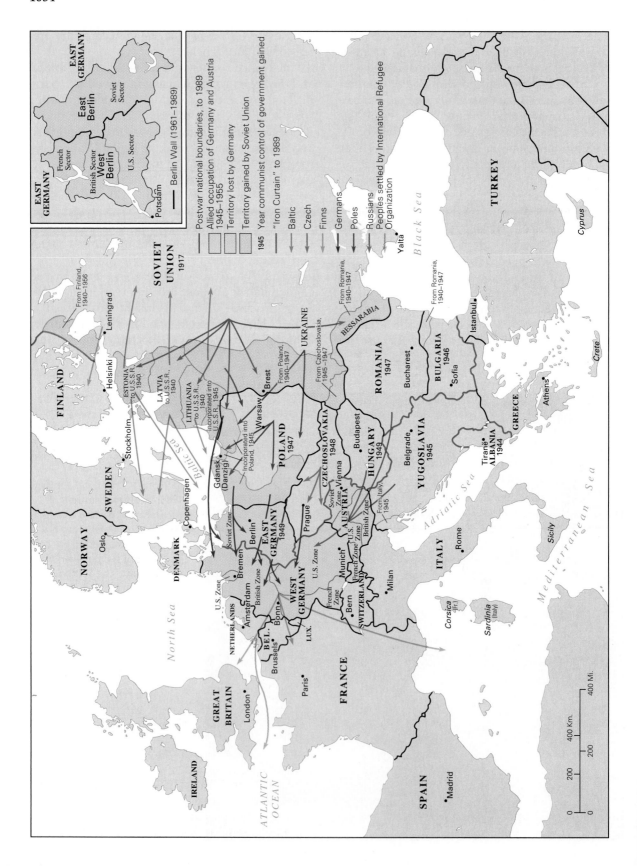

British Empire." It was agreed at Yalta that the British Empire would be exempt from an anticipated measure to bring former colonies under United Nations trusteeship after the war.

Although it was not the only question on the table, the future of the former Axis territories was central to the deliberations at Yalta. By the time of the conference, the division of former Axis territory into spheres of influence among the Allies was already becoming evident, and, in light of the location of Allied troops, the alignment was probably inevitable. In Italy, where U.S. and British troops held sway, the two democracies had successfully resisted Stalin's claim for a share in the administration. In east-central Europe, however, the Soviet army was in control. Still, the United States, with its vision of a new world order, objected to spheres of influence and insisted that democratic principles be applied everywhere. At Yalta this American priority led to an awkward compromise over east-central Europe; the new governments in the area were to be both democratic and friendly to the Soviet Union.

Most important to the Soviets was Poland, with its crucial location between Russia and Germany. Although the Soviets insisted that Communists lead the new Polish government at the outset, they compromised by allowing a role for the noncommunist Polish government-in-exile in London. They also promised free elections in Poland. The three Allies agreed that the Polish-Soviet border would be the line established after World War I. Poland would gain substantial German territory to its west to make up for what it would lose to the U.S.S.R. to its east (Map 28.4).

In addition, the United States and Britain were to have a role in committees set up to engineer the transition to democracy in the rest of east-central Europe. However, only the Soviets had troops in the area, and those committees proved essentially powerless. But though the sources of future tension were already at work at Yalta, they generally

Map 28.4 The Impact of World War II in Europe As a result of World War II the Soviet Union expanded its western borders and Poland shifted westward at the expense of Germany. Territorial changes added to the wartime disruption and produced a flood of refugees. The cold war division of Europe did not depend on immediate territorial changes, but soon Germany itself came to be divided along east-west lines.

remained hidden by the high spirits of approaching victory.

Victory in Europe

Although the tide had turned in 1943, Germany managed to continue the war by exploiting its conquered territories and by more effectively allocating its domestic resources for war production. Thanks partly to the efforts of armaments minister Albert Speer, war production grew sharply between 1941 and 1944, so Germany had plenty of weapons even as the war was ending. But Germany encountered two crucial bottlenecks that finally crippled its military effort: It was running out of military manpower, and it was running out of oil.

Despite making effective use of synthetics, the Nazi war machine depended heavily on oil from Romania. Late in August 1944, however, Soviet troops crossed into Romania, taking control of the oil fields. In addition, beginning in mid-1944, U.S. and British planes successfully bombed German oil installations.

From the start of the war, some, especially among British military leaders, insisted that bombing could destroy the economic and psychological basis of the enemy's ability to wage war. Beginning in 1942, British-led bombing attacks destroyed an average of half the built-up area of seventy German cities, sometimes producing huge firestorms. The bombing of the historic city of Dresden in February 1945 killed more than 135,000 civilians in the most destructive air assault of the war in Europe. But despite this widespread destruction, such bombing did not undermine morale or disrupt production and transport to the extent expected. In the face of steady Allied bombing, Germany increased its war production during 1943 and 1944.

The more precise targeting favored by U.S. strategists proved more effective. In May 1944, the United States began bombing oil fields in Romania and refineries and synthetic oil plants in Germany. Soon Germany lacked enough fuel even to train pilots; by 1945 German industry was producing more aircraft than the German air force could use. Though its proponents consistently overestimated its value, strategic bombing made a significant contribution to the Allied war effort by the end.

Soviet troops moving westward finally met U.S. troops moving eastward at the Elbe River in

Germany on April 26, 1945. With his regime now thoroughly defeated and much of his country in ruins, Hitler committed suicide in his underground military headquarters in Berlin on April 30, 1945. The war in Europe finally ended with the German surrender to General Dwight D. Eisenhower (1890–1969) at Reims, France, on May 7 and to Marshal Zhukov at Berlin on May 8. The world celebrated the end of the fighting in Europe, but an element of uncertainty surrounded the Allied victory because East-West differences were increasingly coming to the fore within the anti-German alliance.

The Potsdam Conference and the Question of Germany

The immediate question for the victorious allies was the fate of Germany, which was bound to be central to the shape of the postwar era. The leaders of the United States, Britain, and the Soviet Union confronted the question at the last of their notable wartime conferences, at Potsdam, just outside Berlin, from July 17 to August 2, 1945. The circumstances were dramatically different from those at Yalta just months before. With Hitler dead and Germany defeated, no common military aim provided unity. And of the three Allied leaders who had been at Yalta, only Stalin remained. President Roosevelt had died in April, so his successor, Harry Truman (1884–1972), represented the United States. In Britain, Churchill's Conservatives lost the general election during the first days of the conference, so Clement Attlee (1883–1967), the new Labour prime minister, assumed the leadership of the British delegation.

At Potsdam, the Allies had to determine how to implement their earlier agreements about Germany, which, devastated by bombing and left without a government, depended on the Allied occupying forces even for its day-to-day survival.

The Soviet Victory in Europe After forcing the Germans back for almost two years, Soviet troops reached Berlin in April 1945. Although it required a day of heavy fighting and bombardment, the Soviets took the Reichstag building, in the heart of the now devastated German capital, on April 30. Here two Soviet sergeants, Yegorov and Kantariya, plant the Soviet flag atop the Reichstag, symbolizing the Soviet victory in the decisive encounter of World War II in Europe. *(ITAR-TAS/Sovfoto)*

The Allies had agreed that Germany was to be forced to surrender unconditionally, but it was not yet clear what would be done with the country over the longer term. For a time U.S. policymakers had even considered destroying Germany's industrial capacity in perpetuity. However, cooler heads understood that the deindustrialization, or "pastoralization," of Germany would not be in anyone's economic interests. Moreover, as the democracies grew increasingly suspicious about Soviet intentions, an economically healthy Germany seemed necessary to help in the balance against the Soviet Union.

For their part, the Soviets had reason to take a much harder line against Germany. Having been invaded—and devastated—by German forces twice within living memory, the Soviet Union wanted to weaken Germany both territorially and economically. But of the three victors, the Soviets had suffered a greatly disproportionate share of the wartime destruction and economic loss, so they also sought to exploit the remaining resources of Germany by exacting heavy reparations. Moreover, the British and the Americans accepted the Soviet proposal that Germany's eastern border with Poland be shifted substantially westward, to the line formed by the Oder and Neisse Rivers. But just as Poland gained at the expense of Germany, the Soviet Union kept a substantial slice of what had been eastern Poland (see Map 28.4).

Each of the three Allies had responsibility for administering a particular zone of occupation, but they were supposed to coordinate their activities in a common policy toward Germany. This effort was to include de-Nazification, demilitarization, and an assault on concentrations of economic power—to root out what seemed the sources of Germany's antidemocratic and aggressive tendencies. But disagreements over economic policy soon undermined the pretense of joint government. Thus East-West differences, already influencing events in east-central Europe, came to affect the settlement in Germany as well.

The Atomic Bomb and the Capitulation of Japan

In the Pacific, Japan had been forced onto the defensive by September 1943, but during 1944 it mounted two major counterattacks to challenge the Americans' newly won naval supremacy. The Japanese wanted especially to prevent American reconquest of the Philippines, which would cut Japan off from its vital raw materials farther south. But the naval battles of 1944 led only to further Japanese defeat. The resulting losses of ships, coupled with increasing shortages of fuel, had virtually crippled the Japanese navy by the end of the year. U.S. forces encountered only token naval resistance when they invaded Okinawa in April 1945 (see Map 28.3).

However, as the situation grew more desperate for Japan, Japanese ground soldiers battled ever more fiercely, often fighting to the death, or taking their own lives, rather than surrendering. Beginning late in 1944, aircraft pilots practiced *kamikaze*, suicidally crashing planes filled with explosives into U.S. targets. The Japanese used this tactic especially as the Americans sought to take Okinawa in the spring of 1945; the U.S. forces finally prevailed in June, but only after the most bitter combat of the entire Pacific war.

In conquering Okinawa, American forces got close enough for air raids on the Japanese home islands. But though the United States was now clearly in control, it seemed likely that an actual invasion of Japan would be necessary to force a Japanese surrender. Some estimated that invasion might cost the United States as many as 1 million additional casualties, because the Japanese could be expected to fight even more desperately to defend their own soil. It was especially for this reason that the Americans decided to try to end the war in an altogether different way, by using an atomic bomb.

In 1939 scientists in several countries, including Germany, had started to advise their governments that new, immensely destructive weapons based on thermonuclear fission were theoretically possible. The German economics ministry began seeking uranium as early as 1939, but Hitler promoted jet- and rocket-propelled terror weaponry instead, especially the V-2 rocket bombs that the Germans began showering on England in the fall of 1944. Still, fear that the Nazis were developing atomic weapons lurked behind the Allied effort to produce an atomic bomb as quickly as possible.

Although the British were the first to initiate an atomic weapons program, by late 1941 the Americans were building on what they knew of British findings to develop their own crash program, known as the Manhattan Project. Constructing an atomic bomb proved far more difficult and costly than most had expected in 1941, and it took a concerted effort by the United States to have atomic weapons ready for use by mid-1945.

The U.S. decision actually to use the atomic bomb, dropping two of them on Japanese civilians, has been one of the most controversial of modern history. The decision fell to the new president, Harry Truman, who had known nothing of the bomb project when Roosevelt died in April 1945. During the next few months, Truman listened to spirited disagreement among American policymakers. Was it necessary actually to drop the bomb to force the Japanese to surrender? Especially because the ultimate victory of the United States was not in doubt, some argued that it would be enough simply to demonstrate the new weapon to the Japanese in a test firing.

By July, when the Allies met at Potsdam, the United States was prepared to use the bomb, but President Truman first warned Japan that if it did not surrender at once, it would be subjected to destruction immeasurably greater than Germany had just suffered. The Japanese decided to ignore the American warning, although the United States had begun area-bombing Japanese cities a few months before. The bombing of Tokyo in March produced a firestorm that gutted one-fourth of the city and killed over 80,000 people. In light of the Japanese refusal to surrender, the use of the atomic bomb could seem the logical next step.

At 8:15 on the morning of August 6, 1945, from a height of 32,000 feet above the Japanese city of Hiroshima, an American pilot released the first atomic bomb to be used against an enemy target. The bomb exploded after 45 seconds, 2000 feet above the ground, killing 80,000 people outright and leaving tens of thousands more to die in the aftermath. Three days later, on August 9, the Americans exploded a second atomic bomb over Nagasaki, killing perhaps 50,000 people. Although sectors of the Japanese military held out for continued resistance, Emperor Hirohito (1901–1989) finally surrendered on August 15. The bombing of civilians had discredited the Japanese military, which not only had proven unable to defend the country but had systematically misled the Japanese people about the country's prospects.

The war in the Pacific ended more suddenly than had seemed possible just a few months before (see Map 28.3). This proved advantageous to the various national liberation or decolonization movements that had developed in Asia during the war, for the Europeans had little opportunity to reassert their control in the colonial territories they had earlier lost to the Japanese.

In Burma and the Dutch East Indies, the Japanese had encouraged anticolonial sentiment, even helping local nationalists create patriotic militias. After the war, the Dutch were never able to reestablish their control against the Indonesian nationalist movement the Japanese had fostered in the East Indies. But even when its target was Japanese occupation, local resistance intensified nationalist feeling and produced hostility to the former colonial masters, as well as to the Japanese. British troops returned to Malaya and Singapore in time to accept the Japanese surrender, but they eventually came into conflict with local forces that they themselves had helped to develop against the Japanese.

Japanese pressure during the war also served the cause of Indian independence. Fearing a Japanese attack on India, the United States pressured Britain into a conciliatory stance toward the growing movement for Indian independence, directed by the charismatic spiritual leader Mohandas Gandhi (see page 1000). In March 1942 the British government pledged that as soon as the war was over, India would be granted independence under a constitution the Indians could devise for themselves. Still, Britain cracked down on Indian dissidents demanding immediate independence during the remainder of the war, so it was not clear what would happen to India once the war was over.

In Asia and the Pacific, then, Japanese occupation and pressure provoked resistance that fed anticolonialism. In 1945 Japan had been defeated, but the war had severely weakened the old Western imperialism in the region. What would follow remained unclear.

Death, Disruption, and the Question of Guilt

World War II left 50 to 60 million people dead—three times as many as World War I. About that same number were left homeless for some length of time, or found themselves forced onto the mercies of others as refugees. The Soviet Union and Germany suffered by far the highest casualty

Reconstruction Begins Shortly after the end of the war, women in Berlin pass pails of rubble along a line to a dump. Wartime bombing had severely damaged cities throughout much of Europe, although destruction was greatest in Germany. *(Hulton-Getty/Tony Stone Images)*

figures; for each, the figure was considerably higher than in World War I. An appalling 23 million Soviet citizens died, of whom 12 to 13 million were civilians. Germany lost 5 to 6 million, including perhaps 2 million civilians.

In contrast, casualty rates for Italy, Britain, and France were lower than in World War I. Italy suffered 200,000 military and 200,000 civilian deaths. Total British losses, including civilians, numbered 450,000, to which must be added 120,000 from the British Empire. Despite its quick defeat, France lost more lives than Britain because of the ravages of German occupation: The 350,000 deaths among French civilians considerably exceeded the British figure, closer to 100,000.

The United States lost 300,000 servicemen and 5,000 civilians. Figures for Japan are problematic, partly because the Japanese claim that 300,000 of those who surrendered to the Soviets in 1945 have remained unaccounted for. Apart from this number, 1,740,000 Japanese servicemen died from 1941 to 1945, more from hunger and disease than from combat, and 300,000 civilians died in Japan, most from U.S. bombing.

But this war was not confined to the major powers. Armed forces in east-central Europe also suffered substantial losses, perhaps 300,000 to 400,000 each for Hungary, Yugoslavia, Poland, Austria, and Romania. In addition, up to 1.5 million from the Yugoslav resistance died in fighting that took on the dimensions of a civil war.

The bombing of Europe destroyed buildings and left huge areas of major cities in rubble by the end of the fighting. This destruction, in turn, left hundreds of thousands homeless and contributed to the unprecedented uprooting of peoples that marked the era of World War II.

During the war, Jews, Poles, and others deemed undesirable by the Nazis had been rounded up and shipped to ghettos or camps, where the great majority had died. Of those Jews who were still alive when the Nazi camps were liberated, almost half died within a few weeks. Even those who managed to return home sometimes faced pogroms when they arrived; forty Jews were killed in the worst of them, at Kielce, in Poland.

The redrawing of Germany's borders contributed to the huge wave of refugees just after the war. To guarantee the permanence of the new territorial configuration of Poland, the Soviets and Poles began expelling ethnic Germans from the historically German areas that were now to become Polish. They constituted the bulk of the estimated 7 million Germans who were rounded up for deportation from reconstituted Poland during the years 1945 and 1946 alone. These Germans were sometimes sent to detention camps, and when they were shipped out, it was often in cattle cars. Some 2 million died in the process. By 1958, perhaps 10 million Germans had been forced out of the new Poland, leaving only about 1 million Germans still living there. Similarly, the Czechs were expelling Germans from the Sudetenland area of Czechoslovakia by 1947. So a flood of German refugees was forced to move west after the war, into the shrunken territory of the new Germany. They were among the 16 million Europeans who were permanently uprooted and transplanted between 1939 and 1947.

As the war was ending, Europeans began attempting to assess guilt and punish those responsible for the disasters of the era. In the climate of violence, resistance forces in France, Italy, and elsewhere often subjected fascists and collaborators to summary justice, sometimes through quick trials in ad hoc courts. In Italy, this process led to 15,000 executions; in France, 10,000. French women accused of sleeping with German soldiers were shamed by having their heads shaved. After the war, governments sought to dispense justice in a more orderly way, but the results differed widely across Europe. In Belgium, 634,000 of a population of 8 million were prosecuted for collaborating with the Nazis, whereas in Austria, with a comparable population, only 9000 were brought to trial.

The most sensitive confrontation with the recent past took place in Germany, where the occupying powers imposed a program of de-Nazification. In the western zones, German citizens were required to attend lectures on the virtues of democracy and to view the corpses of the victims of Nazism. In this context, the allies determined to identify and bring to justice those responsible for the crimes of the Nazi regime. This effort led to the Nuremberg trials of 1945 to 1946, the most famous

of a number of war crimes trials held in Germany and the occupied countries after the war.

Although Hitler, Himmler, and Goebbels had committed suicide, the occupying authorities apprehended for trial twenty-four individuals who had played important but very different roles in Hitler's Third Reich. All but three were convicted of war crimes and "crimes against humanity." Twelve were sentenced to death; two of them committed suicide, and the other ten were executed.

Questions about their legitimacy dogged the Nuremberg trials from the start. To a considerable extent the accused were being judged according to law made after the fact. The notion of "crimes against humanity" remained vague. Moreover, even insofar as a measure of international law was in force, it was arguably binding only on states, not individuals. But in light of the unprecedented atrocities of the Nazi regime, there was widespread agreement among the victors that the Nazi leaders could not be treated simply as defeated adversaries.

The effort to apprehend the perpetrators of Nazi atrocities continued for over a half-century thereafter, resulting in a number of highly publicized trials. But even as the century drew to a close, there remained uncertainty about responsibility and guilt, and about what it would mean to come to terms with the brutality that had marked the era of World War II.

TOWARD THE POSTWAR WORLD

Even after the fighting stopped in 1945, remarkable changes continued as the forces unleashed by the war played themselves out. Most immediately, differences between the Soviets and the Western democracies soon undermined the wartime alliance, producing the division of Germany and a bipolar Europe. Thus the conclusion of World War II led directly to the danger of a third world war, which might involve nuclear weapons and threaten the very survival of life on earth.

In addition to the dramatic changes in Europe, the wider effects of the war brought to the forefront a whole new set of issues, from anticolonialism to the Arab-Israeli conflict to the spread of communism within the non-Western world. These issues would remain central for decades, but by 1949 it was possible to discern the contours of the new postwar world, a world with new sources of hope but also with conflicts and dangers hardly imaginable ten years earlier.

Conflicting Visions and the Coming of the Cold War

Starting with the Atlantic Charter conference of 1941, Roosevelt had sought to assure that the common effort against the Axis powers would lead to a firmer basis for peace, to be framed through a new international organization after the war. At a conference at Dumbarton Oaks in Washington in September 1944, the United States outlined the structure of a new United Nations. Seeking to design a more effective body than the discredited League of Nations, Roosevelt proposed that the United States, Britain, the Soviet Union, and China play a special collective role as permanent members of a Security Council, which would form a directing nucleus for the new international body. At Yalta a few months later, Churchill persuaded Roosevelt that France, too, should have a permanent seat on the Security Council.

By the end of the war, several international meetings had used the United Nations title. In July 1944 the United Nations Monetary and Financial Conference at Bretton Woods, New Hampshire, brought together delegates from forty-four nations to deal with problems of currency and exchange rates. Although it produced only recommendations subject to ratification by the individual states, the conference indicated a new determination to cooperate on the international level after the failures of the interwar period. And the outcome of the conference, the Bretton Woods Agreement, laid the foundation for international economic exchange in the noncommunist world for the crucial quarter-century of economic recovery after the war. In addition, the conference gave birth to the International Monetary Fund and the International Bank for Reconstruction and Development, which became pillars of the global economic order.

At a conference in San Francisco from April to June 1945, delegates from almost fifty anti-Axis countries translated the principles discussed at Dumbarton Oaks into a charter for the new United Nations. As Roosevelt had envisioned, the major powers were given a privileged position in the organization as permanent members of the Security Council, each with veto power. But it was hoped

that the United Nations would institutionalize the spirit of cooperation that had developed among those who had struggled against the Axis during the war. To dramatize its departure from the Geneva-based League of Nations, which the United States had refused to join, the United Nations was headquartered in New York. In July 1945 the American Senate approved U.S. membership in the international body almost unanimously.

The creation of the United Nations afforded hope for the future, but the virtually simultaneous advent of the cold war soon cast a heavy shadow over the new organization. Whereas the United States envisioned a world order based on the ongoing cooperation of the three victors, the Soviet Union gave top priority to creating a buffer zone of friendly states in east-central Europe, especially as a bulwark against Germany. The Soviets were particularly determined to have their own way in Poland, with its central location between the Soviet Union and Germany.

While seeking this sphere of influence in east-central Europe, Stalin gave the British a free hand to settle the civil war between communists and anticommunists in Greece, and he did not push for revolution in western Europe. The strong communist parties that had emerged from the resistance movements in Italy and France were directed to work within broad-based democratic fronts rather than try to take power. Although no formal deal was made, Stalin saw this moderate position in western and southern Europe as a tacit exchange with the West for a free hand in east-central Europe.

The United States refused simply to acquiesce as the Soviets established this sphere of influence in east-central Europe. Whatever the realism of their alternative vision of the postwar world, the American reluctance to abandon the peoples of east-central Europe to unwelcome Soviet hegemony is understandable. But U.S. policymakers failed to grasp the historical and strategic basis for Soviet priorities and assumed the Soviets were trying to spread communism. The cleft between the emerging superpowers widened.

The Division of Germany

The area of greatest potential stress between the Soviets and the democracies was inevitably Germany. At first, the Western Allies were concerned especially to root out the sources of Germany's antidemocratic, aggressive behavior, but that concern faded as communism, not Nazism, came to seem the immediate menace. And it was especially conflict over Germany that cemented the division of Europe.

Disagreements over economic policy proved the major source of the split. Historians differ in apportioning the blame—and in assessing the inevitability of the outcome. Neither side lived up to all its agreements, but in light of the fundamental differences in priorities, cooperation between the democracies and the Soviets was bound to be difficult at best.

At Potsdam, the West had accepted Soviet demands for German reparations, but rather than wait for payment, the Soviets began removing German factories and equipment for reassembly in the Soviet Union. To assure that they got their due, the Soviets wanted access to the economic resources not simply of the Russian occupation zone but of the whole of Germany. The United States and Britain, in contrast, gave priority to economic reconstruction and quickly began integrating the economies of the Western zones for that purpose.

Friction developed from 1945 to 1948 as the West insisted on reduced reparations and a higher level of industrial production than the Soviets wanted. Finally, as part of their effort to spur economic recovery, the United States and Britain introduced a new currency without Soviet consent. Stalin's response, in June 1948, was to blockade the city of Berlin, cutting its western sectors off from the main Western occupation zones, almost two hundred miles west. The Western Allies responded with a massive airlift that kept their sectors of Berlin supplied for almost a year, until May 1949, when the Soviets finally backed down.

The fragile Potsdam agreement concerning Germany had gradually disintegrated. And the pretense of Allied collaboration, sustained for a while after 1945, disappeared altogether by 1948, when two separate states clearly began emerging from the Allied occupation zones. The growing split with the Soviet Union reinforced the determination of the United States and Britain to get the Western zones back on their feet as quickly as possible. Western Germany must become a viable state—economically, politically, and even militarily.

The Western occupying powers began restoring local government immediately after the war,

to create the administrative framework necessary to provide public utilities and food distribution. Gradually a governing structure was built from the ground up in the Western zones, which were increasingly coordinated. By 1949 it was possible to restore government on the national level.

With Allied support, a "parliamentary council" of German leaders met during 1948 and 1949 and produced a document that, when ratified in September 1949, became the "basic law" of a new Federal Republic of Germany. This founding document was termed simply the basic law, as opposed to the constitution, to emphasize the provisional character of the new West German state. For the same reason, the capital was placed in the small, provincial city of Bonn, which was obviously no substitute for Berlin (see Map 28.4). As far as many West Germans were concerned, the advent of a new state limited to the west did not foreclose the future reunification of Germany. But as it became clear that a new state was being created in the Western zones, and that Germany was thus to be at least temporarily divided, the Soviets settled for a new state in their zone, in eastern Germany. Thus the Communist-led German Democratic Republic, with its capital in East Berlin, was born in October 1949.

The "Iron Curtain" and the Emergence of a Bipolar World

In east-central Europe, only Yugoslavia and Albania had achieved liberation on their own, and the communist leaders of their resistance movements had a plausible claim to political power. Elsewhere, the Soviet army had provided liberation, and the Soviet military presence remained the decisive political fact as the war ended. In much of the region, authoritarianism and collaboration had been the rule for a decade or more, so there was no possibility of returning to a clearly legitimate prewar political order. To be sure, each country had local political groups, some representing former governments in exile, that now claimed a governing role, but their standing in relation to the Soviet army was uncertain.

Under these circumstances, the Soviets were able to work with local communists to install new communist-led regimes friendly to the Soviet Union in most of east-central Europe. But though Churchill warned as early as 1946 that "an iron curtain" was descending from the Baltic to the Adriatic, the process of Soviet power consolidation was not easy, and it took place gradually, in discrete steps over several years. (See the box, "Discerning the Iron Curtain.") The Communist-led government of Poland held elections in January 1947—but rigged them to guarantee a favorable outcome. In Czechoslovakia, the communists faced serious losses in upcoming elections and so finally took power outright in 1948. By 1949 there were communist governments, relying on Soviet support, in Poland, Czechoslovakia, East Germany, Hungary, Romania, and Bulgaria, with Yugoslavia and Albania also communist but capable of a more independent line.

Communism might have spread still farther in Europe, and perhaps beyond, but the West drew the line at Greece. There, as in Yugoslavia, an indigenous, communist-led resistance movement had become strong enough to contend for political power by late 1944. But when it sought to oust the monarchical government that had just returned to Greece from exile, the British intervened, helping the monarchy put down the communist uprising. Although Stalin gave the Greek communists little help, communist guerrilla activity continued, thanks partly to support from Tito's Yugoslavia. In 1946 a renewed communist uprising escalated into civil war.

As the cold war developed, both the Soviet Union and the United States began taking a more active interest in the Greek conflict. After the financially strapped Labour government in Britain reduced its involvement early in 1947, the United States stepped in to support the Greek monarchy against the communists. American policymakers feared that communism would progress from the Balkans through Greece to the Middle East. Greece seemed the place to draw the line. Thus, in March 1947, President Truman announced the Truman Doctrine, which committed the United States to the "containment" of communism throughout the world. American advisers now began re-equipping the anticommunist forces in Greece. Faced with this determined opposition from the West, Stalin pulled back, but the Greek communists, with their strong indigenous support, were not defeated until 1949.

Thus the wartime marriage of expediency between the Soviet Union and the Western democracies fell apart in the war's aftermath. Only in Austria, jointly occupied by the Soviets and the Western democracies, were the former Allies able to arrange the postwar transition in a reasonably amicable way. The Soviets acquiesced in the neutralization of a democratic Austria as the occupying powers left in 1954. Elsewhere, Europe was divided into two antagonistic power blocs. The antagonism between the two superpowers became more menacing when the Soviets exploded their first atomic bomb in August 1949, intensifying the postwar arms race. By then, in fact, the United States was on its way to the more destructive hydrogen bomb. The split between these two nations, unmistakable by 1949, established the framework for world affairs for the next forty years. (See the box, "The Soviet View of the Cold War.")

The West and the New World Agenda

At the same time, other dramatic changes around the world suggested that, with or without the cold war, the postwar political scene would be hard to manage. Events in India in 1947, in Israel in 1948, and in China in 1949 epitomized the new hopes and uncertainties that had emerged directly from World War II.

Although the British, under U.S. pressure, had reluctantly promised independence for India in order to elicit Indian support during the war, British authorities and Indian leaders had continued to skirmish. Mohandas Gandhi was twice jailed for resisting British demands and threatening a massive program of nonviolent resistance to British rule. But by 1946 the British lacked the will and the financial resources to maintain their control in India. Thus Britain acquiesced in Indian independence, proclaimed on August 15, 1947. Allowing independence to India, long the jewel of the British Empire, raised questions about Britain's role in the postwar world and portended a wider disintegration of the European colonial system. There would be new countries, many of them poor—and resentful of Western imperialism. What would that mean for the new world order, centering on the United Nations, that Roosevelt had envisioned?

Questions about the fate of the Jews, who had suffered so grievously during World War II, were inevitable as well. Almost two-thirds of the Jews of Europe had been killed, and many of the survivors either had no place to go or had concluded that they could never again live as a minority in

Discerning the Iron Curtain

Winston Churchill, out of office and touring the United States, sought to specify the contours of the postwar international situation in a speech at Westminster College in Fulton, Missouri, on March 5, 1946. To characterize the developing division of Europe, Churchill referred to "an iron curtain," a term that attracted immediate attention and dramatically affected public opinion in both the United States and western Europe. Soviet historians dated the beginning of the cold war from this speech.

A shadow has fallen upon the scenes so lately lighted by the Allied victory. Nobody knows what Soviet Russia and its Communist international organization intends to do in the immediate future, or what are the limits, if any, to their expansive and proselytizing tendencies. . . . We understand the Russian need to be secure on her western frontiers by the removal of all possibility of German aggression. We welcome her to her rightful place among the leading nations of the world. . . . It is my duty, however, to place before you certain facts. . . .

From Stettin in the Baltic to Trieste in the Adriatic, an iron curtain has descended across the Continent. Behind that line lie all the capitals of the ancient states of central and eastern Europe. Warsaw, Berlin, Prague, Vienna, Budapest, Belgrade, Bucharest, and Sofia, all these famous cities and the populations around them lie in what I must call the Soviet sphere, and all are subject in one form or another, not only to Soviet influence but to a very high and, in many cases, increasing measure of control from Moscow. Athens alone—Greece with its immortal glories—is free to decide its future at an election under British, American and French observation. The Russian-dominated Polish Government has been encouraged to make enormous and wrongful inroads upon Germany, and mass expulsions of millions of Germans on a scale grievous and undreamed-of

are now taking place. The Communist parties, which were very small in all these Eastern States of Europe, have been raised to pre-eminence and power far beyond their numbers and are seeking everywhere to obtain totalitarian control. . . .

If now the Soviet Government tries, by separate action, to build up a pro-Communist Germany in their areas, this will cause new serious difficulties in the British and American zones, and will give the defeated Germans the power of putting themselves up to auction between the Soviets and the Western Democracies. Whatever conclusions may be drawn from these facts—and facts they are—this is certainly not the Liberated Europe we fought to build up. Nor is it one which contains the essentials of permanent peace. . . .

. . . I do not believe that Soviet Russia desires war. What they desire is the fruits of war and the indefinite expansion of their power and doctrines. But what we have to consider here to-day while time remains, is the permanent prevention of war and the establishment of the conditions of freedom and democracy as rapidly as possible in all countries. . . .

From what I have seen of our Russian friends and allies during the war, I am convinced that there is nothing they admire so much as strength, and there is nothing for which they have less respect than for weakness, especially military weakness.

Source: Winston S. Churchill, *His Complete Speeches, 1897–1963*, vol. VII, *1943–1949*, ed. Robert Rhodes James (New York: Chelsea House, 1974), pp. 7290–7292.

Europe. Many insisted that they must have a homeland of their own. For decades such Zionist sentiment (see page 943) had centered on the biblical area of Israel, in what had become, after

World War I, the British mandate of Palestine. Jewish immigration to the area accelerated during the interwar period, but it caused increasing friction between Jews and the Palestinian Arabs.

The Soviet View of the Cold War

The first cold war document the Soviet government made available to Western scholars was a telegram that Nikolai Novikov, the Soviet ambassador to the United States, sent from Washington to Soviet Foreign Minister Vyacheslav Molotov on September 27, 1946. Novikov sought to pinpoint the essential features of the new foreign policy the United States seemed to be pursuing after its victory in World War II. In releasing the document in 1990, Soviet authorities contended it had been of central importance in the Soviet effort to understand postwar American intentions and to formulate their own policy in response.

The foreign policy of the United States, which reflects the imperialist tendencies of American monopolistic capital, is characterized in the postwar period by a striving for world supremacy. This is the real meaning of the many statements by President Truman and other representatives of American ruling circles: that the United States has the right to lead the world. All the forces of American diplomacy—the army, the air force, the navy, industry, and science— are enlisted in the service of this foreign policy. For this purpose broad plans for expansion have been developed and are being implemented through diplomacy and the establishment of a system of naval and air bases stretching far beyond the boundaries of the United States, through the arms race, and through the creation of ever newer types of weapons. . . .

. . . [W]e have seen a failure of calculations on the part of U.S. circles which assumed that the Soviet Union would be destroyed in the war or would come out of it so weakened that it would be forced to go begging to the United States for economic assistance. Had that happened, they would have been able to dictate conditions permitting the United States to carry out its expansion in Europe and Asia without hindrance from the USSR. . . .

One of the most important elements in the general policy of the United States, which is directed toward limiting the international role of the USSR in the postwar world, is the policy with regard to Germany. In Germany, the United States is taking measures to strengthen reactionary forces for the purpose of opposing democratic reconstruction. Furthermore, it displays special insistence on accompanying this policy with completely inadequate measures for the demilitarization of Germany. . . .

Careful note should be taken of the fact that the preparation by the United States for a future war is being conducted with the prospect of war against the Soviet Union, which in the eyes of American imperialists is the main obstacle in the path of the United States to world domination. This is indicated by facts such as the tactical training of the American army for war with the Soviet Union as the future opponent, the siting of American strategic bases in regions from which it is possible to launch strikes on Soviet territory, intensified training and strengthening of Arctic regions as close approaches to the USSR, and attempts to prepare Germany and Japan to use those countries in a war against the USSR.

Source: "The Novikov Telegram," *Diplomatic History,* vol. 15, no. 4 (Fall 1991), pp. 527–528, 536–537.

Concerned about access to Middle Eastern oil, the British sought to cultivate good relations with the Arab world after the war. Thus they opposed further immigration of Jews to Palestine, as well as proposals to carve an independent Jewish state from the area. The United States, however, was considerably more sympathetic to the Zionist cause. As tensions built, Jewish terrorists blew up the British headquarters in Jerusalem, and the British decided to abandon what seemed a no-win situation. In September 1947, they announced their intention to withdraw from Palestine, leaving its

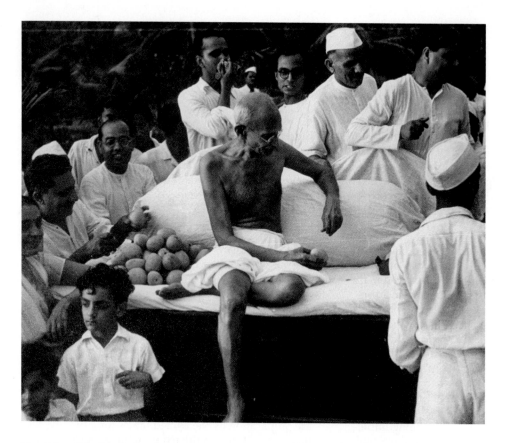

Gandhi and Indian Independence An apostle of nonviolence, Mohandas Gandhi inspired the movement that finally won India's independence from Britain in 1947. He is shown here distributing fruit to children near Bombay in 1944. *(Dinodia Picture Agency/Image Works)*

future to the United Nations. In November the UN voted to partition Palestine, creating both a Jewish and a new Arab Palestinian state (Map 28.5).

Skirmishing between Jews and Arabs became full-scale war in December, and in that context the Jews declared their independence as the new state of Israel on May 14, 1948. When fighting ended in 1949, the Israelis had conquered more territory than had been envisioned in the original partition plan, and the remaining Arab territories fell to Egypt and Jordan, rather than forming an independent Palestinian state. Thus was born the new state of Israel, partly a product of the assault on the Jews during World War II. Yet it was born amid Arab hostility and Western concerns about oil.

In 1949 the communist insurgency in China under Mao Zedong (Mao Tse-tung) (see page 1000) finally triumphed over the Chinese Nationalists under Chiang Kai-shek, who were forced to flee to the island of Taiwan. During the war, the Communists had done better than the Nationalists at identifying themselves with the Chinese cause against both Japanese and Western imperialism. And after their victory, the Chinese Communists enjoyed great prestige among other "national liberation" movements struggling against Western colonialists. To many in the West, however, the outcome in China by 1949 simply intensified fears that communism was poised to spread in the unsettled postwar world.

At the same time, the Chinese revolution undermined Roosevelt's conception of the United Nations. The United States had long supported Chiang Kai-shek as a bulwark against Japan and a source of stability in Asia. And at Roosevelt's insistence, China had been accorded a permanent seat on the UN Security Council as the war was ending. Even after being forced from the mainland in 1949, the militantly anticommunist Chinese Nationalists retained their permanent Security Council seat until 1971, when the communist People's Republic of China was admitted to the UN—and assumed China's seat on the Security Council. The obviously artificial role that the Nationalists played for so long damaged the credibility of the new United Nations.

SUMMARY

By 1949 the division of Europe, the advent of nuclear weapons, and the symptomatic events in India, Israel, and China made it clear that the world's agenda had been radically transformed in the ten years since the beginning of World War II. With the Soviet Union and United States emerging from the war as superpowers, and with the once-dominant European countries weakened and chastened, the center of gravity in the West changed dramatically. Thus the relationship between the West and the world was bound to be radically different. Such was the war's complex and often unexpected legacy.

Although the war opened a new universe of problems and possibilities, it brought to a close an era of European history dominated by fascism. As a result of the war, the two major fascist powers collapsed and fascist forms of politics, with their hostility to democracy and their tendencies toward violence and war, stood at least temporarily discredited. But Nazism and fascism continued to haunt the Western mind, especially with the discovery of the Nazi camps. It was not clear, moreover, whether Germany and Italy, and, for that matter, much of the rest of Europe, would be able to develop effective democratic political systems amid defeat and destruction.

The Soviets had borne the brunt of the war in Europe, and the Soviet Union—and its communist system—emerged with enhanced prestige. At the same time, an overseas war had again drawn the United States, which was prepared in the aftermath, as it had not been after World War I, to play an ongoing leadership role in world affairs. The Soviet Union and the United States offered competing visions of the future, and during the decades that followed their competition helped shape everything from Italian domestic politics to the decolonization struggle in Mozambique.

Map 28.5 The Partition of Palestine and the Birth of the State of Israel In November 1947 the United Nations offered a plan to partition the British mandate of Palestine, but complications immediately arose. The Jews of the area won their own state, Israel, but the Palestinian Arabs did not. Thus tensions continued in the area.

Dwarfed by the two new superpowers, the old European states seemed destined to play a diminished role in world affairs. It quickly became apparent that the costs of the war had left even Britain, a full partner in the Allied victory, too weak to remain a great power. Almost at once, the Europeans began retreating from their long-standing imperial roles, though not without resentment, resistance, and more bloodshed. By 1949 it was clear that non-Western nations would be playing a more prominent role in world affairs in the future.

Whereas there had been, for a while, some illusion of a "return to normal" after World War I, it was obvious after World War II that the old Europe was gone forever and that the relationship between the West and the rest of the world would never be the same. Indeed, much of Europe's proud culture, on the basis of which it had claimed to lead the world, lay in the ruins of war, apparently exhausted. What role could Europe play in Western civilization, and in the wider world, after all that had happened?

NOTES

1. From Farrell's full account as related by General Leslie Groves in his "Memorandum to the Secretary of War," dated July 18, 1945, in Philip L. Cantelon, Richard G. Hewlett, and Robert C. Williams, eds., *The American Atom: A Documentary History of Nuclear Policies from the Discovery of Fission to the Present*, 2d ed. (Philadelphia: University of Pennsylvania Press, 1991), pp. 56–57.
2. Quoted in Karl Dietrich Bracher, *The German Dictatorship: The Origins, Structure, and Effects of National Socialism*, trans. Jean Steinberg (New York: Praeger, 1970), p. 423.

SUGGESTED READING

General Surveys

Calvocoressi, Peter, Guy Wint, and John Pritchard. *Total War: Causes and Courses of the Second World War*, 2d ed., revised. 2 vols. 1989. New edition of a standard, readable work.

Campbell, John, ed. *The Experience of World War II*. 1989. Focusing on the experience of those touched by the war, this collaborative volume covers everything from prisoners of war to the uses of the arts for propaganda purposes. A handsome volume in a large format, with superb illustrations and maps.

Keegan, John. *The Second World War*. 1989. A detailed but readable study featuring military operations. Well illustrated.

Parker, R. A. C. *Struggle for Survival: The History of the Second World War*. 1990. An accessible, comprehensive, and well-balanced survey. Especially good on debates over strategy and the wider implications of the strategies chosen.

Weinberg, Gerhard L. *A World at Arms: A Global History of World War II*. 1994. An enlightening global approach by a leading historian of the period. Stresses the interrelationship among simultaneous events and decisions in the various theaters of the war around the world.

Wright, Gordon. *The Ordeal of Total War, 1939–1945*. 1968. Masterly synthesis of all aspects of the war experience, from the battlefield to the scientific labora-

tory, from the Nazi new order to the coming of the cold war.

Fighting the War

Ellis, John. *On the Front Lines: The Experience of War through the Eyes of the Allied Soldiers in World War II*. 1991. Based partly on oral testimony, a vivid account of the experiences of those who fought the war on the Allied side in Europe, Africa, and the Pacific.

Fussell, Paul. *Wartime: Understanding and Behavior in the Second World War*. 1989. Explores the rationalizations and euphemisms, the contempt and subversion, that enabled U.S. and British fighting men to deal with the horrors of World War II.

Glantz, David M., and Jonathan M. House. *When Titans Clashed: How the Red Army Stopped Hitler*. 1995. Detailed but compelling account of the decisive encounter in World War II, based partly on newly available materials from the former Soviet Union.

Overy, Richard J. *Why the Allies Won*. 1995. Denying that the sheer weight of numbers made the outcome inevitable, this account accents the differences in political, economic, and even moral mobilization to explain why the Allies defeated the Axis powers in World War II.

The Home Front

Harrison, Mark. *Soviet Planning in Peace and War, 1938–1945*. 1985. Shows how Soviet economic planners responded to invasion in 1941, enabling the Soviet Union to defeat Nazi Germany and emerge from the war as a great power.

Milward, Alan S. *War, Economy and Society, 1939–1945*. 1979. A detailed study of the economic adjustments that the war necessitated—and that sustained the long years of fighting.

Overy, R. J. *War and Economy in the Third Reich*. 1994. An important series of essays on the interpenetration of war and economy in Nazi Germany, from rearmament to surrender.

Pelling, Henry. *Winston Churchill*. 1974. Among the best single-volume biographies of Churchill. Balanced and readable.

Summerfield, Penny. *Women Workers in the Second World War: Production and Patriarchy in Conflict*. 1989. Shows how the disruptions of war affected women's opportunities and self-understanding.

Collaboration and Resistance

De Gaulle, Charles. *The Complete War Memoirs of Charles de Gaulle*. 3 vols. in one. 1955, 1959, 1960. Revealing personal account of de Gaulle's remarkable role as leader of the Free French forces during World War II.

Delzell, Charles F. *Mussolini's Enemies: The Italian Anti-Fascist Resistance*. 1961. An exhaustive account of Italian resistance activities, proceeding region by region.

Lacouture, Jean. *De Gaulle*. Vol. 1, *The Rebel, 1890–1944*. 1990. First volume of a standard biography, detailed but accessible. Shows how de Gaulle's maverick qualities enabled him to play his special role during the war.

Paxton, Robert O. *Vichy France: Old Guard and New Order*. 1975. A widely admired study that assesses Vichy claims to have shielded the French from the worst features of Nazi occupation.

The Holocaust

Friedländer, Saul, ed. *Probing the Limits of Representation: Nazism and the "Final Solution."* 1992. Searching essays on the enduring impact of the Holocaust and our uncertain attempts to make sense of it.

Gilbert, Martin. *The Holocaust: A History of the Jews of Europe During the Second World War*. 1986. A comprehensive but straightforward account, making effective use of the testimony of those involved.

Hilberg, Raul. *Perpetrators, Victims, Bystanders: The Jewish Catastrophe, 1933–1945*. 1992. The dean of Holocaust historians offers an accessible, compelling account by weaving capsule portraits delineating the many layers of involvement and responsibility at issue in the Holocaust.

———. *The Destruction of the European Jews*. Revised and definitive ed. 3 vols. 1985. Pioneering, detailed account of the Holocaust, based on exhaustive research. Especially revealing on the administrative mechanics of the process.

Laqueur, Walter. *The Terrible Secret: Suppression of the Truth about Hitler's "Final Solution."* 1982. Raises the gnawing questions about who knew what, and when, about the extermination of the Jews. Without exonerating policymakers who might have responded more effectively, the author shows how difficult it was to comprehend what seemed incomprehensible.

Lifton, Robert Jay. *The Nazi Doctors: Medical Killing and the Psychology of Genocide*. 1986. A major expert on the psychology of extreme situations seeks to understand the large number of German medical doctors who played central roles in Nazi programs of mass killing.

Marrus, Michael. *The Holocaust in History*. 1987. An ideal introduction to the major issues. Readable and balanced.

Yahil, Leni. *The Holocaust: The Fate of European Jewry*. 1990. A clear and comprehensive account that accents the underlying continuity in Nazi policy and assesses the Jewish response.

The Wider Impact of the War

Laqueur, Walter. *A History of Zionism*. 1989. Surveys the five decades of European Zionist activity that helped bring about the establishment of the state of Israel.

Marrus, Michael R. *The Unwanted: European Refugees in the Twentieth Century*. 1985. Pioneering account of the rise of the refugee phenomenon as a major but neglected aspect of modern political disruptions.

Rhodes, Richard. *The Making of the Atomic Bomb*. 1988. An acclaimed study that combines science, politics, and personality in an especially dramatic way.

The Coming of the Cold War

Eisenberg, Carolyn Woods. *Drawing the Line: The American Decision to Divide Germany, 1944–1949*. 1996. A detailed, scholarly account that uses newly available sources to accent the American role in the process that culminated in the division of Germany by 1949.

Gaddis, John Lewis. *We Now Know: Rethinking Cold War History*. 1997. Taking advantage of newly available Russian and Chinese documents, a leading authority reassesses the cold war, from its origins to the Cuban missile crisis of 1962.

Paterson, Thomas G. *On Every Front: The Making and Unmaking of the Cold War*. 1992. Updated edition of a highly regarded survey.

Reynolds, David, ed. *The Origins of the Cold War in Europe: International Perspectives*. 1994. With chapters devoted to individual countries, traces the origins of the cold war and its impact on subsequent development in western Europe. Includes a fine introduction by the editor.

Yergin, Daniel. *Shattered Peace: The Origins of the Cold War*. Revised ed. 1990. Readable, balanced narrative, focusing especially on the bases of American policy.

Weighing the Evidence

HOLOCAUST TESTIMONY

There were loud announcements, but it was all fairly restrained: nobody did anything to us. I followed the crowd: "Men to the right, women and children to the left," we had been told. The women and children disappeared into a barrack further to the left and we were told to undress. One of the SS men—later I knew his name, Küttner—told us in a chatty sort of tone that we were going into a disinfection bath and afterwards would be assigned work. Clothes, he said, could be left in a heap on the floor, and we'd find them again later. . . .

The queue began to move and I suddenly noticed several men fully dressed standing near another barrack further back, and I was wondering who they were. And just then another SS man (Miete was his name) came by me and said, "Come on, you, get back into your clothes, quick, special work." That was the first time I was frightened. Everything was very quiet, you know. And when he said that to me, the others turned around and looked at me—and I thought, my God, why me, why does he pick on me? When I had got back into my clothes, the line had moved on and I noticed that several other young men had also been picked out and were dressing. We were taken through to the "work-barrack," most of which was filled from floor to ceiling with clothes, stacked up in layers. . . . You understand, there was no time, not a moment between the instant we were taken in there and put to work, to talk to anyone, to take stock of what was happening . . . [ellipses in the original] and of course never forget that we had no idea at all what this whole installation was for. One saw these stacks of clothing—I suppose the thought must have entered our minds, where do they come from, what are they? We must have connected them with the clothes all of us had just taken off outside . . . [ellipses in the original] but I cannot remember doing that. I only remember starting work at once making bundles.*

This is the voice of Richard Glazar, recalling when, as a young Jewish student from Prague, he arrived at the Nazi extermination camp at Treblinka in October 1942. Glazar was telling his story in 1972 to the British journalist Gitta Sereny, who had been covering the trial in Germany of the commandant of the Treblinka camp, Franz Stangl. Seeking to understand Stangl, Sereny tracked down a number of those who had come into contact with him, including survivors like Glazar.

Glazar's recollections are part of a rich body of testimony by Jewish survivors of the Holocaust, testimony that is often moving, gripping, terrifying. Some accounts offer direct personal recollections. Others integrate personal remembrance into literature. Still others use the insights of social psychology in an effort to explain the special features of the camp experience.

Even with all this evidence, we wonder if we can ever really grasp what millions of Jews experienced at the hands of the Nazis in the extermination camps. But listening to witnesses like Glazar, we gain some sense of the uncertainty and fear, the suffering and humiliation, that helped define that experience. And we recognize the determination, the affirmation of life, that marked the Jewish response.

We may be surprised at Glazar's insistence that "we had no idea at all what this whole installation was for." Didn't the Jews understand what the camps held for them? In fact, some Jews had a better idea than others, but in most cases only through rumor, and no one could know the whole story as it was unfolding. Over a year before, Glazar's family had sent him to work in the country, where they assumed he would be safe, so he had been relatively isolated. But what one knew, or could surmise, also depended on what one was prepared to believe was possible, what the world could hold. Some simply could not believe the rumors.

Once they were in the camps, however, the Jews could only come to terms with the unprece-

*The testimony of Richard Glazar is from Gitta Sereny, *Into That Darkness: An Examination of Conscience* (New York: Random House, Vintage Books, 1983), pp. 176–179, 183.

**Arrival at the Auschwitz
Extermination Camp**
(*Corbis-Bettmann*)

dented situation as best they could. Let us listen further to Glazar, whose insights into the minds of the SS overseers help us better to grasp the terrible capriciousness of the situation:

> One must not forget their incredible power, their autonomy within their narrow and yet, as far as we were concerned, unlimited field; but also the isolation created by their unique situation and by what they—and hardly anyone else even within the German or Nazi community—had in common. Perhaps if this isolation had been the result of good rather than evil deeds, their own relationship towards each other would have been different. As it was, most of them seemed to hate and despise each other and do anything—almost anything—to "get at" each other. Thus, if one of them selected a man out of a new transport for work, in other words to stay alive at least for a while, it could perfectly easily happen . . . that one of his rivals . . . would come along and kill that man just to spite him. . . . All this created a virtually indescribable atmosphere of fear. The most important thing for a prisoner at Treblinka, you see, was not to make himself conspicuous.

But what, then, can be said about the human attributes that such conditions called forth—and that enabled some, at least, to survive?

> Our daily life? It was in a way very directed, very specific. . . . [I]t was essential to fill oneself completely with a determination to survive; it was es-
> sential to create in oneself a capacity for dissociating oneself to some extent from Treblinka; it was important not to adapt completely to it. . . .
>
> It wasn't *ruthlessness* that enabled an individual to survive—it was an intangible quality, not peculiar to educated or sophisticated individuals. Anyone might have it. It is perhaps best described as an overriding thirst—perhaps, too, a talent for life, and a faith in life.

Glazar, of course, was speaking thirty years later, and despite the engaging spontaneity of his testimony, he may have forgotten things, or the experiences of the intervening years may have colored his memory. Moreover, he could only tell what he recalled through the categories of language, which may be inadequate to convey, to those who were not there, what it was like to be sent to the Nazi extermination camps. Perhaps survivors called upon, years later, to put their recollections into words are bound to impose too much order, even to romanticize, by using categories their listeners can understand—or want to hear. Glazar was clearly stretching to find the words. Does "talent for life" ring true? We will continue to wonder.

As for Glazar himself, he escaped from Treblinka in an uprising in August 1943, and then made his way to Germany, where he managed to survive the war disguised as a foreign laborer. When Sereny reached him in 1972, he was living in Switzerland, working as an engineer. ✦

1071

CHAPTER 29

An Anxious Stability: The Age of the Cold War, 1949–1985

Sampling an American hot dog at a meatpacking plant in Iowa in 1959, the leader of the Soviet Union, Nikita Khrushchev, wryly observed that "we have beaten you to the moon, but you have beaten us in sausage-making." Khrushchev was in the midst of a two-week visit to the United States in response to an invitation from President Dwight Eisenhower. Though the visit included the expected top-level talks and communiqués, it also gave Khrushchev a chance to witness American life, from a Manhattan nightclub to a southern California suburb to an Iowa farm. The Soviet leader grew peevish when, for security reasons, the American authorities would not let him visit recently opened Disneyland, but he found much to praise in American society, and he took every occasion to stress the possibility of "peaceful coexistence." Still, Khrushchev also took it for granted that, in virtually every sphere, competition would continue between the United States, leading the capitalist West, and the Soviet Union, leading the communist East.

Americans were not sure what to make of this robust, plain-spoken leader of the communist world. The large crowd that came out to see his motorcade in New York was, according to one account, "restrained and curious rather than hostile." Some of those who met him provoked heated exchanges by criticizing recent Soviet actions in east-central Europe, or by questioning the treatment of workers in the Soviet Union, or by harping on Khrushchev's remark, a few years earlier, about "burying" the United States. But Khrushchev sought seriously to avoid divisive issues and to

Soviet leader Nikita
Khrushchev (in hat) visiting
an Iowa farm in 1959.

find areas of common ground, even with respect to difficult international issues like the status of Germany.

It was time to recognize, Khrushchev insisted, that each side fervently believed in its own system; hence, there was no point in trying to convince the other. The two sides would simply compete—and the competition could be peaceful. Noting his own humble origins, Khrushchev stressed how far his country had come in its brief period under communism; indeed, it was remarkable that the Soviet Union could now stand head to head with an advanced country like the United States. And if they were not quite up to America in hot dogs and other consumer goods, the Soviets seemed to be setting the pace in significant areas of advanced technology. They had been first in space with an artificial satellite, *Sputnik I*, in 1957, and they had just sent the first unmanned rocket to the moon. Thus Khrushchev's confident appeal to the future: "Let us compete peacefully and let the people be the judges of which system provides greater possibilities." Everything that was not progressive would die away. The ongoing competition between the two superpowers, and the respective socioeconomic systems they represented, did not have to mean an endless arms race and the threat of nuclear annihilation.

But in 1960, less than a year after Khrushchev's visit, the Soviet military shot down a U.S. spy plane over the Soviet Union, partly, it seems, to undercut Khrushchev's effort at better relations with the United States. Soviet hawks found Khrushchev too trusting, too accommodating. The incident wrecked a previously planned summit meeting, and relations between the Soviet Union and the United States cooled. Although they would eventually warm again, ideological competition, mutual suspicion, and a costly and dangerous arms race continued to characterize the postwar era. It seemed possible that, virtually overnight, the cold war could develop into a hot war that could lead to nuclear annihilation. Only as it was ending, more than four decades after World War II, did it become clear that the anxious cold war era had been one of relative stability and peace.

Both halves of Europe had to operate within the bipolar framework, but the Western and Soviet blocs each confronted different challenges and evolved in very different ways. Dependent on U.S. leadership, unable to resist the tide of decoloniza-tion, the countries of Western Europe adjusted to a diminished international role. The change in scale led many to advocate some form of European union, which might eventually enable the Western Europeans to deal with the superpowers on a more equal basis. On the domestic level, the postwar situation was so unsettled at first that no Western European country, not even victorious Britain, could simply apply a prewar model. Postwar reconstruction rested on a new consensus that government must play a more active role in promoting both economic growth and social welfare. By the 1960s the promise of shared prosperity was realized to a remarkable extent. But changing circumstances by the early 1970s threatened the consensus that postwar prosperity had made possible.

Although the Soviet Union had suffered immensely in winning World War II, the communist regime emerged from the war with renewed legitimacy. Having led the country to superpower status, it seemed to offer its citizens a better future, just as Khrushchev emphasized in 1959. During the 1950s and 1960s, the Soviet system achieved some significant successes, but its efforts to outgrow its Stalinist framework were halting. By 1980 the system was becoming rigid and stagnant. Still, it was not until the late 1980s that the terms of the long postwar settlement radically changed, bringing the cold war era to a dramatic close.

THE SEARCH FOR CULTURAL BEARINGS

The events from World War I to the cold war added up to an unprecedented period of disaster for Europe. Europeans were bound to ask what had gone wrong, and what could be salvaged from the ruins of a culture that had made possible the most destructive wars in history, as well as fascism, totalitarianism, and the Holocaust. The cold war framework inevitably affected the answers. Some embraced the Soviet Union or sought a renewed Marxism. Opposition to communism helped stimulate others to return to religious or classical traditions or to embrace new ideas associated with America's recent successes. In Western Europe, at least, this effort to take stock led promptly to the renewed determination and fresh ideas that helped produce the dramatically successful postwar reconstruction.

Absurdity and Commitment in Existentialism

The postwar mood of exhaustion and despair found classic expression in the work of the Irish-born writer Samuel Beckett (1906–1989), especially in his plays *Waiting for Godot* (1952) and *Endgame* (1957). Through Beckett's characters, we see ourselves going through the motions, with nothing worth saying or doing, ludicrously manipulating the husks of a worn-out culture. The only redeeming element is the comic pathos we feel as we watch ourselves.

The same sense of anxiety and despair led to the vogue of existentialism, a movement that marked philosophy, the arts, and popular culture from the later 1940s until well into the 1950s. Existentialism developed from the ideas of the German thinker Martin Heidegger (1889–1976), especially *Being and Time* (1927), one of the most influential philosophical works of the century. Though it was a philosophy of sorts, existentialism was most significant as a broader cultural tendency, finding expression in novels and films. The existentialists explored what it means to be a human being in a world cast adrift from its cultural moorings, with no mutually accepted guideposts, standards, or values.

The most influential postwar existentialists were the Frenchmen Albert Camus (1913–1960) and Jean Paul Sartre (1905–1980), each of whom had been involved in the French resistance, Camus in a particularly central role as editor of an underground newspaper. For both, an authentic human response to a world spinning out of control entailed engagement, commitment, responsibility—even though every action is fraught with risk for the individual. (See the box, "Existentialism and the Loss of Bearings.")

Rather than accept the bleak, ludicrously comic vision of Beckett's plays, Camus sought to show how we might go on living in a positive, affirmative spirit, even in an absurd world, even after all that had happened. Conventional values like friendship and tolerance could be made usable again, based on the simple fact that we human beings are all caught up in this unmasterable situation together. People suffer and die, but as we come together to help as best we can, we might at least learn to stop killing one another.

Camus split from Sartre in a disagreement over the ongoing value of Marxism and the communist experiment in the Soviet Union. Though never an orthodox communist, Sartre found potential for human liberation in the working class, in communist parties, even in the Soviet Union

Sartre and de Beauvoir
Among the most influential intellectual couples of the century, Jean-Paul Sartre and Simone de Beauvoir emerged as leaders of French existentialism by the later 1940s. See the boxes on pages 1076 and 1083. *(Giansant/Sygma)*

Existentialism and the Loss of Bearings

In 1945, in a lecture entitled "Existentialism is a Humanism," Jean Paul Sartre offered the classic explanation of the fundamental existentialist tenet: "Existence precedes essence." In a world in which the traditional sources of order and direction appear to have dissolved, we human beings simply find ourselves existing, without some "human nature" that tells us what we are or might become. But then what?

What do we mean by saying that existence precedes essence? We mean that man first of all exists, encounters himself, surges up in the world—and defines himself afterwards. If man as the existentialist sees him is not definable, it is because to begin with he is nothing. He will not be anything until later, and then he will be what he makes of himself. . . . [M]an is, before all else, something which propels itself towards a future and is aware that it is doing so. . . . If . . . existence is prior to essence, man is responsible for what he is. Thus, the first effect of existentialism is that it puts every man in possession of himself as he is, and places the entire responsibility for his existence squarely upon his own shoulders. And, when we say that man is responsible for himself, we do not mean he is responsible only for his own individuality, but that he is responsible for all men. . . . [N]othing can be better for us unless it is better for all. . . . In fashioning myself I fashion man. . . .

. . . If a voice speaks to me, it is still I myself who must decide whether the voice is or is not that of an angel. If I regard a certain course of action as good, it is only I who choose to say that it is good and not bad. . . .

It is nowhere written that "the good" exists, that one must be honest or must not lie, since we are now upon the plane where there are only men. . . . [M]an . . . cannot find anything to depend upon either within or outside himself. He discovers forthwith, that he is without excuse. For if indeed existence precedes essence, one will never be able to explain one's actions by reference to a given and specific human nature; in other words, there is no determinism—man is free, man is freedom. [W]e have neither behind us, nor before us in a luminous realm of values, any means of justification or excuse. That is what I mean when I say that man is condemned to be free.

Source: Walter Kaufmann, ed., *Existentialism from Dostoevsky to Sartre* (Cleveland: World, Meridian Books, 1956), pp. 290–295. (First pub. in French in 1946; first English ed. 1948.)

itself, which he saw as the strongest alternative to U.S. imperialism. By the 1950s, he was portraying existentialism as fundamentally a way to revitalize Marxism.

By contrast, Camus, who had started as a communist in the 1930s, had grown disillusioned even before the war, and his major political tract, *The Rebel* (1951), was partly an attack on Marxism and communism. Establishing new bases for human happiness and solidarity meant recognizing limits to what human beings could accomplish, limits even to our demands for freedom and justice. These were precisely the limits that the new political movements of the century had so disas-

trously overstepped. Communism, like fascism, was part of the problem, not the solution.

Marxists and Traditionalists

Sartre was among the many European intellectuals who believed that Marxism had won a new lease on life from the wartime resistance. As they saw it, Marxism could be revamped for the West, without the Stalinist excesses of the Soviet Union. Marxism remained a significant strand in the political culture of the West during the cold war era, but it also attracted periodic waves of denunciation.

In Italy, as in France, the communists' major role in the resistance enhanced their prestige, preparing the way for the extraordinary posthumous influence of Antonio Gramsci (1891–1937), a founder of the Italian Communist party who had spent most of the fascist period in prison. His *Prison Notebooks*, published during the late 1940s, became influential throughout the world and helped make Marxism a powerful force in postwar Italian culture. Seeking to learn the lessons of the fascist triumph in Italy, Gramsci pointed Marxists toward a flexible political strategy, attuned to the special historical circumstances of each country.

Loosely Marxist ideas were central to the renewal of political activism in the West by the later 1960s, although Marxism proved more effective as a critique of capitalism than as a blueprint for change. The best-known spokesman for a renewed radicalism on both sides of the Atlantic during the late 1960s and early 1970s was the German-born social thinker Herbert Marcuse (1898–1979), who explored the cultural mechanisms through which capitalism perpetuates itself in *One-Dimensional Man* (1964).

Even during the late 1940s, however, others, like Camus, held that Marxism was inherently flawed and denied that any recasting could overcome its deficiencies. Damaging revelations about the excesses of Stalinism during the 1930s seemed to confirm this view. Such writers as the Hungarian-born Arthur Koestler (1905–1983) and the Italian Ignazio Silone (1900–1978), who had believed in communism during the 1930s, now denounced it as "the God that failed." Whatever its initial promise, Marxism would inevitably lead to the kind of tyranny that had developed in the Soviet Union. In his futuristic novel *Nineteen Eighty-Four*, published in 1949, the British intellectual George Orwell, long a partisan of leftist causes, chillingly portrayed the dehumanization that seemed to threaten from the totalitarian direction that many now associated with communism.

By the mid-1970s, the disturbing portrait of the Stalinist gulag, or forced-labor-camp system, by the exiled Soviet writer Alexander Solzhenitsyn (b. 1918) stimulated another wave of anticommunist thinking. And whether or not Marxism was necessarily Stalinist and repressive in implication, its relevance to the increasingly prosperous industrial democracies of Western Europe was open to question. Did the Marxist understanding of capitalism and class relations illuminate the core social problems and point the way to solutions, or had the progress of the capitalist West rendered Marxist categories irrelevant? By the early 1980s, many had come to believe that Marxism was simply passé.

Those hostile to Marxism often insisted that the West had to reconnect with older traditions if it were to avoid further horrors like those it had just been through. Especially in the first years after the war, many, like the French Catholic thinker Jacques Maritain (1882–1973), held that only a return to religious traditions would suffice. For the American-born British writer T. S. Eliot (1888–1965), the essential return to tradition had to embrace family and locality, as well as religion. Without a return to tradition, Eliot warned, the West could expect more excesses like fascism and totalitarianism in the future.

The Intellectual Migration and Americanism

The extraordinary migration of European artists and intellectuals to the United States to escape persecution during the 1930s and 1940s profoundly affected the cultural life of the postwar period. An array of luminaries arrived on American shores, from the composer Igor Stravinsky to the theoretical physicist Albert Einstein, from the architect Walter Gropius to the radical social theorist Herbert Marcuse.

Before this cross-fertilization, American culture had remained slightly provincial, sometimes proudly and self-consciously so. All the direct contact with the Europeans by the 1940s helped propel the United States into the Western cultural mainstream. No longer could "Western" culture be identified primarily with Europe. In some spheres—painting, for example—Americans were now confident enough to claim the leadership for the first time.

With the abstract expressionism of the later 1940s, American painters began creating visual images the like of which had never been seen in Europe. In comparison with the raw, energetic painting of Jackson Pollock (1912–1956), the work of the Europeans seemed merely "pretty"—and the newly brash Americans were not shy about telling them so. Now New York began to supplant Paris as the art capital of the Western world.

But the American achievement owed something to European existentialism, and it became possible only because so many of the most innovative European painters had come to New York, where the Americans had been able to learn their lessons at first hand. At the same time European painters like Jean Dubuffet (1901–1985) in France and Francis Bacon (1910–1992) in Britain created new forms of their own—sometimes playful, sometimes brutal—as they sought the startling new visual imagery that seemed appropriate to Western culture after the era of fascism and war. Even in the United States, artists began reacting against the deep seriousness of abstract expressionism during the mid-1950s. One new direction led by the early 1960s to "pop art," which was "American" in a different sense, featuring the ordinary objects and mass-produced images of modern consumerist culture. (See the feature, "Weighing the Evidence: Pop Art," on pages 1110–1111.)

Some Europeans were eager to embrace what seemed distinctively American, because America had remained relatively free of the political ideologies that seemed to have led Europe to totalitarianism and ruin. By the 1950s there was much talk of "the end of ideology," with America pointing the way to a healthier alternative, combining technology, value-free social science, and scientific management. Whereas the old European way led either to mere theorizing, to political extremism, or to polarization and impasse, the American approach got results by tackling problems one at a time, so that they could be solved by managerial or technical experts.

Such Americanism fed the notion that Europe needed a clean break based on technological values. If such a break was necessary, however, what was to become of the European tradition, for centuries the center of gravity of the West, and until recently dominant in the world? Did anything

Dubuffet: Spinning Round Seeking to depart from the European tradition of sophisticated, well-made art, Jean Dubuffet developed imagery that was at once crude and primitive, playful and whimsical. *(Dubuffet, Jean,* Spinning Round, *1961. ARS Tate Gallery, London, Great Britain)*

distinctively European remain, or was Europe doomed to lick its wounds in the shadow of America? These questions lurked in the background, but first Europeans faced the difficult task of economic and political restoration.

PROSPERITY, DEMOCRACY, AND THE NEW SOCIAL COMPACT IN WESTERN EUROPE

By 1941 democracy seemed to be dying on the European continent, yet in Western Europe it quickly revived after World War II, taking root more easily than most had thought possible. The bipolar international framework helped. The United States sought actively to encourage democracy, and Europeans nervous about communism and the Soviet Union were happy to follow the American lead. Success at economic reconstruction was important as well. Not only was there greater prosperity, but governments could afford to deliver on promises of enhanced security, social welfare, and equality of opportunity. It also mattered that Western Europeans learned from past mistakes.

From Economic Reconstruction to Economic Miracle

It is hard to imagine how desperate the situation in much of Western Europe had become by 1945. Major cities like Rotterdam, Hamburg, and Le Havre lay largely in ruins, and normal routines suffered radical disruption. Production had declined to perhaps 25 percent of the prewar level in Italy, to 20 percent in France, and to a mere 5 percent in southern Germany. Cigarettes, often gained through barter from American soldiers, served widely as a medium of exchange.

Although the U.S. commitment to help reconstruct Europe was not originally a cold war measure, the developing cold war context made it seem all the more necessary for the United States to help the Europeans get their economies running again as quickly as possible. The key was the Marshall Plan, which U.S. secretary of state General George Marshall outlined in 1947, and which channeled $13.5 billion in aid to Western Europe by 1951. The need to rebuild afforded Europeans a chance to start over, using the most up-to-date methods and technologies. Though rebuilding strategies dif-

fered, the Western European countries made remarkable recoveries.

The new German government cut state aid to business and limited the long-standing power of cartels. The state was permitted to intervene in the economy only to ensure free competition. In France, by contrast, many were determined to use government to modernize the country, thereby overcoming the weakness that had led to defeat. So virtually at once after the war, France adopted a flexible, pragmatic form of government-led economic planning.

In 1946 Jean Monnet (1888–1979) launched the first of the French postwar economic plans, which brought government and business leaders together to agree on production targets. Economic planning enabled France to make especially effec-

Architects of the New Europe Offering decisive leadership in the unsettled postwar world, Jean Monnet (left) spearheaded European economic integration, and Konrad Adenauer (right) guided the new West German democracy. The two greatly admired each other, and the cooperation they fostered between their two countries was crucial to the peace and prosperity in Western Europe after World War II. *(Eclair Mondial/Sipa Press)*

tive use of the capital that the Marshall Plan provided. French industrial production returned to its prewar peak by 1951, and by 1957 it had risen to twice the level of 1938.

Strong and sustained rates of economic growth were achieved throughout much of Western Europe through the mid-1960s. From 1953 to 1964, annual rates of growth averaged 6 percent in Germany, 5.6 percent in Italy, and 4.9 percent in France. Britain, however, lagged considerably, averaging only 2.7 percent growth annually during that same period.

As part of the new postwar consensus, labor was supposed to be brought more fully into economic decision making. Thus, for example, the trade unions participated in the planning process in France. In Germany the co-determination law of 1951 provided for labor participation in management decisions in heavy industry, and labor representatives were given access to company books and full voting memberships on boards of directors. This measure ultimately made little difference in the functioning of the affected firms, but it helped head off any return to trade-union radicalism.

During the first years of rapid economic growth, the labor movement remained fairly passive in Western Europe, even though wages stayed relatively low. After an era of depression, fascist repression, and war, workers were grateful simply to have jobs, free trade unions, and at least the promise of greater prosperity in the future. By the 1960s, however, it seemed time to redeem that promise; labor began demanding—generally with success—to share more fully in the new prosperity. Now, rather abruptly, much of Western Europe assumed the look of a consumer society, with widespread ownership of automobiles, televisions, and other household appliances.

Social Welfare and the Issue of Gender

Western governments began to adopt social welfare measures on a large scale late in the nineteenth century (see page 862), and by the 1940s some degree of governmental responsibility for unemployment insurance, workplace safety, and even old-age pensions was widely accepted. Some Europeans, seeking renewal after the war, found an attractive model in Sweden and Denmark, where the outlines of a welfare state had emerged by the 1930s. Sweden, especially, attracted attention as a "middle way" that avoided the extremes

of both Soviet Marxism, with its coercive statism, and American-style capitalism, with its brash commercialism and selfish individualism.

Sweden's economy remained fundamentally capitalist, based on private ownership; even after World War II, its nationalized, or government-run, sector was not large by European standards. But the system of social insurance in Sweden was the most extensive in Europe, and the government worked actively with business to promote full employment and to steer the economy in directions deemed socially desirable. Moreover, the welfare state came to mean a major role for the Swedish trade unions, which won relatively high wages for workers and even enjoyed a quasi-veto power over legislation.

At the same time, the Swedish government began playing a more active role in spheres of life that had formerly been private, from sexuality to child rearing. Thus, for example, drugstores were required to carry contraceptives beginning in 1946. Sweden was the first country to provide sex education in the public schools—on an optional basis beginning in 1942, then on a compulsory basis in 1955. By 1979 the Swedes were limiting corporal punishment—the right to spank—and prohibiting the sale of war toys. This deprivatization of the family stemmed from a sense, especially pronounced in Sweden, that society is collectively responsible for the well-being of its children.

Although Sweden and the other Scandinavian countries had pioneered the welfare state, Britain's decision to move in the same direction evidenced its widening appeal. Britain had been a major victor in the war and was apparently still a great imperial power. Yet it began constructing a welfare state just after the war, even dumping Winston Churchill in the process.

Churchill's inspired leadership of Britain during the darkest days of the war made him perhaps the most admired Western leader of the twentieth century. But when Britain held its first postwar elections, in July 1945, Churchill's Conservatives suffered a crushing loss to the Labour party, led by Clement Attlee (1883–1967). Even early in the war most Britons came to take it for granted that major socioeconomic changes would follow from victory, and Labour seemed better equipped to deliver on that promise.

Greater collective responsibility for the well-being of all British citizens seemed appropriate

Social Welfare in Sweden
With the state playing a major role, Sweden proved a pioneer in responding to the family and children's issues that became increasingly prominent after World War II. Here children play at a daycare center in Stockholm in 1953. *(Roland Janson/Pressens Bild, Stockholm)*

in light of the shared hardships the war had imposed. Moreover, the successes of government planning and control in response to the wartime emergency suggested that once the war was over, government could assume responsibility for the basic needs of the British people, guaranteeing full employment and providing a national health service. But only after the Labour victory in the 1945 elections did formal legislation begin putting these aspirations into practice, creating the British welfare state.

Although some expected, and others feared, that the result would be a form of socialism, establishing a welfare state did not undermine the capitalist economic system. The Labour government nationalized some key industries, but 80 percent of the British work force remained employed in private firms in 1948. Moreover, even under Labour, the British government did not seek the kind of economic planning role that government was playing in France. Much like the United States, Britain relied on monetary and fiscal policy to coordinate its economy.

The core of the British departure in 1945 was not nationalization but a set of social welfare measures that significantly affected the lives of ordinary people. These included old-age pensions; insurance against unemployment, sickness, and disability; and allowances for pregnancy, child rearing, widowhood, and burial. The heart of the

system was free medical care, to be provided by a National Health Service, created in November 1946 and operating by 1948.

In Britain as elsewhere, gender roles were inevitably at issue as government welfare measures were debated and adopted. Were married women to have access to the welfare system as individual citizens, or as members of a family unit, with special responsibility for child rearing and dependent on their husbands as wage-earning breadwinners? Should government seek to enable women to be both mothers and workers, or should goverment help make it possible for mothers not to have to work outside the home? Women themselves did not always agree on priorities, and there were some instructive differences in accent across national boundaries.

As during the First World War, the percentage of women in the work force had increased significantly during World War II, but in the post–World War II period both women and men showed a more marked tendency to return to the security of traditional domestic patterns. So the war itself did not change gender patterns of work even to the extent that World War I had done. In Britain women made up about 30 percent of the labor force in 1931, 31 percent in 1951. The percentage of women in the U.S. work force increased from 26 to 36 percent during the war years, but by 1947 it had returned to 28 percent. Thus the embrace of welfare measures took place at a time of renewed conservatism in conceptions of gender roles.

British feminists at first welcomed provisions of the British welfare state recognizing the special role of women as mothers. The government was to ease burdens by providing family allowances, to be paid directly to mothers, for more than one child. This seemed a progressive step beyond the long-standing British trade union demand for a "family wage"—a wage high enough to enable the male breadwinner to support a family so that his wife would not have to work. Such a wage was to be paid to all workers, regardless of family status. The new provisions of the British welfare state singled out mothers for benefits and enabled them to stay home with their children. At the same time, however, those provisions reinforced both the traditional assumption that marriage meant economic dependence for women and the actual economic dependence of married British women on their husbands.

In France, which had refused even to grant women the vote after World War I, the very different situation after 1945 stimulated a more innovative response, which eventually made the French approach to gender and family issues a model for others. After the experience of defeat, collaboration, and resistance, the French were determined to pursue both economic dynamism and individual justice. But they also remained concerned with population growth, so they combined incentives to encourage large families with measures to promote equal opportunity and economic independence for women. Thus, as they expanded the role of government after the war, the French tended more than the British to assume that paid employment for women was healthy and desirable. The French did not, however, view work outside the home as incompatible with a special female role in child rearing. They recognized that women had special needs as mothers—even as they also recognized that, in crucial respects, husbands shared the responsibility for parenting. The challenge, then, was to combine equal treatment, including equal employment opportunities, with support for child rearing.

New laws gave French women equal access to civil service jobs and guaranteed equal pay for equal work. In addition, the French welfare system treated women as individual citizens, regardless of marital or economic status. Thus they were equally entitled to pensions, health services, and job-related benefits. Yet the French system also recognized a special motherhood role by providing benefits for women during and after pregnancy. However, there were also family allowances that treated the two parents as equally essential.

Although female participation in the paid labor force declined just after the war, it began rising throughout the West during the 1950s, then accelerated during the 1960s, reaching new highs in the 1970s and 1980s. Thanks partly to the expansion of government, the greatest job growth was in the service sector—in social work, health care, and education, for example—and many of these new jobs went to women. From about 1960 to 1988, the percentage of women aged 25 to 34 in the labor force rose from 38 to 67 in Britain, from 42 to 75 in France, and from 49 to 87 in Germany. These statistics reflected significant changes in women's lives, but even as their choices expanded in some respects, women became more deeply aware of enduring limits to their opportunities. Their awareness served to energize a new feminist movement by the later 1960s (see page 1107). That movement drew intellectual inspiration from *The Second Sex*, a pioneering work published in 1949 by the French existentialist Simone de Beauvoir (1908–1986), who started with the existentialist emphasis on human freedom to show how cultural conventions continued to restrict the range of choices for women. (See the box, "Human Freedom and the Origins of a New Feminism.")

Restoration of Democracy in Germany, France, and Italy

With its turn to a welfare state, Britain was seeking to renew a long-standing democracy after an arduous victory. Much of continental western Europe faced a deeper challenge—to rebuild democracy after defeat and humiliation. With the developing cold war complicating the situation, the outcome of the effort to restore democracy was by no means certain in the late 1940s. Although the division of Germany weakened communism in the new Federal Republic, in France and Italy strong Communist parties had emerged from the wartime resistance and claimed to point the way beyond conventional democracy altogether.

The new Federal Republic of Germany held its first election under the Basic Law in August

Human Freedom and the Origins of a New Feminism

*The renewed feminism that became prominent during the later 1960s took inspiration from **The Second Sex**, a pioneering work by the French existentialist Simone de Beauvoir that was first published in 1949. Even while valuing sexual difference, she showed the scope for opening the full range of human choices to women.*

[T]he nature of things is no more immutably given, once for all, than is historical reality. If woman seems to be the inessential which never becomes the essential, it is because she herself fails to bring about this change. . . .

To decline to be the Other, to refuse to be a party to the deal—this would be for women to renounce all the advantages conferred upon them by their alliance with the superior caste. Man-the-sovereign will provide woman-the-liege with material protection and will undertake the moral justification of her existence; thus she can evade at once both economic risk and the metaphysical risk of a liberty in which ends and aims must be contrived without assistance. Indeed, along with the ethical urge of each individual to affirm his subjective existence, there is also the temptation to forgo liberty and become a thing. . . .

If a caste is kept in a state of inferiority, no doubt it remains inferior; but liberty can break the circle. Let negroes vote, and they become worthy of having the vote; let woman be given responsibilities and she is able to assume them. . . .

. . . [T]here will be some to object that . . . when woman is "the same" as her male, life will lose its salt and spice. . . .

. . . And it is true that the evolution now in progress threatens more than feminine charm alone: in beginning to exist for herself, woman will relinquish the function as double and mediator to which she owes her privileged place in the masculine universe. . . . There is no

denying that feminine dependence, inferiority, woe, give women their special character; assuredly woman's autonomy, if it spares men many troubles, will also deny them many conveniences; assuredly there are certain forms of the sexual adventure which will be lost in the world of tomorrow. But this does not mean that love, happiness, poetry, dream, will be banished from it.

. . . New relations of flesh and sentiment of which we have no conception will arise between the sexes; already, indeed, there have appeared between men and women friendships, rivalries, complicities, comradeships—chaste or sensual—which past centuries could not have conceived. . . .

. . . [T]here will always be certain differences between man and woman; her eroticism, and therefore her sexual world, have a special form of their own and therefore cannot fail to engender a sensuality, a sensitivity, of a special nature. . . .

. . . To emancipate women is to refuse to confine her to the relations she bears to man, not to deny them to her; let her have her independent existence and she will continue none the less to exist for him *also:* mutually recognizing each other as subject, each will yet remain for the other an *other.* . . . [W]hen we abolish the slavery of half of humanity, together with the whole system of hypocrisy that it implies, then the "division" of humanity will reveal its genuine significance and the human couple will find its true form.

Source: Simone de Beauvoir, *The Second Sex* (New York: Random House, Vintage, 1989), pp. xxv, xxvii, 728–731.

1949, launching what proved a successful democracy. Partly to counter the Soviet Union but also to avoid what seemed the disastrous mistake of the harsh peace settlement after World War I, the victors sought to help get Germany back on its feet as quickly as possible. At the same time, German political leaders, determined to avoid the mistakes of the Weimar years, now better understood the need to compromise, to take responsibility for governing the whole nation.

To prevent the instability that had plagued the Weimar Republic, the creators of the new government strengthened the chancellor in relation to the Bundestag, the lower house of parliament. In the same way, the Basic Law helped establish a stable party system by discouraging splinter parties and by allowing the courts to outlaw extremist parties. On that basis, the courts outlawed both the Communist party and a neo-Nazi party during the formative years of the new German democracy.

The new West German republic proved more stable than the earlier Weimar Republic partly because the political party system was now considerably simpler. Two mass parties, the Christian Democratic Union (CDU) and the Social Democratic party (SPD), were immediately predominant, although a third, the much smaller Free Democratic party (FDP), proved important for coalition purposes.

Konrad Adenauer (1876–1967), head of the CDU, the largest party in 1949, immediately emerged as postwar Germany's leading statesman. A Catholic who had been mayor of Cologne under Weimar, he had withdrawn from active politics during the Nazi period, but he re-emerged after the war to lead the council that drafted the Basic Law. As chancellor from 1949 until 1963, he oriented the new German democracy toward Western Europe and the Atlantic bloc, led by the United States.

The new bipolar world confronted West Germany with a cruel choice. By accepting the bipolar framework, the country could become a full partner within the Atlantic bloc. But by trying to straddle the fence instead, it could keep open the possibility that Germany could be reunified as a neutral and disarmed state. The choice was made in the early 1950s when the outbreak of war in Korea intensified the cold war, and the United States pressured West Germany to rearm and join the Western bloc.

Although some West Germans resisted, Adenauer led the Federal Republic into the Atlantic alliance in 1955. This was to accept not only U.S. leadership but also, for the foreseeable future, the division of Germany. Adenauer was eager to anchor the new Federal Republic to the West, partly to buttress the new democracy in West Germany, but also to cement U.S. support for Western Europe in the face of what seemed an ongoing Soviet threat to German security.

By the late 1950s the West German economy was recovering nicely, and the country was a valued member of the Western alliance. Adenauer's CDU seemed so potent that the other major party, the SPD, appeared to be consigned to permanent—and sterile—opposition. Frustrated with its outsider status, the SPD began to shed its Marxist trappings in an effort to widen its appeal. Prominent among those pushing in this direction was Willy Brandt (1913–1992), who became mayor of West Berlin in 1957, and who would become the party's leader in 1963. At its watershed national congress at Bad Godesberg in 1959, the party officially gave up talk of the class struggle and adopted a more moderate program.

Adenauer stepped down in 1963 at the age of 87, after fourteen years as chancellor. The contrast with Weimar, which had known twenty-one different cabinets in a comparable fourteen-year period, could not be more striking. The Adenauer years proved to Germans that liberal democracy could mean stable and effective government, economic prosperity, and foreign policy success. Still, Adenauer had become somewhat authoritarian by his later years, and it was arguable that West Germany had become overly reliant on him and his party.

During the years from 1963 to 1969, the CDU proved it could govern without Adenauer, and the SPD came to seem ever more respectable, even joining as junior partner in a government coalition with the CDU in 1966. Finally, in October 1969, new parliamentary elections brought Brandt to the chancellorship, and the SPD became responsible for governing West Germany for the first time since the war.

Brandt sought to provide a genuine alternative to the CDU without undermining the consensus that had developed around the new regime since 1949. He wanted especially to improve relations between West Germany and the Soviet bloc, but this required a more independent foreign policy than Germany had followed under Adenauer and his successors. Under Adenauer, the Federal Republic had refused to deal with East Germany at all. So for a socialist chancellor seeking to prove his respectability, Brandt's opening to the East, or *Ostpolitik*, was risky, but he pursued it with skill and success.

In treaties with the Soviet Union, Czechoslovakia, and Poland, West Germany accepted the main lines of the postwar settlement. This was to abandon any claim to the former German territory east of the Oder-Neisse line, now in Poland. Brandt also managed to improve relations with East Germany. After the two countries finally agreed to mutual diplomatic recognition, each was admitted to the United Nations in 1973. Brandt's overtures made possible closer economic ties between them, and even broader opportunities for ordinary citizens to interact across the east-west border. His *Ostpolitik* was widely popular and helped deepen the postwar consensus in West Germany.

In France and Italy, unlike West Germany, communists emerged powerful from major roles in wartime resistance movements. Indeed, in either nation they might conceivably have made a bid for power as the war was ending. But Moscow, concerned with the larger picture in Europe, called for the moderate route of participation in coalitions instead, at least partly because the presence of Western troops in these countries gave the leverage to noncommunists. And the United States intervened persistently to minimize the communists' role as new democracies took root in both nations after 1945.

When the first parliamentary elections were held in the new Fourth Republic in France in 1946, the Communists won the largest number of seats, and their support continued to rise until 1949. Partly because of pressure from the United States, however, they were forced out of the coalition government in 1947, and after 1949 their strength began leveling off. During the years that followed, the French Communist party proved particularly inflexible and unimaginative, maintaining strict subservience to the Soviet Union.

As the leader of the overall resistance effort, Charles de Gaulle immediately assumed the dominant political role after the liberation of France in August 1944. But he withdrew, disillusioned, from active politics early in 1946, as political life under the new Fourth Republic seemed to return to the patterns of the old Third Republic. As before, government depended on multiparty coalitions; it required considerable political energy simply to put together a stable majority. The Fourth Republic became something of a laughingstock as governments rose and fell every six months, on the average, over its twelve-year life. Still, governmental decision making changed significantly as the nonpolitical, technocratic side of the French state

The Return of de Gaulle Disillusioned with the political squabbles of the early Fourth Republic, General Charles de Gaulle retired from public life in 1946. But he believed his country would need his leadership again. He returned to power in 1958, with France in turmoil over the Algerian War, and spearheaded the creation of the Fifth Republic. *(Keystone/Sygma)*

gained power in areas such as economic planning. And government technocrats survived the fall of the Fourth Republic in 1958, when de Gaulle returned to politics at a moment of crisis, stemming from France's war to maintain control of Algeria (see page 1089).

Although de Gaulle became prime minister within the Fourth Republic, it was clear that his return signified a change of regime. The French legislature promptly gave his government full powers for six months, including a charge to draft a new constitution, which was then approved by referendum in the fall of 1958. The result was the new Fifth Republic, which featured a stronger executive—and soon a president elected directly by the people and not dependent on the Chamber of

Deputies. It was only in 1958, with the return of de Gaulle and the advent of the Fifth Republic, that government in postwar France began to assume definitive contours.

Italy's political challenge, after more than twenty years of fascism, was even more dramatic than France's. Shortly after the war, the Italians adopted a new democratic constitution and voted to end the monarchy, thereby making modern Italy a republic for the first time. But much depended on the balance of political forces, which quickly crystallized around the Christian Democratic party (DC), oriented toward the Catholic church, and the Communist and Socialist parties. The international context favored the Christian Democrats, who assumed the dominant political role. As the cold war developed, the United States intervened as necessary to support the Christian Democrats as the chief bulwark against the Communists. Many Italian moderates with little attachment to the church supported the DC for the same reason.

Well into the 1970s, the Christian Democrats' share of the vote remained relatively stable at around 40 percent in national parliamentary elections. The DC was invariably the largest single party, yet not a majority, so it was forced to work in coalition with smaller parties. Beginning in the early 1960s, with the much-trumpeted "opening to the left," this could even include the Socialist party (PSI), which typically won 10 to 15 percent of the vote in national elections. This total fell far behind that of the Communist party, which for decades remained the second largest at 25 to 35 percent. The relative strength of the political parties established the framework for the curious combination of surface instability and deeper stability—or immobility—that came to characterize the new Italian democracy. Domination by the Christian Democrats was the fundamental fact of Italian political life until the early 1990s.

Unlike their counterparts in France, the Italian Communists did not settle for a role of opposition and protest. Taking their cue from Gramsci's writings, they sought to make their presence felt in as many areas of Italian life as possible in order gradually to establish their legitimacy. And they had considerable success as they organized profit-making cooperatives for sharecroppers, won local and regional elections, and garnered the support of intellectuals, journalists, and publishers. At one

time or another, they ran many of Italy's local and regional governments, often for years at a time, and they generally did well at it. Heavily communist Bologna, for example, was one of the best-governed cities in Europe.

But as the years after World War II turned to decades, the Italian Communists' successes raised awkward questions. What were the Communists trying to accomplish on the national level, and how long was it supposed to take? Could a communist party function as a governing party within a democratic political system? Because the Italian Communists, unlike the German Social Democrats, never established their credibility as a national governing party, the Christian Democrats grew ever more entrenched, becoming increasingly arrogant and corrupt.

WESTERN EUROPE AND THE WORLD

By the early 1950s, the old Europe seemed dwarfed by the two global superpowers and, for the foreseeable future, divided by the conflict between them. The colonial networks that had symbolized European predominance unraveled rapidly at the same time. One obvious response was some form of European unity. A unified Europe might eventually have the clout to stand as a global superpower in its own right. Although the first steps toward European unity did not go so far as visionaries had hoped, they established lasting foundations by the late 1950s—and they served European prosperity and security well.

NATO and the Atlantic Orientation

As the Soviets tightened their grip on the satellite states of east-central Europe, fears of Soviet expansion into western Europe led to the creation of the North Atlantic Treaty Organization (NATO) under U.S. leadership in April 1949. In pooling the forces of its member countries under a unified command, NATO went beyond the usual peacetime military alliance. This Atlantic bloc assumed definitive shape only in 1955, when it encompassed the newly rearmed West Germany (see Map 29.2). The prospect of German rearmament made the French nervous at first, but by 1954 they had come to agree that the best course for French security was to integrate the western part of a divided Germany into the U.S.-led Western bloc.

NATO was intended specifically to prevent any Soviet expansion in Europe. Yet the Soviets had considerable superiority in conventional forces, which had ready access to western Europe. As a balance, the United States offered its nuclear superiority; indeed, the American nuclear guarantee was the cornerstone of the NATO alliance. Thus it seemed crucial for the United States to maintain its superiority in nuclear weapons, a fact that helped fuel the continuing arms race and nuclear buildup.

However, as the Soviet Union developed the capacity for a nuclear strike at the United States, Europeans began asking whether the Americans could be counted on to respond with nuclear weapons to a conventional Soviet attack on western Europe. The Americans might hesitate, now that the United States was vulnerable to Soviet nuclear retaliation. Did it make sense, then, for western Europeans to rely on the United States as the ultimate guarantor of their defense? Such doubts became especially widespread in France, where President de Gaulle, citing concerns for French sovereignty and security, accelerated the development of a French nuclear force during the 1960s.

The Varieties of Decolonization

The advent of a new world configuration, with a circumscribed place for Europe, found dramatic expression in the rapid disintegration of the European colonial empires after World War II (Map 29.1). The process of decolonization was varied and uneven, partly because the local independence movements differed but also because the interests of Europeans varied. Where there were large numbers of European settlers or their descendants, the remaining colonial powers—Britain, France, Belgium, the Netherlands, and Portugal—were reluctant to yield to independence forces. But everywhere they were more likely to yield if they could negotiate their withdrawal with local moderates, thereby preserving

Ban the Bomb As nuclear tension escalated during the 1950s, some built air-raid shelters; others took to the streets in antinuclear protest. The protest movement was especially prominent in Britain, where the noted philosopher Bertrand Russell (1872–1970) played a central role. Here, seated at right, he awaits arrest during a sit-in demonstration outside the British Defense Ministry. *(Hulton-Getty/Tony Stone Images)*

Date is year independence was achieved.
Shading indicates former ruler.

Great Britain
France
Netherlands
Italy
Belgium
Portugal
United States

property rights and the possibility of continued influence.

The Second World War proved a major catalyst for anticolonialist independence movements throughout the world. In southeast Asia and the Pacific, quick Japanese conquests revealed the vulnerability of France, the Netherlands, and Britain. And it was not colonial reconquest that marked the end of the war, but the atomic bomb and the victory of the United States, which took a dim view of conventional European colonialism.

The effort of the Netherlands to regain control of the Dutch East Indies led to four years of military struggle against the Indonesian nationalist insurgency. Although most independent observers felt they could not win, the Dutch were reluctant to relinquish control of the East Indies, which had been in Dutch hands since the seventeenth century. Especially after the humiliations of defeat and occupation during World War II, the Dutch took pride in their imperial role. The struggle lasted from 1945 to 1949, when the Dutch finally had to yield as their former colony became independent Indonesia.

Unlike the Netherlands, Britain was still a great power in the twentieth century, and its empire had seemed essential to its stature. Although India, the crown jewel of the empire, had won full independence in 1947, many Britons still envisioned extending Commonwealth status to the former British colonies as a way of retaining economic ties and political influence. But the Commonwealth idea proved to have little appeal for Britain's former colonies; the British Commonwealth became little more than a voluntary cooperative association. Despite illusions and hesitations, however, Britain proved the most realistic of the European colonial powers, grasping the need to compromise and work with emerging national leaders.

Nevertheless, even Britain decided to resist in 1956, when it provoked an international crisis over the status of the Suez Canal in Egypt (see Map 28.1 on page 1036). Once a British protectorate, Egypt had remained under heavy British

influence even after nominally becoming sovereign in 1922. But a revolution in 1952 produced a new government of Arab nationalists, led by the able and charismatic Colonel Gamel Abdul Nasser (1918–1970). In 1954 Britain agreed with Egypt to leave the Suez Canal zone within twenty months, though the zone was to be international, not Egyptian, and Britain was to retain special rights there in the event of war. In 1956, however, Nasser announced the nationalization of the canal, partly so that Egypt could use its revenues to finance public works projects.

Led by the Conservative Anthony Eden (1897–1977), Britain decided on a showdown. Eden won the support of Israel and France, each of which had reason to fear the pan-Arab nationalism that Nasser's Egypt was now spearheading. Israel had remained at odds with its Arab neighbors since its founding in 1948, and Nasser was helping the Arabs who were beginning to take up arms against French rule in Algeria.

Late in 1956 Britain, Israel, and France orchestrated a surprise attack on Egypt. After the Israelis invaded, the British and French bombed military targets, then landed troops to take the canal. But the troops met stubborn Egyptian resistance, and the British and French encountered decisive defeat in the diplomatic maneuvering that accompanied the outbreak of fighting. Both the United States and the Soviet Union opposed the Anglo-French-Israeli move, as did world opinion. The old European powers had sought to act on their own, by the old rules, but the outcome of the Suez crisis demonstrated how limited the reach of the Western European states had become. Moreover, nations like Egypt, formerly subservient to Europeans, could be a factor in their own right within the new bipolar framework.

Still, the outcome in 1956 did not convince France to abandon its struggle to retain Algeria. And that struggle proved the most dramatic, wrenching experience that any European country was to have with decolonization. For the French the process started not in North Africa but in Indochina, in southeast Asia, during World War II.

Led by the communist Ho Chi Minh (1890–1969), the Indochinese anticolonialist movement gained strength resisting the Japanese during the war and then, before the French could return, established a political base in northern Vietnam in 1945. Although the French re-established control

Map 29.1 From Colonialism to Independence During a thirty-five-year period after World War II, the European empires in Africa, Asia, and the Pacific gradually came apart as the former colonies became independent nations.

in the south, negotiations between the French and the Vietnamese nationalists seemed at first to be moving toward some form of self-government for Vietnam. However, there was considerable opposition in France, especially within the army, to giving in to the Vietnamese independence movement. In 1946 French authorities in Indochina deliberately provoked an incident to undercut negotiations and start hostilities. Eight years of difficult guerrilla war followed, creating a major drain on the French economy.

With its strongly anticolonialist posture, the United States was unsympathetic to the French cause at first. But the communist takeover in China in 1949 and the outbreak of war in Korea in 1950 made the French struggle in Indochina seem a battle in a larger war against communism in Asia. By 1954 the United States was covering 75 percent of the cost of the French effort in Indochina. Nonetheless, when the fall of the fortified area at Dien Bien Phu in May 1954 signaled a decisive French defeat, the United States decided to pull back and accept a negotiated settlement. Partly at the urging of its European allies, the United States had concluded that the Soviet threat in Europe must remain its principal concern.

France worked out the terms of independence for Vietnam in 1955. The solution, however, entailed north-south partition to separate the communist and anticommunist forces, pending elections to unify the country. The anticommunist regime the United States sponsored in the south resisted holding the elections, so the country remained divided (see Map 29.1). Only in 1975, after a brutal war with the United States, would the communist heirs of those who had led the fight against the French assume the leadership of a unified Vietnam.

In France, the defeat in Indochina left a legacy of bitterness, especially among army officers, many of whom felt that French forces could have won had they not been undercut by politicians at home. When the outcome in Indochina emboldened Arab nationalists in North Africa to take up arms against the French colonial power, the French army was anxious for a second chance— and the French government was willing to give it to them. The French agreed to independence for Tunisia and Morocco by 1956, but only so that they could concentrate their military forces in Algeria, where the stakes seemed high enough for a

showdown. Algeria had been under French control since 1830, and it had a substantial minority of ethnic Europeans, totaling over a million, or 10 percent of the population.

Although France gradually committed 500,000 troops to Algeria, the war bogged down into what threatened to become a lengthy stalemate, with increasing brutality on both sides. As it drained French lives and resources, the war became a highly volatile political issue in France. The situation came to a head during the spring of 1958 when the advent of a new ministry, rumored to favor a compromise settlement, led to violent demonstrations, engineered by the sectors of the French army in Algeria. Military intervention in France itself seemed likely to follow—and with it the danger of civil war.

It was at this moment of genuine emergency that Charles de Gaulle returned to lead the change to the Fifth Republic. Those determined to hold Algeria welcomed de Gaulle as their savior. But de Gaulle fooled them, working out a compromise with the nationalist rebels that ended the war and made Algeria independent in 1962. No doubt only de Gaulle could have engineered this outcome without provoking still deeper political division in France.

The anticolonial movement in Algeria gave rise to a more radical new political order than had been the case in Tunisia and Morocco. The new Algerian government's policy of expropriation and nationalization led most of the French settlers to relocate to France.

All over Europe, the colonialist impulse, which had still been significant immediately after World War II, waned noticeably by the end of the 1950s. The economic successes of Germany and Italy, both free of colonialist expenses, suggested to other Europeans that they would be better off without colonies, particularly if maintaining them required a heavy military burden.

But there remained resistance, and considerable variation, as the colonies of sub-Saharan Africa moved toward independence in the decades following World War II. Outcomes depended on the number and intransigence of white settlers, on the extent to which local elites had emerged, and on the confidence of the Europeans that they could retain their influence if they agreed to independence. Of the major imperial powers in the region, Britain had done best at preparing local leaders and proved the most willing to work with indigenous elites. The two smaller countries, Belgium and Portugal, were less certain they could maintain their influence, and they proved the most reluctant to give up their imperial status.

The transition was smoothest in British West Africa, where the Gold Coast achieved independence as Ghana, first as a Commonwealth dominion in 1957, then as a fully independent republic in 1960. There were few British settlers in that part of Africa, and the small, relatively cohesive African elite favored a moderate transition, not revolution. Where British settlers were relatively numerous, however, as in Kenya or Rhodesia, the transition to independence proved much more difficult. The very presence of Europeans had impeded the development of cohesive local elites, so movements for independence in those areas tended to become more radical, threatening the expropriation of European-held property.

The British had to use 50,000 troops and police to put down a major rebellion in Kenya from 1951 to 1956. This episode helped convince the British that the cost of maintaining colonial rule was simply too high, and they gradually developed a compromise that led to independence for Kenya in 1963. In Southern Rhodesia, however, unyielding European settlers resisted the British government's effort to promote a comparable compromise. A white supremacist government declared its independence from Britain in 1965, fueling a guerrilla war. The Africans won independence as Zimbabwe only in 1980.

Nowhere was decolonization messier than in the two largest Portuguese colonies in Africa, Mozambique and Angola. Portugal had run the most repressive of the African colonial regimes, with elements of the earlier system of forced labor lingering into the 1960s. Portuguese intransigence radicalized the independence movement, which took advantage of help from the communist world to resist the colonizers militarily. Finally, by 1974, sectors of the Portuguese military, weary of a colonial war they lacked the resources to win, engineered a political coup at home. The new government promptly washed its hands of the debilitating colonialist struggle, granting independence to both Mozambique and Angola in 1975. In each of the new countries, communist-supported radicals had won the upper hand within divided anticolonialist movements, but the struggles themselves, and the

DECOLONIZATION	
1919	League of Nations mandate system
	Amritsar massacre in India
	Anti-British insurrection in Egypt
1921	Mohandas Gandhi adopts native Indian attire
1922	British grant formal independence to Egypt
1941	Japanese establish control in French Indochina
1947	India achieves independence from Britain
1949	Indonesia wins independence from the Netherlands
1954	Defeat of France in Vietnam
1955	Bandung conference of non-Western countries in Indonesia
1956	Peace terms in Vietnam yield north-south partition
	Suez crisis; defeat for Britain and France in Egypt
1957	Establishment of independent Ghana (from Gold Coast and British Togoland)
1962	Algerian War results in Algerian independence from France
1965	White supremacist government declares independence of Southern Rhodesia from Britain
1975	Independence of Mozambique and Angola from Portugal
	North Vietnamese defeat of South Vietnam and the United States leads to reunification of Vietnam
1980	End of guerrilla war in Southern Rhodesia; independence of Zimbabwe

sudden departure of the Portuguese, left considerable socioeconomic disarray.

The process of decolonization led to a remarkable transformation in the thirty-five years after World War II. Forms of colonial rule that had been taken for granted before World War I stood discredited, virtually without defenders, by the late twentieth century. But decolonization hardly offered a neat and definitive solution. In formerly

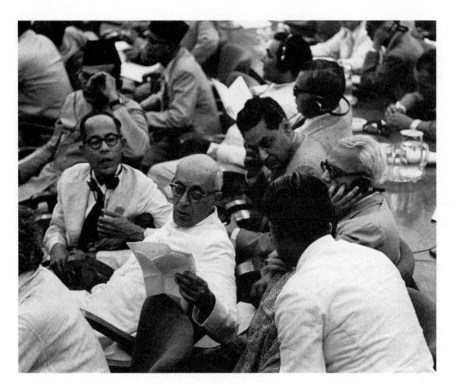

Nonalignment in a Bipolar World At a major conference of Asian and African leaders at Bandung, Indonesia, in 1955, India's Jawaharlal Nehru (center) advocated "nonalignment" for the nations outside the immediate orbits of the United States and the Soviet Union. Although its results were inconclusive, the Bandung conference marked a new level of awareness among Asians and Africans that their nations—many of them new—could work together to play a major role in world affairs. *(Wide World Photos)*

colonial territories, new political boundaries often stemmed from the way Europeans had carved things up, rather than from indigenous ethnic or national patterns. Moreover, questions remained about the longer-term economic relationships between the Europeans and their former colonies.

The leader of Ghana, Kwame Nkrumah (1909–1972), used the term *neocolonialism* to suggest that more subtle forms of Western exploitation had replaced direct colonial rule. But attempts by the former colonies to do without economic ties to the West often proved counterproductive, and in some areas reasonably good relations, compatible with Western economic interests, eventually developed. Generally, postcolonial leaders were highly ambivalent toward the West, where many of them had been educated. Nkrumah, for example, had studied in the United States and England during the 1930s and 1940s, and India's Jawaharlal Nehru had attended some of the best schools in England. These leaders understood the need to learn from the West, but at the same time they claimed their countries could "modernize" without losing the traditions that made them different from the West—and in some ways superior.

At the same time, the context of superpower rivalry afforded new challenges and opportunities

for the postcolonial world. In April 1955 the leaders of twenty-nine Asian and African nations met at Bandung, Indonesia, in a conference that proved a watershed in the self-understanding of what was coming to be called the "Third World." The most influential, like Nehru, Nasser, and Indonesia's Achmed Sukarno (1901–1970), were charismatic nation-builders, at once anti-Western and Westernizing, who understood the scope for postcolonial countries to play major roles in global politics. Along with Tito of Yugoslavia, Nehru was the leading proponent of "nonalignment," of navigating an independent course between the Western and the Soviet blocs. And whether or not their countries were formally nonaligned, Third World leaders often found ways of exploiting the superpower rivalry to their own advantage.

The reaction against Eurocentrism that accompanied the turn from colonialism was not confined to those who had been subjected to European imperialism. It contributed to the vogue of "structuralism," as developed in anthropology by Claude Lévi-Strauss (b. 1908) in such works as *Tristes Tropiques* (1955). While raising deep questions about any notion of Western superiority, Lévi-Strauss also expressed a certain nostalgia for a world untouched by Western influence. There

~ **ENCOUNTERS WITH THE WEST** ~

The Legacy of European Colonialism

In the following passage from **The Wretched of the Earth** *(1961), Frantz Fanon probes the negative consequences of colonialism—for both colonizers and colonized—and tries to show why a radical, even violent break from colonialism was necessary.*

The violence which has ruled over the ordering of the colonial world, which has ceaselessly drummed the rhythm for the destruction of native social forms and broken up without reserve the systems of reference of the economy, the customs of dress and external life, that same violence will be claimed and taken over by the native at the moment when, deciding to embody history in his own person, he surges into the forbidden quarters. . . .

. . . In the colonial context the settler only ends his work of breaking in the native when the latter admits loudly and intelligibly the supremacy of the white man's values. In the period of decolonization, the colonized masses mock at these very values, insult them, and vomit them up.

. . . All that the native has seen in his country is that they can freely arrest him, beat him, starve him: and no professor of ethics, no priest has ever come to be beaten in his place, nor to share their bread with him. As far as the native is concerned, morality is very concrete; it is to silence the settler's defiance, to break his flaunting violence—in a word, to put him out of the picture. . . .

. . . The colonialist bourgeoisie, in its narcissistic dialogue, expounded by the members of its universities, had in fact deeply implanted in the minds of the colonized intellectual that the essential qualities remain eternal in spite of all the blunders men may make: the essential

qualities of the West, of course. . . . Now it so happens that during the struggle for liberation, at the moment that the native intellectual comes into touch again with his people, . . . [a]ll the Mediterranean values—the triumph of the human individual, of clarity, and of beauty— . . . are revealed as worthless, simply because they have nothing to do with the concrete conflict in which the people is engaged.

Individualism is the first to disappear. . . . The colonialist bourgeoisie had hammered into the native's mind the idea of a society of individuals where each person shuts himself up in his own subjectivity, and whose only wealth is individual thought. Now the native who has the opportunity to return to the people during the struggle for freedom will discover the falseness of this theory. The very forms of organization of the struggle will suggest to him a different vocabulary. Brother, sister, friend— these are words outlawed by the colonialist bourgeoisie, because for them my brother is my purse, my friend is part of my scheme for getting on. The native intellectual . . . will . . . discover the substance of village assemblies, the cohesion of people's committees, and the extraordinary fruitfulness of local meetings and groupments. Henceforward, the interests of one will be the interests of all, for in concrete fact *everyone* will be discovered by the troops, *everyone* will be massacred—or *everyone* will be saved.

Source: Frantz Fanon, *The Wretched of the Earth* (New York: Grove, 1968), pp. 40–47.

was also much interest among westerners in the work of Frantz Fanon (1925–1961), a black intellectual from Martinique who became identified especially with the cause of the Algerian rebels. In *The Wretched of the Earth* (1961), Fanon found the West

spiritually exhausted and called on the peoples of the non-Western world to go their own way, based on their own values and traditions. (See the box, "Encounters with the West: The Legacy of European Colonialism.")

Economic Integration and the Coming of the European Union

As the old colonialism increasingly fell into disrepute, many found in European unity the best prospect for the future. Although hopes for full-scale political unity were soon frustrated, the movement for European integration gradually achieved significant fruit in the economic sphere, especially through the European Economic Community (EEC), or Common Market, established in 1957.

The impetus for economic integration came especially from a new breed of "Eurocrats"—technocrats with a supranational, or pan-European, outlook. Two remarkable French leaders, Jean Monnet and Robert Schuman (1886–1963), set the pattern. Schuman came from Lorraine, which had passed between France and Germany four times between 1870 and 1945. After serving as a German officer in World War I, he was elected to the French Chamber of Deputies in 1919 as Lorraine was returned to France. Monnet, by contrast, served as an official of the League of Nations while a young man just after World War I. He quickly became convinced that the League was too much a collection of existing, unequal nations; peace and cooperation required stronger rules and institutions to transcend parochial national interests.

As French foreign minister after World War II, Schuman was responsible for a 1950 plan to coordinate French and German production of coal and steel. The Schuman Plan quickly encompassed Italy and the Benelux countries to become the European Coal and Steel Community (ECSC) in 1951. Monnet served as the ECSC's first president. From this position, he pushed for more thoroughgoing economic integration, and the successes of the ECSC led directly to the Common Market. (See the box, "Practical Thinking and European Integration.")

The quest for European integration was boosted by the 1956 Suez crisis, which dramatized Europe's dependence on Middle Eastern oil. In light of this long-term vulnerability, economic cooperation seemed essential to the very survival of Europe. It helped, too, that in 1957 the Soviet Union launched *Sputnik I,* the first artificial satellite, suggesting that unless the nations of Western Europe could work together, they were in danger of falling ever further behind the superpowers in advanced technology.

In March 1957, leaders of France, Germany, Italy, Belgium, the Netherlands, and Luxembourg signed the Treaty of Rome, establishing the Common Market, or EEC. Subsequently ratified by the parliaments of the member nations, the treaty took effect on January 1, 1958. Over the next four decades the EEC's membership gradually expanded, encompassing Denmark, Ireland, and Britain in 1973, Greece in 1981, Spain and Portugal in 1986, and Austria, Finland, and Sweden in 1995 (Map 29.2).

The immediate aim of the EEC was to facilitate trade by eliminating customs duties within the Common Market and establishing a common tariff on imports from the rest of the world. For each member of the EEC, tariff reduction entailed the advantage of access to wider markets abroad, but also the risks of new competition in its own domestic market. So it was hard to be sure who might gain and who might lose from the move toward a common market. However, the EEC proved advantageous to so many that tariff reduction proceeded well ahead of schedule. By 1968 the last internal tariffs had been eliminated.

With tariffs dropping, trade among the member countries nearly doubled between 1958 and 1962. French exports of automobiles and chemicals to Germany increased more than eightfold. Partly because the increasing competition stimulated initiative and productivity, industrial production within the EEC increased at a robust annual rate of 7.6 percent during those years.

After the merger of the governing institutions of the several European supranational organizations in 1967, the term *European Community* (EC) and later *European Union* (EU) came to replace the "Common Market" to indicate the institutional web that had emerged since the launching of the European Coal and Steel Community in 1951. This broadening of the EEC did not, however, occur without vigorous debate.

The goal of the Common Market—to enable goods, capital, and labor to move freely among the member countries—required some coordination of the social and economic policies of the member states. Thus state sovereignty became an important issue. To what extent was the Common Market to be a new whole, greater than the sum of

Practical Thinking and European Integration

Jean Monnet insisted that European unity would grow not from idealistic pronouncements but from technical solutions to specific problems, taken one at a time. In the following passages from his memoirs, he outlines the thinking that led him to help create the European Coal and Steel Community, which proved a springboard for the Common Market and, eventually, the European Union.

In places like London, New York, and Washington, where the big decisions are made, my first talks have always been with people who cannot afford to make mistakes—bankers, industrialists, lawyers, and newspapermen. What others say may be colored by imagination, ambition, or doctrine. I certainly respect their influence, but I base my judgement on the wisdom of practical men. . . .

By the end of 1949 . . . French production could look forward to a more settled future: but other problems would soon arise out of the very achievements that [the new French planning authority] had helped to make possible. It was at that time, I well remember, that I came to realize the limits of what any one nation could do. The French could not become modern or great by themselves. . . .

Looking back on this mid-century period, one can hardly fail to be struck by the extraordinary ferment in men's minds about the idea of European unity. . . . [I]ndeed, the vocabulary and arguments still used on the subject today were already current then. But they had nothing to do with action . . . , and I found it hard to take much interest. . . .

. . . Experience had taught me that one cannot act in general terms, starting from a vague concept, but that anything becomes possible as soon as one can concentrate on one precise point which leads on to everything else. . . . Unity would gradually be created by the momentum of a first achievement. Our efforts must therefore be concentrated on the very point about which disagreements had come to a head. . . .

If only the French could lose their fear of German industrial domination, then the greatest obstacle to a united Europe would be removed. A solution which would put French industry on the same footing as German industry, while freeing the latter from the discrimination born of defeat—that would restore the economic and political preconditions for the mutual understanding so vital to Europe as a whole. It could, in fact, become the germ of European unity. . . .

The joint resources of France and Germany lay essentially in their coal and steel, distributed unevenly but in complementary fashion over a triangular area artificially divided by historical frontiers. . . . Coal and steel were at once the key to economic power and the raw materials for forging weapons of war. This double role gave them immense symbolic significance. . . . To pool them across frontiers would reduce their malign prestige and turn them instead into a guarantee of peace.

Source: Jean Monnet, *Memoirs* (Garden City, N.Y.: Doubleday, 1978), pp. 271, 277, 282–283, 286, 292–293.

its parts, as opposed to a mere federation of existing states?

In the mid-1960s President de Gaulle of France forced some of the underlying uncertainties about the Common Market to the fore. Though he had willingly turned from the old colonialism, de Gaulle was not prepared to compromise French sovereignty, and he was not persuaded that supranational integration offered the best course for postwar Europe. With the end of the Algerian War in 1962, de Gaulle's France began playing an assertively independent role in international affairs. Thus, for example, de Gaulle developed an independent French nuclear force,

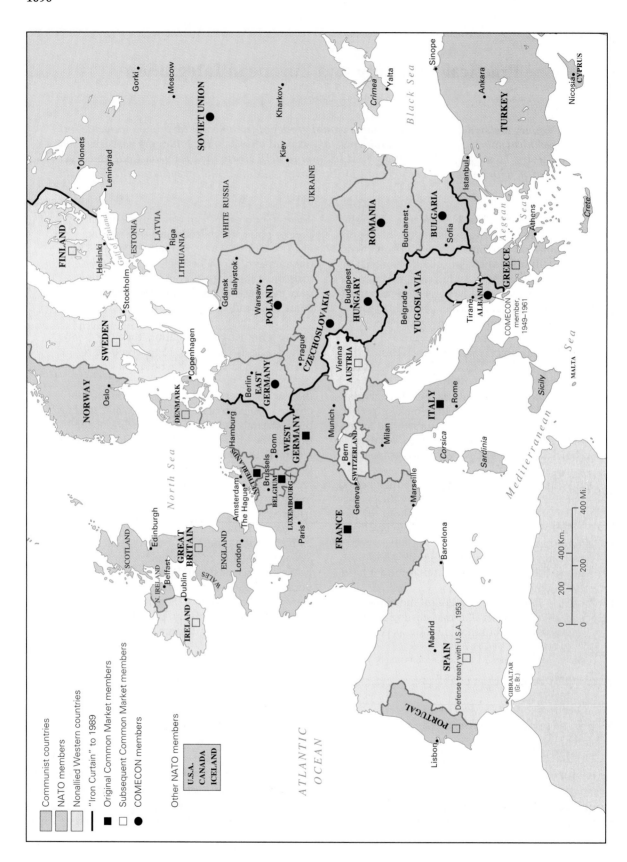

Communist countries

NATO members

Nonallied Western countries

"Iron Curtain" to 1989

■ Original Common Market members

□ Subsequent Common Market members

● COMECON members

Other NATO members

U.S.A.
CANADA
ICELAND

SOVIET UNION

Moscow

Gorki

Olonets

Leningrad

FINLAND

Helsinki

Gulf of Finland

ESTONIA

LATVIA

Riga

LITHUANIA

WHITE RUSSIA

Kiev

Kharkov

UKRAINE

Crimea

Yalta

Black Sea

Sinope

Ankara

TURKEY

Nicosia

CYPRUS

Istanbul

BULGARIA

Sofia

ROMANIA

Bucharest

Aegean Sea

GREECE

Athens

Crete

COMECON
member,
1949–1961

Tiranë
ALBANIA

Belgrade

YUGOSLAVIA

Budapest

HUNGARY

Vienna

AUSTRIA

Prague

CZECHOSLOVAKIA

Warsaw

POLAND

Gdansk

Bialystok

Stockholm

Copenhagen

SWEDEN

NORWAY

Oslo

DENMARK

Berlin

EAST
GERMANY

Hamburg

Munich

Bonn

WEST
GERMANY

Bern

SWITZERLAND

Milan

ITALY

Rome

Corsica

Sardinia

Sicily

MALTA

Mediterranean Sea

Marseille

Geneva

LUXEMBOURG

Paris

FRANCE

Brussels

BELGIUM

NETHERLANDS

Amsterdam

The Hague

North Sea

London

ENGLAND

WALES

GREAT
BRITAIN

Edinburgh

SCOTLAND

Belfast

N. IRELAND

Dublin

IRELAND

ATLANTIC
OCEAN

Barcelona

Madrid

SPAIN

Defense treaty with U.S.A. 1953

GIBRALTAR
(Gr. Br.)

PORTUGAL

Lisbon

400 Mi.

400 Km.

200

200

0

0

curtailed the French role in NATO, and recognized the communist People's Republic of China.

This determination to assert France's sovereignty inevitably led to friction between de Gaulle and the supranational Eurocrats of the Common Market. Matters came to a head in 1965, when a confrontation developed over agricultural policy. The immediate result was a compromise, but de Gaulle's tough stance served to check the increasing supranationalism evident in the Common Market until then. As the economic context became more difficult during the 1970s, it became still harder to maintain the cohesion of the EEC. So though the Common Market proved an important departure, it did not overcome the older forms of national sovereignty or give Western Europe a new world role during the first decades after World War II.

THE SOVIET UNION AND THE COMMUNIST BLOC

By the late 1950s, there were increasing concerns in the West that the Soviet Union, though rigid and inhumane in important respects, might have significant advantages in the race with the capitalist democracies. While still making jokes about goods "made in Japan," Westerners worried about producing enough scientists and engineers to match the Soviets. With the Great Depression still in memory, some economists held that central planning might prove as efficient as capitalism.

Nonetheless, flaws in the political and economic system that had emerged under Stalin continued in the Soviet Union, and its system of satellites in east-central Europe presented new dilemmas. Efforts to make the Soviet system more flexible after Stalin's death in 1953 proved sporadic at best, and the Soviet suppression of the reform movement in Czechoslovakia during the "Prague Spring" of 1968 confirmed the rigidity of the Soviet system.

Dilemmas of the Soviet System in Postwar Europe

The Soviet Union had suffered enormously in leading the victory over Nazi Germany. Especially in the more developed western part of the country, thousands of factories and even whole towns lay destroyed, and there were severe shortages of everything from labor to housing. Yet the developing cold war seemed to require that military spending remain high.

At the same time, the Soviet Union faced the challenge of solidifying the new system of satellite states it had put together in east-central Europe. Most of the region had no desirable interwar past to try to reclaim, and thus there was widespread sentiment for significant change, including nationalization of industry. Even in Czechoslovakia, which had been the most prosperous and democratic state in the region, considerable nationalization was completed *before* the communist takeover in 1948. And whatever integration into the new Soviet bloc might mean politically, it was not clear in the late 1940s that it had to be economically disadvantageous over the long term. The Soviet system seemed to have proven itself in standing up to the Nazis, and many believed that a socialist economic system could be made to work. So a measure of idealism and enthusiasm surrounded postwar reconstruction even in the satellite states of east-central Europe.

Partly in response to U.S. initiatives in Western Europe, the Soviets sought to mold the new communist states into a secure, coordinated bloc of allies. In the economic sphere, the Soviets founded a new organization, COMECON, as part of their effort to lead the economies of the satellite states away from their earlier ties to the West and toward the Soviet Union (see Map 29.2). Thus, for example, whereas only 7 percent of Poland's foreign trade had been with the Soviet Union before the war, by 1951 the figure was 58 percent. Through such mechanisms as artificial pricing of imports and exports, these new economic relationships often entailed outright exploitation of the satellite states for the benefit of the Soviet Union.

Map 29.2 Military Alliances and Multinational Economic Groupings in the Era of the Cold War The cold war split was reflected especially in the two military alliances: NATO, formed in 1949, and the Warsaw Pact, formed in 1955. Each side also had its own multinational economic organization, but the membership of the EEC, or Common Market, was not identical to that of NATO. Although communist, Yugoslavia remained outside Soviet-led organizations, as did Albania for part of the period.

In the military-diplomatic sphere, the Soviets countered NATO in 1955 by bringing the Soviet bloc countries together in a formal alliance, the Warsaw Pact, which provided for a joint military command and mutual military assistance. The Warsaw Pact established a new basis for the continuing presence of Soviet troops in the satellite states, but the tensions within the Soviet-dominated system in east-central Europe soon raised questions about what the pact meant.

From the start, Yugoslavia had been a point of vulnerability for the Soviet system. Communist-led partisans under Tito had liberated Yugoslavia from the Axis on their own, and they had not needed the Red Army to begin constructing a new communist regime. Tito was willing to work with the Soviets, but because he had his own legitimacy, he could be considerably more independent than those elsewhere whose power rested on Soviet support. Thus the Soviets deemed it essential to bring Tito to heel, lest his example encourage too much independence in the other communist states. When Soviet demands, including control of the Yugoslav police and army, became intolerably meddlesome from the Yugoslav point of view, Tito broke with the Soviet Union altogether in 1948. Yugoslavia then began developing a more flexible socialist economic system, with greater scope for local initiatives. Soviet leaders worried that others, too, might seek their own directions, causing the Soviet satellite system to fall apart.

Stalin's initial response to Tito's defection in 1948 was a crackdown on potential opponents throughout the Soviet bloc. In the Soviet Union itself, a major target was the army, which enjoyed great prestige after its victory in World War II. Its top commander, Marshal Georgi Zhukov, was reassigned from Berlin to an obscure post. As during the 1930s, Stalin relied especially on the secret police, which executed those suspected of deviation, inspiring fear even among those closest to him.

As arrest and execution of communist leaders continued in the satellite states, opposition strikes and demonstrations developed as well, finally reaching a crisis point in East Germany in 1953. The East German communist leader, Walter Ulbricht (1893–1973), was worried that the cold war maneuvering of the two superpowers might undermine his regime. As the United States pressed West Germany to rearm and join NATO, some Soviet leaders concluded that Soviet interests would be better served by a reunified but strictly neutral and disarmed Germany than by the integration of West Germany into a military alliance against the Soviet Union. German reunification, however, would entail free elections, which the East German Communists could not hope to win. Seeking to head off any such scenario, Ulbricht intensified the industrial development of East Germany, to make his country too valuable an economic ally for the Soviet Union to sacrifice. The resulting pressure on labor produced growing opposition, which came dramatically to a head in East Berlin in June 1953.

A workers' protest against a provision to increase output or face wage cuts promptly led to political demands, including free elections and the withdrawal of Soviet troops. Disturbances spread from East Berlin to the other major East German cities. Though this spontaneous uprising was not well coordinated, Soviet troops and tanks had to intervene to put down the movement and save the Ulbricht government. The East German example helped stimulate strikes and antigovernment demonstrations elsewhere in the Soviet bloc, convincing Soviet leaders that something had to give. But at this point, shortly after Stalin's death, the leadership of the Soviet Union was still being sorted out.

De-Stalinization Under Khrushchev, 1955–1964

Although a struggle for succession followed Stalin's death, the nature of the struggle itself forecasted a turn from the extremes of Stalinism. The political infighting involved a reasonable degree of give and take, as opposed to terror and violence. To be sure, the contestants quickly ganged up on the hated secret police chief, Lavrenti Beria, who was tried and executed within months, but this was part of their agreed-upon effort to limit the role of the secret police. Moreover, although one of the eventual losers was sent to Siberia to run a power station and the other was made ambassador to Outer Mongolia, it was a major departure that the winner, Nikita Khrushchev (1894–1971), had neither of them exiled or executed.

Although he had not been Stalin's heir apparent, Khrushchev gradually established himself as the new leader by building up patronage networks and playing off factions. Slightly crude, even something of a buffoon, he won out by 1955 partly because his opponents repeatedly underestimated him. Although his period of leadership was brief, it was eventful indeed—and in some ways the Soviet system's best chance for renewal.

At a closed session of the Soviet Communist party's twentieth national congress in February 1956, Khrushchev made a dramatic late-night speech denouncing the criminal excesses of the Stalinist system and the "cult of personality" that had developed around Stalin himself. (See the box, "Denouncing the Crimes of Stalinism.") Khrushchev's immediate aim was to undercut his hard-line rivals, but he also insisted that key features of Stalinism had amounted to an unnecessary deviation from Marxism-Leninism. So the advent of Khrushchev suggested there might be liberalization and reform.

At the same time, however, the growing popular discontent in the satellite states placed the whole system in crisis. In the face of the East German uprising of 1953, the Soviets backed off from hard-line Stalinism, making room for more moderate communists they had previously shunned, like the Hungarian Imre Nagy (1896–1958) and the Pole Wladislaw Gomulka (1905–1982). Khrushchev even sought to patch things up with Tito, exchanging visits with him in 1955 and 1956. In his speech to the party congress in 1956, Khrushchev condemned Stalin's treatment of Tito and suggested that different countries might take different routes to communism.

To keep their new system together, the Soviets apparently had to allow greater flexibility among the satellite states. But could liberalization be contained within the larger framework of Soviet leadership, or were openness and innovation bound to threaten the system itself? In Poland beginning in June 1956, strikes against wage cuts took on a political character, finally provoking the intervention of Soviet troops by October. Nonetheless, the Soviets found they could work with the moderate communist Gomulka, who favored reform within Poland but was quite loyal to the Warsaw Pact as a bulwark against Germany. By the fall of 1956, however, the events in Poland had helped stimulate comparable demonstrations in Hungary, where reformers led by the moderate communist Nagy had taken advantage of the liberalizing atmosphere by mid-1956 to begin making dramatic changes.

THE ERA OF THE COLD WAR

1947	Marshall Plan announced
1949	Formation of NATO
1951	Formation of the European Coal and Steel Community
1953	Death of Stalin
	Workers' revolt in East Germany
1955	West Germany joins NATO
	Warsaw Pact
1956	Khrushchev speech to the twentieth party congress
1956	Suez crisis
	Hungarian reform movement crushed
1957	Sputnik I launched
	Treaty of Rome establishes Common Market
1958	Beginning of Fifth Republic under de Gaulle
1959	Bad Godesberg: reorientation of German socialism
1961	Berlin Wall erected
1962	Cuban missile crisis
1964	Ouster of Nikita Khrushchev
1968	Days of May uprising in France
	Prague Spring reform movement crushed
1969	Willy Brandt becomes West German chancellor
1973	First OPEC oil crisis begins
1978	Kidnapping and assassination of Aldo Moro in Italy
1981	François Mitterand elected French president

The Hungarians dismantled their collective farms and moved toward a multiparty system and democratic coalition government. Then they called for Soviet troops to withdraw, to enable Hungary to leave the Warsaw Pact and become neutral. These were not changes within the system, but changes that would undermine the system itself. So when a democratic coalition government was set up by November, the Soviets used tanks to

Denouncing the Crimes of Stalinism

In his speech to the Soviet Communist party's national congress in 1956, Nikita Khrushchev repeatedly contrasted Stalin with Lenin, seeking to show that Stalinism had been an unfortunate and unnecessary deviation, not the logical outcome of the communist revolution. Khrushchev's denunciation of Stalin produced considerable commotion in the hall.

[I]t is impermissible and foreign to the spirit of Marxism-Leninism to elevate one person, to transform him into a superman possessing supernatural characteristics akin to those of a god. . . .

Such a belief about a man, and specifically about Stalin, was cultivated among us for many years. . . .

While ascribing great importance to the role of the leaders and organizers of the masses, Lenin at the same time mercilessly stigmatized every manifestation of the cult of the individual. . . .

Stalin originated the concept "enemy of the people." This term . . . made possible the usage of the most cruel repression, violating all norms of revolutionary legality, against anyone who in any way disagreed with Stalin, against those who were only suspected of hostile intent, against those who had bad reputations. This concept, "enemy of the people," actually eliminated the possibility of any kind of ideological fight or the making of one's views known on this or that issue, even those of a practical character. In the main, and in actuality, the only proof of guilt used, against all norms of current legal science, was the "confession" of the accused himself; and, as subsequent probing proved, "confessions" were acquired through physical torture against the accused. . . .

Arbitrary behavior by one person encouraged and permitted arbitrariness in others. Mass arrests and deportations of many thousands of people, execution without trial and without normal investigation created conditions of insecurity, fear and even desperation. . . .

Lenin used severe methods only in the most necessary cases, when the exploiting classes were still in existence and were vigorously opposing the revolution, when the struggle for survival was decidedly assuming the sharpest forms, even including a civil war. Stalin, on the other hand, used extreme methods and mass repressions at a time when the revolution was already victorious, when the Soviet state was strengthened, when the exploiting classes were already liquidated. . . . It is clear that here Stalin showed in a whole series of cases his intolerance, his brutality and his abuse of power. . . .

Source: The Anti-Stalin Campaign and International Communism: A Selection of Documents, edited by the Russian Institute, Columbia University (New York: Columbia University Press, 1956), pp. 2, 4, 12–14, 17, 20–21.

crush the Hungarian reform movement. Thousands were killed during the fighting or were executed, and 200,000 Hungarians fled to the West.

Yet even the crackdown in Hungary did not mean a return to the old days of Stalinist rigidity throughout the Soviet bloc. The Soviets understood that the system had to become more palatable, but they had made it clear that liberalization was to be kept within certain limits. It could not challenge the system itself, especially communist monopoly rule and the Warsaw Pact.

Hungary's new leader, János Kádár (b. 1912), collectivized agriculture more fully than before, but he also engineered a measure of economic decentralization, allowing scope for local initiatives and market mechanisms. There was eventually an amnesty for political prisoners, as well as considerable liberalization in cultural life, so that Hungary came to enjoy freer contact with the West than the other satellites.

Even where hard-liners remained predominant, as in East Germany and Romania, differences

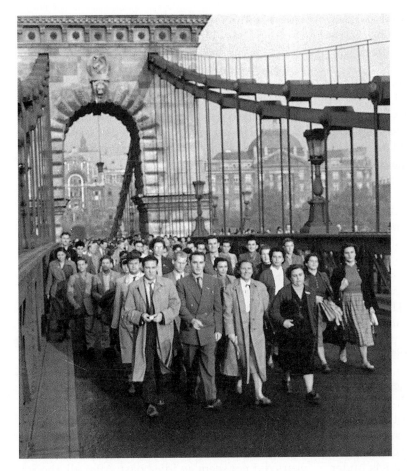

Revolution and Restoration in Hungary
Led by students and faculty from the Karl Marx University of Economics, Hungarians march across the Chain Bridge in Budapest on October 23, 1956, initiating the revolutionary phase of the movement for change in communist Hungary. Within two weeks, a Soviet-led crackdown, including shelling by Soviet tanks, had crushed the revolution, inflicting 27,000 casualties on the Hungarians. *(MTI/Eastfoto/Sovfoto)*

arose. Although Romania under Nicolae Ceausescu (1918–1989) remained one of the most repressive communist states, it grew relatively independent from the Soviet Union in matters of foreign and economic policy. And Ceausescu fostered autonomy by playing up the ethnic difference between the Romanians, Latin in background, and the Slavic peoples of much of the Soviet bloc.

By contrast, East Germany's communist leaders had every reason *not* to try to distance themselves from the Soviets by playing up nationalism and distinctiveness. Walter Ulbricht, who remained in power until his retirement in 1971, concentrated on central planning and heavy industry in orthodox fashion, but he made the East German economy the most successful in the Soviet bloc.

Still, because that economic growth was built on low wages, East German workers were tempted to immigrate to West Germany as the West German economic miracle gleamed ever brighter during the 1950s. The special position of Berlin, in

the heart of East Germany yet still divided among the occupying powers, made such immigration relatively easy, and 2.6 million East Germans left for the west between 1950 and 1962. With a population of only 17.1 million, East Germany could not afford to let this hemorrhaging continue. Thus, in August 1961 the Ulbricht regime erected the Berlin Wall, which would long serve as a grim reminder that despite periodic thaws in East-West relations, the iron curtain remained in place.

From Liberalization to Stagnation

The most intense phase of the cold war ended with Stalin's death in 1953. In his speech to the twentieth party congress in 1956, Khrushchev repudiated the previous Soviet tenet that the very existence of Western capitalist imperialism made a military showdown with the communist world inevitable. During his visit to the United States in 1959, he stressed that the ongoing competition between the two sides could be peaceful. However, despite summit conferences and sporadic efforts at better relations, friction between the Soviet Union and the United States continued.

Indeed, a new peak of tension was reached in October 1962 when the Soviets placed missiles in Cuba, which had developed close ties with the Soviet Union after the 1959 revolution led by Fidel Castro (b. 1926). Although the United States had its own offensive missiles in Turkey, adjacent to the Soviet Union, the Soviet attempt to base missiles in Cuba seemed an intolerable challenge. For several days, military confrontation appeared a distinct possibility, but President John F. Kennedy (1917–1963) managed an effective combination of resistance and restraint in responding to the Soviet move. The Soviets withdrew their missiles in exchange for a U.S. promise not to seek to overthrow the communist government in Cuba. The outcome was essentially a victory for the United States, which retained its offensive missile capacity adjacent to the Soviet Union. The Cuban missile crisis was the closest the superpowers came to direct armed confrontation during the cold war period.

At the same time, it became increasingly clear that international communism was not the monolithic force it had once seemed. The most dramatic indication was the Sino-Soviet split, which developed during the 1950s as the communists under Mao Zedong solidified their regime in China. In the long struggle that led to their victory in 1949, the Chinese communists had often had no choice but to go their own way, and during the 1940s, especially, Stalin had been willing to subordinate any concern for their cause to Soviet national interests. After taking power in 1949, the Chinese communists pursued their own path to development without worrying about the Soviet model. With some justification, the Soviets feared that the independent, innovative Chinese might be prepared to challenge Soviet leadership in international communism. By the early 1960s, the communist Chinese path had become appealing especially in the non-Western world, though it attracted dissident communists in the West as well. The split within world communism, and the antagonism between China and the Soviet Union, added another layer of uncertainty to the cold war era.

As a domestic leader, Khrushchev proved mercurial and erratic, but he was an energetic innovator, willing to experiment. He jettisoned the worst features of the police state apparatus, including some of the infamous Siberian prison camps, and offered several amnesties for prisoners. He also liberalized cultural life and gave workers greater freedom to move from one job to another. The economic planning apparatus was decentralized somewhat, affording more scope for local initiatives and placing greater emphasis on consumer goods. The government expanded medical and educational facilities and, between 1955 and 1964, doubled the nation's housing stock, substantially alleviating a severe housing shortage.

As part of the domestic thaw in the Soviet Union after Stalin, divorce became easier and abortion was legalized. Women received liberal provisions for maternity leave as well as measures to ensure equal access to higher education and the professions. Still, women were concentrated in lower-paying occupations and rarely rose to the top echelons. To be sure, they were prominent in medicine in the Soviet Union, but Soviet doctors did not have the status—or the incomes—their counterparts enjoyed in the West.

Though living standards remained relatively low, Khrushchev's reforms helped improve the lives of ordinary people by the early 1960s. Even his claim in 1961 that the Soviet Union would surpass the Western standard of living within twenty years did not seem an idle boast. After all, the Soviets had launched *Sputnik I* in 1957, assuming the lead in the ensuing space race. They followed by putting the first human into space in 1961. Such achievements suggested that even ordinary Soviet citizens had reason for optimism. More generally, the communist regimes throughout the Soviet bloc entered the 1960s with confidence after having achieved excellent rates of economic growth during the 1950s.

Yet Khrushchev had made enemies with his erratic reform effort, and this led to his forced retirement in October 1964. After the unending experiment in the economy, his opponents wanted to consolidate, to return to stability and predictability. But not until 1968 did it become clear that the liberalization and innovation of the Khrushchev era were over.

By early 1968 a significant reform movement had developed within the Communist party in Prague, the capital of Czechoslovakia. Determined to avoid the fate of the Hungarian effort in 1956, the reformers emphasized that Czechoslovakia was to remain a communist state and a full member of the Warsaw Pact. But within that framework, they felt, it should be possible to invite freer cultural expression, to democratize the Communist party's procedures, and to broaden participation in public life.

However, efforts to reassure the Soviets about the limits of the movement's aims alienated some of its supporters, who stepped up their demands as a result. As earlier in Hungary, the demand for change seemed to outstrip the intentions of the movement's organizers. Finally, Soviet leaders in Moscow decided to crack down. In August 1968 Soviet tanks moved into Prague to crush the reform movement—precisely what its leaders had been seeking to avoid.

The end of the "Prague Spring" closed the era of relative flexibility and cautious innovation in the Soviet bloc that had begun as early as 1953. A period of relative stagnation followed under Leonid Brezhnev (1906–1982), a careful, consensus-seeking bureaucrat. Now setting the tone was the "Brezhnev doctrine," which specified that the Soviet Union would help established communist regimes remain in power against any "counter-revolutionary" threat. This blanket statement helped chill reform hopes during the years that followed. Even as efforts toward détente and arms control made news during the 1970s, this Soviet willingness to intervene, with military force when necessary, in the affairs of the satellite states suggested the ongoing fragility of the whole Soviet system.

Poland, too, experienced a reform effort in 1968, but it was initiated by students and failed to attract the support of workers, who were largely loyal to the communist regime. Though quick to infringe on "bourgeois" civil liberties, the Polish communist government—like others in the Soviet bloc—was eager for working-class support. Thus it provided subsidized food, housing, and medical care. But to pay the bill the government had to borrow from foreigners. The loans were ostensibly to help Poland modernize, and thereby to boost efficiency. But in fact the money was used for immediate consumption, for inefficient state-owned companies, and for bureaucratic graft. Despite the infusion of capital, productivity was actually declining in Poland by the end of the 1970s, and the problem was becoming clear to creditors. So even in Poland, where the communist regime seemed

generally to satisfy the workers, its way of doing so was increasingly artificial—and unsustainable.

After the successes of the 1950s and early 1960s, the Soviet Union was finding it ever harder to match the West in economic growth and technological innovation. And despite periodic efforts at economic reform, the satellite states did not do appreciably better with the central planning model. Ordinary people became increasingly frustrated as the communist economic system proved erratic in providing even the most basic consumer goods.

Frustration grew especially among women, who seemed to bear a disproportionate share of the burdens. Women were more likely to be employed outside the home in the Soviet bloc than in the West. For example, around 90 percent of adult women in the Soviet Union and East Germany had paid jobs outside the home by 1980. In 1984, 50 percent of the East German work force was female, compared with 39 percent in West Germany. Yet not only were women concentrated in jobs with low pay and prestige in the communist countries, but they also still bore the major responsibility for child care, housework, and shopping. They had few of the labor-saving devices available in the West, and they often had to spend hours in line to buy ordinary consumer items. Dissatisfaction among women fed a new underground protest movement that began developing in the Soviet bloc in the mid-1970s—a further indication of the growing strains in the overall system.

But what would it take for these strains to produce a full-scale crisis? Although often secretive and arrogant, the Soviet Union remained preoccupied with its place in the postwar international order. It had long wanted some sort of international conference that would regularize the status of East Germany and confirm the western border of Poland. When, in 1969, Willy Brandt became West Germany's chancellor and began pursuing his *Ostpolitik,* or opening to the East, the Soviets got their chance. But the eventual outcome was hardly what they envisioned.

In 1975, high-level representatives of thirty-five countries, including all of the Soviet bloc, came together in Helsinki, Finland, in the most prominent of the international meetings that Brandt's policy made possible. The parties recognized East Germany and all borders, precisely according to the Soviet script. But they also adopted a detailed agreement on human rights, which came to be known as the Helsinki Accords. And that agreement, merely symbolic in one sense, ended up providing a foundation for forces that would eventually bring the whole Soviet system crashing down.

DEMOCRACY AND ITS DISCONTENTS, 1968 AND AFTER

The year 1968, which saw the end of the "Prague Spring," proved a turning point in Western Europe as well. By this point, a generation after World War II, democracy seemed to have succeeded remarkably, and, indeed, it would win further successes in the 1970s as Greece, Spain, and Portugal turned from authoritarianism to democratic government. But during the late 1960s it became clear that, despite the economic prosperity and political stability, political alienation had been building in Western Europe. And though they came to be exaggerated, the dissatisfactions that began erupting in 1968 fundamentally changed the tone of politics in Europe and the West. The economic difficulties that began in 1973 only added fuel to an already smoldering fire.

Democratic Consolidation and Political Alienation

Observing the success of democracy in the most developed parts of Western Europe, Spain, Portugal, and Greece established workable democracies after periods of dictatorial rule. Following the death of Francisco Franco in 1975, almost forty years after his triumph in the Spanish civil war, democracy returned to Spain more smoothly than most had dared hope. Franco established that a restoration of the monarchy would follow his death, and King Juan Carlos (r. 1975–) served as an effective catalyst in the transition to democracy.

When the first democratic elections in Spain since the civil war were held in 1977, the extremes of both left and right did poorly. The big winners were a democratic centrist party and a moderate socialist party. The Socialists won a parliamentary majority in the next elections, in 1982, and a moderate Socialist replaced the centrist leader as prime minister. The transition suggested that Spain had quickly found its way to an effective two-party system. Meanwhile, the new constitution of 1978 dismantled what was left of the Franco system so

that, for example, Catholicism was no longer recognized as the official religion of the Spanish state.

A comparable transition from military rule to democracy took place in Portugal and Greece. Like Spain, each sought to help cement a long-term commitment to democracy by seeking entry into the European Economic Community, and each was accepted by the end of the 1970s. For all three, EEC membership became a pillar of the solidifying democratic consensus.

At the same time, however, political disaffection threatened the consensus in the more established democracies of the European continent. The most dramatic eruption of radical protest was the "Days of May" uprising that shook France during May 1968. The movement was partly a reaction against the priorities of de Gaulle's Fifth Republic—especially the preoccupation with France's international role. But it was also a response to the unevenness in the modernization effort that had seemed necessary to support that role. The commitment to technocratic values had produced impressive economic growth, but many ordinary people felt left out of France's economic success. Despite all the growth, public services had been neglected, and problems in such areas as housing and education continued—or even worsened.

Higher education in France affords a telling example. Enrollment in French universities more than doubled between 1939 and 1960, then more than doubled again between 1960 and 1967. Apart from a few highly selective *grandes écoles*, the institutions of the state-run university system were open to anyone who passed a standard examination, and it was not considered politically feasible to limit enrollments by restricting access. Instead, the government tried to build to keep up with demand—thereby creating vast, impersonal institutions with professors increasingly inaccessible to students. But overcrowding persisted, and the value of a university degree diminished, leaving graduates with uncertain job prospects.

The uprising of 1968 started with university students, who sought to reach out to others, especially industrial workers, by offering a broad critique of the present system. But union activists and workers generally declined to join the movement, and the students ended up settling for relatively limited concessions. Still, the uprising made it clear that the university system needed a complete overhaul—and that students and faculty had to be involved in the changes. Over the next several years, the Education Ministry carried out reforms, breaking existing institutions into smaller units, with more local control over budgets and instructional methods. At the same time, however, student and faculty participation in institutional governance tended to politicize French universities, some of which became communist strongholds, others bastions of the right. And this caused friction with the education bureaucrats in Paris.

At first glance, the parties of the Marxist left might appear the likely beneficiaries of the popular discontent that emerged during the late 1960s. But the effort to come to terms with the events of 1968 deepened divisions within the Communist party and initiated a renewed disenchantment with Marxism among French intellectuals. Unable to transcend long-standing class categories and to encompass the aspirations of those, like the students, who were newly disaffected, French communism increasingly seemed old and stale. However, the French Socialist party gained dramatically during the 1970s. Claiming the mantle of the new left that had emerged in 1968, the Socialists appealed to those, especially young people, who believed the promise of that year could still be translated into substantial change.

The Oil Crisis and the Changing Economic Framework

As the political situation in Western Europe became more volatile, events outside Europe made it clear how interdependent the world had become—and that the West did not hold all the trump cards. In the fall of 1973, Egypt and Syria attacked Israel, seeking to recover the losses they had suffered in a brief war in 1967. Although the assault failed, the Arab nations of the oil-rich Middle East came together in the aftermath to retaliate against the Western bloc for supporting Israel. By restricting the output and distribution of the oil its members controlled, the Arab-led Organization of Petroleum Exporting Countries (OPEC) produced a sharp increase in oil prices and a severe economic disruption all over the industrialized world. Western Europe, which was heavily dependent on Middle Eastern oil, was especially hard hit. By January 1975 the price of oil was six times what it had been in 1973, before the embargo, and this increase remained a source of inflationary pressure throughout the Western world until the early 1980s.

The immediate European response to the oil embargo dramatized the limits of the economic integration so far achieved through the Common Market. When OPEC imposed especially harsh measures on the Netherlands, which had taken a strong stand in support of Israel, the other nations of the Common Market dealt separately with the cartel rather than stand together.

The 1970s proved to be an unprecedented period of "stagflation"—sharply reduced rates of growth combined with inflation and rising unemployment. The economic miracle that had transformed much of Western Europe had clearly ended, partly because the European economies

Oil, the West, and the World
Led by several oil-rich Arab states, OPEC drove up world oil prices by restricting production during the 1970s. The power of the oil cartel made it clear that decisions by non-Westerners could vitally affect the industrialized West. OPEC delegates are shown here in Algiers in 1975. *(Sygma)*

were subject to growing competition from non-Western countries, most notably Japan. Everywhere the labor movement was suddenly on the defensive in light of increasing global competition, technological change, and high unemployment.

Strains in the Welfare State

A tighter economy made it harder for governments to afford the welfare measures that had helped establish the new political consensus in much of the West since World War II. Although much publicity surrounded the British welfare state, the percentage of the British economy devoted to public expenditure for welfare, housing, and education by the early 1970s—18.2 percent—was about average for the industrialized nations of the West. Sweden had the highest figure at 23.7 percent, and the Swedish case particularly dramatized the problems of managing a welfare state in conditions of economic stringency.

By the early 1970s, 40 percent of Sweden's national income went for taxes to finance the system—the highest rate of taxation in the world. At the same time, Sweden found itself less competitive, both because its wages were so high and because it was not keeping abreast of technological developments. In Sweden, as elsewhere, there were growing doubts that a welfare state could nurture the initiative and productivity needed for success in the increasingly competitive global economy. By 1980 unemployment and efforts to cut government spending led to the most severe labor unrest the country had experienced since the war. Even on the level of everyday life, it seemed that the Swedish model, with its emphasis on societal responsibility, entailed excessive governmental intrusion in the private sphere.

In Britain a dramatic assault on the welfare state began developing at the same time. Until the early 1970s, Britain retained the consensus on the government's role in social welfare that had emerged with the end of the war. But the British economy lagged the others of the industrialized West, then suffered especially during the 1970s. Between 1968 and 1976, the country lost 1 million manufacturing jobs. By the mid-1970s this economic decline threatened to shatter Britain's postwar settlement, because there was no consensus over how to apportion the pain of the necessary austerity measures.

During the 1970s each of Britain's two major political parties made a serious effort to deal with the situation, but neither succeeded, especially because neither could deal effectively with Britain's strong trade unions. The election of the militantly conservative Margaret Thatcher (b. 1925) as Conservative party leader in 1975 proved a turning point, however. When she became prime minister in 1979, it was clear that Britain was embarking on a radically different course.

The Democratic Consensus and Its Limitations

Even where the welfare state was not the immediate bone of contention, discontent with the political consensus led to a variety of new political alignments and expedients, some of them violent. In Italy the Communists responded to economic crisis and political alienation by offering to share power—and responsibility—with the Christian Democrats on the national level for the first time. In 1976, the Communist party's share of the vote in national elections reached an all-time high of 34.4 percent. By the end of the 1970s, however, the Communists' efforts had led nowhere; their share of the vote steadily declined, as did their support among younger people and intellectuals. But the Christian Democrats, too, were losing electoral support by the early 1980s. Their message seemed ever less relevant as Italy became a more secular society. And as the Italian Communists declined, many found it less important to support Christian Democracy as a bulwark against communism.

During the 1970s, frustration with the political immobility that seemed to have neutralized even the established left gave rise to a new wave of terrorism, prominent especially in Italy and Germany. Terrorists in such groups as the Red Brigades in Italy and the Baader-Meinhof gang in Germany assassinated a number of prominent public officials and businessmen, including the long-time Italian Christian Democratic leader Aldo Moro (1916–1978). By the late 1970s, left- and right-wing extremism fed each other, and it was right-wing extremists who were responsible for Italy's most deadly terrorist episode, a bombing in the railway station in Bologna that killed eighty-five people in August 1980.

But political frustration also found productive outlets, as new coalitions developed around newly politicized issues—from abortion to the environment—that had not been associated with the Marxist left. In Germany, the Green movement formed by peace and environmental activists during the late 1970s took pains to avoid acting like a conventional party. Concerned that Germany, with its central location, would end up the devastated battleground in any superpower confrontation, the Greens opposed deployment of additional U.S. missiles on German soil and called for an alternative to the endless arms race. The SPD, as the governing party in an important NATO state, seemed unable to confront this issue and lost members as a result.

Prominent among the new political currents that began emerging around 1968 was the feminist movement, comparable to the earlier movement for women's suffrage. This new movement for "women's liberation" sought equal opportunities for women in education and employment. It was striking, for example, that despite major steps toward equal educational opportunity in postwar France, the country's prestigious engineering schools were still not admitting women in the late 1960s—and would begin doing so only during the 1980s. But feminists also forced new issues onto the political stage, working, for example, to liberalize divorce and abortion laws throughout the Western world. At the same time, women faced new questions after a generation of experience with the activist postwar state. In Britain, where government had sought to free mothers from the necessity of employment outside the home, feminists increasingly saw the welfare state as a major source of what seemed their ongoing second-class status. But the tradeoffs were complex, and a deeper sense of gender issues would become central to public debate and personal choice all over the Western world during the last two decades of the century.

Although the timing varied greatly from country to country, the tendency throughout Western Europe after World War II was toward the consolidation of democracy in some form of two-party system. The domestication of the socialist left was essential to that process. After Willy Brandt became chancellor in 1969, the West German Socialists led the government for thirteen years, finally meeting electoral defeat in 1982. By that point, Socialists and Conservatives agreed on the essentials; there was disagreement only about degrees. The Socialists had completed the turn to moderation that they began in the late 1950s, leaving Germany essentially with a two-party system. The strength of the Green party, which had first seemed to offer a new political direction, leveled off during the 1980s at 10 to 15 percent of the vote—significant, but hardly a breakthrough.

During the early 1980s, revitalized socialist parties in France, Spain, and Italy marginalized the communists and, for a time, even seemed poised to reorient government. In France François Mitterrand (1916–1996) was elected president in 1981, promising to create the first genuinely democratic socialism. But during the 1980s, he gradually abandoned his talk of socialism in the face of economic and political pressures. By the end of the decade, he was questioning the relevance of long-standing socialist tenets and playing up the virtues of entrepreneurship, the profit mechanism, and free-market competition. The key was that France, like the other industrial democracies, had to operate in an increasingly competitive international economy. The Socialists met defeat in the early 1990s, but they had proven they could work within the system, and, despite their immediate discredit, it seemed likely that they would eventually regain power, taking their turn in a two-party democracy.

SUMMARY

In the decades that followed World War II, a bipolar framework, dominated by the United States and the Soviet Union, shaped world affairs. The states of western and central Europe, dominant before 1914 but shaken by World War I, declined in influence, even losing their remaining colonial possessions. The new bipolar framework opened certain possibilities but also limited political options in both halves of newly divided Europe. The Western European states had to follow the U.S. lead, especially in matters of national security, though France under de Gaulle grew especially restive. But this framework enabled Western Europe to achieve remarkable prosperity and even to take significant steps toward multinational integration.

In the communist bloc, Stalin's death in 1953 ended the most repressive features of the Soviet regime, and under his successor, Nikita Khrushchev, the Soviet Union seemed able to compete with the United States in areas from education to economic growth to the exploration of outer space.

But the experiment with various forms of central planning in the Soviet bloc proved ever less successful. At the same time, the fate of a series of opposition and reform efforts, from East Berlin in 1953 to Prague in 1968, made it clear that the Soviets intended to keep their east-central European satellite states on a relatively tight leash. The degree of unity demanded by the Soviet system imposed stability in a potentially volatile part of Europe, keeping long-standing ethnic rivalries in check.

In Western Europe, the shared experience of wartime led to a new social compact based on greater government responsibility for economic well-being and social welfare. The implicit promise of growing prosperity for all made possible a measure of cooperation between business and labor that eroded earlier assumptions of irreconcilable class struggle. And the new consensus provided a foundation for democracy, which became solidly established in Western Europe during the first two decades after the war.

By 1968, however, strains began to appear in the Western democracies, and slower economic growth during the 1970s jeopardized the postwar settlement. Even in the context of increasing prosperity, a diffuse discontent developed among many Western Europeans, who felt left out as the most important decisions were made by party leaders, technocratic planners, EEC Eurocrats, or the executives of multinational corporations. Thus the quest for new forms of political participation that began in 1968 and continued throughout the 1970s.

The bipolar world rested on a kind of balance between the superpowers. And though significant political discontents surfaced in both halves of divided Europe in 1968, Western Europe came to take for granted a substantial measure of prosperity and political legitimacy, while Eastern Europe was not so fortunate. That imbalance threatened to undermine the anxious stability that characterized the era from 1949 to 1985.

SUGGESTED READING

General Surveys and the Cold War Framework

Crockatt, Richard. *The Fifty Years' War: The United States and the Soviet Union in World Politics, 1941–1991.* 1995. A balanced history of U.S.-Soviet relations, showing the global impact of their cold war rivalry.

Gleason, Abbott. *Totalitarianism: The Inner History of the Cold War.* 1995. A Soviet specialist examines the uses

and misuses of the concept of totalitarianism, especially as it helped shape understanding in the West during the cold war period.

Hanrieder, Wolfram F. *Germany, America, Europe: Forty Years of German Foreign Policy.* Updated ed. 1991. A major work on the place of West Germany in the cold war era. Updated edition considers the import of German reunification.

Laqueur, Walter. *Europe in Our Time: A History, 1945–1992.* 1992. A comprehensive, well-balanced survey by a leading authority on twentieth-century Europe.

Maier, Charles S., ed. *The Cold War in Europe: Era of a Divided Continent*, 3d ed. 1996. A series of essays on the implications of the cold war framework for Western European development during the four decades after World War II.

Cultural and Intellectual History

Hughes, H. Stuart. *Between Commitment and Disillusion: The Obstructed Path and the Sea Change, 1930–1965.* 1987. Updated edition of two previously published works by an influential intellectual historian. *The Sea Change* covers the intellectual migration from Europe to America.

Judt, Tony. *Past Imperfect: French Intellectuals, 1944–1956.* 1992. A spirited critique of the apologies for communism that French intellectuals like Sartre and de Beauvoir offered in the years after World War II.

Stromberg, Roland N. *After Everything: Western Intellectual History Since 1945.* 1975. A survey, good on the 1940s and 1950s, less sympathetic on the innovations of the later 1960s and thereafter.

Restabilization, Economic Growth, and Social Change

Ellwood, David W. *Rebuilding Europe: Western Europe, America and Postwar Reconstruction.* 1992. Readable, well-balanced survey of the course of reconstruction in Western Europe in the decade after World War II.

Hogan, Michael J. *The Marshall Plan: America, Britain, and the Reconstruction of Western Europe, 1947–1952.* 1987. Concerned especially with U.S. policy toward Europe; emphasizes the American desire for a neo-capitalist world system based on free trade.

Kuisel, Richard F. *Capitalism and the State in Modern France: Renovation and Economic Management in the Twentieth Century.* 1981. A careful and thorough study tracing the emergence of economic planning and a technocratic ethos in France.

Maier, Charles S. *In Search of Stability.* 1987. Essays on the wider sociopolitical context of economic policies in the twentieth century. Several essays contrast the two postwar periods in illuminating ways.

Milward, Alan S. *The Reconstruction of Western Europe, 1945–51.* 1984. An influential account that emphasizes the importance of European initiatives, as opposed to

American help, in making the postwar economic boom so durable.

Ruggie, Mary. *The State and Working Women: A Comparative Study of Britain and Sweden*. 1984. A sophisticated study that seeks to explain why women achieved greater economic equality in Sweden than in Britain.

Postwar Government and Politics

Bark, Dennis L., and David R. Gress. *A History of West Germany*. Vol. 1, *From Shadow to Substance, 1945–1963*, and Vol. 2, *Democracy and Its Discontents, 1963–1988*. 1989. Offers a favorable account of West Germany's democracy and its Atlantic and European roles in the face of ongoing suspicion and criticism.

Ginsbourg, Paul. *A History of Contemporary Italy: Society and Politics, 1943–1988*. 1990. A comprehensive survey especially good on the radical postwar socioeconomic transformation in Italy.

Larkin, Maurice. *France Since the Popular Front: Government and People, 1936–1986*. 1988. A comprehensive survey that focuses on the interaction between political life and socioeconomic change.

Morgan, Kenneth O. *The People's Peace: British History 1945–1990*. 1992. A thorough survey that seeks to avoid overemphasis on decline and pessimism. Accents the relative peace and stability of the period.

Pulzer, Peter. *German Politics, 1945–1995*. 1995. Brief and clear yet probing account of political developments in both East and West Germany. Also good on the impact of reunification.

Sapelli, Giulio. *Southern Europe Since 1945: Tradition and Modernity in Portugal, Spain, Italy, Greece, and Turkey*. 1995. Using a regional and comparative approach, shows how industrialization led to social change and the consolidation of political democracy in the decades after World War II.

Turner, Henry Ashby, Jr. *Germany from Partition to Reunification*. 1992. A fair-minded treatment of both East and West Germany. Explains the collapse of communism in East Germany and the subsequent German reunification.

Williams, Charles. *The Last Great Frenchman: A Life of Charles de Gaulle*. 1993. Comprehensive, straightforward, balanced account of a remarkable career.

Decolonization

Holland, R. F. *European Decolonization, 1918–1981: An Introductory Survey*. 1985. A sensitive, comprehensive account that gives particular attention to the British experience.

Porter, Bernard. *The Lion's Share: A Short History of British Imperialism, 1850–1995*. 1996. Updated edition of a widely read survey of the British imperial experience, with effective chapters on decolonization and the Commonwealth system that Britain sought to foster as the empire came apart.

Mommsen, Wolfgang J., and Jürgen Osterhammel, eds. *Imperialism and After: Continuities and Discontinuities*. 1986. A collection of essays by leading scholars. Analyzes the informal means through which European influence continued even after the end of formal imperial control.

Von Laue, Theodore H. *The World Revolution of Westernization: The Twentieth Century in Global Perspective*. 1987. A comprehensive, readable, sometimes provocative survey, especially helpful on the transition from decolonization to the new global age.

European Integration and the Common Market

Brinkley, Douglas, and Clifford Hackett, eds. *Jean Monnet: The Path to European Unity*. 1991. A collection of essays on Monnet's central role in the movement toward European integration after World War II.

Dedman, Martin J. *The Origins and Development of the European Union, 1945–95: A History of European Integration*. 1996. A concise and accessible introductory work.

Duchêne, François. *Jean Monnet: The First Statesman of Interdependence*. 1994. A carefully researched and quite readable biography featuring Monnet's role as the architect of European integration.

Hackett, Clifford. *Cautious Revolution: The European Community Arrives*, 2d ed. 1995. An effective blend of history with prescription, suggesting how the European Community could become capable of unified political decision.

Pinder, John. *European Community: The Building of a Union*. 1991. Combines a historical account of the development of EC institutions with a balanced assessment of the prospects for European federation.

The Soviet Union and the Soviet Bloc

Hosking, Geoffrey. *The First Socialist Society: A History of the Soviet Union from Within*. Enlarged ed. 1990. Looks at family, religion, nationality, and the experience of factory workers in an effort to portray the lives of ordinary Soviet citizens.

Linden, Carl A. *Khrushchev and the Soviet Leadership: With an Epilogue on Gorbachev*. Updated ed. 1990. Especially good on the internal political maneuvering that eventually led to Khrushchev's ouster. Includes a useful epilogue on the course from Khrushchev's ambiguous legacy to Gorbachev's reform effort.

Rothschild, Joseph. *Return to Diversity: A Political History of East Central Europe Since World War II*, 2d ed. 1993. A straightforward survey that makes sense of the differences as well as the similarities among the Soviet bloc countries during the cold war.

Stokes, Gale, ed. *From Stalinism to Pluralism: A Documentary History of Eastern Europe Since 1945*, 2d ed. 1991. A collection of documents, with effective commentaries. Includes the disintegration of communism in 1989 and the immediate aftermath.

POP ART

Hamburgers, comic strips, soup-can labels, familiar images of entertainment icons—such was the stuff of "pop art," which burst onto the New York art scene in the early 1960s and came to exert a widespread cultural influence. Indeed, with their imaginative renderings of familiar images and whimsical sculptures of everyday objects, artists like Andy Warhol (1928–1987), Roy Lichtenstein (b. 1923), and Claes Oldenburg (b. 1929) helped shape the experience of the later twentieth century. But was this serious art—or a joke, a parody, a put-on? Were the pop artists poking fun at the triviality of modern society, or were they deepening our encounter with defining aspects of contemporary culture? And whatever their intent, what does the emergence of this striking new art form tell us about the direction of Western culture in the decades after World War II?

The term *pop art* was coined in England in the later 1950s, when a group of artists and critics became interested in bridging the cultural gap between "fine art" and the emerging popular culture of mass media and machine-produced images, of

Oldenburg: Floor Burger, 1962 (*Claus Oldenburg [American, b. 1929], Floor Burger, 1962. Painted sailcloth stuffed with foam, 132.1 × 213.4 cm. Art Gallery of Ontario, Toronto.*)

advertising and automobiles. Like everyone else, they associated that consumerist mass culture with America—the America of Hollywood, Detroit, and Madison Avenue. And they found it more vital than the conventional fine art of the period. The American pop artists were similarly fascinated by the impersonal, mass-produced, often expendable quality of the objects and images that have come to surround us.

Pop art was part of a wider reaction against the deeply serious abstract expressionist painting that emerged in New York just after the Second World War. By the early 1950s, abstract expressionists like Jackson Pollock and Mark Rothko had created images of unprecedented power, whether seeking to forge an artistic identity in the face of nothingness or to transcend selfhood in a cosmic wholeness (see page 1077). In the mid-1950s, however, younger artists "tired of the stink of artists' egos" began reacting against the self-importance of abstract expressionism. For these younger artists, art did not have to be a vehicle for the psychological expression of the artist or a quest for "the tragic and timeless." Although the reaction took several forms, pop art proved the most influential. The pop movement emerged especially in the United States, and it interested Europeans as typically American, fresh and fascinating or garish and vulgar, depending on one's point of view.

Whereas the abstract expressionists had sought to rise above the everyday world, Claes Oldenburg's sculptures played with the scale and context of the most ordinary objects—a mixer, a three-pronged plug, a lipstick, a hamburger—to deepen our involvement with the everyday things that surround us. In this sense, the aim of pop art was not simply to parody or satirize, but to affirm our relationship with the objects and images of ordinary life. Hollywood, Detroit, and Madison Avenue were all right after all; indeed, they had become the centers of Western culture by the later twentieth century.

Warhol: Marilyn Diptych, 1962 *(© Copyright ARS, NY. Tate Gallery, London/Art Resource, NY)*

Though anonymous and impersonal, the modern world of mass production, mass consumption, and mass media is "popular"—its images and objects are accessible to us all. In fact, they bombard us from all directions, giving shared shape and definition to our everyday lives. This is our world, the pop artists were saying, and they were creating the art appropriate to our time. They invite us to relax and enjoy that world, but they also enhance our experience by making art from it, thereby awakening us to its novelty and vitality.

But some viewers have found an element of melancholy, nostalgia, even tragedy just beneath the surface in pop art. In a world of mass media and reproduced images, more of our experience becomes secondhand and literally superficial, for pop subjects, from fast food to billboards, have no deeper meaning, no expressive personal trappings. With his multiplied image of Marilyn Monroe, Andy Warhol dealt not with the actress herself but with the obsessive familiarity of her image. He cultivated a deadpan, detached style that reflected the machine-made quality of his subject matter—the quality that made the images he started with so familiar in the first place. But even as, on one level, he embraced aspects of the new mass culture, Warhol was exploring precisely the emotional detachment—and the accompanying trivialization of emotion—at work in the culture that had produced the images he adapted. Especially in his paintings treating impersonal newspaper images of disaster and death, Warhol bore witness to our indifference—and perhaps to a cosmic meaninglessness as well. One expert has noted that "in Warhol's pictures of the material objects and other false idols that most of us worship, the pain lies just below the bright surfaces of the images and waits passively to engage us."*

The advent of pop art provoked a series of questions that remain without definitive answers. Is the embrace of the mass-produced and commercial, at the expense of traditional "fine-art" values, a symptom of exhaustion or a healthy affirmation of contemporary popular culture, so bound up with the commercial world? Or is pop art perhaps a valuable comment on the emptiness of that culture, with its impersonal conformity, garish commercialism, and mechanical repetition? In the final analysis, were the pop artists abandoning the artist's mission and giving in to the ordinary, or were they the first to show us what "Western civilization" had come to mean by the late twentieth century?

*Eric Shanes, *Warhol* (New York: Portland House, 1991), p. 41.

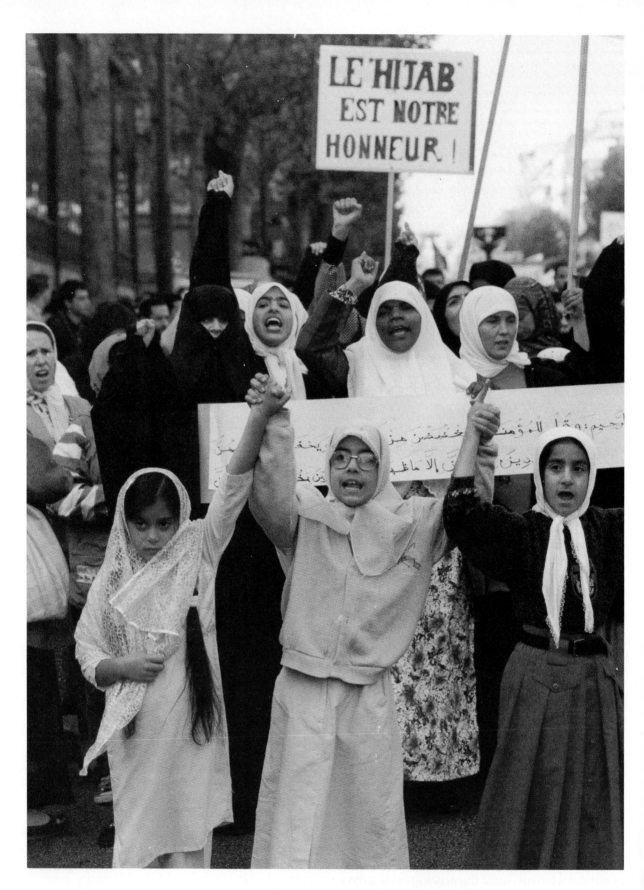

The West and the World in the Late Twentieth Century

During the fall of 1989, three teenaged Muslim girls were suspended from a public school near Paris because they insisted on wearing the headscarves traditional for Islamic women. School authorities cited a law barring religious displays in France's strictly secular state-run school system. The three girls, however, protested that Islamic teaching required women to cover their heads in public as a sign of modesty. Yet in the eyes of some Westerners, that practice simply reflected the second-class status of women in Islamic civilization. The leader of France's largest teachers' union contended that "this flaunting of a clear symbol of women's subordination negates the teaching of human rights in schools." Thus, when the French Minister of Education defended the students' right to wear the scarves, he was widely criticized for condoning the oppression of women in Islam.

In fact, the education minister was not seeking to defend Islamic tradition or cultural diversity, let alone the oppression of women. He wanted simply to keep these girls—and the many others like them—in France's state-run schools, to expose them to secular influence and thereby to promote their assimilation into French culture.

In 1989 Muslims totaled 5 percent of the French population, or 2.7 million people, and this episode prompted many of them to demonstrate for greater pluralism and tolerance in France. Some of France's non-Muslim majority joined in, even wearing scarves in solidarity. Others, in contrast, called for stepped-up efforts to assimilate immigrants and those with foreign backgrounds into the common French civilization.

"The hijab [headscarf] is our honor": Muslim women and girls demonstrate in Paris, October 1989.

France's prestigious Council of State soon ruled that the scarves did not violate the constitutional separation of church and state, as long as they were not worn in an effort to flaunt religion or to prose-lytize. The council left it to local school authorities to decide each case. But the riddles of multicultur-alism at issue in this "affair of the scarves" kept coming up in France and elsewhere by the late twentieth century, as contact between the West and other parts of the world took new forms.

In an increasingly global age, traditional cul-tural boundaries were breaking down. Communi-cations and flow of capital became instantaneous, products like Coca-Cola and McDonald's burgers and fries became familiar worldwide, and a com-mon urban youth culture began to emerge. In spheres from popular music to food, elements from diverse societies seemed to be fusing. Talk of a sin-gle "global village" became commonplace. Yet, as the controversy over the Islamic scarves suggests, in some respects cultural boundaries loomed larger as cultural contact deepened.

Cultural convergence stemmed especially from the process known as modernization, or "Western-ization," though it took varied forms in the non-Western world as it mixed with indigenous tradi-tions. The process entailed, above all, participation in the competitive global market economy that had spread from Europe. Paradoxically, however, West-ernization meant that "the West" was becoming less meaningful as a category or basis for distinc-tion. Western Europe and the United States encoun-tered formidable economic competition first from Japan, and later from other countries of the East Asian Pacific rim, such as Taiwan, Korea, Thailand, and Malaysia. What increasingly mattered, from this perspective, was the difference between the industrialized, relatively affluent "North" and the less developed "South," including much of Africa, Latin America, southern Asia, and the Middle East.

As the population exploded in the less devel-oped world, the gap between rich and poor nations widened. The prosperous countries of the North were increasingly a magnet for the disadvantaged from around the world. The resulting immigration created new social and political pressures that raised questions about citizenship and assimilation, pluralism and diversity, identity and community.

Such questions came to center stage partly be-cause of the end of the cold war, which had over-shadowed all else for decades after World War II.

In 1989, precisely the year of the affair of the scarves in France, dramatic change in the Soviet bloc came to a head, leading to the end of commu-nism and even the dissolution of the Soviet Un-ion. The unraveling of the whole Soviet system brought an abrupt end to the postwar era, which had rested on a tense balance between the com-munist states and the capitalist democracies.

The former communist countries sought to follow the West in pluralistic liberal democracy, but the Western democracies were themselves fac-ing unprecedented economic challenges in the late twentieth century. The pace of technological change, and related changes in the structure of in-ternational capitalism, seemed so rapid that no one could foresee the next stage—and thus no one could feel secure. Moreover, key decisions seemed to be made increasingly by multinational corpora-tions or supranational organizations, beyond democratic control. Some looked to those organi-zations with hope, others with suspicion and re-sentment. By the early 1990s, the apparent limits of government power and, in some countries, the short-sightedness and corruption of politicians bred political disillusionment. Even in the demo-cratic West a new set of anxieties and uncertainties quickly replaced those of the cold war era.

CHALLENGES OF AFFLUENCE IN THE WEST

After the economic dislocations of the 1970s, most of Western Europe again enjoyed strong economic growth by the early 1980s. In Italy a "second eco-nomic miracle" enabled the country to surpass Britain and become the world's fifth largest econ-omy. But in Italy and elsewhere in Western Europe, growth was uneven, confined to certain sectors and regions. By the 1990s prosperity mixed with ongoing worries about international competition, technological unemployment, and environmental constraints in a small and crowded continent.

By the 1980s democracy had become the unchallenged norm in Western Europe, where the radical right was largely discredited and the Marxist left seemed to have been domesticated for good. In important respects, in fact, conservatives and social democrats sounded more and more alike. But at the same time there was a weakening of the postwar consensus about governmental re-sponsibility for social and economic well-being, as

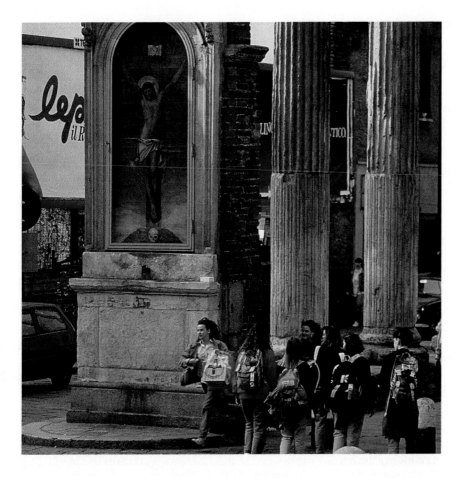

Old and New in Contemporary Europe Especially with the transformation of Europe since World War II, new styles of life intersect with living artifacts from the past to form sometimes ironic combinations. Here, in a neighborhood in Milan, Italy, teenagers wearing blue jeans and backpacks seem oblivious to the legacies of Roman antiquity and Christianity that are prominent around them. *(© 1993 George Steinmetz)*

new questions arose about the scope of the public sphere, the reach of the state.

Many of the trends important in Europe were visible in the United States as well. The widening gap between rich and poor, the weakening of organized labor, the growing prominence of women in the work force, the increasing concern about such family issues as child care—all were characteristic of Western civilization in general by the late twentieth century. But there were some instructive differences in the ways the different nations of the West dealt with these issues.

The Changing Economies: Prosperity, Imbalance, Limitation

By the 1980s there was greater prosperity in the Western democracies, but for a smaller proportion of the people. In Western Europe unemployment reached levels not seen since the Great Depression. Even after solid growth resumed by 1983, unemployment hovered stubbornly at around 10

percent throughout much of the region, with 13 percent the norm in some older industrial areas. These figures would have seemed unimaginable fifteen years before and were much higher than the rates of 5 to 7 percent typical of the United States during the same period. Yet unemployment persisted, even worsening in some areas. By the mid-1990s, it was highest in Spain, at 20 percent, followed by Finland at 17 percent.

This combination of prosperity and unemployment stemmed in part from the technological changes that, during the late twentieth century, produced a "third industrial revolution." (See the box, "Toward a Postindustrial Society.") Based most dramatically on the computer, it encompassed everything from robotics to fiber optics. The advent of new technologies in a context of increasing global competition produced new winners, but it also transformed the workplace and patterns of employment in worrisome ways.

Such technologies created opportunities for new firms able to start from scratch, without the

Toward a Postindustrial Society

The Canadian communications theorist Marshall McLuhan (1911–1980) offered pioneering analyses of the power of the mass media to shape the form, the scale, and even the content of human interaction in the emerging "global village." Writing in 1964, he also sought to outline what automation and the dawning of the computer age—the transition from the mechanical to the "electrical"—would mean for the future. In the offing was not merely the latest phase in the ongoing process of industrialization, but a deeper revolution, comparable to the advent of printing, which McLuhan identified with its fifteenth-century inventor, Johann Gutenberg.

The future of work consists of earning a living in the automation age. This is a familiar pattern in electric technology in general. It ends the old dichotomies between culture and technology, between art and commerce, and between work and leisure. Whereas in the mechanical age of fragmentation leisure had been the absence of work, or mere idleness, the reverse is true in the electric age. As the age of information demands the simultaneous use of all our faculties, we discover that we are most at leisure when we are most intensely involved, very much as with the artists in all ages.

. . . The new kind of interrelation in both industry and entertainment is the result of the electric instant speed. Our new electric technology now extends the instant processing of knowledge by interrelation that has long occurred within our central nervous system. It is that same speed that constitutes "organic unity" and ends the mechanical age that had gone into high gear with Gutenberg. Automation brings in real "mass production," not in terms of size, but of an instant inclusive embrace. Such is also the character of "mass media." They are an indication, not of the size of their audiences, but of the fact that everybody becomes involved in them at the same time. . . .

. . . With the electric technology, the new kinds of instant interdependence and interprocess that take over production also enter the market and social organizations. For this reason, markets and education designed to cope with the products of servile toil and mechanical production are no longer adequate. Our education has long ago acquired the fragmentary and piecemeal character of mechanism. It is now under increasing pressure to acquire the depth and interrelation that are indispensable in the all-at-once world of electric organization.

Paradoxically, automation makes liberal education mandatory. The electric age of servomechanisms suddenly releases men from the mechanical and specialist servitude of the preceding machine age. . . . We are suddenly threatened with a liberation that taxes our inner resources of self-employment and imaginative participation in society. This would seem to be a fate that calls men to the role of artist in society. It has the effect of making most people realize how much they had come to depend on the fragmentalized and repetitive routines of the mechanical era. . . . Men are suddenly nomadic gatherers of knowledge, nomadic as never before, informed as never before, free from fragmentary specialism as never before—but also involved in the total social process as never before; since with electricity we extend our central nervous system globally, instantly interrelating every human experience.

Source: Marshall McLuhan, *Understanding Media: The Extensions of Man* (Cambridge, Mass.: The MIT Press, 1994), pp. 346–347, 349, 357–358.

problems of redundant workers or outmoded plant and equipment that older competitors faced. A good example was Benetton, an Italian clothing firm founded in 1964 that quickly made effective use of computer technology in all aspects of its operation. But Benetton was so successful partly because it needed fewer workers. Manufacturing jobs tended to be lost as competition forced the industrial sector to become more efficient through computers and automation. In the German steel industry, which had spearheaded a remarkable industrial transformation a century before, over half the jobs disappeared during the 1970s and 1980s.

Changing labor patterns reinforced the decline of organized labor, which was decidedly on the defensive throughout Western Europe and the United States by the 1980s. In France, for example, the organized labor movement was at once divided and relatively small, with fewer than 10 percent of workers unionized. The increasing danger of unemployment undercut the leverage of the unions. And as the economy grew more complex, workers were ever less likely to understand themselves as members of a single, unified working class.

Affluence and Secularization

Postwar economic growth created a secular, consumerist society throughout much of Western Europe by the mid-1960s, establishing patterns that would continue into the less secure 1990s. Growing prosperity meant not only paid annual vacations of three to four weeks but also the luxury of spending them away from home, often at crowded beach resorts. Prosperity entailed the democratization of leisure, increasingly enjoyed in the privacy of the home rather than in a public café, pub, or theater. Television was virtually universal in households across Europe by the beginning of the 1980s. Still, spectator sports grew more popular at the same time, with soccer, the undisputed king, drawing rowdy and sometimes violent crowds.

In Western Europe, as in the United States, a remarkable baby boom had followed the end of the war and carried into the early 1960s. The birthrate declined rapidly thereafter, however, so that family size diminished markedly by 1990. In Italy, where changes in lifestyle accompanying the new prosperity were especially dramatic, the number of births in 1987 was barely half the number in 1964, when the postwar baby boom reached its peak. By 1995 the population was not sustaining itself in Italy or Spain.

Secularization diminished the once central role of the churches in popular culture, which had long revolved around religious festivals and holy days. Regular church attendance declined steadily. In assuming responsibility for social welfare, the state had taken over much of the charitable role that the churches had long played. Seeking to change with the times, the Catholic church undertook a notable modernization effort under the popular Pope John XXIII (r. 1958–1963). But under his more conservative successors, the church became caught up in controversy, especially over issues like abortion that women had forced to the fore. By the last decade of the century, its conservative social policy had put the Catholic church on the defensive.

In traditionally Catholic countries like France, Italy, and Spain, many people considered themselves "cultural Catholics" and ignored church rulings they found inappropriate, especially those concerning sexuality, marriage, and gender roles. The easier availability of contraception—especially the birth control pill, widely obtainable by the late 1960s—fostered a sexual revolution that was central to the new secular lifestyle. In referenda in 1974 and 1981, two-thirds of Italians defied the Vatican by voting to legalize divorce and approve abortion rights. Even in heavily Catholic Ireland, the electorate narrowly approved the legalization of divorce in 1995, after defeating it overwhelmingly in a referendum just nine years before. Controversy also developed over the possibility of ordaining women as priests.

Increasing affluence led to rising expectations and demands for still wider opportunity. Such pressure focused especially on access to government-supported higher education, the chief vehicle for upward mobility based on merit. In France, university admission required passing the *baccalauréat* exam at the end of secondary school. The percentage of the age group that reached this threshold grew from 1 percent in 1900 to 5 percent in 1949, then rose to 23 percent by 1974. In Italy the number of university students increased sixfold from the late 1930s to the late 1960s, partly the result of an open enrollment policy. In West Germany higher education was still restrictive, elitist, and authoritarian at the end of the 1960s, but under pressure from the left the university system quadrupled in size by 1975.

The development of a mass-based university system produced new dilemmas. In France, demands for reform of higher education had been central to the uprising of 1968, but subsequent government efforts to decentralize the system produced widespread opposition from students and faculty by the 1980s. The government's proposal to give individual universities the right to choose their own students provoked protests and strikes, the most notable of which, in 1986, involved 400,000 demonstrators and violent clashes with police. Such opposition forced the government to abandon much of its reform effort.

The resistance to reform reflected the reverse side of social mobility—the considerable status anxiety among students and faculty, especially those in the humanities and social sciences. As French universities had become institutions of mass education, the market value of the state diploma had declined substantially, as had the prestige of the faculty. For those who opposed reform, fear of loss outweighed the possibility of gain from a more competitive system. The French experience with university reform made it clear that mobility and security, equality and excellence, opportunity and merit meshed uneasily in the democratic societies of the West.

The Significance of Gender

As the cases of class and religion indicate, long-standing bases of identity were becoming less important as an affluent, secular society emerged. But new ones became central at the same time. A striking example by the 1980s was the growing preoccupation with gender, which, like the concern with higher education, stemmed from the ongoing quest for equality of opportunity to provide the basis for individual self-realization. In this area, too, the pursuit of equality of opportunity— now across gender lines—encountered tensions.

As it matured, the feminist movement that crystalized in the late 1960s found it necessary to expand its focus beyond the quest for equal opportunity. Examining subtle cultural obstacles to equality led feminists to the more general issue of gender—the way societies perceive sexual difference and thereby define social roles. There was much interest in the innovative ideas of the French existentialist Simone de Beauvoir, who had raised in 1949 precisely the issues that came to the fore during the 1980s. (See the box, "Human Freedom and the Origins of a New Feminism," on page 1083.) And as debate expanded from "women's issues" to gender roles, the self-understanding and often the immediate economic advantage of men were at issue as well.

Insofar as differentiated gender roles are "constructed" by particular societies, gender had been important throughout the long history of the West. Indeed, "gendering" had been central to the socialization process whereby young people learn how to function in their societies. But the gender roles dictated by society were usually taken as natural, so gender was only rarely as explicit and controversial an issue as it became in the late twentieth century. By the 1990s the gender issue was central not only to public policy but also to private relationships and to decisions about life choices in much of the Western world.

It was increasingly recognized that, at least implicitly, debates about the welfare state had often centered on gender from the beginning. After World War II, concerns about labor shortage in both East and West led to conflicting impulses in policy discussions and decisions. Should women be encouraged to work or to concentrate on rearing the children who would be the workers of the future? In Western Europe immigration helped ease the labor shortage, so it was especially in the Soviet bloc that this tension was evident in shifting public policy. In 1981, for example, the Soviet Union reversed course by increasing child care payments and adopting measures to reduce the hours that mothers worked outside the home.

With the dramatic slowdown in population growth in Western Europe after the mid-1960s, there was renewed fear about shortages of labor. At the same time, the feminist movement, seeking equal opportunity, sought measures like government-subsidized day care that would enable women to combine paid employment with raising a family. By the 1970s, these impulses had come together in much of Western Europe. Seeking to enhance both equality of opportunity and long-term economic productivity, governments assumed responsibility for combining productive working parents with effective childhood development.

Setting the pace was France, where the government began making quality day care available to all during the 1980s. Government subsidy kept costs within reach for ordinary working families. In addition, 95 percent of French children aged 3 to 6 were enrolled in the free public nursery schools available by the early 1990s. Comparable figures for Italy (85 percent) and Germany (65 to 70 percent) were also high, although Britain lagged at 35 to 40 percent.

The increasing reliance on child care both reflected and reinforced a decline in the socializing role of the traditional family. This trend prompted concern about the long-term consequences for the socialization of children—and thus for the future of society. At issue was the interaction of family roles, economic functions, individual self-realization, and the well-being of children. Even committed feminists disagreed about whether the undoubted biological difference in childbearing and nursing entailed a special role for women—and had implications for public policy. No one could be sure about the longer-term consequences of this departure from traditional family roles, which was a crucial phase of the ongoing experiment in the West.

Still, the French model seemed to work well in combining child support with equal opportunity for paid employment. Moreover, in France social services were delivered with less paperwork and intrusiveness than elsewhere. By the 1990s, the question was simply whether France could still afford such benefits. And this question reflected a wider set of concerns, becoming central everywhere, about the political order and the role of government.

Re-evaluating the Role of Government

Although the welfare state was in question everywhere by the 1980s, the most dramatic and single-minded assault came in Britain after Margaret Thatcher became prime minister in a new conservative government in 1979. Thatcher insisted that Britain could reverse its economic decline only by fostering a new "enterprise culture," restoring the individual initiative that had been sapped, as she saw it, by decades of dependence on government. Thatcher took it for granted that the free market, undistorted by government intervention, produced optimum economic efficiency and thus, in the long term, the greatest social benefit.

Abandoning its paternalistic tendencies and aristocratic vestiges, the Conservative party now appealed especially to the upwardly mobile, entrepreneurial middle class. But in light of the socioeconomic difficulties Britain faced by the late 1970s, Thatcher's message had broad appeal across the social spectrum. With Labour increasingly isolated, identified with decaying inner cities and old industrial regions, Thatcher easily won re-election in 1983 and 1987.

Three immediate priorities followed directly from Thatcher's overall strategy. First, her government made substantial cuts in taxes and corresponding cuts in spending for education, national health, and public housing. Second, the government fostered privatization, selling off an array of state-owned firms from Rolls Royce to British

Thatcher's Conservative Revolution As British prime minister from 1979 to 1990, Margaret Thatcher led an assault on the welfare state and a renewed embrace of free market economics in Britain. Together with U.S. president Ronald Reagan, who greatly admired her, she came to symbolize the retreat from government that marked the 1980s. Thatcher is shown here at a political rally in London in 1987. (*D. Hudson/Sygma*)

Airways. The government even sold public housing to tenants, at as much as 50 percent below market value, a measure that helped Thatcher win considerable working-class support. Third, Thatcher curbed the power of Britain's labor unions, which were already on the defensive in this period of high unemployment.

Several new laws curtailed trade-union power, and Thatcher refused to consult with union leaders as her predecessors had done since the war. A showdown was reached with the yearlong coal miners' strike of 1984 and 1985, one of the most bitter and violent European strikes of the twentieth century. The strike's failure in the face of government intransigence further discredited the labor movement and enhanced Thatcher's prestige. Still, the violent encounters between police and picketing strikers, carried nationwide on TV, indicated the cracks in the relative social harmony that Britain had long enjoyed.

In addition, riots by unemployed youths broke out in several major industrial cities in 1981 and again in 1985. On one issue, however, the Thatcher government managed a meeting of the minds with discontented city dwellers. Even before Thatcher took office, increasing immigration from Britain's former colonies was being blamed for a variety of social ills, from unemployment to urban crime. Taking a hard line on the immigration issue, Thatcher's Conservatives sponsored the Nationality Act of 1982, which restricted emigration from the former British colonies.

With her nationalist bent, Thatcher resisted the growing power of the multinational European Union. But her stance on this issue, coupled with what seemed an increasingly arrogant, strident tone, provoked growing opposition even within her own party, which finally ousted her as party leader, and thus as prime minister, in 1990.

Controversy over the significance of the Thatcher years mounted after her departure. On the plus side, her efforts helped boost the competitiveness of British industry. Productivity grew at an average annual rate of 4.5 percent in Britain from 1979 to 1988, 50 percent above the average of the other industrial democracies. This striking improvement stemmed partly from the attack on the trade unions, which had limited productivity by protecting redundant labor. Even critics admitted that Thatcher's policies, especially her willingness

to curb the unions, had produced a significant change in British attitudes in favor of enterprise and competition. Privatization found increasing approval, while the number of new businesses reflected a revival of entrepreneurship—apparently the basis for better economic performance over the longer term. Whatever the gains during the Thatcher years, however, the gap between rich and poor widened and the old industrial regions of the north were left ever further behind.

Although Thatcher's assault was unequaled, the social and economic role of the state came under scrutiny all over the Western world at the same time. Still, a renewed emphasis on market economics did not always produce a restriction of the welfare state. In Italy reforms during the 1970s made available a wider range of state services than ever before, from kindergarten and medical care to sports and recreational facilities. In France by the mid-1990s, five-week paid vacations were mandatory, with the government sometimes subsidizing the cost of transportation to seaside or mountain resorts. Comparable government subsidies kept the costs of cultural events affordable to ordinary workers. Accustomed to a strong government role in society, Europeans had difficulty understanding how measures like government-sponsored health care could cause such controversy among Americans.

Even as they prospered as never before, however, countries like France and Italy seemed unable to afford, at a time of intensifying economic competition, all the benefits their governments had gradually come to promise. But what the developed countries of the West could afford for pensions, education, welfare, or health care could not be established objectively; at issue, rather, were societal priorities, to be worked out through the political process. As the economy became more ruthlessly competitive and the gap in incomes widened, the winners, and even those holding their own, seemed ever more reluctant to pay for those who were less successful. The growing preoccupation with cost reflected an erosion of the sense of community and fairness that had been essential to the postwar consensus—and that had led to the expanded government role in the first place. That phenomenon raised questions about the long-term health of the democracies that had consolidated themselves after World War II.

ON THE RUINS OF THE COMMUNIST SYSTEM

By the early 1980s, the system hammered out by Stalin and his successors still seemed firmly entrenched in the Soviet Union and its satellites in east-central Europe, despite a lackluster period under the aging leadership of Leonid Brezhnev and his allies. Yet crises were building in both the Soviet Union and the satellite states, producing forces for change that finally engulfed the whole communist bloc. In one sense, the process began in Poland, Hungary, and Czechoslovakia, where new challenges to the communist system emerged during the 1970s. But no one had forgotten the fate of the earlier reform movements in Hungary and Prague; whatever pressures might develop in the satellite states, the outcome would depend on the Soviet response.

So in another sense, the death of Leonid Brezhnev in 1982 and the beginning of a concerted reform effort in the Soviet Union in 1985 were the decisive moments. By the end of the 1980s the forces for change in the Soviet Union and its satellites had intersected, leading the whole communist system to unravel. The dangerous but stable bipolar world that had emerged from World War II had suddenly vanished, and the countries of the former Soviet bloc began seeking to rejoin the rest of Europe.

BEYOND THE COLD WAR	
1979	Margaret Thatcher becomes prime minister of Britain
	First direct elections to European parliament
1980	Formation of Solidarity in Poland
1981	Mitterrand elected president of France
1982	Death of Leonid Brezhnev in the Soviet Union
1985	Gorbachev comes to power in the Soviet Union
1986	Explosion at Chernobyl nuclear power plant
1989	Collapse of communism in east-central Europe
1990	Reunification of Germany
	Persian Gulf War begins
1991	Collapse of communism in the Soviet Union; dissolution of the Soviet Union
	Beginning of fighting in Yugoslavia
	Maastrict agreement expanding scope of the European Union
1996	Peace in Bosnia
	Yeltsin re-elected as Russian president

Crisis and Innovation in the Soviet Bloc

The impressive rates of economic growth achieved in the Soviet Union and several of its satellite states after World War II continued into the 1960s. However, much of that success came from adding labor—women and underemployed peasants—to the industrial work force. By the end of the 1960s that process was reaching its limits, so increasingly the challenge for the Soviet bloc was to boost productivity through technological innovation.

Even compared to those elsewhere in the communist bloc, the command economy the Soviet Union had developed was particularly centralized and inflexible, involving methods of accounting and resource allocation that proved increasingly counterproductive as the economic challenge gradually changed. The results of the agriculture plan

of 1976 to 1980 were especially disappointing. The persistent shortages of many consumer goods, understandable during the transformation to an industrial society, seemed less and less tolerable. And by the late 1970s the Soviet Union was falling behind in high technology, which required the freedom to experiment and exchange ideas that was notably lacking in the rigid Soviet system. As that system bogged down, the expense of the arms race with the United States dragged ever more seriously on the Soviet economy.

In satellite countries like Poland and Hungary, the communist governments managed for a while to win mass support by borrowing from foreign banks so that they could provide meat and other consumer goods at artificially low prices. "Sausage-stuffing," some called it. But as the lending banks came to realize, by the end of the 1970s, that such loans were not being used for their stated purpose of fostering modernization and productivity, these governments found it much harder to borrow. Thus they began having to impose greater austerity.

For all its terrible excesses, Stalin's regime had continued to inspire a measure of genuine idealism during his lifetime. But by the 1970s the Soviet system had settled into narrow routine or outright corruption. Its major functionaries were increasingly a class apart, enjoying access to special shops and other privileges. Brezhnev himself took enormous pleasure in his collection of expensive automobiles.

Brezhnev's death in 1982 made possible the rise of Mikhail Gorbachev (b. 1931), who became party secretary in 1985 and who represented a new generation, beyond those who had been groomed for party careers during the Stalinist 1930s. He quickly charted a reform course—and attracted the admiration of much of the world.

Gorbachev's effort encompassed four intersecting initiatives: arms reduction; liberalization in the satellite states; *glasnost*, or "openness" to discussion and criticism; and *perestroika*, or economic "restructuring." This was to be a reform within the Soviet system. There was no thought of giving up the Communist party's monopoly on power or embracing a free-market economy. The reformers still took it for granted that communism could point the way beyond Western capitalism, with its widespread crime, its illegal drugs, its shallow consumerism. So a measure of idealism guided the reformers' efforts. But they had to make communism work.

Gorbachev understood that "openness" was a prerequisite for "restructuring." The freedom to criticize was essential to check abuses of power, which, in turn, was necessary to overcome the cynicism of the workers and improve productivity. Openness was also imperative to gain the full participation of the country's most creative people, whose contribution was critical if the Soviet Union was to become competitive in advanced technology.

The main thrust of restructuring was to depart from the rigid economic planning mechanism by giving local managers more autonomy. The alternative did not have to entail privatization or a return to free-market capitalism. It could mean, for example, letting workers elect factory managers. But any restructuring was bound to encounter re-

sistance, especially from those with careers tied to the central planning apparatus.

The Crisis of Communism in the Satellite States

Meanwhile, in the Soviet satellites, opposition had continued beneath the surface even after the crushing of the Prague reform effort in 1968. Although the intellectual response in Czechoslovakia would prove significant, Hungary and Poland were the best positioned of the Soviet-bloc countries to respond to the fresh air from the Soviet Union.

For many intellectuals in the Soviet bloc, the Soviet suppression of the Prague Spring in 1968 ended any hope that communism could be made to work. The immediate outcome was a sense of hopelessness and resignation, but by the mid-1970s an opposition movement, centering on underground (or *samizdat*) publications, had begun to take shape in Hungary, Poland, and Czechoslovakia.

In one sense, these dissidents realized, the dominant condition of intellectuals and ordinary people alike was powerlessness in the face of heavy-handed communist government. But they came to argue that there was still scope for individual honesty, for "living the truth," by ceasing to participate in the empty rituals of communist rule. And simple honesty could have political potential, thanks especially to the Helsinki Accords on human rights that the Soviets had accepted in 1975 (see page 1103). By demanding that the communist governments live up to their pretensions, opposition intellectuals could begin to cast doubts upon the legitimacy of the communist regimes. Through various "Helsinki Watch" groups monitoring civil liberties, the opposition managed to assume the moral leadership.

The most significant such group was Charter 77 in Czechoslovakia, which grew from a movement of protest against the arrest of a rock group called "The Plastic People of the Universe." Long-haired and anti-establishment like their counterparts in the West, the Plastic People were deemed filthy, obscene, and disrespectful of society by the repressive Czechoslovak regime. In 1977, protesting the crackdown on the group, 243 individuals signed "Charter 77"—using their own names and addresses, living the truth, acting as if they were free to register such an opinion. Their point was not explicitly political or ideological; rather, in protest-

Power from Below: Living the Truth

Considering the scope for change in the communist world by the late 1970s, Václav Havel imagines a conformist grocer who routinely puts a sign in his window with the slogan "Workers of the world, unite!" simply because it is expected. That same grocer, says Havel, has the power to break the stifling sociopolitical system, which ultimately rests on those innumerable acts of everyday compliance.

[T]he real meaning of the greengrocer's slogan has nothing to do with what the text of the slogan actually says. Even so, this real meaning is quite clear and generally comprehensible because the code is so familiar: the greengrocer declares his loyalty . . . in the only way the regime is capable of hearing; that is, by accepting the prescribed *ritual,* by accepting appearances as reality, by accepting the given rules of the game. In doing so, however, he has himself become a player in the game, thus making it possible for the game to go on, for it to exist in the first place. . . .

Let us now imagine that one day something in our greengrocer snaps and he stops putting up the slogans merely to ingratiate himself. He stops voting in elections he knows are a farce. He begins to say what he really thinks at political meetings. . . . He rejects the ritual and breaks the rules of the game. He discovers once more his suppressed identity and dignity. . . .

. . . He has shown everyone that it *is* possible to live within the truth. Living within the lie can constitute the system only if it is universal.

The principle must embrace and permeate everything. There are no terms whatsoever on which it can coexist with living within the truth, and therefore everyone who steps out of line *denies it in principle and threatens it in its entirety.* . . .

And since all genuine problems and matters of critical importance are hidden beneath a thick crust of lies, it is never quite clear when the proverbial last straw will fall, or what that straw will be. This . . . is why the regime prosecutes, almost as a reflex action preventively, even the most modest attempts to live within the truth.

. . . [T]he crust presented by the life of lies is made of strange stuff. As long as it seals off hermetically the entire society, it appears to be made of stone. But the moment someone breaks through in one place, when one person cries out, "The emperor is naked!"—when a single person breaks the rules of the game, thus exposing it as a game—everything suddenly appears in another light and the whole crust seems then to be made of a tissue on the point of tearing and disintegrating uncontrollably.

Source: Václav Havel et al., *The Power of the Powerless: Citizens Against the State in Central-Eastern Europe* (Armonk, N.Y.: M. E. Sharpe, 1985), pp. 31, 37, 39–40, 42–43.

ing this violation of human rights they at once made clear the scope for basic honesty and called attention to the gulf between honesty and the communist regime.

A leader in Charter 77 was the writer Václav Havel (b. 1936), who noted that after 1968 there was no hope of reforming the state or the Communist party through direct political action. Hopes for change depended on people organizing themselves, outside the structures of the party-state, in diverse, independent social groupings. (See the box, "Power from Below: Living the Truth.") Havel

and a number of his associates were in and out of jail as the government sought to head off this protest movement.

Despite the efforts of Havel and his colleagues, government remained particularly repressive and unimaginative, and ordinary people remained relatively passive, in Czechoslovakia until the late 1980s. For quite different reasons, Hungary and Poland offered greater scope for change.

Even after the failed reform effort of 1956, Hungary proved the most innovative of the European communist countries. Partly because its government allowed small-scale initiatives outside the central planning apparatus, Hungary was relatively prosperous by the end of the 1970s. But like others in the Soviet bloc, it faced difficulties paying off its foreign debt. The Hungarians responded as nowhere else, however, committing the economy to the discipline of the world market by joining the International Monetary Fund and the World Bank in 1982. This move required economic austerity, and Hungarian living standards declined during the early 1980s. But it also entailed, first, some role for reformers within the Communist party and, second, further encouragement of the "second economy," the country's autonomous private sector. Thus, for example, small food-processing enterprises developed, and independent craftsmen began contracting with the state on their own. Even on the collective farms, agricultural workers were allowed to work their particular sector as a family unit. By the mid-1980s various alternative forms of ownership were responsible for one-third of Hungary's economic output.

This openness to experiment in the economy enabled reformers within the Hungarian Communist party to gain the upper hand. Amid growing talk of "socialist pluralism," the Hungarian elections of 1985 introduced an element of genuine democracy. Mikhail Gorbachev's visit to Budapest in 1986 helped embolden the reformers, but by then the course of change in Hungary had developed a momentum of its own. Finally, in 1988, communist reformers ousted the aging János Kádár, who lacked the vision for continued reform. Increasingly open to a variety of viewpoints, the Hungarian communists gradually pulled back from their long-standing claim to a monopoly of power.

With growing concern for the Hungarian minority in Romania helping to galvanize political consciousness, new political clubs proliferated in Hungary. Finally, in June 1989, popular pressure led to the ceremonial reburial of Imre Nagy, who had led the reform effort in 1956. After having been convicted of treason, executed, and buried in obscurity, Nagy had been derided as a counter-revolutionary traitor in official government pronouncements. The significance of his reburial indicated the importance of historical memory—and who controls it. With the reformers' victory in this battle, Hungarians no longer had to live with the official lie about what had happened in 1956.

The reform effort that built gradually in Hungary stemmed especially from reform aspirations within the governing elite. More dramatic was the course of change in Poland, where there was already a tradition of labor militancy, especially among shipyard workers on the Baltic coast. In fact, these workers' demands for independent, genuinely representative trade unions in 1970 had led to a violent crackdown by the government.

It was crucial that, whereas Polish workers had not supported dissident students and intellectuals who had demonstrated in 1968, the two sides managed to come together during the 1970s. When Polish workers struck again in 1976, in response to a cut in food subsidies, intellectuals formed a Committee for the Defense of the Workers, soon expanded to become the Social Self-Defense Committee (KOR). This alliance had become possible because dissident intellectuals in Poland, as in other Soviet-bloc countries, were coming to emphasize the importance of grassroots efforts that challenged the logic of the communist system without attacking it directly.

But an extra ingredient from an unexpected quarter also affected the situation in Poland, perhaps in a decisive way. In 1978 the College of Cardinals of the Roman Catholic church departed from long tradition and, for the first time since 1522, elected a non-Italian pope. But even more startling was the fact that the new pope was from Poland, behind the iron curtain. He was Karol Cardinal Wojtyla (b. 1920), the archbishop of Kracow, who took the name John Paul II.

After World War II, the Polish Catholic church had been unique among the major churches of east-central Europe in maintaining and even enhancing its position. It worked just enough with the ruling communists to be allowed to carve out a measure of autonomy. For many Poles, the church thus remained a tangible institutional alternative to communism and the focus of national self-consciousness in the face of Soviet domination. Thus the new pope's visit to Poland in 1979 had an electrifying effect on ordinary Poles, who took to the streets by the millions to greet him—and found they were not alone. This boost in self-confidence provided the catalyst for the founding of a new trade union, Solidarity, in August 1980.

Led by the remarkable shipyard electrician Lech Walesa (b. 1944), Solidarity emerged most

Lech Walesa and Solidarity A shipyard electrician, Walesa spearheaded the dissident Polish trade union, Solidarity, formed in 1980, and then emerged from prison to lead the movement that eventually toppled the communist regime in Poland in 1989. Here he addresses a rally during a strike at the Lenin shipyards in Gdansk in August 1988. *(Sygma)*

immediately in response to labor discontent in the vast Lenin shipyard in Gdansk, on the Baltic Sea (see Map 30.1). Demanding the right to form their own independent trade unions, 70,000 workers took over the shipyards, winning support both from their intellectual allies and from the Catholic church. Support for Solidarity grew partly because the government, facing the crisis of its "sausage-stuffing" strategy, was cutting subsidies and raising food prices. But the new union developed such force because it placed moral demands first—independent labor organizations, the right to strike, and freedom of expression. Reflecting the wider opposition thinking in east-central Europe, Solidarity was not to be bought off with lower meat prices, even had the government been able to deliver them.

After over a year of negotiation, compromise, and broken promises, the tense situation came to a head in December 1981, when the government under General Wojciech Jaruzelski (b. 1923) declared martial law and outlawed Solidarity, imprisoning its leaders. Strikes in protest were crushed by mil-

itary force. Soviet intervention was a definite possibility—but proved unnecessary.

So much for that, it seemed. Another lost cause, another reform effort colliding with inflexible communist power in east-central Europe, as in 1953, 1956, and 1968. But this time, it was different.

The ideas of Solidarity continued to spread underground. Walesa remained a powerfully effective leader, able to keep the heterogeneous movement together. Then the advent of Gorbachev in 1985 changed the overall framework of the communist bloc, for Gorbachev was convinced that the essential restructuring of the Soviet system required reform in the satellites as well. So as the Polish economy, already in difficulty by 1980, reached a crisis in 1987, Solidarity began stepping up its efforts.

When proposed price increases were rejected in a referendum, the Polish government imposed them by fiat. Strikes demanding the relegalization of Solidarity followed during the spring of 1988. The government again responded with military force, but Solidarity-led strikes in August forced

government leaders to send signals that they might be prepared to negotiate. With the economy nearing collapse, the government recognized that it could no longer govern on its own.

The negotiations that followed early in 1989 proved pivotal. When they began, Walesa and his advisers wanted primarily to regain legalization for Solidarity within the communist-dominated system, still under Jaruzelski. In exchange, they assumed they would have to help legitimate a rigged election to approve painful but necessary economic measures. But as these "Round Table" negotiations proceeded, the government gave ever more in exchange for Solidarity's cooperation. Not only did it consent to legalize Solidarity, but it agreed to make the forthcoming elections free enough for the opposition to participate genuinely.

The elections of June 1989 produced an overwhelming repudiation of Poland's communist government. Even government leaders running unopposed failed to win election as voters crossed out their names. In the aftermath of the elections, President Jaruzelski was forced to give Solidarity a chance to lead. Not all members of the opposition felt it wise to accept government responsibility under such difficult economic circumstances, but finally Tadeusz Mazowiecki (b. 1927), Walesa's choice and one of the movement's most distinguished intellectuals, agreed to form a government.

The chain of events in Poland culminated in one of the extraordinary events of modern history—the negotiated end of communist rule. That a communist government might give up power voluntarily had been utterly unforeseen. It happened partly because the Soviet Union under Gorbachev was seeking reform and thus had become much less likely to intervene militarily. It also mattered that the Polish Catholic church was available to act as mediator, hosting meetings, reminding both sides of their shared responsibilities in the difficult situation facing their country. By some accounts, General Jaruzelski, who seemed for most of the 1980s to be just another military strongman, willing to do the Soviets' bidding, had proven a national hero for his grace, perhaps even ingenu

ity, in yielding power to the opposition. But most important was the courage, the persistence, and the vision of Solidarity itself.

The Anticommunist Revolution, 1989–1991

Although the Hungarians were already breaking out of the communist mold, it was especially the Polish example that suggested to others in the Soviet bloc that the communist system was open to challenge. During 1989, demands for reform and, increasingly, for an end to communist rule spread through east-central Europe by means of the domino effect that had preoccupied the Soviets from the start. By the end of that year, the Soviet satellite system was in ruins (Map 30.1).

Though antigovernment strikes and demonstrations took place throughout the region, the end of the established communist order in Hungary, Czechoslovakia, East Germany, Bulgaria, and Albania was more peaceful than anyone would have dreamed possible a few years before. Starting with Hungary, these countries essentially followed the model established in Poland and negotiated the transfer of power from the Communists to opposition leaders. In Czechoslovakia, the transition was so peaceful that it was promptly dubbed the "Velvet Revolution." The signal exception was Romania, where the communist dictator Nicolae Ceausescu's bloody crackdown on the reform movement provoked an armed revolt that finally overthrew the government. The opposition executed Ceausescu and his wife on Christmas Day 1989.

Though the outcome was relatively peaceful, the possibility of violent repression was never far from the surface. Just months before, in June 1989, the communist leadership in China had used massive force to crush a comparable movement for democracy in Tiananmen Square in Beijing. As the opposition movement grew in East Germany early in the fall, with weekly demonstrations in Leipzig attracting 300,000 people, the East German communist leader Erich Honecker (1912–1994) began preparing for such a "Chinese solution" in his country. But a dramatic appeal for nonviolence by local opposition leaders in Leipzig helped persuade the police to hold off. At the same time, Gorbachev, visiting Honecker in October, called for moderation. Gorbachev still believed that reform offered the best hope for saving the system. Honecker was

Map 30.1 Europe After the Cold War The reunification of Germany and the breakup of the Soviet Union, Yugoslavia, and Czechoslovakia fundamentally altered the map of Europe by the early 1990s.

soon forced out of the East German leadership in favor of communists who desired reform.

A marked increase in illegal emigration from East Germany to the west had been one manifestation that the whole satellite system was starting to unravel. During 1989 the reform-minded Hungarian communists decided to stop impeding East Germans, many of whom vacationed in Hungary, from immigrating to the west at the Hungarian border with Austria. If the communist reformers in East Germany were to have any chance of turning the situation around, they had to relax restrictions on travel and even grant the right to emigrate. Thus they immediately began preparing legislation to both ends, amid a host of reforms intended to save the system. On November 9, 1989, the regime in East Germany did what had long seemed unthinkable: It opened the Berlin Wall, which was promptly dismantled altogether. Germans now traveled freely back and forth between east and west.

This liberalization effort proved too late, however, for by now discontented East Germans envi-sioned not simply reforming the communist system but ending it altogether. As it became possible to contemplate even German reunification, the communist system in the east quickly dissolved. Decisive steps toward reunification followed almost immediately during 1990.

The opening of the Berlin Wall in November 1989 signaled the end of the cold war. The immediate result in the west was euphoria, but few failed to recognize that a still more difficult task lay ahead. To be sure, reformers in the former communist countries claimed to want individual freedom, political democracy, and free-market capitalism. But it would be necessary to build these on the ruins of the now-discredited communist system and its command economy, a task never confronted before.

Meanwhile, in the Soviet Union, what began as a restructuring of the communist system became a struggle for survival of the system itself. The much-trumpeted glasnost produced greater freedom in Soviet culture and politics, but Gorbachev sought to avoid alienating hard-line com-

The Fall of the Wall In November 1989 the dismantling of the Berlin Wall, erected in 1961, marked the dramatic end of the cold war era. Here crowds assemble at the Brandenburg gate in the heart of Berlin to be part of the action as history was made—live on television. *(Corbis-Bettmann)*

munists, so he compromised, watering down the economic reforms essential to perestroika. The result proved a set of half-measures that only made things worse. Because so little was done to force the entrenched Soviet bureaucracy to go along, the pace of economic reform was lethargic. The essential structures of the command economy weakened, but free-market forms of exchange among producers, distributors, and consumers did not emerge to replace them.

In 1986 an accidental explosion at the Soviet nuclear power plant at Chernobyl, in Ukraine, released 200 times as much radiation as the atomic bombs dropped on Hiroshima and Nagasaki combined. The accident contaminated food supplies and forced the abandonment of villages and thousands of square miles of formerly productive land. According to later estimates, the radioactivity released would eventually hasten the death of at least 100,000 Soviet citizens. Despite his commitment to openness, Gorbachev reverted to old-fashioned Soviet secrecy for several weeks after the accident, in an effort to minimize what had happened. As a result, the eventual toll was far greater than it need have been. The accident and its aftermath seemed stark manifestation of all that was wrong with the Soviet system—its arrogance and secrecy, its premium on cutting corners to achieve targets imposed from above.

By the end of the 1980s, Soviet citizens felt betrayed by their earlier faith that Soviet communism was leading to a better future. A popular slogan spoke sarcastically of "seventy years on the road to nowhere." The economic situation was deteriorating, yet people were free to discuss alternatives as never before. As the discussion came to include once unthinkable possibilities like privatization and a market economy, it became clear that the whole communist system was in jeopardy.

The Soviet Communist party began losing members—4 million from January 1990 to July 1991. By mid-1990, moreover, the union of Soviet republics itself tottered on the verge of collapse. Lithuania led the way in calling for outright independence. But the stakes were raised enormously in June 1990 when the Russian republic, the largest and most important in the U.S.S.R., followed Lithuania's lead.

In June 1990 the newly elected chairman of Russia's parliament, Boris Yeltsin (b. 1931), persuaded the Russian republic to declare its sover-

eignty. Yeltsin had grown impatient with the slow pace of economic and political change, and by threatening that Russia might go its own way, he hoped to force Gorbachev's reform effort beyond the present impasse. As a further challenge to Gorbachev, Yeltsin dramatically resigned from the Communist party during the televised twenty-eighth congress in July 1990. When, in June 1991, free elections in the Russian republic offered the first clear contest between communists determined to preserve the system and those seeking to replace it, the anticommunist Yeltsin was elected the republic's president by a surprising margin.

After tilting toward the hard-liners late in 1990, Gorbachev sought a return to reform after Yeltsin's dramatic election as president of Russia in June 1991. Late in July, Gorbachev prepared a new union treaty that would have given substantial powers, including authority over taxation, to the constituent republics. He also engineered a new party charter that jettisoned much of the Marxist-Leninist doctrine that had guided communist practice since the revolution.

These measures promised the radical undoing of the Soviet system, and now the hard-liners finally struck back, initiating a coup in August 1991. They managed to force Gorbachev from power—but only for a few days. As the world held its breath, Yeltsin, supported by ordinary people in Moscow, stood up to the conspirators. Key units of the secret police, charged to arrest Yeltsin and other opposition leaders, refused to follow orders, prompting the Soviet army, already divided, to back off from the conspirators' plan to take Moscow. The coup quickly fizzled, but the episode galvanized the anticommunist movement and radically accelerated the pace of change.

Although Gorbachev was restored as head of the Soviet Union, the winner was Yeltsin, who quickly mounted an effort to dismantle the party apparatus before it could regroup. Spontaneous anticommunist demonstrations across much of the Soviet Union toppled statues of Lenin and dissolved local party networks. In a referendum in December 1991, Ukraine, the second most populous Soviet republic, overwhelmingly voted for independence. Not only the communist system but the Soviet Union itself was simply disintegrating.

Liberating though it was, the dissolution of the Soviet empire brought a new set of problems. What was to become of the 27,000 nuclear

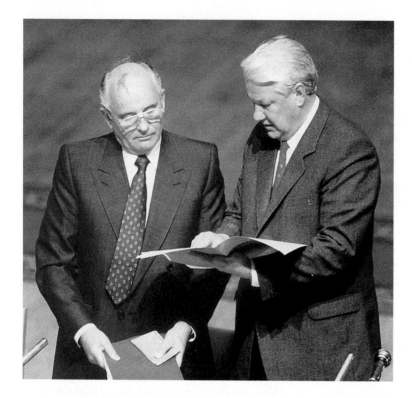

Gorbachev and Yeltsin The two leaders appear together in August 1991, just after the failure of an attempted coup by Soviet hard-liners. After the coup attempt, as it became clear that Gorbachev's effort to reform Soviet communism had stalled, the initiative passed to Yeltsin, who was determined to replace the communist system altogether. *(De Keerle/Grochowiak/Sygma)*

weapons stationed in four of the Soviet republics? Moreover, as the economic situation deteriorated, individual republics began setting up obstacles to economic exchange with the others, keeping what they produced for themselves. Some new form of coordination and unity seemed essential. Thus in December 1991, the leaders of Russia, Ukraine, and Belarus spearheaded the creation of a new Commonwealth of Independent States, which replaced the Soviet Union with a much looser confederation of eleven of the fifteen former Soviet republics. Late in December, Gorbachev finally resigned, paving the way for the official dissolution of the Soviet Union on January 1, 1992 (see Map 30.1).

Life After Communism

All over the formerly communist part of Europe, calls for Western-style democracy accompanied the end of the old order. But the area had little experience with the give and take of democratic politics, and the fragile new political systems found themselves responsible for the difficult transition from a command to a free-market economy. As economic hardship produced backlash and even

nostalgia for the certainties of communist rule, the key question was the staying power of the quest for democracy and a free-market economy in the former communist countries.

Political prospects rested in large part on the success of the economic transition. The economies in the former communist countries were close to chaos as the process began, and the attempt to construct a market economy brought on unemployment, inflation, and widespread corruption. No longer could ordinary people count on the subsidized consumer goods or the welfare safety net that the communist regimes, for all their inadequacies, had provided. While many ordinary citizens suffered great hardship, some former communist functionaries quickly got rich by taking over state-owned companies—and provoked widespread resentment. Still, the transition to a market economy seemed to be working by the mid-1990s, though the course of change varied considerably from one country to the next.

Some of the postcommunist governments concentrated on privatizing existing state-owned concerns while others sought especially to foster entrepreneurship and innovation. In Poland, privatization lagged, but a buoyant new private sector emerged as the Poles proved adept at starting new businesses. By the mid-1990s Poland had a reasonably stable, outward-looking market economy. Privatization, in contrast, was greatest in the Czech Republic under the forceful leadership of Václav Klaus, a passionate partisan of market economics. By the end of 1995, the Czechs had achieved a solid annual economic growth rate of 4 percent with low unemployment and relatively low inflation. But even in this, the most stable of the former communist countries, there was restiveness over corruption and problems in health care and other areas of the public sector.

Privatization was also rapid in Russia, where two-thirds of formerly state-owned industry had been redistributed by mid-1994. However, the fairness of the process was subject to much dispute. Optimists emphasized that thanks to this process, forty million Russians owned shares in newly privatized companies. But even the most optimistic could not deny that in certain sectors, especially natural resources and energy, the process included much insider dealing so that in Russia, more than anywhere else in the former communist world, privatization benefited former Communist party functionaries, some of whom became instant multimillionaires.

In Russia, too, the governmental weakness that accompanied the fall of communism yielded a chilling increase in lawlessness—from ordinary street crime like auto theft to sophisticated, organized crime with a significant role in the nation's economy. Thus in part the nostalgia for the stability of communism that led many Russians to vote Communist in 1995 and 1996. Despite the drama of the anticommunist revolution of 1989–1991, the postcommunist experience made it clear that to adopt democracy and a market economy were but tentative first steps.

In the political sphere, the former communist countries tended first toward political fragmentation—a multiplicity of parties in a weak, divided parliament—which in turn encouraged reliance on a strong leader. Postcommunist Poland's first parliamentary elections in October 1991 produced a parliament splintered among twenty parties, none strong enough to muster more than 12 percent of the vote. This situation seemed to open the way to an ever more authoritarian approach from the president, who, beginning in December 1990, was none other than Lech Walesa himself. Al-

though Walesa, during his five years as president, never became the authoritarian some feared, he was sometimes bullying and intolerant, and his dominant role reflected the wider tendency for a strong leader to emerge in the face of parliamentary fragmentation.

Throughout the formerly communist part of Europe, most were eager to jettison the communist label at first. But by 1992 those in power in Lithuania, Romania, Bulgaria, and the dominant Serbian part of Yugoslavia were former communists whose long-term commitment to democracy remained suspect. And by the mid-1990s, the shock of switching to a market economy was producing a growth in strength or return to power of former communists. Sometimes these communists worked in coalition with nationalists troubled by increasing Western economic penetration as their respective nations joined the international free-market economy. But some one-time communists were more reformed than others, and their electoral successes did not mean the same thing everywhere. Poland and Hungary experienced a tilt to the left by the mid-1990s, but these countries were maturing politically, and even the election of former communists did not mean undercutting democracy or the market economy.

When a charismatic young ex-communist, Alexander Kwasniewski, defeated Walesa in a watershed presidential election in Poland in 1995, it was not a repudiation of the anticommunist revolution that Walesa and Solidarity had spearheaded. By this point, in fact, Walesa was no longer a progressive force. His vote came largely from traditionalist, rural, strongly Catholic parts of Poland, while Kwasniewski attracted Poles interested in expanding the market economy and developing closer ties with Western Europe.

In Russia, communism had far deeper roots than elsewhere in the former Soviet bloc. It had not been imposed by foreigners, and it had been in power far longer than elsewhere. Communist or former communist hard-liners sought to oust not only Gorbachev in 1991 but also Yeltsin in 1993, when the elected parliament, which included many opposed to Yeltsin's free-market reforms, unsuccessfully challenged the president's authority within the new system. By late 1995, when Russia's second postcommunist parliamentary elections took place, the communists, led by Gennady Zyuganov, profited from the unpopularity of reform and the attendant backlash against Yeltsin to win a plurality of seats. Unlike the former communists who had won elections in Lithuania, Hungary, and Poland, these Russian communists had never dropped the communist label and had never fully embraced democratic principles.

When presidential elections followed in 1996, the communists exploited economic discontent and won support especially from workers and older pensioners. But the communist economic platform was riddled with contradictions, and it was hardly clear what a communist victory would have meant. Yeltsin, in contrast, enjoyed the support of Russia's powerful new entrepreneurial class, which opposed any retreat from free-market principles.

An astute, surprisingly resilient politician, Yeltsin capped a remarkable uphill struggle by defeating Zyuganov for president in July 1996. The campaign and election had given Russians their fullest experience of democracy to date, but it remained unclear whether the outcome would prove a turning point in the consolidation of a democratic order in postcommunist Russia.

Although economic reconstruction was paramount, the end of communism opened up divisive new questions across the former Soviet bloc. It quickly became clear that political freedom did not necessarily bring wider rights and liberties. For example, the eclipse of communism in Poland initially promised a major role for the Roman Catholic church, but angry debate followed when, in 1990, the government ordered that children be taught the Catholic religion in school and the head of the Polish church called for an end to the "communist-inspired" separation of church and state. An effort to pass a strong anti-abortion bill in time for a visit by Pope John Paul II in 1991 caused more heated debate; public opinion polls indicated that a majority of Poles favored abortion rights.

Abortion was similarly a major issue as, just after the fall of communism, the former East Germany was incorporated into the Federal Republic of Germany. Abortion law had been more liberal in the communist east than in the west. In the same way, East Germany was considerably more generous than the Federal Republic in providing maternity leaves, day care, and other measures to enable mothers to work outside the home. Though some East German feminists, by the mid-1980s, were accenting gender differences to enable

women to pull back from the workplace, they feared that the difficult transition to capitalism could mean diminished employment opportunities for women. Though a compromise was worked out on the abortion issue, the differences in priorities that surfaced between West and East German feminists made it clear that the end of communism was no panacea.

In the former satellite states, as in several of the republics of the former Soviet Union, autonomy and democracy quickly opened the way to ethnic tensions that occasionally led to outright rebellion. Ethnic repression and conflict were not new to the region, but within the Soviet bloc they had been kept largely submerged.

In Czechoslovakia, which had been widely admired for its peaceful, civilized departure from communism, the Slovak minority broke away to form an independent republic at the beginning of 1993. By 1995 the government was making Slovak the only official language, angering the large Hungarian minority in Slovakia and drawing protests from Hungary. The status of the Hungarian minority in Romania was an ongoing concern as well. But most dramatic—and tragic—was the situation in Yugoslavia, where ethnic and religious conflict produced not only the disintegration of the country but also a brutal, multisided war among Serbs, Croats, and Bosnian Muslims (see Map 30.2). One of the defining events of the 1990s, this war proved a major challenge for the new international order that had emerged from the cold war.

EUROPE AND THE WEST AFTER THE BIPOLAR PEACE

The dissolution of the Soviet system meant the swift, unexpected end of the cold war framework that had defined the era since World War II. Though it seemed only a balance of terror at the time, the cold war had provided a measure of order and security in the years from 1949 to 1989. What sort of international configuration was to follow? Though it could claim, in one sense, to have won the cold war, the United States had also declined in relative strength from the unprecedented pre-eminence it had enjoyed after World War II. Thus the end of the cold war meant not unchallenged U.S. hegemony but a new universe of uncertainties and possibilities.

The new framework seemed to invite Western Europe to become a superpower in its own right, so as the cold war ended, the ongoing push for European integration intensified, producing a more integrated union of fifteen members by the mid-1990s. But obstacles remained, stemming especially from traditional concerns about national sovereignty. And fighting in the former Yugoslavia raised questions about the ability of the European Union, or any international body, to assure stability in the chaotic world that seemed to be emerging after four decades of bipolar peace.

The Changing International Framework

As the potential threat from the Soviet Union dissolved, the United States lost some of its leverage in Europe because American support no longer seemed essential for European security. But despite a renewed military buildup during the 1980s, the Americans, by the early 1990s, could no longer claim the same kind of leadership in any case. The role of superpower had taken its toll on the United States, just as it had on the U.S.S.R. These two had been the big winners of World War II, yet the subsequent arms race burdened the budgets of both countries, while the war's major losers, Germany, Japan, and Italy, pulled back from any great power role to prosper as never before.

The ambiguities of the new international situation came to the fore during the first major international crisis of the post–cold war period, the Persian Gulf War, which the United States led against Iraq in 1990 and 1991. With superpower rivalry no longer an issue, the United States assembled a wide-ranging coalition that reversed an Iraqi takeover of neighboring, oil-rich Kuwait. Though the United States led successfully, it had to pass the hat among its prosperous allies to pay for the Gulf War, and those called on to contribute seemed unlikely to settle for such arrangements again. This was especially true of Japan and Germany, each of which was engaged in reassessing its international role.

The end of the cold war especially affected Germany because the collapse of communism in east-central Europe paved the way for German reunification in 1990. Despite some nervousness, the four postwar occupying powers—the United States, Britain, France, and the Soviet Union—gave their blessing as the Federal Republic simply incorporated the five states of the former East Germany. Although some in West Germany were hesitant about immediate reunification, especially because of the economic costs that seemed likely, West German Chancellor Helmut Kohl (b. 1930) sought to complete the process as quickly as possible. By early 1990 immigration of East Germans to the west had become a flood. West German law treated these Germans as citizens, entitled to social benefits, so their arrival in such numbers presented a considerable financial burden. It seemed imperative for West Germany to regularize the situation as quickly as possible, assuming responsibility for the east and restoring its economy.

Reunification prompted anxiety about the role the new Germany, already a major economic power, might seek to play in Europe and the world. Because 30 percent of the territory of present-day Poland had been taken from Germany after World War II, the Poles were especially concerned. Germany, however, remained eager to prove its good intentions by leading the continuing movement toward European integration. Some worried that the EU would itself become a vehicle for German domination, but the Germans took care to offer reasoned, cautious leadership, with no hint of bullying.

Reunified Germany also encountered new domestic problems that promoted caution. Because reunification proved far more costly than Kohl had expected, his government found it hard to keep some of the promises it had made, in the euphoria of reunification, to Germans in the east. When, in 1993, his government pulled back from its promise of wage equality between east and west, workers in the former East Germany mounted the most serious strikes the Federal Republic had experienced since World War II. Moreover, the strains and costs of reunification contributed to the growing controversy over the role of immigrants in Germany by the early 1990s.

The French were particularly restive about the reunification of Germany, which threatened the leading role on the western Europe continent that France had played since World War II. But France was still willing to act independently—and it could be influential in doing so. When the post–cold war international system fell into discredit with the multisided ethnic fighting in the former Yugoslavia, French pressure, late in 1995,

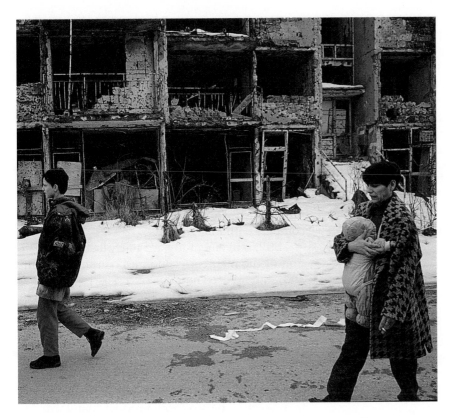

The Agony of Bosnia The wars that accompanied the breakup of Yugoslavia during the 1990s made it tragically clear that the end of the cold war was no guarantee of peace in Europe. The Serb shelling of the Bosnian capital, Sarajevo, from 1992 to 1996 caused widespread destruction and forced many to flee the city. Here Bosnian Muslims return to the Dobrinja area of Sarajevo in March 1996, just after the end of the Serb siege. (*Christopher Morris/Time/Black Star*)

helped bring the situation to a head. President Jacques Chirac's threat to pull France out of the multinational peacekeeping force in the region influenced U.S. President Bill Clinton to step up the U.S. role—with perhaps decisive results. The French initiative in this case manifested the new complexity in relations among the Western allies, but the outcome confirmed the centrality of U.S. leadership in a crucial sense.

The brutality that characterized the fighting in Bosnia, and the halting efforts of the international community in response, brought to an abrupt end the optimism that at first surrounded the end of the cold war. The Serbs, especially, were widely accused of "ethnic cleansing"—brutal forced relocation or killing to rid much of Bosnia of its Muslim inhabitants (Map 30.2). Muslim enclaves in

Map 30.2 Ethnic Conflict in East-Central Europe Much of east-central Europe, and particularly the Balkans, has long been an area of complex ethnic mixture. The end of communist rule opened the way to ethnic conflict, most tragically in what had been Yugoslavia. This map shows ethnic distribution in the region in the early 1990s.

Bosnia suffered grievously under Serb fire. In the Bosnian capital, Sarajevo, a culturally diverse city long known for its tolerant, cosmopolitan atmosphere, more than 10,000 civilians, including 1500 children, were killed by shelling and sniper fire during a Serb siege from 1992 to early 1996.

When a Serb mortar killed thirty-seven civilians in a marketplace in Sarajevo in August 1995, NATO forces responded with air strikes that led to peace accords and the end of four years of fighting by early 1996. The tide turned partly because a Western embargo had devastated the economy of what remained of Yugoslavia, forcing its Serb leader Slobodan Milosevic to cooperate with those seeking a peaceful solution.

But though the peace agreement envisioned a unified Bosnian state, the contending Serbs, Croats, and Bosnian Muslims quickly began carving out separate spheres, violating agreements about repatriation and the rights of minorities as they did so. Traditions of statehood were weak in this part of the Balkans, so it remained unclear whether the forces of disintegration at work in the former Yugoslavia were simply an anomaly in the greater scheme of twentieth-century Western history or an indication of potential, disintegrative forces at loose in Europe and the West. If every ethnic minority were to claim territorial autonomy, the future was uncertain indeed.

Although it was a NATO force that imposed peace in the former Yugoslavia, declining cohesion made NATO's future uncertain as well. The alliance had been formed to check Soviet expansion in Europe; with the apparent end of the Soviet threat, it made sense for its members to rethink their security needs and military priorities. This reconsideration led in several directions, not all of them compatible. Ten leading members of the European Union began developing a common defense mechanism, the Western European Union (WEU), but it remained tied to NATO. Some envisioned expanding NATO to encompass certain of the former Soviet bloc countries, starting with Hungary, Poland, and the Czech Republic. Others suggested that under the new circumstances, each nation would be well advised to look after its own defense. France resumed nuclear testing in the South Pacific in 1995, though in light of the international protest that resulted, it soon promised to cease such testing.

Postcommunist Russia was an especially uncertain player on the international scene. For many Russians, the collapse of communism brought national humiliation, in contrast to the renewed pride and independence to be found in the former satellite states. The role of the West in Bosnia and the prospect of NATO expansion eastward brought home Russia's sudden weakness—and led many Russians to insist that their country still be treated as a great power. Hard-liners began proposing that the now-collapsed "Soviet Union" be revived as a military alliance. Some even favored selling nuclear technology to such countries as Iran, Iraq, and Algeria—to put pressure on the West, especially the United States, which many Russians blamed for their problems. The danger of anti-Western extremism reinforced the support that Yeltsin enjoyed in the West even as it increased pressure at home to take an independent foreign policy line.

The European Union

The end of the cold war added urgency to the process of European integration. From the start, its proponents had hoped that the Common Market could promote greater uniformity in areas like tax policy and business law, in which national differences constituted barriers to economic activity across national borders. Although a full customs union had technically been achieved by the late 1960s, national governments continued to compromise the open market, especially by favoring certain companies to give them a competitive advantage in international competition. For domestic political reasons, governments sometimes confined their purchases to national firms or granted subsidies to domestic producers, thus enabling them to offer artificially lower prices to compete with foreign firms.

Still, movement toward the full-scale integration of the member economies continued by fits and starts. After another oil crisis in 1979, and amid increasing concern about "Eurosclerosis," or lack of innovation and competitiveness, the EEC's twelve members committed themselves in 1985 to the measures necessary to create a true single market with genuinely free competition by the end of 1992. Not only were goods, services, and money to circulate freely among the member countries, but there would be uniform product standards, as well as equal competition for the government contracts of each country.

By the late 1980s, the thrust toward economic integration increasingly assumed a political dimension. A European Parliament had developed from the assembly of the European Coal and Steel Community by 1962, though it had little importance at first. The provision for direct election to this body, which had formerly comprised delegations from the national parliaments, increased its stature when the first such elections were held in 1979. By the mid-1990s the European Union included a network of interlocking institutions, variously seated in Brussels, Strasbourg, and Luxembourg. Among them the European Parliament and the European Court of Justice played increasingly important roles.

Meeting at Maastrict, in the Netherlands, in 1991, the members of the European Union buttressed the powers of the European Parliament, agreed to move toward a common policy of workers' rights, and committed to a common currency and central banking structure by 1999. But this Maastrict agreement required the approval of the EU members, and in one country after another the ensuing debate over European integration proved more divisive than expected. In addition to the fear of German domination, some opponents of further integration saw it as a loss of sovereignty, which would mean entrusting vital decisions to faceless bureaucrats in foreign cities.

Moreover, the creation of an internal customs union, benign though it seemed, did not commit the EU to freer trade with nonmember countries like the United States and Japan. French farmers, especially, relied on a system of government supports that shielded them from U.S. competition. Conversely, high EU agricultural subsidies undercut the chance for Americans to sell their agricultural products in Europe. In 1992 the possibility that the French government would lower those supports, partly in response to pressures from the United States, caused massive demonstrations by French farmers.

Although the EU's members eventually ratified most of the Maastrict agreements, their implementation was not always smooth. Whereas Kohl's Germany continued to try to strengthen the European Commission and the European Parliament, even at the expense of national sovereignties, France and Britain dragged their feet. Citing the danger of terrorism and drug-smuggling, France essentially opted out of a provision to free the movement of people within Europe, whereas Germany found this provision indispensable.

Most controversial, however, was the provision for an Economic and Monetary Union (EMU), based on a common currency, to be in place by 1999. By eliminating the costs of currency exchange, this measure promised significantly to boost trade among the member countries. But to become part of the mechanism, countries had to maintain budget deficits no higher than 3 percent of gross domestic product; to reach that target, most of the member countries would have to decrease their deficits substantially. Governmental efforts to comply with this provision produced conflict on the domestic level, as the thrust toward European Union crashed against the social compact, already under pressure, that had produced high government spending for social welfare measures.

In a televised speech in 1995, President Chirac emphasized his determination to cut the government's budget deficit to enable France to meet the Maastrict criteria for economic and monetary union by 1999. The required austerity would include reducing welfare and pension payments

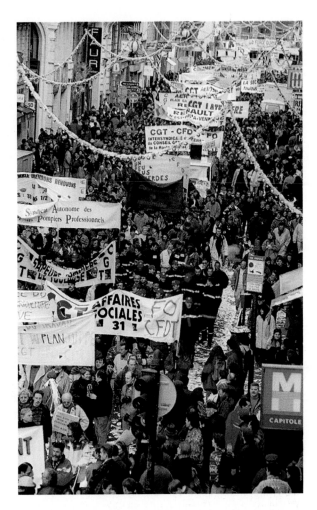

Protesting the New Austerity During the fall of 1995, widespread protest took place in France when the government announced new austerity measures, which it said were necessary to meet the budgetary requirements for membership in the European monetary union. Throughout the fifteen nations of the European Union, uncertainties about the role of government and the allure of further European integration meshed uneasily with the desire for the benefits that governments had come to provide since World War II. *(Wide World Photos)*

and restructuring the debt-plagued state railways. But Chirac's initiative prompted intense popular reaction during the fall of 1995. Railroad workers led the most serious wave of strikes that France had experienced in a decade, including periodic interruptions of public services. Students joined in, insisting that the university system needed more money, not less.

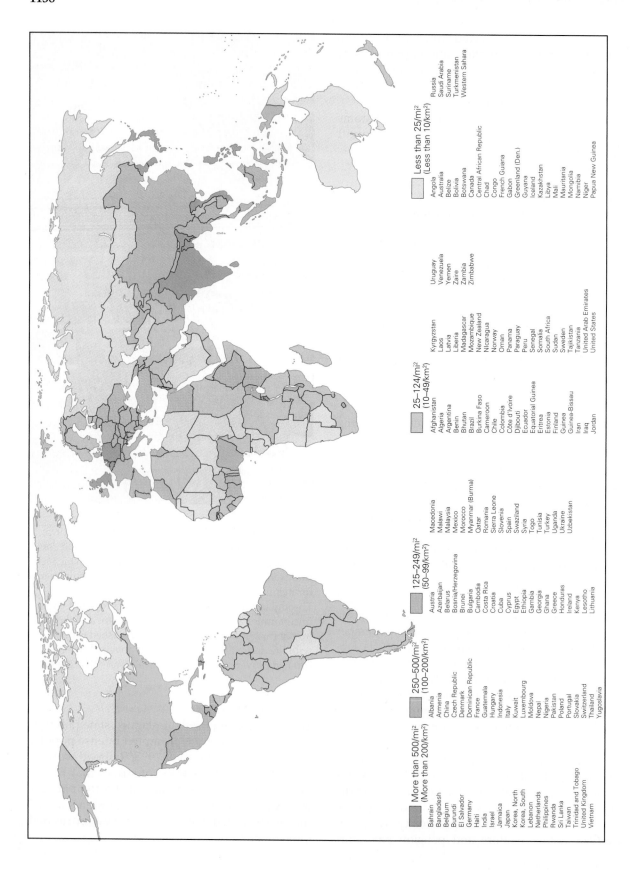

For many in France, embracing the EU seemed to jeopardize the egalitarianism that helped sustain social cohesion among the French. So even as the collapse of communism and the retreat from the interventionist state appeared to leave the field clear for free-market economics, the French response forced new questions about the relationship between social values and market forces. But the outcome of the strikes of 1995 was an awkward, provisional compromise. For France, and for the West, it was not clear how to arrive at a balance, in either economic or political terms.

Supranational Initiatives and Global Issues

Although less visible than the EU, other supranational entities also wielded increasing clout during the late twentieth century, making decisions that deeply affected the lives of ordinary people. Most obvious were multinational corporations, but the World Bank and the International Monetary Fund also played important roles, helping to keep the industrial economies synchronized and the less developed economies on a free-market path. These organizations could strongly influence domestic policies—by refusing, for example, to lend to countries spending heavily on defense. They were also major vehicles for the influence of the wealthy nations, centered in the West, on those from east-central Europe to south-central Africa that were trying to catch up.

At the same time, international cooperation took on greater urgency because growing concern with the global environment intensified the sense of world interdependence. Such problems as global warming, the destruction of rain forests, and the deterioration of the ozone layer were inherently supranational in scope. Yet environmental concerns complicated relations between the industrialized nations and the rest of the world. Countries seeking to industrialize encountered environmental constraints that had not been at issue

when the West industrialized. The challenge for the West was to foster protection of the environment in poorer regions of the globe without imposing unfair limitations on economic growth.

At the same time, changing demographic and economic patterns suggested that "North-South" tensions between the prosperous countries, concentrated in the northern hemisphere, and the poorer ones, more likely to be found farther south, might replace the East-West tensions of the cold war. World population reached 5.5 billion in 1993, having doubled in forty years. This was the fastest rate of world population growth ever, and by the 1990s virtually all of the growth was in Africa, Asia, and Latin America. The population of Europe was growing at only 0.2 percent per year, and in several countries, including Italy, Germany, and Spain, the population would actually have declined without the boost provided by immigration (Map 30.3).

Demographic pressure in the less developed countries contributed to the rising immigration to western Europe that made Africans selling hats, figurines, and sunglasses familiar in European cities by the early 1990s. But such immigration became a divisive political issue as Europeans faced the problems of an increasingly competitive world economy. In France the government's expulsion of illegal African immigrants sparked a major protest in 1996. The question of response to the needs of poorer countries with burgeoning populations had become central to the post–cold war agenda.

The combination of supranational organization, new technologies, and the global economy seemed to hold unprecedented promise, but startling scandals made clear the unprecedented scope for abuse it also allowed. When they came to light in 1991, the activities of the Bank of Credit and Commerce International (BCCI), a multinational bank nominally based in Luxembourg, brought home how vulnerable the world had become in an age of instant communications and global financial networks. For several years BCCI had dealt in drugs, illegal arms, terror, and money-laundering on a colossal international scale, corrupting prominent individuals throughout the world. Revelations of its operations suggested the need for more sophisticated forms of international regulation and accounting, but the pace of technological change seemed to outstrip the capacity of the international community to react.

Map 30.3 World Population Density, mid-1990s Most of Europe remains densely populated, but the explosive population growth of the late twentieth century took place especially in the poorer countries of Asia, Africa, and Latin America. (*Source:* Data from *1997 Information Please Almanac* (Boston: Houghton Mifflin, 1996), pp. 143 ff.)

Moreover, as the European Union and other supranational organizations became more prominent, forces in the opposite direction—subnational, religious, ethnic, tribal—simultaneously grew more powerful, producing conflict from Northern Ireland to Yugoslavia, from Spain to Lithuania. Such subgroup conflict was most tragic in east-central Europe (see Map 30.2), but it grew in western Europe as well, indicating that its sources were deep and widespread. Beginning in 1969, the British had to use troops in Northern Ireland to keep order in the face of ongoing threats from Irish Catholics seeking the end of British rule and unification with the Republic of Ireland. The result was polarization between Protestants and Catholics that defied solution. In Spain the restoration of democracy gave the long-restive Basque and Catalan minorities the chance to press openly for autonomy. Even in Belgium, there was growing antagonism between Flemish-speaking Flemings and French-speaking Walloons during the 1990s.

Immigration and Citizenship

With immigration growing sharply in Western Europe by the 1980s, questions about citizenship became politically central, giving a new twist to the interaction with the non-Western world that had helped define "the West" from the beginning. By 1995 there were 11 million legal resident immigrants living in the countries of the European Union—including, as the largest contingent, 2.6 million Turks. There were also as many as 4 million illegals. As economic pressures grew during the 1980s and 1990s, the tensions surrounding immigrants and foreigners threatened the political consensus in Western Europe.

At issue was not only new immigration, but the status of immigrant families already resident, in many cases for several generations since World War II. Some of those raising questions were not seeking simply to preserve economic advantages by limiting access. Rather, they were concerned about community, diversity, and national identity—about what it meant to belong. Because of differences in tradition, individual countries tended to conceive the alternatives differently.

Germany had actively recruited foreign workers during the decades of economic boom and labor shortage that followed the war. By 1973 noncitizens constituted 2.6 million workers, or 11.9 percent of the work force. At first these "guest workers" were viewed not as immigrants but as temporary, almost migrant, workers. But as they remained in Germany, their family patterns came to approximate those of the rest of the country, though their birthrates were considerably higher. By the 1980s, Germany had a large and increasingly settled population of non-Germans, many of them born and educated there.

In addition, the German Federal Republic had adopted a generous asylum law in an effort to atone for the crimes of the Nazi period. With the turmoil surrounding the end of communism in the Soviet bloc, the newly reunified Germany found 60,000 new arrivals seeking asylum every month by 1993. At that point Germany had a large foreign population of 6.4 million.

The law governing citizenship for immigrants and their descendants had originated in 1913 and reflected a long-standing German assumption that citizenship presupposed German ethnicity—or at least full assimilation. Thus ethnic Germans—over a million of whom moved to Germany from the former Soviet bloc between 1988 and 1991—were immediately accorded German citizenship. But there were many Turks, for example, who had been born in Germany but who could not become citizens. Precisely because citizenship entailed full assimilation, some Germans opposed citizenship for such "foreigners" or immigrants out of respect for cultural diversity.

But as the new wave of immigration from the east swelled the "foreign" population in Germany, more mundane motives came to the fore. Germans subject to economic pressures, especially, felt that foreigners and asylum-seekers were getting a better deal than ordinary citizens such as themselves. In 1992 alone, there were two thousand attacks on foreigners, some of them fatal. Those responsible were sometimes "skinheads," young people with uncertain economic prospects who claimed to admire Nazism. Their violence provoked massive counter-demonstrations by Germans eager to disavow any such ethnic hatred. But as reaction against refugees and foreign workers grew, the German parliament voted in 1993 to restrict the right of asylum.

These issues provoked particular controversy in Germany, but the claims of immigrants and refugees confronted all the Western democracies with difficult questions about the meaning of citizenship. In France the right-wing National Front, led by Jean-Marie LePen, forced the issue to center stage during the 1980s. Unlike the Germans, the French accorded citizenship automatically to second-generation immigrants, assuming that the offspring of immigrants would be readily assimilated into the national community. But as France began to attract rising numbers of immigrants, especially from Algeria and the other Islamic countries of North Africa, critics like LePen attacked the French citizenship law as too loose, charging that too many recent immigrants did not want to assimilate. Whereas the French left defended cultural diversity and its compatibility with citizenship, the right complained that citizenship was being devalued as a mere convenience, requiring no real commitment to the national community. This difference in perspective helps explain the controversy over the Muslim girls' headscarves that gripped France in 1989.

As these issues became ever more central in the West, representatives of twenty-seven Mediterranean countries—some European, some Middle-Eastern, some African—met in Barcelona in 1995 to seek common ground. The Europeans feared a continuing influx of immigrants fleeing poverty or the Islamic fundamentalism that was growing in the Islamic parts of the Mediterranean region. They also associated this wave of immigration with terrorism and illegal drug-dealing. For their part, the non-European countries of the Mediterranean feared that Europeans would begin expelling immigrants, thereby exacerbating the problems these immigrants had fled in the first place. To help limit the flow of immigrants, the Europeans pledged to help the other Mediterranean economies, but the need to protect competing EU agriculture made it hard to deliver. The Barcelona conference dramatized the web of interlocking difficulties that surrounded Western Europe's relations with its neighbors by the late twentieth century.

IN THE SHADOW OF HISTORY: THE EXPERIMENT CONTINUES

The rapid change of the later twentieth century raised new questions for Europeans about the meaning of their distinctive history and traditions. Some worried that prosperity necessarily entailed "Americanization," the unwelcome sameness of mass consumer culture. For the formerly communist countries of east-central Europe, the challenge was to find a positive way of reconnecting with their own national histories after decades of Soviet domination and communist ideology. In some cases, this return of history and memory contributed to the renewed emphasis on ethnic identity, which itself produced conflict and repression.

The collapse of communism in the Soviet bloc seemed to mean the triumph of democratic capitalism. But rapid economic and technological change introduced problems that proved hard to handle within the democratic political sphere. And during the 1990s, divisive issues all over the Western world—from the role of the state to environmental protection to immigration and cultural diversity—threatened to disrupt the political consensus that had crystallized since World War II.

Europe and America, Old and New

The center of gravity of Western civilization had changed before, gradually shifting from the eastern Mediterranean to the North Atlantic, but its location became especially uncertain with the dramatic changes surrounding World War II. Having weakened itself disastrously in the two world wars, Western Europe found itself dependent on the United States, first for its economic recovery, then for its defense. For decades after 1945, Europe seemed to have no choice but to follow the U.S. lead. Such subservience troubled some Europeans, and a kind of love-hate relationship with the United States developed in Western Europe during the later twentieth century.

Even after Europe's postwar economic recovery, the United States continued to set the pace in high-technology industries, prompting concerns that Europe would become a mere economic satellite of the United States. Europe seemed to be caught in a dilemma: To retain its distinctiveness over the long term, it apparently had to become more like America in the short term. The French writer Jean-Jacques Servan-Schreiber (b. 1924) made this case in his widely discussed book *The American Challenge,* first published in France in 1967 and quickly recognized as the classic statement of postwar Europe's ambivalent attitude toward Americanization. Haunted by the decline of earlier civilizations, Servan-Schreiber warned that if Europeans failed to become sufficiently

Kiefer: Osiris and Isis The German artist Anselm Kiefer combined unusual materials to create haunting images that often suggested the horrors of recent history. In this work from 1985 to 1987, the interpenetrating layers of human culture include images of ruin and death, hope and resurrection. *(Anselm Kiefer,* Osiris und Isis, *1985–87. Mixed media on canvas, 150" × 220½" × 6½". San Francisco Museum of Modern Art. Purchased through a gift of Jean Stein by exchange, the Mrs. Paul L. Wattis Fund, and the Doris and Don Fisher Fund. Photo: Ben Blackwell)*

dynamic to compete with the Americans, Europe would gradually sink into decadence without ever understanding why it had happened. (See the box, "Europe and the American Challenge.")

By the 1980s much of Western Europe had caught up with the United States in standard of living, and the Western Europeans set the pace in confronting some of the new problems that resulted from ongoing socioeconomic change. The French day-care system was one prominent example. Nonetheless, concerns about Americanization deepened at the same time. By the late 1980s consumerism and the widening impact of American popular culture—from blue jeans and American TV to shopping malls and theme parks—suggested a growing homogenization in the capi-

talist democracies. A Euro-Disneyland opened in France in 1992 and, after a slow start, proved increasingly popular. Tangible reminders of Europe's distinctive past survived, but the growing "heritage industry" in Britain and elsewhere suggested that they were merely commodities to be packaged like any other.

Although the shadow of fascism and war remained, Europe had experienced a radical transformation in the half-century since World War II, a transformation that in some ways had cut Europeans off from their own tradition. Visible artifacts of Europe's history, including its difficult recent past, lurked as bits and pieces in present experience, and the contemporary relationship to the tradition grew increasingly uncertain, even ironic.

Europe and the American Challenge

Throughout the twentieth century, the complex relationship between Europe and the United States helped to define "the West." Writing in 1967, the French writer Jean-Jacques Servan-Schreiber worried that postwar Western Europe's dependence on America would deprive European civilization of its distinctiveness, vitality, and purpose.

Today's generation faces a . . . clear choice of building an independent Europe or letting it become an annex of the United States. The sheer weight of American power is pushing our hesitant countries along the path of annexation, and the point of no return may be reached before today's ten-year-olds are able to vote.

It is still possible for us to catch up, but there is a great deal of dead weight to overcome. . . . [P]erhaps it is asking too much of Europeans to adapt to global competition, shake themselves loose from entrenched national habits, pull together dispersed resources, adjust to severe new rules of management, and stop wasting precious men and capital. Is it reasonable to ask an old continent to show the vitality of a new nation—especially when the satellization of Europe is accompanied, at least initially, by a rising standard of living and by only a very gradual reduction in our freedom of thought? . . .

There is no way of leaving the "economic area" to the Americans so that we can get on with political, social, and cultural areas in our own way, as some people would like to believe. There is no such compartmentalization in the real world. . . .

A few leading firms, subsidiaries of American corporations, would decide how much European workers would earn and how they would live. . . . American capital and American management will not stop short at the gates of our society.

. . . [T]hese managers . . . will take a majority interest in, and then control, the firms that dominate the market in publishing, the press, phonograph recording, and television production. The formulas, if not all the details, of our cultural "messages" would be imported. . . .

Cairo and Venice were able to keep their social and cultural identities during centuries of economic decline. But it was not such a small world then, and the pace of change was infinitely slower. A dying civilization could linger for a long time on the fragrance left in an empty vase. We will not have that consolation. . . .

There is no excuse for Europeans to be passive or complacent, for they are free to examine the American experience critically. . . .

If Europe decides to do this, she would greatly improve the chances of building a decent world, one that could reconcile the unity of modern industrial society with the variety of national cultures that compose it. A polycentric world would ensure a growing exchange of goods and ideas, and the continuing competition between human societies that has always been the condition of human progress. Would an isolated Egypt, Greece, or Rome have done any better than the Mayas trapped in their jungle?

An independent Europe is essential for orderly world economic development. Is there any group of advanced nations—other than those of the Common Market, together with Britain—that could form a pole of attraction different from both America and Russia? A united Europe could bring about significant changes in the world power balance, and not only from the strength of her ideas. They would come, above all, from the very creation of a third great industrial power with no imperial pretensions—one whose only strategy is to help build a more unified international community.

Source: Jean-Jacques Servan-Schreiber, *The American Challenge* (New York: Avon, 1969), pp. 175–180.

This ambiguous relationship found striking expression in architecture and painting by the last decades of the century.

During the first two decades after World War II, modernist architecture, turning from tradition to embrace the modern industrial age, had triumphed at last, transforming cities throughout the world. By the 1980s, however, architects were turning from modernism to postmodernism, a glitzy way of building with ambiguous or ironic references to a tradition that was still present, even if those living within it were not quite sure what to make of it.

This uneasy contemporary relationship with the past, especially the traumatic past of the earlier twentieth century, took more pointed form in the neoexpressionism prominent in German and Italian painting during the 1980s. Artists like Anselm Kiefer (b. 1945) and Sandro Chia (b. 1946) created striking images that reflect the ongoing search for meaning in the context of an unmastered past.

Technology and the Fragile European Environment

With the disintegration of the Soviet bloc, it became clear that the years of communism had produced environmental degradation on an appalling scale. The Stalinist determination to industrialize quickly had combined with the Marxist faith in human mastery and progress to produce this result, and those who came after were left to clean up as best they could. But in Western Europe as well, the impact of rapid economic growth on the European landscape and cityscape continued to provoke concern.

The number of automobiles in Western Europe increased from 6 million in 1939 to 16 million by 1959 to 42 million by 1969. Almost overnight, traffic and air pollution fundamentally changed the face of Europe's old cities. In 1976 five statues that had supported the Eastern Portico of the Erectheum Temple on the Acropolis in Athens since the fifth century B.C. had to be replaced by replicas and put in a museum to save them from the rapid decay that air pollution was causing. There was talk of the "melancholy of progress" as the dimensions of the conflict between economic prosperity and the tangible monuments of Europe's history became clear.

The natural setting proved just as vulnerable. By the early 1980s acid rain had damaged one-third of the forests of West Germany, including the famous Black Forest of the southwest. Water pollution was a major problem from the Rhine to the Mediterranean to the Black Sea.

During much of the 1970s and 1980s, environmental concerns focused on the difficult question of nuclear power, which solved certain environmental problems while posing the risk of still more serious ones. By the 1990s the West's greatest proponent of nuclear power was France, which was getting 80 percent of its electricity from nuclear plants and was striving for 100 percent, whereas in the United States and Britain the comparable figure was only 20 percent—and shrinking. The French could boast that they had experienced no major safety problems and that by using nuclear power they were avoiding the hazards associated with fossil fuels, from acid rain to global warming. In much of Europe, however, there was decisive movement away from nuclear power, even before the Soviet nuclear accident at Chernobyl in 1986. In Germany the Greens led demonstrations in 1977 that forced the government drastically to decrease its plans for nuclear power. In Austria a referendum banned nuclear power altogether in 1978.

The Uncertain Triumph of Democratic Capitalism

The end of the cold war, the discrediting of communism, and the domestication of socialism all seemed to mean the triumph of political democracy and free-market capitalism. The superiority of both to the Soviet-style alternatives was all but universally recognized by the early 1990s. But though there was a good deal of self-congratulation in the West at first, what followed its victory was not a period of untroubled confidence but a deeper questioning of the capitalist democracy that had triumphed.

In light of the Western political experience so far, few denied that what worked best, and afforded the only basis for political legitimacy, was representative democracy based on universal suffrage within an open, pluralistic society guaranteeing individual freedom. There must be freedom not only to inquire and to criticize but also to pursue in dividual advantage within a market economy. At the same time, that free-market system had to be bounded by some measure of governmental responsibility—for education, for social welfare, for workplace and product safety, and for the environment. But there remained difficult questions about the proper role for government in coordinating, channeling, or balancing market forces. Some emphasized the contrast between the "social market economy" of Germany and the more unrestrained capitalism of the United States and Britain. (See the box, "The Varieties of Liberal Capitalism.")

As the former communist East struggled to catch up to the West, Western affluence increasingly seemed brittle and uncertain. It was largely economic insecurity that made immigration such a volatile issue all over the Western world by the 1990s. High unemployment, the result of technological change and increasing global competition, persisted in Western Europe, even afflicting Germany by the mid-1990s. In the United States, unemployment was considerably lower, but new jobs were often poorly paid, with few health and insurance benefits. Moreover, Americans did not have quite the safety net that the European welfare states provided—in health care, most notably. For most, real wages advanced little between the mid-1970s and the mid-1990s. The widening gap between the well-off and those barely getting by suggested the emergence of a "winner-take-all" society.[1]

Although the socialist left had won reforms that were now central to the consensus around democratic capitalism, it had abandoned much of what it had stood for—from class struggle and revolution to state ownership and a centrally planned economy. Socialism could apparently serve only as the mildly left-leaning party within the framework of capitalist democracy. In France the effort of Socialist President François Mitterrand to create a democratic socialist alternative bogged down by the later 1980s. As French socialism seemed to lose its sense of direction, some leading Socialists got caught up in corruption scandals, and the party met massive defeat at the polls in 1993 and 1995. In Italy, too, the Socialists were central to a corruption scandal that began convulsing the country in 1992, and that quickly spread to discredit the Christian Democrats as well—and indeed the whole entrenched Italian political class.

With the decline of socialism as a political alternative, the new right, which had been associated especially with anti-immigrant sentiment at first, grew in prominence by the mid-1990s as it sought to expand the range of political choices. Although differing considerably in priorities, respectability, and success, right-leaning political leaders—from LePen in France and José Maria Aznar in Spain to Jörg Haider in Austria and Gianfranco Fini in Italy—tapped into the growing political frustration and economic uncertainty.

But what did it mean to be "right wing" or conservative by the late twentieth century? In Italy and Austria, new right politicians criticized the prevailing understanding of the recent past— the era of fascism and the Second World War— playing up the patriotic, anticommunist thrust of the interwar right. But as far as present priorities were concerned, conservatives sometimes differed sharply among themselves. In Britain the Thatcher government had tamed the labor unions and sold state-owned industries, but conservative critics pointed out that it had expanded centralized control over local government, health care, and education. With its ideological agenda, the Thatcher government had been activist and interventionist, not cautious, gradualist, and pragmatic—not truly conservative. In addressing economic anxieties, the new right sometimes articulated problems that mainstream politicians ignored, but it seemed unable to propose viable solutions. Its proponents even disagreed over the relative merits of free trade and protectionism.

Extreme though it was, the Italian corruption scandal of the early 1990s dramatized troubling tendencies in the democratic political system of the later twentieth century. The need for money to finance electioneering and political patronage kept the whole system on the edge of corruption. Democracy seemed to place a premium on short-term advantage over vision and principle. By the early 1990s, declining voter turnout suggested growing political cynicism and disillusionment all over the Western world.

At the same time, participation in national politics came to seem less significant partly because key decisions were often made elsewhere, by multinational corporations or supranational organizations not directly subject to democratic control. As global competition intensified, the logic of capitalism, or the market, seemed increasingly to overwhelm the capacities of democratic politics.

The Varieties of Liberal Capitalism

The collapse of communism during 1989–1991 meant the triumph of capitalism, but it also brought to center stage the choices and trade-offs at work within the advanced capitalist world. Postwar West Germany had achieved remarkable success with its "social market economy," but as renewed under Ronald Reagan and Margaret Thatcher during the 1980s, the more individualistic, entrepreneurial capitalism of the United States and Britain attracted increasing support. Writing in 1991, the French industrialist and government leader Michel Albert offered a spirited critique of Anglo-American capitalism and advocated that France embrace the German "Rhine model" within a more fully integrated European Union.

The rich need no longer feel ashamed of their wealth. Where they once shunned any hint of ostentation, they now display it with an immodesty that the French used to consider shockingly vulgar when they witnessed it in Americans. And this wealth increasingly rubs shoulders with a new poverty of the kind that is flourishing in the USA. France, too, now has its zones of urban blight, dumping-grounds populated by a growing army of the unemployed, those whose benefit has run out, young people seeking their first job, and immigrants—illegal or otherwise. . . .

The Rhine model . . . embodies, on the one hand, capitalism which can provide social security, and on the other, a system in which the company is seen not just as a heap of capital but a group of people. This is exactly what France badly needs. . . .

. . . If the aim is to harness capitalism without impairing its efficiency, it is no longer to the nation state that we must look, but to Europe. And Europe must produce both powerful financial structures . . . and political institutions. . . .

. . . [A] whole new ideology of capitalism had come to power:

[T]he market is good, the state is bad; social welfare provision, once a sign of progress, is blamed for encouraging laziness; taxation, once an indispensable means for reconciling economic development and social justice, is accused (not without reason) of discouraging talent and initiative. . . . Where the nineteenth century saw capitalism challenge the state, but with no thought of replacing it in such areas as health, education or the media . . . , the late twentieth century now proposes to substitute market forces for the state. . . . [I]n the majority of developed countries, more and more services, from broadcasting to rubbish collection and from the water supply to the post office, are being transferred from the public to the private sector. . . .

We Europeans are, more than anyone else on the planet, faced with the question of which sacrifices we shall make, and for which gains. The European Community is the main battleground on which the conflict of capitalism against capitalism will be fought. . . .

1. Either Europeans will fail to understand what is really at stake, and so will not press their leaders to make the imaginative leap towards true political union: in which case, the Single Market will begin to fray and disintegrate before it has begun; the possibility of unity will recede ever further under a cloud of permanent Europessimism; the slide towards the neo-American model will accelerate as the zones of decay and deprivation already staked out on the periphery of our cities continue to swell. . . .

2. Or we will actually begin to build the United States of Europe: in which case, we will have all the means at our disposal to choose the best possible socioeconomic system, that which has already proven its mettle within one part of the continent and which will become the "European model" of capitalism.

Source: Michel Albert, *Capitalism Against Capitalism* (London: Whurr, 1993), pp. 238–240, 244, 247, 253–254, 260.

CONCLUSION: WESTERN CIVILIZATION IN A GLOBAL AGE

By the late twentieth century, the West was part of a world that, in one sense, was dramatically less Eurocentric than it had been a century before, when European imperialism was at its peak. Events in the West competed for attention with OPEC meetings, Japanese economic decisions, or the struggle against apartheid in South Africa. Decisions vitally affecting Europeans or Americans might be made anywhere. A planetary culture, a threatened environment, and an interdependent international economy required people to think and react in global terms as never before.

One of the defining characteristics of the modern period in the West had been a "master narrative"—a conception of all human development—that took the European model as privileged and assumed everyone else to be trying to catch up. Such developmentalist assumptions were linked to the arrogant sense of superiority that had once seemed to justify Western imperialism. There was no question that capitalism had spread from Europe, but even as Westernization continued at the end of the twentieth century, it was increasingly recognized that the West was not necessarily the model, the standard of development.

Although as late as 1965 a distinguished British historian suggested that sub-Saharan Africa had no real history prior to the arrival of Europeans, there was growing interest in the non-Western world and increasing respect for its diverse traditions during the latter part of the century. At the same time, scholars like Edward Said, a Palestinian teaching in the United States, showed how Western images of the non-Western world had been constructed, and become stereotypes, reinforcing assumptions of Western superiority. (See the box, "Encounters with the West: The Case of 'Orientalism.'")

Such insights contributed to the "postmodern" departure from a Eurocentered master narrative as the basis of our historical self-understanding. This departure enabled the West to place cultural differences in more genuinely global, or human, perspective. At the same time, it led some to deny that Western civilization merited privilege as an object of study. After that civilization had been glorified for so long, this stance was no doubt understandable, though it also involved a measure of overreaction. The discussion gradually made it clearer that the point of such study was not to celebrate Western civilization but simply to understand it—as the matrix that continued to shape the West and, less directly, the world. That tradition included much that might be criticized, and its present outcome entailed much that might be changed. But understanding had to come first. The invitation to think freely about the Western tradition, to criticize it, and to build a better future on it rested on precisely that tradition—and remained perhaps its most fundamental legacy.

But as the end of the century approached, the concern about diversity and assimilation throughout much of the Western world suggested that controversy would continue over the significance of the Western tradition in contemporary life. (See the feature, "Weighing the Evidence: The Debate over Western Civilization," on pages 1150–1151.) Concern about immigration was one manifestation, as was the controversy over "multiculturalism" in the United States. There was little agreement even about what an educated person in the West ought to know about the cultures of the world—including the West. At issue was how to do justice to difference and diversity without forgetting the common humanity, the recognition of shared experience, that gives substance to the notion of "the humanities." On that basis, we seek to learn from others, even those, perhaps especially those, with different backgrounds and values, as we also seek to understand the complex, tension-ridden tradition of the West.

A question that dramatized some of the difficulties at work concerned the sources of jazz, the American musical form that moved up the Mississippi River from New Orleans early in the twentieth century and took Europe by storm in the 1920s. Jazz contributed to the more generic American popular music that, in turn, helped nourish the worldwide popular culture emerging by the end of the century. Yet during the mid-1990s there was a divisive debate in the United States over the "ownership" of jazz. Was it a cultural blend, confirming the long-cherished notion that America had been a melting pot, or was it an African creation that the dominant, European-derived culture sought to expropriate? Each side appealed to history to justify its interpretation.

Debate about cultural contributions, even about fusion and expropriation, seems likely to continue. And it invites some measure of ideologi-

∼ **ENCOUNTERS WITH THE WEST** ∼

The Case of "Orientalism"

In his influential book **Orientalism**, *published in 1978, the Palestinian-American scholar Edward Said explored the process through which Westerners had constructed the "Middle East"—as different from the West. Though critical of the West, Said appealed to our common humanity in an effort to overcome the ongoing tendency, which was not confined to the West, to understand oneself as superior by stereotyping others. In the final analysis, he suggested, we all need to learn from one another.*

The Orient is not only adjacent to Europe; it is also the place of Europe's greatest and richest and oldest colonies, the source of its civilizations and languages, its cultural contestant, and one of its deepest and most recurring images of the Other. In addition, the Orient has helped to define Europe (or the West) as its contrasting image, idea, personality, experience. . . .

. . . The relationship between Occident and Orient is a relationship of power, of domination, of varying degrees of a complex hegemony. . . . There is very little consent to be found, for example, in the fact that Flaubert's encounter with an Egyptian courtesan produced a widely influential model of the Oriental woman; she never spoke of herself, she never represented her emotions, presence, or history. *He* spoke for and represented her. He was foreign, comparatively wealthy, male, and these were historical facts of domination that allowed him not only to possess Kuchuk Hanem physically but to speak for her and tell his readers in what way she was "typically Oriental." . . .

. . . [T]here is no avoiding the fact that even if we disregard the Orientalist distinctions between "them" and "us," a powerful series of political and ultimately ideological realities inform scholarship today. No one can escape dealing with, if not the East/West division, then the North/South one, the have/have-not one, the imperialist/anti-imperialist one, the white/colored one. We cannot

get around them all by pretending they do not exist; on the contrary, contemporary Orientalism teaches us a great deal about the intellectual dishonesty of dissembling on that score, the result of which is to intensify the divisions and make them both vicious and permanent. Yet an openly polemical and right-minded "progressive" scholarship can very easily degenerate into dogmatic slumber, a prospect that is not edifying either.

. . . [E]nough is being done today in the human sciences to provide the contemporary scholar with insights, methods, and ideas that could dispense with racial, ideological, and imperialist stereotypes of the sort provided during its historical ascendancy by Orientalism. I consider Orientalism's failure to have been a human as much as an intellectual one; for in having to take up a position of irreducible opposition to a region of the world it considered alien to its own, Orientalism failed to identify with human experience, failed also to see it as human experience. . . . I hope to have shown my reader that the answer to Orientalism is not Occidentalism. No former "Oriental" will be comforted by the thought that having been an Oriental himself he is likely— too likely—to study new "Orientals"—or "Occidentals"—of his own making. If the knowledge of Orientalism has any meaning, it is in being a reminder of the seductive degradation of knowledge, of any knowledge, anywhere, at any time. Now perhaps more than before.

Source: Edward W. Said, *Orientalism* (New York: Random House, Vintage, 1979), pp. 1–2, 4–8, 327–328.

cal or political distortion, from whichever side. Such debate makes it clear that historical study has become more relevant than ever in this era of rapid cultural cross-fertilization, yet history is also

more contested, as the ultimate court of appeal. So the danger is not indifference to history but the opposite—that historical inquiry will become too politicized to allow us genuinely to learn from it.

Such learning is crucial not to enable us to celebrate "who we are," but to deepen our understanding, even to make us more self-critical, so that, continuing the experiment, we may act more effectively—and thereby create a better future.

NOTES

1. Robert H. Frank and Philip J. Cook, *The Winner-Take-All Society* (New York: Free Press, 1995).

SUGGESTED READING

Western Society in the Late Twentieth Century

Ardagh, John. *France Today,* revised ed. 1988. Updated edition of a lively, perceptive survey of the remarkable changes in French life since World War II.

Barkan, Joanne. *Visions of Emancipation: The Italian Workers' Movement Since 1945.* 1984. A sympathetic account of the influential postwar Italian labor movement. Provides a good feel for the experience of factory workers and makes sense of their demands for autonomy.

Bridenthal, Renate, et al., eds. *Becoming Visible: Women in European History.* 1987. A major collection of essays on women's history, including seven that deal with twentieth-century topics. Jane Jenson's "Both Friend and Foe: Women and State Welfare" offers an illuminating comparative study of women and the welfare systems in Britain and France in the post–World War II period.

Brubaker, Rogers. *Citizenship and Nationhood in France and Germany.* 1992. Lucid comparative study showing how very different conceptions of citizenship emerged in these two countries as a result of their contrasting historical experiences over the past two centuries.

Hollifield, James F., and George Ross, eds. *Searching for the New France.* 1991. A collection of essays on topics from political structure and foreign policy to immigration and higher education.

Marwick, Arthur. *British Society Since 1945.* 1990. A lively, comprehensive survey, accenting the change to a consumer culture in the 1960s, but with due emphasis on the conservative transformation of the 1980s.

Mosse, George L. *The Image of Man: The Creation of Modern Masculinity.* 1996. Traces the idea and image of the masculine from the advent of nineteenth century bourgeois society to the late twentieth century, when gender roles were open to discussion as rarely before in the West.

Sorlin, Pierre. *European Cinemas, European Societies 1939–1990.* 1991. Emphasizes the themes of urbanization, immigration, and gender. Contrasts European with U.S. film making.

Questioning the Role of Government

Cheles, Luciano, et al., eds. *The Far Right in Western and Eastern Europe,* 2d ed. 1995. A superior collection of essays on the revival of the extreme right in the 1980s and 1990s.

Jenkins, Simon. *Accountable to None: The Tory Nationalisation of Britain.* 1995. Provocative conservative critique of Margaret Thatcher's revolution in Britain. Argues that Thatcher increased centralization even as she fostered privatization.

Maier, Charles, ed. *Changing Boundaries of the Political: Essays on the Evolving Balance Between the State and Society, Public and Private in Europe.* 1987. Though uneven and sometimes difficult, this is a useful collection of essays on an important and elusive topic. Good, for example, on the changing politics of health care.

Pierson, Paul. *Dismantling the Welfare State? Reagan, Thatcher, and the Politics of Retrenchment.* 1994. A comparative analysis of what worked and what did not in the conservative effort at retreat from the welfare state in the 1980s. Concludes that because of the high political costs of retrenchment, the welfare state remained essentially intact.

Young, Hugo. *The Iron Lady: A Biography of Margaret Thatcher.* 1989. A full-scale, readable biography that challenges Thatcher's consistency and questions her achievement.

The Transformation in Eastern and East-Central Europe

Elster, Jon, ed. *The Roundtable Talks and the Breakdown of Communism.* 1996. Separate essays on the negotiated end to communist rule in five east-central European countries, with an additional essay on the contrasting case of China.

Funk, Nanette, and Magda Mueller, eds. *Gender Politics and Post-Communism: Reflections from Eastern Europe and the Former Soviet Union.* 1993. Country-by-country analysis and critique by feminist scholars from the region, with an effective mixture of outside perspectives.

Garton Ash, Timothy. *The Magic Lantern: The Revolution of '89 Witnessed in Warsaw, Budapest, Berlin, and Prague.* 1990. Firsthand testimony on the fall of communism by a British intellectual with close contacts among anticommunists in east-central Europe.

Goldman, Marshall I. *What Went Wrong with Perestroika.* 1991. Focuses on the incongruity between the successful political restructuring, which went beyond what Gorbachev intended, and the inadequate economic reform.

Havel, Václav. *Disturbing the Peace: A Conversation with Karel Hvížďala.* 1991. Part autobiography, part history, part philosophy, part personal testimony. Demonstrates the moral vision that made Havel so effective as a leader in the Czech opposition to communism.

(continued on page 1152)

THE DEBATE OVER WESTERN CIVILIZATION

A striking theme in Western civilization during the last third of the twentieth century has been the intense debate that has erupted over "Western civilization" itself—its significance, and even its legitimacy as a concept. Why have the points at issue been contested so passionately at this moment in history, and what can we learn from this ongoing debate? The following testimony, from four very different thinkers, raises the central questions.

Jacques Ellul Writing in 1975, this influential French intellectual sought to counter the overreaction that he believed marked the increasing tendency—even in the West—to idealize non-Western cultures and denigrate Western civilization.

I admit, then, all the accusations leveled at the West for its colonialism and imperialism. . . .

Am I therefore to become a masochist and reject everything western, deny all the values of our world? No! . . . I accept responsibility for the evil that has been done, but I deny that only evil has been done. I know our civilization is built on bloodshed and robbery, but I also know that every civilization is built on bloodshed and robbery. . . .

. . . [W]e cannot expect to find justice and innocence "somewhere else." The Chinese and the Africans are not free of the sin we acknowledge in ourselves; they have been colonialists no less than we. . . .

. . . If the Chinese have done away with binding the feet of women, and if the Moroccans, Turks, and Algerians have begun to liberate their women, whence did the impulse to these moves come from? From the West, and nowhere else! Who invented the "rights of man"? The same holds for the elimination of exploitation. . . . The whole of the modern world, for better or for worse, is following a western model; no one imposed it on others, they have adopted it themselves, and enthusiastically. (*Source:* Jacques Ellul, *The Betrayal of the West,* trans. Matthew J. O'Connell [New York: Seabury Press (Continuum), 1978], pp. 7, 9, 11–12, 16–17.)

Silvia Federici Twenty years after Ellul expressed his views, this Italian-American scholar questioned the whole concept of "Western civilization" and the purposes that, over the past two centuries, led some to place such emphasis on it.

[T]he concept of "the West" is highly problematic, since it pretends to be constructed by reference to conven

tional geographical coordinates and yet maps the world in ways that defy "common sense," leaving entire regions in limbo. . . . Worse yet, a genealogy of "Western Civilization" demonstrates that this concept has historically developed in the context of military and ideological warfare, as the label for a political reality that could be conceived as unified only by reference to perceived enemies and contenders. . . .

Only in the aftermath of the nineteenth-century colonial penetration of India, China, and the Middle East did "the West" take on a more prominent political role, as the signifier of Europe's imperial project. It was at this time that it began . . . to merge with the concept of "civilization." . . .

As a synonym for social progress, "civilization" remained throughout the nineteenth century the prime signifier in the anthropological self-presentation of the European elites. Thus, the "civilized"/"savage" ("primitive," "backward") contrast became a standard element in European literature. (*Source:* Silvia Federici, ed., *Enduring Western Civilization: The Construction of the Concept of Western Civilization and Its "Others"* [Westport, Conn.: Praeger, 1995], pp. 65–66.)

Jean Dubuffet Writing in the early 1980s, this well-known French artist did not deny that there is a recognizable Western cultural tradition, but he found it elitist, limiting, even "asphyxiating."

It is naive to think that the few meager deeds and few meager works that happened to be preserved from the past are necessarily the best and most important of the thoughts of these times. Their preservation results only from that fact that a small coterie chose and applauded them, while eliminating all others. Those who celebrate culture do not think enough about the great number of humans and the innumerable character of productions of the mind. . . . The Westerner's idea that culture is the business of books, paintings and monuments is childish. . . .

When I think of these nations that had only an oral culture, and which left us no trace of their thought, it strikes me that the same is true of our nation. For we cannot call the works that form our scholastic material the work of a nation, all of which—writings, paintings, monuments—are products of a very restricted circle— the caste of lords—and of a handful of scholars who work for them. (*Source:* Jean Dubuffet, *Asphyxiating Culture,* trans. Carol Volk (New York: Four Walls Eight Windows, 1988), pp. 17-19.)

V. S. Naipaul Speaking in New York in 1990 on the universal significance of the Western tradition, this influential novelist, born and raised in Trinidad, began by reflecting on his own Indian Hindu family background.

We were a people of ritual and sacred texts. . . . But . . . [o]ur literature, our texts, didn't commit us to an exploration of our world; rather they were cultural markers, giving us a sense of the wholeness of our world, and the alienness of what lay outside. I don't believe that, in his family, anyone before my father would have thought of original literary composition. That idea came to my father in Trinidad with the English language . . . in spite of the colonial discouragements of the place. . . .

    The universal civilization . . . wasn't always as attractive as it is today. The expansion of Europe gave it for at least three centuries a racial tint, which still causes pain. In Trinidad I grew up in the last days of that kind of racialism. And that, perhaps, has given me a greater appreciation of the immense changes that have taken place since the end of [World War II], the extraordinary attempt of this civilization to accommodate the rest of the world. . . .

    . . . [T]he idea of the pursuit of happiness . . . is at the heart of the attractiveness of the civilization to so many outside it or on its periphery. . . . It implies a certain kind of society, a certain kind of awakened spirit. I don't imagine my father's parents would have been able to understand the idea. So much is contained in it: the idea of the individual, responsibility, choice, the life of the intellect, the idea of vocation and perfectibility and achievement. It is an immense human idea. (*Source:* V. S. Naipaul, "Our Universal Civilization," reprinted in *The New York Review of Books*, January 31, 1991, pp. 22, 25.)

Whether or not we find Federici's critique convincing, she formulated the most basic questions—is it legitimate to speak of "the West" at all, and what purposes were at work as the notion of "Western civilization" evolved? Most agree that there is a distinctive cultural tradition in what, despite the obvious geographical imprecision, is usefully termed "the West," though the questions about its value, and the uses or misuses that have been made of it, remain. Dubuffet recognized a coherent Western cultural tradition, but he found it so limited, reflecting the interests of the winners—the powerful—and their intellectual allies, as to be a problem, not a source of sustenance.

    Despite his claim to strike a balance, Ellul was perhaps too eager to have it both ways as he denied the uniqueness of the West's crimes while crediting the West for the values of individualism and freedom. At the very least, his argument suggests the need for cross-cultural historical comparisons. It is striking, however, that Naipaul, from his cross-cultural perspective, associated the West with essentially the same values Ellul emphasized—and similarly found them at once uniquely Western in origin and universal in appeal and significance.

    It first seems ironic that this debate would come to the fore during the decades after World War II, when, according to Naipaul, Western civilization became more open and began more genuinely living up to its ideals. But this was also the period of decolonization and the quantum leap in "globalization," trends that were bound to raise new questions as the West pulled back from the pretense of cultural superiority. The democratization of the era similarly prompted the new line of questioning that we find in the passage from Dubuffet.

    Even those most skeptical, like Federici and Dubuffet, do not simply turn from the Western tradition but invite us to question it afresh, thereby expanding our sense of what it includes and deepening our relationship with it. In the same way, even defenders like Ellul and Naipaul lead us to ask what, in the wider globalization, is best understood as "Westernization"—as opposed to cultural fusion, or ongoing diversity, or renewed exploitation. Moreover, Ellul and Naipaul stress that the contemporary democratic impulse itself grew from within the Western tradition. That impulse has prompted historians to expand their focus to ordinary people and, in the realm of "high" culture, to expand the "canon"—the body of works considered worthy of our attention. The Western tradition has proven flexible enough even to accommodate changes in our understanding of the West's past.

    The debate over Western civilization is itself testimony to the openness and freedom of that tradition. For all of us, the Western tradition entails an invitation, and a responsibility, to question "Western civilization" as part of our effort to learn from the whole human experience. ✄

Hosking, Geoffrey. *The Awakening of the Soviet Union.* Enlarged ed. 1991. Seeks to understand the Gorbachev reform effort from the perspective of ordinary people. Accents the potential for autonomy and initiative that would enable Soviet citizens to carry the reform effort beyond the intent of its leaders.

Laba, Roman. *The Roots of Solidarity.* 1991. Seeks to show that workers, as opposed to the Polish intelligentsia, were the driving force behind the Solidarity movement.

Malia, Martin. *The Soviet Tragedy: A History of Socialism in Russia, 1917–1991.* 1994. A deeply critical assessment of the course of the Soviet experiment from the perspective of its failure by the early 1990s.

Remnick, David. *Lenin's Tomb: The Last Days of the Soviet Empire.* 1994. Acclaimed and compelling account of the fall of the communist regime. Makes effective use of oral testimony.

Skidelsky, Robert. *The Road from Serfdom: The Economic and Political Consequences of the End of Communism.* 1996. Using the collapse of communism as a starting point, a leading economic historian accents the global dimensions of the shift to liberal capitalism in the 1980s and outlines a cautiously optimistic scenario for the future.

Steele, Jonathan. *Eternal Russia: Yeltsin, Gorbachev, and the Mirage of Democracy.* 1994. Places events before and after the fall of communism in useful historical perspective, while criticizing the preoccupation with privatization and the corresponding failure to foster a culture of democracy.

Stokes, Gale. *The Walls Came Tumbling Down: The Collapse of Communism in Eastern Europe.* 1993. Dramatic and comprehensive, the first standard account of the dissolution of communism in east-central Europe.

The New International Situation

Caplan, Richard, and John Feffer, eds. *Europe's New Nationalism: States and Minorities in Conflict.* 1996. Sophisticated essays by international scholars on the renewal of nationalism in Europe after the end of the cold war.

Donia, Robert J., and John V. A. Fine, Jr. *Bosnia and Hercegovina: A Tradition Betrayed.* 1994. Accessible, well-illustrated historical overview leading up to the region's central place in the Wars of Yugoslav Secession, which helped redefine international politics after the end of the cold war. Accenting the long tradition of ethnic and religious toleration in the area, insists that the conflict stemmed from contemporary political and territorial ambitions, not historically rooted ethnic or religious tensions.

Garton Ash, Timothy. *In Europe's Name: Germany and the Divided Continent.* 1993. A searching essay on Germany's place in Europe and the world, from the years of division, to reunification, to the post–cold war order.

Glenny, Misha. *The Fall of Yugoslavia: The Third Balkan War.* 3d revised edition. 1996. Influential account of the disintegration of Yugoslavia, combining historical analysis with dramatic treatment of the multisided ethnic fighting of the 1990s.

Jarausch, Konrad H. *The Rush to German Unity.* 1994. A clear and compelling account of the process of German reunification after the fall of communism in the east, with a careful assessment of the outcome.

Treverton, Gregory. *America, Germany, and the Future of Europe.* 1992. Treats the historical background of European-American relations after the cold war and shows why the United States seems bound to play a diminished role in Europe.

Europeans and Americans

Dean, John, and Jean-Paul Gabillet, eds. *European Readings of American Popular Culture.* 1996. Varied essays by European scholars assessing the impact of American popular culture in postwar Europe.

Diner, Dan. *America in the Eyes of the Germans: An Essay on Anti-Americanism.* 1996. A German-Israeli historian offers a provocative, critical look at the tendency of Germans—and Europeans more generally—to use America as a metaphor for the dark side of modernism.

Kroes, Rob. *If You've Seen One, You've Seen the Mall: Europeans and American Mass Culture.* 1996. Lively, sophisticated essay on the European way of transforming themes from American popular culture.

Kuisel, Richard F. *Seducing the French: The Dilemmas of Americanization.* 1993. Illuminating study of the French response to all things American in the half-century of American hegemony that followed World War II.

Chapter Opener Credits

Text Credits

the Freeing of the Serfs" from *A Sourcebook for Russian History from Early Times to 1917*, Volume 3, edited by George Vernadsky et al. Copyright 1972 by Yale University Press. Reprinted by permission of the publisher.

Chapter 23: Page 872: "Emile Zola on the Novelist as Scientist" from *Movements, Currents, Trends: Aspects of European Thought in the Nineteenth and Twentieth Centuries* by Eugen Weber. Copyright © 1992 by D.C. Heath and Company. Reprinted by permission of Houghton Mifflin Company.

Chapter 24: Page 907: "A Conspiratorial Revolutionary Party" from *Collected Works of Lenin, 1929*. Reprinted by permission of International Publishers.

Chapter 25: Page 924: "Into the Trenches" from *German Students' War Letters*, edited by A. F. Wedd, translated and arranged from the original edition of Dr. Philipp Witkop. London: Methuen 1929. **Page 936:** "The Bolsheviks in Power, November 1917" from *Ten Days that Shook the World* by John Reed. (London: Penguin 1977).

Chapter 26: Page 966: "Doubts About Mass Society" from *The Weimar Republic Sourcebook* by Anton Kaes, Martin Jay, and Ed Dimendberg. Copyright © 1994 by the University of California Press. Reprinted by permission of the Regents of the University of California and the University of California Press. **Page 988:** "Tradition and Women: The Conditions of Independence" from *A Room of One's Own* by Virginia Woolf. Copyright 1929 by Harcourt Brace & Company and renewed 1957 by Leonard Woolf. Reprinted by permission of Harcourt Brace & Company and the Society of Authors as the literary representative of the estate of Virginia Woolf.

Chapter 27: Page 999: "Retreating from 'The New Woman'" in *The Weimar Republic Sourcebook*, edited by Anton Kaes, Martin Jay, and Edward Dimendberg. Copyright © 1994 by the University of California Press. Reprinted by permission of the Regents of the University of California and the University of California Press. **Page 1001:** "Gandhi on Nonviolence" from *The Essential Writings of Mahatma Gandhi*, edited by Raghavan Iyer (Delhi: Oxford University Press, 1991). Copyright 1991 by the Navajivan Trust. Reprinted by permission of the Navajivan Trust. **Page 1003:** "Carrying Out the Stalinist Revolution" from *No Jail for Thought* by Lev Kopelev (London: Secker & Warburg Ltd., 1977. An imprint of Reed Consumer Books). **Page 1008:** "Hitler's World-View: Nature, Race, and Struggle" from *Mein Kampf* by Adolf Hitler, translated by Ralph Manheim. Copyright 1943, renewed 1971 by Houghton Mifflin. Reprinted by permission of Houghton Mifflin Company and Random Century Group UK. All rights reserved.

Chapter 28: Page 1041: "Toward the Nazi New Order" from *Nazism: A History in Documents and Eyewitness Accounts*, edited by Jeremy Noakes and G. Pridham. Copyright © 1988 by Department of History and Archaeology, University of Exeter. Reprinted by permission of Jeremy Noakes. **Page 1045:** "Stalingrad: The Diary of a German Soldier" from *The Battle of Stalingrad* by Vasili I. Chuikov. Copyright © 1964 by HarperCollins Publishers Ltd. Reprinted by permission. **Page 1049:** "Japan's 'Pan-Asian' Mission" from Nagayo Yoshiu, "Our Present War and the Cultural Significance," translated by Mitsuko Iriye in *Modern Asia and Africa*, edited by William H. McNeill and Mitsuko Iriye (Oxford University Press, 1971). Reprinted by permission of William H. McNeill. **Page 1065:** "The Soviet View of the Cold War" from "The Novikov Telegram" in *Diplomatic History*, Vol. 15, No. 4 (Fall 1991). Reprinted by permission of Blackwell Publishers.

Chapter 29: Page 1083: "Human Freedom and the Origins of a New Feminism" from *The Second Sex* by Simone de Beauvoir, translated by H. M. Parshley. Copyright 1952 and renewed 1980 by Alfred A. Knopf Inc. Reprinted by permission of Alfred A. Knopf, the Estate of Simone de Beauvoir, and Jonathan Cape. **Page 1093:** "Legacy of European Colonialism" from *The Wretched of the Earth* by Frantz Fanon, translated by Constance Farrington. Copyright © 1963 by Presence Africaine. Reprinted by permission of Grove/Atlantic, Inc. **Page 1095:** "Practical Thinking and European Integration" from *Memoirs* by Jean Monnet, Introduction by George W. Ball, translated by Richard Mayne. Translation copyright © 1978 by Doubleday, a division of Bantam Doubleday Dell Publishing Group, Inc. Reprinted by permission of the publisher. **Page 1100:** "Denouncing the Crimes of Stalinism" from *The Anti-Stalin Campaign and International Communism*, edited by the Russian Institute. Copyright © 1956 by Columbia University Press. Reprinted by permission of the publisher.

Chapter 30: Page 1116: "Toward a Postindustrial Society" from *Understanding Media: The Extensions of Man* by Marshall McLuhan. Copyright © 1994 by Marshall McLuhan. Reprinted by permission of the MIT Press. **Page 1143:** "Europe and the American Challenge" from *The American Challenge* by Jean-Jacques Servan-Schreiber. Copyright © 1975 by Éditions Denoël. English translation copyright © 1968 by Atheneum House, Inc. Reprinted by permission of Georges Borchardt, Inc., and Éditions Denoël. **Page 1146:** "The Varieties of Liberal Capitalism" from *Capitalism Against Capitalism* by Michel Albert (London: Whurr, 1993). Reprinted by permission of Whurr Publishers Limited. **Page 1148:** "The Case of 'Orientalism'" from *Orientalism* by Edward W. Said. Copyright © 1978 by Edward W. Said. Reprinted by permission of Pantheon Books, a division of Random House, Inc. **Page 1151:** From "Our Universal Civilization" by V. S. Naipul in *New York Review of Books*, January 31, 1991. Copyright © 1991 by V. S. Naipaul. Reprinted by permission of Aitken & Stone Ltd.